The Short Fiction

of

Edgar Allan Poe

The Library of Literature
under the general editorship of
John Henry Raleigh and Ian Watt

The Short Fiction
of
Edgar Allan Poe

an annotated edition
by
Stuart and Susan Levine

The Bobbs-Merrill Company, Inc.
Indianapolis

The Bobbs-Merrill Company, Inc.
4300 West 62nd Street
Indianapolis, Indiana 46268

First Edition
Second Printing 1976
Design: Starr Atkinson

Library of Congress Cataloging in Publication Data

Poe, Edgar Allan, 1809–1849.
  The short fiction of Edgar Allan Poe.

  (The Library of literature)
  Bibliography: p.
  I. Levine, Stuart, ed. II. Levine, Susan, ed.
III. Title.
PZ3.P752Sh   [PS2612]   813'.3   74–12377
ISBN 0–672–51462–1
ISBN 0–672–61032–9 (pbk.)

For Wilma, Jean, and Mac

Contents

List of Pictures, Maps, Charts, and Diagrams   x

Preface   xi

Acknowledgements   xii

Introduction *by* **Stuart Levine (SGL)**   xv

   The New Image of Poe   xv

   Poe's Early Years   xxi

   The Professional Years   xxv

   The Personality   xxix

Bibliography   xxxi

   Works on or by Poe   xxxi

   Other Works Utilized   xxxv

The Short Fiction
of
Edgar Allan Poe

1. Unimpeded Visions

   Preface   3

   The Domain of Arnheim   5

   The Philosophy of Furniture   14

   The Island of the Fay   18

   Landor's Cottage   21

   Morning on the Wissahiccon   29

   Notes   32

2. Salvation Through Terror

   Preface   39

   A Descent into the Maelström   40

   The Pit and the Pendulum   50

   Notes   59

3. The Death of a Beautiful Woman

   Preface   62

   The Oval Portrait   65

Morella   68
Berenice   71
Eleonora   76
Ligeia   79
The Fall of the House of Usher   88
Notes   99

4. Occult Fantasies
Preface   107
The Power of Words   114
The Conversation of Eiros and Charmion   116
The Colloquy of Monos and Una   119
Shadow   124
Silence   126
A Tale of the Ragged Mountains   128
The Facts in the Case of M. Valdemar   134
Mesmeric Revelation   139
Notes   145

5. Detective Stories
Preface   152
The Gold-Bug   155
The Murders in the Rue Morgue   175
The Mystery of Marie Rogêt   197
The Purloined Letter   225
The Oblong Box   236
Notes   244

6. Moral Issues
Preface   251
The Black Cat   254
The Tell-Tale Heart   259
Hop-Frog   262
The Imp of the Perverse   268
William Wilson   271
The Man of the Crowd   283
Notes   290

7. Slapstick Gothic
Preface   294
King Pest   296
Metzengerstein   303
The Premature Burial   308
The Sphinx   316
Notes   319

8. The Rake and the Fop
Preface   323
Thou Art the Man   324
The Spectacles   333
Notes   347

9. Literary Satires
Preface   351
How to Write a Blackwood Article   357
A Predicament   363

Never Bet the Devil Your Head   368
A Tale of Jerusalem   374
The Literary Life of Thingum Bob, Esq.   376
The Duc De L'Omelette   388
Some Passages in the Life of a Lion   390
The Devil in the Belfry   393
Bon-Bon   398
Why the Little Frenchman Wears His Hand in a Sling   407
X-ing a Paragrab   410
Notes   414

10. Political Satires
Preface   438
Four Beasts in One / The Homo-Cameleopard   439
The Man That Was Used Up   443
Notes   449

11. Anti-Aristocratic Tales
Preface   454
Mystification   456
The Masque of the Red Death   461
The Cask of Amontillado   464
Notes   468

12. Multiple Intention
Preface   471
The Assignation   473
Loss of Breath   482
The Angel of the Odd   489
Notes   495

13. Popular Journalism
Preface   502
The Thousand-and-Second Tale of Scheherazade   504
Some Words with a Mummy   512
Diddling Considered As One of the Exact Sciences   522
The Business Man   528
Three Sundays in a Week   533
Notes   537

14. Science, Technology, Oddities
Preface   547
The Balloon-Hoax   549
Hans Pfaal   558
Mellonta Tauta   588
The System of Dr. Tarr and Prof. Fether   596
Von Kempelen and His Discovery   607
Notes   611

15. The Beginning and the End
Preface   622
MS. Found in a Bottle   623
The Light-House   629
Notes   630

Index of Tales   632

Pictures, Maps, Charts, and Diagrams

1.	An Outline of Some Major Events in Poe's Professional Years	xxvii
2.	Claude Lorrain, "A Pastoral"	8
3.	The Plate Which Accompanied Poe's Sketch, "The Island of the Fay"	19
4.	A Mountain Wagon	22
5.	Salvator Rosa, "Tobias and the Angel"	24
6.	The Plate Which Accompanied "The Elk" in its First Appearance	29
7.	A Map of the Area in Which "A Descent into the Maelström" is Set	40
8.	Pentagon and Pentacle	104
9.	Map of Poe's Paris	176
10.	Map: The Last Voyage of the "Independence"	237
11.	The Book That "Does Not Permit Itself to Be Read"	284
12.	Locations of Gabae and Tabae	450
13.	Fleeing the Plague	461
14.	Map of Poe's Venice	474
15.	The Piazzetta	475
16.	The Prison	475
17.	The Ducal Palace	475
18.	San Marco	475
19.	Ponte di Rialto	475
20.	Building Facade, Piazza di Rialto	475
21.	Some Statues of Commodus	478
22.	The Venus de Medici	497
23.	The Fountain at the Bowling Green	521
24.	*The Extra Sun:* Poe's "Balloon Hoax" as it Originally Appeared	551

Preface

The Short Fiction of Edgar Allan Poe represents our attempt to bring together in one convenient edition all of the information one needs to understand Poe's stories. We wanted to do it in a way that would be readable, attractive, and accessible to a general reader or student, but would also be useful to a scholar or specialist. Doing so called for the decisions on procedure and format which are explained in this preface.

The information needed is often highly specialized and hard to come by. Much of it is scattered in the hundred different places in which scholars make their contributions; much of it we generated ourselves through an extensive program of literary sleuthing. We are, of course, responsible for the accuracy and completeness of what appears in this edition. We have tried to make it as nearly definitive as possible, though of course new discoveries will continue to be made by others and by us. This is as it should be; literary knowledge is not static.

Putting Poe in Context. In the notes appears information about each appearance of the tales in American magazines, books, or gift books during Poe's lifetime. We compiled most of our data from Heartman and Canny and other published sources. This information appears in an early note for each tale.

There is a special reason beyond good editorial practice for including such publication information: now that microfilm and microcard files of nineteenth-century American magazines are widely available, readers at thousands of libraries can, if they like, examine the journals in which Poe's work first appeared and thus gain a sense of the literary or sub-literary environment in which these tales were set. Poe's readers have been prone to think of his work as exotic. But seen in the context in which they were first printed, his stories seem much less so.

A Note on the Text. Because Poe published many of his tales more than once and thus had the opportunity to add or delete, tinker, and catch typographical and authorial errors, his stories pose fewer serious textual problems than most nineteenth-century works. Though we now know how maliciously Rufus Griswold tampered with the facts of Poe's life, he seems to have been reasonably scrupulous with most of Poe's texts, and later anthologists have generally accepted either his versions or the last versions which Poe himself supervised. Although some important textual scholarship has been done since it appeared, the "Virginia" or "New York" edition which James A. Harrison edited in 1902 contains the most information about Poe's own revisions, and so we used it more than any other single source.

One important exception is "The Landscape Garden"/"The Domain of Arnheim," which Harrison treated as two separate stories. We saw no reason to do so—this edition is large enough without reprinting identical passages—and so we have collated the two versions to show how Poe expanded a shorter story into a longer one.

On a Few "Obvious" Allusions. If classical education were still the norm, or perhaps even if the "educated reader" could be relied on to be familiar with a reasonable range of "common learnings," a few of the literary and historical allusions which are explained in our notes would be unnecessary. We include them because it seems to us that not to do so involves snobbery: we think it wrong to assume that any reader who does not immediately recognize the connotations, let us say, of a classical reference is unworthy of editorial attention, especially when a simple explanation is generally all that is needed to show him what Poe's allusion implies. We feel, moreover, that the educated reader today—particularly the student—knows fully as much as did his predecessor of decades or centuries ago. It is just that his knowledge is far less predictable. If he has to be told that Milton was a poet, he is liable to know who A. J. Downing was, or who was President when Poe joined the staff of *Graham's Magazine*. It is for the benefit of readers like him that we included small amounts of information which other readers will find unnecessary.

Acknowledgements

During the past eight years a large number of people, scholars, colleagues, librarians, and students have helped us on this edition. We thank them all.

The heaviest burden has fallen upon Carol Boner, our editor at Bobbs-Merrill. She has toiled intelligently on this work for nearly three years. Although we have never met her, we wish to express our gratitude at least this way.

Many Poe scholars helped in various ways, but our indebtedness to Burton Pollin is especially deep. He not only gave important encouragement, injecting his enthusiasm into our project, he also volunteered a number of not-yet-published articles filled with new information we would not have found otherwise, and obtained permission for their use from the scholarly magazines in which they were later published.

Our bibliography identifies the scholars whose works on Poe we used. We have tried to pull together all the fugitive explications we could. Eric Carlson and G. R .Thompson must be thanked especially for their service in keeping Poe specialists in touch with one another, Carlson through correspondence and Thompson through his good journal, *Poe Studies.*

Others helped in specialized ways: Tom Worthen, on Greek and Latin quotations and allusions; Kenneth Rothwell, on "Pop" Emmons; Annamaria Kelley, on Italian; Harold Orel, on Irish dialect; Rabbi Robert Sachs, on Poe's Hebrew; John Whelan of the Seward Observatory and N. S. Hetherington of the University of Kansas, on astronomy; James Seaver, who produced scores and rare recordings of seldom-performed operas; William Pozefsky, for errands in the New York Public Library; Alexandra Mason, who corrected a reading error and aided us in obtaining one of the illustrations; Martin Bailey of The University of London Library, and Frances Wood of the British Museum staff.

Many librarians helped us explicate specific items, but we owe very special thanks to Patricia Turner (now on the library staff of the University of Minnesota), who was in charge of the Humanities Reference Room at the University of Arizona during SGL's tenure as scholar-in-residence there. A masterly scholarly tactician, she repeatedly contributed new angles of approach when information proved elusive. In truth, the entire library staff at Tucson was wonderful, and we direct another special thanks to John C. McKay, the Inter-Library Loan librarian who continued to help us after we had left the university.

The staffs of other libraries we used, too: Watson and Spencer Libraries at The University of Kansas; the Kennedy Library at California State College, Los Angeles; the UCLA Library; and the Benjamin Franklin Library in Mexico City. Extra gratitude to the staff of the microfilm collection at Watson Library and to Barbara Jones of the reference staff. Lewis Armstrong of the Map Collection staff of Spencer Research Library labeled the maps which are reproduced in this edition, and drew those which are original. Herbert Friedson helped by preparing several sketches.

Donna Schafer, Mary Jane Harmon, and Nancy Reichley, student assistants, made useful contributions in the early stages of the work.

For permission to reprint works in their collections, we thank the Yale University Art Gallery, Leonard C. Hanna, Jr. Fund; the Wadsworth Atheneum, Hartford, Ella Gallup Sumner and Mary Catlin Sumner Collections; the American Antiquarian Society, Worcester, Massachusetts; the British Museum; the New York Public Library; and Spencer Research Library of The University of Kansas, the Summerfield Collection. Detailed acknowledgements appear with the plates.

Friends in Mexico helped, too: Cathy and Wayne Siewert, and Ainslie Minor of the American Embassy.

SGL owes thanks, also, to the administrators of the General Research Fund of The University of Kansas, who have several times supported his work on Poe.

Most important, of course, are our scholarly debts; their nature and our system of acknowledgements are explained in the Bibliography.

Introduction:
The New Image of Poe

> History . . . is like those waterholes I have heard of in the wilds of Africa: the most various beasts may drink there side by side with equal nourishment.
>
> John Barth, *The Sot-Weed Factor*

There is much truth in what cynical Henry Burlingame says in Mr. Barth's novel, and it is as true of literary as of social and political history. Surely we remake the past to suit our own needs, waving authors like flags to symbolize our positions, stressing those of their characteristics which we need to have stressed.

But having conceded that literary scholars are no more unbiased observers of the past than are historians, it is important—and reassuring—to note also that there are times when our image of an author or of the past changes because of completely new information. Such is the case for Edgar Poe. The old image of Poe, however, has been slow to disappear. It has a strong hold on the popular imagination; though the facts which should alter it have been known for three decades, it is still with us. So we should begin by looking squarely at it, and then turn to see what has happened to make it implausible.

The Edgar Poe of the old image was easy to visualize: a creepy chap, somewhere in an attic, bats flapping about his head as he sits at his desk, writing. A candle sputters in a wine bottle, perhaps, casting shadows which magnify his size on the cobwebby walls and ceiling. A second bottle on the cluttered desk holds unwholesome-looking liquor. He drinks, coughs, cackles, and writes a line. A gust of wind through the cracked panes of a small window almost extinguishes the candle, then a flash of weird lightning strays from cloud to moving cloud in the stormy sky, and in the unnatural and fitfully sustained brilliance we catch a glimpse of the maddened and eager eyes of the dope addict as he takes a shot of opium, morphine, laudanum, hashish, who-knows-what. He writes another line.

His personal life too has come down to us in images which remind us of late-night T.V. We imagine his chamber: the door opens quietly, and a young girl, hardly a teen-ager, enters. She would be beautiful were not her eyes so round and vacant, and were she not nervously chewing upon a knuckle. Sensing her, the man at the desk turns, and the look of crazed inspiration changes to one of perverted but calculating lust.

As for the relation of the writer to the bustling young republic in which he lived? Some of the most time-worn clichés about the artist in America were applied to Poe. One almost feels that Poe's career, as popularly understood, helped create those clichés. Agony is the key word—the agony of the possessed and sensitive genius, mistreated and misunderstood in the market-place world of an aggressively materialistic vulgar democracy.

The writings themselves were used to document aspects of the strange personality. It was as though every word Poe uttered had come from a patient on the psychiatrist's couch, compulsively pouring out accounts of the spectres which haunted him.

But in the past few decades, new information about Poe has drastically altered the image of Poe in which most literary historians believed. For brevity let us list the key factors which have changed the picture:

1. There is a traditional kind of literary scholarship, called "source studies," in which scholars endeavor to identify works which have influenced authors. Modern source studies of Poe begin to appear in significant numbers in the thirties, and their production accelerates through the following decades. Many source studies are not the work of Poe specialists; characteristically, an English professor who has been teaching Poe as part of a survey happens upon a passage in another work which he is reading which reminds him forcibly of a Poe story he has just taught. He checks to see what are the chances that Poe knew the work and publishes an article in which he assesses the possibility that the other work influenced Poe. Often he can be certain that it did. These studies reach a number of "peaks"; in several instances, whole issues of scholarly journals are given over to them. Finally, there appear on the scene Poe specialists who produce books devoted entirely to source studies, the most notable being *Discoveries in Poe* by Burton Pollin.

Source studies play a respectable role in developing an understanding of literary relationships, but they are, in the case of most authors, of little concern to the non-specialist reader. Poe's case, however, is different. For him they have very important implications, for they convince us that we must discard the familiar idea that Poe wrote "by compulsion." Whatever psychological reasons he may have had for choosing his subjects, forty years of carefully documented source studies establish that Poe's material is not original with him. We know now that Poe's experience with literature and sub-literature is so extensive that the word "immersion" is not too strong to describe it. He read contemporary fiction, good and bad, major and minor works of the more or less recent past, famous and obscure pieces from classical antiquity, and, above all, the British and American magazines of his own era.

We know further that Poe not only knew these works, but systematically went to them for story ideas. While it is true that a man who deals repeatedly with such a macabre subject as burial alive must in some sense be fascinated by it, we see now that Poe's contribution was not the discovery of the psychologically revealing subject, but rather its utilization in a series of carefully-crafted stories. Today we feel that Poe was a far more conscious and methodical a craftsman than we used to think. And this is perfectly congruent with the new things we know about his biography.

2. The scholars in various American universities currently working on Poe like one another, stay in contact with one another's research and criticism, and cooperate admirably. If this seems like a strange factor to mention in a list of important events which have changed our picture of Poe, bear in mind that we understand an author largely in terms of the ways in which "authorities" present him to us. It is embarrassing to report that until quite recently, Poe scholars had a deserved bad reputation for irascibility, mutual hostility and jealousy. They quarreled about who had the right to use given letters or manuscripts and deliberately hid information from one another. The late Thomas Ollive Mabbott told me about one otherwise good scholar who was doing important biographical work on Poe but who refused to use crucial evidence which strengthened his own case simply because doing so would involve his acknowledging the work of a colleague whom he did not like! So far as we know, that kind of nonsense has ceased. One of the reasons that we now have a saner view of Poe is that we have saner people working on him.

Even a casual examination of this edition of Poe's stories will reveal the extent to which we were aided by other Poe scholars, and our pleasant experience is by no means isolated. When Eric Carlson did a good edition of selected portions of Poe's works in 1967, he wrote to us and to other Poe scholars for ideas and suggestions. There is even a well-edited *Poe Newsletter* and an affiliated small journal, *Poe Studies*, which scholars interested in Poe use to communicate with one another. All of this means that one is less likely today to read a book or an article about Poe written by someone whose effort to understand Poe is undermined by his desire to make his scholarly rivals appear fools.

3. In 1941, Arthur Hobson Quinn published the first really reliable biography of Poe. Quinn, with some help from others, had cracked a spectacular literary fraud. Shortly before his death, Poe had told Maria ("Muddy") Clemm that in the event of his death she should take his literary remains to the Reverend Rufus Griswold, who would then serve as his literary executor. Muddy followed Poe's instructions. A year after Poe's death, Griswold began to bring out an edition of Poe's works on which all subsequent editions have, to a large extent, been founded. More than any other single factor, the biographical material in the Griswold edition created the image of the creepy fellow in the attic. The Quinn biography of 1941 demonstrated that Griswold, who had a serious grudge against Poe, had altered facts, lied, forged, tinkered with documents, and, in general, done everything in his power to present an image of Edgar Poe so totally unwholesome yet so plausible that Poe's reputation would never recover. The appearance of the Quinn biography should have discouraged foolish speculation about the sleazy side of Poe's life. That it failed to do so was perhaps the result of its unreliability in other ways: it pur-

ported to be a "critical biography," but the criticism struck most readers as so silly and naive that for some it may have destroyed the credibility of an otherwise very good book.

What Quinn showed was that while we could not prove, for example, that Poe was not a drug addict and an alcoholic, we could not prove that he was, either. Corroborating evidence such as the tremendous volume of work which Poe turned out throughout the years in which, supposedly, he was consistently drugged or inebriated, suggested a very different picture of the man. Quinn figured, on the basis of fairly good evidence, that Poe probably was one of those fellows who shouldn't drink, and who know it—people who begin to behave badly after just a drink or two, and who, therefore, like the vengeful dwarf in the tale "Hop-Frog," make a point of staying away from alcohol. Quinn couldn't prove this, but, again, the other evidence suggests that his guess is reasonable.

4. About the best thing that one could say, years ago, about Poe's relationships with his contemporaries in the literary world of the 1830s and 40s was that perhaps Poe behaved badly because he knew that making himself notorious was good for the circulation of the magazines for which he worked and helped him sell stories to the others. There is no question, by the way, that Poe understood that perfectly well; it is one important reason behind his contentiousness as a critic. But in the last ten or fifteen years a series of books directed at precisely this problem has shown us another dimension.

That Poe was terribly insecure in his craft is true. That some of the fights he picked were unjust is as clear now as it was forty years ago, or a hundred and forty years ago. But for the most part, Poe now appears as champion of higher literary standards than were then prevalent in the American literary world, and for the most part the battles which he waged seem honorable. Caught in a dreadful system in which editors of magazines praised one another's books in advance of publication in order to persuade publishers to take them, Poe tried hard to fight back in the name of purely artistic standards. One can't entirely blame the editors and authors: the United States had not yet ratified the international copyright agreement, and so publishers could simply print English or continental works by established authors without paying a cent in royalty. They were only willing to risk publication of an American book when there was fair assurance that its first edition would sell quite well; the only way to be sure of that was to have the book "puffed" in literary magazines before its publication. And the only way to get one's book "puffed" in that manner was to have good relations with the editors of magazines, or to own a magazine oneself, so that one could swap "puffs" with one's friendly rivals, the proprietors of other journals.

Related to this line of investigation has been a good deal of solid scholarship devoted to specific literary relationships, notorious bits of literary gossip, now mostly forgotten but important at the time, and to the history of American and English magazines and to some extent even newspapers. In the case of most authors, such information would probably be of interest only to scholars and specialists. But Poe is peculiar in that such relatively small-scale events and relationships are the real raison d'être of a good many of his short stories. British magazinists filled *Fraser's, Blackwood's,* and other magazines with ironic, whimsical, sometimes bitter, but always witty editorial dialogue, difficult to follow unless one reads it habitually, but engrossing and entertaining for *aficionados.* Poe often wrote as though his readers were familiar with it all; he entered into the banter as though he were on the staff of one of the Edinburgh journals. The point of many a Poe story will escape every reader who is not either immersed in such material or briefed on it as he reads. The notes and section prefaces of this edition are designed to provide the necessary briefing.

We have a certain amount of sympathy with the familiar student complaint, "You're criticizing this story to death—why not just let us read it?" In the case of most authors, that makes some sense—either the works can stand on their own, or we should probably not bother reading them anymore. But a great many Poe stories can be understood only in the context in which they were written. Present a bright reader with a story such as "A Tale of Jerusalem" and he will come away puzzled; it seems to be a rather offensive and pointless anecdote. Show him, on the other hand, the four-volume bestseller of which it is, in effect, a sort of condensed collage, and he sees the story as hilarious. Similarly, "The Duc De L'Omelette" does not mean very much as a "story" in the usual sense. The reader briefed on the peculiarities of style of a well-known American editor of the day, however, can see what Poe is about and perhaps enjoy the tale.

5. And this brings us to the major revision in our image of Poe as an artist. The line between Poe's so-called "major" and "minor" fiction is becoming increasingly blurred. It used to seem fairly clear that the important works were those most frequently anthologized. Among the short stories, this meant those with the most spectacular theatrical effects and the most macabre subjects. Attention is now being paid to stories which, for example, deal with the strange subjects, but which are relatively cool in tone, a coolness which suggests more artistic detachment than the image of the madman in the garret would allow.

Moreover, as we come to understand it, Poe's satirical fiction seems more important. We see Poe playing with ideas, associations, and language itself not only for satirical purposes but also for the pure joy of creative play. He seems, in these stories, a nineteenth-century precursor not merely of detective stories, science fiction, and the cult of the macabre, but also of major works built on comparable "association" and creative play, by authors such as James Joyce and the popular Latin American writer Julio Cortázar, who, not surprisingly, did a fairly recent Spanish edition of Poe's tales. To cap the effect goes the discovery that this kind of play goes on not only in those strange satirical stories which until just a very few years ago puzzled critics, but also in many of the most familiar tales as well, until it is impossible to tell when Poe is playing games with us and when he is being serious. Our own feeling is that he is playing games with us almost all the time: the two are not really incompatible.

It is true, on the other hand, that sometimes the games which he plays are so private that only a reader who had been following everything that Poe wrote in the various magazines in which he published in any given period, and who had quite a good idea of everything that Poe had been reading, could understand what some of these tales are about. Perhaps for this reason some of them do deserve to be called "minor," but it is only fair to point out that a writer like Joyce can, at times, be rather "private" as well.

6. Scholars began to notice as early as the 1920s and 30s that there was a surprising measure of philosophical consistency in Poe. In the past couple of decades, specialists in American studies, in comparative literature, and in mythological criticism have begun to teach the more conventionally trained literary critics that the Romantic movement is not merely a rebellion of the heart against the head, but an attempt on the part of artists to recapture the kind of power and centrality which artists in non-Western societies have always enjoyed. We are now beginning to understand that the Romantic age is shot through with seriously held occult beliefs, that artists in that period, and many since then, including a great many important contemporaries in all creative fields, believe seriously that the inspired person is quite literally a creator of truth, whose function, if he is to communicate his ineffable wisdom, will combine the roles of scientist, artist, prophet, magician, and priest. As Patrick Quinn suggested, a major reason for the French enthusiasm for Poe which has long puzzled Americans was that many French artists were deeply involved in just this sort of mystical or occult belief, and thought they heard in Poe an inspired voice.

We are all to a great extent children of the Enlightenment and of rationalism in general, and it is difficult for us to take seriously a world-view alien to rationalism. Poe and many other romantic authors were not merely extolling the "irrational" to redress a balance. They were reaffirming a philosophy much older than rationalism. We call it "occultism," and, being rationalists, refuse to take it seriously even when the artists we admire—Melville and the early T. S. Eliot, for instance—say that it is as reputable as any philosophy, or when others—Blake, Shelley, Poe, Emerson, Whitman, many abstract expressionist painters, to name a few—tell us that it is the true view and the one in which they believe.

Perhaps some of these artists don't really believe in it. But they say they do, and some, like Poe, produce much of their art within the context of an occult world-view. To an occultist, the world is alive, sacred, and an organic whole. The Western rational tradition of analysis and specialization is felt to be evil; it compartmentalizes men into professions and sees the world as a series of subdivisions. Art becomes just one more subdivision, and the artist just a specialist producing a commodity, nice to have around, good for the prestige of the community or nation, entertaining and even inspiring if one likes his work, but not really essential. To an occultist, there are no divisions, and the artist cannot be separated from the scientist, the seer, the prophet. He is more like the tribal medicine-man than the writer-in-residence.

Whether or not we choose to take occultism seriously as a viable philosophy for ourselves is less important than our willingness to recognize some simple facts: the occult world-view is, as Poe tells us, as respectable in terms of intellectual history as is any other, and it is by far the most important world-view in terms of longevity or numbers of adherents.

There can be no doubt that Poe understood it fully. One can debate the extent of his commitment to it because sometimes he directs his satire at it. But if we are to take him at his word, he is an occult artist. His longest work, *Eureka*, is literally an attempt to write occult scripture, and the majority of his tales can be seen as enactments of the nature of perceiving the complex and *outré* patterns and associations which he believed led to the core of reality. Our guess is that Poe learned this way of looking at the world quite early in his life. One has only to look at the writings of his favorite classical philosophers to see how explicitly it is spelled out in their works, and at Poe's own writings to see how consistently he refers to them approvingly. We feel that he learned more and more about the mystical underside of Romanticism through the early Romantic writers he knew so intimately, and it is our educated guess that by the last few years of his life, these beliefs constituted his personal and philosophical faith.

In the new picture of Poe, then, the career is no longer an object lesson in the sterility of the American environment. The personal life is a shade less scandalous, but, if anything, more ambiguous because firm evidence of lurid behavior has largely been discredited. We see far stronger ties to his place and age than we used to; we see somewhat less "mad genius" and somewhat more "commercial craftsman." More wit, erudition, and philosophical consistency are evident in the new Poe, and far less compulsion. If we cannot entirely do away with the popular image of guttering candles and circling bats, in short, we should at least be able to point to craftsmanship, detachment, and humor.

Poe's Early Years

Of the general outlines of Poe's life, we have passably good records. We are certain that he was born to David and Elizabeth Poe on or about January 19, 1809. Theatrical records give us a fair feeling for the careers of his actor father and actress mother. If we are not sure of the exact house in which the Poe family lived at that time of Edgar's birth, we are sure of the neighborhood in Boston, between the Common and the Charles River.

Similar records tell us that at the time Poe was nine months old, the family had moved to New York. We know that hard times awaited his family in the new city, in part probably because of his father's limitations as an actor and as a man. We also know that after Mrs. Poe left New York, she acted in a great number of plays in various cities of the South. By then she had appar-

ently separated from David, and was herself in increasingly ill health. Edgar
was not quite two years old when, on December 18, 1811, Elizabeth Arnold
Poe died. She was all of twenty-four. The toddling young Eddie was placed, a
few days later, with Mr. and Mrs. John Allan, and his baby sister Rosalie
went to another Richmond family. His grandfather David Poe took charge of
Edgar's older brother William.

By a stroke of scholarly good luck, it happens that the first reliable biography of Poe was written by a man who was also an authority on the American theater. With a good feel for what the stage was like in America in those
days, Arthur Hobson Quinn concluded that Poe's father must have been
somewhat more talented than we had previously thought: he was simply
given far too many important roles during his six years on the stage to have
been a really weak actor. There was apparently a commanding stage presence,
and if David Poe, Jr., was sometimes nasty as a person, temperamentally unreliable, and at least to an extent alcoholic, there seems to have been enough
discipline in his character to enable him to learn a very great number of difficult roles. The picture we get of his wife is more attractive: a perky and talented little lady who delighted audiences in comic roles and could sing, but
who was also given a wide variety of serious parts. The extent to which Poe's
infant years with such parents shaped his personality has intrigued biographers, as has the possibility that his supposed weakness for alcohol might also
be hereditary. But that's all speculation.

Then come the years with Mr. and Mrs. John Allan in Richmond. In the
old picture of Poe, the childhood years were miserable. Poe's biographers por-
trayed a sensitive and lonely child bullied by an aggressively domineering
foster father whose only real interest was in his business as a merchant. We
now see some far more agreeable things about John Allan, whose letters are
surprisingly witty, who harbored ambitions to be a writer, who really liked
children, and who, so far as recent biographers have determined, accepted the
young Poe generously into his household.

Thirty-four days of the summer of 1815 young Edgar and the Allan family
spent on board ship enroute to England. Although Poe frequently hinted that
he had made other trips to Europe later in his life, this is the only one the
biographers have been able to document and is probably his only foreign experience. These were bad years for the Allan family. England was suffering a
postwar depression, Mrs. Allan was ill, and John Allan's business affairs did
not seem to have been going very well. But the Allans took good care of Poe,
so far as we can tell from the records of the schools he attended. Indeed, the
Reverend John Bransby, whose name Poe used decades later in his tale "William Wilson," reported (perhaps inaccurately) that the Allans tended to spoil
young Edgar.

The Allan family was back in the United States in late July of 1820. There
are indications in the second Richmond period of increasing unhappiness in
the household; Quinn is fairly certain that Poe must have known of his foster
father's infidelity. There is also the hazy matter of Poe's early romantic at-
tachments. We think it is fair enough to say of these and of his later liaisons

with women other than his wife that the evidence is so hazy we had best not jump to conclusions. Our guess is that all of these were nothing more than relatively innocent romantic and sentimental liaisons. A good account of them all appears in Chapter Five of Edward Wagenknecht's biography of Poe. This sensible writer gives samples of the prose of Poe's letters to his ladies, what facts we have, some speculations about Poe's possible motivations, and leaves matters up to the reader's judgment.

As for Poe's education, all the firm evidence we have today suggests that he was a far better student than we used to think. The Reverend Bransby spoke respectfully if somewhat inaccurately of Poe's early accomplishments, and his records at the University of Virginia and at West Point are really quite distinguished up to the point, in both cases, at which his personal situation became so decidedly uncomfortable that his classwork began to deteriorate. Certainly the evidence of his erudition which we encountered in preparing this edition is far more impressive than we had been led to believe. Though some of the learning is faked, most is not. Indeed, some of the faking is learned: Poe read widely to bluff so well.

The University of Virginia, was, in 1826, in only its second year of operation, and it may be that it has never since been as illustrious a school as then: Thomas Jefferson had not only designed the famous campus and practically invented the American state university, he had hand-picked the faculty. Poe's professors were good men, and they liked him.

Just how extravagant Poe was late in his University of Virginia career is not clear. It seems reasonable to speculate, with Poe's best biographers, that he had been brought up to think of himself as something of an aristocrat and that his growing disillusionment with Allan, and Allan's with him, made his foster father unwilling to continue to finance his education and, perhaps, to pay his gambling debts.

At any rate, in 1827 Poe made his way to Boston, in which city he may or may not have made an attempt to pursue a theatrical career. Unhappy days for the college dropout, apparently: he arrived in Boston in April 1827 and enlisted in the army on May 26, lying about his name and age in an apparent effort, as Quinn put it, "to disappear." The summer of 1827 marks the appearance of *Tamerlane and Other Poems* "by a Bostonian." From November 18 until December 11, 1828, he was stationed at Fort Moultrie on the Sullivan's Island which he was to use as the setting for "The Gold-Bug." His artillery battery was transferred to Fortress Monroe in Virginia in mid-December.

The stereotyped Edgar Poe of the older portrait would have been totally miserable in the army, and there is plenty of evidence that by late 1828 Poe wanted out. But it is worth considering that his army career seems to have been completely successful: on New Year's Day of 1829 he was promoted to "sargeant-major." There are some gaps in the record from this period until Poe's appointment in March 1830 to the military academy at West Point. The most important event of these months is the publication of *Al Aaraaf, Tamerlane, and Minor Poems* in 1829. We do know that John Allan forwarded a little more money in response to pleading letters from Poe, but it is the appointment to West Point which interests us most, for it seems strong evidence of a certain amount of conventional solidity in Poe's personality in these years. Apparently his record as an enlisted man in the army was more than respectable, and he seems to have impressed people in positions of power, this despite the rather lukewarm manner in which Allan referred to him whenever Poe wrote to his foster father for letters of recommendation.

Poe's famous departure from West Point is still somewhat puzzling because we lack facts, but biographers can speculate intelligently on what must have happened. Poe may have been drinking, and he may have run up some "gentlemanly debts," but probably just as important was his impatience with the pettiness and routine of a military education. For Poe, already a published poet (if an obscure one) and an army veteran—a top sergeant at that—this side of life at the Point might have seemed especially annoying. Unable to resign because Allan would not give his consent, unable to remain because Allan stopped paying his bills, Poe apparently set about deliberately getting himself expelled. At any rate, he was indeed court-martialed, and he left West Point on February 19, 1831. The older picture of Poe makes us want to think of him as a sensitive and brooding youngster who must have been terribly isolated from what we imagine to have been the earthier and "more normal" cadets at the Point, but the evidence suggests some popularity: his classmates banded together to raise a small sum of money to aid him in the publication of another volume of poems; in April 1831 *Poems by Edgar A. Poe, Second Edition* appeared.

This brings us to the end of what old-fashioned biographers used to call "the formative years." From then until his death in 1849, Poe was continually involved in the literary or sub-literary world of the American magazines. On June 4, 1831, the *Philadelphia Saturday Courier* announced a short story contest, which Poe entered. He failed to win the prize, but had the pleasure of seeing all five of the tales which he submitted printed during the course of 1832: "Metzengerstein," "The Duc De L'Omelette," "A Tale of Jerusalem," "A Decided Loss" ("Loss of Breath"), and "The Bargain Lost" ("Bon-Bon"). The June 15, 1833 issue of the *Baltimore Saturday Visiter* announced another contest; Poe entered again, and this time won. So far as we know, this is the first significant remuneration Poe had received for his efforts as a writer, and from this time forward, it is necessary to think of him as a commercial author trying to make a living with his pen through the medium of the various literary and general magazines, gift books, ladies' books, annuals, gentlemen's magazines, and occasionally, sporting periodicals and humor magazines which were his market.

From about this time also we must date the beginning of Poe's long close association with his aunt, Mrs. Maria Clemm, an association which eventually led to Poe's marrying her daughter Virginia on May 16, 1836. However much modern biographers have been able to "normalize" Poe's biography, there is no getting around the fact that his wife was just thirteen. Freudian scholars speculate luridly about the significance of Poe's marrying a little girl, and they're quite certain that Poe was, at the very least, impotent. It is possible that Poe married Virginia in order to provide himself with some of the comforts of married life without being expected to perform sexually. One can, however, maintain quite the reverse, or that he married Virginia because he was a lecher. Some argue that marriages of very young girls were less uncommon in this period than they are today. The argument is not strong, first because recent studies show that Americans as a whole do not marry later than their ancestors did, and second, because extremely early marriage was certainly not normal in any of the urban social circles with which Poe was in contact. There certainly is something in Quinn's suggestions that Poe married Virginia in order to put his relationship with Mrs. Clemm on a firm and permanent footing.

Poe apparently needed a certain amount of mothering and the stability of an established household; these things Muddy Clemm could provide. What was the precise nature of his feelings toward his young cousin we shall never know. Affection was clearly there, and pity, too, though of exactly what sort we can't be sure. The more sensational biographers of Poe tell us that Virginia was mentally retarded. But there is conflicting testimony as well: some of the visitors to the little house in Fordham spoke very favorably of Virginia and of the household and gave no evidence at all that she was in any way mentally incompetent. There is, moreover, a charming little valentine which she wrote to her husband in 1846. It is by no means great poetry, but hardly the work, either, of a half-wit. The poem is an acrostic; the first letter of the lines spell "EDGAR ALLAN POE." If, as one of my students noticed, Virginia's poem "doesn't scan," that is less proof of mental incompetence than of the indisputable fact that being married to a poet does not make one a poetess. Remember, too, that Virginia was no longer a little girl by that time; she was a young woman old enough, in our day, to have graduated from college.

The Professional Years

For our purposes, facts about Poe's adult and professional years which seem most important can be summarized quickly:

1. Poe seems constantly under financial pressure. To some extent we have this impression because of the evidence of his correspondence: He does not write a letter to a friend to say, "My wife, my aunt, and I have enough money this month to get along." The letters come when things get tight. We would guess that there were times when Poe was less strapped, but there is no denying his poverty.

2. Even today, relatively few "serious" authors make a good living en-

tirely through writing. They teach, they lecture, they have other jobs or money in the family. A modicum of tact and perseverance on Poe's part would have given him the financial underpinning he needed. Other men of modest origins were able to support themselves *and* to write. Even Poe's dream of owning a good magazine could have been realized: a couple of hundred dollars was all it took to found a journal, and Poe, who had a superb sense of how to build circulation without printing trash, could have made one successful. A man of his ability and education could have readily amassed the cash and credit needed to commence operations. Doing so might have required a few months of nonliterary endeavor. Certainly work was available; even during depressions, Poe, for all his reputation for unreliability, was able to find editorial posts, one of them reasonably lucrative. Most people would have known what to do and could have done it without compromising ideals or standards. Poe, so bright in other ways, seems never to have faced the simplest of economic truths.

3. This is not to say Poe was lazy. He ground out great quantities of copy, some of very high quality. Almost all of it gives evidence of what one writer called firm intellectual control. All of this creative energy could have produced a great magazine. Poe never got it focused; to change our image, he never did the necessary spadework first. Even *The Broadway Journal*, the one periodical he came to control, could have been made into the magazine he wanted: he was very famous during the year in which he became its proprietor, and, with a little tact and patience, could have established it solidly and *then* used it as a medium not only for fine fiction, poetry, criticism, and reviews, but also for an attack on the very real abuses of the petty New York literary establishment. Instead he wasted energy in unjust attacks on the innocent—especially Longfellow—failed to "mind the store," and lost it within a year.

4. Many of the people around him were snakes, but others were men and women of high ideals. Their talents were not always contemptible. Many were kind to Poe—aware of his ability, tolerant of his weaknesses, and eager to see him prosper and produce good work. His inability to hold his liquor undoubtedly was part of his problem; the solution, as he well knew, was abstinence, even at the literary receptions which seem to have overwhelmed him following the publication of "The Raven." His lack of tact and social maturity are more important aspects of the same problem. However unsure we are today of the biography, we are certain that we are dealing with a weak man. His failure to flourish cannot be blamed simply on "the American environment."

Major events in Poe's career from the time his publications commence are listed in the accompanying chart. Readers interested in the details of his life should look at the Wagenknecht or A. H. Quinn biographies listed in the Bibliography; for details of his professional life and his literary battles, the two Moss volumes and the books by Jacobs and Michael Allen are cordially recommended. Moss, Jacobs, and Allen are far more reliable in their coverage of literary wars than is A. H. Quinn.

FIGURE ONE. MAJOR EVENTS IN POE'S PROFESSIONAL YEARS

1827 Personal: Poe is in Richmond after leaving the University of Virginia. His engagement to Sarah Elmira Royster is broken. Goes to Boston; enlists in Army.
Publication: *Tamerlane and Other Poems*

1828 Personal: In Army.

1829 Personal: Frances (Mrs. John) Allan dies. Poe leaves Army.
Publication: *Al Aaraaf, Tamerlane and Minor Poems.*

1830 Personal: John Allan marries second wife. Poe enters West Point.

1831 Personal: Poe departs from West Point, lives in New York, and then lives with the Clemms in Baltimore. Virginia Clemm is 8. Poe tries to get teaching job. His brother Henry Poe dies. Poe enters the *Courier* contest.
Publication: *Poems* ("Second Edition").

1832 Publications: *Courier* tales: "Metzengerstein," "The Duc De L'Omelette," "A Tale of Jerusalem," "A Decided Loss" ("Loss of Breath"), and "The Bargain Lost" ("Bon-Bon").

1833 Personal: Poe wins *Visiter* prize. He tries to sell "Epimanes" ("Four Beasts in One") and other "Tales of the Arabesque." His friendship with John Pendleton Kennedy begins.
Publication: "MS. Found in a Bottle."

1834 Personal: John Allan dies.
Publication: "The Visionary" ("The Assignation").

1835 Personal: Poe makes another attempt to obtain a teaching job. He writes a desperate letter to Muddy and Virginia Clemm. He brings them to Richmond.
Editorial: With Kennedy's help, Poe gets *Southern Literary Messenger* job in Richmond.
Publications: portions of *Politian* (a poetic drama set in Italy but based on a famous incident in Kentucky), "Berenice," "Morella," "Hans Pfaall" ("Hans Pfaal"), "Shadow," "King Pest."

1836 Personal: Poe marries Virginia Clemm. Harper & Brothers rejects a book of tales.
Editorial: Poe has troubles with White, the owner of *SLM*. He publishes extensive criticism in *SLM*.
Publication: "Epimanes" ("Four Beasts in One/The Homo-Cameleopard")

1837 Personal: Poe leaves *SLM* and moves to New York, completes *The Narrative of A. Gordon Pym*, but is unable to find good work.
Publications: first chapter of *Pym*, "Von Jung" ("Mystification").

1838 Personal: Poe moves to Philadelphia.
Publications: "Ligeia," "The Psyche Zenobia" ("How to Write a Blackwood Article"), the complete *Pym*.

1839 Editorial: Poe joins *Burton's Gentleman's Magazine* in July.
Publications: "The Man That Was Used Up," "The Fall of the House of Usher," "William Wilson," "The Conversation of Eiros and Charmion," *The Conchologist's First Book*.

1840 Editorial: Poe leaves *Burton's* in May and begins a long series of attempts to found his own magazine. Burton sells out to George R. Graham, who combines *Burton's* with *The Casket*.

Publications: "The Journal of Julius Rodman," "The Philosophy of Furniture," "The Man of the Crowd," *Tales of the Grotesque and Arabesque.*

1841 Editorial: In January, Poe joins the staff of *Graham's Magazine* at $800 per year.
Publications: "The Murders in the Rue Morgue," "A Descent into the Maelström," "The Island of the Fay," "The Colloquy of Monos and Una," and "Eleonora."

1842 Personal: Virginia is ill.
Editorial: Poe leaves *Graham's* in May.
Publications: review of Hawthorne's *Twice-Told Tales,* "The Masque of the Red Death," "The Landscape Garden" ("The Domain of Arnheim"), "The Pit and the Pendulum," "The Mystery of Marie Rogêt" (Nov. and Dec., '42; Feb., '43).

1843 Personal: Poe's "The Gold-Bug" wins the *Dollar Newspaper* contest.
Editorial: Poe negotiates for a position with *The Saturday Museum* but apparently fails to agree to terms.
Publications: "The Tell-Tale Heart," "The Gold-Bug," "The Black Cat," "Raising the Wind" ("Diddling"), *The Prose Romances of EAP.*

1844 Personal: Poe's family moves to New York.
Editorial: Poe joins the staff of the *New York Mirror* in September.
Publications: "The Balloon-Hoax," "A Tale of the Ragged Mountains," "The Premature Burial," "Mesmeric Revelation," "The Oblong Box," "The Purloined Letter," "Thou Art the Man," "The Literary Life of Thingum Bob, Esq."

1845 Personal: Poe gains great fame from "The Raven," first published in the *Evening Mirror,* Jan. 29. In March, he meets Mrs. Frances Osgood and begins a literary flirtation which is made into a scandal by Mrs. Ellet.
Editorial: Poe leaves the *Mirror* in February to join the editorial staff of *The Broadway Journal,* where he continues a literary war with Longfellow begun in the *Mirror.* In July, Poe becomes the sole editor and in October, the proprietor of *The Broadway Journal.* He is listed on the staff of the *Aristidean.*
Publications: "The Raven," "The Power of Words," "The Imp of the Perverse," "The Facts in the Case of M. Valdemar," *Tales,* and *The Raven and Other Poems.*

1846 Personal: Poe moves to the cottage in Fordham. "The Literati" and personal indiscretions ruin his reputation. He receives a sweet and flattering letter from Elizabeth Barrett Browning about his fame in England, and a flattering and friendly letter from Hawthorne. He initiates a civil suit for libel (Poe v. Fuller and Clason) and he gives his famous Boston Lyceum lecture.
Editorial: *The Broadway Journal* dies on January 3. Poe's reviews and criticism appear in *Graham's.*
Publications: "The Literati of New York City," "The Philosophy of Composition," "The Cask of Amontillado."

1847 Personal: Virginia Poe dies. Poe wins his lawsuit and $225 damages. He is at work on *Eureka.*
Publication: "Ulalume." Poe is represented in Griswold's *The Prose Writers of America.*

1848 Personal: Poe allegedly enters into affairs with Mrs. Shew, Mrs. Richmond, and Mrs. Whitman.
Publications: "The Rationale of Verse," *Eureka.*

1849 Personal: Poe dies on October 7, while on a trip to arrange his wedding with Sarah Elmira Royster Shelton.
  Publications: "Hop-Frog," "Von Kempelen and His Discovery," "X-ing a Para-grab," "Landor's Cottage."

1850 Personal: Griswold's forgeries are published in *The Works of the Late Edgar Allan Poe.*
  Publications: "The Poetic Principle" (published posthumously).

The Personality

It is curiously difficult to get close to Americans of Poe's day. One can go back much further in history or come closer to the present and find personalities which, however different from our own, reveal themselves fairly readily. But social historians have trouble with his period, perhaps because the extraordinary economic, social and technological changes which were taking place produced extreme instability. Our literature—possibly for the same reasons—does not give us much sense of social context from the 1820s through mid-century. The novel of social density was not yet on the scene, yet the age of the great diaries was past.

Certainly the personalities of American literary figures of the 1820s, 30s and 40s seem less immediate to us than those of the later century. A scholar who specializes in Washington Irving told me once that after a lifetime of work on Irving he felt less "close" to him than he did to Winthrop, Franklin, Edwards, or to Melville, Whitman, Howells, James—almost any earlier or later figure.

His good biographers seem to have similar problems with Poe; it is not easy to get the fit of his shoes. In an age of people who are hard to come to know, he seems especially difficult and inconsistent. He's insecure in all his roles; he wants to cut a bigger figure than he does, to be wealthy and a literary lion in the eyes of his contemporaries. But he mocks the way to such status and wealth. He's kind, generous, courageous, exceedingly clever, and his mind roams freely and brilliantly over past and present. He's also unreliable and selfish the way only a weak person can be; he's a liar, a plagiarist, a sponge. When embarrassed, he's intolerable and immature. At the height of his public fame and success, he was invited to deliver a lecture in Boston. He faced the prospect in panic, but exactly what occurred in the hall will probably never be known. It upset him so violently that he rushed into print, apparently in a squirming agony of embarrassment, a series of foolish accounts of his behavior and that of the Boston audience in an attempt to rationalize his way out of whatever had transpired.

Poe begs for pity and deserves some. His high literary ideals sometimes got in the way of practical compromises which could have made a hard life more pleasant. But he sometimes violated those ideals, and just as often his trouble stemmed from nonliterary sources. We should not for a moment believe the old French argument that Poe would have been happy had he been born a Frenchman. He would have starved in a garret in Paris as surely as he did in the cottage in Fordham. With a few exceptions, I think his compatriots treated him at least as well as he deserved. He was not a nice person.

He was, moreover, a reactionary, a snob, and a racist whose works give offense to Blacks, to Jews, to American Indian people, to Dutchmen, to Irishmen, to almost anyone who is not Edgar Poe.

Yet his brilliance is indisputable, and his contribution to American and world literature, enormous. The picture of the isolated genius, lonely and misunderstood in a workaday world, however, is nonsense. There never was an author—unless it was Mark Twain—more fascinated by the texture of everyday life in his own time and place and more intrigued by the new science he sometimes mocked, by the new technology he sometimes parodied, by the political scene he lampooned, and by the new wealth he hated and desperately envied.

Stuart Levine

Bibliography

The system of citation used in the notes and section prefaces was designed to provide full bibliographical information without being cumbersome. When we wish to express indebtedness to another scholar, we put his name in parentheses immediately following the information which his work elucidates. Such names appear again here with full citations.

To identify works of scholars who wrote more than one item on our list, we have used a numbering system. Thus "(Pollin 7)" or "(Whipple 2)" in the text refer to the seventh item listed under Burton Pollin's name or the second under William Whipple's in the bibliography.

The peculiarities of Poe's fiction are behind this system. Poe wrote about solving difficult puzzles, but his stories are the most complex puzzles he ever conceived. The tangled and interwoven lines of association which run through them and the thousands of allusions and obscure works which he packed into them must be explained if the reader is to know what Poe is talking about. Most of the sleuthing involved in explication requires highly specialized knowledge. Wherever we could find help in the work of other scholars, we made use of it, and strongly feel that this debt should be acknowledged. Hence our system of citations, which we hope colleagues and readers find acceptable, ethical, and useful.

WORKS ON OR BY POE

Those works on this list which are of general interest to the nonspecialist reader are marked with an asterisk (*). More technical items which we used in locating Poe's references, allusions, and quotations are also included. Further bibliographical information is found in the following works:

Louis Broussard, *The Measure of Poe* contains a sixty-page bibliography.

Eric Carlson, *Introduction to Poe* has a good bibliography which includes many standard discussions of Poe not in our lists.

Esther F. Hyneman, *Edgar Allan Poe: An Annotated Bibliography of Books and Articles in English, 1827–1973*, is large and useful.

Stuart Levine, *Edgar Poe: Seer and Craftsman* contains notes which yield a list heavily slanted to criticism.

Burton Pollin, *Discoveries in Poe* provides much useful information in the notes.

Floyd Stovall, editor, *Eight American Authors* contains a large Poe bibliography compiled by Jay B. Hubbell.

G. R. Thompson, *Poe's Fiction: Romantic Irony in the Gothic Tales* contains very useful notes.

Allen, Hervey. Israfel: *The Life and Times of Edgar Allan Poe.* 2 vols. New York, 1926.   An informative older work, but read A. H. Quinn first.

*Allen, Michael. *Poe and the British Magazine Tradition.* New York, 1969.   One of the good recent works on Poe's intellectual environment.

Bandy, W. T. "More on 'The Angel of the Odd,' " *Poe Newsletter,* III (June 1970), 22.

Barzun, Jacques. "A Note on the Inadequacy of Poe as a Proofreader and of his Editors as French Scholars," *Romantic Review,* LXI (February 1970), 23–27.

Basler, Roy. "Byronism in Poe's 'To One in Paradise,' " *American Literature,* IX (May 1937), 232–236.

Benson, Adolph B. "Scandinavian References in the Works of Poe," *Journal of English and Germanic Philology,* XL (January 1941), 73–90.

Benton, Richard P. (1) "Is Poe's 'The Assignation' a Hoax?" *Nineteenth Century Fiction,* XVIII (September 1963), 193–197.

————. (2) "Poe's 'The System of Dr. Tarr and Prof. Fether': Dickens or Willis?" *Poe Newsletter,* I (April 1968), 7–9.

————. (3) "Poe's 'Lionizing': A Quiz on Willis and Lady Blessington," *Studies in Short Fiction,* V (Spring 1968), 239–244.

————. (4) "Reply to Professor Thompson, " *Studies in Short Fiction,* VI (Fall 1968), 97.

————. (5) "Poe's Acquaintance with Chinese Literature," *Poe Newsletter,* II (April 1969), 14.

Bonaparte, Marie. *The Life and Works of Edgar Allan Poe: A Psycho-Analytical Interpretation.* Translated by John Rodker. London, 1949.   A translation from French of a book from the heyday of Freudian literary studies, 1933.

Broussard, Louis. *The Measure of Poe.* Norman, Okla., 1969.

Campbell, Killis. "Marginalia on Longfellow, Lowell, and Poe," *Modern Language Notes,* XLII (December 1927), 516–521.

Carlson, Eric. (1) *The Recognition of Edgar Allan Poe.* Ann Arbor, Mich., 1966. Reprint (paper), 1970.   An anthology of criticism of Poe from 1829 to present.

*————. (2) *Introduction to Poe: A Thematic Reader,* esp. "Notes to Tales." Glenview, Ill., 1967.   An edition which introduces the reader to the major genres of Poe's work.

Carter, Boyd. "Poe's Debt to Charles Brockden Brown," *Prairie Schooner,* XXVII (Summer 1953), 190–196.

Cherry, Fannye. "The Source of Poe's 'Three Sundays in a Week,' " *American Literature,* II (November 1930), 232–235.

Daughrity, Kenneth L. "Poe's 'Quiz on Willis,' " *American Literature,* V (March 1933), 55–62.

Engstrom, Alfred G. "Chateaubriand's *Itinéraire de Paris à Jerusalem* and Poe's 'The Assignation,' " *Modern Language Notes,* LXIX (November 1954), 506–507.

Fagin, N. Bryllion. *The Histrionic Mr. Poe.* Baltimore, 1949.   Poe as a dramatist of himself.

Forrest, William. *Biblical Allusions in Poe.* New York, 1928.

Glassheim, Eliot. "A Dogged Interpretation of 'Never Bet the Devil Your Head,' " *Poe Newsletter,* II (October 1969), 44–45.

Griffith, Clark. "Poe's 'Ligeia' and the English Romantics," *University of Toronto Quarterly,* XXIV (October 1954), 8–25.

Hall, Thomas. "Poe's Use of a Source," *Poe Newsletter,* I (October 1968), 28.

Hammond, Alexander. "A Reconstruction of Poe's 1833 Tales of the Folio Club," *Poe Studies,* V (December 1972), 25–32.

*Harrison, James A. *The Complete Works of Edgar Allan Poe*. New York, 1902.   The "Virginia" and "New York" edition.

Heartman, Charles and James Canny. *A Bibliography of First Printings of the Writings of Edgar Allan Poe*. Hattiesburg, Mississippi, 1940.   A very valuable work even though it contains minor errors.

Hirsch, David H. "Another Source for Poe's 'The Duc De L'Omelette,' " *American Literature*, XXXVIII (January 1967), 534–536.

Hungerford, Edward. "Poe and Phrenology," *American Literature*, II (November 1930), 209–231.

Jackson, David K. "Poe Notes: 'Pinakidia' and 'Some Ancient Greek Authors,' " *American Literature*, V (November 1933), 258–267.

*Jacobs, Robert D. *Poe: Journalist and Critic*. Baton Rouge, 1969.   Poe in context.

Kaplan, Sidney, ed. *The Narrative of Arthur Gordon Pym*. New York, 1960.   A work containing the famous Poe-as-fundamentalist argument.

King, Lucille. "Notes on Poe's Sources," *University of Texas Studies in English*, X (July 1930), 128–134.

Krappe, Edith S. "A Possible Source for Poe's 'The Tell-Tale Heart' and 'The Black Cat,' " *American Literature*, XII (March 1940), 84–88.

Krutch, Joseph Wood. *Edgar Allan Poe: A Study in Genius*. New York, 1926.   A Freudian reading, intelligent but in need of tempering in the light of more recent data on Poe.

Le Breton, Maurice. "Edgar Poe and Macaulay," *Revue Anglo-Americaine*, XXI (October 1935), 38–42.

Levine, Stuart. (1) "Poe's *Julius Rodman:* Judaism, Plagiarism, and the Wild West," *Midwest Quarterly*, I (Spring 1960), 245–259.

———. (2) "Scholarly Strategy: The Poe Case," *American Quarterly*, XVII (Spring 1965), 133–144.

*———. (3) *Edgar Poe: Seer and Craftsman*. Deland, Fla., 1972.   A critical study of Poe's fiction: structure, philosophy, the magazine environment, the intellectual and scientific environments.

Mabbott, Thomas Ollive. (1) "On Poe's 'Tales of the Folio Club,' " *Sewanee Review*, XXXVI (1928), 171–176.

———. (2) "Origins of 'The Angel of the Odd,' " *Notes & Queries*, CLX (January 1931), 8.

———. (3) "Evidence That Poe Knew Greek," *Notes & Queries*, CLXXXV (July 1943), 39–40.

———. (4) "Poe and Dr. Lardner," *American Notes & Queries*, III (November 1943), 115–117.

———. (5) "The Source of Poe's Motto for the 'Gold-Bug,' " *Notes & Queries*, CXCVIII (February 1953), 68.

———. (6) "Poe's 'The Cask of Amontillado,' " *Explicator*, XXV (November 1966), Item 30.

———. (7) "Poe's 'The Man That Was Used Up,' " *Explicator*, (April 1967), Item 70.

———. (8) "The Books in the House of Usher," *Books at Iowa*, 19 (November 1973).

McCarthy, Kevin M. "Another Source for 'The Raven,' " *Poe Newsletter*, I (October 1968), 29.

McClary, Ben Harris. "Poe's 'Turkish Fig-Pedler,' " *Poe Newsletter*, II (October 1969), 56.

McNeal, Thomas H. "Poe's *Zenobia:* An Early Satire on Margaret Fuller," *Modern Language Quarterly*, XI (June 1950), 205–216.

Miller, Perry. *The Raven and the Whale*. New York, 1956.   A treatment of literary circles in Poe's and Melville's New York. Good in conjunction with the works by Moss and Jacobs.

Mooney, Stephen L. "The Comic in Poe's Fiction," *American Literature*, XXXIII (January 1962), 433–441.

Moore, John Robert. "Poe's Reading of *Anne of Geierstein*," *American Literature*, XXII (January 1951), 493–496.

Moss, Sidney P. (1) "Poe and the Norman Leslie Incident," *American Literature*, XXV (November 1953), 293–306.

————. (2) "Poe and His Nemesis—Lewis Gaylord Clark," *American Literature*, XXVIII (March 1956), 30–46.

*————. (3) *Poe's Literary Battles*. Durham, N. C., 1963.   A very good book. It is difficult to understand the literary world of Poe's America without it.

————. (4) *Poe's Major Crisis*. Durham, N. C., 1970.

Norman, Emma Katherine. "Poe's Knowledge of Latin," *American Literature*, VI (March 1934), 72–77.

Ostrom, John Ward. *The Letters of Edgar Allan Poe*. 2 vols. Cambridge, Mass., 1948.

Pollin, Burton. (1) " 'The Spectacles' of Poe—Sources and Significance," *American Literature*, XXXVIII (May 1965), 185–190.

————. (2) "Bulwer-Lytton and 'The Tell-Tale Heart,' " *American Notes & Queries* (New Haven), IV (September 1965), 7–8.

————. (3) *Dictionary of Names and Titles in Poe's Collected Works*. New York, 1968.   A useful reference tool.

————. (4) "Poe's 'Diddling': The Source of Title and Tale," *The Southern Literary Journal*, II (Fall 1969), 106–111.

*————. (5) *Discoveries in Poe*. Notre Dame, Ind., 1970.   The best of the source studies: not only where Poe got ideas, but how his mind worked.

————. (6) "Poe's Dr. Ollapod," *American Literature*, XLII (March 1970), 80–82.

————. (7) "Figs, Bells, Poe, and Horace Smith," *Poe Newsletter*, III (June 1970), 8–10.

————. (8) "Poe's 'Some Words with a Mummy' Reconsidered," *Emerson Society Quarterly*, No. 60 (Fall 1970), 60–67.

————. (9) "Poe's Use of Material from Bernardin de Saint-Pierre's *Etudes*," *Romance Notes*, XII (Summer 1971), 1–8.

————. (10) "Politics and History in Poe's 'Mellonta Tauta,' " *Studies in Short Fiction*, VIII (Fall 1971), 627–631.

————. (11) "Poe's Literary Use of 'Oppodeldoc' and Other Patent Medicines," *Poe Newsletter*, IV (December 1971), 30–32.

————. (12) "Poe's Tale of Psyche Zenobia: A Reading for Humor and Ingenious Construction." Pp. 92–103 in *Papers on Poe*, ed. Richard Veler. Springfield, Ohio, 1972.

————. (13) "Poe and Thomas Moore," *Emerson Society Quarterly*, No. 63 (June 1972), 166–173.

————. (14) "Poe's 'Mystification': Its Source in Fay's *Norman Leslie*," *Mississippi Quarterly*, XXV (Spring 1972), 111–130.

Posey, Meredith Neill. "Notes on Poe's 'Hans Pfaall,' " *Modern Language Notes*, XLV (December 1930), 501–507.

*Quinn, Arthur Hobson. *Edgar Allan Poe: A Critical Biography*. New York, 1941.   A work critically naive, but biographically indispensable: the book that cracked the Griswold forgery.

*Quinn, Patrick F. *The French Face of Edgar Poe*. Carbondale, Ill., 1957.   Good answers to the old question, "What do the French see in Poe?"

*Rans, Geoffrey. *Edgar Allan Poe*. Edinburgh and London, 1965.

Rein, David. *Edgar Allan Poe: The Inner Pattern*. New York, 1960.   A psychological study of Poe, similar to those of the 1920s and early 1930s, yet with some good insights.

Reiss, Edmund. "The Comic Setting of 'Hans Pfaall,' " *American Literature*, XXIX (November 1957), 306–309.

Richard, Claude. "Arrant Bubbles: Poe's 'The Angel of the Odd,' " *Poe Newsletter*, II (October 1969), 46–48.

Robbins, J. A. "The Poe 'Dictionary,' " *Poe Newsletter*, II (April 1969), 38–39.   Review of Burton Pollin's *Dictionary*. . . .

Rothwell, Kenneth. "A Source for the Motto to Poe's 'William Wilson,' " *Modern Language Notes*, LXXIV (April 1959), 297–298.

St. Armand, Barton Levi. "Usher Unveiled: Poe and the Metaphysic of Gnosticism," *Poe Studies*, V (June 1972), 1–8.

Schuster, Richard. "More on the 'Fig-Pedler,' " *Poe Newsletter*, III (June 1970), 22.

Scudder, Harold H. "Poe's 'Balloon-Hoax,' " *American Literature*, XXI (May 1949), 179–190.

Stovall, Floyd, ed. (1) *Eight American Authors*. New York, 1963.   Contains a forty-seven page bibliography on Poe by Jay B. Hubbell.

———. (2) *The Poems of Edgar Allan Poe*. Charlottesville, Va., 1965.   The best texts of Poe's poems.

Thompson, G. R. (1) "On the Nose—Further Speculation on the Sources and Meaning of Poe's 'Lionizing,' " *Studies in Short Fiction*, VI (Fall 1968), 94–96.

———. (2) "Poe's 'Flawed' Gothic: Absurdist Techniques in 'Metzengerstein' and the *Courier* Satires," *Emerson Society Quarterly*, No. 60 (Fall 1970), 38–58.

———. (3) "Poe and 'Romantic Irony.' " Pp. 28–41 in *Papers on Poe*, ed. Richard Veler. Springfield, Ohio, 1972.

*———. (4) *Poe's Fiction: Romantic Irony in the Gothic Tales*. Madison, Wis., 1973.

Turner, Arlin. "Sources of Poe's 'A Descent into the Maelström,' " *The Journal of English and Germanic Philology*, XLVI (July 1947), 298–301.

Varner, Cornelia. "Notes on Poe's Use of Contemporary Materials in Certain of His Stories," *The Journal of English and Germanic Philology*, XXXII (January 1933), 77–80.

Veler, Richard, ed. *Papers on Poe: Essays in Honor of John Ward Ostrom*. Springfield, Ohio: Chantry Music Press at Wittenberg University, 1972.   A collection of varied articles on Poe, very useful as a survey of the current conflicting interpretations of Poe's fiction.

Vierra, Clifford C. "Poe's 'Oblong Box': Factual Origins," *Modern Language Notes*, LXXIV (December 1959), 693–695.

*Wagenknecht, Edward. *Edgar Allan Poe: The Man Behind the Legend*. New York, 1963.   An intelligent and informed brief biography.

Wetzel, George. "The Source of Poe's 'The Man That Was Used Up,' " *Notes & Queries*, CXCVIII (January 1953), 38.

Whipple, William. (1) "Poe's Two-Edged Satiric Tale," *Nineteenth Century Fiction*, IX (September 1954), 121–133.

———. (2) "Poe's Political Satire," *Texas University Studies in English*, XXXV (1956), 81–95.

———. (3) "Poe, Clark, and 'Thingum Bob,' " *American Literature*, XXIX (November 1957), 312–316.

Wilkinson, Ronald Sterne. "Poe's 'Balloon-Hoax' Once More," *American Literature*, XXXII (November 1960), 313–317.

Wilson, James Southall. "The Devil Was In It," *American Mercury*, XXIV (October 1931), 215–220.

Woodberry, George E. *The Life of Edgar Allan Poe*. 2 vols. Boston, 1909.   An older study which is still useful. But check facts against A. H. Quinn or Wagenknecht.

OTHER WORKS UTILIZED

This list does not include standard—or not-so-standard—reference works, although we used such books very heavily. It omits general encyclopedias, dictionaries of various languages, the *OED*, dictionaries of names and guides to biographies, dictionaries of fictional characters, literary histories, encyclopedias of religion, guides to wines, foods, and costume, histories of science, music and the arts, the *Catalogue* of the British Museum, atlases, and gazetteers. It includes some modern works mentioned in notes or section prefaces, those books which enabled us to reconstruct Poe's lines of allusion or association, and certain works which Poe himself used repeatedly and which, we felt, altered our understanding of Poe's intentions. We made no attempt to provide a complete list of works known to have influenced Poe.

Alger, William Rounseville. *Life of Edwin Forrest*, Vol. I. Philadelphia, 1877.

Arabian Nights. Lane translation. New York, 1927.

Beckford, William. *Vathek*. Samuel Henley translation, 1786.

Brooks, Van Wyck. *The Flowering of New England*. New York, 1937.

Bryant, Jacob. A *New System; or, an Analysis of Ancient Mythology* (1774–1776). We refer to the third edition, London, 1807.

Bulwer, Edward, Lord Lytton. *Pelham or the Adventures of a Gentleman* (1828). A source of various literary and geographical allusions in Poe.

Bury, Lady Charlotte Susan Maria (attr.). *The Exclusives* (1830).

Carlyle, Thomas. *Sartor Resartus: The Life and Opinions of Herr Teufelsdröckh*. Boston, 1836. First published in *Fraser's Magazine* (1833–1834).

Cowper, William. *The Works of William Cowper*. Edited by Robert Southey. London, 1854.

Davenport, A. *See* Hall, Joseph.

Disraeli, Isaac. *Curiosities of Literature*. Various editions of this work, in part or whole, have appeared since the first in 1791. We refer to the New York, 1853 edition containing *Curiosities of Literature* and *The Literary Character Illustrated* by Disraeli with *Curiosities of American Literature* by Rufus W. Griswold, and also to an 1865 edition of *Curiosities*. . . .

Firdausi. *The Shánáma of Firdausi*. 4 vols. Arthur George Warner and Edmond Warner translation. London, 1906.

Griswold, Rufus. *The Prose Writers of America* (1847).

Hall, Joseph. *The Collected Poems of Joseph Hall*, ed. A. Davenport. Liverpool, 1949.

Hardenberg, Georg Friedrich Phillipp von (Novalis). *Novalis: Hymns to the Night and Other Selected Writings*. Indianapolis, 1960. A translation from German of selected works of Novalis.

Hogg, James (and others?). "The Chaldee Manuscript." Added as an appendix to "History of *Blackwood's Magazine*," *Noctes Ambrosianae*, Vol. I. Edited by R. Shelton Mackenzie. New York, 1863. "The Chaldee Manuscript" appeared originally in *Blackwood's Magazine* (October 1817).

Hunt, Leigh. *The Poetical Works of Leigh Hunt*. Edited by H. S. Milford. London, 1923.

———. *The Seer: or, Common-Places Refreshed* (1840–1841). We refer to the 1864 Boston edition.

The Koran. George Sale translation. London, 1734. A version Poe knew.

Linscott, Eloise Hubbard, collector and editor. *Folk Songs of Old New England*. New York, 1939.

Lockhart, John. " 'Letter' from 'Z' to Leigh Hunt, 'King of the Cockneys,' " *Blackwood's Edinburgh Magazine*, III (May 1818), 196–201.

———. "Cockney School of Poetry, No. III," *Blackwood's Edinburgh Magazine*, III (July 1818), 453–456.

———. "Cockney School of Poetry, No. IV," *Blackwood's Edinburgh Magazine*, III (August 1818), 519–524.

Lucan. *Lucan*. J. D. Duff translation. London, 1928.

Lucian. *The Works of Lucian of Samosata*. H. W. and F. G. Fowler translation. Oxford, 1905.

Maginn, William. *A Gallery of Illustrious Literary Characters 1830–1838*. With drawings by Daniel Maclise. William Bates, editor. London, 1873. Republished from *Fraser's Magazine*, where the drawings and accompanying literary sketches appeared between 1830 and 1838.

———. *Miscellanies: Prose and Verse*. 2 vols. Edited by R. W. Montagu. London, 1885. Stories and poems by Maginn which appeared in a variety of literary journals during his lifetime.

Martin, Malachi. "The New Castle: Mecca," *Intellectual Digest*, IV (October 1973), 24–26.

Morgan, Lady Sydney. *Florence Macarthy: An Irish Tale* (1818). 4 vols.

———. *Patriotic Sketches of Ireland* (1807). 2 vols.

Moses, Montrose J. *The Fabulous Forrest*. Boston, 1929.

Nicholson, Marjorie Hope. *Voyages to the Moon*. New York, 1948.

Rees, James (Colly Cibber). *The Life of Edwin Forrest with Reminiscences and Personal Recollections*. Philadelphia, 1874.

Numbers, Ronald L. "The American Kepler: Daniel Kirkwood and His Analogies," *Journal for the History of Astronomy*, IV, Part 1 (1973), 13–21.13.

St. Jerome. *Cartas de San Jerónimo*. Edited by Daniel Ruíz Bueno. Madrid, 1962.

Scott, Walter. *Anne of Geierstein* (1829).

Senior, John. *The Way Down and Out: The Occult in Symbolist Literature*. Ithaca, 1959.

Sherburn, George. "The Restoration and Eighteenth Century," in *A Literary History of England*. Edited by Albert C. Baugh. New York, 1948. The other sections of this work were also very useful to us.

Smith, Horace. *Zillah: A Tale of the Holy City* (1828).

Southey, Robert. *The Doctor* (1834–1847).

Thackeray, William M. *The Book of Snobs* (1848).

Tuckerman, Henry T. *Book of the Artists*. New York, 1867.

Walsh, William S. *Handy-Book of Literary Curiosities*. Philadelphia, 1906.

Wilson, John (Christopher North), William Maginn, John Gibson Lockhart, James Hogg and others. *Noctes Ambrosianae*. This work appeared originally as a series of articles in *Blackwood's* between 1822 and 1835. We refer to the 1863 New York edition in five volumes with "Memoirs and Notes" by R. Shelton Mackenzie.

The Short Fiction
of
Edgar Allan Poe

1. Unimpeded Visions

In many of Poe's stories, a "perceiver" has a "vision," which is usually complex, bizarre, and, to use one of Poe's pet words, "*outré.*" The plots deal largely with what happens to the perceiving character in order to make the visionary experience possible. In this first group of sketches, nothing much happens. The creators of the gardens and rooms do not have to be sick, drugged, or terrified before they can produce the complex and *outré* combinations which Poe calls beautiful. They are, apparently, ideal artists, able to perceive the supernal beauty of the universal order and to approximate it on earth. They are, in short, visionaries or, if you will, occult saints.

The Island of the Fay. The occult world-view is extremely explicit in "The Island of the Fay," where in a single passage we are told that the world is an "animate and sentient whole," that it regards us as we regard the "animalcula" in our own brains, who, in turn, regard us as we regard the universe. In occult thought, the universe is a man, and we are the man. Poe says that the path to the godhead is through understanding that matter is "vital"; the universe is composed of "cycle within cycle without end"; and both the huge—stars, planets, the universe—and the minute—the "clod of the valley" or microorganisms within our bodies—are part of the soul of God. The world, indeed, "thinks" and "enjoys"; thought is godlike; enjoyment is knowledge. The tale exemplifies the world-view; tarns writhe or sleep, lakes contain heaven, the sky yields "sunset fountains" which pour into the valley, "emerald turf" and "crystal dominion" merge, and the Fay, created by the linked analogies of the universe in the mind of the dozing narrator, is no less real than the unities which he has perceived. Thus the world is not merely animate, but sacred, and the key to enlightenment is godlike creation. Our narrator's thoughts and enjoyment create the Fay, as the thoughts of the universe create us.

Note that the adjectives used to describe supernal beauty in "The Island of the Fay" are similar to those in the other tales in this group. Beauty is "multiform," "complex," "radiant," "of eastern figure," "Asphodel-interspersed," "somber" and "spectral." Poe's taste, in short, is not necessarily ours.

The Philosophy of Furniture. This piece tells us how to furnish a bachelor apartment. Poe talks of simplicity and leads the modern reader to expect that an ideal apartment will be simply furnished. But the room we are shown, with all its crimson, silver and gold, Arabesque devices, drapes, carpet, giltwork, paintings, vases, and perfumed lamps, comes as a surprise. Poe uses almost exactly the same language to describe its "beauty" that he uses in "The Island of the Fay" or in "The Domain of Arnheim." If his taste is not ours, then, it is certainly consistent.

Morning on the Wissahiccon. Sketches accompanied by plates were known to be good for magazine circulation, and gift-books followed the commercially attractive precedent of the magazines. Often the plates preceded the prose, and in most cases, the prose was cranked out by the editor in appropriately lofty "magazine-ese" (see pp. 360 ff. for Poe's comments on magazine styles in "How to Write a Blackwood Article"). In this case, Poe did the job for N. P. Willis, and one suspects that the prose came first, because Poe knew the stream in question from walks near Philadelphia (A. H. Quinn).

Landor's Cottage. Stately though he is, the elk in "Morning on the Wissahiccon" turns out to be just a pet. If this suggests something of the artificiality of Poe's vision of ideal beauty, the suggestion is confirmed by "Landor's Cottage," a related sketch which seems to have been based on "Morning on the Wissahiccon." ("Landor's Cottage" appeared in 1849, a few months before Poe's death. "Morning on the Wissahiccon" came out in late 1843 for the 1844 issue of *The Opal*.) In "Landor's Cottage," the deer are fenced in, the birds are in cages, random stones are picked up: even "natural" beauty, in short, must be altered to make it ideal. The effect is less "staged" than that in "The Domain of Arnheim," but as in that piece, the visitor's approach is carefully controlled, and there are special lighting effects, undoubtedly suggested by Poe's familiarity with the theatre.

The Domain of Arnheim. The vision in "Arnheim" is even less "natural." One sees "scarcely a green leaf" and seems to see "rubies, sapphires, opals and golden onyxes" rolling out of the sky. In fact, Poe actually uses the word "artificial."

"The Domain of Arnheim" is probably the most important sketch in this group. Ellison is Poe's prototypical seer-artist. Ellison, indeed, has everything. He is not only the ideal poet, but also has enormous wealth, a lovely wife, and a fine family. He can "create beauty" under ideal conditions. Other creators in Poe are less fortunate; their visions must be induced by sickness, liquor, drugs, terror, or despair. In general, the easier it is for one of the perceptive characters in Poe to perceive, the less complex the plot of the piece in which he appears. So this is hardly a story at all: we're told who Ellison is, what he can do, and what he has. Then we're shown what he created. For comparison, see the difficulties of Roderick Usher in "The Fall of the House of Usher," a tale with a very complex plot.

"Arnheim" also contains a theoretical explanation of the need for artificiality: earthly "nature" is not quite supernal beauty. The inspired seer-artist, however, can alter it to make it intimate the complex patterns of transcendent vision. Taken as a group, these tales form a good introduction to Poe's most frequently stated philosophy and to the "look" of his visions.

The Tales

THE DOMAIN OF ARNHEIM[1]

The garden like a lady fair was cut,
  That lay as if she slumbered in
    delight,
And to the open skies her eyes did shut.
The azure fields of Heaven were
    'sembled right
  In a large round set with the flowers
    of light.
The flowers de luce and the round
    sparks of dew
That hung upon their azure leaves
    did shew
Like twinkling stars that sparkle in the
    evening blue.[2]

                              Giles Fletcher.

[No more remarkable man ever lived than my friend, the young Ellison. He was remarkable in the entire and continuous profusion of good gifts ever lavished upon him by fortune.] From his cradle to his grave a gale of prosperity bore my friend Ellison along. Nor do I use the word prosperity in its mere worldly sense. I mean it as synonymous with happiness. The person of whom I speak seemed born for the purpose of foreshadowing the doctrines of Turgot, Price, Priestley and Condorcet[3]— of exemplifying by individual instance what has been deemed the chimera of the perfectionists. In the brief existence of Ellison I fancy that I have seen refuted the dogma, that in man's very nature lies some hidden principle, the antagonist of bliss. An anxious examination of his career has given me to understand that, in general, from the violation of a few simple laws of humanity arises the wretchedness of mankind—that as a species we have in our possession the as yet unwrought elements of content—and that, even now, in the present darkness and madness of all thought on the great question of the social condition, it is not impossible that man, the individual, under certain unusual and highly fortuitous conditions, may be happy.

With opinions such as these my young friend, too, was fully imbued; and thus it is worthy of observation that the uninterrupted enjoyment which distinguished his life was, in great measure, the result of preconcert. It is, indeed, evident that with less of the instinctive philosophy which, now and then, stands so well in the stead of experience, Mr. Ellison would have found himself precipitated, by the very extraordinary success of his life, into the common vortex of unhappiness which yawns for those of pre-eminent endowments. But it is by no means my object to pen an essay on happiness. The ideas of my friend may be summed up in a few words. He admitted but four elementary principles, or, more strictly, conditions, of bliss. That which he considered chief was (strange to say!) the simple and purely physical one of free exercise in the open air. "The health," he said, "attainable by other means is scarcely worth the name." He instanced the ecstacies of the fox-hunter, and pointed to the tillers of the earth, the only people who, as a class, can be fairly considered happier than others.[4] His second condition was the love of woman. His third, *and most difficult of realization,* was the contempt of ambition. His fourth was an object of unceasing pursuit; and he held that, other things being equal, the extent of attainable happiness was in proportion to the spirituality of this object.

[I have said that] Ellison was remarkable in the continuous profusion of good gifts lavished upon him by fortune. In personal grace and beauty he exceeded all men. His intellect was of that order to which the acquisition of knowledge is less a labor than an intuition and a necessity. His family was one of the most illustrious of the empire. His bride was the loveliest and most devoted of women. His possessions had been always ample; but, on the attainment of his majority, it was discovered that one of those extraordinary freaks of fate had been played in his behalf which startle the whole social world amid which they occur, and seldom fail radically to alter the moral constitution of those who are their objects.

It appears that, about a hundred years before Mr. Ellison's coming of age, there had died, in a remote province, one Mr. Seabright Ellison. This gentleman had amassed a princely fortune, and, having no immediate connections, conceived the whim of suffering his wealth to accumulate for a century after his decease. Minutely and sagaciously directing the various modes of investment, he bequeathed the aggregate amount to the nearest of blood, bearing the name Ellison, who should be alive at the end of the hundred years. Many attempts had been made to set aside this singular bequest; their *ex post facto* character rendered them abortive; but the attention of a jealous government was aroused, and a legislative act finally obtained, forbidding all similar accumulations. This act, however, did not prevent young Ellison from entering into possession, on his twenty-first birth-day, as the heir of his ancestor Seabright, of a fortune of *four hundred and fifty millions of dollars.*[5]

When it had become known that such was the enormous wealth inherited, there were, of course, many speculations as to the mode of its disposal. The magnitude and the immediate availability of the sum bewildered all who thought on the topic. The possessor of any *appreciable* amount of money might have been imagined to perform any one of a thousand things. With riches merely surpassing those of any citizen, it would have been easy to suppose him engaging to supreme excess in the fashionable extravagances of his time—or busying himself with political intrigue—or aiming at ministerial power —or purchasing increase of nobility—or collecting large museums of *virtù*[6]—or playing the munificent patron of letters, of science, of art—or endowing, and bestowing his name upon, extensive institutions of charity. But for the inconceivable wealth in the actual possession of the heir, these objects and all ordinary objects were felt to afford too limited a field. Recourse was had to figures, and these but sufficed to confound. It was seen that, even at three per cent, the annual income of the inheritance amounted to no less that thirteen millions and five hundred thousand dollars; which was one million and one hundred and twenty-five thousand per month; or thirty-six thousand nine hundred and eighty-six per day; or one thousand five hundred and forty-one per hour; or six and twenty dollars for every minute that flew. Thus the usual track of supposition was thoroughly broken up. Men knew not what to imagine. There were some who even conceived that Mr. Ellison would divest himself of at least one half of his fortune, as of utterly superfluous opulence—enriching whole troops of his relatives by division of his superabundance. To the nearest of these he did, in fact, abandon the very unusual wealth which was his own before the inheritance.

I was not surprised, however, to perceive that he had long made up his mind on a point which had occasioned so much discussion to his friends. Nor was I greatly astonished at the nature of his decision. *In regard to individual charities he had satisfied his conscience. In the possibility of any improvement, properly so called, being effected by man himself in the general condition of man, he had (I am sorry to confess it) little faith. Upon the whole, whether happily or unhappily, he was thrown back, in very great measure, upon self.*

In the widest and noblest sense he was a poet. He comprehended, moreover, the true character, the august aims, the supreme majesty and dignity of the poetic sentiment. The *fullest, if not the sole* proper satisfaction of this sentiment he instinctively felt to lie in the creation of novel forms of beauty. Some peculiarities, either in his early education, or in the nature of his intellect, had tinged with what is termed materialism all his ethical speculations; and it was this bias, perhaps, which led him to believe that the most advantageous *at least*, if not the sole legitimate field for the poetic exercise, lies in the creation of novel moods of purely *physical* loveliness. Thus it happened he became neither musician nor poet—if we use this latter term in its every-day acceptation. Or it might have been that he neglected to become either, merely in pursuance of his idea that in contempt of ambition is to be found one of the essential principles of happiness on earth. Is it not, indeed, possible that, while a high order of genius is necessarily ambitious, the highest is above that which is termed ambition? And may it not thus happen that many far greater than Milton have contentedly remained "mute and inglorious?"[7] I believe that the world has never seen—and that, unless through some series of accidents goading the noblest order of mind into distasteful exertion, the world will never see—that full extent of triumphant execution, in the richer domains of art, of which the human nature is absolutely capable.

Ellison became neither musician nor poet; although no man lived more pro-

foundly enamored of music and poetry. Under other circumstances than those which invested him, it is not impossible that he would have become a painter. [The field of] sculpture, although in its nature rigorously poetical, was too limited in its extent and consequences, to have occupied, at any time, much of his attention. And I have now mentioned all the provinces in which the common understanding of the poetic sentiment has declared it capable of expatiating. But Ellison maintained that the richest, the truest and most natural, if not altogether the most extensive province, had been unaccountably neglected. No definition had spoken of the landscape-gardener as of the poet; yet it seemed to my friend that the creation of the landscape-garden offered to the proper Muse the most magnificent of opportunities. Here, indeed, was the fairest field for the display of imagination in the endless combining of forms of novel beauty; the elements to enter into combination being, by a vast superiority, the most glorious which the earth could afford. In the multiform and multicolor of the flower and the trees, he recognised the most direct and energetic efforts of Nature at physical loveliness. And in the direction or concentration of this effort—or, more properly, in its adaptation to the eyes which were to behold it on earth—he perceived that he should be employing the best means—laboring to the greatest advantage—in the fulfillment, *not only* of his *own* destiny as poet, *but of the august purposes for which the Deity had implanted the poetic sentiment in man.*

"Its adaptation to the eyes which were to behold it on earth." In his explanation of this phraseology, Mr. Ellison did much toward solving what has always seemed to me an enigma:—I mean the fact (which none but the ignorant dispute) that no such combination of scenery exists in nature as the painter of genius may produce. No such paradises are to be found in reality as have glowed on the canvas of

Claude. In the most enchanting of natural landscapes there will always be found a defect or an excess—many excesses and defects. While the component parts may defy, individually, the highest skill of the artist, the arrangement of these parts will always be susceptible of improvement. In short, no position can be attained on the wide surface of the *natural* earth, from which an artistical eye, looking steadily, will not find matter of offense in what is termed the "composition" of the landscape. And yet how unintelligible is this! In all other matters we are justly instructed to regard nature as supreme. With her details we shrink from competition. Who shall presume to imitate the colors of the tulip, or to improve the proportions of the lily of the valley? The criticism which says, of sculpture or portraiture, that here nature is to be exalted or ideal-

ized rather than imitated, is in error. No pictorial or sculptural combinations of points of human loveliness do more than approach the living and breathing beauty [as it gladdens our daily path. Byron, who often erred, erred not in saying,

> I've seen more living beauty, ripe
>   and real,
> Than all the nonsense of their
>   stone ideal.][8]

In landscape alone is the principle of the critic true; and, having felt its truth here, it is but the headlong spirit of generalization which has led him to pronounce it true throughout all the domains of art. Having I say, *felt* its truth here; for the feeling is no affectation or chimera. The mathematics afford no more absolute demonstrations than the sentiment of his art yields the artist. He not only believes, but positively knows, that such and such

Figure Two. Claude Lorrain, *A pastoral*. Reproduced with the permission of Yale University Art Gallery, Leonard C. Hanna, Jr., Fund.

apparently arbitrary arrangements of matter constitute and alone constitute the true beauty. His reasons, however, have not yet been matured into expression. It remains for a more profound analysis than the world has yet seen, fully to investigate and express them. Nevertheless he is confirmed in his instinctive opinions by the voice of all his brethren. Let a "composition" be defective; let an emendation be wrought in its mere arrangement of form; let this emendation be submitted to every artist in the world; by each will its necessity be admitted. And even far more than this:—in remedy of the defective composition, each insulated member of the fraternity would have suggested the identical emendation.

I repeat that in landscape arrangements alone is the physical nature susceptible of exaltation, and that, therefore, her susceptibility of improvement at this one point, was a mystery I had been unable to solve. *My own thoughts on the subject had rested in the idea that the primitive intention of nature would have so arranged the earth's surface as to have fulfilled at all points man's sense of perfection in the beautiful, the sublime, or the picturesque; but that this primitive intention had been frustrated by the known geological disturbances—disturbances of form and colour-grouping, in the correction or allaying of which lies the soul of art. The force of this idea was much weakened, however, by the necessity which it involved of considering the disturbances abnormal and unadapted to any purpose. It was Ellison who suggested that they were prognostic of *death*. He thus explained:—Admit the earthly immortality of man to have been the first intention. We have then the primitive arrangement of the earth's surface adapted to his blissful estate, as not existent but designed. The disturbances were the preparations for his subsequently conceived deathful condition.*

"Now," said my friend, "what we regard as exaltation of the landscape may be really such, as respects only the moral or human *point of view*. Each alternation of the natural scenery may possibly effect a blemish in the picture, if we can suppose this picture viewed at large—in mass—from some point distant from the earth's surface, although not beyond the limits of its atmosphere. It is easily understood that what might improve a closely scrutinized detail, may at the same time injure a general or more distantly observed effect. There *may* be a class of beings, human once, but now invisible to humanity, to whom, from afar, our disorder may seem order—our unpicturesqueness picturesque; in a word, the earth-angels, for whose scrutiny more especially than our own, and for whose death-refined appreciation of the beautiful, may have been set in array by God the wide landscape-gardens of the hemispheres."[9]

In the course of discussion, my friend quoted some passages from a writer on landscape-gardening, who has been supposed to have well treated his theme:

There are properly but two styles of landscape-gardening, the natural and the artificial. One seeks to recall the original beauty of the country, by adapting its means to the surrounding scenery; cultivating trees in harmony with the hills or plain of the neighboring land; detecting and bringing into practice those nice relations of size, proportion and colour which, hid from the common observer, are revealed everywhere to the experienced student of nature. The result of the natural style of gardening, is seen rather in the absence of all defects and incongruities—in the prevalence of a healthy harmony and order—than in the creation of any special wonders or miracles. The artificial style has as many varieties as there are different tastes to gratify. It has a certain general relation to the various styles of building. There are the stately avenues and retirements of Versailles[10]; Italian terraces; and a various mixed old English style, which bears some relation to the domestic Gothic or

English Elizabethan architecture. Whatever may be said against the abuses of the artificial landscape-gardening, a mixture of pure art in a garden scene adds to it a great beauty. This is partly pleasing to the eye, by the show of order and design, and partly moral. A terrace, with an old moss-covered balustrade, calls up at once to the eye the fair forms that have passed there in other days. The slightest exhibition of art is an evidence of care and human interest.

"From what I have already observed," said Ellison, "you will understand that I reject the idea, here expressed, of recalling the original beauty of the country. The original beauty is never so great as that which may be introduced. Of course, everything depends on the selection of a spot with capabilities. What is said about detecting and bringing into practice nice relations of size, proportion, and color, is one of those mere vaguenesses of speech which serve to veil inaccuracy of thought. The phrase quoted may mean anything, or nothing, and guides in no degree. That the true result of the natural style of gardening is seen rather in the absence of all defects and incongruities than in the creation of any special wonders or miracles, is a proposition better suited to the grovelling apprehension of the herd than to the fervid dreams of the man of genius. The negative merit suggested appertains to that hobbling criticism which, in letters, would elevate Addison into apotheosis. In truth, while that virtue which consists in the mere avoidance of vice appeals directly to the understanding, and can thus be circumscribed in *rule*, the loftier virtue, which flames in creation, can be apprehended in its results alone. Rule applies but to the merits of denial—to the excellencies which refrain. Beyond these, the critical art can but suggest. We may be instructed to build a "Cato," but we are in vain told *how* to conceive a Parthenon or an "Inferno."[11] The thing done, however; the wonder accomplished;

and the capacity for apprehension becomes universal. The sophists of the negative school who, through inability to create, have scoffed at creation, are now found the loudest in applause. What, in its chrysalis condition of principle, affronted their demure reason, never fails, in its maturity of accomplishment, to extort admiration from their instinct of beauty.

"The author's observations on the artificial style," continued Ellison, "are less objectionable. A mixture of pure art in a garden scene adds to it a great beauty. This is just; as also is the reference to the sense of human interest. The principle expressed is incontrovertible—but there *may* be something beyond it. There may be an object in keeping with the principle —an object unattainable by the means ordinarily possessed by individuals, yet which, if attained, would lend a charm to the landscape-garden far surpassing that which a sense of merely human interest could bestow. A poet, having very unusual pecuniary resources, might, while retaining the necessary idea of art, or culture, or, as our author expresses it, of interest, so imbue his designs at once with extent and novelty of beauty, as to convey the sentiment of spiritual interference. It will be seen that, in bringing about such result, he secures all the advantages of interest or *design*, while relieving his work of the harshness or technicality of the worldly *art*. In the most rugged of wildernesses—in the most savage of the scenes of pure nature—there is apparent the *art* of a creator; yet this art is apparent to reflection only; in no respect has it the obvious force of a feeling. Now let us suppose this sense of the Almighty design to be *one step depressed*[12] —to be brought into something like harmony or consistency with the sense of human art—to form an intermedium between the two:*—let us imagine, for example, a landscape whose combined vastness and definitiveness—whose united beauty, magnificence, and *strangeness*, shall convey the idea of care, or culture, or superintendence, on the part of beings superior, yet akin to humanity—then the sentiment of *interest* is preserved, while the art intervolved is made to assume the air of an intermediate or secondary nature —a nature which is not God, nor an emanation from God, but which still is nature in the sense of the handiwork of the angels that hover between man and God."

It was in devoting his enormous wealth to the embodiment of a vision such as this—in the free exercise in the open air ensured by the personal superintendence of his plans—in the unceasing object which these plans afforded—in the high spirituality of the object—in the contempt of ambition which it enabled him truly to feel—*in the perennial springs with which it gratified, without possibility of satiating, that one master passion of his soul, the thirst for beauty*; above all, it was in the sympathy of a woman, *not unwomanly, whose loveliness and love enveloped his existence in the purple atmosphere of Paradise,* that Ellison thought to find, *and found*, exemption from the ordinary cares of humanity, with a far greater amount of positive happiness than ever glowed in the rapt daydreams of De Staël.[13]

I despair of conveying to the reader any distinct conception of the marvels which my friend did actually accomplish. I wish to describe, but am disheartened by the difficulty of description, and hesitate between detail and generality. Perhaps the better course will be to unite the two in their extremes.

Mr. Ellison's first step regarded, of course, the choice of a locality; and scarcely had he commenced thinking on this point, when the luxuriant nature of the Pacific Islands arrested his attention. In fact, he had made up his mind for a voyage to the South Seas, when a night's reflection induced him to abandon the idea. "Were I misanthropic," he said, "such a *locale* would suit me. The thor-

oughness of its insulation and seclusion, and the difficulty of ingress and egress, would in such case be the charm of charms; but as yet I am not Timon.[14] I wish the composure but not the depression of solitude. There must remain with me a certain control over the extent and duration of my repose. There will be frequent hours in which I shall need, too, the sympathy of the poetic in what I have done. Let me seek, then, a spot not far from a populous city—whose vicinity, also, will best enable me to execute my plans."

In search of a suitable place so situated, Ellison travelled for several years, and I was permitted to accompany him. A thousand spots with which I was enraptured he rejected without hesitation, for reasons which satisfied me, in the end, that he was right. We came at length to an elevated table-land of wonderful fertility and beauty, affording a panoramic prospect very little less in extent than that of Ætna,[15] and, in Ellison's opinion as well as my own, surpassing the far-famed view from that mountain in all the true elements of the picturesque.

"I am aware," said the traveller, as he drew a sigh of deep delight after gazing on this scene, entranced, for nearly an hour, "I know that here, in my circumstances, nine-tenths of the most fastidious of men would rest content. This panorama is indeed glorious, and I should rejoice in it but for the excess of its glory. The taste of all the architects I have ever known leads them, for the sake of 'prospect,' to put up buildings on hill-tops. The error is obvious. Grandeur in any of its moods, but especially in that of extent, startles, excites—and then fatigues, depresses. For the occasional scene nothing can be better—for the constant view nothing worse. And, in the constant view, the most objectionable phase of grandeur is that of extent; the worst phase of extent, that of distance. It is at war with the sentiment and with the sense of *seclusion*—the sentiment and sense which we seek to hu-

mor in 'retiring to the country.' In looking from the summit of a mountain we
cannot help feeling *abroad* in the world.
The heart-sick avoid distant prospects as
a pestilence."

It was not until toward the close of the
fourth year of our search that we found a
locality with which Ellison professed himself satisfied. It is, of course, needless to
say *where* was the locality. The late death
of my friend, in causing his domain to be
thrown open to certain classes of visitors,
has given to *Arnheim* a species of secret
and subdued if not solemn celebrity, similar in kind, although infinitely superior
in degree, to that which so long distinguished Fonthill.[16]

The usual approach to Arnheim was by
the river. The visitor left the city in the
early morning. During the forenoon he
passed between shores of a tranquil and
domestic beauty, on which grazed innumerable sheep, their white fleeces spotting
the vivid green of rolling meadows. By degrees the idea of cultivation subsided into
that of merely pastoral care. This slowly
became merged in a sense of retirement—
this again in a consciousness of solitude.
As the evening approached the channel
grew more narrow; the banks more and
more precipitous; and these latter were
clothed in richer, more profuse, and more
sombre foliage. The water increased in
transparency. The stream took a thousand
turns, so that at no moment could its
gleaming surface be seen for a greater distance than a furlong. At every instant the
vessel seemed imprisoned within an enchanted circle, having insuperable and
impenetrable walls of foliage, a roof of
ultra-marine satin, and *no* floor—the keel
balancing itself with admirable nicety on
that of a phantom bark which, by some
accident having been turned upside down,
floated in constant company with the substantial one, for the purpose of sustaining
it. The channel now became a *gorge*—
although the term is somewhat inapplicable, and I employ it merely because the
language has no word which better repre-

sents the most striking—not the most distinctive—feature of the scene. The character of gorge was maintained only in the
height and parallelism of the shores; it
was lost altogether in their other traits.
The walls of the ravine (through which
the clear water still tranquilly flowed)
arose to an elevation of a hundred and occasionally of a hundred and fifty feet, and
inclined so much toward each other as, in
a great measure, to shut out the light of
day; while the long plume-like moss
which depended densely from the inter-
twining shrubberies overhead, gave the
whole chasm an air of funereal gloom.
The windings became more frequent and
intricate, and seemed often as if returning
in upon themselves, so that the voyager
had long lost all idea of direction. He was,
moreover, enwrapt in an exquisite sense
of the strange.[17] The thought of nature
still remained, but her character seemed
to have undergone modification: there
was a weird symmetry, a thrilling uniformity, a wizard propriety in these her
works. Not a dead branch—not a withered
leaf—not a stray pebble—not a patch of
the brown earth was anywhere visible.
The crystal water welled up against the
clean granite, or the unblemished moss,
with a sharpness of outline that delighted
while it bewildered the eye.

Having threaded the mazes of this
channel for some hours, the gloom deepening every moment, a sharp and unexpected turn of the vessel brought it suddenly, as if dropped from heaven, into a
circular basin of very considerable extent
when compared with the width of the
gorge. It was about two hundred yards in
diameter, and girt in at all points but one
—that immediately fronting the vessel as
it entered—by hills equal in general
height to the walls of the chasm, although
of a thoroughly different character. Their
sides sloped from the water's edge at an
angle of some forty-five degrees, and they
were clothed from base to summit—not a
perceptible point escaping—in a drapery
of the most gorgeous flower-blossoms;

scarcely a green leaf being visible among the sea of odorous and fluctuating color. This basin was of great depth, but so transparent was the water that the bottom, which seemed to consist of a thick mass of small round alabaster pebbles, was distinctly visible by glimpses—that is to say, whenever the eye could permit itself *not* to see, far down in the inverted Heaven, the duplicate blooming of the hills. On these latter there were no trees, nor even shrubs of any size. The impressions wrought on the observer were those of richness, warmth, color, quietude, uniformity, softness, delicacy, daintiness, voluptuousness, and a miraculous extremeness of culture that suggested dreams of a new race of fairies, laborious, tasteful, magnificent and fastidious; but as the eye traced upward the myriad-tinted slope, from its sharp junction with the water to its vague termination amid the folds of overhanging cloud, it became, indeed, difficult not to fancy a panoramic cataract of rubies, sapphires, opals and golden onyxes, rolling silently out of the sky.

The visitor, shooting suddenly into this bay from out the gloom of the ravine, is delighted but astounded by the full orb of the declining sun, which he had supposed to be already far below the horizon, but which now confronts him, and forms the sole termination of an otherwise limitless vista seen through another chasmlike rift in the hills.

But here the voyager quits the vessel which has borne him so far, and descends into a light canoe of ivory, stained with Arabesque[18] devices in vivid scarlet, both within and without. The poop and beak of this boat arise high above the water, with sharp points, so that the general form is that of an irregular crescent. It lies on the surface of the bay with the proud grace of a swan. On its ermined floor reposes a single feathery paddle of satinwood; but no oarsman or attendant is to be seen. The guest is bidden to be of good cheer—that the fates will take care of him. The larger vessel disappears, and he is left alone in the canoe, which lies apparently motionless in the middle of the lake. While he considers what course to pursue, however, he becomes aware of a gentle movement in the fairy bark. It slowly swings itself around until its prow points toward the sun. It advances with a gentle but gradually accelerated velocity, while the slight ripples it creates seem to break about the ivory sides in divinest melody—seem to offer the only possible explanation of the soothing yet melancholy music for whose unseen origin the bewildered voyager looks around him in vain.

The canoe steadily proceeds, and the rocky gate of the vista is approached, so that its depths can be more distinctly seen. To the right arise a chain of lofty hills rudely and luxuriantly wooded. It is observed, however, that the trait of exquisite *cleanness* where the bank dips into the water, still prevails. There is not one token of the usual river *débris*. To the left the character of the scene is softer and more obviously artificial. Here the bank slopes upward from the stream in a very gentle ascent, forming a broad sward of grass of a texture resembling nothing so much as velvet, and of a brilliancy of green which would bear comparison with the tint of the purest emerald. This *plateau* varies in width from ten to three hundred yards; reaching from the river bank to a wall, fifty feet high, which extends, in an infinity of curves, but following the general direction of the river, until lost in the distance to the westward. This wall is of one continuous rock, and has been formed by cutting perpendicularly the once rugged precipice of the stream's southern bank; but no trace of the labor has been suffered to remain. The chiselled stone has the hue of ages and is profusely overhung and overspread with the ivy, the coral honeysuckle, the eglantine, and the clematis. The uniformity of the top and bottom lines of the wall is fully relieved by occasional trees of gigantic height, growing singly or in small groups, both

along the *plateau* and in the domain behind the wall, but in close proximity to
it; so that frequent limbs (of the black
walnut especially) reach over and dip their
pendent extremities into the water. Farther back within the domain, the vision
is impeded by an impenetrable screen of
foliage.

These things are observed during the
canoe's gradual approach to what I have
called the gate of the vista. On drawing
nearer to this, however, its chasm-like appearance vanishes; a new outlet from the
bay is discovered to the left—in which direction the wall is also seen to sweep, still
following the general course of the stream.
Down this new opening the eye cannot
penetrate very far; for the stream, accompanied by the wall, still bends to the left,
until both are swallowed up by the leaves.

The boat, nevertheless, glides magically
into the winding channel; and here the
shore opposite the wall is found to resemble that opposite the wall in the straight
vista. Lofty hills, rising occasionally into
mountains, and covered with vegetation
in wild luxuriance, still shut in the scene.

Floating gently onward, but with a velocity slightly augmented, the voyager,
after many short turns, finds his progress
apparently barred by a gigantic gate or
rather door of burnished gold, elaborately
carved and fretted, and reflecting the direct rays of the now fast-sinking sun with
an effulgence that seems to wreath the
whole surrounding forest in flames. This
gate is inserted in the lofty wall; which
here appears to cross the river at right angles. In a few moments, however, it is
seen that the main body of the water still
sweeps in a gentle and extensive curve to
the left, the wall following it as before,
while a stream of considerable volume,
diverging from the principal one, makes
its way, with a slight ripple, under the
door, and is thus hidden from sight. The
canoe falls into the lesser channel and
approaches the gate. Its ponderous wings
are slowly and musically expanded. The
boat glides between them, and com-

mences a rapid descent into a vast amphitheatre entirely begirt with purple mountains, whose bases are laved by a gleaming
river throughout the full extent of their
circuit. Meantime the whole Paradise of
Arnheim bursts upon the view. There is
a gush of entrancing melody; there is an
oppressive sense of strange sweet odor;—
there is a dream-like intermingling to the
eye of tall slender Eastern trees—bosky
shrubberies—flocks of golden and crimson birds—lily-fringed lakes—meadows
of violets, tulips, poppies, hyacinths and
tuberoses—long intertangled lines of silver streamlets—and, upspringing confusedly from amid all, a mass of semi-Gothic,
semi-Saracenic[19] architecture, sustaining
itself as if by miracle in mid-air, glittering
in the red sunlight with a hundred oriels,
minarets, and pinnacles; and seeming the
phantom handiwork, conjointly, of the
Sylphs, of the Fairies, of the Genii, and of
the Gnomes.

THE PHILOSOPHY OF FURNITURE

In the internal decoration, if not in the
external architecture of their residences,
the English are supreme. The Italians have
but little sentiment beyond marbles and
colors. In France, *meliora probant, de-
teriora sequuntur*[1]—the people are too
much a race of gadabouts to maintain
those household proprieties of which, indeed, they have a delicate appreciation, or
at least the elements of a proper sense.
The Chinese and most of the Eastern
races have a warm but inappropriate
fancy. The Scotch are *poor* decorists. The
Dutch have, perhaps, an indeterminate
idea that a curtain is not a cabbage. In
Spain they are *all* curtains—a nation of
hangmen. The Russians do not furnish.
The Hottentots and Kickapoos are very
well in their way. The Yankees alone are
preposterous.

How this happens, it is not difficult to
see. We have no aristocracy of blood, and

having therefore as a natural, and indeed as an inevitable thing, fashioned for ourselves an aristocracy of dollars, the *display of wealth* has here to take the place and perform the office of the heraldic display in monarchial countries. By a transition readily understood, and which might have been as readily foreseen, we have been brought to merge in simple *show* our notions of taste itself.

To speak less abstractly. In England, for example, no mere parade of costly appurtenances would be so likely as with us, to create an impression of the beautiful in respect to the appurtenances themselves —or of taste as regards the proprietor:— this for the reason, first, that wealth is not, in England, the loftiest object of ambition as constituting a nobility; and secondly, that there, the true nobility of blood, confining itself within the strict limits of legitimate taste, rather avoids than affects that mere costliness in which a *parvenu* rivalry[2] may at any time be successfully attempted.

The people *will* imitate the nobles, and the result is a thorough diffusion of the proper feeling. But in America, the coins current being the sole arms of the aristocracy, their display may be said, in general, to be the sole means of aristocratic distinction; and the populace, looking always upward for models, are insensibly led to confound the two entirely separate ideas of magnificence and beauty. In short, the cost of an article of furniture has at length come to be, with us, nearly the sole test of its merit in a decorative point of view— and this test, once established, has led the way to many analogous errors, readily traceable to the one primitive folly.

There could be nothing more directly offensive to the eye of an artist than the interior of what is termed in the United States—that is to say, in Appalachia[3]—a well-furnished apartment. Its most usual defect is a want of keeping. We speak of the keeping of a room as we would of the keeping of a picture—for both the picture and the room are amenable to those un-deviating principles which regulate all varieties of art; and very nearly the same laws by which we decide on the higher merits of a painting, suffice for decision on the adjustment of a chamber.

A want of keeping is observable sometimes in the character of the several pieces of furniture, but generally in their colours or modes of adaptation to use. *Very* often the eye is offended by their inartistical arrangement. Straight lines are too prevalent—too uninterruptedly continued—or clumsily interrupted at right angles. If curved lines occur, they are repeated into unpleasant uniformity. By undue precision, the appearance of many a fine apartment is utterly spoiled.

Curtains are rarely well disposed, or well chosen in respect to other decorations. With formal furniture, curtains are out of place; and an extensive volume of drapery of any kind is, under any circumstances, irreconcilable with good taste— the proper quantum, as well as the proper adjustment, depending upon the character of the general effect.

Carpets are better understood of late than of ancient days, but we still very frequently err in their patterns and colours. The soul of the apartment is the carpet. From it are deduced not only the hues but the forms of all objects incumbent. A judge at common law may be an ordinary man; a good judge of a carpet *must be* a genius. Yet we have heard discoursing of carpets, with the air *"d'un mouton qui rêve,"* fellows who should not and who could not be entrusted with the management of their own *moustaches.* Every one knows that a large floor *may* have a covering of large figures, and that a small one *must* have a covering of small—yet this is not all the knowledge in the world. As regards texture, the Saxony is alone admissible. Brussels is the preterpluperfect tense of fashion, and Turkey is taste in its dying agonies. Touching pattern—a carpet should *not* be bedizened out like a Riccaree Indian—all red chalk, yellow ochre, and cock's feathers. In brief—dis-

tinct grounds, and vivid circular or cy-
cloid figures, *of no meaning*, are here
Median laws. The abomination of flowers, or representations of well-known objects of any kind, should not be endured
within the limits of Christendom. Indeed,
whether on carpets, or curtains, or tapestry, or ottoman coverings, all upholstery
of this nature should be rigidly Arabesque. As for those antique floor-cloths
still occasionally seen in the dwellings of
the rabble—cloths of huge, sprawling, and
radiating devices, stripe-interspersed, and
glorious with all hues, among which no
ground is intelligible—these are but the
wicked invention of a race of time-servers
and money-lovers—children of Baal and
worshippers of Mammon—Benthams,[4]
who, to spare thought and economize
fancy, first cruelly invented the Kaleido-
scope, and then established joint-stock
companies to twirl it by steam.

Glare is a leading error in the philosophy of American household decoration
—an error easily recognised as deduced
from the perversion of taste just specified.
We are violently enamoured of gas and
of glass. The former is totally inadmissible within doors. Its harsh and unsteady
light offends. No one having both brains
and eyes will use it. A mild, or what artists term a cool light, with its consequent
warm shadows, will do wonders for even
an ill-furnished apartment. Never was a
more lovely thought than that of the astral lamp. We mean, of course, the astral
lamp proper—the lamp of Argand,[5] with
its original plain ground-glass shade, and
its tempered and uniform moonlight rays.
The cut-glass shade is a weak invention
of the enemy. The eagerness with which
we have adopted it, partly on account of
its *flashiness*, but principally on account
of its *greater cost*, is a good commentary
on the proposition with which we began.
It is not too much to say that the deliberate employer of a cut-glass shade is either radically deficient in taste, or blindly
subservient to the caprices of fashion. The
light proceeding from one of these gaudy

abominations is unequal, broken, and
painful. It alone is sufficient to mar a
world of good effect in the furniture subjected to its influence. Female loveliness,
in especial, is more than one-half disen-
chanted beneath its evil eye.

In the matter of glass, generally, we
proceed upon false principles. Its leading
feature is *glitter*—and in that one word
how much of all that is detestable do
we express! Flickering, unquiet lights, are
sometimes pleasing—to children and idiots always so—but in the embellishment
of a room they should be scrupulously
avoided. In truth, even strong *steady*
lights are inadmissible. The huge and unmeaning glass chandeliers, prism cut, gas-
lighted, and without shade, which dangle
in our most fashionable drawing-rooms,
may be cited as the quintessence of all
that is false in taste or preposterous in
folly.

The rage for *glitter*—because its idea
has become, as we before observed, confounded with that of magnificence in the
abstract—has led us, also, to the exaggerated employment of mirrors. We line our
dwellings with great British plates, and
then imagine we have done a fine thing.
Now the slightest thought will be sufficient to convince any one who has an eye
at all, of the ill effect of numerous look-
ing-glasses, and especially of large ones.
Regarded apart from its reflection, the
mirror presents a continuous, flat, colour-
less, unrelieved surface,—a thing always
and obviously unpleasant. Considered as
a reflector, it is potent in producing a
monstrous and odious uniformity: and the
evil is here aggravated, not in merely direct proportion with the augmentation of
its sources, but in a ratio constantly increasing. In fact, a room with four or five
mirrors arranged at random, is, for all purposes of artistic show, a room of no shape
at all. If we add to this evil, the attendant
glitter upon glitter, we have a perfect farrago[6] of discordant and displeasing effects.
The veriest bumpkin, on entering an
apartment so bedizzened, would be in-

stantly aware of something wrong, although he might be altogether unable to assign a cause for his dissatisfaction. But let the same person be led into a room tastefully furnished, and he would be startled into an exclamation of pleasure and surprise.

It is an evil growing out of our republican institutions, that here a man of large purse has usually a very little soul which he keeps in it. The corruption of taste is a portion or a pendant of the dollar-manufacture. As we grow rich, our ideas grow rusty. It is, therefore, not among our aristocracy that we must look (if at all, in Appalachia), for the spirituality of a British *boudoir*. But we have seen apartments in the tenure of Americans of modern means, which, in negative merit at least, might vie with any of the *or-molu'd*[7] cabinets of our friends across the water. Even *now*, there is present to our mind's eye a small and not ostentatious chamber with whose decorations no fault can be found. The proprietor lies asleep on a sofa—the weather is cool—the time is near midnight: we will make a sketch of the room during his slumber.

It is oblong—some thirty feet in length and twenty-five in breadth—a shape affording the best (ordinary) opportunities for the adjustment of furniture. It has but one door—by no means a wide one—which is at one end of the parallelogram, and but two windows, which are at the other. These latter are large, reaching down to the floor—have deep recesses—and open on an Italian *veranda*. Their panes are of a crimson-tinted glass, set in rosewood framings, more massive than usual. They are curtained within the recess, by a thick silver tissue adapted to the shape of the window, and hanging loosely in small volumes. Without the recess are curtains of an exceedingly rich crimson silk, fringed with a deep network of gold, and lined with silver tissue, which is the material of the exterior blind. There are no cornices; but the folds of the whole fabric (which are sharp

rather than massive, and have an airy appearance), issue from beneath a broad entablature of rich giltwork, which encircles the room at the junction of the ceiling and walls. The drapery is thrown open also, or closed, by means of a thick rope of gold loosely enveloping it, and resolving itself readily into a knot; no pins or other such devices are apparent. The colours of the curtains and their fringe—the tints of crimson and gold—appear everywhere in profusion, and determine the *character* of the room. The carpet—of Saxony material—is quite half an inch thick, and is of the same crimson ground, relieved simply by the appearance of a gold cord (like that festooning the curtains) slightly relieved above the surface of the *ground*, and thrown upon it in such a manner as to form a succession of short irregular curves—one occasionally overlaying the other. The walls are prepared with a glossy paper of a silver gray tint, spotted with small Arabesque devices of a fainter hue of the prevalent crimson. Many paintings relieve the expanse of the paper. These are chiefly landscapes of an imaginative cast —such as the fairy grottoes of Stanfield, or the lake of the Dismal Swamp of Chapman. There are, nevertheless, three or four female heads, of an ethereal beauty—portraits in the manner of Sully. The tone of each picture is warm, but dark. There are no "brilliant effects." *Repose* speaks in all. Not one is of small size. Diminutive paintings give that *spotty* look to a room, which is the blemish of so many a fine work of Art overtouched. The frames are broad but not deep, and richly carved, without being *dulled* or filigreed. They have the whole lustre of burnished gold. They lie flat on the walls, and do not hang off with cords. The designs themselves are often seen to better advantage in this latter position, but the general appearance of the chamber is injured. But one mirror—and this is not a very large one—is visible. In shape it is nearly circular—and it is hung so that a reflection of the person can be obtained from it in none of the ordinary sitting-places of the room. Two large low sofas of rosewood and crimson silk, gold-flowered, form the only seats, with the exception of two light conversation chairs, also of rosewood. There is a pianoforte (rosewood, also), without cover, and thrown open. An octagonal table, formed altogether of the richest gold-threaded marble, is placed near one of the sofas. This is also without cover—the drapery of the curtains has been thought sufficient. Four large and gorgeous Sèvres vases, in which bloom a profusion of sweet and vivid flowers, occupy the slightly rounded angles of the room. A tall candelabrum, bearing a small antique lamp with highly perfumed oil, is standing near the head of my sleeping friend. Some light and graceful hanging shelves, with golden edges and crimson silk cords with gold tassels, sustain two or three hundred magnificently bound books. Beyond these things, there is no furniture, if we except an Argand lamp, with a plain crimson-tinted ground-glass shade, which depends from the lofty vaulted ceiling by a single slender gold chain, and throws a tranquil but magical radiance over all.[8]

THE ISLAND OF THE FAY

Nullus enim locus sine genio est.
Servius[1]

"*La musique,*" says Marmontel, in those "*Contes Moraux*" which, in all our translations, we have insisted upon calling "Moral Tales" as if in mockery of their spirit—"*la musique est le seul des talens qui jouissent de lui-même; tous les autres veulent des témoins.*" He here confounds the pleasure derivable from sweet sounds with the capacity for creating them. No more than any other *talent,* is that for music susceptible of complete enjoyment, where there is no second party to appreciate its exercise. And it is only in common with other talents that it pro-

duces *effects* which may be fully enjoyed in solitude. The idea which the *raconteur* has either failed to entertain clearly, or has sacrificed in its expression to his national love of *point,* is, doubtless, the very tenable one that the higher order of music is the most thoroughly estimated when we are exclusively alone. The proposition, in this form, will be admitted at once by those who love the lyre for its own sake, and for its spiritual uses. But there is one pleasure still within the reach of fallen mortality—and perhaps only one—which owes even more than does music to the accessory sentiment of seclusion. I mean the happiness experienced in the contemplation of natural scenery. In truth, the man who would behold aright the glory of God upon earth must in solitude behold that glory. To me, at least, the presence—not of human life only—but of life in any other form than that of the green things which grow upon the soil and are voiceless—is a stain upon the landscape—is at war with the genius of the scene. I love, indeed, to regard the dark valleys, and the grey rocks, and the waters that silently smile, and the forests that sigh in uneasy slumbers, and the proud watchful mountains that look down upon all—I love to regard these as themselves but the colossal members of one vast animate and sentient whole—a whole whose form (that of the sphere) is the most perfect and most inclusive of all; whose path is among associate planets; whose meek handmaiden is the moon; whose mediate sovereign is the sun; whose life is eternity; whose thought is that of a God; whose enjoyment is knowledge; whose destinies are lost in immensity; whose cognizance of ourselves is akin with our own cognizance of the *animalculæ*[2] which infest the brain—a being which we, in consequence, regard as purely inanimate and material, much in the same manner as these *animalculæ* must thus regard us.

Our telescopes, and our mathematical investigations assure us on every hand—

Figure Three. "Island of the Fay." This plate accompanied Poe's sketch in *Graham's*, June 1841.

notwithstanding the cant of the more ignorant of the priesthood—that space, and
therefore that bulk, is an important consideration in the eyes of the Almighty.
The cycles in which the stars move are
those best adapted for the evolution,
without collision of the greatest possible
number of bodies. The forms of those
bodies are accurately such as, within a
given surface, to include the greatest possible amount of matter;—while the surfaces themselves are so disposed as to
accommodate a denser population than
could be accommodated on the same surfaces otherwise arranged. Nor is it any
argument against bulk being an object
with God, that space itself is infinite: for
there may be an infinity of matter to fill
it. And since we see clearly that the en-
dowment of matter with vitality is a
principle—indeed as far as our judgments

extend, the *leading* principle in the operations of Deity—it is scarcely logical to
imagine it confined to the regions of the
minute, where we daily trace it, and not
extending to those of the august. As we
find cycle within cycle without end—yet
all revolving around one far-distant centre which is the Godhead, may we not
analogically suppose, in the same manner, life within life, the less within the
greater, and all within the Spirit Divine?
In short, we are madly erring, through
self-esteem, in believing man, in either
his temporal or future destinies, to be of
more moment in the universe than that
vast "clod of the valley" which he tills
and contemns, and to which he denies a
soul for no more profound reason than
that he does not behold it in operation.[3]
    These fancies, and such as these, have
always given to my meditations among

the mountains, and the forests, by the rivers and the ocean, a tinge of what the everyday world would not fail to term the fantastic. My wanderings amid such scenes have been many, and far-searching, and often solitary; and the interest with which I have strayed through many a dim deep valley, or gazed into the reflected Heaven of many a bright lake, has been an interest greatly deepened by the thought that I have strayed and gazed *alone*. What flippant Frenchman was it who said, in allusion to the well-known work of Zimmerman, that, *"la solitude est une belle chose; mais il faut quelqu'un pour vous dire que la solitude est une belle chose."*[4] The epigram cannot be gainsaid; but the necessity is a thing that does not exist.

It was during one of my lonely journeyings, amid a far-distant region of mountain locked within mountain, and sad rivers and melancholy tarns writhing or sleeping within all—that I chanced upon a certain rivulet and island. I came upon them suddenly in the leafy June, and threw myself upon the turf, beneath the branches of an unknown odorous shrub, that I might doze as I contemplated the scene. I felt that thus only should I look upon it—such was the character of phantasm which it wore.

On all sides—save to the west, where the sun was about sinking—arose the verdant walls of the forest. The little river which turned sharply in its course, and was thus immediately lost to sight, seemed to have no exit from its prison, but to be absorbed by the deep green foliage of the trees to the east—while in the opposite quarter (so it appeared to me as I lay at length and glanced upward) there poured down noiselessly and continuously into the valley, a rich golden and crimson water-fall from the sunset fountains of the sky.

About midway in the short vista which my dreamy vision took in, one small circular island, profusely verdured, reposed upon the bosom of the stream.

So blended bank and shadow there,
That each seemed pendulous in air—

so mirror-like was the glassy water, that it was scarcely possible to say at what point upon the slope of the emerald turf its crystal dominion began.

My position enabled me to include in a single view both the eastern and western extremities of the islet; and I observed a singularly-marked difference in their aspects. The latter was all one radiant harem of garden beauties. It glowed and blushed beneath the eye of the slant sunlight, and fairly laughed with flowers. The grass was short, springy, sweet-scented, and Asphodel-interspersed. The trees were lithe, mirthful, erect—bright, slender, and graceful—of eastern figure and foliage, with bark smooth, glossy, and parti-coloured. There seemed a deep sense of life and joy about all; and although no airs blew from out the Heavens, yet everything had motion through the gentle sweepings to and fro of innumerable butterflies, that might have been mistaken for tulips with wings.[5]

The other or eastern end of the isle was whelmed in the blackest shade. A sombre, yet beautiful and peaceful gloom here pervaded all things. The trees were dark in colour and mournful in form and attitude—wreathing themselves into sad, solemn, and spectral shapes, that conveyed ideas of mortal sorrow and untimely death. The grass wore the deep tint of the cypress, and the heads of its blades hung droopingly, and, hither and thither among it, were many small unsightly hillocks, low, and narrow, and not very long, that had the aspect of graves, but were not; although over and all about them the rue and rosemary clambered. The shade of the trees fell heavily upon the water, and seemed to bury itself therein, impregnating the depths of the element with darkness. I fancied that each shadow, as the sun descended lower and lower separated itself sullenly from the trunk that gave it birth, and thus became absorbed by the stream; while other shadows issued momently from the trees, taking the place of their predecessors thus entombed.

This idea, having once seized upon my fancy, greatly excited it, and I lost myself forthwith in reverie. "If ever island were enchanted,"—said I to myself—"this is it. This is the haunt of the few gentle Fays who remain from the wreck of the race. Are these green tombs theirs—or do they yield up their sweet lives as mankind yield up their own? In dying, do they not rather waste away mournfully; rendering unto God little by little their existence, as these trees render up shadow after shadow, exhausting their substance unto dissolution? What the wasting tree is to the water that imbibes its shade, growing thus blacker by what it preys upon, may not the life of the Fay be to the death which engulfs it?"

As I thus mused, with half-shut eyes, while the sun sank rapidly to rest, and eddying currents careered round and round the island, bearing upon their bosom large, dazzling, white flakes of the bark of the sycamore—flakes which, in their multiform positions upon the water, a quick imagination might have converted into anything it pleased—while I thus mused, it appeared to me that the form of one of those very Fays about whom I had been pondering, made its way slowly into the darkness from out the light at the western end of the island. She stood erect, in a singularly fragile canoe, and urged it with the mere phantom of an oar. While within the influence of the lingering sunbeams, her attitude seemed indicative of joy—but sorrow deformed it as she passed within the shade. Slowly she glided along, and at length rounded the islet and re-entered the region of light. "The revolution which has just been made by the Fay," continued I musingly—"is the cycle of the brief year of her life. She has floated through her winter and through her summer. She is a year nearer unto Death: for I did not fail to see that as she came into the shade, her shadow fell from her, and was swallowed up in the dark water, making its blackness more black."

And again the boat appeared, and the Fay; but about the attitude of the latter there was more of care and uncertainty, and less of elastic joy. She floated again from out the light, and into the gloom (which deepened momently) and again her shadow fell from her into the ebony water, and became absorbed into its blackness. And again and again she made the circuit of the island, (while the sun rushed down to his slumbers) and at each issuing into the light, there was more sorrow about her person, while it grew feebler, and far fainter, and more indistinct; and at each passage into the gloom, there fell from her a darker shade, which became whelmed in a shadow more black. But at length, when the sun had utterly departed, the Fay, now the mere ghost of her former self, went disconsolately with her boat into the region of the ebony flood,—and that she issued thence at all I cannot say,—for darkness fell over all things, and I beheld her magical figure no more.

LANDOR'S COTTAGE

A Pendant to "The Domain of Arnheim"

During a pedestrian tour last summer, through one or two of the river counties of New York, I found myself, as the day declined, somewhat embarrassed about the road I was pursuing. The land undulated very remarkably; and my path, for the last hour, had wound about and about so confusedly, in its effort to keep in the valleys, that I no longer knew in what direction lay the sweet village of B——, where I had determined to stop for the night. The sun had scarcely *shone*— strictly speaking—during the day, which, nevertheless, had been unpleasantly warm. A smoky mist, resembling that of the Indian summer, enveloped all things,

Figure Four. A mountain wagon. Sketch by Herbert Friedson.

and, of course, added to my uncertainty. Not that I cared much about the matter. If I did not hit upon the village before sunset, or even before dark, it was more than possible that a little Dutch farmhouse, or something of that kind, would soon make its appearance—although, in fact, the neighborhood (perhaps on account of being more picturesque than fertile) was very sparsely inhabited. At all events, with my knapsack for a pillow, and my hound as a sentry, a bivouac in the open air was just the thing which would have amused me. I sauntered on, therefore, quite at ease—Ponto taking charge of my gun—until at length, just as I had begun to consider whether the numerous little glades that led hither and thither were intended to be paths at all, I was conducted by one of the most promising of them into an unquestionable carriage-track. There could be no mistaking it. The traces of light wheels were evident; and although the tall shrubberies and overgrown undergrowth met overhead, there was no obstruction whatever below, even to the passage of a Virginian mountain wagon—the most aspiring vehicle, I take it, of its kind. The road, however, except in being open through the wood—if wood be not too weighty a name for such an assemblage of light trees— and except in the particulars of evident wheel-tracks—bore no resemblance to any road I had before seen. The tracks of which I speak were but faintly perceptible—having been impressed upon the firm, yet pleasantly moist surface of— what looked more like green Genoese velvet[1] than anything else. It was grass, clearly—but grass such as we seldom see out of England—so short, so thick, so even, and so vivid in color. Not a single impediment lay in the wheel-route—not even a chip or dead twig. The stones that once obstructed the way had been carefully *placed*—not thrown—along the sides of the lane, so as to define its boundaries at bottom with a kind of half-precise, half-negligent, and wholly picturesque definition. Clumps of wild flowers grew everywhere, luxuriantly, in the interspaces.

What to make of all this, of course I knew not. Here was *art* undoubtedly— *that* did not surprise me—all roads, in the ordinary sense, are works of art; nor can I say that there was much to wonder at in the mere *excess* of art manifested; all that seemed to have been done, might have been done *here*—with such natural "capabilities" (as they have it in the books on Landscape Gardening)—with very little labor and expense. No; it was not the amount but the *character* of the art which caused me to take a seat on one of the blossomy stones and gaze up and down this fairy-like avenue for half an hour or more in bewildered admiration. One thing became more and more evident the longer I gazed: an artist, and one with a most scrupulous eye for form, had superintended all these arrangements. The greatest care had been taken to preserve a due medium between the neat and graceful on the one hand, and the *pittoresco*,[2] in the true sense of the Italian term, on the other. There were few straight, and no long uninterrupted lines. The same effect of curvature or of color, appeared twice, usually, but not oftener, at any one point of view. Everywhere was variety in uniformity. It was a piece of "composition," in which the most fastidiously critical taste could scarcely have suggested an emendation.

I had turned to the right as I entered this road, and now, arising, I continued in the same direction. The path was so serpentine, that at no moment could I trace its course for more than two or three paces in advance. Its character did not undergo any material change.

Presently the murmur of water fell gently upon my ear—and in a few moments afterwards, as I turned with the road somewhat more abruptly than hitherto, I became aware that a building of some kind lay at the foot of a gentle declivity just before me. I could see nothing distinctly on account of the mist which occupied all the little valley below. A gentle breeze, however, now arose, as the sun was about descending; and while I remained standing on the brow of the slope, the fog gradually became dissipated into wreaths, and so floated over the scene.

As it came fully into view—thus *gradually* as I describe it—piece by piece, here a tree, there a glimpse of water, and here again the summit of a chimney, I could scarcely help fancying that the whole was one of the ingenious illusions sometimes exhibited under the name of "vanishing pictures."

By the time, however, that the fog had thoroughly disappeared, the sun had made its way down behind the gentle hills, and thence, as if with a slight *chassez*[3] to the south, had come again fully into sight; glaring with a purplish lustre through a chasm that entered the valley from the west. Suddenly, therefore—and as if by the hand of magic—this whole valley and every thing in it became brilliantly visible.

The first *coup d'œil*,[4] as the sun slid into the position described, impressed me very much as I have been impressed when a boy, by the concluding scene of some well-arranged theatrical spectacle or melodrama. Not even the monstrosity of color was wanting; for the sunlight came out through the chasm, tinted all orange and purple; while the vivid green of the grass in the valley was reflected more or less upon all objects, from the curtain of vapor that still hung overhead, as if loth to take its total departure from a scene so enchantingly beautiful.

The little vale into which I thus peered down from under the fog-canopy, could not have been more than four hundred yards long; while in breadth it varied from fifty to one hundred and fifty, or perhaps two hundred. It was most narrow at its northern extremity, opening out as it tended southwardly, but with no very precise regularity. The widest portion was within eighty yards of the southern extreme. The slopes which encompassed the vale could not fairly be called hills, unless at their northern face. Here a precipitous ledge of granite arose to a height of some ninety feet; and, as I have mentioned, the valley at this point was not more than fifty feet wide; but as the visiter proceeded southwardly from this cliff, he found on his right hand and on his left, declivities at once less high, less precipitous, and less rocky. All, in a word, sloped and softened to the south; and yet the whole vale was engirdled by eminences, more or less high, except at two points. One of these I have already spoken of. It lay considerably to the north of west, and was where the setting sun made its way, as I have before described, into the amphitheatre, through a cleanly cut natural cleft in the granite embankment: this fissure might have been ten yards wide at its widest point, so far as the eye could trace it. It seemed to lead up, up, like a natural causeway, into the recesses of unexplored mountains and forests. The other opening was directly at the southern end of the vale. Here, generally, the slopes were nothing more than gentle inclinations, extending from east to west about one hundred and fifty yards. In the middle of this extent was a depression, level with the ordinary floor of the valley. As regards vegetation, as well as in respect to every thing else, the scene *softened and sloped* to the south. To the north—on the craggy precipice—a few paces from the verge—upsprang the magnificent trunks of numerous hickories, black walnuts, and chestnuts, interspersed with occasional oak; and the strong lateral branches thrown out by the walnuts especially, spread far over the edge of the cliff. Proceeding southwardly, the explorer saw, at first, the same class of trees, but less and less lofty and Salvatorish in character; then he saw the gentler elm, succeeded by the sassafras and locust—these again by the softer linden, red-bud, catalpa, and maple—these yet again by still more graceful and more modest varieties. The whole face of the southern declivity was covered with wild shrubbery alone—an occasional silver willow or white poplar excepted. In the bottom of the valley itself—(for it must be borne in mind that the vegetation hitherto mentioned grew only on the cliffs or hill-sides)—were to be seen three insulated trees. One was an elm of fine size and exquisite form: it stood guard over the southern gate of the vale. Another was a hickory, much larger than the elm, and altogether a much finer tree, although both were exceedingly beautiful: it seemed to have taken charge of the north-western entrance, springing from a group of rocks in the very jaws of the ravine, and throwing its graceful body, at an angle of nearly forty-five degrees, far out into the sunshine of the amphitheatre. About thirty yards east of this tree stood, however, the pride of the valley, and beyond all question the most magnificent tree I have ever seen, unless, perhaps, among the cypresses of the Itchiatuckanee. It was a triple-stemmed tulip tree—the *Liriodendron Tulipiferum*[5]—one of the natural order of magnolias. Its three trunks separated from the parent at about three feet from the soil, and diverging very slightly and gradually, were not more than four feet apart at the point where the largest stem shot out into foliage: this was at an elevation of about eighty feet. The whole height of the principal division was one hundred and

Figure Five. Salvator Rosa, "Tobias and the Angel." Reproduced courtesy of
Wadsworth Atheneum, Hartford, Conn.

twenty feet. Nothing can surpass in beauty the form, or the glossy, vivid green of the leaves of the tulip tree. In the present instance they were fully eight inches wide; but their glory was altogether eclipsed by the gorgeous splendor of the profuse blossoms. Conceive, closely congregated, a million of the largest and most resplendent tulips! Only thus can the reader get any idea of the picture I would convey. And then the stately grace of the clean, delicately-granulated columnar stems, the largest four feet in diameter, at twenty from the ground. The innumerable blossoms, mingling with those of other trees scarcely less beautiful, although infinitely less majestic, filled the valley with more than Arabian perfumes.

The general floor of the amphitheatre was *grass* of the same character as that I had found in the road: if anything, more deliciously soft, thick, velvety, and miraculously green. It was hard to conceive how all this beauty had been attained.

I have spoken of the two openings into the vale. From the one to the north-west issued a rivulet, which came, gently murmuring and slightly foaming, down the ravine, until it dashed against the group of rocks out of which sprang the insulated hickory. Here, after encircling the tree, it passed on a little to the north of east, leaving the tulip tree some twenty feet to the south, and making no decided alteration in its course until it came near the midway between the eastern and western boundaries of the valley. At this point, after a series of sweeps, it turned off at right angles and pursued a generally southern direction—meandering as it went—until it became lost in a small lake of irregular figure (although roughly oval), that lay gleaming near the lower extremity of the vale. This lakelet was, perhaps, a hundred yards in diameter at its widest part. No crystal could be clearer than its waters. Its bottom, which could be distinctly seen, consisted altogether of pebbles brilliantly white. Its banks, of the emerald grass already described, *rounded*,

rather than sloped, off into the clear heaven below; and *so* clear was this heaven, so perfectly, at times, did it reflect all objects above it, that where the true bank ended and where the mimic one commenced, it was a point of no little difficulty to determine. The trout, and some other varieties of fish, with which this pond seemed to be almost inconveniently crowded, had all the appearance of veritable flying-fish. It was almost impossible to believe that they were not absolutely suspended in the air. A light birch canoe that lay placidly on the water, was reflected in its minutest fibres with a fidelity unsurpassed by the most exquisitely polished mirror. A small island, fairly laughing with flowers in full bloom, and affording little more space than just enough for a picturesque little building, seemingly a fowl-house—arose from the lake not far from its northern shore—to which it was connected by means of an inconceivably light-looking and yet very primitive bridge. It was formed of a single, broad and thick plank of the tulip wood. This was forty feet long, and spanned the interval between shore and shore with a slight but very perceptible arch, preventing all oscillation. From the southern extreme of the lake issued a continuation of the rivulet, which, after meandering for, perhaps, thirty yards, finally passed through the "depression" (already described) in the middle of the southern declivity, and tumbling down a sheer precipice of a hundred feet, made its devious and unnoticed way to the Hudson.

The lake was deep—at some points thirty feet—but the rivulet seldom exceeded three, while its greatest width was about eight. Its bottom and banks were as those of the pond—if a defect could have been attributed to them, in point of picturesqueness, it was that of excessive *neatness*.

The expanse of the green turf was relieved, here and there, by an occasional showy shrub, such as the hydrangea, or the common snow-ball, or the aromatic seringa; or, more frequently, by a clump of geraniums blossoming gorgeously in great varieties. These latter grew in pots which were carefully buried in the soil, so as to give the plants the appearance of being indigenous. Besides all this, the lawn's velvet was exquisitely spotted with sheep—a considerable flock of which roamed about the vale, in company with three tamed deer, and a vast number of brilliantly-plumed ducks. A very large mastiff seemed to be in vigilant attendance upon these animals, each and all.

Along the eastern and western cliffs—where, towards the upper portion of the amphitheatre, the boundaries were more or less precipitous—grew ivy in great profusion—so that only here and there could even a glimpse of the naked rock be obtained. The northern precipice, in like manner, was almost entirely clothed by grape-vines of rare luxuriance; some springing from the soil at the base of the cliff, and others from ledges on its face.

The slight elevation which formed the lower boundary of this little domain, was crowned by a neat stone wall, of sufficient height to prevent the escape of the deer. Nothing of the fence kind was observable elsewhere; for nowhere else was an artificial enclosure needed:—any stray sheep, for example, which should attempt to make its way out of the vale by means of the ravine, would find its progress arrested, after a few yards' advance, by the precipitous ledge of rock over which tumbled the cascade that had arrested my attention as I first drew near the domain. In short, the only ingress or egress was through a grate occupying a rocky pass in the road, a few paces below the point at which I stopped to reconnoitre the scene.

I have described the brook as meandering very irregularly through the whole of its course. Its two *general* directions, as I have said, were first from west to east, and then from north to south. At the *turn*, the stream, sweeping backwards, made an almost circular loop so as to form a pen-

insula which was *very* nearly an island, and which included about the sixteenth of an acre. On this peninsula stood a dwelling-house—and when I say that this house, like the infernal terrace seen by Vathek, *"était d'une architecture inconnue dans les annales de la terre,"* I mean, merely, that its *tout ensemble* struck me with the keenest sense of combined novelty and propriety—in a word, of *poetry* —(for, than in the words just employed, I could scarcely give, of poetry in the abstract, a more rigorous definition)—and I do *not* mean that the merely *outré*[6] was perceptible in any respect.

In fact, nothing could well be more simple—more utterly unpretending than this cottage. Its marvellous *effect* lay altogether in its artistic arrangement *as a picture*. I could have fancied, while I looked at it, that some eminent landscape-painter had built it with his brush.

The point of view from which I first saw the valley, was not *altogether*, although it was nearly, the best point from which to survey the house. I will therefore describe it as I afterwards saw it—from a position on the stone wall at the southern extreme of the amphitheatre.

The main building was about twenty-four feet long and sixteen broad—certainly not more. Its total height, from the ground to the apex of the roof, could not have exceeded eighteen feet. To the west end of this structure was attached one about a third smaller in all its proportions:—the line of its front standing back about two yards from that of the larger house; and the line of its roof, of course, being considerably depressed below that of the roof adjoining. At right angles to these buildings, and from the rear of the main one—not exactly in the middle— extended a third compartment, very small —being, in general, one third less than the western wing. The roofs of the two larger were very steep—sweeping down from the ridge-beam with a long concave curve, and extending at least four feet beyond the walls in front, so as to form the roofs of two piazzas. These latter roofs, of course, needed no support; but as they had the *air* of needing it, slight and perfectly plain pillars were inserted at the corners alone. The roof of the northern wing was merely an extension of a portion of the main roof. Between the chief building and western wing arose a very tall and rather slender square chimney of hard Dutch bricks, alternately black and red:—a slight cornice of projecting bricks at the top. Over the gables, the roofs also projected very much:—in the main building about four feet to the east and two to the west. The principal door was not exactly in the main division, being a little to the east—while the two windows were to the west. These latter did not extend to the floor, but were much longer and narrower than usual—they had single shutters like doors—the panes were of lozenge form, but quite large. The door itself had its upper half of glass, also in lozenge panes—a moveable shutter secured it at night. The door to the west wing was in its gable, and quite simple— a single window looked out to the south. There was no external door to the north wing, and it, also, had only one window to the east.[7]

The blank wall of the eastern gable was relieved by stairs (with a balustrade) running diagonally across it—the ascent being from the south. Under cover of the widely projecting eave these steps gave access to a door leading into the garret, or rather loft—for it was lighted only by a single window to the north, and seemed to have been intended as a store-room.

The piazzas of the main building and western wing had no floors, as is usual; but at the doors and at each window, large, flat, irregular slabs of granite lay imbedded in the delicious turf, affording comfortable footing in all weather. Excellent paths of the same material—not *nicely* adapted, but with the velvety sod filling frequent intervals between the stones, led hither and thither from the house, to a crystal spring about five paces

off, to the road, or to one or two outhouses that lay to the north, beyond the brook, and were thoroughly concealed by a few locusts and catalpas.

Not more than six steps from the main door of the cottage stood the dead trunk of a fantastic pear-tree, so clothed from head to foot in the gorgeous bignonia blossoms that one required no little scrutiny to determine what manner of sweet thing it could be. From various arms of this tree hung cages of different kinds. In one, a large wicker cylinder with a ring at top, revelled a mocking bird; in another, an oriole; in a third, the impudent bobolink—while three or four more delicate prisons were loudly vocal with canaries.

The pillars of the piazza were enwreathed in jasmine and sweet honeysuckle; while from the angle formed by the main structure and its west wing, in front, sprang a grape-vine of unexampled luxuriance. Scorning all restraint, it had clambered first to the lower roof—then to the higher; and along the ridge of this latter it continued to writhe on, throwing out tendrils to the right and left, until at length it fairly attained the east gable, and fell trailing over the stairs.

The whole house, with its wings, was constructed of the old-fashioned Dutch shingles—broad, and with unrounded corners. It is a peculiarity of this material to give houses built of it the appearance of being wider at bottom than at top—after the manner of Egyptian architecture; and in the present instance, this exceedingly picturesque effect was aided by numerous pots of gorgeous flowers that almost encompassed the base of the buildings.

The shingles were painted a dull gray; and the happiness with which this neutral tint melted into the vivid green of the tulip tree leaves that partially overshadowed the cottage, can readily be conceived by an artist.

From the position near the stone wall, as described, the buildings were seen at great advantage—for the south-eastern angle was thrown forward—so that the eye took in at once the whole of the two fronts, with the picturesque eastern gable, and at the same time obtained just a sufficient glimpse of the northern wing, with parts of a pretty roof to the spring-house, and nearly half of a light bridge that spanned the brook in the near vicinity of the main buildings.

I did not remain very long on the brow of the hill, although long enough to make a thorough survey of the scene at my feet. It was clear that I had wandered from the road to the village, and I had thus good traveller's excuse to open the gate before me, and inquire my way, at all events; so, without more ado, I proceeded.

The road, after passing the gate, seemed to lie upon a natural ledge, sloping gradually down along the face of the northeastern cliffs. It led me on to the foot of the northern precipice, and thence over the bridge, round by the eastern gable to the front door. In this progress, I took notice that no sight of the out-houses could be obtained.

As I turned the corner of the gable, the mastiff bounded towards me in stern silence, but with the eye and the whole air of a tiger. I held him out my hand, however, in token of amity—and I never yet knew the dog who was proof against such an appeal to his courtesy. He not only shut his mouth and wagged his tail, but absolutely offered me his paw—afterwards extending his civilities to Ponto.

As no bell was discernible, I rapped with my stick against the door, which stood half open. Instantly a figure advanced to the threshold—that of a young woman about twenty-eight years of age —slender, or rather slight, and somewhat above the medium height. As she approached, with a certain *modest decision* of step altogether indescribable, I said to myself, "Surely here I have found the perfection of natural, in contradistinction from artificial *grace*." The second impression which she made on me, but by far the more vivid of the two, was that of

enthusiasm. So intense an expression of *romance*, perhaps I should call it, or of unworldliness, as that which gleamed from her deep-set eyes, had never so sunk into my heart of hearts before. I know not how it is, but this peculiar expression of the eye, wreathing itself occasionally into the lips, is the most powerful, if not absolutely the *sole* spell, which rivets my interest in woman. "*Romance*," provided my readers fully comprehend what I would here imply by the word—"romance" and "womanliness" seem to me convertible terms: and, after all, what man truly *loves* in woman, is, simply, her *womanhood*. The eyes of Annie (I heard some one from the interior call her "Annie, darling!") were "spiritual gray;" her hair, a light chestnut: this is all I had time to observe of her.[8]

At her most courteous of invitations, I entered—passing first into a tolerably wide vestibule. Having come mainly to *observe*, I took notice that to my right as I stepped in, was a window, such as those in front of the house; to the left, a door leading into the principal room; while, opposite me, an *open* door enabled me to see a small apartment, just the size of the vestibule, arranged as a study, and having a large *bow* window looking out to the north.

Passing into the parlor, I found myself with *Mr. Landor*—for this, I afterwards found, was his name. He was civil, even cordial in his manner; but just then, I was more intent on observing the arrangements of the dwelling which had so much interested me, than the personal appearance of the tenant.

The north wing, I now saw, was a bed-chamber: its door opened into the parlor. West of this door was a single window, looking towards the brook. At the west end of the parlor, were a fire-place, and a door leading into the west wing—probably a kitchen.

Nothing could be more rigorously simple than the furniture of the parlor. On the floor was an ingrain carpet, of excellent texture—a white ground, spotted with small circular green figures. At the windows were curtains of snowy white jaconet muslin: they were tolerably full, and hung *decisively*, perhaps rather formally, in sharp, parallel plaits to the floor—*just* to the floor. The walls were papered with a French paper of great delicacy—a silver ground, with a faint green cord running zig-zag throughout. Its expanse was relieved merely by three of Julien's exquisite lithographs *à trois crayons*,[9] fastened to the wall without frames. One of these drawings was a scene of Oriental luxury, or rather voluptuousness; another was a "carnival piece," spirited beyond compare; the third was a Greek female head —a face so divinely beautiful, and yet of an expression so provokingly indeterminate, never before arrested my attention.

The more substantial furniture consisted of a round table, a few chairs (including a large rocking-chair,) and a sofa, or rather "settee:" its material was plain maple painted a creamy white, slightly interstriped with green—the seat of cane. The chairs and table were "to match;" but the *forms* of all had evidently been designed by the same brain which planned "the grounds:" it is impossible to conceive anything more graceful.

On the table were a few books; a large, square, crystal bottle of some novel perfume; a plain, ground-glass *astral* (not solar) lamp,[10] with an Italian shade; and a large vase of resplendently-blooming flowers. Flowers indeed of gorgeous colors and delicate odor, formed the sole mere *decoration* of the apartment. The fire-place was nearly filled with a vase of brilliant geranium. On a triangular shelf in each angle of the room stood also a similar vase, varied only as to its lovely contents. One or two smaller *bouquets* adorned the mantel; and late violets clustered about the open windows.

It is not the purpose of this work to do more than give, in detail, a picture of Mr. Landor's residence—*as I found it.*

Figure Six. This plate accompanied "The Elk" ("Morning on the Wissahiccon") in its first appearance in *The Opal*. See the Section Preface and note 1. Reproduced courtesy of the American Antiquarian Society.

MORNING ON THE WISSAHICCON[1]

The natural scenery of America has often been contrasted, in its general features as well as in detail, with the landscape of the Old World—more especially of Europe—and not deeper has been the enthusiasm, than wide the dissension, of the supporters of each region. The discussion is one not likely to be soon closed, for, although much has been said on both sides, a word more yet remains to be said.

The most conspicuous of the British tourists who have attempted a comparison, seem to regard our northern and eastern seaboard, comparatively speaking, as all of America, at least, as all of the United States, worthy consideration. They say little, because they have seen less, of the gorgeous interior scenery of some of our western and southern districts—of the vast valley of Louisiana, for example,—a

realization of the wildest dreams of paradise. For the most part, these travellers
content themselves with a hasty inspection of the natural *lions* of the land—the
Hudson, Niagara, the Catskills, Harper's
Ferry, the lakes of New York, the Ohio,
the prairies, and the Mississippi. These,
indeed, are objects well worthy the contemplation even of him who has just
clambered by the castellated Rhine, or
roamed

> By the blue rushing of the
> arrowy Rhone;[2]

but these are not *all* of which we can
boast; and, indeed, I will be so hardy as
to assert that there are innumerable quiet,
obscure, and scarcely explored nooks,
within the limits of the United States,
that, by the true artist, or cultivated lover
of the grand and beautiful amid the works
of God, will be preferred to each *and to
all* of the chronicled and better accredited
scenes to which I have referred.

In fact, the real Edens of the land lie far
away from the track of our own most deliberate tourists—how very far, then, beyond the reach of the foreigner, who, having made with his publisher at home
arrangements for a certain amount of
comment upon America, to be furnished
in a stipulated period, can hope to fulfil
his agreement in no other manner than
by steaming it, memorandum-book in
hand, through only the most beaten thoroughfares of the country!

I mentioned, just above, the valley of
Louisiana. Of all extensive areas of natural loveliness, this is perhaps the most
lovely. No fiction has approached it. The
most gorgeous imagination might derive
suggestions from its exuberant beauty.
And *beauty* is, indeed, its sole character.
It has little, or rather nothing, of the sublime.[3] Gentle undulations of soil, inter-
wreathed with fantastic crystallic streams,
banked by flowery slopes, and backed by
a forest vegetation, gigantic, glossy, multi-
coloured, sparkling with gay birds and
burthened with perfume—these features
make up, in the vale of Louisiana, the

most voluptuous natural scenery upon
earth.

But, even of this delicious region, the
sweeter portions are reached only by by-
paths. Indeed, in America generally, the
traveller who would behold the finest
landscapes, must seek them not by the
railroad, nor by the steamboat, nor by the
stage-coach, nor in his private carriage,
nor yet even on horseback—but on foot.
He must *walk*, he must leap ravines, he
must risk his neck among precipices, or
he must leave unseen the truest, the richest, and most unspeakable glories of the
land.

Now in the greater portion of Europe
no such necessity exists. In England it
exists not at all. The merest dandy of a
tourist may there visit every nook worth
visiting without detriment to his silk
stockings; so thoroughly known are all
points of interest, and so well-arranged
are the means of attaining them. This
consideration has never been allowed its
due weight, in comparisons of the natural
scenery of the Old and New Worlds. The
entire loveliness of the former is collated
with only the most noted, and with by no
means the most eminent items in the general loveliness of the latter.

River scenery has, unquestionably,
within itself, all the main elements of
beauty, and, time out of mind, has been
the favourite theme of the poet. But much
of this fame is attributable to the predom-
inance of travel in fluvial over that in
mountainous districts. In the same way,
large rivers, because usually highways,
have, in all countries, absorbed an undue
share of admiration. They are more observed, and, consequently, made more the
subject of discourse, than less important,
but often more interesting streams.

A singular exemplification of my remarks upon this head may be found in
the Wissahiccon,[4] a brook, (for more it
can scarcely be called,) which empties itself into the Schuylkill, about six miles
westward of Philadelphia. Now the Wissahiccon is of so remarkable a loveliness

that, were it flowing in England, it would be the theme of every bard, and the common topic of every tongue, if, indeed, its banks were not parcelled off in lots, at an exorbitant price, as building-sites for the villas of the opulent. Yet it is only within a very few years that any one has more than heard of the Wissahiccon, while the broader and more navigable water into which it flows, has been long celebrated as one of the finest specimens of American river scenery. The Schuylkill, whose beauties have been much exaggerated, and whose banks, at least in the neighborhood of Philadelphia, are marshy like those of the Delaware, is not at all comparable, as an object of picturesque interest, with the more humble and less notorious rivulet of which we speak.

It was not until Fanny Kemble, in her droll book[5] about the United States, pointed out to the Philadelphians the rare loveliness of a stream which lay at their own doors, that this loveliness was more than suspected by a few adventurous pedestrians of the vicinity. But, the "Journal" having opened all eyes, the Wissahiccon, to a certain extent, rolled at once into notoriety. I say "to a certain extent," for, in fact, the true beauty of the stream lies far above the route of the Philadelphian picturesque-hunters, who rarely proceed farther than a mile or two above the mouth of the rivulet—for the very excellent reason that here the carriage-road stops. I would advise the adventurer who would behold its finest points to take the Ridge Road, running westwardly from the city, and, having reached the second lane beyond the sixth mile-stone, to follow this lane to its termination. He will thus strike the Wissahiccon, at one of its best reaches, and, in a skiff, or by clambering along its banks, he can go up or down the stream, as best suits his fancy, and in either direction will meet his reward.

I have already said, or should have said, that the brook is narrow. Its banks are generally, indeed almost universally, precipitous, and consist of high hills, clothed with noble shrubbery near the water, and crowned at a greater elevation, with some of the most magnificent forest trees of America, among which stands conspicuous the liriodendron tulipiferum. The immediate shores, however, are of granite, sharply-defined or moss-covered, against which the pellucid water lolls in its gentle flow, as the blue waves of the Mediterranean upon the steps of her palaces of marble. Occasionally in front of the cliffs, extends a small definite plateau of richly herbaged land, affording the most picturesque position for a cottage and garden which the richest imagination could conceive. The windings of the stream are many and abrupt, as is usually the case where banks are precipitous, and thus the impression conveyed to the voyager's eye, as he proceeds, is that of an endless succession of infinitely varied small lakes, or, more properly speaking, tarns. The Wissahiccon, however, should be visited, not like "fair Melrose,"[6] by moonlight, or even in cloudy weather, but amid the brightest glare of a noonday sun; for the narrowness of the gorge through which it flows, the height of the hills on either hand, and the density of the foliage, conspire to produce a gloominess, if not an absolute dreariness of effect, which, unless relieved by a bright general light, detracts from the mere beauty of the scene.

Not long ago I visited the stream by the route described, and spent the better part of a sultry day in floating in a skiff upon its bosom. The heat gradually overcame me, and, resigning myself to the influence of the scenes and of the weather, and of the gently moving current, I sank into a half slumber, during which my imagination revelled in visions of the Wissahiccon of ancient days—of the "good old days" when the Demon of the Engine was not, when pic-nics were undreamed of, when "water privileges" were neither bought nor sold, and when the red man trod alone, with the elk, upon the ridges that now towered above. And, while gradually these conceits took possession of my mind, the lazy brook had borne me, inch by inch, around one promontory and within full view of another that bounded the prospect at the distance of forty or fifty yards. It was a steep rocky cliff, abutting far into the stream, and presenting much more of the Salvator[7] character than any portion of the shore hitherto passed. What I saw upon this cliff, although surely an object of very extraordinary nature, the place and season considered, at first neither startled nor amazed me—so thoroughly and appropriately did it chime in with the half-slumberous fancies that enwrapped me. I saw, or dreamed that I saw, standing upon the extreme verge of the precipice, with neck outstretched, with ears erect, and the whole attitude indicative of profound and melancholy inquisitiveness, one of the oldest and boldest of those identical elks which had been coupled with the red men of my vision.

I say that, for a few moments, this apparition neither startled nor amazed me. During this interval my whole soul was bound up in intense sympathy alone. I fancied the elk repining, not less than wondering, at the manifest alterations for the worse, wrought upon the brook and its vicinage, even within the last few years, by the stern hand of the utilitarian. But a slight movement of the animal's head at once dispelled the dreaminess which invested me, and aroused me to a full sense of the novelty of the adventure. I arose upon one knee within the skiff, and, while I hesitated whether to stop my career, or let myself float nearer to the object of my wonder, I heard the words "hist!" "hist!" ejaculated quickly but cautiously, from the shrubbery overhead. In an instant afterwards, a negro emerged from the thicket, putting aside the bushes with care, and treading stealthily. He bore in one hand a quantity of salt, and, holding it towards the elk, gently yet steadily approached. The noble animal, although a little fluttered, made no attempt at escape. The negro advanced; offered the salt; and spoke a few words of encouragement or conciliation. Presently, the elk bowed and stamped, and then lay quietly down and was secured with a halter.

Thus ended my romance of the elk. It was a *pet* of great age and very domestic habits, and belonged to an English family occupying a villa in the vicinity.[8]

Notes

The Domain of Arnheim

1. This piece is an expansion of an earlier sketch, "The Landscape Garden," which Poe first published in Snowden's *Ladies' Companion*, October 1842, and again in *The Broadway Journal*, September 20, 1845. The two versions are not identical, as Hervey Allen said they were, but the variations, with one exception, are not important. The brackets enclose some of those passages which appeared in *The Broadway Journal* version, but not in "The Domain of Arnheim" as it appeared in the *Columbian Magazine* of March 1847; asterisks (*) appear before and after some of the passages which are in the later version only. The one important change is that "The Landscape Garden" ends before the explanation of how Ellison put his theory into practice, and the guided tour through the garden itself.

"The Domain of Arnheim" is generally terser and less heavily punctuated and uses shorter paragraphs than the earlier version; we have followed its usage. This book is not a variorum edition, but since this piece had two separate lives, we give the reader an idea of how Poe changed and expanded his own story. Moore convincingly argues that the name and a part of the texture of the story were probably derived from Scott's *Anne of Geierstein*, especially chapters 11 and 21.

2. In this excerpt from Fletcher's "Christ's Victory on Earth" Poe modernized the spelling (Harrison). Note that Poe chose a poem in which the beauty of a woman is equated with the beauty of a garden. He said, in "The Philosophy of Composition," "the death . . . of a beautiful woman is, unquestionably, the most poetical topic in the world." Fletcher's lady is asleep, not dead, but clearly Poe wants the reader to see that his sketch concerns ideal beauty. Several times he tells us that Ellison was happily married to a beautiful woman.

3. Anne Robert Jacques Turgot: French statesman and economist (1727–1781).

Richard Price: English moral and political philosopher (1723–1791).

Joseph Priestley: the English theologian, philosopher and chemist (1733–1804), who fled England for the United States late in his career because of his liberal religious ideas.

Condorcet: Marie Jean de Caritat, the French social philosopher and revolutionist (1743–1794).

Poe's narrator means to suggest that human perfection is indeed possible. Poe was usually contemptuous of such optimism when it was applied to man in society; he was politically conservative. But he did believe that the inspired creator, the poet (or landscape architect) could achieve transcendent inspiration and be "perfect" in that sense. Perhaps this belief accounts for his generosity to liberal theorists here. Later in this piece, indeed, we are told that Ellison himself does not believe that we can improve "the general condition of man."

4. Poe turned this sentence around. "The Landscape Garden" reads, "He pointed to the tillers of the earth—the only people who, as a class, are proverbially more happy than others—and then he instanced. . . ." etc. There are a number of changes of this sort which, henceforth, are not mentioned.

5. An incident, similar in outline to the one here imagined, occurred, not very long ago, in England. The name of the fortunate heir was Thelluson. I first saw an account of this matter in the "Tour" of Prince Pückler-Muskau, who makes the sum inherited *ninety millions of pounds*, and justly observes that "in the contemplation of so vast a sum, and of the services to which it might be applied, there is something even of the sublime." To suit the views of this article I have followed the Prince's statement, although a grossly exaggerated one. The germ, and, in fact, the commencement of the present paper was published many years ago—previous to the issue of the first number of Sue's admirable "*Juif errant*," which may possibly have been suggested to him by Muskau's account [Poe's note].

Marie Joseph Sue (Eugène Sue), French novelist (1804–1857). His novel, *Le Juif errant*, does concern a legacy which, invested, accrues interest over 150 years.

Hermann Ludwig Heinrich Fürst Von Pückler-Muskau, German writer of books of travel (1785–1871).

6. See "Some Passages in the Life of a Lion," note 7.

7. Materialism: Poe means something special by "materialism." He had the idea that inspiration, creativity, and insight were the result ultimately of physical connections which unite the entire universe. In the second paragraph he said that Ellison was lucky to believe in "the instinctive philosophy." Human intuition was capable, in Poe's scheme, of establishing contact with the force that interconnects the world. Poe shared that idea with many romantic writers—Blake, Shelley and Emerson, to name three very different ones—and with occultists in all times and places, who believe that the universe is of a piece and that man is capable of merging his consciousness with it. But unlike most other believers, Poe felt that the connection was not merely spiritual. It was based on physical, material fact, and ultimately we were likely to discover what the "force" or "carrier" was. In *Eureka* he tried to spell out his theory. A very clear example of it appears in the tale "The Power of Words," in which a character literally "speaks" a star into being.

"Mute and inglorious": Poe is alluding to Thomas Gray's "Elegy Written in a Country Churchyard": "Some mute inglorious Milton here may rest . . . ," which is to say, some

potentially great poet who never wrote a
poem.

8. Claude: Claude Lorrain (1600–1682), an
important French landscape painter whose
works strongly influenced many artists of
Poe's day. Poe selected his example well:
Claude Lorrain began with fine topographi-
cal sketches, but his final paintings are not at
all literal records of the places in Italy which
his sketches record. See Figure Two.

Byron . . . *ideal*: Poe has altered lines from
Canto 2, CXVIII of *Don Juan*, part of a description of Haidée, selected because Byron
also compares life to sculpture:

> . . . for she was one
> Fit for the model of a statuary
> (A race of mere imposters,
> when all's done—
> I've seen much finer women,
> ripe and real,
> Than all the nonsense of their
> stone ideal).

9. This paragraph and the one above are
the most heavily rewritten in the piece. Poe
apparently felt that Ellison's point about a
beauty different from the kind mortal artists
know was extremely important. His revisions
do not change his meaning; rather, they explain it and make his point more explicit.
For a fuller discussion of the idea that the design of the earth is intended to reflect man's
mortality, see his lengthy metaphysical discourse *Eureka*: "In the Original Unity of the
First Thing lies the Secondary Cause of All
Things, with the Germ of their Inevitable
Annihilation."

10. healthy: The early version has "beautiful" instead of "healthy." Most minor
changes of this sort are for stylistic reasons
and are not mentioned here, but this one is
interesting. The garden which Ellison creates
is surprisingly artificial, elaborate, un-"natural." It may be that the change here from
"beautiful" to "healthy" is to make the point
that the writer whom Ellison is quoting, in
stressing "healthy" order, is missing the point
that beauty (which we've just been told might
be better perceived after death) may not be a
matter of "health." Ellison says in the first
sentence of the next paragraph that he rejects this writer's ideas.

Versailles: the elaborate French palace and
gardens in the city of Versailles near Paris.

11. fervid: Ellison comes by his creativity
easily, but even his dreams are "fervid." Poe

is telling us what beauty is, and working hard
to destroy any preconceptions we may have
about balance, symmetry, order, or serenity.

Addison: Joseph Addison, the neo-classical
essayist (1672–1719). Poe is attacking neo-
classical notions of beauty by way of preparing us for the very different kind of beauty
embodied in Ellison's garden.

"Cato" . . . "Inferno": Interesting that Poe
uses Addison's tragedy "Cato" (first produced in 1713) to represent the neo-classical
ideals he is attacking, but groups the Parthenon, which is generally considered a triumph
of classicism, with Dante's "Inferno" as an
example of the more unrestrained creativity
he advocated. In the earlier version of the
story he used different examples:

> We may be instructed to build an Od-
> yssey, but it is in vain that we are told
> *how* to conceive a "Tempest," an "In-
> ferno," a "Prometheus Bound," a
> "Nightingale," such as that of Keats, or
> the "Sensitive Plant" of Shelley.

We guess that Poe was unsure of the examples which would illustrate works of the
"negative school." Perhaps it's not entirely
accurate to say that he is attacking classical
ideals, but that his target was simply the idea
of restraint, understood to mean a check on
being "fervid" (see above). We find it hard to
think of the Parthenon as "fervid." The religion which the Parthenon served, of course,
was strongly occult; it might be that Poe was
telling us that there is more to classicism
than restraint and order: if English neo-clas-
sicism (Addison) was urbane, polished, and
orderly, Greek classicism had been magical.

12. Poe tinkered extensively with the sentence structure and wording of this paragraph, mostly to increase clarity and to improve parallelism. At this point, he added a
clause, and changed "*harmonized*" to "*one
step depressed.*"

13. This is the end of "The Landscape Garden." The rest of "The Domain of Arnheim"
is new.

Madame de Staël: (Germaine Necker, 1766–
1817) a French novelist and critic noted for
her belief in a romantic aesthetic. Like Poe,
she contrasts clarity, order, and form with
mystery, emotion, and indefiniteness, and
like him, too, she prefers the latter.

14. Timon of Athens is always used as an
example of misanthropy. There are a Shake-

speare play, "The Life of Timon of Athens," a brief account of him in Plutarch's *Lives*, and a dialogue by Lucian, *Timon, or the Misanthrope.*

15. Etna, the volcano in Sicily.

16. Fonthill Abbey: an early and rather silly example of English interest in reviving Gothic architecture. When a large portion of the building collapsed, its owner is supposed to have been delighted: now he had not only his own Gothic building, but a Gothic ruin.

17. From here to the end of the tale Poe gives us a description of what to him represents ideal beauty. "Funereal gloom," intricacy, and strangeness may not match our preconceptions of the components of beauty, but the passage is important for an understanding of Poe's taste.

18. Poe means "elaborate and intertwined, but non-representational, ornamentation," as in Moorish or Arabian architecture. Much Arabesque ornamentation involves stylized representation of leaves and flowers. The term is important in Poe: see "The Philosophy of Composition" (*Works*, XIV, 205) and discussions of Poe's knowledge of the Schlegels' use of "Arabesque" (Thompson 3, 4). A definition which relates design to philosophical implication is Malachi Martin's:

> A central design extending in curved, angular, straight patterns that in turn generate stars within circles, squares within stars, flowers and fruit and beads linked by fragile stems and stout columns and intertwining twigs that flow into Arabic lettering and double back to rejoin and repeat the central design. Color, rhythm and form tumble and twine in symmetries leading to the asymmetrical. Visual and tactile traceries taper into invisible tracks and then reappear in further traceries. Semicircles bud unexpectedly from the sides of squares. Curves interrupted by jagged points flow into empty spaces, to reappear beyond in aery ellipses as in epigrams of mystery.

19. Saracenic: Arabian. We have now been taken, in our little boat, through a carefully programmed tour of an artificially "augmented" fairyland in which lighting effects are controlled, doors swing open as we approach, and music plays for us. What Poe proposes seems no less artificial and elaborate than Disneyland.

The Philosophy of Furniture

1. "People give lip service to better things but follow after the poorer" (Carlson 2). Poe's Latin phrase is a variant on a passage from Ovid's Metamorphoses (VII, 20):

> *Video meliora proboque,*
> *Deteriora sequor.*

2. Rivalry between the newly wealthy.

3. Literally, the land in and around the Appalachian Mountains, which run from the Gaspé Peninsula in Canada down into Alabama. In contemporary usage, Appalachia usually means the economically depressed southern and border-state mountain areas, and it carries connotations of poverty and backwardness. Until quite recently, the area carried humorous connotations for many Americans—it was the land of hillbillies. Poe means for it to cover all of the heavily settled portions of the United States of his day, but he seems also to want to be snide, which would suggest that even in his time the word carried some connotations of comical "backwardness." We have not encountered it in that context in other writers of his period, however.

4. *d'un mouton qui rêve:* "of a dreaming sheep."

Riccaree: not a tribe we've ever heard of; perhaps an alternative name for the Arikara, an offshoot branch of the Skidi Pawnee who lived in what are now the Dakotas.

Arabesque: see "The Domain of Arnheim," note 18.

Median laws: see "King Pest," note 12.

Baal: there were a number of ancient middle-Eastern gods of this name, but in general usage the word means "false god."

Mammon: the personification of wealth.

Bentham: Jeremy Bentham (1748–1832), an English jurist and philosopher. Very sympathetic to American political ideals, he believed in a society designed to produce the greatest happiness for the greatest number of citizens. Poe was highly skeptical of such ideals.

5. astral lamp: an oil lamp designed so that the reservoir of oil does not produce a dark shadow under the flame.

Argand: Aimé Argand (1755–1803), Swiss scientist.

6. confused mixture.

7. Ormolu refers to any of a number of alloys which look like gold and are used in decorating.

8. *veranda:* portico or balcony.

Stanfield: William Clarkson Stanfield (1794–1867), an English painter.

Chapman: John Gadsby Chapman (1808–1889), an American painter, illustrator, and craftsman whom Poe might have known personally. In Tuckerman there is a description of his studio in New York, the furnishings of which ran largely to props he used in his paintings, and which may have a little to do with this essay.

Sully: Thomas Sully (1783–1872), well-known Philadelphia portraitist whose works Poe could have seen in many places.

Sèvres: a kind of fine porcelain.

Poe published this in *Burton's Gentleman's Magazine* in May 1840, and it is not improper to compare his purposes to those of writers in glossy men's magazines such as *Esquire* or *Playboy* today, who tell one how to decorate one's pad. He reprinted the piece, this time titled "House Furniture," in *The Broadway Journal,* May 3, 1845, a paper in some ways like the modern *New Yorker:* it ran fiction and poetry articles on current art and music, commentary, and reportage. We follow precedent in coupling the *Journal* text to the *Burton's* title.

The Island of the Fay

1. "Each place has its own character." Servius: Probably Maurus Servius Honoratus, fourth-century grammarian and commentator on Virgil. When Poe first published this sketch in *Graham's Magazine* (June 1841), he used a version of his sonnet "To Science," altered to include the fay, and signed "ANON." in *The Broadway Journal* (October 4, 1845), he dropped the sonnet and used the motto. The sonnet reads:

> Science, true daughter of old Time
>   thou art,
> Who alterest all things with thy
>   peering eyes!
> Why prey'st thou thus upon the
>   poet's heart,
> Vulture, whose wings are dull realities?
> How should he love thee, or how deem
>   thee wise

> Who wouldst not leave him, in
>   his wandering,
> To seek for treasure on the
>   jewelled skies,
> Albeit he soared with an
>   undaunted wing?
> Hast thou not dragged Diana from
>   her car?
> And driven the Hamadryad from
>   the wood?
> Hast thou not spoilt a story in
>   each star?
> Hast thou not torn the Naiad from
>   her flood?
> The elfin from the grass?—the
>   dainty *fay,*
> The witch, the sprite, the goblin—
>   where are they?
>   *Anon.*

Except for changes in punctuation, the first ten lines are unaltered. But the last four have been rewritten. The idea of a story in a star appears also in the tale "The Power of Words"; Poe's point is that the world is literally ideas; thought and creativity are the same. The other changes are designed to connect the idea of supernatural beings with the creative process and the animate universe. The four lines in the standard version of the sonnet run,

> To seek a shelter in some happier star?
> Hast thou not torn the Naiad from
>   her flood,
> The elfin from the green grass, and
>   from me
> The summer dream beneath the
>   tamarind tree?

2. "Contes Moraux": Moraux is here derived from *moeurs,* and its meaning is "fashionable," or, more strictly, "of manners" [Poe's note]. The *Contes Moraux* of Jean-Francois Marmontel (1723–1799) appeared from 1755 to 1761.

la musique . . . témoins: "Music is the only one of the talents which is enjoyable for itself; all the others desire witnesses" (Carlson 2).

raconteur: story-teller (Poe is referring to Marmontel).

animalculæ: Poe's error in Latin. The plural of *animalculum* (minute animal) is *animalcula.* The passage is most important; see Section Preface.

3. Speaking of the tides, Pomponius Mela, in his treatise *De Situ Orbis,* says "either the

world is a great animal, or" etc. [Poe's note].

Pomponius Mela: first-century Roman geographer. The passage to which Poe refers was translated as follows by Arthur Golding in 1585: "Neither is it yet certainlie knowne, whether the world cause it [tides] with his panting, and uttereth out on all sides about him the water that he had drawne in with his breath, for (as it seemeth to the learned sort) the world is a lyving wight: or whether there be some hollowe caves in the ground for the ebbing Seas to retire into, and to lyft themselves out againe when they are too full: or whether the Moone be the cause of so great fleetings."

4. What flippant Frenchman: Balzac—in substance—I do not remember the words [Poe's note]. Poe refers to the novelist Honoré de Balzac (1799–1850). We have not found the passage.

Zimmerman: Johann Georg, Ritter Von Zimmerman (1728–1795), a Swiss philosophical writer and physician who wrote "On Solitude," in 1756 and amended and enlarged it in 1784–1785.

la solitude . . . chose: "Solitude is a beautiful thing, but it is necessary for someone to tell you that solitude is a beautiful thing."

5. Florem putares nare per liquidum aethera—P. Commire [Poe's note]. "You would imagine a flower floating through the liquid air." Poe found the quotation in the same item in Disraeli's Curiosities of Literature from which he took the ventum textilum (see "The Spectacles," note 5). Disraeli translates the line, "It FLIES, and swims a flower in liquid air!"

Pere Jean Commire: (1625–1702), a French Jesuit.

Landor's Cottage

1. mountain wagon: a large wagon characterized by an oversized brake. The gear in general is more substantial than in other wagons. Some of these wagons could haul up to 6,500 lbs. (See Figure Four.)

Genoese Velvet: Genoa velvet, an obsolete, very fine, thick, all-silk, weft-pile velvet brocade made on a one up, two down twill ground.

For another tale in which a character gets lost on a hazy, warm, Indian summer day

during a walk in the mountains and has a "vision," see "A Tale of the Ragged Mountains." That story was published first in 1844; this one is the last tale Poe published; it appeared in Flag of Our Union, June 9, 1849. On the artificiality of Poe's ideal "nature," see Section Preface and "The Domain of Arnheim," notes 10 and 19.

2. The English word "picturesque" generally means strikingly or quaintly beautiful. Poe wants us to think of the root of the word, literally, "like a picture," that is, a painted and contrived work of pictorial art.

3. chasse, quick sliding movement, as in a dance step.

4. glance.

5. Salvatorish: like trees in the works of Salvator Rosa (c. 1615–1673). See Figure Five.

Itchiatuckanee: there is an Ichetucknee Springs in north central Florida.

Liriodendron Tulipiferum: a favorite of Poe. See "Morning on the Wissahiccon," note 6, and "The Gold-Bug," note 9.

6. Vathek: the central character of Vathek: An Arabian Tale, a famous, early (1786) gothic novel by William Beckford. The French passage may be translated, "was of an architecture unknown in the annals of the earth."

tout ensemble: total effect.

outré: excessive, strange.

7. A. H. Quinn says that the description of setting and cottage are based on Poe's home in Fordham, highly romanticized. He quotes a description by a visitor to Poe's home: "We found him, and his wife, and his wife's mother—who was his aunt—living in a little cottage at the top of a hill. There was an acre or two of greensward, fenced in about the house, as smooth as velvet and as clean as the best kept carpet. There were some grand old cherry-trees in the yard, that threw a massive shade around them. The house had three rooms—a kitchen, a sitting room, and a bed-chamber over the sitting-room. There was a piazza in front of the house that was a lovely place to sit in in summer, with the shade of cherry-trees before it. There was no cultivation, no flowers—nothing but the smooth greensward and the majestic trees. . . ."

8. One of Poe's letters to Mrs. Charles Richmond (née Nancy Locke Heywood, or "Annie") says that "Landor's Cottage" has,

as Poe puts it, "something about 'Annie' in it. . . ."

9. jaconet muslin: strictly speaking, a contradiction in terms, since "jaconet" and "muslin" refer to cotton cloths originally produced in two different parts of the world. We take it, though, that the combined form was a dry-goods term current at the time which would have been perfectly clear in meaning to a housewife.

Julien: Simon Julien (1736–1800), a French historical painter known as "Julien de Parme" after his patron, the Duke of Parma.

à trois crayons: a chalk drawing done in three colors, almost always red and white chalk and black chalk or charcoal.

10. See "The Philosophy of Furniture," note 5.

Morning on the Wissahiccon

1. When this piece was published in a gift-book called The Opal/A Pure Gift for the Holy Days (dated 1844, but probably published late in 1843 for the Christmas trade), it was called "Morning on the Wissahiccon," a title Poe probably got from a sketch (probably not by Poe) in the December 1833 Southern Literary Messenger (Heartman and Canny). In the Griswold edition of 1850, it is called "The Elk." Poe's authorship of the present piece is certain—he mentions it in a letter to Lowell, May 28, 1844. The Opal that year was edited by Nathaniel Willis (see "The Duc De L'Omelette").

2. From Byron's Childe Harold, III, stanza 71.

3. The word "sublime" carried special connotations in Poe's day—not merely "noble" and "grand," but also "awesome," almost "frightening."

4. The name is now spelled "Wissahickon."

5. Poe refers to the 1835 Journal by Frances Anne Butler (Fanny Kemble). He wrote a review of an 1835 issue of The Edinburgh Review for the Southern Literary Messenger (December 1835); the Edinburgh contained a review of the Kemble Journal, and Poe discussed it at length. Fanny Kemble had been attacked in the United States for her supposed hostility to this country; Poe says the Edinburgh review is correct in saying that she was fair, showed both sides, liked much of what she saw here, and that Americans are much too thin-skinned about foreign criticism.

6. liriodendron tulipiferum: See "The Gold-Bug," note 9, and "Landor's Cottage," note 5.

"fair Melrose": Poe alludes to Sir Walter Scott's The Lay of the Last Minstrel, Canto II, stanza 1:

> If thou would'st view fair
>   Melrose aright,
> go visit it by the pale moonlight.

7. See "Landor's Cottage," note 5.

8. This sketch is similar in many details to "Landor's Cottage," which seems based on it.

2. Salvation Through Terror

A Descent into the Maelström; The Pit and the Pendulum. If, as Poe said, his aim as artist was to create the beautiful effect, and if "A Descent into the Maelström" is characteristic of that desire, then the description of the wild beauty of the interior of the Maelström on this weird and terrible night should be worth comparing with the scenes of "ideal" beauty we noted in "The Landscape Garden" and "The Philosophy of Furniture." Different as this tale is, its "beautiful effect" is strangely similar to those in the first group. We may simply note again the consistency of Poe's taste, or look to philosophical explanations. Mystics in all ages have taught that there are multiple paths to enlightenment and described visions which remind us strongly of these "beautiful effects" in Poe: kaleidoscopic unfoldings of complex luminosity. However we explain them, the effects are present in exceedingly dissimilar stories, and characters perceive them in very different ways. Thus, while Ellison creates his beauty without difficulty, the fisherman must be frightened into the state of supersensitivity which enables him to find beauty in his strange surroundings. Apparently the more difficult the process of perceiving "beauty," the more complex the plot.

Thus we expect and get a complex plot in "The Pit and the Pendulum," another tale of salvation from strange surroundings. The brilliance which the narrator needs to sustain his life does not come as naturally as Ellison's artistic brilliance in "The Domain of Arnheim." It is more like the brilliance of the fisherman in "A Descent into the Maelström." The progression down to despair and insanity and up to insight is what makes him "brilliant." Poe is interested in the varieties of inspired creativity—hence the hint that dreams and fainting fits carry knowledge of eternity; the unconscious mind may know what will be known after death. The person just awakening has dim memories of such knowledge. The narrator, in an abnormal state, tortured and frightened, has glimpses of it while awake.

A troubling weakness in many of Poe's tales shows up in "Maelström": often the language of the "simple fisherman" is not only cool, but also far too erudite to be credible. The sentence at note 18 seems especially inappropriate. The trouble may be, as Poe says, haste (see note 12), or it may be that the repertoire of "magazinists" of his day generally did not include effective dialogue. One can read through whole volumes of the magazines in which he published without finding convincing dialogue; most of the authors' efforts seem to be devoted to description of the fantastic. This strange period and genre in the history of literature is called "magazinism."

The Tales

A DESCENT INTO THE MAELSTRÖM

The ways of God in Nature, as in Providence, are not as our ways; nor are the models that we frame any way commensurate to the vastness, profundity, and unsearchableness of His works, which have a depth in them greater than the well of Democritus.
Joseph Glanvill[1]

We had now reached the summit of the loftiest crag. For some minutes the old man seemed too much exhausted to speak.

"Not long ago," said he at length, "and I could have guided you on this route as well as the youngest of my sons; but, about three years past, there happened to me an event such as never happened before to mortal man—or at least such as no man ever survived to tell of—and the six hours of deadly terror which I then endured have broken me up body and soul. You suppose me a *very* old man—but I am not. It took less than a single day to change these hairs from a jetty black to white, to weaken my limbs, and to unstring my nerves, so that I tremble at the least exertion, and am frightened at a shadow. Do you know I can scarcely look over this little cliff without getting giddy?"

The "little cliff," upon whose edge he had so carelessly thrown himself down to rest that the weightier portion of his body hung over it, while he was only kept from falling by the tenure of his elbow on its extreme and slippery edge—this "little cliff" arose, a sheer unobstructed precipice of black shining rock, some fifteen or sixteen hundred feet from the world of crags beneath us. Nothing would have tempted

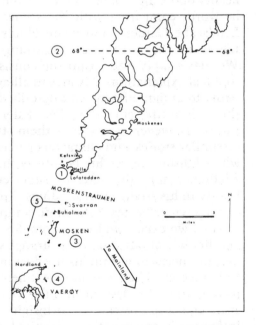

Figure Seven. A map of the area in which Poe's "A Descent into the Maelström" is set, showing places named in the tale:
1. Lofotodden headland, the probable site of the storytelling.
2. The 68° parallel
3. Mosken ("Moskoe")
4. Vaerøy ("Varrgh")
5. Tiny islands mentioned by fisherman
Only Svarvan ("Suarven") and Buholman ("Buckholm") are named on the charts we examined. Map by Lewis Armstrong.

me to be within half a dozen yards of its brink. In truth so deeply was I excited by the perilous position of my companion, that I fell at full length upon the ground, clung to the shrubs around me, and dared not even glance upward at the sky—while I struggled in vain to divest myself of the idea that the very foundations of the mountain were in danger from the fury of the winds. It was long before I could reason myself into sufficient courage to sit up and look out into the distance.

"You must get over these fancies," said the guide, "for I have brought you here that you might have the best possible view of the scene of that event I mentioned—and to tell you the whole story with the spot just under your eye."

"We are now," he continued, in that particularizing manner which distinguished him—"we are now close upon the Norwegian coast—in the sixty-eighth degree of latitude—in the great province of Nordland—and in the dreary district of Lofoden.[2] The mountain upon whose top we sit is Helseggen, the Cloudy. Now raise yourself up a little higher—hold on to the grass if you feel giddy—so—and look out, beyond the belt of vapor beneath us, into the sea."

I looked dizzily, and beheld a wide expanse of ocean, whose waters wore so inky a hue as to bring at once to my mind the Nubian geographer's account of the *Mare Tenebrarum*.[3] A panorama more deplorably desolate no human imagination can conceive. To the right and left, as far as the eye could reach, there lay outstretched, like ramparts of the world, lines of horridly black and beetling cliff, whose character of gloom was but the more forcibly illustrated by the surf which reared high up against it its white and ghastly crest, howling and shrieking for ever. Just opposite the promontory upon whose apex we were placed, and at a distance of some five or six miles out at sea, there was visible a small, bleak-looking island; or, more properly, its position was discernible through the wilderness of surge in which

it was enveloped. About two miles nearer the land, arose another of smaller size, hideously craggy and barren, and encompassed at various intervals by a cluster of dark rocks.

The appearance of the ocean, in the space between the more distant island and the shore, had something very unusual about it. Although, at the time, so strong a gale was blowing landward that a brig in the remote offing lay to under a double-reefed trysail, and constantly plunged her whole hull out of sight, still there was here nothing like a regular swell, but only a short, quick, angry cross dashing of water in every direction—as well in the teeth of the wind as otherwise. Of foam there was little except in the immediate vicinity of the rocks.

"The island in the distance," resumed the old man, "is called by the Norwegians Vurrgh. The one midway is Moskoe. That a mile to the northward is Ambaaren. Yonder are Iflesen, Hoeyholm, Kieldholm, Suarven, and Buckholm. Further off—between Moskoe and Vurrgh—are Otterholm, Flimen, Sandflesen, and Skarholm.[4] These are the true names of the places—but why it has been thought necessary to name them at all, is more than either you or I can understand. Do you hear any thing? Do you see any change in the water?"

We had now been about ten minutes upon the top of Helseggen, to which we had ascended from the interior of Lofoden, so that we had caught no glimpse of the sea until it had burst upon us from the summit. As the old man spoke, I became aware of a loud and gradually increasing sound, like the moaning of a vast herd of buffaloes upon an American prairie;[5] and at the same moment I perceived that what seamen term the *chopping* character of the ocean beneath us, was rapidly changing into a current which set to the eastward. Even while I gazed, this current acquired a monstrous velocity. Each moment added to its speed—to its headlong impetuosity. In five minutes the whole sea, as far as Vurrgh, was lashed into ungovernable fury; but it was between Moskoe and the coast that the main uproar held its sway.[6] Here the vast bed of the waters, seamed and scarred into a thousand conflicting channels, burst suddenly into phrensied convulsion—heaving, boiling, hissing—gyrating in gigantic and innumerable vortices, and all whirling and plunging on to the eastward with a rapidity which water never elsewhere assumes, except in precipitous descents.

In a few minutes more, there came over the scene another radical alteration. The general surface grew somewhat more smooth, and the whirlpools, one by one, disappeared, while prodigious streaks of foam became apparent where none had been seen before. These streaks, at length, spreading out to a great distance, and entering into combination, took unto themselves the gyratory motion of the subsided vortices, and seemed to form the germ of another more vast. Suddenly—very suddenly—this assumed a distinct and definite existence, in a circle of more than half a mile in diameter. The edge of the whirl was represented by a broad belt of gleaming spray; but no particle of this slipped into the mouth of the terrific funnel, whose interior, as far as the eye could fathom it, was a smooth, shining, and jet-black wall of water, inclined to the horizon at an angle of some forty-five degrees, speeding dizzily round and round with a swaying and sweltering motion, and sending forth to the winds an appalling voice, half shriek, half roar, such as not even the mighty cataract of Niagara ever lifts up in its agony to Heaven.

The mountain trembled to its very base, and the rock rocked. I threw myself upon my face, and clung to the scant herbage in an excess of nervous agitation.

"This," said I at length, to the old man —"this *can* be nothing else than the great whirlpool of the Maelström."

"So it is sometimes termed," said he. "We Norwegians call it the Moskoe-ström, from the island of Moskoe in the midway."

The ordinary account of this vortex had by no means prepared me for what I saw. That of Jonas Ramus,[7] which is perhaps the most circumstantial of any, cannot impart the faintest conception either of the magnificence, or of the horror of the scene—or of the wild bewildering sense of *the novel* which confounds the beholder. I am not sure from what point of view the writer in question surveyed it, nor at what time; but it could neither have been from the summit of Helseggen, nor during a storm. There are some passages of his description, nevertheless, which may be quoted for their details, although their effect is exceedingly feeble in conveying an impression of the spectacle.

"Between Lofoden and Moskoe," he says, "the depth of the water is between thirty-six and forty fathoms; but on the other side, toward Ver (Vurrgh) this depth decreases so as not to afford a convenient passage for a vessel, without the risk of splitting on the rocks, which happens even in the calmest weather. When it is flood, the stream runs up the country between Lofoden and Moskoe with a boisterous rapidity; but the roar of its impetuous ebb to the sea is scarce equalled by the loudest and most dreadful cataracts; the noise being heard several leagues off, and the vortices or pits are of such an extent and depth, that if a ship comes within its attraction, it is inevitably absorbed and carried down to the bottom, and there beat to pieces against the rocks; and when the water relaxes, the fragments thereof are thrown up again. But these intervals of tranquillity are only at the turn of the ebb and flood, and in calm weather, and last but a quarter of an hour, its violence gradually returning. When the stream is most boisterous, and its fury heightened by a storm, it is dangerous to come within a Norway mile of it. Boats, yachts, and ships have been carried away by not guarding against it before they were within its reach. It likewise happens frequently, that whales come too near the stream, and are overpowered by its violence; and then it is impossible to describe their howlings and bellowings in their fruitless struggles to disengage themselves. A bear once, attempting to swim from Lofoden to Moskoe, was caught by the stream and borne down, while he roared terribly, so as to be heard on shore. Large stocks of firs and pine trees, after being absorbed by the current, rise again broken and torn to such a degree as if bristles grew upon them. This plainly shows the bottom to consist of craggy rocks, among which they are whirled to and fro. This stream is regulated by the flux and reflux of the sea—it being constantly high and low water every six hours. In the year 1645, early in the morning of Sexagesima Sunday,[8] it raged with such noise and impetuosity that the very stones of the houses on the coast fell to the ground."

In regard to the depth of the water, I could not see how this could have been ascertained at all in the immediate vicinity of the vortex. The "forty fathoms" must have reference only to portions of the channel close upon the shore either of Moskoe or Lofoden. The depth in the centre of the Moskoe-ström must be unmeasurably greater; and no better proof of this fact is necessary than can be obtained from even the sidelong glance into the abyss of the whirl which may be had from the highest crag of Helseggen. Looking down from this pinnacle upon the howling Phlegethon[9] below, I could not help smiling at the simplicity with which the honest Jonas Ramus records, as a matter difficult of belief, the anecdotes of the whales and the bears, for it appeared to me, in fact, a self-evident thing, that the largest ships of the line in existence, coming within the influence of that deadly attraction could, resist it as little as a feather the hurricane, and must disappear bodily and at once.

The attempts to account for the phenomenon—some of which, I remember, seemed to me sufficiently plausible in perusal—now wore a very different and unsatisfactory aspect. The idea generally received is that this, as well as three smaller vortices among the Feroe islands, "have no other cause than the collision of waves rising and falling, at flux and reflux, against a ridge of rocks and shelves, which confines the water so that it precipitates itself like a cataract; and thus the higher the flood rises, the deeper must the fall be, and the natural result of all is a whirlpool or vortex, the prodigious suction of which is sufficiently known by lesser experiments."—These are the words of the Encyclopædia Britannica. Kircher and others imagine that in the centre of the channel of the Maelström is an abyss penetrating the globe, and issuing in some very remote part—the Gulf of Bothnia[10] being somewhat decidedly named in one instance. This opinion, idle in itself, was the one to which, as I gazed, my imagination most readily assented; and, mentioning it to the guide, I was rather surprised to hear him say that, although it was the view almost universally entertained of the subject by the Norwegians, it nevertheless was not his own. As to the former notion he confessed his inability to comprehend it; and here I agreed with him—for, however conclusive on paper, it becomes altogether unintelligible, and even absurd, amid the thunder of the abyss.

"You have had a good look at the whirl now," said the old man, "and if you will creep round this crag, so as to get in its lee, and deaden the roar of the water, I will tell you a story that will convince you I ought to know something of the Moskoeström."

I placed myself as desired, and he proceeded.[11]

"Myself and my two brothers once owned a schooner-rigged smack of about seventy tons burthen, with which we were in the habit of fishing among the islands beyond Moskoe, nearly to Vurrgh. In all violent eddies at sea there is good fishing, at proper opportunities, if one has only the courage to attempt it; but among the whole of the Lofoden coastmen, we three were the only ones who made a regular business of going out to the islands, as I tell you. The usual grounds are a great way lower down to the southward. There fish can be got at all hours, without much risk, and therefore these places are preferred. The choice spots over here among the rocks, however, not only yield the finest variety, but in far greater abundance; so that we often got in a single day, what the more timid of the craft could not scrape together in a week. In fact, we made it a matter of desperate speculation—the risk of life standing instead of labor, and courage answering for capital.

"We kept the smack in a cove about five miles higher up the coast than this; and it was our practice, in fine weather, to take advantage of the fifteen minutes' slack to push across the main channel of the Moskoe-ström, far above the pool, and then drop down upon anchorage somewhere near Otterholm, or Sandflesen, where the eddies are not so violent as elsewhere. Here we used to remain until nearly time for slack-water again, when we weighed and made for home. We never set out upon this expedition without a steady side wind for going and coming—one that we felt sure would not fail us before our return—and we seldom made a miscalculation upon this point. Twice, during six years, we were forced to stay all night at anchor on account of a dead calm, which is a rare thing indeed just about here; and once we had to remain on the grounds nearly a week, starving to death, owing to a gale which blew up shortly after our arrival, and made the channel too boisterous to be thought of. Upon this occasion we should have been driven out to sea in spite of everything, (for the whirlpools threw us round and round so violently, that, at length, we fouled our anchor and dragged it) if it had not been that we drifted into one of the innumerable cross currents—here to-day and gone to-morrow—which drove us un der the lee of Flimen, where, by good luck, we brought up.

"I could not tell you the twentieth part of the difficulties we encountered 'on the ground'—it is a bad spot to be in, even in good weather—but we made shift always to run the gauntlet of the Moskoe-ström itself without accident; although at times my heart has been in my mouth when we happened to be a minute or so behind or before the slack. The wind sometimes was not as strong as we thought it at starting, and then we made rather less way than we could wish, while the current rendered the smack unmanageable. My eldest brother had a son eighteen years old, and I had two stout boys of my own. These would have been of great assistance at such times, in using the sweeps, as well as afterward in fishing—but, somehow, although we ran the risk ourselves, we had not the heart to let the young ones get into the danger—for, after all is said and done, it *was* a horrible danger, and that is the truth.

"It is now within a few days of three years since what I am going to tell you occurred. It was on the tenth of July, 18—, a day which the people of this part of the world will never forget—for it was one in which blew the most terrible hurricane that ever came out of the heavens. And yet all the morning, and indeed until late in the afternoon, there was a gentle and steady breeze from the south-west, while the sun shone brightly, so that the oldest seaman among us could not have foreseen what was to follow.

"The three of us—my two brothers and myself—had crossed over to the islands about two o'clock P.M., and soon nearly loaded the smack with fine fish, which, we all remarked, were more plenty that day than we had ever known them. It was just seven, *by my watch,* when we weighed and started for home, so as to make the worst of the Ström at slack water, which we knew would be at eight.

"We set out with a fresh wind on our starboard quarter, and for some time spanked along at a great rate, never dreaming of danger, for indeed we saw not the slightest reason to apprehend it. All at once we were taken aback by a breeze from over Helseggen. This was most unusual—something that had never happened to us before—and I began to feel a little uneasy, without exactly knowing why. We put the boat on the wind, but could make no headway at all for the eddies, and I was upon the point of proposing to return to the anchorage, when, looking astern, we saw the whole horizon covered with a singular copper-coloured cloud that rose with the most amazing velocity.

"In the meantime the breeze that had headed us off fell away and we were dead becalmed, drifting about in every direction. This state of things, however, did not last long enough to give us time to think about it. In less than a minute the storm was upon us—in less than two the sky was entirely overcast—and what with this and the driving spray, it became suddenly so dark that we could not see each other in the smack.

"Such a hurricane as then blew it is folly to attempt describing. The oldest seaman in Norway never experienced any thing like it. We had let our sails go by the run before it cleverly took us; but, at the first puff, both our masts went by the board as if they had been sawed off—the mainmast taking with it my youngest brother, who had lashed himself to it for safety.[12]

"Our boat was the lightest feather of a thing that ever sat upon water. It had a complete flush deck, with only a small hatch near the bow, and this hatch it had always been our custom to batten down when about to cross the Ström, by way of precaution against the chopping seas. But for this circumstance we should have foundered at once—for we lay entirely buried for some moments. How my elder brother escaped destruction I cannot say, for I never had an opportunity of ascertaining. For my part, as soon as I had let the foresail run, I threw myself flat on deck, with my feet against the narrow gunwale of the bow, and with my hands grasping a ring-bolt near the foot of the foremast. It was mere instinct that prompted me to do this—which was undoubtedly the very best thing I could have done—for I was too much flurried to think.

"For some moments we were completely deluged, as I say, and all this time I held my breath, and clung to the bolt. When I could stand it no longer I raised myself upon my knees, still keeping hold with my hands, and thus got my head clear. Presently our little boat gave herself a shake, just as a dog does in coming out of the water, and thus rid herself, in some measure, of the seas. I was now trying to get the better of the stupor that had come over me, and to collect my senses so as to see what was to be done, when I felt somebody grasp my arm. It was my elder brother, and my heart leaped for joy, for I had made sure that he was overboard—but the next moment all this joy was turned into horror—for he put his mouth close to my ear, and screamed out the word 'Moskoe-ström!'

"No one ever will know what my feelings were at that moment. I shook from head to foot as if I had had the most violent fit of the ague. I knew what he meant by that one word well enough—I knew what he wished to make me understand. With the wind that now drove us on, we were bound for the whirl of the Ström, and nothing could save us!

"You perceive that in crossing the Ström *channel*, we always went a long way up above the whirl, even in the calmest weather, and then had to wait and watch carefully for the slack—but now we were driving right upon the pool itself, and in such a hurricane as this! 'To be sure,' I thought, 'we shall get there just about the slack—there is some little hope in that'—but in the next moment I cursed myself for being so great a fool as to dream of hope at all. I knew very well that we were doomed, had we been ten times a ninety-gun ship.

"By this time the first fury of the tempest had spent itself, or perhaps we did not feel it so much, as we scudded before it, but at all events the seas, which at first had been kept down by the wind, and lay flat and frothing, now got up into absolute mountains. A singular change, too, had come over the heavens. Around in every direction it was still as black as pitch, but nearly overhead there burst out, all at once, a circular rift of clear sky—as clear as I ever saw—and of a deep bright blue—and through it there blazed forth the full moon with a lustre that I never before knew her to wear. She lit up every thing about us with the greatest distinctness—but, oh God, what a scene it was to light up!

"I now made one or two attempts to speak to my brother—but in some manner which I could not understand, the din had so increased that I could not make him hear a single word, although I screamed at the top of my voice in his ear. Presently he shook his head, looking as pale as death, and held up one of his fingers, as if to say 'listen!'

"At first I could not make out what he meant—but soon a hideous thought flashed upon me. I dragged my watch from its fob. It was not going. I glanced at its face by the moonlight, and then burst into tears as I flung it far away into the ocean. *It had run down at seven o'clock! We were behind the time of the slack, and the whirl of the Ström was in full fury!*

"When a boat is well built, properly trimmed, and not deep laden, the waves in a strong gale, when she is going large, seem always to slip from beneath her—which appears strange to a landsman—and this is what is called *riding*, in sea phrase.

"Well, so far we had ridden the swells very cleverly; but presently a gigantic sea happened to take us right under the counter, and bore us with it as it rose—up—

up—as if into the sky, I would not have believed that any wave could rise so high. And then down we came with a sweep, a slide, and a plunge that made me feel sick and dizzy, as if I was falling from some lofty mountain-top in a dream. But while we were up I had thrown a quick glance around—and that one glance was all sufficient. I saw our exact position in an instant. The Moskoe-ström whirlpool was about a quarter of a mile dead ahead—but no more like the every-day Moskoe-ström than the whirl, as you now see it, is like a mill-race. If I had not known where we were, and what we had to expect, I should not have recognised the place at all. As it was, I involuntarily closed my eyes in horror. The lids clenched themselves together as if in a spasm.

"It could not have been more than two minutes afterwards until we suddenly felt the waves subside, and were enveloped in foam. The boat made a sharp half turn to larboard,[13] and then shot off in its new direction like a thunderbolt. At the same moment the roaring noise of the water was completely drowned in a kind of shrill shriek—such a sound as you might imagine given out by the water-pipes of many thousand steam-vessels letting off their steam all together. We were now in the belt of surf that always surrounds the whirl; and I thought, of course, that another moment would plunge us into the abyss—down which we could only see indistinctly on account of the amazing velocity with which we were borne along. The boat did not seem to sink into the water at all, but to skim like an air-bubble upon the surface of the surge. Her starboard side was next the whirl, and on the larboard arose the world of ocean we had left. It stood like a huge writhing wall between us and the horizon.

"It may appear strange, but now, when we were in the very jaws of the gulf, I felt more composed than when we were only approaching it. Having made up my mind to hope no more, I got rid of a great deal of that terror which unmanned me at first.

I suppose it was despair that strung my nerves.

"It may look like boasting—but what I tell you is truth—I began to reflect how magnificent a thing it was to die in such a manner, and how foolish it was in me to think of so paltry a consideration as my own individual life, in view of so wonderful a manifestation of God's power.[14] I do believe that I blushed with shame when this idea crossed my mind. After a little while I became possessed with the keenest curiosity about the whirl itself. I positively felt a *wish* to explore its depths, even at the sacrifice I was going to make; and my principal grief was that I should never be able to tell my old companions on shore about the mysteries I should see. These, no doubt, were singular fancies to occupy a man's mind in such extremity —and I have often thought since, that the revolutions of the boat around the pool might have rendered me a little light-headed.

"There was another circumstance which tended to restore my self-possession; and this was the cessation of the wind, which could not reach us in our present situation—for, as you saw for yourself, the belt of the surf is considerably lower than the general bed of the ocean, and this latter now towered above us, a high, black, mountainous ridge. If you have never been at sea in a heavy gale, you can form no idea of the confusion of mind occasioned by the wind and spray together. They blind, deafen, and strangle you, and take away all power of action or reflection. But we were now, in a great measure, rid of these annoyances —just as death-condemned felons in prison are allowed petty indulgences, forbidden them while their doom is yet uncertain.

"How often we made the circuit of the belt it is impossible to say. We careered round and round for perhaps an hour, flying rather than floating, getting gradually more and more into the middle of the surge, and then nearer and nearer to its horrible inner edge. All this time I had never let go of the ring-bolt. My brother was at the stern, holding on to a large empty water-cask which had been securely lashed under the coop of the counter, and was the only thing on deck that had not been swept overboard when the gale first took us. As we approached the brink of the pit he let go his hold upon this, and made for the ring, from which, in the agony of his terror, he endeavoured to force my hands, as it was not large enough to afford us both a secure grasp. I never felt deeper grief than when I saw him attempt this act—although I knew he was a madman when he did it—a raving maniac through sheer fright. I did not care, however, to contest the point with him. I knew it could make no difference whether either of us held on at all; so I let him have the bolt, and went astern to the cask. This there was no great difficulty in doing; for the smack flew round steadily enough, and upon an even keel —only swaying to and fro with the immense sweeps and swelters of the whirl. Scarcely had I secured myself in my new position, when we gave a wild lurch to starboard, and rushed headlong into the abyss. I muttered a hurried prayer to God, and thought all was over.[15]

"As I felt the sickening sweep of the descent, I had instinctively tightened my hold upon the barrel, and closed my eyes. For some seconds I dared not open them —while I expected instant destruction, and wondered that I was not already in my death-struggles with the water. But moment after moment elapsed. I still lived. The sense of falling had ceased; and the motion of the vessel seemed much as it had been before while in the belt of foam, with the exception that she now lay more along.[16] I took courage and looked once again upon the scene.

"Never shall I forget the sensation of awe, horror, and admiration with which I gazed about me.[17] The boat appeared to be hanging, as if by magic, midway down, upon the interior surface of a funnel vast in circumference, prodigious in depth, and whose perfectly smooth sides might have been mistaken for ebony, but for the bewildering rapidity with which they spun around, and for the gleaming and ghastly radiance they shot forth, as the rays of the full moon, from that circular rift amid the clouds which I have already described, streamed in a flood of golden glory along the black walls, and far away down into the inmost recesses of the abyss.

"At first I was too much confused to observe anything accurately. The general burst of terrific grandeur was all that I beheld. When I recovered myself a little, however, my gaze fell instinctively downward. In this direction I was able to obtain an unobstructed view, from the manner in which the smack hung on the inclined surface of the pool. She was quite upon an even keel—that is to say, her deck lay in a plane parallel with that of the water—but this latter sloped at an angle of more than forty-five degrees, so that we seemed to be lying upon our beamends. I could not help observing, nevertheless, that I had scarcely more difficulty in maintaining my hold and footing in this situation, than if we had been upon a dead level; and this, I suppose, was owing to the speed at which we revolved.

"The rays of the moon seemed to search the very bottom of the profound gulf; but still I could make out nothing distinctly, on account of a thick mist in which everything there was enveloped, and over which there hung a magnificent rainbow, like that narrow and tottering bridge which Musselmen[18] say is the only pathway between Time and Eternity. This mist, or spray, was no doubt occasioned by the clashing of the great walls of the funnel, as they all met together at the bottom—but the yell that went up to the Heavens from out of that mist I dare not attempt to describe.

"Our first slide into the abyss itself, from the belt of foam above, had carried us to a great distance down the slope; but our farther descent was by no means proportionate.[19] Round and round we swept —not with any uniform movement—but in dizzying swings and jerks, that sent us sometimes only a few hundred feet— sometimes nearly the complete circuit of the whirl. Our progress downward, at each revolution, was slow, but very perceptible.

"Looking about me upon the wide waste of liquid ebony on which we were thus borne, I perceived that our boat was not the only object in the embrace of the whirl. Both above and below us were visible fragments of vessels, large masses of building timber and trunks of trees, with many smaller articles, such as pieces of house furniture, broken boxes, barrels and staves. I have already described the unnatural[20] curiosity which had taken the place of my original terrors. It appeared to grow upon me as I drew nearer and nearer to my dreadful doom. I now began to watch, with a strange interest, the numerous things that floated in our company. I *must* have been delirious—for I even sought *amusement* in speculating upon the relative velocities of their several descents toward the foam below. 'This fir tree,' I found myself at one time saying, 'will certainly be the next thing that takes the awful plunge and disappears,'—and then I was disappointed to find that the wreck of a Dutch merchant ship overtook it and went down before. At length, after making several guesses of this nature, and being deceived in all—this fact—the fact of my invariable miscalculation, set me upon a train of reflection that made my limbs again tremble, and my heart beat heavily once more.

"It was not a new terror that thus affected me, but the dawn of a more exciting *hope*. This hope arose partly from memory, and partly from present observation. I called to mind the great variety of buoyant matter that strewed the coast of Lofoden, having been absorbed and then thrown forth by the Moskoe-ström. By far the greater number of the articles were shattered in the most extraordinary way

—so chafed and roughened as to have the appearance of being struck full of splinters—but then I distinctly recollected that there were *some* of them which were not disfigured at all. Now I could not account for this difference except by supposing that the roughened fragments were the only ones which had been *completely absorbed*—that the others had entered the whirl at so late a period of the tide, or, from some reason, had descended so slowly after entering, that they did not reach the bottom before the turn of the flood came, or of the ebb, as the case might be. I conceived it possible, in either instance, that they might thus be whirled up again to the level of the ocean, without undergoing the fate of those which had been drawn in more early or absorbed more rapidly. I made, also, three important observations. The first was, that as a general rule, the larger the bodies were, the more rapid their descent;—the second, that, between two masses of equal extent, the one spherical, and the other *of any other shape,* the superiority in speed of descent was with the sphere;—the third, that, between two masses of equal size, the one cylindrical, and the other of any other shape, the cylinder was absorbed the more slowly. Since my escape, I have had several conversations on this subject with an old school-master of the district; and it was from him that I learned the use of the words 'cylinder' and 'sphere.' He explained to me—although I have forgotten the explanation—how what I observed was, in fact, the natural consequence of the forms of the floating fragments—and showed me how it happened that a cylinder, swimming in a vortex, offered more resistance to its suction, and was drawn in with greater difficulty than an equally bulky body, of any form whatever.[21]

"There was one startling circumstance which went a great way in enforcing these observations, and rendering me anxious to turn them to account, and this was that, at every revolution, we passed something like a barrel, or else the broken yard or the mast of a vessel, while many of these things, which had been on our level when I first opened my eyes upon the wonders of the whirlpool, were now high up above us, and seemed to have moved but little from their original station.[22]

"I no longer hesitated what to do. I resolved to lash myself securely to the water-cask upon which I now held, to cut it loose from the counter, and to throw myself with it into the water. I attracted my brother's attention by signs, pointed to the floating barrels that came near us, and did every thing in my power to make him understand what I was about to do. I thought at length that he comprehended my design—but, whether this was the case or not, he shook his head despairingly, and refused to move from his station by the ring-bolt. It was impossible to force him, the emergency admitted of no delay; and so, with a bitter struggle, I resigned him to his fate, fastened myself to the cask by means of the lashings which secured it to the counter, and precipitated myself with it into the sea, without another moment's hesitation.

"The result was precisely what I had hoped it might be. As it is myself who now tell you this tale—as you see that I *did* escape—and as you are already in possession of the mode in which this escape was effected, and must therefore anticipate all that I have farther to say—I will bring my story quickly to conclusion. It might have been an hour, or thereabout, after my quitting the smack, when, having descended to a vast distance beneath me, it made three or four wild gyrations in rapid succession, and bearing my loved brother with it, plunged headlong, at once and forever, into the chaos of foam below. The barrel to which I was attached sunk very little farther than half the distance between the bottom of the gulf and the spot at which I leaped overboard, before a great change took place in the character of the whirlpool. The slope of the sides of the vast funnel became momently less and less steep. The gyrations of the whirl grew, gradually, less and less violent. By degrees, the froth and the rainbow disappeared, and the bottom of the gulf seemed slowly to uprise. The sky was clear, the winds had gone down, and the full moon was setting radiantly in the west, when I found myself on the surface of the ocean, in full view of the shores of Lofoden, and above the spot where the pool of the Moskoe-ström *had been*. It was the hour of the slack—but the sea still heaved in mountainous waves from the effects of the hurricane. I was borne violently into the channel of the Ström, and in a few minutes, was hurried down the coast into the 'grounds' of the fishermen. A boat picked me up—exhausted from fatigue—and (now that the danger was removed) speechless from the memory of its horror. Those who drew me on board were my old mates and daily companions—but they knew me no more than they would have known a traveller from the spirit-land. My hair, which had been raven-black the day before, was as white as you see it now. They say too that the whole expression of my countenance had changed. I told them my story—they did not believe it. I now tell it to *you*—and I can scarcely expect you to put more faith in it than did the merry fishermen of Lofoden."

THE PIT AND THE PENDULUM

*Impia tortorum longos hic
    turba furores
Sanguinis innocui, non satiata, aluit.
Sospite nunc patriâ, fracto nunc
    funeris antro,
Mors ubi dira fuit vita salusque patent.*
    Quatrain composed for the gates
of a market to be erected upon the site
of the Jacobin Club House at Paris.[1]

I was sick—sick unto death with that long agony; and when they at length unbound me, and I was permitted to sit, I felt that my senses were leaving me. The sentence —the dread sentence of death—was the last of distinct accentuation which reached my ears. After that, the sound of the inquisitorial[2] voices seemed merged in one dreamy indeterminate hum. It conveyed to my soul the idea of *revolution*— perhaps from its association in fancy with the burr of a mill-wheel. This only for a brief period; for presently I heard no more. Yet, for a while, I saw; but with how terrible an exaggeration! I saw the lips of the black-robed judges. They appeared to me white—whiter than the sheet upon which I trace these words— and thin even to grotesqueness; thin with the intensity of their expression of firmness—of immoveable resolution—of stern contempt of human torture. I saw that the decrees of what to me was Fate were still issuing from those lips. I saw them writhe with a deadly locution. I saw them fashion the syllables of my name; and I shuddered because no sound succeeded. I saw, too, for a few moments of delirious horror, the soft and nearly imperceptible waving of the sable draperies which enwrapped the walls of the apartment. And then my vision fell upon the seven tall candles upon the table. At first they wore the aspect of charity, and seemed white slender angels who would save me; but then, all at once, there came a most deadly nausea over my spirit, and I felt every fibre in my frame thrill as if I had touched the wire of a galvanic battery, while the angel forms became meaningless spectres, with heads of flame, and I saw that from them there would be no help. And then there stole into my fancy, like a rich musical note, the thought of what sweet rest there must be in the grave. The thought came gently and stealthily, and it seemed long before it attained full appreciation; but just as my spirit came at length properly to feel and entertain it, the figures of the judges vanished, as if magically, from before me; the tall candles sank into nothingness; their flames went out utterly; the blackness of darkness supervened; all sensations appeared swallowed up in a mad rushing descent as of the soul into Hades.

Then silence, and stillness, and night were the universe.

I had swooned; but still will not say that all of consciousness was lost. What of it there remained I will not attempt to define, or even to describe; yet all was not lost. In the deepest slumber—no! In delirium—no! In a swoon—no! In death—no! even in the grave all *is not* lost. Else there is no immortality for man. Arousing from the most profound of slumbers, we break the gossamer web of *some* dream. Yet in a second afterward, (so frail may that web have been) we remember not that we have dreamed. In the return to life from the swoon there are two stages; first, that of the sense of mental or spiritual; secondly, that of the sense of physical, existence. It seems probable that if, upon reaching the second stage, we could recall the impressions of the first, we should find these impressions eloquent in memories of the gulf beyond. And that gulf is—what? How at least shall we distinguish its shadows from those of the tomb? But if the impressions of what I have termed the first stage, are not, at will, recalled, yet, after long interval, do they not come unbidden, while we marvel whence they come? He who has never swooned, is not he who finds strange palaces and wildly familiar faces in coals that glow; is not he who beholds floating in mid-air the sad visions that the many may not view; is not he who ponders over the perfume of some novel flower—is not he whose brain grows bewildered with the meaning of some musical cadence which has never before arrested his attention.[3]

Amid frequent and thoughtful endeavors to remember; amid earnest struggles to regather some token of the state of seeming nothingness into which my soul had lapsed, there have been moments when I have dreamed of success; there have been brief, very brief periods when I have conjured up remembrances which the lucid reason of a later epoch assures me could have had reference only to that condition of seeming unconsciousness.

These shadows of memory tell, indistinctly, of tall figures that lifted and bore me in silence down—down—still down—till a hideous dizziness oppressed me at the mere idea of the interminableness of the descent. They tell also of a vague horror at my heart, on account of that heart's unnatural stillness. Then comes a sense of sudden motionlessness throughout all things; as if those who bore me (a ghastly train!) had outrun, in their descent, the limits of the limitless, and paused from the wearisomeness of their toil. After this I call to mind flatness and dampness; and then all is *madness*—the madness of a memory which busies itself among forbidden things.

Very suddenly there came back to my soul motion and sound—the tumultuous motion of the heart, and, in my ears, the sound of its beating. Then a pause in which all is blank. Then again sound, and motion, and touch—a tingling sensation pervading my frame. Then the mere consciousness of existence, without thought—a condition which lasted long. Then, very suddenly, *thought*, and shuddering terror, and earnest endeavor to comprehend my true state. Then a strong desire to lapse into insensibility. Then a rushing revival of soul and a successful effort to move. And now a full memory of the trial, of the judges, of the sable draperies, of the sentence, of the sickness, of the swoon. Then entire forgetfulness of all that followed; of all that a later day and much earnestness of endeavour have enabled me vaguely to recall.

So far, I had not opened my eyes. I felt that I lay upon my back, unbound. I reached out my hand, and it fell heavily upon something damp and hard. There I suffered it to remain for many minutes, while I strove to imagine where and *what* I could be. I longed, yet dared not, to employ my vision. I dreaded the first glance at objects around me. It was not that I feared to look upon things horrible, but that I grew aghast lest there should be *nothing* to see. At length, with a wild desperation at heart, I quickly unclosed my eyes. My worst thoughts, then, were confirmed. The blackness of eternal night encompassed me. I struggled for breath. The intensity of the darkness seemed to oppress and stifle me. The atmosphere was intolerably close. I still lay quietly, and made effort to exercise my reason. I brought to mind the inquisitorial proceedings, and attempted from that point to deduce my real condition. The sentence had passed; and it appeared to me that a very long interval of time had since elapsed. Yet not for a moment did I suppose myself actually dead. Such a supposition, notwithstanding what we read in fiction, is altogether inconsistent with real existence;—but where and in what state was I? The condemned to death, I knew, perished usually at the *autos-da-fé*, and one of these had been held on the very night of the day of my trial. Had I been remanded to my dungeon, to await the next sacrifice, which would not take place for many months? This I at once saw could not be. Victims had been in immediate demand. Moreover, my dungeon, as well as all the condemned cells at Toledo[4] had stone floors, and light was not altogether excluded.

A fearful idea now suddenly drove the blood in torrents upon my heart, and for a brief period, I once more relapsed into insensibility. Upon recovering, I at once started to my feet, trembling convulsively in every fibre. I thrust my arms wildly above and around me in all directions. I felt nothing; yet dreaded to move a step, lest I should be impeded by the walls of a *tomb*.[5] Perspiration burst from every pore, and stood in cold big beads upon my forehead. The agony of suspense grew at length intolerable, and I cautiously moved forward, with my arms extended, and my eyes straining from their sockets in the hope of catching some faint ray of light. I proceeded for many paces; but still all was blackness and vacancy. I breathed more freely. It seemed evident that mine was not, at least, the most hideous of fates.

And now, as I still continued to step cautiously onward, there came thronging upon my recollection a thousand vague rumors of the horrors of Toledo. Of the dungeons there had been strange things narrated—fables I had always deemed them,—but yet strange, and too ghastly to repeat, save in a whisper. Was I left to perish of starvation in this subterranean world of darkness; or what fate, perhaps even more fearful, awaited me? That the result would be death, and a death of more than customary bitterness, I knew too well the character of my judges to doubt. The mode and the hour were all that occupied or distracted me.

My outstretched hands at length encountered some solid obstruction. It was a wall, seemingly of stone masonry—very smooth, slimy, and cold. I followed it up; stepping with all the careful distrust with which certain antique narratives had inspired me. This process, however, afforded me no means of ascertaining the dimensions of my dungeon, as I might make its circuit and return to the point whence I set out without being aware of the fact, so perfectly uniform seemed the wall. I therefore sought the knife which had been in my pocket, when led into the inquisitorial chamber; but it was gone; my clothes had been exchanged for a wrapper of coarse serge. I had thought of forcing the blade in some minute crevice of the masonry, so as to identify my point of departure. The difficulty, nevertheless, was but trivial; although, in the disorder of my fancy, it seemed at first insuperable. I tore a part of the hem from the robe and placed the fragment at full length, and at right angles to the wall. In groping my way around the prison, I could not fail to encounter this rag upon completing the circuit. So, at least, I thought; but I had not counted upon the extent of the dungeon, or upon my own weakness. The ground was moist and slippery. I staggered onward for some time, when I stumbled and fell. My excessive fatigue induced me to remain prostrate; and sleep soon overtook me as I lay.

Upon awaking, and stretching forth an arm, I found beside me a loaf and a pitcher with water. I was too much exhausted to reflect upon this circumstance, but ate and drank with avidity. Shortly afterward, I resumed my tour around the prison, and with much toil, came at last upon the fragment of the serge. Up to the period when I fell, I had counted fifty-two paces, and, upon resuming my walk, I had counted forty-eight more—when I arrived at the rag. There were in all, then, a hundred paces; and, admitting two paces to the yard, I presumed the dungeon to be fifty yards in circuit. I had met, however, with many angles in the wall, and thus I could form no guess at the shape of the vault; for vault I could not help supposing it to be.

I had little object—certainly no hope —in these researches; but a vague curiosity prompted me to continue them. Quitting the wall, I resolved to cross the area of the enclosure. At first, I proceeded with extreme caution, for the floor, although seemingly of solid material, was treacherous with slime. At length, however, I took courage, and did not hesitate to step firmly; endeavouring to cross in as direct a line as possible. I had advanced some ten or twelve paces in this manner, when the remnant of the torn hem of my robe became entangled between my legs. I stepped on it, and fell violently on my face.

In the confusion attending my fall, I did not immediately apprehend a somewhat startling circumstance, which yet, in a few seconds afterward, and while I still lay prostrate, arrested my attention. It was this—my chin rested upon the floor of the prison, but my lips, and the upper portion of my head, although seemingly at a less elevation than the chin, touched nothing. At the same time, my forehead seemed bathed in a clammy vapor, and the peculiar smell of decayed fungus arose to my nostrils. I put forward my arm, and shuddered to find that I had fallen at the very brink of a circular pit, whose extent, of course, I had no means of ascertaining at the moment. Groping about the masonry just below the margin, I succeeded in dislodging a small fragment, and let it fall into the abyss. For many seconds I hearkened to its reverberations as it dashed against the sides of the chasm in its descent; at length there was a sullen plunge into water, succeeded by loud echoes. At the same moment, there came a sound resembling the quick opening and as rapid closing of a door overhead, while a faint gleam of light flashed suddenly through the gloom, and as suddenly faded away.

I saw clearly the doom which had been prepared for me, and congratulated myself upon the timely accident by which I had escaped. Another step before my fall, and the world had seen me no more. And the death just avoided was of that very character which I had regarded as fabulous and frivolous in the tales respecting the Inquisition. To the victims of its tyranny, there was the choice of death with its direct physical agonies, or death with its most hideous moral horrors. I had been reserved for the latter. By long suffering my nerves had been unstrung, until I trembled at the sound of my own voice, and had become in every respect a fitting subject for the species of torture which awaited me.

Shaking in every limb, I groped my way back to the wall—resolving there to perish rather than risk the terrors of the wells, of which my imagination now pictured many in various positions about the dungeon. In other conditions of mind, I might have had courage to end my misery at once, by a plunge into one of these abysses; but now I was the veriest of cowards. Neither could I forget what I had read of these pits—that the *sudden* extinction of life formed no part of their most horrible plan.

Agitation of spirit kept me awake for many long hours, but at length I again slumbered. Upon arousing, I found by my side, as before, a loaf and a pitcher of water. A burning thirst consumed me, and I emptied the vessel at a draught. It must have been drugged—for scarcely had I drunk, before I became irresistibly drowsy. A deep sleep fell upon me—a sleep like that of death. How long it lasted of course, I know not; but when, once again, I unclosed my eyes, the objects around me were visible. By a wild, sulphurous lustre, the origin of which I could not at first determine, I was enabled to see the extent and aspect of the prison.

In its size I had been greatly mistaken. The whole circuit of its walls did not exceed twenty-five yards. For some minutes this fact occasioned me a world of vain trouble; vain indeed—for what could be of less importance, under the terrible circumstances which environed me, than the mere dimensions of my dungeon? But my soul took a wild interest in trifles, and I busied myself in endeavours to account for the error I had committed in my measurement. The truth at length flashed upon me. In my first attempt at exploration I had counted fifty-two paces, up to the period when I fell: I must then have been within a pace or two of the fragment of serge; in fact, I had nearly performed the circuit of the vault. I then slept—and, upon waking, I must have returned upon my steps—thus supposing the circuit nearly double what it actually was. My confusion of mind prevented me from observing that I began my tour with the wall to the left, and ended it with the wall to the right.

I had been deceived, too, in respect to the shape of the enclosure. In feeling my way I had found many angles, and thus deduced an idea of great irregularity; so potent is the effect of total darkness upon one arousing from lethargy or sleep! The angles were simply those of a few slight depressions, or niches, at odd intervals. The general shape of the prison was square. What I had taken for masonry seemed now to be iron, or some other metal, in huge plates, whose sutures or joints occasioned the depression. The en-

tire surface of this metallic enclosure was rudely daubed in all the hideous and repulsive devices to which the charnel superstition of the monks has given rise.[6] The figures of fiends in aspects of menace, with skeleton forms, and other more really fearful images, overspread and disfigured the walls. I observed that the outlines of these monstrosities were sufficiently distinct, but that the colors seemed faded and blurred, as if from the effects of a damp atmosphere. I now noticed the floor, too, which was of stone. In the centre yawned the circular pit from whose jaws I had escaped; but it was the only one in the dungeon.

All this I saw indistinctly and by much effort: for my personal condition had been greatly changed during slumber. I now lay upon my back, and at full length, on a species of low framework of wood. To this I was securely bound by a long strap resembling a surcingle.[7] It passed in many convolutions about my limbs and body, leaving at liberty only my head, and my left arm to such extent that I could, by dint of much exertion, supply myself with food from an earthen dish which lay by my side on the floor. I saw, to my horror, that the pitcher had been removed. I say to my horror—for I was consumed with intolerable thirst. This thirst it appeared to be the design of my persecutors to stimulate: for the food in the dish was meat pungently seasoned.

Looking upward, I surveyed the ceiling of my prison. It was some thirty or forty feet overhead, and constructed much as the side walls. In one of its panels a very singular figure riveted my whole attention. It was the painted figure of Time as he is commonly represented, save that, in lieu of a scythe, he held what, at a casual glance, I supposed to be the pictured image of a huge pendulum, such as we see on antique clocks. There was something, however, in the appearance of this machine which caused me to regard it more attentively. While I gazed directly upward at it (for its position was immediately over my own) I fancied that I saw it in motion. In an instant afterward the fancy was confirmed. Its sweep was brief, and of course slow. I watched it for some minutes, somewhat in fear, but more in wonder. Wearied at length with observing its dull movement, I turned my eyes upon the other objects in the cell.

A slight noise attracted my notice, and looking to the floor, I saw several enormous rats traversing it. They had issued from the well which lay just within view to my right. Even then, while I gazed, they came up in troops, hurriedly, with ravenous eyes, allured by the scent of the meat. From this it required much effort and attention to scare them away.

It might have been half an hour, perhaps even an hour, (for I could take but imperfect note of time) before I again cast my eyes upward. What I then saw confounded and amazed me. The sweep of the pendulum had increased in extent by nearly a yard. As a natural consequence, its velocity was also much greater. But what mainly disturbed me was the idea that it had perceptibly *descended*. I now observed—with what horror it is needless to say—that its nether extremity was formed of a crescent of glittering steel, about a foot in length from horn to horn; the horns upward, and the under edge evidently as keen as that of a razor. Like a razor also, it seemed massy and heavy, tapering from the edge into a solid and broad structure above. It was appended to a weighty rod of brass, and the whole *hissed* as it swung through the air.

I could no longer doubt the doom prepared for me by monkish ingenuity in torture. My cognizance of the pit had become known to the inquisitorial agents—*the pit*, whose horrors had been destined for so bold a recusant as myself—*the pit*, typical of hell, and regarded by rumor as the Ultima Thule[8] of all their punishments. The plunge into this pit I had avoided by the merest of accidents, and I knew that surprise, or entrapment into torment, formed an important portion of all the grotesquerie of these dungeon deaths. Having failed to fall, it was no part of the demon plan to hurl me into the abyss; and thus (there being no alternative), a different and a milder destruction awaited me. Milder! I half smiled in my agony as I thought of such application of such a term.

What boots it to tell of the long, long hours of horror more than mortal, during which I counted the rushing vibrations of the steel! Inch by inch—line by line—with a descent only appreciable at intervals that seemed ages—down and still down it came! Days passed—it might have been that many days passed—ere it swept so closely over me as to fan me with its acrid breath. The odor of the sharp steel forced itself into my nostrils. I prayed—I wearied heaven with my prayer for its more speedy descent. I grew frantically mad, and struggled to force myself upward against the sweep of the fearful scimitar. And then I fell suddenly calm, and lay smiling at the glittering death, as a child at some rare bauble.

There was another interval of utter insensibility; it was brief; for, upon again lapsing into life, there had been no perceptible descent in the pendulum. But it might have been long; for I knew there were demons who took note of my swoon, and who could have arrested the vibration at pleasure. Upon my recovery, too, I felt very—oh, inexpressibly sick and weak, as if through long inanition. Even amid the agonies of that period, the human nature craved food. With painful effort I outstretched my left arm as far as my bonds permitted, and took possession of the small remnant which had been spared me by the rats. As I put a portion of it within my lips, there rushed to my mind a half formed thought of joy—of hope. Yet what business had *I* with hope? It was, as I say, a half formed thought—man has many such which are never completed. I felt that it was of joy—of hope; but I felt also that it had perished in its formation. In vain I struggled to perfect—to regain it. Long suffering had nearly annihilated all my ordinary powers of mind. I was an imbecile—an idiot.[9]

The vibration of the pendulum was at right angles to my length. I saw that the crescent was designed to cross the region of the heart. It would fray the serge of my robe—it would return and repeat its operations—again—and again. Notwithstanding its terrifically wide sweep (some thirty feet or more) and the hissing vigor of its descent, sufficient to sunder these very walls of iron, still the fraying of my robe would be all that, for several minutes, it would accomplish. And at this thought I paused. I dared not go further than this reflection. I dwelt upon it with a pertinacity of attention—as if, in so dwelling, I could arrest here the descent of the steel. I forced myself to ponder upon the sound of the crescent as it should pass across the garment—upon the peculiar thrilling sensation which the friction of cloth produces on the nerves. I pondered upon all this frivolity until my teeth were on edge.

Down—steadily down it crept. I took a frenzied pleasure in contrasting its downward with its lateral velocity. To the right —to the left—far and wide—with the shriek of a damned spirit; to my heart with the stealthy pace of the tiger! I alternately laughed and howled, as the one or the other idea grew predominant.

Down—certainly, relentlessly down! It vibrated within three inches of my bosom! I struggled violently, furiously, to free my left arm. This was free only from the elbow to the hand. I could reach the latter, from the platter beside me, to my mouth, with great effort, but no farther. Could I have broken the fastenings above the elbow, I would have seized and attempted to arrest the pendulum. I might as well have attempted to arrest an avalanche!

Down—still unceasingly—still inevitably down! I gasped and struggled at each vibration. I shrunk convulsively at its every sweep. My eyes followed its outward or upward whirls with the eagerness of the most unmeaning despair; they closed themselves spasmodically at the descent, although death would have been a relief, oh! how unspeakable! Still I quivered in every nerve to think how slight a sinking of the machinery would precipitate that keen, glistening axe upon my bosom. It was *hope* that prompted the nerve to quiver—the frame to shrink. It was *hope* —the hope that triumphs on the rack— that whispers to the death-condemned even in the dungeons of the Inquisition.

I saw that some ten or twelve vibrations would bring the steel in actual contact with my robe—and with this observation there suddenly came over my spirit all the keen, collected calmness of despair.[10] For the first time during many hours—or perhaps days—I *thought*. It now occurred to me, that the bandage, or surcingle, which enveloped me, was *unique*. I was tied by no separate cord. The first stroke of the razor-like descent athwart any portion of the band would so detach it that it might be unwound from my person by means of my left hand. But how fearful, in that case, the proximity of the steel! The result of the slightest struggle, how deadly! Was it likely, moreover, that the minions of the torturer had not foreseen and provided for this possibility! Was it probable that the bandage crossed my bosom in the track of the pendulum? Dreading to find my faint, and, as it seemed, my last hope frustrated, I so far elevated my head as to obtain a distinct view of my breast. The surcingle enveloped my limbs and body close in all directions—*save in the path of the destroying crescent*.

Scarcely had I dropped my head back into its original position, when there flashed upon my mind what I cannot better describe than as the unformed half of that idea of deliverance to which I have previously alluded, and of which a moiety only floated indeterminately through my brain when I raised food to my burning lips. The whole thought was now present —feeble, scarcely sane, scarcely definite —but still entire. I proceeded at once, with the nervous energy of despair, to attempt its execution.

For many hours the immediate vicinity of the low framework upon which I lay had been literally swarming with rats. They were wild, bold, ravenous; their red eyes glaring upon me as if they waited but for motionlessness on my part to make me their prey. "To what food," I thought, "have they been accustomed in the well?"

They had devoured, in spite of all my efforts to prevent them, all but a small remnant of the contents of the dish. I had fallen into an habitual see-saw, or wave of the hand about the platter: and, at length, the unconscious uniformity of the movement deprived it of effect. In their voracity, the vermin frequently fastened their sharp fangs in my fingers. With the particles of the oily and spicy viand which now remained, I thoroughly rubbed the bandage wherever I could reach it; then, raising my hand from the floor, I lay breathlessly still.

At first, the ravenous animals were startled and terrified at the change—at the cessation of movement. They shrank alarmedly back; many sought the well. But this was only for a moment. I had not counted in vain upon their voracity. Observing that I remained without motion, one or two of the boldest leaped upon the framework, and smelt at the surcingle. This seemed the signal for a general rush. Forth from the well they hurried in fresh troops. They clung to the wood—they overran it, and leaped in hundreds upon my person. The measured movement of the pendulum disturbed them not at all. Avoiding its strokes, they busied themselves with the anointed bandage. They pressed—they swarmed upon me in ever accumulating heaps. They writhed upon my throat; their cold lips sought my own; I was half stifled by their thronging pressure; disgust, for which the world has no name, swelled my bosom, and chilled, with a heavy clamminess, my heart. Yet one minute, and I felt that the struggle would be over. Plainly I perceived the loosening of the bandage. I knew that in more than one place it must be already severed. With a more than human resolution I lay *still*.

Nor had I erred in my calculations— nor had I endured in vain. I at length felt that I was *free*. The surcingle hung in ribands from my body. But the stroke of the pendulum already pressed upon my bosom. It had divided the serge of the robe. It had cut through the linen beneath. Twice again it swung, and a sharp sense of pain shot through every nerve. But the moment of escape had arrived. At a wave of my hand my deliverers hurried tumultuously away. With a steady movement— cautious, sidelong, shrinking, and slow—I slid from the embrace of the bandage and beyond the reach of the scimitar. For the moment, at least, *I was free.*

Free!—and in the grasp of the Inquisition! I had scarcely stepped from my wooden bed of horror upon the stone floor of the prison, when the motion of the hellish machine ceased, and I beheld it drawn up, by some invisible force, through the ceiling. This was a lesson which I took desperately to heart. My every motion was undoubtedly watched. Free!—I had but escaped death in one form of agony, to be delivered unto worse than death in some other. With that thought I rolled my eyes nervously around on the barriers of iron that hemmed me in. Something unusual —some change which, at first, I could not appreciate distinctly—it was obvious, had taken place in the apartment. For many minutes of a dreamy and trembling abstraction, I busied myself in vain, unconnected conjecture. During this period, I became aware, for the first time, of the origin of the sulphurous light which illumined the cell. It proceeded from a fissure, about half an inch in width, extending entirely around the prison at the base of the walls, which thus appeared, and were, completely separated from the floor. I endeavored, but of course in vain, to look through the aperture.

As I arose from the attempt, the mystery of the alteration in the chamber broke at once upon my understanding. I have observed that, although the outlines of the figures upon the walls were sufficiently distinct, yet the colours seemed blurred and indefinite. These colours had now assumed, and were momentarily assuming, a startling and most intense brilliancy, that gave to the spectral and fiendish portraitures an aspect that might have thrilled even firmer nerves than my own. Demon eyes, of a wild and ghastly vivacity, glared upon me in a thousand directions, where none had been visible before, and gleamed with the lurid lustre of a fire that I could not force my imagination to regard as unreal.

Unreal!—Even while I breathed there came to my nostrils the breath of the vapor of heated iron! A suffocating odour pervaded the prison! A deeper glow settled each moment in the eyes that glared at my agonies! A richer tint of crimson diffused itself over the pictured horrors of blood. I panted! I gasped for breath! There could be no doubt of the design of my tormentors—oh! most unrelenting! oh! most demoniac of men! I shrank from the glowing metal to the centre of the cell. Amid the thought of the fiery destruction that impended, the idea of the coolness of the well came over my soul like balm. I rushed to its deadly brink. I threw my straining vision below. The glare from the enkindled roof illumined its inmost recesses. Yet, for a wild moment, did my spirit refuse to comprehend the meaning of what I saw. At length it forced—it wrestled its way into my soul—it burned itself in upon my shuddering reason.—Oh for a voice to speak!—oh! horror!—oh! any horror but this! With a shriek I rushed from the margin, and buried my face in my hands—weeping bitterly.

The heat rapidly increased, and once again I looked up, shuddering as with a fit of the ague. There had been a second change in the cell—and now the change was obviously in the *form*. As before, it was in vain that I at first endeavoured to appreciate or understand what was taking place. But not long was I left in doubt. The Inquisitorial vengeance had been hurried by my two-fold escape, and there was to be no more dallying with the King of Terrors. The room had been square. I saw that two of its iron angles were now acute —two, consequently, obtuse. The fearful difference quickly increased with a low rumbling or moaning sound. In an instant the apartment had shifted its form into that of a lozenge. But the alteration stopped not here—I neither hoped nor desired it to stop. I could have clasped the red walls to my bosom as a garment of eternal peace. "Death," I said, "any death but that of the pit!" Fool! might I not have known that *into the pit* it was the object of the burning iron to urge me? Could I resist its glow? or, if even that, could I withstand its pressure? And now, flatter and flatter grew the lozenge, with a rapidity that left me no time for contemplation. Its centre, and of course, its greatest width, came just over the yawning gulf. I shrank back—but the closing walls pressed me resistlessly onward. At length for my seared and writhing body there was no longer an inch of foothold on the firm floor of the prison. I struggled no more, but the agony of my soul found vent in one loud, long, and final scream of despair. I felt that I tottered upon the brink—I averted my eyes—

There was a discordant hum of human voices! There was a loud blast as of many trumpets! There was a harsh grating as of a thousand thunders! The fiery walls rushed back! An out-stretched arm caught my own as I fell, fainting, into the abyss. It was that of General Lasalle.[11] The French army had entered Toledo. The Inquisition was in the hands of its enemies.

Notes

A Descent Into the Maelström

1. Joseph Glanvill (1636–1680) was an important English essayist. The quotation is from *Essays on Several Important Subjects in Philosophy and Religion* (1676), and Poe tinkered with his source, as he often did in such quotations. Glanvill's essay reads, "The ways of God in Nature (as in *Providence*) are not as *ours* are: Nor are the Models that we frame any way commensurate to the vastness and profundity of his Works; which have a depth in them greater than the *Well of Democritus*." (A. H. Quinn; Woodberry) Democritus is a materialist philosopher (460–360 B. C. E.) and one of the fathers of atomism ("in reality there is nothing but atoms and space") whose belief in physical causality—he held that even the "soul" is physical—Poe found sympathetic. Compare what Poe says about materialism in "The Domain of Arnheim" and in Agathos's speeches in "The Power of Words." For the "Well of Democritus," see "Ligeia," note 5.

Publications of this tale in the United States in Poe's time: *Graham's*, May 1841; the *Tales* of 1845; *The Broadway Journal* for October 1, 1845; *Boston Museum*, May 26, 1849, and *The Irving Offering* for 1851 (a gift-book).

2. Poe's geography is accurate. The Lofoden (Lofoten) Islands are off the northwest coast of Norway; the 68° line is just above the site on which the fisherman and narrator sit. The hamlet of Helle, a mountain of 601 meters in height, and the Lofotodden headland, a high promontory fronting the sea, are at the lower tip of Moskenes (see Figure Seven).

3. Nubian . . . *Tenebrarum:* Poe's source is a passage in Jacob Bryant's *A New System or, an Analysis of Ancient Mythology* (Vol. IV, 79): "By the Nubian Geographer the Atlantic is uniformly called, according to the present version, Mare Tenebrarum. Aggressi sunt mare tenebrarum quid in eo esset, exploraturi. *They ventured into the sea of darkness, in order to explore what it might contain.*"

Poe uses this quotation in full in "Eleonora." See note 2 of that tale. The Nubian geographer to whom Bryant refers is al Idrisi, author of *Geographia nubiensis*, and not Ptolemy Hephestion, as Poe says in *Eureka*. Bryant does mention Ptolemy Hephæstion, but does not call him "the Nubian geographer." Poe's error in *Eureka* may be deliberate. See "Mellonta Tauta," note 2.

4. Figure Seven (p. 40) locates the places named. Poe got all his data on whirlpools from an encyclopedia article. The story of Poe's borrowings in this tale is good fun; Poe probably would have been pleased to know that, in arguing back against an encyclopedia, he became a "source" himself for a later encyclopedia article on whirlpools (A. H. Quinn, Turner, Benson).

5. A sound Poe had never heard, either: except for a childhood trip to England, his travels were limited, to the best knowledge of his biographers, to the eastern seaboard.

6. Accounts of where the whirlpools form conflict; some say between Mosken and Vaeröy; others say between Mosken and Lofotodden. Modern maps and Poe's narration agree, however. By "coast" Poe means the coast on which his narrator sits, near Helle.

7. Jonas Ramus (1649–1718), author of a book theorizing that Ulysses' experience with Scylla and Charybdis really occurred in the Maelström off the Norwegian coast: *Ulysses et Otinus Unus & idem sive Disquisitio & Historica Geographica* (1702) (Benson). Poe copied Ramus' account from the *Encyclopaedia Britannica*; it, in turn, copied Erich Pontoppidan's *Natural History of Norway* (A. H. Quinn, after Woodberry).

8. second Sunday before Lent.

9. river of fire in Greek mythology.

10. Kircher: Athanasius Kircher (1602–1680).

Gulf of Bothnia: an outlet of the Baltic Sea, between Sweden and Finland.

11. It is enlightening to compare this story

to Coleridge's "The Rime of the Ancient Mariner." We are now at the end of the "frame story." Coleridge's mariner tells his tale to a wedding guest; Poe's fisherman tells his to a tourist.

12. Poe remarked that he had written this tale in haste, which might account for the ineffectiveness of his handling of the personal relations in it. The fisherman's language seems too cool for the situation he is describing; here, the loss of a brother is tossed off in a casual subordinate clause.

13. port, or left (as one faces the bow).

14. Compare to Coleridge's mariner, who, in a moment when he should despair, finds beauty in the creatures of the sea.

15. Again, compare to the behavior of Coleridge's mariner when he blesses the creatures around him.

16. leaned over with a side wind.

17. See Section Preface.

18. Mohammedans.

19. See Section Preface.

20. The key to the brilliance which the fisherman will now display: his state of mind is "unnatural." Coleridge's mariner blesses the beasts and *is* saved; Poe's hero is frightened into brilliance, becomes a kind of intuitive "poet" of natural forces, and can save himself. Compare the process by which the narrator in "The Pit and the Pendulum," in a comparable predicament, turns brilliant and so remains alive to be rescued.

21. See Archimedes, *De Incidentibus in Fluido.*—lib. 2 [Poe's note]. Archimedes is the famous Greek mathematician, c. 287–212 B. C. E. But the work in question says nothing about the behavior of such objects in water (Turner; Campbell).

22. Is Poe right? Experiments by your editors with mixers and blenders are inconclusive.

The Pit and the Pendulum

1. Carlson (2) translates the Latin, "Here an insatiable band of torturers long wickedly nourished their lusts for innocent blood. Saved, now, our homeland; destroyed, the funereal dungeon." The Jacobins were a radical group during the French Revolution, associated with the Reign of Terror. In suggesting a similarity between the Reign of Terror and the Spanish Inquisition (the setting of "The Pit and the Pendulum") Poe associates the excesses of Catholicism with those of political radicalism. Anti-Catholic feeling ran high in Poe's America, and the French Revolution was still a controversial and lively topic, used by conservatives for scare purposes to show the results of too much democracy.

2. The Spanish Inquisition was an independent court of the Roman Catholic Church notorious for cruelty in the prosecution of heretics and of adherents of other religions. Note, however, that Poe dates his story at the point in history in which the Inquisition was discontinued, the Napoleonic conquest of Spain (see note 11).

3. This discussion of the states of sleep and of the nature of fainting "sets up" the procedure on the following pages by which the narrator gradually emerges from his madness to the brilliance which enables him to survive long enough to be rescued from his torturers. Compare this narrator's experiences to those of the Norwegian fisherman in "A Descent into the Maelström." That tale appeared in 1841; this was written in 1842 for the 1843 edition of *The Gift*, and reprinted in *The Broadway Journal*, May 17, 1845.

4. *autos-da-fé:* public announcement and execution of sentence of the Inquisition; in common use, the execution itself, generally by burning at the stake.

Toledo: A. H. Quinn says that Poe had probably been reading a book about the Spanish Inquisition. It suggested to him not only details of setting—the location in the city of Toledo, for example—but also with the idea of the descending pendulum. The idea of the shrinking iron cell might have come from a tale called "The Iron Shroud" in *Blackwood's Magazine* in 1830 (A. H. Quinn); Poe was a regular reader of *Blackwood's.*

5. The buried-alive motif is common in Poe. Some readers may take it as conclusive evidence that Poe suffered an acute psychological condition from fear of such a fate. But Poe observed that burial alive made a good commercial story topic in his day. See also "The Premature Burial."

6. Writing for a Protestant audience, Poe can assume that his readers are familiar with a long tradition of stories of priestly diabolism.

7. a strap around the body; usually, the strap which holds on a horse's saddle.

8. most extreme form; literally, Farthest Thule—in ancient geography, the northernmost habitable region.

9. Modern readers may wonder at the amount of space Poe devotes to describing his narrator's precise state of mind during the ordeal. The commercial reasons for such concern are clearly explained in "How to Write a Blackwood Article": "Should you ever be drowned or hung, be sure and make a note of your sensations—they will be worth to you ten guineas a sheet." Given his theory of inspiration, however, Poe also has philosophical reasons. See Section Preface.

10. the turning point. Cf. "A Descent into the Maelström," note 20.

11. Antoine Chevalier Louis Collinet, Count de La Salle (1775–1809), Napoleonic general who fought brilliantly in Spain in 1808.

3. The Death of a Beautiful Woman

These stories have a few features in common:

First, they are philosophically consistent, and their philosophy is occult: the visionary sees the underlying truths of the universe; the world is sentient; the human mind, which, to the enlightened, is identical with the universe, also creates the universe; and "equivalences" are real and not merely symbolic. One can question Poe's seriousness; at least two tales in this group are also satirical. Mysticism and humor, however, are not incompatible, and Poe's other writings also suggest his commitment to "the perennial philosophy."

Secondly, the psychological connection between death, sexuality, and creativity noted later by Freud is extremely explicit here. The fascination with death in Poe's day is doubtless sick, and deserves the satire which Poe, Hawthorne, and later Twain directed against it. It is, we should note, no stronger in Poe than in other writers of the time: how many sopranos expire gracefully, belting out *da capo* arias in operas of the period? It is perhaps a sign of health that we now regard as unsavory an artistic credo which Poe enunciated in "The Philosophy of Composition": "The death of a beautiful woman is, unquestionably, the most poetical topic in the world. . . ."

And finally, in each tale, Poe provides an escape valve. We see the action through the eyes of narrators who are wounded, drugged, insane, terrified, or a combination of such states. We can, if we wish, read these tales as psychological studies and assume that what occurs in them is not "real," but rather the vision of a deranged intelligence. Or we can say that they reflect the belief common in folklore and occultism that the insane, drugged, or deranged can see truths inaccessible to most of us.

The Oval Portrait. In the final version of "The Oval Portrait," the narrator tells us that he is delirious from his wounds. In the earlier version, he had also taken opium to kill the pain and gone for a week without sleep. Either way, Poe establishes a "margin of credibility": the narrator is in so abnormal a state that the action of the story from note 2 on is ambiguous. The reader can believe it or assume that it is the vision of a very sick man. Poe's ambiguity is deliberate; at note 3 he tells us that the narrator "seemed" to wake up. What follows, then, may be just a dream.

The quasi-ritualistic language in the "quotation" which closes the tale makes explicit the association between art, beauty, creativity, and the death of a beautiful woman.

Morella. Poe's narrator in "Morella" calls German mysticism "the mere dross of the early German literature," says that Fichte is "wild," and generally disparages the mystic's position. The tale, however, shows the narrator wrong. Even as exotic a doctrine as the survival of human identity after death is to be taken seriously.

One gets the distinct impression in reading Poe that as time went on, he came to believe more and more strongly in transcendent experience, mysticism, and the occult. In the first version of this tale, at note 6, he had written,

As I came, she was murmuring in a low under-tone the words of a Catholic hymn:

> *Sancta Maria! turn thine eyes*
> *Upon a sinner's sacrifice*
> *Of fervent prayer, and humble love,*
> *From thy holy throne above.*
>
> *At morn, at noon, at twilight dim,*
> *Maria! thou hast heard my hymn,*
> *In joy and wo, in good and ill,*
> *Mother of God! be with me still.*
>
> *When my hours flew gently by,*
> *And no storms were in the sky,*
> *My soul, lest it should truant be;*
> *Thy love did guide to thine and thee.*
>
> *Now when clouds of Fate o'ercast*
> *All my Present, and my Past,*
> *Let my Future radiant shine*
> *With sweet hopes of thee and thine.*

Poe liked his refreshingly straightforward little hymn, and kept on publishing it after he cut it from "Morella." Its omission strongly suggests his desire to stress the mystical message of the tale by eliminating a conventional religious passage which could dilute it.

Berenice. If the soul can have "previous existence," as Egaeus claims in the third paragraph of "Berenice," and if the "visionary" and apparent worlds can merge in the mind of an illuminated seer, then "Berenice" is a serious philosophical tale. As usual in tales in which a seer perceives a vision, Poe gives the skeptical reader a rational way out. In this tale it is that the narrator is mad. At note 4, we are given a mystical alternative. The "attentive" process described here may be simply a symptom of madness, but it matches very closely one traditional route in mystical religions to psychic realization. Keep in mind the old belief that children and the insane have such powers, the fact that Egaeus' family runs to "visionaries," and that Egaeus says that he believes that he has lived before. The mystic believes that the universe is a whole, that any part of it represents the truth of the whole. Egaeus looks at "frivolous" objects and has unpleasant meditations. At the opening of the story, he tells us that the rainbow, beauty, and joy lead to sorrow, for "misery is manifold." The mystical reading of the tale, in short, is as consistent as the "rational" reading. There is ample evidence that Poe took such beliefs, and this tale, seriously.

Yet much suggests that "Berenice" is an attempt to work up effective fiction from a topic purposely selected for its repulsiveness; the author chuckles up his sleeve. Since Poe's "real" intention is never easy to determine, we are forced to say that the tale is philosophically consistent with his world-view and with his theory of effect and beauty in art, and also that it is, like "Ligeia," at the same time a put-on.

Internal evidence of Poe's intentions is inconclusive. Poe got the name "Egeus" from Shakespeare. In "A Midsummer Night's Dream," Egeus is the father of Hermia. Hermia is in love with Lysander, but Egeus wants her to marry Demetrius. Egeus invokes an Athenian law and calls upon the Duke, Theseus, to enforce it: Hermia must marry Demetrius or be punished by death or by a life in a nunnery. Berenice is not at all like Hermia, and the tone of Poe's tale is totally different from the airy fantasy of Shakespeare. Poe may just have chosen the name because it has a lofty sound (Shakespeare's Egeus *is* of very prominent family). Or he may have had in mind the idea of imposing one's will upon a beautiful woman. In the play, a love potion causes people to fall in love with the wrong partners. But if Poe intended something of the sort, the name would seem more appropriate for the narrator of one of Poe's other tales in this genre, "Morella," in which the daughter of the beautiful but departed woman is, at her own death, replaced by her mother; or "Ligeia," in which the dark Ligeia replaces the dying blonde, Rowena.

Eleonora. The opening paragraph of "Eleonora" utilizes Poe's usual device for establishing the narrator's nervous or even insane temperament as a prop to credibility: the reader then does not have to believe literally the fantastic events of the tale. On the other hand, it sets forth an occult world-view; plentiful evidence suggests that Poe, like many romantics, seriously believed in "the great secret." And the story can be understood as an occult parable.

Ligeia. Poe said several times that this was one of his best stories or even that it was his very best. The suggestion (see note 11) that it is a satire seems incongruous with its apparent seriousness of tone. Yet that suggestion is well argued, and it is not beyond Poe's range of intention to produce a tale at once dead serious in its attempt to create a beautiful effect (see his essay on how he wrote "The Raven"), serious also in its exposition of the mystical doctrine of the reality of the transcendence of the soul, yet satirical in its treatment of contemporary and recent philosophical and literary movements.

The Fall of the House of Usher. "The Fall of the House of Usher" is a philosophical story in that Poe stresses what mystics call "equivalences." Roderick and Madeline are twins who sense one another's feelings as twins are supposed to in folklore; the tarn reflects the house and its gloomy surroundings; the events at the close of the tale reflect the words of the book the narrator reads to Usher; the house represents the family. Note that the narrator senses "equivalences" right at the outset (see note 2). Usher, in his hereditary illness, his drugged state, and his fear, senses the unity of all things. The narrator, by the close of the tale, has come to sense it, too.

This is, then, a tale about perception, and though to perceive here is to fear, we note that, as usual in Poe, the "perceiver" creates beauty. Roderick paints and improvises fantastic music (see note 7). Poe hints that the inspiration involved in the creative process is akin to that which will enable Usher to know that his sister is alive in her coffin.

This is also a "buried alive" story, and a "death of a beautiful woman" story. But before the reader concludes that Poe is as much in the grips of fear as are Usher and the narrator, he should read "The Premature Burial," in which Poe makes healthy fun of morbidness. He should keep in mind also Poe's obvious artistic control: this is no tale written by a madman; it is much too carefully crafted. It will, indeed, "take" specialized philosophical readings, such as a recent careful Gnostic interpretation (St. Armand). Poe even provides a "rational" explanation for what happens: the narrator, as frightened as Usher, may be inventing details (see note 2 again). Poe allows us the possibility that this is a psychological study of the contagion of fear.

The Tales

THE OVAL PORTRAIT

Egli è vivo e parlerebbe se non osservasse la regola del silenzio.
He is alive and would speak were it not for the fact that he must observe the rule of silence.

Inscription beneath an
Italian picture of St. Bruno[1]

[My fever had been excessive and of long duration. All the remedies attainable in this wild Appennine region had been exhausted to no purpose. My valet and sole attendant in the lonely chateau was too nervous and too grossly unskillful to venture upon letting blood—of which indeed I had already lost too much in the affray

with the banditti. Neither could I safely permit him to leave me in search of assistance. At length I bethought me of a little pacquet of opium which lay with my tobacco in the hookah-case; for at Constantinople I had acquired the habit of smoking the weed with the drug. Pedro handed me the case. I sought and found the narcotic. But when about to cut off a portion I felt the necessity of hesitation. In smoking it was a matter of little importance *how much* was employed. Usually I had half filled the bowl of the hookah with opium and tobacco cut and mingled intimately, half and half. Sometimes when I had used the whole of this mixture I experienced no very peculiar effects; at other times I would not have smoked the pipe more than two-thirds out, when symptoms of mental derangement, which were even alarming, warned me to desist. But the effect proceeded with an easy gradation which deprived the indulgence of all danger. Here, however, the case was different. I had never *swallowed* opium before. Laudanum and morphine I had occasionally used, and about *them* should have had no reason to hesitate. But the solid drug I had never seen employed. Pedro knew no more respecting the proper quantity to be taken than myself—and this, in the sad emergency, I was left altogether to conjecture. Still I felt no especial uneasiness; for I resolved to proceed *by degrees.* I would take a *very* small dose in the first instance. Should this prove impotent, I would repeat it; and so on, until I should find an abatement of the fever, or obtain that sleep which was so pressingly requisite, and with which my reeling senses had not been blessed for now more than a week. No doubt it was this very reeling of my senses—it was the dull delirium which already oppressed me—that prevented me from perceiving the incoherence of my reason—which blinded me to the folly of defining any thing as either large or small where I had no preconceived standard of comparison. I had not, at the moment, the faintest idea that what I conceived to be an exceedingly small dose of solid opium might, in fact, be an excessively large one. On the contrary I well remember that I judged confidently of the quantity to be taken by reference to the entire quantity of the lump in possession. The portion which, in conclusion, I swallowed, and swallowed without fear, was no doubt a very small proportion *of the piece which I held in my hand.*]

The chateau in which my valet had ventured to make forcible entrance, rather than permit me, in my desperately wounded condition, to pass a night in the open air, was one of those piles of commingled gloom and grandeur which have so long frowned among the Apennines,

not less in fact than in fancy of Mrs. Radcliffe. To all appearance it had been temporarily and very lately abandoned. We established ourselves in one of the smallest and least sumptuously furnished apartments. It lay in a remote turret of the building. Its decorations were rich, yet tattered and antique. Its walls were hung with tapestry and bedecked with manifold and multiform armorial trophies, together with an unusually great number of very spirited modern paintings in frames of rich golden arabesque. In these paintings, which depended from the walls not only in their main surfaces, but in very many nooks which the bizarre architecture of the chateau rendered necessary—in these paintings my incipient delirium, perhaps, had caused me to take deep interest,[2] so that I bade Pedro to close the heavy shutters of the room—since it was already night—to light the tongues of a tall candelabrum which stood by the head of my bed—and to throw open far and wide the fringed curtains of black velvet which enveloped the bed itself. I wished all this done that I might resign myself, if not to sleep, at least alternately to the contemplation of these pictures, and the perusal of a small volume which had been found upon the pillow, and which purported to criticise and describe them.

Long—long I read—and devoutly, devotedly I gazed. Rapidly and gloriously the hours flew by, and the deep midnight came. The position of the candelabrum displeased me, and outstretching my hand with difficulty, rather than disturb my slumbering valet, I placed it so as to throw its rays more fully upon the book.

But the action produced an effect altogether unanticipated. The rays of the numerous candles (for there were many) now fell within a niche of the room which had hitherto been thrown into deep shade by one of the bed-posts. I thus saw in vivid light a picture all unnoticed before. It was the portrait of a young girl just ripening into womanhood. I glanced at the painting hurriedly, and then closed my eyes.

Why I did this was not at first apparent even to my own perception. But while my lids remained thus shut, I ran over in mind my reason for so shutting them. It was an impulsive movement to gain time for thought—to make sure that my vision had not deceived me—to calm and subdue my fancy for a more sober and more certain gaze. In a very few moments I again looked fixedly at the painting.

That I now saw aright I could not and would not doubt; for the first flashing of the candles upon that canvas had seemed[3] to dissipate the dreamy stupor which was stealing over my senses, and to startle me at once into waking life.

The portrait, I have already said, was that of a young girl. It was a mere head and shoulders, done in what is technically termed a *vignette* manner; much in the style of the favorite heads of Sully. The arms, the bosom and even the ends of the radiant hair, melted imperceptibly into the vague yet deep shadow which formed the background of the whole. The frame was oval, richly gilded and filagreed in *Moresque*.[4] As a thing of art nothing could be more admirable than the painting itself. But it could have been neither the execution of the work, nor the immortal beauty of the countenance, which had so suddenly and so vehemently moved me. Least of all, could it have been that my fancy, shaken from its half slumber, had mistaken the head for that of a living person. I saw at once that the peculiarities of the design, of the *vignetting,* and of the frame, must have instantly dispelled such idea—must have prevented even its momentary entertainment. Thinking earnestly upon these points, I remained, for an hour perhaps, half sitting, half reclining, with my vision riveted upon the portrait. At length, satisfied with the true secret of its effect, I fell back within the bed. I had found the spell of the picture in an absolute *life-likeliness* of expression, which at first startling, finally confounded, subdued and appalled me. With deep and reverent awe I replaced the candelabrum in its former position. The cause of my deep agitation being thus shut from view, I sought eagerly the volume which discussed the paintings and their histories. Turning to the number which designated the oval portrait, I there read the vague and quaint words which follow:

"She was a maiden of rarest beauty, and not more lovely than full of glee. And evil was the hour when she saw, and loved, and wedded the painter. He, passionate, studious, austere, and having already a bride in his Art; she a maiden of rarest beauty, and not more lovely than full of glee; all light and smiles, and frolicksome as the young fawn: loving and cherishing all things: hating only the Art which was her rival: dreading only the palette and brushes and other untoward instruments which deprived her of the countenance of her lover. It was thus a terrible thing for this lady to hear the painter speak of his desire to portray even his young bride. But she was humble and obedient, and sat meekly for many weeks in the dark high turret-chamber where the light dripped upon the pale canvas only from overhead. But he, the painter, took glory in his work, which went on from hour to hour and from day to day. And he was a passionate, and wild and moody man, who became lost in reveries; so that he *would* not see that the light which fell so ghastlily in that lone turret withered the health and the spirits of his bride, who pined visibly to all but him. Yet she smiled on and still on, uncomplainingly, because she saw that the painter, (who had high renown,) took a fervid[5] and burning pleasure in his task, and wrought day and night to depict her who so loved him, yet who grew daily more dispirited and weak. And in sooth some who beheld the portrait spoke of its resemblance in low words, as of a mighty marvel, and a proof not less of the power of the painter than of his deep love for her whom he depicted so surpassingly well. But at length, as the labour drew nearer to its conclusion, there were admitted none into the turret; for the painter had grown wild with the ardor of his work, and turned his eyes from the canvas rarely, even to regard the countenance of his wife. And he *would* not see that the tints which he spread upon the canvas were drawn from the cheeks of her who sate beside him. And when many weeks had passed, and but little remained to do, save one brush upon the mouth and one tint upon the eye, the spirit of the lady again flickered up as the flame within the socket of the lamp. And then the brush was given, and then the tint was placed; and, for one moment, the painter stood entranced before the work which he had wrought; but in the next, while he yet gazed, he grew tremulous and very pallid, and aghast, and crying with a loud voice, 'This is indeed *Life* itself' turned suddenly to regard his beloved:—*She was dead!*"

MORELLA

Αυτο καθ' αυτο μεθ' αυτου, μονο ειδες αιει ον.
Itself, by itself solely, ONE *everlastingly, and single.*
        Plato, *Symposium* [211, XXIX.][1]

With a feeling of deep yet most singular affection I regarded my friend Morella. Thrown by accident into her society many years ago, my soul, from our first meeting, burned with fires it had never before known; but the fires were not of Eros,[2] and bitter and tormenting to my spirit was the gradual conviction that I could in no manner define their unusual meaning, or regulate their vague intensity. Yet we met; and fate bound us together at the altar; and I never spoke of passion, nor thought of love. She, however, shunned society, and attaching herself to me alone, rendered me happy. It is a happiness to wonder;—it is a happiness to dream.

Morella's erudition was profound. As I hope to live, her talents were of no common order—her powers of mind were gigantic. I felt this, and, in many matters, became her pupil. I soon, however, found that, perhaps on account of her Presburg[3]

education, she placed before me a number of those mystical writings which are usually considered the mere dross of the early German literature. These, for what reason I could not imagine, were her favorite and constant study—and that, in process of time they became my own, should be attributed to the single but effectual influence of habit and example.

In all this, if I err not, my reason had little to do. My convictions, or I forget myself, were in no manner acted upon by the ideal, nor was any tincture of the mysticism which I read, to be discovered, unless I am greatly mistaken, either in my deeds or in my thoughts. Persuaded of this, I abandoned myself implicitly to the guidance of my wife, and entered with an unflinching heart into the intricacies of her studies. And then—then, when, poring over forbidden pages, I felt a forbidden spirit enkindling within me—would Morella place her cold hand upon my own, and rake up from the ashes of a dead philosophy some low, singular words, whose strange meaning burned themselves in upon my memory. And then, hour after hour, would I linger by her side, and dwell upon the music of her voice—until, at length, its melody was tainted with terror,—and there fell a shadow upon my soul—and I grew pale, and shuddered inwardly at those too unearthly tones. And thus, joy suddenly faded into horror, and the most beautiful became the most hideous, as Hinnon became Ge-Henna.[4]

It is unnecessary to state the exact character of those disquisitions which, growing out of the volumes I have mentioned, formed, for so long a time, almost the sole conversation of Morella and myself. By the learned in what might be termed theological morality they will be readily conceived, and by the unlearned they would, at all events, be little understood. The wild Pantheism of Fichte; the modified Παλιγγενεσία of the Pythagoreans; and, above all, doctrines of *Identity* as urged by Schelling, were generally the points of discussion presenting the most of beauty to the imaginative Morella. That identity which is termed personal, Mr. Locke,[5] I think, truly defines to consist in the sameness of a rational being. And since by person we understand an intelligent essence having reason, and since there is a consciousness which always accompanies thinking, it is this which makes us all to be that which we call *ourselves*—thereby distinguishing us from other beings that think, and giving us our personal identity. But the *principium individuationis*—the notion of that identity *which at death is or is not lost forever*, was to me—at all times, a consideration of intense interest; not more from the perplexing and exciting nature of its consequences, than from the marked and agitated manner in which Morella mentioned them.

But, indeed, the time had now arrived when the mystery of my wife's manner oppressed me as a spell. I could no longer bear the touch of wan fingers, nor the low tone of her musical language, nor the lustre of her melancholy eyes. And she knew all this, but did not upbraid; she seemed conscious of my weakness or my folly, and, smiling, called it Fate. She seemed, also, conscious of a cause, to me unknown, for the gradual alienation of my regard; but she gave me no hint or token of its nature. Yet was she woman, and pined away daily. In time, the crimson spot settled steadily upon the cheek, and the blue veins upon the pale forehead became prominent; and, one instant, my nature melted into pity, but, in the next, I met the glance of her meaning eyes, and then my soul sickened and became giddy with the giddiness of one who gazes downward into some dreary and unfathomable abyss.

Shall I then say that I longed with an earnest and consuming desire for the moment of Morella's decease? I did; but the fragile spirit clung to its tenement of clay for many days—for many weeks and irksome months—until my tortured nerves obtained the mastery over my mind, and

I grew furious through delay, and, with the heart of a fiend, cursed the days, and the hours, and the bitter moments, which seemed to lengthen and lengthen as her gentle life declined—like shadows in the dying of the day.

But one autumnal evening, when the winds lay still in heaven, Morella called me to her bed-side. There was a dim mist over all the earth, and a warm glow upon the waters, and, amid the rich October leaves of the forest, a rainbow from the firmament had surely fallen.[6]

"It is a day of days," she said, as I approached; "a day of all days either to live or die. It is a fair day for the sons of earth and life—ah, more fair for the daughters of heaven and death!"

I kissed her forehead, and she continued:

"I am dying, yet shall I live."

"Morella!"

"The days have never been when thou couldst love me—but her whom in life thou didst abhor, in death thou shalt adore."

"Morella!"

"I repeat that I am dying. But within me is a pledge of that affection—ah, how little!—which thou didst feel for me, Morella. And when my spirit departs shall the child live—thy child and mine, Morella's. But thy days shall be days of sorrow—that sorrow which is the most lasting of impressions, as the cypress is the most enduring of trees. For the hours of thy happiness are over; and joy is not gathered twice in a life, as the roses of Pæstum twice in a year. Thou shalt no longer, then, play the Teian with time, but, being ignorant of the myrtle and the vine, thou shalt bear about with thee thy shroud on the earth, as do the Moslemin at Mecca."[7]

"Morella!" I cried, "Morella! how knowest thou this?"—but she turned away her face upon the pillow, and, a slight tremor coming over her limbs, she thus died, and I heard her voice no more.

Yet, as she had foretold, her child—to

which in dying she had given birth, and
which breathed not until the mother
breathed no more—her child, a daughter,
lived. And she grew strangely in stature
and intellect, and was the perfect resemblance of her who had departed, and I
loved her with a love more fervent than
I had believed it possible to feel for any
denizen of earth.

But, ere long, the heaven of this pure
affection became darkened, and gloom,
and horror, and grief, swept over it in
clouds. I said the child grew strangely
in stature and intelligence. Strange indeed
was her rapid increase in bodily size—but
terrible, oh! terrible were the tumultuous
thoughts which crowded upon me while
watching the development of her mental
being. Could it be otherwise, when I daily
discovered in the conceptions of the child
the adult powers and faculties of the
woman?—when the lessons of experience
fell from the lips of infancy? and when
the wisdom or the passions of maturity
I found hourly gleaming from its full and
speculative eye? When, I say, all this became evident to my appalled senses—
when I could no longer hide it from my
soul, nor throw it off from those perceptions which trembled to receive it—is it
to be wondered at that suspicions, of a
nature fearful and exciting, crept in upon
my spirit, or that my thoughts fell back
aghast upon the wild tales and thrilling
theories of the entombed Morella? I
snatched from the scrutiny of the world
a being whom destiny compelled me to
adore and in the rigorous seclusion of my
home, watched with an agonizing anxiety
over all which concerned the beloved.

And, as years rolled away, and I gazed,
day after day, upon her holy, and mild,
and eloquent face, and pored over her ma-
turing form, day after day did I discover
new points of resemblance in the child
to her mother, the melancholy and the
dead. And, hourly, grew darker these shadows of similitude, and more full, and more
definite, and more perplexing, and more
hideously terrible in their aspect. For that

her smile was like her mother's I could
bear; but then I shuddered at its too perfect *identity*—that her eyes were like Morella's I could endure; but then they too
often looked down into the depths of my
soul with Morella's own intense and bewildering meaning. And in the contour of
the high forehead, and in the ringlets of
the silken hair, and in the wan fingers
which buried themselves therein, and in
the sad musical tones of her speech, and
above all—oh, above all—in the phrases
and expressions of the dead on the lips of
the loved and the living, I found food for
consuming thought and horror—for a
worm that *would* not die.

Thus passed away two lustra of her life,
and, as yet, my daughter remained nameless upon the earth. "My child" and "my
love" were the designations usually
prompted by a father's affection, and the
rigid seclusion of her days precluded all
other intercourse. Morella's name died
with her at her death. Of the mother I
had never spoken to the daughter;—it
was impossible to speak. Indeed, during
the brief period of her existence the latter
had received no impressions from the outward world save such as might have been
afforded by the narrow limits of her privacy. But at length the ceremony of baptism presented to my mind, in its unnerved and agitated condition, a present
deliverance from the terrors of my destiny. And at the baptismal font I hesitated
for a name. And many titles of the wise
and beautiful, of old and modern times, of
my own and foreign lands, came thronging to my lips, with many, many fair
titles of the gentle, and the happy, and
the good. What prompted me, then, to
disturb the memory of the buried dead?
What demon urged me to breathe that
sound, which, in its very recollection was
wont to make ebb the purple blood in
torrents from the temples to the heart?
What fiend spoke from the recesses of my
soul, when, amid those dim aisles, and in
the silence of the night, I whispered
within the ears of the holy man the syl-

lables—Morella? What more than fiend convulsed the features of my child, and overspread them with hues of death, as starting at that scarcely audible sound, she turned her glassy eyes from the earth to heaven, and, falling prostrate on the black slabs of our ancestral vault, responded—"I am here!"

Distinct, coldly, calmly distinct, fell those few simple sounds within my ear, and thence, like molten lead, rolled hissingly into my brain. Years—years may pass away, but the memory of that epoch —never! Nor was I indeed ignorant of the flowers and the vine—but the hemlock and the cypress overshadowed me night and day. And I kept no reckoning of time or place, and the stars of my fate faded from heaven, and therefore the earth grew dark, and its figures passed by me, like flitting shadows, and among them all I beheld only—Morella. The winds of the firmament breathed but one sound within my ears, and the ripples upon the sea murmured evermore—Morella. But she died; and with my own hands I bore her to the tomb; and I laughed with a long and bitter laugh as I found no traces of the first, in the charnel where I laid the second—Morella.

BERENICE

Dicebant mihi sodales, si sepulchrum amicæ visitarem, curas meas aliquantulum fore levatas.

Ebn Zaiat[1]

Misery is manifold. The wretchedness of earth is multiform. Overreaching the wide horizon as the rainbow, its hues are as various as the hues of that arch,—as distinct too, yet as intimately blended. Overreaching the wide horizon as the rainbow! How is it that from beauty I have derived a type of unloveliness?—from the covenant of peace a simile of sorrow? But as, in ethics, evil is a consequence of good, so, in fact, out of joy is sorrow born. Either the memory of past bliss is the anguish of

to-day, or the agonies which *are* have their origin in the ecstasies which *might have been.*

My baptismal name is Egæus; that of my family I will not mention. Yet there are no towers in the land more time-honored than my gloomy, gray, hereditary halls. Our line has been called a race of visionaries; and in many striking particulars—in the character of the family mansion—in the frescos of the chief saloon —in the tapestries of the dormitories—in the chiselling of some buttresses in the armory—but more especially in the gallery of antique paintings—in the fashion of the library chamber—and, lastly, in the very peculiar nature of the library's contents, there is more than sufficient evidence to warrant the belief.[2]

The recollections of my earliest years are connected with that chamber, and with its volumes—of which latter I will say no more. Here died my mother. Herein was I born. But it is mere idleness to say that I had not lived before—that the soul has no previous existence. You deny it? —let us not argue the matter. Convinced myself, I seek not to convince. There is, however, a remembrance of aërial forms— of spiritual and meaning eyes—of sounds, musical yet sad—a remembrance which will not be excluded; a memory like a shadow, vague, variable, indefinite, unsteady; and like a shadow, too, in the impossibility of my getting rid of it while the sunlight of my reason shall exist.

In that chamber was I born. Thus awaking from the long night of what seemed, but was not, nonentity, at once into the very regions of fairy-land—into a palace of imagination—into the wild dominions of monastic thought and erudition—it is not singular that I gazed around me with a startled and ardent eye—that I loitered away my boyhood in books, and dissipated my youth in reverie; but it *is* singular that as years rolled away, and the noon of manhood found me still in the mansion of my fathers—it *is* wonderful what stagnation there fell upon the springs of my life—wonderful how total an inversion took place in the character of my commonest thought. The realities of the world affected me as visions, and as visions only, while the wild ideas of the land of dreams became, in turn,—not the material of my everyday existence—but in very deed that existence utterly and solely in itself.

Berenice and I were cousins, and we grew up together in my paternal halls. Yet differently we grew—I ill of health, and buried in gloom—she agile, graceful, and overflowing with energy; hers the ramble on the hill-side—mine the studies of the cloister—I living within my own heart, and addicted body and soul to the most intense and painful meditation—she roaming carelessly through life with no thought of the shadows in her path, or the silent flight of the raven-winged hours. Berenice!—I call upon her name—Berenice!—and from the gray ruins of memory a thousand tumultuous recollections are startled at the sound! Ah! vividly is her image before me now, as in the early days of her light-heartedness and joy! Oh! gorgeous yet fantastic beauty! Oh! sylph amid the shrubberies of Arnheim![3]—Oh! Naiad among its fountains!—and then—then all is mystery and terror, and a tale which should not be told. Disease—a fatal disease—fell like the simoom upon her frame, and, even while I gazed upon her, the spirit of change swept over her, pervading her mind, her habits, and her character, and, in a manner the most subtle and terrible, disturbing even the identity of her person! Alas! the destroyer came and went, and the victim—where was she? I knew her not—or knew her no longer as Berenice.

Among the numerous train of maladies superinduced by that fatal and primary one which effected a revolution of so horrible a kind in the moral and physical being of my cousin, may be mentioned as the most distressing and obstinate in its nature, a species of epilepsy not unfre-

quently terminating in *trance* itself—trance very nearly resembling positive dissolution, and from which her manner of recovery was, in most instances, startlingly abrupt. In the mean time my own disease—for I have been told that I should call it by no other appellation—my own disease, then, grew rapidly upon me, and assumed finally a monomaniac character of a novel and extraordinary form—hourly and momently gaining vigor—and at length obtaining over me the most incomprehensible ascendancy. This monomania, if I must so term it, consisted in a morbid irritability of those properties of the mind in metaphysical science termed the *attentive*. It is more than probable that I am not understood; but I fear, indeed, that it is in no manner possible to convey to the mind of the merely general reader, an adequate idea of that nervous *intensity of interest* with which, in my case, the powers of meditation (not to speak technically) busied and buried themselves, in the contemplation of even the most ordinary objects of the universe.

To muse for long unwearied hours with my attention riveted to some frivolous device on the margin, or in the typography of a book; to become absorbed for the better part of a summer's day, in a quaint shadow falling aslant upon the tapestry, or upon the door; to lose myself for an entire night in watching the steady flame of a lamp, or the embers of a fire; to dream away whole days over the perfume of a flower; to repeat monotonously some common word, until the sound, by dint of frequent repetition, ceased to convey any idea whatever to the mind; to lose all sense of motion or physical existence, by means of absolute bodily quiescence long and obstinately persevered in;—such were a few of the most common and least pernicious vagaries induced by a condition of the mental faculties, not, indeed, altogether unparalleled, but certainly bidding defiance to anything like analysis or explanation.

Yet let me not be misapprehended.—

The undue, earnest, and morbid attention thus excited by objects in their own nature frivolous, must not be confounded in character with that ruminating propensity common to all mankind, and more especially indulged in by persons of ardent imagination. It was not even, as might be at first supposed, an extreme condition, or exaggeration of such propensity, but primarily and essentially distinct and different. In the one instance, the dreamer, or enthusiast, being interested by an object usually *not* frivolous, imperceptibly loses sight of this object in a wilderness of deductions and suggestions issuing therefrom, until, at the conclusion of a day dream *often replete with luxury,* he finds the *incitamentum* or first cause of his musings entirely vanished and forgotten. In my case the primary object was *invariably frivolous,* although assuming, through the medium of my distempered vision, a refracted and unreal importance. Few deductions, if any, were made; and those few pertinaciously returning in upon the original object as a centre. The meditations were *never* pleasurable; and, at the termination of the reverie, the first cause, so far from being out of sight, had attained that supernaturally exaggerated interest which was the prevailing feature of the disease. In a word, the powers of mind more particularly exercised were, with me, as I have said before, the *attentive,* and are, with the day-dreamer, the *speculative.*[4]

My books, at this epoch, if they did not actually serve to irritate the disorder, partook, it will be perceived, largely, in their imaginative and inconsequential nature, of the characteristic qualities of the disorder itself. I well remember, among other, the treatise of the noble Italian Cœlius Secundus Curio *"de Amplitudine Beati Regni Dei;"* St. Austin's great work, the "City of God;" and Tertullian *"de Carne Christi,"* in which the paradoxical sentence *"Mortuus est Dei filius; credibile est quia ineptum est: et sepultus resurrexit; certum est quia impossibile est"*[5]

occupied my undivided time, for many weeks of laborious and fruitless investigation.

Thus it will appear that, shaken from its balance only by trivial things, my reason bore resemblance to that ocean-crag spoken of by Ptolemy Hephestion, which steadily resisting the attacks of human violence, and the fiercer fury of the waters and the winds, trembled only to the touch of the flower called Asphodel.[6] And although, to a careless thinker, it might appear a matter beyond doubt, that the alteration produced by her unhappy malady, in the *moral* condition of Berenice, would afford me many objects for the exercise of that intense and abnormal meditation whose nature I have been at some trouble in explaining, yet such was not in any degree the case. In the lucid intervals of my infirmity, her calamity, indeed, gave me pain, and, taking deeply to heart that total wreck of her fair and gentle life, I did not fail to ponder frequently and bitterly upon the wonder-working means by which so strange a revolution had been so suddenly brought to pass. But these reflections partook not of the idiosyncrasy of my disease, and were such as would have occurred, under similar circumstances, to the ordinary mass of mankind. True to its own character, my disorder revelled in the less important but more startling changes wrought in the *physical* frame of Berenice—in the singular and most appalling distortion of her personal identity.

During the brightest days of her unparalleled beauty, most surely I had never loved her. In the strange anomaly of my existence, feelings with me *had never been* of the heart, and my passions *always were* of the mind. Through the gray of the early morning—among the trellissed shadows of the forest at noonday—and in the silence of my library at night, she had flitted by my eyes, and I had seen her—not as the living and breathing Berenice, but as the Berenice of a dream—not as a being of the earth, earthy, but as the abstraction of such a being—not as a thing to admire, but to analyze—not as an object of love, but as the theme of the most abstruse although desultory speculation. And *now*—now I shuddered in her presence, and grew pale at her approach; yet bitterly lamenting her fallen and desolate condition, I called to mind that she had loved me long, and, in an evil moment, I spoke to her of marriage.

And at length the period of our nuptials was approaching, when, upon an afternoon in the winter of the year,—one of those unseasonably warm, calm, and misty days which are the nurse of the beautiful Halcyon,[7]—I sat, (and sat, as I thought, alone,) in the inner apartment of the library. But uplifting my eyes I saw that Berenice stood before me.

Was it my own excited imagination—or the misty influence of the atmosphere—or the uncertain twilight of the chamber—or the gray draperies which fell around her figure—that caused in it so vacillating and indistinct an outline? I could not tell. She spoke no word, and I—not for worlds could I have uttered a syllable. An icy chill ran through my frame; a sense of insufferable anxiety oppressed me; a consuming curiosity pervaded my soul; and sinking back upon the chair, I remained for some time breathless and motionless, with my eyes riveted upon her person. Alas! its emaciation was excessive, and not one vestige of the former being lurked in any single line of the contour. My burning glances at length fell upon the face.

The forehead was high, and very pale, and singularly placid; and the once jetty hair fell partially over it, and overshadowed the hollow temples with innumerable ringlets now of a vivid yellow, and jarring discordantly, in their fantastic character, with the reigning melancholy of the countenance. The eyes were lifeless, and lustreless, and seemingly pupilless, and I shrank involuntarily from their glassy stare to the contemplation of the thin and shrunken lips. They parted; and in a smile of peculiar meaning, *the teeth* of the changed Berenice disclosed themselves slowly to my view. Would to God that I had never beheld them, or that, having done so, I had died!

The shutting of a door disturbed me, and, looking up, I found that my cousin had departed from the chamber. But from the disordered chamber of my brain, had not, alas! departed, and would not be driven away, the white and ghastly *spectrum* of the teeth. Not a speck on their surface—not a shade on their enamel—not an indenture in their edges—but what that period of her smile had sufficed to brand in upon my memory. I saw them *now* even more unequivocally than I beheld them *then*. The teeth!—the teeth! —they were here, and there, and every where, and visibly and palpably before me; long, narrow, and excessively white, with the pale lips writhing about them, as in the very moment of their first terrible development. Then came the full fury of my *monomania*, and I struggled in vain against its strange and irresistible influence. In the multiplied objects of the external world I had no thoughts but for the teeth. For these I longed with a phrenzied desire. All other matters and all different interests became absorbed in their single contemplation. They—they alone were present to the mental eye, and they, in their sole individuality, became the essence of my mental life. I held them in every light. I turned them in every attitude. I surveyed their characteristics. I dwelt upon their peculiarities. I pondered upon their conformation. I mused upon the alteration in their nature. I shuddered as I assigned to them in imagination a sensitive and sentient power, and even when unassisted by the lips, a capability of moral expression. Of Mad'selle Sallé it has been well said, "*que tous ses pas étaient des sentiments,*" and of Berenice I more seriously believe *que toutes ses dents étaient des idées.*[8] *Des idées!*—ah here was the idiotic thought that destroyed me! *Des idées!*—ah *therefore* it was that I coveted them so madly! I felt that their possession could alone ever restore me to peace, in giving me back to reason.

And the evening closed in upon me thus—and then the darkness came, and tarried, and went—and the day again dawned—and the mists of a second night were now gathering around—and still I sat motionless in that solitary room; and still I sat buried in meditation, and still the *phantasma* of the teeth maintained its terrible ascendancy as, with the most vivid and hideous distinctness, it floated about amid the changing lights and shadows of the chamber. At length there broke in upon my dreams a cry as of horror and dismay; and thereunto, after a pause, succeeded the sound of troubled voices, intermingled with many low moanings of sorrow, or of pain. I arose from my seat and, throwing open one of the doors of the library, saw standing out in the antechamber a servant maiden, all in tears, who told me that Berenice was—no more. She had been seized with epilepsy in the early morning, and now, at the closing in of the night, the grave was ready for its tenant, and all the preparations for the burial were completed.[9]

I found myself sitting in the library, and again sitting there alone. It seemed that I had newly awakened from a confused and exciting dream. I knew that it was now midnight, and I was well aware that since the setting of the sun Berenice had been interred. But of that dreary period which intervened I had no positive —at least no definite comprehension. Yet its memory was replete with horror—horror more horrible from being vague, and terror more terrible from ambiguity. It was a fearful page in the record of my existence, written all over with dim, and hideous, and unintelligible recollections. I strived to decypher them, but in vain; while ever and anon, like the spirit of a departed sound, the shrill and piercing shriek of a female voice seemed to be ringing in my ears. I had done a deed—what was it? I asked myself the question aloud, and the whispering echoes of the chamber answered me, *"what was it?"*

On the table beside me burned a lamp, and near it lay a little box. It was of no remarkable character, and I had seen it frequently before, for it was the property of the family physician; but how came it *there,* upon my table, and why did I shudder in regarding it? These things were in no manner to be accounted for, and my eyes at length dropped to the open pages of a book, and to a sentence underscored therein. The words were the singular but simple ones of the poet Ebn Zaiat, *"Dicebant mihi sodales, si sepulchrum amicæ visitarem, curas meas aliquantulum fore levatas."* Why then, as I perused them, did the hairs of my head erect themselves on end, and the blood of my body become congealed within my veins?

There came a light tap at the library door, and pale as the tenant of a tomb, a menial entered upon tiptoe. His looks were wild with terror, and he spoke to me in a voice tremulous, husky, and very low. What said he?—some broken sentences I heard. He told of a wild cry disturbing the silence of the night—of the gathering together of the household—of a search in the direction of the sound;—and then his tones grew thrillingly distinct as he whispered me of a violated grave—of a disfigured body enshrouded, yet still breathing, still palpitating, still *alive!*

He pointed to my garments;—they were muddy and clotted with gore. I spoke not, and he took me gently by the hand;—it was indented with the impress of human nails. He directed my attention to some object against the wall;—I looked at it for some minutes;—it was a spade. With a shriek I bounded to the table, and grasped the box that lay upon it. But I could not force it open; and in my tremor it slipped from my hands, and fell heavily, and burst into pieces; and from it, with a rattling sound, there rolled out some instruments of dental surgery, intermingled with thirty-two small, white and ivory-looking substances that were scattered to and fro about the floor.

ELEONORA

Sub conservatione formæ specificæ salva anima.
—Raymond Lully.[1]

I am come of a race noted for vigor of fancy and ardor of passion. Men have called me mad; but the question is not yet settled, whether madness is or is not the loftiest intelligence—whether much that is glorious—whether all that is profound —does not spring from disease of thought —from *moods* of mind exalted at the expense of the general intellect. They who dream by day are cognizant of many things which escape those who dream only by night. In their gray visions they obtain glimpses of eternity, and thrill, in awaking, to find that they have been upon the verge of the great secret. In snatches, they learn something of the wisdom which is of good, and more of the mere knowledge which is of evil. They penetrate, however rudderless or compassless, into the vast ocean of the "light ineffable" and again, like the adventurers of the Nubian geographer, "*agressi sunt mare tenebrarum, quid in eo esset exploraturi.*"[2]

We will say, then, that I am mad. I grant, at least, that there are two distinct conditions of my mental existence—the condition of a lucid reason, not to be disputed, and belonging to the memory of events forming the first epoch of my life —and a condition of shadow and doubt, appertaining to the present, and to the recollection of what constitutes the second great era of my being. Therefore, what I shall tell of the earlier period, believe; and to what I may relate of the later time, give only such credit as may seem due; or doubt it altogether; or, if doubt it ye cannot, then play unto its riddle the Oedipus.[3]

She whom I loved in youth, and of whom I now pen calmly and distinctly these remembrances, was the sole daughter of the only sister of my mother long departed. Eleonora was the name of my cousin. We had always dwelled together, beneath a tropical sun, in the Valley of the Many-Coloured Grass. No unguided footstep ever came upon that vale; for it lay far away up among a range of giant hills that hung beetling around about it, shutting out the sunlight from its sweetest recesses. No path was trodden in its vicinity; and, to reach our happy home, there was need of putting back, with force, the foliage of many thousands of forest trees, and of crushing to death the glories of many millions of fragrant flowers. Thus it was that we lived all alone, knowing nothing of the world without the valley,—I, and my cousin, and her mother.[4]

From the dim regions beyond the mountains at the upper end of our encircled domain, there crept out a narrow and deep river, brighter than all save the eyes of Eleonora; and, winding stealthily about in mazy courses, it passed away, at length, through a shadowy gorge, among hills still dimmer than those whence it had issued. We called it the "River of Silence"; for there seemed to be a hushing influence in its flow. No murmur arose from its bed, and so gently it wandered along, that the pearly pebbles upon which we loved to gaze, far down within its bosom, stirred not at all, but lay in a motionless content, each in its own old station, shining on gloriously forever.

The margin of the river, and of the many dazzling rivulets that glided, through devious ways, into its channel, as well as the spaces that extended from the margins away down into the depths of the streams until they reached the bed of pebbles at the bottom,—these spots, not less than the whole surface of the valley, from the river to the mountains that girdled it in, were carpeted all by a soft green grass, thick, short, perfectly even, and vanilla-perfumed, but so besprinkled throughout with the yellow buttercup, the white daisy, the purple violet, and the ruby-red asphodel, that its exceeding beauty spoke to our hearts, in loud tones, of the love and of the glory of God.

And, here and there, in groves about this grass, like wildernesses of dreams, sprang up fantastic trees, whose tall slender stems stood not upright, but slanted gracefully towards the light that peered at noon-day into the centre of the valley. Their bark was speckled with the vivid alternate splendor of ebony and silver, and was smoother than all save the cheeks of Eleonora; so that but for the brilliant green of the huge leaves that spread from their summits in long tremulous lines, dallying with the Zephyrs, one might have fancied them giant serpents of Syria doing homage to their Sovereign the Sun.[5]

Hand in hand about his valley, for fifteen years, roamed I with Eleonora before Love entered within our hearts. It was one evening at the close of the third lustrum of her life, and of the fourth of my own, that we sat, locked in each other's embrace, beneath the serpent-like trees, and looked down within the waters of the River of Silence at our images therein. We spoke no words during the rest of that sweet day; and our words even upon the morrow were tremulous and few. We had drawn the god Eros from that wave, and now we felt that he had enkindled within us the fiery souls of our forefathers. The passions which had for centuries distinguished our race, came thronging with the fancies for which they had been equally noted, and together breathed a delirious bliss over the Valley of the Many-Coloured Grass. A change fell upon all things. Strange brilliant flowers, star-shaped, burst out upon the trees where no flowers had been known before. The tints of the green carpet deepened; and when, one by one, the white daisies shrank away, there sprang up, in place of them, ten by ten of the ruby-red asphodel. And life arose in our paths; for the tall flamingo, hitherto unseen, with all gay glowing birds, flaunted his scarlet plumage before us. The golden and silver fish haunted the river, out of the bosom of which issued, little by little, a murmur that swelled, at length, into a lulling melody more divine than that of the harp of Æolus—sweeter than all save the voice of Eleonora. And now, too, a voluminous cloud, which we had long watched in the regions of Hesper,[6] floated out thence, all gorgeous in crimson and gold, and settling in peace above us, sank, day by day, lower and lower, until its edges rested upon the tops of the mountains, turning all their dimness into magnificence, and shutting us up, as if forever, within a magic prison-house of grandeur and of glory.

The loveliness of Eleonora was that of the Seraphim; but she[7] was a maiden artless and innocent as the brief life she had led among the flowers. No guile disguised the fervor of love which animated her heart, and she examined with me its inmost recesses as we walked together in the Valley of the Many-Coloured Grass, and discoursed of the mighty changes which had lately taken place therein.

At length, having spoken one day, in tears, of the last sad change which must befall Humanity, she thenceforward dwelt only upon this one sorrowful theme, interweaving it into all our converse, as, in the songs of the bard of Schiraz,[8] the same images are found occurring, again and again, in every impressive variation of phrase.

She had seen that the finger of Death was upon her bosom—that, like the ephemeron, she had been made perfect in loveliness only to die; but the terrors of the grave, to her, lay solely in a consideration which she revealed to me, one evening at twilight, by the banks of the River of Silence. She grieved to think that, having entombed her in the Valley of the Many-Coloured Grass, I would quit forever its happy recesses, transferring the love which now was so passionately her own to some maiden of the outer and every-day world. And, then and there, I threw myself hurriedly at the feet of Eleonora, and offered up a vow, to herself and to Heaven, that I would never bind myself in marriage to any daughter of Earth—that I would in no manner prove recreant to her dear memory, or to the memory of the devout affection with which she had blessed me. And I called the Mighty Ruler of the Universe to witness the pious solemnity of my vow. And the curse which I invoked of *Him* and of her, a saint in Helusion,[9] should I prove traitorous to that promise, involved a penalty the exceeding great horror of which will not permit me to make record of it here. And the bright eyes of Eleonora grew brighter at my words; and she sighed as if a deadly burthen had been taken from her breast; and she trembled and very bitterly wept; but she made acceptance of the vow, (for what was she but a child?) and it made easy to her the bed of her death. And she said to me, not many days afterwards, tranquilly dying, that, because of what I had done for the comfort of her spirit, she would watch over me in that spirit when departed, and, if so it were permitted her, return to me visibly in the watches of the night; but, if this thing were, indeed, beyond the power of the souls in Paradise, that she would, at least, give me frequent indications of her presence; sighing upon me in the evening winds, or filling the air which I breathed with perfume from the censers of the angels. And, with these words upon her lips, she yielded up her innocent life, putting an end to the first epoch of my own.

Thus far I have faithfully said. But as I pass the barrier in Time's path formed by the death of my beloved, and proceed with the second era of my existence, I feel that a shadow gathers over my brain, and I mistrust the perfect sanity of the record. But let me on.—Years dragged themselves along heavily, and still I dwelled within the Valley of the Many-Coloured Grass;—but a second change had come upon all things. The star-shaped flowers shrank into the stems of the trees,

and appeared no more. The tints of the green carpet faded; and, one by one, the ruby-red asphodels withered away; and there sprang up, in place of them, ten by ten, dark eye-like violets that writhed uneasily and were ever encumbered with dew.[10] And Life departed from our paths; for the tall flamingo flaunted no longer his scarlet plumage before us, but flew sadly from the vale into the hills, with all the gay glowing birds that had arrived in his company. And the golden and silver fish swam down through the gorge at the lower end of our domain and bedecked the sweet river never again. And the lulling melody that had been softer than the wind-harp of Æolus and more divine than all save the voice of Eleonora, it died little by little away, in murmurs growing lower and lower, until the stream returned, at length, utterly, into the solemnity of its original silence. And then, lastly the voluminous cloud uprose, and, abandoning the tops of the mountains to the dimness of old, fell back into the regions of Hesper, and took away all its manifold golden and gorgeous glories from the Valley of the Many-Coloured Grass.

Yet the promises of Eleonora were not forgotten; for I heard the sounds of the swinging of the censers of the angels; and streams of a holy perfume floated ever and ever about the valley; and at lone hours, when my heart beat heavily, the winds that bathed my brow came unto me laden with soft sighs; and indistinct murmurs filled often the night air; and once—oh, but once only! I was awakened from a slumber like the slumber of death by the pressing of spiritual lips upon my own.

But the void within my heart refused, even thus, to be filled. I longed for the love which had before filled it to overflowing. At length the valley *pained* me through its memories of Eleonora, and I left it forever for the vanities and the turbulent triumphs of the world.

*   *   *

I found myself within a strange city, where all things might have served to blot from recollection the sweet dreams I had dreamed so long in the Valley of the Many-Coloured Grass. The pomps and pageantries of a stately court, and the mad clangor of arms, and the radiant loveliness of woman, bewildered and intoxicated my brain. But as yet my soul had proved true to its vows, and the indications of the presence of Eleonora were still given me in the silent hours of the night. Suddenly, these manifestations they ceased; and the world grew dark before mine eyes; and I stood aghast at the burning thoughts which possessed—at the terrible temptations which beset me; for there came from some far, far distant and unknown land, into the gay court of the king I served, a maiden to whose beauty my whole recreant heart yielded at once—at whose footstool I bowed down without a struggle, in the most ardent, in the most abject worship of love. What indeed was my passion for the young girl of the valley in comparison with the fervor, and the delirium, and the spirit-lifting ecstasy of adoration with which I poured out my whole soul in tears at the feet of the ethereal Ermengarde?— Oh bright was the seraph Ermengarde! and in that knowledge I had room for none other.—Oh divine was the angel Ermengarde! and as I looked down into the depths of her memorial eyes I thought only of them—and *of her*.[11]

I wedded;—nor dreaded the curse I had invoked; and its bitterness was not visited upon me. And once—but once again in the silence of the night, there came through my lattice the soft sighs which had forsaken me; and they modelled themselves into familiar and sweet voice, saying:

"Sleep in peace!—for the Spirit of Love reigneth and ruleth, and, in taking to thy passionate heart her who is Ermengarde, thou art absolved, for reasons which shall be made known to thee in Heaven, of thy vows unto Eleonora."

LIGEIA[1]

And the will therein lieth, which dieth not. Who knoweth the mysteries of the will, with its vigor? For God is but a great will pervading all things by nature of its intentness. Man doth not yield himself to the angels, nor unto death utterly, save only through the weakness of his feeble will.

Joseph Glanvill.[2]

I cannot, for my soul, remember how, when, or even precisely where, I first became acquainted with the lady Ligeia. Long years have since elapsed, and my memory is feeble through much suffering. Or, perhaps, I cannot *now* bring these points to mind, because, in truth, the character of my beloved, her rare learning, her singular yet placid cast of beauty, and the thrilling and enthralling eloquence of her low musical language, made their way into my heart by paces so steadily and stealthily progressive that they have been unnoticed and unknown. Yet I believe that I met her first and most frequently in some large, old, decaying city near the Rhine. Of her family—I have surely heard her speak. That it is of a remotely ancient date cannot be doubted. Ligeia! Ligeia! Buried in studies of a nature more than all else adapted to deaden impressions of the outward world, it is by that sweet word alone—by Ligeia—that I bring before mine eyes in fancy the image of her who is no more. And now, while I write, a recollection flashes upon me that I have *never known* the paternal name of her who was my friend and my betrothed, and who became the partner of my studies, and finally the wife of my bosom. Was it a playful charge on the part of my Ligeia? or was it a test of my strength of affection, that I should institute no inquiries upon this point? or was it rather a caprice of my own—a wildly romantic offering on the shrine of the most passionate devotion? I but indistinctly recall the fact itself—what wonder that I have utterly forgotten the circumstances which originated or attended it? And, indeed, if ever that spirit which is entitled *Romance*—if ever she, the wan and the misty-winged *Ashtophet*[3] of idolatrous Egypt, presided, as they tell, over marriages ill-omened, then most surely she presided over mine.

There is one dear topic, however, on which my memory fails me not. It is the *person* of Ligeia. In stature she was tall, somewhat slender, and, in her latter days, even emaciated. I would in vain attempt to portray the majesty, the quiet ease of her demeanor, or the incomprehensible lightness and elasticity of her foot-fall. She came and departed as a shadow. I was never made aware of her entrance into my closed study save by the dear music of her low sweet voice, as she placed her marble hand upon my shoulder. In beauty of face no maiden ever equalled her. It was the radiance of an opium-dream—an airy and spirit-lifting vision more wildly divine than the phantasies which hovered about the slumbering souls of the daughters of Delos. Yet her features were not of that regular mould which we have been falsely taught to worship in the classical labours of the heathen. "There is no exquisite beauty," says Bacon, Lord Verulam, speaking truly of all the forms and *genera* of beauty, "without some *strangeness* in the proportion." Yet, although I saw that the features of Ligeia were not of a classic regularity—although I perceived that her loveliness was indeed "exquisite," and felt that there was much of "strangeness" pervading it, yet I have tried in vain to detect the irregularity and to trace home my own perception of "the strange." I examined the contour of the lofty and pale forehead —it was faultless—how cold indeed that word when applied to a majesty so divine!—the skin rivalling the purest ivory, the commanding extent and repose, the gentle prominence of the regions above the temples; and then the raven-black, the glossy, the luxuriant and naturally-curling tresses, setting forth the full force of the Homeric epithet, "hyacinthine!" I looked at the delicate outlines of the nose —and nowhere but in the graceful me-

dallions of the Hebrews had I beheld a similar perfection. There were the same luxurious smoothness of surface, the same scarcely perceptible tendency to the aquiline, the same harmoniously curved nostrils speaking the free spirit. I regarded the sweet mouth. Here was indeed the triumph of all things heavenly—the magnificent turn of the short upper lip—the soft, voluptuous slumber of the under—the dimples which sported, and the colour which spoke—the teeth glancing back, with a brilliancy almost startling, every ray of the holy light which fell upon them in her serene and placid yet most exultingly radiant of all smiles. I scrutinized the formation of the chin—and, here too, I found the gentleness of breadth, the softness and the majesty, the fullness and the spirituality, of the Greek—the contour which the god Apollo revealed but in a dream, to Cleomenes,[4] the son of the Athenian. And then I peered into the large eyes of Ligeia.

For eyes we have no models in the remotely antique. It might have been, too, that in these eyes of my beloved lay the secret to which Lord Verulam alludes. They were, I must believe, far larger than the ordinary eyes of our own race. They were even fuller than the fullest of the gazelle eyes of the tribe of the valley of Nourjahad. Yet it was only at intervals— in moments of intense excitement—that this peculiarity became more than slightly noticeable in Ligeia. And at such moments was her beauty—in my heated fancy thus it appeared perhaps—the beauty of beings either above or apart from the earth—the beauty of the fabulous Houri of the Turk. The hue of the orbs was the most brilliant of black, and, far over them, hung jetty lashes of great length. The brows, slightly irregular in outline, had the same tint. The "strangeness," however, which I found in the eyes, was of a nature distinct from the formation, or the colour, or the brilliancy of the features, and must, after all, be referred to the *expression*. Ah, word of no meaning! behind whose vast latitude of mere sound we intrench our ignorance of so much of the spiritual. The expression of the eyes of Ligeia! How for long hours have I pondered upon it! How have I, through the whole of a midsummer night, struggled to fathom it! What was it —that something more profound than the well of Democritus—which lay far within the pupils of my beloved? What *was* it? I was possessed with a passion to discover. Those eyes! those large, those shining, those divine orbs! they became to me twin stars of Leda,[5] and I to them devoutest of astrologers.

There is no point, among the many incomprehensible anomalies of the science of mind, more thrillingly exciting than the fact—never, I believe, noticed in the schools—that in our endeavours to recall to memory something long forgotten, we often find ourselves *upon the very verge* of remembrance, without being able, in the end, to remember. And thus how frequently, in my intense scrutiny of Ligeia's eyes, have I felt approaching the full knowledge of their expression—felt it approaching—yet not quite be mine—and so at length entirely depart! And (strange, oh strangest mystery of all!) I found, in the commonest objects of the universe, a circle of analogies to that expression. I mean to say that, subsequently to the period when Ligeia's beauty passed into my spirit, there dwelling as in a shrine, I derived, from many existences in the material world, a sentiment such as I felt always aroused, within me, by her large and luminous orbs. Yet not the more could I define that sentiment, or analyze, or even steadily view it. I recognized it, let me repeat, sometimes in the survey of a rapidly growing vine—in the contemplation of a moth, a butterfly, a chrysalis, a stream of running water. I have felt it in the ocean; in the falling of a meteor. I have felt it in the glances of unusually aged people. And there are one or two stars in heaven—(one especially, a star of the sixth magnitude, double and changeable, to be found near the large star in Lyra) in a telescopic scrutiny of which I have been made aware of the feeling.[6] I have been filled with it by certain sounds from stringed instruments, and not unfrequently by passages from books. Among innumerable other instances, I well remember something in a volume of Joseph Glanvill, which (perhaps from its quaintness—who shall say?) never failed to inspire me with the sentiment;—"And the will therein lieth, which dieth not. Who knoweth the mysteries of the will, with its vigor? For God is but a great will pervading all things by nature of its intentness. Man doth not yield him to the angels, nor unto death utterly, save only through the weakness of his feeble will."

Length of years, and subsequent reflection, have enabled me to trace, indeed, some remote connection between this passage in the English moralist and a portion of the character of Ligeia. An *intensity* in thought, action, or speech, was possibly, in her, a result, or at least an index, of that gigantic volition which, during our long intercourse, failed to give other and more immediate evidence of its existence. Of all the women whom I have ever known, she, the outwardly calm, the ever-placid Ligeia, was the most violently a prey to the tumultuous vultures of stern passion. And of such passion I could form no estimate, save by the miraculous expansion of those eyes which at once so delighted and appalled me—by the almost magical melody, modulation, distinctness, and placidity of her very low voice—and by the fierce energy (rendered doubly effective by contrast with her manner of utterance) of the wild words which she habitually uttered.

I have spoken of the learning of Ligeia; it was immense—such as I have never known in woman. In the classical tongues was she deeply proficient, and as far as my own acquaintance extended in regard to the modern dialects of Europe, I have never known her at fault. Indeed upon any theme of the most admired, because simply the most abstruse of the boasted erudition of the academy, have I *ever* found Ligeia at fault? How singularly— how thrillingly, this one point in the nature of my wife has forced itself, at this late period only, upon my attention! I said her knowledge was such as I have never known in woman—but where breathes the man who has traversed, and successfully, *all* the wide areas of moral, physical, and mathematical science? I saw not then what I now clearly perceive, that the acquisitions of Ligeia were gigantic, were astounding; yet I was sufficiently aware of her infinite supremacy to resign myself, with a child-like confidence, to her guidance through the chaotic world of metaphysical investigation at which I was most busily occupied during the earlier years of our marriage. With how vast a triumph—with how vivid a delight—with how much of all that is ethereal in hope —did I *feel,* as she bent over me in studies but little sought—but less known—that delicious vista by slow degrees expanding before me, down whose long, gorgeous, and all untrodden path, I might at length pass onward to the goal of a wisdom too divinely precious not to be forbidden!

How poignant, then, must have been the grief with which, after some years, I beheld my well-grounded expectations take wings to themselves and fly away! Without Ligeia I was but as a child groping benighted. Her presence, her readings alone, rendered vividly luminous the many mysteries of the transcendentalism in which we were immersed. Wanting the radiant lustre of her eyes, letters, lambent and golden, grew duller than Saturnian lead. And now those eyes shone less and less frequently upon the pages over which I pored. Ligeia grew ill. The wild eyes blazed with a too—too glorious effulgence; the pale fingers became of the transparent waxen hue of the grave; and the blue veins upon the lofty forehead swelled and sank impetuously with the tides of the most gentle emotion. I saw that she must die—and I struggled desperately in spirit with the grim Azrael.[7] And the struggles of the passionate wife were, to my astonishment, even more energetic than my own. There had been much in her stern nature to impress me with the belief that, to her, death would have come without its terrors; but not so. Words are impotent to convey any just idea of the fierceness of resistance with which she wrestled with the Shadow. I groaned in anguish at the pitiable spectacle. I would have soothed —I would have reasoned; but, in the intensity of her wild desire for life,—for life —*but* for life—solace and reason were alike the uttermost of folly. Yet not until the last instance, amid the most convulsive writhings of her fierce spirit, was shaken the external placidity of her demeanor. Her voice grew more gentle— grew more low—yet I would not wish to dwell upon the wild meaning of the quietly uttered words. My brain reeled as I hearkened entranced, to a melody more than mortal—to assumptions and aspirations which mortality had never before known.

That she loved me I should not have doubted; and I might have been easily aware that, in a bosom such as hers, love would have reigned no ordinary passion. But in death only was I fully impressed with the strength of her affection. For long hours, detaining my hand, would she pour out before me the overflowing of a heart whose more than passionate devotion amounted to idolatry. How had I deserved to be so blessed by such confessions?—how had I deserved to be so cursed with the removal of my beloved in the hour of her making them? But upon this subject I cannot bear to dilate. Let me say only, that in Ligeia's more than womanly abandonment to a love, alas! all unmerited, all unworthily bestowed, I at length recognized the principle of her longing with so wildly earnest a desire for the life which was now fleeting so rapidly away. It is this wild longing—it is this eager vehemence of desire for life—*but* for life —that I have no power to portray—no utterance capable of expressing.

At high noon of the night in which she departed, beckoning me, peremptorily, to her side, she bade me repeat certain verses composed by herself not many days before. I obeyed her.—They were these:

Lo! 'tis a gala night
    Within the lonesome latter years!
An angel throng, bewinged, bedight
    In veils, and drowned in tears,
Sit in a theatre, to see
    A play of hopes and fears,
While the orchestra breathes fitfully
    The music of the spheres.

Mimes, in the form of God on high.
    Mutter and mumble low,
And hither and thither fly—
    Mere puppets they, who come and go
At bidding of vast formless things
    That shift the scenery to and fro.
Flapping from out their Condor wings
    Invisible Wo!

That motley drama!—oh, be sure
    It shall not be forgot!
With its Phantom chased forever more,
    By a crowd that seize it not,
Through a circle that ever returneth in
    To the self-same spot,
And much of Madness and more of Sin
    And Horror the soul of the plot.

But see, amid the mimic rout,
    A crawling shape intrude!
A blood-red thing that writhes
        from out
    The scenic solitude!
It writhes!—it writhes!—with
        mortal pangs
The mimes become its food,
And the seraphs sob at vermin fangs
    In human gore imbued.

Out—out are the lights—out all!
    And over each quivering form,
The curtain, a funeral pall,
    Comes down with the rush of
        a storm,
And the angels, all pallid and wan,
    Uprising, unveiling, affirm
That the play is the tragedy, "Man,"
    And its hero the Conqueror Worm.[8]

"O God!" half shrieked Ligeia, leaping to her feet and extending her arms aloft with a spasmodic movement, as I made an end of these lines—"O God! O Divine Father!—shall these things be undeviatingly so?—shall this Conqueror be not once conquered? Are we not part and parcel in Thee? Who—who knoweth the mysteries of the will with its vigor? Man doth not yield him to the angels, *nor unto death utterly*, save only through the weakness of his feeble will."

And now, as if exhausted with emotion, she suffered her white arms to fall, and returned solemnly to her bed of death. And as she breathed her last sighs, there came mingled with them a low murmur from her lips. I bent to them my ear, and distinguished, again, the concluding words of the passage in Glanvill—"*Man doth not yield him to the angels, nor unto death utterly, save only through the weakness of his feeble will.*"

She died;—and I, crushed into the very dust with sorrow, could no longer endure the lonely desolation of my dwelling in the dim and decaying city by the Rhine. I had no lack of what the world calls wealth. Ligeia had brought me far more, very far more than ordinarily falls to the lot of mortals. After a few months, therefore, of weary and aimless wandering, I purchased, and put in some repair, an abbey, which I shall not name, in one of the wildest and least frequented portions of fair England. The gloomy and dreary grandeur of the building, the almost savage aspect of the domain, the many melancholy and time-honored memories connected with both, had much in unison with the feelings of utter abandonment which had driven me into that remote and unsocial region of the country. Yet although the external abbey, with its verdant decay hanging about it, suffered but little alteration, I gave way, with a childlike perversity, and perchance with a faint hope of alleviating my sorrows, to a display of more than regal magnificence within.—For such follies, even in childhood, I had imbibed a taste, and now they came back to me as if in the dotage of grief. Alas, I feel how much even of incipient madness might have been discovered in the gorgeous and fantastic draperies, in the solemn carvings of Egypt, in the wild cornices and furniture, in the Bedlam patterns of the carpets of tufted gold! I had become a bounden slave in the trammels of opium, and my labors and orders had taken a colouring from my dreams.[9] But these absurdities I must not pause to detail. Let me speak only of that one chamber, ever accursed, whither, in a moment of mental alienation, I led from the altar as my bride—as the successor of the unforgotten Ligeia—the fair-haired and blue-eyed Lady Rowena Trevanion, of Tremaine.

There is no individual portion of the architecture and decoration of that bridal chamber which is not now visibly before me. Where were the souls of the haughty family of the bride, when, through thirst of gold, they permitted to pass the threshold of an apartment so bedecked, a maiden and a daughter so beloved? I have said that I minutely remember the details of the chamber—yet I am sadly forgetful on topics of deep moment—and here there was no system, no keeping, in the fantastic display, to take hold upon the memory. The room lay in a high turret of the castellated abbey, was pentagonal in shape, and of capacious size. Occupying the whole southern face of the pentagon was the sole window—an immense sheet of unbroken glass from Venice—a single pane, and tinted of a leaden hue, so that the rays of either the sun or moon, passing through it, fell with a ghastly lustre on the objects within. Over the upper portion of this huge window, extended the trellis-work of an aged vine, which clambered up the massy walls of the turret. The ceiling, of gloomy-looking oak, was excessively lofty, vaulted, and elaborately fretted with the wildest and most grotesque specimens of a semi-Gothic, semi-Druidical device. From out the most central recess of this melancholy vaulting, depended, by a single chain of gold with long links, a huge censer of the same metal, Saracenic[10] in pattern, and with many perforations so contrived that there writhed in and out of them, as if endued with a serpent vitality,

a continual succession of parti-colored fires.

Some few ottomans and golden candelabra, of Eastern figure, were in various stations about—and there was the couch, too—the bridal couch—of an Indian model, and low, and sculptured of solid ebony, with a pall-like canopy above. In each of the angles of the chamber stood on end a gigantic sarcophagus of black granite, from the tombs of the kings over against Luxor, with their aged lids full of immemorial sculpture. But in the draping of the apartment lay, alas! the chief phantasy of all. The lofty walls, gigantic in height—even unproportionably so—were hung from summit to foot, in vast folds, with a heavy and massive-looking tapestry —tapestry of a material which was found alike as a carpet on the floor, as a covering for the ottomans and the ebony bed, as a canopy for the bed and as the gorgeous volutes of the curtains which partially shaded the window. The material was the richest cloth of gold. It was spotted all over, at irregular intervals, with arabesque figures, about a foot in diameter, and wrought upon the cloth in patterns of the most jetty black. But these figures partook of the true character of the arabesque only when regarded from a single point of view. By a contrivance now common, and indeed traceable to a very remote period of antiquity, they were made changeable in aspect. To one entering the room, they bore the appearance of simple monstrosities; but upon a farther advance, this appearance gradually departed; and step by step, as the visiter moved his station in the chamber, he saw himself surrounded by an endless succession of the ghastly forms which belong to the superstition of the Norman, or arise in the guilty slumbers of the monk. The phantasmagoric effect was vastly heightened by the artificial introduction of a strong continual current of wind behind the draperies—giving a hideous and uneasy animation to the whole.[11]

In halls such as these—in a bridal chamber such as this—I passed, with the Lady of Tremaine, the unhallowed hours of the first month of our marriage—passed them with but little disquietude. That my wife dreaded the fierce moodiness of my temper—that she shunned me and loved me but little—I could not help perceiving; but it gave me rather pleasure than otherwise. I loathed her with a hatred belonging more to demon than to man. My memory flew back (oh, with what intensity of regret!) to Ligeia, the beloved, the august, the beautiful, the entombed. I revelled in recollections of her purity, of her wisdom, of her lofty, her ethereal nature, of her passionate, her idolatrous love. Now, then, did my spirit fully and freely burn with more than all the fires of her own. In the excitement of my opium dreams (for I was habitually fettered in the shackles of the drug) I would call aloud upon her name, during the silence of the night, or among the sheltered recesses of the glens by day, as if, through the wild eagerness, the solemn passion, the consuming ardor of my longing for the departed, I could restore her to the pathways she had abandoned—ah, *could* it be forever?—upon the earth.

About the commencement of the second month of the marriage, the Lady Rowena was attacked with sudden illness, from which her recovery was slow. The fever which consumed her rendered her nights uneasy; and in her perturbed state of half-slumber, she spoke of sounds, and of motions, in and above the chamber of the turret, which I concluded had no origin save in the distemper of her fancy, or perhaps in the phantasmagoric influences of the chamber itself. She became at length convalescent—finally well. Yet but a brief period elapsed, ere a second more violent disorder again threw her upon a bed of suffering; and from this attack her frame, at all times feeble, never altogether recovered. Her illnesses were, after this epoch, of alarming character, and of more alarming recurrence, defying alike the knowledge and the great exertions of her physicians. With the increase of the chronic disease which had thus, apparently, taken too sure hold upon her constitution to be eradicated by human means, I could not fail to observe a similar increase in the nervous irritation of her temperament, and in her excitability by trivial causes of fear. She spoke again, and now more frequently and pertinaciously, of the sounds—of the slight sounds—and of the unusual motions among the tapestries, to which she had formerly alluded.

One night, near the closing in of September, she pressed this distressing subject with more than usual emphasis upon my attention. She had just awakened from an unquiet slumber, and I had been watching, with feelings half of anxiety, half of vague terror, the workings of her emaciated countenance. I sat by the side of her ebony bed, upon one of the ottomans of India. She partly arose, and spoke, in an earnest low whisper, of sounds which she *then* heard, but which I could not hear —of motions which she *then* saw, but which I could not perceive. The wind was rushing hurriedly behind the tapestries, and I wished to show her (what, let me confess it, I could not *all* believe) that those almost inarticulate breathings, and those very gentle variations of the figures upon the wall, were but the natural effects of that customary rushing of the wind. But a deadly pallor, overspreading her face, had proved to me that my exertions to reassure her would be fruitless. She appeared to be fainting, and no attendants were within call. I remembered where was deposited a decanter of light wine which had been ordered by her physicians, and hastened across the chamber to procure it. But, as I stepped beneath the light of the censer, two circumstances of a startling nature attracted my attention. I had felt that some palpable although invisible object had passed lightly by my person; and I saw that there lay upon the golden carpet, in the very middle of the rich lustre thrown from the censer, a shadow—a faint, indefinite shadow of angelic aspect—such as might be fancied for the shadow of a shade. But I was wild with the excitement of an immoderate dose of opium, and heeded these things but little, nor spoke of them to Rowena. Having found the wine, I recrossed the chamber, and poured out a goblet-ful, which I held to the lips of the fainting lady. She had now partially recovered, however, and took the vessel herself, while I sank upon an ottoman near me, with my eyes fastened upon her person. It was then that I became distinctly aware of a gentle footfall upon the carpet, and near the couch; and in a second thereafter, as Rowena was in the act of raising the wine to her lips, I saw, or may have dreamed that I saw, fall within the goblet, as if from some invisible spring in the atmosphere of the room, three or four large drops of a brilliant and ruby colored fluid.[12] If this I saw—not so Rowena. She swallowed the wine unhesitatingly, and I forbore to speak to her of a circumstance which must, after all, I considered, have been but the suggestion of a vivid imagination, rendered morbidly active by the terror of the lady, by the opium, and by the hour.

Yet I cannot conceal it from my own perception that, immediately subsequent to the fall of the ruby-drops, a rapid change for the worse took place in the disorder of my wife; so that, on the third subsequent night, the hands of her menials prepared her for the tomb, and on the fourth, I sat alone, with her shrouded body, in that fantastic chamber which had received her as my bride.—Wild visions, opium-engendered, flitted, shadowlike, before me. I gazed with unquiet eye upon the sarcophagi in the angles of the room,[13] upon the varying figures of the drapery, and upon the writhing of the parti-colored fires in the censer overhead. My eyes then fell, as I called to mind the circumstances of a former night, to the spot beneath the glare of the censer where I had seen the faint traces of the shadow. It was there, however, no longer; and breathing with

greater freedom, I turned my glances to the pallid and rigid figure upon the bed. Then rushed upon me a thousand memories of Ligeia—and then came back upon my heart, with the turbulent violence of a flood, the whole of that unutterable wo with which I had regarded *her* thus enshrouded. The night waned; and still, with a bosom full of bitter thoughts of the one only and supremely beloved, I remained gazing upon the body of Rowena.

It might have been midnight, or perhaps earlier, or later, for I had taken no note of time, when a sob, low, gentle, but very distinct, startled me from my revery. I *felt* that it came from the bed of ebony—the bed of death. I listened in an agony of superstitious terror—but there was no repetition of the sound. I strained my vision to detect any motion in the corpse—but there was not the slightest perceptible. Yet I could not have been deceived. I *had* heard the noise, however faint, and my soul was awakened within me. I resolutely and perseveringly kept my attention riveted upon the body. Many minutes elapsed before any circumstance occurred tending to throw light upon the mystery. At length it became evident that a slight, a very feeble, and barely noticeable tinge of colour had flushed up within the cheeks, and along the sunken small veins of the eyelids. Through a species of unutterable horror and awe, for which the language of mortality has no sufficiently energetic expression, I felt my heart cease to beat, my limbs grow rigid where I sat. Yet a sense of duty finally operated to restore my self-possession. I could no longer doubt that we had been precipitate in our preparations—that Rowena still lived. It was necessary that some immediate exertion be made; yet the turret was altogether apart from the portion of the abbey tenanted by the servants—there were none within call —I had no means of summoning them to my aid without leaving the room for many minutes—and this I could not venture to do. I therefore struggled alone in my endeavours to call back the spirit still hovering. In a short period it was certain, however, that a relapse had taken place; the colour disappeared from both eyelid and cheek, leaving a wanness even more than that of marble; the lips became doubly shrivelled and pinched up in the ghastly expression of death; a repulsive clamminess and coldness overspread rapidly the surface of the body; and all the usual rigorous stiffness immediately supervened. I fell back with a shudder upon the couch from which I had been so startlingly aroused, and again gave myself up to passionate waking visions of Ligeia.

An hour thus elapsed when (could it be possible?) I was a second time aware of some vague sound issuing from the region of the bed. I listened—in extremity of horror. The sound came again—it was a sigh. Rushing to the corpse, I saw—distinctly saw—a tremor upon the lips. In a minute afterward they relaxed, disclosing a bright line of the pearly teeth. Amazement now struggled in my bosom with the profound awe which had hitherto reigned there alone. I felt that my vision grew dim, that my reason wandered; and it was only by a violent effort that I at length succeeded in nerving myself to the task which duty thus once more had pointed out. There was now a partial glow upon the forehead and upon the cheek and throat; a perceptible warmth pervaded the whole frame; there was even a slight pulsation at the heart. The lady *lived*; and with redoubled ardor I betook myself to the task of restoration. I chafed and bathed the temples and the hands, and used every exertion which experience, and no little medical reading, could suggest. But in vain. Suddenly, the colour fled, the pulsation ceased, the lips resumed the expression of the dead, and, in an instant afterward, the whole body took upon itself the icy chilliness, the livid hue, the intense rigidity, the sunken outline, and all the loathsome peculiarities of that which has been, for many days, a tenant of the tomb.

And again I sunk into visions of Ligeia —and again, (what marvel that I shudder while I write?) *again* there reached my ears a low sob from the region of the ebony bed. But why shall I minutely detail the unspeakable horrors of that night? Why shall I pause to relate how, time after time, until near the period of the gray dawn, this hideous drama of revivification was repeated; how each terrific relapse was only into a sterner and apparently more irredeemable death; how each agony wore the aspect of a struggle with some invisible foe; and how each struggle was succeeded by I know not what of wild change in the personal appearance of the corpse? Let me hurry to a conclusion.

The greater part of the fearful night had worn away, and she who had been dead once again stirred—and now more vigorously than hitherto, although arousing from a dissolution more appalling in its utter hopelessness than any. I had long ceased to struggle or to move, and remained sitting rigidly upon the ottoman, a helpless prey to a whirl of violent emotions, of which extreme awe was perhaps the least terrible, the least consuming. The corpse, I repeat, stirred, and now more vigorously than before. The hues of life flushed up with unwonted energy into the countenance—the limbs relaxed— and, save that the eyelids were yet pressed heavily together, and that the bandages and draperies of the grave still imparted their charnel character to the figure, I might have dreamed that Rowena had indeed shaken off, utterly, the fetters of Death. But if this idea was not, even then, altogether adopted, I could at least doubt no longer, when, arising from the bed, tottering, with feeble steps, with closed eyes, and with the manner of one bewildered in a dream, the thing that was enshrouded advanced boldly and palpably into the middle of the apartment.

I trembled not—I stirred not—for a crowd of unutterable fancies connected with the air, the stature, the demeanor of the figure, rushing hurriedly through my brain, had paralyzed—had chilled me into stone. I stirred not—but gazed upon the apparition. There was a mad disorder in my thoughts—a tumult unappeasable. Could it, indeed, be the *living* Rowena who confronted me? Could it, indeed, be Rowena *at all*—the fair-haired, the blue-eyed Lady Rowena Trevanion of Tremaine? Why, *why* should I doubt it? The bandage lay heavily about the mouth—but then might it not be the mouth of the breathing Lady of Tremaine? And the cheeks—there were the roses as in her noon of life—yes, these might indeed be the fair cheeks of the living Lady of Tremaine. And the chin, with its dimples, as in health, might it not be hers?—but *had she then grown taller since her malady?* What inexpressible madness seized me with that thought? One bound, and I had reached her feet! Shrinking from my touch, she let fall from her head, unloosened, the ghastly cerements which had confined it, and there streamed forth into the rushing atmosphere of the chamber huge masses of long and dishevelled hair; *it was blacker than the raven wings of midnight!* And now slowly opened *the eyes* of the figure which stood before me. "Here then, at least," I shrieked aloud, "can I never—can I never be mistaken—these are the full, and the black, and the wild eyes—of my lost love—of the Lady —of the LADY LIGEIA!"

THE FALL OF
THE HOUSE OF USHER

Son cœur est un luth suspendu;
Sitôt qu'on le touche il résonne.
De Béranger.[1]

During the whole of a dull, dark, and soundless day in the autumn of the year, when the clouds hung oppressively low in the heavens, I had been passing alone, on horseback, through a singularly dreary tract of country, and at length found myself, as the shades of the evening drew on, within view of the melancholy House of Usher. I know not how it was—but, with the first glimpse of the building, a sense

of insufferable gloom pervaded my spirit. I say insufferable; for the feeling was unrelieved by any of that half-pleasurable, because poetic, sentiment, with which the mind usually receives even the sternest natural images of the desolate or terrible. I looked upon the scene before me—upon the mere house, and the simple landscape features of the domain—upon the bleak walls—upon the vacant eye-like windows —upon a few rank sedges—and upon a few white trunks of decayed trees—with an utter depression of soul which I can compare to no earthly sensation more properly than to the after-dream of the reveller upon opium—the bitter lapse into every-day life—the hideous dropping off of the veil. There was an iciness, a sinking, a sickening of the heart—an unredeemed dreariness of thought which no goading of the imagination could torture into aught of the sublime. What was it— I paused to think—what was it that so unnerved me in the contemplation of the House of Usher? It was a mystery all insoluble; nor could I grapple with the shadowy fancies that crowded upon me as I pondered. I was forced to fall back upon the unsatisfactory conclusion, that while, beyond doubt, there *are* combinations of very simple natural objects which have the power of thus affecting us, still the analysis of this power lies among considerations beyond our depth. It was possible, I reflected, that a mere different arrangement of the particulars of the scene, of the details of the picture, would be sufficient to modify, or perhaps to annihilate its capacity for sorrowful impression; and, acting upon this idea, I reined my horse to the precipitous brink of a black and lurid tarn[2] that lay in unruffled lustre by the dwelling, and gazed down —but with a shudder even more thrilling than before—upon the remodelled and inverted images of the gray sedge, and the ghastly tree-stems, and the vacant and eye-like windows.

Nevertheless, in this mansion of gloom I now proposed to myself a sojourn of some weeks. Its proprietor, Roderick Usher, had been one of my boon companions in boyhood; but many years had elapsed since our last meeting. A letter, however, had lately reached me in a distant part of the country—a letter from him—which, in its wildly importunate nature, had admitted of no other than a personal reply. The MS. gave evidence of nervous agitation. The writer spoke of acute bodily illness—of a mental disorder which oppressed him—and of an earnest desire to see me, as his best, and indeed his only personal friend, with a view of attempting, by the cheerfulness of my society, some alleviation of his malady. It was the manner in which all this, and much more, was said—it was the apparent *heart* that went with his request—which allowed me no room for hesitation; and I accordingly obeyed forthwith what I still considered a very singular summons.

Although, as boys, we had been even intimate associates, yet I really knew little of my friend. His reserve had been always excessive and habitual. I was aware, however, that his very ancient family had been noted, time out of mind, for a peculiar sensibility of temperament, displaying itself, through long ages, in many works of exalted art, and manifested, of late, in repeated deeds of munificent yet unobtrusive charity, as well as in a passionate devotion to the intricacies, perhaps even more than to the orthodox and easily recognizable beauties, of musical science. I had learned, too, the very remarkable fact, that the stem of the Usher race, all time-honoured as it was, had put forth, at no period, any enduring branch; in other words, that the entire family lay in the direct line of descent, and had always, with very trifling and very temporary variation, so lain. It was this deficiency, I considered, while running over in thought the perfect keeping of the character of the premises with the accredited character of the people, and while speculating upon the possible influence which the one, in the long lapse of centuries, might have

exercised upon the other—it was this deficiency, perhaps of collateral issue, and the consequent undeviating transmission, from sire to son, of the patrimony with the name, which had, at length, so identified the two as to merge the original title of the estate in the quaint and equivocal apellation of the "House of Usher"—an appellation which seemed to include, in the minds of the peasantry who used it, both the family and the family mansion.

I have said that the sole effect of my somewhat childish experiment—that of looking down within the tarn—had been to deepen the first singular impression. There can be no doubt that the consciousness of the rapid increase of my superstition—for why should I not so term it? —served mainly to accelerate the increase itself. Such, I have long known, is the paradoxical law of all sentiments having terror as a basis. And it might have been for this reason only, that, when I again uplifted my eyes to the house itself, from its image in the pool, there grew in my mind a strange fancy—a fancy so ridiculous, indeed, that I but mention it to show the vivid force of the sensations which oppressed me. I had so worked upon my imagination as really to believe that about the whole mansion and domain there hung an atmosphere peculiar to themselves and their immediate vicinity—an atmosphere which had no affinity with the air of heaven, but which had reeked up from the decayed trees, and the gray wall, and the silent tarn—a pestilent and mystic vapour, dull, sluggish, faintly discernible, and leaden-hued.

Shaking off from my spirit what *must* have been a dream, I scanned more narrowly the real aspect of the building. Its principal feature seemed to be that of an excessive antiquity. The discoloration of ages had been great. Minute fungi overspread the whole exterior, hanging in a fine tangled web-work from the eaves. Yet all this was apart from an extraordinary dilapidation. No portion of the masonry had fallen; and there appeared to be a wild inconsistency between its still perfect adaptation of parts, and the crumbling condition of the individual stones. In this there was much that reminded me of the specious totality of the old woodwork which has rotted for long years in some neglected vault, with no disturbance from the breath of the external air. Beyond this indication of extensive decay, however, the fabric gave little token of instability. Perhaps the eye of a scrutinizing observer might have discovered a barely perceptible fissure, which, extending from the roof of the building in front, made its way down the wall in a zigzag direction, until it became lost in the sullen waters of the tarn.

Noticing these things, I rode over a short causeway to the house. A servant in waiting took my horse, and I entered the Gothic archway of the hall. A valet, of stealthy step, thence conducted me, in silence, through many dark and intricate passages in my progress to the .studio of his master. Much that I encountered on the way contributed, I know not how, to heighten the vague sentiments of which I have already spoken. While the objects around me—while the carvings of the ceilings, the sombre tapestries of the walls, the ebon blackness of the floors, and the phantasmagoric armorial trophies which rattled as I strode, were but matters to which, or to such as which, I had been accustomed from my infancy—while I hesitated not to acknowledge how familiar was all this—I still wondered to find how unfamiliar were the fancies which ordinary images were stirring up. On one of the staircases, I met the physician of the family. His countenance, I thought, wore a mingled expression of low cunning and perplexity. He accosted me with trepidation and passed on. The valet now threw open a door and ushered me into the presence of his master.

The room in which I found myself was very large and lofty. The windows were long, narrow, and pointed, and at so vast a distance from the black oaken floor as to be altogether inaccessible from within. Feeble gleams of encrimsoned light made their way through the trellised panes, and served to render sufficiently distinct the more prominent objects around; the eye, however, struggled in vain to reach the remoter angles of the chamber, or the recesses of the vaulted and fretted ceiling. Dark draperies hung upon the walls. The general furniture was profuse, comfortless, antique, and tattered. Many books and musical instruments lay scattered about, but failed to give any vitality to the scene. I felt that I breathed an atmosphere of sorrow. An air of stern, deep, and irredeemable gloom hung over and pervaded all.

Upon my entrance, Usher arose from a sofa on which he had been lying at full length, and greeted me with a vivacious warmth which had much in it, I at first thought, of an overdone cordiality—of the constrained effort of the *ennuyé* man of the world. A glance, however, at his countenance convinced me of his perfect sincerity. We sat down; and for some moments, while he spoke not, I gazed upon him with a feeling half of pity, half of awe. Surely, man had never before so terribly altered, in so brief a period, as had Roderick Usher! It was with difficulty that I could bring myself to admit the identity of the wan being before me with the companion of my early boyhood. Yet the character of his face had been at all times remarkable. A cadaverousness of complexion; an eye large, liquid, and luminous beyond comparison; lips somewhat thin and very pallid, but of a surpassingly beautiful curve; a nose of a delicate Hebrew model, but with a breadth of nostril unusual in similar formations; a finely moulded chin, speaking, in its want of prominence, of a want of moral energy; hair of a more than web-like softness and tenuity; these features, with an inordinate expansion above the regions of the temple, made up altogether a countenance not easily to be forgotten. And now in the mere exaggeration of the prevailing character of these features, and of the expression they were wont to convey, lay so much of change that I doubted to whom I spoke. The now ghastly pallor of the skin, and the now miraculous lustre of the eye, above all things startled and even awed me. The silken hair, too, had been suffered to grow all unheeded, and as, in its wild gossamer texture, it floated rather than fell about the face, I could not, even with effort, connect its Arabesque[3] expression with any idea of simple humanity.

In the manner of my friend I was at once struck with an incoherence—an inconsistency; and I soon found this to arise from a series of feeble and futile struggles to overcome an habitual trepidancy—an excessive nervous agitation. For something of this nature I had indeed been prepared, no less by his letter, than by reminiscences of certain boyish traits, and by conclusions deduced from his peculiar physical conformation and temperament. His action was alternately vivacious and sullen. His voice varied rapidly from a tremulous indecision (when the animal spirits seemed utterly in abeyance) to that species of energetic concision—that abrupt, weighty, unhurried, and hollow-sounding enunciation—that leaden, self-balanced, and perfectly modulated guttural utterance, which may be observed in the lost drunkard, or the irreclaimable eater of opium, during the periods of his most intense excitement.[4]

It was thus that he spoke of the object of my visit, of his earnest desire to see me, and of the solace he expected me to afford him. He entered, at some length, into what he conceived to be the nature of his malady. It was, he said, a constitutional and a family evil, and one for which he despaired to find a remedy—a mere nervous affection, he immediately added, which would undoubtedly soon pass off. It displayed itself in a host of unnatural sensations. Some of these, as he detailed them, interested and bewildered me; although, perhaps, the terms and the general manner of their narration had their

weight. He suffered much from a morbid acuteness of the senses; the most insipid food was alone endurable; he could wear only garments of certain texture; the odours of all flowers were oppressive; his eyes were tortured by even a faint light; and there were but peculiar sounds, and these from stringed instruments, which did not inspire him with horror.

To an anomalous species of terror I found him a bounden slave. "I shall perish," said he, "I *must* perish in this deplorable folly. Thus, thus, and not otherwise, shall I be lost. I dread the events of the future, not in themselves, but in their results. I shudder at the thought of any, even the most trivial, incident, which may operate upon this intolerable agitation of soul. I have, indeed, no abhorrence of danger, except in its absolute effect—in terror. In this unnerved—in this pitiable condition—I feel that the period will sooner or later arrive when I must abandon life and reason together, in some struggle with the grim phantasm, FEAR."

I learned, moreover, at intervals, and through broken and equivocal hints, another singular feature of his mental condition. He was enchained by certain superstitious impressions in regard to the dwelling which he tenanted, and whence, for many years, he had never ventured forth—in regard to an influence whose supposititious force was conveyed in terms too shadowy here to be re-stated—an influence which some peculiarities in the mere form and substance of his family mansion had, by dint of long sufferance, he said, obtained over his spirit—an effect which the *physique* of the gray wall and turrets, and of the dim tarn into which they all looked down, had, at length, brought about upon the *morale* of his existence.

He admitted, however, although with hesitation, that much of the peculiar gloom which thus afflicted him could be traced to a more natural and far more palpable origin—to the severe and long-continued illness—indeed to the evidently approaching dissolution—of a tenderly beloved sister, his sole companion for long years, his last and only relative on earth. "Her decease," he said, with a bitterness which I can never forget, "would leave him (him the hopeless and the frail) the last of the ancient race of the Ushers." While he spoke, the lady Madeline (for so was she called) passed slowly through a remote portion of the apartment, and, without having noticed my presence, disappeared. I regarded her with an utter astonishment not unmingled with dread —and yet I found it impossible to account for such feelings. A sensation of stupor oppressed me, as my eyes followed her retreating steps. When a door, at length, closed upon her, my glance sought instinctively and eagerly the countenance of the brother—but he had buried his face in his hands, and I could only perceive that a far more than ordinary wanness had overspread the emaciated fingers through which trickled many passionate tears.

The disease of the lady Madeline had long baffled the skill of her physicians. A settled apathy, a gradual wasting away of the person, and frequent although transient affections of a partially cataleptical character were the unusual diagnosis. Hitherto she had steadily borne up against the pressure of her malady, and had not betaken herself finally to bed; but on the closing in of the evening of my arrival at the house, she succumbed (as her brother told me at night with inexpressible agitation) to the prostrating power of the destroyer; and I learned that the glimpse I had obtained of her person would thus probably be the last I should obtain—that the lady, at least while living, would be seen by me no more.

For several days ensuing, her name was unmentioned by either Usher or myself: and during this period I was busied in earnest endeavours to alleviate the melancholy of my friend. We painted and read together, or I listened, as if in a dream, to the wild improvisations of his speaking guitar.[5] And thus, as a closer and still closer intimacy admitted me more unreservedly into the recesses of his spirit, the more bitterly did I perceive the futility of all attempt at cheering a mind from which darkness, as if an inherent positive quality, poured forth upon all objects of the moral and physical universe in one unceasing radiation of gloom.

I shall ever bear about me a memory of the many solemn hours I thus spent alone with the master of the House of Usher. Yet I should fail in any attempt to convey an idea of the exact character of the studies, or of the occupations, in which he involved me, or led me the way. An excited and highly distempered ideality threw a sulphureous lustre over all. His long improvised dirges will ring forever in my ears. Among other things, I hold painfully in mind a certain singular perversion and amplification of the wild air of the last waltz of Von Weber. From the paintings over which his elaborate fancy brooded, and which grew, touch by touch, into vagueness at which I shuddered the more thrillingly, because I shuddered knowing not why:—from these paintings (vivid as their images now are before me) I would in vain endeavour to educe more than a small portion which should lie within the compass of merely written words. By the utter simplicity, by the nakedness of his designs, he arrested and overawed attention. If ever mortal painted an idea, that mortal was Roderick Usher. For me at least—in the circumstances then surrounding me—there arose out of the pure abstractions which the hypochondriac contrived to throw upon his canvas, an intensity of intolerable awe, no shadow of which I felt ever yet in the contemplation of the certainly glowing yet too concrete reveries of Fuseli.[6]

One of the phantasmagoric conceptions of my friend, partaking not so rigidly of the spirit of abstraction, may be shadowed forth, although feebly, in words. A small picture presented the interior of an immensely long and rectangular vault or tunnel, with low walls, smooth, white, and without interruption or device. Certain accessory points of the design served well to convey the idea that this excavation lay at an exceeding depth below the surface of the earth. No outlet was observed in any portion of its vast extent, and no torch or other artificial source of light was discernible; yet a flood of intense rays rolled throughout, and bathed the whole in a ghastly and inappropriate splendour.

I have just spoken of that morbid condition of the auditory nerve which rendered all music intolerable to the sufferer, with the exception of certain effects of stringed instruments. It was, perhaps, the narrow limits to which he thus confined himself upon the guitar, which gave birth, in great measure, to the fantastic character of his performance. But the fervid *facility* of his *impromptus*[7] could not be so accounted for. They must have been, and were, in the notes, as well as in the words of his wild fantasias (for he not unfrequently accompanied himself with rhymed verbal improvisations), the result of that intense mental collectedness and concentration to which I have previously alluded as observable only in particular moments of the highest artificial excitement. The words of one of these rhapsodies I have easily remembered. I was, perhaps, the more forcibly impressed with it, as he gave it, because, in the under or mystic current of its meaning, I fancied that I perceived, and for the first time, a full consciousness on the part of Usher, of the tottering of his lofty reason upon her throne. The verses, which were entitled "The Haunted Palace," ran very nearly, if not accurately, thus:

I.

In the greenest of our valleys,
  By good angels tenanted,
Once a fair and stately palace—
  Radiant palace—reared its head.
In the monarch Thought's dominion—
  It stood there!
Never seraph spread a pinion
  Over fabric half so fair.

II.

Banners yellow, glorious, golden,
  On its roof did float and flow;
(This—all this—was in the olden
  Time long ago)
And every gentle air that dallied,
  In that sweet day,
Along the ramparts plumed and pallid,
  A winged odour went away.

III.

Wanderers in that happy valley
  Through two luminous windows saw
Spirits moving musically
  To a lute's well-tunéd law,
Round about a throne, where sitting
  (Porphyrogene!)
In state his glory well befitting,
  The ruler of the realm was seen.

IV.

And all with pearl and ruby glowing
  Was the fair palace door,
Through which came flowing,
  flowing, flowing
And sparkling evermore,
A troop of Echoes whose sweet duty
  Was but to sing,
In voices of surpassing beauty,
  The wit and wisdom of their king.

V.

But evil things, in robes of sorrow,
  Assailed the monarch's high estate;
(Ah, let us mourn, for never morrow
  Shall dawn upon him, desolate!)
And, round about his home, the glory
  That blushed and bloomed
Is but a dim-remembered story
  Of the old time entombed.

VI.

And travellers now within that valley,
  Through the red-litten windows see
Vast forms that move fantastically
  To a discordant melody;
While, like a rapid ghastly river,
  Through the pale door,
A hideous throng rush out forever,
  And laugh—but smile no more.[8]

I well remember that suggestions arising from this ballad led us into a train of thought wherein there became manifest an opinion of Usher's which I mention not so much on account of its novelty (for other men[9] have thought thus,) as on account of the pertinacity with which he maintained it. This opinion, in its general form, was that of the sentience of all vegetable things. But, in his disordered fancy, the idea had assumed a more daring character, and trespassed, under certain conditions, upon the kingdom of inorganization. I lack words to express the full extent, or the earnest *abandon* of his persuasion. The belief, however, was connected (as I have previously hinted) with the gray stones of the home of his forefathers. The conditions of the sentience had been here, he imagined, fulfilled in the method of collocation of these stones —in the order of their arrangement, as well as in that of the many *fungi* which overspread them, and of the decayed trees which stood around—above all, in the long undisturbed endurance of this. arrangement, and in its reduplication in the still waters of the tarn. Its evidence—the evidence of the sentience—was to be seen, he said (and I here started as he spoke), in the gradual yet certain condensation of an atmosphere of their own about the waters and the walls. The result was discoverable, he added, in that silent yet importunate and terrible influence which for centuries had moulded the destinies of his family, and which made *him* what I now saw him—what he was. Such opinions need no comment, and I will make none.

Our books—the books which, for years, had formed no small portion of the mental existence of the invalid—were, as might be supposed, in strict keeping with his character of phantasm. We pored together over such works as the Ververt et Chartreuse of Gresset; the Belphegor of Machiavelli; the Heaven and Hell of Swedenborg; the Subterranean Voyage of Nicholas Klimm of Holberg; the Chiromancy of Robert Flud, of Jean D'Indaginé, and of De la Chambre; the Journey into the Blue Distance of Tieck; and the City of the Sun of Campanella. One favourite volume was a small octavo edition of the *Directorium Inquisitorum,* by the Dominican Eymeric de Gironne; and there were passages in Pomponius Mela, about the old African Satyrs and Ægipans, over which Usher would sit dreaming for hours. His chief delight, however, was found in the perusal of an exceedingly

rare and curious book in quarto Gothic—the manual of a forgotten church—the *Vigiliæ Mortuorum secundum Chorum Ecclesiæ Maguntinæ.*[10]

I could not help thinking of the wild ritual of this work, and of its probable influence upon the hypochondriac, when, one evening, having informed me abruptly that the lady Madeline was no more, he stated his intention of preserving her corpse for a fortnight, (previously to its final interment,) in one of the numerous vaults within the main walls of the building. The worldly reason, however, assigned for this singular proceeding, was one which I did not feel at liberty to dispute. The brother had been led to his resolution (so he told me) by consideration of the unusual character of the malady of the deceased, of certain obtrusive and eager inquiries on the part of her medical men, and of the remote and exposed situation of the burial-ground of the family. I will not deny that when I called to mind the sinister countenance of the person whom I met upon the staircase, on the day of my arrival at the house, I had no desire to oppose what I regarded as at best but a harmless, and by no means an unnatural, precaution.

At the request of Usher, I personally aided him in the arrangements for the temporary entombment. The body having been encoffined, we two alone bore it to its rest. The vault in which we placed it (and which had been so long unopened that our torches, half smothered in its oppressive atmosphere, gave us little opportunity for investigation) was small, damp, and entirely without means of admission for light; lying, at great depth, immediately beneath that portion of the building in which was my own sleeping apartment. It had been used, apparently, in remote feudal times, for the worst purposes of a donjon-keep, and, in later days, as a place of deposit for powder, or some other highly combustible substance, as a portion of its floor, and the whole interior of a long archway through which we reached it, were carefully sheathed with copper. The door, of massive iron, had been, also, similarly protected. Its immense weight caused an unusually sharp grating sound, as it moved upon its hinges.

Having deposited our mournful burden upon tressels[11] within this region of horror, we partially turned aside the yet unscrewed lid of the coffin, and looked upon the face of the tenant. A striking similitude between the brother and sister now first arrested my attention; and Usher, divining, perhaps, my thoughts, murmured out some few words from which I learned that the deceased and himself had been twins, and that sympathies of a scarcely intelligible nature had always existed between them. Our glances, however, rested not long upon the dead—for we could not regard her unawed. The disease which had thus entombed the lady in the maturity of youth, had left, as usual in all maladies of a strictly cataleptical character, the mockery of a faint blush upon the bosom and the face, and that suspiciously lingering smile upon the lip which is so terrible in death. We replaced and screwed down the lid, and, having secured the door of iron, made our way, with toil, into the scarcely less gloomy apartments of the upper portion of the house.

And now, some days of bitter grief having elapsed, an observable change came over the features of the mental disorder of my friend. His ordinary manner had vanished. His ordinary occupations were neglected or forgotten. He roamed from chamber to chamber with hurried, unequal, and objectless step. The pallor of his countenance had assumed, if possible, a more ghastly hue—but the luminousness of his eye had utterly gone out. The once occasional huskiness of his tone was heard no more; and a tremulous quaver, as if of extreme terror, habitually characterized his utterance. There were times, indeed, when I thought his unceasingly agitated mind was labouring with some oppressive secret, to divulge which he struggled for the necessary courage. At times, again, I was obliged to resolve all into the mere inexplicable vagaries of madness, for I beheld him gazing upon vacancy for long hours, in an attitude of the profoundest attention, as if listening to some imaginary sound. It was no wonder that his condition terrified—that it infected me. I felt creeping upon me, by slow yet certain degrees, the wild influences of his own fantastic yet impressive superstitions.

It was, especially, upon retiring to bed late in the night of the seventh or eighth day after the placing of the lady Madeline within the donjon, that I experienced the full power of such feelings. Sleep came not near my couch—while the hours waned and waned away. I struggled to reason off the nervousness which had dominion over me. I endeavoured to believe that much, if not all of what I felt, was due to the bewildering influence of the gloomy furniture of the room—of the dark and tattered draperies, which, tortured into motion by the breath of a rising tempest, swayed fitfully to and fro upon the walls, and rustled uneasily about the decorations of the bed. But my efforts were fruitless. An irrepressible tremour gradually pervaded my frame; and, at length, there sat upon my very heart an incubus of utterly causeless alarm.[12] Shaking this off with a gasp and a struggle, I uplifted myself upon the pillows, and, peering earnestly within the intense darkness of the chamber, hearkened—I know not why, except that an instinctive spirit prompted me—to certain low and indefinite sounds which came, through the pauses of the storm, at long intervals, I knew not whence. Overpowered by an intense sentiment of horror, unaccountable yet unendurable, I threw on my clothes with haste, (for I felt that I should sleep no more during the night), and endeavoured to arouse myself from the pitiable condition into which I had fallen, by pacing rapidly to and fro through the apartment.

I had taken but few turns in this manner, when a light step on an adjoining staircase arrested my attention. I presently recognised it as that of Usher. In an instant afterward he rapped, with a gentle touch, at my door, and entered, bearing a lamp. His countenance was, as usual, cadaverously wan—but, moreover, there was a species of mad hilarity in his eyes —an evidently restrained *hysteria* in his whole demeanour. His air appalled me— but anything was preferable to the solitude which I had so long endured, and I even welcomed his presence as a relief.

"And you have not seen it?" he said abruptly, after having stared about him for some moments in silence—"you have not then seen it?—but, stay! you shall." Thus speaking, and having carefully shaded his lamp, he hurried to one of the casements, and threw it freely open to the storm.

The impetuous fury of the entering gust nearly lifted us from our feet. It was, indeed, a tempestuous yet sternly beautiful night, and one wildly singular in its terror and its beauty. A whirlwind had apparently collected its force in our vicinity; for there were frequent and violent alterations in the direction of the wind; and the exceeding density of the clouds (which hung so low as to press upon the turrets of the house) did not prevent our perceiving the life-like velocity with which they flew careering from all points against each other, without passing away into the distance. I say that even their exceeding density did not prevent our perceiving this —yet we had no glimpse of the moon or stars—nor was there any flashing forth of the lightning. But the under surfaces of the huge masses of agitated vapour, as well as all terrestrial objects immediately around us, were glowing in the unnatural light of a faintly luminous and distinctly visible gaseous exhalation which hung about and enshrouded the mansion.

"You must not—you shall not behold this!" said I, shudderingly, to Usher, as I led him, with a gentle violence, from the window to a seat. "These appearances, which bewilder you, are merely electrical phenomena not uncommon—or it may be that they have their ghastly origin in the rank miasma[13] of the tarn. Let us close this casement;—the air is chilling and dangerous to your frame. Here is one of your favourite romances. I will read, and you shall listen;—and so we will pass away this terrible night together."

The antique volume which I had taken up was the "Mad Trist" of Sir Launcelot Canning;[14] but I had called it a favourite of Usher's more in sad jest than in earnest; for, in truth, there is little in its uncouth and unimaginative prolixity which could have had interest for the lofty and spiritual ideality of my friend. It was, however, the only book immediately at hand; and I indulged a vague hope that the excitement which now agitated the hypochondriac might find relief (for the history of mental disorder is full of similar anomalies) even in the extremeness of the folly which I should read. Could I have judged, indeed, by the wild overstrained air of vivacity with which he hearkened, or apparently hearkened, to the words of the tale, I might well have congratulated myself upon the success of my design.

I had arrived at that well-known portion of the story where Ethelred, the hero of the Trist, having sought in vain for peaceable admission into the dwelling of the hermit, proceeds to make good an entrance by force. Here, it will be remembered, the words of the narrative run thus:[15]

"And Ethelred, who was by nature of a doughty heart, and who was now mighty withal, on account of the powerfulness of the wine which he had drunken, waited no longer to hold parley with the hermit, who, in sooth, was of an obstinate and maliceful turn, but, feeling the rain upon his shoulders, and fearing the rising of the tempest, uplifted his mace outright, and, with blows, made quickly room in the plankings of the door for his gauntleted hand; and now pulling therewith sturdily, he so cracked, and ripped, and tore all asunder, that the noise of the dry and hollow-sounding wood alarmed and reverberated throughout the forest."

At the termination of this sentence I started and, for a moment, paused; for it appeared to me (although I at once concluded that my excited fancy had deceived me)—it appeared to me that, from some very remote portion of the mansion, there came, indistinctly, to my ears, what might have been, in its exact similarity of character, the echo (but a stifled and dull one certainly) of the very cracking and ripping sound which Sir Launcelot had so particularly described. It was, beyond doubt, the coincidence alone which had arrested my attention; for, amid the rattling of the sashes of the casements, and the ordinary commingled noises of the still increasing storm, the sound, in itself, had nothing, surely, which should have interested or disturbed me. I continued the story:

"But the good champion Ethelred, now entering within the door, was sore enraged and amazed to perceive no signal of the maliceful hermit; but, in the stead thereof, a dragon of a scaly and prodigious demeanour, and of a fiery tongue, which sate in guard before a palace of gold, with a floor of silver; and upon the wall there hung a shield of shining brass with this legend enwritten—

Who entereth herein, a conqueror hath bin;
Who slayeth the dragon, the shield he shall win.

And Ethelred uplifted his mace, and struck upon the head of the dragon, which fell before him, and gave up his pesty breath, with a shriek so horrid and harsh, and withal so piercing, that Ethelred had fain to close his ears with his hands against the dreadful noise of it, the like whereof was never before heard."

Here again I paused abruptly, and now with a feeling of wild amazement—for there could be no doubt whatever that, in this instance, I did actually hear (although from what direction it proceeded I found it impossible to say) a low and apparently distant, but harsh, protracted, and most unusual screaming or grating sound—the exact counterpart of what my fancy had already conjured up for the dragon's unnatural shriek as described by the romancer.

Oppressed, as I certainly was, upon the occurrence of the second and most extraordinary coincidence, by a thousand conflicting sensations, in which wonder and extreme terror were predominant, I still retained sufficient presence of mind to avoid exciting, by any observation, the sensitive nervousness of my companion. I was by no means certain that he had noticed the sounds in question; although, assuredly, a strange alteration had, during the last few minutes, taken place in his demeanour. From a position fronting my own, he had gradually brought round his chair, so as to sit with his face to the door of the chamber; and thus I could but partially perceive his features, although I saw that his lips trembled as if he were murmuring inaudibly. His head had dropped upon his breast—yet I knew that he was not asleep, from the wide and rigid opening of the eye as I caught a glance of it in profile. The motion of his body, too, was at variance with this idea—for he rocked from side to side with a gentle yet constant and uniform sway. Having rapidly taken notice of all this, I resumed the narrative of Sir Launcelot, which thus proceeded:

"And now, the champion, having escaped from the terrible fury of the dragon, bethinking himself of the brazen shield, and of the breaking up of the enchantment which was upon it, removed the carcass from out of the way before him, and approached valorously over the silver pavement of the castle to where the shield was upon the wall; which in sooth tarried not for his full coming, but fell down at his feet upon the silver floor, with a mighty great and terrible ringing sound."

No sooner had these syllables passed my lips, than—as if a shield of brass had indeed, at the moment, fallen heavily upon a floor of silver—I became aware of a distinct, hollow, metallic, and clangorous, yet apparently muffled reverberation. Completely unnerved, I leaped to my feet; but the measured rocking movement of Usher was undisturbed. I rushed to the chair in which he sat. His eyes were bent fixedly before him, and throughout his whole countenance there reigned a stony rigidity. But, as I placed my hand upon his shoulder, there came a strong shudder over his whole person; a sickly smile quivered about his lips; and I saw that he spoke in a low, hurried, and gibbering murmur, as if unconscious of my presence. Bending closely over him, I at length drank in the hideous import of his words.

"Not hear it?—yes, I hear it, and *have* heard it. Long—long—long—many minutes, many hours, many days, have I heard it—yet I dared not—oh, pity me, miserable wretch that I am!—I dared not —I *dared* not speak! *We have put her living in the tomb!* Said I not that my senses were acute? I *now* tell you that I heard her first feeble movements in the hollow coffin. I heard them—many, many days ago—yet I dared not—I *dared not speak!* And now—to-night—Ethelred—ha! ha!— the breaking of the hermit's door, and the death-cry of the dragon, and the clangour of the shield!—say, rather, the rending of her coffin, and the grating of the iron hinges of her prison, and her struggles within the coppered archway of the vault! Oh whither shall I fly? Will she not be here anon? Is she not hurrying to upbraid me for my haste? Have I not heard her footsteps on the stair? Do I not distinguish that heavy and horrible beating of her heart? MADMAN!"—here he sprang furiously to his feet, and shrieked out his syllables, as if in the effort he were giving up his soul—"MADMAN! I TELL YOU THAT SHE NOW STANDS WITHOUT THE DOOR!"

As if in the superhuman energy of his utterance there had been found the potency of a spell—the huge antique panels to which the speaker pointed, threw slowly back, upon the instant, their ponderous and ebony jaws. It was the work of the rushing gust—but then without those doors there *did* stand the lofty and enshrouded figure of the lady Madeline of Usher. There was blood upon her white robes, and the evidence of some bitter struggle upon every portion of her emaciated frame. For a moment she remained trembling and reeling to and fro upon the threshold, then, with a low moaning cry, fell heavily inward upon the person of her brother, and in her violent and now final death-agonies, bore him to the floor a corpse, and a victim to the terrors he had anticipated.

From that chamber, and from that mansion, I fled aghast. The storm was still abroad in all its wrath as I found myself crossing the old causeway. Suddenly there shot along the path a wild light, and I turned to see whence a gleam so unusual could have issued; for the vast house and its shadows were alone behind me. The radiance was that of the full, setting, and blood-red moon, which now shone vividly through that once barely discernible fissure, of which I have before spoken as extending from the roof of the building, in a zigzag direction, to the base. While I gazed, this fissure rapidly widened—there came a fierce breath of the whirlwind— the entire orb of the satellite burst at once upon my sight—my brain reeled as I saw the mighty walls rushing asunder—there was a long tumultuous shouting sound like the voice of a thousand waters[16]—and the deep and dank tarn at my feet closed sullenly and silently over the fragments of the "HOUSE OF USHER."

Notes

The Oval Portrait

1. Poe changed the title of this tale when he republished it. In *Graham's Magazine* in April 1842 it was called "Life in Death." In *The Broadway Journal* (April 26, 1845), the title is "The Oval Portrait." The early version had a motto and an introductory paragraph which Poe cut from the 1845 version. In 1845, Poe apparently thought that it was enough for his narrator to be injured and feverish; in 1842, he had also been sleepless and drugged. The omitted material includes the motto, in which Harrison corrected Poe's Italian, and the long (bracketed) first paragraph.

motto: The quotation combines the idea of the picture so life-like it might speak, with the vow of silence of the Carthusian order of monks. St. Bruno of Cologne (c. 1030–1101) founded the order.

2. Ann Radcliffe (1764–1823): a Gothic novelist long on horror, creepy atmosphere, and scary sounds, albeit short on characterization. A student of Poe would do well to examine the works of writers of her sort, because Poe utilizes a great many of the conventions of the Gothic fiction industry.

arabesque: ornament of the elaborate and stylized sort used in Moorish architecture. Compare this room with the one described in "The Philosophy of Furniture" and with the garden which Ellison creates in "The Domain of Arnheim" for an indication of Poe's taste. See "The Domain of Arnheim," note 18.

incipient delirium . . . interest: See Section Preface.

3. See Section Preface.

4. Thomas Sully: very well-known American portraitist (1783–1872) who worked in Philadelphia, and whose works Poe could have seen in many places.

Moresque: a kind of stylized decoration, complex and ornate, yet generally symmetrical, often characterized by great energy, richness and beauty. Many Moresque decorations

seem to radiate out in decorative zones from a center (which might be a stylized flower) much in the manner of this story: the beauty of the girl, then the painting which the "fervid" artist created, its frame, the book of comments, then the feverish and drugged narrator who perceived it all, and, if you wish, Poe himself creating yet another "frame" around the whole.

5. fervid: a favorite word of Poe's when he is describing the artistic process. Compare what Ellison says about art in "The Domain of Arnheim."

Morella

1. Poe's quotation is from a speech which is attributed to "a woman of Mantinea," the topic of which is the advisability of moving from the love of beauty in transitory things to the love of beautiful pursuits, from those to the love of "beautiful domains of science," and from those to the love of "eternal beauty in itself," "beauty absolute." The passage supports the mystical reading of the tale: the beauty of the single object is, to the illumined, identical with the beauty of the universe, and wisdom consists of the ability to see the unity. The quotation appears as Poe gives it in *The Broadway Journal.* His Greek is correct but without accents. He uses an alternative spelling of one word and makes two words of a compound adjective. A modern text reads: αὐτὸ καθ' αὐτο μεθ' αὐτοῦ μονοειδὲς ἀεὶ ὄν. . . .

Poe published this first in the April 1835 *Southern Literary Messenger,* then in the November 1839 *Burton's Gentleman's Magazine,* the 1840 *Tales of the Grotesque and Arabesque,* and the June 21, 1845 *The Broadway Journal.*

2. Love. Poe's meaning is broader than just "erotic love." See his "Politian—A Tragedy," in which Lalage invites Politian to flee with her to America where ". . . Care shall be forgotten, and sorrow shall be no more, and Eros be all."

3. Pressburg, or Bratislava, a city "once renowned as a center of study of the occult sciences" (Pollin 3).

4. Hinnom is a valley near Jerusalem used in Biblical times to dump refuse. Gehenna is the same place, but in the New Testament, the word is used to mean "hell."

5. Johann Gottlieb Fichte (1762–1842), German philosopher whose pantheism posits a God of infinite essence.

Friedrich Wilhelm Joseph von Schelling (1775–1854), German philosopher, influenced by Fichte. His *Identitatsphilosophie* argued the identity of nature and spirit.

Παλιγγενεσία: the Greek word means "rebirth" or "palingenesis." Poe actually writes palingenesia; which is the more normal Greek form. The Pythagoreans believed we would be reborn as either people or animals (or even plants).

John Locke (1632–1704). Poe refers to Book Two, Chapter 27 in Locke's *Essay Concerning Human Understanding*, "in which Locke spends many pages on the distinction between a man (a creature having the *accidental* features of a rational man) speaking gibberish and an animal (a creature having the *accidental* features of a creature below man) speaking coherent words and sentences" (McCarthy).

6. See Section Preface.

7. Paestum: an ancient Greek colony in what is now Italy. Virgil, Ovid, Martial, and other classical authors mention that its roses bloom twice a year.

Teian: pertaining to the city of Teos, where Anacreon was born. The poet Anacreon is noted for songs of love and wine; perhaps Poe means that the narrator shall no longer enjoy life. Poe's famous contemporary, the poet Thomas Moore (1779–1852), bore the nickname Anacreon.

"shroud . . . Mecca": Moslem pilgrims to Mecca put on *ihram* garments consisting of two white seamless sheets, one around the loins and another for the upper body.

Berenice

1. "My companions said that my troubles would be appreciably relieved if I should visit the tomb of my sweetheart" (Carlson 2). Pollin (3) says that Ebn Zaiat is an Arabian biographer.

2. Egæus: See Section Preface.

Our line . . . belief: By hinting that the family is "a race of visionaries" and that Egæus is mad, Poe establishes a margin of credibility. The reader can now assume, if he prefers, that what follows is largely imagined.

3. For the connotations of this word in Poe, see "The Domain of Arnheim."

4. In a word . . . *speculative:* See Section Preface.

5. Coelius Secundus Curio: (1503–1569), Italian author and philosopher. In *De Amplitudine beati Regni Dei* (1550) the author attempts to prove that Heaven has more inhabitants than Hell.

St Austin: St Augustine (354–430). The *City of God* illustrates God's plan for human history, in which the City of Man will pass away, to be replaced by the City of God on earth.

Tertullian (c. 165–220): zealous and aggressive church father who fought heresy, paganism, and Judaism, and then became a heretic himself. The quotation translates "The Son of God is dead, a thing believable because absurd; and he who was entombed is risen again, a thing true because impossible" (Carlson 2). It is part of Tertullian's argument that "the more absurd an idea appeared to the unaided human reason, so much the more meritorious it was in the eyes of God to believe it" (Easton, *The Heritage of the Ancient World*).

6. Ptolemy Hephestion: Ptolemy Chennos, son of Hephestion (Pollin 3) (Fl. c. 100), Alexandrian author.

Asphodel: a flower often associated with death (Carlson 2).

7. For as Jove, during the winter season, gives twice seven days of warmth, men have called this clement and temperate time the nurse of the beautiful Halcyon—Simonides [Poe's note].

Halcyon: in legend, the bird which could charm the wind and sea into mildness so that it could breed in a nest on the water. There were supposed to be fourteen mild days surrounding the winter solstice.

Simonides of Ceos: a Greek poet (c. 556–c. 469 B.C.E.). In keeping with his mystical theme of horror out of beauty, Poe sets

Egæus' discovery of Berenice's teeth on an unseasonably lovely day.

8. Not a speck. . . . moral expression: Poe's subject is so *outré* (to use a word he liked) that it is difficult to take seriously, but it's worth noting that what Egæus says is good mystical doctrine: any object is "sentient" because the world is sensate and sacred.

Mad'selle Sallé (de Sallé): A French dancer, friend and protégée of Voltaire. Louis Fuzelier said (translated) "that all her steps were sentiments." Egæus' adaptation means "that all her teeth were ideas" (Carlson 2).

9. Poe published "Berenice" three times, first in March 1835, in the *Southern Literary Messenger*, again in 1840 in his book *Tales of the Grotesque and Arabesque*, and finally in *The Broadway Journal*, April 5, 1845 during the period in which he was associate editor of that paper. Our text follows that last version, which omits one horrific paragraph critics agree is better omitted. Here it is:

> With a heart full of grief, yet reluctantly, and oppressed with awe, I made my way to the bed-chamber of the departed. The room was large, and very dark, and at every step within its gloomy precincts I encountered the paraphernalia of the grave. The coffin, so a menial told me, lay surrounded by the curtains of yonder bed, and in that coffin, he whisperingly assured me, was all that remained of Berenice. Who was it asked me would I not look upon the corpse? I had seen the lips of no one move, yet the question had been demanded, and the echo of the syllables still lingered in the room. It was impossible to refuse; and with a sense of suffocation I dragged myself to the side of the bed. Gently I uplifted the sable draperies of the curtains. As I let them fall they descended upon my shoulders, and shutting me thus out from the living, enclosed me in the strictest communion with the deceased. The very atmosphere was redolent of death. The peculiar smell of the coffin sickened me; and I fancied a deleterious odor was already exhaling from the body. I would have given worlds to escape—to fly from the pernicious influence of mortality—to breathe once again the pure air of the eternal heavens. But I had no longer the power to move—my knees tottered beneath me—and I remained rooted to the spot, and gazing upon the frightful length of the rigid body as it lay outstretched in the dark coffin without a lid. God of heaven!—is it possible? Is it my brain that reeled—or was it indeed the finger of the enshrouded dead that stirred in the white cerement that bound it? Frozen with unutterable awe I slowly raised my eyes to the countenance of the corpse. There had been a band around the jaws, but, I know not how, it was broken asunder. The livid lips were wreathed in a species of smile, and, through the enveloping gloom, once again there glared upon me in too palpable a reality, the white and glistening, and ghastly teeth of Berenice. I sprang convulsively from the bed, and, uttering no word, rushed forth a maniac from that apartment of triple horror, and mystery, and death.

Eleonora

1. "In the preservation of its specific life form lies the safety of the spirit of life," from Raimon Lull (c. 1235–1315): scholastic philosopher and logician (Carlson 2). Poe took the quotation from a Victor Hugo novel he was reading; Hugo got it from Henri Sauval; Sauval said he used Raimon Lull, but the passage is probably not really from Lull (Pollin 5). Poe's own (faulty) translation is: "Under the conservation/protection of specific forms the soul is safe" (Pollin 5).

This tale appeared "first" in the *Boston Notion* for September 4, 1841, and in the *New York Weekly Tribune* for September 18, 1841 (Vol. I, 1), both times with a line saying it was from the *Gift* for 1842. The *Gift* was one of a number of fancy annual magazines intended for the Christmas trade. They were published late in the year preceding their title-date so that people could give them as presents. Their intended audience, like that of many of the magazines for which Poe wrote, was feminine, but because they paid rather better than most periodicals, they attracted a certain number of "known" writers, whose productions appeared surrounded by the more sentimental effusions of the minor ones. The volume of the *Gift* containing "Eleonora" was issued in September 1841. Poe also saw the story in print in *Roberts Semi-Monthly Magazine for Town and Country*, September 15, 1841; *New York* (Daily) *Tribune*, Vol. 1, 139, September 20, 1841; *The Literary Souvenir*, November 13, 1841, and again on July 9, 1842; and *The Broadway Journal*, May 24, 1845.

2. Nubian . . . *exploraturi*: see "A Descent into the Maelström," note 3, for identification, translation, and Poe's source.

3. See "Thou Art the Man," note 1. Poe says, in effect, "solve it as Oedipus solved his riddle."

4. Poe's wife was his cousin, and his mother died when he was an infant. After the marriage, the Poes did, in fact, live with Virginia's mother. Virginia Poe, his wife, died in 1847, long after the publication of "Eleonora." But the story has nevertheless often been taken as autobiographical, a kind of prose-poem to his love for his young wife, who by January 1842 clearly had tuberculosis. Poe's fiancée, Sarah Helen Whitman, was in his mind by 1848. He gave her a copy of the 1845 reprinting of the story (Pollin 5.)

5. Nature embodies "the glory of God"; trees do homage to the sun; Eleonora's beauty is nature's; all religions are fragmentary versions of a perennial philosophy which alone is true: conventional romantic assumptions, but also good occult doctrine: man, the heavens and earth are a whole, and the wholeness is revealed to the seer. See Section Preface.

6. Eros: the Greek god of love. See "Morella" note 2.

the harp of Æolus: Æolus is the Greek god of the winds. An Aeolian harp plays when wind strikes it.

Hesper: the evening star; usually refers to Venus.

7. When Poe revised the *Gift* version of "Eleonora" for use again, he cut out an interesting passage: Poe had,

> —and here, as in all things referring to this epoch, my memory is vividly distinct. In stature she was tall, and slender even to fragility; the exceeding delicacy of her frame, as well as of the hues of her cheek, speaking painfully of the feeble tenure by which she held existence. The lilies of the valley were not more fair. With the nose, lips, and chin of the Greek Venus, she had the majestic forehead, the naturally-waving auburn hair, and the large luminous eyes of her kindred. Her beauty, nevertheless, was of that nature which leads the heart to wonder not less than to love. The grace of her motion was surely ethereal. Her fantastic step left no impress upon the asphodel—and I

could not but dream as I gazed, enrapt, upon her alternate moods of melancholy and of mirth, that two separate souls were enshrined within her. So radical were the changes of countenance, that at one instant I fancied her possessed by some spirit of smiles, at another by some demon of tears. She. . . .

8. Carlson (2) says, "Probably refers to Saadi (1184?–1291?), a venerated Persian poet born in Shiraz. He wrote symbolic poetry of exceptional beauty. Shiraz was also the birthplace of Hafiz, a poet of more vehement verse (d. 1389?)."

9. Helusion: Poe's spelling of Elysium, the portion of Hades reserved, in Greek myth, for the blessed dead. See "Shadow," note 3.

10. In Poe's day, "flower books" and articles, in which flowers symbolized human characteristics or even personalities, were very popular. In one, hand-colored steel engravings of a flower and a girl appear on left-hand pages, and prose sketches about Rose, Daisy, Violet, or Petunia are printed on the right-hand pages. The mood of such productions was, of course, extremely sentimental, but surprisingly tough-minded authors—notably Hawthorne—were attracted to the idea of utilizing this insipid symbolism in their fiction. The key to their interest is probably the popularity of "flower books"—an author could count on his readers' understanding what he was about.

11. Here Poe cut a passage which had appeared in the *Gift* version of the tale:

> I looked down into the blue depths of her meaning eyes, and I thought only of her. Oh, lovely was the lady Ermengarde! and in that knowledge I had room for none other. Oh, glorious was the wavy flow of her auburn tresses! and I clasped them in a transport of joy to my bosom. And I found rapture in the fantastic grace of her step—and there was a wild delirium in the love I bore her when I started to see upon her countenance the identical transition from tears to smiles that I had wondered at in the long-lost Eleonora.
> I forgot—I despised the horrors of the curse I had so blindly invoked, and I wedded the lady Ermengarde.

This passage and the one noted in note 7 above deal with changes in mood; Poe evidently decided that such changes were extraneous and detracted from the strong unified effect he believed was a prime aesthetic goal of short fiction. Dropping this latter passage also removed a jarring Latinate locution—"identical transition"—which certainly had hurt the earlier version.

Ligeia

1. In Poe's long (264-line), unfinished poem "Al Aaraaf" appears Nesace's song to Ligeia whom A. H. Quinn calls "the soul of beauty" and Carlson (2) "the goddess of harmony." The poem itself is mystical in message: only intuitive creativity can achieve cosmic and supernal beauty. Scientific knowledge is a lesser path; its "Truth is Falsehood."

2. Scholars have failed to find this passage in the writings of Joseph Glanvill (1636–1680). Poe's choice of Glanvill is apt, however. Though he is best-remembered in the literary histories for his philosophical skepticism and for his contribution to modernizing and simplifying English prose style, Carlson (2) speaks of his "intuitional idealism and cabalism." This is, in fact, an occult story, if we are to take Ligeia's study of mystic texts, the doctrine of the "will," and the final transformation seriously. See Section Preface.

3. Pollin (3) and Carlson (2) think Poe means Ashtoreth, Egyptian goddess of fertility.

4. Delos: The Greek island in which Apollo and Artemis were supposed to have been born (Carlson 2).

"There is . . . proportion": Poe slightly misquotes his source, Francis Bacon (1561–1626), the great English essayist. In Bacon's "Of Beauty," the line reads, "There is no excellent beauty that hath not some strangeness in the proportion."

Cleomenes: the Greek sculptor of the Venus of Medici. Carlson (2) reports that the dream sent by Apollo is not part of Greek myth; apparently Poe made it up.

5. Nourjahad: "An allusion to Francis Sheridan's *The History of Nourjahad,* an oriental novel" (Carlson 2). Our reading of the novel, however, failed to reveal any "gazelle eyes." Poe might have had the *Arabian Nights* in mind; gazelle eyes are mentioned there.

Houri: In Muslim belief, those who attain Paradise enjoy the favors of beautiful young virgins called "houri."

the well of Democritus: Poe's frequent allusions to this well are actually to a proverbial saying attributed to Democritus and current in many renderings by different authors. Democritus actually said, "Of a truth we know nothing, for truth is in an abyss" (ἐν βύθῳ). Since Poe had Bacon in mind as he wrote this tale (see note 4, above), he was probably reminded of the saying by Bacon's version, "The truth of nature lieth hid in certain deep mines and caves." Regarding "Democritus" see "A Descent into the Maelström," note 1.

Leda: in Greek legend, the wife of Tyndareus, King of Sparta, and the mother of Clytemnestra. In one legend, Zeus, in the form of a swan, fathered Helen (in one egg) and Castor and Pollux (in another) by her.

6. The "circle of analogies" in this paragraph is orthodox occultism. In occult religions—the subjects of Ligeia's studies—analogies are not understood as "representing" similarities between two or more objects or ideas; rather, since the universe is one, a whole, all parts of which partake of the holy unity, they are interpreted literally. They don't *represent,* they *are.* The narrator is on the verge of transcendent realization. The transformations at the close of the story and the theme of the power of the will are further examples of the "linked analogies" (to use Melville's phrase) which underlie all creation and ideality. See "The Power of Words" for an unusually clear exposition of Poe's use of occult beliefs.

Lyra: a constellation, "the Lyre" or "the Harp."

7. Saturnus is the alchemical name for lead. Alchemy, usually described simply as the primitive precursor of modern chemistry, or as a persistently foolish effort to transmute lead into gold, was, in point of fact, an occult discipline in which the "transmutations" were intended to bring the practitioner into transcendent illumination.

Azrael: the angel of death.

8. Poe first published this poem separately, in *Graham's Magazine,* January 1843. The story had already appeared in the September 1838 *American Museum* and the 1840 *Tales of the Grotesque and Arabesque.* In the February 1845 *New World* the poem (usually titled "The Conqueror Worm") was first included as part of the story (Stovall 2). Poe

used the story with the poem again in the September 27, 1845 issue of *The Broadway Journal.*

9. Poe frequently provided readers with an alternative "rational" way of accounting for the fantastic. In "Ligeia," the narrator's "incipient madness" and his addiction to opium provide the needed margin of credibility: all that follows may be an illusion. Note, however, that madness and drugs are traditionally believed to be routes to transcendent truth. One chooses one's own interpretation.

10. pentagonal: The pentagon is the five-sided figure contained within the pentagram or pentacle, the "star of five lines" in occultism. It is part of an occult system for "getting through" to the power inherent in transcendent knowledge.

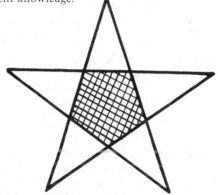

Figure Eight. Pentagon and Pentacle. The shaded area is the pentagon.

semi-Gothic, semi-Druidical; Saracenic: See notes 18 and 19, "The Domain of Arnheim."

11. The bridal chamber merges the black and dark imagery connected with Ligeia with the gold imagery connected with Rowena (who is purchased from her parents). Griffith argues quite convincingly that Poe's real intention in the tale is satirical, and that its targets are the two schools of romantic transcendentalism, German (Ligeia and the dark imagery) and English (Rowena and the gold).

12. One critic suggests that in reality the narrator poisons Rowena's wine, deluding himself, in his drugged state, into believing in spiritual intervention and the transformation which ends the tale.

13. The association between sexuality and death is a favorite theme for Freudian critics. Their theory, briefly, is that in prudish ages, there takes place an imaginative substitution of death for sex. Hence the female corpses in bridal dress laid out upon their wedding beds, and, in this tale, the deathly bridal chamber.

The Fall of the House of Usher

1. His heart is a pendant lute
Which resounds the moment touched.

Pierre-Jean de Béranger (1780–1857), among the best-known and respected poets of the period, now considered minor. Poe published this story in *Burton's Gentleman's Magazine* in September 1839, and reprinted it in his books of 1840 and 1845. Poe also saw it in print in a London magazine called *Bentley's Miscellany,* in August 1840, in the American edition of the same periodical later in 1840, in the *Boston Notion* issue for September 5, 1840, and in Rufus Griswold's immensely successful anthology, *The Prose Writers of America* (1847).

2. I know not. . . . the veil: Outer reality and states of mind are associated right at the opening of the tale, to give the reader a "margin of credibility." Poe is saying, in effect, that what "happens" and what his narrator feels may be so closely related that the reader who is unwilling to believe given parts of the action may view them as reflections of the processes of his narrator's mind.

tarn: mountain lake.

3. *ennuyé:* bored.

Arabesque: See "The Domain of Arnheim," note 18 for the implications of the word. Its use here is odd, and the sentence somewhat ambiguous: is it the hair or the face that is "Arabesque"? Grammatically, it is the hair, yet can hair have "expression"? A guess: among the connotations of "Arabesque" for Poe is exoticism, a quality which, along with brilliance, creativity, and mental illness, he wanted associated with Usher. The reference of the word is less important than its inclusion.

4. Now both Usher and the narrator have been associated with drugs and with marginal states of consciousness.

5. Mental illness and creativity are associated frequently in Poe, and beauty is always exotic, *outré,* "Arabesque." Madness, apparently, is one way to achieve contact with transcendent sources of inspiration. For an alternate route to the same kind of beauty, see "The Domain of Arnheim."

6. Von Weber: Carl Maria Friedrich Ernst von Weber (1786–1826), German composer. The "Last Waltz" is, according to Carlson (2), "No. 5 of the *Danses Brillantes* by Karl Reissiger (1798–1859), based on the last waltz of Carl von Weber."

Fuseli: John Henry Fuseli (1741–1825), Swiss-English painter of the fantastic, who was famous in his own time.

7. An "impromptu" is a musical work of an extemporized nature (though in point of fact there are *written* impromptus). Usher, in his high "excitement" creates beautiful and strange works. Note that the "intense . . . collectedness of concentration" is also a sign of insanity. Poe plays on the folk belief that the insane see the world of spirit.

8. Poe had published this poem earlier (in the *American Museum*, April 1839), and after the story was published, the poem was reprinted both as a part of "Usher" and on its own. "Law" in stanza III has the sense of patterned accompaniment, but its precise meaning is not clear to us. Poe might intend "law" in the sense of "rules" or "foundation" for the dancing spirits. "Porphyrogene" is also a puzzler. Porphyry is a kind of rock; its connotations of stolidity don't seem appropriate to the ruler of this still happy palace. Or the word might refer to Malchus Porphyrius or Porphyry (c. 233–c. 305), a neo-Platonic philosopher, in which case "Porphyrogene" might imply "like a great philosopher." But Porphyry's anti-Christian writings, though distinguished by moderation and wisdom, would probably have been offensive to Poe. Poe's own credo is both mystical and Platonic, as was the religious view Porphyry defended, but in his most public statements, Poe generally took a conventional Christian stance; certainly he never attacked Christianity except indirectly via the occult worldview of many of his tales.

9. Watson, Dr. Percival, Spallanzani, and especially the Bishop of Landaff—See "Chemical Essays," vol. V [Poe's note]. Richard Watson, Bishop of Landaff (1737–1819) was an English chemist. James Gates Percival (1795–1856) was an American physician and poet. Abée Lazzaro Spallanzani (1729–1799) was professor of natural history at the University of Pavia.

10. Usher says he fears fear, and Poe has selected a library of dark works with which Usher can scare himself. Jean-Baptiste-Louis

Gresset (1709–1777), for example, wrote some works dealing with the theme of the delectation of evil. His "Vert-Vert" (1734), however, is a poem light in tone. Carlson (2) says that *Vairvert* and *Ma Chartreuse* are "satirical, anti-clerical, and licentious" poems.

Niccoló Machiavelli: the Florentine writer and political figure (1469–1527), whose name is synonymous with the amoral approach to political power. The novel to which Poe refers is a satire on marriage, but it includes a demon (Belfagor) who could have frightened Usher.

Emanuel Swedenborg: mystic, philosopher, and scientist (1688–1772), very influential on romantic authors of Poe's day. His supposed clairvoyance is relevant to Usher's. (Usher supposedly has mystical ties to his sister Madeline.)

Ludwig Holberg (1684–1754): Danish dramatist, historian, and novelist (Carlson 2). His *Iter Subterraneum* is about a "country inside the earth where the people are trees who walk and talk" (Mabbott 8).

Chiromancy: the ancient pseudo-science of palm-reading. It is, as Poe implies, an occult system in origin.

Robert Flud (1574–1637): "English physician, mystic philosopher (sometimes called 'The English Rosicrucian'), scientific experimenter, and writer on pseudo-science" (Carlson 2). His *Tractatus de Geomantia* is about geomancy—divination by "marking the earth with a pointed stick" (Mabbott 8).

Jean D'Indaginé: writer on palmistry, author of *Chiromantia* (1522), (Carlson 2).

Maria Cireau de la Chambre (1594–1669): another writer on palmistry (Carlson, 2), author of *Principes de la Chiromancie* (1653), (Mabbott 8).

Ludwig Tieck: German writer and critic (1773–1853). Carlson (2) says that the book to which Poe refers deals with a journey into another world. So does "The City of the Sun" (*Civitas Solis*) by Tomasso Campanella (1568–1639), "a utopian work suggesting the ideal state in the world beyond" (Carlson 2).

Nicholas Eymeric de Gironne: inquisitor-general of Castille in Spain in 1356, wrote *Directorium Inquisitorium* (1503). He gives "instructions to priests examining heretics" and "a list of forbidden books" (Mabbott 8).

Pomponius Mela: "a first-century Roman Geographer, whose widely used textbook often described strange beasts" (Carlson 2). The passage which Poe has in mind is quoted in Mabbott (8).

Satyrs: Greek woodland deities, generally human in appearance, but with goat's legs, pointed ears, small horns, and wanton ways.

Ægipans: a name for Pan, the god of forests, flocks, and shepherds. He, too, had goat's horns and hoofs; Carlson (2) ventures the guess that Poe thought Pan a type of satyr.

Vigiliæ Mortuorum: " 'The Watches of the Dead according to the Choir of the Church of Mayence [Mainz],' printed in Basel, c. 1500" (Carlson 2).

11. Trestles.

12. See Section Three Preface.

13. Unwholesome gas or atmosphere.

14. Pollin (3) says there is no "Sir Launcelot Canning," but that Poe coined the name from a name in the works of Thomas Chatterton (1752–1770), William Canynge. Chatterton undoubtedly caught Poe's imagination.

A gifted youngster, he created pseudo-archaic poems, failed to achieve fame or financial rewards, and killed himself at the age of 17. There was also a well-known political leader and satiric writer, George Canning (1770–1827) whose fame might have put the name in Poes' head. Poe used the name also in his prospectus for The Stylus, a magazine he tried to found; on the title-page of the prospectus appear three lines which he attributes to "Launcelot Canning."

15. Poe seems to have made up the story. For a century before Poe wrote "Usher," authors had been inventing pseudo-archaic epics, tales, and ballads; by using familiar elements and characters, Poe suggests that this is either such a work or the real thing, an ancient tale. There were two real kings named Ethelred who ruled from 866 to 871 and from 978 to 1016, respectively. A trist (tryst) is a meeting; the encounter with a hermit is a common element in tales of questing.

16. Poe's language is probably an echo of Psalm 93. See "The Balloon-Hoax," note 9.

4. Occult Fantasies

There is no way to separate the "serious" Poe from the playful Poe or the commercial Poe. "Silence" is supposed to be a satire—we have Poe's own word (see note 1) for that—yet its evocative and ritualistic language works so well that we think of it less as a satire than as Poe's demonstration that he could use another author's materials better than the author could. "Valdemar" contains very high-grade commercial Gothic horror; it capitalizes on topics of current interest, and is even a hoax. But what it says about transcendence is too central in Poe's philosophy not to be taken seriously.

Indeed, these stories are philosophically consistent in that each contains an occult vision. But Poe's emphasis upon the vision varies from one story to the next. For understanding Poe's philosophy and Romanticism in general, there is no more important document than "The Power of Words." In "A Tale of the Ragged Mountains," on the other hand, the mystical "equivalences" are obvious, but might be present primarily to make the plot seem clever.

The Power of Words. Carlyle's essay on "Boswell's Life of Johnson" dates from 1832, and Poe's "The Power of Words" appeared in print in 1835. The essay could well provide a motto for the tale: "Nothing dies, nothing can die. No idlest word thou speakest but is a seed cast into Time, and grows through all Eternity!" Poe knew Carlyle's work well, and this particular idea is consistent with Poe's most frequently held philosophical stance. The quasi-scriptural tone of the Carlyle passage also may have its echoes in Poe.

For the reader who wants to understand Poe's metaphysics, this is his most important story. The passage at note 6 is the center of the story and in a sense the center of the romantic movement in literature. Modern critics generally make the mistake Oinos makes. Seeing a literary symbol, they interpret it as simile—it is "like" what it represents. Even when they interpret it as a metaphor, they assume that it merely "represents." But romantics of Poe's sort, men as different as Blake, Shelley, and Whitman, were attempting to restore to art its ancient properties of science, magic, and prophecy. Oinos is about to learn that the flowers are not *like* "a fairy dream"; the volcanoes are not *like* "the passions of a turbulent heart." They *are* literally "unfulfilled dreams" and "passions." That romantic authors are serious when they say such things is hard for us as Western rationalists to grasp, but Poe is unerringly consistent in the matter, and other authors have always taken him seriously. This is the basic reason, for example, for the enthusiasm for Poe among French symbolist poets. If the idea is hard to grasp, your editors recommend John Senior's admirable book *The Way Down and Out: The Occult in Symbolist Literature* (Cornell University Press, 1959) as a reliable introduction to the field.

The Conversation of Eiros and Charmion. Modern Western societies distinguish art clearly from science, and both from religion. But the scriptural "poet" was at once priest, prophet, artist, and scientist, a position for the artist which Poe and many of his contemporaries—notably Shelley—wanted to restore. Thus it is not surprising to find Poe writing a story about the literal truth of biblical prophecy, complete even to a "scientific" account of the mechanism by which the earth is to be destroyed by fire. The fact that there was a great deal of popular scientific discussion of comets in Poe's day undoubtedly played its part in suggesting the subject to Poe; Halley's comet had been seen in 1835. As usual, in short, the serious Poe and the commercial Poe turn out to be the same man.

Critics of Poe have recently been making the point that Poe is a "fundamentalist." We agree only up to a point. This story does argue that a biblical prophecy is literally true, but one must remember Poe's context: first, prophecy is and always has been a gift of true poets; second, the fulfillment of prophecy and, indeed, any understanding of the workings of the universe will be based on "materialistic" grounds. There will, in short, be a physical explanation for all that happens. Note also the absence in this tale of any explicitly "fundamentalist" or even Christian theological concern. Neither Eiros nor Charmion says anything about being saved because of belief in Jesus; indeed, Poe selected names which suggest the occult religions of Roman times. Iras and Charmion (see note 1) called on Egyptian gods. Poe was, however, skeptical of modern religious liberalism with its optimistic view of human nature.

What this story says about reason and inspiration is important: reason is wrong. "Superstition," to the extent to which it is based upon inspiration, is more likely to be right. The approach of the comet, Eiros tells us, made all men respect reason and made learned men "pant" for truth. But this did no good; reason alone will not solve problems. Compare this story to the detective stories involving Dupin. His rival, the Prefect of Police, uses only deductive logic and gets nowhere. Dupin retires to his study, puffs his pipe, and *intuits* the truth. The present tale, operating on a more cosmic scale, also argues the role of inspiration. Compare also the satires on nineteenth-century pride in the accomplishments of rational science and technology—for example, "The Thousand-and-Second Tale of Scheherazade" or "Mellonta Tauta."

The Colloquy of Monos and Una. Note 3 locates a key passage for understanding Poe's philosophical point of view. The poetic intellect, responding with imagination to analogy, is the real source of truth about the universe; "the unaided reason," in contrast, is impotent. "Progress" is illusory. Poe daringly calls the biblical story of Eden a "mystic parable" because an occultist or mystic believes that real truth cannot be *told* or "explained." The initiate must have the experience himself: it is not something which can be codified, but rather the total perception of the unity and sanctity of the world. Hence mystical scripture speaks in parable, not scientific prose. Critics who argue that Poe is a fundamentalist tend to ignore passages such as this.

The paragraph above note 4 seems to attack "Art." We must note first that by "Art" Poe here means not the fine arts but rather human skill in "dominion" over nature and, second, that Poe feels that our culture defines the role of the artist (in the usual sense of the word) too narrowly. In cultures which view the universe as sacred, the "artist" is also priest, prophet, and scientist. This is why Poe, when he describes a golden age (in the paragraph at note 3), speaks of a time when the human view was unitary, not compartmentalized.

The detailed record of sensations after death in the passage above note 8 is consistent with Poe's philosophy. Two other factors should be mentioned, however, because they also play a part: (1) Poe's contemporaries were obsessed with death. A tale which assumes that consciousness goes on beyond death is thus potentially comforting and even inspiring. The more details the better. (2) Poe says playfully in "How to Write a Blackwood Article" that if you should ever get killed, be sure to take good notes of your sensations, because they will make valuable magazine copy. Both Poe's serious intentions—artistic and philosophical—and his commercial attitude must be kept in mind before deciding what to make of his fiction.

Shadow. Pollin (12) demonstrates that "Shadow" is built on a chapter of Thomas Moore's *The Epicureans;* one can call it a satire. But that word is used too loosely in Poe criticism: as Pollin notes, the tale's poetic evocation of the voices of the departed is too "beautifully wrought" not to be compelling even for the reader who knows what game Poe is playing. We think Poe here, as in "Silence," is deliberately writing a virtuoso piece, demonstrating how well he can take another man's materials and make them work for him.

The other basic source of "Shadow" suggests as much: Jacob Bryant's *Mythology.* We are certain that Poe connects Bryant to this story (see note 3 especially); he also praises Bryant elsewhere. Bryant's work presents, in its analysis of ancient myth, the philosophical and mythical framework of Poe's tale; it also contains much of Poe's language and even the proper names Poe uses—including the "foul Charonian canal" which has hitherto puzzled scholars.

"Zoilus" is likely Poe's rendition of Jacob Bryant's "Coilus" which ". . . in the original aceptation certainly signified heavenly. . . . [Coilus] was . . . a sacred or heavenly person" (Bryant, Vol. I, 140).

Bryant also seems to be the source of the name Oinos. In a complicated explanation, he equates the Dove from the Ark with Ion, Ionah [Jonah], and Oinas of the Greeks, "the interpreter of the will of the Gods to man." Bryant identifies Oinas with Eanus (Janus), whom he consequently equates with other deities—Apollo, Diana, Helius, Dionysus, and Saturn.

Bryant describes Janus as having "two faces"—one toward the past and one toward the future—and as representing "the end and the beginning of all things." He presides, Bryant says, "over everything that could be shut or opened; and . . . [is] the guardian of the doors of Heaven." In rites in honor of both the gods Saturn and Dionysus, originally a sacrifice was made, representing the end of one period and the beginning of another. (Dionysus is, in fact, listed in Greek dictionaries as one of the meanings of οἶνος.) The name Oinos, its form in Poe, is identical to an archaic Latin form for the modern *unus*, "one." With or without the classical word-play, clearly Poe had in mind the idea in Dionysian rites that life and death lead into each other as one.

If the names Oinos and Zoilus are given meanings based on references in Bryant, "Shadow," like "Eiros and Charmion," and "Monos and Una" may be read as a myth of rebirth. The reading might go as follows: Zoilus, the heavenly one, is dead. The planets are in a period of Saturnian darkness. Oinos (and possibly the seven men as a whole, if we take into account the magical properties of the number seven) is perhaps equated with Dionysus—the new representation of a God—or with the Dove which reveals God's will. In this dark period the group is passing "through the Valley," the abyss (symbolically represented in the story by the bottomless image reflected in the surface of the ebony table), Hell, "Helusion," the place from whence the Shadow comes and from whence the voices of the dead are heard, and is suffering the rite of purification which, as we see in "The Colloquy of Monos and Una" must be endured before resurrection. Death leads to life. The motto added to the story in its 1840 version suggests that another beginning is to take place. Death must be experienced but is not to be feared because there is "something" beyond—a continuation.

Another possibility, given Poe's capacity for irony, is that Poe, while he admires Bryant's erudition, also sees the humor in the seemingly unending chain of connections which Bryant is able to make from any given proper name. In "Four Beasts in One," a story first published just six months after the first publication of "Shadow," Poe first makes jokes based upon antiquarian etymologies and then concludes "—what great fools are antiquarians!" The time was ripe for making fun of Bryant. In Chapter 176 of *The Doctor* by Robert Southey, Doctor Daniel Dove was delighted ". . . when in perusing Jacob Bryant's Analysis of ancient Mythology, he found that so many of the most illustrious personages of antiquity proved to be Doves, when their names were truly interpreted or properly understood!" Southey carries the derivation of the name Dove through Bryant's explanation to its comical extremes. Poe could not have seen the passage: he was probably reading the first two volumes of the novel at about the time he wrote "Shadow," for his review of it appeared soon after, but the version of it Poe read did not contain the Bryant passage. What this proves is the intimacy of Poe's ties to the intellectual world of the British magazines.

Silence. The Folio Club tales were to have been the work of "Dunderheads." "Silence," like the others, uses material from then-current prose. Its tone seems undeniably serious; we would suggest that Poe's intention is not so simple. Poe does not seem just to be making fun of his sources or using them to tease popular editors or authors. A number of scholars noticed, for example, that Bulwer's "Monos and Daimonos, A Legend" is a source for "Silence." Many elements in "Silence"—even whole sentences—come from Bulwer. The Bulwer story is about a man whose father lived on a rock; it contains a sentence which begins, "As the Lord liveth, I believe the tale that I shall tell you . . ." while Poe writes, "As Allah liveth, that fable which the Demon told me . . . ," and so forth, Yet "Silence is not only a spoof of Bulwer's "Monos and Daimonos"; it is at least partially a lesson in how powerful a tale one could produce from the same materials Bulwer used.

Moreover, the Bulwer story is not all that Poe uses; clear echoes of Jacob Bryant's *Mythology* (See Preface to "Shadow") are audible, too: (1) Bryant explains the ancient custom of worshipping on a stone or upon high places: ". . . there is in the history of every oracular temple some legend about a stone; some reference to the word Petra." "Petra," indeed is in the "first ages" a name for the Sun Deity, Bryant explains, later applied to the Deity's temple, then to the other temples, then to temples erected on a rock, and finally to the rock itself. (2) Bryant says, ". . . the whole religion of the ancients consisted in . . . the worship of Daemons: . . . the souls of men deceased." These demons were supposed to have existed in the time of Cronus and were "guardians of mankind." (3) Poe's hippopotamus and water lilies (the lotus is a water lily) are explained in Bryant: "Hence the crocodile and the hippopotamus, were emblems of the Ark; because during the inundation of the Nile they rose with the waters, and were superior to the flood. The Lotus, that peculiar plant of the Nile, was reverenced upon the same account. . . ." (4) In related Egyptian rites, according to Bryant, there is "a person preserved in the midst of waters." (5) Many other details—"Libya," "Dodona," "Magi" and "Sybils" —as well as those named above are discussed prominently in Bryant. By themselves they would not be convincing, since they might appear in any book on myth and ancient religion. In conjunction with the others, they are. Poe both admired and poked fun at such antiquarianism: see "Four Beasts in One" for a good example of humor based on such teasing.

One must be careful in claiming that one work is the "source" of another. The poetic fragment from which Poe takes his motto seems a sure source of Poe's ideas, but in fact Poe originally used a motto from a poem of his own which also matches the ideas in "Silence." (See note 2 for details.) The Alcman quotation might be the source of both. Poe, when he wrote "Silence," might not have had it handy, and decided for other reasons to use his own equally appropriate lines. Or he might have found Alcman later, been struck by its appropriateness, or attracted by the chance to show erudition, and replaced his with it.

We conclude first that the idea was in circulation, and second, that one must be very cautious in interpreting all aspects of "Silence."

Different scholars reach different conclusions about which member of the Folio Club tells this tale. Hammond thinks it was Poe himself, possibly because, among other things, "Siope" (Poe's first title, Greek for "Silence") is an anagram: "is Poe," and because "Silence" uses imagery from Poe's own poetry.

A Tale of the Ragged Mountains. Perhaps the equivalences at the close of this tale seem too "tricky" to us, and make the story less effective. But if we take them seriously, this tale is another working-out of a mystic's cosmology. Physical death is less important an event in many non-rationalistic cultures; to the mystic, prior incarnation is no more remarkable than any other kind of "equivalence." Note that Poe sets his tale partially in India and that he writes at a time when literary magazines were filling their pages with accounts of oriental beliefs.

Bedloe's ambiguous age—he seems young, yet, the narrator says, at times could pass for very old—is mentioned as part of a passage designed to set up the idea of his prior incarnation as Oldeb. This is, however, another of those odd recurring ideas in Poe; he says pretty much the same thing about his character Ritzner Von Jung in "Mystification."

Boyd Carter points out that many details in "A Tale of the Ragged Mountains" are similar to details in Charles Brockden Brown's *Edgar Huntley* (1799). G. R. Thompson, a critic who does not take the equivalences at the close of Poe's tale seriously, uses Carter's observations as evidence that Poe is likely "burlesquing, even parodying, *Edgar Huntley*" in much the same way that he parodies other works (Thompson 4).

"A Tale of the Ragged Mountains" also contains a plagiarized passage. Poe had read Thomas Macaulay's review in the October 1841 *Edinburgh Review* of the *Memoirs of the Life of Warren Hastings, First Governor-General of Bengal*, compiled by G. R. Gleig, and he swiped a number of passages from it almost *verbatim* for his description of the fight in Benares (Pollin 5; Le Breton).

The Facts in the Case of M. Valdemar. The cool tone of Poe's narrator at the opening of this tale is designed to heighten credibility. In a sense, the story is a hoax; Poe would be pleased if the reader considered it true or at least suspended judgment until Poe brought off his big effect, the rotting of M. Valdemar. Poe has going for him a number of factors:

1. The magazines in which he published contained articles as well as stories and generally did not distinguish one from the other through format. It was possible to fool the reader by pretending, as Poe did here, that a story was an article.

2. Interest in science was very high, and literary magazines often ran articles on science, especially when they touched on issues which had to do with certain philosophical matters. In this story, for instance, the possibility that scientific proof has at last been found of the existence of life after death would have been of great interest, not merely on theological grounds, but also because romantic artists wanted to believe that there was "something out there" with which the inspired mind was in contact. In the back of the minds of many romantic artists was the idea that science was on the verge of discovering the force that unifies the universe, thus giving "inspiration" a physical

basis (see note 2, "magnetic"). Many thought it electrical in nature. Thus a literary magazine, for instance, carried accounts of the work of the French researcher Magendie on electrical stimulation of the brain, and others noted in 1837 that Andrew Crosse of the London Electrical Society seemed to have created life through the application of electricity to "silicate of potash," HCl, and iron oxide.

3. The line between science and pseudo-science was often ill-defined. Phrenology (reading personality and analyzing psychological problems through examination of the shape of the head) and mesmerism (hypnotism) were both taken seriously. When both "sciences" fell into the hands of quacks, phrenology died peacefully. Mesmerism, as hypnotism, is still very much with us as a serious field of investigation although it is much less prominent in the popular press than it was in Poe's time.

4. Poe's care in "documentation," as in the passage at note 5: Poe and other magazinists frequently claim to be quoting from diaries, notebooks, and other sources. Poe, having pretended that he's out just to set the "facts" straight, and having "identified" Valdemar and diagnosed his symptoms, brings in not one but two doctors, two nurses, and an intern as witnesses, and then "copies" from the intern's notes.

When the story was published in England in 1846, the publishers sought to capitalize on its credibility. They changed the title to

Mesmerism
"In Articulo Mortis"
An
Astounding and Horrifying Narrative
Shewing the Extraordinary Power of Mesmerism
in Arresting the
Progress of Death

and included an "Advertisement" which suggested that the events described were believed to be true.

As for the horror itself: the passage following note 8 is perhaps Poe's deepest penetration into what is called "Gothic horror." There can be no doubt that sensationalism, the "vivid effect" and horror are his main concerns here, but note that the tale is philosophically consistent with his other fiction and with his aesthetic aims in short fiction; and that his detachment from the horrid materials he is using is very clear: he "plays games" with Valdemar's identity, fusses with story-telling devices to maintain credibility, and uses to the end a vocabulary and sentence structure more scholarly than passionate.

The last paragraph is as gruesome as anything in Poe. But before concluding that the man was mad to concern himself with such subjects, (1) Examine the contents of magazines of his day to see how common such episodes were in articles and in fiction (though Poe was far more craftsmanlike than most peddlers of horror); (2) Note that the tale is presented in the language of an eighteenth-century scientific paper; (3) Consider the care with which the mechanics of credibility and the "hoax" are handled; (4) Compare the tale to what seem to your editors to be much more deeply-felt passages of horror in, say, Hawthorne and Melville; for example, the scene in *The House of the Seven Gables* in which a fly walks across the open eye of a corpse, or that in Melville's *White Jacket* in which a character pretends to relish the taste of cancer tissue.

Mesmeric Revelation. If the use of mesmerism in this tale is more evidence of Poe's response to topics of popular interest, the tale's mysticism shows as clearly his ties to romanticism, and the seriousness of his occult beliefs. Compare this story to "The Facts in the Case of Mr. Valdemar"—in the latter, Poe tantalizes us with the possibilities of using hypnosis to explore the afterlife; in this, he actually does so.

The Tales

THE POWER OF WORDS

Oinos. Pardon. Agathos,[1] the weakness of a spirit new-fledged with immortality!

Agathos. You have spoken nothing, my Oinos, for which pardon is to be demanded. Not even here is knowledge a thing of intuition.[2] For wisdom ask of the angels freely, that it may be given!

Oinos. But in this existence, I dreamed that I should be at once cognizant of all things, and thus at once be happy in being cognizant of all.

Agathos. Ah, not in knowledge is happiness, but in the acquisition of knowledge! In for ever knowing, we are for ever blessed; but to know all, were the curse of a fiend.

Oinos. But does not The Most High know all?

Agathos. That (since he is The Most Happy) must be still the *one* thing unknown even to HIM.

Oinos. But, since we grow hourly in knowledge, must not *at last* all things be known?

Agathos. Look down into the abysmal distances!—attempt to force the gaze down the multitudinous vistas of the stars, as we sweep slowly through them thus— and thus—and thus! Even the spiritual vision, is it not at all points arrested by the continuous golden walls of the universe?—the walls of the myriads of the shining bodies that mere number has appeared to blend into unity?

Oinos. I clearly perceive that the infinity of matter is no dream.

Agathos. There are *no* dreams in Aidenn—but it is here whispered that, of this infinity of matter, the *sole* purpose is to afford infinite springs, at which the soul may allay the thirst *to know* which is for ever unquenchable within it—since to quench it, would be to extinguish the soul's self. Question me then, my Oinos, freely and without fear. Come! we will leave to the left the loud harmony of the Pleiades,[3] and swoop outward from the throne into the starry meadows beyond Orion, where, for pansies and violets, and heart's-ease, are the beds of the triplicate and triple-tinted suns.

Oinos. And now, Agathos, as we proceed, instruct me!—speak to me in the earth's familiar tones! I understood not what you hinted to me, just now, of the modes or of the methods of what, during mortality, we were accustomed to call Creation. Do you mean to say that the Creator is not God?

Agathos. I mean to say that the Deity does not create.

Oinos. Explain!

Agathos. In the beginning *only*, he created. The seeming creatures which are now, throughout the universe, so perpetually springing into being, can only be considered as the mediate or indirect, not as the direct or immediate results of the Divine creative power.

Oinos. Among men, my Agathos, this idea would be considered heretical in the extreme.

Agathos. Among angels, my Oinos, it is seen to be simply true.

Oinos. I can comprehend you thus far —that certain operations of what we term Nature, or the natural laws, will, under certain conditions, give rise to that which has all the *appearance* of creation. Shortly before the final overthrow of the earth, there were, I well remember, many very successful experiments in what some philosophers were weak enough to denominate the creation of animalcula.[4]

Agathos. The cases of which you speak were, in fact, instances of the secondary creation—and of the *only* species of creation which has ever been, since the first word spoke into existence the first law.

Oinos. Are not the starry worlds that, from the abyss of nonentity, burst hourly forth into the heavens—are not these stars, Agathos, the immediate handiwork of the King?

Agathos. Let me endeavor, my Oinos, to lead you, step by step, to the conception I intend. You are well aware that, as no thought can perish, so no act is without infinite result. We moved our hands, for example, when we were dwellers on the earth, and, in so doing, we gave vibration to the atmosphere which engirdled it. This vibration was indefinitely extended, till it gave impulse to every particle of the earth's air, which thenceforward, *and for ever*, was actuated by the one movement of the hand. This fact the mathematicians of our globe well knew. They made the special effects, indeed, wrought in the fluid by special impulses, the subject of exact calculation—so that it became easy to determine in what precise period an impulse of given extent would engirdle the orb, and impress (for ever) every atom of the atmosphere circumambient. Retrograding, they found no difficulty, from a given effect, under given conditions, in determining the value of the original impulse. Now the mathematicians who saw that the results of any given impulse were absolutely endless—and who saw that a portion of these results were accurately traceable through the agency of algebraic analysis —who saw, too, the facility of the retrogradation—these men saw, at the same time, that this species of analysis itself, had within itself a capacity for indefinite progress—that there were no bounds conceivable to its advancement and applicability, except within the intellect of him who advanced or applied it. But at this point our mathematicians paused.

Oinos. And why, Agathos, should they have proceeded?

Agathos. Because there were some considerations of deep interest beyond. It was deducible from what they knew, that to a being of infinite understanding—one to whom the *perfection* of the algebraic analysis lay unfolded—there could be no difficulty in tracing every impulse given the air—and the ether through the air—to the remotest consequences at any even infinitely remote epoch of time. It is indeed demonstrable that every such impulse *given the air*, must, *in the end*, impress every individual thing that exists *within the universe;*—and the being of infinite understanding—the being whom we have imagined—might trace the remote undulations of the impulse—trace them upward and onward in their influences upon all particles of all matter—

upward and onward for ever in their modifications of old forms—or, in other words, *in their creation of new*—until he found them reflected—unimpressive *at last*—back from the throne of the Godhead. And not only could such a being do this, but at any epoch, should a given result be afforded him—should one of these numberless comets, for example, be presented to his inspection—he could have no difficulty in determining, by the analytic retrogradation, to what original impulse it was due. This power of retrogradation in its absolute fulness and perfection—this faculty of referring at *all* epochs, *all* effects to *all* causes—is of course the prerogative of the Deity alone—but in every variety of degree, short of the absolute perfection, is the power itself exercised by the whole host of the Angelic intelligences.

Oinos. But you speak merely of impulses upon the air.

Agathos. In speaking of the air, I referred only to the earth; but the general proposition has reference to impulses upon the ether[5]—which, since it pervades, and alone pervades all space, is thus the great medium of *creation*.

Oinos. Then all motion, of whatever nature, creates?

Agathos. It must: but a true philosophy has long taught that the source of all motion is thought—and the source of all thought is—

Oinos. God.

Agathos. I have spoken to you, Oinos, as to a child of the fair Earth which lately perished—of impulses upon the atmosphere of the Earth.

Oinos. You did.

Agathos. And while I thus spoke, did there not cross your mind some thought of the *physical power of words?* Is not every word an impulse on the air?

Oinos. But why, Agathos, do you weep —and why—oh why do your wings droop as we hover above this fair star—which is the greenest and yet most terrible of all we have encountered in our flight? Its brilliant flowers look like a fairy dream —but its fierce volcanoes like the passions of a turbulent heart.[6]

Agathos. They *are!*—they *are!* This wild star—it is now three centuries since, with clasped hands, and with streaming eyes, at the feet of my beloved—I spoke it —with a few passionate sentences—into birth. Its brilliant flowers *are* the dearest of all unfulfilled dreams, and its raging volcanoes *are* the passions of the most turbulent and unhallowed of hearts.

THE CONVERSATION OF EIROS AND CHARMION

Πῦρ σοι προσοίσω.
I will bring fire to thee.
                    Euripides, *Andromache*[1]

Eiros. Why do you call me Eiros?

Charmion. So henceforward will you always be called. You must forget, too, *my* earthly name, and speak to me as Charmion.

Eiros. This is indeed no dream!

Charmion. Dreams are with us no more;—but of these mysteries anon. I rejoice to see you looking life-like and rational. The film of the shadow has already passed from off your eyes. Be of heart, and fear nothing. Your allotted days of stupor have expired; and, to-morrow, I will myself induct you into the full joys and wonders of your novel existence.

Eiros. True—I feel no stupor—none at all. The wild sickness and the terrible darkness have left me, and I hear no longer that mad, rushing, horrible sound, like the "voice of many waters."[2] Yet my senses are bewildered, Charmion, with the keenness of their perception of *the new*.

Charmion. A few days will remove all this;—but I fully understand you, and feel for you. It is now ten earthly years since I underwent what you undergo—yet the remembrance of it hangs by me still. You have now suffered all of pain, however, which you will suffer in Aidenn.[3]

Eiros. In Aidenn?

Charmion. In Aidenn.

Eiros. Oh God!—pity me, Charmion!—I am over-burthened with the majesty of all things—of the unknown now known—of the speculative Future merged in the august and certain Present.

Charmion. Grapple not now with such thoughts. To-morrow we will speak of this. Your mind wavers, and its agitation will find relief in the exercise of simple memories. Look not around, nor forward—but back. I am burning with anxiety to hear the details of that stupendous event which threw you among us. Tell me of it. Let us converse of familiar things, in the old familiar language of the world which has so fearfully perished.

Eiros. Most fearfully, fearfully!—this is indeed no dream.

Charmion. Dreams are no more. Was I much mourned, my Eiros?

Eiros. Mourned, Charmion?—oh deeply. To that last hour of all, there hung a cloud of intense gloom and devout sorrow over your household.

Charmion. And that last hour—speak of it. Remember that, beyond the naked fact of the catastrophe itself, I know nothing. When, coming out from among mankind, I passed into Night through the Grave—at that period, if I remember aright, the calamity which overwhelmed you was utterly unanticipated. But, indeed, I knew little of the speculative philosophy of the day.

Eiros. The individual calamity was, as you say, entirely unanticipated; but analogous misfortunes had been long a subject of discussion with astronomers. I need scarce tell you, my friend, that, even when you left us, men had agreed to understand those passages in the most holy writings[4] which speak of the final destruction of all things by fire, as having reference to the orb of the earth alone. But in regard to the immediate agency of the ruin, speculation had been at fault from that epoch in astronomical knowledge in which the comets were divested of the terrors of flame. The very moderate density of these bodies had been well established. They had been ob-

served to pass among the satellites of Jupiter, without bringing about any sensible alteration either in the masses or in the orbits of these secondary planets. We had long regarded the wanderers as vapory creations of inconceivable tenuity, and as altogether incapable of doing injury to our substantial globe, even in the event of contact. But contact was not in any degree dreaded; for the elements of all the comets were accurately known. That among *them* we should look for the agency of the threatened fiery destruction had been for many years considered an inadmissible idea. But wonders and wild fancies had been, of late days, strangely rife among mankind; and, although it was only with a few of the ignorant that actual apprehension prevailed, upon the announcement by astronomers of a *new* comet, yet this announcement was generally received with I know not what of agitation and mistrust.

The elements of the strange orb were immediately calculated, and it was at once conceded by all observers, that its path, at perihelion,[5] would bring it into very close proximity with the earth. There were two or three astronomers, of secondary note, who resolutely maintained that a contact was inevitable. I cannot very well express to you the effect of this intelligence upon the people. For a few short days they would not believe an assertion which their intellect, so long employed among worldly considerations, could not in any manner grasp. But the truth of a vitally important fact soon makes its way into the understanding of even the most stolid. Finally, all men saw that astronomical knowledge lied not, and they awaited the comet. Its approach was not, at first, seemingly rapid; nor was its appearance of very unusual character. It was of a dull red, and had little perceptible train. For seven or eight days we saw no material increase in its apparent diameter, and but a partial alteration in its color. Meantime, the ordinary affairs of men were discarded, and all interests absorbed in a growing discussion, instituted by the philosophic, in respect to the cometary nature. Even the grossly ignorant aroused their sluggish capacities to such considerations. The learned *now* gave their intellect—their soul—to no such points as the allaying of fear, or to the sustenance of loved theory. They sought—they panted for right views. They groaned for perfected knowledge. *Truth* arose in the purity of her strength and exceeding majesty, and the wise bowed down and adored.

That material injury to our globe or to its inhabitants would result from the apprehended contact, was an opinion which hourly lost ground among the wise; and the wise were now freely permitted to rule the reason and the fancy of the crowd. It was demonstrated, that the density of the comet's *nucleus* was far less than that of our rarest gas; and the harmless passage of a similar visitor among the satellites of Jupiter was a point strongly insisted upon, and which served greatly to allay terror. Theologists, with an earnestness fear-enkindled, dwelt upon the biblical prophecies, and expounded them to the people with a directness and simplicity of which no previous instance had been known. That the final destruction of the earth must be brought about by the agency of fire, was urged with a spirit that enforced everywhere conviction; and that the comets were of no fiery nature (as all men now knew) was a truth which relieved all, in a great measure, from the apprehension of the great calamity foretold. It is noticeable that the popular prejudices and vulgar errors in regard to pestilence and wars—errors which were wont to prevail upon every appearance of a comet—were now altogether unknown. As if by some sudden convulsive exertion, reason had at once hurled superstition from her throne.[6] The feeblest intellect had derived vigor from excessive interest.

What minor evils might arise from the contact were points of elaborate question. The learned spoke of slight geological disturbances, of probable alterations in climate, and consequently in vegetation; of possible magnetic and electric influences. Many held that no visible or perceptible effect would in any manner be produced. While such discussions were going on, their subject gradually approached, growing larger in apparent diameter, and of a more brilliant lustre. Mankind grew paler as it came. All human operations were suspended.

There was an epoch in the course of the general sentiment when the comet had attained, at length, a size surpassing that of any previously recorded visitation. The people now, dismissing any lingering hope that the astronomers were wrong, experienced all the certainty of evil. The chimerical aspect of their terror was gone. The hearts of the stoutest of our race beat violently within their bosoms. A very few days sufficed, however, to merge even such feelings in sentiments more unendurable. We could no longer apply to the strange orb any *accustomed* thoughts. Its *historical* attributes had disappeared. It oppressed us with a hideous *novelty* of emotion. We saw it not as an astronomical phenomenon in the heavens, but as an incubus upon our hearts, and a shadow upon our brains. It had taken, with inconceivable rapidity, the character of a gigantic mantle of rare flame, extending from horizon to horizon.

Yet a day, and men breathed with greater freedom. It was clear that we were already within the influence of the comet; yet we lived. We even felt an unusual elasticity of frame and vivacity of mind. The exceeding tenuity of the object of our dread was apparent; for all heavenly objects were plainly visible through it. Meantime, our vegetation had perceptibly altered; and we gained faith, from this predicted circumstance, in the foresight of the wise. A wild luxuriance of foliage, utterly unknown before, burst out upon every vegetable thing.

Yet another day—and the evil was not altogether upon us. It was now evident that its nucleus would first reach us. A wild change had come over all men; and the first sense of *pain* was the wild signal for general lamentation and horror. This first sense of pain lay in a rigorous constriction of the breast and lungs, and an insufferable dryness of the skin. It could not be denied that our atmosphere was radically affected; the conformation of this atmosphere and the possible modifications to which it might be subjected, were now the topics of discussion. The result of investigation sent an electric thrill of the intensest terror through the universal heart of man.

It had been long known that the air which encircled us was a compound of oxygen and nitrogen gases, in the proportion of twenty-one measures of oxygen, and seventy-nine of nitrogen, in every one hundred of the atmosphere. Oxygen, which was the principle of combustion, and the vehicle of heat, was absolutely necessary to the support of animal life, and was the most powerful and energetic agent in nature.[7] Nitrogen, on the contrary, was incapable of supporting either animal life or flame. An unnatural excess of oxygen would result, it had been ascertained, in just such an elevation of the animal spirits as we had latterly experienced. It was the pursuit, the extension of the idea, which had engendered awe. What would be the result of a total extraction of the nitrogen? A combustion irresistible, all-devouring, omniprevalent, immediate;—the entire fulfilment, in all their minute and terrible details, of the fiery and horror-inspiring denunciations of the prophecies of the Holy Book.

Why need I paint, Charmion, the now disenchained frenzy of mankind? That tenuity in the comet which had previously inspired us with hope, was now the source of the bitterness of despair. In its impalpable gaseous character we clearly perceived the consummation of Fate. Meantime a day again passed—bearing away with it the last shadow of Hope. We gasped in the rapid modification of the air. The red blood bounded tumultuously

through its strict channels. A furious delirium possessed all men; and, with arms rigidly outstretched towards the threatening heavens, they trembled and shrieked aloud. But the nucleus of the destroyer was now upon us;—even here in Aidenn, I shudder while I speak. Let me be brief —brief as the ruin that overwhelmed. For a moment there was a wild lurid light alone, visiting and penetrating all things. Then let us bow down, Charmion, before the excessive majesty of the great God!— then, there came a shouting and pervading sound, as if from the mouth itself of HIM; while the whole incumbent mass of ether in which we existed, burst at once into a species of intense flame, for whose surpassing brilliancy and all-fervid heat even the angels in the high Heaven of pure knowledge have no name. Thus ended all.

THE COLLOQUY OF MONOS AND UNA

Μέλλοντα ταῦτα
These things are in the near future.
                Sophocles, *Antigone*[1]

Una. "Born again?"

Monos. Yes, fairest and best beloved Una, "born again." These were the words upon whose mystical meaning I had so long pondered, rejecting the explanation of the priesthood, until Death himself resolved for me the secret.

Una. Death!

Monos. How strangely, sweet Una, you echo my words! I observe, too, a vacillation in your step—a joyous inquietude in your eyes. You are confused and oppressed by the majestic novelty[2] of the Life Eternal. Yes, it was of Death I spoke. And here how singularly sounds that word which of old was wont to bring terror to all hearts—throwing a mildew upon all pleasures!

Una. Ah, Death, the spectre which sate at all feasts! How often, Monos, did we lose ourselves in speculations upon its nature! How mysteriously did it act as a check to human bliss—saying unto it "thus far, and no farther!" That earnest mutual love, my own Monos, which burned within our bosoms—how vainly did we flatter ourselves, feeling happy in its first upspringing, that our happiness would strengthen with its strength! Alas! as it grew, so grew in our hearts the dread of that evil hour which was hurrying to separate us forever! Thus, in time, it became painful to love. Hate would have been mercy then.

Monos. Speak not here of these griefs, dear Una—mine, mine forever now!

Una. But the memory of past sorrow —is it not present joy? I have much to say yet of the things which have been. Above all, I burn to know the incidents of your own passage through the dark Valley and Shadow.

Monos. And when did the radiant Una ask any thing of her Monos in vain? I will be minute in relating all—but at what point shall the weird narrative begin?

Una. At what point?

Monos. You have said.

Una. Monos, I comprehend you. In Death we have both learned the propensity of man to define the indefinable. I will not say, then, commence with the moment of life's cessation—but commence with that sad, sad instant when, the fever having abandoned you, you sank into a breathless and motionless torpor, and I pressed down your pallid eyelids with the passionate fingers of love.

Monos. One word first, my Una, in regard to man's general condition at this epoch. You will remember that one or two of the wise among our forefathers— wise in fact, although not in the world's esteem—had ventured to doubt the propriety of the term "improvement," as applied to the progress of our civilization. There were periods in each of the five or six centuries immediately preceding our dissolution, when arose some vigorous intellect, boldly contending for those principles whose truth appears now, to our disenfranchised reason, so utterly obvious

—principles which should have taught our race to submit to the guidance of the natural laws, rather than attempt their control. At long intervals some masterminds appeared, looking upon each advance in practical science as a retrogradation in the true utility. Occasionally the poetic intellect—that intellect which we now feel to have been the most exalted of all—since those truths to us were of the most enduring importance and could only be reached by that *analogy* which speaks in proof-tones to the imagination alone, and to the unaided reason bears no weight —occasionally did this poetic intellect proceed a step farther in the evolving of the vague idea of the philosophic, and find in the mystic parable[3] that tells of the tree of knowledge, and of its forbidden fruit, death-producing, a distinct intimation that knowledge was not meet for man in the infant condition of his soul. And these men, the poets, living and perishing amid the scorn of the "utilitarians"—of rough pedants, who arrogated to themselves a title which could have been properly applied only to the scorned—these men, the poets, ponder piningly, yet not unwisely, upon the ancient days when our wants were not more simple than our enjoyments were keen—days when *mirth* was a word unknown, so solemnly deeptoned was happiness—holy, august, and blissful days, when blue rivers ran undammed, between hills unhewn, into far forest solitudes, primæval, odorous, and unexplored.

Yet these noble exceptions from the general misrule served but to strengthen it by opposition. Alas! we had fallen upon the most evil of all our evil days. The great "movement"—that was the cant term—went on: a diseased commotion, moral and physical. Art—the Arts—arose supreme, and, once enthroned, cast chains upon the intellect which had elevated them to power. Man, because he could not but acknowledge the majesty of Nature, fell into childish exultation at his acquired and still-increasing dominion over her elements. Even while he stalked a God in his own fancy, an infantine imbecility came over him. As might be supposed from the origin of his disorder, he grew infected with system, and with abstraction. He enwrapped himself in generalities. Among other odd ideas, that of universal equality gained ground; and in the face of analogy and of God—in despite of the loud warning voice of the laws of *gradation* so visibly pervading all things in Earth and Heaven—wild attempts at an omniprevalent Democracy were made. Yet this evil sprang necessarily from the leading evil—Knowledge. Man could not both know and succumb. Meantime huge smoking cities arose, innumerable. Green leaves shrank before the hot breath of furnaces. The fair face of Nature was deformed as with the ravages of some loathsome disease. And methinks, sweet Una, even our slumbering sense of the forced and of the far-fetched might have arrested us here. But now it appears that we had worked out our own destruction in the perversion of our *taste,* or rather in the blind neglect of its culture in the schools. For, in truth, it was at this crisis that taste alone—that faculty which, holding a middle position between the pure intellect and the moral sense, could never safely have been disregarded—it was now that taste alone could have led us gently back to Beauty, to Nature, and to Life. But alas for the pure contemplative spirit and majestic intuition of Plato! Alas for the μουσική which he justly regarded as an all sufficient education for the soul! Alas for him and for it!—since both were most desperately needed when both were most entirely forgotten or despised.[4]

Pascal, a philosopher whom we both love, has said, how truly!—"*que tout notre raisonnement se réduit à céder au sentiment*"; and it is not impossible that the sentiment of the natural, had time permitted it, would have regained its old ascendancy over the harsh mathematical reason of the schools. But this thing was not to be. Prematurely induced by intemperance of knowledge, the old age of the world drew on. This the mass of mankind saw not, or, living lustily although unhappily, affected not to see. But, for myself, the Earth's records had taught me to look for widest ruin as the price of highest civilization. I had imbibed a prescience of our Fate from comparison of China the simple and enduring, with Assyria the architect, with Egypt the astrologer, with Nubia, more crafty than either, the turbulent mother of all Arts. In history of these regions I met with a ray from the Future. The individual artificialities of the three latter were local diseases of the Earth, and in their individual overthrows we had seen local remedies applied; but for the infected world at large I could anticipate no regeneration save in death. That man, as a race, should not become extinct, I saw that he must be "*born again.*"[5]

And now it was, fairest and dearest, that we wrapped our spirits, daily, in dreams. Now it was that, in twilight, we discoursed of the days to come, when the Art-scarred surface of the Earth, having undergone that purification which alone could efface its rectangular obscenities, should clothe itself anew in the verdure and the mountain-slopes and the smiling waters of Paradise, and be rendered at length a fit dwelling-place for man:—for man the Death-purged—for man to whose now exalted intellect there should be poison in knowledge no more—for the redeemed, regenerated, blissful, and now immortal, but still for the *material,*[6] man.

Una. Well do I remember these conversations, dear Monos; but the epoch of the fiery overthrow was not so near at hand as we believed, and as the corruption you indicate did surely warrant us in believing. Men lived; and died individually. You yourself sickened, and passed into the grave; and thither your constant Una speedily followed you. And though the century which has since elapsed, and whose conclusion brings us thus together once more, tortured our slumbering senses with no impatience of duration, yet, my Monos, it was a century still.

Monos. Say, rather, a point in the vague infinity. Unquestionably, it was in the Earth's dotage that I died. Wearied at heart with anxieties which had their origin in the general turmoil and decay, I succumbed to the fierce fever. After some few days of pain, and many of dreamy delirium replete with ecstasy, the manifestations of which you mistook for pain, while I longed but was impotent to undeceive you—after some days there came upon me, as you have said, a breathless and motionless torpor; and this was termed *Death* by those who stood around me.

Words are vague things. My condition did not deprive me of sentience. It appeared to me not greatly dissimilar to the extreme quiescence of him, who, having slumbered long and profoundly, lying motionless and fully prostrate in a midsummer noon, begins to steal slowly back into consciousness, through the mere sufficiency of his sleep, and without being awakened by external disturbances.

I breathed no longer. The pulses were still. The heart had ceased to beat. Volition had not departed, but was powerless. The senses were unusually active, although eccentrically so—assuming often each other's functions at random.[7] The taste and the smell were inextricably confounded, and became one sentiment, abnormal and intense. The rosewater with which your tenderness had moistened my lips to the last, affected me with sweet fancies of flowers—fantastic flowers, far more lovely than any of the old Earth, but whose prototypes we have here blooming around us. The eyelids, transparent and bloodless, offered no complete impediment to vision. As volition was in abeyance, the balls could not roll in their sockets—but all objects within the range of the visual hemisphere were seen with more or less distinctness; the rays which fell upon the external retina, or into the corner of the eye, producing a more vivid

effect than those which struck the front or anterior surface. Yet, in the former instance, this effect was so far anomalous that I appreciated it only as *sound*—sound sweet or discordant as the matters presenting themselves at my side were light or dark in shade—curved or angular in outline. The hearing at the same time, although excited in degree, was not irregular in action—estimating real sounds with an extravagance of precision, not less than of sensibility. Touch had undergone a modification more peculiar. Its impressions were tardily received, but pertinaciously retained, and resulted always in the highest physical pleasure. Thus the pressure of your sweet fingers upon my eyelids, at first only recognized through vision, at length, long after their removal, filled my whole being with a sensual delight immeasurable. I say with a sensual delight. *All* my perceptions were purely sensual. The materials furnished the passive brain by the senses were not in the least degree wrought into shape by the deceased understanding. Of pain there was some little; of pleasure there was much; but of moral pain or pleasure none at all. Thus your wild sobs floated into my ear with all their mournful cadences, and were appreciated in their every variation of sad tone; but they were soft musical sounds and no more; they conveyed to the extinct reason no intimation of the sorrows which gave them birth; while the large and constant tears which fell upon my face, telling the bystanders of a heart which broke, thrilled every fibre of my frame with ecstasy alone. And this was in truth the *Death* of which these bystanders spoke reverently, in low whispers —you, sweet Una, gaspingly, with loud cries.

They attired me for the coffin—three or four dark figures which flitted busily to and fro. As these crossed the direct line of my vision they affected me as *forms*; but upon passing to my side their images impressed me with the idea of shrieks, groans, and other dismal expressions of terror, of horror, or of woe. You alone, habited in a white robe, passed in all directions musically about me.

The day waned; and, as its light faded away, I became possessed by a vague uneasiness—an anxiety such as the sleeper feels when sad real sounds fall continuously within his ear—low distant bell tones, solemn, at long but equal intervals, and commingling with melancholy dreams. Night arrived; and with its shadows a heavy discomfort. It oppressed my limbs with the oppression of some dull weight, and was palpable. There was also a moaning sound, not unlike the distant reverberation of surf, but more continuous, which, beginning with the first twilight, had grown in strength with the darkness. Suddenly lights were brought into the room, and this reverberation became forthwith interrupted into frequent unequal bursts of the same sound, but less dreary and less distinct. The ponderous oppression was in a great measure relieved; and, issuing from the flame of each lamp (for there were many), there flowed unbrokenly into my ears a strain of melodious monotone. And when now, dear Una, approaching the bed upon which I lay outstretched, you sat gently by my side, breathing odor from your sweet lips, and pressing them upon my brow, there arose tremulously within my bosom, and mingling with the merely physical sensations which circumstances had called forth, a something akin to sentiment itself—a feeling that, half appreciating, half responded to your earnest love and sorrow; but this feeling took no root in the pulseless heart, and seemed indeed rather a shadow than a reality, and faded quickly away, first into extreme quiescence, and then into a purely sensual pleasure as before.[8]

And now, from the wreck and the chaos of the usual senses, there appeared to have arisen within me a sixth, all perfect. In its exercise I found a wild delight—yet a delight still physical, inasmuch as the understanding in it had no part. Motion in the animal frame had fully ceased. No muscle quivered; no nerve thrilled; no artery throbbed. But there seemed to have sprung up in the brain, *that* of which no words could convey to the merely human intelligence even an indistinct conception. Let me term it a mental pendulous pulsation. It was the moral embodiment of man's abstract idea of *Time*. By the absolute equalization of this movement—or of such as this—had the cycles of the firmamental orbs themselves, been adjusted. By its aid I measured the irregularities of the clock upon the mantel, and of the watches of the attendants. Their tickings came sonorously to my ears. The slightest deviation from the true proportion—and these deviations were omniprevalent—affected me just as violations of abstract truth are wont, on earth, to affect the moral sense. Although no two of the timepieces in the chamber struck individual seconds accurately together, yet I had no difficulty in holding steadily in mind the tones, and the respective momentary errors of each. And this—this keen, perfect, self-existing sentiment of *duration*—this sentiment existing (as man could not possibly have conceived it to exist) independently of any succession of events—this idea—this sixth sense, upspringing from the ashes of the rest, was the first obvious and certain step of the intemporal soul upon the threshold of the temporal Eternity.

It was midnight; and you still sat by my side. All others had departed from the chamber of Death. They had deposited me in the coffin. The lamps burned flickeringly; for this I knew by the tremulousness of the monotonous strains. But, suddenly these strains diminished in distinctness and in volume. Finally they ceased. The perfume in my nostrils died away. Forms affected my vision no longer. The oppression of the Darkness uplifted itself from my bosom. A dull shock like that of electricity pervaded my frame, and was followed by total loss of the idea of contact. All of what man has termed sense was merged in the sole consciousness of entity, and in the one abiding sentiment of duration. The mortal body had been at length stricken with the hand of the deadly *Decay*.

Yet had not all of sentience departed; for the consciousness and the sentiment remaining supplied some of its functions by a lethargic intuition. I appreciated the direful change now in operation upon the flesh, and, as the dreamer is sometimes aware of the bodily presence of one who leans over him, so, sweet Una, I still dully felt that you sat by my side. So, too, when the noon of the second day came, I was not unconscious of those movements which displaced you from my side, which confined me within the coffin, which deposited me within the hearse, which bore me to the grave, which lowered me within it, which heaped heavily the mould upon me, and which thus left me, in blackness and corruption, to my sad and solemn slumbers with the worm.

And here, in the prison-house which has few secrets to disclose, there rolled away days and weeks and months; and the soul watched narrowly each second as it flew, and, without effort, took record of its flight—without effort and without object.

A year passed. The consciousness of *being* had grown hourly more indistinct, and that of mere *locality* had, in great measure, usurped its position. The idea of entity was becoming merged in that of *place*. The narrow space immediately surrounding what had been the body, was now going to be the body itself. At length, as often happens to the sleeper (by sleep and its world alone is *Death* imaged)—at length, as sometimes happened on Earth to the deep slumberer, when some flitting light half startled him into awaking, yet left him half enveloped in dreams—so to me, in the strict embrace of the *Shadow*, came *that* light which alone might have had power to startle—the light of enduring *Love*. Men toiled at the grave in which I lay darkling. They upthrew the damp

earth. Upon my mouldering bones there descended the coffin of Una.

And now again all was void. That nebulous light had been extinguished. That feeble thrill had vibrated itself into quiescence. Many *lustra*[9] had supervened. Dust had returned to dust. The worm had food no more. The sense of being had at length utterly departed, and there reigned in its stead—instead of all things—dominant and perpetual—the autocrats *Place* and *Time*. For *that* which *was not*—for that which had no form—for that which had no thought—for that which had no sentience—for that which was soulless, yet of which matter formed no portion—for all this nothingness, yet for all this immortality, the grave was still a home, and the corrosive hours, co-mates.

SHADOW

A Parable

Yea! though I walk through the valley of the Shadow:
                              Psalm of David[1]

Ye who read are still among the living: but I who write shall have long since gone my way into the region of shadows. For indeed strange things shall happen, and secret things be known, and many centuries shall pass away, ere these memorials be seen of men. And, when seen, there will be some to disbelieve, and some to doubt, and yet a few who will find much to ponder upon in the characters here graven with a stylus of iron.

The year had been a year of terror, and of feelings more intense than terror for which there is no name upon the earth. For many prodigies and signs had taken place, and far and wide, over sea and land, the black wings of the Pestilence were spread abroad. To those, nevertheless, cunning in the stars, it was not unknown that the heavens wore an aspect of ill; and to me, the Greek Oinos, among others, it was evident that now had arrived the alternation of that seven hundred and ninety-fourth year when, at the entrance of Aries, the planet Jupiter is conjoined with the red ring of the terrible Saturnus.[2] The peculiar spirit of the skies, if I mistake not greatly, made itself manifest, not only in the physical orb of the earth, but in the souls, imaginations, and meditations of mankind.

Over some flasks of the red Chian wine, within the walls of a noble hall, in a dim city called Ptolemais, we sat, at night, a company of seven. And to our chamber there was no entrance save by a lofty door of brass: and the door was fashioned by the artizan Corinnos, and, being of rare workmanship, was fastened from within. Black draperies, likewise, in the gloomy room, shut out from our view the moon, the lurid stars, and the peopleless streets —but the boding and the memory of Evil, they would not be so excluded. There were things around us and about of which I can render no distinct account—things material and spiritual—heaviness in the atmosphere—a sense of suffocation—anxiety—and, above all, that terrible state of existence which the nervous experience when the senses are keenly living and awake, and meanwhile the powers of thought lie dormant. A dead weight hung upon us. It hung upon our limbs—upon the household furniture—upon the goblets from which we drank; and all things were depressed, and borne down thereby —all things save only the flames of the seven iron lamps which illumined our revel. Uprearing themselves in tall slender lines of light, they thus remained burning all pallid and motionless; and in the mirror which their lustre formed upon the round table of ebony at which we sat, each of us there assembled beheld the pallor of his own countenance, and the unquiet glare in the downcast eyes of his companions. Yet we laughed and were merry in our proper way—which was hysterical; and sang the songs of Anacreon—which are madness; and drank deeply—although the purple wine reminded us of blood. For

there was yet another tenant of our chamber in the person of young Zoilus. Dead, and at full length he lay, enshrouded;— the genius and the demon of the scene. Alas! he bore no portion in our mirth, save that his countenance, distorted with the plague, and his eyes in which Death had but half extinguished the fire of the pestilence, seemed to take such interest in our merriment as the dead may haply take in the merriment of those who are to die. But although I, Oinos, felt that the eyes of the departed were upon me, still I forced myself not to perceive the bitterness of their expression, and, gazing down steadily into the depths of the ebony mirror, sang with a loud and sonorous voice the songs of the son of Teios. But gradually my songs they ceased, and their echoes, rolling afar off among the sable draperies of the chamber, became weak, and undistinguishable, and so faded away. And lo! from among those sable draperies where the sounds of the song departed, there came forth a dark and undefined shadow—a shadow such as the moon, when low in heaven, might fashion from the figure of a man: but it was the shadow neither of man, nor of God, nor of any familiar thing. And, quivering awhile among the draperies of the room, it at length rested in full view upon the surface of the door of brass. But the shadow was vague, and formless, and indefinite, and was the shadow neither of man, nor of God—neither God of Greece, nor God of Chaldæa, nor any Egyptian God. And the shadow rested upon the brazen doorway, and under the arch of the entablature of the door, and moved not, nor spoke any word, but there became stationary and remained. And the door whereupon the shadow rested was, if I remember aright, over against the feet of the young Zoilus enshrouded. But we, the seven there assembled, having seen the shadow as it came out from among the draperies, dared not steadily behold it, but cast down our eyes, and gazed continually into the depths of the mirror of ebony. And at length I, Oinos, speaking some low words, demanded of the shadow its dwelling and its appellation. And the shadow answered, "I am shadow, and my dwelling is near to the Catacombs of Ptolemais, and hard by those dim plains of Helusion which border upon the foul Charonian canal."[3] And then did we, the seven, start from our seats in horror, and stand trembling, and shuddering, and aghast: for the tones in the voice of the shadow were not the tones of any one being, but of a multitude of beings, and, varying in their cadences from syllable to syllable, fell duskily upon our ears in the well remembered and familiar accents of many thousand departed friends.

SILENCE

A Fable[1]

Εὔδουσιν δ' ὀρέων κορυφαί τε καὶ φάραγγες
Πρώονές τε καὶ χαράδραι.
The mountain pinnacles slumber; valleys, crags and caves **are silent.**
                    Alcman.[2]

"Listen to *me*," said the Demon, as he placed his hand upon my head. "The region of which I speak is a dreary region in Libya, by the borders of the river Zäire.[3] And there is no quiet there, nor silence.

"The waters of the river have a saffron and sickly hue; and they flow not onwards to the sea, but palpitate forever and forever beneath the red eye of the sun with a tumultuous and convulsive motion. For many miles on either side of the river's oozy bed is a pale desert of gigantic water-lilies.[4] They sigh one unto the other in that solitude, and stretch towards the heaven their long and ghastly necks, and nod to and fro their everlasting heads. And there is an indistinct murmur which cometh out from among them like the rushing of subterrene water. And they sigh one unto the other.

"But there is a boundary to their realm —the boundary of the dark, horrible, lofty forest. There, like the waves about the Hebrides, the low underwood is agitated continually. But there is no wind throughout the heaven. And the tall primeval trees rock eternally hither and thither with a crashing and mighty sound. And from their high summits, one by one, drop everlasting dews. And at the roots strange poisonous flowers lie writhing in perturbed slumber. And overhead, with a rustling and loud noise, the gray clouds rush westwardly forever, until they roll, a cataract, over the fiery wall of the horizon. But there is no wind throughout the heaven. And by the shores of the river Zäire there is neither quiet nor silence.

"It was night, and the rain fell; and, falling, it was rain, but, having fallen, it was blood. And I stood in the morass among the tall lilies, and the rain fell upon my head—and the lilies sighed one unto the other in the solemnity of their desolation.

"And, all at once, the moon arose through the thin ghastly mist, and was crimson in colour. And mine eyes fell upon a huge gray rock which stood by the shore of the river, and was lighted by the light of the moon. And the rock was gray, and ghastly, and tall,—and the rock was gray. Upon its front were characters engraven in the stone; and I walked through the morass of water-lilies, until I came close unto the shore, that I might read the characters upon the stone. But I could not decypher them. And I was going back into the morass, when the moon shone with a fuller red, and I turned and looked again upon the rock, and upon the characters;—and the characters were desolation.

"And I looked upwards, and there stood a man upon the summit of the rock; and I hid myself among the water-lilies that I might discover the actions of the man. And the man was tall and stately in form, and was wrapped up from his shoulders to his feet in the toga of old Rome. And the outlines of his figure were indistinct —but his features were the features of a deity; for the mantle of the night, and of the mist, and of the moon, and of the dew, had left uncovered the features of his face. And his brow was lofty with thought, and his eye wild with care; and, in the few furrows upon his cheek I read the fables of sorrow, and weariness, and disgust with mankind, and a longing after solitude.[5]

"And the man sat upon the rock, and leaned his head upon his hand, and looked out upon the desolation. He looked down into the low unquiet shrubbery, and up into the tall primeval trees, and up higher at the rustling heaven, and into the crimson moon. And I lay close within shelter of the lilies, and observed the actions of the man. And the man trembled in the solitude;—but the night waned, and he sat upon the rock.

"And the man turned his attention from the heaven, and looked out upon the dreary river Zäire, and upon the yellow ghastly waters, and upon the pale legions of the water-lilies. And the man listened to the sighs of the water-lilies, and to the murmur that came up from among them. And I lay close within my covert and observed the actions of the man. And the man trembled in the solitude;—but the night waned and he sat upon the rock.

"Then I went down into the recesses of the morass, and waded afar in among the wilderness of the lilies, and called unto the hippopotami which dwelt among the fens in the recesses of the morass. And the hippopotami heard my call, and came, with the behemoth,[6] unto the foot of the rock, and roared loudly and fearfully beneath the moon. And I lay close within my covert and observed the actions of the man. And the man trembled in the solitude;—but the night waned and he sat upon the rock.

"Then I cursed the elements with the curse of tumult; and a frightful tempest gathered in the heaven where, before, there had been no wind. And the heaven became livid with the violence of the tempest—and the rain beat upon the head of the man—and the floods of the river came down—and the river was tormented into foam—and the water-lilies shrieked within their beds—and the forest crumbled before the wind—and the thunder rolled—and the lightning fell—and the rock rocked to its foundation. And I lay close within my covert and observed the actions of the man. And the man trembled in the solitude;—but the night waned and he sat upon the rock.

"Then I grew angry and cursed, with the curse of *silence*, the river, and the lilies, and the wind, and the forest, and the heaven, and the thunder, and the sighs of the water-lilies. And they became accursed, and *were still*. And the moon ceased to totter up its pathway to heaven—and the thunder died away—and the lightning did not flash—and the clouds hung motionless—and the waters sunk to their level and remained—and the trees ceased to rock—and the water-lilies sighed no more—and the murmur was heard no longer from among them, nor any shadow of sound throughout the vast illimitable desert. And I looked upon the characters of the rock, and they were changed;—and the characters were SILENCE.[7]

"And mine eyes fell upon the countenance of the man, and his countenance was wan with terror. And, hurriedly, he raised his head from his hand, and stood forth upon the rock and listened. But there was no voice throughout the vast illimitable desert, and the characters upon the rock were SILENCE. And the man shuddered, and turned his face away, and fled afar off, in haste, so that I beheld him no more."

Now there are fine tales in the volumes of the Magi—in the iron-bound, melancholy volumes of the Magi. Therein, I say, are glorious histories of the Heaven, and of the Earth, and of the mighty sea—and of the Genii that over-ruled the sea, and the earth, and the lofty heaven. There was much lore too in the sayings which were said by the Sybils; and holy, holy things were heard of old by the dim leaves that trembled around Dodona—but, as Allah liveth, that fable which the Demon told me as he sat by my side in the shadow of the tomb, I hold to be the most wonderful of all! And as the Demon made an end of his story, he fell back within the cavity of the tomb and laughed. And I could not laugh with the Demon, and he cursed me because I could not laugh. And the lynx[8] which dwelleth forever in the tomb, came out therefrom, and lay down at the feet of the Demon, and looked at him steadily in the face.

A TALE OF
THE RAGGED MOUNTAINS

During the fall of the year 1827, while residing near Charlottesville, Virginia, I casually made the acquaintance of Mr. Augustus Bedloe.[1] This young gentleman was remarkable in every respect, and excited in me a profound interest and curiosity. I found it impossible to comprehend him either in his moral or his physical relations. Of his family I could obtain no satisfactory account. Whence he came, I never ascertained. Even about his age—although I call him a young gentleman—there was something which perplexed me in no little degree. He certainly *seemed* young—and he made a point of speaking about his youth—yet there were moments when I should have had little trouble in imagining him a hundred years of age. But in no regard was he more peculiar than in his personal appearance. He was singularly tall and thin. He stooped much. His limbs were exceedingly long and emaciated. His forehead was broad and low. His complexion was absolutely bloodless. His mouth was large and flexible, and his teeth were more wildly uneven, although sound, than I had ever before seen teeth in a human head. The expression of his smile, however, was by no means unpleasing, as might be supposed; but it had no variation whatever.

It was one of profound melancholy—of a phaseless and unceasing gloom. His eyes were abnormally large, and round like those of a cat. The pupils, too, upon any accession or diminution of light, underwent contraction or dilation, just such as is observed in the feline tribe. In moments of excitement the orbs grew bright to a degree almost inconceivable; seeming to emit luminous rays, not of a reflected, but of an intrinsic lustre, as does a candle or the sun; yet their ordinary condition was so totally vapid, filmy and dull, as to convey the idea of the eyes of a long-interred corpse.

These peculiarities of person appeared to cause him much annoyance, and he was continually alluding to them in a sort of half explanatory, half apologetic strain, which, when I first heard it, impressed me very painfully. I soon, however, grew accustomed to it, and my uneasiness wore off. It seemed to be his design rather to insinuate than directly to assert that, physically, he had not always been what he was—that a long series of neuralgic attacks had reduced him from a condition of more than usual personal beauty, to that which I saw. For many years past he had been attended by a physician, named Templeton—an old gentleman, perhaps seventy years of age—whom he had first encountered at Saratoga,[2] and from whose attention, while there, he either received, or fancied that he received, great benefit. The result was that Bedloe, who was wealthy, had made an arrangement with Doctor Templeton, by which the latter, in consideration of a liberal annual allowance, had consented to devote his time and medical experience exclusively to the care of the invalid.

Doctor Templeton had been a traveller in his younger days, and, at Paris, had become a convert, in great measure, to the doctrines of Mesmer. It was altogether by means of magnetic remedies that he had succeeded in alleviating the acute pains of his patient; and this success had very naturally inspired the latter with a certain degree of confidence in the opinions from which the remedies had been educed. The Doctor, however, like all enthusiasts, had struggled hard to make a thorough convert of his pupil, and finally so far gained his point as to induce the sufferer to submit to numerous experiments.—By a frequent repetition of these, a result had arisen, which of late days has become so common as to attract little or no attention, but which, at the period of which I write, had very rarely been known in America. I mean to say, that between Doctor Templeton and Bedloe there had grown up, little by little, a very distinct and strongly marked *rapport*,[3] or magnetic relation. I am not prepared to assert, however, that this *rapport* extended beyond the limits of the simple sleep-producing power; but this power itself had attained great intensity. At the first attempt to induce the magnetic somnolency, the mesmerist entirely failed. In the fifth or sixth he succeeded very partially, and after long continued effort. Only at the twelfth was the triumph complete. After this the will of the patient succumbed rapidly to that of the physician, so that, when I first became acquainted with the two, sleep was brought about almost instantaneously, by the mere volition of the operator, even when the invalid was unaware of his presence. It is only now, in the year 1845, when similar miracles are witnessed daily by thousands, that I dare venture to record this apparent impossibility as a matter of serious fact.

The temperament of Bedloe was, in the highest degree, sensitive, excitable, enthusiastic. His imagination was singularly vigorous and creative; and no doubt it derived additional force from the habitual use of morphine, which he swallowed in great quantity, and without which he would have found it impossible to exist.[4] It was his practice to take a very large dose of it immediately after breakfast, each morning—or rather immediately after a cup of strong coffee, for he ate nothing in the forenoon—and then set forth alone, or attended only by a dog, upon a long ramble among the chain of wild and dreary hills that lie westward and southward of Charlottesville, and are there dignified by the title of the Ragged Mountains.

Upon a dim, warm, misty day, towards the close of November, and during the strange *interregnum* of the seasons which in America is termed the Indian Summer, Mr. Bedloe departed, as usual, for the hills. The day passed, and still he did not return.

About eight o'clock at night, having become seriously alarmed at his protracted absence, we were about setting out in search of him, when he unexpectedly made his appearance, in health no worse than usual, and in rather more than ordinary spirits. The account which he gave of his expedition, and of the events which had detained him, was a singular one indeed.

"You will remember," said he, "that it was about nine in the morning when I left Charlottesville. I bent my steps immediately to the mountains, and, about ten, entered a gorge which was entirely new to me. I followed the windings of this pass with much interest.—The scenery which presented itself on all sides, although scarcely entitled to be called grand, had about it an indescribable, and to me, a delicious aspect of dreary desolation. The solitude seemed absolutely virgin. I could not help believing that the green sods and the gray rocks upon which I trod, had been trodden never before by the foot of a human being. So entirely secluded, and in fact inaccessible, except through a series of accidents, is the entrance of the ravine, that it is by no means impossible that I was indeed the first adventurer—the very first and sole adventurer who had ever penetrated its recesses.

"The thick and peculiar mist, or smoke, which distinguishes the Indian Summer, and which now hung heavily over all objects, served, no doubt, to deepen the vague impressions which these objects created. So dense was this pleasant fog, that I could at no time see more than a dozen yards of the path before me. This path[5] was excessively sinuous, and as the sun could not be seen, I soon lost all idea of the direction in which I journeyed. In the meantime the morphine had its customary effect—that of enduing all the external world with an intensity of interest. In the quivering of a leaf—in the hue of a blade of grass—in the shape of a trefoil —in the humming of a bee—in the gleaming of a dew-drop—in the breathing of the wind—in the faint odors that came from the forest—there came a whole universe of suggestion—a gay and motly train of rhapsodical and immethodical thought.

"Busied in this, I walked on for several hours, during which the mist deepened around me to so great an extent, that at length I was reduced to an absolute groping of the way. And now an indescribable uneasiness possessed me—a species of nervous hesitation and tremor.—I feared to tread, lest I should be precipitated into some abyss. I remembered, too, strange stories told about these Ragged Hills, and of the uncouth and fierce races of men who tenanted their groves and caverns. A thousand vague fancies oppressed and disconcerted me—fancies the more distressing because vague. Very suddenly my attention was arrested by the loud beating of a drum.

"My amazement was, of course, extreme. A drum in these hills was a thing unknown. I could not have been more surprised at the sound of the trump of the Archangel. But a new and still more astounding source of interest and perplexity arose. There came a wild rattling or jingling sound, as if of a bunch of large keys—and upon the instant a dusky-visaged and half-naked man rushed past me with a shriek. He came so close to my person that I felt his hot breath upon my face. He bore in one hand an instrument composed of an assemblage of steel rings,

and shook them vigorously as he ran. Scarcely had he disappeared in the mist, before, panting after him, with open mouth and glaring eyes, there darted a huge beast. I could not be mistaken in its character. It was a hyena.

"The sight of this monster rather relieved than heightened my terrors—for I now made sure that I dreamed, and endeavored to arouse myself to waking consciousness. I stepped boldly and briskly forward. I rubbed my eyes. I called aloud. I pinched my limbs. A small spring of water presented itself to my view, and here, stooping, I bathed my hands and my head and neck. This seemed to dissipate the equivocal sensations which had hitherto annoyed me. I arose, as I thought, a new man, and proceeded steadily and complacently on my unknown way.

"At length, quite overcome by exertion, and by a certain oppressive closeness of the atmosphere, I seated myself beneath a tree. Presently there came a feeble gleam of sunshine, and the shadow of the leaves of the tree fell faintly but definitely upon the grass. At this shadow I gazed wonderingly for many minutes. Its character stupified me with astonishment. I looked upward. The tree was a palm.

"I now arose hurriedly, and in a state of fearful agitation—for the fancy that I dreamed would serve me no longer. I saw —I felt that I had perfect command of my senses—and these senses now brought to my soul a world of novel and singular sensation. The heat became all at once intolerable. A strange odor loaded the breeze.—A low continuous murmur, like that arising from a full, but gently-flowing river, came to my ears, intermingled with the peculiar hum of multitudinous human voices.

"While I listened in an extremity of astonishment which I need not attempt to describe, a strong and brief gust of wind bore off the incumbent fog as if by the wand of an enchanter.[6]

"I found myself at the foot of a high mountain, and looking down into a vast plain, through which wound a majestic river. On the margin of this river stood an Eastern-looking city, such as we read of in the Arabian Tales, but of a character even more singular than any there described. From my position, which was far above the level of the town, I could perceive its every nook and corner, as if delineated on a map. The streets seemed innumerable, and crossed each other irregularly in all directions, but were rather long winding alleys than streets, and absolutely swarmed with inhabitants. The houses were wildly picturesque. On every hand was a wilderness of balconies, of verandahs, of minarets, of shrines, and fantastically carved oriels. Bazaars abounded; and in these were displayed rich wares in infinite variety and profusion—silks, muslins, the most dazzling cutlery, the most magnificent jewels and gems. Besides these things, were seen, on all sides, banners and palanquins, litters with stately dames close veiled, elephants gorgeously caparisoned, idols grotesquely hewn, drums, banners and gongs, spears, silver and gilded maces. And amid the crowd, and the clamor, and the general intricacy and confusion—amid the million of black and yellow men, turbaned and robed, and of flowing beard, there roamed a countless multitude of holy filleted[7] bulls, while vast legions of the filthy but sacred ape clambered, chattering and shrieking, about the cornices of the mosques, or clung to the minarets and oriels. From the swarming streets to the banks of the river, there descended innumerable flights of steps leading to bathing places, while the river itself seemed to force a passage with difficulty through the vast fleets of deeply-burthened ships that far and wide encumbered its surface. Beyond the limits of the city arose, in frequent majestic groups, the palm and the cocoa, with other gigantic and weird trees of vast age; and here and there might be seen a field of rice, the thatched hut of a peasant, a tank, a stray temple, a gypsy camp, or a solitary graceful maiden taking her way, with a pitcher upon her head, to the banks of the magnificent river.

"You will say now, of course, that I dreamed; but not so. What I saw—what I heard—what I felt—what I thought—had about it nothing of the unmistakeable idiosyncrasy of the dream. All was rigorously self-consistent. At first, doubting that I was really awake, I entered into a series of tests, which soon convinced me that I really was. Now, when one dreams, and, in the dream, suspects that he dreams, the suspicion *never fails to confirm itself,* and the sleeper is almost immediately aroused.—Thus Novalis errs not in saying that 'we are near waking when we dream that we dream.'[8] Had the vision occurred to me as I describe it, without my suspecting it as a dream, then a dream it might absolutely have been, but, occurring as it did, and suspected and tested as it was, I am forced to class it among other phenomena."

"In this I am not sure that you are wrong," observed Dr. Templeton, "but proceed. You arose and descended into the city."

"I arose," continued Bedloe, regarding the Doctor with an air of profound astonishment, "I arose, as you say, and descended into the city. On my way, I fell in with an immense populace, crowding, through every avenue, all in the same direction, and exhibiting in every action the wildest excitement. Very suddenly, and by some inconceivable impulse, I became intensely imbued with personal interest in what was going on. I seemed to feel that I had an important part to play, without exactly understanding what it was. Against the crowd which environed me, however, I experienced a deep sentiment of animosity. I shrank from amid them, and, swiftly, by a circuitous path, reached and entered the city. Here all was the wildest tumult and contention. A small party of men, clad in garments half-Indian, half European, and officered by gentlemen in a uniform partly British, were engaged, at great odds, with the swarming rabble of the alleys. I joined the weaker party, arming myself with the weapons of a fallen officer, and fighting I knew not whom with the nervous ferocity of despair. We were soon overpowered by numbers, and driven to seek refuge in a species of kiosk. Here we barricaded ourselves, and, for the present, were secure. From a loop-hole near the summit of the kiosk, I perceived a vast crowd, in furious agitation, surrounding and assaulting a gay palace that overhung the river. Presently, from an upper window of this palace, there descended an effeminate-looking person, by means of a string made of the turbans of his attendants. A boat was at hand, in which he escaped to the opposite bank of the river.

"And now a new object took possession of my soul. I spoke a few hurried but energetic words to my companions, and, having succeeded in gaining over a few of them to my purpose, made a frantic sally from the kiosk. We rushed amid the crowd that surrounded it. They retreated, at first, before us. They rallied, fought madly, and retreated again. In the mean time we were borne far from the kiosk, and became bewildered and entangled among the narrow streets of tall overhanging houses, into the recesses of which the sun had never been able to shine. The rabble pressed impetuously upon us, harassing us with their spears, and overwhelming us with flights of arrows. These latter were very remarkable, and resembled in some respects the writing creese[9] of the Malay. They were made to imitate the body of a creeping serpent, and were long and black, with a poisoned barb. One of them struck me upon the right temple. I reeled and fell. An instantaneous and dreadful sickness seized me. I struggled—I gasped—I died."

"You will hardly persist *now*," said I, smiling, "that the whole of your adventure was not a dream. You are not prepared to maintain that you are dead?"

When I said these words, I of course expected some lively sally from Bedloe in reply; but, to my astonishment, he hesitated, trembled, became fearfully pallid, and remained silent. I looked towards Templeton. He sat erect and rigid in his chair—his teeth chattered, and his eyes were starting from their sockets. "Proceed!" he at length said hoarsely to Bedloe.

"For many minutes," continued the latter, "my sole sentiment—my sole feeling —was that of darkness and nonentity, with the consciousness of death. At length, there seemed to pass a violent and sudden shock through my soul, as if of electricity. With it came the sense of elasticity and of light. This latter I felt—not saw. In an instant I seemed to rise from the ground. But I had no bodily, no visible, audible, or palpable presence. The crowd had departed. The tumult had ceased. The city was in comparative repose. Beneath me lay my corpse, with the arrow in my temple, the whole head greatly swollen and disfigured. But all these things I felt—not saw. I took interest in nothing. Even the corpse seemed a matter in which I had no concern. Volition I had none, but appeared to be impelled into motion, and flitted buoyantly out of the city, retracing the circuitous path by which I had entered it. When I had attained that point of the ravine in the mountains, at which I had encountered the hyena, I again experienced a shock as of a galvanic battery; the sense of weight, of volition, of substance, returned. I became my original self, and bent my steps eagerly homewards—but the past had not lost the vividness of the real—and not now even for an instant, can I compel my understanding to regard it as a dream."

"Nor was it," said Templeton, with an air of deep solemnity, "yet it would be difficult to say how otherwise it should be termed. Let us suppose only, that the soul of the man of to-day is upon the verge of some stupendous psychal discoveries.[10] Let us content ourselves with this supposition. For the rest I have some explanation to make. Here is a water-colour drawing, which I should have shown you before, but which an unaccountable sentiment of horror has hitherto prevented me from showing."

We looked at the picture which he presented. I saw nothing in it of an extraordinary character; but its effect upon Bedloe was prodigious. He nearly fainted as he gazed. And yet it was but a miniature portrait—a miraculously accurate one, to be sure—of his own very remarkable features. At least this was my thought as I regarded it.

"You will perceive," said Templeton, "the date of this picture—it is here, scarcely visible, in this corner—1780. In this year was the portrait taken. It is the likeness of a dead friend—a Mr. Oldeb—to whom I became much attached at Calcutta, during the administration of Warren Hastings.[11] I was then only twenty years old.—When I first saw you, Mr. Bedloe, at Saratoga, it was the miraculous similarity which existed between yourself and the painting, which induced me to accost you, to seek your friendship, and to bring about those arrangements which resulted in my becoming your constant companion. In accomplishing this point, I was urged partly, and perhaps principally, by a regretful memory of the deceased, but also, in part, by an uneasy, and not altogether horrorless curiosity respecting yourself.

"In your detail of the vision which presented itself to you amid the hills, you have described, with the minutest accuracy, the Indian city of Benares, upon the Holy River. The riots, the combats, the massacre, were the actual events of the insurrection of Cheyte Sing, which took place in 1780, when Hastings was put in imminent peril of his life. The man escaping by the string of turbans, was Cheyte Sing himself. The party in the kiosk were sepoys[12] and British officers, headed by Hastings. Of this party I was one, and did all I could to prevent the

rash and fatal sally of the officer who fell, in the crowded alleys, by the poisoned arrow of a Bengalee. That officer was my dearest friend. It was Oldeb. You will perceive by these manuscripts," (here the speaker produced a note-book in which several pages appeared to have been freshly written) "that at the very period in which you fancied these things amid the hills, I was engaged in detailing them upon paper here at home."

In about a week after this conversation, the following paragraphs appeared in a Charlottesville paper.

"We have the painful duty of announcing the death of Mr. AUGUSTUS BEDLO, a gentleman whose amiable manners and many virtues have long endeared him to the citizens of Charlottesville.

"Mr. B., for some years past, has been subject to neuralgia, which has often threatened to terminate fatally; but this can be regarded only as the mediate cause of his decease. The proximate cause was one of especial singularity. In an excursion to the Ragged Mountains, a few days since, a slight cold and fever were contracted, attended with great determination of blood to the head. To relieve this, Dr. Templeton resorted to topical bleeding. Leeches were applied to the temples. In a fearfully brief period the patient died, when it appeared that, in the jar containing the leeches, had been introduced, by accident, one of the venomous vermicular sangsues[13] which are now and then found in the neighboring ponds. This creature fastened itself upon a small artery in the right temple. Its close resemblance to the medicinal leech caused the mistake to be overlooked until too late.

"N.B. The poisonous sangsue of Charlottesville may always be distinguished from the medicinal leech by its blackness, and especially by its writhing or vermicular motions, which very nearly resemble those of a snake."

I was speaking with the editor of the paper in question, upon the topic of this remarkable accident, when it occurred to me to ask how it happened that the name of the deceased had been given as Bedlo.

"I presume," said I, "you have authority for this spelling, but I have always supposed the name to be written with an *e* at the end."

"Authority?—no," he replied. "It is a mere typographical error. The name is Bedlo with an *e*, all the world over, and I never knew it to be spelt otherwise in my life."

"Then," said I mutteringly, as I turned upon my heel, "then indeed has it come to pass that one truth is stranger than any fiction—for Bedlo, without the *e*, what is it but Oldeb conversed? And this man tells me it is a typographical error."

THE FACTS IN THE CASE OF M. VALDEMAR[1]

Of course I shall not pretend to consider it any matter for wonder, that the extraordinary case of M. Valdemar has excited discussion. It would have been a miracle had it not—especially under the circumstances. Through the desire of all parties concerned, to keep the affair from the public, at least for the present, or until we had farther opportunities for investigation—through our endeavours to effect this—a garbled or exaggerated account made its way into society, and became the source of many unpleasant misrepresentations, and, very naturally, of a great deal of disbelief.

It is now rendered necessary that I give the *facts*—as far as I comprehend them myself. They are, succinctly, these:

My attention for the last three years, had been repeatedly drawn to the subject of Mesmerism; and, about nine months ago, it occurred to me, quite suddenly, that in the series of experiments made hitherto, there had been a very remarkable and most unaccountable omission:—no person had as yet been mesmerized *in articulo mortis*. It remained to be seen, first, whether, in such condition, there

existed in the patient any susceptibility to the magnetic[2] influence; secondly, whether, if any existed, it was impaired or increased by the condition; thirdly, to what extent, or for how long a period, the encroachments of Death might be arrested by the process. There were other points to be ascertained, but these most excited my curiosity—the last in especial, from the immensely important character of its consequences.

In looking around me for some subject by whose means I might test these particulars, I was brought to think of my friend, M. Ernest Valdemar, the well-known compiler of the "Bibliotheca Forensica," and author (under the *nom de plume* of Issachar Marx) of the Polish version of "Wallenstein" and "Gargantua." M. Valdemar, who has resided principally at Harlaem, N.Y., since the year 1839, is (or was) particularly noticeable for the extreme spareness of his person —his lower limbs much resembling those of John Randolph; and, also, for the whiteness of his whiskers, in violent contrast to the blackness of his hair—the latter, in consequence, being very generally mistaken for a wig. His temperament was markedly nervous, and rendered him a good subject for mesmeric experiment. On two or three occasions I had put him to sleep with little difficulty, but was disappointed in other results which his peculiar constitution had naturally led me to anticipate. His will was at no period positively, or thoroughly, under my control, and in regard to *clairvoyance*, I could accomplish with him nothing to be relied upon. I always attributed my failure at these points to the disordered state of his health. For some months previous to my becoming acquainted with him, his physicians had declared him in a confirmed phthisis.[3] It was his custom, indeed, to speak calmly of his approaching dissolution, as of a matter neither to be avoided nor regretted.

When the ideas to which I have alluded first occurred to me, it was of course very natural that I should think of M. Valdemar. I knew the steady philosophy of the man too well to apprehend any scruples from *him*; and he had no relatives in America who would be likely to interfere. I spoke to him frankly upon the subject; and, to my surprise, his interest seemed vividly excited. I say to my surprise; for, although he had always yielded his person freely to my experiments, he had never before given me any tokens of sympathy with what I did. His disease was of that character which would admit of exact calculation in respect to the epoch of its termination in death; and it was finally arranged between us that he would send for me about twenty-four hours before the period announced by his physicians as that of his decease.

It is now rather more than seven months since I received, from M. Valdemar himself, the subjoined note:

MY DEAR P——,
    You may as well come *now*. D—— and F—— are agreed that I cannot hold out beyond to-morrow midnight; and I think they have hit the time very nearly.
                                   VALDEMAR.

I received this note within half an hour after it was written, and in fifteen minutes more I was in the dying man's chamber. I had not seen him for ten days, and was appalled by the fearful alteration which the brief interval had wrought in him. His face wore a leaden hue; the eyes were utterly lustreless; and the emaciation was so extreme that the skin had been broken through by the cheek-bones. His expectoration was excessive. The pulse was barely perceptible. He retained, nevertheless, in a very remarkable manner, both his mental power and a certain degree of physical strength. He spoke with distinctness— took some palliative medicines without aid—and, when I entered the room, was occupied in penciling memoranda in a pocket-book. He was propped up in the bed by pillows. Doctors D—— and F—— were in attendance.

After pressing Valdemar's hand, I took these gentlemen aside, and obtained from them a minute account of the patient's condition. The left lung had been for eighteen months in a semi-osseous or cartilaginous state, and was, of course, entirely useless for all purposes of vitality. The right, in its upper portion, was also partially, if not thoroughly, ossified, while the lower region was merely a mass of purulent tubercles, running one into another. Several extensive perforations existed; and, at one point, permanent adhesion to the ribs had taken place. These appearances in the right lobe were of comparatively recent date. The ossification had proceeded with very unusual rapidity; no sign of it had been discovered a month before, and the adhesion had only been observed during the three previous days. Independently of the phthisis, the patient was suspected of aneurism of the aorta;[4] but on this point the osseous symptoms rendered an exact diagnosis impossible. It was the opinion of both physicians that M. Valdemar would die about midnight on the morrow (Sunday). It was then seven o'clock on Saturday evening.

On quitting the invalid's bed-side to hold conversation with myself, Doctors D—— and F—— had bidden him a final farewell. It had not been their intention to return; but, at my request, they agreed to look in upon the patient about ten the next night.

When they had gone, I spoke freely with M. Valdemar on the subject of his approaching dissolution, as well as, more particularly, of the experiment proposed. He still professed himself quite willing and even anxious to have it made, and urged me to commence it at once. A male and a female nurse were in attendance; but I did not feel myself altogether at liberty to engage in a task of this character with no more reliable witnesses than these people, in case of sudden accident, might prove. I therefore postponed operations until about eight the next night, when the arrival of a medical student with whom I had some acquaintance, (Mr. Theodore L——l,) relieved me from farther embarrassment. It had been my design, originally, to wait for the physicians; but I was induced to proceed, first, by the urgent entreaties of M. Valdemar, and secondly, by my conviction that I had not a moment to lose, as he was evidently sinking fast.

Mr. L——l was so kind as to accede to my desire that he would take notes of all that occurred; and it is from his memoranda that what I now have to relate is, for the most part, either condensed or copied *verbatim*.[5]

It wanted about five minutes of eight when, taking the patient's hand, I begged him to state, as distinctly as he could, to Mr. L——l, whether he (M. Valdemar) was entirely willing that I should make the experiment of mesmerizing him in his then condition.

He replied feebly, yet quite audibly, "Yes, I wish to be mesmerized"—adding immediately afterwards, "I fear you have deferred it too long."

While he spoke thus, I commenced the passes which I had already found most effectual in subduing him. He was evidently influenced with the first lateral stroke of my hand across his forehead; but although I exerted all my powers, no farther perceptible effect was induced until some minutes after ten o'clock, when Doctors D—— and F—— called, according to appointment. I explained to them, in a few words, what I designed, and as they opposed no objection, saying that the patient was already in the death agony, I proceeded without hesitation—exchanging, however, the lateral passes for downward ones, and directing my gaze entirely into the right eye of the sufferer.

By this time his pulse was imperceptible and his breathing was stertorous,[6] and at intervals of half a minute.

This condition was nearly unaltered for a quarter of an hour. At the expiration of this period, however, a natural although a very deep sigh escaped the bosom of the dying man, and the stertorous breathing ceased—that is to say, its stertorousness was no longer apparent; the intervals were undiminished. The patient's extremities were of an icy coldness.

At five minutes before eleven I perceived unequivocal signs of the mesmeric influence. The glassy roll of the eye was changed for that expression of uneasy *inward* examination which is never seen except in cases of sleep-waking, and which it is quite impossible to mistake. With a few rapid lateral passes I made the lids quiver, as in incipient sleep, and with a few more I closed them altogether. I was not satisfied, however, with this, but continued the manipulations vigorously, and with the fullest exertion of the will, until I had completely stiffened the limbs of the slumberer, after placing them in a seemingly easy position. The legs were at full length; the arms were nearly so, and reposed on the bed at a moderate distance from the loins. The head was very slightly elevated.

When I had accomplished this, it was fully midnight, and I requested the gentlemen present to examine M. Valdemar's condition. After a few experiments, they admitted him to be in an unusually perfect state of mesmeric trance. The curiosity of both the physicians was greatly excited. Dr. D—— resolved at once to remain with the patient all night, while Dr. F—— took leave with a promise to return at daybreak. Mr. L——l and the nurses remained.

We left M. Valdemar entirely undisturbed until about three o'clock in the morning, when I approached him and found him in precisely the same condition as when Dr. F—— went away—that is to say, he lay in the same position; the pulse was imperceptible; the breathing was gentle (scarcely noticeable, unless through the application of a mirror to the lips); the eyes were closed naturally; and the limbs were as rigid and as cold as marble. Still, the general appearance was certainly not that of death.

As I approached M. Valdemar I made a kind of half effort to influence his right arm into pursuit of my own, as I passed the latter gently to and fro above his person. In such experiments with this patient I had never perfectly succeeded before, and assuredly I had little thought of succeeding now; but to my astonishment, his arm very readily, although feebly, followed every direction I assigned it with mine. I determined to hazard a few words of conversation.

"M. Valdemar," I said, "are you asleep?" He made no answer, but I perceived a tremor about the lips, and was thus induced to repeat the question, again and again. At its third repetition, his whole frame was agitated by a very slight shivering; the eyelids unclosed themselves so far as to display a white line of the ball; the lips moved sluggishly, and from between them, in a barely audible whisper, issued the words:

"Yes;—asleep now. Do not wake me! —let me die so!"

I here felt the limbs and found them as rigid as ever. The right arm, as before, obeyed the direction of my hand. I questioned the sleep-waker again:

"Do you still feel pain in the breast, M. Valdemar?"

The answer now was immediate, but even less audible than before:

"No pain—I am dying."

I did not think it advisable to disturb him farther just then, and nothing more was said or done until the arrival of Dr. F——, who came a little before sunrise, and expressed unbounded astonishment at finding the patient still alive. After feeling the pulse and applying a mirror to the lips, he requested me to speak to the sleep-waker again. I did so, saying:

"M. Valdemar, do you still sleep?"

As before, some minutes elapsed ere a reply was made; and during the interval the dying man seemed to be collecting his energies to speak. At my fourth repetition of the question, he said very faintly, almost inaudibly:

"Yes; still asleep—dying."

It was now the opinion, or rather the wish, of the physicians, that M. Valdemar should be suffered to remain undisturbed in his present apparently tranquil condition, until death should supervene—and this, it was generally agreed, must now take place within a few minutes. I concluded, however, to speak to him once more, and merely repeated my previous question.

While I spoke, there came a marked change over the countenance of the sleep-waker. The eyes rolled themselves slowly open, the pupils disappearing upwardly; the skin generally assumed a cadaverous hue, resembling not so much parchment as white paper; and the circular hectic spots which, hitherto, had been strongly defined in the centre of each cheek, *went out* at once. I use this expression, because the suddenness of their departure put me in mind of nothing so much as the extinguishment of a candle by a puff of the breath. The upper lip, at the same time, writhed itself away from the teeth, which it had previously covered completely; while the lower jaw fell with an audible jerk, leaving the mouth widely extended, and disclosing in full view the swollen and blackened tongue. I presume that no member of the party then present had been unaccustomed to death-bed horrors; but so hideous beyond conception was the appearance of M. Valdemar at this moment, that there was a general shrinking back from the region of the bed.

I now feel that I have reached a point of this narrative at which every reader will be startled into positive disbelief. It is my business, however, simply to proceed.

There was no longer the faintest sign of vitality in M. Valdemar; and concluding him to be dead, we were consigning him to the charge of the nurses, when a strong vibratory motion was observable in the tongue. This continued for perhaps a minute. At the expiration of this period, there issued from the distended and motionless jaws a voice—such as it would be madness in me to attempt describing. There are, indeed, two or three epithets which might be considered as applicable to it in part; I might say, for example, that the sound was harsh, and broken and hollow; but the hideous whole is indescribable, for the simple reason that no similar sounds have ever jarred upon the ear of humanity. There were two particulars, nevertheless, which I thought then, and still think, might fairly be stated as characteristic of the intonation—as well adapted to convey some idea of its unearthly peculiarity. In the first place, the voice seemed to reach our ears—at least mine—from a vast distance, or from some deep cavern within the earth. In the second place, it impressed me (I fear, indeed, that it will be impossible to make myself comprehended) as gelatinous or glutinous matters impress the sense of touch.

I have spoken both of "sound" and of "voice." I mean to say that the sound was one of distinct—of even wonderfully, thrillingly distinct—syllabification. M. Valdemar *spoke*—obviously in reply to the question I had propounded to him a few minutes before. I had asked him, it will be remembered, if he still slept. He now said:

"Yes;—no;—I *have been* sleeping—and now—now—*I am dead.*"

No person present even affected to deny, or attempted to repress, the unutterable, shuddering horror which these few words, thus uttered, were so well calculated to convey. Mr. L——l (the student) swooned.[7] The nurses immediately left the chamber, and could not be induced to return. My own impressions I would not pretend to render intelligible to the reader. For nearly an hour, we busied ourselves, silently—without the utterance of a word—in endeavours to revive Mr. L——l. When he came to himself, we addressed ourselves again to an investigation of M. Valdemar's condition.

It remained in all respects as I have last described it, with the exception that the

mirror no longer afforded evidence of respiration. An attempt to draw blood from the arm failed. I should mention, too, that this limb was no farther subject to my will. I endeavoured in vain to make it follow the direction of my hand. The only real indication, indeed, of the mesmeric influence, was now found in the vibratory movement of the tongue, whenever I addressed M. Valdemar a question. He seemed to be making an effort to reply, but had no longer sufficient volition. To queries put to him by any other person than myself he seemed utterly insensible—although I endeavoured to place each member of the company in mesmeric *rapport* with him. I believe that I have now related all that is necessary to an understanding of the sleep-waker's state at this epoch. Other nurses were procured; and at ten o'clock I left the house in company with the two physicians and Mr. L——l.

In the afternoon we all called again to see the patient. His condition remained precisely the same. We had now some discussion as to the propriety and feasibility of awakening him; but we had little difficulty in agreeing that no good purpose would be served by so doing. It was evident that, so far, death (or what is usually termed death) had been arrested by the mesmeric process. It seemed clear to us all that to awaken M. Valdemar would be merely to insure his instant, or at least his speedy dissolution.

From this period until the close of last week—*an interval of nearly seven months*—we continued to make daily calls at M. Valdemar's house, accompanied, now and then, by medical and other friends. All this time the sleep-waker remained *exactly* as I have last described him. The nurses' attentions were continual.

It was on Friday last that we finally resolved to make the experiment of awakening, or attempting to awaken him; and it is the (perhaps) unfortunate result of this latter experiment which has given rise to so much discussion in private circles—to so much of what I cannot help thinking unwarranted popular feeling.

For the purpose of relieving M. Valdemar from the mesmeric trance, I made use of the customary passes. These, for a time, were unsuccessful. The first indication of revival was afforded by a partial descent of the iris. It was observed, as especially remarkable, that this lowering of the pupil was accompanied by the profuse outflowing of a yellowish ichor[8] (from beneath the lids) of a pungent and highly offensive odor.

It was now suggested that I should attempt to influence the patient's arm, as heretofore. I made the attempt and failed. Dr. F—— then intimated a desire to have me put a question. I did so, as follows:

"M. Valdemar, can you explain to us what are your feelings or wishes now?"

There was an instant return of the hectic circles on the cheeks; the tongue quivered, or rather rolled violently in the mouth (although the jaws and lips remained rigid as before;) and at length the same hideous voice which I have already described, broke forth:

"For God's sake!—quick!—quick!—put me to sleep—or, quick!—waken me!—quick!—*I say to you that I am dead!*"

I was thoroughly unnerved, and for an instant remained undecided what to do. At first I made an endeavour to re-compose the patient; but, failing in this through total abeyance of the will, I retraced my steps and as earnestly struggled to awaken him. In this attempt I soon saw that I should be successful—or at least I soon fancied that my success would be complete—and I am sure that all in the room were prepared to see the patient awaken.

For what really occurred, however, it is quite impossible that any human being could have been prepared.

As I rapidly made the mesmeric passes, amid ejaculations of "dead! dead!" absolutely *bursting* from the tongue and not from the lips of the sufferer, his whole frame at once—within the space of a single minute, or even less, shrunk—crumbled—absolutely *rotted* away beneath my hands. Upon the bed, before that whole company, there lay a nearly liquid mass of loathsome—of detestable putridity.

MESMERIC REVELATION

Whatever doubt may still envelop the *rationale* of mesmerism, its startling *facts* are now almost universally admitted. Of these latter, those who doubt, are your mere doubters by profession—an unprofitable and disreputable tribe. There can be no more absolute waste of time than the attempt to *prove*, at the present day, that man, by mere exercise of will, can so impress his fellow, as to cast him into an abnormal condition, in which the phenomena resemble very closely those of *death*, or at least resemble them more nearly than they do the phenomena of any other normal condition within our cognizance; that, while in this state, the person so impressed employs only with effort, and then feebly, the external organs of sense, yet perceives, with keenly refined perception, and through channels supposed unknown, matters beyond the scope of the physical organs; that, moreover, his intellectual faculties are wonderfully exalted and invigorated; that his sympathies with the person so impressing him are profound; and, finally, that his susceptibility to the impression increases with its frequency, while, in the same proportion, the peculiar phenomena elicited are more extended and more *pronounced*.

I say that these—which are the laws of mesmerism in its general features—it would be supererogation to demonstrate; nor shall I inflict upon my readers so needless a demonstration to-day. My purpose at present is a very different one indeed. I am impelled, even in the teeth of a world of prejudice, to detail, without comment, the very remarkable substance of a colloquy occurring between a sleep-waker and myself.

I had been long in the habit of mesmer-izing the person in question (Mr. Van-kirk,) and the usual acute susceptibility and exaltation of the mesmeric percep-tion had supervened. For many months he had been labouring under confirmed phthisis,[1] the more distressing effects of which had been relieved by my manipu-lations; and on the night of Wednesday, the fifteenth instant, I was summoned to his bedside.

The invalid was suffering with acute pain in the region of the heart, and breathed with great difficulty, having all the ordinary symptoms of asthma. In spasms such as these he had usually found relief from the application of mustard to the nervous centres, but to-night this had been attempted in vain.

As I entered his room he greeted me with a cheerful smile, and although evi-dently in much bodily pain, appeared to be, mentally, quite at ease.

"I sent for you to-night," he said, "not so much to administer to my bodily ail-ment, as to satisfy me concerning certain psychal impressions which, of late, have occasioned me much anxiety and surprise. I need not tell you how sceptical I have hitherto been on the topic of the soul's immortality. I cannot deny that there has always existed, as if in that very soul which I have been denying, a vague half-sentiment of its own existence. But this half-sentiment at no time amounted to conviction. With it my reason had noth-ing to do. All attempts at logical inquiry resulted, indeed, in leaving me more scep-tical than before. I had been advised to study Cousin. I studied him in his own works as well as in those of his European and American echoes. The 'Charles El-wood' of Mr. Brownson, for example, was placed in my hands. I read it with pro-found attention. Throughout I found it logical, but the portions which were not *merely* logical were unhappily the initial arguments of the disbelieving hero of the book. In his summing up it seemed evi-dent to me that the reasoner had not even succeeded in convincing himself. His end had plainly forgotten his beginning, like the government of Trinculo.[2] In short, I was not long in perceiving that if man is to be intellectually convinced of his own immortality, he will never be so con-vinced by the mere abstractions which have been so long the fashion of the mor-alists of England, of France, and of Ger-many. Abstractions may amuse and exer-cise, but take no hold on the mind. Here upon earth, at least, philosophy, I am per-suaded, will always in vain call upon us to look upon qualities as things. The will may assent—the soul—the intellect, never.

"I repeat, then, that I only half felt, and never intellectually believed. But latterly there has been a certain deepening of the feeling, until it has come so nearly to re-semble the acquiescence of reason, that I find it difficult to distinguish between the two. I am enabled, too, plainly to trace this effect to the mesmeric influence. I cannot better explain my meaning than by the hypothesis that the mesmeric ex-altation enables me to perceive a train of ratiocination which, in my abnormal ex-istence, convinces, but which, in full ac-cordance with the mesmeric phenomena, does not extend, except through its *effect*, into my normal condition. In sleep-wak-ing, the reasoning and its conclusion—the cause and its effect—are present together. In my natural state, the cause vanishing, the effect only, and perhaps only partially, remains.

"These considerations have led me to think that some good results might ensue from a series of well-directed questions propounded to me while mesmerized. You have often observed the profound self-cognizance evinced by the sleep-waker—the extensive knowledge he displays upon all points relating to the mesmeric condi-tion itself; and from this self-cognizance may be deduced hints for the proper con-duct of a catechism."

I consented of course to make this experiment. A few passes threw Mr. Vankirk into the mesmeric sleep. His breathing became immediately more easy, and he seemed to suffer no physical uneasiness. The following conversation then ensued:—*V.* in the dialogue representing the patient, and *P.* myself.

P. Are you asleep?

V. Yes—no; I would rather sleep more soundly.

P. *[After a few more passes.]* Do you sleep now?

V. Yes.

P. How do you think your present illness will result?

V. *[After a long hesitation and speaking as if with effort.]* I must die.

P. Does the idea of death afflict you?

V. *[Very quickly.]* No—no!

P. Are you pleased with the prospect?

V. If I were awake I should like to die, but now it is no matter. The mesmeric condition is so near death as to content me.

P. I wish you would explain yourself, Mr. Vankirk.

V. I am willing to do so, but it requires more effort than I feel able to make. You do not question me properly.

P. What then shall I ask?

V. You must begin at the beginning.

P. The beginning! But where is the beginning?

V. You know that the beginning is GOD. *[This was said in a low, fluctuating tone, and with every sign of the most profound veneration.]*

P. What, then, is God?

V. *[Hesitating for many minutes.]* I cannot tell.

P. Is not God spirit?

V. While I was awake I knew what you meant by "spirit," but now it seems only a word—such, for instance, as truth, beauty—a quality, I mean.

P. Is not God immaterial?

V. There is no immateriality; it is a mere word. That which is not matter, is not at all—unless qualities are things.

P. Is God, then, material?

V. No. *[This reply startled me' very much.]*

P. What, then, is he?

V. *[After a long pause, and mutteringly.]* I see—but it is a thing difficult to tell. *[Another long pause.]* He is no spirit, for he exists. Nor is he matter, *as you understand it.* But there are *gradations* of matter of which man knows nothing; the grosser impelling the finer, the finer pervading the grosser. The atmosphere, for example, impels the electric principle, while the electric principle permeates the atmosphere. These gradations of matter increase in rarity or fineness, until we arrive at a matter *unparticled*—without particles—indivisible—*one*; and here the law of impulsion and permeation is modified. The ultimate or unparticled matter not only permeates all things, but impels all things; and thus *is* all things within itself. This matter is God. What men attempt to embody in the word "thought," is this matter in motion.[3]

P. The metaphysicians maintain that all action is reducible to motion and thinking, and that the latter is the origin of the former.

V. Yes; and I now see the confusion of idea. Motion is the action of *mind,* not of *thinking.* The unparticled matter, or God, in quiescence, is (as nearly as we can conceive it) what men call mind. And the power of self-movement (equivalent in effect to human volition) is, in the unparticled matter, the result of its unity and omniprevalence; *how,* I know not, and now clearly see that I shall never know. But the unparticled matter, set in motion by a law or quality existing within itself, is thinking.

P. Can you give me no more precise idea of what you term the unparticled matter?

V. The matters of which man is cognizant escape the senses in gradation. We have, for example, a metal, a piece of wood, a drop of water, the atmosphere, a gas, caloric,[4] electricity, the luminiferous

ether. Now, we call all these things matter, and embrace all matter in one general
definition; but in spite of this, there can
be no two ideas more essentially distinct
than that which we attach to a metal, and
that which we attach to the luminiferous
ether. When we reach the latter, we feel
an almost irresistible inclination to class
it with spirit, or with nihility. The only
consideration which restrains us is our
conception of its atomic constitution; and
here, even, we have to seek aid from our
notion of an atom, as something possessing in infinte minuteness, solidity, palpability, weight. Destroy the idea of the
atomic constitution and we should no
longer be able to regard the ether as an
entity, or, at least, as matter. For want of
a better word we might term it spirit.
Take, now, a step beyond the luminiferous ether; conceive a matter as much more
rare than the ether, as this ether is more
rare than the metal, and we arrive at once
(in spite of all the school dogmas) at a
unique mass—an unparticled matter. For
although we may admit infinite littleness
in the atoms themselves, the infinitude
of littleness in the spaces between them is
an absurdity. There will be a point—there
will be a degree of rarity at which, if the
atoms are sufficiently numerous, the interspaces must vanish, and the mass absolutely coalesce. But the consideration of
the atomic constitution being now taken
away, the nature of the mass inevitably
glides into what we conceive of spirit. It
is clear, however, that it is as fully matter
as before. The truth is, it is impossible to
conceive spirit, since it is impossible to
imagine what is not. When we flatter ourselves that we have formed its conception,
we have merely deceived our understanding by the consideration of infinitely rar-
ified matter.

P. There seems to me an insurmount-
able objection to the idea of absolute coalescence;—and that is the very slight
resistance experienced by the heavenly
bodies in their revolutions through space
—a resistance now ascertained, it is true,

to exist in *some* degree, but which is, nevertheless, so slight as to have been quite
overlooked by the sagacity even of Newton. We know that the resistance of bodies
is, chiefly, in proportion to their density.
Absolute coalescence is absolute density.
Where there are no interspaces, there can
be no yielding. An ether, absolutely dense,
would put an infinitely more effectual
stop to the progress of a star than would
an ether of adamant or of iron.

V. Your objection is answered with
an ease which is nearly in the ratio of
its apparent unanswerability.—As regards
the progress of the star, it can make no
difference whether the star passes through
the ether *or the ether through it.* There is
no astronomical error more unaccountable than that which reconciles the
known retardation of the comets with the
idea of their passage through an ether; for,
however rare this ether be supposed, it
would put a stop to all sidereal revolution
in a very far briefer period than has been
admitted by those astronomers who have
endeavoured to slur over a point which
they found it impossible to comprehend.
The retardation actually experienced is,
on the other hand, about that which
might be expected from the *friction* of
the ether in the instantaneous passage
through the orb. In the one case, the retarding force is momentary and complete
within itself—in the other it is endlessly
accumulative.[5]

P. But in all this—in this identification of mere matter with God—is there
nothing of irreverence? [*I was forced to
repeat this question before the sleep-
waker fully comprehended my meaning.*]

V. Can you say *why* matter should be
less reverenced than mind? But you forget
that the matter of which I speak is, in all
respects, the very "mind" or "spirit" of
the schools, so far as regards its high capacities, and is, moreover, the "matter" of
these schools at the same time. God, with
all the powers attributed to spirit, is but
the perfection of matter.

P. You assert, then, that the unparticled matter, in motion, is thought.

V. In general, this motion is the universal thought of the universal mind. This thought creates. All created things are but the thoughts of God.

P. You say, "in general."

V. Yes. The universal mind is God. For new individualities, *matter* is necessary.

P. But you now speak of "mind" and "matter" as do the metaphysicians.

V. Yes—to avoid confusion. When I say "mind," I mean the unparticled or ultimate matter; by "matter," I intend all else.

P. You were saying that "for new individualities matter is necessary."

V. Yes: for mind, existing unincorporate, is merely God. To create individual, thinking beings, it was necessary to incarnate portions of the divine mind. Thus man is individualized. Divested of corporate investiture, he were God. Now the particular motion of the incarnated portions of the unparticled matter is the thought of man; as the motion of the whole is that of God.

P. You say that divested of the body man will be God?

V. [*After much hesitation.*] I could not have said this; it is an absurdity.

P. [*Referring to my notes.*] You *did* say that "divested of corporate investiture man were God."

V. And this is true. Man thus divested *would* be God—would be unindividualized.[6] But he can never be thus divested —at least never *will be*—else we must imagine an action of God returning upon itself—a purposeless and futile action. Man is a creature. Creatures are thoughts of God. It is the nature of thought to be irrevocable.

P. I do not comprehend. You say that man will never put off the body?

V. I say that he will never be bodiless.

P. Explain.

V. There are two bodies—the rudimental and the complete, corresponding with the two conditions of the worm and the butterfly. What we call "death," is but the painful metamorphosis. Our present incarnation is progressive, preparatory, temporary. Our future is perfected, ultimate, immortal. The ultimate life is the full design.

P. But of the worm's metamorphosis we are palpably cognizant.

V. *We*, certainly—but not the worm. The matter of which our rudimental body is composed, is within the ken of the organs of that body; or, more distinctly, our rudimental organs are adapted to the matter of which is formed the rudimental body; but not to that of which the ultimate is composed. The ultimate body thus escapes our rudimental senses, and we perceive only the shell which falls, in decaying, from the inner form; not that inner form itself; but this inner form, as well as the shell, is appreciable by those who have already acquired the ultimate life.

P. You have often said that the mesmeric state very nearly resembles death. How is this?

V. When I say that it resembles death, I mean that it resembles the ultimate life; for when I am entranced the senses of my rudimental life are in abeyance, and I perceive external things directly, without organs, through a medium which I shall employ in the ultimate, unorganized life.

P. Unorganized?

V. Yes; organs are contrivances by which the individual is brought into sensible relation with particular classes and forms of matter, to the exclusion of other classes and forms. The organs of man are adapted to his rudimental condition, and to that only; his ultimate condition, being unorganized, is of unlimited comprehension in all points but one—the nature of the volition of God—that is to say, the motion of the unparticled matter. You will have a distinct idea of the ultimate body by conceiving it to be entire brain. This it is *not*; but a conception of this nature will bring you near a comprehension of what it *is*. A luminous body imparts vibration to the luminiferous ether. The vibrations generate similar ones within the retina; these again communicate similar ones to the optic nerve. The nerve conveys similar ones to the brain; the brain, also, similar ones to the unparticled matter which permeates it. The motion of this latter is thought, of which perception is the first undulation. This is the mode by which the mind of the rudimental life communicates with the external world; and this external world is, to the rudimental life, limited, through the idiosyncrasy of its organs. But in the ultimate, unorganized life, the external world reaches the whole body, (which is of a substance having affinity to brain, as I have said,) with no other intervention than that of an infinitely rarer ether than even the luminiferous; and to this ether—in unison with it—the whole body vibrates, setting in motion the unparticled matter which permeates it. It is to the absence of idiosyncratic organs, therefore, that we must attribute the nearly unlimited perception of the ultimate life. To rudimental beings, organs are the cages necessary to confine them until fledged.

P.   You speak of rudimental "beings." Are there other rudimental thinking beings than man?

V.   The multitudinous conglomeration of rare matter into nebulæ, planets, suns, and other bodies which are neither nebulæ, suns, nor planets, is for the sole purpose of supplying *pabulum*[7] for the idiosyncrasy of the organs of an infinity of rudimental beings. But for the necessity of the rudimental, prior to the ultimate life, there would have been no bodies such as these. Each of these is tenanted by a distinct variety of organic, rudimental, thinking creatures. In all, the organs vary with the features of the place tenanted. At death, or metamorphosis, these creatures, enjoying the ultimate life—immortality—and cognizant of all secrets but *the one*, act all things and pass everywhere by mere volition:—indwelling, not

the stars, which to us seem the sole palpabilities, and for the accommodation of which we blindly deem space created—but that SPACE itself—that infinity of which the truly substantive vastness swallows up the star-shadows—blotting them out as nonentities from the perception of the angels.

P.   You say that "but for the *necessity* of the rudimental life, there would have been no stars." But why this necessity?

V.   In the inorganic life, as well as in the inorganic matter generally, there is nothing to impede the action of one simple *unique* law—the Divine Volition. With the view of producing impediment, the organic life and matter (complex, substantial, and law-encumbered) were contrived.

P.   But again—why need this impediment have been produced?

V.   The result of law inviolate is perfection—right—negative happiness. The result of law violate is imperfection, wrong, positive pain. Through the impediments afforded by the number, complexity, and substantiality of the laws of organic life and matter, the violation of law is rendered, to a certain extent, practicable. Thus pain, which in the inorganic life is impossible, is possible in the organic.

P.   But to what good end is pain thus rendered possible?

V.   All things are either good or bad by comparison. A sufficient analysis will show that pleasure, in all cases, is but the contrast of pain. *Positive* pleasure is a mere idea. To be happy at any one point we must have suffered at the same. Never to suffer would have been never to have been blessed. But it has been shown that, in the inorganic life, pain cannot be; thus the necessity for the organic. The pain of the primitive life of Earth, is the sole basis of the bliss of the ultimate life of Heaven.

P.   Still, there is one of your expressions which I find it impossible to comprehend—"the truly *substantive* vastness of infinity."

V.   This, probably, is because you have no sufficiently generic conception of the term *"substance"* itself. We must not regard it as a quality, but as a sentiment:—it is the perception, in thinking beings, of the adaptation of matter to their organization. There are many things on the Earth, which would be nihility to the inhabitants of Venus—many things visible and tangible in Venus, which we could not be brought to appreciate as existing at all. But to the inorganic beings—to the angels—the whole of the unparticled matter is substance; that is to say, the whole of what we term "space," is to them the truest substantiality;—the stars, meantime, through what we consider their materiality, escaping the angelic sense, just in proportion as the unparticled matter, through

what we consider its immateriality, eludes the organic.

As the sleep-waker pronounced these latter words, in a feeble tone, I observed on his countenance a singular expression, which somewhat alarmed me, and induced me to awake him at once. No sooner had I done this, than, with a bright smile irradiating all his features, he fell back upon his pillow and expired. I noticed that in less than a minute afterward his corpse had all the stern rigidity of stone. His brow was of the coldness of ice. Thus, ordinarily, should it have appeared, only after long pressure from Azrael's[8] hand. Had the sleep-waker, indeed, during the latter portion of his discourse, been addressing me from out the region of the shadows?

Notes

The Power of Words

1. "Oinos" is the Greek word for wine but can also mean "one," and "Agathos" means "good." A character named "Oinos" narrates another Poe story, "Shadow—A Parable," and identifies himself as Greek, so one would guess that Poe intended those meanings. One wonders whether Poe didn't intend a bilingual pun. "Oinos" is pronounced ē-nos; Enos is a Hebrew name derived from the Hebrew word for "man." "Good" and "man" (or "one") make much more sense in this tale than "good" and "wine." See also "Shadow," note 2, and Section Preface, pp. 109–112.

2. This statement is difficult to square with Poe's general theory of inspiration and with the explicit mysticism of this story. Perhaps all Poe means by "intuition" here is guesswork, which he would feel would not lead to knowledge. He insists so many times that knowledge *does* arise from inspired intuition, from the perception of consistency via analogies, from a combination of intellection and imagination (but not from intellection alone)

that some such qualification of Agathos' assertion seems necessary.

3. Aidenn: from the Arabic form Aden or Adn for Eden—a paradise not precisely equivalent to the Hebrew Garden of Eden. An instance of the "Ai" spelling used by an author known to Poe is in William Maginn's poem "Cork is an Aiden for you, love and me." Poe used the word also in "The Conversation of Eiros and Charmion" (1839) and in the poem "The Raven" (1845). For Poe's reasons for alluding to Arabic elements, see "The Domain of Arnheim," note 18.

harmony of the Pleiades: Poe is playing with the medieval idea of the music of the spheres (the idea that the perfect mathematics of the universe is a kind of "music") and also with the idea that after death, or in a state of heightened awareness, the senses merge or are confounded, an idea he uses in several other stories (see, for example, "Mesmeric Revelation"). Accounts by people who have used the so-called "mind-expanding" drugs often speak of similar sensations. To Poe, who seemed to believe that the consistency of the universe would be perceived in such states, this justified interest in such states, whether induced by illness, drugs, or insanity, or present naturally (as in the case of Ellison in "The Domain of Arnheim"). An enlightened spirit in "Aidenn" would have it as a matter of course.

4. A matter of considerable speculation and excitement in Poe's day. This story was first published in 1845 (in the June *United States Magazine and Democratic Review*; it was reprinted in *The Broadway Journal*, October 25, 1845); in 1837, Andrew Crosse performed a series of experiments which seemed to many scientists of the time to have resulted in the creation of living microorganisms, which were even classified by genus.

5. Whether or not an "ether" exists was a matter of scientific debate for centuries. The ether was understood to be the "stuff" of the universe, a perfectly elastic medium which pervades all of space. Poe needs some such stuff to make his materialistic theory work. If all thought and action has physical consequences, there has to be a "carrier." The earth's atmosphere will do for manual actions so far as it extends; beyond that, and for thought, he had to have another "carrier," so he used the idea of ether. His "materialism" is an attempt to ground the idea of spirituality in physical fact.

6. See Section Preface.

The Conversation of Eiros and Charmion

1. motto: Harrison locates the quotation at line 257.

Eiros and Charmion: Poe's most likely source for these names is Jacob Bryant. Bryant says, "The two female attendants upon Cleopatra . . . were named Eiras and Charmion; which I should interpret the Rainbow, and Dove." He describes the Rainbow and the Dove as the two aspects of the heavenly wonder—signs from God after the Flood. Both are symbols of rebirth. For evidence that Poe has rebirth specifically in mind, see "The Colloquy of Monos and Una," note 5. In Shakespeare's "Antony and Cleopatra" are three characters with similar names. Eros is an ex-slave so deeply devoted to Antony that, when Antony, in grief, orders Eros to kill him, Eros kills himself instead. Iras and Charmian are a pair of attendants to Queen Cleopatra. At the

opening of the play (Act I, Scene 2), in the scene with the soothsayer, Shakespeare gives them some of the bawdiest lines he ever assigned to female characters, but at the close, Iras dies of heartbreak on being kissed by her disconsolate queen, and Charmian, after Cleopatra's suicide, applies the asp to herself. The names probably suggested themselves to Poe because of their association with death at a time when "the whole world was coming apart"—in Shakespeare, the fragile world of Antony and Cleopatra's love and to some extent the military and political structure of the Roman Empire; in Poe, literally the whole earth.

The story appeared first in the December 1839 *Gentleman's Magazine*, then in the 1840 *Tales of the Grotesque and Arabesque*, the April 1, 1843 *Saturday Museum* (under the title "The Destruction of the World") and the 1845 *Tales*.

2. Poe has in mind a passage from Psalm 93:

> The floods have lifted up their voice;
> The floods lift up their roaring.
> Above the voices of many waters,
> The mighty breakers of the sea
> The Lord on high is mighty.

The same psalm, however, says "Now is the earth firmly established. It shall not be moved." See also "The Balloon-Hoax," note 9.

3. See "The Power of Words," note 3.

4. See Section Preface.

5. The point in its orbit at which a planet or comet is nearest the sun.

6. See Section Preface.

7. Poe's "scientific" terms and facts in this tale are imprecise, according to the knowledge of his day, or ours.

The Colloquy of Monos and Una

1. Monos and Una: Both suggest "one." Poe seems to want to make a masculine and a feminine character name out of the idea of "one." There is, incidentally, an "Una" in Spenser's "The Faerie Queene."

This story appeared first in *Graham's Magazine*, August 1841, and in the 1845 *Tales*.

motto: a quotation Poe liked: he used it as the title of another story ("Mellonta Tauta"). It appears in line 1334 of the play: the chorus consoles the king, telling him not to worry about his Future—"These things will be [that is, they are in the hands of the gods]. Deal with what is at hand now. Others will take care of the future." The context suggests that Poe is being ironic.

2. "Novelty" strikes the modern reader as a cheap word to use to describe something as solemn as the concept of the afterlife, but its choice is not careless. Poe uses it also in the same context in "The Conversation of Eiros and Charmion." For Poe's discussion of what he meant by it, see "The Philosophy of Composition."

3. See Section Preface.

4. wild attempts . . . were made: Poe is consistently skeptical of democracy.

But alas . . . despised: "It will be hard to discover a better [method of education] than that which the experience of so many ages has already discovered; and this may be summed up as consisting in gymnastics for the body, and music for the soul."—Repub. lib. 2. "For this reason is a musical education most essential; since it causes Rhythm and Harmony to penetrate most intimately into the soul, taking the strongest hold upon it, filling it with *beauty* and making the man *beautiful-minded.* . . . He will praise and admire the *beautiful,* will receive it with joy into his soul, will feed upon it, and *assimilate his own condition with it."*—*Ibid.* lib. 3. Music (μουσική) had, however, among the Athenians, a far more comprehensive signification than with us. It included not only the harmonies of time and of tune, but the poetic diction, sentiment, and creation, each in its widest sense. The study of *music* was with them, in fact, the general cultivation of the taste—of that which recognizes the beautiful —in contradistinction from reason, which deals only with the true [Poe's note].

5. Pascal . . . *au sentiment:* Blaise Pascal (1623–1662) the French scientist, mathematician, philosopher and author, whose career reflects Poe's ideas in that he did become dissatisfied with "hard science" and moved to philosophy. His view that man *should* use his reason to seek truth and that God would enable him to feel truth, is also reasonably close to Poe's belief. Like Poe, he was hostile to the view that reason *alone* would lead to full understanding. The quotation translates, "That all our rationality be made to surrender to sentiment." It is from Pascal's *Pensées,* section IV.

history: "History," from ἱστορεῖν, to contemplate [Poe's note].

but . . . *"born again.":* This passage and the paragraph which follows suggest that Poe has in mind resurrection myth in these tales; see also "The Conversation of Eiros and Charmion," note 1. As to when the characters are reborn: Una explains the tale's chronology in her speech following note 6.

6. purification: The word seems to be used with reference to its root in the Greek πῦρ, fire [Poe's note].

material: Poe's "materialism" amounts to a belief that the spiritual order has a physical basis. In "The Power of Words," for instance, an "angel" explains that every act, thought, or word "moves" the "ether" and literally changes the world. So, says the angel, he once "spoke" a star into being.

7. A concept common in Poe, in the writings of mystics, and in the literature of drug users: the idea seems to be that the senses become one sense (one "sees" music, for example) because the universe (to the mystic, at any rate) is one, a whole. The names Monos and Una suggest this, as do the hints of biblical prophecy: Poe reminds us that the world is supposed to end in fire; we also recall that there is to come a time when the world will be one, and God's name one.

8. See Section Preface.

9. A "lustrum" is five years.

Shadow

1. The verse, from Psalm 23, reads, "Yea, though I walk through the valley of the shadow of death, I will fear no evil: for thou art with me; thy rod and thy staff they comfort me." Poe added the motto when he revised the 1840 *Tales of the Grotesque and Arabesque,* hoping to publish another selection. The tale had first appeared in the September 1835 *Southern Literary Messenger* (where it was called "Shadow/A Fable"), and Poe used it last in the May 31, 1845 *The Broadway Journal.*

2. Oinos: See Section Preface and "The Power of Words," note 1. In Bryant's *Mythology,* one of Poe's sources, see Vol. III, pp. 81–90 and *passim.*

alternation . . . Saturnus: An astronomer friend kindly checked out Poe's figures for us, and reports that Poe is correct. Not knowing what values Poe used for the orbital periods of Jupiter and Saturn, he used "P" to represent Poe's values and worked an equation to find "P." "J" represents Jupiter; and "S" Saturn.

$$794 \text{ years} = 67P_{JP} = 27P_{SP}$$

Modern values turn out very close to Poe's: modern Jupiter is 11.8622 years; Poe's Jupiter is 11.8507 years. Modern Saturn is 29.4577 years; Poe's Saturn is 29.4074 years. Either way, Jupiter and Saturn will be in the same position with respect to the sun every 794 years, as Poe says. Poe's "the entrance of Aires" means "Spring." The planets were in this position during Poe's lifetime—Spring, 1822. Simple subtraction thus gives us possible dates for the setting of the story: 1028, 234, 560 B.C.E., 1354 B.C.E., and so forth.

3. Chian wine: wine from Chios in the Aegean Sea. Bryant points out, in Vol. V, p. 176, that it is famous for its wine. See Section Preface.

city called Ptolemais: Three ancient cities bear this name: one in Cyrenaica, one on the west coast of the Red Sea, and the town now called Acre, in Israel.

the artizan Corinnos: a made-up name, apparently, intended to suggest an artisan from Corinth, famous for its metalwork in ancient times.

seven iron lamps: Curious that Poe uses approximately the same lighting fixtures here as in his other tale of plague-terror, "The Masque of the Red Death." Perhaps because both share details based on Moore's The Epicurean, Poe associates the two tales in his mind. He also seems to associate iron lamps with the Devil: see "Bon-Bon," note 11.

Anacreon: Greek poet (c. 563–c. 478 B.C.E.) associated with celebration of love and wine. See Teios, below. Pollin (12) points out that if Poe is parodying "pseudo-poetic transcendental fictions" as G. R. Thompson (2) says he seems to be, Thomas Moore is a likely butt of the parody. Moore was often referred to as "Anacreon" Moore, and his The Epicurean contains a section which Pollin (12) feels is the basis of Poe's tale.

Zoilus: Poe uses the name of a fourth-century B.C.E. Greek rhetorician famous for his dislike for Homer; the epics he felt too fabulous. In general usage, a "Zoilus" is an over-critical critic. But we feel Poe's source is Bryant's Mythology. See Section Preface.

Teios: Τέως, town in Ionia where Anacreon was born. It should be spelled Teos.

Catacombs . . . canal: Poe's source is Bryant's discussion of places of Amonian worship in Vol. I, p. 34 of Mythology, "The Elysian plain, near the Catacombs in Egypt, stood upon the foul Charonian canal; which was so noisome, that every fetid ditch and cavern was from it called Charonian." "Helusion" is Poe's spelling of Ἡλύσιον, Elysium, Bryant's Elysian plain. Bryant's word "Charonian" evokes Charon, who in Greek myth, ferried the dead to Hades over the River Styx. However, Bryant's use of the word suggests that he might have had a specific place in mind.

Silence

1. Poe's original name for this tale was "Siope/In the Manner of the Psychological Autobiographists." He published it first in a gift book, The Baltimore Book, for 1838; it was called "Silence/A Fable" in the 1840 Tales of the Grotesque and Arabesque and the September 6, 1845 issue of The Broadway Journal. Poe wrote it earlier; we know this because of his MS. copy of material for the Folio Club. Bulwer and De Quincey (see for Bulwer "Thou Art the Man," note 6; for De Quincey note 5 below, and "How to Write a Blackwood Article," note 7) are among the psychological autobiographists. This was to have been one of the satirical "Tales of the Folio Club." See Section Preface.

2. The first version of the story used a motto from Poe's "Al Aaraaf":

> Ours is a world of words: Quiet we call
> "Silence"—which is the merest word
> of all.

The later motto is from the work of Alcman, a poet believed active in Sparta in the mid-seventh century B.C.E., whose work survives only in a few fragments, saved often because other writers quoted his work. A burst of classical archeological discoveries connected with the Egyptological work in the early nineteenth century (See Figure 24, for instance) had brought several new fragments to light. Poe's lines come from a fragment which survived because Apollonius, a Greek lexicographer of the first century B.C.E., quoted it in his Homeric Lexicon and commented on it. Curiously, none of the modern translations we examined uses the idea of silence which Poe emphasizes in his free translation of the first two of the fragment's seven lines. But the idea appears in a translation by the Scottish poet Thomas Campbell (1777–1854) whose work Poe knew. Campbell's translation reads,

> The mountain summits sleep: glens, cliffs, and caves
> Are silent— . . . .

The entire fragment is relevant to the tale; the remainder of Campbell's version reads,

> . . . all the black earth's reptile brood—
> The bees—the wild beasts of the mountain wood:
> In depths beneath the dark red ocean's waves
> Its monsters rest, whilst wrapt in bower and spray
> Each bird is hush'd that stretch'd its pinions to the day.

Beyond the concept of busy nature now stilled, Poe might also have responded to Alcman's "monsters" because of his own use of the "behemoth" (see note 6). Indeed, Apollonius' comment on the fragment has to do with what Alcman means by the words "beasts" and "monsters." Poe certainly saw that; he also may well have remembered that Aristotle mentions Alcman as an example of a famous man who died of "this disease [morbus pedicularis] when the body contains too much moisture," an idea which ironically echoes the mythological theme from Bryant (see Section Preface) of the "person preserved in the midst of waters." Moreover, Campbell's translation speaks of a red ocean (other versions make it purple brine) which suggests the rain of blood in the fourth paragraph of this story. So the lines of ancient poetry were a superb choice, so good that had they been in the tale's first version, scholars would argue that "Silence" is an imaginative expansion of the Alcman fragment. Our Greek follows David Campbell, *Greek Lyric Poetry* (N.Y., 1967). Poe's is identical but without accents.

3. Demon: See Section Preface.

Libya: In old Greek usage, "Libya" meant simply "Africa." See Section Preface.

Zaire: the old name for the Congo, now in use again.

4. See Section Preface.

5. rock: See Section Preface.

solitude: Major writers said a great deal about solitude in Poe's day; see Poe's tale "The Lighthouse" for a character with similar yearnings. Poe knew Isaac Disraeli's essay on solitude in *Curiosities of Literature*. He did not know a passage in De Quincey's *Suspiria de Profundis* because it appeared in 1845, but it certainly illustrates how frequently the idea appears, and how close one writer is to another in what he says about it. De Quincey calls solitude "silent as light" and "a secret heiroglyphic from God." His passage forcibly suggests "Silence" because it connects supernatural writing with the idea of solitude, and because De Quincey is a psychological autobiographist (see note 1).

6. Then: Poe's use of "and" and "then" to begin so many of his sentences is part of his attempt to create a scriptural tone. Whimsy and a scriptural tone are not incompatible, however. A notable scriptural parody, "The Chaldee Manuscript," made fun of Edinburgh magazinists and used a similar tone. Poe certainly knew it: it was published first in Blackwood's in 1817, and its principal author, James Hogg, appears frequently in Poe's writing. Poe probably considered Hogg a psychological autobiographist as well as poet and satirist. See also note 8, lynx.

behemoth: See Job 40: 15–24; See Section Preface and note 2.

7. A passage in Thomas Carlyle's *Sartor Resartus/The Life and Opinions of Herr Teufelsdröckh* (1831), which Poe knew well, concludes, "Speech is of time, Silence is of Eternity" (Book III, Chapter 3). The idea of words changing Poe could have taken from William Beckford (See "Landor's Cottage," note 6); as Mabbott points out, this happens to characters inscribed on a cliff, in *Vathek*.

8. Magi: Persian priests. See Section Preface.

Genii: magical beings in near-Eastern lore.

Sybils: prophetesses in Greek and Roman belief. See Section Preface.

Dodona: site of a sacred grove at which a priest and priestess read oracular meanings in the sounds of rustling leaves. See Section Preface.

lynx: one of the symbolic animals representing writers in "The Chaldee Manuscript" (see note 6).

A Tale of the Ragged Mountains

1. Charlottesville: Poe went to college here at the University of Virginia and knew the area.

Bedloe: Poe picked up this name from a review by Thomas B. Macaulay in the October 1841 *Edinburgh Review*, in which it appears in close proximity with the name "Oats" (". . . Oatses, and Bedloes . . ."). This probably suggested the palindrome "Bedlo[e]-Oldeb" (Pollin 5). Poe's use of the name "Oldeb" also undoubtedly stems from his acquaintance with *Edgar Huntley*. See Section Preface.

Poe published the story first in *Godey's Lady's Book* for April 1844 and used it again in *The Broadway Journal*, November 29, 1845.

2. the health spa in New York State.

3. Mesmer: See Section Preface, pp. 112–114, and "Some Words with A Mummy," note 21.

rapport: The "*rapport*" with Dr. Templeton is intended to provide a more-or-less rational alternate means of explaining the "wonder," Bedloe's vision. The reader unwilling to believe in reincarnation will perhaps believe that Bedloe shares Templeton's memories.

4. Bedloe follows the pattern of perceiving characters in Poe: nervous, ill, and often, drugged.

5. If Bedloe is the first to walk here, why is there a path?

6. Illness, drugs, mesmerism, then fog provide the "margin of credibility"; Poe proceeds now to the "vision." See the Section Preface to the group of tales labelled "Unimpeded Visions."

7. palanquins: covered litters, borne on poles.

filleted: tied with ribbons.

8. Novalis is German poet Georg Friedrich Phillipp von Hardenberg (1772–1801). The quotation is from "Blütenstaub" ("Pollen"), a group of aphoristic writings first published in 1798. In format, "Pollen" resembles Poe's "Pinakidia" and "Marginalia" and, like those series by Poe, first appeared in a magazine. See "The Mystery of Marie Rogêt," note 2.

9. dagger with a wavy-edged blade.

10. Templeton's statement represents not an extreme view but practically a consensus opinion among educated people of the period. An enormous scientific breakthrough which would provide firm physical foundation for belief in transcendent spirituality seemed to be impending. It was generally supposed that it would be electrical in nature, hence Bedloe's mention of the galvanic shocks he felt.

11. Warren Hastings (1732–1818), first Governor-General of India (from 1774 to 1784). See Section Preface.

12. Cheyte Sing: resistance of the Raja of Benares, Chait Sinh, to demands made by Governor Hastings led to a rebellion.

sepoy: An Indian serving in the British Indian Army.

13. Poe made up this species of leech and borrowed the French word *sangsue* from a passage in Victor Hugo's *Notre-Dame de Paris* (Pollin 5).

The Facts in the Case of M. Valdemar

1. The title was "The Facts of M. Valdemar's Case" when Poe published this first in the *American (Whig) Review*, in December 1845. He ran it the same month in his own magazine, *The Broadway Journal*, on December 20, 1845 under its present title. It was published in England in 1846 (see Section Preface), and in the *Boston Museum*, August 18, 1849.

2. *in articulo mortis:* in the grasp of death.

magnetic: Hypnosis seemed to imply a "force" between subject and hypnotist, often called "magnetism" (see Section Preface).

3. "Bibliotheca Forensica," "Issachar Marx," "Wallenstein," "Gargantua": Poe is playing games with his fictitious "well-known" character, Valdemar. Genesis 49:14 tells us that Issachar "is a strong ass crouching down between two burdens." The burdens seem to be translating Rabelais' *Gargantua* and Schiller's *Wallenstein* into Polish (Carlson 2). "Bibliotheca Forensica" would be a collection of legal works.

nom de plume: pen name.

John Randolph: John Randolph of Roanoke (1773–1833) whose liberal political writings served as a standard point of reference for Democratic politicians. Poe is still playing games with Valdemar's identity—"You know Valdemar," he says in effect, "he's the fellow who translates books into Polish. He looks a lot like—well, his lower legs look like John Randolph's."

clairvoyance: Poe's chatter about the technical aspects of mesmerism is largely intended as a prop to credibility, but he may have inserted the business about clairvoyance to excuse the fact that Valdemar is not going to report much of what he sees beyond death.

phthisis: state of tuberculosis.

4. *aneurism:* a condition marked by the dilation of the wall of an artery. A pulsating sac forms, and the victim usually suffers pain. One wonders, considering the snide fun he has in describing Valdemar, whether Poe knew that one cause of aneurism is syphilis.

aorta: the main artery from the left ventricle of the heart.

5. the credibility game again. See Section Preface.

6. He snored when he breathed.

7. a squeamish lot, these interns. See Section Preface.

8. a watery, acrid fluid discharged from sores.

Mesmeric Revelation

1. See "The Facts in the Case of M. Valdemar," note 3.

2. Cousin: Victor Cousin (1792–1867), French philosopher of spiritualist leanings. Mr. Brownson: Orestes Brownson (1803–1876), American editor, social thinker, philosopher, politician, and novelist. *Charles Elwood* (1834, published 1840), a fictionalized account of Brownson's own intellectual flirtation with skepticism, was, as Poe says, influenced by Cousin; Brownson, rereading his own book years later, when he had undergone major changes in his religious point of view, said so himself. Poe seems to have understood Brownson intimately; there is a most perceptive paragraph on him in his series of brief estimates of contemporary men-of-letters, the "Autography."

Trinculo: the jester in Shakespeare's *The Tempest* who plots with Caliban and Stefano to take over Prospero's island. They end up, however, discovered, rebuked, and reeking with the stench of a horse pool into which Ariel, "a spirit of the pure air" who does Prospero's bidding, has led them: an inglorious end to grand illusions.

3. This is one of a series of passages in various works in which Poe attempts a physical explanation of spirituality. See, for example, "The Power of Words," and the cosmological essay, *Eureka*.

4. A scientific concept already discarded by Poe's day, caloric had been thought to be the "stuff" or "principle" involved in burning or oxidation.

5. This tale appeared in *Columbian Magazine* in August 1844, and in the 1845 *Tales by Edgar A. Poe*. Poe says it was also printed in *The Dollar Weekly*, presumably late in 1844 (he mentions it in a letter dated January 4, 1845). This printing is not listed in Heartman and Canny, who also list the October 4, 1845 *Star of Bethlehem* and the *Saturday Museum* for August 31, 1844. Poe added this paragraph and most of the one before it (from the word "there" in the third sentence) when he revised the tale for the 1845 *Tales*, another strong indication that he was seriously attracted to the idea of providing a scientific and physical basis for spirituality (see note 3, above).

6. Compare Poe's idea with the idea found in many oriental religions that the goal of the enlightened soul is merger with the world-spirit. The significant differences are that Poe searches for a materialistic explanation of such transcendence, and that Poe stops short of belief in total merger with the godhead: man's essential nature turns out to be a "thought" of God. Note also Poe's interest in similar ideas in Plato: see, for instance, "Morella," note 1.

7. nourishment.

8. the angel of death.

5. Detective Stories

These "tales of ratiocination" are so popular and familiar that one is apt to miss the very considerable extent to which they exemplify Edgar Poe's philosophy of beauty, creativity, and perception. But the usual pattern is here; to perceive the complex pattern, one must be hypersensitive, almost to the point of madness, or extraordinarily gifted.

The Gold-Bug. M. Legrand's instability is not as serious as the narrator imagines, of course; Legrand knows what he is about. He is an impecunious scientific amateur who has been bitten by a gold-bug different from the one Jupiter imagines. But the hint of mental instability, the high excitement under which he operates on his quest, and the brilliance of his solution are clearly early indicators of Poe's usual pattern—creativity is associated with madness. Note also that the relationship between the narrator and Legrand is very similar to that between the narrator and Dupin in the Parisian detective tales: the narrator is a friend who plays "straight man."

Poe's stereotype of the ex-slave Jupiter is in his usual manner, part of the illiberal line which Kaplan feels culminates in a racist allegory at the close of Poe's novel, *The Narrative of Arthur Gordon Pym*. But the treatment is at least good humored here, rather in the vein of Poe's treatment of the black character in his incomplete novel *The Journal of Julius Rodman*. Jupiter is loyal, superstitious, and talks funny; his misunderstandings produce some bad puns. Yet he is unafraid of a skull ("somebody bin lef him head up de tree") or of climbing an enormous yellow poplar ("tulip tree").

Some critics of Poe believe that he deliberately sustained a reputation as a kind of wizard by way of a nineteenth-century public-relations "image." Magazines of the period were filled with puzzles and curiosities, and Poe exploited popular interest in them in numerous ways, among them an article in *Alexander's Weekly Messenger* (December 18, 1839) in which he offered to decipher cryptograms, and a follow-up piece in *Graham's* (July 1841), in which he claimed to have solved all but one of the hundred or so submitted. His fibbing does not obscure his sure sense of reader interest; popular magazines and literary reviews still tantalize subscribers with puzzles of the same sort.

The Murders in the Rue Morgue. Dupin, we are to learn, is truly analytical. His powers increase as the Dupin stories develop. In "The Murders in the Rue Morgue," Dupin is superior to the Prefect of Police in that he is analytical; indeed, he *almost* appears to be intuiting truth (see the first paragraph). In "The Mystery of Marie Rogêt" and "The Purloined Letter," Poe goes further; Dupin actually uses what looks like artistic inspiration to solve the problems posed by crime and intrigue.

No one seems able to explain exactly what Poe means by "the old philosophy of the Bi-Part Soul," and the "fancy of a double Dupin . . . creative and resolvent" (page 180). Numerous ancient philosophies use the concept of a dual soul: it appears, for example, in Egypt and, in different form, seems an underlying concept in the Homeric epics (one part or soul is associated with breath, the other with blood). But we have never found the parts called "creative and resolvent." We suspect that Poe borrowed the concept from an as-yet-unlocated passage in his reading (we have searched likely places most diligently), or that he made up the two properties out of Dupin's characteristics.

If the secluded hideout shared by Dupin and the narrator seems familiar, it is because subsequent writers have made it so. The idea of the hero's hidden quarters has passed into popular culture; it is present in pulp and comic book material. Poe invented a great deal of the claptrap and many of the conventions of the modern commercial detective and "super-hero" fiction, as A. Conan Doyle and later writers have acknowledged. Sherlock Holmes, he said, owed much to Dupin, as did the detective-heroes of other writers: "If every man who receives a cheque for a story which owes its springs to Poe were to pay tithe to a monument for the Master, he would have a pyramid as big as that of Cheops."

Since Poe didn't really know Paris, we wondered where he got the texture of his Parisian setting. We are quite sure we now know: from Chapter 23 of Bulwer-Lytton's *Pelham; or Adventures of a Gentleman* (1828). Our reasons:

1. The references to Rousseau's *La Nouvelle Héloïse* appear in both places. Indeed, in "Loss of Breath," Poe refers to exactly the same passage cited by Bulwer-Lytton.
2. The references to Crébillon appear in both places.
3. Pelham loves the Faubourg St.-Germain, and for the same reasons—its antiquity, its quaintness, its "true" feel of old France—which lead Dupin and the narrator to rent quarters for themselves there.

The Mystery of Marie Rogêt. The relationship of Poe's "The Mystery of Marie Rogêt" to the Rogers murder is not as simple as his footnote makes it sound. There is, for instance, some evidence to indicate that as facts about the Rogers murder came to light Poe altered his tale to make it appear that he had predicted what would be found out. Poe, as we noted in discussing "The Gold-Bug," liked to pose as a great solver of puzzles; he had, in 1841, done a series on cryptography, in which he claimed to be able to solve cryptograms submitted by readers. Dupin, however, sometimes does more than solve puzzles; at his best, he thinks creatively and imaginatively.

Modern readers bored by Poe's interminable dissection of the illogic of journalistic accounts of a sensational murder should bear in mind several special circumstances: First, there is Poe's pose as a great logician. Second, Poe took the role of reformer of literary and journalistic cliques in New York, which were guilty of numerous unethical practices as well as sloppy workmanship. This tale serves as a sort of textbook in logic and composition or as an essay on the reporter's craft. Finally, we need to remember that Poe is trying to capitalize on Dupin's character. He hopes readers will be interested enough in his detective's mind to follow the intricacy of his analysis, and so produces a tale almost totally devoid of action. Dupin and the narrator sit home and think; unlike most detective-story heroes, Dupin here does not confront a guilty party, travel about accumulating evidence, foil a plot, or even, so far as we can tell, move from his chair. He lectures us on what's wrong with newspapermen.

Note that Poe speaks in his own voice in this tale; indeed, he identifies himself as the narrator and as Dupin's side-kick.

The Purloined Letter. The categories in which we have grouped Poe's tales are largely arbitrary. Though it is famous as a detective tale, "The Purloined Letter" is also one of Poe's vengeance stories; Dupin has scores personal and political to settle with his friend the mathematician-poet-minister. The tone of the closing paragraphs of the tale is bitter, and the final allusion literally bloodthirsty. Compare this tale with other vengeance stories, such as "Hop-Frog" and "The Cask of Amontillado."

The Oblong Box. By the same token, this story could be placed elsewhere: Poe told James Russell Lowell in a letter of July 2, 1844 that he wrote it and "Thou Art the Man" at about the same time for *Godey's Lady's Book.* In point of fact, he tried to peddle "The Oblong Box" to Willis' *New York Mirror* first. The two are similar in that each is, in a way, a "tale of ratiocination," each is in some ways a horror story, and each is, despite the presence of horror, very cool in tone—more evidence that whether Poe's horror is "from Germany" or "of the soul," he could turn it on and off at will.

We put "The Oblong Box" here—though the reader should compare it to "Thou Art the Man"—because its narrator seems so normal when compared to the feverish Legrand or the inscrutable Dupin. His investigations of Wyatt's puzzling behavior are motivated not by madness, hypersensitivity, drugs, or anything else morbid, but simply by curiosity and "too much strong green tea." Moreover, his "ratiocination" fails to solve the mystery. He's dead wrong.

Note also that, when the puzzle is solved, Wyatt's motives turn out to be normal, and, if we forgive Poe his theatrical exaggeration of emotion, understandable. This is less a morbid story or even a clever story than it is a very sad one.

The Tales

THE GOLD-BUG

*What ho! what ho! this fellow is
    dancing mad!
He hath been bitten by the Tarantula.*
                    All in the Wrong.[1]

Many years ago, I contracted an intimacy with a Mr. William Legrand. He was of an ancient Huguenot family, and had once been wealthy; but a series of misfortunes had reduced him to want. To avoid the mortification consequent upon his disasters, he left New Orleans, the city of his forefathers, and took up his residence at Sullivan's Island, near Charleston, South Carolina.

This Island is a very singular one. It consists of little else than the sea sand, and is about three miles long. Its breadth at no point exceeds a quarter of a mile. It is separated from the main land by a scarcely perceptible creek, oozing its way through a wilderness of reeds and slime, a favorite resort of the marsh-hen. The vegetation, as might be supposed, is scant, or at least dwarfish. No trees of any magnitude are to be seen. Near the western extremity, where Fort Moultrie stands, and where are some miserable frame buildings, tenanted, during summer, by the fugitives from Charleston dust and fever, may be found, indeed, the bristly palmetto; but the whole island, with the exception of this western point, and a line of hard, white beach on the seacoast, is covered with a dense undergrowth of the sweet myrtle, so much prized by the horticulturists of England. The shrub here often attains the height of fifteen or twenty feet, and forms an almost impenetrable coppice, burthening the air with its fragrance.

In the inmost recesses of this coppice, not far from the eastern or more remote end of the island, Legrand had built himself a small hut, which he occupied when I first, by mere accident, made his acquaintance. This soon ripened into friendship—for there was much in the recluse to excite interest and esteem. I found him well educated, with unusual powers of mind, but infected with misanthropy, and subject to perverse moods of alternate enthusiasm and melancholy. He had with him many books, but rarely employed them. His chief amusements were gunning and fishing, or sauntering along the beach and through the myrtles, in quest of shells or entomological specimens;—his collection of the latter might have been envied by a Swammerdamm.[2] In these excursions he was usually accompanied by an old negro, called Jupiter, who had been manumitted before the reverses of the family, but who could be induced, neither by threats nor by promises, to abandon what he considered his right of attendance upon the footsteps of his young "Massa Will." It is not improbable that the relatives of Legrand, conceiving him to be somewhat unsettled in intellect, had contrived to instil this obstinacy into Jupiter, with a view to the supervision and guardianship of the wanderer.

The winters in the latitude of Sullivan's Island are seldom very severe, and in the fall of the year it is a rare event indeed when a fire is considered necessary. About the middle of October, 18—, there occurred, however, a day of remarkable chilliness. Just before sunset I scrambled my way through the evergreens to the hut of my friend, whom I had not visited for several weeks—my residence being, at that time, in Charleston, a distance of nine miles from the Island, while the facilities of passage and re-passage were very far behind those of the present day. Upon reaching the hut I rapped, as was my custom, and getting no reply, sought for the key where I knew it was secreted, unlocked the door and went in. A fine fire was blazing upon the hearth. It was a novelty, and by no means an ungrateful one. I threw off an overcoat, took an armchair by the crackling logs, and awaited patiently the arrival of my hosts.

Soon after dark they arrived, and gave me a most cordial welcome. Jupiter, grinning from ear to ear, bustled about to prepare some marsh-hens for supper. Legrand was in one of his fits—how else shall I term them?—of enthusiasm. He had found an unknown bivalve, forming a new genus, and, more than this, he had hunted down and secured, with Jupiter's assistance, a *scarabæus*[3] which he believed to be totally new, but in respect to which he wished to have my opinion on the morrow.

"And why not to-night?" I asked, rubbing my hands over the blaze, and wishing the whole tribe of *scarabæi* at the devil.

"Ah, if I had only known you were here!" said Legrand, "but it's so long since I saw you; and how could I foresee that you would pay me a visit this very night of all others? As I was coming home I met Lieutenant G——, from the fort,[4] and, very foolishly, I lent him the bug; so it will be impossible for you to see it until morning. Stay here to-night, and I will send Jup down for it at sunrise. It is the loveliest thing in creation!"

"What?—sunrise?"

"Nonsense! no!—the bug. It is of a brilliant gold color—about the size of a large hickory-nut—with two jet black spots near one extremity of the back, and another, somewhat longer, at the other. The *antennæ* are—"

"Dey aint *no* tin in him, Massa Will, I keep a tellin on you," here interrupted Jupiter; "de bug is a goole bug, solid, ebery bit of him, inside and all, sep him wing—neber feel half so hebby a bug in my life."

"Well, suppose it is, Jup," replied Legrand, somewhat more earnestly, it seemed to me, than the case demanded, "is that any reason for your letting the birds burn? The color"—here he turned to me—"is really almost enough to warrant Jupiter's idea. You never saw a more brilliant metallic lustre than the scales emit—but of this you cannot judge till to-morrow. In the mean time I can give you some idea of the shape." Saying this, he seated himself at a small table, on which were a pen and ink, but no paper. He looked for some in a drawer, but found none.

"Never mind," said he at length, "this will answer;" and he drew from his waistcoat pocket a scrap of what I took to be very dirty foolscap, and made upon it a rough drawing with the pen. While he did this, I retained my seat by the fire, for I was still chilly. When the design was complete, he handed it to me without rising. As I received it, a loud growl was heard, succeeded by a scratching at the door. Jupiter opened it, and a large Newfoundland, belonging to Legrand, rushed in, leaped upon my shoulders, and loaded me with caresses; for I had shown him much attention during previous visits. When his gambols were over, I looked at the paper, and, to speak the truth, found myself not a little puzzled at what my friend had depicted.

"Well!" I said, after contemplating it for some minutes, "this *is* a strange *scarabæus*, I must confess: new to me: never saw anything like it before—unless it was a skull, or a death's-head—which it more nearly resembles than anything else that has come under *my* observation."

"A death's-head!" echoed Legrand—"Oh—yes—well, it has something of that appearance upon paper, no doubt. The two upper black spots look like eyes, eh?

and the longer one at the bottom like a mouth—and then the shape of the whole is oval."

"Perhaps so," said I; "but, Legrand, I fear you are no artist. I must wait until I see the beetle itself, if I am to form any idea of its personal appearance."

"Well, I don't know," said he, a little nettled, "I draw tolerably—*should* do it at least—have had good masters, and flatter myself that I am not quite a blockhead."

"But, my dear fellow, you are joking then," said I, "this is a very passable *skull* —indeed, I may say that it is a very *excellent* skull, according to the vulgar notions about such specimens of physiology —and your *scarabæus* must be the queerest *scarabæus* in the world if it resembles it. Why, we may get up a very thrilling bit of superstition upon this hint. I presume you will call the bug *scarabæus caput hominis*,[5] or something of that kind —there are many similar titles in the Natural Histories. But where are the *antennæ* you spoke of?"

"The *antennæ!*" said Legrand, who seemed to be getting unaccountably warm upon the subject; "I am sure you must see the *antennæ*. I made them as distinct as they are in the original insect, and I presume that is sufficient."

"Well, well," I said, "perhaps you have —still I don't see them;" and I handed him the paper without additional remark, not wishing to ruffle his temper; but I was much surprised at the turn affairs had taken; his ill humor puzzled me—and, as for the drawing of the beetle, there were positively *no antennæ* visible, and the whole *did* bear a very close resemblance to the ordinary cuts of a death's-head.

He received the paper very peevishly, and was about to crumple it, apparently to throw it in the fire, when a casual glance at the design seemed suddenly to rivet his attention. In an instant his face grew violently red—in another as excessively pale. For some minutes he continued to scrutinize the drawing minutely where he sat. At length he arose, took a candle from the table, and proceeded to seat himself upon a sea-chest in the farthest corner of the room. Here again he made an anxious examination of the paper; turning it in all directions. He said nothing, however, and his conduct greatly astonished me; yet I thought it prudent not to exacerbate the growing moodiness of his temper by any comment. Presently he took from his coat pocket a wallet, placed the paper carefully in it, and deposited both in a writing-desk, which he locked. He now grew more composed in his demeanor; but his original air of enthusiasm had quite disappeared. Yet he seemed not so much sulky as abstracted. As the evening wore away he became more and more absorbed in reverie, from which no sallies of mine could arouse him. It had been my intention to pass the night at the hut, as I had frequently done before, but, seeing my host in this mood, I deemed it proper to take leave. He did not press me to remain, but, as I departed, he shook my hand with even more than his usual cordiality.

It was about a month after this (and during the interval I had seen nothing of Legrand) when I received a visit, at Charleston, from his man, Jupiter. I had never seen the good old negro look so dispirited, and I feared that some serious disaster had befallen my friend.

"Well, Jup," said I, "what is the matter now?—how is your master?"

"Why, to speak de troof, massa, him not so berry well as mought be."

"Not well! I am truly sorry to hear it. What does he complain of?"

"Dar! dat's it!—him neber plain of notin—but him berry sick for all dat."

"*Very* sick, Jupiter!—why didn't you say so at once? Is he confined to bed?"

"No, dat he aint!—he aint find nowhar —dat's just whar de shoe pinch—my mind is got to be berry hebby bout poor Massa Will."

"Jupiter, I should like to understand what it is you are talking about. You say your master is sick. Hasn't he told you what ails him?"

"Why, massa, taint worf while for to git mad bout de matter—Massa Will say noffin at all aint de matter wid him—but den what make him go about looking dis here way, wid he head down and he soldiers up, and as white as a gose? And den he keep a syphon all de time—"

"Keeps a what, Jupiter?"

"Keeps a syphon wid de figgurs on de slate—de queerest figgurs I ebber did see. Ise gittin to be skeered, I tell you. Hab for to keep mighty tight eye pon him noovers. Todder day he gib me slip fore de sun up and was gone de whole ob de blessed day. I had a big stick ready cut for to gib him d——d good beating when he did come —but Ise sich a fool dat I hadn't de heart arter all—he look so berry poorly."

"Eh?—what?—ah yes!—upon the whole I think you had better not be too severe with the poor fellow—don't flog him, Jupiter—he can't very well stand it—but can you form no idea of what has occasioned this illness, or rather this change of conduct? Has anything unpleasant happened since I saw you?"

"No, massa, dey aint bin noffin onpleasant *since* den—'t was *fore* den I'm feared—'t was de berry day you was dare."

"How? what do you mean?"

"Why, massa, I mean de bug—dare now."

"The what?"

"De bug—I'm berry sartain dat Massa Will bin bit somewhere bout de head by dat goole-bug."

"And what cause have you, Jupiter, for such a supposition?"

"Claws enuff, massa, and mouff too. I nebber did see sich a d——d bug—he kick and he bite ebery ting what cum near him. Massa Will cotch him fuss, but had for to let him go gin mighty quick, I tell you— den was de time he must ha got de bite. I didn't like de look ob de bug mouff, myself, no how, so I wouldn't take hold ob him wid my finger, but I cotch him wid a piece ob paper dat I found. I rap

him up in de paper and stuff piece ob it in he mouff—dat was de way."

"And you think, then, that your master was really bitten by the beetle, and that the bite made him sick?"

"I don't tink noffin about it—I nose it. What make him dream bout de goole so much, if taint cause he bit by de goole-bug? Ise heerd bout dem goole-bugs fore dis."

"But how do you know he dreams about gold?"

"How I know? why cause he talk about it in he sleep—dat's how I nose."

"Well, Jup, perhaps you are right; but to what fortunate circumstance am I to attribute the honor of a visit from you to-day?"

"What de matter, massa?"

"Did you bring any message from Mr. Legrand?"

"No, massa, I bring dis here pissel;" and here Jupiter handed me a note which ran thus:

MY DEAR ——

Why have I not seen you for so long a time? I hope you have not been so foolish as to take offence at any little *brusquerie*[6] of mine; but no, that is improbable.

Since I saw you I have had great cause for anxiety. I have something to tell you, yet scarcely know how to tell it, or whether I should tell it at all.

I have not been quite well for some days past, and poor old Jup annoys me, almost beyond endurance, by his well-meant attentions. Would you believe it?—he had prepared a huge stick, the other day, with which to chastise me for giving him the slip, and spending the day, *solus*,[7] among the hills on the main land. I verily believe that my ill looks alone saved me a flogging.

I have made no addition to my cabinet since we met.

If you can, in any way, make it convenient, come over with Jupiter. *Do* come. I wish to see you *to-night*,

upon business of importance. I assure you that it is of the *highest* importance.
Ever yours,
WILLIAM LEGRAND.

There was something in the tone of this note which gave me great uneasiness. Its whole style differed materially from that of Legrand. What could he be dreamof? What new crotchet possessed his excitable brain? What "business of the highest importance" could *he* possibly have to transact? Jupiter's account of him boded no good. I dreaded lest the continued pressure of misfortune had, at length, fairly unsettled the reason of my friend. Without a moment's hesitation, therefore, I prepared to accompany the negro.

Upon reaching the wharf, I noticed a scythe and three spades, all apparently new, lying in the bottom of the boat in which we were to embark.

"What is the meaning of all this, Jup?" I inquired.

"Him syfe, massa, and spade."

"Very true; but what are they doing here?"

"Him de syfe and de spade what Massa Will sis pon my buying for him in de town, and de debbil's own lot of money I had to gib for em."

"But what, in the name of all that is mysterious, is your 'Massa Will' going to do with scythes and spades?"

"Dat's more dan *I* know, and debbil take me if I don't blieve 't is more dan he know, too. But it's all cum ob de bug."

Finding that no satisfaction was to be obtained of Jupiter, whose whole intellect seemed to be absorbed by "de bug," I now stepped into the boat and made sail. With a fair and strong breeze we soon ran into the little cove to the northward of Fort Moultrie, and a walk of some two miles brought us to the hut. It was about three in the afternoon when we arrived. Legrand had been awaiting us in eager expectation. He grasped my hand with a nervous *empressment*[8] which alarmed me

and strengthened the suspicions already entertained. His countenance was pale even to ghastliness, and his deep-set eyes glared with unnatural lustre. After some inquiries respecting his health, I asked him, not knowing what better to say, if he had yet obtained the *scarabæus* from Lieutenant G——.

"Oh, yes," he replied, coloring violently, "I got it from him the next morning. Nothing should tempt me to part with that *scarabæus*. Do you know that Jupiter is quite right about it?"

"In what way?" I asked, with a sad foreboding at heart.

"In supposing it to be a bug of *real gold*." He said this with an air of profound seriousness, and I felt inexpressibly shocked.

"This bug is to make my fortune," he continued, with a triumphant smile, "to reinstate me in my family possessions. Is it any wonder, then, that I prize it? Since Fortune has thought fit to bestow it upon me, I have only to use it properly and I shall arrive at the gold of which it is the index. Jupiter, bring me that *scarabæus!*"

"What! de bug, massa? I'd rudder not go fer trubble dat bug—you mus git him for your own self." Hereupon Legrand arose, with a grave and stately air, and brought me the beetle from a glass case in which it was enclosed. It was a beautiful *scarabæus*, and, at that time, unknown to naturalists—of course a great prize in a scientific point of view. There were two round, black spots near one extremity of the back, and a long one near the other. The scales were exceedingly hard and glossy, with all the appearance of burnished gold. The weight of the insect was very remarkable, and, taking all things into consideration, I could hardly blame Jupiter for his opinion respecting it; but what to make of Legrand's agreement with that opinion, I could not, for the life of me, tell.

"I sent for you," said he, in a grandiloquent tone, when I had completed my examination of the beetle, "I sent for you, that I might have your counsel and assistance in furthering the views of Fate and of the bug"—

"My dear Legrand," I cried, interrupting him, "you are certainly unwell, and had better use some little precautions. You shall go to bed, and I will remain with you a few days, until you get over this. You are feverish and"—

"Feel my pulse," said he.

I felt it, and, to say the truth, found not the slightest indication of fever.

"But you may be ill and yet have no fever. Allow me this once to prescribe for you. In the first place, go to bed. In the next"—

"You are mistaken," he interposed, "I am as well as I can expect to be under the excitement which I suffer. If you really wish me well, you will relieve this excitement."

"And how is this to be done?"

"Very easily. Jupiter and myself are going upon an expedition into the hills, upon the main land, and, in this expedition, we shall need the aid of some person in whom we can confide. You are the only one we can trust. Whether we succeed or fail, the excitement which you now perceive in me will be equally allayed."

"I am anxious to oblige you in any way," I replied; "but do you mean to say that this infernal beetle has any connection with your expedition into the hills?"

"It has."

"Then, Legrand, I can become a party to no such absurd proceeding."

"I am sorry—very sorry—for we shall have to try it by ourselves."

"Try it by yourselves! The man is surely mad!—but stay!—how long do you propose to be absent?"

"Probably all night. We shall start immediately, and be back, at all events, by sunrise."

"And will you promise me, upon your honor, that when this freak of yours is over, and the bug business (good God!) is

settled to your satisfaction, you will then return home and follow my advice implicitly, as that of your physician?"

"Yes; I promise; and now let us be off, for we have no time to lose."

With a heavy heart I accompanied my friend. We started about four o'clock—Legrand, Jupiter, the dog, and myself. Jupiter had with him the scythe and spades—the whole of which he insisted upon carrying—more through fear, it seemed to me, of trusting either of the implements within reach of his master, than from any excess of industry or complaisance. His demeanor was dogged in the extreme, and "dat d——d bug" were the sole words which escaped his lips during the journey. For my own part, I had charge of a couple of dark lanterns, while Legrand contented himself with the *scarabæus*, which he carried attached to the end of a bit of whip-cord; twirling it to and fro, with the air of a conjuror, as he went. When I observed this last, plain evidence of my friend's aberration of mind, I could scarcely refrain from tears. I thought it best, however, to humor his fancy, at least for the present, or until I could adopt some more energetic measures with a chance of success. In the mean time I endeavored, but all in vain, to sound him in regard to the object of the expedition. Having succeeded in inducing me to accompany him, he seemed unwilling to hold conversation upon any topic of minor importance, and to all my questions vouchsafed no other reply than "we shall see!"

We crossed the creek at the head of the island by means of a skiff, and, ascending the high grounds on the shore of the main land, proceeded in a northwesterly direction, through a tract of country excessively wild and desolate, where no trace of a human footstep was to be seen. Legrand led the way with decision; pausing only for an instant, here and there, to consult what appeared to be certain landmarks of his own contrivance upon a former occasion.

In this manner we journeyed for about two hours, and the sun was just setting when we entered a region infinitely more dreary than any yet seen. It was a species of table land, near the summit of an almost inaccessible hill, densely wooded from base to pinnacle, and interspersed with huge crags that appeared to lie loosely upon the soil, and in many cases were prevented from precipitating themselves into the valleys below, merely by the support of the trees against which they reclined. Deep ravines, in various directions, gave an air of still sterner solemnity to the scene.

The natural platform to which we had clambered was thickly overgrown with brambles, through which we soon discovered that it would have been impossible to force our way but for the scythe; and Jupiter, by direction of his master, proceeded to clear for us a path to the foot of an enormously tall tulip-tree, which stood, with some eight or ten oaks, upon the level, and far surpassed them all, and all other trees which I had then ever seen, in the beauty of its foliage and form, in the wide spread of its branches, and in the general majesty of its appearance. When we reached this tree, Legrand turned to Jupiter, and asked him if he thought he could climb it. The old man seemed a little staggered by the question, and for some moments made no reply. At length he approached the huge trunk, walked slowly around it, and examined it with minute attention. When he had completed his scrutiny, he merely said,

"Yes, massa, Jup climb any tree he ebber see in he life."

"Then up with you as soon as possible, for it will soon be too dark to see what we are about."

"How far mus go up, massa?" inquired Jupiter.

"Get up the main trunk first, and then I will tell you which way to go—and here —stop! take this beetle with you."

"De bug, Massa Will!—de goole bug!" cried the negro, drawing back in dismay —"what for mus tote de bug way up de tree?—d——n if I do!"

"If you are afraid, Jup, a great big negro like you, to take hold of a harmless little dead beetle, why you can carry it up by this string—but, if you do not take it up with you in some way, I shall be under the necessity of breaking your head with this shovel."

"What de matter now, massa?" said Jup, evidently shamed into compliance; "always want for to raise fuss wid old nigger. Was only funnin any how. *Me* feered de bug! what I keer for de bug?" Here he took cautiously hold of the extreme end of the string, and, maintaining the insect as far from his person as circumstances would permit, prepared to ascend the tree.

In youth, the tulip-tree, or *Liriodendron Tulipiferum*,[9] the most magnificent of American foresters, has a trunk peculiarly smooth, and often rises to a great height without lateral branches; but, in its riper age, the bark becomes gnarled and uneven, while many short limbs make their appearance on the stem. Thus the difficulty of ascension, in the present case, lay more in semblance than in reality. Embracing the huge cylinder, as closely as possible, with his arms and knees, seizing with his hands some projections, and resting his naked toes upon others, Jupiter, after one or two narrow escapes from falling, at length wriggled himself into the first great fork, and seemed to consider the whole business as virtually accomplished. The *risk* of the achievement was, in fact, now over, although the climber was some sixty or seventy feet from the ground.

"Which way mus go now, Massa Will?" he asked.

"Keep up the largest branch—the one on this side," said Legrand. The negro obeyed him promptly, and apparently with but little trouble; ascending higher and higher, until no glimpse of his squat figure could be obtained through the dense foliage which enveloped it. Presently his voice was heard in a sort of halloo.

"How much fudder is got for go?"

"How high up are you?" asked Legrand.

"Ebber so fur," replied the negro; "can see de sky fru de top ob de tree."

"Never mind the sky, but attend to what I say. Look down the trunk and count the limbs below you on this side. How many limbs have you passed?"

"One, two, tree, four, fibe—I done pass fibe big limb, massa, pon dis side."

"Then go one limb higher."

In a few minutes the voice was heard again, announcing that the seventh limb was attained.

"Now, Jup," cried Legrand, evidently much excited, "I want you to work your way out upon that limb as far as you can. If you see anything strange, let me know."

By this time what little doubt I might have entertained of my poor friend's insanity, was put finally at rest. I had no alternative but to conclude him stricken with lunacy, and I became seriously anxious about getting him home. While I was pondering upon what was best to be done, Jupiter's voice was again heard.

"Mos feerd for to ventur pon dis limb berry far—tis dead limb putty much all de way."

"Did you say it was a *dead* limb, Jupiter?" cried Legrand in a quavering voice.

"Yes, massa, him dead as de door-nail —done up for sartain—done departed dis here life."

"What in the name of heaven shall I do?" asked Legrand, seemingly in the greatest distress.

"Do!" said I, glad of an opportunity to interpose a word, "why come home and go to bed. Come now!—that's a fine fellow. It's getting late, and, besides, you remember your promise."

"Jupiter," cried he, without heeding me in the least, "do you hear me?"

"Yes, Massa Will, hear you ebber so plain."

"Try the wood well, then, with your knife, and see if you think it *very* rotten."

"Him rotten, massa, sure nuff," replied the negro in a few moments, "but not so berry rotten as mought be. Mought ventur out leetle way pon de limb by myself, dat's true."

"By yourself!—what do you mean?"

"Why I mean de bug. 'T is *berry* hebby bug. Spose I drop him down fuss, and den de limb won't break wid just de weight ob one nigger."

"You infernal scoundrel!" cried Legrand, apparently much relieved, "what do you mean by telling me such nonsense as that? As sure as you let that beetle fall! —I'll break your neck. Look here, Jupiter! do you hear me?"

"Yes, massa, needn't hollo at poor nigger dat style."

"Well! now listen!—if you will venture out on the limb as far as you think safe, and not let go the beetle, I'll make you a present of a silver dollar as soon as you get down."

"I'm gwine, Massa Will—deed I is," replied the negro very promptly—"mos out to de eend now."

"*Out to the end!*" here fairly screamed Legrand, "do you say you are out to the end of that limb?"

"Soon be to de eend, massa,— o-o-o-o-oh! Lor-gol-a-marcy! what *is* dis here pon de tree?"

"Well!" cried Legrand, highly delighted, "what is it?"

"Why taint noffin but a skull—somebody bin lef him head up de tree, and de crows done gobble ebery bit ob de meat off."

"A skull, you say!—very well!—how is it fastened to the limb?—what holds it on?"

"Sure nuff, massa; mus look. Why dis berry curous sarcumstance, pon my word —dare's a great big nail in de skull, what fastens ob it on to de tree."

"Well now, Jupiter, do exactly as I tell you—do you hear?"

"Yes, massa."

"Pay attention, then!—find the left eye of the skull."

"Hum! hoo! dat's good! why dar aint no eye lef at all."

"Curse your stupidity! do you know your right hand from your left?"

"Yes I nose dat—nose all bout dat—tis my left hand what I chops de wood wid."

"To be sure! you are left-handed; and your left eye is on the same side as your left hand. Now, I suppose, you can find the left eye of the skull, or the place where the left eye has been. Have you found it?"

Here was a long pause. At length the negro asked,

"Is de lef eye of de skull pon de same side as de lef hand of de skull, too?—cause de skull aint got not a bit ob a hand at all—nebber mind! I got de lef eye now—here the lef eye! what mus do wid it?"

"Let the beetle drop through it, as far as the string will reach—but be careful and not let go your hold of the string."

"All dat done, Massa Will; mighty easy ting for to put de bug fru de hole—look out for him dar below!"

During this colloquy no portion of Jupiter's person could be seen; but the beetle, which he had suffered to descend, was now visible at the end of the string, and glistened, like a globe of burnished gold, in the last rays of the setting sun, some of which still faintly illumined the eminence upon which we stood. The scarabæus hung quite clear of any branches, and, if allowed to fall, would have fallen at our feet. Legrand immediately took the scythe, and cleared with it a circular space, three or four yards in diameter, just beneath the insect, and, having accomplished this, ordered Jupiter to let go the string and come down from the tree.

Driving a peg, with great nicety, into the ground, at the precise spot where the beetle fell, my friend now produced from his pocket a tape-measure. Fastening one end of this at that point of the trunk of the tree which was nearest the peg, he unrolled it till it reached the peg, and thence farther unrolled it, in the direction already established by the two points of the tree and the peg, for the distance of fifty feet—Jupiter clearing away the brambles with the scythe. At the spot thus attained a second peg was driven, and about this, as a centre, a rude circle, about four feet in diameter, described. Taking now a spade himself, and giving one to Jupiter and one to me, Legrand begged us to set about digging as quickly as possible.

To speak the truth, I had no especial relish for such amusement at any time, and, at that particular moment, would most willingly have declined it; for the night was coming on, and I felt much fatigued with the exercise already taken; but I saw no mode of escape, and was fearful of disturbing my poor friend's equanimity by a refusal. Could I have depended, indeed, upon Jupiter's aid, I would have had no hesitation in attempting to get the lunatic home by force; but I was too well assured of the old negro's disposition, to hope that he would assist me, under any circumstances, in a personal contest with his master. I made no doubt that the latter had been infected with some of the innumerable Southern superstitions about money buried, and that his phantasy had received confirmation by the finding of the scarabæus, or, perhaps, by Jupiter's obstinacy in maintaining it to be "a bug of real gold." A mind disposed to lunacy would readily be led away by such suggestions—especially if chiming in with favorite preconceived ideas—and then I called to mind the poor fellow's speech about the beetle's being "the index of his fortune." Upon the whole, I was sadly vexed and puzzled, but, at length, I concluded to make a virtue of necessity—to dig with a good will, and thus the sooner to convince the visionary, by ocular demonstration, of the fallacy of the opinions he entertained.

The lanterns having been lit, we all fell to work with a zeal worthy a more rational cause; and, as the glare fell upon our persons and implements, I could not help thinking how picturesque a group we composed, and how strange and suspicious our labors must have appeared to any interloper who, by chance, might have stumbled upon our whereabouts.

We dug very steadily for two hours. Little was said; and our chief embarrassment lay in the yelpings of the dog, who took exceeding interest in our proceedings. He, at length, became so obstreperous that we grew fearful of his giving the alarm to some stragglers in the vicinity;—or, rather, this was the apprehension of Legrand;—for myself, I should have rejoiced at any interruption which might have enabled me to get the wanderer home. The noise was, at length, very effectually silenced by Jupiter, who, getting out of the hole with a dogged air of deliberation, tied the brute's mouth up with one of his suspenders, and then returned, with a grave chuckle, to his task.

When the time mentioned had expired, we had reached a depth of five feet, and yet no signs of any treasure became manifest. A general pause ensued, and I began to hope that the farce was at an end. Legrand, however, although evidently much disconcerted, wiped his brow thoughtfully and recommenced. We had excavated the entire circle of four feet diameter, and now we slightly enlarged the limit, and went to the farther depth of two feet. Still nothing appeared. The gold-seeker, whom I sincerely pitied, at length clambered from the pit, with the bitterest disappointment imprinted upon every feature, and proceeded, slowly and reluctantly, to put on his coat, which he had thrown off at the beginning of his labor. In the mean time I made no remark. Jupiter, at a signal from his master, began to gather up his tools. This done, and the dog having been unmuzzled, we turned in profound silence towards home.

We had taken, perhaps, a dozen steps in this direction, when, with a loud oath, Legrand strode up to Jupiter, and seized him by the collar. The astonished negro opened his eyes and mouth to the fullest extent, let fall the spades, and fell upon his knees.

"You scoundrel," said Legrand, hissing out the syllables from between his clenched teeth—"you infernal black villain!—speak, I tell you!—answer me this instant, without prevarication!—which—which is your left eye?"

"Oh, my golly, Massa Will! aint dis here my lef eye for sartain?" roared the terrified Jupiter, placing his hand upon his *right* organ of vision, and holding it there with a desperate pertinacity, as if in immediate dread of his master's attempt at a gouge.

"I thought so!—I knew it!—hurrah!" vociferated Legrand, letting the negro go, and executing a series of curvets and caracols,[10] much to the astonishment of his valet, who, arising from his knees, looked, mutely, from his master to myself, and then from myself to his master.

"Come! we must go back," said the latter, "the game's not up yet;" and he again led the way to the tulip-tree.

"Jupiter," said he, when we reached its foot, "come here! was the skull nailed to the limb with the face outward, or with the face to the limb?"

"De face was out, massa, so dat de crows could get at de eyes good, widout any trouble."

"Well, then, was it this eye or that through which you let the beetle fall?"—here Legrand touched each of Jupiter's eyes.

" 'T was dis eye, massa—de lef eye—jis as you tell me," and here it was his right eye that the negro indicated.

"That will do—we must try it again."

Here my friend, about whose madness I now saw, or fancied that I saw, certain indications of method, removed the peg which marked the spot where the beetle fell, to a spot about three inches to the westward of its former position. Taking, now, the tape-measure from the nearest point of the trunk to the peg, as before, and continuing the extension in a straight line to the distance of fifty feet, a spot was indicated, removed, by several yards, from the point at which we had been digging.

Around the new position a circle, somewhat larger than in the former instance, was now described, and we again set to work with the spades. I was dreadfully weary, but, scarcely understanding what had occasioned the change in my thoughts, I felt no longer any great aversion from the labor imposed. I had become most unaccountably interested—nay, even excited. Perhaps there was something, amid all the extravagant demeanor of Legrand—some air of forethought, or of deliberation, which impressed me. I dug eagerly, and now and then caught myself actually looking, with something that very much resembled expectation, for the fancied treasure, the vision of which had demented my unfortunate companion. At a period when such vagaries of thought most fully possessed me, and when we had been at work perhaps an hour and a half, we were again interrupted by the violent howlings of the dog. His uneasiness, in the first instance, had been, evidently, but the result of playfulness or caprice, but he now assumed a bitter and serious tone. Upon Jupiter's again attempting to muzzle him, he made furious resistance, and, leaping into the hole, tore up the mould frantically with his claws. In a few seconds he had uncovered a mass of human bones, forming two complete skeletons, intermingled with several buttons of metal, and what appeared to be the dust of decayed woollen. One or two strokes of a spade upturned the blade of a large Spanish knife, and, as we dug farther, three or four loose pieces of gold and silver coin came to light.

At sight of these the joy of Jupiter could scarcely be restrained, but the countenance of his master wore an air of extreme disappointment. He urged us, however, to continue our exertions, and the words were hardly uttered when I stumbled and fell forward, having caught the toe of my boot in a large ring of iron that lay half buried in the loose earth.

We now worked in earnest, and never did I pass ten minutes of more intense excitement. During this interval we had fairly unearthed an oblong chest of wood, which, from its perfect preservation, and wonderful hardness, had plainly been subjected to some mineralizing process—perhaps that of the Bi-chloride of Mercury.[11] This box was three feet and a half long, three feet broad, and two and a half feet deep. It was firmly secured by bands of wrought iron, riveted, and forming a kind of trellis-work over the whole. On each side of the chest, near the top, were three rings of iron—six in all—by means of which a firm hold could be obtained by six persons. Our utmost united endeavors served only to disturb the coffer very slightly in its bed. We at once saw the impossibility of removing so great a weight. Luckily, the sole fastenings of the lid consisted of two sliding bolts. These we drew back—trembling and panting with anxiety. In an instant, a treasure of incalculable value lay gleaming before us. As the rays of the lanterns fell within the pit, there flashed upwards, from a confused heap of gold and of jewels, a glow and a glare that absolutely dazzled our eyes.

I shall not pretend to describe the feelings with which I gazed. Amazement was, of course, predominant. Legrand appeared exhausted with excitement, and spoke very few words. Jupiter's countenance wore, for some minutes, as deadly a pallor as it is possible, in the nature of things, for any negro's visage to assume. He seemed stupified—thunder-stricken. Presently he fell upon his knees in the pit, and, burying his naked arms up to the elbows in gold, let them there remain, as if enjoying the luxury of a bath. At length, with a deep sigh, he exclaimed, as if in a soliloquy,

"And dis all cum ob de goole-bug! de putty goole-bug! de poor little goole-bug, what I boosed in dat sabage kind ob style! Aint you shamed ob yourself, nigger?— answer me dat!"

It became necessary, at last, that I should arouse both master and valet to the expediency of removing the treasure. It was growing late, and it behooved us to make exertion, that we might get every thing housed before daylight. It was difficult to say what should be done; and much time was spent in deliberation—so confused were the ideas of all. We, finally, lightened the box by removing two thirds of its contents, when we were enabled, with some trouble, to raise it from the hole. The articles taken out were deposited among the brambles, and the dog left to guard them, with strict orders from Jupiter neither, upon any pretence, to stir from the spot, nor to open his mouth until our return. We then hurriedly made for home with the chest; reaching the hut in safety, but after excessive toil, at one o'clock in the morning. Worn out as we were, it was not in human nature to do more just then. We rested until two, and had supper; starting for the hills immediately afterwards, armed with three stout sacks, which, by good luck, were upon the premises. A little before four we arrived at the pit, divided the remainder of the booty, as equally as might be, among us, and, leaving the holes unfilled, again set out for the hut, at which, for the second time, we deposited our golden burthens, just as the first streaks of the dawn gleamed from over the tree-tops in the East.

We were now thoroughly broken down; but the intense excitement of the time denied us repose. After an unquiet slumber of some three or four hours' duration, we arose, as if by preconcert, to make examination of our treasure.

The chest had been full to the brim, and we spent the whole day, and the greater part of the next night, in a scrutiny of its contents. There had been nothing like order or arrangement. Every thing had been heaped in promiscuously. Having assorted all with care, we found ourselves possessed of even vaster wealth than we had at first supposed. In coin there was rather more than four hundred and fifty thousand dollars—estimating the value of the pieces, as accurately as we could, by the tables of the period. There was not a particle of silver. All was gold of antique date and of great variety—French, Spanish, and German money, with a few English guineas, and some counters, of which we had never seen specimens before. There were several very large and heavy coins, so worn that we could make nothing of their inscriptions. There was no American money. The value of the jewels we found more difficulty in estimating. There were diamonds—some of them exceedingly large and fine—a hundred and ten in all, and not one of them small; eighteen rubies of remarkable brilliancy;—three hundred and ten emeralds, all very beautiful; and twenty-one sapphires, with an opal. These stones had all been broken from their settings and thrown loose in the chest. The settings themselves, which we picked out from among the other gold, appeared to have been beaten up with hammers, as if to prevent identification. Besides all this, there was a vast quantity of solid gold ornaments;—nearly two hundred massive finger and ear rings;—rich chains—thirty of these, if I remember;—eighty-three very large and heavy crucifixes;—five gold censers of great value;—a prodigious golden punch-bowl, ornamented with richly chased vine-leaves and Bacchanalian figures; with two sword-handles exquisitely embossed, and many other smaller articles which I cannot recollect. The weight of these valuables exceeded three hundred and fifty pounds avoirdupois; and in this estimate I have not included one hundred and ninety-seven superb gold watches; three of the number being worth each five hundred dollars, if one. Many of them were very old, and as time keepers valueless; the works having suffered, more or less, from corrosion—but all were richly jewelled and in cases of great worth. We estimated the entire contents of the chest, that night, at a million and a half of dollars; and, upon the subsequent disposal of the trinkets and jewels (a few being retained for our own use), it was found that we had greatly undervalued the treasure.

When, at length, we had concluded our examination, and the intense excitement of the time had, in some measure, subsided, Legrand, who saw that I was dying with impatience for a solution of this most extraordinary riddle, entered into a full detail of all the circumstances connected with it.

"You remember," said he, "the night when I handed you the rough sketch I had made of the *scarabæus*. You recollect also, that I became quite vexed at you for insisting that my drawing resembled a death's-head. When you first made this assertion I thought you were jesting; but afterwards I called to mind the peculiar spots on the back of the insect, and admitted to myself that your remark had some little foundation in fact. Still, the sneer at my graphic powers irritated me —for I am considered a good artist—and, therefore, when you handed me the scrap of parchment, I was about to crumple it up and throw it angrily into the fire."

"The scrap of paper, you mean," said I.

"No; it had much of the appearance of paper, and at first I supposed it to be such, but when I came to draw upon it, I discovered it, at once, to be a piece of very thin parchment. It was quite dirty, you remember. Well, as I was in the very act of crumpling it up, my glance fell upon the sketch at which you had been looking, and you may imagine my astonishment when I perceived, in fact, the figure of a death's-head just where, it seemed to me, I had made the drawing of the beetle. For a moment I was too much amazed to think with accuracy. I knew that my design was very different in detail from this —although there was a certain similarity in general outline. Presently I took a candle, and seating myself at the other end of the room, proceeded to scrutinize the parchment more closely. Upon turning it over, I saw my own sketch upon the reverse, just as I had made it. My first idea, now, was mere surprise at the really remarkable similarity of outline—at the singular coincidence involved in the fact, that unknown to me, there should have been a skull upon the other side of the parchment, immediately beneath my figure of the *scarabæus*, and that this skull, not only in outline, but in size, should so closely resemble my drawing. I say the singularity of this coincidence absolutely stupified me for a time. This is the usual effect of such coincidences. The mind struggles to establish a connection—a sequence of cause and effect—and, being unable to do so, suffers a species of temporary paralysis. But, when I recovered from this stupor, there dawned upon me gradually a conviction which startled me even far more than the coincidence. I began distinctly, positively, to remember that there had been *no* drawing on the parchment when I made my sketch of the *scarabæus*. I became perfectly certain of this; for I recollected turning up first one side and then the other, in search of the cleanest spot. Had the skull been then there, of course I could not have failed to notice it. Here was indeed a mystery which I felt it impossible to explain; but, even at that early moment, there seemed to glimmer, faintly, within the most remote and secret chambers of my intellect, a glow-worm-like conception of that truth which last night's adventure brought to so magnificent a demonstration. I arose at once, and putting the parchment securely away, dismissed all farther reflection until I should be alone.

"When you had gone, and when Jupiter was fast asleep, I betook myself to a more methodical investigation of the affair. In the first place I considered the manner in which the parchment had come into my possession. The spot where we discovered the *scarabæus* was on the coast of the main land, about a mile eastward of the island, and but a short distance above high water mark. Upon my taking hold of it, it gave me a sharp bite, which caused me to let it drop. Jupiter, with his accustomed caution, before seizing the insect, which had flown towards him, looked about him for a leaf, or something of that nature, by which to take hold of it. It was at this moment that his eyes, and mine also, fell upon the scrap of parchment, which I then supposed to be paper. It was lying half buried in the sand, a corner sticking up. Near the spot where we found it, I observed the remnants of the hull of what appeared to have been a ship's long boat. The wreck seemed to have been there for a very great while; for the resemblance to boat timbers could scarcely be traced.

"Well, Jupiter picked up the parchment, wrapped the beetle in it, and gave it to me. Soon afterwards we turned to go home, and on the way met Lieutenant G——. I showed him the insect, and he begged me to let him take it to the fort. On my consenting, he thrust it forthwith into his waistcoat pocket, without the parchment in which it had been wrapped, and which I had continued to hold in my hand during his inspection. Perhaps he dreaded my changing my mind, and thought it best to make sure of the prize at once—you know how enthusiastic he is on all subjects connected with Natural History. At the same time, without being conscious of it, I must have deposited the parchment in my own pocket.

"You remember that when I went to the table, for the purpose of making a sketch of the beetle, I found no paper where it was usually kept. I looked in the drawer, and found none there. I searched my pockets, hoping to find an old letter—and then my hand fell upon the parchment. I thus detail the precise mode in which it came into my possession; for the circumstances impressed me with peculiar force.

"No doubt you will think me fanciful—but I had already established a kind of connection. I had put together two links of a great chain. There was a boat lying on a sea-coast, and not far from the boat was a parchment—not a paper—with a skull depicted on it. You will, of course,

ask 'where is the connection?' I reply that the skull, or death's-head, is the well-known emblem of the pirate. The flag of the death's-head is hoisted in all engagements.

"I have said that the scrap was parchment, and not paper. Parchment is durable—almost imperishable. Matters of little moment are rarely consigned to parchment; since, for the mere ordinary purposes of drawing or writing, it is not nearly so well adapted as paper. This reflection suggested some meaning—some relevancy—in the death's-head. I did not fail to observe, also, the form of the parchment. Although one of its corners had been, by some accident, destroyed, it could be seen that the original form was oblong. It was just such a slip, indeed, as might have been chosen for a memorandum—for a record of something to be long remembered and carefully preserved."

"But," I interposed, "you say that the skull was not upon the parchment when you made the drawing of the beetle. How then do you trace any connection between the boat and the skull—since this latter, according to your own admission, must have been designed (God only knows how or by whom) at some period subsequent to your sketching the scarabæus?"

"Ah, hereupon turns the whole mystery; although the secret, at this point, I had comparatively little difficulty in solving. My steps were sure, and could afford but a single result. I reasoned, for example, thus: When I drew the scarabæus, there was no skull apparent on the parchment. When I had completed the drawing, I gave it to you, and observed you narrowly until you returned it. You, therefore, did not design the skull, and no one else was present to do it. Then it was not done by human agency. And nevertheless it was done.

"At this stage of my reflections I endeavored to remember, and did remember, with entire distinctness, every incident which occurred about the period in question. The weather was chilly (oh rare and happy accident!), and a fire was blazing on the hearth. I was heated with exercise and sat near the table. You, however, had drawn a chair close to the chimney. Just as I placed the parchment in your hand, and as you were in the act of inspecting it, Wolf, the Newfoundland, entered, and leaped upon your shoulders. With your left hand you caressed him and kept him off, while your right, holding the parchment, was permitted to fall listlessly between your knees, and in close proximity to the fire. At one moment I thought the blaze had caught it, and was about to caution you, but, before I could speak, you had withdrawn it, and were engaged in its examination. When I considered all these particulars, I doubted not for a moment that *heat* had been the agent in bringing to light, on the parchment, the skull which I saw designed on it. You are well aware that chemical preparations exist, and have existed time out of mind, by means of which it is possible to write on either paper or vellum, so that the characters shall become visible only when subjected to the action of fire. Zaffre, digested in *aqua regia*, and diluted with four times its weight of water, is sometimes employed; a green tint results. The regulus[12] of cobalt, dissolved in spirit of nitre, gives a red. These colors disappear at longer or shorter intervals after the material written on cools, but again become apparent upon the re-application of heat.

"I now scrutinized the death's-head with care. Its outer edges—the edges of the drawing nearest the edge of the vellum —were far more *distinct* than the others. It was clear that the action of the caloric[13] had been imperfect or unequal. I immediately kindled a fire, and subjected every portion of the parchment to a glowing heat. At first, the only effect was the strengthening of the faint lines in the skull; but, on persevering in the experiment, there became visible, at the corner of the slip, diagonally opposite to the spot in which the death's-head was delineated, the figure of what I at first supposed to be

a goat. A closer scrutiny, however, satisfied me that it was intended for a kid."

"Ha! ha!" said I, "to be sure I have no right to laugh at you—a million and a half of money is too serious a matter for mirth—but you are not about to establish a third link in your chain—you will not find any especial connexion between your pirates and a goat—pirates, you know, have nothing to do with goats; they appertain to the farming interest."

"But I have just said that the figure was *not* that of a goat."

"Well, a kid then—pretty much the same thing."

"Pretty much, but not altogether," said Legrand. "You may have heard of one *Captain* Kidd. I at once looked on the figure of the animal as a kind of punning or hieroglyphical signature. I say signature; because its position on the vellum suggested this idea. The death's-head at the corner diagonally opposite, had, in the same manner, the air of a stamp, or seal. But I was sorely put out by the absence of all else—of the body to my imagined instrument—of the text for my context."

"I presume you expected to find a letter between the stamp and the signature."

"Something of that kind. The fact is, I felt irresistibly impressed with a presentiment of some vast good fortune impending. I can scarcely say why. Perhaps, after all, it was rather a desire than an actual belief;—but do you know that Jupiter's silly words, about the bug being of solid gold, had a remarkable effect on my fancy? And then the series of accidents and coincidences—these were so *very* extraordinary. Do you observe how mere an accident it was that these events should have occurred on the *sole* day of all the year in which it has been, or may be, sufficiently cool for fire, and that without the fire, or without the intervention of the dog at the precise moment in which he appeared, I should never have become aware of the death's-head, and so never the possessor of the treasure?"

"But proceed—I am all impatience."

"Well; you have heard, of course, the many stories current—the thousand vague rumors afloat about money buried, somewhere on the Atlantic coast, by Kidd and his associates. These rumors must have had some foundation in fact. And that the rumors have existed so long and so continuously could have resulted, it appeared to me, only from the circumstance of the buried treasure still *remaining* entombed. Had Kidd concealed his plunder for a time, and afterwards reclaimed it, the rumors would scarcely have reached us in their present unvarying form. You will observe that the stories told are all about money-seekers, not about money-finders. Had the pirate recovered his money, there the affair would have dropped. It seemed to me that some accident—say the loss of a memorandum indicating its locality—had deprived him of the means of recovering it, and that this accident had become known to his followers, who otherwise might never have heard that treasure had been concealed at all, and who, busying themselves in vain, because unguided attempts, to regain it, had given first birth, and then universal currency, to the reports which are now so common. Have you ever heard of any important treasure being unearthed along the coast?"

"Never."

"But that Kidd's accumulations were immense, is well known. I took it for granted, therefore, that the earth still held them; and you will scarcely be surprised when I tell you that I felt a hope, nearly amounting to certainty, that the parchment so strangely found, involved a lost record of the place of deposit."

"But how did you proceed?"

"I held the vellum again to the fire, after increasing the heat; but nothing appeared. I now thought it possible that the coating of dirt might have something to do with the failure; so I carefully rinsed the parchment by pouring warm water over it, and, having done this, I placed it in a tin pan, with the skull downwards, and put the pan upon a furnace of lighted charcoal.

In a few minutes, the pan having become thoroughly heated, I removed the slip, and, to my inexpressible joy, found it spotted, in several places, with what appeared to be figures arranged in lines. Again I placed it in the pan, and suffered it to remain another minute. On taking it off, the whole was just as you see it now."

Here Legrand, having re-heated the parchment, submitted it to my inspection. The following characters were rudely traced, in a red tint, between the death's-head and the goat:

53‡‡†305))6*;4826)4‡)4‡);806*;48
†8¶60))85;]8*:‡*8†83(88)5*†;46(;88*
96*?;8)*‡(;485);5*†2:*‡(;4956*2(5*
—4)8¶8*;4069285);)6†8)4‡‡;1(‡9;48
081;8:8†1;48†85;4)485†528806*81(‡
9;48;(88;4(‡?34;48)4‡;161;:188;‡?;

"But," said I, returning him the slip, "I am as much in the dark as ever. Were all the jewels of Golconda[14] awaiting me on my solution of this enigma, I am quite sure that I should be unable to earn them."

"And yet," said Legrand, "the solution is by no means so difficult as you might be led to imagine from the first hasty inspection of the characters. These characters, as any one might readily guess, form a cipher—that is to say, they convey a meaning; but then, from what is known of Kidd, I could not suppose him capable of constructing any of the more abstruse cryptographs. I made up my mind, at once, that this was of a simple species—such, however, as would appear, to the crude intellect of the sailor, absolutely insoluble without the key."

"And you really solved it?"

"Readily; I have solved others of an abstruseness ten thousand times greater. Circumstances, and a certain bias of mind, have led me to take interest in such riddles, and it may well be doubted whether human ingenuity can construct an enigma of the kind which human ingenuity may not, by proper application, resolve. In fact, having once established connected and legible characters, I scarcely gave a thought to the mere difficulty of developing their import.

"In the present case—indeed in all cases of secret writing—the first question regards the *language* of the cipher; for the principles of solution, so far, especially, as the more simple ciphers are concerned, depend on, and are varied by, the genius of the particular idiom. In general, there is no alternative but experiment (directed by probabilities) of every tongue known to him who attempts the solution, until the true one be attained. But, with the cipher now before us, all difficulty is removed by the signature. The pun on the word 'Kidd' is appreciable in no other language than the English. But for this consideration I should have begun my attempts with the Spanish and French, as the tongues in which a secret of this kind would most naturally have been written by a pirate of the Spanish main. As it was, I assumed the cryptograph to be English.

"You observe there are no divisions between the words. Had there been divisions, the task would have been comparatively easy. In such case I should have commenced with a collation and analysis of the shorter words, and, had a word of a single letter occurred, as is most likely, (a or I, for example,) I should have considered the solution as assured. But, there being no division, my first step was to ascertain the predominant letters, as well as the least frequent. Counting all, I constructed a table, thus:

Of the character 8 there are 33.
; " 26.
4 " 19.
‡) " 16.
* " 13.
5 " 12.
6 " 11.
† 1 " 8.
0 " 6.
9 2 " 5.
: 3 " 4.
? " 3.
¶ " 2.
] — " 1.

"Now, in English, the letter which most frequently occurs is *e*. Afterwards, the succession runs thus: *a o i d h n r s t u y c f g l m w b k p q x z.* E however predominates so remarkably that an individual sentence of any length is rarely seen, in which it is not the prevailing character.

"Here, then, we have, in the very beginning, the groundwork for something more than a mere guess. The general use which may be made of the table is obvious —but, in this particular cipher, we shall only very partially require its aid. As our predominant character is 8, we will commence by assuming it as the *e* of the natural alphabet. To verify the supposition, let us observe if the 8 be seen often in couples—for *e* is doubled with great frequency in English—in such words, for example, as 'meet,' 'fleet,' 'speed,' 'seen,' 'been,' 'agree,' &c. In the present instance we see it doubled no less than five times, although the cryptograph is brief.

"Let us assume 8, then, as *e*. Now, of all *words* in the language, 'the' is most usual; let us see, therefore, whether there are not repetitions of any three characters, in the same order of collocation, the last of them being 8. If we discover repetitions of such letters, so arranged, they will most probably represent the word 'the.' On inspection, we find no less than seven such arrangements, the characters being ;48. We may, therefore, assume that the semicolon represents *t*, that 4 represents *h*, and that 8 represents *e*—the last being now well confirmed. Thus a great step has been taken.

"But, having established a single word, we are enabled to establish a vastly important point; that is to say, several commencements and terminations of other words. Let us refer, for example, to the last instance but one, in which the combination ;48 occurs—not far from the end of the cipher. We know that the semicolon immediately ensuing is the commencement of a word, and, of the six characters succeeding this 'the,' we are cognizant of no less than five. Let us set these characters down, thus, by the letters we know them to represent, leaving a space for the unknown—

t eeth.

"Here we are enabled, at once, to discard the '*th*,' as forming no portion of the word commencing with the first *t*; since, by experiment of the entire alphabet for a letter adapted to the vacancy we perceive that no word can be formed of which this *th* can be a part. We are thus narrowed into

t ee,

and, going through the alphabet, if necessary, as before, we arrive at the word '*tree*,' as the sole possible reading. We thus gain another letter, *r*, represented by (, with the words '*the tree*' in juxtaposition.

"Looking beyond these words, for a short distance, we again see the combination ;48, and employ it by way of *termination* to what immediately precedes. We have thus this arrangement:

the tree ;4(‡?34 the,

or, substituting the natural letters, where known, it reads thus:

the tree thr‡?3h the.

"Now, if, in place of the unknown characters, we leave blank spaces, or substitute dots, we read thus:

the tree thr...h the,

when the word '*through*' makes itself evident at once. But this discovery gives us three new letters, *o*, *u* and *g*, represented by ‡ ? and 3.

"Looking now, narrowly, through the cipher for combinations of known characters, we find, not very far from the beginning, this arrangement,

83(88, or egree,

which, plainly, is the conclusion of the word '*degree*,' and gives us another letter, *d*, represented by †.

"Four letters beyond the word '*degree*,' we perceive the combination

;46(;88*.

"Translating the known characters, and representing the unknown by dots, as before, we read thus:

th.rtee.

an arrangement immediately suggestive of the word '*thirteen*,' and again furnishing us with two new characters, *i* and *n*, represented by 6 and *.

"Referring, now, to the beginning of the cryptograph, we find the combination,

53‡‡†.

"Translating, as before, we obtain

.good,

which assures us that the first letter is *A*, and that the first two words are '*A good*.'

"To avoid confusion, it is now time that we arrange our key, as far as discovered, in a tabular form. It will stand thus:

5 represents		a
†	"	d
8	"	e
3	"	g
4	"	h
6	"	i
*	"	n
‡	"	o
(	"	r
;	"	t

"We have, therefore, no less than ten of the most important letters represented, and it will be unnecessary to proceed with the details of the solution. I have said enough to convince you that ciphers of this nature are readily soluble, and to give you some insight into the *rationale* of their development. But be assured that the specimen before us appertains to the very simplest species of cryptograph. It now only remains to give you the full translation of the characters upon the parchment, as unriddled. Here it is:

'*A good glass in the bishop's hostel in the devil's seat twenty-one degrees and thirteen minutes northeast and by north main branch seventh limb east side shoot from the left eye of the death's-head a bee line from the tree through the shot fifty feet out.*'"

"But," said I, "the enigma seems still in as bad a condition as ever. How is it possible to extort a meaning from all this jargon about 'devil's seats,' 'death's-heads,' and 'bishop's hotels?'"

"I confess," replied Legrand, "that the matter still wears a serious aspect, when regarded with a casual glance. My first endeavor was to divide the sentence into the natural division intended by the cryptographist."

"You mean, to punctuate it?"

"Something of that kind."

"But how was it possible to effect this?"

"I reflected that it had been a *point* with the writer to run his words together without division, so as to increase the difficulty of solution. Now, a not over-acute man, in pursuing such an object, would be nearly certain to overdo the matter. When, in the course of his composition, he arrived at a break in his subject which would naturally require a pause, or a point, he would be exceedingly apt to run his characters, at this place, more than usually close together. If you will observe the MS., in the present instance, you will easily detect five such cases of unusual crowding. Acting on this hint, I made the division thus:

'A good glass in the Bishop's hostel in the Devil's seat—twenty-one degrees and thirteen minutes—northeast and by north—main branch seventh limb east side—shoot from the left eye of the death's-head—a bee-line from the tree through the shot fifty feet out.'"

"Even this division," said I, "leaves me still in the dark."

"It left me also in the dark," replied Legrand, "for a few days; during which I made diligent inquiry, in the neighborhood of Sullivan's Island, for any building which went by the name of the 'Bishop's Hotel;' for, of course, I dropped the obsolete word 'hostel.' Gaining no information on the subject, I was on the point of extending my sphere of search, and proceeding in a more systematic manner, when, one morning, it entered into my head, quite suddenly, that this 'Bishop's Hostel' might have some reference to an old family, of the name of Bessop, which, time out of mind, had held possession of an ancient manor-house, about four miles to the northward of the Island. I accordingly went over to the plantation, and re-instituted my inquiries among the older negroes of the place. At length one of the most aged of the women said that she had heard of such a place as *Bessop's Castle*, and thought that she could guide me to it, but that it was not a castle, nor a tavern, but a high rock.

"I offered to pay her well for her trouble, and, after some demur, she consented to accompany me to the spot. We found it without much difficulty, when, dismissing her, I proceeded to examine the place. The 'castle' consisted of an irregular assemblage of cliffs and rocks—one of the latter being quite remarkable for its height as well as for its insulated and artificial appearance. I clambered to its apex, and then felt much at a loss as to what should be next done.

"While I was busied in reflection, my eyes fell upon a narrow ledge in the eastern face of the rock, perhaps a yard below the summit on which I stood. This ledge projected about eighteen inches, and was not more than a foot wide, while a niche in the cliff just above it, gave it a rude resemblance to one of the hollow-backed chairs used by our ancestors. I made no doubt that here was the 'devil's-seat' alluded to in the MS., and now I seemed to grasp the full secret of the riddle.

"The 'good glass,' I knew, could have reference to nothing but a telescope; for the word 'glass' is rarely employed in any other sense by seamen. Now here, I at once saw, was a telescope to be used, and a definite point of view, *admitting no variation*, from which to use it. Nor did I hesitate to believe that the phrases, 'twenty-one degrees and thirteen minutes,' and 'northeast and by north,' were intended as directions for the levelling of the glass. Greatly excited by these discoveries, I hurried home, procured a telescope, and returned to the rock.

"I let myself down to the ledge, and found that it was impossible to retain a seat on it unless in one particular position. This fact confirmed my preconceived idea. I proceeded to use the glass. Of course, the 'twenty-one degrees and thirteen minutes' could allude to nothing but elevation above the visible horizon, since the horizontal direction was clearly indicated by the words, 'northeast and by north.' This latter direction I at once established by means of a pocket-compass; then, pointing the glass as nearly at an angle of twenty-one degrees of elevation as I could do it by guess, I moved it cautiously up or down, until my attention was arrested by a circular rift or opening in the foliage of a large tree that overtopped its fellows in the distance. In the centre of this rift I perceived a white spot, but could not, at first, distinguish what it was. Adjusting the focus of the telescope, I again looked, and now made it out to be a human skull.

"On this discovery I was so sanguine as to consider the enigma solved; for the phrase 'main branch, seventh limb, east side,' could refer only to the position of the skull on the tree, while 'shoot from the left eye of the death's-head' admitted, also, of but one interpretation, in regard to a search for buried treasure. I perceived that the design was to drop a bullet from the left eye of the skull, and that a beeline, or, in other words, a straight line, drawn from the nearest point of the trunk through 'the shot,' (or the spot where the bullet fell,) and thence extended to a distance of fifty feet, would indicate a definite point—and beneath this point I thought it at least *possible* that a deposit of value lay concealed."

"All this," I said, "is exceedingly clear, and, although ingenious, still simple and explicit. When you left the Bishop's Hotel, what then?"

"Why, having carefully taken the bearings of the tree, I turned homewards. The instant that I left 'the devil's seat,' however, the circular rift vanished; nor could I get a glimpse of it afterwards, turn as I would. What seems to me the chief ingenuity in this whole business, is the fact (for repeated experiment has convinced

me it *is* a fact) that the circular opening in question is visible from no other attainable point of view than that afforded by the narrow ledge on the face of the rock.

"In this expedition to the 'Bishop's Hotel' I had been attended by Jupiter, who had, no doubt, observed, for some weeks past, the abstraction of my demeanor, and took especial care not to leave me alone. But, on the next day, getting up very early, I contrived to give him the slip, and went into the hills in search of the tree. After much toil I found it. When I came home at night my valet proposed to give me a flogging. With the rest of the adventure I believe you are as well acquainted as myself."

"I suppose," said I, "you missed the spot, in the first attempt at digging, through Jupiter's stupidity in letting the bug fall through the right instead of through the left eye of the skull."

"Precisely. This mistake made a difference of about two inches and a half in the 'shot'—that is to say, in the position of the peg nearest the tree; and had the treasure been *beneath* the 'shot,' the error would have been of little moment; but 'the shot,' together with the nearest point of the tree, were merely two points for the establishment of a line of direction; of course the error, however trivial in the beginning, increased as we proceeded with the line, and by the time we had gone fifty feet, threw us quite off the scent. But for my deep-seated convictions that treasure was here somewhere actually buried, we might have had all our labor in vain."

"I presume the fancy of *the skull*, of letting fall a bullet through the skull's eye —was suggested to Kidd by the piratical flag. No doubt he felt a kind of poetical consistency in recovering his money through this ominous insignium."

"Perhaps so; still I cannot help thinking that common-sense had quite as much to do with the matter as poetical consistency. To be visible from the devil's-seat, it was necessary that the object, if small, should be white; and there is nothing like your human skull for retaining and even increasing its whiteness under exposure to all vicissitudes of weather."

"But your grandiloquence, and your conduct in swinging the beetle—how excessively odd! I was sure you were mad. And why did you insist on letting fall the bug, instead of a bullet, from the skull?"

"Why, to be frank, I felt somewhat annoyed by your evident suspicions touching my sanity, and so resolved to punish you quietly, in my own way, by a little bit of sober mystification.[15] For this reason I swung the beetle, and for this reason I let it fall from the tree. An observation of yours about its great weight suggested the latter idea."

"Yes, I perceive; and now there is only one point which puzzles me. What are we to make of the skeletons found in the hole?"

"That is a question I am no more able to answer than yourself. There seems, however, only one plausible way of accounting for them—and yet it is dreadful to believe in such atrocity as my suggestion would imply. It is clear that Kidd —if Kidd indeed secreted this treasure, which I doubt not—it is clear that he must have had assistance in the labor. But, the worst of this labor concluded, he may have thought it expedient to remove all participants in his secret. Perhaps a couple of blows with a mattock were sufficient, while his coadjutors were busy in the pit; perhaps it required a dozen—who shall tell?"

THE MURDERS
IN THE RUE MORGUE[1]

What song the Syrens sang, or what name Achilles assumed when he hid himself among women, although puzzling questions are not beyond all conjecture.
Sir Thomas Brown, *Urn-Burial.*[2]

The mental features discoursed of as the analytical, are, in themselves, but little susceptible of analysis. We appreciate them only in their effects. We know of them, among other things, that they are always to their possessor, when inordinately possessed, a source of the liveliest enjoyment. As the strong man exults in his physical ability, delighting in such exercises as call his muscles into action, so glories the analyst in that moral activity which *disentangles*. He derives pleasure from even the most trivial occupations bringing his talents into play. He is fond of enigmas, of conundrums, of hieroglyphics; exhibiting in his solutions of each a degree of *acumen* which appears to the ordinary apprehension preternatural. His results, brought about by the very soul and essence of method, have, in truth, the whole air of intuition. The faculty of re-solution is possibly much invigorated by mathematical study, and especially by that highest branch of it which, unjustly, and merely on account of its retrograde operations, has been called, as if *par excellence*, analysis. Yet to calculate is not in itself to analyze. A chess-player, for example, does the one without effort at the other. It follows that the game of chess, in its effects upon mental character, is greatly misunderstood. I am not now writing a treatise, but simply prefacing a somewhat peculiar narrative by observations very much at random; I will, therefore, take occasion to assert that the higher powers of the reflective intellect are more decidedly and more usefully tasked by the unostentatious game of draughts[3] than by all the elaborate frivolity of chess. In this latter, where the pieces have different and *bizarre* motions, with various and variable values, what is only complex is mistaken (a not unusual error) for what is profound. The *attention* is here called powerfully into play. If it flag for an instant, an oversight is committed, resulting in injury or defeat. The possible moves being not only manifold but involute, the chances of such oversights are multiplied; and in nine cases out of ten it is the more concentrative rather than the

PARIS

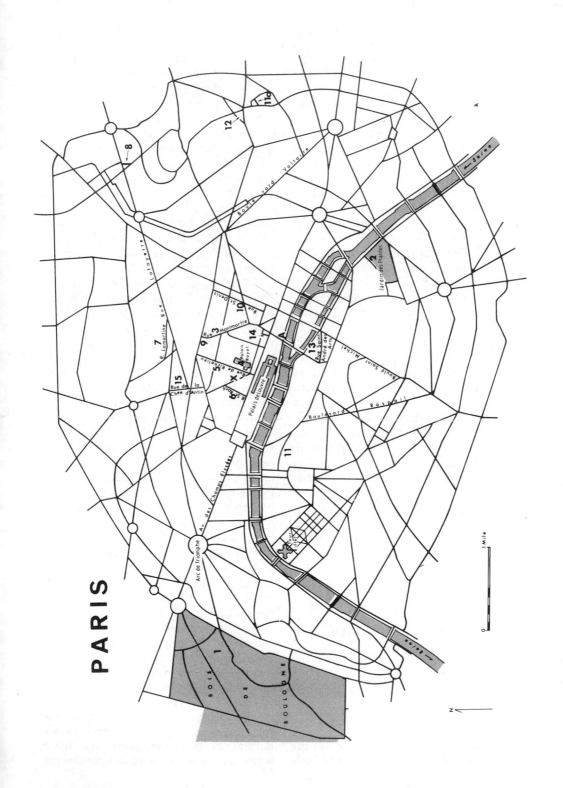

KEY

"The Murders in the Rue Morgue"
1. Bois de Boulogne.
2. Jardin des Plantes.
3. Rue Montmartre.
4. Palais Royal.
5. Rue (de) Richelieu.
6. Rue St.-Roch.
7. Lamartine (alley): Current maps show no such alley; our map shows the narrow street, Rue Lamartine. Poe may be joking—he disliked Lamartine's work (Lombard).
8. Rue Deloraine: If this street existed in Poe's day, it is no longer on maps of Paris. Our map locates the Rue de Loraine.
9. Theatre des Varietes.
10. Rue St. Denis.
11. "Faubourg St.-Germain": There are three possible locations: (1) The area near St.-Germain-des-Prés on the West Bank (left of 13 on our map) is the most likely location. This is the area in which the character Pelham in Bulwer's novel *Pelham* would like to live, and Bulwer calls it "Faubourg St.-Germain." Also, Poe took much of his Parisian texture from Bulwer (see Section Preface). Number 11 on the map locates the Rue Saint-Dominique where an acquaintance of Pelham lives; (2) St.-Germain-l'Auxerrois in the Arrondissement Louvre (across the street from the Louvre just above "A"); (3) near area 11 on our map, marked "11A." Since "Faubourg" means "suburb" and since the other two possibilities are in central Paris, this may be the real location. See number 12 for another reason for believing 11A is the location.
12. Rue Dubourg: We were unable to obtain a street index of pre-Haussman Paris, so we are uncertain as to whether there was a Rue Dubourg. Dupin mentions it to a sailor who does not know Paris well and, since there is a character in the story named Pauline Dubourg, it is possible that

Poe made it up. Dupin, wanting a fictitious street name, could have had the name in mind. Poe, moreover, had known some people named "Dubourg" when he was in England with the Allans. Two sisters by that name kept a boarding school he attended, and their brother worked for John Allan. There is, however, a Cité Dubourg, located at number 12, which is a fairly likely site because, as Dupin says, it is "just by" his home. If "11A" above is correct, "12" probably is as well.

X. Rue Morgue: We are told no such street exists. Poe says it runs from Rue St.-Roch to the Rue (de) Richelieu. The area he had in mind, then, is near the modern Avenue de l'Opera. "X" marks the spot.

"The Mystery of Marie Rogêt"
13. Rue Pavée Saint André: This is located on our map at the Rue Saint André des Arts (Number 14).
14. Rue du Roule. Numbers 13 and 14 are opposite one another across the river Seine, as Poe says, but he chooses an odd location for the body to be found: there were then, and are now, far more prominent landmarks. We assume that by "Quartier of the Rue Saint André" and "the neighborhood of the Barrière du Roule" he intends the areas immediately around those streets.
Rue des Drômes: We were unable to locate such a street.
A. Approximate location of Marie's body. (See numbers 13 and 14).

"The Purloined Letter"
Rue Dunôt: Its location should be near number 11 (see explanation there), but no such street seems to exist now.

"The Duc De L'Omelette"
15. Rue de la Chaussée d'Antin.

Figure Nine. Poe's Paris. Places mentioned in "The Murders in the Rue Morgue" are listed first, then "The Mystery of Marie Rogêt," "The Purloined Letter," and "The Duc De l'Omelette." Some modern landmarks are shown to help orient the reader. Map drawn by Lewis Armstrong.

more acute player who conquers. In draughts, on the contrary, where the moves are *unique* and have but little variation, the probabilities of inadvertence are diminished, and the mere attention being left comparatively unemployed, what advantages are obtained by either party are obtained by superior *acumen*. To be less abstract—Let us suppose a game of draughts where the pieces are reduced to four kings, and where, of course, no oversight is to be expected. It is obvious that here the victory can be decided (the players being at all equal) only by some *recherché*[4] movement, the result of some strong exertion of the intellect. Deprived of ordinary resources, the analyst throws himself into the spirit of his opponent, identifies himself therewith, and not unfrequently sees thus, at a glance, the sole methods (sometimes indeed absurdly simple ones) by which he may seduce into error or hurry into miscalculation.

Whist has long been noted for its influence upon what is termed the calculating power; and men of the highest order of intellect have been known to take an apparently unaccountable delight in it, while eschewing chess as frivolous. Beyond doubt there is nothing of a similar nature so greatly tasking the faculty of analysis. The best chess-player in Christendom *may* be little more than the best player of chess; but proficiency in whist implies capacity for success in all these more important undertakings where mind struggles with mind. When I say proficiency, I mean that perfection in the game which includes a comprehension of *all* the sources whence legitimate advantage may be derived. These are not only manifold but multiform, and lie frequently among recesses of thought altogether inaccessible to the ordinary understanding. To observe attentively is to remember distinctly; and, so far, the concentrative chess-player will do very well at whist; while the rules of Hoyle[5] (themselves based upon the mere mechanism of the game) are sufficiently and generally comprehensible. Thus to have a retentive memory, and to proceed by "the book," are points commonly regarded as the sum total of good playing. But it is in matters beyond the limits of mere rule that the skill of the analyst is evinced. He makes, in silence, a host of observations and inferences. So, perhaps, do his companions; and the difference in the extent of the information obtained, lies not so much in the validity of the inference as in the quality of the observation. The necessary knowledge is that of *what* to observe. Our player confines himself not at all; nor, because the game is the object, does he reject deductions from things external to the game. He examines the countenance of his partner, comparing it carefully with that of each of his opponents. He considers the mode of assorting the cards in each hand; often counting trump by trump, and honor by honor, through the glances bestowed by their holders upon each. He notes every variation of face as the play progresses, gathering a fund of thought from the differences in the expression of certainty, of surprise, of triumph, or chagrin. From the manner of gathering up a trick he judges whether the person taking it can make another in the suit. He recognizes what is played through feint, by the air with which it is thrown upon the table. A casual or inadvertent word; the accidental dropping or turning of a card, with the accompanying anxiety or carelessness in regard to its concealment; the counting of the tricks, with the order of their arrangement; embarrassment, hesitation, eagerness or trepidation—all afford, to his apparently intuitive perception, indications of the true state of affairs. The first two or three rounds having been played, he is in full possession of the contents of each hand, and thenceforward puts down his cards with as absolute a precision of purpose as if the rest of the party had turned outward the faces of their own.

The analytical power should not be

confounded with simple ingenuity; for while the analyst is necessarily ingenious, the ingenious man is often remarkably incapable of analysis. The constructive or combining power, by which ingenuity is usually manifested, and to which the phrenologists (I believe erroneously) have assigned a separate organ, supposing it a primitive faculty,[6] has been so frequently seen in those whose intellect bordered otherwise upon idiocy, as to have attracted general observation among writers on morals. Between ingenuity and the analytic ability there exists a difference far greater, indeed, than that between the fancy and the imagination, but of a character very strictly analogous. It will be found, in fact, that the ingenious are always fanciful, and the *truly* imaginative never otherwise than analytic.

The narrative which follows will appear to the reader somewhat in the light of a commentary upon the propositions just advanced.

Residing in Paris during the spring and part of the summer of 18—, I there became acquainted with a Monsieur C. Auguste Dupin.[7] This young gentleman was of an excellent—indeed of an illustrious family, but, by a variety of untoward events, had been reduced to such poverty that the energy of his character succumbed beneath it, and he ceased to bestir himself in the world, or to care for the retrieval of his fortunes. By courtesy of his creditors, there still remained in his possession a small remnant of his patrimony; and, upon the income arising from this, he managed, by means of a rigorous economy, to procure the necessaries of life, without troubling himself about its superfluities. Books, indeed, were his sole luxuries, and in Paris these are easily obtained. Our first meeting was at an obscure library in the Rue Montmartre, where the accident of our both being in search of the same very rare and very remarkable volume, brought us into closer communion. We saw each other again and again. I was

deeply interested in the little family history which he detailed to me with all that candor which a Frenchman indulges whenever mere self is the theme. I was astonished, too, at the vast extent of his reading; and, above all, I felt my soul enkindled within me by the wild fervor, and the vivid freshness of his imagination. Seeking in Paris the objects I then sought, I felt that the society of such a man would be to me a treasure beyond price; and this feeling I frankly confided to him. It was at length arranged that we should live together during my stay in the city; and as my worldly circumstances were somewhat less embarrassed than his own, I was permitted to be at the expense of renting, and furnishing in a style which suited the rather fantastic gloom of our common temper, a time-eaten and grotesque mansion, long deserted through superstitions into which we did not inquire, and tottering to its fall in a retired and desolate portion of the Faubourg St. Germain.

Had the routine of our life at this place been known to the world, we should have been regarded as madmen—although, perhaps, as madmen of a harmless nature. Our seclusion was perfect. We admitted no visitors. Indeed the locality of our retirement had been carefully kept a secret from my own former associates; and it had been many years since Dupin had ceased to know or be known in Paris. We existed within ourselves alone.

It was a freak of fancy in my friend (for what else shall I call it?) to be enamored of the Night for her own sake; and into this *bizarrerie*, as into all his others, I quietly fell; giving myself up to his wild whims with a perfect *abandon*. The sable divinity would not herself dwell with us always; but we could counterfeit her presence. At the first dawn of the morning we closed all the massy shutters of our old building; lighted a couple of tapers which, strongly perfumed, threw out only the ghastliest and feeblest of rays. By the aid of these we then buried our souls in dreams—reading, writing, or conversing, until warned by the clock of the advent of the true Darkness. Then we sallied forth into the streets, arm and arm, continuing the topics of the day, or roaming far and wide until a late hour, seeking, amid the wild lights and shadows of the populous city, that infinity of mental excitement which quiet observation can afford.

At such times I could not help remarking and admiring (although from his rich ideality I had been prepared to expect it) a peculiar analytic ability in Dupin. He seemed, too, to take an eager delight in its exercise—if not exactly in its display—and did not hesitate to confess the pleasure thus derived. He boasted to me, with a low chuckling laugh, that most men, in respect to himself, wore windows in their bosoms, and was wont to follow up such assertions by direct and very startling proofs of his intimate knowledge of my own. His manner at these moments was frigid and abstract; his eyes were vacant in expression; while his voice, usually a rich tenor, rose into a treble which would have sounded petulantly but for the deliberateness and entire distinctness of the enunciation. Observing him in these moods, I often dwelt meditatively upon the old philosophy of the Bi-Part Soul, and amused myself with the fancy of a double Dupin—the creative and the resolvent.

Let it not be supposed, from what I have just said, that I am detailing any mystery, or penning any romance. What I have described in the Frenchman, was merely the result of an excited, or perhaps of a diseased intelligence.[8] But of the character of his remarks at the periods in question an example will best convey the idea.

We were strolling one night down a long dirty street, in the vicinity of the Palais Royal. Being both, apparently, occupied with thought, neither of us had spoken a syllable for fifteen minutes at least. All at once Dupin broke forth with these words:—

"He is a very little fellow, that's true, and would do better for the *Théâtre des Variétés.*"

"There can be no doubt of that," I replied unwittingly, and not at first observing (so much had I been absorbed in reflection) the extraordinary manner in which the speaker had chimed in with my meditations. In an instant afterward I recollected myself, and my astonishment was profound.

"Dupin," said I, gravely, "this is beyond my comprehension. I do not hesitate to say that I am amazed, and can scarcely credit my senses. How was it possible you should know I was thinking of——?" Here I paused, to ascertain beyond a doubt whether he really knew of whom I thought.

—— "of Chantilly," said he, "why do you pause? You were remarking to yourself that his diminutive figure unfitted him for tragedy."

This was precisely what had formed the subject of my reflections. Chantilly was a *quondam* cobbler of the Rue St. Denis, who, becoming stage-mad, had attempted the *rôle* of Xerxes, in Crébillon's tragedy so called, and been notoriously Pasquinaded for his pains.[9]

"Tell me, for Heaven's sake," I exclaimed, "the method—if method there is—by which you have been enabled to fathom my soul in this matter." In fact I was even more startled than I would have been willing to express.

"It was the fruiterer," replied my friend, "who brought you to the conclusion that the mender of soles was not of sufficient height for Xerxes *et id genus omne.*"[10]

"The fruiterer!—you astonish me—I know no fruiterer whomsoever."

"The man who ran up against you as we entered the street—it may have been fifteen minutes ago."

I now remembered that, in fact, a fruiterer, carrying upon his head a large basket of apples, had nearly thrown me down, by accident, as we passed from the Rue C—— into the thoroughfare where we stood; but what this had to do with Chantilly I could not possibly understand.

There was not a particle of *charlatanerie* about Dupin. "I will explain," he said, "and that you may comprehend all clearly, we will first retrace the course of your meditations, from the moment in which I spoke to you until that of the *rencontre* with the fruiterer in question. The larger links of the chain run thus— Chantilly, Orion, Dr. Nichols, Epicurus, Stereotomy, the street stones, the fruiterer."

There are few persons who have not, at some period of their lives, amused themselves in retracing the steps by which particular conclusions of their own minds have been attained. The occupation is often full of interest; and he who attempts it for the first time is astonished by the apparently illimitable distance and incoherence between the starting-point and the goal. What, then, must have been my amazement when I heard the Frenchman speak what he had just spoken, and when I could not help acknowledging that he had spoken the truth. He continued:

"We had been talking of horses, if I remember aright, just before leaving the Rue C——. This was the last subject we discussed. As we crossed into this street, a fruiterer, with a large basket upon his head, brushing quickly past us, thrust you upon a pile of paving-stones collected at a spot where the causeway is undergoing repair. You stepped upon one of the loose fragments, slipped, slightly strained your ankle, appeared vexed or sulky, muttered a few words, turned to look at the pile, and then proceeded in silence. I was not particularly attentive to what you did; but observation has become with me, of late, a species of necessity.

"You kept your eyes upon the ground —glancing, with a petulant expression, at the holes and ruts in the pavement, (so that I saw you were still thinking of the stones,) until we reached the little alley called Lamartine, which has been paved, by way of experiment, with the overlapping and riveted blocks. Here your countenance brightened up, and, perceiving your lips move, I could not doubt that you murmured the word 'stereotomy,' a term very affectedly applied to this species of pavement. I knew that you could not say to yourself 'stereotomy' without being brought to think of atomies, and thus of the theories of Epicurus; and since, when we discussed this subject not very long ago, I mentioned to you how singularly, yet with how little notice, the vague guesses of that noble Greek had met with confirmation in the late nebular cosmogony, I felt that you could not avoid casting your eyes upward to the great *nebula* in Orion, and I certainly expected that you would do so. You did look up; and I was now assured that I had correctly followed your steps. But in that bitter *tirade* upon Chantilly, which appeared in yesterday's 'Musée,' the satirist, making some disgraceful allusions to the cobbler's change of name upon assuming the buskin, quoted a Latin line about which we have often conversed. I mean the line

Perdidit antiquum litera prima sonum.

I had told you that this was in reference to Orion, formerly written Urion; and, from certain pungencies connected with this explanation, I was aware that you could not have forgotten it. It was clear, therefore, that you would not fail to combine the two ideas of Orion and Chantilly.[11] That you did combine them I saw by the character of the smile which passed over your lips. You thought of the poor cobbler's immolation. So far, you had been stooping in your gait; but now I saw you draw yourself up to your full height. I was then sure that you reflected upon the diminutive figure of Chantilly. At this point I interrupted your meditations to remark that as, in fact, he *was* a very little fellow—that Chantilly—he would do better at the *Théâtre des Variétés*."

Not long after this, we were looking over an evening edition of the "Gazette des Tribunaux," when the following paragraphs arrested our attention.

"EXTRAORDINARY MURDERS. — This morning, about three o'clock, the inhabitants of the Quartier St. Roch were aroused from sleep by a succession of terrific shrieks, issuing, apparently, from the fourth story of a house in the Rue Morgue, known to be in the sole occupancy of one Madame L'Espanaye, and her daughter, Mademoiselle Camille L'Espanaye. After some delay, occasioned by a fruitless attempt to procure admission in the usual manner, the gateway was broken in with a crowbar, and eight or ten of the neighbors entered, accompanied by two *gendarmes*. By this time the cries had ceased; but, as the party rushed up the first flight of stairs, two or more rough voices, in angry contention, were distinguished, and seemed to proceed from the upper part of the house. As the second landing was reached, these sounds, also, had ceased, and everything remained perfectly quiet. The party spread themselves, and hurried from room to room. Upon arriving at a large back chamber in the fourth story, (the door of which, being found locked, with the key inside, was forced open,) a spectacle presented itself which struck every one present not less with horror than with astonishment.

"The apartment was in the wildest disorder—the furniture broken and thrown about in all directions. There was only one bedstead; and from this the bed had been removed, and thrown into the middle of the floor. On a chair lay a razor, besmeared with blood. On the hearth were two or three long and thick tresses of gray human hair, also dabbled in blood, and seeming to have been pulled out by the roots. Upon the floor were found four Napoleons, an ear-ring of topaz, three large silver spoons, three smaller of *métal d'Alger*,[12] and two bags, containing nearly four thousand francs in gold. The drawers of a *bureau*, which stood in one corner, were open, and had been, apparently, rifled, although many articles still remained

in them. A small iron safe was discovered under the *bed* (not under the bedstead). It was open, with the key still in the door. It had no contents beyond a few old letters, and other papers of little consequence.

"Of Madame L'Espanaye no traces were here seen; but an unusual quantity of soot being observed in the fire-place, a search was made in the chimney, and (horrible to relate!) the corpse of the daughter, head downward, was dragged therefrom; it having been thus forced up the narrow aperture for a considerable distance. The body was quite warm. Upon examining it, many excoriations were perceived, no doubt occasioned by the violence with which it had been thrust up and disengaged. Upon the face were many severe scratches, and, upon the throat, dark bruises, and deep indentations of finger nails, as if the deceased had been throttled to death.

"After a thorough investigation of every portion of the house, without farther discovery, the party made its way into a small paved yard in the rear of the building, where lay the corpse of the old lady, with her throat so entirely cut that, upon an attempt to raise her, the head fell off. The body, as well as the head, was fearfully mutilated—the former so much so as scarcely to retain any semblance of humanity.

"To this horrible mystery there is not as yet, we believe, the slightest clew."

The next day's paper had these additional particulars.

"*The Tragedy in the Rue Morgue.* Many individuals have been examined in relation to this most extraordinary and frightful affair." [The word '*affaire*' has not yet, in France, that levity of import which it conveys with us,] "but nothing whatever has transpired to throw light upon it. We give below all the material testimony elicited.

"*Pauline Dubourg*, laundress, deposes that she has known both the deceased for three years, having washed for them during that period. The old lady and her daughter seemed on good terms—very affectionate towards each other. They were excellent pay. Could not speak in regard to their mode or means of living. Believed that Madame L. told fortunes for a living. Was reputed to have money put by. Never met any persons in the house when she called for the clothes or took them home. Was sure that they had no servant in employ. There appeared to be no furniture in any part of the building except in the fourth story.

"*Pierre Moreau*, tobacconist, deposes that he has been in the habit of selling small quantities of tobacco and snuff to Madame L'Espanaye for nearly four years. Was born in the neighborhood, and has always resided there. The deceased and her daughter had occupied the house in which the corpses were found, for more than six years. It was formerly occupied by a jeweller, who under-let the upper rooms to various persons. The house was the property of Madame L. She became dissatisfied with the abuse of the premises by her tenant, and moved into them herself, refusing to let any portion. The old lady was childish. Witness had seen the daughter some five or six times during the six years. The two lived an exceedingly retired life—were reputed to have money. Had heard it said among the neighbours that Madame L. told fortunes—did not believe it. Had never seen any person enter the door except the old lady and her daughter, a porter once or twice, and a physician some eight or ten times.

"Many other persons, neighbours, gave evidence to the same effect. No one was spoken of as frequenting the house. It was not known whether there were any living connexions of Madame L. and her daughter. The shutters of the front windows were seldom opened. Those in the rear were always closed, with the exception of the large back room, fourth story. The house was a good house—not very old.

"*Isodore Musèt, gendarme,* deposes that he was called to the house about three o'clock in the morning, and found some twenty or thirty persons at the gateway, endeavouring to gain admittance. Forced it open, at length, with a bayonet—not with a crowbar. Had but little difficulty in getting it open, on account of its being a double or folding gate, and bolted neither at bottom nor top. The shrieks were continued until the gate was forced—and then suddenly ceased. They seemed to be screams of some person (or persons) in great agony—were loud and drawn out, not short and quick. Witness led the way up stairs. Upon reaching the first landing, heard two voices in loud and angry contention—the one a gruff voice, the other much shriller—a very strange voice. Could distinguish some words of the former, which was that of a Frenchman. Was positive that it was not a woman's voice. Could distinguish the words '*sacré*' and '*diable.*' The shrill voice was that of a foreigner. Could not be sure whether it was the voice of a man or of a woman. Could not make out what was said, but believed the language to be Spanish. The state of the room and of the bodies was described by this witness as we described them yesterday.

"*Henri Duval,* a neighbor, and by trade a silversmith, deposes that he was one of the party who first entered the house. Corroborates the testimony of Musèt in general. As soon as they forced an entrance, they reclosed the door, to keep out the crowd, which collected very fast, notwithstanding the lateness of the hour. The shrill voice, the witness thinks, was that of an Italian. Was certain it was not French. Could not be sure that it was a man's voice. It might have been a woman's. Was not acquainted with the Italian language. Could not distinguish the words, but was convinced by the intonation that the speaker was an Italian. Knew Madame L. and her daughter. Had conversed with both frequently. Was sure that the shrill voice was not that of either of the deceased.

"—— *Odenheimer, restaurateur.* This

witness volunteered his testimony. Not speaking French, was examined through an interpreter. Is a native of Amsterdam. Was passing the house at the time of the shrieks. They lasted for several minutes —probably ten. They were long and loud —very awful and distressing. Was one of those who entered the building. Corroborated the previous evidence in every respect but one. Was sure that the shrill voice was that of a man—of a Frenchman. Could not distinguish the words uttered. They were loud and quick—unequal— spoken apparently in fear as well as in anger. The voice was harsh—not so much shrill as harsh. Could not call it a shrill voice. The gruff voice said repeatedly 'sacré,' 'diable' and once 'mon Dieu.'[13]

"*Jules Mignaud*, banker, of the firm of Mignaud et Fils, Rue Deloraine. Is the elder Mignaud. Madame L'Espanaye had some property. Had opened an account with his banking house in the spring of the year————(eight years previously). Made frequent deposits in small sums. Had checked for nothing until the third day before her death, when she took out in person the sum of 4000 francs. This sum was paid in gold, and a clerk sent home with the money.

"*Adolphe Le Bon*, clerk to Mignaud et Fils, deposes that on the day in question, about noon, he accompanied Madame L'Espanaye to her residence with the 4000 francs, put up in two bags. Upon the door being opened, Mademoiselle L. appeared and took from his hands one of the bags, while the old lady relieved him of the other. He then bowed and departed. Did not see any person in the street at the time. It is a bye-street—very lonely.

"*William Bird*, tailor, deposes that he was one of the party who entered the house. Is an Englishman. Has lived in Paris two years. Was one of the first to ascend the stairs. Heard the voices in contention. The gruff voice was that of a Frenchman. Could make out several words, but cannot now remember all. Heard distinctly 'sacré' and 'mon Dieu.'

There was a sound at the moment as if of several persons struggling—a scraping and scuffling sound. The shrill voice was very loud—louder than the gruff one. Is sure that it was not the voice of an Englishman. Appeared to be that of a German. Might have been a woman's voice. Does not understand German.

"Four of the above-named witnesses, being recalled, deposed that the door of the chamber in which was found the body of Mademoiselle L. was locked on the inside when the party reached it. Every thing was perfectly silent—no groans or noises of any kind. Upon forcing the door no person was seen. The windows, both of the back and front room, were down and firmly fastened from within. A door between the two rooms was closed, but not locked. The door leading from the front room into the passage was locked, with the key on the inside. A small room in the front of the house, on the fourth story, at the head of the passage, was open, the door being ajar. This room was crowded with old beds, boxes, and so forth. These were carefully removed and searched. There was not an inch of any portion of the house which was not carefully searched. Sweeps were sent up and down the chimneys. The house was a four story one, with garrets (*mansardes*). A trap-door on the roof was nailed down very securely—did not appear to have been opened for years. The time elapsing between the hearing of the voices in contention and the breaking open of the room door, was variously stated by the witnesses. Some made it as short as three minutes—some as long as five. The door was opened with difficulty.

"*Alfonzo Garcio*, undertaker, deposes that he resides in the Rue Morgue. Is a native of Spain. Was one of the party who entered the house. Did not proceed up stairs. Is nervous, and was apprehensive of the consequences of agitation. Heard the voices in contention. The gruff voice was that of a Frenchman. Could not distinguish what was said. The shrill voice was that of an Englishman—is sure of this. Does not understand the English language, but judges by the intonation.

"*Alberto Montani*, confectioner, deposes that he was among the first to ascend the stairs. Heard the voices in question. The gruff voice was that of a Frenchman. Distinguished several words. The speaker appeared to be expostulating. Could not make out the words of the shrill voice. Spoke quick and unevenly. Thinks it the voice of a Russian. Corroborates the general testimony. Is an Italian. Never conversed with a native of Russia.

"Several witnesses, recalled, here testified that the chimneys of all the rooms on the fourth story were too narrow to admit the passage of a human being. By 'sweeps' were meant cylindrical sweeping-brushes, such as are employed by those who clean chimneys. These brushes were passed up and down every flue in the house. There is no back passage by which any one could have descended while the party proceeded up stairs. The body of Mademoiselle L'Espanaye was so firmly wedged in the chimney that it could not be got down until four or five of the party united their strength.

"*Paul Dumas*, physician, deposes that he was called to view the bodies about day-break. They were both then lying on the sacking of the bedstead in the chamber where Mademoiselle L. was found. The corpse of the young lady was much bruised and excoriated. The fact that it had been thrust up the chimney would sufficiently account for these appearances. The throat was greatly chafed. There were several deep scratches just below the chin, together with a series of livid spots which were evidently the impression of fingers. The face was fearfully discolored, and the eye-balls protruded. The tongue had been partially bitten through. A large bruise was discovered upon the pit of the stomach, produced, apparently, by the pressure of a knee. In the opinion of M. Dumas, Mademoiselle L'Espanaye had been throt-

tled to death by some person or persons unknown. The corpse of the mother was horribly mutilated. All the bones of the right leg and arm were more or less shattered. The left *tibia*[14] much splintered, as well as all the ribs of the left side. Whole body dreadfully bruised and discolored. It was not possible to say how the injuries had been inflicted. A heavy club of wood, or a broad bar of iron—a chair—any large, heavy, and obtuse weapon would have produced such results, if wielded by the hands of a very powerful man. No woman could have inflicted the blows with any weapon. The head of the deceased, when seen by witness, was entirely separated from the body, and was also greatly shattered. The throat had evidently been cut with some very sharp instrument—probably with a razor.

"*Alexandre Etienne*, surgeon, was called with M. Dumas to view the bodies. Corroborated the testimony, and the opinions of M. Dumas.

"Nothing farther of importance was elicited, although several other persons were examined. A murder so mysterious, and so perplexing in all its particulars, was never before committed in Paris—if indeed a murder has been committed at all. The police are entirely at fault—an unusual occurrence in affairs of this nature. There is not, however, the shadow of a clew apparent."

The evening edition of the paper stated that the greatest excitement still continued in the Quartier St. Roch—that the premises in question had been carefully re-searched, and fresh examinations of witnesses instituted, but all to no purpose. A postscript, however, mentioned that Adolphe Le Bon had been arrested and imprisoned—although nothing appeared to criminate him, beyond the facts already detailed.

Dupin seemed singularly interested in the progress of this affair—at least so I judged from his manner, for he made no comments. It was only after the announcement that Le Bon had been imprisoned, that he asked me my opinion respecting the murders.

I could merely agree with all Paris in considering them an insoluble mystery. I saw no means by which it would be possible to trace the murderer.

"We must not judge of the means," said Dupin, "by this shell of an examination. The Parisian police, so much extolled for *acumen*, are cunning, but no more. There is no method in their proceedings, beyond the method of the moment. They make a vast parade of measures; but, not unfrequently, these are so ill adapted to the objects proposed, as to put us in mind of Monsieur Jourdain's calling for his *robe-de-chambre—pour mieux entendre la musique*.[15] The results attained by them are not unfrequently surprising, but, for the most part, are brought about by simple diligence and activity. When these qualities are unavailing, their schemes fail. Vidocq, for example, was a good guesser, and a persevering man. But, without educated thought, he erred continually by the very intensity of his investigations. He impaired his vision by holding the object too close. He might see, perhaps, one or two points with unusual clearness, but in so doing he, necessarily, lost sight of the matter as a whole. Thus there is such a thing as being too profound. Truth is not always in a well.[16] In fact, as regards the more important knowledge, I do believe that she is invariably superficial. The truth lies not in the valleys where we seek her, but upon the mountain-tops where she is found. The modes and sources of this kind of error are well typified in the contemplation of the heavenly bodies. To look at a star by glances—to view it in a side-long way, by turning toward it the exterior portions of the *retina* (more susceptible of feeble impressions of light than the interior), is to behold the star distinctly—is to have the best appreciation of its lustre—a lustre which grows dim just in proportion as we turn our vision *fully* upon it. A greater number of rays actually fall upon the eye in the latter case, but, in the former, there is the more refined capacity for comprehension. By undue profundity we perplex and enfeeble thought; and it is possible to make even Venus herself vanish from the firmament by a scrutiny too sustained, too concentrated, or too direct.

"As for these murders, let us enter into some examinations for ourselves, before we make up an opinion respecting them. An inquiry will afford us amusement," [I thought this an odd term, so applied, but said nothing] "and, besides, Le Bon once rendered me a service for which I am not ungrateful. We will go and see the premises with our own eyes. I know G——, the Prefect of Police, and shall have no difficulty in obtaining the necessary permission."

The permission was obtained, and we proceeded at once to Rue Morgue. This is one of those miserable thoroughfares which intervene between the Rue Richelieu and the Rue St. Roch. It was late in the afternoon when we reached it; as this quarter is at a great distance from that in which we resided. The house was readily found; for there were still many persons gazing up at the closed shutters, with an objectless curiosity, from the opposite side of the way. It was an ordinary Parisian house, with a gateway, on one side of which was a glazed watch-box, with a sliding panel in the window, indicating a *loge de concierge*.[17] Before going in we walked up the street, turned down an alley, and then, again turning, passed in the rear of the building—Dupin, meanwhile, examining the whole neighbourhood, as well as the house, with a minuteness of attention for which I could see no possible object.

Retracing our steps, we came again to the front of the dwelling, rang, and, having shown our credentials, were admitted by the agents in charge. We went up stairs —into the chamber where the body of Mademoiselle L'Espanaye had been found, and where both the deceased still lay. The disorders of the room had, as usual, been suffered to exist. I saw nothing beyond what had been stated in the "Gazette des Tribunaux." Dupin scrutinized every thing—not excepting the bodies of the victims. We then went into the other rooms, and into the yard; a *gendarme* accompanying us throughout. The examination occupied us until dark, when we took our departure. On our way home my companion stopped in for a moment at the office of one of the daily papers.

I have said that the whims of my friend were manifold, and that *Je les ménageais:*[18]—for this phrase there is no English equivalent. It was his humor, now, to decline all conversation on the subject of the murder, until about noon the next day. He then asked me, suddenly, if I had observed any thing *peculiar* at the scene of the atrocity.

There was something in his manner of emphasizing the word "peculiar," which caused me to shudder, without knowing why.

"No, nothing *peculiar*," I said; "nothing more, at least, than we both saw stated in the paper."

"The 'Gazette,'" he replied, "has not entered, I fear, into the unusual horror of the thing. But dismiss the idle opinions of this print. It appears to me that this mystery is considered insoluble, for the very reason which should cause it to be regarded as easy of solution—I mean for the *outré*[19] character of its features. The police are confounded by the seeming absence of motive—not for the murder itself —but for the atrocity of the murder. They are puzzled, too, by the seeming impossibility of reconciling the voices heard in contention, with the facts that no one was discovered up stairs but the assassinated Mademoiselle L'Espanaye, and that there were no means of egress without the notice of the party ascending. The wild disorder of the room; the corpse thrust, with the head downward, up the chimney; the frightful mutilation of the body of the old lady; these considerations, with those just mentioned, and others which I need not

mention, have sufficed to paralyze the powers, by putting completely at fault the boasted *acumen*, of the government agents. They have fallen into the gross but common error of confounding the unusual with the abstruse. But it is by these deviations from the plane of the ordinary, that reason feels its way, if at all, in its search for the true. In investigations such as we are now pursuing, it should not be so much asked 'what has occurred,' as 'what has occurred that has never occurred before.' In fact, the facility with which I shall arrive, or have arrived, at the solution of this mystery, is in the direct ratio of its apparent insolubility in the eyes of the police."

I stared at the speaker in mute astonishment.

"I am now awaiting," continued he, looking toward the door of our apartment —"I am now awaiting a person who, although perhaps not the perpetrator of these butcheries, must have been in some measure implicated in their perpetration. Of the worst portion of the crimes committed, it is probable that he is innocent. I hope that I am right in this supposition; for upon it I build my expectation of reading the entire riddle. I look for the man here—in this room—every moment. It is true that he may not arrive; but the probability is that he will. Should he come, it will be necessary to detain him. Here are pistols; and we both know how to use them when occasion demands their use."

I took the pistols, scarcely knowing what I did, or believing what I heard, while Dupin went on, very much as if in a soliloquy. I have already spoken of his abstract manner at such times. His discourse was addressed to myself; but his voice, although by no means loud, had that intonation which is commonly employed in speaking to some one at a great distance. His eyes, vacant in expression, regarded only the wall.

"That the voices heard in contention," he said, "by the party upon the stairs, were not the voices of the women themselves, was fully proved by the evidence. This relieves us of all doubt upon the question whether the old lady could have first destroyed the daughter, and afterward have committed suicide. I speak of this point chiefly for the sake of method; for the strength of Madame L'Espanaye would have been utterly unequal to the task of thrusting her daughter's corpse up the chimney as it was found; and the nature of the wounds upon her own person entirely preclude the idea of self-destruction. Murder, then, has been committed by some third party; and the voices of this third party were those heard in contention. Let me now advert—not to the whole testimony respecting these voices —but to what was *peculiar* in that testimony. Did you observe anything peculiar about it?"

I remarked that, while all the witnesses agreed in supposing the gruff voice to be that of a Frenchman, there was much disagreement in regard to the shrill, or, as one individual termed it, the harsh voice.

"That was the evidence itself," said Dupin, "but it was not the peculiarity of the evidence. You have observed nothing distinctive. Yet there *was* something to be observed. The witnesses, as you remark, agreed about the gruff voice; they were here unanimous. But in regard to the shrill voice, the peculiarity is—not that they disagreed—but that, while an Italian, an Englishman, a Spaniard, a Hollander, and a Frenchman attempted to describe it, each one spoke of it as that *of a foreigner*. Each is sure that it was not the voice of one of his own countrymen. Each likens it—not to the voice of an individual of any nation with whose language he is conversant—but the converse. The Frenchman supposes it the voice of a Spaniard, and 'might have distinguished some words *had he been acquainted with the Spanish*.' The Dutchman maintains it to have been that of a Frenchman; but we find it stated that '*not understanding*

French this witness was examined through an interpreter.' The Englishman thinks it the voice of a German, and '*does not understand German*.' The Spaniard 'is sure' that it was that of an Englishman, but 'judges by the intonation' altogether, '*as he has no knowledge of the English*.' The Italian believes it the voice of a Russian, but '*has never conversed with a native of Russia*.' A second Frenchman differs, moreover, with the first, and is positive that the voice was that of an Italian; but, *not being cognizant of that tongue*, is, like the Spaniard, 'convinced by the intonation.' Now, how strangely unusual must that voice have really been, about which such testimony as this *could* have been elicited!—in whose *tones*, even, denizens of the five great divisions of Europe could recognise nothing familiar! You will say that it might have been the voice of an Asiatic—of an African. Neither Asiatics nor Africans abound in Paris; but, without denying the inference, I will now merely call your attention to three points. The voice is termed by one witness 'harsh rather than shrill.' It is represented by two others to have been 'quick and *unequal*.' No words—no sounds resembling words—were by any witness mentioned as distinguishable.

"I know not," continued Dupin, "what impression I may have made, so far, upon your own understanding; but I do not hesitate to say that legitimate deductions even from this portion of the testimony —the portion respecting the gruff and shrill voices—are in themselves sufficient to engender a suspicion which should give direction to all farther progress in the investigation of the mystery. I said 'legitimate deductions'; but my meaning is not thus fully expressed. I designed to imply that the deductions are the *sole* proper ones, and that the suspicions arise *inevitably* from them as the single result. What the suspicion is, however, I will not say just yet. I merely wish you to bear in mind that, with myself, it was sufficiently forcible to give a definite form—a certain tendency—to my inquiries in the chamber.

"Let us now transport ourselves, in fancy, to this chamber. What shall we first seek here? The means of egress employed by the murderers. It is not too much to say that neither of us believe in præternatural events. Madame and Mademoiselle L'Espanaye were not destroyed by spirits. The doers of the deed were material, and escaped materially. Then how? Fortunately, there is but one mode of reasoning upon the point, and that mode *must* lead us to a definite decision.—Let us examine, each by each, the possible means of egress. It is clear that the assassins were in the room where Mademoiselle L'Espanaye was found, or at least in the room adjoining, when the party ascended the stairs. It is then only from these two apartments that we have to seek issues. The police have laid bare the floors, the ceilings, and the masonry of the walls, in every direction. No *secret* issues could have escaped their vigilance. But, not trusting to *their* eyes, I examined with my own. There were, then, *no* secret issues. Both doors leading from the rooms into the passage were securely locked, with the keys inside. Let us turn to the chimneys. These, although of ordinary width for some eight or ten feet above the hearths, will not admit, throughout their extent, the body of a large cat. The impossibility of egress, by means already stated, being thus absolute, we are reduced to the windows. Through those of the front room no one could have escaped without notice from the crowd in the street. The murderers *must* have passed, then, through those of the back room. Now, brought to this conclusion in so unequivocal a manner as we are, it is not our part, as reasoners, to reject it on account of apparent impossibilities. It is only left for us to prove that these apparent 'impossibilities' are, in reality, not such.

"There are two windows in the chamber. One of them is unobstructed by furniture, and is wholly visible. The lower portion of the other is hidden from view by the head of the unwieldy bedstead which is thrust close up against it. The former was found securely fastened from within. It resisted the utmost force of those who endeavored to raise it. A large gimlet-hole had been pierced in its frame to the left, and a very stout nail was found fitted therein, nearly to the head. Upon examining the other window, a similar nail was seen similarly fitted in it; and a vigorous attempt to raise this sash, failed also. The police were now entirely satisfied that egress had not been in these directions. And, *therefore,* it was thought a matter of supererogation to withdraw the nails and open the windows.

"My own examination was somewhat more particular, and was so for the reason I have just given—because here it was, I knew, that all apparent impossibilities *must* be proved to be not such in reality.

"I proceeded to think thus—*à posteriori.*[20] The murderers *did* escape from one of these windows. This being so, they could not have re-fastened the sashes from the inside, as they were found fastened; —the consideration which put a stop, through its obviousness, to the scrutiny of the police in this quarter. Yet the sashes *were* fastened. They *must,* then, have the power of fastening themselves. There was no escape from this conclusion. I stepped to the unobstructed casement, withdrew the nail with some difficulty, and attempted to raise the sash. It resisted all my efforts, as I had anticipated. A concealed spring must, I now knew, exist; and this corroboration of my idea convinced me that my premises, at least, were correct, however mysterious still appeared the circumstances attending the nails. A careful search soon brought to light the hidden spring. I pressed it, and, satisfied with the discovery, forebore to upraise the sash.

"I now replaced the nail and regarded it attentively. A person passing out through this window might have reclosed it, and the spring would have caught—

but the nail could not have been replaced. The conclusion was plain, and again narrowed in the field of my investigations. The assassins *must* have escaped through the other window. Supposing, then, the springs upon each sash to be the same, as was probable, there *must* be found a difference between the nails, or at least between the modes of their fixture. Getting upon the sacking of the bedstead, I looked over the head-board minutely at the second casement. Passing my hand behind the board, I readily discovered and pressed the spring, which was, as I had supposed, identical in character with its neighbour. I now looked at the nail. It was as stout as the other, and apparently fitted in the same manner—driven in nearly up to the head.

"You will say that I was puzzled; but, if you think so, you must have misunderstood the nature of the inductions. To use a sporting phrase, I had not been once 'at fault.' The scent had never for an instant been lost. There was no flaw in any link of the chain. I had traced the secret to its ultimate result,—and that result was *the nail*. It had, I say, in every respect, the appearance of its fellow in the other window; but this fact was an absolute nullity (conclusive as it might seem to be) when compared with the consideration that here, at this point, terminated the clew. 'There *must* be something wrong,' I said, 'about the nail.' I touched it; and the head, with about a quarter of an inch of the shank, came off in my fingers. The rest of the shank was in the gimlet-hole, where it had been broken off. The fracture was an old one (for its edges were incrusted with rust), and had apparently been accomplished by the blow of a hammer, which had partially imbedded, in the top of the bottom sash, the head portion of the nail. I now carefully replaced this head portion in the indentation whence I had taken it, and the resemblance to a perfect nail was complete—the fissure was invisible. Pressing the spring, I gently raised the sash for a few inches; the head

went up with it, remaining firm in its bed. I closed the window, and the semblance of the whole nail was again perfect.

"The riddle, so far, was now unriddled. The assassin had escaped through the window which looked upon the bed. Dropping of its own accord upon his exit (or perhaps purposely closed), it had become fastened by the spring; and it was the retention of this spring which had been mistaken by the police for that of the nail,—farther inquiry being thus considered unnecessary.

"The next question is that of the mode of descent. Upon this point I had been satisfied in my walk with you around the building. About five feet and a half from the casement in question there runs a lightning-rod. From this rod it would have been impossible for any one to reach the window itself, to say nothing of entering it. I observed, however, that the shutters of the fourth story were of the peculiar kind called by Parisian carpenters *ferrades* —a kind rarely employed at the present day, but frequently seen upon very old mansions at Lyons and Bordeaux. They are in the form of an ordinary door, (a single, not a folding door) except that the upper half is latticed or worked in open trellis—thus affording an excellent hold for the hands. In the present instance these shutters are fully three feet and a half broad. When we saw them from the rear of the house, they were both about half open—that is to say, they stood off at right angles from the wall. It is probable that the police, as well as myself, examined the back of the tenement; but, if so, in looking at these *ferrades* in the line of their breadth (as they must have done), they did not perceive this great breadth itself, or, at all events, failed to take it into due consideration. In fact, having once satisfied themselves that no egress could have been made in this quarter, they would naturally bestow here a very cursory examination. It was clear to me, however, that the shutter belonging to the window at the head of the bed, would, if swung fully back to the wall, reach to within two feet of the lightning-rod. It was also evident that, by exertion of a very unusual degree of activity and courage, an entrance into the window, from the rod, might have been thus effected.—By reaching to the distance of two feet and a half (we now suppose the shutter open to its whole extent) a robber might have taken a firm grasp upon the trellis-work. Letting go, then, his hold upon the rod, placing his feet securely against the wall, and springing boldly from it, he might have swung the shutter so as to close it, and, if we imagine the window open at the time, might even have swung himself into the room.

"I wish you to bear especially in mind that I have spoken of a *very* unusual degree of activity as requisite to success in so hazardous and so difficult a feat. It is my design to show you, first, that the thing might possibly have been accomplished:—but, secondly and *chiefly*, I wish to impress upon your understanding the *very extraordinary*—the almost præternatural character of that agility which could have accomplished it.

"You will say, no doubt, using the language of the law, that 'to make out my case' I should rather undervalue, than insist upon a full estimation of the activity required in this matter. This may be the practice in law, but it is not the usage of reason. My ultimate object is only the truth. My immediate purpose is to lead you to place in juxta-position that *very unusual* activity of which I have just spoken, with that *very peculiar* shrill (or harsh) and *unequal* voice, about whose nationality no two persons could be found to agree, and in whose utterance no syllabification could be detected."

At these words a vague and half-formed conception of the meaning of Dupin flitted over my mind. I seemed to be upon the verge of comprehension, without power to comprehend—as men, at times, find themselves upon the brink of remembrance, without being able, in the end, to remember. My friend went on with his discourse.

"You will see," he said, "that I have shifted the question from the mode of egress to that of ingress. It was my design to suggest that both were effected in the same manner, at the same point. Let us now revert to the interior of the room. Let us survey the appearances here. The drawers of the bureau, it is said, had been rifled, although many articles of apparel still remained within them. The conclusion here is absurd. It is a mere guess—a very silly one—and no more. How are we to know that the articles found in the drawers were not all these drawers had originally contained? Madame L'Espanaye and her daughter lived an exceedingly retired life—saw no company—seldom went out—had little use for numerous changes of habiliment. Those found were at least of as good quality as any likely to be possessed by these ladies. If a thief had taken any, why did he not take the best—why did he not take all? In a word, why did he abandon four thousand francs in gold to encumber himself with a bundle of linen? The gold *was* abandoned. Nearly the whole sum mentioned by Monsieur Mignaud, the banker, was discovered, in bags, upon the floor. I wish you, therefore, to discard from your thoughts the blundering idea of *motive*, engendered in the brains of the police by that portion of the evidence which speaks of money delivered at the door of the house. Coincidences ten times as remarkable as this (the delivery of the money, and murder committed within three days upon the party receiving it), happen to all of us every hour of our lives, without attracting even momentary notice. Coincidences, in general, are great stumbling-blocks in the way of that class of thinkers who have been educated to know nothing of the theory of probabilities—that theory to which the most glorious objects of human research are indebted for the most glorious of illustration. In the present instance, had the gold been gone, the fact of its delivery three days before would have formed something more than a coincidence. It would have been corroborative of this idea of motive. But, under the real circumstances of the case, if we are to suppose gold the motive of this outrage, we must also imagine the perpetrator so vacillating an idiot as to have abandoned his gold and his motive together.

"Keeping now steadily in mind the points to which I have drawn your attention—that peculiar voice, that unusual agility, and that startling absence of motive in a murder so singularly atrocious as this—let us glance at the butchery itself. Here is a woman strangled to death by manual strength, and thrust up a chimney, head downward. Ordinary assassins employ no such modes of murder as this. Least of all, do they thus dispose of the murdered. In the manner of thrusting the corpse up the chimney, you will admit that there was something *excessively outré*—something altogether irreconcilable with our common notions of human action, even when we suppose the actors the most depraved of men. Think, too, how great must have been that strength which could have thrust the body *up* such an aperture so forcibly that the united vigor of several persons was found barely sufficient to drag it *down!*

"Turn, now, to other indications of the employment of a vigor most marvellous. On the hearth were thick tresses—very thick tresses—of gray human hair. These had been torn out by the roots. You are aware of the great force necessary in tearing thus from the head even twenty or thirty hairs together. You saw the locks in question as well as myself. Their roots (a hideous sight!) were clotted with fragments of the flesh of the scalp—sure token of the prodigious power which had been exerted in uprooting perhaps half a million of hairs at a time. The throat of the old lady was not merely cut, but the head absolutely severed from the body: the instrument was a mere razor. I wish you also to look at the *brutal* ferocity of these

deeds. Of the bruises upon the body of Madame L'Espanaye I do not speak. Monsieur Dumas, and his worthy coadjutor Monsieur Etienne, have pronounced that they were inflicted by some obtuse instrument; and so far these gentlemen are very correct. The obtuse instrument was clearly the stone pavement in the yard, upon which the victim had fallen from the window which looked in upon the bed. This idea, however simple it may now seem, escaped the police for the same reason that the breadth of the shutters escaped them—because, by the affair of the nails, their perceptions had been hermetically sealed against the possibility of the windows having ever been opened at all.

"If now, in addition to all these things, you have properly reflected upon the odd disorder of the chamber, we have gone so far as to combine the ideas of an agility astounding, a strength superhuman, a ferocity brutal, a butchery without motive, a *grotesquerie* in horror absolutely alien from humanity, and a voice foreign in tone to the ears of men of many nations, and devoid of all distinct or intelligible syllabification. What result, then, has ensued? What impression have I made upon your fancy?"

I felt a creeping of the flesh as Dupin asked me the question. "A madman," I said, "has done this deed—some raving maniac, escaped from a neighboring *Maison de Santé.*"[21]

"In some respects," he replied, "your idea is not irrelevant. But the voices of madmen, even in their wildest paroxysms, are never found to tally with that peculiar voice heard upon the stairs. Madmen are of some nation, and their language, however incoherent in its words, has always the coherence of syllabification. Besides, the hair of a madman is not such as I now hold in my hand. I disentangled this little tuft from the rigidly clutched fingers of Madame L'Espanaye. Tell me what you can make of it."

"Dupin!" I said, completely unnerved;

"this hair is most unusual—this is no *human* hair."

"I have not asserted that it is," said he; "but, before we decide this point, I wish you to glance at the little sketch I have here traced upon this paper. It is a *fac-simile* drawing of what has been described in one portion of the testimony as 'dark bruises, and deep indentations of finger nails,' upon the throat of Mademoiselle L'Espanaye, and in another, (by Messrs. Dumas and Etienne,) as a 'series of livid spots, evidently the impression of fingers.'

"You will perceive," continued my friend, spreading out the paper upon the table before us, "that this drawing gives the idea of a firm and fixed hold. There is no *slipping* apparent. Each finger has retained—possibly until the death of the victim—the fearful grasp by which it originally imbedded itself. Attempt, now, to place all your fingers, at the same time, in the respective impressions as you see them."

I made the attempt in vain.

"We are possibly not giving this matter a fair trial," he said. "The paper is spread out upon a plane surface; but the human throat is cylindrical. Here is a billet of wood, the circumference of which is about that of the throat. Wrap the drawing around it, and try the experiment again."

I did so; but the difficulty was even more obvious than before.

"This," I said, "is the mark of no human hand."

"Read now," replied Dupin, "this passage from Cuvier."[22]

It was a minute anatomical and generally descriptive account of the large fulvous Ourang-Outang of the East Indian Islands. The gigantic stature, the prodigious strength and activity, the wild ferocity, and the imitative propensities of these mammalia are sufficiently well known to all. I understood the full horrors of the murder at once.

"The description of the digits," said I, as I made an end of reading, "is in exact accordance with this drawing. I see that no animal but an Ourang-Outang, of the species here mentioned, could have impressed the indentations as you have traced them. This tuft of tawny hair, too, is identical in character with that of the beast of Cuvier. But I cannot possibly comprehend the particulars of this frightful mystery. Besides, there were *two* voices heard in contention, and one of them was unquestionably the voice of a Frenchman."

"True; and you will remember an expression attributed almost unanimously, by the evidence, to this voice,—the expression, '*mon Dieu!*' This, under the circumstances, has been justly characterized by one of the witnesses (Montani, the confectioner,) as an expression of remonstrance or expostulation. Upon these two words, therefore, I have mainly built my hopes of a full solution of the riddle. A Frenchman was cognizant of the murder. It is possible—indeed it is far more than probable—that he was innocent of all participation in the bloody transactions which took place. The Ourang-Outang may have escaped from him. He may have traced it to the chamber; but, under the agitating circumstances which ensued, he could never have re-captured it. It is still at large. I will not pursue these guesses—for I have no right to call them more—since the shades of reflection upon which they are based are scarcely of sufficient depth to be appreciable by my own intellect, and since I could not pretend to make them intelligible to the understanding of another. We will call them guesses then, and speak of them as such. If the Frenchman in question is indeed, as I suppose, innocent of this atrocity, this advertisement, which I left last night, upon our return home, at the office of 'Le Monde,' (a paper devoted to the shipping interest, and much sought by sailors,) will bring him to our residence."

He handed me a paper, and I read thus:

CAUGHT—*In the Bois de Boulogne, early in the morning of the* ——

inst., (the morning of the murder,)
a very large, tawny Ourang-Outang
of the Bornese species. The owner,
(who is ascertained to be a sailor, be-
longing to a Maltese vessel,) may
have the animal again, upon identi-
fying it satisfactorily, and paying a
few charges arising from its capture
and keeping. Call at No. ——, Rue
——, Faubourg St. Germain—au
troisième.

"How was it possible," I asked, "that
you should know the man to be a sailor,
and belonging to a Maltese vessel?"

"I do *not* know it," said Dupin. "I am
not *sure* of it. Here, however, is a small
piece of ribbon, which from its form, and
from its greasy appearance, has evidently
been used in tying the hair in one of those
long *queues* of which sailors are so fond.
Moreover, this knot is one which few besides sailors can tie, and is peculiar to the
Maltese. I picked the ribbon up at the foot
of the lightning-rod. It could not have
belonged to either of the deceased. Now
if, after all, I am wrong in my induction
from this ribbon, that the Frenchman was
a sailor belonging to a Maltese vessel, still
I can have done no harm in saying what
I did in the advertisement. If I am in error,
he will merely suppose that I have been
misled by some circumstance into which
he will not take the trouble to inquire.
But if I am right, a great point is gained.
Cognizant although innocent of the murder, the Frenchman will naturally hesitate
about replying to the advertisement—
about demanding the Ourang-Outang. He
will reason thus:—'I am innocent; I am
poor; my Ourang-Outang is of great value
—to one in my circumstances a fortune
of itself—why should I lose it through
idle apprehensions of danger? Here it is,
within my grasp. It was found in the Bois
de Boulogne—at a vast distance from the
scene of that butchery. How can it ever
be suspected that a brute beast should
have done the deed? The police are at
fault—they have failed to procure the
slightest clew. Should they even trace the

animal, it would be impossible to prove
me cognizant of the murder, or to implicate me in guilt on account of that cognizance. Above all, *I am known.* The advertiser designates me as the possessor of
the beast. I am not sure to what limit his
knowledge may extend. Should I avoid
claiming a property of so great value,
which it is known that I possess, I will
render the animal, at least, liable to suspicion. It is not my policy to attract attention either to myself or to the beast. I will
answer the advertisement, get the Ourang-
Outang, and keep it close until this matter has blown over.' "

At this moment we heard a step upon
the stairs.

"Be ready," said Dupin, "with your pistols, but neither use them nor show them
until at a signal from myself."

The front of the house had been left
open, and the visitor had entered, without
ringing, and advanced several steps upon
the staircase. Now, however, he seemed
to hesitate. Presently we heard him descending. Dupin was moving quickly to
the door, when we again heard him coming up. He did not turn back a second
time, but stepped up with decision and
rapped at the door of our chamber.

"Come in," said Dupin, in a cheerful
and hearty tone.

A man entered. He was a sailor, evidently,—a tall, stout, and muscular-look-
ing person, with a certain dare-devil expression of countenance, not altogether
unprepossessing. His face, greatly sun-
burnt, was more than half hidden by
whisker and *mustachio.* He had with him
a huge oaken cudgel, but appeared to
be otherwise unarmed. He bowed awkwardly, and bade us "good evening," in
French accents, which, although somewhat Neufchatelish,[23] were still sufficiently indicative of a Parisian origin.

"Sit down, my friend," said Dupin. "I
suppose you have called about the
Ourang-Outang. Upon my word, I almost
envy you the possession of him; a remarkably fine, and no doubt a very valu-

able animal. How old do you suppose him to be?"

The sailor drew a long breath, with the air of a man relieved of some intolerable burden, and then replied, in an assured tone:

"I have no way of telling—but he can't be more than four or five years old. Have you got him here?"

"Oh no; we had no conveniences for keeping him here. He is at a livery stable in the Rue Dubourg, just by. You can get him in the morning. Of course you are prepared to identify the property?"

"To be sure I am, sir."

"I shall be sorry to part with him," said Dupin.

"I don't mean that you should be at all this trouble for nothing, sir," said the man. "Couldn't expect it. Am very willing to pay a reward for the finding of the animal—that is to say, any thing in reason."

"Well," replied my friend, "that is all very fair, to be sure. Let me think!—what should I have? Oh! I will tell you. My reward shall be this. You shall give me all the information in your power about these murders in the Rue Morgue."

Dupin said the last words in a very low tone, and very quietly. Just as quietly, too, he walked toward the door, locked it, and put the key in his pocket. He then drew a pistol from his bosom and placed it, without the least flurry, upon the table.

The sailor's face flushed up as if he were struggling with suffocation. He started to his feet and grasped his cudgel; but the next moment he fell back into his seat, trembling violently, and with the countenance of death itself. He spoke not a word. I pitied him from the bottom of my heart.

"My friend," said Dupin, in a kind tone, "you are alarming yourself unnecessarily—you are indeed. We mean you no harm whatever. I pledge you the honor of a gentleman, and of a Frenchman, that we intend you no injury. I perfectly well know that you are innocent of the atrocities in the Rue Morgue. It will not do,

however, to deny that you are in some measure implicated in them. From what I have already said, you must know that I have had means of information about this matter—means of which you could never have dreamed. Now the thing stands thus. You have done nothing which you could have avoided—nothing, certainly, which renders you culpable. You were not even guilty of robbery, when you might have robbed with impunity. You have nothing to conceal. You have no reason for concealment. On the other hand, you are bound by every principle of honor to confess all you know. An innocent man is now imprisoned, charged with that crime of which you can point out the perpetrator."

The sailor had recovered his presence of mind, in a great measure, while Dupin uttered these words; but his original boldness of bearing was all gone.

"So help me God," said he, after a brief pause, "I *will* tell you all I know about this affair;—but I do not expect you to believe one half I say—I would be a fool indeed if I did. Still, I *am* innocent, and I will make a clean breast if I die for it."

What he stated was, in substance, this. He had lately made a voyage to the Indian Archipelago. A party, of which he formed one, landed at Borneo, and passed into the interior on an excursion of pleasure. Himself and a companion had captured the Ourang-Outang. This companion dying, the animal fell into his own exclusive possession. After great trouble, occasioned by the intractable ferocity of his captive during the home voyage, he at length succeeded in lodging it safely at his own residence in Paris, where, not to attract toward himself the unpleasant curiosity of his neighbours, he kept it carefully secluded, until such time as it should recover from a wound in the foot, received from a splinter on board ship. His ultimate design was to sell it.

Returning home from some sailors' frolic on the night, or rather in the morning of the murder, he found the beast occupying his own bed-room, into which it had broken from a closet adjoining, where it had been, as was thought, securely confined. Razor in hand, and fully lathered, it was sitting before a looking-glass, attempting the operation of shaving, in which it had no doubt previously watched its master through the key-hole of the closet. Terrified at the sight of so dangerous a weapon in the possession of an animal so ferocious, and so well able to use it, the man, for some moments, was at a loss what to do. He had been accustomed, however, to quiet the creature, even in its fiercest moods, by the use of a whip, and to this he now resorted. Upon sight of it, the Ourang-Outang sprang at once through the door of the chamber, down the stairs, and thence, through a window, unfortunately open, into the street.

The Frenchman followed in despair; the ape, razor still in hand, occasionally stopping to look back and gesticulate at its pursuer, until the latter had nearly come up with it. It then again made off. In this manner the chase continued for a long time. The streets were profoundly quiet, as it was nearly three o'clock in the morning. In passing down an alley in the rear of the Rue Morgue, the fugitive's attention was arrested by a light gleaming from the open window of Madame L'Espanaye's chamber, in the fourth story of her house. Rushing to the building, it perceived the lightning-rod, clambered up with inconceivable agility, grasped the shutter, which was thrown fully back against the wall, and, by its means, swung itself directly upon the headboard of the bed. The whole feat did not occupy a minute. The shutter was kicked open again by the Ourang-Outang as it entered the room.

The sailor, in the meantime, was both rejoiced and perplexed. He had strong hopes of now recapturing the brute, as it could scarcely escape from the trap into which it had ventured, except by the rod, where it might be intercepted as it came down. On the other hand, there was much cause for anxiety as to what it might do in the house. This latter reflection urged the man still to follow the fugitive. A lightning-rod is ascended without difficulty, especially by a sailor; but, when he had arrived as high as the window, which lay far to his left, his career was stopped; the most that he could accomplish was to reach over so as to obtain a glimpse of the interior of the room. At this glimpse he nearly fell from his hold through excess of horror. Now it was that those hideous shrieks arose upon the night, which had startled from slumber the inmates of the Rue Morgue. Madame L'Espanaye and her daughter, habited in their night clothes, had apparently been arranging some papers in the iron chest already mentioned, which had been wheeled into the middle of the room. It was open, and its contents lay beside it on the floor. The victims must have been sitting with their backs toward the window; and, from the time elapsing between the ingress of the beast and the screams, it seems probable that it was not immediately perceived. The flapping-to of the shutter would naturally have been attributed to the wind.

As the sailor looked in, the gigantic animal had seized Madame L'Espanaye by the hair, (which was loose, as she had been combing it,) and was flourishing the razor about her face, in imitation of the motions of a barber. The daughter lay prostrate and motionless; she had swooned. The screams and struggles of the old lady (during which the hair was torn from her head) had the effect of changing the probably pacific purposes of the Ourang-Outang into those of wrath. With one determined sweep of its muscular arm it nearly severed her head from her body. The sight of blood inflamed its anger into phrenzy. Gnashing its teeth, and flashing fire from its eyes, it flew upon the body of the girl, and imbedded its fearful talons in her throat, retaining its grasp until she expired. Its wandering and wild glances fell at this moment upon the head of the bed, over which the face of its master, rigid with horror, was just discernible. The fury of the beast, who no doubt bore still in mind the dreaded whip, was instantly converted into fear. Conscious of having deserved punishment, it seemed desirous of concealing its bloody deeds, and skipped about the chamber in an agony of nervous agitation; throwing down and breaking the furniture as it moved, and dragging the bed from the bedstead. In conclusion, it seized first the corpse of the daughter, and thrust it up the chimney, as it was found; then that of the old lady, which it immediately hurled through the window headlong.

As the ape approached the casement with its mutilated burden, the sailor shrank aghast to the rod, and, rather gliding than clambering down it, hurried at once home—dreading the consequences of the butchery, and gladly abandoning, in his terror, all solicitude about the fate of the Ourang-Outang. The words heard by the party upon the staircase were the Frenchman's exclamations of horror and affright, commingled with the fiendish jabberings of the brute.

I have scarcely anything to add. The Ourang-Outang must have escaped from the chamber, by the rod, just before the breaking of the door. It must have closed the window as it passed through it. It was subsequently caught by the owner himself, who obtained for it a very large sum at the *Jardin des Plantes*. Le Bon was instantly released, upon our narration of the circumstances (with some comments from Dupin) at the *bureau* of the Prefect of Police. This functionary, however well disposed to my friend, could not altogether conceal his chagrin at the turn which affairs had taken, and was fain to indulge in a sarcasm or two, about the propriety of every person minding his own business.

"Let them talk," said Dupin, who had not thought it necessary to reply. "Let him discourse; it will ease his conscience.

I am satisfied with having defeated him in his own castle. Nevertheless, that he failed in the solution of this mystery, is by no means that matter for wonder which he supposes it; for, in truth, our friend the Prefect is somewhat too cunning to be profound. In his wisdom is no *stamen*. It is all head and no body, like the pictures of the Goddess Laverna—or, at best, all head and shoulders, like a codfish. But he is a good creature after all. I like him especially for one master stroke of cant, by which he has attained his reputation for ingenuity. I mean the way he has '*de nier ce qui est, et d'expliquer ce qui n'est pas.*' "[24]

THE MYSTERY OF MARIE ROGÊT[1]

A Sequel to "The Murders in the Rue Morgue"

Es giebt eine Reihe idealischer Begebenheiten, die der Wirklichkeit parallel läuft. Selten fallen sie zusammen. Menschen und Zufälle modificiren gewöunlich die idealische Begebenheit, so dass sie unvollkommen erscheint, und ihre Folgen gleichfalls unvollkommen sind. So bei der Reformation: statt des Protestantismus kam das Lutherthum hervor.

There are ideal series of events which run parallel with the real ones. They rarely coincide. Men and circumstances generally modify the ideal train of events, so that it seems imperfect, and its consequences are 'equally imperfect. Thus with the Reformation; instead of Protestantism came Lutheranism.

Novalis,[2] *Moralische Ansichten.*

There are few persons, even among the calmest thinkers, who have not occasionally been startled into a vague yet thrilling half-credence in the supernatural, by *co-incidences* of so seemingly marvellous a character that, as *mere* coincidences, the intellect has been unable to receive them. Such sentiments—for the half-credences of which I speak have never the full force of *thought*—are seldom thoroughly stifled unless by reference to the doctrine of chance, or, as it is technically termed, the Calculus of Probabilities. Now this Calculus is, in its essence, purely mathematical; and thus we have the anomaly of the most rigidly exact in science applied to the shadow and spirituality of the most intangible in speculation.

The extraordinary details which I am now called upon to make public, will be found to form, as regards sequence of time, the primary branch of a series of scarcely intelligible *coincidences*, whose secondary or concluding branch will be recognized by all readers in the late murder of MARY CECILIA ROGERS, at New York.

When, in an article entitled "The Murders in the Rue Morgue,"[3] I endeavored, about a year ago, to depict some very remarkable features in the mental character of my friend, the Chevalier C. Auguste Dupin, it did not occur to me that I should ever resume the subject. This depicting of character constituted my design; and this design was fulfilled in the train of circumstances brought to instance Dupin's idiosyncrasy. I might have adduced other examples, but I should have proven no more. Late events, however, in their surprising development, have startled me into some farther details, which will carry with them the air of extorted confession. Hearing what I have lately heard, it would be indeed strange should I remain silent in regard to what I both heard and saw so long ago.

Upon the winding up of the tragedy involved in the deaths of Madame L'Espanaye and her daughter,[4] the Chevalier dismissed the affair at once from his attention, and relapsed into his old habits of moody reverie. Prone, at all times, to abstraction, I readily fell in with his humor; and, continuing to occupy our chambers in the Faubourg Saint Germain, we gave the Future to the winds, and slumbered tranquilly in the Present, weaving the dull world around us into dreams.

But these dreams were not altogether uninterrupted. It may readily be supposed that the part played by my friend, in the drama at the Rue Morgue, had not failed of its impression upon the fancies of the Parisian police. With its emissaries, the name of Dupin had grown into a household word. The simple character of those inductions[5] by which he had disentangled the mystery never having been explained even to the Prefect, or to any other individual than myself, of course it is not surprising that the affair was regarded as little less than miraculous, or that the Chevalier's analytical abilities acquired for him the credit of intuition. His frankness would have led him to disabuse every inquirer of such prejudice; but his indolent humor forbade all farther agitation of a topic whose interest to himself had long ceased. It thus happened that he found himself the cynosure of the policial eyes; and the cases were not few in which attempt was made to engage his services at the Prefecture. One of the most remarkable instances was that of the murder of a young girl named Marie Rogêt.

This event occurred about two years after the atrocity in the Rue Morgue. Marie, whose Christian and family name will at once arrest attention from their resemblance to those of the unfortunate "cigar-girl," was the only daughter of the widow Estelle Rogêt. The father had died during the child's infancy, and from the period of his death, until within eighteen months before the assassination which forms the subject of our narrative, the mother and daughter had dwelt together in the Rue Pavée Saint André; Madame there keeping a *pension,* assisted by Marie. Affairs went on thus until the latter had attained her twenty-second year, when her great beauty attracted the notice of a perfumer, who occupied one of the shops in the basement of the Palais Royal, and whose custom lay chiefly among the desperate adventurers infesting that neighborhood. Monsieur Le Blanc[6] was not unaware of the advantages to be derived from the attendance of the fair Marie in his perfumery; and his liberal proposals were accepted eagerly by the girl, although with somewhat more of hesitation by Madame.

The anticipations of the shopkeeper were realized, and his rooms soon became notorious through the charms of the sprightly *grisette*.[7] She had been in his employ about a year, when her admirers were thrown into confusion by her sudden disappearance from the shop. Monsieur Le Blanc was unable to account for her absence, and Madame Rogêt was distracted with anxiety and terror. The public papers immediately took up the theme, and the police were upon the point of making serious investigations, when, one fine morning, after the lapse of a week, Marie, in good health, but with a somewhat saddened air, made her re-appearance at her usual counter in the perfumery. All inquiry, except that of a private character, was of course immediately hushed. Monsieur Le Blanc professed total ignorance, as before. Marie, with Madame, replied to all questions, that the last week had been spent at the house of a relation in the country. Thus the affair died away, and was generally forgotten; for the girl, ostensibly to relieve herself from the impertinence of curiosity, soon bade a final adieu to the perfumer, and sought the shelter of her mother's residence in the Rue Pavée Saint André.

It was about three years after this return home, that her friends were alarmed by her sudden disappearance for the second time. Three days elapsed, and nothing was heard of her. On the fourth her corpse was found floating in the Seine, near the shore which is opposite the Quartier of the Rue Saint André, and at a point not very far distant from the secluded neighborhood of the Barrière du Roule.[8]

The atrocity of this murder, (for it was at once evident that murder had been committed,) the youth and beauty of the victim, and, above all, her previous notoriety, conspired to produce intense excitement in the minds of the sensitive Parisians. I can call to mind no similar occurrence producing so general and so intense an effect. For several weeks, in the discussion of this one absorbing theme, even the momentous political topics of the day were forgotten. The Prefect made unusual exertions; and the powers of the whole Parisian police were, of course, tasked to the utmost extent.

Upon the first discovery of the corpse, it was not supposed that the murderer would be able to elude, for more than a very brief period, the inquisition which was immediately set on foot. It was not until the expiration of a week that it was deemed necessary to offer a reward; and even then this reward was limited to a thousand francs. In the mean time the investigation proceeded with vigor, if not always with judgment, and numerous individuals were examined to no purpose; while, owing to the continual absence of all clue to the mystery, the popular excitement greatly increased. At the end of the tenth day it was thought advisable to double the sum originally proposed; and, at length, the second week having elapsed without leading to any discoveries, and the prejudice which always exists in Paris against the Police having given vent to itself in several serious *émeutes*,[9] the Prefect took it upon himself to offer the sum of twenty thousand francs "for the conviction of the assassin," or, if more than one should prove to have been implicated, "for the conviction of any one of the assassins." In the proclamation setting forth this reward, a full pardon was promised to any accomplice who should come forward in evidence against his fellow; and to the whole was appended, wherever it appeared, the private placard of a committee of citizens, offering ten thousand francs, in addition to the amount proposed by the Prefecture. The entire reward thus stood at no less than thirty thousand francs, which will be regarded as an extraordinary sum when we consider the humble condition of the girl, and the great frequency, in large cities, of such atrocities as the one described.

No one doubted now that the mystery of this murder would be immediately brought to light. But although, in one or two instances, arrests were made which promised elucidation, yet nothing was elicited which could implicate the parties suspected; and they were discharged forthwith. Strange as it may appear, the third week from the discovery of the body had passed, without any light being thrown upon the subject, before even a rumor of the events which had so agitated the public mind, reached the ears of Dupin and myself. Engaged in researches which had absorbed our whole attention, it had been nearly a month since either of us had gone abroad, or received a visiter, or more than glanced at the leading political articles in one of the daily papers. The first intelligence of the murder was brought us by G——, in person. He called upon us early in the afternoon of the thirteenth of July, 18—, and remained with us until late in the night. He had been piqued by the failure of all his endeavors to ferret out the assassins. His reputation—so he said with a peculiarly Parisian air—was at stake. Even his honor was concerned. The eyes of the public were upon him; and there was really no sacrifice which he would not be willing to make for the development of the mystery. He concluded a somewhat droll speech with a compliment upon what he was pleased to term the *tact* of Dupin, and made him a direct, and certainly a liberal proposition, the precise nature of which I do not feel myself at liberty to disclose, but which has no bearing upon the proper subject of my narrative.

The compliment my friend rebutted as best he could, but the proposition he accepted at once, although its advantages were altogether provisional. This point being settled, the Prefect broke forth at once into explanations of his own views, interspersing them with long comments upon the evidence; of which latter we were not yet in possession. He discoursed much, and beyond doubt, learnedly; while

I hazarded an occasional suggestion as the night wore drowsily away. Dupin, sitting steadily in his accustomed arm-chair, was the embodiment of respectful attention. He wore spectacles during the whole interview; and an occasional glance beneath their green glasses, sufficed to convince me that he slept not the less soundly, because silently, throughout the seven or eight leaden-footed hours which immediately preceded the departure of the Prefect.

In the morning, I procured, at the Prefecture, a full report of all the evidence elicited, and, at the various newspaper offices, a copy of every paper in which, from first to last, had been published any decisive information in regard to this sad affair. Freed from all that was positively disproved, this mass of information stood thus:

Marie Rogêt left the residence of her mother, in the Rue Pavée St. André, about nine o'clock in the morning of Sunday, June the twenty-second, 18—. In going out, she gave notice to a Monsieur Jacques St. Eustache,[10] and to him only, of her intention to spend the day with an aunt who resided in the Rue des Drômes. The Rue des Drômes is a short and narrow but populous thoroughfare, not far from the banks of the river, and, at a distance of some two miles, in the most direct course possible, from the *pension* of Madame Rogêt. St. Eustache was the accepted suitor of Marie, and lodged, as well as took his meals, at the *pension*. He was to have gone for his betrothed at dusk, and to have escorted her home. In the afternoon, however, it came on to rain heavily; and, supposing that she would remain all night at her aunt's, (as she had done under similar circumstances before,) he did not think it necessary to keep his promise. As night drew on, Madame Rogêt (who was an infirm old lady, seventy years of age,) was heard to express a fear "that she should never see Marie again;" but this observation attracted little attention at the time.

On Monday, it was ascertained that the girl had not been to the Rue des Drômes; and when the day elapsed without tidings of her, a tardy search was instituted at several points in the city, and its environs. It was not, however, until the fourth day from the period of her disappearance that any thing satisfactory was ascertained respecting her. On this day, (Wednesday, the twenty-fifth day of June,) a Monsieur Beauvais,[11] who, with a friend, had been making inquiries for Marie near the Barrière du Roule, on the shore of the Seine which is opposite the Rue Pavée St. André, was informed that a corpse had just been towed ashore by some fishermen, who had found it floating in the river. Upon seeing the body, Beauvais, after some hesitation, identified it as that of the perfumery-girl. His friend recognized it more promptly.

The face was suffused with dark blood, some of which issued from the mouth. No foam was seen, as in the case of the merely drowned. There was no discoloration in the cellular tissue. About the throat were bruises and impressions of fingers. The arms were bent over on the chest and were rigid. The right hand was clenched; the left partially open. On the left wrist were two circular excoriations, apparently the effect of ropes, or of a rope in more than one volution. A part of the right wrist, also, was much chafed, as well as the back throughout its extent, but more especially at the shoulder-blades. In bringing the body to the shore the fishermen had attached to it a rope; but none of the excoriations had been effected by this. The flesh of the neck was much swollen. There were no cuts apparent, or bruises which appeared the effect of blows. A piece of lace was found tied so tightly around the neck as to be hidden from sight; it was completely buried in the flesh, and was fastened by a knot which lay just under the left ear. This alone would have sufficed to produce death. The medical testimony spoke confidently of the virtuous character of the deceased. She had been subjected, it said, to brutal violence. The corpse was in such condition when found, that there could have been no difficulty in its recognition by friends.

The dress was much torn and otherwise disordered. In the outer garment, a slip, about a foot wide, had been torn upward from the bottom hem to the waist, but not torn off. It was wound three times around the waist, and secured by a sort of hitch in the back. The dress immediately beneath the frock was of fine muslin; and from this a slip eighteen inches wide had been torn entirely out—torn very evenly and with great care. It was found around her neck, fitting loosely, and secured with a hard knot. Over this muslin slip and the slip of lace, the strings of a bonnet were attached; the bonnet being appended. The knot by which the strings of the bonnet were fastened, was not a lady's, but a slip or sailor's knot.

After the recognition of the corpse, it was not, as usual, taken to the Morgue, (this formality being superfluous,) but hastily interred not far from the spot at which it was brought ashore. Through the exertions of Beauvais, the matter was industriously hushed up, as far as possible; and several days had elapsed before any public emotion resulted. A weekly paper,[12] however, at length took up the theme; the corpse was disinterred, and a re-examination instituted; but nothing was elicited beyond what has been already noted. The clothes, however, were now submitted to the mother and friends of the deceased, and fully identified as those worn by the girl upon leaving home.

Meantime, the excitement increased hourly. Several individuals were arrested and discharged. St. Eustache fell especially under suspicion; and he failed, at first, to give an intelligible account of his whereabouts during the Sunday on which Marie left home. Subsequently, however, he submitted to Monsieur G——, affidavits, accounting satisfactorily for every hour of the day in question. As time passed and no discovery ensued, a thousand contradictory rumors were circulated, and journalists busied themselves in *suggestions*. Among these, the one which attracted the most notice, was the idea that Marie Rogêt still lived—that the corpse found in the Seine was that of some other unfortunate. It will be proper that I submit to the reader some passages which embody the suggestion alluded to. These passages are *literal* translations from L'Etoile,[13] a paper conducted, in general, with much ability.

"Mademoiselle Rogêt left her mother's house on Sunday morning, June the twenty-second, 18—, with the ostensible purpose of going to see her aunt or some other connexion, in the Rue des Drômes. From that hour, nobody is proved to have seen her. There is no trace or tidings of her at all. . . . There has no person, whatever, come forward, so far, who saw her at all, on that day, after she left her mother's door. . . . Now, though we have no evidence that Marie Rogêt was in the land of the living after nine o'clock on Sunday, June the twenty-second, we have proof that, up to that hour, she was alive. On Wednesday noon, at twelve, a female body was discovered afloat on the shore of the Barrière du Roule. This was, even if we presume that Marie Rogêt was thrown into the river within three hours after she left her mother's house, only three days from the time she left her home—three days to an hour. But it is folly to suppose that the murder, if murder was committed on her body, could have been consummated soon enough to have enabled her murderers to throw the body into the river before midnight. Those who are guilty of such horrid crimes, choose darkness rather than light. . . . Thus we see that if the body found in the river *was* that of Marie Rogêt, it could only have been in the water two and a half days, or three at the outside. All experience has shown that drowned bodies, or bodies thrown into the water immediately after death by violence, require from six to ten days for sufficient decomposition to take

place to bring them to the top of the water. Even where a cannon is fired over a corpse, and it rises before at least five or six days' immersion, it sinks again, if let alone. Now, we ask, what was there in this case to cause a departure from the ordinary course of nature? . . . If the body had been kept in its mangled state on shore until Tuesday night, some trace would be found on shore of the murderers. It is a doubtful point, also, whether the body would be so soon afloat, even were it thrown in after having been dead two days. And, furthermore, it is exceedingly improbable that any villains who had committed such a murder as is here supposed, would have thrown the body in without weight to sink it, when such a precaution could have so easily been taken."

The editor here proceeds to argue that the body must have been in the water "not three days merely, but, at least, five times three days," because it was so far decomposed that Beauvais had great difficulty in recognizing it. This latter point, however, was fully disproved. I continue the translation:

"What, then, are the facts on which M. Beauvais says that he has no doubt the body was that of Marie Rogêt? He ripped up the gown sleeve, and says he found marks which satisfied him of the identity. The public generally supposed those marks to have consisted of some description of scars. He rubbed the arm and found *hair* upon it—something as indefinite, we think, as can readily be imagined—as little conclusive as finding an arm in the sleeve. M. Beauvais did not return that night, but sent word to Madame Rogêt, at seven o'clock, on Wednesday evening, that an investigation was still in progress respecting her daughter. If we allow that Madame Rogêt, from her age and grief, could not go over, (which is allowing a great deal,) there certainly must have been some one who would have thought it worth while to go over and attend the investigation, if they thought the body was that of Marie. Nobody went over. There was nothing said or heard about the matter in the Rue Pavée St. André, that reached even the occupants of the same building. M. St. Eustache, the lover and intended husband of Marie, who boarded in her mother's house, deposes that he did not hear of the discovery of the body of his intended until the next morning, when M. Beauvais came into his chamber and told him of it. For an item of news like this, it strikes us it was very coolly received."

In this way the journal endeavored to create the impression of an apathy on the part of the relatives of Marie, inconsistent with the supposition that these relatives believed the corpse to be hers. Its insinuations amount to this:—that Marie, with the connivance of her friends, had absented herself from the city for reasons involving a charge against her chastity; and that these friends, upon the discovery of a corpse in the Seine, somewhat resembling that of the girl, had availed themselves of the opportunity to impress the public with the belief of her death. But L'Etoile was again over hasty. It was distinctly proved that no apathy, such as was imagined, existed; that the old lady was exceedingly feeble, and so agitated as to be unable to attend to any duty; that St. Eustache, so far from receiving the news coolly, was distracted with grief, and bore himself so frantically, that M. Beauvais prevailed upon a friend and relative to take charge of him, and prevent his attending the examination at the disinterment. Moreover, although it was stated by L'Etoile, that the corpse was re-interred at the public expense—that an advantageous offer of private sepulture was absolutely declined by the family— and that no member of the family attended the ceremonial:—although, I say, all this was asserted by L'Etoile in furtherance of the impression it designed to convey—yet all this was satisfactorily disproved. In a subsequent number of the paper, an attempt was made to throw suspicion upon Beauvais himself. The editor says:

"Now, then, a change comes over the matter. We are told that, on one occasion, while a Madame B—— was at Madame Rogêt's house, M. Beauvais, who was going out, told her that a gendarme was expected there, and that she, Madame B., must not say anything to the gendarme until he returned, but let the matter be for him. . . . In the present posture of affairs, M. Beauvais appears to have the whole matter locked up in his head. A single step cannot be taken without M. Beauvais; for, go which way you will, you run against him. . . . For some reason, he determined that nobody shall have any thing to do with the proceedings but himself, and he has elbowed the male relatives out of the way, according to their representations, in a very singular manner. He seems to have been very much averse to permitting the relatives to see the body."

By the following fact, some color was given to the suspicion thus thrown upon Beauvais. A visiter at his office, a few days prior to the girl's disappearance, and during the absence of its occupant, had observed a rose in the key-hole of the door, and the name "Marie" inscribed upon a slate which hung near at hand.

The general impression, so far as we were enabled to glean it from the newspapers, seemed to be, that Marie had been the victim of a gang of desperadoes —that by these she had been borne across the river, maltreated and murdered. Le Commerciel,[14] however, a print of extensive influence, was earnest in combating this popular idea. I quote a passage or two from its columns:

"We are persuaded that pursuit has hitherto been on a false scent, so far as it has been directed to the Barrière du Roule. It is impossible that a person so well known to thousands as this young woman was, should have passed three blocks without some one having seen her; and any one who saw her would have remembered it, for she interested all who knew her. It was when the streets were full of people, when she went out. . . . It is impossible that she could have gone to the Barrière du Roule, or to the Rue des Drômes, without being recognized by a dozen persons; yet no one has come forward who saw her outside of her mother's door, and there is no evidence, except the testimony concerning her *expressed intentions*, that she did go out at all. Her gown was torn, bound round her, and tied; and by that the body was carried as a bundle. If the murder had been committed at the Barrière du Roule, there would have been no necessity for any such arrangement. The fact that the body was found floating near the Barrière, is no proof as to where it was thrown into the water. . . . A piece of one of the unfortunate girl's petticoats, two feet long and one foot wide, was torn out and tied under her chin around the back of her head, probably to prevent screams. This was done by fellows who had no pocket-handkerchiefs."

A day or two before the Prefect called upon us, however, some important information reached the police, which seemed to overthrow, at least, the chief portion of Le Commerciel's argument. Two small boys, sons of a Madame Deluc, while roaming among the woods near the Barrière du Roule, chanced to penetrate a close thicket, within which were three or four large stones, forming a kind of seat, with a back and footstool. On the upper stone lay a white petticoat; on the second a silk scarf. A parasol, gloves, and a pocket-handkerchief were also here found. The handkerchief bore the name "Marie Rogêt." Fragments of dress were discovered on the brambles around. The earth was trampled, the bushes were broken, and there was every evidence of a struggle. Between the thicket and the river, the fences were found taken down, and the ground bore evidence of some heavy burthen having been dragged along it.

A weekly paper, Le Soleil,[15] had the following comments upon this discovery

—comments which merely echoed the sentiment of the whole Parisian press:

"The things had all evidently been there at least three or four weeks; they were all mildewed down hard with the action of the rain, and stuck together from mildew. The grass had grown around and over some of them. The silk on the parasol was strong, but the threads of it were run together within. The upper part, where it had been doubled and folded, was all mildewed and rotten, and tore on its being opened. . . . The pieces of her frock torn out by the bushes were about three inches wide and six inches long. One part was the hem of the frock, and it had been mended; the other piece was part of the skirt, not the hem. They looked like strips torn off, and were on the thorn bush, about a foot from the ground. . . . There can be no doubt, therefore, that the spot of this appalling outrage has been discovered."

Consequent upon this discovery, new evidence appeared. Madame Deluc testified that she keeps a roadside inn not far from the bank of the river, opposite the Barrière du Roule. The neighborhood is secluded—particularly so. It is the usual Sunday resort of blackguards from the city, who cross the river in boats. About three o'clock, in the afternoon of the Sunday in question, a young girl arrived at the inn, accompanied by a young man of dark complexion. The two remained here for some time. On their departure, they took the road to some thick woods in the vicinity. Madame Deluc's attention was called to the dress worn by the girl, on account of its resemblance to one worn by a deceased relative. A scarf was particularly noticed. Soon after the departure of the couple, a gang of miscreants made their appearance, behaved boisterously, ate and drank without making payment, followed in the route of the young man and girl, returned to the inn about dusk, and re-crossed the river as if in great haste.

It was soon after dark, upon this same

evening, that Madame Deluc, as well as her eldest son, heard the screams of a female in the vicinity of the inn. The screams were violent but brief. Madame D. recognized not only the scarf which was found in the thicket, but the dress which was discovered upon the corpse. An omnibus-driver, Valence,[16] now also testified that he saw Marie Rogêt cross a ferry on the Seine, on the Sunday in question, in company with a young man of dark complexion. He, Valence, knew Marie, and could not be mistaken in her identity. The articles found in the thicket were fully identified by the relatives of Marie.

The items of evidence and information thus collected by myself, from the newspapers, at the suggestion of Dupin, embraced only one more point—but this was a point of seemingly vast consequence. It appears that, immediately after the discovery of the clothes as above described, the lifeless, or nearly lifeless body of St. Eustache, Marie's betrothed, was found in the vicinity of what all now supposed the scene of the outrage. A phial labelled "laudanum,"[17] and emptied, was found near him. His breath gave evidence of the poison. He died without speaking. Upon his person was found a letter, briefly stating his love for Marie, with his design of self-destruction.

"I need scarcely tell you," said Dupin, as he finished the perusal of my notes, "that this is a far more intricate case than that of the Rue Morgue; from which it differs in one important respect. This is an *ordinary*, although an atrocious instance of crime. There is nothing peculiarly *outré* about it. You will observe that, for this reason, the mystery has been considered easy, when, for this reason, it should have been considered difficult, of solution. Thus, at first, it was thought unnecessary to offer a reward. The myrmidons of G—— were able at once to comprehend how and why such an atrocity *might have been* committed. They could picture to their imaginations a mode—

many modes—and a motive—many motives; and because it was not impossible that either of these numerous modes and motives *could* have been the actual one, they have taken it for granted that one of them *must*. But the ease with which these variable fancies were entertained, and the very plausibility which each assumed, should have been understood as indicative rather of the difficulties than of the facilities which must attend elucidation. I have before observed that it is by prominences above the plane of the ordinary, that reason feels her way, if at all, in her search for the true, and that the proper question in cases such as this, is not so much 'what has occurred?' as 'what has occurred that has never occurred before?' In the investigations at the house of Madame L'Espanaye,[18] the agents of G—— were discouraged and confounded by that very *unusualness* which, to a properly regulated intellect, would have afforded the surest omen of success; while this same intellect might have been plunged in despair at the ordinary character of all that met the eye in the case of the perfumery-girl, and yet told of nothing but easy triumph to the functionaries of the Prefecture.

"In the case of Madame L'Espanaye and her daughter, there was, even at the beginning of our investigation, no doubt that murder had been committed. The idea of suicide was excluded at once. Here, too, we are freed, at the commencement, from all supposition of self-murder. The body found at the Barrière du Roule, was found under such circumstances as to leave us no room for embarrassment upon this important point. But it has been suggested that the corpse discovered, is not that of the Marie Rogêt for the conviction of whose assassin, or assassins, the reward is offered, and respecting whom, solely, our agreement has been arranged with the Prefect. We both know this gentleman well. It will not do to trust him too far. If, dating our inquiries from the body found, and thence tracing a murderer, we yet discover this body to be that of some other individual than Marie; or, if starting from the living Marie, we find her, yet find her unassassinated—in either case we lose our labor; since it is Monsieur G—— with whom we have to deal. For our own purpose, therefore, if not for the purpose of justice, it is indispensable that our first step should be the determination of the identity of the corpse with the Marie Rogêt who is missing.

"With the public the arguments of L'Etoile have had weight; and that the journal itself is convinced of their importance would appear from the manner in which it commences one of its essays upon the subject—'Several of the morning papers of the day,' it says, 'speak of the *conclusive* article in Monday's Etoile.' To me, this article appears conclusive of little beyond the zeal of its inditer.[19] We should bear in mind that, in general, it is the object of our newspapers rather to create a sensation—to make a point—than to further the cause of truth. The latter end is only pursued when it seems coincident with the former. The print which merely falls in with ordinary opinion (however well founded this opinion may be) earns for itself no credit with the mob. The mass of the people regard as profound only him who suggests *pungent contradictions* of the general idea. In ratiocination, not less than in literature, it is the *epigram* which is the most immediately and the most universally appreciated. In both, it is of the lowest order of merit.

"What I mean to say is, that it is the mingled epigram and melodrame of the idea, that Marie Rogêt still lives, rather than any true plausibility in this idea, which have suggested it to L'Etoile, and secured it a favorable reception with the public. Let us examine the heads of this journal's argument; endeavoring to avoid the incoherence with which it is originally set forth.

"The first aim of the writer is to show, from the brevity of the interval between Marie's disappearance and the finding of the floating corpse, that this corpse cannot be that of Marie. The reduction of this interval to its smallest possible dimension, becomes thus, at once, an object with the reasoner. In the rash pursuit of this object, he rushes into mere assumption at the outset. 'It is folly to suppose,' he says, 'that the murder, if murder was committed on her body, could have been consummated soon enough to have enabled her murderers to throw the body into the river before midnight.' We demand at once, and very naturally, *why?* Why is it folly to suppose that the murder was committed *within five minutes* after the girl's quitting her mother's house? Why is it folly to suppose that the murder was committed at any given period of the day? There have been assassinations at all hours. But, had the murder taken place at any moment between nine o'clock in the morning of Sunday, and a quarter before midnight, there would still have been time enough 'to throw the body into the river before midnight.' This assumption, then, amounts precisely to this —that the murder was not committed on Sunday at all—and, if we allow L'Etoile to assume this, we may permit it any liberties whatever. The paragraph beginning 'It is folly to suppose that the murder, etc.,' however it appears as printed in L'Etoile, may be imagined to have existed actually *thus* in the brain of its inditer— 'It is folly to suppose that the murder, if murder was committed on the body, could have been committed soon enough to have enabled her murderers to throw the body into the river before midnight; it is folly, we say, to suppose all this, and to suppose at the same time, (as we are resolved to suppose,) that the body was *not* thrown in until *after* midnight'—a sentence sufficiently inconsequential in itself, but not so utterly preposterous as the one printed.

"Were it my purpose," continued Dupin, "merely to *make out a case* against this passage of L'Etoile's argument, I might safely leave it where it is. It is not, however, with L'Etoile that we have to do, but with the truth. The sentence in question has but one meaning, as it stands; and this meaning I have fairly stated: but it is material that we go behind the mere words, for an idea which these words have obviously intended, and failed to convey. It was the design of the journalist to say that, at whatever period of the day or night of Sunday this murder was committed, it was improbable that the assassins would have ventured to bear the corpse to the river before midnight. And herein lies, really, the assumption of which I complain. It is assumed that the murder was committed at such a position, and under such circumstances, that *the bearing it* to the river became necessary. Now, the assassination might have taken place upon the river's brink, or on the river itself; and, thus, the throwing the corpse in the water might have been resorted to, at any period of the day or night, as the most obvious and most immediate mode of disposal. You will understand that I suggest nothing here as probable, or as coincident with my own opinion. My design, so far, has no reference to the *facts* of the case. I wish merely to caution you against the whole tone of L'Etoile's *suggestion*, by calling your attention to its *ex parte*[20] character at the outset.

"Having prescribed thus a limit to suit its own preconceived notions; having assumed that, if this were the body of Marie, it could have been in the water but a very brief time; the journal goes on to say:

'All experience has shown that drowned bodies, or bodies thrown into the water immediately after death by violence, require from six to ten days for sufficient decomposition to take place to bring them to the top of the water. Even when a cannon is fired over a corpse, and it rises before at least five or six days' immersion, it sinks again if let alone.'

"These assertions have been tacitly received by every paper in Paris, with the exception of Le Moniteur.[21] This latter print endeavors to combat that portion of the paragraph which has reference to 'drowned bodies' only, by citing some five or six instances in which the bodies of individuals known to be drowned were found floating after the lapse of less time than is insisted upon by L'Etoile. But there is something excessively unphilosophical in the attempt on the part of Le Moniteur, to rebut the general assertion of L'Etoile, by a citation of particular instances militating against that assertion. Had it been possible to adduce fifty instead of five examples of bodies found floating at the end of two or three days, these fifty examples could still have been properly regarded only as exceptions to L'Etoile's rule, until such time as the rule itself should be confuted. Admitting the rule, (and this Le Moniteur does not deny, insisting merely upon its exceptions,) the argument of L'Etoile is suffered to remain in full force; for this argument does not pretend to involve more than a question of the *probability* of the body having risen to the surface in less than three days; and this probability will be in favor of L'Etoile's position until the instances so childishly adduced shall be sufficient in number to establish an antagonistical rule.

"You will see at once that all argument upon this head should be urged, if at all, against the rule itself; and for this end we must examine the *rationale* of the rule. Now the human body, in general, is neither much lighter nor much heavier than the water of the Seine; that is to say, the specific gravity of the human body, in its natural condition, is about equal to the bulk of fresh water which it displaces. The bodies of fat and fleshy persons, with small bones, and of women generally, are lighter than those of the lean and large-boned, and of men; and the specific gravity of the water of a river is somewhat influenced by the presence of the tide from sea. But, leaving this tide out of question, it may be said that *very* few human bodies will sink at all, even in fresh water, *of their own accord.* Almost any one, falling into a river, will be enabled to float, if he suffer the specific gravity of the water fairly to be adduced in comparison with his own—that is to say, if he suffer his whole person to be immersed, with as little exception as possible. The proper position for one who cannot swim, is the upright position of the walker on land, with the head thrown fully back, and immersed; the mouth and nostrils alone remaining above the surface.[22] Thus circumstanced, we shall find that we float without difficulty and without exertion. It is evident, however, that the gravities of the body, and of the bulk of water displaced, are very nicely balanced, and that a trifle will cause either to preponderate. An arm, for instance, uplifted from the water, and thus deprived of its support, is an additional weight sufficient to immerse the whole head, while the accidental aid of the smallest piece of timber will enable us to elevate the head so as to look about. Now, in the struggles of one unused to swimming, the arms are invariably thrown upwards, while an attempt is made to keep the head in its usual perpendicular position. The result is the immersion of the mouth and nostrils, and the inception, during efforts to breathe while beneath the surface, of water into the lungs. Much is also received into the stomach, and the whole body becomes heavier by the difference between the weight of the air originally distending these cavities, and that of the fluid which now fills them. This difference is sufficient to cause the body to sink, as a general rule; but is insufficient in the cases of individuals with small bones and an abnormal quantity of flaccid or fatty matter. Such individuals float even after drowning.

"The corpse, being supposed at the bottom of the river, will there remain until, by some means, its specific gravity again becomes less than that of the bulk of water which it displaces. This effect is brought about by decomposition, or otherwise. The result of decomposition is the generation of gas, distending the cellular tissues and all the cavities, and giving the *puffed* appearance which is so horrible. When this distension has so far progressed that the bulk of the corpse is materially increased without a corresponding increase of *mass* or weight, its specific gravity becomes less than that of the water displaced, and it forthwith makes its appearance at the surface. But decomposition is modified by innumerable circumstances—is hastened or retarded by innumerable agencies; for example, by the heat or cold of the season, by the mineral impregnation or purity of the water, by its depth or shallowness, by its currency or stagnation, by the temperament of the body, by its infection or freedom from disease before death. Thus it is evident that we can assign no period, with any thing like accuracy, at which the corpse shall rise through decomposition. Under certain conditions this result would be brought about within an hour; under others, it might not take place at all. There are chemical infusions by which the animal frame can be preserved *forever* from corruption; the Bi-chloride of Mercury[23] is one. But, apart from decomposition, there may be, and very usually is, a generation of gas within the stomach, from the acetous fermentation of vegetable matter (or within other cavities from other causes) sufficient to induce a distension which will bring the body to the surface. The effect produced by the firing of a cannon is that of simple vibration. This may either loosen the corpse from the soft mud or ooze in which it is imbedded, thus permitting it to rise when other agencies have already prepared it for so doing; or it may overcome the tenacity of some putrescent portions of the cellular tissue; allowing the cavities to distend under the influence of the gas.

"Having thus before us the whole philosophy of this subject, we can easily test by it the assertions of L'Etoile. 'All experience shows,' says this paper, 'that drowned bodies, or bodies thrown into the water immediately after death by violence, require from six to ten days for sufficient decomposition to take place to bring them to the top of the water. Even when a cannon is fired over a corpse, and it rises before at least five or six days' immersion, it sinks again if let alone.'

"The whole of this paragraph must now appear a tissue of inconsequence and incoherence. All experience does *not* show that 'drowned bodies' *require* from six to ten days for sufficient decomposition to take place to bring them to the surface. Both science and experience show that the period of their rising is, and necessarily must be, indeterminate. If, moreover, a body has risen to the surface through firing of cannon, it will *not* 'sink again if let alone,' until decomposition has so far progressed as to permit the escape of the generated gas. But I wish to call your attention to the distinction which is made between 'drowned bodies,' and 'bodies thrown into the water immediately after death by violence.' Although the writer admits the distinction, he yet includes them all in the same category. I have shown how it is that the body of a drowning man becomes specifically heavier than its bulk of water, and that he would not sink at all, except for the struggles by which he elevates his arms above the surface, and his gasps for breath while beneath the surface—gasps which supply by water the place of the original air in the lungs. But these struggles and these gasps would not occur in the body 'thrown into the water immediately after death by violence.' Thus, in the latter instance, *the body, as a general rule, would not sink at all*—a fact of which L'Etoile is evidently ignorant. When decomposition had proceeded to a very great extent—when the flesh had in a great measure left the bones—then, indeed, but not *till* then, should we lose sight of the corpse.

"And now what are we to make of the argument, that the body found could not be that of Marie Rogêt, because, three days only having elapsed, this body was found floating? If drowned, being a woman, she might never have sunk; or having sunk, might have re-appeared in twenty-four hours, or less. But no one supposes her to have been drowned; and, dying before being thrown into the river, she might have been found floating at any period afterwards whatever.

" 'But,' says L'Etoile, 'if the body had been kept in its mangled state on shore until Tuesday night, some trace would be found on shore of the murderers.' Here it is at first difficult to perceive the intention of the reasoner. He means to anticipate what he imagines would be an objection to his theory—viz.: that the body was kept on shore two days, suffering rapid decomposition—*more* rapid than if immersed in water. He supposes that, had this been the case, it *might* have appeared at the surface on the Wednesday, and thinks that *only* under such circumstances it could so have appeared. He is accordingly in haste to show that it *was not* kept on shore; for, if so, 'some trace would be found on shore of the murderers.' I presume you smile at the *sequitur.*[24] You cannot be made to see how the mere *duration* of the corpse on the shore could operate to *multiply traces* of the assassins. Nor can I.

" 'And furthermore it is exceedingly improbable,' continues our journal, 'that any villains who had committed such a murder as is here supposed, would have thrown the body in without weight to sink it, when such a precaution could have so easily been taken.' Observe, here, the laughable confusion of thought! No one—not even L'Etoile—disputes the murder committed *on the body found*. The marks of violence are too obvious. It is our reasoner's object merely to show that this body is not Marie's. He wishes to prove that *Marie* is not assassinated—not that the corpse was not. Yet his observation proves only the latter point. Here is a corpse without weight attached. Murderers, casting it in, would not have failed to attach a weight. Therefore it was not thrown in by murderers. This is all which is proved, if any thing is. The question of identity is not even approached, and L'Etoile has been at great pains merely to gainsay now what it has admitted only a moment before. 'We are perfectly convinced,' it says, 'that the body found was that of a murdered female.'

"Nor is this the sole instance, even in this division of his subject, where our reasoner unwittingly reasons against himself. His evident object, I have already said, is to reduce, as much as possible, the interval between Marie's disappearance and the finding of the corpse. Yet we find him *urging* the point that no person saw the girl from the moment of her leaving her mother's house. 'We have no evidence,' he says, 'that Marie Rogêt was in the land of the living after nine o'clock on Sunday, June the twenty-second.' As his argument is obviously an *ex parte* one, he should, at least, have left this matter out of sight; for had any one been known to see Marie, say on Monday, or on Tuesday, the interval in question would have been much reduced, and, by his own ratiocination, the probability much diminished of the corpse being that of the *grisette*. It is, nevertheless, amusing to observe that L'Etoile insists upon its point in the full belief of its furthering its general argument.

"Reperuse now that portion of this argument which has reference to the identification of the corpse by Beauvais. In regard to the *hair* upon the arm, L'Etoile has been obviously disingenuous. M. Beauvais, not being an idiot, could never have urged, in identification of the corpse, simply *hair upon its arm*. No arm is *without* hair. The *generality* of the expression of L'Etoile is a mere perversion of the witness' phraseology. He must have spoken of some *peculiarity* in this hair. It must have been a peculiarity of color, of quantity, of length, or of situation.

" 'Her foot,' says the journal, 'was small —so are thousands of feet. Her garter is no proof whatever—nor is her shoe—for shoes and garters are sold in packages.

The same may be said of the flowers in her hat. One thing upon which M. Beauvais strongly insists is, that the clasp on the garter found, had been set back to take it in. This amounts to nothing; for most women find it proper to take a pair of garters home and fit them to the size of the limbs they are to encircle, rather than to try them in the store where they purchase.' Here it is difficult to suppose the reasoner in earnest. Had M. Beauvais, in his search for the body of Marie, discovered a corpse corresponding in general size and appearance to the missing girl, he would have been warranted (without reference to the question of habiliment at all) in forming an opinion that his search had been successful. If, in addition to the point of general size and contour, he had found upon the arm a peculiar hairy appearance which he had observed upon the living Marie, his opinion might have been justly strengthened; and the increase of positiveness might well have been in the ratio of the peculiarity, or unusualness, of the hairy mark. If, the feet of Marie being small, those of the corpse were also small, the increase of probability that the body was that of Marie would not be an increase in a ratio merely arithmetical, but in one highly geometrical, or accumulative. Add to all this shoes such as she had been known to wear upon the day of her disappearance, and, although these shoes may be 'sold in packages,' you so far augment the probability as to verge upon the certain. What of itself, would be no evidence of identity, becomes through its corroborative position, proof most sure. Give us, then, flowers in the hat corresponding to those worn by the missing girl, and we seek for nothing farther. If only *one* flower, we seek for nothing farther—what then if two or three, or more? Each successive one is multiple evidence—proof not *added* to proof, but *multiplied* by hundreds or thousands. Let us now discover, upon the deceased, garters such as the living used, and it is almost folly to proceed. But these garters are found to be tightened, by the setting back of a clasp, in just such a manner as her own had been tightened by Marie, shortly previous to her leaving home. It is now madness or hypocrisy to doubt. What L'Etoile says in respect to this abbreviation of the garter's being an usual occurrence, shows nothing beyond its own pertinacity in error. The elastic nature of the clasp-garter is self-demonstration of the *unusualness* of the abbreviation. What is made to adjust itself must of necessity require foreign adjustment but rarely. It must have been by an accident, in its strictest sense, that these garters of Marie needed the tightening described. They alone would have amply established her identity. But it is not that the corpse was found to have the garters of the missing girl, or found to have her shoes, or her bonnet, or the flowers of her bonnet, or her feet, or a peculiar mark upon the arm, or her general size and appearance—it is that the corpse had each, and *all collectively*. Could it be proved that the editor of L'Etoile *really* entertained a doubt, under the circumstances, there would be no need, in his case, of a commission *de lunatico inquirendo*. He has thought it sagacious to echo the small talk of the lawyers, who, for the most part, content themselves with echoing the rectangular precepts of the courts. I would here observe that very much of what is rejected as evidence by a court, is the best of evidence to the intellect. For the court, guiding itself by the general principles of evidence—the recognized and *booked* principles—is averse from swerving at particular instances. And this steadfast adherence to principle, with rigorous disregard of the conflicting exception, is a sure mode of attaining the *maximum* of attainable truth, in any long sequence of time. The practise, *in mass*, is therefore philosophical; but it is not the less certain that it engenders vast individual error.[25]

"In respect to the insinuations levelled at Beauvais, you will be willing to dismiss them in a breath. You have already fathomed the true character of this good gentleman. He is a *busy-body*, with much of romance and little of wit. Any one so constituted will readily so conduct himself, upon occasion of *real* excitement, as to render himself liable to suspicion on the part of the over-acute, or the ill-disposed. M. Beauvais (as it appears from your notes) had some personal interviews with the editor of L'Etoile, and offended him by venturing an opinion that the corpse, notwithstanding the theory of the editor, was, in sober fact, that of Marie. 'He persists,' says the paper, 'in asserting the corpse to be that of Marie, but cannot give a circumstance, in addition to those which we have commented upon, to make others believe.' Now, without re-adverting to the fact that stronger evidence 'to make others believe,' could *never* have been adduced, it may be remarked that a man may very well be understood to believe, in a case of this kind, without the ability to advance a single reason for the belief of a second party. Nothing is more vague than impressions of individual identity. Each man recognizes his neighbor, yet there are few instances in which any one is prepared *to give a reason* for his recognition. The editor of L'Etoile had no right to be offended at M. Beauvais' unreasoning belief.

"The suspicious circumstances which invest him, will be found to tally much better with my hypothesis of *romantic busy-bodyism*, than with the reasoner's suggestion of guilt. Once adopting the more charitable interpretation, we shall find no difficulty in comprehending the rose in the key-hole; the 'Marie' upon the slate; the 'elbowing the male relatives out of the way;' the 'aversion to permitting them to see the body;' the caution given to Madame B——, that she must hold no conversation with the *gendarme* until his return (Beauvais'); and, lastly, his apparent determination 'that nobody should have anything to do with the proceedings except himself.' It seems to me unquestionable that Beauvais was a suitor of Marie's; that she coquetted with him; and that he was ambitious of being thought to enjoy her fullest intimacy and confidence. I shall say nothing more upon this point; and, as the evidence fully rebuts the assertion of L'Etoile, touching the matter of *apathy* on the part of the mother and other relatives—an apathy inconsistent with the supposition of their believing the corpse to be that of the perfumery-girl—we shall now proceed as if the question of *identity* were settled to our perfect satisfaction."

"And what," I here demanded, "do you think of the opinions of Le Commerciel?"

"That, in spirit, they are far more worthy of attention than any which have been promulgated upon the subject. The deductions from the premises are philosophical and acute; but the premises, in two instances, at least, are founded in imperfect observation. Le Commerciel wishes to intimate that Marie was seized by some gang of low ruffians not far from her mother's door. 'It is impossible,' it urges, 'that a person so well known to thousands as this young woman was, should have passed three blocks without some one having seen her.' This is the idea of a man long resident in Paris—a public man—and one whose walks to and fro in the city, have been mostly limited to the vicinity of the public offices. He is aware that *he* seldom passes so far as a dozen blocks from his own *bureau*, without being recognized and accosted. And, knowing the extent of his personal acquaintance with others, and of others with him, he compares his notoriety with that of the perfumery-girl, finds no great difference between them, and reaches at once the conclusion that she, in her walks, would be equally liable to recognition with himself in his. This could only be the case were her walks of the same unvarying, methodical character, and within the same *species* of limited region as are his own. He passes to and fro, at regular intervals, within a confined periphery, abounding in individuals who are led to observation of his person through interest in the kindred nature of his occupation with their own. But the walks of Marie may, in general, be supposed discursive. In this particular instance, it will be understood as most probable, that she proceeded upon a route of more than average diversity from her accustomed ones. The parallel which we imagine to have existed in the mind of Le Commerciel would only be sustained in the event of the two individuals traversing the whole city. In this case, granting the personal acquaintances to be equal, the chances would be also equal that an equal number of personal rencounters would be made. For my own part, I should hold it not only as possible, but as very far more than probable, that Marie might have proceeded, at any given period, by any one of the many routes between her own residence and that of her aunt, without meeting a single individual whom she knew, or by whom she was known. In viewing this question in its full and proper light, we must hold steadily in mind the great disproportion between the personal acquaintances of even the most noted individual in Paris, and the entire population of Paris itself.

"But whatever force there may still appear to be in the suggestion of Le Commerciel, will be much diminished when we take into consideration *the hour* at which the girl went abroad. 'It was when the streets were full of people,' says Le Commerciel, 'that she went out.' But not so. It was nine o'clock in the morning. Now at nine o'clock of every morning in the week, *with the exception of Sunday*, the streets of the city are, it is true, thronged with people. At nine on Sunday, the populace are chiefly within doors *preparing for church*. No observing person can have failed to notice the peculiarly deserted air of the town, from about eight until ten on the morning of every Sabbath.[26] Between ten and eleven the streets are thronged, but not at so early a period as that designated.

"There is another point at which there seems a deficiency of *observation* on the part of Le Commerciel. 'A piece,' it says, 'of one of the unfortunate girl's petticoats, two feet long, and one foot wide, was torn out and tied under her chin, and around the back of her head, probably to prevent screams. This was done by fellows who had no pocket-handkerchiefs.' Whether this idea is, or is not well founded, we will endeavor to see hereafter; but by 'fellows who have no pocket-handkerchiefs,' the editor intends the lowest class of ruffians. These, however, are the very description of people who will always be found to have handkerchiefs even when destitute of shirts. You must have had occasion to observe how absolutely indispensable, of late years, to the thorough blackguard, has become the pocket-handkerchief."

"And what are we to think," I asked, "of the article in Le Soleil?"

"That it is a pity its inditer was not born a parrot—in which case he would have been the most illustrious parrot of his race. He has merely repeated the individual items of the already published opinion; collecting them, with a laudable industry, from this paper and from that. 'The things had all *evidently* been there,' he says, 'at least, three or four weeks, and there can be *no doubt* that the spot of this appalling outrage has been discovered.' The facts here re-stated by Le Soleil, are very far indeed from removing my own doubts upon this subject, and we will examine them more particularly hereafter in connexion with another division of the theme.

"At present we must occupy ourselves with other investigations. You cannot fail to have remarked the extreme laxity of the examination of the corpse. To be sure, the question of identity was readily determined, or should have been; but there were other points to be ascertained. Had the body been in any respect *despoiled?* Had the deceased any articles of jewelry about her person upon leaving home? If so, had she any when found? These are important questions utterly untouched by the evidence; and there are others of equal moment, which have met with no attention. We must endeavor to satisfy ourselves by personal inquiry. The case of St. Eustache must be re-examined. I have no suspicion of this person; but let us proceed methodically. We will ascertain beyond a doubt the validity of the *affidavits* in regard to his whereabouts on the Sunday. Affidavits of this character are readily made matter of mystification. Should there be nothing wrong here, however, we will dismiss St. Eustache from our investigations. His suicide, however corroborative of suspicion, were there found to be deceit in the affidavits, is, without such deceit, in no respect an unaccountable circumstance, or one which need cause us to deflect from the line of ordinary analysis.

"In that which I now propose, we will discard the interior points of this tragedy, and concentrate our attention upon its outskirts. Not the least usual error, in investigations such as this, is the limiting of inquiry to the immediate, with total disregard of the collateral or circumstantial events. It is the mal-practice of the courts to confine evidence and discussion to the bounds of apparent relevancy. Yet experience has shown, and a true philosophy will always show, that a vast, perhaps the larger portion of truth, arises from the seemingly irrelevant. It is through the spirit of this principle, if not precisely through its letter, that modern science has resolved to *calculate upon the unforeseen.* But perhaps you do not comprehend me. The history of human knowledge has so uninterruptedly shown that to collateral, or incidental, or accidental events we are indebted for the most numerous and most valuable discoveries, that it has at length become necessary, in any prospective view of improvement, to make not only large, but the largest allowances for inventions that shall arise by chance, and quite out of the range of ordinary expectation. It is no longer philosophical to base, upon what has been, a vision of what is to be. *Accident* is admitted as a portion of the substructure. We make chance a matter of absolute calculation. We subject the unlooked for and unimagined, to the mathematical *formulæ* of the schools.

"I repeat that it is no more than fact, that the *larger* portion of all truth has sprung from the collateral; and it is but in accordance with the spirit of the principle involved in this fact, that I would divert inquiry, in the present case, from the trodden and hitherto unfruitful ground of the event itself, to the cotemporary circumstances which surround it. While you ascertain the validity of the affidavits, I will examine the newspapers more generally than you have as yet done. So far, we have only reconnoitred the field of investigation; but it will be strange indeed if a comprehensive survey, such as I propose, of the public prints, will not afford us some minute points which shall establish a *direction* for inquiry."

In pursuance of Dupin's suggestion, I made scrupulous examination of the affair of the affidavits. The result was a firm conviction of their validity, and of the consequent innocence of St. Eustache. In the mean time my friend occupied himself, with what seemed to me a minuteness altogether objectless, in a scrutiny of the various newspaper files. At the end of a week he placed before me the following extracts:

"About three years and a half ago, a disturbance very similar to the present, was caused by the disappearance of this same Marie Rogêt, from the *parfumerie* of Monsieur Le Blanc, in the Palais Royal. At the end of a week, however, she re-appeared at her customary *comptoir* as well as ever, with the exception of a slight paleness not altogether usual. It was given out by Monsieur Le Blanc and her mother, that she had merely been on a visit to some friend in the country; and the affair was speedily hushed up. We presume that the present absence is a freak of the same nature, and that, at the expiration of a week, or perhaps of a month, we shall have her among us again."—*Evening Paper—Monday, June* 23.[27]

"An evening journal of yesterday, refers to a former mysterious disappearance of Mademoiselle Rogêt. It is well known that, during the week of her absence from Le Blanc's *parfumerie*, she was in the company of a young naval officer, much noted for his debaucheries. A quarrel, it is supposed, providentially led to her return home. We have the name of the Lothario in question, who is, at present, stationed in Paris, but, for obvious reasons, forbear to make it public."—*Le Mercure—Tuesday Morning, June* 24.[28]

"An outrage of the most atrocious character was perpetrated near this city the day before yesterday. A gentleman, with his wife and daughter, engaged, about dusk, the services of six young men, who were idly rowing a boat to and fro near the banks of the Seine, to convey him across the river. Upon reaching the opposite shore, the three passengers stepped out, and had proceeded so far as to be beyond the view of the boat, when the daughter discovered that she had left in it her parasol. She returned for it, was seized by the gang, carried out into the stream, gagged, brutally treated, and finally taken to the shore at a point not far from that at which she had originally entered the boat with her parents. The villains have escaped for the time, but the police are upon their trail, and some of them will soon be taken."—*Morning Paper—June* 25.[29]

"We have received one or two communications, the object of which is to fasten the crime of the late atrocity upon Mennais; but as this gentleman has been fully exonerated by a legal inquiry, and as the arguments of our several correspondents appear to be more zealous than profound, we do not think it advisable to make them public."—*Morning Paper—June* 28.[30]

"We have received several forcibly written communications, apparently from various sources, and which go far to render it a matter of certainty that the unfortunate Marie Rogêt has become a victim of one of the numerous bands of blackguards which infest the vicinity of the city upon Sunday. Our own opinion is decidedly in favor of this supposition. We shall endeavor to make room for some of these arguments hereafter."—*Evening Paper.— Tuesday, June* 31.[31]

"On Monday, one of the bargemen connected with the revenue service, saw an empty boat floating down the Seine. Sails were lying in the bottom of the boat. The bargeman towed it under the barge office. The next morning it was taken from thence, without the knowledge of any of the officers. The rudder is now at the barge office."—*La Diligence—Thursday, June* 26.[32]

Upon reading these various extracts, they not only seemed to me irrelevant, but I could perceive no mode in which any one of them could be brought to bear upon the matter in hand. I waited for some explanation from Dupin.

"It is not my present design," he said, "to *dwell* upon the first and second of these extracts. I have copied them chiefly to show you the extreme remissness of the police, who, as far as I can understand from the Prefect, have not troubled themselves, in any respect, with an examination of the naval officer alluded to. Yet it is mere folly to say that between the first and second disappearance of Marie, there is no *supposable* connection. Let us admit the first elopement to have resulted in a quarrel between the lovers, and the return home of the betrayed. We are now prepared to view a second *elopement* (if we *know* that an elopement has again taken place) as indicating a renewal of the betrayer's advances, rather than as the result of new proposals by a second individual—we are prepared to regard it as a 'making up' of the old *amour*, rather than as the commencement of a new one. The chances are ten to one, that he who had once eloped with Marie, would again propose an elopement, rather than that

she to whom proposals of elopement had been made by one individual, should have them made to her by another. And here let me call your attention to the fact, that the time elapsing between the first ascertained, and the second supposed elopement, is a few months more than the general period of the cruises of our men-of-war. Had the lover been interrupted in his first villany by the necessity of departure to sea, and had he seized the first moment of his return to renew the base designs not yet altogether accomplished— or not yet altogether accomplished *by him?* Of all these things we know nothing.

"You will say, however, that, in the second instance, there was *no* elopement as imagined. Certainly not—but are we prepared to say that there was not the frustrated design? Beyond St. Eustache, and perhaps Beauvais, we find no recognized, no open, no honorable suitors of Marie. Of none other is there any thing said. Who, then, is the secret lover, of whom the relatives (*at least most of them*) know nothing, but whom Marie meets upon the morning of Sunday, and who is so deeply in her confidence, that she hesitates not to remain with him until the shades of the evening descend, amid the solitary groves of the Barrière du Roule? Who is that secret lover, I ask, of whom, at least, *most* of the relatives know nothing? And what means the singular prophecy of Madame Rogêt on the morning of Marie's departure?—'I fear that I shall never see Marie again.'

"But if we cannot imagine Madame Rogêt privy to the design of elopement, may we not at least suppose this design entertained by the girl? Upon quitting home, she gave it to be understood that she was about to visit her aunt in the Rue des Drômes, and St. Eustache was requested to call for her at dark. Now, at first glance, this fact strongly militates against my suggestion;—but let us reflect. That she *did* meet some companion, and proceed with him across the river, reaching the Barrière du Roule at so late an hour as three o'clock in the afternoon, is known. But in consenting so to accompany this individual, *(for whatever purpose—to her mother known or unknown,)* she must have thought of her expressed intention when leaving home, and of the surprise and suspicion aroused in the bosom of her affianced suitor, St. Eustache, when, calling for her, at the hour appointed, in the Rue des Drômes, he should find that she had not been there, and when, moreover, upon returning to the *pension* with this alarming intelligence, he should become aware of her continued absence from home. She must have thought of these things, I say. She must have foreseen the chagrin of St. Eustache, the suspicion of all. She could not have thought of returning to brave this suspicion; but the suspicion becomes a point of trivial importance to her, if we suppose her *not* intending to return.

"We may imagine her thinking thus— 'I am to meet a certain person for the purpose of elopement, or for certain other purposes known only to myself. It is necessary that there be no chance of interruption—there must be sufficient time given us to elude pursuit—I will give it to be understood that I shall visit and spend the day with my aunt at the Rue des Drômes—I will tell St. Eustache not to call for me until dark—in this way, my absence from home for the longest possible period, without causing suspicion or anxiety, will be accounted for, and I shall gain more time than in any other manner. If I bid St. Eustache call for me at dark, he will be sure not to call before; but, if I wholly neglect to bid him call, my time for escape will be diminished, since it will be expected that I return the earlier, and my absence will the sooner excite anxiety. Now, if it were my design to return *at all*—if I had in contemplation merely a stroll with the individual in question —it would not be my policy to bid St. Eustache call; for, calling, he will be *sure* to ascertain that I have played him false— a fact of which I might keep him for ever

in ignorance, by leaving home without notifying him of my intention, by returning before dark, and by then stating that I had been to visit my aunt in the Rue des Drômes. But, as it is my design *never* to return—or not for some weeks—or not until certain concealments are effected— the gaining of time is the only point about which I need give myself any concern.'

"You have observed, in your notes, that the most general opinion in relation to this sad affair is, and was from the first, that the girl had been the victim of *a gang* of blackguards. Now, the popular opinion, under certain conditions, is not to be disregarded. When arising of itself —when manifesting itself in a strictly spontaneous manner—we should look upon it as analogous with that *intuition* which is the idiosyncrasy of the individual man of genius. In ninety-nine cases from the hundred I would abide by its decision. But it is important that we find no palpable traces of *suggestion*. The opinion must be rigorously *the public's own;* and the distinction is often exceedingly difficult to perceive and to maintain. In the present instance, it appears to me that this 'public opinion,' in respect to *a gang,* has been superinduced by the collateral event which is detailed in the third of my extracts. All Paris is excited by the discovered corpse of Marie, a girl young, beautiful and notorious. This corpse is found, bearing marks of violence, and floating in the river. But it is now made known that, at the very period, or about the very period, in which it is supposed that the girl was assassinated, an outrage similar in nature to that endured by the deceased, although less in extent, was perpetrated, by a gang of young ruffians, upon the person of a second young female. Is it wonderful that the one known atrocity should influence the popular judgment in regard to the other unknown? This judgment awaited direction, and the known outrage seemed so opportunely to afford it! Marie, too, was found in the river; and upon this very river was this known outrage committed. The connexion of the two events had about it so much of the palpable, that the true wonder would have been a *failure* of the populace to appreciate and to seize it. But, in fact, the one atrocity, known to be so committed, is, if any thing, evidence that the other, committed at a time nearly coincident, was *not* so committed. It would have been a miracle indeed, if, while a gang of ruffians were perpetrating, at a given locality, a most unheard-of wrong, there should have been another similar gang, in a similar locality, in the same city, under the same circumstances, with the same means and appliances, engaged in a wrong of precisely the same aspect, at precisely the same period of time! Yet in what, if not in this marvellous train of coincidence, does the accidentally *suggested* opinion of the populace call upon us to believe?

"Before proceeding farther, let us consider the supposed scene of the assassination, in the thicket at the Barrière du Roule. This thicket, although dense, was in the close vicinity of a public road. Within were three or four large stones, forming a kind of seat with a back and footstool. On the upper stone was discovered a white petticoat; on the second, a silk scarf. A parasol, gloves, and a pocket-handkerchief, were also here found. The handkerchief bore the name, 'Marie Rogêt.' Fragments of dress were seen on the branches around. The earth was trampled, the bushes were broken, and there was every evidence of a violent struggle.

"Notwithstanding the acclamation with which the discovery of this thicket was received by the press, and the unanimity with which it was supposed to indicate the precise scene of the outrage, it must be admitted that there was some very good reason for doubt. That it *was* the scene, I may or I may not believe—but there was excellent reason for doubt. Had the *true* scene been, as Le Commerciel suggested, in the neighborhood of the Rue Pavée St. André, the perpetrators of the crime, supposing them still resident in Paris, would naturally have been stricken with terror at the public attention thus acutely directed into the proper channel; and, in certain classes of minds, there would have arisen, at once, a sense of the necessity of some exertion to redivert this attention. And thus, the thicket of the Barrière du Roule having been already suspected, the idea of placing the articles where they were found, might have been naturally entertained. There is no real evidence, although Le Soleil so supposes, that the articles discovered had been more than a very few days in the thicket; while there is much circumstantial proof that they could not have remained there, without attracting attention, during the twenty days elapsing between the fatal Sunday and the afternoon upon which they were found by the boys. 'They were all *mildewed* down hard,' says Le Soleil, adopting the opinions of its predecessors, 'with the action of the rain, and stuck together from *mildew*. The grass had grown around and over some of them. The silk of the parasol was strong, but the threads of it were run together within. The upper part, where it had been doubled and folded, was all *mildewed* and rotten, and tore on being opened.' In respect to the grass having 'grown around and over some of them,' it is obvious that the fact could only have been ascertained from the words, and thus from the recollections, of two small boys; for these boys removed the articles and took them home before they had been seen by a third party. But grass will grow, especially in warm and damp weather, (such as was that of the period of the murder,) as much as two or three inches in a single day. A parasol lying upon a newly turfed ground, might, in a week, be entirely concealed from sight by the upspringing grass. And touching that *mildew* upon which the editor of Le Soleil so pertinaciously insists, that he employs the word no less than three times in the brief paragraph just quoted, is he really unaware of the nature of this *mildew?* Is he to be told that it is one of the many classes of *fungus,* of which the most ordinary feature is its up-springing and decadence within twenty-four hours?

"Thus we see, at a glance, that what has been most triumphantly adduced in support of the idea that the articles had been 'for at least three or four weeks' in the thicket, is most absurdly null as regards any evidence of that fact. On the other hand, it is exceedingly difficult to believe that these articles could have remained in the thicket specified, for a longer period than a single week—for a longer period than from one Sunday to the next. Those who know any thing of the vicinity of Paris, know the extreme difficulty of finding *seclusion,* unless at a great distance from its suburbs. Such a thing as an un-explored, or even an unfrequently visited recess, amid its woods or groves, is not for a moment to be imagined. Let any one who, being at heart a lover of nature, is yet chained by duty to the dust and heat of this great metropolis—let any such one attempt, even during the week-days, to slake his thirst for solitude amid the scenes of natural loveliness which immediately surround us. At every second step, he will find the growing charm dispelled by the voice and personal intrusion of some ruffian or party of carousing black-guards. He will seek privacy amid the densest foliage, all in vain. Here are the very nooks where the unwashed most abound—here are the temples most dese-crate. With sickness of the heart the wan-derer will flee back to the polluted Paris as to a less odious because less incongru-ous sink of pollution. But if the vicinity of the city is so beset during the working days of the week, how much more so on the Sabbath! It is now especially that, re-leased from the chains of labor, or de-prived of the customary opportunities of crime, the town blackguard seeks the pre-cincts of the town, not through love of the rural, which in his heart he despises, but by way of escape from the restraints and conventionalities of society. He de-sires less the fresh air and the green trees, than the utter *license* of the country. Here, at the road-side inn, or beneath the foliage of the woods, he indulges, un-checked by any eye except those of his boon companions, in all the mad excess of a counterfeit hilarity—the joint off-spring of liberty and of rum. I say nothing more than what must be obvious to every dispassionate observer, when I repeat that the circumstance of the articles in ques-tion having remained undiscovered, for a longer period than from one Sunday to another, in *any* thicket in the immediate neighborhood of Paris, is to be looked upon as little less than miraculous.

"But there are not wanting other grounds for the suspicion that the articles were placed in the thicket with the view of diverting attention from the real scene of the outrage. And, first, let me direct your notice to the *date* of the discovery of the articles. Collate this with the date of the fifth extract made by myself from the newspapers. You will find that the discovery followed, almost immediately, the urgent communications sent to the evening paper. These communications, al-though various, and apparently from vari-ous sources, tended all to the same point —viz., the directing of attention to *a gang* as the perpetrators of the outrage, and to the neighborhood of the Barrière du Roule as its scene. Now here, of course, the sus-picion is not that, in consequence of these communications, or of the public atten-tion by them directed, the articles were found by the boys; but the suspicion might and may well have been, that the articles were not *before* found by the boys, for the reason that the articles had not before been in the thicket; having been deposited there only at so late a pe-riod as at the date, or shortly prior to the date of the communications, by the guilty authors of these communications them-selves.

"This thicket was a singular—an ex-ceedingly singular one. It was unusually dense. Within its naturally walled enclosure were three extraordinary stones, *forming a seat with a back and footstool.* And this thicket, so full of a natural art, was in the immediate vicinity, *within a few rods,* of the dwelling of Madame Deluc, whose boys were in the habit of closely examining the shrubberies about them in search of the bark of the sassafras. Would it be a rash wager—a wager of one thousand to one—that *a day* never passed over the heads of these boys without finding at least one of them ensconced in the umbrageous[33] hall, and enthroned upon its natural throne? Those who would hesitate at such a wager, have either never been boys themselves, or have forgotten the boyish nature. I repeat—it is exceedingly hard to comprehend how the articles could have remained in this thicket undiscovered, for a longer period than one or two days; and that thus there is good ground for suspicion, in spite of the dogmatic ignorance of Le Soleil, that they were, at a comparatively late date, deposited where found.

"But there are still other and stronger reasons for believing them so deposited, than any which I have as yet urged. And, now, let me beg your notice to the highly artificial arrangement of the articles. On the *upper* stone lay a white petticoat; on the *second* a silk scarf; scattered around, were a parasol, gloves, and a pocket-handkerchief bearing the name, 'Marie Rogêt.' Here is just such an arrangement as would *naturally* be made by a not-over-acute person wishing to dispose the articles *naturally.* But it is by no means a *really* natural arrangement. I should rather have looked to see the things *all* lying on the ground and trampled under foot. In the narrow limits of that bower, it would have been scarcely possible that the petticoat and scarf should have retained a position upon the stones, when subjected to the brushing to and fro of many struggling persons. 'There was evidence,' it is said, 'of a struggle; and the earth was trampled, the bushes were broken,'—but the petticoat and the scarf are found deposited as if upon shelves. 'The pieces of the frock torn out by the bushes were about three inches wide and six inches long. One part was the hem of the frock and it had been mended. They *looked like strips torn off.*' Here, inadvertently, Le Soleil has employed an exceedingly suspicious phrase. The pieces, as described, do indeed 'look like strips torn off;' but purposely and by hand. It is one of the rarest of accidents that a piece is 'torn off,' from any garment such as is now in question, by the agency *of a thorn.* From the very nature of such fabrics, a thorn or nail becoming entangled in them, tears them rectangularly—divides them into two longitudinal rents, at right angles with each other, and meeting at an apex where the thorn enters—but it is scarcely possible to conceive the piece 'torn off.' I never so knew it, nor did you. To tear a piece *off* from such fabric, two distinct forces, in different directions, will be, in almost every case, required. If there be two edges to the fabric —if, for example, it be a pocket-handkerchief, and it is desired to tear from it a slip, then, and then only, will the one force serve the purpose. But in the present case the question is of a dress, presenting but one edge. To tear a piece from the interior, where no edge is presented, could only be effected by a miracle through the agency of thorns, and no *one* thorn could accomplish it. But, even where an edge is presented, two thorns will be necessary, operating, the one in two distinct directions, and the other in one. And this in the supposition that the edge is unhemmed. If hemmed, the matter is nearly out of the question. We thus see the numerous and great obstacles in the way of pieces being 'torn off' through the simple agency of 'thorns;' yet we are required to believe not only that one piece but that many have been so torn. 'And one part,' too, '*was the hem of the frock!*' Another piece was '*part of the skirt, not the hem,*' —that is to say, was torn completely out, through the agency of thorns, from the unedged interior of the dress! These, I say, are things which one may well be pardoned for disbelieving; yet, taken collectedly, they form, perhaps, less of reasonable ground for suspicion, than the one startling circumstance of the articles having been left in this thicket at all, by any *murderers* who had enough precaution to think of removing the corpse. You will not have apprehended me rightly, however, if you suppose it my design to *deny* this thicket as the scene of the outrage. There might have been a wrong *here*, or, more possibly, an accident at Madame Deluc's. But, in fact, this is a point of minor importance. We are not engaged in an attempt to discover the scene, but to produce the perpetrators of the murder. What I have adduced, notwithstanding the minuteness with which I have adduced it, has been with the view, first, to show the folly of the positive and headlong assertions of Le Soleil, but secondly and chiefly, to bring you, by the most natural route, to a further contemplation of the doubt whether this assassination has, or has not been, the work of *a gang*.

"We will resume this question by mere allusion to the revolting details of the surgeon examined at the inquest. It is only necessary to say that his published *inferences*, in regard to the number of the ruffians, have been properly ridiculed as unjust and totally baseless, by all the reputable anatomists of Paris. Not that the matter *might not* have been as inferred, but that there was no ground for the inference:—was there not much for another?

"Let us reflect now upon 'the traces of a struggle;' and let me ask what these traces have been supposed to demonstrate. A gang. But do they not rather demonstrate the absence of a gang? What *struggle* could have taken place—what struggle so violent and so enduring as to have left its 'traces' in all directions—between a weak and defenceless girl and the *gang* of ruffians imagined? The silent grasp of a few rough arms and all would have

been over. The victim must have been absolutely passive at their will. You will bear in mind that the arguments urged against the thicket as the scene, are applicable, in chief part, only against it as the scene of an outrage committed by *more than a single individual.* If we imagine but *one* violator, we can conceive, and thus only conceive, the struggle of so violent and so obstinate a nature as to have left the 'traces' apparent.

"And again. I have already mentioned the suspicion to be excited by the fact that the articles in question were suffered to remain *at all* in the thicket where discovered. It seems almost impossible that these evidences of guilt should have been accidentally left where found. There was sufficient presence of mind (it is supposed) to remove the corpse; and yet a more positive evidence than the corpse itself (whose features might have been quickly obliterated by decay,) is allowed to lie conspicuously in the scene of the outrage—I allude to the handkerchief with the *name* of the deceased. If this was accident, it was not the accident *of a gang*. We can imagine it only the accident of an individual. Let us see. An individual has committed the murder. He is alone with the ghost of the departed. He is appalled by what lies motionless before him. The fury of his passion is over, and there is abundant room in his heart for the natural awe of the deed. His is none of that confidence which the presence of numbers inevitably inspires. He is *alone* with the dead. He trembles and is bewildered. Yet there is a necessity for disposing of the corpse. He bears it to the river, but leaves behind him the other evidences of guilt; for it is difficult, if not impossible to carry all the burthen at once, and it will be easy to return for what is left. But in his toilsome journey to the water his fears redouble within him. The sounds of life encompass his path. A dozen times he hears or fancies the step of an observer. Even the very lights from the city bewilder him. Yet, in time, and by long and frequent pauses of deep agony, he reaches the river's brink, and disposes of his ghastly charge—perhaps through the medium of a boat. But *now* what treasure does the world hold—what threat of vengeance could it hold out—which would have power to urge the return of that lonely murderer over that toilsome and perilous path, to the thicket and its blood-chilling recollections? He returns *not*, let the consequences be what they may. He *could* not return if he would. His sole thought is immediate escape. He turns his back *forever* upon those dreadful shrubberies, and flees as from the wrath to come.

"But how with a gang? Their number would have inspired them with confidence; if, indeed, confidence is ever wanting in the breast of the arrant blackguard; and of arrant blackguards alone are the supposed *gangs* ever constituted. Their number, I say, would have prevented the bewildering and unreasoning terror which I have imagined to paralyze the single man. Could we suppose an oversight in one, or two, or three, this oversight would have been remedied by a fourth. They would have left nothing behind them; for their number would have enabled them to carry *all* at once. There would have been no need of *return*.

"Consider now the circumstances that, in the outer garment of the corpse when found, 'a slip, about a foot wide, had been torn upward from the bottom hem to the waist, wound three times round the waist, and secured by a sort of hitch in the back.' This was done with the obvious design of affording *a handle* by which to carry the body. But would any *number* of men have dreamed of resorting to such an expedient? To three or four, the limbs of the corpse would have afforded not only a sufficient, but the best possible hold. The device is that of a single individual; and this brings us to the fact that 'between the thicket and the river, the rails of the fences were found taken down, and the ground bore evident traces of some heavy burden having been dragged along it!' But

would a *number* of men have put themselves to the superfluous trouble of taking down a fence, for the purpose of dragging through it a corpse which they might have *lifted over* any fence in an instant? Would a *number* of men have so *dragged* a corpse at all as to have left evident *traces* of the dragging?

"And here we must refer to an observation of Le Commerciel; an observation upon which I have already, in some measure, commented. 'A piece,' says this journal, 'of one of the unfortunate girl's petticoats was torn out and tied under her chin, and around the back of her head, probably to prevent screams. This was done by fellows who had no pocket-handkerchiefs.'

"I have before suggested that a genuine blackguard is never *without* a pocket-handkerchief. But it is not to this fact that I now especially advert. That it was not through want of a handkerchief for the purpose imagined by Le Commerciel, that this bandage was employed, is rendered apparent by the handkerchief left in the thicket; and the object was not 'to prevent screams' appears, also, from the bandage having been employed in preference to what would so much better have answered the purpose. But the language of the evidence speaks of the strip in question as 'found around the neck, fitting loosely, and secured with a hard knot.' These words are sufficiently vague, but differ materially from those of Le Commerciel. The slip was eighteen inches wide, and therefore, although of muslin, would form a strong band when folded or rumpled longitudinally. And thus rumpled it was discovered. My inference is this. The solitary murderer, having borne the corpse, for some distance, (whether from the thicket or elsewhere) by means of the bandage *hitched* around its middle, found the weight, in this mode of procedure, too much for his strength. He resolved to drag the burthen—the evidence goes to show that it *was* dragged. With this object in view, it became necessary to attach something like a rope to one of the extremities. It could be best attached about the neck, where the head would prevent its slipping off. And, now, the murderer bethought him, unquestionably, of the bandage about the loins. He would have used this, but for its volution about the corpse, the *hitch* which embarrassed it, and the reflection that it had not been 'torn off' from the garment. It was easier to tear a new slip from the petticoat. He tore it, made it fast about the neck, and so *dragged* his victim to the brink of the river. That this 'bandage,' only attainable with trouble and delay, and but imperfectly answering its purpose—that this bandage was employed *at all*, demonstrates that the necessity for its employment sprang from circumstances arising at a period when the handkerchief was no longer attainable—that is to say, arising, as we have imagined, after quitting the thicket, (if the thicket it was), and on the road between the thicket and the river.

"But the evidence, you will say, of Madame Deluc, (!) points especially to the presence of *a gang*, in the vicinity of the thicket, at or about the epoch of the murder. This I grant. I doubt if there were not a *dozen* gangs, such as described by Madame Deluc, in and about the vicinity of the Barrière du Roule at or about the period of this tragedy. But the gang which has drawn upon itself the pointed animadversion, although the somewhat tardy and very suspicious evidence of Madame Deluc, is the *only* gang which is represented by that honest and scrupulous old lady as having eaten her cakes and swallowed her brandy, without putting themselves to the trouble of making her payment. *Et hinc illæ iræ?*[34]

"But what *is* the precise evidence of Madame Deluc? 'A gang of miscreants made their appearance, behaved boisterously, ate and drank without making payment, followed in the route of the young man and girl, returned to the inn *about dusk*, and recrossed the river as if in great haste.'

"Now this 'great haste' very possibly seemed *greater* haste in the eyes of Madame Deluc, since she dwelt lingeringly and lamentingly upon her violated cakes and ale—cakes and ale for which she might still have entertained a faint hope of compensation. Why, otherwise, since it was *about dusk*, should she make a point of the *haste?* It is no cause for wonder, surely, that even a gang of blackguards should make *haste* to get home, when a wide river is to be crossed in small boats, when storm impends, and when night *approaches*.

"I say *approaches;* for the night had *not yet arrived*. It was only *about dusk* that the indecent haste of these 'miscreants' offended the sober eyes of Madame Deluc. But we are told that it was upon this very evening that Madame Deluc, as well as her eldest son, 'heard the screams of a female in the vicinity of the inn.' And in what words does Madame Deluc designate the period of the evening at which these screams were heard? 'It was *soon after dark*,' she says. But 'soon *after* dark,' is, at least, *dark;* and '*about dusk*' is as certainly daylight. Thus it is abundantly clear that the gang quitted the Barrière du Roule *prior* to the screams overheard (?) by Madame Deluc. And although, in all the many reports of the evidence, the relative expressions in question are distinctly and invariably employed just as I have employed them in this conversation with yourself, no notice whatever of the gross discrepancy has, as yet, been taken by any of the public journals, or by any of the Myrmidons of police.

"I shall add but one to the arguments against *a gang;* but this *one* has, to my own understanding at least, a weight altogether irresistible. Under the circumstances of large reward offered, and full pardon to any King's evidence, it is not to be imagined, for a moment, that some member of *a gang* of low ruffians, or of any body of men, would not long ago have betrayed his accomplices. Each one of a gang so placed, is not so much greedy of reward, or anxious for escape, as *fearful of betrayal*. He betrays eagerly and early that *he may not himself be betrayed*. That the secret has not been divulged, is the very best of proof that it is, in fact, a secret. The horrors of this dark deed are known only to *one*, or two, living human beings, and to God.

"Let us sum up now the meagre yet certain fruits of our long analysis. We have attained the idea either of a fatal accident under the roof of Madame Deluc, or of a murder perpetrated, in the thicket at the Barrière du Roule, by a lover, or at least by an intimate and secret associate of the deceased. This associate is of swarthy complexion. This complexion, the 'hitch' in the bandage, and the 'sailor's knot,' with which the bonnet-ribbon is tied, point to a seaman. His companionship with the deceased, a gay, but not an abject young girl, designates him as above the grade of the common sailor. Here the well written and urgent communications to the journals are much in the way of corroboration. The circumstance of the first elopement, as mentioned by Le Mercure, tends to blend the idea of this seaman with that of the 'naval officer' who is first known to have led the unfortunate into crime.

"And here, most fitly, comes the consideration of the continued absence of him of the dark complexion. Let me pause to observe that the complexion of this man is dark and swarthy; it was no common swarthiness which constituted the *sole* point of remembrance, both as regards Valence and Madame Deluc. But why is this man absent? Was he murdered by the gang? If so, why are there only *traces* of the assassinated *girl*? The scene of the two outrages will naturally be supposed identical. And where is his corpse? The assassins would most probably have disposed of both in the same way. But it may be said that this man lives, and is deterred from making himself known, through dread of being charged with the murder.

This consideration might be supposed to operate upon him now—at this late period—since it has been given in evidence that he was seen with Marie—but it would have had no force at the period of the deed. The first impulse of an innocent man would have been to announce the outrage, and to aid in identifying the ruffians. This, *policy* would have suggested. He had been seen with the girl. He had crossed the river with her in an open ferry-boat. The denouncing of the assassins would have appeared, even to an idiot, the surest and sole means of relieving himself from suspicion. We cannot suppose him, on the night of the fatal Sunday, both innocent himself and incognizant of an outrage committed. Yet only under such circumstances is it possible to imagine that he would have failed, if alive, in the denouncement of the assassins.

"And what means are ours, of attaining the truth? We shall find these means multiplying and gathering distinctness as we proceed. Let us sift to the bottom this affair of the first elopement. Let us know the full history of 'the officer,' with his present circumstances, and his whereabouts at the precise period of the murder. Let us carefully compare with each other the various communications sent to the evening paper, in which the object was to inculpate *a gang*. This done, let us compare these communications, both as regards style and MS., with those sent to the morning paper, at a previous period, and insisting so vehemently upon the guilt of Mennais. And, all this done, let us again compare these various communications with the known MSS. of the officer. Let us endeavor to ascertain, by repeated questionings of Madame Deluc and her boys, as well as of the omnibus-driver, Valence, something more of the personal appearance and bearing of the 'man of dark complexion.' Queries, skilfully directed, will not fail to elicit, from some of these parties, information on this particular point (or upon others)—information which the parties themselves may not even be aware of possessing. And let us now trace *the boat* picked up by the bargeman on the morning of Monday the twenty-third of June, and which was removed from the barge-office, without the cognizance of the officer in attendance, and *without the rudder,* at some period prior to the discovery of the corpse. With a proper caution and perseverance we shall infallibly trace this boat; for not only can the bargeman who picked it up identify it, but the *rudder is at hand.* The rudder *of a sail-boat* would not have been abandoned, without inquiry, by one altogether at ease in heart. And here let me pause to insinuate a question. There was no *advertisement* of the picking up of this boat. It was silently taken to the barge-office, and as silently removed. But its owner or employer—how *happened* he, at so early a period as Tuesday morning, to be informed, without the agency of advertisement, of the locality of the boat taken up on Monday, unless we imagine some connexion with the *navy*—some personal permanent connexion leading to cognizance of its minute interests—its petty local news?

"In speaking of the lonely assassin dragging his burden to the shore, I have already suggested the probability of his availing himself *of a boat.* Now we are to understand that Marie Rogêt *was* precipitated from a boat. This would naturally have been the case. The corpse could not have been trusted to the shallow waters of the shore. The peculiar marks on the back and shoulders of the victim tell of the bottom ribs of a boat. That the body was found without weight is also corroborative of the idea. If thrown from the shore a weight would have been attached. We can only account for its absence by supposing the murderer to have neglected the precaution of supplying himself with it before pushing off. In the act of consigning the corpse to the water, he would unquestionably have noticed his oversight; but then no remedy would have

been at hand. Any risk would have been preferred to a return to that accursed shore. Having rid himself of his ghastly charge, the murderer would have hastened to the city. There, at some obscure wharf, he would have leaped on land. But the boat—would he have secured it? He would have been in too great haste for such things as securing a boat. Moreover, in fastening it to the wharf, he would have felt as if securing evidence against himself. His natural thought would have been to cast from him, as far as possible, all that had held connection with his crime. He would not only have fled from the wharf, but he would not have permitted *the boat* to remain. Assuredly he would have cast it adrift. Let us pursue our fancies.—In the morning, the wretch is stricken with unutterable horror at finding that the boat has been picked up and detained at a locality which he is in the daily habit of frequenting—at a locality, perhaps, which his duty compels him to frequent. The next night, *without daring to ask for the rudder,* he removes it. Now *where* is that rudderless boat? Let it be one of our first purposes to discover. With the first glimpse we obtain of it, the dawn of our success shall begin. This boat shall guide us, with a rapidity which will surprise even ourselves, to him who employed it in the midnight of the fatal Sabbath. Corroboration will rise upon corroboration, and the murderer will be traced."

[For reasons which we shall not specify, but which to many readers will appear obvious, we have taken the liberty of here omitting, from the MSS. placed in our hands, such portion as details the *following up* of the apparently slight clew obtained by Dupin. We feel it advisable only to state, in brief, that the result desired was brought to pass; and that the Prefect fulfilled punctually, although with reluctance, the terms of his compact with the Chevalier. Mr. Poe's article concludes with the following words.—*Eds.*[35]]

It will be understood that I speak of coincidences *and no more.* What I have said above upon this topic must suffice. In my own heart there dwells no faith in præter-nature. That Nature and its God are two, no man who thinks, will deny. That the latter, creating the former, can, at will, control or modify it, is also unquestionable. I say "at will;" for the question is of will, and not, as the insanity of logic has assumed, of power. It is not that the Deity *cannot* modify his laws, but that we insult him in imagining a possible necessity for modification. In their origin these laws were fashioned to embrace *all* contingencies which *could* lie in the Future. With God all is *Now*.

I repeat, then, that I speak of these things only as of coincidences. And farther: in what I relate it will be seen that between the fate of the unhappy Mary Cecilia Rogers, so far as that fate is known, and the fate of one Marie Rogêt up to a certain epoch in her history, there has existed a parallel in the contemplation of whose wonderful exactitude the reason becomes embarrassed. I say all this will be seen. But let it not for a moment be supposed that, in proceeding with the sad narrative of Marie from the epoch just mentioned, and in tracing to its *dénouement* the mystery which enshrouded her, it is my covert design to hint at an extension of the parallel, or even to suggest that the measures adopted in Paris for the discovery of the assassin of a grisette, or measures founded in any similar ratiocination, would produce any similar result.[36]

For, in respect to the latter branch of the supposition, it should be considered that the most trifling variation in the facts of the two cases might give rise to the most important miscalculations, by diverting thoroughly the two courses of events; very much as, in arithmetic, an error which, in its own individuality, may be inappreciable, produces, at length, by dint of multiplication at all points of the process, a result enormously at variance with truth. And, in regard to the former branch, we must not fail to hold in view that the very Calculus of Probabilities to which I have referred, forbids all idea of the extension of the parallel:—forbids it with a positiveness strong and decided just in proportion as this parallel has already been long-drawn and exact. This is one of those anomalous propositions which, seemingly appealing to thought altogether apart from the mathematical, is yet one which only the mathematician can fully entertain. Nothing, for example, is more difficult than to convince the merely general reader that the fact of sixes having been thrown twice in succession by a player at dice, is sufficient cause for betting the largest odds that sixes will not be thrown in the third attempt. A suggestion to this effect is usually rejected by the intellect at once. It does not appear that the two throws which have been completed, and which lie now absolutely in the Past, can have influence upon the throw which exists only in the Future. The chance for throwing sixes seems to be precisely as it was at any ordinary time—that is to say, subject only to the influence of the various other throws which may be made by the dice. And this is a reflection which appears so exceedingly obvious that attempts to controvert it are received more frequently with a derisive smile than with anything like respectful attention. The error here involved —a gross error redolent of mischief—I cannot pretend to expose within the limits assigned me at present; and with the philosophical it needs no exposure. It may be sufficient here to say that it forms one of an infinite series of mistakes which arise in the path of Reason through her propensity for seeking truth *in detail*.[37]

THE PURLOINED LETTER

Nil sapientiæ odiosius acumine nimio.
Seneca[1]

At Paris, just after dark one gusty evening in the autumn of 18—, I was enjoying the twofold luxury of meditation and a meerschaum, in company with my friend

C. Auguste Dupin, in his little back library, or book-closet, *au troisième, No. 33, Rue Dunôt, Faubourg St. Germain.* For one hour at least we had maintained a profound silence; while each, to any casual observer, might have seemed intently and exclusively occupied with the curling eddies of smoke that oppressed the atmosphere of the chamber. For myself, however, I was mentally discussing certain topics which had formed matter for conversation between us at an earlier period of the evening; I mean the affair of the Rue Morgue, and the mystery attending the murder of Marie Rogêt. I looked upon it, therefore, as something of a coincidence,[2] when the door of our apartment was thrown open and admitted our old acquaintance, Monsieur G——, the Prefect of the Parisian police.

We gave him a hearty welcome; for there was nearly half as much of the entertaining as of the contemptible about the man, and we had not seen him for several years. We had been sitting in the dark, and Dupin now arose for the purpose of lighting a lamp, but sat down again, without doing so, upon G.'s saying that he had called to consult us, or rather to ask the opinion of my friend, about some official business which had occasioned a great deal of trouble.

"If it is any point requiring reflection," observed Dupin, as he forbore to enkindle the wick, "we shall examine it to better purpose in the dark."

"That is another of your odd notions," said the Prefect, who had a fashion of calling every thing "odd" that was beyond his comprehension, and thus lived amid an absolute legion of "oddities."

"Very true," said Dupin, as he supplied his visiter with a pipe, and rolled towards him a comfortable chair.

"And what is the difficulty now?" I asked. "Nothing more in the assassination way, I hope?"

"Oh no; nothing of that nature. The fact is, the business is *very* simple indeed, and I make no doubt that we can manage it sufficiently well ourselves; but then I thought Dupin would like to hear the details of it, because it is so excessively *odd.*"

"Simple and odd," said Dupin.

"Why, yes; and not exactly that either. The fact is, we have all been a good deal puzzled because the affair *is* so simple, and yet baffles us altogether."

"Perhaps it is the very simplicity of the thing which puts you at fault," said my friend.[3]

"What nonsense you *do* talk!" replied the Prefect, laughing heartily.

"Perhaps the mystery is a little *too* plain," said Dupin.

"Oh, good heavens! who ever heard of such an idea?"

"A little *too* self-evident."

"Ha! ha! ha!—ha! ha! ha!—ho! ho! ho!" —roared our visiter, profoundly amused, "oh, Dupin, you will be the death of me yet!"

"And what, after all, *is* the matter on hand?" I asked.

"Why, I will tell you," replied the Prefect, as he gave a long, steady, and contemplative puff, and settled himself in his chair. "I will tell you in a few words; but, before I begin, let me caution you that this is an affair demanding the greatest secrecy, and that I should most probably lose the position I now hold, were it known that I confided it to any one."

"Proceed," said I.

"Or not," said Dupin.

"Well, then; I have received personal information, from a very high quarter, that a certain document of the last importance has been purloined from the royal apartments. The individual who purloined it is known; this beyond a doubt; he was seen to take it. It is known, also, that it stills remains in his possession."

"How is this known?" asked Dupin.

"It is clearly inferred," replied the Prefect, "from the nature of the document, and from the non-appearance of certain results which would at once arise from its passing *out* of the robber's possession;—

that is to say, from his employing it as he must design in the end to employ it."

"Be a little more explicit," I said.

"Well, I may venture so far as to say that the paper gives its holder a certain power in a certain quarter where such power is immensely valuable." The Prefect was fond of the cant of diplomacy.

"Still I do not quite understand," said Dupin.

"No? Well; the disclosure of the document to a third person, who shall be nameless, would bring in question the honour of a personage of most exalted station; and this fact gives the holder of the document an ascendancy over the illustrious personage whose honor and peace are so jeopardized."

"But this ascendancy," I interposed, "would depend upon the robber's knowledge of the loser's knowledge of the robber. Who would dare—"

"The thief," said G., "is the Minister D——, who dares all things, those unbecoming as well as those becoming a man. The method of the theft was not less ingenious than bold. The document in question—a letter, to be frank—had been received by the personage robbed while alone in the royal *boudoir*. During its perusal she was suddenly interrupted by the entrance of the other exalted personage from whom especially it was her wish to conceal it. After a hurried and vain endeavour to thrust it in a drawer, she was forced to place it, open it was, upon a table. The address, however, was uppermost, and, the contents thus unexposed, the letter escaped notice. At this juncture enters the Minister D——. His lynx eye immediately perceives the paper, recognizes the handwriting of the address, observes the confusion of the personage addressed, and fathoms her secret. After some business transactions, hurried through in his ordinary manner, he produces a letter somewhat similar to the one in question, opens it, pretends to read it, and then places it in close juxtaposition to the other. Again he converses, for some

fifteen minutes, upon the public affairs. At length, in taking leave, he takes also from the table the letter to which he had no claim. Its rightful owner saw, but, of course, dared not call attention to the act, in the presence of the third personage who stood at her elbow. The minister decamped; leaving his own letter—one of no importance—upon the table."

"Here, then," said Dupin to me, "you have precisely what you demand to make the ascendancy complete—the robber's knowledge of the loser's knowledge of the robber."

"Yes," replied the Prefect; "and the power thus attained has, for some months past, been wielded, for political purposes, to a very dangerous extent. The personage robbed is more thoroughly convinced, every day, of the necessity of reclaiming her letter. But this, of course, cannot be done openly. In fine, driven to despair, she has committed the matter to me."

"Than whom," said Dupin, amid a perfect whirlwind of smoke, "no more sagacious agent could, I suppose, be desired, or even imagined."

"You flatter me," replied the Prefect; "but it is possible that some such opinion may have been entertained."

"It is clear," said I, "as you observe, that the letter is still in the possession of the minister; since it is this possession, and not any employment of the letter, which bestows the power. With the employment the power departs."

"True," said G.; "and upon this conviction I proceeded. My first care was to make thorough search of the minister's hotel; and here my chief embarrassment lay in the necessity of searching without his knowledge. Beyond all things, I have been warned of the danger which would result from giving him reason to suspect our design."

"But," said I, "you are quite *au fait*[4] in these investigations. The Parisian police have done this thing often before."

"O yes; and for this reason I did not despair. The habits of the minister gave me, too, a great advantage. He is frequently absent from home all night. His servants are by no means numerous. They sleep at a distance from their master's apartment, and being chiefly Neapolitans, are readily made drunk. I have keys, as you know, with which I can open any chamber or cabinet in Paris. For three months a night has not passed, during the greater part of which I have not been engaged, personally, in ransacking the D—— Hôtel. My honor is interested, and, to mention a great secret, the reward is enormous. So I did not abandon the search until I had become fully satisfied that the thief is a more astute man than myself. I fancy that I have investigated every nook and corner of the premises in which it is possible that the paper can be concealed."

"But is it not possible," I suggested, "that although the letter may be in the possession of the minister, as it unquestionably is, he may have concealed it elsewhere than upon his own premises?"

"This is barely possible," said Dupin. "The present peculiar condition of affairs at court, and especially of those intrigues in which D—— is known to be involved, would render the instant availability of the document—its susceptibility of being produced at a moment's notice—a point of nearly equal importance with its possession."

"Its susceptibility of being produced?" said I.

"That is to say, of being *destroyed*," said Dupin.

"True," I observed; "the paper is clearly then upon the premises. As for its being upon the person of the minister, we may consider that as out of the question."

"Entirely," said the Prefect. "He had been twice waylaid, as if by foot-pads, and his person rigorously searched under my own inspection."

"You might have spared yourself this trouble," said Dupin. "D——, I presume, is not altogether a fool, and, if not, must have anticipated these waylayings, as a matter of course."

"Not *altogether* a fool," said G., "but then he is a poet, which I take to be only one remove from a fool."

"True," said Dupin, after a long and thoughtful whiff from his meerschaum, "although I have been guilty of certain doggerel myself."

"Suppose you detail," said I, "the particulars of your search."

"Why the fact is, we took our time, and we searched *every where*. I have had long experience in these affairs. I took the entire building, room by room; devoting the nights of a whole week to each. We examined, first, the furniture of each apartment. We opened every possible drawer; and I presume you know that, to a properly trained police agent, such a thing as a *secret* drawer is impossible. Any man is a dolt who permits a 'secret' drawer to escape him in a search of this kind. The thing is *so* plain. There is a certain amount of bulk—of space—to be accounted for in every cabinet. Then we have accurate rules. The fiftieth part of a line could not escape us. After the cabinets we took the chairs. The cushions we probed with the fine long needles you have seen me employ. From the tables we removed the tops."

"Why so?"

"Sometimes the top of a table, or other similarly arranged piece of furniture, is removed by the person wishing to conceal an article; then the leg is excavated, the article deposited within the cavity, and the top replaced. The bottoms and tops of bedposts are employed in the same way."

"But could not the cavity be detected by sounding?" I asked.

"By no means, if, when the article is deposited, a sufficient wadding of cotton be placed around it. Besides, in our case, we were obliged to proceed without noise."

"But you could not have removed—you could not have taken to pieces *all* articles of furniture in which it would have been possible to make a deposit in the manner you mention. A letter may be compressed into a thin spiral roll, not differing much in shape or bulk from a large knitting-needle, and in this form it might be inserted into the rung of a chair, for example. You did not take to pieces all the chairs?"

"Certainly not; but we did better—we examined the rungs of every chair in the hotel, and indeed the jointings of every description of furniture, by the aid of a most powerful microscope. Had there been any traces of recent disturbance we should not have failed to detect it instantly. A single grain of gimlet-dust, for example, would have been as obvious as an apple. Any disorder in the glueing—any unusual gaping in the joints—would have sufficed to insure detection."

"I presume you looked to the mirrors, between the boards and the plates, and you probed the beds and the bed-clothes, as well as the curtains and carpets."

"That of course; and when we had absolutely completed every particle of the furniture in this way, then we examined the house itself. We divided its entire surface into compartments, which we numbered, so that none might be missed; then we scrutinized each individual square inch throughout the premises, including the two houses immediately adjoining, with the microscope as before."

"The two houses adjoining!" I exclaimed; "you must have had a great deal of trouble."

"We had; but the reward offered is prodigious."

"You include the grounds about the houses?"

"All the grounds are paved with brick. They gave us comparatively little trouble. We examined the moss between the bricks, and found it undisturbed."

"You looked among D——'s papers, of course, and into the books of the library?"

"Certainly; we opened every package and parcel; we not only opened every book, but we turned over every leaf in each volume, not contenting ourselves with a mere shake, according to the fash-

ion of some of our police officers. We also measured the thickness of every book-cover, with the most accurate admeasurement, and applied to each the most jealous scrutiny of the microscope. Had any of the bindings been recently meddled with, it would have been utterly impossible that the fact should have escaped observation. Some five or six volumes, just from the hands of the binder, we carefully probed, longitudinally, with the needles."

"You explored the floors beneath the carpets?"

"Beyond doubt. We removed every carpet, and examined the boards with the microscope."

"And the paper on the walls?"

"Yes."

"You looked into the cellars?"

"We did."

"Then," I said, "you have been making a miscalculation, and the letter is not upon the premises as you suppose."

"I fear you are right there," said the Prefect. "And now, Dupin, what would you advise me to do?"

"To make a thorough re-search of the premises."

"That is absolutely needless," replied G——. "I am not more sure that I breathe than I am that the letter is not at the Hôtel."

"I have no better advice to give you," said Dupin. "You have, of course, an accurate description of the letter?"

"Oh, yes!"—And here the Prefect, producing a memorandum-book, proceeded to read aloud a minute account of the internal, and especially of the external, appearance of the missing document. Soon after finishing the perusal of this description, he took his departure, more entirely depressed in spirits than I had ever known the good gentleman before.

In about a month afterward he paid us another visit, and found us occupied very nearly as before. He took a pipe and a chair and entered into some ordinary conversation. At length I said;—

"Well, but G——, what of the purloined letter? I presume you have at last made up your mind that there is no such thing as overreaching the Minister?"

"Confound him, say I—yes; I made the re-examination, however, as Dupin suggested—but it was all labour lost, as I knew it would be."

"How much was the reward offered, did you say?" asked Dupin.

"Why, a very great deal—a *very* liberal reward—I don't like to say how much, precisely; but one thing I *will* say, that I wouldn't mind giving my individual check for fifty thousand francs to any one who could obtain me that letter. The fact is, it is becoming of more and more importance every day; and the reward has been lately doubled. If it were trebled, however, I could do no more than I have done."

"Why, yes," said Dupin, drawlingly, between the whiffs of his meerschaum, "I really—think, G——, you have not exerted yourself—to the utmost in this matter. You might—do a little more, I think, eh?"

"How?—in what way?"

"Why—puff, puff,—you might—puff, puff—employ counsel in the matter, eh? —puff, puff, puff. Do you remember the story they tell of Abernethy?"

"No; hang Abernethy!"

"To be sure! hang him and welcome. But, once upon a time, a certain rich miser conceived the design of spunging upon this Abernethy for a medical opinion. Getting up, for this purpose, an ordinary conversation in a private company, he insinuated his case to the physician, as that of an imaginary individual.

" 'We will suppose,' said the miser, 'that his symptons are such and such; now, doctor, what would *you* have directed him to take?'

" 'Take!' said Abernethy, 'why, take *advice*, to be sure.' "

"But," said the Prefect, a little discomposed, "I am *perfectly* willing to take advice, and to pay for it. I would *really* give fifty thousand francs to any one who would aid me in the matter."

"In that case," replied Dupin, opening a drawer, and producing a check-book, "you may as well fill me up a check for the amount you mentioned. When you have signed it, I will hand you the letter."

I was astounded. The Prefect appeared absolutely thunder-stricken. For some minutes he remained speechless and motionless, looking incredulously at my friend with open mouth, and eyes that seemed starting from their sockets; then, apparently recovering himself in some measure, he seized a pen, and after several pauses and vacant stares, finally filled up and signed a check for fifty thousand francs, and handed it across the table to Dupin. The latter examined it carefully and deposited it in his pocket-book; then, unlocking an *escritoire*,[5] took thence a letter and gave it to the Prefect. This functionary grasped it in a perfect agony of joy, opened it with a trembling hand, cast a rapid glance at its contents, and then, scrambling and struggling to the door, rushed at length unceremoniously from the room and from the house, without having uttered a syllable since Dupin had requested him to fill up the check.

When he had gone, my friend entered into some explanations.

"The Parisian police," he said, "are exceedingly able in their way. They are persevering, ingenious, cunning, and thoroughly versed in the knowledge which their duties seem chiefly to demand. Thus, when G—— detailed to us his mode of searching the premises at the Hôtel D——, I felt entire confidence in his having made a satisfactory investigation—so far as his labours extended."

"So far as his labours extended?" said I.

"Yes," said Dupin. "The measures adopted were not only the best of their kind, but carried out to absolute perfection. Had the letter been deposited within the range of their search, these fellows would, beyond a question, have found it."

I merely laughed—but he seemed quite serious in all that he said.

"The measures, then," he continued, "were good in their kind, and well executed; their defect lay in their being inapplicable to the case, and to the man. A certain set of highly ingenious resources are, with the Prefect, a sort of Procrustean bed,[6] to which he forcibly adapts his designs. But he perpetually errs by being too deep or too shallow, for the matter in hand; and many a schoolboy is a better reasoner than he. I knew one about eight years of age, whose success at guessing in the game of 'even and odd' attracted universal admiration. This game is simple, and is played with marbles. One player holds in his hand a number of these toys, and demands of another whether that number is even or odd. If the guess is right, the guesser wins one; if wrong, he loses one. The boy to whom I allude won all the marbles of the school. Of course he had some principle of guessing; and this lay in mere observation and admeasurement of the astuteness of his opponents. For example, an arrant simpleton is his opponent, and, holding up his closed hand, asks: 'Are they even or odd?' Our schoolboy replies, 'Odd,' and loses; but upon the second trial he wins, for he then says to himself, 'The simpleton had them even upon the first trial, and his amount of cunning is just sufficient to make him have them odd upon the second; I will therefore guess odd;'—he guesses odd, and wins. Now, with a simpleton a degree above the first, he would have reasoned thus: 'This fellow finds that in the first instance I guessed odd, and, in the second, he will propose to himself upon the first impulse, a simple variation from even to odd, as did the first simpleton; but then a second thought will suggest that this is too simple a variation, and finally he will decide upon putting it even as before. I will therefore guess even;'—he guesses even, and wins. Now this mode of reasoning in the schoolboy, whom his fellows termed 'lucky,'—what, in its last analysis, is it?"

"It is merely," I said, "an identification of the reasoner's intellect with that of his opponent."

"It is," said Dupin; "and, upon inquiring of the boy by what means he effected the *thorough* identification in which his success consisted, I received answer as follows: 'When I wish to find out how wise, or how stupid, or how good, or how wicked is any one, or what are his thoughts at the moment, I fashion the expression on my face, as accurately as possible, in accordance with the expression of his, and then wait to see what thoughts or sentiments arise in my mind or heart, as if to match or correspond with the expression.' This response of the schoolboy lies at the bottom of all the spurious profundity which has been attributed to Rochefoucault, to La Bougive, to Machiavelli, and to Campanella."[7]

"And the identification," I said, "of the reasoner's intellect with that of his opponent, depends, if I understand you aright, upon the accuracy with which the opponent's intellect is admeasured."

"For its practical value it depends upon this," replied Dupin; "and the Prefect and his cohort fail so frequently, first, by default of this identification, and secondly, by ill-admeasurement, or rather through non-admeasurement, of the intellect with which they are engaged. They consider only their *own* ideas of ingenuity; and, in searching for anything hidden, advert only to the modes in which *they* would have hidden it. They are right in this much—that their own ingenuity is a faithful representative of that of *the mass*; but when the cunning of the individual felon is diverse in character from their own, the felon foils them, of course. This always happens when it is above their own, and very usually when it is below. They have no variation of principle in their investigations; at best, when urged by some unusual emergency—by some extraordinary reward—they extend or exaggerate their old modes of *practice*, without touching their principles. What, for example, in this case of D——, has been done to vary the principle of action? What is all this boring, and probing, and sounding, and scrutinizing with the microscope, and dividing the surface of the building into registered square inches—what is it all but an exaggeration *of the application* of one principle or set of principles of search, which are based upon the one set of notions regarding human ingenuity, to which the Prefect, in the long routine of his duty, has been accustomed? Do you not see he has taken it for granted that *all* men proceed to conceal a letter,—not exactly in a gimlet-hole bored in a chair-leg —but, at least, in *some* out-of-the-way hole or corner suggested by the same tenor of thought which would urge a man to secrete a letter in a gimlet-hole bored in a chair-leg? And do you not see also, that such *recherchés*[8] nooks for concealment are adapted only for ordinary occasions, and would be adopted only by ordinary intellects; for, in all cases of concealment, a disposal of the article concealed—a disposal of it in this *recherché* manner—is, in the very first instance, presumable and presumed; and thus its discovery depends, not at all upon the acumen, but altogether upon the mere care, patience, and determination of the seekers; and where the case is of importance—or, what amounts to the same thing in the policial eyes, when the reward is of magnitude,—the qualities in question have *never* been known to fail. You will now understand what I meant in suggesting that, had the purloined letter been hidden anywhere within the limits of the Prefect's examination—in other words, had the principle of its concealment been comprehended within the principles of the Prefect—its discovery would have been a matter altogether beyond question. This functionary, however, has been thoroughly mystified; and the remote source of his defeat lies in the supposition that the Minister is a fool, because he has acquired renown as a poet. All fools are poets; this the Prefect *feels*; and he is merely guilty of a *non*

distributio medii[9] in thence inferring that all poets are fools.

"But is this really the poet?" I asked. "There are two brothers, I know; and both have attained reputation in letters. The Minister I believe has written learnedly on the Differential Calculus. He is a mathematician, and no poet."

"You are mistaken; I know him well: he is both. As poet *and* mathematician, he would reason well; as mere mathematician, he could not have reasoned at all, and thus would have been at the mercy of the Prefect."

"You surprise me," I said, "by these opinions, which have been contradicted by the voice of the world. You do not mean to set at naught the well-digested idea of centuries. The mathematical reason has long been regarded as *the* reason *par excellence*."

" 'Il y a à parier,' " replied Dupin, quoting from Chamfort, " 'que toute idée publique, toute convention reçue, est une sottise, car elle a convenu au plus grand nombre.'[10] The mathematicians, I grant you, have done their best to promulgate the popular error to which you allude, and which is none the less an error for its promulgation as truth. With an art worthy a better cause, for example, they have insinuated the term 'analysis' into application to algebra. The French are the originators of this particular deception; but if a term is of any importance—if words derive any value from applicability—then 'analysis' conveys 'algebra' about as much as, in Latin, 'ambitus' implies 'ambition,' 'religio' 'religion,' or 'homines honesti,' a set of *honourable* men."[11]

"You have a quarrel on hand, I see," said I, "with some of the algebraists of Paris; but proceed."

"I dispute the availability, and thus the value, of that reason which is cultivated in any especial form other than the abstractly logical. I dispute, in particular, the reason educed by mathematical study. The mathematics are the science of form and quantity; mathematical reasoning is merely logic applied to observation upon form and quantity. The great error lies in supposing that even the truths of what is called *pure* algebra, are abstract or general truths. And this error is so egregious that I am confounded at the universality with which it has been received. Mathematical axioms are *not* axioms of general truth. What is true of *relation*—of form and quantity—is often grossly false in regard to morals, for example. In this latter science it is very usually *untrue* that the aggregated parts are equal to the whole. In chemistry also the axiom fails. In the consideration of motive it fails; for two motives, each of a given value, have not, necessarily, a value when united, equal to the sum of their values apart. There are numerous other mathematical truths which are only truths within the limits of *relation*. But the mathematician argues from his *finite truths*, through habit, as if they were of an absolutely general applicability—as the world indeed imagines them to be. Bryant, in his very learned 'Mythology,' mentions an analogous source of error, when he says that 'although the Pagan fables are not believed, yet we forget ourselves continually, and make inferences from them as existing realities.' With the algebraists, however, who are Pagans themselves, the 'Pagan fables' *are* believed, and the inferences are made, not so much through lapse of memory as through an unaccountable addling of the brains. In short, I never yet encountered the mere mathematician who would be trusted out of equal roots, or one who did not clandestinely hold it as a point of his faith that $x^2 + px$ was absolutely and unconditionally equal to q.[12] Say to one of these gentlemen, by way of experiment, if you please, that you believe occasions may occur where $x^2 + px$ is *not* altogether equal to q, and having made him understand what you mean, get out of his reach as speedily as convenient, for, beyond doubt, he will endeavour to knock you down.

"I mean to say," continued Dupin, while I merely laughed at his last observations, "that if the Minister had been no more than a mathematician, the Prefect would have been under no necessity of giving me this check. I knew him, however, as both mathematician and poet, and my measures were adapted to his capacity, with reference to the circumstances by which he was surrounded. I knew him as a courtier, too, and as a bold *intriguant*.[13] Such a man, I considered, could not fail to be aware of the ordinary policial modes of action. He could not have failed to anticipate—and events have proved that he did not fail to anticipate—the waylayings to which he was subjected. He must have foreseen, I reflected, the secret investigations of his premises. His frequent absences from home at night, which were hailed by the Prefect as certain aids to his success, I regarded only as *ruses*, to afford opportunity for thorough search to the police, and thus the sooner to impress them with the conviction to which G——, in fact, did finally arrive—the conviction that the letter was not upon the premises. I felt, also, that the whole train of thought, which I was at some pains in detailing to you just now, concerning the invariable principle of policial action in searches for articles concealed—I felt that this whole train of thought would necessarily pass through the mind of the Minister. It would imperatively lead him to despise all the ordinary *nooks* of concealment. *He* could not, I reflected, be so weak as not to see that the most intricate and remote recess of his hotel would be as open as his commonest closets to the eyes, to the probes, to the gimlets, and to the microscopes of the Prefect. I saw, in fine, that he would be driven, as a matter of course, to simplicity, if not deliberately induced to it as a matter of choice. You will remember, perhaps, how desperately the Prefect laughed when I suggested, upon our first interview, that it was just possible this mystery troubled him so much on account of its being so *very* self-evident."

"Yes," said I, "I remember his merriment well. I really thought he would have fallen into convulsions."

"The material world," continued Dupin, "abounds with very strict analogies to the immaterial; and thus some color of truth has been given to the rhetorical dogma, that metaphor, or simile, may be made to strengthen an argument as well as to embellish a description. The principle of the *vis inertiæ*,[14] for example, seems to be identical in physics and metaphysics. It is not more true in the former, that a large body is with more difficulty set in motion than a smaller one, and that its subsequent *momentum* is commensurate with this difficulty, than it is, in the latter, that intellects of the vaster capacity, while more forcible, more constant, and more eventful in their movements than those of inferior grade, are yet the less readily moved, and more embarrassed and full of hesitation in the first few steps of their progress. Again: have you ever noticed which of the street signs, over the shop doors, are the most attractive of attention?"

"I have never given the matter a thought," I said.

"There is a game of puzzles," he resumed, "which is played upon a map. One party playing requires another to find a given word—the name of town, river, state, or empire—any word, in short, upon the motley and perplexed surface of the chart. A novice in the game generally seeks to embarrass his opponents by giving them the most minutely lettered names; but the adept selects such words as stretch, in large characters, from one end of the chart to the other. These, like the over-largely lettered signs and placards of the street, escape observation by the dint of being excessively obvious; and here the physical oversight is precisely analogous with the moral inapprehension by which the intellect suffers to pass unnoticed those considerations which are too obtrusively and too palpably self-evident. But this is a point, it appears, somewhat above or beneath the understanding of the Prefect. He never once thought it probable, or possible, that the Minister had deposited the letter immediately beneath the nose of the whole world, by way of best preventing any portion of that world from perceiving it.

"But the more I reflected upon the daring, dashing, and discriminating ingenuity of D——; upon the fact that the document must always have been *at hand*, if he intended to use it to good purpose; and upon the decisive evidence, obtained by the Prefect, that it was not hidden within the limits of that dignitary's ordinary search—the more satisfied I became that, to conceal this letter, the Minister had resorted to the comprehensive and sagacious expedient of not attempting to conceal it at all.

"Full of these ideas, I prepared myself with a pair of green spectacles, and called one fine morning, quite by accident, at the Ministerial hotel. I found D—— at home, yawning, lounging, and dawdling, as usual, and pretending to be in the last extremity of *ennui*. He is, perhaps, the most really energetic human being now alive—but that is only when nobody sees him.

"To be even with him, I complained of my weak eyes, and lamented the necessity of the spectacles, under cover of which I cautiously and thoroughly surveyed the whole apartment, while seemingly intent only upon the conversation of my host.

"I paid especial attention to a large writing-table near which he sat, and upon which lay confusedly, some miscellaneous letters and other papers, with one or two musical instruments and a few books. Here, however, after a long and very deliberate scrutiny, I saw nothing to excite particular suspicion.

"At length my eyes, in going the circuit of the room, fell upon a trumpery filigree card-rack of pasteboard, that hung dangling by a dirty blue ribbon, from a little brass knob just beneath the middle of the mantel-piece. In this rack, which had three or four compartments, were five or six visiting cards and a solitary letter. This last was much soiled and crumpled. It was torn nearly in two, across the middle—as if a design, in the first instance, to tear it entirely up as worthless, had been altered, or stayed, in the second. It had a large black seal, bearing the D—— cipher *very* conspicuously, and was addressed, in a diminutive female hand, to D——, the minister, himself. It was thrust carelessly, and even, as it seemed, contemptuously, into one of the upper divisions of the rack.

"No sooner had I glanced at this letter than I concluded it to be that of which I was in search. To be sure, it was, to all appearance, radically different from one of which the Prefect had read us so minute a description. Here the seal was large and black, with the D—— cipher; there it was small and red, with the ducal arms of the S—— family. Here, the address, to the Minister, was diminutive and feminine; there the superscription, to a certain royal personage, was markedly bold and decided; the size alone formed a point of correspondence. But, then, the *radicalness* of these differences, which was excessive; the dirt; the soiled and torn condition of the paper, so inconsistent with the *true* methodical habits of D——, and so suggestive of a design to delude the beholder into an idea of the worthlessness of the document; these things, together with the hyperobtrusive situation of this document, full in the view of every visiter, and thus exactly in accordance with the conclusions to which I had previously arrived; these things, I say, were strongly corroborative of suspicion, in one who came with the intention to suspect.

"I protracted my visit as long as possible, and, while I maintained a most animated discussion with the Minister, upon a topic which I knew well had never failed to interest and excite him, I kept my attention really riveted upon the letter. In this examination, I committed to memory its external appearance and ar-

rangement in the rack; and also fell, at length, upon a discovery which set at rest whatever trivial doubt I might have entertained. In scrutinizing the edges of the paper, I observed them to be more *chafed* than seemed necessary. They presented the *broken* appearance which is manifested when a stiff paper, having been once folded and pressed with a folder, is refolded in a reversed direction, in the same creases or edges which had formed the original fold. This discovery was sufficient. It was clear to me that the letter had been turned, as a glove, inside out, re-directed, and re-sealed. I bade the Minister good morning, and took my departure at once, leaving a gold snuff-box upon the table.

"The next morning I called for the snuff-box, when we resumed, quite eagerly, the conversation of the preceding day. While thus engaged, however, a loud report, as if of a pistol, was heard immediately beneath the windows of the hotel, and was succeeded by a series of fearful screams, and the shoutings of a mob. D—— rushed to a casement, threw it open, and looked out. In the meantime I stepped to the card-rack, took the letter, put it in my pocket, and replaced it by a *fac-simile,* (so far as regards externals) which I had carefully prepared at my lodgings; imitating the D—— cipher, very readily, by means of a seal formed of bread.

"The disturbance in the street had been occasioned by the frantic behaviour of a man with a musket. He had fired it among a crowd of women and children. It proved, however, to have been without ball, and the fellow was suffered to go his way as a lunatic or a drunkard. When he had gone, D—— came from the window, whither I had followed him immediately upon securing the object in view. Soon afterward I bade him farewell. The pretended lunatic was a man in my own pay."

"But what purpose had you," I asked, "in replacing the letter by a *fac-simile?* Would it not have been better, at the first visit, to have seized it openly, and departed?"

"D——," replied Dupin, "is a desperate man, and a man of nerve. His hotel, too, is not without attendants devoted to his interests. Had I made the wild attempt you suggest, I might never have left the Ministerial presence alive. The good people of Paris might have heard of me no more. But I had an object apart from these considerations. You know my political prepossessions. In this matter, I act as a partisan of the lady concerned. For eighteen months the Minister has had her in his power. She has now him in hers; since, being unaware that the letter is not in his possession, he will proceed with his exactions as if it was. Thus will he inevitably commit himself, at once, to his political destruction. His downfall, too, will not be more precipitate than awkward. It is all very well to talk about the *facilis descensus Averni*; but in all kinds of climbing, as Catalani said of singing, it is far more easy to get up than to come down. In the present instance I have no sympathy—at least no pity—for him who descends. He is that *monstrum horrendum*,[15] an unprincipled man of genius. I confess, however, that I should like very well to know the precise character of his thoughts, when, being defied by her whom the Prefect terms 'a certain personage,' he is reduced to opening the letter which I left for him in the card-rack."

"How? did you put any thing particular in it?"

"Why—it did not seem altogether right to leave the interior blank—that would have been insulting. D——, at Vienna once, did me an evil turn, which I told him, quite good-humoredly, that I should remember. So, as I knew he would feel some curiosity in regard to the identity of the person who had outwitted him, I thought it a pity not to give him a clue. He is well acquainted with my MS., and I just copied into the middle of the blank sheet the words—

——Un dessein si funeste,
S'il n'est digne d'Atrée, est digne
de Thyeste.

They are to be found in Crébillon's 'Atrée.' "[16]

THE OBLONG BOX[1]

Some years ago, I engaged passage from Charleston, S.C., to the city of New York, in the fine packet-ship "Independence,"[2] Captain Hardy. We were to sail on the fifteenth of the month (June,) weather permitting; and, on the fourteenth, I went on board to arrange some matters in my state-room.

I found that we were to have a great many passengers, including a more than usual number of ladies. On the list were several of my acquaintances; and, among other names, I was rejoiced to see that of Mr. Cornelius Wyatt,[3] a young artist, for whom I entertained feelings of warm friendship. He had been with me a fellow student at C—— University, where we were very much together. He had the ordinary temperament of genius, and was a compound of misanthropy, sensibility, and enthusiasm. To these qualities he united the warmest and truest heart which ever beat in a human bosom.

I observed that his name was carded upon *three* state-rooms; and, upon again referring to the list of passengers, I found that he had engaged passage for himself, wife, and two sisters—his own. The state-rooms were sufficiently roomy, and each had two berths, one above the other. These berths, to be sure, were so exceedingly narrow as to be insufficient for more than one person; still, I could not comprehend why there were *three* state-rooms for these four persons. I was, just at that epoch, in one of those moody frames of mind which make a man abnormally inquisitive about trifles: and I confess, with shame, that I busied myself in a variety of ill-bred and preposterous conjectures about this matter

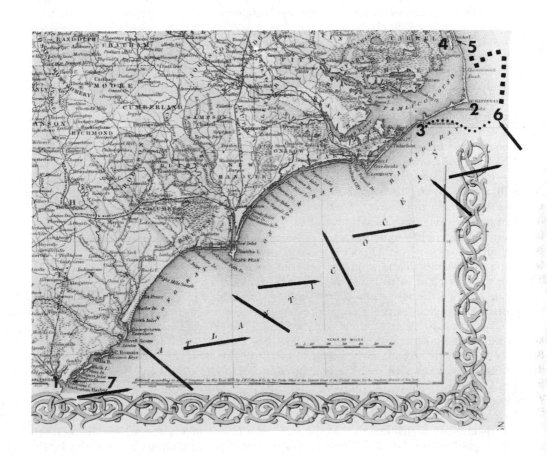

KEY

◀━━━ Route of the "Independence," tacking against strong winds.

● ● ● ● Route of the long-boat.

■ ■ ■ ■ Route of the jolly-boat.

"The Oblong Box"

1. Charleston.
2. Cape Hatteras.
3. Ocracoke Inlet.
4. Roanoke Island.

5. The beach opposite Roanoke Island.
6. Sinking of the "Independence."
"The Gold-Bug"
7. Sullivan's Island.

Figure Ten. The Last Voyage of the "Independence." Map from *Colton's Atlas of the World* (New York, 1857).

of the supernumerary state-room. It was no business of mine, to be sure; but with none the less pertinacity did I occupy myself in attempts to resolve the enigma. At last I reached a conclusion which wrought in me great wonder why I had not arrived at it before. "It is a servant, of course," I said; "what a fool I am, not sooner to have thought of so obvious a solution!" And then I again repaired to the list—but here I saw distinctly that *no* servant was to come with the party; although, in fact, it had been the original design to bring one —for the words "and servant" had been first written and then overscored. "Oh, extra baggage to be sure," I now said to myself—"something he wishes not to be put in the hold—something to be kept under his own eye—ah, I have it—a painting or so—and this is what he has been bargaining about with Nicolino, the Italian Jew."[4] This idea satisfied me, and I dismissed my curiosity for the nonce.

Wyatt's two sisters I knew very well, and most amiable and clever girls they were. His wife he had newly married, and I had never yet seen her. He had often talked about her in my presence, however, and in his usual style of enthusiasm. He described her as of surpassing beauty, wit, and accomplishment. I was, therefore, quite anxious to make her acquaintance.

On the day in which I visited the ship, (the fourteenth), Wyatt and party were also to visit it—so the captain informed me—and I waited on board an hour longer than I had designed, in hope of being presented to the bride; but then an apology came. "Mrs. W. was a little indisposed, and would decline coming on board until to-morrow, at the hour of sailing."

The morrow having arrived, I was going from my hotel to the wharf, when Captain Hardy met me and said that, "owing to circumstances" (a stupid but convenient phrase,) "he rather thought the 'Independence' would not sail for a day or two, and that when all was ready, he would send up and let me know." This I

thought strange, for there was a stiff southerly breeze; but as "the circumstances" were not forthcoming, although I pumped for them with much perseverance, I had nothing to do but to return home and digest my impatience at leisure.[5]

I did not receive the expected message from the captain for nearly a week. It came at length, however, and I immediately went on board. The ship was crowded with passengers, and everything was in the bustle attendant upon making sail. Wyatt's party arrived in about ten minutes after myself. There were the two sisters, the bride, and the artist—the latter in one of his customary fits of moody misanthropy. I was too well used to these however, to pay them any special attention. He did not even introduce me to his wife;—this courtesy devolving, per force, upon his sister Marian, a very sweet and intelligent girl, who, in a few hurried words, made us acquainted.

Mrs. Wyatt had been closely veiled; and when she raised her veil, in acknowledging my bow, I confess that I was very profoundly astonished. I should have been much more so, however, had not long experience advised me not to trust, with too implicit a reliance, the enthusiastic descriptions of my friend, the artist, when indulging in comments upon the loveliness of woman. When beauty was the theme, I well knew with what facility he soared into the regions of the purely ideal.

The truth is, I could not help regarding Mrs. Wyatt as a decidedly plain-looking woman. If not positively ugly, she was not, I think, very far from it. She was dressed, however, in exquisite taste—and then I had no doubt that she had captivated my friend's heart by the more enduring graces of the intellect and soul. She said very few words, and passed at once into her state-room with Mr. W.

My old inquisitiveness now returned. There was *no* servant—*that* was a settled point. I looked, therefore, for the extra baggage. After some delay, a cart arrived at the wharf, with an oblong pine box, which was everything that seemed to be expected. Immediately upon its arrival we made sail, and in a short time were safely over the bar and standing out to sea.

The box in question was, as I say, oblong. It was about six feet in length by two and a half in breadth;—I observed it attentively, and like to be precise. Now this shape was *peculiar*; and no sooner had I seen it, than I took credit to myself for the accuracy of my guessing. I had reached the conclusion, it will be remembered, that the extra baggage of my friend, the artist, would prove to be pictures, or at least a picture; for I knew he had been for several weeks in conference with Nicolino:—and now here was a box which, from its shape, *could* possibly contain nothing in the world but a copy of Leonardo's "Last Supper;" and a copy of this very "Last Supper," done by Rubini the younger, at Florence, I had known, for some time, to be in the possession of Nicolino. This point, therefore, I considered as sufficiently settled. I chuckled excessively when I thought of my acumen. It was the first time I had ever known Wyatt to keep from me any of his artistical secrets; but here he evidently intended to steal a march upon me, and smuggle a fine picture to New York, under my very nose; expecting me to know nothing of the matter. I resolved to quizz[6] him *well*, now and hereafter.

One thing, however, annoyed me not a little. The box did *not* go into the extra state-room. It was deposited in Wyatt's own; and there, too, it remained, occupying very nearly the whole of the floor—no doubt to the exceeding discomfort of the artist and his wife;—this the more especially as the tar or paint with which it was lettered in sprawling capitals, emitted a strong, disagreeable, and, to *my* fancy, a peculiarly disgusting odor. On the lid were painted the words—*"Mrs. Adelaide Curtis, Albany, New York. Charge of Cornelius Wyatt, Esq. This side up. To be handled with care."*

Now, I was aware that Mrs. Adelaide Curtis, of Albany, was the artist's wife's mother;—but then I looked upon the whole address as a mystification, intended especially for myself. I made up my mind, of course, that the box and contents would never get farther north than the studio of my misanthropic friend, in Chambers Street,[7] New York.

For the first three or four days we had fine weather, although the wind was dead ahead; having chopped round to the northward, immediately upon our losing sight of the coast. The passengers were consequently in high spirits, and disposed to be social. I *must* except, however, Wyatt and his sisters, who behaved stiffly, and, I could not help thinking, uncourteously to the rest of the party. *Wyatt's* conduct I did not so much regard. He was gloomy, even beyond his usual habit—in fact, he was *morose*—but in him I was prepared for eccentricity. For the sisters, however, I could make no excuse. They secluded themselves in their state-rooms during the greater part of the passage, and absolutely refused, although I repeatedly urged them, to hold communication with any person on board.

Mrs. Wyatt herself, was far more agreeable. That is to say, she was *chatty*; and to be chatty is no slight recommendation at sea. She became *excessively* intimate with most of the ladies; and, to my profound astonishment, evinced no equivocal disposition to coquet with the men. She amused us all very much. I say *"amused"* —and scarcely know how to explain myself. The truth is, I soon found that Mrs. W. was far oftener laughed *at* than *with*. The gentlemen said little about her; but the ladies, in a little while, pronounced her "a good-hearted thing, rather indifferent-looking, totally uneducated, and decidedly vulgar." The great wonder was, how Wyatt had been entrapped into such a match. Wealth was the general solution —but this I knew to be no solution at all; for Wyatt had told me that she neither brought him a dollar nor had any expectations from any source whatever. "He had married," he said, "for love, and for love only; and his bride was far more than worthy of his love." When I thought of these expressions, on the part of my friend, I confess that I felt indescribably puzzled. Could it be possible that he was taking leave of his senses? What else could I think? *He*, so refined, so intellectual, so fastidious, with so exquisite a perception of the faulty, and so keen an appreciation of the beautiful! To be sure, the lady seemed especially fond of *him*— particularly so in his absence—when she made herself ridiculous by frequent quotations of what had been said by her "beloved husband, Mr. Wyatt." The word "husband" seemed forever—to use one of her own delicate expressions—forever "on the tip of her tongue." In the meantime, it was observed by all on board, that he avoided *her* in the most pointed manner, and, for the most part, shut himself up alone in his state-room, where, in fact, he might have been said to live altogether, leaving his wife at full liberty to amuse herself as she thought best, in the public society of the main cabin.

My conclusion, from what I saw and heard, was, that the artist, by some unaccountable freak of fate, or perhaps in some fit of enthusiastic and fanciful passion, had been induced to unite himself with a person altogether beneath him, and that the natural result, entire and speedy disgust, had ensued. I pitied him from the bottom of my heart—but could not, for that reason, quite forgive his incommunicativeness in the matter of the "Last Supper." For this I resolved to have my revenge.

One day he came upon deck, and, taking his arm as had been my wont, I sauntered with him backwards and forwards. His gloom, however, (which I considered quite natural under the circumstances,) seemed entirely unabated. He said little, and that moodily, and with evident effort. I ventured a jest or two, and he made a sickening attempt at a smile. Poor fellow! —as I thought of *his wife*, I wondered that he could have heart to put on even the semblance of mirth. At last I ventured a home thrust. I determined to commence a series of covert insinuations, or innuendoes, about the oblong box—just to let him perceive, gradually, that I was *not* altogether the butt, or victim, of his little bit of pleasant mystification. My first observation was by way of opening a masked battery.[8] I said something about the "peculiar shape of *that* box;" and, as I spoke the words, I smiled knowingly, winked, and touched him gently with my fore-finger in the ribs.

The manner in which Wyatt received this harmless pleasantry, convinced me, at once, that he was mad. At first he stared at me as if he found it impossible to comprehend the witticism of my remark; but as its point seemed slowly to make its way into his brain, his eyes, in the same proportion seemed protruding from their sockets. Then he grew very red—then hideously pale—then, as if highly amused with what I had insinuated, he began a loud and boisterous laugh, which, to my astonishment, he kept up, with gradually increasing vigor, for ten minutes or more. In conclusion, he fell flat and heavily upon the deck. When I ran to uplift him, to all appearance he was *dead*.

I called assistance, and, with much difficulty, we brought him to himself. Upon reviving he spoke incoherently for some time. At length we bled him and put him to bed. The next morning he was quite recovered, so far as regarded his mere bodily health. Of his mind I say nothing, of course. I avoided him during the rest of the passage, by advice of the captain, who seemed to coincide with me altogether in my views of his insanity, but cautioned me to say nothing on this head to any person on board.

Several circumstances occurred immediately after this fit of Wyatt's which contributed to heighten the curiosity with which I was already possessed. Among other things, this: I had been nervous— drank too much strong green tea, and slept ill at night—in fact, for two nights I could not be properly said to sleep at all. Now, my state-room opened into the main cabin, or dining-room, as did those of all the single men on board. Wyatt's three rooms were in the after-cabin, which was separated from the main one by a slight sliding door, never locked even at night. As we were almost constantly on a wind, and the breeze was not a little stiff, the ship heeled to leeward very considerably; and whenever her starboard side was to leeward, the sliding door between the cabins slid open, and so remained, nobody taking the trouble to get up and shut it. But my berth was in such a position, that when my own state-room door was open, as well as the sliding door in question, (and my own door was *always* open on account of the heat) I could see into the after cabin quite distinctly, and just at that portion of it, too, where were situated the state-rooms of Mr. Wyatt. Well, during two nights (*not* consecutive) while I lay awake, I clearly saw Mrs. W., about eleven o'clock upon each night, steal cautiously from the state-room of Mr. W. and enter the extra room, where she remained until daybreak, when she was called by her husband and went back. That they were virtually separated was clear. They had separate apartments—no doubt in contemplation of a more permanent divorce; and here, after all, I thought, was the mystery of the extra state-room.

There was another circumstance, too, which interested me much. During the two wakeful nights in question, and immediately after the disappearance of Mrs. Wyatt into the extra state-room, I was attracted by certain singular, cautious, subdued noises in that of her husband. After listening to them for some time, with thoughtful attention, I at length succeeded perfectly in translating their import. They were sounds occasioned by the artist in prying open the oblong box, by means of a chisel and mallet—the latter being apparently muffled, or deadened,

by some soft woollen or cotton substance in which its head was enveloped.

In this manner I fancied I could distinguish the precise moment when he fairly disengaged the lid—also, that I could determine when he removed it altogether, and when he deposited it upon the lower berth in his room; this latter point I knew, for example, by certain slight taps which the lid made in striking against the wooden edges of the berth, as he endeavored to lay it down *very* gently—there being no room for it on the floor. After this there was a dead stillness, and I heard nothing more, upon either occasion, until nearly daybreak; unless, perhaps, I may mention a low sobbing, or murmuring sound, so very much suppressed as to be nearly inaudible—if, indeed, the whole of this latter noise were not rather produced by my own imagination. I say it seemed to *resemble* sobbing or sighing—but, of course, it could not have been either. I rather think it was a ringing in my own ears. Mr. Wyatt, no doubt, according to custom, was merely giving the rein to one of his hobbies—indulging in one of his fits of artistic enthusiasm. He had opened his oblong box, in order to feast his eyes on the pictorial treasure within. There was nothing in this, however, to make him *sob*. I repeat, therefore, that it must have been simply a freak of my own fancy, distempered by good Captain Hardy's green tea. Just before dawn, on each of the two nights of which I speak, I distinctly heard Mr. Wyatt replace the lid upon the oblong box, and force the nails into their old places, by means of the muffled mallet. Having done this, he issued from his state-room, fully dressed, and proceeded to call Mrs. W. from hers.

We had been at sea seven days, and were now off Cape Hatteras, when there came a tremendously heavy blow from the southwest. We were, in a measure, prepared for it, however, as the weather had been holding out threats for some time. Everything was made snug, alow and aloft; and as the wind steadily freshened, we lay to, at length, under spanker and foretopsail, both double-reefed.[9]

In this trim, we rode safely enough for forty-eight hours—the ship proving herself an excellent sea boat, in many respects, and shipping no water of any consequence. At the end of this period, however, the gale had freshened into a hurricane, and our after-sail split into ribbons, bringing us so much in the trough of the water that we shipped several prodigious seas, one immediately after the other. By this accident we lost three men over-board, with the caboose, and nearly the whole of the larboard bulwarks. Scarcely had we recovered our senses, before the foretopsail went into shreds, when we got up a storm stay-sail,[10] and with this did pretty well for some hours, the ship heading the sea much more steadily than before.

The gale still held on, however, and we saw no signs of its abating. The rigging was found to be ill-fitted, and greatly strained; and on the third day of the blow, about five in the afternoon, our mizzenmast, in a heavy lurch to windward, went by the board. For an hour or more, we tried in vain to get rid of it, on account of the prodigious rolling of the ship; and, before we had succeeded, the carpenter came aft and announced four feet of water in the hold. To add to our dilemma, we found the pumps choked and nearly useless.

All was now confusion and despair—but an effort was made to lighten the ship by throwing overboard as much of her cargo as could be reached, and by cutting away the two masts that remained. This we at last accomplished—but we were still unable to do anything at the pumps; and, in the meantime, the leak gained on us very fast.

At sundown, the gale had sensibly diminished in violence, and, as the sea went down with it, we still entertained faint hopes of saving ourselves in the boats. At eight, P. M., the clouds broke away to windward, and we had the advantage of

a full moon—a piece of good fortune which served wonderfully to cheer our drooping spirits.

After incredible labor we succeeded, at length, in getting the long-boat over the side without material accident, and into this we crowded the whole of the crew and most of the passengers. This party made off immediately, and, after undergoing much suffering, finally arrived, in safety, at Ocracoke Inlet,[11] on the third day after the wreck.

Fourteen passengers, with the Captain, remained on board, resolving to trust their fortunes to the jolly-boat at the stern. We lowered it without difficulty, although it was only by a miracle that we prevented it from swamping as it touched the water. It contained, when afloat, the captain and his wife, Mr. Wyatt and party, a Mexican officer, wife, four children, and myself, with a negro valet.

We had no room, of course, for anything except a few positively necessary instruments, some provision, and the clothes upon our backs. No one had thought of even attempting to save anything more. What must have been the astonishment of all then, when, having proceeded a few fathoms from the ship, Mr. Wyatt stood up in the stern-sheets, and coolly demanded of Captain Hardy that the boat should be put back for the purpose of taking in his oblong box!

"Sit down, Mr. Wyatt," replied the Captain, somewhat sternly; "you will capsize us if you do not sit quite still. Our gunwale is almost in the water now."

"The box!" vociferated Mr. Wyatt, still standing—"the box, I say! Captain Hardy, you cannot, you *will* not refuse me. Its weight will be but a trifle—it is nothing —mere nothing. By the mother who bore you—for the love of Heaven—by your hope of salvation, I *implore* you to put back for the box!"

The Captain, for a moment, seemed touched by the earnest appeal of the artist, but he regained his stern composure, and merely said—

"Mr. Wyatt, you are *mad*. I cannot listen to you. Sit down, I say, or you will swamp the boat. Stay—hold him—seize him!—he is about to spring overboard! There—I knew it—he is over!"

As the Captain said this, Mr. Wyatt, in fact, sprang from the boat, and, as we were yet in the lee of the wreck, succeeded, by almost superhuman exertion, in getting hold of a rope which hung from the fore-chains. In another moment he was on board, and rushing frantically down into the cabin.

In the meantime, we had been swept astern of the ship, and being quite out of her lee,[12] were at the mercy of the tremendous sea which was still rushing. We made a determined effort to put back, but our little boat was like a feather in the breath of the tempest. We saw at a glance that the doom of the unfortunate artist was sealed.

As our distance from the wreck rapidly increased, the madman (for as such only could we regard him) was seen to emerge from the companion-way, up which, by dint of a strength that appeared gigantic, he dragged, bodily, the oblong box. While we gazed in the extremity of astonishment, he passed, rapidly, several turns of a three-inch rope, first around the box and then around his body. In another instant both body and box were in the sea—disappearing suddenly, at once and forever.

We lingered awhile sadly upon our oars, with our eyes riveted upon the spot. At length we pulled away. The silence remained unbroken for an hour. Finally, I hazarded a remark.

"Did you observe, Captain, how suddenly they sank? Was not that an exceedingly singular thing? I confess that I entertained some feeble hope of his final deliverance, when I saw him lash himself to the box, and commit himself to the sea."

"They sank, as a matter of course," replied the Captain, "and that like a shot. They will soon rise again, however—*but not till the salt melts*."

"The salt!" I ejaculated.

"Hush!" said the Captain, pointing to the wife and sisters of the deceased. "We must talk of these things at some more appropriate time."

———

We suffered much, and made a narrow escape; but fortune befriended *us*, as well as our mates in the long boat. We landed, in fine, more dead than alive, after four days of intense distress, upon the beach opposite Roanoke Island.[13] We remained here a week, were not ill-treated by the wreckers, and at length obtained a passage to New York.

About a month after the loss of the "Independence," I happened to meet Captain Hardy in Broadway. Our conversation turned, naturally, upon the disaster, and especially upon the sad fate of poor Wyatt. I thus learned the following particulars.

The artist had engaged passage for himself, wife, two sisters and a servant. His wife was, indeed, as she had been represented, a most lovely, and most accomplished woman. On the morning of the fourteenth of June, (the day in which I first visited the ship,) the lady suddenly sickened and died. The young husband was frantic with grief—but circumstances imperatively forbade the deferring his voyage to New York. It was necessary to take to her mother the corpse of his adored wife, and on the other hand, the universal prejudice which would prevent his doing so openly, was well known. Nine-tenths of the passengers would have abandoned the ship rather than take passage with a dead body.

In this dilemma, Captain Hardy arranged that the corpse, being first partially embalmed, and packed, with a large quantity of salt,[14] in a box of suitable dimensions, should be conveyed on board as merchandize. Nothing was to be said of the lady's decease; and, as it was well understood that Mr. Wyatt had engaged passage for his wife, it became necessary that some person should personate her during the voyage. This the deceased's lady's-maid was easily prevailed on to do. The extra state-room, originally engaged for this girl, during her mistress' life, was now merely retained. In this state-room the pseudo wife slept, of course, every night. In the day-time she performed, to the best of her ability, the part of her mistress—whose person, it had been carefully ascer-tained, was unknown to any of the pas-sengers on board.

My own mistakes arose, naturally enough, through too careless, too inquisi-tive, and too impulsive a temperament. But of late, it is a rare thing that I sleep soundly at night. There is a countenance which haunts me, turn as I will. There is an hysterical laugh which will forever ring within my ears.

Notes

The Gold-Bug

1. There is a play by this name by Arthur Murphy (1730–1805), but these lines are not in it; indeed, the play is in prose (Carlson 2; Pollin 3). T. O. Mabbott (5) thinks Poe wrote the lines himself, basing them on his mem-ories of Frederick Reynold's comedy, *The Democrat* (1789), which Poe quoted else-where. A tarantula bite is "supposed to cause a mania for dancing" (Carlson).

2. Jan Swammerdam (1637–1680), Dutch entomologist.

3. Beetle. A. H. Quinn says Poe's bug might be a combination of the characteristics of two insects which inhabit the area, one a large gold and green beetle, the other a common click beetle which has the spots described in the tale. The real "gold-bug," *Callichroma splendidum*, can bite, as Jupiter says, though it is not of the family scarabaeus.

4. Fort Moultrie, on the western end of the island. Poe served there in the army from late 1827 to late 1828. See map accompanying "The Oblong Box." The story was not pub-lished until June 21 and 28, 1843, when it appeared serially in *The Dollar Newspaper* of Philadelphia. Poe had sold it to *Graham's* but asked for it back so he could enter it in a prize competition in *The Dollar Newspa-per*, which it won. The same paper reprinted it in its "Supplement" of July 12, 1843. *The Volunteer* (Montrose, Pa.) ran it in three in-stallments, August 3, 10, and 17, 1843; Poe used it in his 1845 *Tales by Edgar A. Poe*. It appeared twice in 1848: in the June 22 *Bos-ton Museum*, and in the July 1 and 8 *Satur-day Courier*.

5. "Man-head beetle."

6. brusqueness, bluntness.

7. alone.

8. earnestness.

9. *Liriodendron tulipifera*, the yellow pop-lar or tulip tree (Carlson 2). See "Landor's Cottage," note 5 and "Morning on the Wissahiccon," note 6.

10. These are terms of horsemanship; Legrand in effect kicks up his heels. The usual English spelling is "caracoles."

11. HgCl$_2$, mercuric chloride, used to pre-serve museum specimens and wood.

12. zaffre: zaffer, a blue pigment made from cobalt ore.

aqua regia: a mixture of nitric and hydro-chloric acids, which gets its name—"royal water"—from its ability to dissolve gold.

regulus: "metallic mass that sinks to the bot-tom when ore is treated" (Carlson 2).

13. In archaic chemical usage, caloric was a subtle fluid which produced heat.

14. A city in India "famous in the six-teenth century for its diamond-cutting and polishing" (Carlson 2).

15. For the exact connotations of this word in Poe, see the story "Mystification."

The Murders in the Rue Morgue

1. The "Rue Morgue" doesn't seem to be a real place (Carlson 2). But for a discussion of

the "Morque" (Morgue) of Paris and the Quartier in which it was located see "Posthumous Letters of Charles Edwards, Esq. No. IV" in Blackwood's (December 1824), pp. 669–670. For other Parisian locations, see map. To the best of anyone's knowledge, Poe had never been to France. This "first of the modern detective stories" ran first in the April 1841 number of Graham's Magazine. Poe published it again in his abortive pamphlet-edition of his stories, the Prose Romances, and finally in 1845 in the Tales. .

2. Hydriotaphia, or Urn-Burial: a famous and beautifully written essay by Sir Thomas Browne (1605–1682), English physician and essayist. Poe would have found many aspects of Browne's point of view sympathetic. Browne has religious faith, yet believes that reason need not conflict with it; his opinion of man is low (hell, he says, is in his own heart, and men grow more sinful as they grow older). The point of the quotation is that conjecture—in this story, inspired guess-work—can be helpful when pure logic fails. Browne's name was very much in the public mind when Poe's story was published, for in 1840 his coffin was opened and his skull stolen and sold. Poor Browne got his head back in 1922.

3. checkers.

4. rare, exquisite, choice.

5. whist: a card game, an ancestor of the modern bridge.

Hoyle: Sir Edmund Hoyle (1672–1769), who published in 1742 Short Treatise on the Game of Whist and later a number of books on other games.

6. It was not yet clear in Poe's day that phrenology, the science of studying personality through examination of the shape of the head, was a scientific dead-end. Though the field rapidly fell into the hands of quacks, the pioneers in the area had been serious scientists. Phrenology made use of the concepts of "faculty psychology": it assumed that each inherent power of the mind was located in a specific portion of one's head. It was hoped that once phrenologists were sure which "faculties" were basic, they could examine subjects' crania and produce what we would perhaps call personality or aptitude profiles. The concept is not in nature different from the assumptions of twentieth-century work on the physiology of the brain.

7. Poe's detective hero. He seems to have borrowed the name from a character in some articles about the French Minister of Police, Francois Eugene Vidocq (1775–1857) which appeared in Burton's Gentleman's Magazine in 1838 (A. H. Quinn). Poe's Dupin is the hero of three detective stories, "Rue Morgue," "The Mystery of Marie Rogêt," and "The Purloined Letter."

8. A hint that Dupin ultimately has more than analytical ability, that some "faculty" unnamed by the narrator (who, like Holmes' friend Dr. Watson, never really understands his friend) is present.

9. quondam: former.

Crébillon: Prosper Jolyot de Crébillon (1674–1762), French dramatist who wrote a number of plays on classical subjects. The narrator is amused by the thought of the cobbler playing an heroic character based on Xerxes the Great (c. 519–c. 465 B.C.E.), Persian king whom the Greeks defeated at Salamis in 480 B.C.E.

Pasquinaded: ridiculed or lampooned.

10. "and all of that sort."

11. stereotomy: the art of cutting solids, especially stones, as in masonry or, here, paving.

Epicurus: (341–270 B.C.E.) Greek philosopher who did, in fact, follow Democritus in the matter of atomism.

nebular cosmogony: probably a reference to Charles de Laplace's 1796 postulation of "a cosmogony of the solar system with the planets developing from rings abandoned by a rotating, contracting nebula." Poe knew of Laplace's work; interestingly, American scientific writers in Poe's day often did not (Numbers).

buskin: a type of boot associated with actors in tragedies.

Perdidit . . . sonum: may be translated, "The first letter has lost its ancient sound."

Chantilly: The cobbler's change of name on becoming an actor and the change in spelling suggest other changes and associations: cobbler—hobbler (bad actor); Orion, a giant and a great hunter in Greek mythology and the diminutive Chantilly; and, possibly, an association in Poe's mind between cobblestone and a cobbler which could have suggested the whole business.

12. métal d'Alger or Metal of Algiers is a

combination of pewter, lead, and antimony.

13. literally, "holy," "devil," and "my God." Poe intends for the reader to understand that the witnesses heard fragments of French expletives.

14. shin bone.

15. A "robe-de-chambre" is a dressing gown. The joke, however, turns on the word "chambre," chamber. In Moliere's Le Bourgeois Gentilhomme, the nouveau riche M. Jourdain, in order to listen to chamber music better, wants his "chamber robe." He says to his servants, "Donnez-moi ma robe pour mieux entendre. . . ." Poe completed the sentence by adding the words, "la musique."

16. Vidocq: See note 7. Contemporary accounts of Vidocq do not suggest that he was notable for the qualities Poe assigns to him.

Truth . . . well: See "Ligeia," note 5.

17. a doorkeeper's apartment.

18. I handled them tactfully.

19. strange, odd.

20. "after the fact"—that is, beginning by assuming that I was correct.

21. insane asylum.

22. Baron Georges Cuvier (1769–1832), great French naturalist whose classification of animals was one of the standard guides to the subject until Darwin.

23. Neufchâtel is a town in northern France. "Neufchâtelish" implies "Swiss-French."

24. the Goddess Laverna: the patroness of thieves in ancient Roman religion.

'de nier . . . n'est pas': Rousseau, Nouvelle Héloïse [Poe's note]. Jean Jacques Rousseau's Julie ou La Nouvelle Héloïse (1760). The French may be translated, "of denying that which is, and of explaining that which is not."

The Mystery of Marie Rogêt

1. On the original publication of "Marie Rogêt," the foot-notes now appended were considered unnecessary; but the lapse of several years since the tragedy upon which the tale is based, renders it expedient to give them, and also to say a few words in explanation of the general design. A young girl, Mary Cecilia Rogers, was murdered in the vicinity of New York; and, although her death occasioned an intense and long-enduring excitement, the mystery attending it had

remained unsolved at the period when the present paper was written and published (November, 1842). Herein, under pretence of relating the fate of a Parisian grisette, the author has followed, in minute detail, the essential, while merely paralleling the inessential facts of the real murder of Mary Rogers. Thus all argument founded upon the fiction is applicable to the truth; and the investigation of the truth was the object.

The "Mystery of Marie Rogêt" was composed at a distance from the scene of the atrocity, and with no other means of investigation than the newspapers afforded. Thus much escaped the writer of which he could have availed himself had he been on the spot, and visited the localities. It may not be improper to record, nevertheless, that the confessions of two persons, (one of them the Madame Deluc of the narrative) made, at different periods, long subsequent to the publication, confirmed, in full, not only the general conclusion, but absolutely all the chief hypothetical details by which that conclusion was attained [Poe's note]. See Section Preface.

2. The nom de plume of Von Hardenberg [Poe's note].

Georg Friedrich Phillipp von Hardenberg (1772–1801), German poet and aphorist.

3. "Marie Rogêt" was published first in serial form in Snowden's Ladies' Companion, November and December 1842 and February 1843, and again in Tales, 1845. "Rue Morgue" was published first in April 1841.

4. The two women murdered by an ourang-outang in "The Murders in the Rue Morgue."

5. inductions, not deductions. Dupin leaves it to the Prefect of Police to deduce.

6. Rue . . . André: Nassau Street [Poe's note].

pension: boarding house.

Monsieur Le Blanc: Anderson [Poe's note].

7. a French working-girl. The word carries connotations of prettiness and flirtatiousness.

8. Seine: The Hudson [Poe's note].

Barrière du Roule: Weehawken [Poe's note].

9. uprisings or riots.

10. Payne [Poe's note].

11. Crommelin [Poe's note].

12. The "N. Y. Mercury" [Poe's note].

13. The "N. Y. Brother Jonathan," edited by H. Hastings Weld, Esq. [Poe's note].

14. N. Y. "Journal of Commerce" [Poe's note].

15. Phil. "Sat. Evening Post," edited by C. J. Peterson, Esq. [Poe's note].

16. Adam [Poe's note].

17. drug containing opium.

18. *outré*: weird, strange, unusual.

myrmidons: faithful followers; in this usage, "agents" or "troops."

Madame L'Espanaye: See notes 3 and 4 above.

19. This slap at the editor of "L'Etoile" (which Poe identifies as the *New York Brother Jonathan*) is interesting. Rufus Griswold, who was to ruin Poe's reputation for almost a century through bitter slander in the form of an obituary and a memoir, was one of the editors of that paper, which was notorious for stealing authors' work under the weak copyright situation of the time. Although Poe apparently named Griswold his literary executor, he and Griswold had fought on and off for years, and the dig at "L'Etoile" might be aimed at his antagonist. See Introduction, p. xvii.

20. one-sided.

21. The "N. Y. Commercial Advertiser," edited by Col. Stone [Poe's note].

22. Poe is on solid ground—or rather, floating clear—here. The position he recommends is identical with that currently recommended by safety authorities for non-swimmers who find themselves in deep water.

23. See "The Gold-Bug," note 11.

24. A *non sequitur* is a conclusion which doesn't follow from the evidence presented. Dupin's short form is best rendered "logic" or "reasoning"—". . . you smile at the bad reasoning."

25. commission *de lunatico inquirendo*: a committee to investigate the madman (or mad act).

And this . . . individual error: "A theory based on the qualities of an object, will prevent its being unfolded according to its objects; and he who arranges topics in reference to their causes, will cease to value them according to their results. Thus the jurisprudence of every nation will show that, when law becomes a science and a system, it ceases to be justice. The errors into which a blind devotion to *principles* of classification has led the common law, will be seen by observing how often the legislature has been obliged

to come forward to restore the equity its scheme had lost."—*Landor* [Poe's note]. (Pollin [3] identifies the quotation as follows: William Landor for Horace Binney Wallace.) Wallace (1817–1852) was an author who contributed to the literature of law.

26. Dupin's logic here fits Protestant early nineteenth-century New York better than it does Catholic and cosmopolitan Paris. Even in urban Catholic neighborhoods in which church attendance is high, there is less uniformity of schedules because of the usual parish practice of multiple masses at different hours. Moreover, the neighborhood which Poe describes at the start of the tale does not sound particularly family and church oriented.

27. *comptoir*: cashier's desk.

Evening . . . 23: "N. Y. Express" [Poe's note].

28. "N. Y. Herald" [Poe's note].

29. "N. Y. Courier and Inquirer" [Poe's note].

30. Mennais: Mennais was one of the parties originally suspected and arrested, but discharged through total lack of evidence [Poe's note].

Morning . . . 28: "N. Y. Courier and Inquirer" [Poe's note].

31. "N. Y. Evening Post" [Poe's note].

32. "N. Y. Standard" [Poe's note].

33. shady.

34. Hence her fury?

35. Of the Magazine in which the article was originally published [Poe's note]. Poe added the footnote when he revised the piece for republication in 1845. The note in brackets in the text, of course, is by Poe, not by the editors of *Snowden's Ladies' Companion*. It is clearly a cop-out.

36. *dénouement*: conclusion.

to suggest . . . result: Poe is covering all possibilities now by disclaiming what he had claimed in a letter to Dr. J. E. Snodgrass dated June 4, 1842: ". . . I really believe, not only that I have demonstrated the falsity of the idea that the girl was the victim of a gang, but have *indicated the assassin*."

37. Poe's logic is consistent insofar as it deals with the matter of coincidence, discussed here and at the start of the tale. But it makes little sense in terms of Dupin's argument as he analyzes the evidence detail by detail.

The Purloined Letter

1. "Nothing is more distasteful to good sense than too much cunning" (Carlson 2). Carlson says that the quotation, in point of fact, is not from Seneca. There are any number of similar sayings: Samuel Johnson's "They who cannot be wise are almost always cunning," Francis Bacon's "Cunning is . . . a sinister or crooked wisdom" and "Nothing doth more hurt in a state, than that cunning men pass for wise." Poe's "quotation," indeed is so close in spirit to Bacon's essay "Of Cunning" that it could serve as its conclusion.

A shorter version of this story appeared in the November 30, 1844 issue of *Chamber's Edinburgh Journal*. The present version was published first in late 1844 in *The Gift* (dated 1845), and the same year in *Tales*.

2. *au troisième:* third (fourth) floor. For the probable location of Dupin's apartment, see the map "Poe's Paris," pp. 176–177.

something of a coincidence: so it seems to the narrator, but the hint is that our thoughts and events are really connected. Since the story is about the capacity to project oneself "poetically" into another's personality, Poe hints that the arrival of the Prefect as the narrator thinks about him is no coincidence. For further evidence of Poe's belief in the power of the mind to create, literally, the world around one, see "The Power of Words" and *Eureka*.

3. Dupin's solution appears before he even knows the nature of the problem.

4. well-informed.

5. writing desk.

6. In Greek mythology, the giant Procrustes tied travellers to an iron bed; he made them fit by stretching or amputating their limbs.

7. Rochefoucault: François, Duc de la Rochefoucauld (1613–1680), Prince de Marsillac, celebrated French moralist and courtier, whose *Réflexions, ou Sentences et Maximes Morales* (1665) argues that self-love is the chief motive in human actions.

La Bougive: Neither we nor scholars we have consulted have been able to identify the author to whom Poe refers. Barzun is sure Poe means LaBruyère (Jean de la Bruyère, 1645–1696); he notes that Poe's French is untrustworthy.

Machiavelli: Niccoló Machiavelli (1469–1527), the Italian statesman and writer whose name is synonymous with the idea of cold calculation in diplomacy.

Campanella: Tommaso Campanella (1568–1639), Italian philosopher and Dominican monk, whose *Philosophy Demonstrated by the Senses* (1591) caused his imprisonment for heresy.

Poe's list is of writers who assume all human behavior is to be understood simply in selfish terms.

8. rare, strange.

9. "The undistributed middle" is an error in logic. The syllogism would run,

> *All fools are poets.*
> *The minister is a poet.*
> *Therefore, the minister is a fool.*

The conclusion is illogical because the syllogism does not rule out the possibility that some poets aren't fools. A proper syllogism would run,

> *All poets are fools.*
> *The minister is a poet.*
> *Therefore, the minister is a fool.*

Dupin cheats a little in his argument here, because the Prefect really said that poets are "only one remove" from fools. He has no way of knowing that, had the Prefect actually thought out a syllogism, even one with as dubious a premise as either of these, he would have used the incorrect version.

10. *'Il y a . . . nombre':* "The odds are that every popular idea, every accepted convention, is nonsense, because it has suited itself to the majority" (Carlson 2). The quotation is from *Maximes et Pensées*.

Chamfort: Sebastian Roch Nicholas Chamfort (1741–1794).

11. Each of the Latin words is the source of the English word, but Poe is correct; their meanings were quite different in classical times.

ambitus: In classical times, it referred to "going around," as in going around seeking office or going around soliciting votes (by paying for them).

religio: This referred to anything you were bound to do—such as religious observance or just obeying your conscience. It could apply to anything from "superstition" to "conscience."

homines honesti: honestus, of which *honesti* is the plural, meant just "distinguished"; it had no moral connotations.

12. Bryant: Poe refers to Jacob Bryant (1715–1804), a learned English antiquarian. Poe's quotation is from his *A New System, or an Analysis of Antient Mythology* (1774–1776). In the London, 1807 edition, it appears in Volume II, p. 173. Poe knew Bryant well—see also "Eleonora," "Shadow," "Four Beasts in One." The present passage Poe quotes also in his philosophical "prose-poem" *Eureka* and in the *Pinakidia,* a collection of literary odds and ends which Poe assembled in 1836.

$x^2 + px \ldots = q$: Poe's formula is not a standard equation for anything; as it stands, it has no special meaning.

13. intriguer.

14. the power of inertia.

15. *facilis descensus Averni*: When Aeneas, in Virgil's *Aeneid,* asks the Sibyl of Cumae to allow him to descend into the underworld to visit his father, she warns him, "Easy is the descent into hell [Avernus]; all night and day the gate of dark Dis stands open, but to recall thy steps and issue to upper air, this is the task, this the burden." Avernus is a smouldering crater in Italy, so foreboding in appearance it was considered an entrance to the underworld. Carlson (2) notices that Poe has the quotation wrong: for "Averni" the original reads "Avernus."

Catalani: Angelica Catalani (1780–1849) was a famous Italian operatic singer. For evidence of Poe's familiarity with opera, see "The Spectacles."

monstrum horrendum: also from Virgil; the phrase means "horrible monster."

16. "A plot so deadly, if not worthy of Atreus is worthy of Thyestes," from *Atrée et Thyeste* by Prosper Jolyot de Crébillon (1674–1762). The play, dated 1707, is a "revenge tragedy." Thyestes seduces his brother's wife and plans to murder him. Atreus, his brother, kills Thyestes' three sons and makes them the main dish at a banquet for their father. Poe seems to associate Dupin with Crébillon: see "The Murders in the Rue Morgue," note 9.

The Oblong Box

1. First published in *Godey's Lady's Book,* September 1844. Used again in *The Broadway Journal,* December 13, 1845, during Poe's period as proprietor.

2. A real ship, launched 1834, and famous for a record-breaking fast crossing to Liverpool in 1836 (Vierra), bore this name, but its history differs from that of Poe's packet-ship.

3. There is, according to Pollin (3), no "Cornelius Wyatt," but the name Wyatt was a good choice because of the number of English artists with that name.

4. Poe's art dealer is probably made up, but there are several "known" figures with similar names: Antonio Niccolini (1772–1850), for example, was a painter best known for his theatre decorations, and Poe might have known the name.

5. Poe describes an experience familiar to travelers-by-sea in the nineteenth century. Ship departures were notoriously irregular, though, as his narrator implies, late departure was a little unusual for a packet-ship.

6. Leonardo's "Last Supper": Leonardo da Vinci's famous painting, about 1497, on a wall of the refectory of Santa Maria delle Grazie, Milan. Before the days of good color reproduction, skillful copies of masterworks were far more important, and since this painting had deteriorated badly even in Leonardo's lifetime, early copies are *very* valuable: they are closer to the original than the original. But Poe's idea that a copy would fit in a casket-shaped box is wrong; the painting's dimensions are 15' 1⅛" × 28' 10½".

Rubini the younger: It's hard to tell which painter Poe has in mind, or even whether he has a specific one in mind at all. Vigilio Rubini, active 1583–1608, is a "younger" in that he is the son of Lorenzo Rubini, also a "known" artist, but Vigilio Rubini is a sculptor. Three "known" painters who could have copied the painting are named Rubini: Andrea Rubini, a late 16th and early 17th century Italian, Giovanni-Battista Rubini, who died about 1752, and Pietro Rubini, c. 1700–after 1765. No source we have examined speaks of any of them as "the younger." All four men named here are fairly obscure; Poe may simply have picked "Rubini" as an Italian name with a fairly familiar ring: Poe liked to show his knowledge of opera, and there was, in his day, a very great Italian tenor named Giovanni Rubini (1795–1854) whose fame may well have put the name in Poe's head. How Rubini *fils* executed in Florence a copy of a notably unmovable painting in Milan is less than clear.

quizz: As Poe used it, the word does not mean ask, but rather fool, trick or tease.

7. Chambers Street is a real street in New York, running ESE from the Hudson across 9th Avenue, crossing Greenwich, West Broadway, Church, Broadway, by City Hall, and ending at or just beyond Chatham. Most of its length runs between Reed and Warren. The area today is way downtown, an easy walk from the Battery.

8. military language. To open a masked battery is to commence using an emplaced cannon or group of cannons of which the enemy was unaware.

9. Cape Hatteras: See Figure Ten map.

spanker . . . double-reefed: The ship was faced into the wind to ride out the storm. The spanker and foretopsail are the two sails Captain Hardy used to maintain his position;

"double-reefed" means "with a considerable part of the sails tucked in to reduce their effective size."

10. caboose: galley.

stay-sail: The safest position for a sailing ship in a storm is headed into the wind. To maintain that position, small sails are needed. Hence the concern when the two small sails in use are destroyed, and the quick rigging of a substitute, the small and probably triangular stay-sail.

11. a sea passage which connects Pamlico Sound with the ocean. See map.

12. the area near the ship, sheltered from the storm.

13. See Figure Ten map.

14. Poe probably based this detail on a famous murder case: John Colt killed Samuel Adams, a printer, on September 17, 1841, packed the corpse in salt, put it in an oblong box, and shipped it off by sea (Vierra).

6. Moral Issues

Grouped together here are tales of crime and punishment. Another editor, looking over the group, might choose to call them "Tales of Gothic Horror," for each is gothic and contains horror: twelve murders in six stories. We choose to emphasize not the strange details with which Poe created his "effects," but rather the surprisingly simple and conventional moral underpinnings which support those effects: guilt will out; loss of human contact means spiritual death; conscience must be heeded; and so forth.

This group is unusual for its relative freedom from literary allusions and for the fact that, though each tale deals in one way or another with abnormal psychological states, each contains some surprisingly strong tie to the "normal" world.

The Black Cat. In this story for instance, we are told that the narrator is happily married; we know a bit about his childhood; he seems to have been a nice person. His downfall he attributes to intemperance, homely enough as a vice in an age when temperance propaganda was quite inescapable in American society. We would argue that even what the narrator calls "perverseness" is really conscience. Guilt about his alcoholism seems to him the "perverseness" which maims and kills the first cat; guilt about those acts produces the murder of his wife—who, after all, showed him the gallows on the second cat's breast. He says, we notice, that the "incarnate Night-Mare" was "incumbent eternally upon . . . his heart." For all its intensity, then, the tale serves as a corrective to those readings of Poe which insist upon Poe's "unreality" and his isolation from the workaday environment around him. All this tale says is that the capacity for violence and horror is within even the nicest of us: compassionate people who like goldfish, dogs, and cats.

The Tell-Tale Heart. Again we are reminded not to take horror in Poe too autobiographically. Krappe points out that a Dickens tale uses very similar ideas. So many of Poe's tales borrow plot and texture from popular authors whose works Poe knew that it is probably safe to say that Poe's real contribution to the short story form was manner, not matter.

Hop-Frog. Given what we now know about Poe's dependence upon his sources for story ideas and details, it is perilous to attach strong psychological significance to his subject matter. "Hop-Frog" was produced at a time when he was very "commercial-minded," writing cheery notes to friends about how much material he was selling and how well he knew the market for prose.

To the critics who read Poe into Hop-Frog, Poe is rationalizing his own difficulties with alcohol by claiming, through the story, that people "force" drinks upon him. Certainly his use of one of his own failings does suggest involvement. So does the fact that the sensitive cripple is in a way an "artist," dragged from his homeland to entertain the "fat headed" establishment— exactly what Poe calls the king and his ministers—in return for crumbs from their table. (See notes 5 and 7.) If the mention of liquor, in other words, suggests that Poe is feeling sorry for himself, and the treatment of the dwarf as a mistreated artist suggests a complaint about the status of the artist in society, then the dwarf's capacity for love and vengeance is an assertion of the artist's human dignity and manliness. But why, then, is the vengeance so hideous? Probably because Poe believed that every tale should create a strong effect, bizarre, grotesque, outré.

Note the ending of the tale: Trippetta and Hop-Frog "live happily ever after." Poe seems to have a fairy-tale effect in mind. He is extremely vague about date, as though he wanted this kingdom to be some timeless Never-Never-Land. The narrator speaks of a time when jesters were still common (implying "a long time ago"), but also of "great continental 'powers,' " a relatively modern development. He says that he was present when the events of the story occurred, implying the relatively recent past, yet that orang-utans were hardly known in the civilized world, implying a date at least before the age of exploration. Since Poe intends for his story to have some of the qualities of a folk-tale or even a parable, this vagueness seems deliberate. Note also the paucity of foreign phrases or quotations and explicit literary references; Poe seems concerned more than usual with keeping things simple. The place in which his tale was to appear might have influenced his decision (see note 1).

The Imp of the Perverse. This story depends for its effectiveness on the vagueness of the line which distinguished story from article in the periodicals of Poe's day. The story is in a way a hoax: it pretends to be a "normal" article, then turns into a story. The reader has no way of knowing that this witty and philosophical "essay" is a work of fiction until he is well into it—indeed, only in the last nine paragraphs do we discover that our narrator is a "character" and that we are to have a "plot." One has to reread the opening to see that the narrator's argument is specious when he says that science should cease trying to locate characteristics man should have, and start instead by observing characteristics which he *does* have. The narrator's first point is perfectly good: phrenology can be seen as a branch of metaphysics, and metaphysicians have erred through moralistic assumptions. The trouble is that there is no such thing as the "perverseness" of which he speaks. He is not perverse; he is criminally insane. His examples of perversity before he begins to tell his own story show a crescendo of intensity, culminating in a passage on suicidal desire which is a miniature horror-story in itself; they serve to transfer us from the "essay" to the "story." And our narrator continues to see his "perverseness" in his confession, not in the murder itself. "The Imp of the Perverse" turns out to be conscience.

William Wilson. Here Poe establishes credibility in two ways: first, through the usual passage about how Wilson comes from an "imaginative and easily excitable race," and second, through a very rare and uncharacteristically "realistic" description of childhood. (See paragraphs above note 6.) The only other child developed in any detail is Arthur Gordon Pym in Poe's one completed novel.

Poe admired Hawthorne, and, in this most Hawthornian of his tales, used Hawthorne's usual technique for suggesting the incredible while maintaining credibility: he made the strangest occurrences in his story ambiguous. Wilson says that he could only "with difficulty shake off the belief" that he had known his double in a prior life; often the double appears when Wilson is "madly flushed" by liquor or excitement. We see the double as conscience and note that Wilson sometimes welcomes the interruptions. Those facts and Wilson's hereditary imaginativeness give us room to interpret the tale either literally or as the creation of a guilt-ridden and diseased mind.

Note that Wilson is shown to be arrogant and aristocratic; he is, for instance, ashamed of his "common" name and regards institutions of higher learning as playgrounds for the elite. The usually undemocratic Poe, in certain tales which deal with moral issues, plays on his audience's anti-aristocratic biases: compare "The Masque of the Red Death."

The Man of the Crowd. It is not easy to say exactly what this strange and wonderful story means: its vision of some unnamed horror in the heart of the city reminds one of the descent into New York in Melville's *Pierre*; its catalogue of social classes is Whitmanesque; and its refusal to moralize is very modern—one thinks of Hemingway's "A Clean Well-Lighted Place" and other visions of urban loneliness. We group it with "Moral Issues" not because it moralizes—it does not—but because it contains, along with the usual condescension and racism, a refreshing dose of compassion: Poe pities the poor, the prostitutes, the city's underdogs.

The old cliché about Poe's otherworldliness crumbles before passages of almost Dickensian genre characterization such as the long special catalogue which begins in paragraph five. Poe, we must remember, was an urban man, who, if he did not know the London in which this story is supposedly set, knew Philadelphia and New York very well. Poe the artist seems generally far greater than Poe the man, but this tale suggests that he was capable of spiritual as well as literary growth.

Critics from 1847 on have noted the apparent implausibility of the events of "The Man of the Crowd"; they ignore the paragraph indicated by note 4, in which the narrator tells us that he has been ill—indeed, is still recuperating —and is in a strange and hyperacute state. This is the familiar Poe device of providing a "margin of credibility" through a peculiar state of mind: we can believe what happens, or assume that it is partially a delusion, the result of the narrator's illness.

The likely source of Poe's tale is William Maginn's sketch "The Night Walker," published first in *Blackwood's Edinburgh Magazine* in November 1823. The narrator takes the reader on a tour of the busy places in London throughout the night; we begin in the theatre district and move through less respectable forms of entertainment. As in the Poe story, too, there are catalogues of trades and occupations and a telling of the hours; Maginn tells us which people are seen at each hour.

The Tales

THE BLACK CAT

For the most wild, yet most homely narrative which I am about to pen, I neither expect nor solicit belief. Mad indeed would I be to expect it, in a case where my very senses reject their own evidence. Yet, mad am I not—and very surely do I not dream. But to-morrow I die, and to-day I would unburthen my soul. My immediate purpose is to place before the world, plainly, succinctly, and without comment, a series of mere household events. In their consequences, these events have terrified—have tortured—have destroyed me. Yet I will not attempt to expound them. To me, they have presented little but Horror—to many they will seem less terrible than *baroques*.[1] Hereafter, perhaps, some intellect may be found which will reduce my phantasm to the common-place—some intellect more calm, more logical, and far less excitable than my own, which will perceive, in the circumstances I detail with awe, nothing more than an ordinary succession of very natural causes and effects.

From my infancy I was noted for the docility and humanity of my disposition.

My tenderness of heart was even so conspicuous as to make me the jest of my companions. I was especially fond of animals, and was indulged by my parents with a great variety of pets. With these I spent most of my time, and never was so happy as when feeding and caressing them. This peculiarity of character grew with my growth, and, in my manhood, I derived from it one of my principal sources of pleasure. To those who have cherished an affection for a faithful and sagacious dog, I need hardly be at the trouble of explaining the nature or the intensity of the gratification thus derivable. There is something in the unselfish and self-sacrificing love of a brute, which goes directly to the heart of him who has had frequent occasion to test the paltry friendship and gossamer fidelity of mere *Man*.

I married early, and was happy to find in my wife a disposition not uncongenial with my own. Observing my partiality for domestic pets, she lost no opportunity of procuring those of the most agreeable kind. We had birds, gold fish, a fine dog, rabbits, a small monkey, and *a cat*.

This latter was a remarkably large and

beautiful animal, entirely black, and saga-cious to an astonishing degree.[2] In speak-ing of his intelligence, my wife, who at heart was not a little tinctured with super-stition, made frequent allusion to the an-cient popular notion, which regarded all black cats as witches in disguise. Not that she was ever *serious* upon this point—and I mention the matter at all for no better reason than that it happens, just now, to be remembered.

Pluto—this was the cat's name—was my favorite pet and playmate. I alone fed him, and he attended me wherever I went about the house. It was even with diffi-culty that I could prevent him from fol-lowing me through the streets.

Our friendship lasted, in this manner, for several years, during which my gen-eral temperament and character—through the instrumentality of the Fiend Intem-perance—had (I blush to confess it) expe-rienced a radical alteration for the worse. I grew, day by day, more moody, more irritable, more regardless of the feelings of others. I suffered myself to use intemper-ate language to my wife. At length, I even offered her personal violence. My pets, of course, were made to feel the change in my disposition. I not only neglected, but ill-used them. For Pluto, however, I still retained sufficient regard to restrain me from maltreating him, as I made no scru-ple of maltreating the rabbits, the mon-key, or even the dog, when by accident, or through affection, they came in my way. But my disease grew upon me—for what disease is like Alcohol!—and at length even Pluto, who was now becom-ing old, and consequently somewhat pee-vish—even Pluto began to experience the effects of my ill temper.

One night, returning home, much in-toxicated, from one of my haunts about town, I fancied that the cat avoided my presence. I seized him; when, in his fright at my violence, he inflicted a slight wound upon my hand with his teeth. The fury of a demon instantly possessed me. I knew myself no longer. My original soul

seemed, at once, to take its flight from my body; and a more than fiendish malevo-lence, gin-nurtured, thrilled every fibre of my frame. I took from my waistcoat-pocket a pen-knife, opened it, grasped the poor beast by the throat, and deliberately cut one of its eyes from the socket! I blush, I burn, I shudder, while I pen the damnable atrocity.

When reason returned with the morn-ing—when I had slept off the fumes of the night's debauch—I experienced a sen-timent half of horror, half of remorse, for the crime of which I had been guilty; but it was, at best, a feeble and equivocal feel-ing, and the soul remained untouched. I again plunged into excess, and soon drowned in wine all memory of the deed.

In the meantime the cat slowly recov-ered. The socket of the lost eye presented, it is true, a frightful appearance, but he no longer appeared to suffer any pain. He went about the house as usual, but, as might be expected, fled in extreme terror at my approach. I had so much of my old heart left, as to be at first grieved by this evident dislike on the part of a creature which had once so loved me. But this feeling soon gave place to irritation. And then came, as if to my final and irrevoca-ble overthrow, the spirit of PERVERSENESS. Of this spirit philosophy takes no account. Yet I am not more sure that my soul lives, than I am that perverseness is one of the primitive impulses of the human heart—one of the indivisible primary faculties, or sentiments, which give direction to the character of Man. Who has not, a hun-dred times, found himself committing a vile or a silly action, for no other reason than because he knows he should *not*? Have we not a perpetual inclination, in the teeth of our best judgment, to violate that which is *Law*, merely because we un-derstand it to be such? This spirit of per-verseness, I say, came to my final over-throw. It was this unfathomable longing of the soul *to vex itself*—to offer violence to its own nature—to do wrong for the wrong's sake only—that urged me to continue and finally to consummate the injury I had inflicted upon the unoffending brute. One morning, in cool blood, I slipped a noose about its neck and hung it to the limb of a tree;—hung it with the tears streaming from my eyes, and with the bitterest remorse at my heart;—hung it *because* I knew that it had loved me, and *because* I felt it had given me no reason of offence;—hung it *because* I knew that in so doing I was committing a sin —a deadly sin that would so jeopardize my immortal soul as to place it—if such a thing were possible—even beyond the reach of the infinite mercy of the Most Merciful and Most Terrible God.

On the night of the day on which this cruel deed was done, I was aroused from sleep by the cry of fire. The curtains of my bed were in flames. The whole house was blazing. It was with great difficulty that my wife, a servant, and myself, made our escape from the conflagration. The destruction was complete. My entire worldly wealth was swallowed up, and I resigned myself thenceforward to despair.

I am above the weakness of seeking to establish a sequence of cause and effect, between the disaster and the atrocity. But I am detailing a chain of facts—and wish not to leave even a possible link imperfect. On the day succeeding the fire, I visited the ruins. The walls, with one exception, had fallen in. This exception was found in a compartment wall, not very thick, which stood about the middle of the house, and against which had rested the head of my bed. The plastering had here, in great measure, resisted the action of the fire—a fact which I attributed to its having been recently spread. About this wall a dense crowd were collected, and many persons seemed to be examining a particular portion of it with very minute and eager attention. The words "strange!" "singular!" and other similar expressions, excited my curiosity. I approached and saw, as if graven in *bas relief* upon the white surface, the figure of a gigantic cat. The impression was given

with an accuracy truly marvellous. There was a rope about the animal's neck.

When I first beheld this apparition— for I could scarcely regard it as less—my wonder and my terror were extreme. But at length reflection came to my aid. The cat, I remembered, had been hung in a garden adjacent to the house. Upon the alarm of fire, this garden had been immediately filled by the crowd—by some one of whom the animal must have been cut from the tree and thrown, through an open window, into my chamber. This had probably been done with the view of arousing me from sleep. The falling of other walls had compressed the victim of my cruelty into the substance of the freshly-spread plaster; the lime of which, with the flames, and the *ammonia* from the carcass, had then accomplished the portraiture as I saw it.

Although I thus readily accounted to my reason, if not altogether to my conscience, for the startling fact just detailed, it did not the less fail to make a deep impression upon my fancy. For months I could not rid myself of the phantasm of the cat; and, during this period, there came back into my spirit a half-sentiment that seemed, but was not, remorse. I went so far as to regret the loss of the animal, and to look about me, among the vile haunts which I now habitually frequented, for another pet of the same species, and of somewhat similar appearance, with which to supply its place.

One night as I sat, half stupified, in a den of more than infamy, my attention was suddenly drawn to some black object, reposing upon the head of one of the immense hogsheads of Gin, or of Rum, which constituted the chief furniture of the apartment. I had been looking steadily at the top of this hogshead for some minutes, and what now caused me surprise was the fact that I had not sooner perceived the object thereupon. I approached it, and touched it with my hand. It was a black cat—a very large one—fully as large as Pluto, and closely resembling him in every respect but one. Pluto had not a white hair upon any portion of his body; but this cat had a large, although indefinite splotch of white, covering nearly the whole region of the breast.

Upon my touching him, he immediately arose, purred loudly, rubbed against my hand, and appeared delighted with my notice. This, then, was the very creature of which I was in search. I at once offered to purchase it of the landlord; but this person made no claim to it—knew nothing of it—had never seen it before.

I continued my caresses, and, when I prepared to go home, the animal evinced a disposition to accompany me. I permitted it to do so; occasionally stooping and patting it as I proceeded. When it reached the house it domesticated itself at once, and became immediately a great favorite with my wife.

For my own part, I soon found a dislike to it arising within me. This was just the reverse of what I had anticipated; but I know not how or why it was—its evident fondness for myself rather disgusted and annoyed. By slow degrees, these feelings of disgust and annoyance rose into the bitterness of hatred. I avoided the creature; a certain sense of shame, and the remembrance of my former deed of cruelty, preventing me from physically abusing it. I did not, for some weeks, strike, or otherwise violently ill use it; but gradually—very gradually—I came to look upon it with unutterable loathing, and to flee silently from its odious presence, as from the breath of a pestilence.

What added, no doubt, to my hatred of the beast, was the discovery, on the morning after I brought it home, that, like Pluto, it also had been deprived of one of its eyes. This circumstance, however, only endeared it to my wife, who, as I have already said, possessed, in a high degree, that humanity of feeling which had once been my distinguishing trait, and the source of many of my simplest and purest pleasures.

With my aversion to this cat, however, its partiality for myself seemed to increase. It followed my footsteps with a pertinacity which it would be difficult to make the reader comprehend. Whenever I sat, it would crouch beneath my chair, or spring upon my knees, covering me with its loathsome caresses. If I arose to walk it would get between my feet and thus nearly throw me down, or, fastening its long and sharp claws in my dress, clamber, in this manner, to my breast. At such times, although I longed to destroy it with a blow, I was yet withheld from so doing, partly by a memory of my former crime, but chiefly—let me confess it at once—by absolute *dread* of the beast.

This dread was not exactly a dread of physical evil—and yet I should be at a loss how otherwise to define it. I am almost ashamed to own—yes, even in this felon's cell, I am almost ashamed to own—that the terror and horror with which the animal inspired me, had been heightened by one of the merest chimæras it would be possible to conceive. My wife had called my attention, more than once, to the character of the mark of white hair, of which I have spoken, and which constituted the sole visible difference between the strange beast and the one I had destroyed. The reader will remember that this mark, although large, had been originally very indefinite; but, by slow degrees—degrees nearly imperceptible, and which for a long time my Reason struggled to reject as fanciful—it had, at length, assumed a rigorous distinctness of outline. It was now the representation of an object that I shudder to name—and for this, above all, I loathed, and dreaded, and would have rid myself of the monster *had I dared*—it was now, I say, the image of a hideous—of a ghastly thing—of the GALLOWS!—oh, mournful and terrible engine of Horror and of Crime—of Agony and of Death!

And now was I indeed wretched beyond the wretchedness of mere Humanity. And *a brute beast*—whose fellow I had contemptuously destroyed—*a brute beast* to work out for *me*—for me a man, fashioned in the image of the High God—so much of insufferable wo! Alas! neither by day nor by night knew I the blessing of Rest any more! During the former the creature left me no moment alone; and, in the latter, I started, hourly, from dreams of unutterable fear, to find the hot breath of *the thing* upon my face, and its vast weight—an incarnate Night-Mare that I had no power to shake off—incumbent eternally upon my *heart!*

Beneath the pressure of torments such as these, the feeble remnant of the good within me succumbed. Evil thoughts became my sole intimates—the darkest and most evil of thoughts. The moodiness of my usual temper increased to hatred of all things and of all mankind; while, from the sudden, frequent, and ungovernable outbursts of a fury to which I now blindly abandoned myself, my uncomplaining wife, alas! was the most usual and the most patient of sufferers.

One day she accompanied me, upon some household errand, into the cellar of the old building which our poverty compelled us to inhabit. The cat followed me down the steep stairs, and, nearly throwing me headlong, exasperated me to madness. Uplifting an axe, and forgetting, in my wrath, the childish dread which had hitherto stayed my hand, I aimed a blow at the animal which, of course, would have proved instantly fatal had it descended as I wished. But this blow was arrested by the hand of my wife. Goaded, by the interference, into a rage more than demoniacal, I withdrew my arm from her grasp and buried the axe in her brain. She fell dead upon the spot, without a groan.

This hideous murder accomplished, I set myself forthwith, and with entire deliberation, to the task of concealing the body. I knew that I could not remove it from the house, either by day or by night, without the risk of being observed by the neighbors. Many projects entered my mind. At one period I thought of cutting the corpse into minute fragments, and

destroying them by fire. At another, I resolved to dig a grave for it in the floor of the cellar. Again, I deliberated about casting it in the well in the yard—about packing it in a box, as if merchandize, with the usual arrangements, and so getting a porter to take it from the house. Finally I hit upon what I considered a far better expedient than either of these. I determined to wall it up in the cellar—as the monks of the middle ages are recorded to have walled up their victims.

For a purpose such as this the cellar was well adapted. Its walls were loosely constructed, and had lately been plastered throughout with a rough plaster, which the dampness of the atmosphere had prevented from hardening. Moreover, in one of the walls was a projection, caused by a false chimney, or fireplace, that had been filled up, and made to resemble the rest of the cellar. I made no doubt that I could readily displace the bricks at this point, insert the corpse, and wall the whole up as before, so that no eye could detect anything suspicious.

And in this calculation I was not deceived. By means of a crow-bar I easily dislodged the bricks, and, having carefully deposited the body against the inner wall, I propped it in that position, while, with little trouble, I re-laid the whole structure as it originally stood. Having procured mortar, sand, and hair, with every possible precaution, I prepared a plaster which could not be distinguished from the old, and with this I very carefully went over the new brick-work. When I had finished, I felt satisfied that all was right. The wall did not present the slightest appearance of having been disturbed. The rubbish on the floor was picked up with the minutest care. I looked around triumphantly, and said to myself—"Here at least, then, my labor has not been in vain."

My next step was to look for the beast which had been the cause of so much wretchedness; for I had, at length, firmly resolved to put it to death. Had I been able to meet with it, at the moment, there could have been no doubt of its fate; but it appeared that the crafty animal had been alarmed at the violence of my previous anger, and forebore to present itself in my present mood. It is impossible to describe, or to imagine, the deep, the blissful sense of relief which the absence of the detested creature occasioned in my bosom. It did not make its appearance during the night—and thus for one night at least, since its introduction into the house, I soundly and tranquilly slept; aye, *slept* even with the burden of murder upon my soul!

The second and the third day passed, and still my tormentor came not. Once again I breathed as a freeman. The monster, in terror, had fled the premises forever! I should behold it no more! My happiness was supreme! The guilt of my dark deed disturbed me but little. Some few inquiries had been made, but these had been readily answered. Even a search had been instituted—but of course nothing was to be discovered. I looked upon my future felicity as secured.

Upon the fourth day of the assassination, a party of the police came, very unexpectedly, into the house, and proceeded again to make rigorous investigation of the premises. Secure, however, in the inscrutability of my place of concealment, I felt no embarrassment whatever. The officers bade me accompany them in their search. They left no nook or corner unexplored. At length, for the third or fourth time, they descended into the cellar. I quivered not in a muscle. My heart beat calmly as that of one who slumbers in innocence. I walked the cellar from end to end. I folded my arms upon my bosom, and roamed easily to and fro. The police were thoroughly satisfied and prepared to depart. The glee at my heart was too strong to be restrained. I burned to say if but one word, by way of triumph, and to render doubly sure their assurance of my guiltlessness.

"Gentlemen," I said at last, as the party

ascended the steps, "I delight to have allayed your suspicions. I wish you all health, and a little more courtesy. By the bye, gentlemen, this—this is a very well constructed house." [In the rabid desire to say something easily, I scarcely knew what I uttered at all.]—"I may say an *excellently* well constructed house. These walls—are you going, gentlemen?—these walls are solidly put together;" and here, through the mere phrenzy of bravado, I rapped heavily, with a cane which I held in my hand, upon that very portion of the brick-work behind which stood the corpse of the wife of my bosom.

But may God shield and deliver me from the fangs of the Arch-Fiend! No sooner had the reverberation of my blows sunk into silence, than I was answered by a voice from within the tomb!—by a cry, at first muffled and broken, like the sobbing of a child, and then quickly swelling into one long, loud, and continuous scream, utterly anomalous and inhuman —a howl—a wailing shriek, half of horror and half of triumph, such as might have arisen only out of hell, conjointly from the throats of the damned in their agony and of the demons that exult in the damnation.

Of my own thoughts it is folly to speak. Swooning, I staggered to the opposite wall. For one instant the party upon the stairs remained motionless, through extremity of terror and of awe. In the next, a dozen stout arms were toiling at the wall. It fell bodily. The corpse, already greatly decayed and clotted with gore, stood erect before the eyes of the spectators. Upon its head, with red extended mouth and solitary eye of fire, sat the hideous beast whose craft had seduced me into murder, and whose informing voice had consigned me to the hangman. I had walled the monster up within the tomb!

THE TELL-TALE HEART

True!—nervous—very, very dreadfully nervous I had been and am; but why *will* you say that I am mad? The disease had sharpened my senses—not destroyed—not dulled them. Above all was the sense of hearing acute. I heard all things in the heaven and in the earth. I heard many things in hell. How, then, am I mad? Hearken! and observe how healthily— how calmly I can tell you the whole story.[1]

It is impossible to say how first the idea entered my brain; but once conceived, it haunted me day and night. Object there was none. Passion there was none. I loved the old man. He had never wronged me. He had never given me insult. For his gold I had no desire. I think it was his eye! yes, it was this! He had the eye of a vulture—a pale blue eye, with a film over it. Whenever it fell upon me, my blood ran cold; and so by degrees—very gradually—I made up my mind to take the life of the old man, and thus rid myself of the eye forever.

Now this is the point. You fancy me mad. Madmen know nothing. But you should have seen me. You should have seen how wisely I proceeded—with what caution—with what foresight—with what dissimulation I went to work! I was never kinder to the old man than during the whole week before I killed him. And every night, about midnight, I turned the latch of his door and opened it—oh so gently! And then, when I had made an opening sufficient for my head, I put in a dark lantern, all closed, closed, so that no light shone out, and then I thrust in my head. Oh, you would have laughed to see how cunningly I thrust it in! I moved it slowly—very, very slowly, so that I might not disturb the old man's sleep. It took me an hour to place my whole head within the opening so far that I could see him as he lay upon his bed. Ha!—would a madman have been so wise as this? And then, when my head was well in the room, I undid the lantern cautiously—oh, so cautiously—cautiously (for the hinges creaked)—I undid it just so much that a single thin ray fell upon the vulture eye.

And this I did for seven long nights— every night just at midnight—but I found the eye always closed; and so it was impossible to do the work; for it was not the old man who vexed me, but his Evil Eye. And every morning, when the day broke, I went boldly into the chamber, and spoke courageously to him, calling him by name in a hearty tone, and inquiring how he had passed the night. So you see he would have been a very profound old man, indeed, to suspect that every night, just at twelve, I looked in upon him while he slept.

Upon the eighth night I was more than usually cautious in opening the door. A watch's minute hand moves more quickly than did mine. Never before that night, had I *felt* the extent of my own powers —of my sagacity. I could scarcely contain my feelings of triumph. To think that there I was, opening the door, little by little, and he not even to dream of my secret deeds or thoughts. I fairly chuckled at the idea; and perhaps he heard me; for he moved on the bed suddenly, as if startled. Now you may think that I drew back—but no. His room was as black as pitch with the thick darkness, (for the shutters were close fastened, through fear of robbers,) and so I knew that he could not see the opening of the door, and I kept pushing it on steadily, steadily.

I had my head in, and was about to open the lantern, when my thumb slipped upon the tin fastening, and the old man sprang up in bed, crying out—"Who's there?"

I kept quite still and said nothing. For a whole hour I did not move a muscle, and in the meantime I did not hear him lie down. He was still sitting up in the bed listening;—just as I have done, night after night, hearkening to the death watches in the wall.

Presently I heard a slight groan, and I knew it was the groan of mortal terror. It was not a groan of pain or of grief—oh, no!—it was the low stifled sound that arises from the bottom of the soul when overcharged with awe. I knew the sound well. Many a night, just at midnight, when all the world slept, it has welled up from my own bosom, deepening, with its dreadful echo, the terrors that distracted me. I say I knew it well. I knew what the old man felt, and pitied him, although I chuckled at heart. I knew that he had been lying awake ever since the first slight noise, when he had turned in the bed. His fears had been ever since growing upon him. He had been trying to fancy them causeless, but could not. He had been saying to himself—"It is nothing but the wind in the chimney—it is only a mouse crossing the floor," or "it is merely a cricket which has made a single chirp." Yes, he had been trying to comfort himself with these suppositions: but he had found all in vain. *All in vain;* because Death, in approaching him had stalked with his black shadow before him, and enveloped the victim. And it was the mournful influence of the unperceived shadow that caused him to feel—although he neither saw nor heard—to *feel* the presence of my head within the room.

When I had waited a long time, very patiently, without hearing him lie down, I resolved to open a little—a very, very little crevice in the lantern. So I opened it—you cannot imagine how stealthily, stealthily—until, at length a simple dim ray, like the thread of the spider, shot from out the crevice and fell full upon the vulture eye.

It was open—wide, wide open—and I grew furious as I gazed upon it. I saw it with perfect distinctness—all a dull blue, with a hideous veil over it that chilled the very marrow in my bones; but I could see nothing else of the old man's face or person: for I had directed the ray as if by instinct, precisely upon the damned spot.

And have I not told you that what you mistake for madness is but over acuteness of the senses?—now, I say, there came to my ears a low, dull, quick sound, such as a watch makes when enveloped in cotton. I knew *that* sound well, too. It was the beating of the old man's heart. It increased my fury, as the beating of a drum stimulates the soldier into courage.

But even yet I refrained and kept still. I scarcely breathed. I held the lantern motionless. I tried how steadily I could maintain the ray upon the eye. Meantime the hellish tattoo of the heart increased. It grew quicker and quicker, and louder and louder every instant. The old man's terror *must* have been extreme! It grew louder, I say, louder every moment!—do you mark me well? I have told you that I am nervous: so I am. And now at the dead hour of the night, amid the dreadful silence of that old house, so strange a noise as this excited me to uncontrollable terror. Yet, for some minutes longer I refrained and stood still. But the beating grew louder, louder! I thought the heart must burst. And now a new anxiety seized me —the sound would be heard by a neighbour! The old man's hour had come! With a loud yell, I threw open the lantern and leaped into the room. He shrieked once —once only. In an instant I dragged him to the floor, and pulled the heavy bed over him. I then smiled gaily, to find the deed so far done. But, for many minutes, the heart beat on with a muffled sound. This, however, did not vex me; it would not be heard through the wall. At length it ceased. The old man was dead. I removed the bed and examined the corpse. Yes, he was stone, stone dead. I placed my hand upon the heart and held it there many minutes. There was no pulsation. He was stone dead. His eye would trouble me no more.

If still you think me mad, you will think so no longer when I describe the wise precautions I took for the concealment of the body. The night waned, and I worked hastily, but in silence. First of all I dismembered the corpse. I cut off the head and the arms and the legs.

I then took up three planks from the flooring of the chamber, and deposited all between the scantlings. I then replaced the boards so cleverly, so cunningly, that no human eye—not even *his*—could have detected any thing wrong. There was nothing to wash out—no stain of any kind —no blood-spot whatever. I had been too wary for that. A tub had caught all—ha! ha!

When I had made an end of these labors, it was four o'clock—still dark as midnight. As the bell sounded the hour, there came a knocking at the street door. I went down to open it with a light heart, —for what had I *now* to fear? There entered three men, who introduced themselves, with perfect suavity, as officers of the police. A shriek had been heard by a neighbour during the night; suspicion of foul play had been aroused; information had been lodged at the police office, and they (the officers) had been deputed to search the premises.

I smiled,—for *what* had I to fear? I bade the gentlemen welcome. The shriek, I said, was my own in a dream. The old man, I mentioned, was absent in the country. I took my visitors all over the house. I bade them search—search *well*. I led them, at length, to *his* chamber. I showed them his treasures, secure, undisturbed. In the enthusiasm of my confidence, I brought chairs into the room, and desired them *here* to rest from their fatigues, while I myself, in the wild audacity of my perfect triumph, placed my own seat upon the very spot beneath which reposed the corpse of the victim.

The officers were satisfied. My *manner* had convinced them. I was singularly at ease. They sat, and while I answered cheerily, they chatted of familiar things. But, ere long, I felt myself getting pale and wished them gone. My head ached, and I fancied a ringing in my ears: but still they sat and still chatted. The ringing became more distinct:—it continued and became more distinct: I talked more freely to get rid of the feeling: but it continued and gained definiteness—until, at length, I found that the noise was *not* within my ears.

No doubt I now grew *very* pale;—but I talked more fluently, and with a heightened voice. Yet the sound increased—and what could I do? It was *a low, dull, quick sound—much such a sound as a watch makes when enveloped in cotton.* I gasped for breath—and yet the officers heard it not. I talked more quickly—more vehemently; but the noise steadily increased. I arose and argued about trifles, in a high key and with violent gesticulations; but the noise steadily increased. Why *would* they not be gone? I paced the floor to and fro with heavy strides, as if excited to fury by the observations of the men—but the noise steadily increased. Oh God! what *could* I do? I foamed—I raved—I swore! I swung the chair upon which I had been sitting, and grated it upon the boards, but the noise arose over all and continually increased. It grew louder—louder—*louder!* And still the men chatted pleasantly, and smiled. Was it possible they heard not? Almighty God!—no, no! They heard!— they suspected!—they *knew!*—they were making a mockery of my horror!—this I thought, and this I think. But anything was better than this agony! Anything was more tolerable than this derision! I could bear those hypocritical smiles no longer! I felt that I must scream or die! and now —again!—hark! louder! louder! louder! *louder!*

"Villains!" I shrieked, "dissemble no more! I admit the deed!—tear up the planks! here, here!—it is the beating of his hideous heart!"

HOP-FROG
or
THE EIGHT CHAINED OURANG-OUTANGS[1]

I never knew any one so keenly alive to a joke as the king was. He seemed to live only for joking. To tell a good story of the joke kind, and to tell it well, was the surest road to his favor. Thus it happened that his seven ministers were all noted for their accomplishments as jokers. They all took after the king, too, in being large, corpulent, oily men, as well as inimitable jokers. Whether people grow fat by joking, or whether there is something in fat itself which predisposes to a joke, I have never been quite able to determine; but certain it is that a lean joker is a *rara avis in terris.*[2]

About the refinements, or, as he called them, the "ghosts" of wit, the king troubled himself very little. He had an especial admiration for *breadth* in a jest, and would often put up with *length,* for the sake of it. Over-niceties wearied him. He would have preferred Rabelais's "Gargantua," to the "Zadig" of Voltaire:[3] and, upon the whole, practical jokes suited his taste far better than verbal ones.

At the date of my narrative, professing jesters had not altogether gone out of fashion at court.[4] Several of the great continental "powers" still retained their "fools," who wore motley, with caps and bells, and who were expected to be always ready with sharp witticisms, at a moment's notice, in consideration of the crumbs that fell from the royal table.

Our king, as a matter of course, retained his "fool." The fact is, he *required* something in the way of folly—if only to counterbalance the heavy wisdom of the seven wise men who were his ministers—not to mention himself.

His fool, or professional jester, was not *only* a fool, however. His value was trebled in the eyes of the king, by the fact of his being also a dwarf and a cripple. Dwarfs were as common at court, in those days, as fools; and many monarchs would have found it difficult to get through their days (days are rather longer at court than elsewhere) without both a jester to laugh *with,* and a dwarf to laugh *at.* But, as I have already observed, your jesters, in ninety-nine cases out of a hundred, are fat, round and unwieldy—so that it was no small source of self-gratulation with our king that, in Hop-Frog (this was the fool's name,) he possessed a triplicate treasure in one person.

I believe the name "Hop-Frog" was *not* given to the dwarf by his sponsors at baptism, but it was conferred upon him, by general consent of the seven ministers, on account of his inability to walk as other men do. In fact, Hop-Frog could only get along by a sort of interjectional gait—something between a leap and a wriggle—a movement that afforded illimitable amusement, and of course consolation, to the king, for (notwithstanding the protuberance of his stomach and a constitutional swelling of the head) the king, by his whole court, was accounted a capital figure.

But although Hop-Frog, through the distortion of his legs, could move only with great pain and difficulty along a road or floor, the prodigious muscular power which nature seemed to have bestowed upon his arms, by way of compensation for deficiency in the lower limbs, enabled him to perform many feats of wonderful dexterity, where trees or ropes were in question, or anything else to climb. At such exercises he certainly much more resembled a squirrel, or a small monkey, than a frog.

I am not able to say, with precision, from what country Hop-Frog originally came. It was from some barbarous region, however, that no person ever heard of—a vast distance from the court of our king. Hop-Frog, and a young girl very little less dwarfish than himself (although of exquisite proportions, and a marvellous dancer,) had been forcibly carried off from their respective homes in adjoining provinces, and sent as presents to the king, by one of his ever-victorious generals.

Under these circumstances, it is not to be wondered at that a close intimacy arose between the two little captives. Indeed, they soon became sworn friends. Hop-Frog, who, although he made a great deal of sport, was by no means popular, had it not in his power to render Trippetta many services; but *she,* on account of her grace and exquisite beauty (although a dwarf,) was universally admired and petted: so she possessed much influence; and never failed to use it, whenever she could, for the benefit of Hop-Frog.

On some grand state occasion—I forget what—the king determined to have a masquerade; and whenever a masquerade, or anything of that kind, occurred at our court, then the talents both of Hop-Frog and Trippetta were sure to be called in play. Hop-Frog, in especial, was so inventive in the way of getting up pageants, suggesting novel characters, and arranging costume, for masked balls, that nothing could be done, it seems, without his assistance.

The night appointed for the *fête* had arrived. A gorgeous hall had been fitted up, under Trippetta's eye, with every kind of device which could possibly give *éclat* to a masquerade. The whole court was in a fever of expectation. As for costumes and characters, it might well be supposed that everybody had come to a decision on such points. Many had made up their minds (as to what *rôles* they should assume) a week, or even a month, in advance; and, in fact, there was not a particle of indecision anywhere—except in the case of the king and his seven ministers. Why *they* hesitated I never could tell, unless they did it by way of a joke. More probably, they found it difficult, on account of being so fat, to make up their minds. At all events, time flew; and, as a last resource, they sent for Trippetta and Hop-Frog.

When the two little friends obeyed the summons of the king, they found him sitting at his wine with the seven members of his cabinet council; but the monarch appeared to be in a very ill humor. He knew that Hop-Frog was not fond of wine; for it excited the poor cripple almost to madness; and madness is no comfortable feeling.[5] But the king loved his practical jokes, and took pleasure in forcing Hop-Frog to drink and (as the king called it) "to be merry."

"Come here, Hop-Frog," said he, as the jester and his friend entered the room;

"swallow this bumper to the health of your absent friends [here Hop-Frog sighed,] and then let us have the benefit of your invention. We want characters—*characters*, man—something novel—out of the way. We are wearied with this everlasting sameness. Come drink! the wine will brighten your wits."

Hop-Frog endeavoured, as usual, to get up a jest in reply to these advances from the king; but the effort was too much. It happened to be the poor dwarf's birthday, and the command to drink to his "absent friends" forced the tears to his eyes. Many large, bitter drops fell into the goblet as he took it, humbly, from the hand of the tyrant.

"Ah! ha! ha! ha!" roared the latter, as the dwarf reluctantly drained the beaker. "See what a glass of good wine can do! Why, your eyes are shining already!"

Poor fellow, his large eyes *gleamed*, rather than shone; for the effect of wine on his excitable brain was not more powerful than instantaneous. He placed the goblet nervously on the table, and looked round upon the company with a half-insane stare. They all seemed highly amused at the success of the king's "*joke*."

"And now to business," said the prime minister, a *very* fat man.

"Yes," said the king; "come, Hop-Frog, lend us your assistance. Characters, my fine fellow; we stand in need of characters —all of us—ha! ha! ha!" and as this was seriously meant for a joke, his laugh was chorused by the seven.

Hop-Frog also laughed, although feebly and somewhat vacantly.

"Come, come," said the king, impatiently, "have you nothing to suggest?"

"I am endeavouring to think of something *novel*," replied the dwarf, abstractedly, for he was quite bewildered by the wine.

"Endeavouring!" cried the tyrant, fiercely; "what do you mean by *that*? Ah, I perceive. You are sulky, and want more wine. Here, drink this!" and he poured out another goblet full and offered it to the cripple, who merely gazed at it, gasping for breath.

"Drink, I say!" shouted the monster, "or by the fiends—"

The dwarf hesitated. The king grew purple with rage. The courtiers smirked. Trippetta, pale as a corpse, advanced to the monarch's seat, and, falling on her knees before him, implored him to spare her friend.

The tyrant regarded her, for some moments, in evident wonder at her audacity. He seemed quite at a loss what to do or say—how most becomingly to express his indignation. At last, without uttering a syllable, he pushed her violently from him, and threw the contents of the brimming goblet in her face.

The poor girl got up as best she could, and, not daring even to sigh, resumed her position at the foot of the table.

There was a dead silence for about a half a minute, during which the falling of a leaf, or of a feather might have been heard. It was interrupted by a low, but harsh and protracted *grating* sound which seemed to come at once from every corner of the room.

"What—what—*what* are you making that noise for?" demanded the king, turning furiously to the dwarf.

The latter seemed to have recovered, in great measure from his intoxication, and looking fixedly but quietly into the tyrant's face, merely ejaculated:

"I—I? How could it have been me?"

"The sound appeared to come from without," observed one of the courtiers. "I fancy it was the parrot at the window, whetting his bill upon his cage-wires."

"True," replied the monarch, as if much relieved by the suggestion; "but, on the honour of a knight, I could have sworn that it was the gritting of this vagabond's teeth."[6]

Hereupon the dwarf laughed (the king was too confirmed a joker to object to any one's laughing), and displayed a set of large, powerful, and very repulsive teeth. Moreover, he avowed his perfect willingness to swallow as much wine as desired. The monarch was pacified; and having drained another bumper with no very perceptible ill effect, Hop-Frog entered at once, and with spirit, into the plans for the masquerade.

"I cannot tell what was the association of idea," observed he, very tranquilly, and as if he had never tasted wine in his life, "but *just after* your majesty had struck the girl and thrown the wine in her face —*just after* your majesty had done this, and while the parrot was making that odd noise outside the window, there came into my mind a capital diversion—one of my own country frolics[7]—often enacted among us, at our masquerades: but here it will be new altogether. Unfortunately, however, it requires a company of eight persons, and—"

"Here we *are!*" cried the king, laughing at his acute discovery of the coincidence; "eight to a fraction—I and my seven ministers. Come! what is the diversion?"

"We call it," replied the cripple, "the Eight Chained Ourang-Outangs, and it really is excellent sport if well enacted."

"*We* will enact it," remarked the king, drawing himself up, and lowering his eyelids.

"The beauty of the game," continued Hop-Frog, "lies in the fright it occasions among the women."

"Capital!" roared in chorus the monarch and his ministry.

"I will equip you as ourang-outangs," proceeded the dwarf; "leave all that to me. The resemblance shall be so striking, that the company of masqueraders will take you for real beasts—and, of course, they will be as much terrified as astonished."

"O, this is exquisite!" exclaimed the king. "Hop-Frog! I will make a man of you."

"The chains are for the purpose of increasing the confusion by their jangling. You are supposed to have escaped, *en masse*, from your keepers. Your majesty cannot conceive the *effect* produced at a masquerade, by eight chained ourang-outangs, imagined to be real ones by most of the company; and rushing in with savage cries, among the crowd of delicately and gorgeously habited men and women. The *contrast* is inimitable."

"It *must* be," said the king: and the council arose hurriedly (as it was growing late), to put in execution the scheme of Hop-Frog.

His mode of equipping the party as ourang-outangs was very simple, but effective enough for his purposes. The animals in question had, at the epoch of my story, very rarely been seen in any part of the civilized world; and as the imitations made by the dwarf were sufficiently beast-like and more than sufficiently hideous, their truthfulness to nature was thus thought to be secured.

The king and his ministers were first encased in tight-fitting stockinet[8] shirts and drawers. They were then saturated with tar. At this stage of the process, some one of the party suggested feathers; but the suggestion was at once overruled by the dwarf, who soon convinced the eight, by ocular demonstration, that the hair of such a brute as the ourang-outang was much more efficiently represented by *flax*. A thick coating of the latter was accordingly plastered upon the coating of tar. A long chain was now procured. First, it was passed about the waist of the king, *and tied*; then about another of the party, and also tied; then about all successively, in the same manner. When this chaining arrangement was complete, and the party stood as far apart from each other as possible, they formed a circle; and to make all things appear natural, Hop-Frog passed the residue of the chain, in two diameters, at right angles, across the circle, after the fashion adopted, at the present day, by those who capture Chimpanzees, or other large apes, in Borneo.

The grand saloon in which the masquerade was to take place, was a circular room, very lofty, and receiving the light of the sun only through a single window at top. At night (the season for which the apartment was especially designed,) it was illuminated principally by a large chandelier, depending by a chain from the centre of the sky-light, and lowered, or elevated, by means of a counter-balance as usual; but (in order not to look unsightly) this latter passed outside the cupola and over the roof.

The arrangements of the room had been left to Trippetta's superintendence; but, in some particulars, it seems, she had been guided by the calmer judgment of her friend the dwarf. At his suggestion it was that, on this occasion, the chandelier was removed. Its waxen drippings (which, in weather so warm, it was quite impossible to prevent,) would have been seriously detrimental to the rich dresses of the guests, who, on account of the crowded state of the saloon, could not *all* be expected to keep from out its centre—that is to say, from under the chandelier. Additional sconces were set in various parts of the hall, out of the way; and a flambeau, emitting sweet odor, was placed in the right hand of each of the Caryatides[9] that stood against the wall—some fifty or sixty altogether.

The eight ourang-outangs, taking Hop-Frog's advice, waited patiently until midnight (when the room was thoroughly filled with masqueraders) before making their appearance. No sooner had the clock ceased striking, however, than they rushed, or rather rolled in, all together—for the impediment of their chains caused most of the party to fall, and all to stumble as they entered.

The excitement among the masqueraders was prodigious, and filled the heart of the king with glee. As had been anticipated, there were not a few of the guests who supposed the ferocious-looking creatures to be beasts of *some* kind in reality, if not precisely ourang-outangs. Many of the women swooned with affright; and had not the king taken precaution to exclude all weapons from the saloon, his party might soon have expiated their frolic in their blood. As it was, a general rush was made for the doors; but the king had ordered them to be locked immediately upon his entrance; and, at the dwarf's suggestion, the keys had been deposited with *him*.

While the tumult was at its height, and each masquerader attentive only to his own safety—(for, in fact, there was much *real* danger from the pressure of the excited crowd,)—the chain by which the chandelier ordinarily hung, and which had been drawn up on its removal, might have been seen very gradually to descend, until its hooked extremity came within three feet of the floor.

Soon after this, the king and his seven friends, having reeled about the hall in all directions, found themselves, at length, in its centre, and, of course, in immediate contact with the chain. While they were thus situated, the dwarf, who had followed closely at their heels, inciting them to keep up the commotion, took hold of their own chain at the intersection of the two portions which crossed the circle diametrically and at right angles. Here, with the rapidity of thought, he inserted the hook from which the chandelier had been wont to depend; and, in an instant, by some unseen agency, the chandelier-chain was drawn so far upward as to take the hook out of reach, and, as an inevitable consequence, to drag the ourang-outangs together in close connection, and face to face.

The masqueraders, by this time, had recovered, in some measure, from their alarm; and beginning to regard the whole matter as a well-contrived pleasantry, set up a loud shout of laughter at the predicament of the apes.

"Leave them to *me!*" now screamed Hop-Frog, his shrill voice making itself easily heard through all the din. "Leave them to *me*. I fancy *I* know them. If I can only get a good look at them, *I* can soon tell who they are."

Here, scrambling over the heads of the crowd, he managed to get to the wall; when, seizing a flambeau from one of the Caryatides, he returned, as he went, to the centre of the room—leaped, with the agility of a monkey, upon the king's head —and thence clambered a few feet up the chain—holding down the torch to examine the group of ourang-outangs, and still screaming, "I shall soon find out who they are!"

And now, while the whole assembly (the apes included) were convulsed with laughter, the jester suddenly uttered a shrill whistle; when the chain flew violently up for about thirty feet—dragging with it the dismayed and struggling ourang-outangs, and leaving them suspended in mid-air between the sky-light and the floor. Hop-Frog, clinging to the chain as it rose, still maintained his relative position in respect to the eight maskers, and still (as if nothing were the matter) continued to thrust his torch down towards them, as though endeavoring to discover who they were.

So thoroughly astonished were the whole company at this ascent, that a dead silence, of about a minute's duration, ensued. It was broken by just such a low, harsh, *grating* sound, as had before attracted the attention of the king and his councillors, when the former threw the wine in the face of Trippeta. But, on the present occasion, there could be no question as to *whence* the sound issued. It came from the fang-like teeth of the dwarf, who ground them and gnashed them as he foamed at the mouth, and glared, with an expression of maniacal rage, into the upturned countenances of the king and his seven companions.

"Ah, ha!" said at length the infuriated jester. "Ah, ha! I begin to see who these people *are*, now!" Here, pretending to scrutinize the king more closely, he held the flambeau to the flaxen coat which enveloped him, and which instantly burst into a sheet of vivid flame. In less than half a minute the whole eight ourang-outangs were blazing fiercely, amid the shrieks of the multitude who gazed at them from below, horror-stricken, and without the power to render them the slightest assistance.

At length the flames, suddenly increasing in virulence, forced the jester to climb higher up the chain, to be out of their reach; and, as he made this movement, the crowd again sank, for a brief instant, into silence. The dwarf seized his opportunity, and once more spoke:

"I now see *distinctly*," he said, "what manner of people these maskers are. They are a great king and his seven privy-councillors—a king who does not scruple to strike a defenceless girl, and his seven councillors who abet him in the outrage. As for myself, I am simply Hop-Frog, the jester—and *this is my last jest*."

Owing to the high combustibility of both the flax and the tar to which it adhered, the dwarf had scarcely made an end of his brief speech before the work of vengeance was complete. The eight corpses swung in their chains, a fetid, blackened, hideous, and indistinguishable mass. The cripple hurled his torch at them, clambered leisurely to the ceiling, and disappeared through the sky-light.

It is supposed that Trippetta, stationed on the roof of the saloon, had been the accomplice of her friend in his fiery revenge, and that, together, they effected their escape to their own country: for neither was seen again.

THE IMP OF THE PERVERSE

In the consideration of the faculties and impulses—of the *prima mobilia* of the human soul, the phrenologists have failed to make room for a propensity which, although obviously existing as a radical, primitive, irreducible sentiment, has been equally overlooked by all the moralists who have preceded them. In the pure arrogance of the reason, we have all overlooked it. We have suffered its existence to escape our senses, solely through want of belief—of faith;—whether it be faith in Revelation, or faith in the Kabbala. The idea of it has never occurred to us, simply because of its supererogation. We saw no *need* of the impulse—for the propensity. We could not perceive its necessity. We could not understand, that is to say, we could not have understood, had the notion of this *primum mobile* ever obtruded itself;—we could not have understood in what manner it might be made to further the objects of humanity, either temporal or eternal. It cannot be denied that phrenology, and in good measure, all metaphysicianism have been concocted *à priori*. The intellectual or logical man, rather than the understanding or observant man, set himself to imagine designs—to dictate purposes to God. Having thus fathomed to his satisfaction the intentions of Jehovah, out of these intentions he built his innumerable systems of mind. In the matter of phrenology, for example, we first determined, naturally enough, that it was the design of the Deity that man should eat. We then assigned to man an organ of alimentiveness, and this organ is the scourge with which the Deity compels man, will-I, nill-I, into eating. Secondly, having settled it to be God's will that man should continue his species, we discovered an organ of amativeness, forthwith. And so with combativeness, with ideality, with causality, with constructiveness,—so, in short, with every organ, whether representing a propensity, a moral sentiment, or a faculty of the pure intellect. And in these arrangements of the *principia* of human action, the Spurzheimites,[1] whether right or wrong, in part, or upon the whole, have but followed, in principle, the footsteps of their predecessors; deducing and establishing every thing from the preconceived destiny of man, and upon the ground of the objects of his Creator.

It would have been wiser, it would have been safer to classify, (if classify we must,) upon the basis of what man usually or occasionally did, and was always occasionally doing, rather than upon the basis of what we took it for granted the

Deity intended him to do. If we cannot comprehend God in his visible works, how then in his inconceivable thoughts, that call the works into being! If we cannot understand him in his objective creatures, how then in his substantive moods and phases of creation?

Induction, *à posteriori*, would have brought phrenology to admit, as an innate and primitive principle of human action, a paradoxical something, which we may call *perverseness*, for want of a more characteristic term. In the sense I intend, it is, in fact, a *mobile* without motive, a motive not *motivirt*.[2] Through its promptings we act without comprehensible object; or, if this shall be understood as a contradiction in terms, we may so far modify the proposition as to say, that through its promptings we act, for the reason that we should *not*. In theory, no reason can be more unreasonable; but, in fact, there is none more strong. With certain minds, under certain conditions, it becomes absolutely irresistible. I am not more certain that I breathe, than that the assurance of the wrong or error of any action is often the one unconquerable *force* which impels us, and alone impels us to its prosecution. Nor will this overwhelming tendency to do wrong for the wrong's sake, admit of analysis, or resolution into ulterior elements. It is a radical, a primitive impulse—elementary. It will be said, I am aware, that when we persist in acts because we feel we should *not* persist in them, our conduct is but a modification of that which ordinarily springs from the *combativeness* of phrenology. But a glance will show the fallacy of this idea. The phrenological combativeness has for its essence, the necessity of self-defence. It is our safeguard against injury. Its principle regards our well-being; and thus the desire to be well, is excited simultaneously with its development. It follows, that the desire to be well must be excited simultaneously with any principle which shall be merely a modification of combativeness, but in the case of that something which I term

perverseness, the desire to be well is not only not aroused, but a strongly antagonistical sentiment exists.

An appeal to one's own heart is, after all, the best reply to the sophistry just noticed. No one who trustingly consults and thoroughly questions his own soul, will be disposed to deny the entire radicalness of the propensity in question. It is not more incomprehensible than distinctive. There lives no man who at some period has not been tormented, for example, by an earnest desire to tantalize a listener by circumlocution. The speaker is aware that he displeases; he has every intention to please; he is usually curt, precise, and clear; the most laconic and luminous language is struggling for utterance upon his tongue; it is only with difficulty that he restrains himself from giving it flow; he dreads and deprecates the anger of him whom he addresses; yet, the thought strikes him, that by certain involutions and parentheses, this anger may be engendered. That single thought is enough. The impulse increases to a wish, the wish to a desire, the desire to an uncontrollable longing, and the longing, (to the deep regret and mortification of the speaker, and in defiance of all consequences,) is indulged.[3]

We have a task before us which must be speedily performed. We know that it will be ruinous to make delay. The most important crisis of our life calls, trumpet-tongued, for immediate energy and action. We glow, we are consumed with eagerness to commence the work, with the anticipation of whose glorious result our whole souls are on fire. It must, it shall be undertaken to-day, and yet we put it off until to-morrow; and why? There is no answer, except that we feel *perverse*, using the word with no comprehension of the principle. To-morrow arrives, and with it a more impatient anxiety to do our duty, but with this very increase of anxiety arrives, also, a nameless, a positively fearful, because unfathomable, craving for delay. This craving gathers strength as the moments fly. The last hour for action is at hand. We tremble with the violence of the conflict within us,—of the definite with the indefinite—of the substance with the shadow. But, if the contest have proceeded thus far, it is the shadow which prevails,—we struggle in vain. The clock strikes, and is the knell of our welfare. At the same time, it is the chanticleer-note to the ghost that has so long overawed us. It flies—it disappears—we are free. The old energy returns. We will labor *now*. Alas, it is *too late!*

We stand upon the brink of a precipice. We peer into the abyss—we grow sick and dizzy. Our first impulse is to shrink from the danger. Unaccountably we remain. By slow degrees our sickness, and dizziness, and horror, become merged in a cloud of unnameable feeling. By gradations, still more imperceptible, this cloud assumes shape, as did the vapor from the bottle out of which arose the genius[4] in the Arabian Nights. But out of this *our* cloud upon the precipice's edge, there grows into palpability, a shape, far more terrible than any genius, or any demon of a tale, and yet it is but a thought, although a fearful one, and one which chills the very marrow of our bones with the fierceness of the delight of its horror. It is merely the idea of what would be our sensations during the sweeping precipitancy of a fall from such a height. And this fall—this rushing annihilation—for the very reason that it involves that one most ghastly and loathsome of all the most ghastly and loathsome images of death and suffering which have ever presented themselves to our imagination—for this very cause do we now the most vividly desire it. And because our reason violently deters us from the brink, *therefore,* do we the most impetuously approach it. There is no passion in nature so demoniacally impatient, as that of him, who shuddering upon the edge of a precipice, thus meditates a plunge. To indulge for a moment, in any attempt at *thought,* is to be inevitably lost; for reflection but urges us to forbear,

and *therefore* it is, I say, that we *cannot.* If there be no friendly arm to check us, or if we fail in a sudden effort to prostrate ourselves backward from the abyss, we plunge, and are destroyed.

Examine these and similar actions as we will, we shall find them resulting solely from the spirit of the *Perverse.* We perpetrate them merely because we feel that we should *not.* Beyond or behind this, there is no intelligible principle: and we might, indeed, deem this perverseness a direct instigation of the arch-fiend, were it not occasionally known to operate in furtherance of good.

I have said thus much, that in some measure I may answer your question— that I may explain to you why I am here —that I may assign to you something that shall have at least the faint aspect of a cause for my wearing these fetters, and for my tenanting this cell of the condemned. Had I not been thus prolix, you might either have misunderstood me altogether, or, with the rabble, have fancied me mad. As it is, you will easily perceive that I am one of the many uncounted victims of the Imp of the Perverse.

It is impossible that any deed could have been wrought with a more thorough deliberation. For weeks, for months, I pondered upon the means of the murder. I rejected a thousand schemes, because their accomplishment involved a *chance* of detection. At length, in reading some French memoirs, I found an account of a nearly fatal illness that occurred to Madam Pilau,[5] through the agency of a candle accidentally poisoned. The idea struck my fancy at once. I knew my victim's habit of reading in bed. I knew, too, that his apartment was narrow and ill-ventilated. But I need not vex you with impertinent details. I need not describe the easy artifices by which I substituted, in his bedroom candle-stand, a wax-light of my own making, for the one which I there found. The next morning he was discovered dead in his bed, and the coroner's verdict was, —"Death by the visitation of God."

Having inherited his estate, all went well with me for years. The idea of detection never once entered my brain. Of the remains of the fatal taper, I had myself carefully disposed. I had left no shadow of a clue by which it would be possible to convict, or even to suspect, me of the crime. It is inconceivable how rich a sentiment of satisfaction arose in my bosom as I reflected upon my absolute security. For a very long period of time, I was accustomed to revel in this sentiment. It afforded me more real delight than all the mere worldly advantages accruing from my sin. But there arrived at length an epoch, from which the pleasurable feeling grew, by scarcely perceptible gradations, into a haunting and harassing thought. It harassed because it haunted. I could scarcely get rid of it for an instant. It is quite a common thing to be thus annoyed with the ringing in our ears, or rather in our memories, of the burthen of some ordinary song, or some unimpressive snatches from an opera. Nor will we be the less tormented if the song itself be good, or the opera air meritorious. In this manner, at last, I would perpetually catch myself pondering upon my security, and repeating, in a low under-tone, the phrase, "I am safe."

One day, while sauntering along the streets, I arrested myself in the act of murmuring, half aloud, these customary syllables. In a fit of petulance, I re-modelled them thus:—"I am safe—I am safe —yes—if I be not fool enough to make open confession!"

No sooner had I spoken these words, than I felt an icy chill creep to my heart. I had had some experience in these fits of perversity, (whose nature I have been at some trouble to explain,) and I remembered well, that in no instance, I had successfully resisted their attacks. And now my own casual self-suggestion, that I might possibly be fool enough to confess the murder of which I had been guilty, confronted me, as if the very ghost of him

whom I had murdered—and beckoned me on to death.

At first, I made an effort to shake off this nightmare of the soul. I walked vigorously—faster—still faster—at length I ran. I felt a maddening desire to shriek aloud. Every succeeding wave of thought overwhelmed me with new terror, for, alas! I well, too well, understood that to *think*, in my situation, was to be lost. I still quickened my pace. I bounded like a madman through the crowded thoroughfares. At length, the populace took the alarm, and pursued me. I felt *then* the consummation of my fate. Could I have torn out my tongue, I would have done it—but a rough voice resounded in my ears—a rougher grasp seized me by the shoulder. I turned—I gasped for breath. For a moment, I experienced all the pangs of suffocation; I became blind, and deaf, and giddy; and then, some invisible fiend, I thought, struck me with his broad palm upon the back. The long-imprisoned secret burst forth from my soul.[6]

They say that I spoke with a distinct enunciation, but with marked emphasis and passionate hurry, as if in dread of interruption before concluding the brief but pregnant sentences that consigned me to the hangman and to hell.

Having related all that was necessary for the fullest judicial conviction. I fell prostrate in a swoon.

But why shall I say more? To-day I wear these chains, and am *here!* To-morrow I shall be fetterless!—*but where?*

WILLIAM WILSON

What say of it? what say [of]
CONSCIENCE *grim,*
That spectre in my path?
Chamberlayne's
Pharronida[1]

Let me call myself, for the present, William Wilson. The fair page now lying before me need not be sullied with my real appellation. This has been already too much an object for the scorn—for the horror—for the detestation of my race. To the uttermost regions of the globe have not the indignant winds bruited its unparalleled infamy? Oh, outcast of all outcasts most abandoned!—to the earth art thou not forever dead? to its honors, to its flowers, to its golden aspirations?—and a cloud, dense, dismal, and limitless, does it not hang eternally between thy hopes and heaven?

I would not, if I could, here or to-day, embody a record of my later years of unspeakable misery, and unpardonable crime. This epoch—these later years—took unto themselves a sudden elevation in turpitude, whose origin alone it is my present purpose to assign. Men usually grow base by degrees. From me, in an instant, all virtue dropped bodily as a mantle. From comparatively trivial wickedness I passed, with the stride of a giant, into more than the enormities of an Elah-Gabalus.[2] What chance—what one event brought this evil thing to pass, bear with me while I relate. Death approaches; and the shadow which foreruns him has thrown a softening influence over my spirit. I long, in passing through the dim valley, for the sympathy—I had nearly said for the pity—of my fellow men. I would fain have them believe that I have been, in some measure, the slave of circumstances beyond human control. I would wish them to seek out for me, in the details I am about to give, some little oasis of *fatality* amid a wilderness of error. I would have them allow—what they cannot refrain from allowing—that, although temptation may have erewhile existed as great, man was never *thus*, at least, tempted before—certainly, never *thus* fell. And is it therefore that he has never thus suffered? Have I not indeed been living in a dream? And am I not now dying a victim to the horror and the mystery of the wildest of all sublunary visions?

I am the descendant of a race whose imaginative and easily excitable temperament has at all times rendered them re-markable; and, in my earliest infancy, I gave evidence of having fully inherited the family character. As I advanced in years it was more strongly developed; becoming, for many reasons, a cause of serious disquietude to my friends, and of positive injury to myself. I grew self-willed, addicted to the wildest caprices, and a prey to the most ungovernable passions. Weak-minded, and beset with constitutional infirmities akin to my own, my parents could do but little to check the evil propensities which distinguished me. Some feeble and ill-directed efforts resulted in complete failure on their part, and, of course, in total triumph on mine. Thenceforward my voice was a household law; and at an age when few children have abandoned their leading-strings, I was left to the guidance of my own will, and became, in all but name, the master of my own actions.

My earliest recollections of a school-life, are connected with a large, rambling, Elizabethan house, in a misty-looking village of England, where were a vast number of gigantic and gnarled trees, and where all the houses were excessively ancient. In truth, it was a dream-like and spirit-soothing place, that venerable old town. At this moment, in fancy, I feel the refreshing chilliness of its deeply-shadowed avenues, inhale the fragrance of its thousand shrubberies, and thrill anew with undefinable delight, at the deep hollow note of the church-bell, breaking, each hour, with sullen and sudden roar, upon the stillness of the dusky atmosphere in which the fretted Gothic steeple lay imbedded and asleep.

It gives me, perhaps, as much of pleasure as I can now in any manner experience, to dwell upon minute recollections of the school and its concerns. Steeped in misery as I am—misery, alas! only too real—I shall be pardoned for seeking relief, however slight and temporary, in the weakness of a few rambling details. These, moreover, utterly trivial, and even ridiculous in themselves, assume, to my fancy, adventitious importance, as connected with a period and a locality when and where I recognise the first ambiguous monitions of the destiny which afterwards so fully overshadowed me. Let me then remember.

The house, I have said, was old and irregular. The grounds were extensive, and a high and solid brick wall, topped with a bed of mortar and broken glass, encompassed the whole. This prison-like rampart formed the limit of our domain; beyond it we saw but thrice a week—once every Saturday afternoon, when, attended by two ushers, we were permitted to take brief walks in a body through some of the neighbouring fields—and twice during Sunday, when we were paraded in the same formal manner to the morning and evening service in the one church of the village. Of this church the principal of our school was pastor. With how deep a spirit of wonder and perplexity was I wont to regard him from our remote pew in the gallery, as, with step solemn and slow, he ascended the pulpit! This reverend man, with countenance so demurely benign, with robes so glossy and so clerically flowing, with wig so minutely powdered, so rigid and so vast,—could this be he who, of late, with sour visage, and in snuffy habiliments, administered, ferule in hand, the Draconian laws of the academy? Oh, gigantic paradox, too utterly monstrous for solution!

At an angle of the ponderous wall frowned a more ponderous gate. It was riveted and studded with iron bolts, and surmounted with jagged iron spikes. What impressions of deep awe did it inspire! It was never opened save for the three periodical egressions and ingressions already mentioned; then, in every creak of its mighty hinges, we found a plenitude of mystery—a world of matter for solemn remark, or for more solemn meditation.

The extensive enclosure was irregular in form, having many capacious recesses. Of these, three or four of the largest constituted the play-ground. It was level, and covered with fine hard gravel. I well remember it had no trees, nor benches, nor anything similar within it. Of course it was in the rear of the house. In front lay a small parterre, planted with box and other shrubs; but through this sacred division we passed only upon rare occasions indeed—such as a first advent to school or final departure thence, or perhaps, when a parent or friend having called for us, we joyfully took our way home for the Christmas or Midsummer holy-days.

But the house!—how quaint an old building was this!—to me how veritably a palace of enchantment! There was really no end to its windings—to its incomprehensible subdivisions. It was difficult, at any given time, to say with certainty upon which of its two stories one happened to be. From each room to every other there were sure to be found three or four steps either in ascent or descent. Then the lateral branches were innumerable—inconceivable—and so returning in upon themselves, that our most exact ideas in regard to the whole mansion were not very far different from those with which we pondered upon infinity. During the five years of my residence here, I was never able to ascertain with precision, in what remote locality lay the little sleeping apartment assigned to myself and some eighteen or twenty other scholars.

The school-room was the largest in the house—I could not help thinking, in the world. It was very long, narrow, and dismally low, with pointed Gothic windows and a ceiling of oak. In a remote and terror-inspiring angle was a square enclosure of eight or ten feet, comprising the *sanctum*, "during hours," of our principal, the Reverend Dr. Bransby. It was a solid structure, with massy door, sooner than open which in the absence of the "Dominie," we would all have willingly perished by the *peine forte et dure*.[3] In other angles were two other similar boxes, far less reverenced, indeed, but still greatly matters of awe. One of these was the pulpit of the "classical" usher, one of the

"English and mathematical." Interspersed about the room, crossing and recrossing in endless irregularity, were innumerable benches and desks, black, ancient, and time-worn, piled desperately with much-bethumbed books, and so beseamed with initial letters, names at full length, grotesque figures, and other multiplied efforts of the knife, as to have entirely lost what little of original form might have been their portion in days long departed. A huge bucket with water stood at one extremity of the room, and a clock of stupendous dimensions at the other.

Encompassed by the massy walls of this venerable academy, I passed, yet not in tedium or disgust, the years of the third lustrum of my life. The teeming brain of childhood requires no external world of incident to occupy or amuse it; and the apparently dismal monotony of a school was replete with more intense excitement than my riper youth has derived from luxury, or my full manhood from crime. Yet I must believe that my first mental development had in it much of the uncommon—even much of the *outré*. Upon mankind at large the events of very early existence rarely leave in mature age any definite impression. All is gray shadow— a weak and irregular remembrance—an indistinct regathering of feeble pleasures and phantasmagoric pains. With me this is not so. In childhood I must have felt with the energy of a man what I now find stamped upon memory in lines as vivid, as deep, and as durable as the *exergues*[4] of the Carthaginian medals.

Yet in fact—in the fact of the world's view—how little was there to remember! The morning's awakening, the nightly summons to bed; the connings, the recitations; the periodical half-holidays, and perambulations; the play-ground, with its broils, its pastimes, its intrigues;—these, by a mental sorcery long forgotten, were made to involve a wilderness of sensation, a world of rich incident, an universe of varied emotion, of excitement the most

passionate and spirit-stirring. *"Oh, le bon temps, que ce siècle de fer!"*[5]

In truth, the ardor, the enthusiasm, and the imperiousness of my disposition, soon rendered me a marked character among my schoolmates, and by slow, but natural gradations, gave me an ascendancy over all not greatly older than myself;—over all with a single exception. This exception was found in the person of a scholar, who, although no relation, bore the same Christian and surname as myself;—a circumstance, in fact, little remarkable; for, notwithstanding a noble descent, mine was one of those everyday appellations which seem, by prescriptive right, to have been, time out of mind, the common property of the mob. In this narrative I have therefore designated myself as William Wilson,—a fictitious title not very dissimilar to the real. My namesake alone, of those who in school phraseology constituted "our set," presumed to compete with me in the studies of the class —in the sports and broils of the play-ground—to refuse implicit belief in my assertions, and submission to my will— indeed, to interfere with my arbitrary dictation in any respect whatsoever. If there is on earth a supreme and unqualified despotism, it is the despotism of a master mind in boyhood over the less energetic spirits of its companions.[6]

Wilson's rebellion was to me a source of the greatest embarrassment;—the more so as, in spite of the bravado with which in public I made a point of treating him and his pretensions, I secretly felt that I feared him, and could not help thinking the equality which he maintained so easily with myself, a proof of his true superiority; since not to be overcome cost me a perpetual struggle. Yet this superiority —even this equality—was in truth acknowledged by no one but myself; our associates, by some unaccountable blindness, seemed not even to suspect it. Indeed, his competition, his resistance, and especially his impertinent and dogged interference with my purposes, were not more pointed than private. He appeared to be destitute alike of the ambition which urged, and of the passionate energy of mind which enabled me to excel. In his rivalry he might have been supposed actuated solely by a whimsical desire to thwart, astonish, or mortify myself; although there were times when I could not help observing, with a feeling made up of wonder, abasement, and pique, that he mingled with his injuries, his insults, or his contradictions, a certain most inappropriate, and assuredly most unwelcome *affectionateness* of manner. I could only conceive this singular behavior to arise from a consummate self-conceit assuming the vulgar airs of patronage and protection.

Perhaps it was this latter trait in Wilson's conduct, conjoined with our identity of name, and the mere accident of our having entered the school upon the same day, which set afloat the notion that we were brothers, among the senior classes in the academy. These do not usually inquire with much strictness into the affairs of their juniors. I have before said, or should have said, that Wilson was not, in the most remote degree, connected with my family. But assuredly if we *had* been brothers we must have been twins; for, after leaving Dr. Bransby's, I casually learned that my namesake was born on the nineteenth of January, 1813[7]—and this is a somewhat remarkable coincidence; for the day is precisely that of my own nativity.

It may seem strange that in spite of the continual anxiety occasioned me by the rivalry of Wilson, and his intolerable spirit of contradiction, I could not bring myself to hate him altogether. We had, to be sure, nearly every day a quarrel in which, yielding me publicly the palm of victory, he, in some manner, contrived to make me feel that it was he who had deserved it; yet a sense of pride on my part, and a veritable dignity on his own, kept us always upon what are called "speaking terms," while there were many points of strong congeniality in our tempers, operating to awake in me a sentiment which our position alone, perhaps, prevented from ripening into friendship. It is difficult, indeed, to define, or even to describe, my real feelings towards him. They formed a motley and heterogeneous admixture;—some petulant animosity, which was not yet hatred, some esteem, more respect, much fear, with a world of uneasy curiosity. To the moralist it will be unnecessary to say, in addition, that Wilson and myself were the most inseparable of companions.

It was no doubt the anomalous state of affairs existing between us, which turned all my attacks upon him, (and they were many, either open or covert) into the channel of banter or practical joke (giving pain while assuming the aspect of mere fun) rather than into a more serious and determined hostility. But my endeavours on this head were by no means uniformly successful, even when my plans were the most wittily concocted; for my namesake had much about him, in character, of that unassuming and quiet austerity which, while enjoying the poignancy of its own jokes, has no heel of Achilles[8] in itself, and absolutely refuses to be laughed at. I could find, indeed, but one vulnerable point, and that, lying in a personal peculiarity, arising, perhaps, from constitutional disease, would have been spared by any antagonist less at his wit's end than myself;—my rival had a weakness in the faucial or guttural organs, which precluded him from raising his voice at any time *above a very low whisper*. Of this defect I did not fail to take what poor advantage lay in my power.

Wilson's retaliations in kind were many; and there was one form of his practical wit that disturbed me beyond measure. How his sagacity first discovered at all that so petty a thing would vex me, is a question I never could solve; but, having discovered, he habitually practised the annoyance. I had always felt aversion to my uncourtly patronymic, and its very common, if not plebeian prænomen. The words were venom in my ears; and when, upon the day of my arrival, a second William Wilson came also to the academy, I felt angry with him for bearing the name, and doubly disgusted with the name because a stranger bore it, who would be the cause of its twofold repetition, who would be constantly in my presence, and whose concerns, in the ordinary routine of the school business, must inevitably, on account of the detestable coincidence, be often confounded with my own.

The feeling of vexation thus engendered grew stronger with every circumstance tending to show resemblance, moral or physical, between my rival and myself. I had not then discovered the remarkable fact that we were of the same age; but I saw that we were of the same height, and I perceived that we were even singularly alike in general contour of person and outline of feature. I was galled, too, by the rumor touching a relationship, which had grown current in the upper forms.[9] In a word, nothing could more seriously disturb me, (although I scrupulously concealed such disturbance,) than any allusion to a similarity of mind, person, or condition existing between us. But, in truth, I had no reason to believe that (with the exception of the matter of relationship, and in the case of Wilson himself,) this similarity had ever been made a subject of comment, or even observed at all by our schoolfellows. That *he* observed it in all its bearings, and as fixedly as I, was apparent; but that he could discover in such circumstances so fruitful a field of annoyance, can only be attributed, as I said before, to his more than ordinary penetration.

His cue, which was to perfect an imitation of myself, lay both in words and in actions; and most admirably did he play his part. My dress it was an easy matter to copy; my gait and general manner were, without difficulty, appropriated; in spite of his constitutional defect, even my voice did not escape him. My louder tones were, of course, unattempted, but then the key, it was identical; *and his singular whisper, it grew the very echo of my own.*

How greatly this most exquisite portraiture harassed me, (for it could not justly be termed a caricature,) I will not now venture to describe. I had but one consolation—in the fact that the imitation, apparently, was noticed by myself alone, and that I had to endure only the knowing and strangely sarcastic smiles of my namesake himself. Satisfied with having produced in my bosom the intended effect, he seemed to chuckle in secret over the sting he had inflicted, and was characteristically disregardful of the public applause which the success of his witty endeavours might have so easily elicited. That the school, indeed, did not feel his design, perceive its accomplishment, and participate in his sneer, was, for many anxious months, a riddle I could not resolve. Perhaps the *gradation* of his copy rendered it not so readily perceptible; or, more possibly, I owed my security to the masterly air of the copyist, who, disdaining the letter, (which in a painting is all the obtuse can see,) gave but the full spirit of his original for my individual contemplation and chagrin.

I have already more than once spoken of the disgusting air of patronage which he assumed toward me, and of his frequent officious interference with my will. This interference often took the ungracious character of advice; advice not openly given, but hinted or insinuated. I received it with a repugnance which gained strength as I grew in years. Yet, at this distant day, let me do him the simple justice to acknowledge that I can recall no occasion when the suggestions of my rival were on the side of those errors or follies so usual to his immature age and seeming inexperience; that his moral sense, at least, if not his general talents and worldly wisdom, was far keener than my own; and that I might, to-day, have been a better, and thus a happier man, had I less frequently rejected the counsels embodied in those meaning whispers which I then but too cordially hated and too bitterly despised.

As it was, I at length grew restive in the extreme under his distasteful supervision, and daily resented more and more openly what I considered his intolerable arrogance. I have said that, in the first years of our connexion as schoolmates, my feelings in regard to him might have been easily ripened into friendship: but, in the latter months of my residence at the academy, although the intrusion of his ordinary manner had, beyond doubt, in some measure, abated, my sentiments, in nearly similar proportion, partook very much of positive hatred. Upon one occasion he saw this, I think, and afterwards avoided, or made a show of avoiding me.

It was about the same period, if I remember aright, that, in an altercation of violence with him, in which he was more than usually thrown off his guard, and spoke and acted with an openness of demeanor rather foreign to his nature, I discovered, or fancied I discovered, in his accent, his air, and general appearance, a something which first startled, and then deeply interested me, by bringing to mind dim visions of my earliest infancy—wild, confused and thronging memories of a time when memory herself was yet unborn. I cannot better describe the sensation which oppressed me than by saying that I could with difficulty shake off the belief of my having been acquainted with the being who stood before me, at some epoch very long ago—some point of the past even infinitely remote. The delusion, however, faded rapidly as it came; and I mention it at all but to define the day of the last conversation I there held with my singular namesake.

The huge old house, with its countless subdivisions, had several large chambers communicating with each other, where slept the greater number of the students. There were, however, (as must necessarily happen in a building so awkwardly planned,) many little nooks or recesses, the odds and ends of the structure; and these the economic ingenuity of Dr. Bransby had also fitted up as dormitories; although, being the merest closets, they were capable of accommodating but a single individual. One of these small apartments was occupied by Wilson.

One night, about the close of my fifth year at the school, and immediately after the altercation just mentioned, finding every one wrapped in sleep, I arose from bed, and, lamp in hand, stole through a wilderness of narrow passages from my own bedroom to that of my rival. I had long been plotting one of those ill-natured pieces of practical wit at his expense in which I had hitherto been so uniformly unsuccessful. It was my intention, now, to put my scheme in operation, and I resolved to make him feel the whole extent of the malice with which I was imbued. Having reached his closet, I noiselessly entered, leaving the lamp, with a shade over it, on the outside. I advanced a step, and listened to the sound of his tranquil breathing. Assured of his being asleep, I returned, took the light, and with it again approached the bed. Close curtains were around it, which, in the prosecution of my plan, I slowly and quietly withdrew, when the bright rays fell vividly upon the sleeper, and my eyes, at the same moment, upon his countenance. I looked;—and a numbness, an iciness of feeling instantly pervaded my frame. My breast heaved, my knees tottered, my whole spirit became possessed with an objectless yet intolerable horror. Gasping for breath, I lowered the lamp in still nearer proximity to the face. Were these—*these* the lineaments of William Wilson? I saw, indeed, that they were his, but I shook as if with a fit of the ague in fancying they were not. What *was* there about them to confound me in this manner? I gazed;—while my brain reeled with a multitude of incoherent thoughts.

Not thus he appeared—assuredly not *thus* —in the vivacity of his waking hours. The same name! the same contour of person! the same day of arrival at the academy! And then his dogged and meaningless imitation of my gait, my voice, my habits, and my manner! Was it, in truth, within the bounds of human possibility, that *what I now saw* was the result, merely, of the habitual practice of this sarcastic imitation? Awe-stricken, and with a creeping shudder, I extinguished the lamp, passed silently from the chamber, and left, at once, the halls of that old academy, never to enter them again.

After a lapse of some months, spent at home in mere idleness, I found myself a student at Eton. The brief interval had been sufficient to enfeeble my remembrance of the events at Dr. Bransby's, or at least to effect a material change in the nature of the feelings with which I remembered them. The truth—the tragedy —of the drama was no more. I could now find room to doubt the evidence of my senses; and seldom called up the subject at all but with wonder at the extent of human credulity, and a smile at the vivid force of the imagination which I hereditarily possessed. Neither was this species of scepticism likely to be diminished by the character of the life I led at Eton. The vortex of thoughtless folly into which I there so immediately and so recklessly plunged, washed away all but the froth of my past hours, engulfed at once every solid or serious impression, and left to memory only the veriest levities of a former existence.

I do not wish, however, to trace the course of my miserable profligacy here— a profligacy which set at defiance the laws, while it eluded the vigilance of the institution. Three years of folly, passed without profit, had but given me rooted habits of vice, and added, in a somewhat unusual degree, to my bodily stature, when, after a week of soulless dissipation, I invited a small party of the most dissolute students to a secret carousal in my chambers. We

met at a late hour of the night; for our debaucheries were to be faithfully protracted until morning. The wine flowed freely, and there were not wanting other and perhaps more dangerous seductions; so that the grey dawn had already faintly appeared in the east, while our delirious extravagance was at its height. Madly flushed with cards and intoxication, I was in the act of insisting upon a toast of more than wonted profanity, when my attention was suddenly diverted by the violent, although partial unclosing of the door of the apartment, and by the eager voice of a servant from without. He said that some person, apparently in great haste, demanded to speak with me in the hall.

Wildly excited with wine, the unexpected interruption rather delighted than surprised me. I staggered forward at once, and a few steps brought me to the vestibule of the building. In this low and small room there hung no lamp; and now no light at all was admitted, save that of the exceedingly feeble dawn which made its way through the semi-circular window. As I put my foot over the threshold, I became aware of the figure of a youth about my own height, and habited in a white kerseymere morning frock, cut in the novel fashion of the one I myself wore . at the moment. This the faint light enabled me to perceive; but the features of his face I could not distinguish. Upon my entering he strode hurriedly up to me, and, seizing me by the arm with a gesture of petulant impatience, whispered the words "William Wilson!" in my ear.

I grew perfectly sober in an instant.

There was that in the manner of the stranger, and in the tremulous shake of his uplifted finger, as he held it between my eyes and the light, which filled me with unqualified amazement; but it was not this which had so violently moved me. It was the pregnancy of solemn admonition in the singular, low, hissing utterance; and, above all, it was the character, the tone, *the key*, of those few, simple, and familiar, yet whispered syllables, which came with a thousand thronging memories of by-gone days, and struck upon my soul with the shock of a galvanic battery. Ere I could recover the use of my senses he was gone.

Although this event failed not of a vivid effect upon my disordered imagination, yet was it evanescent as vivid. For some weeks, indeed, I busied myself in earnest inquiry, or was wrapped in a cloud of morbid speculation. I did not pretend to disguise from my perception the identity of the singular individual who thus perseveringly interfered with my affairs, and harassed me with his insinuated counsel. But who and what was this Wilson? —and whence came he?—and what were his purposes? Upon neither of these points could I be satisfied; merely ascertaining, in regard to him, that a sudden accident in his family had caused his removal from Dr. Bransby's academy on the afternoon of the day in which I myself had eloped. But in a brief period I ceased to think upon the subject; my attention being all absorbed in a contemplated departure for Oxford. Thither I soon went; the uncalculating vanity of my parents furnishing me with an outfit and annual establishment, which would enable me to indulge at will in the luxury already so dear to my heart,—to vie in profuseness of expenditure with the haughtiest heirs of the wealthiest earldoms in Great Britain.

Excited by such appliances to vice, my constitutional temperament broke forth with redoubled ardor, and I spurned even the common restraints of decency in the mad infatuation of my revels. But it were absurd to pause in the detail of my extravagance. Let it suffice, that among spendthrifts I out-Heroded Herod, and that, giving name to a multitude of novel follies, I added no brief appendix to the long catalogue of vices then usual in the most dissolute university of Europe.[10]

It could hardly be credited, however, that I had, even here, so utterly fallen from the gentlemanly estate, as to seek acquaintance with the vilest arts of the gambler by profession, and, having become an adept in his despicable science, to practise it habitually as a means of increasing my already enormous income at the expense of the weak-minded among my fellow-collegians. Such, nevertheless, was the fact. And the very enormity of this offence against all manly and honourable sentiment proved, beyond doubt, the main if not the sole reason of the impunity with which it was committed. Who, indeed, among my most abandoned associates, would not rather have disputed the clearest evidence of his senses, than have suspected of such courses, the gay, the frank, the generous William Wilson —the noblest and most liberal commoner at Oxford—him whose follies (said his parasites) were but the follies of youth and unbridled fancy —whose errors but inimitable whim—whose darkest vice but a careless and dashing extravagance?

I had been now two years successfully busied in this way, when there came to the university a young *parvenu* nobleman, Glendinning—rich, said report, as Herodes Atticus[11]—his riches, too, as easily acquired. I soon found him of weak intellect, and, of course, marked him as a fitting subject for my skill. I frequently engaged him in play, and contrived, with the gambler's usual art, to let him win considerable sums, the more effectually to entangle him in my snares. At length, my schemes being ripe, I met him (with the full intention that this meeting should be final and decisive) at the chambers of a fellow-commoner, (Mr. Preston,) equally intimate with both, but who, to do him justice, entertained not even a remote suspicion of my design. To give to this a better colouring, I had contrived to have assembled a party of some eight or ten, and was solicitously careful that the introduction of cards should appear accidental, and originate in the proposal of my contemplated dupe himself. To be brief upon a vile topic, none of the low finesse was omitted, so customary upon similar occasions that it is a just matter for wonder how any are still found so besotted as to fall its victim.

We had protracted our sitting far into the night, and I had at length effected the manœuvre of getting Glendinning as my sole antagonist. The game, too, was my favorite écarté.[12] The rest of the company, interested in the extent of our play, had abandoned their own cards, and were standing around us as spectators. The parvenu, who had been induced by my artifices in the early part of the evening, to drink deeply, now shuffled, dealt, or played, with a wild nervousness of manner for which his intoxication, I thought, might partially, but could not altogether account. In a very short period he had become my debtor to a large amount, when, having taken a long draught of port, he did precisely what I had been coolly anticipating—he proposed to double our already extravagant stakes. With a well-feigned show of reluctance, and not until after my repeated refusal had seduced him into some angry words which gave a color of pique to my compliance, did I finally comply. The result, of course, did but prove how entirely the prey was in my toils; in less than an hour he had quadrupled his debt. For some time his countenance had been losing the florid tinge lent it by the wine; but now, to my astonishment, I perceived that it had grown to a pallor truly fearful. I say to my astonishment. Glendinning had been represented to my eager inquiries as immeasurably wealthy; and the sums which he had as yet lost, although in themselves vast, could not, I supposed, very seriously annoy, much less so violently affect him. That he was overcome by the wine just swallowed, was the idea which most readily presented itself; and, rather with a view to the preservation of my own character in the eyes of my associates, than from any less interested motive, I was about to insist, peremptorily, upon a discontinuance of the play, when some expressions at my elbow from among the company, and an ejaculation evincing utter despair on the part of Glendinning, gave me to understand that I had effected his total ruin under circumstances which, rendering him an object for the pity of all, should have protected him from the ill offices even of a fiend.

What now might have been my conduct it is difficult to say. The pitiable condition of my dupe had thrown an air of embarrassed gloom over all; and, for some moments, a profound silence was maintained, during which I could not help feeling my cheeks tingle with the many burning glances of scorn or reproach cast upon me by the less abandoned of the party. I will even own that an intolerable weight of anxiety was for a brief instant lifted from my bosom by the sudden and extraordinary interruption which ensued. The wide, heavy folding doors of the apartment were all at once thrown open, to their full extent, with a vigorous and rushing impetuosity that extinguished, as if by magic, every candle in the room. Their light, in dying, enabled us just to perceive that a stranger had entered, about my own height, and closely muffled in a cloak. The darkness, however, was now total; and we could only *feel* that he was standing in our midst. Before any one of us could recover from the extreme astonishment into which this rudeness had thrown all, we heard the voice of the intruder.

"Gentlemen," he said, in a low, distinct, and never-to-be-forgotten *whisper* which thrilled to the very marrow of my bones, "Gentlemen, I make no apology for this behaviour, because in thus behaving, I am but fulfilling a duty. You are, beyond doubt, uninformed of the true character of the person who has to-night won at écarté a large sum of money from Lord Glendinning. I will therefore put you upon an expeditious and decisive plan of obtaining this very necessary information. Please to examine, at your leisure, the inner linings of the cuff of his left sleeve, and the several little packages which may be found in the somewhat capacious pockets of his embroidered morning wrapper."

While he spoke, so profound was the stillness that one might have heard a pin drop upon the floor. In ceasing, he departed at once, and as abruptly as he had entered. Can I—shall I describe my sensations?—must I say that I felt all the horrors of the damned? Most assuredly I had little time given for reflection. Many hands roughly seized me upon the spot, and lights were immediately reprocured. A search ensued. In the lining of my sleeve were found all the court cards essential in *écarté*, and, in the pockets of my wrapper, a number of packs, fac-similes of those used at our sittings, with the single exception that mine were of the species called, technically, *arrondées*;[13] the honours being slightly convex at the ends, the lower cards slightly convex at the sides. In this disposition, the dupe who cuts, as customary, at the length of the pack, will invariably find that he cuts his antagonist an honor; while the gambler, cutting at the breadth, will, as certainly, cut nothing for his victim which may count in the records of the game.

Any burst of indignation upon this discovery would have affected me less than the silent contempt, or the sarcastic composure, with which it was received.

"Mr. Wilson," said our host, stooping to remove from beneath his feet an exceedingly luxurious cloak of rare furs, "Mr. Wilson, this is your property." (The weather was cold; and, upon quitting my own room, I had thrown a cloak over my dressing wrapper, putting it off upon reaching the scene of play.) "I presume it is supererogatory to seek here (eyeing the folds of the garment with a bitter smile) for any farther evidence of your skill. Indeed, we have had enough. You will see the necessity, I hope, of quitting Oxford—at all events, of quitting instantly my chambers."

Abased, humbled to the dust as I then was, it is probable that I should have resented this galling language by immediate personal violence, had not my whole attention been at the moment arrested by a fact of the most startling character. The cloak which I had worn was of a rare description of fur; how rare, how extravagantly costly, I shall not venture to say. Its fashion, too, was of my own fantastic invention; for I was fastidious to an absurd degree of coxcombry, in matters of this frivolous nature. When, therefore, Mr. Preston reached me that which he had picked up upon the floor, and near the folding doors of the apartment, it was with an astonishment nearly bordering upon terror, that I perceived my own already hanging on my arm, (where I had no doubt unwittingly placed it,) and that the one presented me was but its exact counterpart in every, in even the minutest possible particular. The singular being who had so disastrously exposed me, had been muffled, I remembered, in a cloak; and none had been worn at all by any of the members of our party with the exception of myself. Retaining some presence of mind, I took the one offered me by Preston; placed it, unnoticed, over my own; left the apartment with a resolute scowl of defiance; and, next morning ere dawn of day, commenced a hurried journey from Oxford to the continent, in a perfect agony of horror and of shame.

I fled in vain. My evil destiny pursued me as if in exultation, and proved, indeed, that the exercise of its mysterious dominion had as yet only begun. Scarcely had I set foot in Paris ere I had fresh evidence of the detestable interest taken by this Wilson in my concerns. Years flew, while I experienced no relief. Villain!—at Rome, with how untimely, yet with how spectral an officiousness, stepped he in between me and my ambition! At Vienna, too—at Berlin—and at Moscow! Where, in truth, had I *not* bitter cause to curse him within my heart? From his inscrutable tyranny did I at length flee, panic-stricken, as from a pestilence; and to the very ends of the earth *I fled in vain.*

And again, and again, in secret communion with my own spirit, would I demand the questions "Who is he?—whence came he?—and what are his objects?" But no answer was there found. And then I scrutinized, with a minute scrutiny, the forms, and the methods, and the leading traits of his impertinent supervision. But even here there was very little upon which to base a conjecture. It was noticeable, indeed, that, in no one of the multiplied instances in which he had of late crossed my path, had he so crossed it except to frustrate those schemes, or to disturb those actions, which, if fully carried out, might have resulted in bitter mischief. Poor justification this, in truth, for an authority so imperiously assumed! Poor indemnity for natural rights of self-agency so pertinaciously, so insultingly denied!

I had also been forced to notice that my tormentor, for a very long period of time, (while scrupulously and with miraculous dexterity maintaining his whim of an identity of apparel with myself,) had so contrived it, in the execution of his varied interference with my will, that I saw not, at any moment, the features of his face. Be Wilson what he might, *this*, at least, was but the veriest of affectation, or of folly. Could he, for an instant, have supposed that, in my admonisher at Eton— in the destroyer of my honor at Oxford, —in him who thwarted my ambition at Rome, my revenge at Paris, my passionate love at Naples, or what he falsely termed my avarice in Egypt,—that in this, my arch-enemy and evil genius, I could fail to recognise the William Wilson of my school boy days,—the namesake, the companion, the rival,—the hated and dreaded rival at Dr. Bransby's? Impossible!—But let me hasten to the last eventful scene of the drama.

Thus far I had succumbed supinely to this imperious domination. The sentiment of deep awe with which I habitually regarded the elevated character, the majestic wisdom, the apparent omnipresence and omnipotence of Wilson, added to a feeling of even terror, with which certain other traits in his nature and assumptions inspired me, had operated, hitherto, to impress me with an idea of my own utter weakness and helplessness, and to suggest an implicit, although bitterly reluctant submission to his arbitrary will. But, of late days, I had given myself up entirely to wine; and its maddening influence upon my hereditary temper rendered me more and more impatient of control. I began to murmur,—to hesitate,—to resist. And was it only fancy which induced me to believe that, with the increase of my own firmness, that of my tormentor underwent a proportional diminution? Be this as it may, I now began to feel the inspiration of a burning hope, and at length nurtured in my secret thoughts a stern and desperate resolution that I would submit no longer to be enslaved.

It was at Rome, during the Carnival of 18—, that I attended a masquerade in the palazzo of the Neapolitan Duke Di Broglio. I had indulged more freely than usual in the excesses of the wine-table; and now the suffocating atmosphere of the crowded rooms irritated me beyond endurance. The difficulty, too, of forcing my way through the mazes of the company contributed not a little to the ruffling of my temper; for I was anxiously seeking, (let me not say with what unworthy motive) the young, the gay, the beautiful wife of the aged and doting Di Broglio. With a too unscrupulous confidence she had previously communicated to me the secret of the costume in which she would be habited, and now, having caught a glimpse of her person, I was hurrying to make my way into her presence.—At this moment I felt a light hand placed upon my shoulder, and that ever-remembered, low, damnable *whisper* within my ear.

In an absolute phrenzy of wrath, I turned at once upon him who had thus interrupted me, and seized him violently by the collar. He was attired, as I had expected, in a costume altogether similar to my own; wearing a Spanish cloak of blue velvet, begirt about the waist with a crimson belt sustaining a rapier. A mask of black silk entirely covered his face.

"Scoundrel!" I said, in a voice husky with rage, while every syllable I uttered seemed as new fuel to my fury, "scoundrel! impostor! accursed villain! you shall not—you *shall not* dog me unto death! Follow me, or I stab you where you stand!"—and I broke my way from the ball-room into a small ante-chamber adjoining—dragging him unresistingly with me as I went.

Upon entering, I thrust him furiously from me. He staggered against the wall, while I closed the door with an oath, and commanded him to draw. He hesitated but for an instant; then, with a slight sigh, drew in silence, and put himself upon his defence.

The contest was brief indeed. I was frantic with every species of wild excitement, and felt within my single arm the energy and power of a multitude. In a few seconds I forced him by sheer strength against the wainscoting, and thus, getting him at mercy, plunged my sword, with brute ferocity, repeatedly through and through his bosom.

At that instant some person tried the latch of the door. I hastened to prevent an intrusion, and then immediately returned to my dying antagonist. But what human language can adequately portray *that* astonishment, *that* horror which possessed me at the spectacle then presented to view? The brief moment in which I averted my eyes had been sufficient to produce, apparently, a material change in the arrangements at the upper or farther end of the room. A large mirror,—so at first it seemed to me in my confusion—now stood where none had been perceptible before; and, as I stepped up to it in extremity of terror, mine own image, but with features all pale and dabbled in blood, advanced to meet me with a feeble and tottering gait.

Thus it appeared, I say, but was not. It was my antagonist—it was Wilson, who then stood before me in the agonies of his dissolution. His mask and cloak lay, where he had thrown them, upon the floor. Not a thread in all his raiment—not a line in all the marked and singular lineaments of his face which was not, even in the most absolute identity, *mine own!*

It was Wilson; but he spoke no longer in a whisper, and I could have fancied that I myself was speaking while he said:

"You have conquered, and I yield. Yet, henceforward art thou also dead—dead to the World, to Heaven and to Hope! In me didst thou exist—and, in my death, see by this image, which is thine own, how utterly thou hast murdered thyself."

THE MAN OF THE CROWD[1]

Ce grand malheur, de ne pouvoir être seul.

La Bruyère[2]

It was well said of a certain German book that *"es lässt sich nicht lesen"*—it does not permit itself to be read.[3] There are some secrets which do not permit themselves to be told. Men die nightly in their beds, wringing the hands of ghostly confessors, and looking them piteously in the eyes—die with despair of heart and convulsion of throat, on account of the hideousness of mysteries which will not *suffer themselves* to be revealed. Now and then, alas, the conscience of man takes up a burden so heavy in horror that it can be thrown down only into the grave. And thus the essence of all crime is undivulged.

Not long ago, about the closing in of an evening in autumn, I sat at the large bow window of the D—— Coffee-House in London. For some months I had been ill in health, but was now convalescent, and, with returning strength, found myself in one of those happy moods which are so precisely the converse of *ennui*—moods of the keenest appetency, when the film from the mental vision departs—the ἀχλὺς ἣ πρὶν ἐπῆεν—and the intellect, electrified, surpasses as greatly its every-day condi-

Figure Eleven. The book that "does not permit itself to be read": Poe learned of it from Isaac Disraeli's *Curiosities of Literature* in which an article on tasteless and obscene religious illustrations cites Grunninger's volume as especially obnoxious. (See note 16 for details; the title means "little garden of the soul," and the spelling varies from one edition to the next.) If such a book exists, two colleagues searching the British Museum collection could not find it: Grunninger and others printed many volumes of this title around 1500, but their plates are characteristic religious engravings of the age. Even the "strangest" of them, shown here, uses traditional iconography; the "odd" facial expressions are ordinary in German graphic art of the time. It may be that the book which Disraeli saw has disappeared, but pending the discovery of offensive plates, we conclude that the skeptical humanist Disraeli, suspicious even of the "superstitious" aspects of his ancestoral Judaism, was showing up—or pretending to show up —the crudities and banalities of Christianity. If he was fibbing or exaggerating, the joke is on Poe. The colophon reads, "printed at the expense of . . . Johann Koberger . . . Nuremberg . . . Frederick Peypus the printer, 1518, 12 December." Plates courtesy of the British Museum.
Copyright, the British Museum.

tion, as does the vivid yet candid reason of Leibnitz, the mad and flimsy rhetoric of Gorgias. Merely to breathe was enjoyment; and I derived positive pleasure even from many of the legitimate sources of pain. I felt a calm but inquisitive interest in every thing. With a cigar in my mouth and a newspaper in my lap, I had been amusing myself for the greater part of the afternoon, now in poring over advertisements, now in observing the promiscuous company in the room, and now in peering through the smoky panes into the street.[4]

This latter is one of the principal thoroughfares of the city, and had been very much crowded during the whole day. But, as the darkness came on, the throng momently increased; and, by the time the lamps were well lighted, two dense and continuous tides of population were rushing past the door. At this particular period of the evening I had never before been in a similar situation, and the tumultuous sea of human heads filled me, therefore, with a delicious novelty of emotion. I gave up, at length, all care of things within the hotel, and became absorbed in contemplation of the scene without.

At first my observations took an abstract and generalizing turn. I looked at the passengers in masses, and thought of them in their aggregate relations. Soon, however, I descended to details, and regarded with minute interest the innumerable varieties of figure, dress, air, gait, visage, and expression of countenance.

By far the greater number of those who went by had a satisfied business-like demeanour, and seemed to be thinking only of making their way through the press. Their brows were knit, and their eyes rolled quickly; when pushed against by fellow-wayfarers they evinced no symptom of impatience, but adjusted their clothes and hurried on. Others, still a numerous class, were restless in their movements, had flushed faces, and talked and gesticulated to themselves, as if feeling in solitude on account of the very denseness of the company around. When impeded in their progress, these people suddenly ceased muttering, but redoubled their gesticulations, and awaited, with an absent and overdone smile upon the lips, the course of the persons impeding them. If jostled, they bowed profusely to the jostlers, and appeared overwhelmed with confusion.—There was nothing very distinctive about these two large classes beyond what I have noted. Their habiliments belonged to that order which is pointedly termed the decent. They were undoubtedly noblemen, merchants, attorneys, tradesmen, stock-jobbers—the Eupatrids[5] and the commonplaces of society —men of leisure and men actively engaged in affairs of their own—conducting business upon their own responsibility. They did not greatly excite my attention.

The tribe of clerks was an obvious one; and here I discerned two remarkable divisions. There were the junior clerks of flash houses—young gentlemen with tight coats, bright boots, well-oiled hair, and supercilious lips. Setting aside a certain dapperness of carriage, which may be termed *deskism* for want of a better word, the manner of these persons seemed to me an exact facsimile of what had been the perfection of *bon ton*[6] about twelve or eighteen months before. They wore the cast-off graces of the gentry;—and this, I believe, involves the best definition of the class.

The division of the upper clerks of staunch firms, or of the "steady old fellows," it was not possible to mistake. These were known by their coats and pantaloons of black or brown, made to sit comfortably, with white cravats and waistcoats, broad solid-looking shoes, and thick hose or gaiters.—They had all slightly bald heads, from which the right ears, long used to pen-holding, had an odd habit of standing off on end. I observed that they always removed or settled their hats with both hands, and wore watches, with short gold chains of a substantial and ancient pattern. Theirs was the affectation of respectability;—if indeed there be an affectation so honorable.[7]

There were many individuals of dashing appearance, whom I easily understood as belonging to the race of swell pickpockets, with which all great cities are infested. I watched these gentry with much inquisitiveness, and found it difficult to imagine how they should ever be mistaken for gentlemen by gentlemen themselves. Their voluminousness of wristband, with an air of excessive frankness, should betray them at once.

The gamblers, of whom I descried not a few, were still more easily recognisable. They wore every variety of dress, from that of the desperate thimble-rig[8] bully, with velvet waistcoat, fancy neckerchief, gilt chains, and filigreed buttons, to that of the scrupulously inornate clergyman than which nothing could be less liable to suspicion. Still all were distinguished by a certain sodden swarthiness of complexion, a filmy dimness of eye, and pallor and compression of lip. There were two other traits, moreover, by which I could always detect them;—a guarded lowness of tone in conversation, and a more than ordinary extension of the thumb in a direction at right angles with the fingers. —Very often, in company with these sharpers, I observed an order of men somewhat different in habits, but still birds of a kindred feather. They may be defined as the gentlemen who live by their wits. They seem to prey upon the public in two battalions—that of the dandies and that of the military men. Of the first grade the leading features are long locks and smiles; of the second, frogged coats and frowns.

Descending in the scale of what is termed gentility, I found darker and deeper themes for speculation. I saw Jew pedlars, with hawk eyes flashing from countenances whose every other feature wore only an expression of abject humility; sturdy professional street beggars scowling upon mendicants of a better stamp, whom despair alone had driven forth into the night for charity; feeble and ghastly invalids, upon whom death had placed a sure hand, and who sidled and tottered through the mob, looking every one beseechingly in the face, as if in search of some chance consolation, some lost hope; modest young girls returning from long and late labor to a cheerless home, and shrinking more tearfully than indignantly from the glances of ruffians, whose direct contact, even, could not be avoided; women of the town of all kinds and of all ages—the unequivocal beauty in the prime of her womanhood, putting one in mind of the statue in Lucian, with the surface of Parian marble, and the interior filled with filth—the loathsome and utterly lost leper in rags— the wrinkled, bejewelled and paint-begrimmed beldame, making a last effort at youth—the mere child of immature form, yet, from long association, an adept in the dreadful coquetries of her trade, and burning with a rabid ambition to be ranked the equal of her elders in vice; drunkards innumerable and indescribable —some in shreds and patches, reeling, inarticulate, with bruised visage and lacklustre eyes—some in whole although filthy garments, with a slightly unsteady swagger, thick sensual lips, and heartylooking rubicund faces—others clothed in materials which had once been good, and which even now were scrupulously well brushed—men who walked with a more than naturally firm and springy step, but whose countenances were fearfully pale, whose eyes were hideously wild and red, and who clutched with quivering fingers, as they strode through the crowd, at every object which came within their reach; beside these, pie-men, porters, coal-heavers, sweeps; organ-grinders, monkey-exhibitors and ballad-mongers, those who vended with those who sang; ragged artizans and exhausted labourers of every description, and all full of a noisy and inordinate vivacity which jarred discordantly upon the ear, and gave an aching sensation to the eye.[9]

As the night deepened, so deepened to me the interest of the scene; for not only did the general character of the crowd materially alter (its gentler features retiring in the gradual withdrawal of the more orderly portion of the people, and its harsher ones coming out into bolder relief, as the late hour brought forth every species of infamy from its den,) but the rays of the gas-lamps, feeble at first in their struggle with the dying day, had now at length gained ascendancy, and threw over every thing a fitful and garish lustre. All was dark yet splendid—as that ebony to which has been likened the style of Tertullian.[10]

The wild effects of the light enchained me to an examination of individual faces; and although the rapidity with which the world of light flitted before the window, prevented me from casting more than a glance upon each visage, still it seemed that, in my then peculiar mental state, I could frequently read, even in that brief interval of a glance, the history of long years.

With my brow to the glass, I was thus occupied in scrutinizing the mob, when suddenly there came into view a countenance (that of a decrepid old man, some sixty-five or seventy years of age,)—a countenance which at once arrested and absorbed my whole attention, on account of the absolute idiosyncrasy of its expression. Any thing even remotely resembling that expression I had never seen before. I well remember that my first thought, upon beholding it, was that Retszch,[11] had he viewed it, would have greatly preferred it to his own pictural incarnations of the fiend. As I endeavoured, during the brief minute of my original survey, to form some analysis of the meaning conveyed, there arose confusedly and paradoxically within my mind, the ideas of vast mental power, of caution, of penuriousness, of avarice, of coolness, of malice, of blood-thirstiness, of triumph, of merriment, of excessive terror, of intense—of extreme despair. I felt singularly aroused, startled,

fascinated. "How wild a history," I said to myself, "is written within that bosom!" Then came a craving desire to keep the man in view—to know more of him. Hurriedly putting on an overcoat, and seizing my hat and cane, I made my way into the street, and pushed through the crowd in the direction which I had seen him take; for he had already disappeared. With some little difficulty I at length came within sight of him, approached, and followed him closely, yet cautiously, so as not to attract his attention.

I had now a good opportunity of examining his person. He was short in stature, very thin, and apparently very feeble. His clothes, generally, were filthy and ragged; but as he came, now and then, within the strong glare of a lamp, I perceived that his linen, although dirty, was of beautiful texture; and my vision deceived me, or, through a rent in a closely-buttoned and evidently second-hand *roquelaire*[12] which enveloped him, I caught a glimpse both of a diamond and of a dagger. These observations heightened my curiosity, and I resolved to follow the stranger whithersoever he should go.

It was now fully night-fall, and a thick humid fog hung over the city, soon ending in a settled and heavy rain. This change of weather had an odd effect upon the crowd, the whole of which was at once put into new commotion, and overshadowed by a world of umbrellas. The waver, the jostle, and the hum increased in a tenfold degree. For my own part I did not much regard the rain—the lurking of an old fever in my system rendering the moisture somewhat too dangerously pleasant. Tying a handkerchief about my mouth, I kept on. For half an hour the old man held his way with difficulty along the great thoroughfare; and I here walked close at his elbow through fear of losing sight of him. Never once turning his head to look back, he did not observe me. By and bye he passed into a cross street, which, although densely filled with people, was not quite so much thronged as the main one he had quitted. Here a change in his demeanour became evident. He walked more slowly and with less object than before—more hesitatingly. He crossed and re-crossed the way repeatedly without apparent aim; and the press was still so thick, that, at every such movement, I was obliged to follow him closely. The street was a narrow and long one, and his course lay within it for nearly an hour, during which the passengers had gradually diminished to about that number which is ordinarily seen at noon on Broadway near the Park—so vast a difference is there between a London populace and that of the most frequented American city.[13] A second turn brought us into a square, brilliantly lighted, and overflowing with life. The old manner of the stranger re-appeared. His chin fell upon his breast, while his eyes rolled wildly from under his knit brows, in every direction, upon those who hemmed him in. He urged his way steadily and perseveringly. I was surprised, however, to find, upon his having made the circuit of the square, that he turned and retraced his steps. Still more was I astonished to see him repeat the same walk several times—once nearly detecting me as he came round with a sudden movement.

In this exercise he spent another hour, at the end of which we met with far less interruption from passengers than at first. The rain fell fast; the air grew cool; and the people were retiring to their homes. With a gesture of impatience, the wanderer passed into a by-street comparatively deserted. Down this, some quarter of a mile long, he rushed with an activity I could not have dreamed of seeing in one so aged, and which put me to much trouble in pursuit. A few minutes brought us to a large and busy bazaar, with the localities of which the stranger appeared well acquainted, and where his original demeanour again became apparent, as he forced his way to and fro, without aim, among the host of buyers and sellers.

During the hour and a half, or there-abouts, which we passed in this place, it required much caution on my part to keep him within reach without attracting his observation. Luckily I wore a pair of caoutchouc[14] over-shoes, and could move about in perfect silence. At no moment did he see that I watched him. He entered shop after shop, priced nothing, spoke no word, and looked at all objects with a wild and vacant stare. I was now utterly amazed at his behaviour, and firmly resolved that we should not part until I had satisfied myself in some measure respecting him.

A loud-toned clock struck eleven, and the company were fast deserting the bazaar. A shop-keeper, in putting up a shutter, jostled the old man, and at the instant I saw a strong shudder come over his frame. He hurried into the street, looked anxiously around him for an instant, and then ran with incredible swiftness through many crooked and people-less lanes, until we emerged once more upon the great thoroughfare whence we had started—the street of the D—— Hotel. It no longer wore, however, the same aspect. It was still brilliant with gas; but the rain fell fiercely, and there were few persons to be seen. The stranger grew pale. He walked moodily some paces up the once populous avenue, then, with a heavy sigh, turned in the direction of the river, and, plunging through a great variety of devious ways, came out, at length, in view of one of the principal theatres. It was about being closed, and the audience were thronging from the doors. I saw the old man gasp as if for breath while he threw himself amid the crowd; but I thought that the intense agony of his countenance had, in some measure, abated. His head again fell upon his breast; he appeared as I had seen him at first. I observed that he now took the course in which had gone the greater number of the audience—but, upon the whole, I was at a loss to comprehend the waywardness of his actions.

As he proceeded, the company grew more scattered, and his old uneasiness and vacillation were resumed. For some time he followed closely a party of some ten or twelve roisterers; but from this number one by one dropped off, until three only remained together, in a narrow and gloomy lane little frequented. The stranger paused, and, for a moment, seemed lost in thought; then, with every mark of agitation, pursued rapidly a route which brought us to the verge of the city, amid regions very different from those we had hitherto traversed. It was the most noisome quarter of London, where everything wore the worst impress of the most deplorable poverty, and of the most desperate crime.[15] By the dim light of an accidental lamp, tall, antique, worm-eaten, wooden tenements were seen tottering to their fall, in directions so many and capricious that scarce the semblance of a passage was discernible between them. The paving-stones lay at random, displaced from their beds by the rankly growing grass. Horrible filth festered in the dammed-up gutters. The whole atmosphere teemed with desolation. Yet, as we proceeded, the sounds of human life revived by sure degrees, and at length large bands of the most abandoned of a London populace were seen reeling to and fro. The spirits of the old man again flickered up, as a lamp which is near its death-hour. Once more he strode onward with elastic tread. Suddenly a corner was turned, a blaze of light burst upon our sight, and we stood before one of the huge suburban temples of Intemperance—one of the palaces of the fiend, Gin.

It was now nearly day-break; but a number of wretched inebriates still pressed in and out of the flaunting entrance. With a half shriek of joy the old man forced a passage within, resumed at once his original bearing, and stalked backward and forward, without apparent object, among the throng. He had not been thus long occupied, however, before a rush to the doors gave token that the host was closing them for the night. It was something even more intense than despair that I then observed upon the countenance of the singular being whom I had watched so pertinaciously. Yet he did not hesitate in his career, but, with a mad energy, retraced his steps at once, to the heart of the mighty London. Long and swiftly he fled, while I followed him in the wildest amazement, resolute not to abandon a scrutiny in which I now felt an interest all-absorbing. The sun arose while we proceeded, and, when we had once again reached that most thronged mart of the populous town, the street of the D—— Hotel, it presented an appearance of human bustle and activity scarcely inferior to what I had seen on the evening before. And here, long, amid the momently increasing confusion, did I persist in my pursuit of the stranger. But, as usual, he walked to and fro, and during the day did not pass from out the turmoil of that street. And, as the shades of the second evening came on, I grew wearied unto death, and, stopping fully in front of the wanderer, gazed at him steadfastly in the face. He noticed me not, but resumed his solemn walk, while I, ceasing to follow, remained absorbed in contemplation. "This old man," I said at length, "is the type and the genius of deep crime. He refuses to be alone. *He is the man of the crowd.* It will be in vain to follow; for I shall learn no more of him, nor of his deeds. The worst heart of the world is a grosser book than the 'Hortulus Animæ,'[16] and perhaps it is but one of the great mercies of God that 'es lässt sich nicht lesen.'"

Notes

The Black Cat

1. *baroques:* a deceptive sentence. Poe has used the plural form of the French word *baroque*, to make it agree with "they" (events). It reads more easily in English, where the agreement problem does not appear: ". . . less terrible than baroque."

Published first in the *United States Saturday Post (The Saturday Evening Post)* for August 19, 1843, in the 1845 *Tales*, and again in the *Pictorial National Library* (November 1848).

2. The cat may have been real. In *Alexander's Weekly Messenger* (January 29, 1840), Poe describes a black cat he says he owns which has "not a white hair about her," which is very intelligent, and which is, like all black cats, a witch. That cat, though, is female.

The Tell-Tale Heart

1. The narrator's "nervousness" is a version of Poe's frequently used device of establishing plausibility and tone through heightened states of consciousness. Poe published this first in James Russell Lowell's *The Pioneer* for January 1843 and used it again in *The Broadway Journal*, August 23, 1845.

Hop-Frog

1. Poe published this story not in a literary journal, ladies' magazine, gift book, but in a frankly commercial "sporting magazine," *The Flag of our Union* (March 17, 1849), saying of his decision that this was "not a *very* respectable journal, perhaps, in a literary point of view, but one that pays . . . high prices. . . ." See Section Six Preface. The title given is from that first publication.

2. rare bird upon the earth (from Juvenal).

3. *Gargantua* (1534) is a satirical romance about a peace-loving giant prince with a vast appetite. François Rabelais (c. 1494–c. 1553), French humorist and satirist, is noted for the boisterous, bawdy, and energetic nature of his work. Voltaire (François-Marie Arouet, 1694–1778), in contrast, is noted more for cleverness and wit. *Zadig, ou la destinée* (1747) is a sophisticated and bitter satire. Poe's contrast is between broad and pointed comedy.

4. In other words, "Once upon a time." See Section Preface.

5. Some critics, knowing that Poe was unable to hold his liquor, read Poe into "Hop-Frog." See Section Preface and note 7.

6. Hop-Frog now creates a "brilliant" vision of revenge—complex, in other words, for all its horror, "beautiful," or in Poe's aesthetic, bizarre and outré. Apparently the wine and the king's cruelty, the "madness," and the gnashing of his teeth are necessary to produce the state of "inspiration" in which "Hop-Frog" devises his weird plan. Compare the process to that which inspired characters undergo. See especially "The Domain of Arnheim" and "The Fall of the House of Usher."

7. Hop-Frog, remember, is from a remote province (the South?) He describes the "diversion" as a "country frolic" from his home. It is, in fact, tarring-and-feathering or, to be accurate, tarring-and-flaxing.

8. an elastic knitted fabric.

9. supporting columns made in the form of female figures.

The Imp of the Perverse

1. *prima mobilia:* prime movers, first causes.

phrenologists: Poe's tale appeared in *Graham's Magazine* for July 1845, and in *The May Flower* the same year (dated 1846), during a period in which it was becoming clear that most phrenologists were quacks. But phrenology had been founded as a serious science. The idea behind it was that it seemed reasonable to assume that different portions of the human mind served different functions and that, once one knew their locations, their relative development ought to be reflected in the shape of the head. Serious studies were done of the *crania* of men noted for various characteristics. The skulls of notable leaders, geniuses, madmen, and even criminals were often exhumed for measurement and examination, and attempts were made to apply clinically what had been learned. Science historians report that serious and sensitive practicing phrenologists functioned much in the way psychologists do today. A troubled bookkeeper might be told, after examination of the "bumps" on his head, that a source of his trouble was his profession: his head showed that those "faculties" or "organs" connected with calculation were relatively small, while those connected with, say, creativity were well developed. A change of profession might clear up his problem, as it sometimes did. Intelligent people in the 1840s still argued that if the quacks could be kept out of the profession, phrenology could redeem its promise as an approach to understanding personality.

primum mobile: prime mover.

à priori: the logical process of proceeding from a cause to its effect.

organ: See "phrenologists," above.

principia: principles.

Spurzheimites: Johann Kaspar Spurzheim (1776–1832) was one of the popularizers of phrenology in the period when it was still taken seriously as a science.

2. *à posteriori:* the logical opposite of *à priori* reasoning: moving from facts to principles, or from evidence to cause.

motivirt: motivated.

3. The narrator's first example is mild; the reader still thinks he is being addressed by a witty and observant essayist. Note that the succeeding examples grow in intensity and in the seriousness of the "perverseness" displayed until the narrator steps forth to identify his own case. See Section Preface.

4. genius: jinni, genie.

5. Madame Pilau: An item entitled "Madame Pilau: an Oddity of the Seventeenth Century" by C. F. Gore appeared in *The New Monthly Magazine* in 1839. Presumably, it relates the incident to which Poe refers.

6. See Section Preface. The narrator's "sanest" act, confession, seems to him "perverse."

William Wilson

1. William Chamberlayne's *Pharonnida* (1659) is a lengthy verse romance, but this "quotation" is not in it. A passage much like it, however, appears in Chamberlayne's *Love's Victory* (1658), which was printed with *Pharonnida* in an 1820 edition Poe probably knew. He probably scrambled them together as he did quotations in other stories (Rothwell).

2. Heliogabalus (204–222), Roman Emperor (218–222). See "Four Beasts in One," note 7.

3. Dr. Bransby: a real person. Poe spent part of his childhood in England, at a school run by the Reverend John Bransby. Wilson's lengthy description of the school's complexities and windings is intended to associate it with a child's memories ("Let me then remember").

peine forte et dure: "long and hard pain"—a medieval torture.

4. lustrum: five-year period. Poe was at the Manor House School in Stoke Newington from 1817 to 1820, so he was younger than Wilson.

outré: strange.

exergues: a numismatics term for the area on the reverse of a medal or a coin, beneath the picture or design, in which information is imprinted.

5. connings: Students studied by "conning over lessons," which usually meant reading them over and over softly to themselves.

"Oh, le bon temps, que ce siècle de fer!": "Oh! what a good time is this century of iron!" (in the sense of Industrial Age). The quotation is from Voltaire's "Le Mondain" (1736), line 21, and is ironic; the poet speaks sarcastically about those who refer to the good old times or the golden age.

6. See Section Preface.

7. Poe was born on January 19, 1809. He did sometimes give 1813 as his birth-year (Carlson 2).

8. Achilles, the epic protagonist of Homer's *Iliad*, had according to tradition been made invulnerable except in the heel by which his mother held him when, as a baby, he was given the magical dunking which conferred godly protection.

9. classes.

10. Poe has pet phrases. He uses "out-

Heroded Herod" in several stories. See for example "Metzengerstein," note 8 and "The Masque of the Red Death," note 7. Forrest lists Matthew 2:16 as the source of the phrase. In "Mystification," Poe says Göttingen is the most dissolute university in Europe.

11. *parvenu:* a newly-rich person.

Herodes Atticus: Athenian orator and statesman (c. 110–c. 185), very wealthy and very famous as a large-scale benefactor of several Greek cities.

12. card game for two people.

13. rounded.

The Man of the Crowd

1. First published in December 1840 in the newly combined *Gentleman's Magazine* ("Burton's") and *Graham's Magazine* (formerly *Casket*). Poe, who had been with *Burton's*, would shortly become editor of *Graham's*. Poe used it again in his 1845 collection *Tales by Edgar A. Poe;* this is the version which was very favorably reviewed in the November 1847 *Blackwood's Edinburgh Magazine* (A. H. Quinn).

2. "This great misfortune of not being able to be alone." Poe's line is from "De L'Homme" in *Les Caractères* by Jean de la Bruyère (1645–1696). The original reads, "*Tout notre mal vient de ne pouvoir être seuls. . . .*" Compare "Metzengerstein," note 4. Poe probably saw the line in Bulwer Lytton's novel *Pelham* (1828), where it appears as the motto of chapter 42.

3. Poe later said this of another book. See his "Fifty Suggestions," number 46. See also note 16.

4. ἀχλὺς ἥ πρὶν ἐπῆεν: In Book V of *The Iliad*, Athena says to Diomedes, "Take heart in battle, for I have removed *the mist from your eyes that was there before,* so that you will be able to tell gods from men." The translation of Poe's quotation appears in italics. Editors alter the case to match the passage to its grammatical context in the English sentence.

Gottfried Wilhelm Leibnitz (1646–1716); Gorgias (c. 483–375 B. C. E.): Poe contrasts the two philosophers: Leibnitz, the eternal reconciler, lover of unity, order and relationships; Gorgias, by repute so great a rhetorician that rhetoric became an end in itself, even at the expense of logic.

For comments on the importance of this paragraph for the plausibility of the tale, see Section Preface.

5. aristocrats. Note how Poe's great catalogue of people seen from the coffee-house window is organized—it begins with the most prosperous and descends through clerks, criminals, gamblers, etc. The "dregs and lees" of society—what we would today more sympathetically call "people of the inner city" —ultimately give birth to the Man of the Crowd. Fear of him is largely fear of the city itself.

6. flash houses: firms engaged in new, showy, and speculative lines of business.

bon ton: fashionable style.

7. See Section Preface for comments on Poe's categories of genre.

8. The thimble-rig is the old name for the shell-game—the victim is supposed to guess under which "thimble" the pea is hidden.

9. statue in Lucian: In "The Cock," the Greek satiric writer Lucian (c. 125–c. 200) has the cock say, speaking of himself as a ruler, "I was like those colossal statues, the work of Phidias, Myron or Praxiteles: they too look extremely well from outside: 'tis Posidon with his trident, Zeus with his thunderbolt, all ivory and gold: but take a peep inside, and what have we? One tangle of bars, bolts, nails, planks, wedges, with pitch and mortar and everything that is unsightly; not to mention a possible colony of rats or mice. There you have royalty" (Fowler translation). Poe alludes to the passage again in "Fifty Suggestions."

Parian marble: marble from Paros, in the Cyclades, famous in the ancient world as a fine white statuary marble.

Poe's economic and racial stereotypes are offensive and should be so labeled. Most writers of his day seem unable to transcend the fear with which the impoverished or the persecuted were regarded, and Poe is usually more racist or condescending than other major authors. This paragraph is exceptional in that it shows a certain compassion and even social concern.

10. ebony . . . Tertullian: "Ebony" was a name by which other writers for *Blackwood's* referred to William Blackwood: ebony is "black wood." (See "How to Write a Blackwood Article," note 6.) Tertullian is Quintus

Septimius Florens Tertullianus (c. 150–after 220), an important church writer noted for the vigor and vehemence of his denunciation of worldliness. He is said by the *Catholic Encyclopedia* to be "the most difficult of all Latin prose writers." Another source says that he wrote in "the Asiatic manner," a fashionable "modern" style of his day characterized by short paratactical sentences adorned with play on sounds and words; a style "personal, pregnant, terse and not free from obscurity," yet "powerful and passionate." We would suggest a search of Lactantius, St. Jerome, or Gibbon, three writers of different ages who have commented on his dense but polished ("ebony"?) style. Poe intends a wry comment on the *Blackwood's* style, and on his own story, certainly "dark yet splendid," and whose basic source may be traced to *Blackwood's*. See Section Preface.

11. Retzsch: Moritz Retzsch (1779–1857), a German painter, etcher, and designer, noted for his etchings in outline to illustrate Goethe, Schiller, Shakespeare, and others.

12. Short cloak: See "The Cask of Amontillado," note 6. Poe spelled the word "*roque-laure*" in the 1840 version.

13. too dangerously pleasant: Poe reminds us of the sickness as we approach the portion of the tale—the long "chase"—which critics consider implausible. See note 4 and Section Preface.

American City: Poe is of course right; London was enormous compared to the American cities Poe's readers knew. But he mentions the size partly to play on the traditional American fear of the large city, an agrarian bias which, urban dweller though he was, he as a Virginian may have felt. American magazines by the 1830s ran articles on problems posed by urban growth; Poe, who followed all the notable journals, certainly had read such pieces. In the 1840s, indeed, Poe himself would comment on A. J. Downing's suburban residential ideas, which grow directly out of this fear of the urban environment. See "Mellonta Tauta," note 2.

14. rubber: See "Mellonta Tauta," note 5.

15. Poe's tour of the city parallels his catalogue of its inhabitants; we move from the prosperous to the most desperate.

16. Poe refers to the *Hortulus Animæ cum Oratiiunculis Aliquibus Superadditis quae in prioribus Libris non habentur* (1500) of John Grunninger (c. 1455–c. 1533). Poe probably learned of this work in Isaac Disraeli's *Curiosities of Literature*, a work he used frequently. Disraeli says it is exceedingly obnoxious, not so much for the text, as for the illustrations. See Figure Eleven.

7. Slapstick Gothic

Our old picture of Poe composing in a cobwebby attic, bats flapping about his lofty brow, does not square very well with what modern scholarship has discovered about tales such as those in this little group. Poe snickering up his sleeve is more like it. If Poe is abnormally afraid of the plague, why is "King Pest" a political allegory? And why does he mock such fear in "The Sphinx"? If he is "haunted" by gothicism, how can he parody it uproariously in "Metzengerstein"? And if fear of entombment alive is the result of a deep psychic scar inflicted in infancy, as Marie Bonaparte tells us, why does the narrator of "The Premature Burial" tell us to open our windows, let in the fresh air, fling out our morbid books, and enjoy life?

King Pest. A. H. Quinn says that "King Pest" is funny only if the reader is familiar with Chapter 1, Book 6 of Disraeli's *Vivian Grey* (1826), of which it is a burlesque.

William Whipple (2) thinks first, that Poe may have used cholera because Baltimore and Washington had epidemics during the election campaign of 1832; second, that the drinking scene might parody an extremely wet banquet on January 8, 1835, honoring both President Jackson, on the anniversary of his victory at the Battle of New Orleans, and the abolition of the national debt; third, that Poe may have thought of an undertaker's parlor because of the attempted assassination of Jackson on January 30, 1835.

Whipple (2) identifies the "allegorical" characters as follows: King Pest the First = Jackson; Queen Pest = Rachel Jackson; the Arch Duchess Ana-Pest = Peggy Eaton; the man with the bandaged leg and cheeks on his shoulders = Colonel Thomas Hart Benton; the thin man with the alcoholic tremor = Francis Blair of the *Globe*; the paralyzed man in the coffin could be either Amos Kendall or William H. Crawford; Tarpaulin = Martin Van Buren; Legs might be Major Jack Downing. Our explication strongly suggests that the identification is valid: see notes 1, 2, 5, 7, and 11.

"King Pest" has an energy of its own, however, which has carried along generations of readers unaware of allegorical meaning.

Metzengerstein. This Folio Club story was probably told by "Mr. Horribile Dictu" (Thompson 2, 4). This means that Poe is not serious about its gothi cism; indeed, A. H. Quinn, Thompson, and others see it as a satire on the gothic mode. Certainly the story spends a good deal of its space telling us of its own absurdity, and Thompson (2, 4) catalogues ironic and contradictory elements within it: everything is so complicated and cockeyed that Poe must be joking. Incongruities abound, too, as when Poe tells us that "near neighbors are seldom friends," and places castle and palace so close together that the families can look into one another's windows, a modern urban phenomenon comically cozy for such rural and aristocratic protagonists. Readers who are unfamiliar with gothic literature or who have trouble understanding Poe's joke are urged to read Thompson's good essay, which spells out Poe's hoax in detail. The essay and an expanded discussion of its ideas appear in his book, *Poe's Fiction: Romantic Irony in the Gothic Tales.*

We suggest comparing this tale first with "Mystification," to see how Poe handles "meaninglessness," and second with some of his more serious gothic efforts, such as "The Fall of the House of Usher" or "The Pit and the Pendulum." Poe never ceases to "put us on," of course; there are hoaxes and little jokes hidden in all types of stories. But "Usher" and "The Pit" lack the peculiar itchy quality of this tale; it seems clear that here Poe's primary intention is humor.

The Premature Burial. Three points need to be made about this important story:

1. It pretends to be an article, not a work of fiction. The narrator does not become important until more than half the story is over. This is, in short, a hoax.

2. The narrator's worst nightmare emphasizes not horror and terror, but woe and compassion.

3. Horror is clearly not in control of Poe. The "article" portion of the story is rather like a *Reader's Digest* piece, a string of related strange anecdotes; the "tale" portion mocks fear of premature entombment. Poe's penultimate paragraph, indeed, argues for a healthy attitude, for breathing "the free air of heaven," and for avoiding creepy books and "charnel apprehensions."

The Sphinx. This story should be compared with "The Masque of the Red Death" to make the point that fear of epidemics is something Poe turned on and off and not a lifelong obsession, for this tale is as cool as the other is heated. It should also be compared with any of the stories told by an excitable narrator, to make clear that the narrator who says "men have called me mad" is not Poe. This narrator has all the usual characteristics, but Poe clearly is detached from him. Indeed, Poe makes fun of him—the fellow is silly enough to scare himself with a bug. His state of "heightened consciousness" makes the "vision" possible, but there is no ambiguity; the wild vision is *not* real; he saw a bug, nothing more.

The Tales

KING PEST

A Tale Containing an Allegory

*The gods do bear and well allow
     in kings
The things which they abhor in
     rascal routes.*
                    Buckhurst's Tragedy of
                         Ferrex and Porrex[1]

About twelve o'clock, one night in the month of October, and during the chivalrous reign of the third Edward, two seamen belonging to the crew of the "Free and Easy," a trading schooner plying between Sluys and the Thames, and then at anchor in that river, were much astonished to find themselves seated in the taproom of an ale-house in the parish of St. Andrews,[2] London—which ale-house bore for sign the portraiture of a "Jolly Tar."

The room, although ill-contrived, smoke-blackened, low-pitched, and in every other respect agreeing with the general character of such places at the period —was nevertheless, in the opinion of the grotesque groups scattered here and there within it, sufficiently well adapted to its purpose.

Of these groups our two seamen formed, I think, the most interesting if not the most conspicuous.

The one who appeared to be the elder, and whom his companion addressed by the characteristic appellation of "Legs," was at the same time much the taller of the two. He might have measured six feet and a half, and an habitual stoop in the shoulders seemed to have been the necessary consequence of an altitude so enormous. Superfluities in height were, however, more than accounted for by de-

ficiencies in other respects. He was exceedingly thin; and might, as his associates asserted, have answered, when drunk, for a pennant at the mast-head, or, when sober, have served for a jib-boom. But these jests, and others of a similar nature, had evidently produced, at no time, any effect upon the cachinnatory muscles of the tar. With high cheek-bones, a large hawk-nose, retreating chin, fallen under-jaw, and huge protruding white eyes, the expression of his countenance, although tinged with a species of dogged indifference to matters and things in general, was not the less utterly solemn and serious beyond all attempts at imitation or description.

The younger seaman was, in all outward appearance, the converse of his companion. His stature could not have exceeded four feet. A pair of stumpy bowlegs supported his squat, unwieldy figure, while his unusually short and thick arms, with no ordinary fists at their extremities, swung off dangling from his sides like the fins of a sea-turtle. Small eyes, of no particular colour, twinkled far back in his head. His nose remained buried in the mass of flesh which enveloped his round, full, and purple face; and his thick upper-lip rested upon the still thicker one beneath with an air of complacent self-satisfaction, much heightened by the owner's habit of licking them at intervals. He evidently regarded his tall shipmate with a feeling half-wondrous, half-quizzical; and stared up occasionally in his face as the red setting sun stares up at the crags of Ben Nevis.[3]

Various and eventful, however, had been the peregrinations of the worthy couple in and about the different tap-houses of the neighborhood during the earlier hours of the night. Funds even the most ample, are not always everlasting: and it was with empty pockets our friends had ventured upon the present hostelrie.

At the precise period, then, when this history properly commences, Legs, and his fellow, Hugh Tarpaulin, sat, each with both elbows resting upon the large oaken table in the middle of the floor, and with a hand upon either cheek. They were eyeing, from behind a huge flagon of unpaid-for "humming-stuff," the portentous words, "No Chalk,"[4] which to their indignation and astonishment were scored over the door-way by means of that very mineral whose presence they purported to deny. Not that the gift of decyphering written characters—a gift among the commonalty of that day considered little less cabalistical than the art of inditing—could, in strict justice, have been laid to the charge of either disciple of the sea; but there was, to say the truth, a certain twist in the formation of the letters—an indescribable lee-lurch about the whole—which foreboded, in the opinion of both seamen, a long run of dirty weather; and determined them at once, in the allegorical words of Legs himself, to "pump ship, clew up all sail, and scud before the wind."

Having accordingly disposed of what remained of the ale, and looped up the points of their short doublets, they finally made a bolt for the street. Although Tarpaulin rolled twice into the fireplace, mistaking it for the door, yet their escape was at length happily effected—and half after twelve o'clock found our heroes ripe for mischief, and running for life down a dark alley in the direction of St. Andrew's Stair,[5] hotly pursued by the landlady of the "Jolly Tar."

At the epoch of this eventful tale, and periodically, for many years before and after, all England, but more especially the metropolis, resounded with the fearful cry of "Plague!" The city was in a great measure depopulated—and in those horrible regions, in the vicinity of the Thames, where, amid the dark, narrow, and filthy lanes and alleys, the Demon of Disease was supposed to have had his nativity, Awe, Terror, and Superstition were alone to be found stalking abroad.

By authority of the king such districts were placed *under ban*, and all persons forbidden, under pain of death, to intrude upon their dismal solitude. Yet neither the mandate of the monarch, nor the huge barriers erected at the entrances of the streets, nor the prospect of that loathsome death which, with almost absolute certainty, overwhelmed the wretch whom no peril could deter from the adventure, prevented the unfurnished and untenanted dwellings from being stripped, by the hand of nightly rapine, of every article, such as iron, brass, or lead-work, which could in any manner be turned to a profitable account.

Above all, it was usually found, upon the annual winter opening of the barriers, that locks, bolts, and secret cellars had proved but slender protection to those rich stores of wines and liquors which, in consideration of the risk and trouble of removal, many of the numerous dealers having shops in the neighborhood had consented to trust, during the period of exile, to so insufficient a security.

But there were very few of the terror-stricken people who attributed these doings to the agency of human hands. Pest-spirits, plague-goblins, and fever-demons were the popular imps of mischief; and tales so bloodchilling were hourly told, that the whole mass of forbidden buildings was, at length, enveloped in terror as in a shroud, and the plunderer himself was often scared away by the horrors his own depredations had created; leaving the entire vast circuit of prohibited district to gloom, silence, pestilence, and death.

It was by one of the terrific barriers already mentioned, and which indicated the region beyond to be under the Pest-ban, that, in scrambling down an alley, Legs and the worthy Hugh Tarpaulin found their progress suddenly impeded. To return was out of the question, and no time was to be lost, as their pursuers were close upon their heels. With thorough-bred seamen to clamber up the roughly fashioned plank-work was a trifle; and, maddened with the twofold excitement of exercise and liquor, they leaped unhesitatingly down within the enclosure, and holding on their drunken course with shouts and yellings, were soon bewildered in its noisome and intricate recesses.

Had they not, indeed, been intoxicated beyond moral sense, their reeling footsteps must have been palsied by the horrors of their situation. The air was cold and misty. The paving-stones, loosened from their beds, lay in wild disorder amid the tall, rank grass, which sprang up around the feet and ankles. Fallen houses choked up the streets. The most fetid and poisonous smells everywhere prevailed; —and by the aid of that ghastly light which, even at midnight, never fails to emanate from a vapory and pestilential atmosphere, might be discerned lying in the by-paths and alleys, or rotting in the windowless habitations, the carcass of many a nocturnal plunderer arrested by the hand of the plague in the very perpetration of his robbery.

But it lay not in the power of images, or sensations, or impediments such as these, to stay the course of men who, naturally brave, and at that time especially, brimful of courage and of "humming-stuff," would have reeled, as straight as their condition might have permitted, undauntedly into the very jaws of Death. Onward—still onward stalked the grim Legs, making the desolate solemnity echo and reecho with yells like the terrific war-whoop of the Indian; and onward, still onward rolled the dumpy Tarpaulin, hanging on to the doublet of his more active companion, and far surpassing the latter's most strenuous exertions in the way of vocal music, by bull-roarings in *basso*,[6] from the profundity of his stentorian lungs.

They had now evidently reached the stronghold of the pestilence. Their way at every step or plunge grew more noisome and more horrible—the paths more narrow and more intricate. Huge stones and beams falling momently from the decaying roofs above them, gave evidence, by their sullen and heavy descent, of the vast height of the surrounding houses; and while actual exertion became necessary to force a passage through frequent heaps of rubbish, it was by no means seldom that the hand fell upon a skeleton or rested upon a more fleshly corpse.

Suddenly, as the seamen stumbled against the entrance of a tall and ghastly-looking building, a yell more than usually shrill from the throat of the excited Legs, was replied to from within, in a rapid succession of wild, laughter-like, and fiendish shrieks. Nothing daunted at sounds which, of such a nature, at such a time, and in such a place, might have curdled the very blood in hearts less irrevocably on fire, the drunken couple rushed headlong against the door, burst it open, and staggered into the midst of things with a volley of curses.

The room within which they found themselves proved to be the shop of an undertaker; but an open trap-door, in a corner of the floor near the entrance, looked down upon a long range of wine-cellars, whose depths the occasional sound of bursting bottles proclaimed to be well stored with their appropriate contents. In the middle of the room stood a table—in the centre of which again arose a huge tub of what appeared to be punch. Bottles of various wines and cordials, together with jugs, pitchers, and flagons of every shape and quality, were scattered profusely upon the board. Around it, upon coffin-tressels, was seated a company of six. This company I will endeavour to delineate one by one.

Fronting the entrance, and elevated a little above his companions, sat a personage who appeared to be the president of the table. His stature was gaunt and tall, and Legs was confounded to behold in him a figure more emaciated than himself. His face was as yellow as saffron—but no feature excepting one alone, was sufficiently marked to merit a particular description. This one consisted in a forehead so unusually and hideously lofty, as to have the appearance of a bonnet or crown of flesh superadded upon the natural head.[7] His mouth was puckered and dimpled into an expression of ghastly affability, and his eyes, as indeed the eyes of all at table, were glazed over with the fumes of intoxication. This gentleman was clothed from head to foot in a richly-embroidered black silk-velvet pall, wrapped negligently around his form after the fashion of a Spanish cloak. His head was stuck full of sable hearse-plumes, which he nodded to and fro with a jaunty and knowing air; and, in his right hand, he held a huge human thigh-bone, with which he appeared to have been just knocking down some member of the company for a song.

Opposite him, and with her back to the door, was a lady of no whit the less extraordinary character. Although quite as tall as the person just described, she had no right to complain of his unnatural emaciation. She was evidently in the last stage of a dropsy; and her figure resembled nearly that of the huge puncheon of October beer which stood, with the head driven in, close by her side, in a corner of the chamber. Her face was exceedingly round, red, and full; and the same peculiarity, or rather want of peculiarity, attached itself to her countenance, which I before mentioned in the case of the president—that is to say, only one feature of her face was sufficiently distinguished to need a separate characterization: indeed the acute Tarpaulin immediately observed that the same remark might have applied to each individual person of the party; every one of whom seemed to possess a monopoly of some particular portion of physiognomy. With the lady in question this portion proved to be the mouth. Commencing at the right ear, it swept with a terrific chasm to the left—the short pendants which she wore in either auricle continually bobbing into the aperture. She made, however, every exertion to keep her mouth closed and look dignified, in a dress consisting of a newly starched and ironed shroud coming up close under her chin, with a crimpled ruffle of cambric muslin. At her right hand sat a diminutive young lady whom she appeared to patronize. This delicate little creature, in the trembling of her wasted fingers, in the livid hue of her lips, and in the slight hectic spot which tinged her otherwise leaden complexion, gave evident indications of a galloping consumption. An air of extreme *haut ton*, however, pervaded her whole appearance; she wore in a graceful and *dégagé*[8] manner, a large and beautiful winding-sheet of the finest India lawn; her hair hung in ringlets over her neck; a soft smile played about her mouth; but her nose, extremely long, thin, sinuous, flexible, and pimpled, hung down far below her under-lip, and, in spite of the delicate manner in which she now and then moved it to one side or the other with her tongue, gave to her countenance a somewhat equivocal expression.

Over against her, and upon the left of the dropsical lady, was seated a little puffy, wheezing, and gouty old man, whose cheeks reposed upon the shoulders of their owner, like two huge bladders of Oporto[9] wine. With his arms folded, and with one bandaged leg deposited upon the table, he seemed to think himself entitled to some consideration. He evidently prided himself much upon every inch of his personal appearance, but took more especial delight in calling attention to his gaudy-coloured surtout. This, to say the truth, must have cost him no little money, and was made to fit him exceedingly well—being fashioned from one of the curiously embroidered silken covers appertaining to those glorious escutcheons which, in England and elsewhere, are customarily hung up, in some conspicuous place, upon the dwellings of departed aristocracy.

Next to him, and at the right hand of the president, was a gentleman in long white hose and cotton drawers. His frame shook, in a ridiculous manner, with a fit of what Tarpaulin called "the horrors." His jaws, which had been newly shaved, were tightly tied up by a bandage of muslin; and his arms being fastened in a similar way at the wrists, prevented him from helping himself too freely to the liquors upon the table; a precaution rendered necessary, in the opinion of Legs, by the peculiarly sottish and wine-bibbing cast of his visage. A pair of prodigious ears, nevertheless, which it was no doubt found impossible to confine, towered away into the atmosphere of the apartment, and were occasionally pricked up in a spasm, at the sound of the drawing of a cork.

Fronting him, sixthly and lastly, was situated a singularly stiff-looking personage, who, being afflicted with paralysis, must, to speak seriously, have felt very ill at ease in his unaccommodating habiliments. He was habited, somewhat uniquely, in a new and handsome mahogany coffin. Its top or head-piece pressed upon the skull of the wearer, and extended over it in the fashion of a hood, giving to the entire face an air of indescribable interest. Arm-holes had been cut in the sides for the sake not more of elegance than of convenience; but the dress, nevertheless, prevented its proprietor from sitting as erect as his associates; and as he lay reclining against his tressel, at an angle of forty-five degrees, a pair of huge goggle eyes rolled up their awful whites toward the ceiling in absolute amazement at their own enormity.

Before each of the party lay a portion of a skull, which was used as a drinking-cup. Overhead was suspended a human skeleton, by means of a rope tied round one of the legs and fastened to a ring in the ceiling. The other limb, confined by no such fetter, stuck off from the body at right angles, causing the whole loose and rattling frame to dangle and twirl about at the caprice of every occasional puff of wind which found its way into the apartment. In the cranium of this hideous thing lay a quantity of ignited charcoal, which threw a fitful but vivid light over the entire scene; while coffins, and other wares appertaining to the shop of an undertaker, were piled high up around the room, and against the windows, preventing any ray from escaping into the street.

At sight of this extraordinary assembly, and of their still more extraordinary paraphernalia, our two seamen did not conduct themselves with that degree of decorum which might have been expected. Legs, leaning against the wall near which he happened to be standing, dropped his lower jaw still lower than usual, and spread open his eyes to their fullest extent; while Hugh Tarpaulin, stooping down so as to bring his nose upon a level with the table, and spreading out a palm upon either knee, burst into a long, loud, and obstreperous roar of very ill-timed and immoderate laughter.

Without, however, taking offence at behavior so excessively rude, the tall president smiled very graciously upon the intruders—nodded to them in a dignified manner with his head of sable plumes—and, arising, took each by an arm, and led him to a seat which some others of the company had placed in the meantime for his accommodation. Legs to all this offered not the slightest resistance, but sat down as he was directed; while the gallant Hugh, removing his coffin-tressel from its station near the head of the table, to the vicinity of the little consumptive lady in the winding-sheet, plumped down by her side in high glee, and pouring out a skull of red wine, quaffed it to their better acquaintance. But at this presumption the stiff gentleman in the coffin seemed exceedingly nettled; and serious consequences might have ensued, had not the president, rapping upon the table with his truncheon, diverted the attention of all present to the following speech:

"It becomes our duty upon the present happy occasion——"

"Avast there!" interrupted Legs, looking very serious, "avast there a bit, I say, and tell us who the devil ye all are, and what business ye have here, rigged off like the foul fiends, and swilling the snug blue ruin stowed away for the winter by my honest shipmate, Will Wimble,[10] the undertaker!"

At this unpardonable piece of ill-breeding, all the original company half-started to their feet, and uttered the same rapid succession of wild fiendish shrieks which had before caught the attention of the seamen. The president, however, was the first to recover his composure, and at length, turning to Legs with great dignity, recommenced:

"Most willingly will we gratify any reasonable curiosity on the part of guests so illustrious, unbidden though they be. Know then that in these dominions I am monarch, and here rule with undivided empire under the title of 'King Pest the First.'

"This apartment, which you no doubt profanely suppose to be the shop of Will Wimble the undertaker—a man whom we know not, and whose plebeian appellation has never before this night thwarted our royal ears—this apartment, I say, is the Dais-Chamber of our Palace, devoted to the councils of our kingdom, and to other sacred and lofty purposes.

"The noble lady who sits opposite is Queen Pest, our Serene Consort. The other exalted personages whom you behold are all of our family, and wear the insignia of the blood royal under the respective titles of 'His Grace the Arch Duke Pest-Iferous'—'His Grace the Duke Pest-Ilential'—'His Grace the Duke Tem-Pest' —and 'Her Serene Highness the Arch Duchess Ana-Pest.'[11]

"As regards," continued he, "your demand of the business upon which we sit here in council, we might be pardoned for replying that it concerns, and concerns *alone*, our own private and regal interest, and is in no manner important to any other than ourself. But in consideration of those rights to which as guests and strangers you may feel yourselves entitled, we will furthermore explain that we are here this night, prepared by deep research and accurate investigation, to examine, analyze, and thoroughly determine the indefinable spirit—the incomprehensible qualities and nare—of those inestimable treasures of the palate, the wines, ales, and liqueurs of this goodly metropolis: by so doing to advance not more our own designs than the true welfare of that unearthly sovereign whose reign is over us all, whose dominions are unlimited, and whose name is 'Death.'"

"Whose name is Davy Jones!" ejaculated Tarpaulin, helping the lady by his side to a skull of liqueur, and pouring out a second for himself.

"Profane varlet!" said the president, now turning his attention to the worthy Hugh, "profane and execrable wretch!—we have said, that in consideration of those rights which, even in thy filthy person, we feel no inclination to violate, we have condescended to make reply to thy rude and unreasonable inquiries. We nevertheless, for your unhallowed intrusion upon our councils, believe it our duty to mulct thee and thy companion in each a gallon of Black Strap—having imbibed which to the prosperity of our kingdom —at a single draught—and upon your bended knees—ye shall be forthwith free either to proceed upon your way, or remain and be admitted to the privileges of our table, according to your respective and individual pleasures."

"It would be a matter of utter impossibility," replied Legs, whom the assumptions and dignity of King Pest the First had evidently inspired with some feelings of respect, and who arose and steadied himself by the table as he spoke—"it would, please your majesty, be a matter of utter impossibility to stow away in my hold even one fourth part of that same liquor which your majesty has just mentioned.

To say nothing of the stuffs placed on board in the forenoon by way of ballast, and not to mention the various ales and liqueurs shipped this evening at different sea-ports, I have, at present, a full cargo of 'humming-stuff' taken in and duly paid for at the sign of the 'Jolly Tar.' You will, therefore, please your majesty, be so good as to take the will for the deed—for by no manner of means either can I or will I swallow another drop—least of all a drop of that villainous bilge-water that answers to the hail of 'Black Strap.' "

"Belay that!" interrupted Tarpaulin, astonished not more at the length of his companion's speech than at the nature of his refusal—"Belay that, you lubber!— and I say, Legs, none of your palaver. *My* hull is still light, although I confess you yourself seem to be a little topheavy; and as far as the matter of your share of the cargo, why rather than raise a squall I would find stowage-room for it myself, but"——

"This proceeding," interposed the President, "is by no means in accordance with the terms of the mulct or sentence, which is in its nature Median,[12] and not to be altered or recalled. The conditions we have imposed must be fulfilled to the letter, and that without a moment's hesitation—in failure of which fulfilment we decree that you do here be tied neck and heels together, and duly drowned as rebels in yon hogshead of October beer!"

"A sentence!—a sentence!—a righteous and just sentence!—a glorious decree!—a most worthy and upright, and holy condemnation!" shouted the Pest family altogether. The king elevated his forehead into innumerable wrinkles; the gouty little old man puffed like a pair of bellows; the lady of the winding-sheet waved her nose to and fro; the gentleman in the cotton drawers pricked up his ears; she of the shroud gasped like a dying fish; and he of the coffin looked stiff and rolled up his eyes.

"Ugh! ugh! ugh!" chuckled Tarpaulin without heeding the general excitation, "ugh! ugh! ugh!—ugh! ugh! ugh! ugh!— ugh! ugh! ugh!—I was saying," said he, —"I was saying when Mr. King Pest poked in his marlin-spike, that as for the matter of two or three gallons more or less of Black Strap, it was a trifle to a tight sea-boat like myself not overstowed—but when it comes to drinking the health of the Devil (whom God assoilzie)[13] and going down upon my marrow bones to his ill-favored majesty there, whom I know, as well as I know myself to be a sinner, to be nobody in the whole world but Tim Hurlygurly the stage-player—why! it's quite another guess sort of a thing, and utterly and altogether past my comprehension."

He was not allowed to finish this speech in tranquility. At the name of Tim Hurlygurly the whole assembly leaped from their seats.

"Treason!" shouted his Majesty King Pest the First.

"Treason!" said the little man with the gout.

"Treason!" screamed the Arch Duchess Ana-Pest.

"Treason!" muttered the gentleman with his jaws tied up.

"Treason!" growled he of the coffin.

"Treason! treason!" shrieked her majesty of the mouth; and, seizing by the hinder part of his breeches the unfortunate Tarpaulin, who had just commenced pouring out for himself a skull of liqueur, she lifted him high into the air, and let him fall without ceremony into the huge open puncheon of his beloved ale. Bobbing up and down, for a few seconds, like an apple in a bowl of toddy, he, at length, finally disappeared amid the whirlpool of foam which, in the already effervescent liquor, his struggles easily succeeded in creating.

Not tamely, however, did the tall seaman behold the discomfiture of his companion. Jostling King Pest through the open trap, the valiant Legs slammed the door down upon him with an oath, and strode toward the centre of the room. Here tearing down the skeleton which swung over the table, he laid it about him with so much energy and good will, that, as the last glimpses of light died away within the apartment, he succeeded in knocking out the brains of the little gentleman with the gout. Rushing then with all his force against the fatal hogshead full of October ale and Hugh Tarpaulin, he rolled it over and over in an instant. Out burst a deluge of liquor so fierce—so impetuous—so overwhelming—that the room was flooded from wall to wall—the loaded table was overturned—the tressels were thrown upon their backs—the tub of punch into the fire-place—and the ladies into hysterics. Piles of death-furniture floundered about. Jugs, pitchers, and carboys mingled promiscuously in the *mêlée*, and wicker flagons encountered desperately with bottles of junk. The man with the horrors was drowned upon the spot—the little stiff gentleman floated off in his coffin—and the victorious Legs, seizing by the waist the fat lady in the shroud, rushed out with her into the street, and made a bee-line for the "Free and Easy," followed under easy sail by the redoubtable Hugh Tarpaulin, who, having sneezed three or four times, panted and puffed after him with the Arch Duchess Ana-Pest.

METZENGERSTEIN

Pestis eram vivus—moriens tua mors ero.
Martin Luther[1]

Horror and fatality have been stalking abroad in all ages. Why then give a date to the story I have to tell?[2] Let it suffice to say, that at the period of which I speak, there existed, in the interior of Hungary, a settled although hidden belief in the doctrines of the Metempsychosis.[3] Of the doctrines themselves—that is, of their falsity, or of their probability—I say nothing. I assert, however, that much of our incredulity (as La Bruyère says of all our unhappiness) *"vient de ne pouvoir être seuls."*[4]

But there were some points in the Hungarian superstition which were fast verging to absurdity. They—the Hungarians—differed very essentially from their Eastern authorities. For example. *"The soul,"* said the former—I give the words of an acute and intelligent Parisian—*"ne demeure qu'une seule fois dans un corps sensible: au reste—un cheval, un chien, un homme même, n'est que la ressemblance peu tangible de ces animaux."*[5]

The families of Berlifitzing and Metzengerstein had been at variance for centuries. Never before were two houses so illustrious, mutually embittered by hostility so deadly. The origin of this enmity seems to be found in the words of an ancient prophecy—"A lofty name shall have a fearful fall when, as the rider over his horse, the mortality of Metzengerstein shall triumph over the immortality of Berlifitzing."[6]

To be sure the words themselves had little or no meaning. But more trivial causes have given rise—and that no long while ago—to consequences equally eventful. Besides, the estates, which were contiguous, had long exercised a rival influence in the affairs of a busy government. Moreover, near neighbors are seldom friends; and the inhabitants of the Castle Berlifitzing might look, from their lofty buttresses, into the very windows of the Palace Metzengerstein.[7] Least of all had the more than feudal magnificence thus discovered a tendency to allay the irritable feelings of the less ancient and less wealthy Berlifitzings. What wonder, then, that the words, however silly, of that prediction, should have succeeded in setting and keeping at variance two families already predisposed to quarrel by every instigation of hereditary jealousy? The prophecy seemed to imply—if it implied anything—a final triumph on the part of the already more powerful house; and was of course remembered with the more bitter animosity by the weaker and less influential.

Wilhelm, Count Berlifitzing, although loftily descended, was, at the epoch of this narrative, an infirm and doting old man, remarkable for nothing but an inordinate and inveterate personal antipathy to the family of his rival, and so passionate a love of horses, and of hunting, that neither bodily infirmity, great age, nor mental incapacity, prevented his daily participation in the dangers of the chase.

Frederick, Baron Metzengerstein, was, on the other hand, not yet of age. His father, the Minister G——, died young. His mother, the Lady Mary, followed him quickly. Frederick was, at that time, in his eighteenth year. In a city, eighteen years are no long period: but in a wilderness— in so magnificent a wilderness as that old principality, the pendulum vibrates with a deeper meaning.

From some peculiar circumstances attending the administration of his father, the young Baron, at the decease of the former, entered immediately upon his vast possessions. Such estates were seldom held before by a nobleman of Hungary. His castles were without number. The chief in point of splendor and extent was the "Palace Metzengerstein." The boundary line of his dominions was never clearly defined; but his principal park embraced a circuit of fifty miles.

Upon the succession of a proprietor so young, with a character so well known, to a fortune so unparalleled, little speculation was afloat in regard to his probable course of conduct. And, indeed, for the space of three days, the behaviour of the heir out-heroded Herod,[8] and fairly surpassed the expectations of his most enthusiastic admirers. Shameful debaucheries —flagrant treacheries—unheard-of atrocities—gave his trembling vassals quickly to understand that no servile submission on their part—no punctilios of conscience on his own—were thenceforward to prove

any security against the remorseless fangs of a petty Caligula.[9] On the night of the fourth day, the stables of the Castle Berlifitzing were discovered to be on fire; and the unanimous opinion of the neighborhood added the crime of the incendiary to the already hideous list of the Baron's misdemeanors and enormities.

But during the tumult occasioned by this occurrence, the young nobleman himself, sat apparently buried in meditation, in a vast and desolate upper apartment of the family palace of Metzengerstein. The rich although faded tapestry hangings which swung gloomily upon the walls, represented the shadowy and majestic forms of a thousand illustrious ancestors. *Here*, rich-ermined priests, and pontifical dignitaries, familiarly seated with the autocrat and the sovereign, put a veto on the wishes of a temporal king, or restrained with the fiat of papal supremacy the rebellious sceptre of the Arch-enemy. *There*, the dark, tall statures of the Princes Metzengerstein—their muscular war-coursers plunging over the carcasses of fallen foes—startled the steadiest nerves with their vigorous expression: and *here*, again, the voluptuous and swan-like figures of the dames of days gone by, floated away in the mazes of an unreal dance to the strains of imaginary melody.

But as the Baron listened, or affected to listen, to the gradually increasing uproar in the stables of Berlifitzing—or perhaps pondered upon some more novel, some more decided act of audacity—his eyes were turned unwittingly to the figure of an enormous, and unnaturally coloured horse, represented in the tapestry as belonging to a Saracen ancestor of the family of his rival. The horse itself, in the foreground of the design, stood motionless and statue-like—while, farther back, its discomfited rider perished by the dagger of a Metzengerstein.

On Frederick's lip arose a fiendish expression, as he became aware of the direction which his glance had, without his consciousness, assumed. Yet he did not remove it. On the contrary, he could by no means account for the overwhelming anxiety which appeared falling like a pall upon his senses. It was with difficulty that he reconciled his dreamy and incoherent feelings with the certainty of being awake. The longer he gazed, the more absorbing became the spell—the more impossible did it appear that he could ever withdraw his glance from the fascination of that tapestry. But the tumult without becoming suddenly more violent, with a compulsory exertion he diverted his attention to the glare of ruddy light thrown full by the flaming stables upon the windows of the apartment.

The action, however, was but momentary; his gaze returned mechanically to the wall. To his extreme horror and astonishment, the head of the gigantic steed had, in the meantime, altered its position. The neck of the animal, before arched, as if in compassion, over the prostrate body of its lord, was now extended, at full length, in the direction of the Baron. The eyes, before invisible, now wore an energetic and human expression, while they gleamed with a fiery and unusual red; and the distended lips of the apparently enraged horse left in full view his sepulchral and disgusting teeth.

Stupefied with terror, the young nobleman tottered to the door. As he threw it open, a flash of red light, streaming far into the chamber, flung his shadow with a clear outline against the quivering tapestry; and he shuddered to perceive that shadow—as he staggered awhile upon the threshold—assuming the exact position, and precisely filling up the contour, of the relentless and triumphant murderer of the Saracen Berlifitzing.

To lighten the depression of his spirits, the Baron hurried into the open air. At the principal gate of the palace he encountered three equerries. With much difficulty, and at the imminent peril of their lives, they were restraining the convulsive plunges of a gigantic and fiery-coloured horse.

"Whose horse? Where did you get him?" demanded the youth, in a querulous and husky tone, as he became instantly aware that the mysterious steed in the tapestried chamber was the very counterpart of the furious animal before his eyes.

"He is your own property, sire," replied one of the equerries, "at least he is claimed by no other owner. We caught him flying, all smoking and foaming with rage, from the burning stables of the Castle Berlifitzing. Supposing him to have belonged to the old Count's stud of foreign horses, we led him back as an estray. But the grooms there disclaim any title to the creature; which is strange, since he bears evident marks of having made a narrow escape from the flames."

"The letters W. V. B. are also branded very distinctly on his forehead," interrupted a second equerry; "I supposed them, of course, to be the initials of Wilhelm Von Berlifitzing—but all at the castle are positive in denying any knowledge of the horse."

"Extremely singular!" said the young Baron, with a musing air, and apparently unconscious of the meaning of his words. "He is, as you say, a remarkable horse—a prodigious horse! although, as you very justly observe, of a suspicious and untractable character; let him be mine, however," he added, after a pause, "perhaps a rider like Frederick of Metzengerstein, may tame even the devil from the stables of Berlifitzing."

"You are mistaken, my lord; the horse, as I think we mentioned, is *not* from the stables of the Count. If such had been the case, we know our duty better than to bring him into the presence of a noble of your family."

"True!" observed the Baron, drily; and at that instant a page of the bed-chamber came from the palace with a heightened color, and a precipitate step. He whispered into his master's ear an account of the sudden disappearance of a small portion of the tapestry, in an apartment which he designated; entering, at the same time, into particulars of a minute and circumstantial character; but from the low tone of voice in which these latter were communicated, nothing escaped to gratify the excited curiosity of the equerries.

The young Frederick, during the conference, seemed agitated by a variety of emotions. He soon, however, recovered his composure, and an expression of determined malignancy settled upon his countenance, as he gave peremptory orders that the apartment in question should be immediately locked up, and the key placed in his own possession.

"Have you heard of the unhappy death of the old hunter Berlifitzing?" said one of his vassals to the Baron, as, after the departure of the page, the huge steed which that nobleman had adopted as his own, plunged and curveted, with redoubled fury, down the long avenue which extended from the palace to the stables of Metzengerstein.

"No!" said the Baron, turning abruptly towards the speaker, "dead! say you?"

"It is indeed true, my lord; and, to the noble of your name, will be, I imagine, no unwelcome intelligence."

A rapid smile shot over the countenance of the listener. "How died he?"

"In his rash exertions to rescue a favorite portion of his hunting stud, he has himself perished miserably in the flames."

"I—n—d—e—e—d—!" ejaculated the Baron, as if slowly and deliberately impressed with the truth of some exciting idea.

"Indeed;" repeated the vassal.

"Shocking!" said the youth, calmly, and turned quietly into the palace.

From this date a marked alteration took place in the outward demeanor of the dissolute young Baron Frederick Von Metzengerstein. Indeed, his behaviour disappointed every expectation, and proved little in accordance with the views of many a manœuvring mamma; while his habits and manners, still less than formerly, offered anything congenial with those of the neighboring aristocracy. He was never to be seen beyond the limits of his own domain, and, in this wide and social world, was utterly companionless —unless, indeed, that unnatural, impetuous, and fiery-coloured horse, which he henceforward continually bestrode, had any mysterious right to the title of his friend.

Numerous invitations on the part of the neighborhood for a long time, however, periodically came in. "Will the Baron honor our festivals with his presence?" "Will the Baron join us in a hunting of the boar?"—"Metzengerstein does not hunt;" "Metzengerstein will not attend," were the haughty and laconic answers.

These repeated insults were not to be endured by an imperious nobility. Such invitations became less cordial—less frequent—in time they ceased altogether. The widow of the unfortunate Count Berlifitzing was even heard to express a hope "that the Baron might be at home when he did not wish to be at home, since he disdained the company of his equals; and ride when he did not wish to ride, since he preferred the society of a horse." This to be sure was a very silly explosion of hereditary pique; and merely proved how singularly unmeaning our sayings are apt to become, when we desire to be unusually energetic.

The charitable, nevertheless, attributed the alteration in the conduct of the young nobleman to the natural sorrow of a son for the untimely loss of his parents;—forgetting, however, his atrocious and reckless behaviour during the short period immediately succeeding that bereavement. Some there were, indeed, who suggested a too haughty idea of self-consequence and dignity. Others again (among whom may be mentioned the family physician) did not hesitate in speaking of morbid melancholy, and hereditary ill-health; while dark hints, of a more equivocal nature, were current among the multitude.

Indeed, the Baron's perverse attachment to his lately-acquired charger—an attachment which seemed to attain new strength from every fresh example of the animal's ferocious and demonlike propensities—at length became, in the eyes of all reasonable men, a hideous and unnatural fervor. In the glare of noon—at the dead hour of night—in sickness or in health[10]—in calm or in tempest—the young Metzengerstein seemed riveted to the saddle of that colossal horse, whose intractable audacities so well accorded with his own spirit.

There were circumstances, moreover, which, coupled with late events, gave an unearthly and portentous character to the mania of the rider, and to the capabilities of the steed. The space passed over in a single leap had been accurately measured, and was found to exceed by an astounding difference, the wildest expectations of the most imaginative. The Baron, besides, had no particular *name* for the animal, although all the rest in his collection were distinguished by characteristic appellations. His stable, too, was appointed at a distance from the rest; and with regard to grooming and other necessary offices, none but the owner in person had ventured to officiate, or even to enter the enclosure of that horse's particular stall. It was also to be observed, that although the three grooms, who had caught the steed as he fled from the conflagration at Berlifitzing, had succeeded in arresting his course, by means of a chain-bridle and noose—yet no one of the three could with any certainty affirm that he had, during that dangerous struggle, or at any period thereafter, actually placed his hand upon the body of the beast. Instances of peculiar intelligence in the demeanor of a noble and high-spirited horse are not to be supposed capable of exciting unreasonable attention, but there were certain circumstances which intruded themselves per force upon the most skeptical and phlegmatic; and it is said there were times when the animal caused the gaping crowd who stood around to recoil in horror from

the deep and impressive meaning of his terrible stamp—times when the young Metzengerstein turned pale and shrunk away from the rapid and searching expression of his earnest and human-looking eye.

Among the retinue of the Baron, however, none were found to doubt the ardor of that extraordinary affection which existed on the part of the young nobleman for the fiery qualities of his horse; at least, none but an insignificant and misshapen little page, whose deformities were in everybody's way, and whose opinions were of the least possible importance. He (if his ideas are worth mentioning at all,) had the effrontery to assert that his master never vaulted into the saddle, without an unaccountable and almost imperceptible shudder; and that, upon his return from every long-continued and habitual ride, an expression of triumphant malignity distorted every muscle in his countenance.

One tempestuous night, Metzengerstein, awaking from heavy slumber, descended like a maniac from his chamber, and, mounting in hot haste, bounded away into the mazes of the forest. An occurrence so common attracted no particular attention, but his return was looked for with intense anxiety on the part of his domestics, when, after some hours' absence, the stupendous and magnificent battlements of the Palace Metzengerstein, were discovered crackling and rocking to their very foundation, under the influence of a dense and livid mass of ungovernable fire.

As the flames, when first seen, had already made so terrible a progress that all efforts to save any portion of the building were evidently futile, the astonished neighborhood stood idly around in silent, if not apathetic wonder. But a new and fearful object soon riveted the attention of the multitude, and proved how much more intense is the excitement wrought in the feelings of a crowd by the contemplation of human agony, than that brought about by the most appalling spectacles of inanimate matter.

Up the long avenue of aged oaks which led from the forest to the main entrance of the Palace Metzengerstein,[11] a steed, bearing an unbonneted and disordered rider, was seen leaping with an impetuosity which outstripped the very Demon of the Tempest.

The career of the horseman was indisputably, on his own part, uncontrollable. The agony of his countenance, the convulsive struggle of his frame, gave evidence of superhuman exertion; but no sound, save a solitary shriek, escaped from his lacerated lips, which were bitten through and through in the intensity of terror. One instant, and the clattering of hoofs resounded sharply and shrilly above the roaring of the flames and the shrieking of the winds—another, and, clearing at a single plunge the gate-way and the moat, the steed bounded far up the tottering staircases of the palace, and, with its rider, disappeared amid the whirlwind of chaotic fire.

The fury of the tempest immediately died away, and a dead calm sullenly succeeded. A white flame still enveloped the building like a shroud, and, streaming far away into the quiet atmosphere, shot forth a glare of preternatural light; while a cloud of smoke settled heavily over the battlements in the distinct colossal figure of—a horse.

THE PREMATURE BURIAL

There are certain themes of which the interest is all-absorbing, but which are too entirely horrible for the purposes of legitimate fiction. These the mere romanticist must eschew, if he do not wish to offend, or to disgust. They are with propriety handled, only when the severity and majesty of Truth sanctify and sustain them. We thrill, for example, with the most intense of "pleasurable pain," over the accounts of the Passage of the Beresina, of the Earthquake at Lisbon, of the Plague at London, of the Massacre of St. Bartholomew, or of the stifling of the hundred and twenty-three prisoners in the Black Hole at Calcutta.[1] But, in these accounts, it is the fact—it is the reality—it is the history which excites. As inventions, we should regard them with simple abhorrence.

I have mentioned some few of the more prominent and august calamities on record; but, in these, it is the extent, not less than the character of the calamity, which so vividly impresses the fancy. I need not remind the reader that, from the long and weird catalogue of human miseries, I might have selected many individual instances more replete with essential suffering than any of these vast generalities of disaster. The true wretchedness, indeed— the ultimate woe—is particular, not diffuse. That the ghastly extremes of agony are endured by man the unit, and never by man the mass—for this let us thank a merciful God!

To be buried while alive, is, beyond question, the most terrific of these extremes which has ever fallen to the lot of mere mortality. That it has frequently, very frequently, so fallen, will scarcely be denied by those who think. The boundaries which divide Life from Death, are at best shadowy and vague. Who shall say where the one ends, and where the other begins? We know that there are diseases in which occur total cessations of all the apparent functions of vitality, and yet in which these cessations are merely suspensions, properly so called. They are only temporary pauses in the incomprehensible mechanism. A certain period elapses, and some unseen mysterious principle again sets in motion the magic pinions and the wizard wheels. The silver cord was not for ever loosed, nor the golden bowl irreparably broken. But where, meantime, was the soul?

Apart, however, from the inevitable conclusion, à priori,[2] that such causes must produce such effects—that the well known occurrence of such cases of suspended animation must naturally give rise, now and then, to premature interments—apart from this consideration, we have the direct testimony of medical and ordinary experience, to prove that a vast number of such interments have actually taken place. I might refer at once, if necessary, to a hundred well authenticated instances. One of very remarkable character, and of which the circumstances may be fresh in the memory of some of my readers, occurred, not very long ago, in the neighboring city of Baltimore, where it occasioned a painful, intense, and widely extended excitement. The wife of one of the most respectable citizens—a lawyer of eminence and a member of Congress—was seized with a sudden and unaccountable illness, which completely baffled the skill of her physicians. After much suffering she died, or was supposed to die. No one suspected, indeed, or had reason to suspect, that she was not actually dead. She presented all the ordinary appearances of death. The face assumed the usual pinched and sunken outline. The lips were of the usual marble pallor. The eyes were lustreless. There was no warmth. Pulsation had ceased. For three days the body was preserved unburied, during which it had acquired a stony rigidity. The funeral, in short, was hastened, on account of the rapid advance of what was supposed to be decomposition.

The lady was deposited in her family vault, which, for three subsequent years, was undisturbed. At the expiration of this term, it was opened for the reception of a sarcophagus;—but, alas! how fearful a shock awaited the husband, who, personally, threw open the door. As its portals swung outwardly back, some white-apparelled object fell rattling within his arms. It was the skeleton of his wife in her yet unmouldered shroud.

A careful investigation rendered it evident that she had revived within two days after her entombment—that her struggles within the coffin had caused it to fall from a ledge, or shelf, to the floor, where it was so broken as to permit her escape. A lamp which had been accidentally left, full of oil, within the tomb, was found empty; it might have been exhausted, however, by evaporation. On the uppermost of the steps which led down into the dread chamber, was a large fragment of the coffin, with which it seemed that she had endeavored to arrest attention, by striking the iron door. While thus occupied, she probably swooned, or possibly died, through sheer terror; and, in falling, her shroud became entangled in some iron-work which projected interiorly. Thus she remained, and thus she rotted, erect.

In the year 1810, a case of living inhumation happened in France, attended with circumstances which go far to warrant the assertion that truth is, indeed, stranger than fiction. The heroine of the story was a Mademoiselle Victorine Lafourcade,[3] a young girl of illustrious family, of wealth, and of great personal beauty. Among her numerous suitors was Julien Bossuet, a poor *littérateur*, or journalist, of Paris. His talents and general amiability had recommended him to the notice of the heiress, by whom he seems to have been truly beloved; but her pride of birth decided her, finally, to reject him, and to wed a Monsieur Rénelle, a banker, and a diplomatist of some eminence. After marriage, however, this gentleman neglected, and, perhaps, even more positively ill-treated her. Having passed with him some wretched years, she died,—at least her condition so closely resembled death as to deceive every one who saw her. She was buried—not in a vault—but in an ordinary grave in the village of her nativity. Filled with despair, and still inflamed by the memory of a profound attachment, the lover journeys from the capital to the remote province in which the village lies, with the romantic purpose of disinterring the corpse, and possessing himself of its luxuriant tresses. He reaches the grave. At midnight he unearths the coffin, opens it, and is in the act of detaching the hair, when he is arrested by the unclosing of the beloved eyes. In fact, the lady had been buried alive. Vitality had not altogether departed; and she was aroused, by the caresses of her lover, from the lethargy which had been mistaken for death. He bore her frantically to his lodgings in the village. He employed certain powerful restoratives suggested by no little medical learning. In fine, she revived. She recognized her preserver. She remained with him until, by slow degrees, she fully recovered her original health. Her woman's heart was not adamant, and this last lesson of love sufficed to soften it. She bestowed it upon Bossuet. She returned no more to her husband, but concealing from him her resurrection, fled with her lover to America. Twenty years afterwards, the two returned to France, in the persuasion that time had so greatly altered the lady's appearance that her friends would be unable to recognize her. They were mistaken, however; for, at the first meeting, Monsieur Rénelle did actually recognize and make claim to his wife. This claim she resisted; and a judicial tribunal sustained her in her resistance; deciding that the peculiar circumstances, with the long lapse of years, had extinguished, not only equitably but legally, the authority of the husband.

The "Chirurgical Journal" of Leipsic[4] —a periodical, of high authority and merit, which some American bookseller would do well to translate and republish —records, in a late number, a very distressing event of the character in question.

An officer of artillery, a man of gigantic stature and of robust health, being thrown from an unmanageable horse, received a very severe contusion upon the head, which rendered him insensible at once; the skull was slightly fractured; but no immediate danger was apprehended. Trepanning[5] was accomplished successfully. He was bled, and many other of the ordinary means of relief were adopted. Gradually, however, he fell into a more and

more hopeless state of stupor; and, finally, it was thought that he died.

The weather was warm; and he was buried, with indecent haste, in one of the public cemeteries. His funeral took place on Thursday. On the Sunday following, the grounds of the cemetery were, as usual, much thronged with visiters; and, about noon, an intense excitement was created by the declaration of a peasant that, while sitting upon the grave of the officer, he had distinctly felt a commotion of the earth, as if occasioned by some one struggling beneath. At first little attention was paid to the man's asseveration; but his evident terror, and the dogged obstinacy with which he persisted in his story, had, at length, their natural effect upon the crowd. Spades were hurriedly procured, and the grave, which was shamefully shallow, was, in a few minutes, so far thrown open that the head of its occupant appeared. He was then, seemingly, dead; but he sat nearly erect within his coffin, the lid of which, in his furious struggles, he had partially uplifted.

He was forthwith conveyed to the nearest Hospital, and there pronounced to be still living, although in an asphytic[6] condition. After some hours he revived, recognized individuals of his acquaintance, and, in broken sentences, spoke of his agonies in the grave.

From what he related, it was clear that he must have been conscious of life for more than an hour, while inhumed, before lapsing into insensibility. The grave was carelessly and loosely filled with an exceedingly porous soil; and thus some air was necessarily admitted. He heard the footsteps of the crowd overhead, and endeavored to make himself heard in turn. It was the tumult within the grounds of the cemetery, he said, which appeared to awaken him from a deep sleep—but no sooner was he awake than he became fully aware of the awful horrors of his position.

This patient, it is recorded, was doing well, and seemed to be in a fair way of ultimate recovery, but fell a victim to the quackeries of medical experiment. The galvanic battery was applied;[7] and he suddenly expired in one of those ecstatic paroxysms which, occasionally, it superinduces.

The mention of the galvanic battery, nevertheless, recalls to my memory a well known and very extraordinary case in point, where its action proved the means of restoring to animation a young attorney of London who had been interred for two days. This occurred in 1831, and created, at the time, a very profound sensation wherever it was made the subject of converse.

The patient, Mr. Edward Stapleton,[8] had died, apparently, of typhus fever, accompanied with some anomalous symptoms which had excited the curiosity of his medical attendants. Upon his seeming decease, his friends were requested to sanction a *post mortem* examination, but declined to permit it. As often happens when such refusals are made, the practitioners resolved to disinter the body and dissect it at leisure, in private. Arrangements were easily effected with some of the numerous corps of body-snatchers with which London abounds; and, upon the third night after the funeral, the supposed corpse was unearthed from a grave eight feet deep, and deposited in the operating chamber of one of the private hospitals.

An incision of some extent had been actually made in the abdomen, when the fresh and undecayed appearance of the subject suggested an application of the battery. One experiment succeeded another, and the customary effects supervened, with nothing to characterize them in any respect, except, upon one or two occasions, a more than ordinary degree of life-likeness in the convulsive action.

It grew late. The day was about to dawn; and it was thought expedient, at length, to proceed at once to the dissection. A student, however, was especially desirous of testing a theory of his own, and insisted upon applying the battery to one of the pectoral muscles. A rough gash was made, and a wire hastily brought in contact; when the patient, with a hurried but quite unconvulsive movement, arose from the table, stepped into the middle of the floor, gazed about him uneasily for a few seconds, and then—spoke. What he said was unintelligible; but words were uttered; the syllabification was distinct. Having spoken, he fell heavily to the floor.

For some moments all were paralyzed with awe—but the urgency of the case soon restored them their presence of mind. It was seen that Mr. Stapleton was alive, although in a swoon. Upon exhibition of ether he revived and was rapidly restored to health, and to the society of his friends —from whom, however, all knowledge of his resuscitation was withheld, until a relapse was no longer to be apprehended. Their wonder—their rapturous astonishment—may be conceived.

The most thrilling peculiarity of this incident, nevertheless, is involved in what Mr. S. himself asserts. He declares that at no period was he altogether insensible— that, dully and confusedly, he was aware of every thing which happened to him, from the moment in which he was pronounced *dead* by his physicians, to that in which he fell swooning to the floor of the Hospital. "I am alive" were the uncomprehended words which, upon recognizing the locality of the dissecting-room, he had endeavored, in his extremity, to utter.

It were an easy matter to multiply such histories as these—but I forbear—for, indeed, we have no need of such to establish the fact that premature interments occur. When we reflect how very rarely, from the nature of the case, we have it in our power to detect them, we must admit that they may *frequently* occur without our cognizance. Scarcely, in truth, is a graveyard ever encroached upon, for any purpose, to any great extent, that skeletons are not found in postures which suggest the most fearful of suspicions.

Fearful indeed the suspicion—but more

fearful the doom! It may be asserted, without hesitation, that *no* event is so terribly well adapted to inspire the supremeness of bodily and of mental distress, as is burial before death. The unendurable oppression of the lungs—the stifling fumes from the damp earth—the clinging of the death garments—the rigid embrace of the narrow house—the blackness of the absolute Night—the silence like a sea that overwhelms—the unseen but palpable presence of the Conqueror Worm[9]—these things, with thoughts of the air and grass above, with memory of dear friends who would fly to save us if but informed of our fate, and with consciousness that of this fate they can *never* be informed— that our hopeless portion is that of the really dead—these considerations, I say, carry into the heart, which still palpitates, a degree of appalling and intolerable horror from which the most daring imagination must recoil. We know of nothing so agonizing upon Earth—we can dream of nothing half so hideous in the realms of the nethermost Hell. And thus all narratives upon this topic have an interest profound; an interest, nevertheless, which, through the sacred awe of the topic itself, very properly and very peculiarly depends upon our conviction of the *truth* of the matter narrated. What I have now to tell, is of my own actual knowledge—of my own positive and personal experience.

For several years I had been subject to attacks of the singular disorder which physicians have agreed to term catalepsy, in default of a more definitive title. Although both the immediate and the predisposing causes, and even the actual diagnosis, of this disease, are still mysteries, its obvious and apparent character is sufficiently well understood. Its variations seem to be chiefly of degree. Sometimes the patient lies, for a day only, or even for a shorter period, in a species of exaggerated lethargy. He is senseless and externally motionless; but the pulsation of the heart is still faintly perceptible; some traces of warmth remain; a slight color

lingers within the centre of the cheek; and, upon application of a mirror to the lips, we can detect a torpid, unequal, and vacillating action of the lungs. Then again the duration of the trance is for weeks— even for months; while the closest scrutiny, and the most rigorous medical tests, fail to establish any material distinction between the state of the sufferer and what we conceive of absolute death. Very usually, he is saved from premature interment solely by the knowledge of his friends that he has been previously subject to catalepsy, by the consequent suspicion excited, and, above all, by the nonappearance of decay. The advances of the malady are, luckily, gradual. The first manifestations, although marked, are unequivocal. The fits grow successively more and more distinctive, and endure each for a longer term than the preceding. In this lies the principal security from inhumation. The unfortunate whose *first* attack should be of the extreme character which is occasionally seen, would almost inevitably be consigned alive to the tomb.

My own case differed in no important particular from those mentioned in medical books. Sometimes, without any apparent cause, I sank, little by little, into a condition of hemi-syncope, or half swoon; and, in this condition, without pain, without ability to stir, or, strictly speaking, to think, but with a dull lethargic consciousness of life and of the presence of those who surrounded my bed, I remained, until the crisis of the disease restored me, suddenly, to perfect sensation. At other times I was quickly and impetuously smitten. I grew sick, and numb, and chilly, and dizzy, and so fell prostrate at once. Then, for weeks, all was void, and black, and silent, and Nothing became the universe. Total annihilation could be no more. From these latter attacks I awoke, however, with a gradation slow in proportion to the suddenness of the seizure. Just as the day dawns to the friendless and houseless beggar who roams the streets throughout the long desolate winter night

—just so tardily—just so wearily—just so cheerily came back the light of the Soul to me.

Apart from the tendency to trance, however, my general health appeared to be good; nor could I perceive that it was at all affected by the one prevalent malady —unless, indeed, an idiosyncrasy in my ordinary *sleep* may be looked upon as superinduced. Upon awaking from slumber, I could never gain, at once, thorough possession of my senses, and always remained, for many minutes, in much bewilderment and perplexity;—the mental faculties in general, but the memory in especial, being in a condition of absolute abeyance.

In all that I endured there was no physical suffering, but of moral distress an infinitude. My fancy grew charnel. I talked "of worms, of tombs and epitaphs." I was lost in reveries of death, and the idea of premature burial held continual possession of my brain. The ghastly Danger to which I was subjected, haunted me day and night. In the former, the torture of meditation was excessive—in the latter, supreme. When the grim Darkness overspread the Earth, then, with very horror of thought, I shook—shook as the quivering plumes upon the hearse. When Nature could endure wakefulness no longer, it was with a struggle that I consented to sleep[10]—for I shuddered to reflect that, upon awaking, I might find myself the tenant of a grave. And when, finally, I sank into slumber, it was only to rush at once into a world of phantasms, above which, with vast, sable, overshadowing wings, hovered, predominant, the one sepulchral Idea.

From the innumerable images of gloom which thus oppressed me in dreams, I select for record but a solitary vision. Methought I was immersed in a cataleptic trance of more than usual duration and profundity. Suddenly there came an icy hand upon my forehead, and an impatient, gibbering voice whispered the word "Arise!" within my ear.

I sat erect. The darkness was total. I could not see the figure of him who had aroused me. I could call to mind neither the period at which I had fallen into the trance, nor the locality in which I then lay. While I remained motionless, and busied in endeavors to collect my thoughts, the cold hand grasped me fiercely by the wrist, shaking it petulantly, while the gibbering voice said again:

"Arise! did I not bid thee arise?"

"And who," I demanded, "art thou?"

"I have no name in the regions which I inhabit," replied the voice mournfully; "I was mortal, but am fiend. I was merciless, but am pitiful. Thou dost feel that I shudder.—My teeth chatter as I speak, yet it is not with the chilliness of the night —of the night without end. But this hideousness is insufferable. How canst *thou* tranquilly sleep? I cannot rest for the cry of these great agonies. These sights are more than I can bear. Get thee up! Come with me into the outer Night, and let me unfold to thee the graves. Is not this a spectacle of woe?—Behold!"

I looked; and the unseen figure, which still grasped me by the wrist, had caused to be thrown open the graves of all mankind; and from each issued the faint phosphoric radiance of decay; so that I could see into the innermost recesses, and there view the shrouded bodies in their sad and solemn slumbers with the worm. But, alas! the real sleepers were fewer, by many millions, than those who slumbered not at all; and there was a feeble struggling; and there was a general sad unrest; and from out the depths of the countless pits there came a melancholy rustling from the garments of the buried. And, of those who seemed tranquilly to repose, I saw that a vast number had changed, in a greater or less degree, the rigid and uneasy position in which they had originally been entombed. And the voice again said to me, as I gazed:

"Is it not—oh, is it *not* a pitiful sight?" —but, before I could find words to reply, the figure had ceased to grasp my wrist, the phosphoric lights expired, and the graves were closed with a sudden violence, while from out them arose a tumult of despairing cries, saying again— "Is it not—oh, God! is it *not* a very pitiful sight?"

Phantasies such as these, presenting themselves at night, extended their terrific influence far into my waking hours. —My nerves became thoroughly unstrung, and I fell a prey to perpetual horror. I hesitated to ride, or to walk, or to indulge in any exercise that would carry me from home. In fact, I no longer dared trust myself out of the immediate presence of those who were aware of my proneness to catalepsy, lest, falling into one of my usual fits, I should be buried before my real condition could be ascertained. I doubted the care, the fidelity of my dearest friends. I dreaded that, in some trance of more than customary duration, they might be prevailed upon to regard me as irrecoverable. I even went so far as to fear that, as I occasioned much trouble, they might be glad to consider any very protracted attack as sufficient excuse for getting rid of me altogether. It was in vain they endeavored to reassure me by the most solemn promises. I exacted the most sacred oaths, that under no circumstances they would bury me until decomposition had so materially advanced as to render farther preservation impossible. And, even then, my mortal terrors would listen to no reason—would accept no consolation. I entered into a series of elaborate precautions. Among other things, I had the family vault so remodelled as to admit of being readily opened from within. The slightest pressure upon a long lever that extended far into the tomb would cause the iron portals to fly back. There were arrangements also for the free admission of air and light, and convenient receptacles for food and water, within immediate reach of the coffin intended for my reception. This coffin was warmly and softly padded, and was provided with a lid, fashioned upon the principle of the vault-door, with the addition of springs so contrived that the feeblest movement of the body would be sufficient to set it at liberty. Besides all this, there was suspended from the roof of the tomb, a large bell, the rope of which, it was designed, should extend through a hole in the coffin, and so be fastened to one of the hands of the corpse. But, alas! what avails the vigilance against the Destiny of man? Not even these well contrived securities sufficed to save from the uttermost agonies of living inhumation, a wretch to these agonies foredoomed!

There arrived an epoch—as often before there had arrived—in which I found myself emerging from total unconsciousness into the first feeble and indefinite sense of existence.—Slowly—with a tortoise gradation—approached the faint gray dawn of the psychal day. A torpid uneasiness. An apathetic endurance of dull pain. No care—no hope—no effort. Then, after long interval, a ringing in the ears; then, after a lapse still longer, a pricking or tingling sensation in the extremities; then a seemingly eternal period of pleasurable quiescence, during which the awakening feelings are struggling into thought; then a brief re-sinking into nonentity; then a sudden recovery. At length the slight quivering of an eyelid, and immediately thereupon, an electric shock of a terror, deadly and indefinite, which sends the blood in torrents from the temples to the heart. And now the first positive effort to think. And now the first endeavor to remember. And now a partial and evanescent success. And now the memory has so far regained its dominion that, in some measure, I am cognizant of my state.[11] I feel that I am not awaking from ordinary sleep. I recollect that I have been subject to catalepsy. And now, at last, as if by the rush of an ocean, my shuddering spirit is overwhelmed by the one grim Danger—by the one spectral and ever-prevalent Idea.

For some minutes after this fancy possessed me, I remained without motion. And why? I could not summon courage to move. I dared not make the effort which was to satisfy me of my fate—and yet there was something at my heart which whispered me *it was sure.* Despair —such as no other species of wretchedness ever calls into being—despair alone urged me, after long irresolution, to uplift the heavy lids of my eyes. I uplifted them. It was dark—all dark. I knew that the fit was over. I knew that the crisis of my disorder had long passed. I knew that I had now fully recovered the use of my visual faculties—and yet it was dark— all dark—the intense and utter raylessness of the Night that endureth for evermore.

I endeavored to shriek; and my lips and my parched tongue moved convulsively together in the attempt—but no voice issued from the cavernous lungs, which, oppressed as if by the weight of some incumbent mountain, gasped and palpitated, with the heart, at every elaborate and struggling inspiration.

The movement of the jaws, in this effort to cry aloud, showed me that they were bound up, as is usual with the dead. I felt, too, that I lay upon some hard substance; and by something similar my sides were, also, closely compressed. So far, I had not ventured to stir any of my limbs—but now I violently threw up my arms, which had been lying at length, with the wrists crossed. They struck a solid wooden substance, which extended above my person at an elevation of not more than six inches from my face. I could no longer doubt that I reposed within a coffin at last.

And now, amid all my infinite miseries, came sweetly the cherub Hope—for I thought of my precautions. I writhed, and made spasmodic exertions to force open the lid: it would not move. I felt my wrists for the bell-rope: it was not to be found. And now the Comforter fled forever, and a still sterner Despair reigned triumphant; for I could not help perceiv-

ing the absence of the paddings which I had so carefully prepared—and then, too, there came suddenly to my nostrils the strong peculiar odor of moist earth. The conclusion was irresistible. I was *not* within the vault. I had fallen into a trance while absent from home—while among strangers—when, or how, I could not remember—and it was they who had buried me as a dog—nailed up in some common coffin—and thrust, deep, deep, and forever, into some ordinary and nameless *grave.*

As this awful conviction forced itself, thus, into the innermost chambers of my soul, I once again struggled to cry aloud. And in this second endeavor I succeeded. A long, wild, and continuous shriek, or yell, of agony, resounded through the realms of the subterrene Night.

"Hillo! hillo, there!" said a gruff voice in reply.

"What the devil's the matter now?" said a second.

"Get out o' that!" said a third.

"What do you mean by yowling in that ere kind of style, like a cattymount?"[12] said a fourth; and hereupon I was seized and shaken without ceremony, for several minutes, by a junto of very rough-looking individuals. They did not arouse me from slumber—for I was wide awake when I screamed—but they restored me to the full possession of my memory.

This adventure occurred near Richmond, in Virginia. Accompanied by a friend, I had proceeded, upon a gunning expedition, some miles down the banks of James River. Night approached, and we were overtaken by a storm. The cabin of a small sloop lying at anchor in the stream, and laden with garden mould, afforded us the only available shelter. We made the best of it, and passed the night on board. I slept in one of the only two berths in the vessel—and the berths of a sloop of sixty or seventy tons, need scarcely be described. That which I occupied had no bedding of any kind. Its extreme width was eighteen inches. The distance of its bottom from the deck over-head, was precisely the same. I found it a matter of exceeding difficulty to squeeze myself in. Nevertheless, I slept soundly; and the whole of my vision—for it was no dream, and no nightmare—arose naturally from the circumstances of my position—from my ordinary bias of thought—and from the difficulty, to which I have al-luded, of collecting my senses, and espe-cially of regaining my memory, for a long time after awaking from slumber. The men who shook me were the crew of the sloop, and some laborers engaged to un-load it. From the load itself came the earthy smell. The bandage about the jaws was a silk handkerchief in which I had bound up my head, in default of my cus-tomary nightcap.

The tortures endured, however, were indubitably quite equal, for the time, to those of actual sepulture. They were fear-fully—they were inconceivably hideous; but out of Evil proceeded Good; for their very excess wrought in my spirit an in-evitable revulsion. My soul acquired tone —acquired temper. I went abroad. I took vigorous exercise. I breathed the free air of Heaven. I thought upon other subjects than Death. I discarded my medical books. "Buchan" I burned. I read no "Night Thoughts"[13]—no fustian about church-yards—no bugaboo tales—*such as this*. In short, I became a new man, and lived a man's life. From that memorable night, I dismissed forever my charnel apprehen-sions, and with them vanished the cata-leptic disorder, of which, perhaps, they had been less the consequence than the cause.

There are moments when, even to the sober eye of Reason, the world of our sad Humanity may assume the semblance of a Hell—but the imagination of man is no Carathis, to explore with impunity its ev-ery cavern. Alas! the grim legion of sepul-chral terrors cannot be regarded as alto-gether fanciful—but, like the Demons in whose company Afrasiab made his voyage down the Oxus,[14] they must sleep, or they will devour us—they must be suffered to slumber, or we perish.

THE SPHINX

During the dread reign of the Cholera in New York, I had accepted the invitation of a relative to spend a fortnight with him in the retirement of his *cottage orné*[1] on the banks of the Hudson. We had here around us all the ordinary means of sum-mer amusement; and what with rambling in the woods, sketching, boating, fishing, bathing, music and books, we should have passed the time pleasantly enough, but for the fearful intelligence which reached us every morning from the populous city. Not a day elapsed which did not bring us news of the decease of some acquaintance. Then, as the fatality increased, we learned to expect daily the loss of some friend. At length we trembled at the approach of every messenger. The very air from the South seemed to us redolent with death. That palsying thought, indeed, took en-tire possession of my soul. I could neither speak, think, nor dream of anything else. My host was of a less excitable tempera-ment, and, although greatly depressed in spirits, exerted himself to sustain my own. His richly philosophical intellect was not at any time affected by unrealities. To the substances of terror he was sufficiently alive, but of its shadows he had no appre-hension.

His endeavors to arouse me from the condition of abnormal gloom into which I had fallen, were frustrated in great mea-sure, by certain volumes which I had found in his library. These were of a char-acter to force into germination whatever seeds of hereditary superstition lay latent in my bosom. I had been reading these books without his knowledge, and thus he was often at a loss to account for the forc-ible impressions which had been made upon my fancy.

A favorite topic with me was the popu-lar belief in omens—a belief which, at this one epoch of my life, I was almost seriously disposed to defend. On this subject we had long and animated discussions —he maintaining the utter groundlessness of faith in such matters—I contending that a popular sentiment arising with absolute spontaneity—that is to say, without apparent traces of suggestion—had in itself the unmistakable elements of truth, and was entitled to much respect.

The fact is, that soon after my arrival at the cottage, there had occurred to myself an incident so entirely inexplicable, and which had in it so much of the portentous character, that I might well have been excused for regarding it as an omen. It appalled, and at the same time so confounded and bewildered me, that many days elapsed before I could make up my mind to communicate the circumstance to my friend.

Near the close of an exceedingly warm day, I was sitting, book in hand, at an open window, commanding, through a long vista of the river banks, a view of a distant hill, the face of which nearest my position, had been denuded, by what is termed a land-slide, of the principal portion of its trees. My thoughts had been long wandering from the volume before me to the gloom and desolation of the neighboring city. Uplifting my eyes from the page, they fell upon the naked face of the hill, and upon an object—upon some living monster of hideous conformation, which very rapidly made its way from the summit to the bottom, disappearing finally in the dense forest below. As this creature first came in sight, I doubted my own sanity—or at least the evidence of my own eyes; and many minutes passed before I succeeded in convincing myself that I was neither mad nor in a dream. Yet when I describe the monster, (which I distinctly saw, and calmly surveyed through the whole period of its progress,) my readers, I fear, will feel more difficulty in being convinced of these points than even I did myself.

Estimating the size of the creature by comparison with the diameter of the large trees near which it passed—the few giants of the forest which had escaped the fury of the land-slide—I concluded it to be far larger than any ship of the line in existence. I say ship of the line, because the shape of the monster suggested the idea —the hull of one of our seventy-fours[2] might convey a very tolerable conception of the general outline. The mouth of the animal was situated at the extremity of a proboscis some sixty or seventy feet in length, and about as thick as the body of an ordinary elephant. Near the root of this trunk was an immense quantity of black shaggy hair—more than could have been supplied by the coats of a score of buffaloes; and projecting from this hair downwardly and laterally, sprang two gleaming tusks not unlike those of the wild boar, but of infinitely greater dimension. Extending forward, parallel with the proboscis, and on each side of it, was a gigantic staff, thirty or forty feet in length, formed seemingly of pure crystal, and in shape a perfect prism:—it reflected in the most gorgeous manner the rays of the declining sun. The trunk was fashioned like a wedge with the apex to the earth. From it there were outspread two pairs of wings—each wing nearly one hundred yards in length—one pair being placed above the other, and all thickly covered with metal scales; each scale apparently some ten or twelve feet in diameter. I observed that the upper and lower tiers of wings were connected by a strong chain. But the chief peculiarity of this horrible thing, was the representation of a *Death's Head*, which covered nearly the whole surface of its breast, and which was as accurately traced in glaring white, upon the dark ground of the body, as if it had been there carefully designed by an artist. While I regarded this terrific animal, and more especially the appearance on its breast, with a feeling of horror and awe—with a sentiment of forthcoming evil, which I found it impossible to quell by any effort of the reason, I perceived the huge jaws at the extremity of the proboscis, suddenly expand themselves, and from them there proceeded a sound so loud and so expressive of wo, that it struck upon my nerves like a knell, and as the monster disappeared at the foot of the hill, I fell at once, fainting, to the floor.

Upon recovering, my first impulse of course was, to inform my friend of what I had seen and heard—and I can scarcely explain what feeling of repugnance it was, which, in the end, operated to prevent me.

At length, one evening, some three or four days after the occurrence, we were sitting together in the room in which I had seen the apparition—I occupying the same seat at the same window, and he lounging on a sofa near at hand. The association of the place and time impelled me to give him an account of the phenomenon. He heard me to the end—at first laughed heartily—and then lapsed into an excessively grave demeanor, as if my insanity was a thing beyond suspicion. At this instant I again had a distinct view of the monster—to which, with a shout of absolute terror, I now directed his attention. He looked eagerly—but maintained that he saw nothing—although I designated minutely the course of the creature, as it made its way down the naked face of the hill.

I was now immeasurably alarmed, for I considered the vision either as an omen of my death, or, worse, as the forerunner of an attack of mania. I threw myself passionately back in my chair, and for some moments buried my face in my hands. When I uncovered my eyes, the apparition was no longer visible.

My host, however, had in some degree resumed the calmness of his demeanor, and questioned me very rigorously in respect to the conformation of the visionary creature. When I had fully satisfied him on this head, he sighed deeply, as if relieved of some intolerable burden, and went on to talk, with what I thought a cruel calmness, of various points of speculative philosophy, which had heretofore formed subject of discussion between us. I remember his insisting very especially (among other things) upon the idea that the principal source of error in all human investigations, lay in the liability of the understanding to under-rate or to over-value the importance of an object, through mere misadmeasurement of its propinquity. "To estimate properly, for example," he said, "the influence to be exercised on mankind at large by the thorough diffusion of Democracy, the distance of the epoch at which such diffusion may possibly be accomplished, should not fail to form an item in the estimate. Yet can you tell me one writer on the subject of government, who has ever thought this particular branch of the subject worthy of discussion at all?"

He here paused for a moment, stepped to a bookcase, and brought forth one of the ordinary synopses of Natural History. Requesting me then to exchange seats with him, that he might better distinguish the fine print of the volume, he took my arm-chair at the window, and, opening the book, resumed his discourse very much in the same tone as before.

"But for your exceeding minuteness," he said, "in describing the monster, I might never have had it in my power to demonstrate to you what it was. In the first place, let me read to you a school-boy account of the genus *Sphinx*, of the family *Crepuscularia*, of the order *Lepidoptera*, of the class of *Insecta*—or insects. The account runs thus:

"Four membraneous wings covered with little colored scales of a metallic appearance; mouth forming a rolled proboscis, produced by an elongation of the jaws, upon the sides of which are found the rudiments of mandibles and downy palpi; the inferior wings retained to the superior by a stiff hair; antennæ in the form of an elongated club, prismatic; abdomen pointed. The Death's-headed Sphinx has occasioned much terror among the vulgar, at times, by the melancholy kind of cry which it utters, and the in-signia of death which it wears upon its corslet."[3]

He here closed the book and leaned forward in the chair, placing himself ac-curately in the position which I had occu-pied at the moment of beholding "the monster."

"Ah, here it is!" he presently exclaimed —"it is reascending the face of the hill, and a very remarkable looking creature, I admit it to be. Still, it is by no means so large or so distant as you imagined it; for the fact is that, as it wriggles its way up this thread, which some spider has wrought along the window-sash, I find it to be about the sixteenth of an inch in its extreme length, and also about the six-teenth of an inch distant from the pupil of my eye."[4]

Notes

King Pest

1. Poe confuses his authors. "Buckhurst" is Charles Sackville, Lord Buckhurst (1637–1706 —Earl of Dorset after 1677), but the author of a portion of the "Tragedy of Ferrex and Por-rex" is Thomas Sackville (1536–1608). He wrote the last two acts; Poe's quotation is from Act 2, Scene 1, believed to be written by Thomas Norton (1532–1584), whose name appears as author of three of the five acts on the title page of the 1565 edition. The lines are spoken by Herman, confidant of Ferrex, one of the two sons of Gorboduc, the aged king who has unwisely decided to divide En-gland between his heirs. Badly advised, the sons war; one kills the other, the vengeful mother kills the survivor, and the wrathful Britons rise to slaughter Gorboduc and queen. Then come fifty years of "tumults, rebellions, armes and civill warres . . . as fell in the realme of great Brittayne, which by the space of fiftie yeares and more continwd in civill warre betweene the nobilitie after the death of king Gorboduc, and of his issues, for want of certayne limitacion in succession of the crowne. . . ."

Since Poe's real target is Jacksonian politics, the quotation is stunningly relevant even though Poe erred in his attribution. Note also that the quotation is not especially germane to the literal plot of the story; it makes sense only if the tale is, as Poe says, allegorical, a warning against misrule. "King Pest" was first published in the September 1835 South-ern Literary Messenger as "King Pest the First," then in the 1840 book Tales of the Grotesque and Arabesque, and in the Octo-ber 18, 1845, issue of The Broadway Journal.

2. the third Edward: Edward III, reigned 1327–1377. Several dreadful visitations of the plague hit England during his reign, in 1348–1349, 1361–1362, and 1369.

"Free and Easy": perhaps a dig at Jacksonian policies.

"Sluys and the Thames": Sluys (Sluis): town in southwest Holland, on the Belgian border, near which in 1340 Edward III defeated a French fleet.

Thames: literally, of course, the river in En-gland. But Poe names it because Richard M. Johnson, congressman from Kentucky and later Vice President, became famous in the Battle of the Thames in Canada in 1813. See Section Preface; Johnson is the target of Poe's satire "The Man That Was Used Up." The Democratic convention which nominated him for Vice President had been held in Bal-timore in May 1835 while Poe was in the city; "King Pest" appeared in September.

"St. Andrews": President Jackson's first name was Andrew. See Section Preface.

3. a high mountain in Scotland.

4. "humming-stuff": strong liquor or ale called "hum;" the OED conjectures that

"humming" refers to the sound it produces in the head.

"No Chalk" no credit.

5. probably located near St. Andrew's Church near the Thames, which was destroyed in the great fire. See note 2.

6. in a bass voice.

7. president of the table: A hint at his identity. See Section Preface.

forehead . . . head: Portraits of Jackson show an unusually high forehead, often exaggerated in newspaper caricatures.

8. *haut ton:* High tone.

degagé: Free and easy.

9. Port.

10. Poe would have known the name from Joseph *The Spectator* essays, where he is "a country gentleman extremely well versed in all the little handcrafts of an idle man." Poe uses here, however, for its connotations. One meaning of "Wimble" is a kind of drill for boring in soft earth; Poe's adaptation is a name of the same sort as "Digger O'Dell," the radio undertaker of a few decades ago, or Wimble the undertaker in the current comic strip "Tumbleweed."

11. Jacksonian government, in other words, is a plague on the nation. The grotesque characters are close to newspaper cartoon representations of Jackson and other leaders; there are allusions to Jackson's defense of Peggy Eaton and to her supposedly scandalous involvement with prominent men, and so forth. See Section Preface.

12. median: Unchangeable, like those of "A Median kingdom whose laws never know change." Forrest gives the Biblical reference Daniel 6:8.

13. absolve.

Metzengerstein

1. "I was your plague, living; dying, I will be your death" (Carlson 2). Martin Luther (1483–1546) spoke these words when Pope Clement VII summoned the Council of Trent in 1526: "O Pope, if I live I shall be a pestilence to thee, and if I die I shall be thy death."

2. Good reason to give a date: this is Poe's first known published story. It appeared in the *Philadelphia Saturday Courier,* January 14, 1832. In January 1836, when he used it in the *Southern Literary Messenger,* Poe added

a subtitle, "A Tale in Imitation of the German." In the 1840 *Tales of the Grotesque and Arabesque* the subtitle was dropped. In 1842, Poe tried to publish another collection of tales, to be titled "Phantasy Pieces"; in that, he changed the title altogether, to "The Horse-Shade." Harrison and Carlson (2) follow the 1850 Griswold edition, presumably based on Poe's last revisions; we do, too.

3. Metempsychosis: belief in the transmigration of the human soul.

4. Mercier, in *L'an deux mille quatre cent quarante* seriously maintains the doctrines of the Metempsychosis, and I. D'Israeli says that "no system is so simple and so little repugnant to the understanding." Colonel Ethan Allen, the "Green Mountain Boy," is also said to have been a serious metempsychosist [Poe's Note].

The information about Mercier and D'Israeli (Disraeli) is from an article entitled "Metempsychosis" in Disraeli's *Curiosities of Literature,* a book Poe leaned on heavily throughout his career as a short-story writer. Disraeli's book did not appear in its modern forms until 1839 and later, but the portions Poe uses here were in print at least as early as 1817.

Mercier: Louis Sebastien Mercier (1740–1814), French writer and politician. His *L'an 2440* is "a work of prophetic imagination."

Ethan Allen, the Revolutionary hero (1737–1789), caused considerable theological excitement through his vocal Deism and his authorship of "Ethan Allen's Bible" (*Reason the Only Oracle of Man,* 1789), a Deist tract, but he did not, so far as we know, believe in Metempsychosis. His Deism was of the usual rationalistic sort.

"vient de ne pouvoir être seuls": "comes from not being able to be alone." See "The Man of the Crowd," note 2.

5. Poe apparently wrote this "quotation" himself, for the French is faulty in grammar and vague in reference: "[the soul] resides only once in a sensate body: besides, a horse, a dog, even a man is [are] nothing more than a faint resemblance of such animals."

6. one of many places where Poe hints that the tale itself is not serious. Note his comments on absurdity in the paragraph above; see Section Preface.

7. See Section Preface.

8. a phrase Poe used repeatedly. Cf. "William Wilson," note 10.

9. Caligula (12–41), famously cruel Roman emperor (37–41), "wanted to make his *horse* a consul" (Thompson 2; Mabbott 1).

10. To point out all of Poe's sly gags in this tale would be to fill the page with footnotes. This one, however, is easy to miss and especially funny: as Thompson noticed, "in sickness or in health" comes from the Prayer Book Marriage Ceremony.

11. A. H. Quinn believes this passage is based on Poe's memory of a real place, the approach to the estate "Oakland," Christ Church Parish, South Carolina.

The Premature Burial

1. Passage of the Beresina: An episode in the Napoleonic War in Russia. Generals Ney and Oudinot used 8,500 men to force a passage against 25,000 on November 26–28, 1812. From that point on, the French retreat became an awful and chaotic rout. By December 13, when the 100,000 French survivors crossed the Niemen, an estimated 300,000 Napoleonic troops had been killed and 100,000 more captured.

Earthquake at Lisbon: On November 1, 1755, 30,000 people died in the Portuguese capital.

Plague at London: The most famous plague was that of April 1665, but Poe also has in mind Daniel Defoe's *A Journal of the Plague Year* (1722), for it raises precisely the issue he is discussing in his opening paragraph, namely that we will accept in a factual essay that which would be abhorrent in fiction. Defoe was only five when the plague he describes took place, yet his "journal" pretends to be a factual record of events, not fiction.

Massacre of St. Bartholomew: The slaughter of about 30,000 Huguenots in France, August 23–24, 1572.

Black Hole at Calcutta: Siráj-ud-Daulá, Nawáb of Bengal, quarreled with the English, seized Calcutta, and imprisoned 146 people in a room 18 feet square on June 29, 1756. Only 23 lived till the next morning.

2. from cause to effect.

3. Poe's examples of burials alive seem to have been based on cases of which he had read. Killis Campbell located this one in an item Poe read in the September 1827 issue of *The Philadelphia Casket*, for example.

4. Chirugical: surgical.

Leipsic: Leipzig.

5. surgery on the skull, generally to remove a piece of bone and hence relieve pressure.

6. suffocated, deprived of oxygen.

7. Compare to "Loss of Breath," note 14, and to "Some Words with A Mummy."

8. A. H. Quinn thinks this anecdote imaginary, though it parallels a story in the October 1821 *Blackwood's.*

9. Poe's poem of this title appeared in *Graham's Magazine* for January 1843, so Poe's capitalizing the words is a subtle form of advertising. "The Premature Burial" was published first in the *Dollar Newspaper*, July 31, 1844. Fragments of it appeared in *The Rover* for August 17, 1844. Poe used it again in *The Broadway Journal*, June 14, 1845.

10. "of worms . . . epitaphs": Poe alludes to and slightly alters a line from Shakespeare's *Richard II*, III, ii:

> Let's talk of graves, of worms, and epitaphs. . . .

When nature . . . sleep: Friends who are subjected to occasional "fits" tell us that Poe's narrator is doing precisely the wrong thing: the seizures, they report, increase in frequency with fatigue.

11. The fascination of artists in Poe's day with marginal states of consciousness accounts for this detailed account of the narrator's awakening.

12. catamount, mountain lion.

13. Buchan: Poe could have intended any of a number of authors of this name. If he has in mind medical books, William Buchan (1729–1805) was the author of an immensely influential *Domestic Medicine* (1769) which was still being reprinted in Poe's day. If he means "creepy books in general," Peter Buchan (1790–1854), the well-known collector of ballads, had written in 1826 *Witchcraft Detected and Prevented, or the School of Black Art Newly Opened.*

"Night Thoughts": *Night Thoughts* (1742–1745) by Edward Young (1683–1765) is "an exercise in Christian appologetics, but its appeal . . . lies in its concentration on death, on its macabre detail" (George Sherburn).

14. Carathis: In William Beckford's *Vathek* (1786), Carathis is the mother of Vathek. Like her son, she seeks dark knowledge and is ulti-

mately allowed to explore the caverns and alleys of Hell, after which she is punished by having her heart set ablaze.

Afrasiab: In the Persian epic *Sháhnáma* by Abul Kasim Mansur Firdausi (c. 950–c. 1020), Afrasiab, a king of Turan who was against the kings of Iran, is killed by Kaikhosru. Though much of the epic is "historical," Afrasiab lives through all four volumes of the edition we read, covering centuries, and thus seems a symbolic evil force, not a real king.

Oxus: the old name of Amu Darya, a river in Asia near which a large number of battles and events in the *Sháhnáma* take place.

The Sphinx

1. For Poe's familiarity with epidemics, see "The Masque of the Red Death." There had been cholera epidemics in eastern American cities around the turn of the century.

cottage orné (properly, *ornée*): A small villa in a free and semi-rustic style. This was the age of the "cottage style" movement in American architecture; see "Mellonta Tauta," note 2.

2. ship of the line: a full-sized battleship, usually a seventy-four.

seventy-fours: Warships were rated by the number of guns they carried. A "seventy-four" was a big ship.

3. Poe got his description from Thomas Wyatt, *A Synopsis of Natural History* (Philadelphia, 1839), a book which he probably ghost-wrote himself, having been hired by Professor Wyatt (Heartman and Canny).

4. This ending is unusually implausible for Poe. Perhaps the comment a few paragraphs back about the diffusion of democracy is more important to Poe than is his plot. Or perhaps he did not take too seriously the periodical for which he wrote the tale, *Arthur's Ladies Magazine* (January 1846). "The Sphinx" appeared again in the 1851 *The American Keepsake*. Two factors bother the reader: depth-of-field (the eye cannot simultaneously keep in focus extremely close and distant objects, and can't focus on an object $\frac{1}{16}$ of an inch away anyway) and the spider's strand of thread. If a bug could wiggle up it without becoming entangled, a thread $\frac{1}{16}$ of an inch from one's pupil would touch one's face and be fouled in one's eyelashes.

8. The Rake and the Fop

We group these tales together because they are good antidotes to melodramatic biographies of Poe: "Thou Art the Man" because its hero shares many of Poe's problems, and "The Spectacles" because of what it says about romantic love.

Thou Art the Man. This is one of a number of stories outside the general pattern of Poe tales. It is, in one sense, another of the detective stories ("tales of ratiocination"), but it is also a satire on small-town manners and gullibility. And although critics who like to guess at Poe's personality through analysis of his tales generally stick to tales of terror and horror, they might learn more from this one, in which the above-board "nice guy," Old Charley Goodfellow, turns out to be a liar and a murderer, while the wealthy young rake, Pennifeather, turns out worthy and innocent. Pennifeather, the misunderstood and maligned young dandy, makes more sense as a mask for Poe than most of the more spectacularly depraved characters of the better-known stories.

The fairy-tale formula "happily ever afterwards" underlies the reversal of expectations. Pennifeather, having sown his wild oats, reforms. The moral seems to be that rakish young men can be nice guys, while the cronies of the establishment are liable to be scoundrels.

The Spectacles. Were this a light theatrical comedy instead of a short story, we would be comfortable with its foolish hero and would recognize him as the sort of silly romantic youth to whom Gilbert and Sullivan generally assigned their tenors. Many comedies and operettas of the past century were built upon such characters. They poke fun at romantic illusions about love: the "electrical" love-at-first-sight, the idea of one-true-love-and-no-other, the infatuated hero who will die if separated from his beloved, and so forth. Since these characteristics were for more than a century attached to Poe by his biographers when they dealt with his supposed liaisons with lady poets and old flames, this tale is important for suggesting a kind of detachment Poe was not supposed to have (see Introduction, pages xxii, xxiii, xxviii).

A number of Poe tales are about elaborate ruses—see, for instance, "Mystification." Magazines of his period seemed to welcome such material, for other authors contributed such stories as well. If they strike the modern reader as tedious, it is apparently because tastes have changed. To the extent that they remind us of theatrical conventions, they serve to point Poe's close interest in the stage, and the number of his tales which seem inspired by theatre. The plot of "The Spectacles" is no more absurd than that of many popular comedies; somehow we seem more willing to laugh at the working out of elaborate and improbable fantasies of this sort on stage than in print. But the conventions of short story form were by no means securely established in 1844 when Poe wrote this. Poe, who is often said to have invented and codified the short story, also tried a number of experiments with short prose which puzzle us because short fiction has for the most part followed certain short story conventions. For a twentieth-century author, strongly influenced by Poe, who still experiments the way Poe did with absurd and grotesque short fiction, see the works of the brilliant Argentine author Jorge Luis Borges.

The Tales

THOU ART THE MAN

I will now play the Œdipus to the Rattleborough enigma. I will expound to you as I alone can—the secret of the enginery that effected the Rattleborough[1] miracle —the one, the true, the admitted, the undisputed, the indisputable miracle, which put a definite end to infidelity among the Rattleburghers, and converted to the orthodoxy of the grandames all the carnal-minded who had ventured to be sceptical before.

This event—which I should be sorry to discuss in a tone of unsuitable levity— occurred in the summer of 18—. Mr. Barnabas Shuttleworthy,[2] one of the wealthiest and most respectable citizens of the borough, had been missing for several days under circumstances which gave rise to suspicion of foul play. Mr. Shuttleworthy had set out from Rattleborough very early one Saturday morning on horseback, with the avowed intention of proceeding to the city of —— about fifteen miles distant, and of returning the night of the same day. Two hours after his departure, however, his horse returned without him, and without the saddle-bags which had been strapped on his back at starting. The animal was wounded, too, and covered with mud. These circumstances naturally gave rise to much alarm among the friends of the missing man, and when it was found, on Sunday morning, that he had not yet made his appearance, the whole borough arose en masse to go and look for his body.

The foremost and most energetic in instituting this search was the bosom friend of Mr. Shuttleworthy—a Mr. Charles Goodfellow,[3] or, as he was universally called, "Charley Goodfellow," or "Old Charley Goodfellow.'" Now, whether it is a marvellous coincidence, or whether it is that the name itself has an imperceptible effect upon the character, I have never yet been able to ascertain; but the fact is unquestionable, that there never yet was any person named Charles who was not an open, manly, honest, good-natured and frank-hearted fellow, with a rich, clear voice, that did you good to hear it, and an eye that looked you always straight in the face, as much as to say, "I have a clear conscience myself; am afraid of no man, and am altogether above doing a mean action." And thus all the hearty, careless, "walking gentlemen" of the stage are very certain to be called Charles.

Now "Old Charley Goodfellow," although he had been in Rattleborough not longer than six months or thereabouts, and although nobody knew any thing about him before he came to settle in the neighbourhood, had experienced no difficulty in the world in making the acquaintance of all the respectable people in the borough. Not a man of them but would have taken his bare word for a thousand at any moment; and as for the women, there is no saying what they would not have done to oblige him. And all this came of his having been christened Charles, and of his possessing, in consequence, that ingenuous face which is proverbially the very "best letter of recommendation."

I have already said that Mr. Shuttleworthy was one of the most respectable, and, undoubtedly, he was the most wealthy man in Rattleborough, while "Old Charley Goodfellow" was upon as intimate terms with him as if he had been his own brother. The two old gentlemen were next-door neighbours, and although Mr. Shuttleworthy seldom, if ever, visited "Old Charley," and never was known to take a meal in his house, still this did not prevent the two friends from being exceedingly intimate, as I have just observed; for "Old Charley" never let a day pass without stepping in three or four times to see how his neighbour came on, and very often he would stay to breakfast or tea, and almost always to dinner; and then the amount of wine that was made way with by the two cronies at a sitting, it would really be a difficult thing to ascertain. Old Charley's favorite beverage was *Château Margaux*,[4] and it appeared to do Mr. Shuttleworthy's heart good to see the old fellow swallow it, as he did, quart after quart; so that, one day, when the wine was *in* and the wit, as a natural consequence, somewhat *out*, he said to his crony, as he slapped him upon the back —"I tell you what it is, Old Charley, you are, by all odds, the heartiest old fellow I ever came across in all my born days; and, since you love to guzzle the wine at that fashion, I'll be darned if I don't have to make thee a present of a big box of the Château Margaux. Od rot me,"—(Mr. Shuttleworthy had a sad habit of swearing, although he seldom went beyond "Od rot me," or "By gosh," or "By the jolly golly,")—"Od rot me," says he, "if I don't send an order to town this very afternoon for a double box of the best that can be got, and I'll make ye a present of it, I will! —ye needn't say a word, now—I *will*, I tell ye, and there's an end of it; so look out for it—it will come to hand some of these fine days, precisely when ye are looking for it the least." I mention this little bit of liberality on the part of Mr. Shuttleworthy, just by way of showing you how *very* intimate an understanding existed between the two friends.

Well, on the Sunday morning in question, when it came to be fairly understood that Mr. Shuttleworthy had met with foul play, I never saw any one so profoundly affected as "Old Charley Goodfellow." When he first heard that the horse had come home without his master, and without his master's saddle-bags, and all bloody from a pistol-shot that had gone clean through and through the poor animal's chest without quite killing him; when he heard all this, he turned as pale as if the missing man had been his own dear brother or father, and shivered and shook all over as if he had had a fit of the ague.

At first, he was too much overpowered with grief to be able to do any thing at all, or to decide upon any plan of action; so that for a long time he endeavoured to dissuade Mr. Shuttleworthy's other friends from making a stir about the matter, thinking it best to wait awhile—say for a week or two, or a month or two—to see if something would n't turn up, or if Mr. Shuttleworthy would n't come in the natural way, and explain his reasons for sending his horse on before. I dare say you have often observed this disposition to temporize, or to procrastinate in people who are labouring under any very poignant sorrow. Their powers of mind seem to be rendered torpid, so that they have a horror of any thing like action, and like nothing in the world so well as to lie quietly in bed and "nurse their grief," as the old ladies express it—that is to say, ruminate over their trouble.

The people of Rattleborough had, indeed, so high an opinion of the wisdom and discretion of "Old Charley," that the greater part of them felt disposed to agree with him, and not make a stir in the business "until something should turn up," as the honest old gentleman worded it; and I believe that, after all, this would have been the general determination but for the very suspicious interference of Mr. Shuttleworthy's nephew, a young man of very dissipated habits, and otherwise of rather bad character. This nephew, whose name was Pennifeather, would listen to nothing like reason in the matter of "lying quiet," but insisted upon making immediate search for the "corpse of the murdered man." This was the expression he employed; and Mr. Goodfellow acutely remarked at the time, that it was "a *singular* expression, to say no more." This remark of Old Charley's, too, had great effect upon the crowd; and one of the party was heard to ask, very impressively, "how it happened that young Mr. Pennifeather was so intimately cognizant of all the circumstances connected with his wealthy uncle's disappearance, as to feel authorized to assert, distinctly and unequivocally, that his uncle *was* 'a murdered man.' " Hereupon some little squibbing and bickering occurred among various members of the crowd, and especially between "Old Charley" and Mr. Penni-

feather—although this latter occurrence was, indeed, by no means a novelty, for no good will had subsisted between the parties for the last three or four months; and matters had even gone so far that Mr. Pennifeather had actually knocked down his uncle's friend for some alleged excess of liberty that the latter had taken in the uncle's house, of which the nephew was an inmate. Upon this occasion, "Old Charley" is said to have behaved with exemplary moderation and Christian charity. He arose from the blow, adjusted his clothes, and made no attempt at retaliation at all—merely muttering a few words about "taking summary vengeance at the first convenient opportunity,"—a natural and very justifiable ebullition of anger, which meant nothing, however, and, beyond doubt, was no sooner given vent to than forgotten.

However these matters may be, (which have no reference to the point now at issue,) it is quite certain that the people of Rattleborough, principally through the persuasion of Mr. Pennifeather, came at length to the determination of dispersing over the adjacent country in search of the missing Mr. Shuttleworthy. I say they came to this determination in the first instance. After it had been fully resolved that a search should be made, it was considered almost a matter of course that the seekers should disperse—that is to say, distribute themselves in parties—for the more thorough examination of the region round about. I forget, however, by what ingenious train of reasoning it was that "Old Charley" finally convinced the assembly that this was the most injudicious plan that could be pursued. Convince them, however, he did—all except Mr. Pennifeather; and, in the end, it was arranged that a search should be instituted carefully and very thoroughly by the burghers *en masse*, "Old Charley" himself leading the way.

As for the matter of that, there could have been no better pioneer than "Old Charley," whom every body knew to have the eye of a lynx; but, although he led them into all manner of out-of-the-way holes and corners, by routes that nobody had ever suspected of existing in the neighbourhood, and although the search was incessantly kept up day and night for nearly a week, still no trace of Mr. Shuttleworthy could be discovered. When I say no trace, however, I must not be understood to speak literally; for trace, to some extent, there certainly was. The poor gentleman had been tracked, by his horse's shoes, (which were peculiar,) to a spot about three miles to the east of the borough, on the main road leading to the city. Here the track made off into a by-path through a piece of woodland—the path coming out again into the main road, and cutting off about half a mile of the regular distance. Following the shoe-marks down this lane, the party came at length to a pool of stagnant water, half hidden by the brambles, to the right of the lane, and opposite this pool all vestige of the track was lost sight of. It appeared, however, that a struggle of some nature had here taken place, and it seemed as if some large and heavy body, much larger and heavier than a man, had been dragged from the by-path to the pool. This latter was carefully dragged twice, but nothing was found; and the party were upon the point of going away, in despair of coming to any result, when Providence suggested to Mr. Goodfellow the expediency of draining the water off altogether. This project was received with cheers and many high compliments to "Old Charley" upon his sagacity and consideration. As many of the burghers had brought spades with them, supposing that they might possibly be called upon to disinter a corpse, the drain was easily and speedily effected; and no sooner was the bottom visible than right in the middle of the mud that remained was discovered a black silk velvet waistcoat, which nearly every one present immediately recognized as the property of Mr. Pennifeather. This waistcoat was much torn, and stained with blood, and

there were several persons among the party who had a distinct remembrance of its having been worn by its owner on the very morning of Mr. Shuttleworthy's departure for the city; while there were others, again, ready to testify upon oath, if required, that Mr. P. did *not* wear the garment in question at any period during the *remainder* of that memorable day; nor could any one be found to say that he had seen it upon Mr. P.'s person at any period at all subsequent to Mr. Shuttleworthy's disappearance.

Matters now wore a very serious aspect for Mr. Pennifeather, and it was observed, as an indubitable confirmation of the suspicions which were excited against him, that he grew exceedingly pale, and when asked what he had to say for himself, was utterly incapable of saying a word. Hereupon, the few friends his riotous mode of living had left him deserted him at once to a man, and were even more clamorous than his ancient and avowed enemies for his instantaneous arrest. But, on the other hand, the magnanimity of Mr. Goodfellow shone forth with only the more brilliant lustre through contrast. He made a warm and intensely eloquent defence of Mr. Pennifeather, in which he alluded more than once to his own sincere forgiveness of that wild young gentleman—"the heir of the worthy Mr. Shuttleworthy,"—for the insult which he (the young gentleman) had, no doubt in the heat of passion, thought proper to put upon him (Mr. Goodfellow.) "He forgave him for it," he said, "from the very bottom of his heart; and for himself (Mr. Goodfellow), so far from pushing the suspicious circumstances to extremity, which, he was sorry to say, really *had* arisen against Mr. Pennifeather, he (Mr. Goodfellow) would make every exertion in his power, would employ all the little eloquence in his possession to—to—to—soften down, as much as he could conscientiously do so, the worst features of this really exceedingly perplexing piece of business."

Mr. Goodfellow went on for some half

hour longer in this strain, very much to the credit both of his head and of his heart; but your warm-hearted people are seldom apposite in their observations— they run into all sorts of blunders, *contretemps* and *mal àproposisms*,[5] in the hotheadedness of their zeal to serve a friend —thus, often with the kindest intentions in the world, doing infinitely more to prejudice his cause than to advance it.

So, in the present instance, it turned out with all the eloquence of "Old Charley;" for, although he laboured earnestly in behalf of the suspected, yet it so happened, somehow or other, that every syllable he uttered of which the direct but unwitting tendency was not to exalt the speaker in the good opinion of his audience had the effect to deepen the suspicion already attached to the individual whose cause he pleaded, and to arouse against him the fury of the mob.

One of the most unaccountable errors committed by the orator was his allusion to the suspected as "the heir of the worthy old gentleman Mr. Shuttleworthy." The people had really never thought of this before. They had only remembered certain threats of disinheritance uttered a year or two previously by the uncle, (who had no living relative except the nephew;) and they had, therefore, always looked upon this disinheritance as a matter that was settled—so single-minded a race of beings were the Rattleburghers; but the remark of "Old Charley" brought them at once to a consideration of this point, and thus gave them to see the possibility of the threats having been nothing *more* than a threat. And straightway, hereupon, arose the natural question of *cui bono?*— a question that tended even more than the waistcoat to fasten the terrible crime upon the young man. And here, lest I be misunderstood, permit me to digress for one moment merely to observe that the exceedingly brief and simple Latin phrase which I have employed, is invariably mistranslated and misconceived. "*Cui bono,*" in all the crack novels and elsewhere,—

in those of Mrs. Gore, for example, (the author of "Cecil,") a lady who quotes all tongues from the Chaldæn to Chickasaw, and is helped to her learning, "as needed," upon a systematic plan, by Mr. Beckford, —in *all* the crack novels, I say, from those of Bulwer and Dickens to those of Turnapenny and Ainsworth,[6] the two little Latin words *cui bono* are rendered "to what purpose," or, (as if *quo bono,*) "to what good." Their true meaning, nevertheless, is "for whose advantage." *Cui,* to whom; *bono,* is it for a benefit. It is a purely legal phrase, and applicable precisely in cases such as we have now under consideration, where the probability of the doer of a deed hinges upon the probability of the benefit accruing to this individual or to that from the deed's accomplishment. Now, in the present instance, the question *cui bono* very pointedly implicated Mr. Pennifeather. His uncle had threatened him, after making a will in his favour, with disinheritance. But the threat had not been actually kept; the original will, it appeared, had not been altered. *Had* it been altered, the only supposable motive for murder on the part of the suspected would have been the ordinary one of revenge; and even this would have been counteracted by the hope of reinstation into the good graces of the uncle. But the will being unaltered, while the threat to alter remained suspended over the nephew's head, there appears at once the very strongest possible inducement for the atrocity: and so concluded, very sagaciously, the worthy citizens of the borough of Rattle.

Mr. Pennifeather was, accordingly, arrested upon the spot, and the crowd, after some farther search, proceeded homewards, having him in custody. On the route, however, another circumstance occurred tending to confirm the suspicion entertained. Mr. Goodfellow, whose zeal led him to be always a little in advance of the party, was seen suddenly to run forward a few paces, stoop, and then apparently to pick up some small object from the grass. Having quickly examined it, he was observed, too, to make a sort of half attempt at concealing it in his coat pocket; but this action was noticed, as I say, and consequently prevented, when the object picked up was found to be a Spanish knife, which a dozen persons at once recognized as belonging to Mr. Pennifeather. Moreover, his initials were engraved upon the handle. The blade of this knife was open and bloody.

No doubt now remained of the guilt of the nephew, and immediately upon reaching Rattleborough he was taken before a magistrate for examination.

Here matters again took a most unfavourable turn. The prisoner, being questioned as to his whereabouts on the morning of Mr. Shuttleworthy's disappearance, had absolutely the audacity to acknowledge that on that very morning he had been out with his rifle deer-stalking, in the immediate neighbourhood of the pool where the blood-stained waistcoat had been discovered through the sagacity of Mr. Goodfellow.

This latter now came forward, and, with tears in his eyes, asked permission to be examined. He said that a stern sense of the duty he owed to his Maker, not less than to his fellow men, would permit him no longer to remain silent. Hitherto, the sincerest affection for the young man (notwithstanding the latter's ill treatment of himself, Mr. Goodfellow), had induced him to make every hypothesis which imagination could suggest, by way of endeavouring to account for what appeared suspicious in the circumstances that told so seriously against Mr. Pennifeather; but these circumstances were now altogether *too* convincing—*too* damning; he would hesitate no longer—he would tell all he knew, although his heart (Mr. Goodfellow's) should absolutely burst asunder in the effort. He then went on to state that, on the afternoon of the day previous to Mr. Shuttleworthy's departure for the city, that worthy old gentleman had mentioned to his nephew, in *his* hearing, (Mr. Good-

fellow's,) that his object in going to town on the morrow was to make a deposit of an unusually large sum of money in the "Farmers' and Mechanics' Bank," and that, then and there the said Mr. Shuttleworthy had distinctly avowed to the said nephew his irrevocable determination of rescinding the will originally made, and of cutting him off with a shilling. He (the witness) now solemnly called upon the accused to state whether what he (the witness) had just stated was or was not the truth in every substantial particular. Much to the astonishment of every one present, Mr. Pennifeather frankly admitted that *it was.*

The magistrate now considered it his duty to send a couple of constables to search the chamber of the accused in the house of his uncle. From this search they almost immediately returned with the well known steel-bound, russet leather pocket-book which the old gentleman had been in the habit of carrying for years. Its valuable contents, however, had been abstracted, and the magistrate in vain endeavoured to extort from the prisoner the use which had been made of them, or the place of their concealment. Indeed, he obstinately denied all knowledge of the matter. The constables, also, discovered, between the bed and sacking of the unhappy man, a shirt and neck-handkerchief both marked with the initials of his name, and both hideously besmeared with the blood of the victim.

At this juncture, it was announced that the horse of the murdered man had just expired in the stable from the effects of the wound he had received, and it was proposed by Mr. Goodfellow that a *post mortem* examination of the beast should be immediately made, with the view, if possible, of discovering the ball. This was accordingly done; and, as if to demonstrate beyond a question the guilt of the accused, Mr. Goodfellow, after considerable searching in the cavity of the chest, was enabled to detect and to pull forth a bullet of very extraordinary size, which, upon trial, was found to be exactly adapted to the bore of Mr. Pennifeather's rifle, while it was far too large for that of any other person in the borough or its vicinity. To render the matter even surer yet, however, this bullet was discovered to have a flaw or seam at right angles to the usual suture; and upon examination, this seam corresponded precisely with an accidental ridge or elevation in a pair of moulds acknowledged by the accused himself to be his own property. Upon the finding of this bullet, the examining magistrate refused to listen to any farther testimony, and immediately committed the prisoner for trial—declining resolutely to take any bail in the case, although against this severity Mr. Goodfellow very warmly remonstrated, and offered to become surety in whatever amount might be required. This generosity on the part of "Old Charley" was only in accordance with the whole tenour of his amiable and chivalrous conduct during the entire period of his sojourn in the borough of Rattle. In the present instance, the worthy man was so entirely carried away by the excessive warmth of his sympathy, that he seemed to have quite forgotten, when he offered to go bail for his young friend, that he himself (Mr. Goodfellow) did not possess a single dollar's worth of property upon the face of the earth.

The result of the committal may be readily foreseen. Mr. Pennifeather, amid the loud execrations of all Rattleborough, was brought to trial at the next criminal sessions, when the chain of circumstantial evidence (strengthened as it was by some additional damning facts, which Mr. Goodfellow's sensitive conscientiousness forbade him to withhold from the court), was considered so unbroken and so thoroughly conclusive, that the jury, without leaving their seats, returned an immediate verdict of *"Guilty of murder in the first degree."* Soon afterwards the unhappy wretch received sentence of death, and was remanded to the county jail to await the inexorable vengeance of the law.

In the mean time, the noble behaviour of "Old Charley Goodfellow" had doubly endeared him to the honest citizens of the borough. He became ten times a greater favourite than ever; and, as a natural result of the hospitality with which he was treated, he relaxed, as it were, perforce, the extremely parsimonious habits which his poverty had hitherto impelled him to observe, and very frequently had little *réunions* at his own house, when wit and jollity reigned supreme—dampened a little, *of course,* by the occasional remembrance of the untoward and melancholy fate which impended over the nephew of the late lamented bosom friend of the generous host.

One fine day, this magnanimous old gentleman was agreeably surprised at the receipt of the following letter:—

"*Charles Goodfellow, Esquire—*

"*Dear Sir*—In conformity with an order transmitted to our firm about two months since, by our esteemed correspondent, Mr. Barnabas Shuttleworthy, we have the honour of forwarding this morning, to your address, a double box of Château-Margaux, of the antelope brand, violet seal. Box numbered and marked as per margin.
    "We remain, sir,
        "Your most ob'nt ser'ts,
            HOGGS, FROGS, BOGS & Co.[7]
    "City of —— June 21st, 18—.

"*P. S.*—The box will reach you, by wagon, on the day after your receipt of this letter. Our respects to Mr. Shuttleworthy. H. F. B. & Co."

[marginal note, read vertically:] Charles Goodfellow, Esq., Rattleborough. From H. F. B. & Co.—No. 1—6 doz. bottles (½ Gross). Chât. Mar. A—

The fact is, that Mr. Goodfellow had, since the death of Mr. Shuttleworthy, given over all expectation of ever receiving the promised Château-Margaux; and he, therefore, looked upon it *now* as a sort of especial dispensation of Providence in his behalf. He was highly delighted, of course, and, in the exuberance of his joy, invited a large party of friends to a *petit souper*[8] on the morrow, for the purpose of broaching the good old Mr. Shuttleworthy's present. Not that he *said* any thing about "the good old Mr. Shuttleworthy" when he issued the invitations. The fact is, he thought much and concluded to say nothing at all. He did *not* mention to any one—if I remember aright—that he had received a *present* of Château-Margaux. He merely asked his friends to come and help him drink some, of a remarkably fine quality and rich flavour, that he had ordered up from the city a couple of months ago, and of which he would be in the receipt upon the morrow. I have often puzzled myself to imagine *why* it was that "Old Charley" came to the conclusion to say nothing about having received the wine from his old friend, but I could never precisely understand his reason for the silence, although he had *some* excellent and very magnanimous reason, no doubt.

The morrow at length arrived, and with it a very large and highly respectable company at Mr. Goodfellow's house. Indeed, half the borough was there—I myself among the number—but, much to the vexation of the host, the Château-Margaux did not arrive until a late hour, and when the sumptuous supper supplied by "Old Charley" had been done very ample justice by the guests. It came at length, however,—a monstrously big box of it there was, too,—and as the whole party were in excessively good humour, it was decided, *nem. con.*,[9] that it should be lifted upon the table and its contents disemboweled forthwith.

No sooner said than done. I lent a helping hand; and, in a trice, we had the box upon the table, in the midst of all the bottles and glasses, not a few of which were demolished in the scuffle. "Old Charley," who was pretty much intoxicated, and excessively red in the face, now took a seat, with an air of mock dignity, at the head of the board, and thumped furiously upon it with a decanter, calling upon the company to keep order "during the ceremony of disinterring the treasure."

After some vociferation, quiet was at length fully restored, and, as very often happens in similar cases, a profound and remarkable silence ensued. Being then requested to force open the lid, I complied, of course, "with an infinite deal of pleasure." I inserted a chisel, and giving it a few slight taps with a hammer, the top of the box flew suddenly and violently off, and, at the same instant, there sprang up into a sitting position, directly facing the host, the bruised, bloody and nearly putrid corpse of the murdered Mr. Shuttleworthy himself. It gazed for a few moments, fixedly and sorrowfully, with its decaying and lack-lustre eyes, full into the countenance of Mr. Goodfellow; uttered slowly, but clearly and impressively, the words—"Thou art the man!" and then, falling over the side of the chest as if thoroughly satisfied, stretched out its limbs quiveringly upon the table.

The scene that ensued is altogether beyond description. The rush for the doors and windows was terrific, and many of the most robust *men* in the room fainted outright through sheer horror. But after the first wild, shrieking burst of affright, all eyes were directed to Mr. Goodfellow. If I live a thousand years, I can never forget the more than mortal agony which was depicted in that ghastly face of his, so lately rubicund with triumph and wine. For several minutes, he sat rigidly as a statue of marble; his eyes seeming, in the intense vacancy of their gaze, to be turned inwards and absorbed in the contemplation of his own miserable, murderous soul. At length, their expression appeared to flash suddenly out into the external world, when with a quick leap, he sprang from his chair, and, falling heavily with his head and shoulders upon the table, and in contact with the corpse, poured out rapidly and vehemently a detailed confession of the hideous crime for which Mr. Pennifeather was then imprisoned and doomed to die.

What he recounted was, in substance, this:—He followed his victim to the vicinity of the pool; there shot his horse with a pistol; despatched the rider with its butt end; possessed himself of the pocket-book; and, supposing the horse dead, dragged it with great labour to the brambles by the pond. Upon his own beast he slung the corpse of Mr. Shuttleworthy, and thus bore it to a secure place of concealment a long distance off through the woods.

The waistcoat, the knife, the pocket-book and the bullet, had been placed by himself where found with the view of avenging himself upon Mr. Pennifeather. He had also contrived the discovery of the stained handkerchief and shirt.

Towards the end of the blood-chilling recital, the words of the guilty wretch faltered and grew hollow. When the record was finally exhausted, he arose, staggered backwards from the table, and fell —*dead*.

————

The means by which this happily-timed confession was extorted, although efficient, were simple indeed. Mr. Goodfellows' excess of frankness had disgusted me, and excited my suspicions from the first. I was present when Mr. Pennifeather had struck him, and the fiendish expression which then arose upon his countenance, although momentary, assured me that his threat of vengeance would, if possible, be rigidly fulfilled. I was thus prepared to view the *manœuvring* of "Old Charley" in a very different light from that in which it was regarded by the good citizens of Rattleborough. I saw at once that all the criminating discoveries arose, either directly, or indirectly, from himself. But the fact which clearly opened my eyes to the true state of the case, was the affair of the bullet, *found* by Mr. G. in the carcass of the horse. *I* had not forgotten, although the Rattleburghers *had*, that there was a hole where the ball had entered the horse, and another where it *went out*. If it were found in the animal then, after having made its exit, I saw clearly that it must have been deposited by the person who found it. The bloody shirt and handkerchief confirmed the idea suggested by the bullet; for the blood upon examination proved to be capital claret, and no more. When I came to think of these things, and also of the late increase of liberality and expenditure on the part of Mr. Goodfellow, I entertained a suspicion which was none the less strong because I kept it altogether to myself.

In the mean time, I instituted a rigorous private search for the corpse of Mr. Shuttleworthy, and, for good reasons, searched in quarters as divergent as possible from those to which Mr. Goodfellow conducted his party. The result was that, after some days, I came across an old dry well, the mouth of which was nearly hidden by brambles; and here, at the bottom, I discovered what I sought.

Now it so happened that I had overheard the colloquy between the two cronies, when Mr. Goodfellow had contrived to cajole his host into the promise of a box of Château-Margaux. Upon this hint I acted. I procured a stiff piece of whalebone, thrust it down the throat of the corpse, and deposited the latter in an old wine box—taking care so to double the body up as to double the whalebone with it In this manner I had to press forcibly upon the lid to keep it down while I secured it with nails; and I anticipated, of course, that as soon as these latter were removed, the top would fly *off* and the body *up*.

Having thus arranged the box, I marked, numbered and addressed it as already told; and then writing a letter in the name of the wine merchants with whom Mr. Shuttleworthy dealt, I gave instructions to my servant to wheel the box to Mr. Goodfellow's door, in a barrow, at a given signal from myself. For the words which I intended the corpse to speak, I confidently depended upon my ventriloquial abilities; for their effect, I counted upon the conscience of the murderous wretch.

I believe there is nothing more to be explained. Mr. Pennifeather was released upon the spot, inherited the fortune of his uncle, profited by the lessons of experience, turned over a new leaf, and led happily ever afterwards a new life.

THE SPECTACLES

Many years ago, it was the fashion to ridicule the idea of "love at first sight;" but those who think, not less than those who feel deeply, have always advocated its existence. Modern discoveries, indeed, in what may be termed ethical magnetism or magnetœsthetics,[1] render it probable that the most natural, and, consequently the truest and most intense of the human affections, are those which arise in the heart as if by electric sympathy—in a word, that the brightest and most enduring of the psychal fetters are those which are riveted by a glance. The confession I am about to make will add another to the already almost innumerable instances of the truth of the position.

My story requires that I should be somewhat minute. I am still a very young man —not yet twenty-two years of age. My name, at present, is a very usual and rather plebeian one—Simpson. I say "at present;" for it is only lately that I have been so called—having legislatively adopted this surname within the last year, in order to receive a large inheritance left me by a distant male relative, Adolphus Simpson, Esq. The bequest was conditioned upon my taking the name of the testator;—the family, not the Christian name; my Christian name is Napoleon Buonaparte[2]—or, more properly, these are my first and middle appellations.

I assumed the name, Simpson, with some reluctance, as in my true patronym, Froissart, I felt a very pardonable pride; believing that I could trace a descent from the immortal author of the "Chronicles." While on the subject of names, by the bye, I may mention a singular coincidence of sound attending the names of some of my immediate predecessors. My father was a Monsieur Froissart, of Paris. His wife, my mother, whom he married at fifteen, was a Mademoiselle Croissart, eldest daughter of Croissart the banker; whose wife, again, being only sixteen when married, was the eldest daughter of one Victor Voissart. Monsieur Voissart, very singularly, had married a lady of similar name—a Mademoiselle Moissart. She, too, was quite a child when married; and her mother, also, Madame Moissart, was only fourteen when led to the altar. These early marriages are usual in France. Here, however, are Moissart, Voissart, Croissart, and Froissart,[3] all in the direct line of descent. My own name, though, as I say, became Simpson, by act of Legislature, and with so much repugnance on my part that, at one period, I actually hesitated about accepting the legacy with the useless and annoying *proviso* attached.

As to personal endowments I am by no means deficient. On the contrary, I believe that I am well made, and possess what nine tenths of the world would call a handsome face. In height I am five feet eleven. My hair is black and curling. My nose is sufficiently good. My eyes are large and gray; and although, in fact, they are weak to a very inconvenient degree, still no defect in this regard would be suspected from their appearance. The weakness, itself, however, has always much annoyed me, and I have resorted to every remedy—short of wearing glasses. Being youthful and good-looking, I naturally dislike these, and have resolutely refused to employ them. I know nothing, indeed, which so disfigures the countenance of a young person, or so impresses every feature with an air of demureness, if not altogether of sanctimoniousness and of age. An eye-glass, on the other hand, has a savor of downright foppery and affectation. I have hitherto managed as well as I could without either. But something too much of these merely personal details, which, after all, are of little importance. I will content myself with saying, in addition, that my temperament is sanguine, rash, ardent, enthusiastic—and that all my life I have been a devoted admirer of the women.

One night, last winter, I entered a box at the P—— theatre, in company with a friend, Mr. Talbot. It was an opera night, and the bills presented a very rare attraction, so that the house was excessively crowded. We were in time, however, to obtain the front seats which had been reserved for us, and into which, with some little difficulty, we elbowed our way.

For two hours, my companion, who was a musical *fanatico,* gave his undivided attention to the stage; and, in the meantime, I amused myself by observing the audience, which consisted, in chief part, of the very *élite* of the city. Having satisfied myself upon this point, I was about turning my eyes to the *prima donna,*[4] when they were arrested and riveted by a figure in one of the private boxes which had escaped my observation.

If I live a thousand years, I can never forget the intense emotion with which I regarded this figure. It was that of a female, the most exquisite I had ever beheld. The face was so far turned towards the stage that, for some minutes, I could not obtain a view of it—but the form was *divine*—no other word can sufficiently express its magnificent proportion, and even the term "divine" seems ridiculously feeble as I write it.

The magic of a lovely form in woman —the necromancy of female gracefulness —was always a power which I had found it impossible to resist; but here was grace personified, incarnate, the *beau idéal* of my wildest and most enthusiastic visions. The figure, almost all of which the construction of the box permitted to be seen, was somewhat above the medium height, and nearly approached, without positively reaching, the majestic. Its perfect fulness and *tournure* were delicious. The head, of which only the back was visible, rivalled in outline that of the Greek Psyche, and was rather displayed than concealed by an elegant cap of *gaze aérienne*, which put me in mind of the *ventum textilem* of

Apuleius. The right arm hung over the balustrade of the box, and thrilled every nerve of my frame with its exquisite symmetry. Its upper portion was draperied by one of the loose open sleeves now in fashion. This extended but little below the elbow. Beneath it was worn an under one of some frail material, close-fitting, and terminated by a cuff of rich lace which fell gracefully over the top of the hand, revealing only the delicate fingers, upon one of which sparkled a diamond ring which I at once saw was of extraordinary value. The admirable roundness of the wrist was well set off by a bracelet which encircled it, and which also was ornamented and clasped by a magnificent *aigrette*[5] of jewels—telling, in words that could not be mistaken, at once of the wealth and fastidious taste of the wearer.

I gazed at this queenly apparition for at least half an hour, as if I had been suddenly converted to stone; and, during this period, I felt the full force and truth of all that has been said or sung concerning "love at first sight." My feelings were totally different from any which I had hitherto experienced, in the presence of even the most celebrated specimens of female loveliness. An unaccountable, and what I am compelled to consider a *magnetic* sympathy of soul for soul, seemed to rivet, not only my vision, but my whole powers of thought and feeling upon the admirable object before me. I saw—I felt —I knew[6] that I was deeply, madly, irrevocably in love—and this even before seeing the face of the person beloved. So intense, indeed, was the passion that consumed me, that I really believe it would have received little if any abatement had the features, yet unseen, proved of merely ordinary character; so anomalous is the nature of the only true love—of the love at first sight—and so little really dependent is it upon the external conditions which only seem to create and control it.

While I was thus wrapped in admiration of this lovely vision, a sudden disturbance among the audience caused her to turn her head partially towards me, so that I beheld the entire profile of the face. Its beauty even exceeded my anticipations—and yet there was something about it which disappointed me without my being able to tell exactly what it was. I said "disappointed," but this is not altogether the word. My sentiments were at once quieted and exalted. They partook less of transport and more of calm enthusiasm—of enthusiastic repose. This state of feeling arose, perhaps, from the Madonna-like and matronly air of the face; and yet I at once understood that it could not have arisen entirely from this. There was something else—some mystery which I could not develope—some expression about the countenance which slightly disturbed me while it greatly heightened my interest. In fact, I was just in that condition of mind which prepares a young and susceptible man for any act of extravagance. Had the lady been alone, I should undoubtedly have entered her box and accosted her at all hazards; but, fortunately, she was attended by two companions—a gentleman, and a strikingly beautiful woman, to all appearance a few years younger than herself.

I revolved in my mind a thousand schemes by which I might obtain, hereafter, an introduction to the elder lady, or, for the present, at all events, a more distinct view of her beauty. I would have removed my position to one nearer her own; but the crowded state of the theatre rendered this impossible, and the stern decrees of Fashion had, of late, imperatively prohibited the use of the opera-glass, in a case such as this, even had I been so fortunate as to have one with me—but I had not, and was thus in despair.

At length I bethought me of applying to my companion.

"Talbot," I said, "*you* have an opera-glass. Let me have it."

"An opera-glass! no! what do you suppose *I* would be doing with an opera-glass?" Here he turned impatiently towards the stage.

"But, Talbot," I continued, pulling him by the shoulder, "listen to me, will you? Do you see the stage-box?—there! no, the next—did you ever behold as lovely a woman?"

"She is very beautiful, no doubt," he said.

"I wonder who she can be!"

"Why, in the name of all that is angelic, don't you *know* who she is? 'Not to know her argues yourself unknown.'[7] She is the celebrated Madame Lalande—the beauty of the day *par excellence*, and the talk of the whole town. Immensely wealthy, too—a widow, and a great match—has just arrived from Paris."

"Do you know her?"

"Yes; I have the honor."

"Will you introduce me?"

"Assuredly; with the greatest pleasure; when shall it be?"

"To-morrow, at one, I will call upon you at B——'s."

"Very good: and now *do* hold your tongue, *if* you can."

In this latter respect I was forced to take Talbot's advice; for he remained obstinately deaf to every further question or suggestion, and occupied himself exclusively for the rest of the evening, with what was transacting upon the stage.

In the mean time I kept my eyes riveted on Madame Lalande, and at length had the good fortune to obtain a full front view of her face. It was exquisitely lovely—this, of course, my heart had told me before, even had not Talbot fully satisfied me upon the point—but still the unintelligible something disturbed me. I finally concluded that my senses were impressed by a certain air of gravity, sadness, or still more properly, of weariness, which took something from the youth and freshness of the countenance, only to endow it with a seraphic tenderness and majesty, and thus, of course, to my enthusiastic and romantic temperament, with an interest tenfold.

While I thus feasted my eyes, I perceived, at last, to my great trepidation, by an almost imperceptible start on the part of the lady, that she had become suddenly aware of the intensity of my gaze. Still, I was absolutely fascinated, and could not withdraw it, even for an instant. She turned aside her face, and again I saw only the chiselled contour of the back portion of the head. After some minutes, as if urged by curiosity to see if I was still looking, she gradually brought her face again around and again encountered my burning gaze. Her large dark eyes fell instantly, and a deep blush mantled her cheek. But what was my astonishment at perceiving that she not only did not a second time avert her head, but that she actually took from her girdle a double eye-glass—elevated it —adjusted it—and then regarded me through it, intently and deliberately, for the space of several minutes.

Had a thunderbolt fallen at my feet I could not have been more thoroughly astounded—astounded *only*—not offended or disgusted in the slightest degree; although an action so bold in any other woman, would have been likely to offend or disgust. But the whole thing was done with so much quietude—so much *nonchalance*—so much repose—with so evident an air of the highest breeding, in short—that nothing of mere effrontery was perceptible, and my sole sentiments were those of admiration and surprise.

I observed that, upon her first elevation of the glass, she had seemed satisfied with a momentary inspection of my person, and was withdrawing the instrument, when, as if struck by a second thought, she resumed it, and so continued to regard me with fixed attention for the space of several minutes—for five minutes, at the very least, I am sure.

This action, so remarkable in an American theatre, attracted very general observation, and gave rise to an indefinite movement, or *buzz*, among the audience, which for a moment filled me with confusion, but produced no visible effect upon the countenance of Madame Lalande.

Having satisfied her curiosity—if such it was—she dropped the glass, and quietly gave her attention again to the stage; her profile now being turned toward myself, as before. I continued to watch her unremittingly, although I was fully conscious of my rudeness in so doing. Presently I saw the head slowly and slightly change its position; and soon I became convinced that the lady, while pretending to look at the stage was, in fact, attentively regarding myself. It is needless to say what effect this conduct, on the part of so fascinating a woman, had upon my excitable mind.

Having thus scrutinized me for perhaps a quarter of an hour, the fair object of my passion addressed the gentleman who attended her, and, while she spoke, I saw distinctly, by the glances of both, that the conversation had reference to myself.

Upon its conclusion, Madame Lalande again turned towards the stage, and, for a few minutes, seemed absorbed in the performances. At the expiration of this period, however, I was thrown into an extremity of agitation by seeing her unfold, for the second time, the eye-glass which hung at her side, fully confront me as before, and, disregarding the renewed buzz of the audience, survey me, from head to foot, with the same miraculous composure which had previously so delighted and confounded my soul.

This extraordinary behaviour, by throwing me into a perfect fever of excitement —into an absolute delirium of love— served rather to embolden than to disconcert me. In the mad intensity of my devotion, I forgot everything but the presence and the majestic loveliness of the vision which confronted my gaze. Watching my opportunity, when I thought the audience were fully engaged with the opera, I at length caught the eyes of Madame Lalande, and, upon the instant, made a slight but unmistakeable bow.

She blushed very deeply—then averted her eyes—then slowly and cautiously looked around, apparently to see if my rash action had been noticed—then leaned over towards the gentleman who sat by her side.

I now felt a burning sense of the impropriety I had committed, and expected nothing less than instant exposure; while a vision of pistols upon the morrow floated rapidly and uncomfortably through my brain. I was greatly and immediately relieved, however, when I saw the lady merely hand the gentleman a play-bill, without speaking; but the reader may form some feeble conception of my astonishment—of my profound amazement—my delirious bewilderment of heart and soul—when, instantly afterwards, having again glanced furtively around, she allowed her bright eyes to settle fully and steadily upon my own, and then, with a faint smile, disclosing a bright line of her pearly teeth, made two distinct, pointed and unequivocal affirmative inclinations of the head.

It is useless, of course, to dwell upon my joy—upon my transport—upon my illimitable ecstasy of heart. If ever man was mad with excess of happiness, it was myself at that moment. I loved. This was my *first* love—so I felt it to be. It was love supreme—indescribable. It was "love at first sight;" and at first sight too, it had been appreciated and—*returned*.

Yes, returned. How and why should I doubt it for an instant? What other construction could I possibly put upon such conduct, on the part of a lady so beautiful—so wealthy—evidently so accomplished—of so high breeding—of so lofty a position in society—in every regard so entirely respectable as I felt assured was Madame Lalande? Yes, she loved me—she returned the enthusiasm of my love, with an enthusiasm as blind—as uncompromising—as uncalculating—as abandoned—and as utterly unbounded as my own! These delicious fancies and reflections, however, were now interrupted by the falling of the drop-curtain. The audience arose; and the usual tumult immediately supervened. Quitting Talbot abruptly, I made every effort to force my way into closer proximity with Madame Lalande. Having failed in this, on account of the crowd, I at length gave up the chase, and bent my steps homewards; consoling myself for my disappointment in not having been able to touch even the hem of her robe, by the reflection that I should be introduced by Talbot, in due form, upon the morrow.

This morrow at last came; that is to say, a day finally dawned upon a long and weary night of impatience; and then the hours until "one" were snail-paced, dreary and innumerable. But even Stamboul,[8] it is said, shall have an end, and there came an end to this long delay. The clock struck. As the last echo ceased, I stepped into B——'s and enquired for Talbot.

"Out," said the footman—Talbot's own.

"Out!" I replied, staggering back half a dozen paces—"let me tell you, my fine fellow, that this thing is thoroughly impossible and impracticable; Mr. Talbot is *not* out. What do you mean?"

"Nothing, sir; only Mr. Talbot is not in. That's all. He rode over to S——, immediately after breakfast, and left word that he would not be in town again for a week."

I stood petrified with horror and rage. I endeavored to reply, but my tongue refused its office. At length I turned on my heel, livid with wrath, and inwardly consigning the whole tribe of the Talbots to the innermost regions of Erebus. It was evident that my considerate friend, *il fanatico*,[9] had quite forgotten his appointment with myself—had forgotten it as soon as it was made. At no time was he a very scrupulous man of his word. There was no help for it; so smothering my vexation as well as I could, I strolled moodily up the street, propounding futile inquiries about Madame Lalande to every male acquaintance I met. By report she was known, I found, to all—to many by sight—but she had been in town only a few weeks, and there were very few, therefore, who claimed her personal acquaintance. These few, being still comparatively strangers, could not, or would not, take the liberty of introducing me through the formality of a morning call. While I stood thus, in despair, conversing with a trio of friends upon the all absorbing subject of my heart, it so happened that the subject itself passed by.

"As I live, there she is!" cried one.

"Surpassingly beautiful!" exclaimed a second.

"An angel upon earth!" ejaculated a third.

I looked; and, in an open carriage which approached us, passing slowly down the street, sat the enchanting vision of the opera, accompanied by the younger lady who had occupied a portion of her box.

"Her companion also wears remarkably well," said the one of my trio who had spoken first.

"Astonishingly," said the second; "still quite a brilliant air; but art will do wonders. Upon my word, she looks better than she did at Paris five years ago. A beautiful woman still;—don't you think so, Froissart?—Simpson, I mean."

"Still!" said I, "and why shouldn't she be? But compared with her friend she is as a rushlight to the evening star—a glowworm to Antares."[10]

"Ha! ha! ha!—why, Simpson, you have an astonishing tact at making discoveries—original ones, I mean." And here we separated, while one of the trio began humming a gay vaudeville, of which I caught only the lines—

> Ninon, Ninon, Ninon à bas—
> A bas Ninon De L'Enclos![11]

During this little scene, however, one thing had served greatly to console me, although it fed the passion by which I was consumed. As the carriage of Madame Lalande rolled by our group, I had observed that she recognized me; and more than this, she had blessed me, by the most seraphic of all imaginable smiles, with no equivocal mark of the recognition.

As for an introduction, I was obliged to abandon all hope of it, until such time as Talbot should think proper to return from the country. In the meantime I perseveringly frequented every reputable place of public amusement; and, at length, at the theatre, where I first saw her, I had the supreme bliss of meeting her, and of exchanging glances with her once again. This did not occur, however, until the lapse of a fortnight. Every day, in the interim, I had inquired for Talbot at his hotel, and every day had been thrown into a spasm of wrath by the everlasting "Not come home yet" of his footman.

Upon the evening in question, therefore, I was in a condition little short of madness. Madame Lalande, I had been told, was a Parisian—had lately arrived from Paris—might she not suddenly return?—return before Talbot came back—and might she not be thus lost to me forever? The thought was too terrible to bear. Since my future happiness was at issue, I resolved to act with a manly decision. In a word, upon the breaking up of the play, I traced the lady to her residence, noted the address, and the next morning sent her a full and elaborate letter, in which I poured out my whole heart.

I spoke boldly, freely—in a word, I spoke with passion. I concealed nothing—nothing even of my weakness. I alluded to the romantic circumstances of our first meeting—even to the glances which had passed between us. I went so far as to say that I felt assured of her love; while I offered this assurance, and my own intensity of devotion, as two excuses for my otherwise unpardonable conduct. As a third, I spoke of my fear that she might quit the city before I could have the opportunity of a formal introduction. I concluded the most wildly enthusiastic epistle ever penned, with a frank declaration of my worldly circumstances—of my affluence—and with an offer of my heart and of my hand.

In an agony of expectation I awaited the reply. After what seemed the lapse of a century it came.

Yes, *actually came*. Romantic as all this may appear, I really received a letter from Madame Lalande—the beautiful, the wealthy, the idolized Madame Lalande.— Her eyes—her magnificent eyes—had not belied her noble heart. Like a true French-woman, as she was, she had obeyed the frank dictates of her reason—the gener-ous impulses of her nature—despising the conventional pruderies of the world. She had *not* scorned my proposals. She had *not* sheltered herself in silence. She had *not* returned my letter unopened. She had even sent me, in reply, one penned by her own exquisite fingers. It ran thus:

> Monsieur Simpson vill pardonne me for not compose de butefulle tong of his contrée so vell as might. It is only de late dat I am arrive, and not yet ave de opportunité for to— l'étudier.
>
> Vid dis apologie for de manière, I vill now say dat, hélas![12]—Mon-sieur Simpson ave guess but de too true. Need I say de more? Hélas! am I not ready speak de too moshe?
>
> EUGÉNIE LALANDE.

This noble-spirited note I kissed a mil-lion times, and committed, no doubt, on its account, a thousand other extrava-gances that have now escaped my mem-ory. Still Talbot *would* not return. Alas! could he have formed even the vaguest idea of the suffering his absence occa-sioned his friend, would not his sympa-thizing nature have flown immediately to my relief? Still, however, he came *not*. I wrote. He replied. He was detained by urgent business—but would shortly re-turn. He begged me not to be impatient —to moderate my transports—to read soothing books—to drink nothing stronger than Hock[13]—and to bring the consola-tions of philosophy to my aid. The fool! if he could not come himself, why, in the name of every thing rational, could he not have enclosed me a letter of presenta-tion? I wrote again, entreating him to forward one forthwith. My letter was re-turned by *that* footman, with the follow-ing endorsement in pencil. The scoundrel had joined his master in the country:

> Left S—— yesterday, for parts unknown—did not say where—or when be back—so thought best to return letter, knowing your hand-writing, and as how you is always, more or less, in a hurry.—
>
> Yours, sincerely,
> STUBBS.

After this, it is needless to say, that I devoted to the infernal deities both mas-ter and valet;—but there was little use in anger, and no consolation at all in com-plaint.

But I had yet a resource left, in my constitutional audacity. Hitherto it had served me well, and I now resolved to make it avail me to the end. Besides, after the correspondence which had passed be-tween us, what act of mere informality *could* I commit, within bounds, that ought to be regarded as indecorous by Ma-dame Lalande? Since the affair of the let-ter, I had been in the habit of watching her house, and thus discovered that, about twilight, it was her custom to promenade, attended only by a negro in livery, in a public square overlooked by her windows. Here, amid the luxuriant and shadowing groves, in the gray gloom of a sweet mid-summer evening, I observed my opportu-nity and accosted her.

The better to deceive the servant in at-tendance, I did this with the assured air of an old and familiar acquaintance. With a presence of mind truly Parisian, she took the cue at once, and, to greet me, held out the most bewitchingly little of hands. The valet at once fell into the rear; and now, with hearts full to overflowing, we discoursed long and unreservedly of our love.

As Madame Lalande spoke English even

less fluently than she wrote it, our conversation was necessarily in French. In this sweet tongue, so adapted to passion, I gave loose to the impetuous enthusiasm of my nature, and with all the eloquence I could command, besought her consent to an immediate marriage.

At this impatience she smiled. She urged the old story of decorum—that bugbear which deters so many from bliss until the opportunity for bliss has forever gone by. I had most imprudently made it known among my friends, she observed, that I desired her acquaintance—thus that I did not possess it—thus, again, there was no possibility of concealing the date of our first knowledge of each other. And then she adverted, with a blush, to the extreme recency of this date. To wed immediately would be improper—would be indecorous—would be *outré*.[14]—All this she said with a charming air of *naïveté* which enraptured while it grieved and convinced me. She went even so far as to accuse me, laughingly, of rashness—of imprudence. She bade me remember that I really even knew not who she was—what were her prospects, her connexions, her standing in society. She begged me, but with a sigh, to reconsider my proposal, and termed my love an infatuation—a will o' the wisp—a fancy or fantasy of the moment—a baseless and unstable creation rather of the imagination than of the heart. These things she uttered as the shadows of the sweet twilight gathered darkly and more darkly around us—and then, with a gentle pressure of her fairy-like hand, overthrew, in a single sweet instant, all the argumentative fabric she had reared.

I replied as best I could—as only a true lover can. I spoke at length, and perseveringly, of my devotion, of my passion—of her exceeding beauty, and of my own enthusiastic admiration. In conclusion, I dwelt, with a convincing energy, upon the perils that encompass the course of love —that course of true love that never did run smooth, and thus deduced the mani

fest danger of rendering that course unnecessarily long.

This latter argument seemed finally to soften the rigor of her determination. She relented; but there was yet an obstacle, she said, which she felt assured I had not properly considered. This was a delicate point—for a woman to urge, especially so; in mentioning it, she saw that she must make a sacrifice of her feelings; still, for *me*, every sacrifice should be made. She alluded to the topic of *age*. Was I aware —was I fully aware of the discrepancy between us? That the age of the husband should surpass by a few years—even by fifteen or twenty—the age of the wife, was regarded by the world as admissible, and, indeed, as even proper; but she had always entertained the belief that the years of the wife should *never* exceed in number those of the husband. A discrepancy of this unnatural kind gave rise, too frequently, alas! to a life of unhappiness. Now she was aware that my own age did not exceed two and twenty; and I, on the contrary, perhaps, was *not* aware that the years of my Eugénie extended very considerably beyond that sum.

About all this there was a nobility of soul—a dignity of candor—which delighted—which enchanted me—which eternally rivetted my chains. I could scarcely restrain the excessive transport which possessed me.

"My sweetest Eugénie," I cried, "what is all this about which you are discoursing? Your years surpass in some measure my own. But what then? The customs of the world are so many conventional follies. To those who love as ourselves, in what respect differs a year from an hour? I am twenty-two, you say; granted: indeed you may as well call me, at once, twenty-three. Now you yourself, my dearest Eugénie, can have numbered no more than—can have numbered no more than —no more than—than—than—than—"

Here I paused for an instant, in the expectation that Madame Lalande would interrupt me by supplying her true age. But a Frenchwoman is seldom direct, and has always, by way of answer to an embarrassing query, some little practical reply of her own. In the present instance Eugénie, who, for a few moments past, had seemed to be searching for something in her bosom, at length let fall upon the grass a miniature, which I immediately picked up and presented to her.

"Keep it!" she said, with one of her most ravishing smiles. "Keep it for my sake—for the sake of her whom it too flatteringly represents. Besides, upon the back of the trinket, you may discover, perhaps, the very information you seem to desire. It is now, to be sure, growing rather dark—but you can examine it at your leisure in the morning. In the meantime, you shall be my escort home tonight. My friends are about holding a little musical levée.[15] I can promise you, too, some good singing. We French are not nearly so punctilious as you Americans, and I shall have no difficulty in smuggling you in, in the character of an old acquaintance."

With this, she took my arm, and I attended her home. The mansion was quite a fine one, and, I believe, furnished in good taste. Of this latter point, however, I am scarcely qualified to judge; for it was just dark as we arrived; and in American mansions of the better sort, lights seldom, during the heat of summer, make their appearance at this, the most pleasant period of the day. In about an hour after my arrival, to be sure, a single shaded solar lamp[16] was lit in the principal drawing-room; and this apartment, I could thus see, was arranged with unusual good taste and even splendor; but two other rooms of the suite, and in which the company chiefly assembled, remained, during the whole evening, in a very agreeable shadow. This is a well conceived custom, giving the party at least a choice of light or shade, and one which our friends over the water could not do better than immediately adopt.

The evening thus spent was unquestionably the most delicious of my life. Madame Lalande had not overrated the musical abilities of her friends; and the singing I here heard I had never heard excelled in any private circle out of Vienna. The instrumental performers were many and of superior talents. The vocalists were chiefly ladies, and no individual sang less than well. At length, upon a peremptory call for "Madame Lalande," she arose at once, without affectation or demur, from the *chaise longue* upon which she had sate by my side, and, accompanied by one or two gentlemen and her female friend of the opera, repaired to the piano in the main drawing-room. I would have escorted her myself; but felt that, under the circumstances of my introduction to the house, I had better remain unobserved where I was. I was thus deprived of the pleasure of seeing, although not of hearing her, sing.

The impression she produced upon the company seemed electrical—but the effect upon myself was something even more. I know not how adequately to describe it. It arose in part, no doubt, from the sentiment of love with which I was imbued; but chiefly from my conviction of the extreme sensibility of the singer. It is beyond the reach of art to endow either air or recitative with more impassioned *expression* than was hers. Her utterance of the romance in Otello—the tone with which she gave the words "*Sul mio sasso*," in the Capuletti—is ringing in my memory yet. Her lower tones were absolutely miraculous. Her voice embraced three complete octaves, extending from the contralto D to the D upper soprano, and, though sufficiently powerful to have filled the San Carlos, executed, with the minutest precision, every difficulty of vocal composition—ascending and descending scales, cadences, or *fioriture*. In the finale of the Sonnambula, she brought about a most remarkable effect at the words—

Ah! non giunge uman pensiero
Al contento ond 'io son piena.[17]

Here, in imitation of Malibran,[18] she modified the original phrase of Bellini, so as to let her voice descend to the tenor G, when, by a rapid transition, she struck the G above the treble stave, springing over an interval of two octaves.

Upon rising from the piano after these miracles of vocal execution, she resumed her seat by my side; when I expressed to her, in terms of the deepest enthusiasm, my delight at her performance. Of my surprise I said nothing, and yet was I most unfeignedly surprised; for a certain feebleness, or rather a certain tremulous indecision of voice in ordinary conversation, had prepared me to anticipate that, in singing, she would not acquit herself with any remarkable ability.

Our conversation was now long, earnest, uninterrupted, and totally unreserved. She made me relate many of the earlier passages of my life, and listened with breathless attention, to every word of the narrative. I concealed nothing—I felt that I had a right to conceal nothing from her confiding affection. Encouraged by her candor upon the delicate point of her age, I entered, with perfect frankness, not only into a detail of my many minor vices, but made full confession of those moral and even of those physical infirmities, the disclosure of which, in demanding so much higher a degree of courage, is so much surer an evidence of love. I touched upon my college indiscretions —upon my extravagances—upon my carousals—upon my debts—upon my flirtations. I even went so far as to speak of a slightly hectic cough with which, at one time, I had been troubled—of a chronic rheumatism—of a twinge of hereditary gout—and, in conclusion, of the disagreeable and inconvenient, but hitherto carefully concealed, weakness of my eyes.

"Upon this latter point," said Madame Lalande, laughingly, "you have been surely injudicious in coming to confession; for, without the confession, I take it for granted that no one would have accused you of the crime. By the by" she continued, "have you any recollection"— and here I fancied that a blush, even through the gloom of the apartment, became distinctly visible upon her cheek— "have you any recollection, *mon cher ami,*[19] of this little ocular assistant which now depends from my neck?"

As she spoke she twirled in her fingers the identical double eye-glass, which had so overwhelmed me with confusion at the opera.

"Full well—alas! do I remember it," I exclaimed, pressing passionately the delicate hand which offered the glasses for my inspection. They formed a complex and magnificent toy, richly chased and filagreed, and gleaming with jewels, which, even in the deficient light, I could not help perceiving were of high value.

"*Eh bien! mon ami,*" she resumed with a certain *empressement*[20] of manner that rather surprised me—"*Eh bien, mon ami,* you have earnestly besought of me a favor which you have been pleased to denominate priceless. You have demanded of me my hand upon the morrow. Should I yield to your entreaties—and, I may add, to the pleadings of my own bosom—would I not be entitled to demand of you a very —a very little boon in return?"

"Name it!" I exclaimed with an energy that had nearly drawn upon us the observation of the company, and restrained by their presence alone from throwing myself impetuously at her feet. "Name it, my beloved, my Eugénie, my own!— name it!—but alas it is already yielded ere named."

"You shall conquer then, *mon ami,*" she said, "for the sake of the Eugénie whom you love, this little weakness which you have last confessed—this weakness more moral than physical—and which, let me assure you, is so unbecoming the nobility of your real nature—so inconsistent with the candor of your usual character—and which, if permitted farther control, will assuredly involve you, sooner or later, in some very disagreeable scrape. You shall conquer, for my sake, this affectation which leads you, as you yourself acknowledge, to the tacit or implied denial of your infirmity of vision. For, this infirmity you virtually deny, in refusing to employ the customary means for its relief. You will understand me to say, then, that I wish you to wear spectacles:—ah, hush!—you have already consented to wear them, *for my sake*. You shall accept the little toy which I now hold in my hand, and which, though admirable as an aid to vision, is really of no very immense value as a gem. You perceive that, by a trifling modification thus—or thus—it can be adapted to the eyes in the form of spectacles, or worn in the waistcoat pocket as an eye-glass. It is in the former mode, however, and habitually, that you have already consented to wear it *for my sake*."

This request—must I confess it?—confused me in no little degree. But the condition with which it was coupled rendered hesitation, of course, a matter altogether out of the question.

"It is done!" I cried, with all the enthusiasm that I could muster at the moment. "It is done—it is most cheerfully agreed. I sacrifice every feeling for your sake. To-night I wear this dear eye-glass, *as* an eye-glass, and upon my heart; but with the earliest dawn of that morning which gives me the pleasure of calling you wife, I will place it upon my—upon my nose—and there wear it ever afterwards, in the less romantic, and less fashionable, but certainly in the more serviceable form which you desire."

Our conversation now turned upon the details of our arrangements for the morrow. Talbot, I learned from my betrothed, had just arrived in town. I was to see him at once, and procure a carriage. The soirée[21] would scarcely break up before two; and by this hour the vehicle was to be at the door; when, in the confusion occasioned by the departure of the company, Madame L. could easily enter it unobserved. We were then to call at the house of a clergyman who would be in waiting; there be married, drop Talbot, and proceed on a short tour to the East; leaving the fashionable world at home to make whatever comments upon the matter it thought best.

Having planned all this, I immediately took leave, and went in search of Talbot, but, on the way, I could not refrain from stepping into a hotel, for the purpose of inspecting the miniature; and this I did by the powerful aid of the glasses. The countenance was a surpassingly beautiful one! Those large luminous eyes!—that proud Grecian nose!—those dark luxuriant curls!—"Ah!" said I exultingly to myself, "this is indeed the speaking image of my beloved!" I turned the reverse, and discovered the words—"Eugénie Lalande —aged twenty-seven years and seven months."

I found Talbot at home, and proceeded at once to acquaint him with my good fortune. He professed excessive astonishment, of course, but congratulated me most cordially, and proffered every assistance in his power. In a word, we carried out our arrangement to the letter; and, at two in the morning, just ten minutes after the ceremony, I found myself in a close carriage with Madame Lalande—with Mrs. Simpson, I should say—and driving at a great rate out of town, in a direction North-east and by North, half-North.

It had been determined for us by Talbot, that, as we were to be up all night, we should make our first stop at C——, a village about twenty miles from the city, and there get an early breakfast and some repose, before proceeding upon our route. At four precisely, therefore, the carriage drew up at the door of the principal inn. I handed my adored wife out, and ordered breakfast forthwith. In the mean time we were shown into a small parlor and sate down.

It was now nearly if not altogether daylight; and, as I gazed, enraptured, at the angel by my side, the singular idea came, all at once, into my head, that this was really the very first moment since my ac-

quaintance with the celebrated loveliness
of Madame Lalande, that I had enjoyed
a near inspection of that loveliness by
daylight, at all.

"And now, *mon ami*," said she taking
my hand, and so interrupting this train
of reflection, "and now, *mon cher ami*,
since we are indissolubly one—since I
have yielded to your passionate entreaties,
and performed my portion of our agreement—I presume you have not forgotten
that you also have a little favor to bestow
—a little promise which it is your intention to keep. Ah!—let me see! Let me remember! Yes; full easily do I call to mind
the precise words of the dear promise you
made to Eugénie last night. Listen! You
spoke thus: 'It is done!—it is most cheerfully agreed! I sacrifice every feeling for
your sake. To-night I wear this dear eye-
glass *as* an eye-glass, and upon my heart;
but with the earliest dawn of that morning which gives me the privilege of calling
you wife, I will place it upon my—upon
my nose—and there wear it, ever afterwards, in the less romantic, and less fashionable, but certainly in the more serviceable form which you desire.' These were
the exact words, my beloved husband,
were they not?"

"They were," I said; "you have an excellent memory; and assuredly, my beautiful Eugénie, there is no disposition on
my part to evade the performance of the
trivial promise they imply. See! Behold!
They are becoming—rather—are they
not?" And here, having arranged the
glasses in the ordinary form of spectacles,
I applied them gingerly in their proper
position; while Madame Simpson, adjusting her cap, and folding her arms, sat bolt
upright in her chair, in a somewhat stiff
and prim, and indeed in a somewhat undignified position.

"Goodness gracious me!" I exclaimed
almost at the very instant that the rim of
the spectacles had settled upon my nose
—"*My!* goodness gracious me!—why
what *can* be the matter with these
glasses?" and taking them quickly off, I

wiped them carefully with a silk handkerchief, and adjusted them again.

But if, in the first instance, there had
occurred something which occasioned me
surprise, in the second, this surprise became elevated into astonishment; and this
astonishment was profound—was extreme
—indeed I may say it was horrific. What,
in the name of everything hideous, did
this mean? Could I believe my eyes?—
could I?—that was the question. Was that
—was that—was that *rouge*? And were
those—were those—were those *wrinkles*,
upon the visage of Eugénie Lalande?—
And oh, Jupiter! and every one of the
gods and goddesses, little and big!—what
—what—what—*what* had become of her
teeth? I dashed the spectacles violently
to the ground, and, leaping to my feet,
stood erect in the middle of the floor, confronting Mrs. Simpson, with my arms set
a-kimbo, and grinning and foaming, but,
at the same time utterly speechless and
helpless with terror and with rage.

Now I have already said that Madame
Eugénie Lalande—that is to say, Simpson
—spoke the English language but very
little better than she wrote it: and for this
reason she very properly never attempted
to speak it upon ordinary occasions. But
rage will carry a lady to any extreme; and
in the present case it carried Mrs. Simpson
to the very extraordinary extreme of attempting to hold a conversation in a
tongue that she did not altogether understand.

"Vell, Monsieur," said she, after surveying me, in great apparent astonishment, for some moments—"Vell, Monsieur!—and vat den?—vat de matter now?
Is it de dance of de Saint Vitusse dat you
ave? If not like me, vat for vy buy de pig
in de poke?"

"You wretch!" said I, catching my
breath—"you—you—you villainous old
hag!"

"Ag?—ole?—me not so *ver* ole, after
all! me not one single day more dan de
eighty-doo."

"Eighty-two!" I ejaculated, staggering to

the wall—"eighty-two hundred thousand baboons! The miniature said twenty-seven years and seven months!"

"To be sure!—dat is so!—ver true! but den de portraite has been take for dese fifty-five year. Ven I go marry my segonde usbande, Monsieur Lalande, at dat time I had de portraite take for my daughter by my first usbande, Monsieur Moissart."

"Moissart!" said I.

"Yes, Moissart, Moissart;" said she, mimicking my pronunciation, which, to speak the truth, was none of the best; "and vat den? Vat *you* know bout de Moissart?"

"Nothing, you old fright!—I know nothing about him at all;—only I had an ancestor of that name, once upon a time."

"Dat name! and vat you ave for say to dat name?—'T is ver *goot* name; and so is Voissart—*dat* is ver goot name, too. My daughter, Mademoiselle Moissart, she marry von Monsieur Voissart; and de name is bote *ver* respectaable name."

"Moissart!" I exclaimed, "and Voissart! why what is it you mean?"

"Vat I mean?—I mean Moissart and Voissart; and for de matter of dat, I mean Croissart and Froissart, too, if I only tink proper to mean it. My daughter's daughter, Mademoiselle Voissart, she marry von Monsieur Croissart, and, den agin, my daughter's grande daughter, Mademoiselle Croissart, she marry von Monsieur Froissart; and I suppose you say dat *dat* is not von *ver* respectaable name."

"Froissart!" said I, beginning to faint, "why surely you don't say Moissart, and Voissart, and Croissart, and Froissart?"

"Yes," she replied, leaning fully back in her chair, and stretching out her lower limbs at great length; "yes, Moissart, and Voissart, and Croissart, and Froissart. But Monsieur Froissart, he vas von *ver* big vat you call fool—he vas von ver great big donce like yourself—for he lef *la belle France* for come to dis stupide Amérique —and ven he get here he vent and ave von *ver* stupide, von *ver*, *ver* stupide sonn, so I hear, dough I not yet av ad de plaisir

to meet vid him—neither me nor my companion, de Madame Stéphanie Lalande. He is name de Napoléon Bonaparte Froissart, and I suppose you say dat *dat*, too, is not von *ver* respectaable name."

Either the length or the nature of this speech, had the effect of working up Mrs. Simpson into a very extraordinary passion indeed; and as she made an end of it, with great labor, she jumped up from her chair like somebody bewitched, dropping upon the floor an entire universe of bustle as she jumped. Once upon her feet, she gnashed her gums, brandished her arms, rolled up her sleeves, shook her fist in my face, and concluded the performance by tearing the cap from her head, and with it an immense wig of the most valuable and beautiful black hair, the whole of which she dashed upon the ground with a yell, and there trampled and danced a fandango upon it, in an absolute ecstasy and agony of rage.

Meantime I sank aghast into the chair which she had vacated. "Moissart and Voissart!" I repeated, thoughtfully, as she cut one of her pigeon-wings, and "Croissart and Froissart!" as she completed another—"Moissart and Voissart and Croissart and Napoléon Bonaparte Froissart! —why, you ineffable old serpent, that's *me*—that's *me*—d'ye hear?—that's *me*"— here I screamed at the top of my voice —"that's *me e e! I* am Napoleon Bonaparte Froissart! and if I havn't married my great, great, grandmother, I wish I may be everlastingly confounded!"

Madame Eugénie Lalande, *quasi* Simpson—formerly Moissart—was, in sober fact, my great, great, grandmother. In her youth she had been beautiful, and even at eighty-two, retained the majestic height, the sculptural contour of head, the fine eyes and the Grecian nose of her girlhood. By the aid of these, of pearl-powder, of rouge, of false hair, false teeth, and false *tournure*, as well as of the most skilful modistes of Paris, she contrived to hold a respectable footing among the beauties *un peu passées* of the French metropolis. In this respect, indeed, she might have been regarded as little less than the equal of the celebrated Ninon De L'Enclos.[22]

She was immensely wealthy, and being left, for the second time, a widow without children, she bethought herself of my existence in America, and, for the purpose of making me her heir, paid a visit to the United States, in company with a distant and exceedingly lovely relative of her second husband's—a Madame Stéphanie Lalande.

At the opera, my great, great, grandmother's attention was arrested by my notice; and, upon surveying me through her eye-glass, she was struck with a certain family resemblance to herself. Thus interested, and knowing that the heir she sought was actually in the city, she made inquiries of her party respecting me.—The gentleman who attended her knew my person, and told her who I was. The information thus obtained induced her to renew her scrutiny; and this scrutiny it was which so emboldened me that I behaved in the absurd manner already detailed. She returned my bow, however, under the impression that, by some odd accident, I had discovered her identity. When, deceived by my weakness of vision, and the arts of the toilet, in respect to the age and charms of the strange lady, I demanded so enthusiastically of Talbot who she was, he concluded that I meant the younger beauty, as a matter of course, and so informed me, with perfect truth, that she was "the celebrated widow, Madame Lalande."

In the street, next morning, my great, great, grandmother encountered Talbot, an old Parisian acquaintance; and the conversation, very naturally, turned upon myself. My deficiencies of vision were then explained; for these were notorious, although I was entirely ignorant of their notoriety; and my good old relative discovered, much to her chagrin, that she had been deceived in supposing me aware of her identity, and that I had been merely making a fool of myself, in making open

love, in a theatre, to an old woman unknown. By way of punishing me for this imprudence, she concocted with Talbot a plot. He purposely kept out of my way, to avoid giving me the introduction. My street inquiries about "the lovely widow, Madame Lalande," were supposed to refer to the younger lady, of course; and thus the conversation with the three gentlemen whom I encountered shortly after leaving Talbot's hotel, will be easily explained, as also their allusion to Ninon De L'Enclos. I had no opportunity of seeing Madame Lalande closely during daylight; and, at her musical *soirée*, my silly weakness in refusing the aid of glasses, effectually prevented me from making a discovery of her age. When "Madame Lalande" was called upon to sing, the younger lady was intended; and it was she who arose to obey the call; my great, great, grandmother, to further the deception, arising at the same moment, and accompanying her to the piano in the main drawing-room. Had I decided upon escorting her thither, it had been her design to suggest the propriety of my remaining where I was; but my own prudential views rendered this unnecessary. The songs which I so much admired, and which so confirmed my impression of the youth of my mistress, were executed by Madame Stéphanie Lalande. The eye-glass was presented by way of adding a reproof to the hoax—a sting to the epigram of the deception. Its presentation afforded an opportunity for the lecture upon affectation with which I was so especially edified. It is almost superfluous to add that the glasses of the instrument, as worn by the old lady, had been exchanged by her for a pair better adapted to my years. They suited me, in fact, to a т.

The clergyman, who merely pretended to tie the fatal knot, was a boon companion of Talbot's, and no priest.—He was an excellent "whip," however; and having doffed his cassock to put on a great coat, he drove the hack which conveyed the "happy couple" out of town. Talbot took a seat at his side. The two scoundrels were thus "in at the death," and, through a half open window of the back parlor of the inn, amused themselves in grinning at the *dénouement*[23] of the drama. I believe I shall be forced to call them both out.

Nevertheless, I am *not* the husband of my great, great, grandmother; and this is a reflection which affords me infinite relief;—but I *am* the husband of Madame Lalande—of Madame Stéphanie Lalande —with whom my good old relative, besides making me her sole heir when she dies—if she ever does—has been at the trouble of concocting me a match. In conclusion: I am done forever with *billets doux*,[24] and am never to be met without SPECTACLES.

Notes

Thou Art the Man

1. Title: When David displeases God, Nathan comes to warn him with a parable, appropriate to this tale, and the ultimate source of the phrase "Thou art the man" (II Samuel 12:7). Poe's immediate source is probably the passage in Edward Bulwer-Lytton's *The Last Days of Pompeii* in which Olinthus, falsely accused of murder, extends his right arm toward the murderer Arbaces and says, "in a deep and loud voice . . . 'thou art the man.'"

Oedipus . . . enigma: In Greek legend, Oedipus became King of Thebes by solving the riddle of the Sphinx. The answer to the riddle bears on the story title, too: the Sphinx asks what animal goes on four feet in the morning, two at noon and three in the evening; recognizing that the times of day represent ages, Oedipus answers, "Man."

Rattleborough: Several eastern small towns bear similar-sounding names: Brattleboro, Vt. ("Brattle" means clattering noise), Attleboro, Mass. etc. Poe's tale, published in *Godey's Lady's Book* for November 1844, is one of the earliest American satires on the small-town mentality.

2. Barnabus was one of the apostles; having some land, he sold it and contributed cash to the apostles' communal hoard. "Shuttleworthy" implies that the old man made his money in textiles. So the name implies, "a wealthy and generous mill-owner."

3. The name suggests Robin Goodfellow, another name for Puck. The connotations are mischief, pranks, jests, and practical jokes.

4. a red Bordeaux wine. Poe may have learned of it in one of his favorite idea-mines, Bulwer-Lytton's *Pelham*, where a good pun is made of it with the name Margot in Chapter 17.

5. accidental blunders and misuses of language.

6. Mrs. Gore: Catherine Gore (1799–1861), exceedingly prolific popular novelist. Her *Cecil, or the Adventures of a Coxcomb* (1841), because of its intimate revelations of club life, was, in Poe's day, assumed to be the work of a man.

Beckford: See "Landor's Cottage," note 6.

Bulwer: Edward Lytton Bulwer (1803–1873), British novelist. See "Silence," notes 1 and 5; "Loss of Breath," note 5; "Some Passages in the Life of a Lion," note 10; Section Preface to "The Murders in the Rue Morgue."

Dickens: See "Loss of Breath," note 21; "The Literary Life of Thingum Bob, Esq.," note 25.

Turnapenny: i.e., a writer who writes for cash.

Poe's long interruption to discuss *cui bono* has less to do with his tale than with an extensive and amusing literary exchange, too complicated to go into here, among a number of British authors. Suffice it to say that, among other things, Byron was known as the *cui bono* poet.

Ainsworth: William Harrison Ainsworth (1805–1882). See "The Balloon-Hoax."

7. "antelope brand, violet seal": Before labels came into general use, a colored wax seal was used to protect the cork on a bottle of wine. Some merchants used steel dyes to stamp information on the wax before it cooled.

HOGGS, FROGS, BOGS & CO.: For our educated guess at the meaning of Poe's nonsensical firm-name, see "X-ing a Paragrab," note 8; See also "Mellonta Tauta," note 8.

8. ordinary evening meal.

9. a contraction for *nemine contradicente*, which is faulty Latin for *nullo contradicente*, i.e., no one contradicting. See "The Business Man," note 9.

The Spectacles

1. For romantic hope that science would prove spirituality, see "Mesmeric Revelation," note 3, and the Section Preface to "The Facts in the Case of M. Valdemar." Though Poe would probably have liked to see such matters proved, and was obviously fascinated by them, he also, at times, made fun of them and of their implications. Here, in a satirical tale, he is *not* being serious. His narrator, we will soon learn, is a fool, and the connections between love-at-first-sight, "ethical magnetism," and "electric sympathy," while they do present one way of explaining his falling in love with so improbable a lady, are not meant seriously. They are one of a number of indications that "Simpson" is a "simp" who will make a "spectacle" of himself.

"The Spectacles" appeared first in *The Dollar Newspaper*, March 27, 1844, and was reprinted in *The Broadway Journal*, November 22, 1845.

2. plebeian . . . Simpson: Compare what the narrator of the story "William Wilson" says about *his* name. As so often in Poe, the same devices, ideas, or language show up in serious tales or in satires. Pollin (1) notices another group of parallels: The idea of a sudden large inheritance must have intrigued poor Poe, cut off by his wealthy foster father. It appears here, in "The Landscape Garden" and "The Domain of Arnheim," in "The Gold-Bug" ("Legrand" and "Lalande" are similar names, as are "Ellison" and "Simpson"), in "Von Kempelen and his Discovery," and

the poem "Eldorado." Name and identity changes also recur here and in "William Wilson," "Ligeia," and "A Tale of the Ragged Mountains." See note 3 below.

Napoleon Buonaparte: Poe employs a nineteenth-century gag, the combination of an illustrious name with a common one. Compare "Plotinus Plinlimmon" in Melville's *Pierre* and Martin Van Buren Mavis in "Mellonta Tauta." See also IX, 187–190 of the Harrison edition of Poe. Note Poe's spelling of B[u]onaparte is inconsistent.

3. Froissart . . . "Chronicles": Jean Froissart (c. 1347–1404), author of the *Chroniques*, a history of feats of arms and valor from 1325 to 1400.

Moissart . . . Froissart: Donna E. Schafer has figured out what Poe was up to in this seemingly pointless passage about names. The first sentence of the story speaks of seeing (" 'love at first sight' "), thinking, and feeling deeply. The names involved in this passage are Moissart, Voissart, and Croissart. Remove the last syllable, which the three have in common, and three French meanings are suggested: *moi*, me or I; *vois*, from the verb *voir*, to see; *crois*, from the verb *croire*, to believe (or "feel deeply"). Since the tale is about the difference between appearance and reality —about not seeing too well—Miss Schafer's postulation of a hidden motto, something to the effect of "seeing is believing only if you see clearly," makes good sense and is worthy of Dupin. Also, the narrator's name, Froissart, could relate to the verb *froisser*: "to crumple, to bruise, to ruffle, to offend, to hurt," which suggests why he speaks of "the direct line of descent." See also note 6.

4. *fanatico*: fanatic, fan.

prima donna: the leading female singer.

5. *beau idéal*: highest kind of beauty.

tournure: shape or figure.

gaze aérienne: light and transparent cloth of silk, linen, etc.

ventum textilem of Apuleius: Poe's source for this phrase is Isaac Disraeli's *Curiosities of Literature* where it is translated, "woven air." Disraeli says that Apuleius is describing neckerchiefs which "in veiling, discover the beautiful bosom of a woman." Curiously, the words do not appear to be in Apuleius. The story of Psyche (see earlier in this paragraph) in Apuleius' *Metamorphosis or the Golden Ass* does contain a reference to filmy garments. The term *ventum textilem* appears in the *Satyricon* of Titus Petronius Arbiter: Trimalchio, praising the works of Pubilius Syrus, quotes these lines (which may not really be by Pubilius):

> *Aequum est induere nuptam*
> *ventum textilem,*
> *palam prostare nudam in nebula*
> *linea?* (LV)

Michael Heseltine translates them:

> Thy bride might as well clothe herself with a garment of the wind as stand forth publicly naked under her clouds of muslin.

A French translation, published in 1842, which included both works, might be the reason for Disraeli's error: he might have confused the two Latin authors because he had recently read them in the same volume: *Pétrone, Apulée, Aulu-Gelle, oeuvres complètes avec la traduction en français publiées sous la direction de M. Nisard.* Paris, J. J. Dubochet et compagnie, editeurs, 1842. See also "The Island of the Fay," note 5, which explains why we know that Disraeli is Poe's source.

aigrette: a piece of jewelry in the form of a tuft.

6. Poe's word game again—Moissart, Voissart, Croissart. See note 3.

7. Poe alters a line from Milton's *Paradise Lost* (IV, 830): "Not to know me argues yourself unknown."

8. Istanbul, formerly Constantinople, in ancient times Byzantium.

9. Erebus: Poe means "hell," though strictly speaking, Erebus was, in Greek mythology, the dark region a shade had to pass through on the way to hell.

il fanatico: The fanatic—Talbot, that is.

10. a very bright star.

11. *vaudeville:* street song, topical song, or satirical song.

Anne de Ninon de Lenclos (1620–1705) was a famous courtesan noted not only for her liaisons with distinguished men, but also her brains, charm, and wit. Simpson's friend, once he realizes that it is the old lady, not the young, whom Simpson admires, sings an appropriate song. Even the disparity in age is appropriate. The courtesan of the song knew La Fontaine, Racine, Molière and others, but late in her life befriended the young Voltaire.

> *Ninon, Ninon, down with Ninon*
> *Down with Ninon de Lenclos!*

12. *l'étudier:* Study it.

hélas: alas.

13. white Rhine wine.

14. strange, odd, abnormal.

15. a reception or party.

16. an Argand Lamp (after the inventor Aimé Argand); a lamp with a tubular wick which admits a current of air inside as well as outside of the flame.

17. air or recitative: Traditional operas use two different modes of solo singing, aria (or "air") and recitative. The aria is songlike ("air" is, in some usage, just another word for "song"), structured, melodic, and often very elaborate. Recitative, in contrast, is closer to the patterns of normal speech. Characteristically, it serves to move the plot along, while the aria expresses emotionally important moments and provides a showpiece for the singer's skills.

romance: a lyrical but not elaborate piece.

Otello: "Otelo," the 1816 opera by Rossini (the more famous Verdi opera was not written until 1887).

Capuletti: Bellini's opera "The Capulets and Montagues" (1830), based on Shakespeare's *Romeo and Juliet*.

"*Sul mio sasso*": "On my gravestone." Sung by Romeo (both Romeo and Giulietta are sung by sopranos) in the last duet in the work.

three . . . octaves: An octave in music is the distance from one note to the next note higher or lower which bears the same name. If one sings up a major scale, it will be the eighth note sung. Each octave doubles the number of vibrations per second. When one hears an orchestra "tune up" to an A, the A is about 440 vps. Three octaves is a very large range—almost anyone can produce three octaves, but not with good tonal quality. Women's voices are categorized according to their best range, and Poe claims that Stéphanie Lalande's covers from the contralto register, the lowest female voice, to high in the range of the soprano.

San Carlos: The famous opera house in Naples, Italy.

The Sonnambula: "La Sonnambula" ("The Sleepwalker"), the Bellini opera of 1831.

Ah! . . . piena: "Let no human thought come near to the contentment with which I am full," from a fast aria, "Capaletta," at the close of the opera after the sleepwalker is rescued from the mill-wheel.

18. Maria Felicita Malibran (1808–1836), a very famous singer who, like Stéphanie, was a soprano with enormous range. Vocal gymnastics of the sort Poe mentions often were known to have been originated by specific singers and sometimes became traditional; singers doing the part a century later often used the same unwritten devices. The specific information about Malibran Poe culled from two sources located by Pollin (1)—an article in an issue of the 1836 *New Monthly Belle Assemblée* which we know Poe read and a book on Malibran which Poe reviewed for *Burton's Gentleman's Magazine* in May 1840 (*Works*, X, 91–96).

19. my dear friend.

20. "*Eh bien! mon ami*": All right, my friend.

empressement: animated earnestness.

21. party.

22. modistes: purveyors of fashionable clothing.

un peu passées: a flattering way of implying "a little on the old side."

Ninon De L'Enclos: See note 10.

23. "whip": a man who drives a hack or coach.

dénouement: final unraveling of the plot.

24. Love letters. This is an interesting point on which to end the tale, because Ninon de Lenclos wrote a famous *billet* to a lover named La Chatre when he went into the army. She promised in it to be faithful to him, a vow she promptly broke, saying, "*Le bon billet qu'à La Chatre*"—"The nice letter that La Chatre has,"—an expression which became a proverb meaning a promise one doesn't expect to keep.

9. Literary Satires

We do not yet fully understand Poe's humor, but in recent years scholars have made progress in figuring out many of his most puzzling comic tales. Buried allusions, parodies, private jokes, and puns appear in all sorts of his tales, but in the literary satires they are so dense that they almost seem to be the main point.

Once one knows the books Poe is referring to, the literary quarrels he has in mind, the manner in which topic A reminds him of article B, the way he cues the readers who recognize a line from his own work or that of an author he has reviewed, and then uses the cue to construct an implied comparison between, for example, a literary antagonist and an absurd character in fiction, these puzzling tales come alive.

Indeed, they resonate. Stories which had seemed interesting only for their apparent absurdity become genuinely funny to the reader who has just read the material on which they are based. However surprising the comparison, we find this side of Poe reminding us forcibly of James Joyce: very few major authors have operated in quite this way—Poe and the British magazinists, Joyce and to a lesser extent Nabokov.

The objects of Poe's satires were often unclear, not only to his readers, but to his editors and colleagues as well, some of whom advised him that he was being too subtle or obscure. Most of the stories in this section Poe had intended to include in his projected "Tales of the Folio Club," each supposedly prepared for a meeting of the club—"a Junto of Dunderheadism"—by one of the members. But the collection was never published. Exactly which tales Poe included in it, as well as the identities of the author-members of his club, are still unclear, even after decades of scholarly investigation. (See especially Mabbott (1), Wilson, Thompson (2), and Hammond).

Nor have our efforts and those of other scholars ferreted out all the jokes embedded in Poe's prose. Our best hope here is to give the reader a general idea of what Poe was up to and to give the scholar some leads to follow.

How to Write a Blackwood Article. This tale is a satire on style, and Pollin (12) has identified many of Poe's targets. For our purposes, suffice it to say that Poe is after pretension, bombast, and false erudition. Mr. Blackwood's advice to Zenobia parodies specific passages in works Poe knew. The tale is also a satire on the important magazine named in its title. McNeal, working on circumstantial evidence, identifies Zenobia as a caricature of Margaret Fuller, scholar, literary critic, and "leading female light" among the Transcendentalists of Boston, Cambridge, and Concord at whom Poe sniped whenever the opportunity arose.

A Predicament. "The Signora Zenobia" produces this tale following "Mr. Blackwood's" recipe. Poe always published the two together. Zenobia tries hard to stress sensations, to use the commercially attractive "tones," and to show her erudition by working in the exotic tidbits of information and the foreign language quotations. Poe points them all out in "How to Write A Blackwood Article."

The parody of the commercial writer is important because Poe himself "followed these instructions" in his own most serious work. The language of "A Predicament" reminds one of the language of many of his tales and even of at least one poem; like Zenobia, he paraded his (sometimes pretended) erudition and built many of his stories around a careful recording of "sensations."

Never Bet the Devil Your Head. This tale should be compared to "How to Write a Blackwood Article," in that it makes fun of the various popular magazine styles (stiles), ties the Transcendentalists of America to those of Europe, and associates both with the gifted groups of writers who produced *Blackwood's*.

A Tale of Jerusalem. James Southall Wilson demonstrated in 1931 that Poe's early burlesques were quite literally parodies of specific works. Of "A Tale of Jerusalem," he wrote, " 'Zillah, a Tale of Jerusalem' by Horace Smith [1779–1849] was a popular novel in 1829 and Poe not only burlesqued episodes in the story, such as the siege of the city, but lifted for ridicule whole sentences and phrases from its text, such as 'true as the Pentateuch,' and 'bigger than the letter Jod.' " (One edition of the novel is dated London, 1828, and the title reads *Zillah; A Tale of the Holy City*. The running-head, however, reads "Zillah; A tale of Jerusalem.") "He filled his tale with El Emanu! Booshoh-he! and El Elohim! and closed it with words from Smith's book: 'it is the unutterable flesh.' "

Poe's story is more than a parody; it is literally a collage of snatches of the Smith novel, cut out and pasted together in a new order. Read immediately after *Zillah*, it is very funny. Read without *Zillah* it is merely a puzzling and even offensive anecdote.

In reading *Zillah,* which deserves parody (though Poe in general seems to have admired Smith), we came upon the very incident on which Poe bases his story. Dinah, Zillah's nurse, narrates:

"... when the Holy city was besieged, not many years agone, they let down in
a basket, every day, over the walls, so much money as would buy lambs for the

daily sacrifices, which lambs they drew up again in the same basket. But an Israelite, who spoke Greek, having acquainted the besiegers that so long as the sacrifices were offered, the city could not be taken, the profane villains popped a hog in the basket instead of the usual victim, and from that time we have been accustomed to curse every one that could speak Greek" (I, 219).

Wilson says that Poe's tale burlesques "episodes in the story Zillah, such as the siege of the city." Actually, there are three sieges involved. The episode in Zillah is the siege involving the conquest of Jerusalem by Herod in 40 B. C. E. Poe doesn't directly burlesque that. An earlier siege, the source of Smith's pig anecdote and Poe's tale, occurred during a complex civil war ending in Roman dominance about 63 B.C.E. And Poe sets his tale in 181 of the common era, a puzzling date, because the last major Jewish uprising, Bar Kochba's rebellion, ended in 135. Minor rebellions did continue until about 200.

Poe knew well the works of the Blackwood's group of writers. One had in 1827 produced a satire on another Smith novel: Whitehall: or, the Days of George IV by William Maginn (1793–1842). Poe knew Maginn's work well enough that one scholar (Hammond) thinks Poe intended for readers to recognize Maginn as one of the "authors" of his Folio Club tales (see Preface to Section Nine). Poe had, then, good literary precedent: an exceedingly clever writer had satirized Smith.

The Literary Life of Thingum Bob, Esq. This tale pokes fun at the little literary world of the magazines. Fiercely competitive, insecure about their own artistic worth, limited in popularity and influence, the American literary magazines of Poe's day had to create an illusion of importance in order to survive at all, and their editors were, indeed, guilty of the faults which Poe exaggerates in Thingum Bob, such as the tendency to see "the Literary History of America" in terms of their own careers. Whipple (3) has figured out one specific target of Poe's sarcasm. Lewis Gaylord Clark began in 1844 publication of the Literary Remains of the Late Willis Gaylord Clark, his twin brother. Thingum Bob represents Willis, but, since Willis is dead, Poe's real target is Lewis and the system of "You scratch my back and I'll scratch yours" which prevailed in magazine and book publishing circles of Poe's day. Note the similarity in titles. Thingum is still alive (Whipple errs here), but Poe gets the word "late" (i.e. deceased) into his subtitle to make it clear to the reader that he has the Clarks' Literary Remains in mind.

There is another related target: Poe's dispute with Lewis Clark stems largely from Poe's famous hostile review of Theodore Fay's Norman Leslie. Fay fought back in a satire which, Pollin shows, was aimed at Poe: He called Poe "Bulldog," made him editor of "The Southern Literary Passenger," and said that Poe hated successful novelists because his own works were rejected by publishers. And Poe responded with this tale. Pollin (14) spells out the relationship between it and the piece by Fay:

Fay's "The Successful Novel"	Poe's answer to it ("Thingum Bob")
1. Fay was a lawyer, politician, poet, and editor	1. See text at note 5: these are the careers Thingum considers
2. The name "Thingum"	2. "Thingum Bob"
3. "Capias"	3. "Slyass"
4. "Toadeater"	4. "Toad"
5. "Goosequill"	5. "Goosetherumfoodle"
6. "Bumble-Bee"	6. "Gad-Fly"
7. "Rosewater"	7. "Oil of Bob"

Pollin's case is strong; we can't summarize it here. Clearly Poe had Fay in mind as well as the Clark brothers, and clearly the tale is one of Poe's multiple-targeted forays against the New York literary cliques.

The Duc De L'Omelette. Daughrity has figured out what "The Duc De L'Omelette" is about: N. P. Willis at the time was editor of *The American Monthly Magazine* and wrote for it a column called the "Editor's Table" in which he invited the reader to share the pleasures of his office: two dogs, a pet "South American trulian" (a bird of his own invention, apparently), perfume for the quill of his pen, crimson curtains, all manner of exotic lounges, ottomans, and divans, olives, japonica flowers, and a bottle of Rudesheimer.

Willis was attacked and teased for these affectations; they were well enough known so that James Paulding, in explaining that a group of Poe's tales was rejected because the targets of Poe's satires would be missed by most readers, also said that this story was one of the exceptions—everyone would understand it. Twentieth-century scholars caught on first to a second joke buried in the tale: the Duc's affectations come from *The Young Duke* by Benjamin Disraeli. Hirsch informed us of another quite private joke: Poe probably never even read the Disraeli novel. Our explication (see note 2) adds still another: Poe hadn't read all of his other "sources," either.

Some Passages in the Life of a Lion. Since Nathaniel Parker Willis had quickly become a literary lion, hobnobbed with the famous in London and Scotland, and filled his editorial columns with evidences of his erudition, it had been assumed that this story was, in J. K. Paulding's phrase, a "quiz [i.e. satire] on Willis." Daughrity argues against this reading, but Benton convinces us that Willis and literary lionizing in general are Poe's main targets. Poe wrote "Some Passages . . ." early in his career. Later evidence shows that he liked Willis's work, though he continued to remember that Willis's fame rested not only on his ability as a writer, but also on his contacts in literary circles.

An alternate, but not contradictory, interpretation is Marie Bonaparte's: there is an old and vulgar association in folklore of "nose" with "penis." Jones becomes famous because of the size of his sexual apparatus, and Poe, whose humor does frequently take a nasty turn, is the author of a dirty tale. Thompson offers a sensible alternative—though he agrees that, since Poe is often vulgar, the nose-penis joke is probably deliberate. an item in the June

1827 *Edinburgh Review* reads, "In literature . . . , 'every man,' says Lessing, 'has his own style, like his own nose.' True, there are noses of wonderful dimensions; but no nose can be justly amputated by the public. . . ." "Nose," then, means "style," and Bulwer and Willis become examples of authors who became lions through style alone.

Though Poe, early in his career, parodied the literary lion, it is clear enough from biographical data that he himself enjoyed notoriety and wished that he could cut a larger figure even in the modest literary circles of America in his day.

The Devil in the Belfry. Whipple (2) sees "The Devil in the Belfry" as another political satire:

> If we steep ourselves in the political atmosphere of the late eighteen thirties, we no longer find the allusions in "The Devil in the Belfry" obscure. We see in the little devil who bows and pirouettes, whose hair is tied in curlpapers, who is constantly smiling and seems so self-satisfied, a delightful parody of Van Buren's dandyism and consciously acquired courtly mannerisms. We are reminded of the nickname Flying Dutchman when this stranger pigeon-wings up to the belfry. When the devil claps the *chapeau de bras* (hat of power) on the belfry keeper we think of the Regency's control . . . of . . . politics. ["The Regency" is a nickname for Van Buren's political machine.] The pigs with the repeaters tied to their tails are a clear allusion to New York's machine politics. [A "repeater" is a voter paid to vote several times. According to a persistent but undocumented story, incidentally, Poe's death in Baltimore came after intoxication and exposure brought on by accepting drinks in return for voting as a "repeater" on election day.] . . . The stranger's sitting on the belfry keeper and fiddling a double jig, "Paddy O'Rafferty," [is] for the delight of the Irish riffraff . . . [who were the base of Van Buren's political power in New York]. The hooked nose of the devil [Van Buren had one, too], the gold snuff-box [Van Buren was famous for his use of snuff], and the people's deference to the steeple clock [at "Fivepoints," the center of the old-world villagelike Irish district in New York, the Hall steeple contained a bell] all corroborate evidence that Poe was satirizing a particular individual, President Martin Van Buren.

Poe said, however, that in satirical tales such as this, he hit out in all directions, and he has characteristically hidden in this story a large number of allusions to Thomas Carlyle's *Sartor Resartus*. The two lines of satire coalesce in the Irish jig at the end, for Carlyle's book devotes one of its last chapters (Book III, Ch. 10) largely to the Irish and concludes with a paragraph about "all too Irish mirth and madness." This line of imagery is not exactly a private joke, for Poe could expect some of his readers to know Carlyle, just as he could expect most to know Van Buren. To minimize footnotes, we can note some congruences here: in *Sartor Resartus* Book II, Ch. 4 Carlyle speaks of "Peace and War against the Time-Prince *(Zeitfürst)* or Devil. . . ."; the identification of time and Devil occurs also in II, 1 and III, 12. Teufelsdröckh lives in a "watch-tower" (I, 3), the highest in a town with an absurd "German" name ("Weissnichtwo"). Teufelsdröckh, indeed, appears in the light-blue cloak so common to Poe's grotesque characters, and even looks like a "little blue Belfry" (II, 8). And so on. *Sartor Resartus* provides Poe's readers with a running joke through a number of satiric tales, but seems so close to the surface in this story that it is fair to say that Poe is playing with it as he played, to a greater extent, with *Zillah* in "A Tale of Jerusalem."

Bon-Bon. For all Poe's mockery of Carlyle, one distinctly feels that Poe was strongly influenced by him, and even envied him. "Bon-Bon" grows from some kernels Poe probably picked up in *Sartor Resartus*, especially in Chapter 7, "The Everlasting No," in which Teufelsdröckh undergoes an important change of heart: "Soul is *not* synonymous with Stomach." A passage put into Teufelsdröckh's mouth could serve as a motto for the Poe story:

> Not on Morality, but on Cookery, let us build our stronghold: there brandishing our frying-pan, as censer, let us offer sweet incense to the Devil, and live at ease in the fat things *he* has provided for his Elect.

Another hint Poe took:

> . . . in our age of Down-pulling and Disbelief, the very Devil has been pulled down, you cannot so much as believe in a Devil.

Why the Little Frenchman Wears His Hand in a Sling. Following a clue in Wilson, we checked out Poe's interest in Irish dialect humor and Lady Morgan, because "Why the Little Frenchman Wears His Hand in a Sling" seems to have been intended as a burlesque of her work for Poe's oft-revised and never completed "Tales of the Folio Club" project.

In 1836, Poe "used up" Colonel Stone for a novel called *Ups and Downs.* Poe wrote,

> . . . in Chapter XII, his wife affronts the scholars by swearing by the powers she would be after clearing them out—the spalpeens!—that's what she would, honies!

This review is late in date compared to the composition of most of the Folio Club tales, but since no publication of the story has been found before 1840, it is possible that Poe wrote one tale later than the others. At any rate, he had stage-Irish in mind as late as 1836.

In Lady Morgans' *Florence Macarthy: An Irish Tale* occurs a scene close enough to "Why the Little Frenchman . . ." to have given Poe the idea of non-communication between an Irishman and a Frenchman. Mr. De Vere arrives in Dublin with a French valet. The valet is approached by an Irishman who wants to help with the baggage. As the two go along together and try to talk, each sentence results in a misunderstanding. The Irishman parodies French he doesn't understand, and, mimicking the Frenchman's bow, says, "troth, you do your dancing master every justice, whoever he was" (London, 1818, Vol. I, p. 30). All of those elements appear in Poe's tale.

Lady Morgan, moreover, was known for an over-fondness for French in her work, which could also account for Poe's decision to build his story around an argument between a Frenchman and an Irishman. In "Blue-Stocking Revels," Leigh Hunt wrote of her,

> So he kissed her, and called her "eternal good wench";
> But asked, why the devil she spoke so much French?

Pollin (13) points to another possible source for some elements in this tale, Thomas Moore's *The Fudges in England* (1835); Moore sometimes employs similar humorous dialect in it. (For Poe's familiarity with this source, see "Some Passages in the Life of a Lion.")

X-ing a Paragrab. To our knowledge, "X-ing a Paragrab" remains unsolved. Probably it has some fairly specific target over which no Poe scholar has yet stumbled. The petty rivalry, literally a tempest in a *Tea-Pot*, between dunderhead editors reminds one of "Lionizing," but the allusions to Boston and the hint that the piece makes fun of a specific Transcendentalist editor who went west suggest a more specific interpretation. Perhaps notes 2 and 3 will provide clues for a future scholar. The portion of the tale which deals with the late-night troubles of Bob, the twelve-year-old printer's devil, on the other hand, seems straightforward enough; Poe knew his way around printshops, and the tale he tells is only a slight exaggeration of the kinds of things which sometimes happen in such establishments. Writers close to the world of journalism often work the printing process into their works, and most, like Poe, have been victimized now and then by errors accidental or deliberate.*

The Tales

HOW TO WRITE A BLACKWOOD ARTICLE[1]

"In the name of the Prophet—figs!!"
Cry of the Turkish fig-peddler[2]

I presume everybody has heard of me. My name is the Signora Psyche Zenobia. This I know to be a fact. Nobody but my enemies ever calls me Suky Snobbs. I have been assured that Suky is but a vulgar corruption of Psyche, which is good Greek, and means "the soul" (that's me, I'm *all* soul) and sometimes "a butterfly," which latter meaning undoubtedly alludes to my appearance in my new crimson satin dress, with the sky-blue Arabian *mantelet*, and the trimmings of green *agraffas*, and the seven flounces of orange-colored *auriculas*. As for Snobbs—any person who should look at me would be instantly aware that my name wasn't Snobbs. Miss Tabitha Turnip propagated that report through sheer envy. Tabitha Turnip indeed! Oh the little wretch! But what can we expect from a turnip? Won-

---

* *cf.* Mark Twain's *Huckleberry Finn*, a novel in which a rogue who knows printing "borrows" a print shop for his own uses and sets some bad poetry of his own by way of payment. Then, in the printing of the novel itself, Twain himself was victimized by a printer's employee who scratched some extra lines into an engraving, making it obscene.

der if she remembers the old adage about "blood out of a turnip," etc.? [Mem: put her in mind of it the first opportunity.] [Mem again—pull her nose.] Where was I? Ah! I have been assured that Snobbs is a mere corruption of Zenobia, and that Zenobia was a queen—(So am I. Dr. Moneypenny always calls me the Queen of Hearts)—and that Zenobia, as well as Psyche, is good Greek, and that my father was "a Greek,"[3] and that consequently I have a right to our patronymic, which is Zenobia, and not by any means Snobbs. Nobody but Tabitha Turnip calls me Suky Snobbs. I am the Signora Psyche Zenobia.

As I said before, everybody has heard of me. I am that very Signora Psyche Zenobia, so justly celebrated as corresponding secretary to the "*Philadelphia, Regular, Exchange, Tea, Total, Young, Belles, Lettres, Universal, Experimental, Bibliographical, Association, To, Civilize, Humanity.*" Dr. Moneypenny made the title for us, and says he chose it because it sounded big like an empty rum-puncheon. (A vulgar man that sometimes —but he's deep.) We all sign the initials of the society after our names, in the fashion of the R. S. A., Royal Society of Arts —the S. D. U. K., Society for the Diffusion of Useful Knowledge, etc., etc. Dr. Moneypenny says that S stands for *stale,* and that D. U. K. spells duck, (but it don't) and that S. D. U. K. stands for Stale Duck, and not for Lord Brougham's society[4]— but then Dr. Moneypenny is such a queer man that I am never sure when he is telling me the truth. At any rate we always add to our names the initials P. R. E. T. T. Y. B. L. U. E. B. A. T. C. H.—that is to say, Philadelphia, Regular, Exchange, Tea, Total, Young, Belles, Lettres, Universal, Experimental, Bibliographical, Association, To, Civilize, Humanity—one letter for each word, which is a decided improvement upon Lord Brougham. Dr. Moneypenny will have it that our initials give our true character—but for my life I can't see what he means.

Notwithstanding the good offices of the

Doctor, and the strenuous exertions of the association to get itself into notice, it met with no very great success until I joined it. The truth is, the members indulged in too flippant a tone of discussion. The papers read every Saturday evening were characterized less by depth than buffoonery. They were all whipped syllabub. There was no investigation of first causes, first principles. There was no investigation of anything at all. There was no attention paid to that great point, the "fitness of things." In short there was no fine writing like this. It was all low—very! No profundity, no reading, no metaphysics— nothing which the learned call spirituality, and which the unlearned choose to stigmatize as cant. [Dr. M. says I ought to spell "cant" with a capital K[5]—but I know better.]

When I joined the society it was my endeavor to introduce a better style of thinking and writing, and all the world knows how well I have succeeded. We get up as good papers now in the P. R. E. T. T. Y. B. L. U. E. B. A. T. C. H. as any to be found even in *Blackwood*. I say, *Blackwood,* because I have been assured that the finest writing, upon every subject, is to be discovered in the pages of that justly celebrated Magazine. We now take it for our model upon all themes, and are getting into rapid notice accordingly. And, after all, it's not so very difficult a matter to compose an article of the genuine *Blackwood* stamp, if one only goes properly about it. Of course I don't speak of the political articles. Everybody knows how *they* are managed, since Dr. Moneypenny explained it. Mr. Blackwood has a pair of tailor's-shears, and three apprentices who stand by him for orders. One hands him the *Times,* another the *Examiner* and a third a "Gulley's New Compendium of Slang-Whang."[6] Mr. B. merely cuts out and intersperses. It is soon done —nothing but *Examiner,* "Slang-Whang," and *Times*—then *Times,* "Slang-Whang," and *Examiner*—and then *Times, Examiner, and "Slang-Whang."*

But the chief merit of the Magazine lies in its miscellaneous articles; and the best of these come under the head of what Dr. Moneypenny calls the *bizarreries* (whatever that may mean) and what everybody else calls the *intensities*. This is a species of writing which I have long known how to appreciate, although it is only since my late visit to Mr. Blackwood (deputed by the society) that I have been made aware of the exact method of composition. This method is very simple, but not so much so as the politics. Upon my calling at Mr. B's, and making known to him the wishes of the society, he received me with great civility, took me into his study, and gave me a clear explanation of the whole process.

"My dear madam," said he, evidently struck with my majestic appearance, for I had on the crimson satin, with the green *agraffas*, and orange-colored *auriculas*. "My *dear* madam," said he, "sit down. The matter stands thus: In the first place your writer of intensities must have very black ink, and a very big pen, with a very blunt nib. And, mark me, Miss Psyche Zenobia!" he continued, after a pause, with the most expressive energy and solemnity of manner, "mark me!—*that pen—must—never be mended!* Herein, madam, lies the secret, the soul, of intensity. I assume upon myself to say, that no individual, of however great genius, ever wrote with a good pen,—understand me, —a good article. You may take it for granted, that when manuscript can be read it is never worth reading. This is a leading principle in our faith, to which if you cannot readily assent, our conference is at an end."

He paused. But, of course, as I had no wish to put an end to the conference, I assented to a proposition so very obvious, and one, too, of whose truth I had all along been sufficiently aware. He seemed pleased, and went on with his instructions.

"It may appear invidious in me, Miss Psyche Zenobia, to refer you to an article, or set of articles, in the way of model or study; yet perhaps I may as well call your attention to a few cases. Let me see. There was 'The Dead Alive,' a capital thing!— the record of a gentleman's sensations when entombed before the breath was out of his body—full of taste, terror, sentiment, metaphysics, and erudition. You would have sworn that the writer had been born and brought up in a coffin. Then we had the 'Confessions of an Opium-eater'—fine, very fine!—glorious imagination—deep philosophy—acute speculation—plenty of fire and fury, and a good spicing of the decidedly unintelligible. That was a nice bit of flummery, and went down the throats of the people delightfully. They would have it that Coleridge wrote the paper—but not so. It was composed by my pet baboon, Juniper, over a rummer of Hollands and water, 'hot, without sugar.' " [This I could scarcely have believed had it been anybody but Mr. Blackwood, who assured me of it.] "Then there was 'The Involuntary Experimentalist,' all about a gentleman who got baked in an oven, and came out alive and well, although certainly done to a turn. And then there was 'The Diary of a Late Physician,' where the merit lay in good rant, and indifferent Greek—both of them taking things with the public. And then there was 'The Man in the Bell,'[7] a paper by-the-by, Miss Zenobia, which I cannot sufficiently recommend to your attention. It is the history of a young person who goes to sleep under the clapper of a church bell, and is awakened by its tolling for a funeral. The sound drives him mad, and, accordingly, pulling out his tablets, he gives a record of his sensations. Sensations are the great things after all. Should you ever be drowned or hung, be sure and make a note of your sensations—they will be worth to you ten guineas a sheet. If you wish to write forcibly, Miss Zenobia, pay minute attention to the sensations."

"That I certainly will, Mr. Blackwood," said I.

"Good!" he replied. "I see you are a pupil after my own heart. But I must put you *au fait* to[8] the details necessary in composing what may be denominated a genuine *Blackwood* article of the sensation stamp—the kind which you will understand me to say I consider the best for all purposes.

"The first thing requisite is to get yourself into such a scrape as no one ever got into before. The oven, for instance,—that was a good hit. But if you have no oven, or big bell, at hand, and if you cannot conveniently tumble out of a balloon, or be swallowed up in an earthquake, or get stuck fast in a chimney, you will have to be contented with simply imagining some similar misadventure. I should prefer, however, that you have the actual fact to bear you out. Nothing so well assists the fancy, as an experimental knowledge of the matter in hand. 'Truth is strange,' you know, 'stranger than fiction'—besides being more to the purpose."

Here I assured him I had an excellent pair of garters, and would go and hang myself forthwith.

"Good!" he replied, "do so;—although hanging is somewhat hackneyed. Perhaps you might do better. Take a dose of Brandreth's pills,[9] and then give us your sensations. However, my instructions will apply equally well to any variety of misadventure, and on your way home you may easily get knocked in the head, or run over by an omnibus, or bitten by a mad dog, or drowned in a gutter. But to proceed.

"Having determined upon your subject, you must next consider the tone, or manner, of your narration. There is the tone didactic, the tone enthusiastic, the tone natural—all commonplace enough. But then there is the tone laconic, or curt, which has lately come much into use. It consists in short sentences. Somehow thus: Can't be too brief. Can't be too snappish. Always a full stop. And never a paragraph.

"Then there is the tone elevated, diffusive, and interjectional. Some of our best novelists patronize this tone. The words must be all in a whirl, like a humming-top, and make a noise very similar, which answers remarkably well instead of meaning. This is the best of all possible styles where the writer is in too great a hurry to think.

"The tone metaphysical is also a good one. If you know any big words this is your chance for them. Talk of the Ionic and Eleatic schools—of Archytas, Gorgias, and Alcmæon. Say something about objectivity and subjectivity. Be sure and abuse a man called Locke. Turn up your nose at things in general, and when you let slip any thing a little *too* absurd, you need not be at the trouble of scratching it out, but just add a foot-note and say that you are indebted for the above profound observation to the '*Kritik der reinen Vernunft*,' or to the '*Metaphysische Anfangsgründe der Naturwissenschaft*.'[10] This will look erudite and—and—and frank.

"There are various other tones of equal celebrity, but I shall mention only two more—the tone transcendental and the tone heterogeneous. In the former the merit consists in seeing into the nature of affairs a very great deal farther than anybody else. This second sight is very efficient when properly managed. A little reading of the *Dial* will carry you a great way. Eschew, in this case, big words; get them as small as possible, and write them upside down. Look over Channing's poems and quote what he says about a 'fat little man with a delusive show of Can.'[11] Put in something about the Supernal Oneness. Don't say a syllable about the Infernal Twoness. Above all, study innuendo. Hint everything—assert nothing. If you feel inclined to say 'bread and butter,' do not by any means say it outright. You may say any thing and every thing *approaching* to 'bread and butter.' You may hint at buck-wheat cake, or you may even go so far as to insinuate oat-meal porridge, but if bread and butter be your real meaning, be cautious, my *dear* Miss Psyche, not on any account to say 'bread and butter'!''

I assured him that I should never say it again as long as I lived. He kissed me and continued:

"As for the tone heterogeneous, it is merely a judicious mixture, in equal proportions, of all the other tones in the world, and is consequently made up of every thing deep, great, odd, piquant, pertinent, and pretty.

"Let us suppose now you have determined upon your incidents and tone. The most important portion—in fact, the soul of the whole business, is yet to be attended to,—I allude to *the filling up.* It is not to be supposed that a lady, or gentleman either, has been leading the life of a book-worm. And yet above all things it is necessary that your article have an air of erudition, or at least afford evidence of extensive general reading. Now I'll put you in the way of accomplishing this point. See here!'' (pulling down some three or four ordinary-looking volumes, and opening them at random). "By casting your eye down almost any page of any book in the world, you will be able to perceive at once a host of little scraps of either learning or *bel-esprit-ism*,[12] which are the very thing for the spicing of a *Blackwood* article. You might as well note down a few while I read them to you. I shall make two divisions: first, *Piquant Facts for the Manufacture of Similes;* and second, *Piquant Expressions to be introduced as occasion may require.* Write now!—'' and I wrote as he dictated.

"Piquant Facts for Similes. 'There were originally but three Muses—Melete, Mneme, Aœde—meditation, memory, and singing.' You may make a good deal of that little fact if properly worked. You see it is not generally known, and looks *recherché*. You must be careful and give

the thing with a downright improviso air.[13]

"Again. 'The river Alpheus[14] passed beneath the sea, and emerged without injury to the purity of its waters.' Rather stale that, to be sure, but, if properly dressed and dished up, will look quite as fresh as ever.

"Here is something better. 'The Persian Iris[15] appears to some persons to possess a sweet and very powerful perfume, while to others it is perfectly scentless.' Fine that, and very delicate! Turn it about a little, and it will do wonders. We'll have some thing else in the botanical line. There's nothing goes down so well, especially with the help of a little Latin. Write!

" '*The Epidendrum Flos Aeris*,[16] of Java, bears a very beautiful flower, and will live when pulled up by the roots. The natives suspend it by a cord from the ceiling, and enjoy its fragrance for years.' That's capital! That will do for the similes. Now for the Piquant Expressions.

"Piquant Expressions. '*The Venerable Chinese novel Ju-Kiao-Li.*'[17] Good! By introducing these few words with dexterity you will evince your intimate acquaintance with the language and literature of the Chinese. With the aid of this you may possibly get along without either Arabic, or Sanscrit, or Chickasaw. There is no passing muster, however, without Spanish, Italian, German, Latin, and Greek. I must look you out a little specimen of each. Any scrap will answer, because you must depend upon your own ingenuity to make it fit into your article. Now write!

" '*Aussi tendre que Zaïre*'—as tender as Zaïre—French. Alludes to the frequent repetition of the phrase, *la tendre Zaïre*, in the French tragedy of that name.[18] Properly introduced, will show not only your knowledge of the language, but your general reading and wit. You can say, for instance, that the chicken you were eating (write an article about being choked to death by a chicken-bone) was not altogether *aussi tendre que Zaïre*. Write!

> '*Ven muerte tan escondida.*
> *Que no te sienta venir,*
> *Porque el plazer del morir,*
> *No me torne a dar la vida.*'[19]

"That's Spanish—from Miguel de Cervantes. 'Come quickly, O death! but be sure and don't let me see you coming, lest the pleasure I shall feel at your appearance should unfortunately bring me back again to life.' This you may slip in quite *à propos* when you are struggling in the last agonies with the chicken-bone. Write!

> '*Il pover' huomo che non sen'era*
> *accorto,*
> *Andava combattendo, ed era morto.*'[20]

"That's Italian, you perceive—from Ariosto. It means that a great hero, in the heat of combat, not perceiving that he had been fairly killed, continued to fight valiantly, dead as he was. The application of this to your own case is obvious—for I trust, Miss Psyche, that you will not neglect to kick for at least an hour and a half after you have been choked to death by that chicken-bone. Please to write!

> '*Und sterb'ich doch, so sterb'ich denn*
> *Durch sie—durch sie!*'[21]

"That's German—from Schiller. 'And if I die, at least I die—for thee—for thee!' Here it is clear that you are apostrophizing the *cause* of your disaster, the chicken. Indeed what gentleman (or lady either) of sense, *wouldn't* die, I should like to know, for a well fattened capon of the right Molucca breed, stuffed with capers and mushrooms, and served up in a salad-bowl, with orange-jellies *en mosaïques*. Write! (You can get them that way at Tortoni's,[22])— Write, if you please!

"Here is a nice little Latin phrase, and rare too (one can't be too *recherché* or brief in one's Latin, it's getting so common,)—*ignoratio elenchi*. He has committed an *ignoratio elenchi*—that is to say, he

has understood the words of your proposition, but not the idea. The man was *a fool*, you see. Some poor fellow whom you address while choking with that chicken-bone, and who therefore didn't precisely understand what you were talking about. Throw the *ignoratio elenchi* in his teeth, and, at once, you have him annihilated. If he dares to reply, you can tell him from Lucan (here it is) that speeches are mere *anemonœ verborum*, anemone words. The anemone, with great brilliancy, has no smell. Or, if he begins to bluster, you may be down upon him with *insomnia Jovis*, reveries of Jupiter—a phrase which Silius Italicus[23] (see here!) applies to thoughts pompous and inflated. This will be sure and cut him to the heart. He can do nothing but roll over and die. Will you be kind enough to write?

"In Greek we must have some thing pretty—from Demosthenes, for example. Ἀνὴρ ὁ φεύγων καὶ πάλιν μαχήσεται. [Aner o pheugon kai palin makesetai.] There is a tolerably good translation of it in Hudibras—

> *For he that flies may fight again,*
> *Which he can never do that's slain.*[24]

In a *Blackwood* article nothing makes so fine a show as your Greek. The very letters have an air of profundity about them. Only observe, madam, the astute look of that Epsilon! That Phi ought certainly to be a bishop! Was ever there a smarter fellow than that Omicron? Just twig that Tau! In short, there is nothing like Greek for a genuine sensation-paper. In the present case your application is the most obvious thing in the world. Rap out the sentence, with a huge oath, and by way of *ultimatum* at the good-for-nothing dunder-headed villain who couldn't understand your plain English in relation to the chicken-bone. He'll take the hint and be off, you may depend upon it."

These were all the instructions Mr. B. could afford me upon the topic in question, but I felt they would be entirely sufficient. I was, at length, able to write a genuine Blackwood article, and determined to do it forthwith. In taking leave of me, Mr. B. made a proposition for the purchase of the paper when written; but as he could offer me only fifty guineas a sheet, I thought it better to let our society have it, than sacrifice it for so paltry a sum. Notwithstanding this niggardly spirit, however, the gentleman showed his consideration for me in all other respects, and indeed treated me with the greatest civility. His parting words made a deep impression upon my heart, and I hope I shall always remember them with gratitude.

"My dear Miss Zenobia," he said, while the tears stood in his eyes, "is there *any* thing else I can do to promote the success of your laudable undertaking? Let me reflect! It is just possible that you may not be able, so soon as convenient, to—to—get yourself drowned, or—choked with a chicken-bone, or—or hung,—or—bitten by a—but stay! Now I think me of it, there are a couple of very excellent bulldogs in the yard—fine fellows, I assure you—savage, and all that—indeed just the thing for your money—they'll have you eaten up, *auriculas* and all, in less than five minutes (here's my watch!)—and then only think of the sensations! Here! I say —Tom!—Peter!—Dick, you villain!—let out those"—but as I was really in a great hurry, and had not another moment to spare, I was reluctantly forced to expedite my departure, and accordingly took leave *at once*—somewhat more abruptly, I admit, than strict courtesy would have otherwise allowed.

It was my primary object, upon quitting Mr. Blackwood, to get into some immediate difficulty, pursuant to his advice, and with this view I spent the greater part of the day in wandering about Edinburgh, seeking for desperate adventures—adventures adequate to the intensity of my feelings, and adapted to the vast character of the article I intended to write. In this excursion I was attended by one negroservant Pompey, and my little lap-dog

Diana, whom I had brought with me from Philadelphia. It was not, however, until late in the afternoon that I fully succeeded in my arduous undertaking. An important event then happened, of which the following Blackwood article, in the tone heterogeneous, is the substance and result.

A PREDICAMENT[1]

What chance, good lady, hath bereft
you thus!
                                        Comus[2]

It was a quiet and still afternoon when I strolled forth in the goodly city of Edina. The confusion and bustle in the streets were terrible. Men were talking. Women were screaming. Children were choking. Pigs were whistling. Carts they rattled. Bulls they bellowed. Cows they lowed. Horses they neighed. Cats they caterwauled. Dogs they danced. *Danced!* Could it then be possible? *Danced!* Alas, thought I, *my* dancing days are over! Thus it is ever. What a host of gloomy recollections will ever and anon be awakened in the mind of genius and imaginative contemplation, especially of a genius doomed to the everlasting, and eternal, and continual, and, as one might say, the—*continued* —yes, the *continued and continuous*, bitter, harassing, disturbing, and, if I may be allowed the expression, the *very* disturbing influence of the serene, and godlike, and heavenly, and exalted, and elevated, and purifying effect of what may be rightly termed the most enviable, the most *truly* enviable—nay! the most benignly beautiful, the most deliciously ethereal, and, as it were, the most *pretty* (if I may use so bold an expression) *thing* (pardon me, gentle reader!) in the world—but I am always led away by my feelings. In *such* a mind, I repeat, what a host of recollections are stirred up by a trifle! The dogs danced! I—I *could* not! They frisked —I wept. They capered—I sobbed aloud. Touching circumstances! which cannot fail to bring to the recollection of the classical reader that exquisite passage in relation to the fitness of things, which is to be found in the commencement of the third volume of that admirable and venerable Chinese novel the *Jo-Go-Slow*.

In my solitary walk through the city I had two humble but faithful companions. Diana, my poodle! sweetest of creatures! She had a quantity of hair over her one eye, and a blue ribband tied fashionably around her neck. Diana was not more than five inches in height, but her head was somewhat bigger than her body, and her tail being cut off exceedingly close, gave an air of injured innocence to the interesting animal which rendered her a favorite with all.

And Pompey, my negro!—sweet Pompey! how shall I ever forget thee? I had taken Pompey's arm. He was three feet in height (I like to be particular) and about seventy, or perhaps eighty, years of age. He had bow-legs and was corpulent. His mouth should not be called small, nor his ears short. His teeth, however, were like pearl, and his large full eyes were deliciously white. Nature had endowed him with no neck, and had placed his ankles (as usual with that race) in the middle of the upper portion of the feet. He was clad with a striking simplicity. His sole garments were a stock of nine inches in height, and a nearly-new drab overcoat which had formerly been in the service of the tall, stately, and illustrious Dr. Moneypenny. It was a good overcoat. It was well cut. It was well made. The coat was nearly new. Pompey held it up out of the dirt with both hands.

There were three persons in our party, and two of them have already been the subject of remark. There was a third—that person was myself. I am the Signora Psyche Zenobia. I am *not* Suky Snobbs. My appearance is commanding. On the memorable occasion of which I speak I was habited in a crimson satin dress, with a sky-blue Arabian mantelet. And the dress had trimmings of green agraffas, and

seven graceful flounces of the orange-colored auricula. I thus formed the third of the party. There was the poodle. There was Pompey. There was myself. We were *three*. Thus it is said there were originally but three Furies—Melty, Nimmy, and Hetty—Meditation, Memory, and Fiddling.

Leaning upon the arm of the gallant Pompey, and attended at a respectful distance by Diana, I proceeded down one of the populous and very pleasant streets of the now deserted Edina. On a sudden, there presented itself to view a church—a Gothic cathedral—vast, venerable, and with a tall steeple, which towered into the sky. What madness now possessed me? Why did I rush upon my fate? I was seized with an uncontrollable desire to ascend the giddy pinnacle, and then survey the immense extent of the city. The door of the cathedral stood invitingly open. My destiny prevailed. I entered the ominous archway. Where then was my guardian angel?—if indeed such angels there be. *If!* Distressing monosyllable! what a world of mystery,[3] and meaning, and doubt, and uncertainty is there involved in thy two letters! I entered the ominous archway! I entered; and, without injury to my orange-colored auriculas, I passed beneath the portal, and emerged within the vestibule. Thus it is said the immense river Alfred passed, unscathed, and unwetted, beneath the sea.

I thought the staircase would never have an end. *Round!* Yes, they went round and up, and round and up and round and up, until I could not help surmising, with the sagacious Pompey, upon whose supporting arm I leaned in all the confidence of early affection[4]—I *could* not help surmising that the upper end of the continuous spiral ladder had been accidentally, or perhaps designedly, removed. I paused for breath; and, in the meantime, an accident occurred of too momentous a nature in a moral, and also in a metaphysical point of view, to be passed over without notice. It appeared to me—indeed I was quite confident of the fact—I could not be mistaken—no! I had, for some moments, carefully and anxiously observed the motions of my Diana—I say that *I could not be* mistaken—Diana *smelt a rat!* At once I called Pompey's attention to the subject, and he—he agreed with me. There was then no longer any reasonable room for doubt. The rat had been smelled—and by Diana. Heavens! shall I ever forget the intense excitement of the moment? Alas! what is the boasted intellect of man? The rat!—it was there—that is to say, it was somewhere. Diana smelled the rat. I—*I could* not! Thus it is said the Prussian Isis has, for some persons, a sweet and very powerful perfume, while to others it is perfectly scentless.

The staircase had been surmounted, and there were now only three or four more upward steps intervening between us and the summit. We still ascended, and now only one step remained. One step! One little, little step! Upon one such little step in the great staircase of human life how vast a sum of human happiness or misery depends![5] I thought of myself, then of Pompey, and then of the mysterious and inexplicable destiny which surrounded us. I thought of Pompey!—alas, I thought of love! I thought of my many false *steps* which have been taken, and may be taken again. I resolved to be more cautious, more reserved. I abandoned the arm of Pompey, and, without his assistance, surmounted the one remaining step, and gained the chamber of the belfry. I was followed immediately afterward by my poodle. Pompey alone remained behind. I stood at the head of the staircase, and encouraged him to ascend. He stretched forth to me his hand, and unfortunately in so doing was forced to abandon his firm hold upon the overcoat. Will the gods never cease their persecution? The overcoat is dropped, and, with one of his feet, Pompey stepped upon the long and trailing skirt of the overcoat. He stumbled and fell—this consequence was inevitable. He fell forward, and, with his accursed head,

striking me full in the—in the breast, precipitated me headlong, together with himself, upon the hard, filthy, and detestable floor of the belfry. But my revenge was sure, sudden, and complete. Seizing him furiously by the wool with both hands, I tore out a vast quantity of black, and crisp, and curling material, and tossed it from me with every manifestation of disdain. It fell among the ropes of the belfry and remained. Pompey arose, and said no word. But he regarded me piteously with his large eyes, and—sighed. Ye Gods —that sigh! It sunk into my heart. And the hair—the wool! Could I have reached that wool I would have bathed it with my tears, in testimony of regret. But alas! it was now far beyond my grasp. As it dangled among the cordage of the bell, I fancied it alive. I fancied that it stood on end with indignation. Thus the *happy-dandy Flos Aeris* of Java bears, it is said, a beautiful flower, which will live when pulled up by the roots. The natives suspend it by a cord from the ceiling and enjoy its fragrance for years.

Our quarrel was now made up, and we looked about the room for an aperture through which to survey the city of Edina. Windows there were none. The sole light admitted into the gloomy chamber proceeded from a square opening, about a foot in diameter, at a height of about seven feet from the floor. Yet what will the energy of true genius not effect? I resolved to clamber up to this hole. A vast quantity of wheels, pinions, and other cabalistic-looking machinery stood opposite the hole, close to it; and through the hole there passed an iron rod from the machinery. Between the wheels and the wall where the hole lay there was barely room for my body—yet I was desperate, and determined to persevere. I called Pompey to my side.

"You perceive that aperture, Pompey. I wish to look through it. You will stand here just beneath the hole—so. Now, hold out one of your hands, Pompey, and let me step upon it—thus. Now, the other hand, Pompey, and with its aid I will get upon your shoulders."

He did every thing I wished, and I found, upon getting up, that I could easily pass my head and neck through the aperture. The prospect was sublime. Nothing could be more magnificent. I merely paused a moment to bid Diana behave herself, and assure Pompey that I would be considerate and bear as lightly as possible upon his shoulders. I told him I would be tender of his feelings—*ossi tender que beefsteak.* Having done this justice to my faithful friend, I gave myself up with great zest and enthusiasm to the enjoyment of the scene which so obligingly spread itself out before my eyes.

Upon this subject, however, I shall forbear to dilate. I will not describe the city of Edinburgh. Every one has been to the city of Edinburgh. Every one has been to Edinburgh—the classic Edina. I will confine myself to the momentous details of my own lamentable adventure. Having, in some measure, satisfied my curiosity in regard to the extent, situation, and general appearance of the city, I had leisure to survey the church in which I was, and the delicate architecture of the steeple. I observed that the aperture through which I had thrust my head was an opening in the dial-plate of a gigantic clock, and must have appeared, from the street, as a large key-hole, such as we see in the face of the French watches. No doubt the true object was to admit the arm of an attendant, to adjust, when necessary, the hands of the clock from within. I observed also, with surprise, the immense size of these hands, the longest of which could not have been less than ten feet in length, and, where broadest, eight or nine inches in breadth. They were of solid steel apparently, and their edges appeared to be sharp. Having noticed these particulars, and some others, I again turned my eyes upon the glorious prospect below, and soon became absorbed in contemplation.

From this, after some minutes, I was aroused by the voice of Pompey, who declared that he could stand it no longer, and requested that I would be so kind as to come down. This was unreasonable, and I told him so in a speech of some length. He replied, but with an evident misunderstanding of my ideas upon the subject. I accordingly grew angry, and told him in plain words, that he was a fool, that he had committed an *ignoramus e-clench-eye,* that his notions were mere *insommary Bovis,* and his words little better than *an ennemywerrybor'em.* With this he appeared satisfied, and I resumed my contemplations.

It might have been half an hour after this altercation when, as I was deeply absorbed in the heavenly scenery beneath me, I was startled by something very cold which pressed with a gentle pressure on the back of my neck. It is needless to say that I felt inexpressibly alarmed. I knew that Pompey was beneath my feet, and that Diana was sitting, according to my explicit directions, upon her hind legs, in the farthest corner of the room. What could it be? Alas! I but too soon discovered. Turning my head gently to one side, I perceived, to my extreme horror, that the huge, glittering, scimetar-like minute-hand of the clock had, in the course of its hourly revolution, *descended upon my neck.*[6] There was, I knew, not a second to be lost. I pulled back at once—but it was too late. There was no chance of forcing my head through the mouth of that terrible trap in which it was so fairly caught, and which grew narrower and narrower with a rapidity too horrible to be conceived. The agony of that moment is not to be imagined. I threw up my hands and endeavored, with all my strength, to force upward the ponderous iron bar. I might as well have tried to lift the cathedral itself. Down, down, down it came, closer and yet closer. I screamed to Pompey for aid; but he said that I had hurt his feelings by calling him "an ignorant old squint-eye." I yelled to Diana; but she only said "bow-wow-wow," and that "I had told her on no account to stir from the corner." Thus I had no relief to expect from my associates.

Meantime the ponderous and terrific *Scythe of Time* (for I now discovered the literal import of that classical phrase) had not stopped, nor was it likely to stop, in its career. Down and still down, it came. It had already buried its sharp edge a full inch in my flesh, and my sensations grew indistinct and confused. At one time I fancied myself in Philadelphia with the stately Dr. Moneypenny, at another in the back parlor of Mr. Blackwood receiving his invaluable instructions. And then again the sweet recollection of better and earlier times came over me, and I thought of that happy period when the world was not all a desert, and Pompey not altogether cruel.

The ticking of the machinery amused me. *Amused me,* I say, for my sensations now bordered upon perfect happiness, and the most trifling circumstances afforded me pleasure. The eternal *click-clak, click-clak, click-clak* of the clock was the most melodious of music in my ears, and occasionally even put me in mind of the graceful sermonic harangues of Dr. Ollapod.[7] Then there were the great figures upon the dial-plate—how intelligent, how intellectual, they all looked! And presently they took to dancing the Mazurka, and I think it was the figure V who performed the most to my satisfaction. She was evidently a lady of breeding. None of your swaggerers, and nothing at all indelicate in her motions. She did the pirouette to admiration—whirling round upon her apex. I made an endeavour to hand her a chair, for I saw that she appeared fatigued with her exertions—and it was not until then that I fully perceived my lamentable situation. Lamentable indeed! The bar had buried itself two inches in my neck. I was aroused to a sense of exquisite pain. I prayed for death, and, in the agony of the moment, could not help

repeating those exquisite verses of the poet Miguel De Cervantes:

Vanny Buren, tan escondida
Query no te senty venny
Pork and pleasure, delly morry
Nommy, torny, darry, widdy!

But now a new horror presented itself, and one indeed sufficient to startle the strongest nerves. My eyes, from the cruel pressure of the machine, were absolutely starting from their sockets. While I was thinking how I should possibly manage without them, one actually tumbled out of my head, and, rolling down the steep side of the steeple, lodged in the rain gutter which ran along the eaves of the main building. The loss of the eye was not so much as the insolent air of independence and contempt with which it regarded me after it was out. There it lay in the gutter just under my nose, and the airs it gave itself would have been ridiculous had they not been disgusting. Such a winking and blinking were never before seen. This behavior on the part of my eye in the gutter was not only irritating on account of its manifest insolence and shameful ingratitude, but was also exceedingly inconvenient on account of the sympathy which always exists between two eyes of the same head, however far apart. I was forced, in a manner, to wink and to blink, whether I would or not, in exact concert with the scoundrelly thing that lay just under my nose. I was presently relieved, however, by the dropping out of the other eye. In falling it took the same direction (possibly a concerted plot) as its fellow. Both rolled out of the gutter together, and in truth I was very glad to get rid of them.

The bar was now four inches and a half deep in my neck, and there was only a little bit of skin to cut through. My sensations were those of entire happiness, for I felt that in a few minutes, at farthest, I should be relieved from my disagreeable situation. And in this expectation I was

not at all deceived. At twenty-five minutes past five in the afternoon, precisely,
the huge minute-hand had proceeded sufficiently far on its terrible revolution to
sever the small remainder of my neck. I
was not sorry to see the head which had
occasioned me so much embarrassment
at length make a final separation from my
body. It first rolled down the side of the
steeple, then lodged, for a few seconds, in
the gutter, and then made its way, with
a plunge, into the middle of the street.

I will candidly confess that my feelings
were now of the most singular—nay, of
the most mysterious, the most perplexing and incomprehensible character. My
senses were here and there at one and the
same moment. With my head I imagined,
at one time, that I, the head, was the real
Signora Psyche Zenobia—at another I felt
convinced that myself, the body, was the
proper identity. To clear my ideas on this
topic I felt in my pocket for my snuff-box,
but, upon getting it, and endeavouring to
apply a pinch of its grateful contents in
the ordinary manner, I became immediately aware of my peculiar deficiency, and
threw the box at once down to my head.
It took a pinch with great satisfaction, and
smiled me an acknowledgement in return. Shortly afterward it made me a
speech, which I could hear but indistinctly without ears. I gathered enough,
however, to know that it was astonished
at my wishing to remain alive under such
circumstances. In the concluding sentences it quoted the noble words of
Ariosto—

> Il pover hommy che non sera corty
> And have a combat tenty erry morty,

thus comparing me to the hero who, in
the heat of the combat, not perceiving
that he was dead, continued to contest the
battle with inextinguishable valor. There
was nothing now to prevent my getting
down from my elevation, and I did so.
What it was that Pompey saw so very
peculiar in my appearance I have never
yet been able to find out. The fellow

opened his mouth from ear to ear, and
shut his two eyes as if he were endeavouring to crack nuts between the lids. Finally,
throwing off his overcoat he made one
spring for the staircase and disappeared. I
hurled after the scoundrel these vehement
words of Demosthenes—

> Andrew O'Phlegethon, you really
> make haste to fly,

and then turned to the darling of my
heart, to the one-eyed! the shaggy-haired
Diana. Alas! what a horrible vision affronted my eyes? Was that a rat I saw
skulking into his hole? Are these the
picked bones of the little angel who has
been cruelly devoured by the monster?
Ye gods! and what do I behold—is that
the departed spirit, the shade, the ghost,
of my beloved puppy, which I perceive
sitting with a grace so melancholy, in the
corner? Hearken! for she speaks, and,
heavens! it is in the German of Schiller—

> "Unt stubby duk, so stubby dun
> Duk she! duk she!"

Alas! and are not her words too true?

> "And if I died, at least I died
> For thee—for thee."

Sweet creature! she too has sacrificed herself in my behalf. Dogless, niggerless,
headless, what now remains for the unhappy Signora Psyche Zenobia? Alas—
nothing! I have done.

NEVER BET THE DEVIL YOUR HEAD

A Tale with a Moral[1]

"Con tal que las costumbres de un autor,"
says Don Thomas De Las Torres, in the
preface to his "Amatory Poems," "sean
puras y castas, importa muy poco que no
sean igualmente severas sus obras"—
meaning, in plain English, that, provided
the morals of an author are pure, person-

ally, it signifies nothing what are the morals of his books. We presume that Don Thomas is now in Purgatory for the assertion. It would be a clever thing, too, in the way of poetical justice, to keep him there until his "Amatory Poems" get out of print, or are laid definitely upon the shelf through lack of readers. Every fiction *should have* a moral; and, what is more to the purpose, the critics have discovered that every fiction *has*. Philip Melancthon, some time ago, wrote a commentary upon the "Batrachomyomachia" and proved that the poet's object was to excite a distaste for sedition. Pierre La Seine, going a step farther, shows that the intention was to recommend to young men temperance in eating and drinking. Just so, too, Jacobus Hugo has satisfied himself that, by Euenis, Homer meant to insinuate John Calvin; by Antinous, Martin Luther; by the Lotophagi, Protestants in general; and, by the Harpies, the Dutch. Our more modern Scholiasts are equally acute. These fellows demonstrate a hidden meaning in "The Antediluvians," a parable in "Powhatan," new views in "Cock Robin" and transcendentalism in "Hop O' My Thumb." In short, it has been shown that no man can sit down to write without a very profound design. Thus to authors in general much trouble is spared. A novelist, for example, need have no care of his moral. It is there—that is to say it is somewhere—and the moral and the critics can take care of themselves. When the proper time arrives, all that the gentleman intended, and all that he did not intend, will be brought to light, in the "Dial," or the "Down-Easter,"[2] together with all that he ought to have intended, and the rest that he clearly meant to intend:—so that it will all come very straight in the end.

There is no just ground, therefore, for the charge brought against me by certain ignoramuses—that I have never written a moral tale, or, in more precise words, a tale with a moral. They are not the critics predestined to bring me out, and *develop*

my morals:—that is the secret. By and by the "North American Quarterly Humdrum" will make them ashamed of their stupidity. In the meantime, by way of staying execution—by way of mitigating the accusations against me—I offer the sad history appended;—a history about whose obvious moral there can be no question whatever, since he who runs may read it in the large capitals which form the title of the tale. I should have credit for this arrangement—a far wiser one than that of La Fontaine[3] and others, who reserve the impression to be conveyed until the last moment, and thus sneak it in at the fag end of their fables.

Defuncti injuriâ ne afficiantur was a law of the twelve tables, and *De mortuis nil nisi bonum* is an excellent injunction —even if the dead in question be nothing but dead small beer. It is not my design, therefore, to vituperate my deceased friend, Toby Dammit. He was a sad dog,[4] it is true, and a dog's death it was that he died; but he himself was not to blame for his vices. They grew out of a personal defect in his mother. She did her best in the way of flogging him while an infant—for duties to her well-regulated mind were always pleasures, and babies, like tough steaks, or the modern Greek olive trees, are invariably the better for beating—but, poor woman! she had the misfortune to be left-handed, and a child flogged left-handedly had better be left unflogged. The world revolves from right to left. It will not do to whip a baby from left to right. If each blow in the proper direction drives an evil propensity out, it follows that every thump in an opposite one knocks its quota of wickedness in. I was often present at Toby's chastisements, and, even by the way in which he kicked, I could perceive that he was getting worse and worse every day. At last I saw, through the tears in my eyes, that there was no hope of the villain at all, and one day when he had been cuffed until he grew so black in the face that one might have mistaken him for a little African, and no effect had been produced beyond that of making him wriggle himself into a fit, I could stand it no longer, but went down upon my knees forthwith, and, up-lifting my voice, made prophecy of his ruin.

The fact is that his precocity in vice was awful. At five months of age he used to get into such passions that he was unable to articulate. At six months, I caught him gnawing a pack of cards. At seven months he was in the constant habit of catching and kissing the female babies. At eight months he peremptorily refused to put his signature to the Temperance pledge.[5] Thus he went on increasing in iniquity, month after month, until, at the close of the first year, he not only insisted upon wearing *moustaches*, but had contracted a propensity for cursing and swearing, and for backing his assertions by bets.

Through this latter most ungentle-manly practice, the ruin which I had pre-dicted to Toby Dammit overtook him at last. The fashion had "grown with his growth and strengthened with his strength,"[6] so that, when he came to be a man, he could scarcely utter a sentence without interlarding it with a proposition to gamble. Not that he actually *laid* wa-gers—no. I will do my friend the justice to say that he would as soon have laid eggs. With him the thing was a mere for-mula—nothing more. His expressions on this head had no meaning attached to them whatever. They were simple if not altogether innocent expletives—imagina-tive phrases wherewith to round off a sen-tence. When he said "I'll bet you so and so," nobody ever thought of taking him up; but still I could not help thinking it my duty to put him down. The habit was an immoral one, and so I told him. It was a vulgar one—this I begged him to believe. It was discountenanced by society—here I said nothing but the truth. It was forbid-den by act of Congress—here I had not the slightest intention of telling a lie. I remonstrated—but to no purpose. I dem-

onstrated—in vain. I entreated—he smiled. I implored—he laughed. I preached—he sneered. I threatened—he swore. I kicked him—he called for the police. I pulled his nose—he blew it, and offered to bet the Devil his head that I would not venture to try that experiment again.

Poverty was another vice which the pe-culiar physical deficiency of Dammit's mother had entailed upon her son. He was detestably poor; and this was the reason, no doubt, that his expletive expressions about betting seldom took a pecuniary turn. I will not be bound to say that I ever heard him make use of such a figure speech as "I'll bet you a dollar." It was usually "I'll bet you what you please," or "I'll bet you what you dare," or "I'll bet you a trifle," or else, more significantly still, *"I'll bet the Devil my head."*

This latter form seemed to please him best:—perhaps because it involved the least risk; for Dammit had become exces-sively parsimonious. Had any one taken him up, his head was small, and thus his loss would have been small too. But these are my own reflections, and I am by no means sure that I am right in attributing them to him. At all events the phrase in question grew daily in favor, notwith-standing the gross impropriety of a man betting his brains like banknotes:—but this was a point which my friend's per-versity of disposition would not permit him to comprehend. In the end, he aban-doned all other forms of wager, and gave himself up to *"I'll bet the Devil my head,"* with a pertinacity and exclusiveness of devotion that displeased not less than it surprised me. I am always displeased by circumstances for which I cannot account. Mysteries force a man to think, and so in-jure his health. The truth is, there was something in *the air* with which Mr. Dammit was wont to give utterance to his offensive expression—something in his *manner* of enunciation—which at first in-terested, and afterwards made me very uneasy—something which, for want of a more definite term at present, I must be permitted to call *queer;* but which Mr. Coleridge would have called mystical, Mr. Kant pantheistical, Mr. Carlyle twistical, and Mr. Emerson hyperquizzitistical. I began not to like it at all. Mr. Dammit's soul was in a perilous state. I resolved to bring all my eloquence into play to save it. I vowed to serve him as St. Patrick, in the Irish chronicle, is said to have served the toad,[7] that is to say, "awaken him to a sense of his situation." I addressed myself to the task forthwith. Once more I betook myself to remonstrance. Again I collected my energies for a final attempt at expostulation.

When I had made an end of my lecture, Mr. Dammit indulged himself in some very equivocal behaviour. For some moments he remained silent, merely looking me inquisitively in the face. But presently he threw his head to one side, and elevated his eyebrows to great extent. Then he spread out the palms of his hands and shrugged up his shoulders. Then he winked with the right eye. Then he repeated the operation with the left. Then he shut them both up very tight. Then he opened them both so very wide that I became seriously alarmed for the consequences. Then, applying his thumb to his nose, he thought proper to make an indescribable movement with the rest of his fingers. Finally, setting his arms a-kimbo, he condescended to reply.

I can call to mind only the heads of his discourse. He would be obliged to me if I would hold my tongue. He wished none of my advice. He despised all my insinuations. He was old enough to take care of himself. Did I still think him baby Dammit? Did I mean to say anything against his character? Did I intend to insult him? Was I a fool? Was my maternal parent aware, in a word, of my absence from the domiciliary residence? He would put this latter question to me as to a man of veracity, and he would bind himself to abide

by my reply. Once more he would demand explicitly if my mother knew that I was out. My confusion, he said, betrayed me, and he would be willing to bet the Devil his head that she did not.

Mr. Dammit did not pause for my rejoinder. Turning upon his heel, he left my presence with undignified precipitation. It was well for him that he did so. My feelings had been wounded. Even my anger had been aroused. For once I would have taken him up upon his insulting wager. I would have won for the Arch-Enemy Mr. Dammit's little head—for the fact is, my mamma *was* very well aware of my merely temporary absence from home.

But *Khoda shefa midêhed*—Heaven gives relief—as the Musselmen say when you tread upon their toes. It was in pursuance of my duty that I had been insulted, and I bore the insult like a man. It now seemed to me, however, that I had done all that could be required of me, in the case of this miserable individual, and I resolved to trouble him no longer with my counsel, but to leave him to his conscience and himself. But although I forebore to intrude with my advice, I could not bring myself to give up his society altogether. I even went so far as to humor some of his less reprehensible propensities; and there were times when I found myself lauding his wicked jokes, as epicures do mustard, with tears in my eyes.[8] —so profoundly did it grieve me to hear his evil talk.

One fine day, having strolled out together arm in arm, our route led us in the direction of a river. There was a bridge, and we resolved to cross it. It was roofed over, by way of protection from the weather, and the arch-way, having but few windows, was thus very uncomfortably dark. As we entered the passage, the contrast between the external glare, and the interior gloom, struck heavily upon my spirits. Not so upon those of the unhappy Dammit, who offered to bet the Devil his head that I was hipped. He seemed to be in an unusual good humor. He was excessively lively—so much so that I entertained I know not what of uneasy suspicion. It is not impossible that he was affected with the transcendentals. I am not well enough versed, however, in the diagnosis of this disease to speak with decision upon the point; and unhappily there were none of my friends of the "Dial" present. I suggest the idea, nevertheless, because of a certain species of austere Merry-Andrewism which seemed to beset my poor friend, and caused him to make quite a Tom-Fool of himself. Nothing would serve him but wriggling and skipping about under and over everything that came in his way; now shouting out, and now lisping out, all manner of odd little and big words, yet preserving the gravest face in the world all the time. I really could not make up my mind whether to kick or to pity him. At length, having passed nearly across the bridge, we approached the termination of the footway, when our progress was impeded by a turnstile of some height. Through this I made my way quietly, pushing it around as usual. But this turn would not serve the turn of Mr. Dammit. He insisted upon leaping the stile, and said he could cut a pigeon-wing over it in the air. Now this, conscientiously speaking, I did not think he could do. The best pigeon-winger over all kinds of style, was my friend Mr. Carlyle,[9] and as I knew *he* could not do it, I would not believe that it could be done by Toby Dammit. I therefore told him, in so many words, that he was a braggadocio, and could not do what he said. For this, I had reason to be sorry afterwards;—for he straightway offered to *bet the Devil his head* that he could.

I was about to reply, notwithstanding my previous resolutions, with some remonstrance against his impiety, when I heard, close at my elbow, a slight cough, which sounded very much like the ejaculation *"ahem!"* I started, and looked about me in surprise. My glance at length fell into a nook of the frame-work of the bridge, and upon the figure of a little lame old gentleman of venerable aspect. Nothing could be more reverend than his whole appearance; for, he not only had on a full suit of black, but his shirt was perfectly clean and the collar turned very neatly down over a white cravat, while his hair was parted in front like a girl's. His hands were clasped pensively together over his stomach, and his two eyes were carefully rolled up into the top of his head.

Upon observing him more closely, I perceived that he wore a black silk apron over his small-clothes; and this was a thing which I thought very odd. Before I had time to make any remark, however, upon so singular a circumstance, he interrupted me with a second *"ahem!"*

To this observation I was not immediately prepared to reply. The fact is, remarks of this laconic nature are nearly unanswerable. I have known a Quarterly Review *non-plused* by the word *"Fudge!"*[10] I am not ashamed to say, therefore, that I turned to Mr. Dammit for assistance.

"Dammit," said I, "what are you about? don't you hear?—the gentleman says *'ahem!'* " I looked sternly at my friend while I thus addressed him; for to say the truth, I felt particularly puzzled, and when a man is particularly puzzled he must knit his brows and look savage, or else he is pretty sure to look like a fool.

"Dammit," observed I—although this sounded very much like an oath, than which nothing was farther from my thoughts—"Dammit," I suggested—"the gentleman says *'ahem!'* "

I do not attempt to defend my remark on the score of profundity; I did not think it profound myself; but I have noticed that the effect of our speeches is not always proportionate with their importance in our own eyes; and if I had shot Mr. D. through and through with a Paixhan bomb, or knocked him in the head with the "Poets and Poetry of America,"[11] he could hardly have been more discomfited than when I addressed him with those simple words—"Dammit, what are you about?—don't you hear?—the gentleman says *'ahem!'*"

"You don't say so?" gasped he at length, after turning more colors than a pirate runs up,[12] one after the other, when chased by a man-of-war. "Are you quite sure he said *that?* Well, at all events I am in for it now, and may as well put a bold face upon the matter. Here goes, then—*ahem!*"

At this the little old gentleman seemed pleased—God only knows why. He left his station at the nook of the bridge, limped forward with a gracious air, took Dammit by the hand and shook it cordially, looking all the while straight up in his face with an air of the most unadulterated benignity which it is possible for the mind of man to imagine.

"I am quite sure you will win it, Dammit," said he with the frankest of all smiles, "but we are obliged to have a trial you know, for the sake of mere form."

"Ahem!" replied my friend, taking off his coat with a deep sigh, tying a pocket-handkerchief around his waist, and producing an unaccountable alteration in his countenance by twisting up his eyes, and bringing down the corners of his mouth—"ahem!" And "ahem," said he again, after a pause; and not another word more than "ahem!" did I ever know him to say after that. "Aha!" thought I, without expressing myself aloud—"this is quite a remarkable silence on the part of Toby Dammit, and is no doubt a consequence of his verbosity upon a previous occasion. One extreme induces another. I wonder if he has forgotten the many unanswerable questions which he propounded to me so fluently on the day when I gave him my last lecture? At all events, he is cured of the transcendentals."

"Ahem!" here replied Toby, just as if he had been reading my thoughts, and looking like a very old sheep in a reverie.

The old gentleman now took him by the arm, and led him more into the shade of the bridge—a few paces back from the turnstile. "My good fellow," said he, "I make it a point of conscience to allow you this much run. Wait here, till I take my place by the stile, so that I may see whether you go over it handsomely, and transcendentally, and don't omit any flourishes of the pigeon-wing. A mere form, you know. I will say 'one, two, three, and away.' Mind you start at the word 'away.'" Here he took his position by the stile, paused a moment as if in profound reflection, then *looked up* and, I thought, smiled very slightly, then tightened the strings of his apron, then took a long look at Dammit, and finally gave the word as agreed upon—

One—two—three—and away!

Punctually, at the word "away," my poor friend set off in a strong gallop. The stile was not very high, like Mr. Lord's—nor yet very low, like that of Mr. Lord's reviewers, but upon the whole I made sure that he would clear it. And then what if he did not?—ah, that was the question—what if he did not? "What right," said I, "had the old gentleman to make any other gentleman jump? The little old dot-and-carry-one![13] who is *he?* If he asks *me* to jump, I won't do it, that's flat, and I don't care who *the devil he is.*" The bridge, as I say, was arched and covered in, in a very ridiculous manner, and there was a most uncomfortable echo about it at all times—an echo which I never before so particularly observed as when I uttered the four last words of my remark.

But what I said, or what I thought, or what I heard, occupied only an instant. In less than five seconds from his starting, my poor Toby had taken the leap. I saw him run nimbly, and spring grandly from the floor of the bridge, cutting the most awful flourishes with his legs as he went up. I saw him high in the air, pigeon-winging it to admiration just over the top of the stile; and of course I thought it an unusually singular thing that he did not *continue* to go over. But the whole leap was the affair of a moment, and, before I had a chance to make any profound reflections, down came Mr. Dammit on the flat of his back, on the same side of the stile from which he had started. In the same instant I saw the old gentleman limping off at the top of his speed, having caught and wrapped up in his apron something that fell heavily into it from the darkness of the arch just over the turnstile. At all this I was much astonished; but I had no leisure to think, for Mr. Dammit lay particularly still, and I concluded that his feelings had been hurt, and that he stood in need of my assistance. I hurried up to him and found that he had received what might be termed a serious injury. The truth is, he had been deprived of his head, which after a close search I could not find anywhere;—so I determined to take him home, and send for the homœopathists. In the mean time a thought struck me, and I threw open an adjacent window of the bridge; when the sad truth flashed upon me at once. About five feet just above the top of the turnstile, and crossing the arch of the foot-path so as to constitute a brace, there extended a flat iron bar,[14] lying with its breadth horizontally, and forming one of a series that served to strengthen the structure throughout its extent. With the edge of this brace it appeared evident that the neck of my unfortunate friend had come precisely in contact.

He did not long survive his terrible loss. The homœopathists did not give him little enough physic, and what little they did give him he hesitated to take. So in the end he grew worse, and at length died, a lesson to all riotous livers. I bedewed his grave with my tears, worked a *bar* sinister[15] on his family escutcheon, and, for the general expenses of his funeral, sent in my very moderate bill to the transcendentalists. The scoundrels refused to pay it, so I had Mr. Dammit dug up at once, and sold him for dog's meat.

A TALE OF JERUSALEM

Intonsos rigidam in frontem ascendere canos Passus erat ——————

LUCAN

—————— *a bristly* bore.
Translation[1]

"Let us hurry to the walls," said Abel-Phittim to Buzi-Ben-Levi and Simeon the Pharisee, on the tenth day of the month Thammuz, in the year of the world three thousand nine hundred and forty-one— "let us hasten to the ramparts adjoining the gate of Benjamin, which is in the city of David, and overlooking the camp of the uncircumcised; for it is the last hour of the fourth watch, being sunrise; and the idolaters, in fulfilment of the promise of Pompey,[2] should be awaiting us with the lambs for the sacrifices."

Simeon, Abel-Phittim, and Buzi-Ben-Levi were the Gizbarim,[3] or sub-collectors of the offering, in the holy city of Jerusalem.

"Verily," replied the Pharisee, "let us hasten: for this generosity in the heathen is unwonted; and fickle-mindedness has ever been an attribute of the worshippers of Baal."[4]

"That they are fickle-minded and treacherous is as true as the Pentateuch," said Buzi-Ben-Levi, "but that is only towards the people of Adonai. When was it ever known that the Ammonites[5] proved wanting to their own interests? Methinks it is no great stretch of generosity to allow us lambs for the altar of the Lord, receiving in lieu thereof thirty silver shekels per head!"

"Thou forgettest, however, Ben-Levi," replied Abel-Phittim, "that the Roman Pompey, who is now impiously besieging the city of the Most High, has no assurity that we apply not the lambs thus purchased for the altar, to the sustenance of the body, rather than of the spirit."

"Now, by the five corners of my beard," shouted the Pharisee, who belonged to the sect called The Dashers[6] (that little knot of saints whose manner of *dashing* and lacerating the feet against the pavement was long a thorn and a reproach to less zealous devotees—a stumbling-block to less gifted perambulators)—"by the five corners of that beard which as a priest I am forbidden to shave!—have we lived to see the day when a blaspheming and idolatrous upstart of Rome shall accuse us of appropriating to the appetites of the flesh the most holy and consecrated elements? Have we lived to see the day when"——

"Let us not question the motives of the Philistine," interrupted Abel-Phittim, "for to-day we profit for the first time by his avarice or by his generosity; but rather let us hurry to the ramparts, lest offerings should be wanting for that altar whose fire the rains of heaven cannot extinguish, and whose pillars of smoke no tempest can turn aside."

That part of the city to which our worthy Gizbarim now hastened, and which bore the name of its architect King David, was esteemed the most strongly fortified district of Jerusalem; being situated upon the steep and lofty hill of Zion. Here a broad, deep, circumvallatory trench, hewn from the solid rock, was defended by a wall of great strength erected upon its inner edge. This wall was adorned, at regular interspaces, by square towers of white marble; the lowest sixty, and the highest one hundred and twenty cubits in height. But, in the vicinity of the gate of Benjamin, the wall arose by no means from the margin of the fosse. On the contrary, between the level of the ditch and the basement of the rampart, sprang up a perpendicular cliff of two hundred and fifty cubits; forming part of the precipitous Mount Moriah. So that when Simeon and his associates arrived on the summit of the tower called Adoni-Bezek—the loftiest of all the turrets around about Jerusalem, and the usual place of conference with the besieging army—they looked down upon the camp of the enemy from an eminence excelling, by many feet, that of the Pyramid of Cheops, and, by several, that of the temple of Belus.[7]

"Verily," sighed the Pharisee, as he peered dizzily over the precipice, "the uncircumcised are as the sands by the seashore—as the locusts in the wilderness! The valley of The King hath become the valley of Adommin."[8]

"And yet," added Ben-Levi, "thou canst not point me out a Philistine—no, not one—from Aleph to Tau—from the wilderness to the battlements—who seemeth any bigger than the letter Jod!"[9]

"Lower away the basket with the shekels of silver!" here shouted a Roman soldier in a hoarse, rough voice, which appeared to issue from the regions of Pluto—"lower away the basket with the accursed coin which it has broken the jaw of a noble Roman to pronounce! Is it thus you evince your gratitude to our master Pompeius, who, in his condescension, has thought fit to listen to your idolatrous importunities? The god Phœbus, who is a true god, has been charioted for an hour—and were you not to be on the ramparts by sunrise? Ædepol![10] do you think that we, the conquerors of the world, have nothing better to do than stand waiting by the walls of every kennel, to traffic with the dogs of the earth? Lower away! I say—and see that your trumpery be bright in color, and just in weight!"

"El Elohim!" ejaculated the Pharisee, as the discordant tones of the centurion rattled up the crags of the precipice, and fainted away against the temple—"El Elohim!—who is the God Phœbus?—whom doth the blasphemer invoke? Thou, Buzi-Ben-Levi! who art read in the laws of the Gentiles, and hast sojourned among them who dabble with the Teraphim!—is it Nergal of whom the idolator speaketh?—or Ashimah?—or Nibhaz?—or Tartak?—or Adramalech? or Anamalech?—or Succoth-Benith?—or Dagon?—or Belial?—or Baal-Perith?—or Baal-Peor?—or Baal-Zebub?"[11]

"Verily it is neither—but beware how

thou lettest the rope slip too rapidly through thy fingers; for should the wicker-work chance to hang on the projection of yonder crag, there will be a woful outpouring of the holy things of the sanctuary."

By the assistance of some rudely constructed machinery, the heavily laden basket was now carefully lowered down among the multitude; and, from the giddy pinnacle, the Romans were seen gathering confusedly round it; but owing to the vast height and the prevalence of a fog, no distinct view of their operations could be obtained.

Half an hour had already elapsed.

"We shall be too late," sighed the Pharisee, as at the expiration of this period, he looked over into the abyss—"we shall be too late! we shall be turned out of office by the Katholim."[12]

"No more," responded Abel-Phittim, "no more shall we feast upon the fat of the land—no longer shall our beards be odorous with frankincense—our loins girded up[13] with fine linen from the Temple."

"Raca!"[14] swore Ben-Levi, "Raca! do they mean to defraud us of the purchase money? or, Holy Moses! are they weighing the shekels of the tabernacle?"

"They have given the signal at last," cried the Pharisee, "they have given the signal at last!—pull away, Abel-Phittim! —and thou, Buzi-Ben-Levi, pull away!— for verily the Philistines have either still hold upon the basket, or the Lord hath softened their hearts to place therein a beast of good weight!" And the Gizbarim pulled away, while their burthen swung heavily upwards through the still increasing mist.

*   *   *

"Booshoh he!"[15]—as, at the conclusion of an hour, some object at the extremity of the rope became indistinctly visible— "Booshoh he!" was the exclamation which burst from the lips of Ben-Levi.

"Booshoh he!—for shame!—it is a ram from the thickets of Engedi, and as rugged as the valley of Jehosaphat!"[16]

"It is a firstling of the flock," said Abel-Phittim, "I know him by the bleating of his lips, and the innocent folding of his limbs. His eyes are more beautiful than the jewels of the Pectoral,[17] and his flesh is like the honey of Hebron."

"It is a fatted calf from the pastures of Bashan," said the Pharisee, "the heathen have dealt wonderfully with us!—let us raise up our voices in a psalm!—let us give thanks on the shawm and on the psaltery —on the harp and on the huggab—on the cythern and on the sackbut!"[18]

It was not until the basket had arrived within a few feet of the Gizbarim, that a low grunt betrayed to their perception a *hog* of no common size.

"Now El Emanu!" slowly, and with upturned eyes ejaculated the trio, as, letting go their hold, the emancipated porker tumbled headlong among the Philistines, "El Emanu!—God be with us!—*it is the unutterable flesh!*"[19]

THE LITERARY LIFE OF THINGUM BOB, ESQ.

Late Editor of the 'Goosetherumfoodle'[1]

BY HIMSELF

I am now growing in years, and—since I understand that Shakespeare and Mr. Emmons[2] are deceased—it is not impossible that I may even die. It has occurred to me, therefore, that I may as well retire from the field of Letters and repose upon my laurels. But I am ambitious of signalizing my abdication of the literary sceptre by some important bequest to posterity; and, perhaps, I cannot do a better thing than just pen for it an account of my earlier career. My name, indeed, has been so long and so constantly before the public eye, that I am not only willing to admit the naturalness of the interest which it has everywhere excited, but ready to satisfy the extreme curiosity which it has inspired. In fact it is no more than the duty of him who achieves greatness, to leave behind him, in his ascent, such landmarks as may guide others to be great. I propose, therefore, in the present paper, (which I had some idea of calling "Memoranda to serve for the Literary History of America,") to give a detail of those important, yet feeble and tottering first steps, by which, at length, I attained the high road to the pinnacle of human renown.

Of one's *very* remote ancestors it is superfluous to say much. My father, Thomas Bob, Esq., stood for many years at the summit of his profession, which was that of a merchant-barber, in the city of Smug. His warehouse was the resort of all the principal people of the place, and especially of the editorial corps—a body which inspires all about it with profound veneration and awe. For my own part, I regarded them as Gods, and drank in with avidity the rich wit and wisdom which continuously flowed from their august mouths during the process of what is styled "lather." My first moment of positive inspiration must be dated from that ever-memorable epoch, when the brilliant conductor of the "Gad-Fly," in the intervals of the important process just mentioned, recited aloud, before a conclave of our apprentices, an inimitable poem in honor of the "Only Genuine Oil-of-Bob," (so called from its talented inventor, my father,) and for which effusion the editor of the "Fly" was remunerated with a regal liberality, by the firm of Thomas Bob and company, merchant barbers.[3]

The genius of the stanzas to the "Oil-of-Bob" first breathed into me, I say, the divine *afflatus*.[4] I resolved at once to become a great man and to commence by becoming a great poet. That very evening I fell upon my knees at the feet of my father.

"Father," I said, "pardon me!—but I have a soul above lather. It is my firm intention to cut the shop. I would be an edi-

tor—I would be a poet—I would pen stanzas to the 'Oil-of-Bob.' Pardon me and aid me to be great!"

"My dear Thingum," replied my father, (I had been christened Thingum after a wealthy relative so surnamed,) "My dear Thingum," he said, raising me from my knees by the ears—"Thingum, my boy, you're a trump, and take after your father in having a soul. You have an immense head, too, and it must hold a great many brains. This I have long seen, and therefore had thoughts of making you a lawyer. The business, however, has grown ungenteel, and that of a politician don't pay. Upon the whole you judge wisely;—the trade of editor is best:—and if you can be a poet at the same time,—as most of the editors are, by the by,—why you will kill two birds with one stone.[5] To encourage you in the beginning of things, I will allow you a garret; pen, ink and paper; a rhyming dictionary; and a copy of the 'Gad-Fly.' I suppose you would scarcely demand any more."

"I would be an ungrateful villain if I did," I replied with enthusiasm. "Your generosity is boundless. I will repay it by making you the father of a genius."

Thus ended my conference with the best of men, and immediately upon its termination, I betook myself with zeal to my poetical labors; as upon these, chiefly, I founded my hopes of ultimate elevation to the editorial chair.

In my first attempts at composition I found the stanzas to "The Oil-of-Bob" rather a draw-back than otherwise. Their splendor more dazzled than enlightened me. The contemplation of their excellence tended, naturally, to discourage me by comparison with my own abortions; so that for a long time I labored in vain. At length there came into my head one of those exquisitely original ideas which now and then *will* permeate the brain of a man of genius. It was this:—or, rather, thus was it carried into execution. From the rubbish of an old book-stall, in a very remote corner of the town, I got together several antique and altogether unknown or forgotten volumes. The bookseller sold them to me for a song. From one of these, which purported to be a translation of one Dante's "Inferno," I copied with remarkable neatness a long passage about a man named Ugolino, who had a parcel of brats. From another which contained a good many old plays by some person whose name I forget, I extracted in the same manner, and with the same care, a great number of lines about "angels" and "ministers saying grace," and "goblins damned," and more besides of that sort. From a third, which was the composition of some blind man or other, either a Greek or a Choctaw—I cannot be at the pains of remembering every trifle exactly —I took about fifty verses beginning with "Achilles' wrath," and "grease," and something else. From a fourth, which I recollect was also the work of a blind man, I selected a page or two all about "hail" and "holy light;" and although a blind man has no business to write about light, still the verses were sufficiently good in their way.[6]

Having made fair copies of these poems I signed every one of them "Oppodeldoc," (a fine sonorous name,) and, doing each up nicely in a separate envelope, I despatched one to each of the four principal Magazines, with a request for speedy insertion and prompt pay. The result of this well conceived plan, however, (the success of which would have saved me much trouble in after life,) served to convince me that some editors are not to be bamboozled, and gave the *coup-de-grâce* (as they say in France,) to my nascent hopes, (as they say in the city of the transcendentals.)[7]

The fact is, that each and every one of the Magazines in question, gave Mr. "Oppodeldoc" a complete using-up, in the "Monthly Notices to Correspondents." The "Hum-Drum" gave him a dressing after this fashion:

" 'Oppodeldoc,' (whoever he is,) has sent us a long *tirade* concerning a bed-

lamite whom he styles 'Ugolino,' who had a great many children that should have been all whipped and sent to bed without their suppers. The whole affair is exceedingly tame—not to say *flat*. 'Oppodeldoc,' (whoever he is,) is entirely devoid of imagination—and imagination, in our humble opinion, is not only the soul of POESY, but also its very heart. 'Oppodeldoc,' (whoever he is,) has the audacity to demand of us, for his twattle, a 'speedy insertion and prompt pay.' We neither insert nor purchase any stuff of the sort. There can be no doubt, however, that he would meet with a ready sale for all the balderdash he can scribble, at the office of either the 'Rowdy-Dow,' the 'Lollipop,' or the 'Goosetherumfoodle.' "[8]

All this, it must be acknowledged, was very severe upon "Oppodeldoc"—but the unkindest cut was putting the word POESY in small caps. In those five preëminent letters what a world of bitterness is there not involved![9]

But "Oppodeldoc" was punished with equal severity in the "Rowdy-Dow," which spoke thus:

"We have received a most singular and insolent communication from a person, (whoever he is,) signing himself 'Oppodeldoc'—thus desecrating the greatness of the illustrious Roman Emperor so named. Accompanying the letter of 'Oppodeldoc,' (whoever he is,) we find sundry lines of most disgusting and unmeaning rant about 'angels and ministers of grace'—rant such as no madman short of a Nat Lee,[10] or an 'Oppodeldoc,' could possibly perpetrate. And for this trash of trash, we are modestly requested to 'pay promptly.' No sir—no! We pay for nothing of *that* sort. Apply to the 'Hum-Drum,' the 'Lollipop,' or the 'Goosetherumfoodle.' These *periodicals* will undoubtedly accept any literary offal you may send them—and as undoubtedly *promise* to pay for it."

This was bitter indeed upon poor "Oppodeldoc;" but, in this instance, the weight of the satire falls upon the "Hum-

Drum," the "Lollipop," and the "Goose-therumfoodle," who are pungently styled *"periodicals"*—in Italics, too—a thing that must have cut them to the heart.

Scarcely less savage was the "Lollipop," which thus discoursed:

"Some *individual*, who repoices in the appellation 'Oppodeldoc' (to what low uses are the names of the illustrious dead too often applied!) has enclosed us some fifty or sixty *verses*, commencing after this fashion:

> Achilles' wrath, to Greece the
> direful spring
> Of woes unnumbered, &c., &c.,
> &c., &c.

" 'Oppodeldoc,' (whoever he is) is respectfully informed that there is not a printer's devil in our office who is not in the daily habit of composing better *lines*. Those of 'Oppodeldoc' will not *scan*. 'Oppodeldoc' should learn to *count*. But why he should have conceived the idea that we, (of all others, *we!*) would disgrace our pages with his ineffable nonsense, is utterly beyond comprehension. Why, the absurd twattle is scarcely good enough for the 'Hum-Drum,' the 'Rowdy-Dow,' the 'Goosetherumfoodle'—things that are in the practice of publishing 'Mother Goose's Melodies' as original lyrics. And 'Oppodeldoc,' (whoever he is,) has even the assurance to demand *pay* for this drivel. Does 'Oppodeldoc,' (whoever he is,) know —is he aware that we could not be paid to insert it?"[11]

As I perused this I felt myself growing gradually smaller and smaller, and when I came to the point at which the editor sneered at the poem as *"verses,"* there was little more than an ounce of me left. As for "Oppodeldoc" I began to experience *compassion* for the poor fellow. But the "Goosetherumfoodle" showed, if possible, less mercy than the "Lollipop." It was the "Goosetherumfoodle" that said:

"A wretched poetaster, who signs himself 'Oppodeldoc,' is silly enough to fancy that *we* will print and *pay for* a medley of incoherent and ungrammatical bombast which he has transmitted to us, and which commences with the following most *intelligible* line:

> 'Hail, Holy Light! Offspring of Heaven,
> first born.'

"We say, 'most *intelligible*.' 'Oppodeldoc,' (whoever he is,) will be kind enough to tell us, perhaps, how *'hail'* can be *'holy light.'* We always regarded it as *frozen rain*. Will he inform us, also, how frozen rain can be, at one and the same time, both 'holy light,' (whatever that is,) and an 'offspring?'—which latter term, (if *we* understand any thing about English,) is only employed, with propriety, in reference to small babies of about six weeks old. But it is preposterous to descant upon such absurdity—although 'Oppodeldoc,' (whoever he is,) has the unparalleled effrontery to suppose that we will not only 'insert' his ignorant ravings, but (absolutely) *pay for them!*

"Now this is fine—it is rich!—and we have half a mind to punish this young scribbler for his egotism, by really publishing his effusion, *verbatim et literatim*,[12] as he has written it. We could inflict no punishment so severe, and we *would* inflict it, but for the boredom which we should cause our readers in so doing.

"Let 'Oppodeldoc,' (whoever he is,) send any future *composition* of like character to the 'Hum-Drum,' the 'Lollipop,' or the 'Rowdy-Dow.' *They* will 'insert' it. *They* 'insert' every month just such stuff. Send it to them. WE are not to be insulted with impunity."[13]

This made an end of me; and as for the "Hum-Drum," the "Rowdy-Dow," and the "Lollipop," I never could comprehend how they survived it. The putting *them* in the smallest possible *minion*, (that was the rub—thereby insinuating their lowness their baseness,) while WE stood looking down upon them in gigantic capitals!—oh it was *too* bitter!—it was wormwood—it was gall. Had I been either of these periodicals I would have spared no pains to have the "Goosetherumfoodle" prosecuted. It might have been done under the Act for the "Prevention of Cruelty to Animals." As for "Oppodeldoc," (whoever he was,) I had by this time lost all patience with the fellow, and sympathized with him no longer. He was a fool, beyond doubt, (whoever he was,) and got not a kick more than he deserved.

The result of my experiment with the old books, convinced me, in the first place, that "honesty is the best policy," and, in the second, that if I could not write better than Mr. Dante, and the two blind men, and the rest of the old set, it would, at least, be a difficult matter to write worse. I took heart, therefore, and determined to prosecute the "entirely original," (as they say on the covers of the magazines,) at whatever cost of study and pains. I again placed before my eyes as a model, the brilliant stanzas on "The Oil-of-Bob," by the editor of the "Gad-Fly," and resolved to construct an Ode on the same sublime theme, in rivalry of what had already been done.

With my first verse I had no material difficulty. It ran thus:

To pen an Ode upon the "Oil-of-Bob."

Having carefully looked out, however, all the legitimate rhymes to "Bob," I found it impossible to proceed. In this dilemma I had recourse to paternal aid; and, after some hours of mature thought, my father and myself thus constructed the poem:

To pen an Ode upon the "Oil-of-Bob"
Is all sorts of a job.
　　　　(Signed,)　　　　SNOB.

To be sure this composition was of no very great length—but I "have yet to learn" as they say in the Edinburgh Review, that the mere extent of a literary work has any thing to do with its merit. As for the Quarterly cant about "sustained effort," it is impossible to see the sense of it. Upon the whole, therefore, I was satisfied with the success of my maiden attempt, and now the only question regarded the disposal I should make of it. My father suggested that I should send it to the "Gad-Fly"—but there were two reasons which operated to prevent me from so doing. I dreaded the jealousy of the editor—and I had ascertained that he did not pay for original contributions. I therefore, after due deliberation, consigned the article to the more dignified pages of the "Lollipop," and awaited the event in anxiety, but with resignation.

In the very next published number I had the proud satisfaction of seeing my poem printed at length, as the leading article, with the following significant words, prefixed in italics and between brackets:

["We call the attention of our readers to the subjoined admirable stanzas on 'The Oil-of-Bob.' We need say nothing of their sublimity, or of their pathos:—it is impossible to peruse them without tears. Those who have been nauseated with a sad dose on the same august topic from the goose-quill of the editor of the 'Gad-Fly,' will do well to compare the two compositions.

P. S. We are consumed with anxiety to probe the mystery which envelops the evident pseudonym 'Snob.' May we hope for a personal interview?"]

All this was scarcely more than justice, but it was, I confess, rather more than I had expected:—I acknowledge this, be it observed, to the everlasting disgrace of my country and of mankind. I lost no time, however, in calling upon the editor of the "Lollipop," and had the good fortune to find this gentleman at home. He saluted me with an air of profound respect, slightly blended with a fatherly and patronizing admiration, wrought in him, no doubt, by my appearance of extreme youth and inexperience. Begging me to be seated, he entered at once upon the subject of my poem;—but modesty will ever forbid me to repeat the thousand compliments which he lavished upon me. The eulogies of Mr. Crab, (such was the editor's name,) were, however, by no means fulsomely indiscriminate. He analyzed my composition with much freedom and great ability —not hesitating to point out a few trivial defects—a circumstance which elevated him highly in my esteem. The "Gad-Fly" was, of course, brought upon the *tapis*, and I hope never to be subjected to a criticism so searching, or to rebukes so withering, as were bestowed by Mr. Crab upon that unhappy effusion. I had been accustomed to regard the editor of the "Gad-Fly" as something superhuman; but Mr. Crab soon disabused me of that idea. He set the literary as well as the personal character of the Fly (so Mr. C. satirically designated the rival editor,) in its true light. He, the Fly, was very little better than he should be. He had written infamous things. He was a penny-a-liner,[14] and a buffoon. He was a villain. He had composed a tragedy which set the whole country in a guffaw, and a farce which deluged the universe in tears. Besides all this, he had the impudence to pen what he meant for a lampoon upon himself, (Mr. Crab,) and the temerity to style him "an ass." Should I at any time wish to express my opinion of Mr. Fly, the pages of the "Lollipop," Mr. Crab assured me, were at my unlimited disposal. In the meantime, as it was very certain that I would be attacked in the Fly for my attempt at composing a rival poem on the "Oil-of-Bob," he (Mr. Crab,) would take it upon himself to attend, pointedly, to my private and personal interests. If I were not made a man of at once, it should not be the fault of himself, (Mr. Crab.)

Mr. Crab having now paused in his discourse, (the latter portion of which I found it impossible to comprehend,) I ventured to suggest something about the remuneration which I had been taught to expect for my poem, by an announcement on the cover of the "Lollipop," declaring that it, (the "Lollipop,") "insisted upon being permitted to pay exorbitant prices for all accepted contributions;—fre-

quently expending more money for a single brief poem than the whole annual cost of the 'Hum-Drum,' the 'Rowdy-Dow,' and the 'Goosetherumfoodle' combined."[15]

As I mentioned the word "remuneration," Mr. Crab first opened his eyes, and then his mouth, to quite a remarkable extent; causing his personal appearance to resemble that of a highly-agitated elderly duck in the act of quacking;—and in this condition he remained, (ever and anon pressing his hands tightly to his forehead, as if in a state of desperate bewilderment) until I had nearly made an end of what I had to say.

Upon my conclusion, he sank back into his seat, as if much overcome, letting his arms fall lifelessly by his side, but keeping his mouth still rigorously open, after the fashion of the duck. While I remained in speechless astonishment at behaviour so alarming, he suddenly leaped to his feet and made a rush at the bell-rope; but just as he reached this, he appeared to have altered his intention, whatever it was, for he dived under a table and immediately re-appeared with a cudgel. This he was in the act of uplifting, (for what purpose I am at a loss to imagine,) when, all at once, there came a benign smile over his features, and he sank placidly back in his chair.

"Mr. Bob," he said, (for I had sent up my card before ascending myself,) "Mr. Bob, you are a young man, I presume— *very?*"

I assented; adding that I had not yet concluded my third lustrum.[16]

"Ah!" he replied, "very good! I see how it is—say no more! Touching this matter of compensation, what you observe is very just: in fact it is excessively so. But—ah —ah—the *first* contribution—the *first*, I say—it is never the Magazine custom to pay for—you comprehend, eh? The truth is, we are usually the *recipients* in such case." [Mr. Crab smiled blandly as he emphasized the word "recipients."] "For the most part, we are *paid* for the insertion of a maiden attempt—especially in verse. In the second place, Mr. Bob, the Magazine rule is never to disburse what we term in France the *argent comptant:*[17]—I have no doubt you understand. In a quarter or two after publication of the article—or in a year or two—we make no objection to giving our note at nine months:—provided always that we can so arrange our affairs as to be quite certain of a 'burst up' in six. I really *do* hope, Mr. Bob, that you will look upon this explanation as satisfactory." Here Mr. Crab concluded, and the tears stood in his eyes.

Grieved to the soul at having been, however innocently, the cause of pain to so eminent and so sensitive a man, I hastened to apologize, and to reassure him, by expressing my perfect coincidence with his views, as well as my entire appreciation of the delicacy of his position. Having done all this in a neat speech, I took leave.

One fine morning, very shortly afterwards, "I awoke and found myself famous." The extent of my renown will be best estimated by reference to the editorial opinions of the day. These opinions, it will be seen, were embodied in critical notices of the number of the "Lollipop" containing my poem, and are perfectly satisfactory, conclusive and clear with the exception, perhaps, of the hieroglyphical marks, "*Sep.* 15—1 t."[18] appended to each of the critiques.

The "Owl," a journal of profound sagacity, and well known for the deliberate gravity of its literary decisions—the "Owl," I say, spoke as follows:

" 'THE LOLLIPOP!' The October number of this delicious Magazine surpasses its predecessors, and sets competition at defiance. In the beauty of its typography and paper—in the number and excellence of its steel plates—as well as in the literary merit of its contributions—the 'Lollipop' compares with its slow-paced rivals as Hyperion with a Satyr. The 'Hum-Drum,' the 'Rowdy-Dow,' and the 'Goosetherumfoodle,' excel, it is true, in braggadocio,

but, in all other points, give us the 'Lollipop!' How this celebrated journal can sustain its evidently tremendous expenses, is more than we can understand. To be sure, it has a circulation of 100,000,[19] and its subscription-list has increased one fourth during the last month: but, on the other hand, the sums it disburses constantly for contributions are inconceivable. It is reported that Mr. Slyass received no less than thirty-seven and a half cents for his inimitable paper on 'Pigs.' With Mr. CRAB, as editor, and with such names upon the list of contributors as SNOB and Slyass, there can be no such word as 'fail' for the 'Lollipop.' Go and subscribe. *Sep.* 15—1 t."

I must say that I was gratified with this high-toned notice from a paper so respectable as the "Owl." The placing my name —that is to say my *nom de guerre*[20]—in priority of station to that of the great Slyass, was a compliment as happy as I felt it to be deserved.

My attention was next arrested by these paragraphs in the "Toad"—a print highly distinguished for its uprightness, and independence—for its entire freedom from sycophancy and subservience to the givers of dinners:

"The 'Lollipop' for October is out in advance of all its contemporaries, and infinitely surpasses them, of course, in the splendor of its embellishments, as well as in the richness of its literary contents. The 'Hum-Drum,' the 'Rowdy-Dow,' and the 'Goosetherumfoodle' excel, we admit, in braggadocio, but, in all other points, give us the 'Lollipop.' How this celebrated Magazine can sustain its evidently tremendous expenses, is more than we can understand. To be sure, it has a circulation of 200,000, and its subscription list has increased one third during the last fortnight, but on the other hand, the sums it disburses, monthly, for contributions, are fearfully great. We learn that Mr. Mumblethumb received no less than fifty cents for his late 'Monody in a Mud-Puddle.'[21]

"Among the original contributors to the

present number we notice, (besides the eminent editor, Mr. CRAB,) such men as SNOB, Slyass, and Mumblethumb. Apart from the editorial matter, the most valuable paper, nevertheless, is, we think, a poetical gem by 'Snob,' on the 'Oil-of-Bob' —but our readers must not suppose, from the title of this incomparable *bijou*,[22] that it bears any similitude to some balderdash on the same subject by a certain contemptible individual whose name is unmentionable to ears polite. The *present* poem 'On the Oil-of-Bob,' has excited universal anxiety and curiosity in respect to the owner of the evident pseudonym, 'Snob'—a curiosity which, happily, we have it in our power to satisfy. 'Snob' is the *nom-de-plume* of Mr. Thingum Bob, of this city,—a relative of the great Mr. Thingum, (after whom he is named,) and otherwise connected with the most illustrious families of the State. His father, Thomas Bob, Esq., is an opulent merchant in Smug. *Sep. 15—1 t.*"

This generous approbation touched me to the heart—the more especially as it emanated from a source so avowedly—so proverbially pure as the "Toad." The word "balderdash," as applied to the "Oil-of-Bob" of the Fly, I considered singularly pungent and appropriate. The words "gem" and "*bijou*," however, used in reference to my composition, struck me as being, in some degree, feeble. They seemed to me to be deficient in force. They were not sufficiently *prononcés*,[23] (as we have it in France.)

I had hardly finished reading the "Toad," when a friend placed in my hands a copy of the "Mole," a daily, enjoying high reputation for the keenness of its perception about matters in general, and for the open, honest, above-ground style of its editorials. The "Mole" spoke of the "Lollipop" as follows:

"We have just received the 'Lollipop' for October, and *must* say that never before have we perused any single number of any periodical which afforded us a felicity so supreme. We speak advisedly. The 'Hum-Drum,' the 'Rowdy-Dow' and the 'Goosetherumfoodle' must look well to their laurels. These prints, no doubt, surpass every thing in loudness of pretension, but, in all other points, give us the 'Lollipop!' How this celebrated Magazine can sustain its evidently tremendous expenses, is more than we can comprehend. To be sure, it has a circulation of 300,000; and its subscription-list has increased one half within the last week, but then the sum it disburses, monthly, for contributions, is astoundingly enormous. We have it upon good authority, that Mr. Fatquack received no less than sixty-two cents and a half for his late Domestic Nouvelette, the 'Dish-Clout.'"[24]

"The contributors to the number before us are Mr. CRAB, (the eminent editor,) SNOB, Mumblethumb, Fatquack and others; but, after the inimitable compositions of the editor himself, we prefer a diamond-like effusion from the pen of a rising poet who writes over the signature 'Snob'—a *nom de guerre* which we predict will one day extinguish the radiance of 'Boz.'[25] 'SNOB,' we learn, is a Mr. THINGUM BOB, sole heir of a wealthy merchant of this city, Thomas Bob, Esq., and a near relative of the distinguished Mr. Thingum. The title of Mr. B's admirable poem is the 'Oil-of-Bob'—a somewhat unfortunate name, by-the-bye, as some contemptible vagabond connected with the penny press has already disgusted the town with a great deal of drivel upon the same topic. There will be no danger, however, of confounding the compositions. *Sep. 15—1 t.*"

The generous approbation of so clear-sighted a journal as the "Mole" penetrated my soul with delight. The only objection which occurred to me was, that the terms "contemptible vagabond" might have been better written "*odious and* contemptible, *wretch, villain* and vagabond." This would have sounded more gracefully, I think. "Diamond-like," also, was scarcely, it will be admitted, of sufficient intensity to express what the "Mole" evidently *thought* of the brilliancy of the "Oil-of-Bob."

On the same afternoon in which I saw these notices in the "Owl," the "Toad," and the "Mole," I happened to meet with a copy of the "Daddy-Long-Legs," a periodical proverbial for the extreme extent of its understanding. And it was the "Daddy-Long-Legs" which spoke thus:

"The 'Lollipop!!' This gorgeous Magazine is already before the public for October. The question of pre-eminence is forever put to rest, and hereafter it will be excessively preposterous in the 'Hum-Drum,' the 'Rowdy-Dow,' or the 'Goosetherumfoodle,' to make any farther spasmodic attempts at competition. These journals may excel the 'Lollipop' in outcry, but, in all other points, give us the 'Lollipop!' How this celebrated Magazine can sustain its evidently tremendous expenses, is past comprehension. To be sure it has a circulation of precisely half a million, and its subscription-list has increased seventy-five per cent. within the last couple of days; but then the sums it disburses, monthly, for contributions, are scarcely credible; we are cognizant of the fact, that Mademoiselle Cribalittle received no less than eighty-seven cents and a half for her late valuable Revolutionary Tale, entitled 'The York-Town Katy-Did, and the Bunker-Hill Katy-Didn't.'

"The most able papers in the present number, are, of course, those furnished by the editor, (the eminent Mr. CRAB,) but there are numerous magnificent contributions from such names as SNOB; Mademoiselle Cribalittle; Slyass; Mrs. Fibalittle; Mumblethumb; Mrs. Squibalittle; and last, though not least, Fatquack. The world may well be challenged to produce so rich a galaxy of genius.

"The poem over the signature 'SNOB' is, we find, attracting universal commendation, and, we are constrained to say, deserves, if possible, even more applause than it has received. The 'Oil-of-Bob' is the title of this masterpiece of eloquence and art. One or two of our readers *may* have a *very*

faint, although sufficiently disgusting recollection of a poem (?) similarly entitled, the perpetration of a miserable penny-a-liner, mendicant, and cut-throat, connected in the capacity of scullion, we believe, with one of the indecent prints about the purlieus of the city; we beg them, for God's sake, not to confound the compositions. The author of *the* 'Oil-of-Bob' is, we hear, THINGUM BOB, Esq., a gentleman of high genius, and a scholar. 'Snob' is merely a *nom-de-guerre. Sept. 15 —1 t.*"

I could scarcely restrain my indignation while I perused the concluding portions of this diatribe. It was clear to me that the yea-nay manner—not to say the gentleness—the positive forbearance with which the "Daddy-Long-Legs" spoke of that pig, the editor of the "Gad-Fly"—it was evident to me, I say, that this gentleness of speech could proceed from nothing else than a partiality for the Fly—whom it was clearly the intention of the "Daddy-Long-Legs" to elevate into reputation at my expense. Any one, indeed, might perceive, with half an eye, that, had the real design of the "Daddy" been what it wished to appear, it, (the "Daddy,") might have expressed itself in terms more direct, more pungent, and altogether more to the purpose. The words "penny-a-liner," "mendicant," "scullion," and "cut-throat," were epithets so intentionally inexpressive and equivocal, as to be worse than nothing when applied to the author of the very worst stanzas ever penned by one of the human race. We all know what is meant by "damning with faint praise," and, on the other hand, who could fail seeing through the covert purpose of the "Daddy"—that of glorifying with feeble abuse?

What the "Daddy" chose to say of the Fly, however, was no business of mine. What is said of myself *was*. After the noble manner in which the "Owl," the "Toad," the "Mole," had expressed themselves in respect to my ability, it was rather too much to be coolly spoken of by a thing like the "Daddy-Long-Legs," as merely "a gentleman of high genius and a scholar." Gentleman indeed! I made up my mind, at once, either to get a written apology from the "Daddy-Long-Legs," or to call it out.

Full of this purpose, I looked about me to find a friend whom I could entrust with a message to his Daddyship, and, as the editor of the "Lollipop" had given me marked tokens of regard, I at length concluded to seek assistance upon the present occasion.

I have never yet been able to account, in a manner satisfactory to my own understanding, for the *very* peculiar countenance and demeanor with which Mr. Crab listened to me, as I unfolded to him my design. He again went through the scene of the bell-rope and cudgel, and did not omit the duck. At one period I thought he really intended to quack. His fit, nevertheless, finally subsided as before, and he began to act and speak in a rational way. He declined bearing the cartel, however, and in fact, dissuaded me from sending it at all; but was candid enough to admit that the "Daddy-Long-Legs" had been disgracefully in the wrong—more especially in what related to the epithets "gentleman and scholar."

Towards the end of this interview with Mr. Crab, who really appeared to take a paternal interest in my welfare, he suggested to me that I might turn an honest penny and, at the same time, advance my reputation, by occasionally playing Thomas Hawk for the "Lollipop."

I begged Mr. Crab to inform me who was Mr. Thomas Hawk, and how it was expected that I should play him.

Here Mr. Crab again "made great eyes," (as we say in Germany,)[26] but at length, recovering himself from a profound attack of astonishment, he assured me that he employed the words "Thomas Hawk" to avoid the colloquialism, Tommy, which was low—but that the true idea was Tommy Hawk—or tomahawk—and that by "playing tomahawk" he referred to

scalping, brow-beating and otherwise using-up the herd of poor-devil authors.

I assured my patron that, if this was all, I was perfectly resigned to the task of playing Thomas Hawk. Hereupon Mr. Crab desired me to use-up the editor of the "Gad-Fly" forthwith, in the fiercest style within the scope of my ability, and as a specimen of my powers. This I did, upon the spot, in a review of the original "Oil-of-Bob," occupying thirty-six pages of the "Lollipop." I found playing Thomas Hawk, indeed, a far less onerous occupation than poetizing; for I went upon *system* altogether, and thus it was easy to do the thing thoroughly and well. My practice was this. I bought auction copies (cheap) of "Lord Brougham's Speeches," "Cobbett's Complete Works," the "New Slang-Syllabus," the "Whole Art of Snubbing," "Prentice's Billingsgate," (folio edition,) and "Lewis G. Clarke on Tongue." These works I cut up thoroughly with a curry-comb, and then, throwing the shreds into a sieve, sifted out carefully all that might be thought decent, (a mere trifle): reserving the hard phrases, which I threw into a large tin pepper-castor with longitudinal holes, so that an entire sentence could get through without material injury. The mixture was then ready for use. When called upon to play Thomas Hawk, I anointed a sheet of fools-cap with the white of a gander's egg;[27] then, shredding the thing to be reviewed as I had previously shredded the books,—only with more care, so as to get every word separate—I threw the latter shreds in with the former, screwed on the lid of the castor, gave it a shake, and so dusted out the mixture upon the egg'd foolscap; where it stuck. The effect was beautiful to behold. It was captivating. Indeed the reviews I brought to pass by this simple expedient have never been approached, and were the wonder of the world. At first, through bashfulness—the result of inexperience—I was a little put out by a certain inconsistency—a certain air of the *bizarre*, (as we say in France,) worn by the composition as a whole. All the phrases did not *fit*, (as we say in the Anglo-Saxon.) Many were quite awry. Some, even, were up-side-down; and there were none of them which were not, in some measure, injured, in regard to effect, by this latter species of accident, when it occurred:—with the exception of Mr. Lewis Clarke's paragraphs, which were so vigorous, and altogether stout, that they seemed not particularly disconcerted by any extreme of position, but looked equally happy and satisfactory, whether on their heads, or on their heels.

What became of the editor of the "Gad-Fly," after the publication of my criticism on his "Oil-of-Bob," it is somewhat difficult to determine. The most reasonable conclusion is, that he wept himself to death. At all events he disappeared instantaneously from the face of the earth, and no man has seen even the ghost of him since.

This matter having been properly accomplished, and the Furies appeased, I grew at once into high favor with Mr. Crab. He took me into his confidence, gave me a permanent situation as Thomas Hawk of the "Lollipop," and as, for the present, he could afford me no salary[28] allowed me to profit, at discretion, by his advice.

"My Dear Thingum," said he to me one day after dinner, "I respect your abilities and love you as a son. You shall be my heir. When I die I will bequeath you the 'Lollipop.' In the meantime I will make a man of you—I *will*—provided always that you follow my counsel. The first thing to do is to get rid of the old bore."

"Boar?" said I inquiringly—"pig, eh?—*aper?*[29] (as we say in Latin)—who?—where?"

"Your father," said he.

"Precisely," I replied,—"pig."

"You have your fortune to make, Thingum," resumed Mr. Crab, "and that governor of yours is a millstone about your neck. We must cut him at once." [Here I took out my knife.] "We must cut

him," continued Mr. Crab, "decidedly and forever. He won't do—he *won't*. Upon second thoughts, you had better kick him, or cane him, or something of that kind."

"What do you say," I suggested modestly, "to my kicking him in the first instance, caning him afterwards, and winding up by tweaking his nose?"

Mr. Crab looked at me musingly for some moments, and then answered:

"I think, Mr. Bob, that what you propose would answer sufficiently well—indeed remarkably well—that is to say, as far as it went—but barbers are exceedingly hard to cut, and I think, upon the whole, that, having performed upon Thomas Bob the operations you suggest, it would be advisable to blacken, with your fists, both his eyes, very carefully and thoroughly, to prevent his ever seeing you again in fashionable promenades. After doing this, I really do not perceive that you can do any more. However—it might be just as well to roll him once or twice in the gutter, and then put him in charge of the police. Any time the next morning you can call at the watch-house and swear an assault."

I was much affected by the kindness of feeling towards me personally, which was evinced in this excellent advice of Mr. Crab, and I did not fail to profit by it forthwith. The result was, that I got rid of the old bore, and began to feel a little independent and gentleman-like. The want of money, however, was, for a few weeks, a source of some discomfort; but at length, by carefully putting to use my two eyes, and observing how matters went just in front of my nose, I perceived how the thing was to be brought about. I say "thing"—be it observed—for they tell me the Latin for it is *rem*. By the way, talking of Latin, can any one tell me the meaning of *quocunque*—or what is the meaning of *modo?*[30]

My plan was exceedingly simple. I bought, for a song, a sixteenth of the "Snapping-Turtle:"—that was all. The thing was *done*, and I put money in my purse. There were some trivial arrangements afterwards, to be sure; but these formed no portion of the plan. They were a consequence—a result. For example, I bought pen, ink and paper, and put them into furious activity. Having thus completed a Magazine article, I gave it, for appellation, "FOL-LOL, *by the Author of* 'THE OIL-OF-BOB,' " and enveloped it to the "Goosetherumfoodle." That journal, however, having pronounced it "twattle" in the "Monthly Notices to Correspondents," I reheaded the paper " 'Hey-Diddle-Diddle' by THINGUM BOB, Esq., Author of the Ode on 'The Oil-of-Bob,' *and* Editor of the 'Snapping-Turtle.' " With this amendment, I reenclosed it to the "Goosetherumfoodle," and, while I awaited a reply, published daily, in the "Turtle," six columns of what may be termed philosophical and analytical investigation of the literary merits of the "Goosetherumfoodle," as well as of the personal character of the editor of the "Goosetherumfoodle." At the end of a week the "Goosetherumfoodle" discovered that it had, by some odd mistake, "confounded a stupid article, headed 'Hey-Diddle-Diddle' and composed by some unknown ignoramus, with a gem of resplendent lustre similarly entitled, the work of Thingum Bob, Esq., the celebrated author of 'The Oil-of-Bob.' " The "Goosetherumfoodle" deeply "regretted this very natural accident," and promised, moreover, an insertion of the *genuine* "Hey-Diddle-Diddle" in the very next number of the Magazine.

The fact is I *thought*—I *really* thought—I thought at the time—I thought *then*—and have no reason for thinking otherwise *now*—that the "Goosetherumfoodle" *did* make a mistake. With the best intentions in the world, I never knew any thing that made as many singular mistakes as the "Goosetherumfoodle." From that day I took a liking to the "Goosetherumfoodle," and the result was I soon saw into the very depths of its literary merits, and did not fail to expatiate upon them, in

the "Turtle," whenever a fitting opportunity occurred. And it is to be regarded as a very peculiar coincidence—as one of those positively *remarkable* coincidences which set a man to serious thinking—that just such a total revolution of opinion —just such entire *bouleversement*,[31] (as we say in French,)—just such thorough *topsiturviness*, (if I may be permitted to employ a rather forcible term of the Choctaws,) as happened, *pro* and *con*, between myself on the one part, and the "Goosetherumfoodle" on the other, did actually again happen, in a brief period afterwards, and with precisely similar circumstances, in the case of myself and the "Rowdy-Dow," and in the case of myself and the "Hum-Drum."

Thus it was that, by a master-stroke of genius, I at length consummated my triumphs by "putting money in my purse" and thus may be said really and fairly to have commenced that brilliant and eventful career which rendered me illustrious, and which now enables me to say, with Chateaubriand, "I have made history"— "*J'ai fait l'histoire.*"[32]

I have indeed "made history." From the bright epoch which I now record, my actions—my works—are the property of mankind. They are familiar to the world. It is, then, needless for me to detail how, soaring rapidly, I fell heir to the "Lollipop"—how I merged this journal in the "Hum-Drum"—how again I made purchase of the "Rowdy-Dow," thus combining the three periodicals—how, lastly, I effected a bargain for the sole remaining rival, and united all the literature of the country in one magnificent Magazine, known everywhere as the

"Rowdy-Dow, Lollipop, Hum-Drum,

and

GOOSETHERUMFOODLE."

Yes; I have made history. My fame is universal. It extends to the uttermost ends of the earth. You cannot take up a common newspaper in which you shall not see some allusion to the immortal THINGUM BOB. It is Mr. Thingum Bob said so, and Mr. Thingum Bob wrote this, and Mr. Thingum Bob did that. But I am meek and expire with an humble heart. After all, what is it?—this indescribable something which men will persist in terming "genius"? I agree with Buffon—with Hogarth[33]—it is but *diligence* after all.

Look at *me!*—how I labored—how I toiled—how I wrote! Ye Gods, did I *not* write? I knew not the word "ease." By day I adhered to my desk, and at night, a pale student, I consumed the midnight oil. You should have seen me—you *should*. I leaned to the right. I leaned to the left. I sat forward. I sat backward. I sat upon end. I sat *tête baissée*, (as they have it in the Kickapoo,) bowing my head close to the alabaster page. And, through all, I—wrote. Through joy and through sorrow, I, —wrote. Through hunger and through thirst, I—wrote. Through good report and through ill report, I—wrote. Through sunshine and through moonshine, I—wrote. *What* I wrote it is unnecessary to say. The *style!*—that was the thing. I caught it from Fatquack—whizz!—fizz!—and I am giving you a specimen of it now.[34]

THE DUC DE L'OMELETTE

And stepped at once into a
cooler clime.
                Cowper[1]

Keats fell by a criticism. Who was it died of *"The Andromache?"* Ignoble souls!— De L'Omelette perished of an ortolan. *L'histoire en est brève.* Assist me, Spirit of Apicius![2]

A golden cage bore the little winged wanderer, enamored, melting, indolent, to the *Chaussée D'Antin*, from its home in far Peru. From its queenly possessor La Bellissima,[3] to the Duc De L'Omelette, six peers of the empire conveyed the happy bird.

That night the Duc was to sup alone. In the privacy of his bureau he reclined languidly on that ottoman for which he sacrificed his loyalty in outbidding his king,—the notorious ottoman of Cadêt.[4]

He buries his face in the pillow. The clock strikes! Unable to restrain his feelings, his Grace swallows an olive. At this moment the door gently opens to the sound of soft music, and lo! the most delicate of birds is before the most enamored of men! But what inexpressible dismay now overshadows the countenance of the Duc?—"Horreur!—chien!—Baptiste! —l'oiseau! ah, bon Dieu! cet oiseau modeste que tu as déshabillé de ses plumes, et que tu as servi sans papier!"[5] It is superfluous to say more:—the Duc expired in a paroxysm of disgust.

*   *   *

"Ha! ha! ha!" said his Grace on the third day after his decease.

"He! he! he!" replied the Devil faintly, drawing himself up with an air of *hauteur*.[6]

"Why, surely you are not serious," retorted De L'Omelette. "I have sinned— *c'est vrai*[7]—but, my good sir, consider!— you have no actual intention of putting such—such—barbarous threats into execution."

"No *what?*" said his majesty—"come, sir, strip!"

"Strip, indeed!—very pretty i' faith!— no, sir, I shall *not* strip. Who are you, pray, that I, Duc De L'Omelette, Prince de Foie-Gras, just come of age, author of the 'Mazurkiad,' and Member of the Academy, should divest myself at your bidding of the sweetest pantaloons ever made by Bourdon, the daintiest *robe-de-chambre* ever put together by Rombêrt[8]—to say nothing of the taking my hair out of paper —not to mention the trouble I should have in drawing off my gloves?"

"Who am I?—ah, true! I am Baal-Zebub, Prince of the Fly. I took thee, just now, from a rose-wood coffin inlaid with ivory. Thou wast curiously scented, and labelled as per invoice. Belial[9] sent thee, —my Inspector of Cemeteries. The pantaloons, which thou sayest were made by

Bourdon, are an excellent pair of linen drawers, and thy *robe-de-chambre* is a shroud of no scanty dimensions."

"Sir!" replied the Duc, "I am not to be insulted with impunity![10]—Sir! I shall take the earliest opportunity of avenging this insult!—Sir! you shall hear from me! In the meantime *au revoir!*"—and the Duc was bowing himself out of the Satanic presence, when he was interrupted and brought back by a gentleman in waiting. Hereupon his Grace rubbed his eyes, yawned, shrugged his shoulders, reflected. Having become satisfied of his identity, he took a bird's eye view of his whereabouts.

The apartment was superb. Even De L'Omelette pronounced it *bien comme il faut*. It was not its length nor its breadth, —but its height—ah, that was appalling! —There was no ceiling—certainly none— but a dense whirling mass of fiery-colored clouds. His Grace's brain reeled as he glanced upwards. From above, hung a chain of an unknown blood-red metal— its upper end lost, like the city of Boston, *parmi les nues*. From its nether extremity swung a large cresset. The Duc knew it to be a ruby; but from it there poured a light so intense, so still, so terrible, Persia never worshipped such—Gheber[11] never imagined such—Mussulman never dreamed of such when, drugged with opium, he has tottered to a bed of poppies, his back to the flowers, and his face to the God Apollo. The Duc muttered a slight oath, decidedly approbatory.

The corners of the room were rounded into niches.—Three of these were filled with statues of gigantic proportions. Their beauty was Grecian, their deformity Egyptian, their *tout ensemble*[12] French. In the fourth niche the statue was veiled; it was *not* colossal. But then there was a taper ankle, a sandalled foot. De L'Omelette pressed his hand upon his heart, closed his eyes, raised them, and caught his Satanic Majesty—in a blush.

But the paintings!—Kupris! Astarte! Astoreth!—a thousand and the same! And Rafaelle has beheld them! Yes, Rafaelle has been here; for did he not paint the——?[13] and was he not consequently damned? The paintings!—the paintings! O luxury! O love!—who, gazing on those forbidden beauties, shall have eyes for the dainty devices of the golden frames that besprinkle, like stars, the hyacinth and the porphyry walls?

But the Duc's heart is fainting within him. He is not, however, as you suppose, dizzy with magnificence, nor drunk with the ecstatic breath of those innumerable censers. *C'est vrai que de toutes ces choses il a pensé beaucoup—mais!*[14] The Duc De L'Omelette is terror-stricken; for, through the lurid vista which a single uncurtained window is affording, lo! gleams the most ghastly of all fires!

Le pauvre Duc! He could not help imagining that the glorious, the voluptuous, the never-dying melodies which pervaded that hall, as they passed filtered and transmuted through the alchemy of the enchanted window-panes, were the wailings and the howlings of the hopeless and the damned! And there, too!—there!—upon that ottoman!—who could *he* be?—he, the *petit-maitre*—no, the Deity—who sat as if carved in marble, *et qui sourit*, with his pale countenance, *si amèrement?*[15]

Mais il faut agir,—that is to say, a Frenchman never faints outright. Besides, his Grace hated a scene—De L'Omelette is himself again. There were some foils upon a table—some points also. The Duc had studied under B——; *il avait tué ses six hommes.* Now, then, *il peut s'échapper.*[16] He measures two points, and, with a grace inimitable, offers his Majesty the choice. *Horreur!* his Majesty does not fence!

Mais il joue!—how happy a thought! —but his Grace had always an excellent memory. He had dipped in the *"Diable"* of the Abbé Gualtier. Therein it is said *"que le Diable n'ose pas refuser un jeu d'écarté."*[17]

But the chances—the chances! True— desperate; but scarcely more desperate than the Duc. Besides, was he not in the secret?—had he not skimmed over Père Le Brun?—was he not a member of the Club Vingt-un? *"Si je perds,"* said he, *"je serai deux fois perdu*—I shall be double damned—*voilà tout!* (Here his Grace shrugged his shoulders.) *Si je gagne, je reviendrai à mes ortolans—que les cartes soient préparées!"*[18]

His Grace was all care, all attention— his Majesty all confidence. A spectator would have thought of Francis and Charles.[19] His Grace thought of his game. His Majesty did not think; he shuffled. The Duc cut.

The cards are dealt. The trump is turned —it is—it is—the king! No—it was the queen. His Majesty cursed her masculine habiliments. De L'Omelette placed his hand upon his heart.

They play. The Duc counts. The hand is out. His Majesty counts heavily, smiles, and is taking wine. The Duc slips a card.

"C'est à vous à faire," said his Majesty, cutting. His Grace bowed, dealt, and arose from the table *en présentant le Roi.*[20]

His Majesty looked chagrined.

Had Alexander not been Alexander, he would have been Diogenes; and the Duc assured his antagonist in taking leave, *"que s'il n'eût pas été De L'Omelette il n'aurait point d'objection d'être le Diable."*[21]

SOME PASSAGES IN THE LIFE OF A LION

——— *All people went*
Upon their ten toes in wild
wonderment.
Bishop Hall's Satires.[1]

I am—that is to say I *was*—a great man; but I am neither the author of Junius nor the man in the mask; for my name, I believe, is Robert Jones, and I was born somewhere in the city of Fum-Fudge.[2]

The first action of my life was the taking hold of my nose with both hands. My mother saw this and called me a genius;

—my father wept for joy and presented me with a treatise on Nosology. This I mastered before I was breeched.

I now began to feel my way in the science; and soon came to understand that, provided a man had a nose sufficiently conspicuous, he might, by merely following it, arrive at a Lionship. But my attention was not confined to theories alone. Every morning I gave my proboscis a couple of pulls and swallowed a half dozen of drams.

When I came of age my father asked me, one day, if I would step with him into his study.

"My son," said he, when we were seated, "what is the chief end of your existence?"

"My father," I answered, "it is the study of Nosology."

"And what, Robert," he inquired, "is Nosology?"

"Sir," I said, "it is the Science of Noses."

"And can you tell me," he demanded, "what is the meaning of a nose?"

"A nose, my father," I replied, greatly softened, "has been variously defined by about a thousand different authors." [Here I pulled out my watch.] "It is now noon or thereabouts—We shall have time enough to get through with them all before midnight. To commence then:—The nose, according to Bartholinus,[3] is that protuberance—that bump—that excrescence—that——"

—"Will do, Robert," interrupted the good old gentleman. "I am thunderstruck at the extent of your information—I am positively—upon my soul." [Here he closed his eyes and placed his hand upon his heart.] "Come here." [Here he took me by the arm.] "Your education may now be considered as finished—it is high time you should scuffle for yourself—and you cannot do a better thing than merely follow your nose—so—so—so—" [Here he kicked me down stairs and out of the door.]—"so get out of my house and God bless you!"

As I felt within me the divine *afflatus,*[4]

I considered this accident rather fortunate than otherwise. I resolved to be guided by the paternal advice. I determined to follow my nose. I gave it a pull or two upon the spot, and wrote a pamphlet on Nosology forthwith.

All Fum-Fudge was in an uproar.

"Wonderful genius!" said the Quarterly.

"Superb physiologist!" said the Westminster.

"Clever fellow!" said the Foreign.

"Fine writer!" said the Edinburgh.

"Profound thinker!" said the Dublin.

"Great man!" said Bentley.

"Divine soul!" said Fraser.

"One of us!" said Blackwood.

"Who can he be?" said Mrs. Bas-Bleu.[5]

"What can he be?" said big Miss Bas-Bleu.

"Where can he be?" said little Miss Bas-Bleu.—But I paid these people no attention whatever—I just stepped into the shop of an artist.

The Duchess of Bless-my-soul[6] was sitting for her portrait; the Marquis of So-and-So was holding the Duchess' poodle; the Earl of This-and-That was flirting with her salts; and his Royal Highness of Touch-me-Not was leaning upon the back of her chair.

I approached the artist and turned up my nose.

"Oh, beautiful!" sighed her Grace.

"Oh my!" lisped the Marquis.

"Oh shocking!" groaned the Earl.

"Oh abominable!" growled his Royal Highness.

"What will you take for it?" asked the artist.

"For his *nose!*" shouted her Grace.

"A thousand pounds," said I, sitting down.

"A thousand pounds?" inquired the artist, musingly.

"A thousand pounds," said I.

"Beautiful!" said he, entranced.

"A thousand pounds," said I.

"Do you warrant it?" he asked, turning the nose to the light.

"I do," said I, blowing it well.

"Is it *quite* original?" he inquired, touching it with reverence.

"Humph!" said I, twisting it to one side.

"Has *no* copy been taken?" he demanded, surveying it through a microscope.

"None," said I, turning it up.

"*Admirable!*" he ejaculated, thrown quite off his guard by the beauty of the manœuvre.

"A thousand pounds," said I.

"A *thousand* pounds?" said he.

"Precisely," said I.

"A thousand *pounds?*" said he.

"Just so," said I.

"You shall have them," said he, "what a piece of *virtù!*"—So he drew me a check upon the spot, and took a sketch of my nose. I engaged rooms in Jermyn street,[7] and sent her Majesty the ninety-ninth edition of the "Nosology" with a portrait of the proboscis. That sad little rake, the Prince of Wales, invited me to dinner.

We were all lions and *recherchés*.[8]

There was a modern Platonist. He quoted Porphyry, Iamblicus, Plotinus, Proclus, Hierocles, Maximus Tyrius, and Syrianus.[9]

There was a human-perfectibility man. He quoted Turgot, Price, Priestley, Condorcet, De Staël, and the "Ambitious Student in Ill Health."[10]

There was Sir Positive Paradox. He observed that all fools were philosophers, and that all philosophers were fools.[11]

There was Æstheticus Ethix. He spoke of fire, unity, and atoms; bi-part and pre-existent soul; affinity and discord; primitive intelligence and homoömeria.[12]

There was Theologos Theology. He talked of Eusebius and Arianus; heresy and the Council of Nice; Puseyism and consubstantialism; Homoousios and Homoouioisios.[13]

There was Fricassée from the Rocher de Cancale. He mentioned Muriton of red tongue; cauliflowers with *velouté* sauce; veal *à la* St. Menehoult; marinade *à la*

St. Florentin; and orange jellies *en mosaïques*.[14]

There was Bibulus O'Bumper. He touched upon Latour and Markbrünen; upon Mousseux and Chambertin; upon Richebourg and St. George; upon Haubrion, Léonville, and Médoc; upon Barac and Preignac; upon Grâve, and upon St. Péray. He shook his head at Clos de Vougeot, and told, with his eyes shut, the difference between Sherry and Amontillado.[15]

There was Signor Tintontintino from Florence. He discoursed of Cimabué, Arpino, Carpaccio, and Argostino—of the gloom of Caravaggio, of the amenity of Albano, of the colors of Titian, of the frows of Rubens, and of the waggeries of Jan Steen.[16]

There was the President of the Fum Fudge University. He was of opinion that the moon was called Bendis in Thrace, Bubastis in Egypt, Dian in Rome, and Artemis in Greece.[17]

There was a Grand Turk from Stamboul. He could not help thinking that the angels were horses, cocks and bulls; that somebody in the sixth heaven had seventy thousand heads; and that the earth was supported by a sky-blue cow with an incalculable number of green horns.[18]

There was Delphinus Polyglott. He told us what had become of the eighty-three lost tragedies of Æschylus; of the fifty-four orations of Isæus; of the three hundred and ninety-one speeches of Lysias; of the hundred and eighty treatises of Theophrastus; of the eighth book of the Conic Sections of Apollonius; of Pindar's hymns and dithyrambics; and of the five and forty tragedies of Homer Junior.[19]

There was Ferdinand Fitz-Fossillus Feltspar. He informed us all about internal fires and tertiary formations; about aeriforms, fluidiforms, and solidiforms; about quartz and marl; about schist and schorl; about gypsum and trap; about talc and calc; about blende and horn-blende; about mica-slate and pudding-stone; about cyanite and lepidolite; about hæmatite and tremolite; about antimony and chalcedony; about manganese and whatever you please.

There was myself. I spoke of myself;—of myself, of myself, of myself;—of Nosology[,] of my pamphlet, and of myself. I turned up my nose and spoke of myself.

"Marvellous clever man!" said the Prince.

"Superb!" said his guests; and next morning her Grace of Bless-my-soul paid me a visit.

"Will you go to Almacks,[20] pretty creature?" she said, tapping me under the chin.

"Upon honor," said I.

"Nose and all?" she asked.

"As I live," I replied.

"Here then is a card, my life, shall I say you *will* be there?"

"Dear Duchess, with all my heart."

"Pshaw, no!—but with all your nose?"

"Every bit of it, my love," said I:—so I gave it a twist or two, and found myself at Almacks.

The rooms were crowded to suffocation.

"He is coming!" said somebody on the staircase.

"He is coming!" said somebody farther up.

"He is coming!" said somebody farther still.

"He is come!" exclaimed the Duchess —"he is come, the little love!"—and seizing me firmly by both hands, she kissed me thrice upon the nose.[21]

A marked sensation immediately ensued.

"*Diavolo!*"[22] cried Count Capricornutti.

"*Dios guarda!*"[23] muttered Don Stiletto.

"*Mille tonnerres!*"[24] ejaculated the Prince de Grenouille.

"*Tausend teufel!*" growled the Elector of Bluddennuff.[25]

It was not to be borne. I grew angry. I turned short upon Bluddennuff.

"Sir!" said I to him, "you are a baboon."

"Sir," he replied, after a pause, "*Donner und Blitzen!*"

This was all that could be desired. We

exchanged cards. At Chalk-Farm,[26] the next morning, I shot off his nose—and then called upon my friends.

"*Bête!*"[27] said the first.

"Fool!" said the second.

"Dolt!" said the third.

"Ass!" said the fourth.

"Ninny!" said the fifth.

"Noodle!" said the sixth.

"Be off!" said the seventh.

At all this I felt mortified, and so called upon my father.

"Father," I asked, "what is the chief end of my existence?"

"My son," he replied, "it is still the study of Nosology; but in hitting the Elector upon the nose you have overshot your mark. You have a fine nose, it is true; but then Bluddennuff has none. You are damned, and he has become the hero of the day. I grant you that in Fum-Fudge the greatness of a lion is in proportion to the size of his proboscis—but, Good Heavens! there is no competing with a lion who has no proboscis at all."

THE DEVIL IN THE BELFRY[1]

What o'clock is it?
Old Saying.

Everybody knows, in a general way, that the finest place in the world is—or, alas, *was*—the Dutch borough of Vondervotteimittiss. Yet, as it lies some distance from any of the main roads, being in a somewhat out of the way situation, there are, perhaps, very few of my readers who have ever paid it a visit. For the benefit of those who have *not*, therefore, it will be only proper that I should enter into some account of it. And this is, indeed, the more necessary, as with the hope of enlisting public sympathy in behalf of the inhabitants, I design here to give a history of the calamitous events which have so lately occurred within its limits. No one who knows me will doubt that the duty thus self-imposed will be executed to the best of my ability, with all that rigid im-

partiality, all that cautious examination into facts, and diligent collation of authorities which should ever distinguish him who aspires to the title of historian.

By the united aid of medals, manuscripts, and inscriptions, I am enabled to say, positively, that the borough of Vondervotteimittiss has existed, from its origin, in precisely the same condition which it at present preserves. Of the date of this origin, however, I grieve that I can only speak with that species of indefinite definiteness which mathematicians are, at times, forced to put up with in certain algebraic formulæ. The date, I may thus say, in regard to the remoteness of its antiquity, cannot be less than any assignable quantity whatsoever.

Touching the derivation of the name Vondervotteimittiss, I confess myself, with sorrow, equally at fault.—Among a multitude of opinions upon this delicate point, some acute, some learned, some sufficiently the reverse, I am able to select nothing which ought to be considered satisfactory. Perhaps the idea of Grogswigg, nearly coincident with that of Kroutaplenttey, is to be cautiously preferred. It runs:—"*Vondervotteimittiss—Vonder, lege Donder—Votteimittiss, quasi und Bleitziz—Bleitziz obsol: pro Blitzen.*" This derivation, to say the truth, is still countenanced by some traces of the electric fluid evident on the summit of the steeple of the House of the Town-Council. I do not choose, however, to commit myself on a theme of such importance, and must refer the reader desirous of information, to the "*Oratiunculæ de Rebus Præter-Veteris,*" of Dundergutz. See, also, Blunderbuzzard "*De Derivationibus,*" pp. 27 to 5010, Folio Gothic edit., Red and Black character, Catch-word and No Cypher;[2]—wherein consult, also, marginal notes in the autograph of Stuffundpuff, with the Sub-Commentaries of Gruntundguzzell.

Notwithstanding the obscurity which thus envelops the date of the foundation of Vondervotteimittiss, and the derivation of its name, there can be no doubt, as I said before, that it has always existed as we find it at this epoch. The oldest man in the borough can remember not the slightest difference in the appearance of any portion of it; and, indeed, the very suggestion of such a possibility is considered an insult. The site of the village is in a perfectly circular valley, about a quarter of a mile in circumference, and entirely surrounded by gentle hills, over whose summit the people have never yet ventured to pass. For this they assign the very good reason that they do not believe there is anything at all on the other side.

Round the skirts of the valley, (which is quite level, and paved throughout with flat tiles,) extends a continuous row of sixty little houses. These, having their backs on the hills, must look, of course, to the centre of the plain, which is just sixty yards from the front door of each dwelling. Every house has a small garden before it, with a circular path, a sun-dial, and twenty-four cabbages. The buildings themselves are so precisely alike, that one can in no manner be distinguished from the other. Owing to the vast antiquity, the style of architecture is somewhat odd, but it is not for that reason the less strikingly picturesque. They are fashioned of hard-burned little bricks, red, with black ends, so that the walls look like a chess-board upon a great scale. The gables are turned to the front, and there are cornices, as big as all the rest of the house, over the eaves and over the main doors. The windows are narrow and deep, with very tiny panes and a great deal of sash. On the roof is a vast quantity of tiles with long curly ears. The woodwork, throughout, is of a dark hue, and there is much carving about it, with but a trifling variety of pattern; for, time out of mind, the carvers of Vondervotteimittiss have never been able to carve more than two objects—a time-piece and a cabbage.[3] But these they do exceedingly well, and intersperse them, with singular ingenuity, wherever they find room for the chisel.

The dwellings are as much alike inside as out, and the furniture is all upon one plan. The floors are of square tiles, the chairs and tables of black-looking wood with thin crooked legs and puppy feet. The mantel-pieces are wide and high, and have not only time-pieces and cabbages sculptured over the front, but a real time-piece, which makes a prodigious ticking, on the top in the middle, with a flower-pot containing a cabbage standing on each extremity by way of outrider. Between each cabbage and the time-piece again, is a little china man having a large stomach with a great round hole in it, through which is seen the dial-plate of a watch.

The fire-places are large and deep, with fierce crooked-looking fire-dogs. There is constantly a rousing fire, and a huge pot over it full of sauer-kraut and pork, to which the good woman of the house is always busy in attending. She is a little fat old lady, with blue eyes and a red face, and wears a huge cap like a sugar-loaf, ornamented with purple and yellow ribbons. Her dress is of orange-colored linsey-woolsey made very full behind and very short in the waist—and indeed very short in other respects, not reaching below the middle of her leg. This is somewhat thick, and so are her ankles, but she has a fine pair of green stockings to cover them. Her shoes, of pink leather, are fastened each with a bunch of yellow ribbons puckered up in the shape of a cabbage. In her left hand she has a little heavy Dutch watch; in her right she wields a ladle for the sauer-kraut and pork. By her side there stands a fat tabby cat, with a gilt toy repeater tied to its tail, which "the boys" have there fastened by way of a quiz.[4]

The boys themselves are, all three of them, in the garden attending the pig. They are each two feet in height. They have three-cornered cocked hats, purple waistcoats reaching down to their thighs, buckskin knee-breeches, red woollen stockings, heavy shoes with big silver buckles, and long surtout coats with large buttons of mother of pearl. Each, too, has a pipe in his mouth, and a little dumpy watch in his right hand. He takes a puff and a look, and then a look and a puff. The pig, which is corpulent and lazy, is occupied now in picking up the stray leaves that fall from the cabbages, and now in giving a kick behind at the gilt repeater, which the urchins have also tied to *his* tail, in order to make him look as handsome as the cat.

Right at the front door, in a high-backed leather-bottomed armed chair, with crooked legs and puppy feet like the tables, is seated the old man of the house himself.—He is an exceedingly puffy little old gentleman, with big circular eyes and a huge double chin. His dress resembles that of the boys, and I need say nothing farther about it. All the difference is that his pipe is somewhat bigger than theirs, and he can make a greater smoke. —Like them, he has a watch, but he carries his watch in his pocket. To say the truth, he has something of more importance than a watch to attend to, and what that is I shall presently explain. He sits with his right leg upon his left knee, wears a grave countenance, and always keeps one of his eyes, at least, resolutely bent upon a certain remarkable object in the centre of the plain.

This object is situated in the steeple of the House of the Town-Council. The Town-Council are all very little, round, oily, intelligent men, with big saucer eyes and fat double chins, and have their coats much longer and their shoe-buckles much bigger than the ordinary inhabitants of Vondervotteimittiss. Since my sojourn in the borough they have had several special meetings, and have adopted these three important resolutions:

"That it is wrong to alter the good old course of things—"

"That there is nothing tolerable out of Vondervotteimittiss—" and

"That we will stick by our clocks and our cabbages."

Above the session room of the Council is the steeple, and in the steeple is the belfry, where exists, and has existed time out of mind, the pride and wonder of the village—the great clock of the borough of Vondervotteimittiss. And this is the object to which the eyes of the old gentlemen are turned who sit in the leather-bottomed arm chairs.

The great clock has seven faces—one in each of the seven sides of the steeple —so that it can be readily seen from all quarters. Its faces are large and white, and its hands heavy and black. There is a belfry-man whose sole duty is to attend to it; but this duty is the most perfect of sinecures, for the clock of Vondervotteimittiss was never yet known to have anything the matter with it.—Until lately the bare supposition of such a thing was considered heretical. From the remotest period of antiquity to which the archives have reference, the hours have been regularly struck by the big bell. And, indeed, the case was just the same with all the other clocks and watches in the borough. Never was such a place for keeping the true time. When the large clapper thought proper to say "twelve o'clock!" all its obedient followers opened their throats simultaneously, and responded like a very echo. In short the good burghers were fond of their sauer-kraut, but then they were proud of their clocks.

All people who hold sinecure offices are held in more or less respect, and as the belfry-man of Vondervotteimittiss has the most perfect of sinecures, he is the most perfectly respected of any man in the world. He is the chief dignitary of the borough, and the very pigs look up to him with a sentiment of reverence. His coat-tail is *very* far longer—his pipe, his shoe-buckles, his eyes, and his stomach, *very* far bigger than those of any other old gentleman in the village; and as to his chin, it is not only double but triple.

I have thus painted the happy estate of Vondervotteimittiss: alas, that so fair a picture should ever experience a reverse!

There has been long a saying among the wisest inhabitants that "no good can come from over the hills," and it really seemed that the words had in them something of the spirit of prophecy. It wanted five minutes of noon, on the day before yesterday, when there appeared a very odd-looking object on the summit of the ridge to the eastward. Such an occurrence, of course, attracted universal attention, and every little old gentleman who sat in a leather-bottomed arm-chair, turned one of his eyes with a stare of dismay upon the phenomenon, still keeping the other upon the clock in the steeple.

By the time that it wanted only three minutes to noon, the droll object in question was perceived to be a very diminutive foreign-looking young man. He descended the hills at a great rate, so that everybody had soon a good look at him. He was really the most finnicky little personage that had ever been seen in Vondervotteimittiss. His countenance was of a dark snuff-colour, and he had a long hooked nose, pea eyes, a wide mouth, and an excellent set of teeth, which latter he seemed anxious of displaying, as he was grinning from ear to ear. What with mustachios and whiskers there was none of the rest of his face to be seen. His head was uncovered, and his hair neatly done up in *papillotes*. His dress was a tight-fitting swallow-tailed black coat (from one of whose pockets dangled a vast length of white handkerchief,) black kerseymere knee-breeches, black stockings, and stumpy-looking pumps, with huge bunches of black satin ribbon for bows. Under one arm he carried a huge *chapeau-de-bras*,[5] and under the other a fiddle nearly five times as big as himself. In his left hand was a gold snuff-box, from which, as he capered down the hill, cutting all manner of fantastical steps, he took snuff incessantly with an air of the greatest possible self-satisfaction. God bless me! here was a sight for the honest burghers of Vondervotteimittiss!

To speak plainly, the fellow had, in spite of his grinning, an audacious and sinister kind of face; and as he curvetted right into the village, the odd stumpy appearance of his pumps excited no little suspicion, and many a burgher who beheld him that day would have given a trifle for a peep beneath the white cambric handkerchief which hung so obtrusively from the pocket of his swallow-tailed coat. But what mainly occasioned a righteous indignation was, that the scoundrelly popinjay, while he cut a fandango here, and a whirligig there, did not seem to have the remotest idea in the world of such a thing as *keeping time*[6] in his steps.

The good people of the borough had scarcely a chance, however, to get their eyes thoroughly open, when, just as it wanted half a minute of noon, the rascal bounced, as I say, right into the midst of them; gave a *chassez* here and a *balancez* there; and then, after a *pirouette* and a *pas-de-zéphyr*, pigeon-winged[7] himself right up into the belfry of the House of the Town-Council, where the wonder-stricken belfry-man sat smoking in a state of dignity and dismay. But the little chap seized him at once by the nose; gave it a swing and a pull; clapped the big *chapeau-de-bras* upon his head; knocked it down over his eyes and mouth; and then, lifting up the big fiddle, beat him with it so long and so soundly, that what with the belfry-man being so fat, and the fiddle being so hollow, you would have sworn that there was a regiment of double-bass drummers all beating the devil's tattoo up in the belfry of the steeple of Vondervotteimittiss.

There is no knowing to what desperate act of vengeance this unprincipled attack might have aroused the inhabitants, but for the important fact that it now wanted only half a second of noon. The bell was about to strike, and it was a matter of absolute and pre-eminent necessity that everybody should look well at his watch. It was evident, however, that just at this moment, the fellow in the steeple was doing something that he had no business to do with the clock. But as it now began to strike, nobody had any time to attend to his manœuvres, for they had all to count the strokes of the bell as it sounded.

"One!" said the clock.

"Von!" echoed every little old gentleman in every leather-bottomed arm-chair in Vondervotteimittiss—"Von!" said his watch also; "von!" said the watch of his vrow[8] and "von!" said the watches of the boys, and the little gilt repeaters on the tails of the cat and pig.

"Two!" continued the big bell; and

"Doo!" repeated all the repeaters.

"Three! Four! Five! Six! Seven! Eight! Nine! Ten!" said the bell.

"Dree! Vour! Fibe! Sax! Seben! Aight! Noin! Den!" answered the others.

"Eleven!" said the big one.

"Eleben!" assented the little fellows.

"Twelve!" said the bell.

"Dvelf!" they replied, perfectly satisfied, and dropping their voices.

"Und dvelf it iss!" said all the little old gentlemen, putting up their watches. But the big bell had not done with them yet.

"Thirteen!" said he.

"Der Teufel!"[9] gasped the little old gentlemen, turning pale, dropping their pipes, and putting down all their right legs from over their left knees.

"Der Teufel!" groaned they, "Dirteen! Dirteen!!—Mein Gott, it is—it is Dirteen o'clock!!"

Why attempt to describe the terrible scene which ensued? All Vondervotteimittiss flew at once into a lamentable state of uproar.

"Vot is cum'd to mein pelly?" roared all the boys,—"I've been ongry for dis hour!"

"Vot is cum'd to mein kraut?" screamed all the vrows, "It has been done to rags for dis hour!"

"Vot is cum'd to mein pipe?" swore all the little old gentlemen, "Donder and Blitzen! it has been smoked out for dis hour!"—and they filled them up again in a great rage, and, sinking back in their arm-chairs, puffed away so fast and so fiercely that the whole valley was immediately filled with impenetrable smoke.

Meantime the cabbages all turned very red in the face, and it seemed as if old Nick himself had taken possession of everything in the shape of a time-piece. The clocks carved upon the furniture took to dancing as if bewitched, while those upon the mantel-pieces could scarcely contain themselves for fury, and kept such a continual striking of thirteen, and such a frisking and wriggling of their pendulums as was really horrible to see.—But, worse than all, neither the cats nor the pigs could put up any longer with the behaviour of the little repeaters tied to their tails, and resented it by scampering all over the place, scratching and poking, and squeaking and screeching, and caterwauling and squalling, and flying into the faces, and running under the petticoats of the people, and creating altogether the most abominable din and confusion which it is possible for a reasonable person to conceive. And to make matters still more distressing, the rascally little scapegrace in the steeple was evidently exerting himself to the utmost.—Every now and then one might catch a glimpse of the scoundrel through the smoke. There he sat in the belfry upon the belfry-man, who was lying flat upon his back. In his teeth the villain held the bell-rope, which he kept jerking about with his head, raising such a clatter that my ears ring again even to think of it. On his lap lay the big fiddle at which he was scraping out of all time and tune, with both hands, making a great show, the nincompoop! of playing "Judy O'Flannagan and Paddy O'Rafferty."[10]

Affairs being thus miserably situated, I left the place in disgust, and now appeal for aid to all lovers of correct time and fine kraut. Let us proceed in a body to the borough, and restore the ancient order of things in Vondervotteimittiss by ejecting that little fellow from the steeple.

BON-BON[1]

Quand un bon vin meuble
    mon estomac,
Je suis plus savant que Balzac—
Plus sage que Pibrac;
Mon bras seul faisant l'attaque
De la nation Cossaque,
La mettroit au sac;
De Charon je passerois le lac
En dormant dans son bac;
J'irois au fier Eac,
Sans que mon cœur fît tic ni tac,
Présenter du tabac.
                French Vaudeville.[2]

That Pierre Bon-Bon was a *restaurateur* of uncommon qualifications, no man who, during the reign of ——, frequented the little Café in the cul-de-sac Le Febvre at Rouen, will, I imagine, feel himself at liberty to dispute. That Pierre Bon-Bon was, in an equal degree, skilled in the philosophy of that period is, I presume, still more especially undeniable. His *pâtés à la foie* were beyond doubt immaculate: but what pen can do justice to his essays *sur la Nature*—his thoughts *sur l'Ame*—his observations *sur l'Esprit?* If his *omelettes*—if his *fricandeaux* were inestimable, what *littérateur* of that day would not have given twice as much for an *"Idée de Bon-Bon"* as for all the trash of all the *"Idées"* of all the rest of the *savants?* Bon-Bon had ransacked libraries which no other man had ransacked—had read more than any other would have entertained a notion of reading—had understood more than any other would have conceived the possibility of understanding; and although, while he flourished, there were not wanting some authors at Rouen to assert "that his *dicta* evinced neither the purity of the Academy, nor the depth of the Lyceum"—although, mark me, his doctrines were by no means very generally comprehended, still it did not follow that they were difficult of comprehension. It was, I think, on account of their self-evidency that many persons were led to consider them abstruse. It is to Bon-Bon—but let this go no farther—it is to Bon-Bon that Kant himself is mainly indebted for his metaphys-ics. The former was indeed not a Platonist, nor strictly speaking an Aristotelian—nor did he, like the modern Leibnitz, waste those precious hours which might be employed in the invention of a *fricassée,* or, *facili gradu,* the analysis of a sensation, in frivolous attempts at reconciling the obstinate oils and waters of ethical discussion. Not at all. Bon-Bon was Ionic—Bon-Bon was equally Italic. He reasoned *à priori.*—He reasoned also *à posteriori.* His ideas were innate—or otherwise. He believed in George of Trebizond—He believed in Bossarion.[3] Bon-Bon was emphatically a—Bon-Bonist.

I have spoken of the philosopher in his capacity of *restaurateur.* I would not, however, have any friend of mine imagine that, in fulfilling his hereditary duties in that line, our hero wanted a proper estimation of their dignity and importance. Far from it. It was impossible to say in which branch of his profession he took the greater pride. In his opinion the powers of the intellect held intimate connection with the capabilities of the stomach. I am not sure, indeed, that he greatly disagreed with the Chinese, who hold that the soul lies in the abdomen. The Greeks at all events were right, he thought, who employed the same word for the mind and the diaphragm. By this I do not mean to insinuate a charge of gluttony, or indeed any other serious charge to the prejudice of the metaphysician. If Pierre Bon-Bon had his failings—and what great man has not a thousand?—if Pierre Bon-Bon, I say, had his failings, they were failings of very little importance—faults indeed which, in other tempers, have often been looked upon rather in the light of virtues. As regards one of these foibles, I should not even have mentioned it in this history but for the remarkable prominency —the extreme *alto rilievo*[4]—in which it jutted out from the plane of his general disposition.—He could never let slip an opportunity of making a bargain.

Not that he was avaricious—no. It was by no means necessary to the satisfaction of the philosopher, that the bargain should be to his own proper advantage. Provided a trade could be effected—a trade of any kind, upon any terms, or under any circumstances—a triumphant smile was seen for many days thereafter to enlighten his countenance, and a knowing wink of the eye to give evidence of his sagacity.

At any epoch it would not be very wonderful if a humor so peculiar as the one I have just mentioned, should elicit attention and remark. At the epoch of our narrative, had this peculiarity *not* attracted observation, there would have been room for wonder indeed. It was soon reported that, upon all occasions of the kind, the smile of Bon-Bon was wont to differ widely from the downright grin with which he would laugh at his own jokes, or welcome an acquaintance. Hints were thrown out of an exciting nature; stories were told of perilous bargains made in a hurry and repented of at leisure; and instances were adduced of unaccountable capacities, vague longings, and unnatural inclinations implanted by the author of all evil for wise purposes of his own.

The philosopher had other weaknesses —but they are scarcely worthy our serious examination. For example, there are few men of extraordinary profundity who are found wanting in an inclination for the bottle. Whether this inclination be an exciting cause, or rather a valid proof, of such profundity, it is a nice thing to say. Bon-Bon, as far as I can learn, did not think the subject adapted to minute investigation;—nor do I. Yet in the indulgence of a propensity so truly classical, it is not to be supposed that the *restaurateur* would lose sight of that intuitive discrimination which was wont to characterise, at one and the same time, his *essais* and his *omelettes*. In his seclusions the Vin de Bourgogne had its allotted hour, and there were appropriate moments for the Côtes du Rhone. With him Sauterne was to Médoc what Catullus was to Homer. He would sport with a syllogism in sipping St. Péray, but unravel an argument over

Clos de Vougeot, and upset a theory in a torrent of Chambertin. Well had it been if the same quick sense of propriety had attended him in the peddling propensity to which I have formerly alluded—but this was by no means the case. Indeed, to say the truth, *that* trait of mind in the philosophic Bon-Bon *did* begin at length to assume a character of strange intensity and mysticism, and appeared deeply tinctured with the *diablerie*[5] of his favorite German studies.

To enter the little *Café* in the *Cul-de-Sac* Le Febvre was, at the period of our tale, to enter the *sanctum* of a man of genius. Bon-Bon was a man of genius. There was not a *sous-cuisinier*[6] in Rouen, who could not have told you that Bon-Bon was a man of genius. His very cat knew it, and forebore to whisk her tail in the presence of the man of genius. His large water-dog was acquainted with the fact, and upon the approach of his master, betrayed his sense of inferiority by a sanctity of deportment, a debasement of the ears, and a dropping of the lower jaw not altogether unworthy of a dog. It is, however, true that much of this habitual respect might have been attributed to the personal appearance of the metaphysician. A distinguished exterior will, I am constrained to say, have its weight even with a beast; and I am willing to allow much in the outward man of the *restaurateur* calculated to impress the imagination of the quadruped. There is a peculiar majesty about the atmosphere of the little great— if I may be permitted so equivocal an expression—which mere physical bulk alone will be found at all times inefficient in creating. If, however, Bon-Bon was barely three feet in height, and if his head was diminutively small, still it was impossible to behold the rotundity of his stomach without a sense of magnificence nearly bordering upon the sublime. In its size both dogs and men must have seen a type of his acquirements—in its immensity a fitting habitation for his immortal soul.

I might here—if it so pleased me—dilate upon the matter of habiliment, and other mere circumstances of the external metaphysician. I might hint that the hair of our hero was worn short, combed smoothly over his forehead, and surmounted by a conical-shaped white flannel cap and tassels—that his pea-green jerkin was not after the fashion of those worn by the common class of *restaurateurs* at that day—that the sleeves were something fuller than the reigning costume permitted—that the cuffs were turned up, not as usual in that barbarous period, with cloth of the same quality and color as the garment, but faced in a more fanciful manner with the particolored velvet of Genoa—that his slippers were of a bright purple, curiously filagreed, and might have been manufactured in Japan, but for the exquisite pointing of the toes, and the brilliant tints of the binding and embroidery—that his breeches were of the yellow satin-like material called *aimable*—that his sky-blue cloak, resembling in form a dressing-wrapper, and richly bestudded all over with crimson devices, floated cavalierly upon his shoulders like a mist of the morning—and that his *tout ensemble* gave rise to the remarkable words of Benevenuta,[7] the Improvisatrice of Florence, "that it was difficult to say whether Pierre Bon-Bon was indeed a bird of Paradise, or the rather a very Paradise of perfection."—I might, I say, expatiate upon all these points if I pleased;—but I forbear:—merely personal details may be left to historical novelists;—they are beneath the moral dignity of matter-of-fact.

I have said that "to enter the *Café* in the *Cul-de-Sac* Le Febvre was to enter the *sanctum* of a man of genius"—but then it was only the man of genius who could duly estimate the merits of the *sanctum.* A sign consisting of a vast folio swung before the entrance. On one side of the volume was painted a bottle; on the reverse a *pâté.* On the back were visible in large letters Œuvres de Bon-Bon.[8] Thus was delicately shadowed forth the two-fold occupation of the proprietor.

Upon stepping over the threshold the whole interior of the building presented itself to view. A long, low-pitched room, of antique construction, was indeed all the accommodation afforded by the *Café.* In a corner of the apartment stood the bed of the metaphysician. An array of curtains, together with a canopy *à la Grecque,* gave it an air at once classic and comfortable. In the corner diagonally opposite, appeared, in direct family communion, the properties of the kitchen and the *bibliothèque.* A dish of polemics stood peacefully upon the dresser. Here lay an oven-full of the latest ethics—there a kettle of duodecimo *mélanges.* Volumes of German morality were hand and glove with the gridrion—a toasting fork might be discovered by the side of Eusebius[9]— Plato reclined at his ease in the frying pan —and contemporary manuscripts were filed away upon the spit.

In other respects the *Café de Bon-Bon* might be said to differ little from the usual *restaurants* of the period. A large fireplace yawned opposite the door. On the right of the fire-place an open cupboard displayed a formidable array of labelled bottles.

It was here, about twelve o'clock one night, during the severe winter of ——, that Pierre Bon-Bon, after having listened for some time to the comments of his neighbours upon his singular propensity —that Pierre Bon-Bon, I say, having turned them all out of his house, locked the door upon them with an oath, and betook himself in no very pacific mood to the comforts of a leather-bottomed armchair, and a fire of blazing faggots.

It was one of those terrific nights which are only met with once or twice during a century. It snowed fiercely, and the house tottered to its centre with the floods of wind that, rushing through the crannies in the wall, and pouring impetuously down the chimney, shook awfully the curtains of the philosopher's bed, and disorganised the economy of his pâté-pans and papers. The huge folio sign that swung without, exposed to the fury of the tempest, creaked ominously, and gave out a moaning sound from its stanchions of solid oak.

It was in no placid temper, I say, that the metaphysician drew up his chair to its customary station by the hearth. Many circumstances of a perplexing nature had occurred during the day, to disturb the serenity of his meditations. In attempting des œufs à la Princesse he had unfortunately perpetrated an omelette à la Reine;[10] the discovery of a principle in ethics had been frustrated by the overturning of a stew; and last, not least, he had been thwarted in one of those admirable bargains which he at all times took such especial delight in bringing to a successful termination. But in the chafing of his mind at these unaccountable vicissitudes, there did not fail to be mingled some degree of that nervous anxiety which the fury of a boisterous night is so well calculated to produce. Whistling to his more immediate vicinity the large black water-dog we have spoken of before, and settling himself uneasily in his chair, he could not help casting a wary and unquiet eye towards those distant recesses of the apartment whose inexorable shadows not even the red fire-light itself could more than partially succeed in overcoming. Having completed a scrutiny whose exact purpose was perhaps unintelligible to himself, he drew close to his seat a small table covered with books and papers, and soon became absorbed in the task of retouching a voluminous manuscript, intended for publication on the morrow.

He had been thus occupied for some minutes, when "I am in no hurry, Monsieur Bon-Bon," suddenly whispered a whining voice in the apartment.

"The devil!" ejaculated our hero, starting to his feet, overturning the table at his side, and staring around him in astonishment.

"Very true," calmly replied the voice. "Very true!—what is very true?—how came you here?" vociferated the metaphysician, as his eye fell upon something which lay stretched at full length upon the bed.

"I was saying," said the intruder, without attending to the interrogatories, "I was saying that I am not at all pushed for time—that the business upon which I took the liberty of calling is of no pressing importance—in short that I can very well wait until you have finished your Exposition."

"My Exposition!—there now!—how do you know?—how came you to understand that I was writing an exposition?—good God!"

"Hush!" replied the figure, in a shrill under tone: and, arising quickly from the bed, he made a single step towards our hero, while an iron lamp that depended overhead swung convulsively back from his approach.[11]

The philosopher's amazement did not prevent a narrow scrutiny of the stranger's dress and appearance. The outlines of a figure, exceedingly lean, but much above the common height, were rendered minutely distinct by means of a faded suit of black cloth which fitted tight to the skin, but was otherwise cut very much in the style of a century ago. These garments had evidently been intended for a much shorter person than their present owner. His ankles and wrists were left naked for several inches. In his shoes, however, a pair of very brilliant buckles gave the lie to the extreme poverty implied by the other portions of his dress. His head was bare, and entirely bald, with the exception of the hinder part, from which depended a queue of considerable length. A pair of green spectacles, with side glasses, protected his eyes from the influence of the light, and at the same time prevented our hero from ascertaining either their color or their conformation. About the entire person there was no evidence of a shirt; but a white cravat, of filthy appearance, was tied with extreme precision around the throat, and the ends, hanging down formally side by side, gave (although I dare say unintentionally) the idea of an ecclesiastic. Indeed, many other points both in his appearance and demeanour might have very well sustained a conception of that nature. Over his left ear, he carried, after the fashion of a modern clerk, an instrument resembling the *stylus* of the ancients. In a breast-pocket of his coat appeared conspicuously a small black volume fastened with clasps of steel. This book, whether accidentally or not, was so turned outwardly from the person as to discover the words *"Rituel Catholique"*[12] in white letters upon the back. His entire physiognomy was interestingly saturnine —even cadaverously pale. The forehead was lofty, and deeply furrowed with the ridges of contemplation. The corners of the mouth were drawn down into an expression of the most submissive humility. There was also a clasping of the hands, as he stepped towards our hero—a deep sigh—and altogether a look of such utter sanctity as could not have failed to be unequivocally prepossessing. Every shadow of anger faded from the countenance of the metaphysician, as, having completed a satisfactory survey of his visiter's person, he shook him cordially by the hand, and conducted him to a seat.

There would however be a radical error in attributing this instantaneous transition of feeling in the philosopher, to any one of those causes which might naturally be supposed to have had an influence. Indeed Pierre Bon-Bon, from what I have been able to understand of his disposition, was of all men the least likely to be imposed upon by any speciousness of exterior deportment. It was impossible that so accurate an observer of men and things should have failed to discover, upon the moment, the real character of the personage who had thus intruded upon his hospitality. To say no more, the conformation of his visiter's feet was sufficiently

remarkable—he maintained lightly upon his head an inordinately tall hat—there was a tremulous swelling about the hinder part of his breeches—and the vibration of his coat tail was a palpable fact. Judge then with what feelings of satisfaction our hero found himself thrown thus at once into the society of a person for whom he had at all times entertained the most unqualified respect. He was, however, too much of the diplomatist to let escape him any intimation of his suspicions in regard to the true state of affairs. It was not his cue to appear at all conscious of the high honor he thus unexpectedly enjoyed, but by leading his guest into conversation, to elicit some important ethical ideas, which might, in obtaining a place in his contemplated publication, enlighten the human race, and at the same time immortalize himself— ideas which, I should have added, his visiter's great age, and well known proficiency in the science of morals, might very well have enabled him to afford.

Actuated by these enlightened views, our hero bade the gentleman sit down, while he himself took occasion to throw some faggots upon the fire, and place upon the now re-established table some bottles of *Mousseux*. Having quickly completed these operations, he drew his chair *vis-à-vis*[13] to his companion's and waited until the latter should open the conversation. But plans even the most skillfully matured are often thwarted in the outset of their application, and the *restaurateur* found himself *nonplussed* by the very first words of his visiter's speech.

"I see you know me, Bon-Bon," said he: "ha! ha! ha!—he! he! he!—hi! hi! hi!— ho! ho! ho!—hu! hu! hu!"—and the devil, dropping at once the sanctity of his demeanour, opened to its fullest extent a mouth from ear to ear, so as to display a set of jagged and fang-like teeth, and throwing back his head, laughed long, loudly, wickedly, and uproariously, while the black dog, crouching down upon his haunches, joined lustily in the chorus, and the tabby cat, flying off at a tangent, stood up on end and shrieked in the farthest corner of the apartment.

Not so the philosopher; he was too much a man of the world either to laugh like the dog, or by shrieks to betray the indecorous trepidation of the cat. It must be confessed, he felt a little astonishment to see the white letters which formed the words "*Rituel Catholique*" on the book in his guest's pocket, momently changing both their color and their import, and in a few seconds, in place of the original title, the words *Regître des Condamnés*[14] blaze forth in characters of red. This startling circumstance, when Bon-Bon replied to his visiter's remark, imparted to his manner an air of embarrassment which probably might not otherwise have been observed.

"Why, sir," said the philosopher, "why, sir, to speak sincerely—I believe you are —upon my word—the d——dest—that is to say I think—I imagine—I *have* some faint—some *very* faint idea—of the remarkable honor——"

"Oh!—ah!—yes!—very well!" interrupted his Majesty; "say no more—I see how it is." And hereupon, taking off his green spectacles, he wiped the glasses carefully with the sleeve of his coat, and deposited them in his pocket.

If Bon-Bon had been astonished at the incident of the book, his amazement was now much increased by the spectacle which here presented itself to view. In raising his eyes, with a strong feeling of curiosity to ascertain the color of his guest's, he found them by no means black, as he had anticipated—nor gray, as might have been imagined—nor yet hazel nor blue—nor indeed yellow nor red—nor purple—nor white—nor green—nor any other color in the heavens above, or in the earth beneath, or in the waters under the earth. In short Pierre Bon-Bon not only saw plainly that his Majesty had no eyes whatsoever, but could discover no indications of their having existed at any previous period; for the space where eyes should naturally have been, was, I am constrained to say, simply a dead level of flesh.

It was not in the nature of the metaphysician to forbear making some inquiry into the sources of so strange a phenomenon, and the reply of his Majesty was at once prompt, dignified, and satisfactory.

"Eyes! my dear Bon-Bon, eyes! did you say?—oh! ah!—I perceive! The ridiculous prints, eh? which are in circulation, have given you a false idea of my personal appearance. Eyes!!!—true. Eyes, Pierre Bon-Bon, are very well in their proper place —*that*, you would say, is the head?—right —the head of a worm. To *you* likewise these optics are indispensable—yet I will convince you that my vision is more penetrating than your own. There is a cat, I see in the corner—a pretty cat—look at her!—observe her well! Now, Bon-Bon, do you behold the thoughts—the thoughts, I say—the ideas—the reflections—which are being engendered in her pericranium? There it is now!—you do not. She is thinking we admire the length of her tail and the profundity of her mind. She has just concluded that I am the most distinguished of ecclesiastics, and that you are the most superfluous of metaphysicians. Thus you see I am not altogether blind: but to one of my profession the eyes you speak of would be merely an encumbrance, liable at any time to be put out by a toasting iron or a pitchfork. To you, I allow, these optical affairs are indispensable. Endeavor, Bon-Bon, to use them well;—*my* vision is the soul."

Hereupon the guest helped himself to the wine upon the table, and pouring out a bumper for Bon-Bon, requested him to drink it without scruple, and make himself perfectly at home.

"A clever book that of yours, Pierre," resumed his Majesty, tapping our friend knowingly upon the shoulder, as the latter put down his glass after a thorough compliance with his visiter's injunction. "A clever book that of yours, upon my honor. It's a work after my own heart.

Your arrangement of matter, I think, however, might be improved, and many of your notions remind me of Aristotle. That philosopher was one of my most intimate acquaintances. I liked him as much for his terrible ill temper, as for his happy knack at making a blunder. There is only one solid truth in all that he has written, and for that I gave him the hint out of pure compassion for his absurdity. I suppose, Pierre Bon-Bon, you very well know to what divine moral truth I am alluding?"

"Cannot say that I——"

"Indeed!—why it was I who told Aristotle, that by sneezing men expelled superfluous ideas through the proboscis."[15]

"Which is—hiccup!—undoubtedly the case," said the metaphysician, while he poured out for himself another bumper of Mousseux, and offered his snuff-box to the fingers of his visiter.

"There was Plato, too," continued his Majesty, modestly declining the snuff-box and the compliment it implied, "there was Plato, too, for whom I, at one time, felt all the affection of a friend. You knew Plato, Bon-Bon?—ah! no, I beg a thousand pardons. He met me at Athens, one day, in the Parthenon, and told me he was distressed for an idea. I bade him write down that ὁ νοῦς ἐστιν αὐλός. He said that he would do so, and went home, while I stepped over to the pyramids. But my conscience smote me for having uttered a truth, even to aid a friend, and hastening back to Athens, I arrived behind the philosopher's chair as he was inditing the 'αὐλός.' Giving the lambda a fillip with my finger I turned it upside down. So the sentence now reads 'ὁ νοῦς ἐστιν αὐγός,'[16] and is, you perceive, the fundamental doctrine in his metaphysics."

"Were you ever at Rome?" asked the restaurateur as he finished his second bottle of Mousseux, and drew from the closet a larger supply of Chambertin.

"But once, Monsieur Bon-Bon, but once. There was a time"—said the devil, as if reciting some passage from a book— "there was a time when occurred an an-

archy of five years, during which the republic, bereft of all its officers, had no magistracy besides the tribunes of the people, and these were not legally vested with any degree of executive power—at that time, Monsieur Bon-Bon—at that time only I was in Rome, and I have no earthly acquaintance, consequently, with any of its philosophy."[17]

"What do you think of—what do you think of—hiccup!—Epicurus?"[18]

"What do I think of whom?" said the devil in astonishment, "you cannot surely mean to find any fault with Epicurus! What do I think of Epicurus! Do you mean me, sir?—I am Epicurus. I am the same philosopher who wrote each of the three hundred treatises commemorated by Diogenes Laertes."[19]

"That's a lie!" said the metaphysician, for the wine had gotten a little into his head.

"Very well!—very well, sir!—very well indeed, sir!" said his Majesty, apparently much flattered.

"That's a lie!" repeated the restaurateur dogmatically, "that's a—hiccup!—a lie!"

"Well, well! have it your own way," said the devil pacifically: and Bon-Bon, having beaten his Majesty at an argument, thought it his duty to conclude a second bottle of Chambertin.

"As I was saying," resumed the visiter, "as I was observing a little while ago, there are some very outré[20] notions in that book of yours, Monsieur Bon-Bon. What, for instance, do you mean by all that humbug about the soul? Pray, sir, what is the soul?"

"The—hiccup!—soul," replied the metaphysician, referring to his MS., "is undoubtedly"——

"No, sir!"

"Indubitably"——

"No, sir!"

"Indisputably"——

"No, sir!"

"Evidently"——

"No, sir!"

"Incontrovertibly"——

"No, sir!"
"Hiccup!"——
"No, sir!"
"And beyond all question a"——
"No, sir! the soul is no such thing."
(Here, the philosopher looking daggers, took occasion to make an end, upon the spot, of his third bottle of Chambertin.)
"Then—hic-cup!—pray, sir—what—what is it?"
"That is neither here nor there, Monsieur Bon-Bon," replied his Majesty, musingly. "I have tasted—that is to say, I have known some very bad souls, and some too—pretty good ones." Here he smacked his lips, and, having unconsciously let fall his hand upon the volume in his pocket, was seized with a violent fit of sneezing.[21]

He continued:

"There was the soul of Cratinus—passable: Aristophanes—racy: Plato—exquisite—not *your* Plato, but Plato the comic poet; your Plato would have turned the stomach of Cerberus—faugh! Then let me see! there were Naevius, and Andronicus, and Plautus, and Terentius. Then there were Lucilius, and Catullus, and Naso, and Quintus Flaccus,—dear Quinty! as I called him when he sung a *seculare* for my amusement, while I toasted him, in pure good humor, on a fork. But they want *flavor* these Romans. One fat Greek is worth a dozen of them, and besides will *keep*, which cannot be said of a Quirite.[22] —Let us taste your Sauterne."

Bon-Bon had by this time made up his mind to the *nil admirari*,[23] and endeavored to hand down the bottles in question. He was, however, conscious of a strange sound in the room like the wagging of a tail. Of this, although extremely indecent in his Majesty, the philosopher took no notice:—simply kicking the dog, and requesting him to be quiet. The visiter continued:

"I found that Horace tasted very much like Aristotle;—you know I am fond of variety. Terentius I could not have told from Menander. Naso, to my astonish-

ment, was Nicander in disguise. Virgilius had a strong twang of Theocritus. Martial put me much in mind of Archilochus—and Titus Livius was positively Polybius[24] and none other."

"Hic-cup!" here replied Bon-Bon, and his Majesty proceeded:

"But if I *have* a *penchant*, Monsieur Bon-Bon—if I *have* a *penchant*, it is for a philosopher. Yet, let me tell you, sir, it is not every dev—I mean it is not every gentleman who knows how to *choose* a philosopher. Long ones are *not* good; and the best, if not carefully shelled, are apt to be a little rancid on account of the gall."

"Shelled!!"
"I mean taken out of the carcass."
"What do you think of a—hic-cup!—physician?"
"*Don't* mention them!—ugh! ugh!" (Here his Majesty retched violently.) "I never tasted but one—that rascal Hippocrates!—smelt of asafœtida—ugh! ugh! ugh!—caught a wretched cold washing him in the Styx—and after all he gave me the cholera morbus."[25]

"The—hiccup!—wretch!" ejaculated Bon-Bon, "the—hiccup!—abortion of a pill-box!"—and the philosopher dropped a tear.

"After all," continued the visiter, "after all, if a dev—if a gentleman wishes to *live*, he must have more talents than one or two; and with us a fat face is an evidence of diplomacy."

"How so?"
"Why we are sometimes exceedingly pushed for provisions. You must know that, in a climate so sultry as mine, it is frequently impossible to keep a spirit alive for more than two or three hours; and after death, unless pickled immediately, (and a pickled spirit is *not* good,) they will—smell—you understand, eh? Putrefaction is always to be apprehended when the souls are consigned to us in the usual way."

"Hiccup!—hiccup!—good God! how *do* you manage?"

Here the iron lamp commenced swing-ing with redoubled violence, and the devil half started from his seat;—however, with a slight sigh, he recovered his composure, merely saying to our hero in a low tone, "I tell you what, Pierre Bon-Bon, we *must* have no more swearing."

The host swallowed another bumper, by way of denoting thorough comprehen-sion and acquiescence, and the visiter continued:

"Why there are *several* ways of manag-ing. The most of us starve: some put up with the pickle: for my part I purchase my spirits *vivente corpore,*[26] in which case I find they keep very well."

"But the body!—hiccup!—the body!!!"

"The body, the body—well, what of the body?—oh! ah! I perceive. Why, sir, the body is not *at all* affected by the transac-tion. I have made innumerable purchases of the kind in my day, and the parties never experienced any inconvenience. There were Cain and Nimrod, and Nero, and Caligula, and Dionysius, and Pisistra-tus, and—and a thousand others, who never knew what it was to have a soul during the latter part of their lives; yet, sir, these men adorned society. Why isn't there A——,[27] now, whom you know as well as I? Is *he* not in possession of all his faculties, mental and corporeal? Who writes a keener epigram? Who reasons more wittily? Who——but, stay! I have his agreement in my pocket-book."

Thus saying, he produced a red leather wallet, and took from it a number of pa-pers. Upon some of these Bon-Bon caught a glimpse of the letters *Machi—Maza—Robesp*—with the words *Caligula, George, Elizabeth.*[28] His Majesty selected a nar-row slip of parchment, and from it read aloud the following words:

"In consideration of certain mental en-dowments which it is unnecessary to spec-ify, and in farther consideration of one thousand louis d'or, I, being aged one year and one month, do hereby make over to the bearer of this agreement all my right, title, and appurtenance in the shadow

called my soul." (Signed) A. . . . . (Here his Majesty repeated a name which I do not feel myself justified in indicating more unequivocally.)

"A clever fellow that," resumed he; "but like you, Monsieur Bon-Bon, he was mistaken about the soul. The soul a shadow truly! The soul a shadow! Ha! ha! ha!—he! he! he!—hu! hu! hu! Only think of a fricasséed shadow!"

"*Only* think—hiccup!—of a fricasséed shadow!" exclaimed our hero, whose fac-ulties were becoming much illuminated by the profundity of his Majesty's dis-course.

"Only think of a—hiccup!—fricas-séed shadow!! Now, damme!—hiccup!—humph! If *I* would have been such a —hiccup!—nincompoop. My soul, Mr.—humph!"

"*Your* soul, Monsieur Bon-Bon?"

"Yes, sir—hiccup!—my soul is"—

"What, sir?"

"*No* shadow, damme!"

"Did not mean to say"—

"Yes, sir, *my* soul is—hiccup!—humph! —yes, sir."

"Did not intend to assert"—

"*My* soul is—hiccup!—peculiarly qual-ified for—hiccup!—a"—

"What, sir?"

"Stew."

"Ha!"

"Soufflée."

"Eh?"

"Fricassée."

"Indeed!"

"Ragoût and fricandeau[29]—and see here, my good fellow! I'll let you have it —hiccup!—a bargain." Here the philoso-pher slapped his Majesty upon the back.

"Couldn't think of such a thing," said the latter calmly, at the same time rising from his seat. The metaphysician stared.

"Am supplied at present," said his Maj-esty.

"Hiccup!—e-h?" said the philosopher.

"Have no funds on hand."

"What?"

"Besides, very unhandsome in me"—

"Sir!"

"To take advantage of"—

"Hiccup!"

"Your present disgusting and ungentlemanly situation."

Here the visiter bowed and withdrew —in what manner could not precisely be ascertained—but in a well-concerted effort to discharge a bottle at "the villain," the slender chain was severed that depended from the ceiling, and the metaphysician prostrated by the downfall of the lamp.

WHY THE LITTLE FRENCHMAN WEARS HIS HAND IN A SLING[1]

It's on my wisiting cards sure enough (and it's them that's all o' pink satin paper) that inny gintleman that plases may behould the intheristhin words, "Sir Patrick O'Grandison, Barronitt, 39 Southampton Row, Russell Square, Parrish o' Bloomsbury." And shud ye be wantin to diskiver who is the pink of purliteness quite, and the laider of the hot tun in the houl city o' Lonon—why it's jist mesilf. And fait that same is no wonder at all at all, (so be plased to stop curlin your nose,) for every inch o' the six wakes that I've been a gintleman, and left aff wid the bog-throthing to take up wid the Barronissy, it's Pathrick that's been living like a houly imperor, and gitting the iddication and the graces. Och! and wouldn't it be a blessed thing for your sperrits if ye cud lay your two peepers jist upon Sir Pathrick O'Grandison, Barronitt, when he is all riddy drissed for the hopperer, or stipping into the Brisky for the drive into the Hyde Park.—But it's the iligant big figgur that I ave, for the rason o' which all the ladies fall in love wid me. Isn't it my own swate silf now that'll missure the six fut, and the three inches more nor that, in me stockings, and that am excadingly will proportioned all over to match? And is it ralelly more than the three fut and a bit that there is, inny how, of the little

ould furrener Frinchman that lives jist over the way, and that's a oggling and a goggling the houl day, (and bad luck to him,) at the purty widdy Misthress Tracle that's my own nixt door neighbor, (God bliss her) and a most particuller frind and acquintance? You percave the little spalpeen is summat[2] down in the mouth, and wears his lift hand in a sling; and it's for that same thing, by yur lave, that I'm going to give you the good rason.

The truth of the houl matter is jist simple enough; for the very first day that I com'd from Connaught, and showd my swate little silf in the strait to the widdy, who was looking through the windy, it was a gone case althegither wid the heart o' the purty Misthress Tracle. I percaved it, ye see, all at once, and no mistake, and that's God's thruth. First of all it was up wid the windy in a jiffy, and thin she threw open her two peepers to the itmost, and thin it was a little gould spy-glass that she clapped tight to one o' thim, and divil may burn me if it didn't spake to me as plain as a peeper cud spake, and says it, through the spy-glass, "Och! the tip o' the mornin to ye, Sir Patrick O'Grandison, Barronitt, mavourneen; and it's a nate gintleman that ye are, sure enough, and it's mesilf and me fortin jist that'll be at yur sarvice, dear, inny time o' day at all at all for the asking." And it's not mesilf ye wud have to be bate in the purliteness; so I made her a bow that wud ha broken yur heart althegither to behould, and thin I pulled aff me hat with a flourish, and thin I winked at her hard wid both eyes, as much as to say, "Thrue for you, yer a swate little crature, Mrs. Tracle, me darlint, and I wish I may be drownthed dead in a bog, if it's not mesilf, Sir Patrick O'Grandison, Barronitt, that'll make a houl bushel o' love to yur leddyship, in the twinkling o' the eye of a Londonderry purraty."[3]

And it was the nixt mornin, sure, jist as I was making up me mind whither it wouldn't be the purlite thing to sind a bit o' writin to the widdy by way of a love-litter, when up cum'd the delivery sarvant wid an illigant card, and he tould me that the name on it (for I niver cud rade the copper-plate printin on account of being lift handed) was all about Mounseer, the Count, A Goose, Look-aisy, Maiter-di-dauns,[4] and that the houl of the divilish lingo was the spalpeeny long name of the little ould furrener Frinchman as lived over the way.

And jist wid that in cum'd the little willian himsilf, and thin he made me a broth of a bow, and thin he said he had ounly taken the liberty of doing me the honor of the giving me a call, and thin he went on to palaver at a great rate, and divil the bit did I comprehind what he wud be afther the tilling me at all at all, excipting and saving that he said "pully wou, woolly wou," and tould me, among a bushel o' lies, bad luck to him, that he was mad for the love o' my widdy Mis-thress Tracle, and that my widdy Mrs. Tracle had a puncheon[5] for *him*.

At the hearin of this, ye may swear, though, I was as mad as a grasshopper, but I remimbered that I was Sir Pathrick O'Grandison, Barronitt, and that it wasn't althegither gentaal to lit the anger git the upper hand o' the purliteness, so I made light o' the matter and kipt dark, and got quite sociable wid the little chap, and afther a while what did he do but ask me to go wid him to the widdy's, saying he wud give me the feshionable introduc-tion to her leddyship.

"Is it there ye are?" said I thin to me-silf, "and it's thrue for you, Pathrick, that ye're the fortunnittest mortal in life. We'll soon see now whither it's your swate silf, or whither it's little Mounseer Maiter-di-dauns, that Misthress Tracle is head and ears in the love wid."

Wid that we wint aff to the widdy's, next door, and ye may well say it was an illigant place; so it was. There was a car-pet all over the floor, and in one corner there was a forty-pinny[6] and a jews-harp and the divil knows what ilse, and in an-other corner was a sofy, the beautifullest thing in all natur, and sitting on the sofy, sure enough, there was the swate little an-gel, Misthress Tracle.

"The tip o' the morning to ye," says I, "Mrs. Tracle," and thin I made sich an illigant obaysance that it wud ha quite althegither bewildered the brain o' ye.

"Wully woo, pully woo, plump in the mud,"[7] says the little furrenner Frinch-man, "and sure Mrs. Tracle," says he, that he did, "isn't this gintleman here jist his riverence Sir Pathrick O'Grandison, Bar-ronitt, and isn't he althegither and en-tirely the most purticular frind and ac-quintance that I have in the houl world?"

And wid that the widdy, she gits up from the sofy, and makes the swatest curtchy nor iver was seen; and thin down she sits like an angel; and thin, by the powers, it was that little spalpeen Moun-seer Maiter-di-dauns that plumped his silf right down by the right side of her. Och hon![8] I ixpicted the two eyes o' me wud ha cum'd out of my head on the spot, I was so dispirate mad! Howiver, "Bait who!" says I, after a while. "Is it there ye are, Mounseer Maiter-di-dauns?" and so down I plumped on the lift side of her leddyship, to be aven wid the willain. Botheration! it wud ha done your heart good to percave the illigant double wink that I gived her jist thin right in the face wid both eyes.

But the little ould Frinchman he niver beginned to suspict me at all at all, and disperate hard it was he made the love to her leddyship. "Woully wou," says he, "Pully wou," says he, "Plump in the mud," says he.

"That's all to no use, Mounseer Frog,[9] mavourneen," thinks I; and I talked as hard and as fast as I could all the while, and throth it was mesilf jist that divarted her leddyship complately and intirely, by rason of the illigant conversation that I kipt up wid her all about the dear bogs of Connaught. And by and by she gived me such a swate smile, from one ind of her mouth to the ither, that it made me as bould as a pig, and I jist took hould of the ind of her little finger in the most dillikit-test manner in natur, looking at her all the while out o' the whites of my eyes.

And then ounly percave the cuteness of the swate angel, for no sooner did she obsarve that I was afther the squazing of her flipper, than she up wid it in a jiffy, and put it away behind her back, jist as much as to say, "Now thin, Sir Pathrick O'Grandison, there's a bitther chance for ye, mavourneen, for it's not altogether the gentaal thing to be afther the squazing of my flipper right full in the sight of that little furrenner Frinchman, Mounseer Maiter-di-dauns."

Wid that I giv'd her a big wink jist to say, "lit Sir Pathrick alone for the likes o' them thricks," and thin I wint aisy to work, and you'd have died wid the divar-sion to behould how cliverly I slipped my right arm betwane the back o' the sofy, and the back of her leddyship, and there, sure enough, I found a swate little flipper all a waiting to say, "the tip o' the mornin to ye, Sir Pathrick O'Grandison, Barron-itt." And wasn't it mesilf, sure, that jist giv'd it the laste little bit of a squaze in the world, all in the way of a commince-ment, and not to be too rough wid her leddyship? and och, botheration, wasn't it the gentaalest and dilikittest of all the lit-tle squazes that I got in return? "Blood and thunder, Sir Pathrick, mavourneen," thinks I to mesilf, "fait it's jist the moth-er's son of you, and nobody else at all at all, that's the handsomest and the fortu-nittest young bogthrotter that ever cum'd out of Connaught!" And wid that I giv'd the flipper a big squaze, and a big squaze it was, by the powers, that her leddyship giv'd to me back. But it would ha split the seven sides o' you wid the laffin to be-hould, jist thin all at once, the concated[10] behaviour of Mounseer Maiter-di-dauns. The likes o' sich a jabbering, and a smirk-ing, and a parley-wouing as he begin'd wid her leddyship, niver was known be-fore upon arth; and divil may burn me if it wasn't me own very two peepers that cotch'd him tipping her the wink out of one eye. Och hon! if it wasn't mesilf thin that was mad as a Kilkenny cat I shud like to be tould who it was!

"Let me infarm you, Mounseer Maiter-di-dauns," said I, as purlite as iver ye seed, "that it's not the gintaal thing at all at all, and not for the likes o' you inny how, to be afther the oggling and a goggling at her leddyship in that fashion," and jist wid that such another squaze as it was I giv'd her flipper, all as much as to say, "isn't it Sir Pathrick now, my jewel, that'll be able to the proticting o' you, my dar-lint?" and then there cum'd another squaze back, all by way of the answer. "Thrue for you, Sir Pathrick," it said as plain as iver a squaze said in the world, "Thrue for you, Sir Pathrick, mavourneen, and it's a proper nate gintleman ye are —that's God's truth," and wid that she opened her two beautiful peepers till I belaved they wud ha com'd out of her hid althegither and intirely, and she looked first as mad as a cat at Mounseer Frog, and thin as smiling as all out o' doors at mesilf.

"Thin," says he, the willian, "Och hon! and a wolly-wou, polly-wou," and thin wid that he shoved up his two shoulders till the divil the bit of his hid was to be diskivered, and thin he let down the two corners of his purraty-trap,[11] and thin not a haporth more of the satisfaction could I git out o' the spalpeen.

Belave me, my jewel, it was Sir Pathrick that was unrasonable mad thin, and the more by token that the Frinchman kipt an wid his winking at the widdy; and the widdy she kipt an wid the squazing of my flipper, as much as to say, "At him again Sir Pathrick O'Grandison, mavourneen;" so I jist ripped out with a big oath, and says I,

"Ye little spalpeeny frog of a bog-throt-ting son of a bloody noun!"[12]—and jist thin what d'ye think it was that her leddy-ship did? Troth she jumped up from the sofy as if she was bit, and made off through the door, while I turned my head round after her, in a complate bewilderment and botheration, and followed her wid me two peepers. You percave I had a rason of my own for knowing that she couldn't git down the stairs althegither and entirely; for I knew very well that I had hould of her hand, for divil the bit had I iver lit it go. And says I,

"Isn't it the laste little bit of a mistake in the world that ye've been afther the making, yer leddyship? Come back now, that's a darlint, and I'll give ye yur flipper." But aff she wint down the stairs like a shot, and then I turned round to the little Frinch furrenner. Och hon! if it wasn't his spalpeeny little paw that I had hould of in my own—why thin—thin it wasn't—that's all.

And maybe it wasn't mesilf that jist died then outright wid the laffin, to behould the little chap when he found out that it wasn't the widdy at all at all that he had had hould of all the time, but only Sir Pathrick O'Grandison. The ould divil himsilf niver behild sich a long face as he pet an! As for Sir Pathrick O'Grandison, Barronitt, it wasn't for the likes of his riverence to be afther the minding of a thrifle of a mistake. Ye may jist say, though (for it's God's thruth) that afore I lift hould of the flipper of the spalpeen, (which was not till afther her leddyship's futmen had kicked us both down the stairs), I gived it such a nate little broth of a squaze, as made it all up into raspberry jam.

"Wouly-wou," says he, "pully-wou," says he—"Cot tam!"

And that's jist the thruth of the rason why he wears his lift hand in a sling.

X-ING A PARAGRAB[1]

As it is well known that the "wise men" came "from the East," and as Mr. Touch-and-go Bullet-head came from the East, it follows that Mr. Bullet-head was a wise man; and if collateral proof of the matter be needed, here we have it—Mr. B. was an editor. Irascibility was his sole foible;

for in fact the obstinacy of which men accused him was anything but his *foible,* since he justly considered it his *forte.* It was his strong point—his virtue; and it would have required all the logic of a Brownson[2] to convince him that it was "anything else."

I have shown that Touch-and-go Bullet-head was a wise man; and the only occasion on which he did not prove infallible, was when, abandoning that legitimate home for all wise men, the East, he migrated to the city of Alexander-the-Great-o-nopolis,[3] or some place of a similar title, out West.

I must do him the justice to say, however, that when he made up his mind finally to settle in that town, it was under the impression that no newspaper, and consequently no editor, existed in that particular section of the country. In establishing "The Tea-Pot," he expected to have the field all to himself. I feel confident he never would have dreamed of taking up his residence in Alexander-the-Great-o-nopolis, had he been aware that, in Alexander-the-Great-o-nopolis, there lived a gentleman named John Smith (if I rightly remember), who, for many years, had there quietly grown fat in editing and publishing the "Alexander-the-Great-o-nopolis Gazette." It was solely, therefore, on account of having been misinformed, that Mr. Bullet-head found himself in Alex—suppose we call it Nopolis, "for short"—but, as he *did* find himself there, he determined to keep up his character for obst[4]—for firmness, and remain. So remain he did; and he did more; he unpacked his press, type, etc., etc., rented an office exactly opposite to that of the "Gazette," and, on the third morning after his arrival, issued the first number of "The Alexan"—that is to say, of "The Nopolis Tea-Pot:"—as nearly as I can recollect, this was the name of the new paper.

The leading article, I must admit, was brilliant—not to say severe. It was especially bitter about things in general—and as for the editor of "The Gazette," he was torn all to pieces in particular. Some of Bullet-head's remarks were really so fiery that I have always, since that time, been forced to look upon John Smith, who is still alive, in the light of a salamander.[5] I cannot pretend to give *all* the Tea-Pot's paragraphs *verbatim*, but one of them runs thus:

"Oh, yes!—Oh, we perceive! Oh, no doubt! The editor over the way is a genius —O, my! Oh, goodness, gracious!—what *is* this world coming to? *Oh, tempora! Oh, Moses!*"[6]

A philippic at once so caustic and so classical, alighted like a bombshell among the hitherto peaceful citizens of Nopolis. Groups of excited individuals gathered at the corners of the streets. Every one awaited, with heartfelt anxiety, the reply of the dignified Smith. Next morning it appeared, as follows:

"We quote from 'The Tea-Pot' of yesterday the subjoined paragraph:—'Oh, yes! *Oh,* we perceive! *Oh,* no doubt! *Oh,* my! *Oh,* goodness! *Oh,* tempora! *Oh,* Moses!' Why, the fellow is all O! That accounts for his reasoning in a circle, and explains why there is neither beginning nor end to him, nor to anything that he says. We really do not believe the vagabond can write a word that hasn't an O in it. Wonder if this O-ing is a habit of his? By the by, he came away from Down-East in a great hurry. Wonder if he *O's* as much there as he does here? '*O!* it is pitiful.' "

The indignation of Mr. Bullet-head at these scandalous insinuations, I shall not attempt to describe. On the eel-skinning principle, however, he did not seem to be so much incensed at the attack upon his integrity as one might have imagined. It was the sneer at his *style* that drove him to desperation. What!—*he* Touch-and-go Bullet-head!—not able to write a word without an O in it! He would soon let the jackanapes see that he was mistaken. Yes! he would let him see how *much* he was mistaken, the puppy! He, Touch-and-go Bullet-head, of Frogpondium, would let

Mr. John Smith perceive that he, Bullet-head, could indite, if it so pleased him, a whole paragraph—ay! a whole article— in which that contemptible vowel should not *once*—not even *once*—make its appearance.[7] But no;—that would be yielding a point to the said John Smith. *He,* Bullet-head, would make *no* alteration in his style, to suit the caprices of any Mr. Smith in Christendom. Perish so vile a thought! The O forever! He would persist in the O. He would be as O-wy as O-wy could be.

Burning with the chivalry of this determination, the great Touch-and-go, in the next "Tea-Pot," came out merely with this simple but resolute paragraph, in reference to this unhappy affair:

"The editor of the 'Tea-Pot' has the *honor* of advising the editor of 'The Gazette' that he, (the 'Tea-Pot,') will take an opportunity in to-morrow morning's paper, of convincing him (the 'Gazette,') that he (the 'Tea-Pot,') both can and will be *his own master,* as regards style;—he (the 'Tea-Pot') intending to show him, (the 'Gazette,') the supreme, and indeed the withering contempt with which the criticism of him (the 'Gazette,') inspires the independent bosom of him (the 'Tea-Pot,') by composing for the especial gratification (?) of him, (the 'Gazette,') a leading article, of some extent, in which the beautiful vowel—the emblem of Eternity —yet so inoffensive to the hyper-exquisite delicacy of him, (the 'Gazette,') shall most certainly *not be avoided* by his (the 'Gazette's') most obedient, humble servant, the 'Tea-Pot.' 'So much for Buckingham!' "[8]

In fulfilment of the awful threat thus darkly intimated rather than decidedly enunciated, the great Bullet-head, turning a deaf ear to all entreaties for "copy," and simply requesting his foreman to "go to the d——l," when he (the foreman) assured him (the "Tea-Pot!") that it was high time to "go to press:" turning a deaf ear to everything, I say, the great Bullet-head sat up until day-break, consuming the midnight oil, and absorbed in the composition of the really unparalleled paragraph, which follows:

"So ho, John! how now? Told you so, you know. Don't crow, another time, before you're out of the woods! Does your mother *know* you're out? Oh, no, no!—so go home at once, now, John, to your odious old woods of Concord! Go home to your woods, old owl,—go! You won't? Oh, poh, poh, John, don't do so! You've *got* to go, you know! So go at once, and don't go slow; for nobody owns you here, you know. Oh, John, John, if you *don't* go you're no *homo*—no! You're only a fowl, an owl; a cow, a sow; a doll, a poll; a poor, old, good-for-nothing-to-nobody, log, dog, hog, or frog,[9] come out of a Concord bog. Cool, now—cool! *Do* be cool, you fool! None of your crowing, old cock! Don't frown so—don't! Don't hollo, nor howl, nor growl, nor bow-wow-wow! Good Lord, John, how you *do* look! Told you so, you know—but stop rolling your goose of an old poll about so, and go and drown your sorrows in a bowl!"

Exhausted, very naturally, by so stupendous an effort, the great Touch-and-go could attend to nothing farther that night. Firmly, composedly, yet with an air of conscious power, he handed his MS. to the devil[10] in waiting, and then, walking leisurely home, retired, with ineffable dignity, to bed.

Meantime the devil to whom the copy was entrusted, ran up stairs to his "case,"[11] in an unutterable hurry, and forthwith made a commencement at "setting" the MS. "up."

In the first place, of course,—as the opening word was "So"—he made a plunge into the capital S hole and came out in triumph with a capital S. Elated by this success, he immediately threw himself upon the little-*o* box with a blindfold impetuosity—but who shall describe his horror when his fingers came up without the anticipated letter in their clutch? who shall paint his astonishment and rage at perceiving, as he rubbed his knuckles, that

he had been only thumping them to no purpose, against the bottom of an *empty* box. Not a single little-*o* was in the little-*o* hole; and, glancing fearfully at the capital-O partition, he found *that,* to his extreme terror, in a precisely similar predicament. Awe-stricken, his first impulse was to rush to the foreman.

"Sir!" said he, gasping for breath, "I can't never set up nothing without no o's."

"*What* do you mean by that?" growled the foreman, who was in a very ill-humor at being kept up so late.

"Why, sir, there beant an *o* in the office, neither a big un nor a little un!"

"What—what the d——l has become of all that were in the case?"

"*I* don't know, sir," said the boy, "but one of them ere G'zette devils is bin prowling bout here all night, and I spect *he's* gone and cabbaged em every one."

"Dod rot him! I haven't a doubt of it," replied the foreman, getting purple with rage—"but I tell you what you do, Bob, that's a good boy—you go over the first chance you get and hook every one of their i's and (d——n them!) their izzards."[12]

"Jist so," replied Bob, with a wink and a frown—"*I'll* be into em, *I'll* let em know a thing or two; but in de meantime, that ere paragrab? *Mus* go in to-night, you know—else there'll be the d——l to pay, and—"

"And not a *bit* of pitch hot,"[13] interrupted the foreman, with a deep sigh and an emphasis on the "bit." "Is it a *very* long paragraph, Bob?"

"Shouldn't call it a *wery* long paragrab," said Bob.

"Ah, well, then! do the best you can with it! we *must* get to press," said the foreman, who was over head and ears in work; "just stick in some other letter for *o,* nobody's going to read the fellow's trash, any how."

"*Wery* well," replied Bob, "here goes it!" and off he hurried to his case, muttering as he went—"Considdeble vell, them ere expressions, perticcler for a man as doese n't swar. So I's to gouge out all their eyes, eh? and d——n all their gizzards! Vell! this here's the chap as is jist able *for* to do it." The fact is, that although Bob was but twelve years old and four feet high, he was equal to any amount of fight, in a small way.

The exigency here described is by no means of rare occurrence in printing-offices; and I cannot tell how to account for it, but the fact is indisputable, that when the exigency *does* occur, it almost always happens that x is adopted as a substitute for the letter deficient. The true reason, perhaps, is that x is rather the most superabundant letter in the cases, or at least *was* so in old times—long enough to render the substitution in question an habitual thing with printers. As for Bob, he would have considered it heretical to employ any other character, in a case of this kind, than the x to which he had been accustomed.

"I *shell* have to x this ere paragrab," said he to himself, as he read it over in astonishment, "but it's jest about the aw-fulest o-wy paragrab I ever *did* see:" so x it he did, unflinchingly, and to press it went x-*ed*.[14]

Next morning the population of Nop-olis were taken all aback by reading, in "The Tea-Pot" the following extraordi-nary leader:

"Sx hx, Jxhn! hxw nxw; Txld yxu sx, yxu knxw. Dxn't crxw, anxther time, be-fxre yxu're xut xf the wxxds! Dxes yxur mxther *knxw* yxur're xut? Xh, nx, nx! sx gx hxme at xnce, nxw, Jxhn, tx yxur xdi-xus xld wxxds xf Cxncxrd! Gx hxme tx yxur wxxds, xld xwl,—gx! Yxu wxn't? Xh, pxh, pxh, Jxhn, dxn't dx sx! Yxu've *gxt* tx gx, yxu knxw! sx gx at xnce, and dxn't gx slxw; fxr nxbxdy xwns yxu here, yxu knxw. Xh, Jxhn, Jxhn, if yxu *dxn't* gx yxu're nx *hxmx*—nx! Yxu're xnly a fxwl, an xwl; a cxw, a sxw; a dxll, a pxll; a pxxr xld gxxd-fxr-nxthing-tx-nxbxdy lxg, dxg, hxg, xr frxg, cxme xut xf a Cxncxrd bxg.

Cxxl, nxw—cxxl! Dx be cxxl, yxu fxxl! Nxne xf yxur crxwing, xld cxck! Dxn't frxwn sx—dxn't! Dxn't hxllx, nxr hxwl, nxr grxwl, nxr bxw-wxw-wxw! Gxxd Lxrd, Jxhn, hxw yxu *dx* lxxk! Txld yxu sx, yxu knxw, but stxp rxlling yxur gxxse xf an xld pxll abxut sx, and gx and drxwn yxur sxrrxws in a bxwl!"

The uproar occasioned by this mystical and cabalistical article, is not to be con-ceived. The first definite idea entertained by the populace was, that some diabolical treason lay concealed in the hieroglyph-ics; and there was a general rush to Bul-let-head's residence, for the purpose of riding him on a rail; but that gentleman was nowhere to be found. He had van-ished, no one could tell how; and not even the ghost of him has ever been seen since.

Unable to discover its legitimate object, the popular fury at length subsided; leav-ing behind it, by way of sediment, quite a medley of opinion about this unhappy affair.

One gentleman thought the whole an X-ellent joke.

Another said that, indeed, Bullet-head had shown much X-uberance of fancy.

A third admitted him X-entric, but no more.

A fourth could only suppose it the Yankee's design to X-press, in a general way, his X-asperation.

"Say, rather, to set an X-ample to pos-terity," suggested a fifth.

That Bullet-head had been driven to an extremity, was clear to all; and in fact, since *that* editor could not be found, there was some talk about lynching the other one.

The more common conclusion, how-ever, was, that the affair was, simply, X-traordinary and in-X-plicable. Even the town mathematician confessed that he could make nothing of so dark a prob-lem. X, everybody knew, was an unknown quantity; but in this case (as he properly observed), there was an unknown quan-tity of X.

The opinion of Bob, the devil (who kept dark "about his having X-ed the paragrab"), did not meet with so much attention as I think it deserved, although it was very openly and very fearlessly expressed. He said that, for his part, he had no doubt about the matter at all, that it was a clear case, that Mr. Bullet-head never *could* be "persvaded fur to drink like other folks, but vas *continually* a-svigging o' that ere blessed XXX ale, and, as a naiteral consekvence, it just puffed him up savage, and made him X (cross) in the X-treme."[15]

Notes

How to Write a Blackwood Article

1. When this tale first appeared, Poe called it "The Psyche Zenobia" (*The American Museum of Science, Literature, and the Arts*, November 1838). In the 1840 *Tales of the Grotesque and Arabesque* he called it "The Signora Zenobia," and in *The Broadway Journal* for July 12, 1845, "How to Write a Blackwood Article."

2. Poe took his motto from a parody of Dr. Johnson in James and Horace Smith's *Rejected Addresses:*

> "He that is most assured of success will make the fewest appeals to favor, and where nothing is claimed that is undue, nothing that is due will be withheld. A swelling opening is too often succeeded by an insignificant conclusion. Parturient mountains have ere now produced muscipular abortions; and the auditor who compares incipient grandeur with final vulgarity is reminded of the pious hawkers of Constantinople, who solemnly perambulate her streets, exclaiming 'In the name of the Prophet—figs' " (Pollin 7; Schuster).

3. Zenobia: Margaret Fuller was noted for her love of finery and for her imperious ways. Poe probably got the name Zenobia from an 1837 novel by William Ware; Queen Zenobia in the novel is *not* a parody of Miss Fuller, though she is " 'a true New England woman born too soon' " (McNeal quoting Van Wyck Brooks). Hawthorne's Zenobia, in *The Blithesdale Romance* (1852) is unquestionably modeled loosely on Miss Fuller, whom he knew well and who, by then, had died tragically.

McNeal is sure that Hawthorne knew both Ware's Zenobia and Poe's.

Suky: not, as Zenobia says, a corruption of Psyche, but rather a lower class nickname for Susan. Its connotations are vulgar. See, for instance, Gay's "The Beggars' Opera."

sky-blue . . . *mantelet:* A mantelet is a short cloak. Poe dressed many of his absurd characters in sky-blue cloaks. See "The Devil in the Belfry," Section Preface; "Bon-Bon," note 7.

agraffas: ornamental clasps. Pollin (12) writes, "One suspects that he really meant colored 'aigrettes' or ornamental tufts of feathers."

auriculas: flowers of the primrose family ("bear's-ears"). Pollin (12) guesses Poe is referring to sleeves but that he "invents" his own word for the occasion.

Dr. Moneypenny: Emerson (McNeal).

my father was "a Greek": Miss Fuller learned Greek from her father, but McNeal thinks this points to Timothy Fuller or more likely to Bronson Alcott. She taught at Alcott's Temple School in 1837.

4. R. S. A.: a British society founded in 1754.

S. D. U. K. and Lord Brougham: Henry Brougham (1778–1868), political, social and educational reformer, long connected with *The Edinburgh Review*. His famous defense of J. and J. L. Hunt on a libel charge for an article on military flogging they wrote in 1811 for the *Examiner* (see note 6) probably connected him and the *Examiner* in Poe's mind. In 1825, as part of his large-scale reform and educational activities, Brougham established the Society for the Diffusion of Useful Knowledge to provide cheap and useful publications on useful topics; he wrote the first volume himself in 1827. Also see "The Literary Life of Thingum Bob, Esq.," note 27 and "The System of Dr. Tarr and Professor Fether," note 18.

5. syllabub (or sillabub): a dish made by mixing milk or cream with wine or cider, and then whipping it into a froth or boiling it until solid.

Dr. M.: This abbreviation of Moneypenny McNeal takes as a pun on Em-erson.

"cant" . . . K: See note 10.

6. "Mr. Blackwood": William Blackwood (1776–1834) gave his name to *Blackwood's* but here Poe uses the name in a more general sense.

Times: The most distinguished London paper of this period.

Examiner: See note 4, above.

Gully: John Gully (1783–1863) the remarkable English boxer, legislator (via a pocket borough), rare-horse owner, and colliery proprietor. His humble antecedents (at 21 he was in prison for debts) are the basis for Poe's joke. So far as we know, he never wrote a book.

Slang-Whang: Poe got the name from a fable in *The New York Mirror;* Slang-Whang is a Chinese editor who hits the brandy bottle, and may, indeed, be Poe himself, since the *Mirror* at the time bore him a grudge (Pollin 14). See "Mystification" for more on his feud with the *Mirror*.

7. "The Dead Alive": A tale by this name appeared in *Fraser's Magazine*, IX (1833), 411.

"Confessions of an Opium-eater": *The Confessions of an English Opium-Eater* (1822) by Thomas DeQuincey (1785–1859) actually published first not in *Blackwood's* (though DeQuincey had been connected with that journal), but rather in *The London Magazine* for September and October of 1821.

Coleridge wrote the paper: DeQuincey published *Confessions* anonymously, but the secret was not well kept.

rummer: a glass or cup, generally a tall glass without a stem; it can also mean what's in the glass.

Hollands: a variety of gin, made by adding the juniper to the mash instead of to the distilled spirits.

"The Involuntary Experimentalist": a piece about "a physician who falls into a large cauldron at a burning brewery and describes his sensations as the walls begin to glow" (Pollin 12).

"The Diary of a Late Physician": Samuel Warren (1807–1877) published in *Blackwood's* a number of short stories, later published in book form as *Passages from the Diary of a Late Physician* (1838).

"The Man in the Bell": a work by William Maginn, a member of *Blackwood's* team of writers.

8. put you *au fait* to: Inform you of. Poe is probably making a joke of the use of French in the works of American and British authors of his day with this strange construction.

9. See "Some Words with a Mummy," note 27.

10. Ionic: Founded by Thales of Miletus in Asiatic Ionia, it was the first of the ancient sects of philosophers.

Eleatic: The Eleatic philosophers were attractive to romantic authors because of their belief in the universal unity underlying creation. Cf. Mr. Blackwood's comments below about "The Supernal Oneness."

Archytas: eminent Greek philosopher of the Pythagorean sect, a mathematician and general who lived about 350 B.C.E.

Gorgias: Sicilian orator and sophist of the fifth century B.C.E.; a character in one of Plato's dialogues.

Alcmaeon: a natural philosopher, native of Crotona, who lived in the sixth century B.C.E. and was a pupil of Pythagoras.

Locke: See "Morella," note 5.

Kritik der reinen Vernunft: Critique of Pure Reason (1781) by the German philosopher Immanuel Kant (1724–1804).

Metaphysische Anfangsgründe der Naturwissenschaft: Metaphysical Foundations of Natural Science (1786), also by Kant. If critics are correct in assuming that Poe knew little German, it is very doubtful that Poe had read this work; an English translation did not appear until long after his death.

11. *Dial:* The *Dial* was the journal of the Concord Transcendentalists, and Margaret Fuller became, in 1840, its first editor. This

paragraph and the one above are substantially new: Poe added them for the 1845 version of his story. See also "Never Bet the Devil Your Head," at note 2.

Channing: Poe had written for *Graham's Magazine* in August 1843, a wickedly scathing attack on William Ellery Channing (II)'s newly published *Poems*. Channing (1818–1901) was the nephew of William Ellery Channing, the admired essayist of Emerson's group. McNeal points out that to make matters worse, Channing was by the time of Poe's last publication of "How to Write a Blackwood Article" Margaret Fuller's brother-in-law, and Emerson, in an article in the October 1840 *Dial*, had found some encouraging things to say about young Channing's poetry. Hence Poe, who attacked Transcendentalists every chance he got, includes a gratuitous pot-shot at the unoffending amateur poet.

"fat . . . Can": Poe misquotes the line. In his own review, he quoted Channing:

> Thou meetest a common man
> With a delusive show of can.

See also "The Angel of the Odd," note 6.

12. Poe adds the English ending "ism" to the French words *bel esprit*, meaning "wit" or "genius," and uses his new word in the sense of "witticism."

13. Melete, Mneme, Aoede: In one account, the muses were three daughters of Zeus and Mnemosyne: Aoede (song), Melete (meditation), and Mneme (memory).

recherché: refined, studied.

improviso: an obsolete word meaning "unforeseen" or "unexpected."

14. Alpheus: a reference to Coleridge, who writes in "Kubla Kahn":

> In Xanadu did Kubla Kahn
> A stately pleasure-dome decree:
> Where Alph, the sacred river, ran
> Through caverns measureless to
>   man
>   Down to a sunless sea.

15. A variety of Iris called "Persian Iris" does exist. It has white upper petals and brown speckled lower petals. We have not located a reference to the peculiar qualities which Poe mentions.

16. Pollin (12) guesses this reference came from the work by Patrick Keith cited in "Scheherazade." Varner refers us to an item in the *Philadelphia Public Ledger* for July

22, 1839, in which the "*Epidendrum* or air plant" is mentioned.

17. *Yu Chiao Li (The Beautiful Couple)*, a late-Ming Dynasty novel (whose author is unknown) which had been translated into French, German, and English in the 1820s, and discussed in a number of places (Benton 5). Pollin (12) writes: "Poe's source of information was a paper by Philip Pendleton Cooke that Poe, as editor, had published in the *Southern Literary Messenger* of April 1836, 'Leaves from My Scrap Book, Part II.' Cooke is commenting on the plagiarism from the 'Chinese novel, *Yu-Kiao-Li*,' in a motto written by E. Irving."

18. *Zaïre* (1732), a play by François Mariet Arouet (Voltaire).

19. This quotation is from, but not by, Miguel de Cervantes (1547–1616): Cervantes was quoting Juan Escriva (Robbins). The lines occur in a poem which appeared in the 1511 edition of the *Cancionero* de Hernando del Castillo. Poe used the epigram elsewhere in his column "Pinakidia."

20. The lines are from Berni's *Orlando Innamorato* LIII, 60. Poe probably became confused because of the similarity of the title of Berni's work to Ariosto's *Orlando Furioso*. This seems to be an honest mistake. The passage also occurs in Poe's "Pinakidia," where he attributes it correctly.

21. This time Poe's error is deliberate; the lines are from Goethe (Robbins).

22. Molucca: We find no mention of a variety of capon from Molucca. Pollin (12) says that Poe may have deliberately or accidentally confused Molucca with Minorca. Minorcan chickens were a delicacy.

en mosaïques: In *The French Cook* Ude includes an article on "Mosaic Jelly" (Pollin 12).

Tortoni's: a Parisian café which has by now disappeared.

23. *ignoratio elenchi*: ignorance of the point under discussion.

anemonae verborum: Not from Marcus Annaeus Lucanus (39–65), a Roman epic poet, but rather from the "Lexiphones" of Lucian (125–200) (Norman). Translated by H. W. and F. C. Fowler as "unsubstantial flowers of speech." Poe's source, as so often, is Isaac Disraeli, who writes, "Lucian happily describes the works of those who abound with the most luxuriant language void of ideas. He calls their unmeaning verbosity 'anemone-words;' for anemonies are flowers, which however brilliant, only please the eye, leaving no fragrance."

insomnia Jovis: "Poe correctly attributes the phrase . . . to Silius Italicus" (Norman). Pollin (12), discussing Poe's knowledge of Longinus, mentions that in the first version of this story, Poe attributed the words to Longinus.

24. Poe probably copied this information from the footnotes to an edition of Samuel Butler's *Hudibras.* We examined one edition done ten years after Poe's death which is supposed to reprint the best notes of earlier editions. The lines Poe quotes are from Part 3, Canto 3, lines 243–244, and the note explains that Butler did not write

> He that fights and runs away,
> May live to fight another day.

The idea, the note goes on, "appears to be as old as Demosthenes, who, being approached for running away from Philip of Macedonia, at the battle of Chaeronea, replied, 'Aνὴρ ὁ . . . (etc.). The note goes on to give other examples of the idea in sixteenth and seventeenth-century writers. Poe put in the bracketed transliteration so that readers who didn't know Greek could get the joke when "Zenobia," in "A Predicament," "quotes Demosthenes": "Andrew O'Phlegethon, you really make haste to fly." Pollin (12) points out that A. H. Quinn located the "Demosthenes quotation, with its *Hudibras* translation, in the sixth chapter of the 'Scriblerus' papers."

A Predicament

1. Note that this tale is meant to be read after "How to Write a Blackwood Article." Our notes do not explicate the blunders of the heroine/narrator because they are explained in the first story.

Poe's first title for this portion of his two-part spoof was "The Scythe of Time." For his publications of this piece, see "How to Write A Blackwood Article," note 1. Poe used the idea again in "The Pit and the Pendulum," in which his narrator, seeing the diabolical apparatus which is intended to cut him in two, says, "It was the painted figure of Time as he is commonly represented, save that, in lieu of a scythe, he held . . . a huge pendulum." See also note 6.

2. From John Milton's masque "Comus" (1634), line 277. The Lady answers, "Dim darkness and this leavy labyrinth."

3. *If:* In his "Fifty Suggestions" (*Graham's Magazine,* May, June 1845), Poe, making a pun on the name of Mirabeau's dwelling, writes, "Mirabeau, I fancy, acquired his wonderful tact at foreseeing and meeting *contingencies,* during his residence in the stronghold of *If.*"

what a world of mystery: In his poem "The Bells" (1849), which also deals with bells and bell-towers, Poe echoes this phrase. See "The Literary Life of Thingum Bob," note 9, and note 5, below.

4. There is no point in trying to hide Poe's offensive racism. References to Blacks in his works are almost universally stereotyped, condescending, or even sneering. The suggestion that Zenobia/Margaret Fuller is in love with a black man could also be a snide allusion to the outspoken liberalism of most of the Transcendentalists.

5. Poe echoes his humorous writing in his serious. Compare "how vast a sum of human happiness or misery depends!" with such lines in "The Bells" as "What a world of solemn thought their monody compels!"

6. Pollin (12) notes the similarity of this situation to that in Poe's "The Pit and the Pendulum" (1842).

7. Dr. Ollapod was a character in George Colman, Jr.'s very popular farce *The Poor Gentleman.* William Burton, for a time Poe's employer (Burton's *Gentleman's Magazine*), had played the part and became popularly identified with it, so Poe, during his association with Burton, changed "Dr. Ollapod" to "Dr. Morphine." Poe and Burton never got on well, and in the 1845 version, Poe changed the name back to "Ollapod." The character in the play is a charlatan who wants to overdose everyone with cathartics (see the allusion to Brandreth's pills in "How to Write A Blackwood Article"). "Ollapod" is from the Spanish "olla podrida," hodgepodge (Pollin 6). Willis Clark's pen name in *The Knickerbocker* magazine was "Ollapod" (Whipple 3). See "The Literary Life of Thingum Bob."

Never Bet the Devil Your Head

1. Poe's title for this story when he first published it in *Graham's* (September 1841)

was "Never Bet Your Head"; the present title appeared in *The Broadway Journal* version of August 16, 1845. Glassheim points out the bad pun on "head" and "tail."

2. Don Thomas De Las Torres: Possibly Tomás Hermenegildo de Las Torres, author of *Cuentos en verso castellano* (Zaragosa, 1828 and Valencia, 1830?).

provided . . . books: Literally, the Spanish is translated: "Provided that the habits of an author are pure and chaste, it matters very little that his works are not equally severe."

"Every fiction . . . has": Poe is remembered in literary history as the first American author to *avoid* moralizing. He insists, in "The Poetic Principle," for example, that poetry is *"The Rhythmical Creation of Beauty,"* and "has no concern whatever either with Duty or with Truth."

Philip Melancthon: (Philipp Schwarzerd, 1497–1560), famous German theologian and religious reformer, Luther's literary colleague.

"Batrachomyomachia": a Greek comic poem, "The Battle of the Frogs and Mice" by Pigres of Caria (if Plutarch is correct).

Pierre La Seine: Italian scholar, died 1636, author of *Homeri Nepaethes seu de abolendo locter liber* (1624).

Jacobus Hugo: The Jacobus Hugo who seems best to fit Poe's allusion is the subject of a poem by Jean Dorat (1517–1588), one of a group of French poets known as the *Pleiades*; evidence in other works shows Poe's familiarity with the school. The poem, *AD OB-SERVANDISSIMVM PATREM, F. IACOBVM HVGONEM,* refers to Hugo's status as a Doctor of Theology and as a writer of epigrams on Parisian doctors. The little volume in which it appears seems to have been put together to honor a young doctor and is subtitled (in translation from the Latin), *The Antiquities of Medicine from the most ancient of poets, Homer, described allegorically.* This probably accounts for Poe's use of Hugo as a writer who gave far-fetched interpretations of Homer.

Euenis: Euneus, a prince of Lemnos, who helped rescue his mother from slavery, gave the captured Trojan prince Lycaon a silver bowl, and supplied the Greeks at Troy with wine. (*Iliad,* VII, 468; XXIII, 741 etc.) Or: Evenus, who, wanting to keep his daughter

a virgin, challenged suitors to race chariots with him, and cut off their heads on defeating them (*Iliad* II, 692; IX, 557).

John Calvin: French Protestant reformer (1509–1564).

Antinous: the most obnoxious of Penelope's suitors in the *Odyssey.*

Martin Luther: German monk, theologian and reformer (1483–1546).

Lotophagi: the "lotus eaters" of coastal Africa whom Odysseus visits in the *Odyssey,* book IX: eating the fruit made one lose the desire to return home.

Harpies: repulsive winged monsters who served, in Greek myth, to bring divine vengeance, punish the guilty, and carry off the souls of the dead.

"The Antidiluvians": A few months before he published this tale in *Graham's,* Poe unfavorably reviewed Dr. James McHenry's narrative poem of this title (*Graham's,* February 1841).

"Powhatan": "A Metrical Romance in Seven Cantos" by Seba Smith (Jack Downing). Poe panned it in the July 1841 *Graham's.*

"Cock Robin": the nursery-rhyme "Who killed cock robin?"

"Hop O'My Thumb": nursery tale?

"Dial": *The Dial,* the Transcendentalist organ. See "How to Write a Blackwood Article," note 11.

"Down-Easter": In another context Poe uses the phrase "Down-East Review" to mean *The Yankee and Boston Literary Gazette* (Hammond). Poe means the same periodical here; the clinching evidence is that John Neal (see "Diddling," note 2) wrote a novel called *The Down-Easters* (1833). The reasonable guess by Pollin (3) that Poe means *The North American Review* is therefore incorrect: Poe gets to *that* journal in the next paragraph. See note 3.

3. "North American Quarterly Humdrum": *The North American Review,* with which staid periodical Poe quarreled steadily. In "The Poetic Principle" he connects it with the "heresy of The Didactic," and says that Americans in general and Bostonians in particular are guilty of seeing literature as morality.

La Fontaine: French poet and fabulist (1621–

1695), author of *Fables choisies* (1668–1694), collection of satiric fables based on classical material.

4. *Defuncti injuriâ ne afficiantur:* Don't slander the dead.

De mortuis nil nisi bonum: "Of the dead be nothing said but good," a familiar Latin quotation which gained currency in a Latin translation of the life of Chilo by Diogenes Laertius. It was originally a Greek proverb.

dog: Glassheim thinks that Toby is literally a dog, and points to numerous details in Poe's tale which suggest caninity.

5. Good little boys in Poe's day did, in fact, sign pledges against alcoholic beverages; the temperance movement had, by the 1840s, gained sufficient strength among housewives to drive men out of the home and lead to the founding of the saloon as a national institution.

6. Poe quotes and slightly alters a line from Pope's *Essay on Man,* Epistle II, line 136:

> As Man, perhaps, the moment of his
>   breath,
> Receives the lurking principle of death;
> The young disease, that must subdue at
>   length,
> Grows with his growth, and strengthens
>   with his strength.

7. Mr. Coleridge . . . Mr. Kant . . . Mr. Carlyle . . . Mr. Emerson: Poe lists the four most immediately-recognizable transcendental authors. Note, however, that his narrator, who thinks in terms of morality as an act of Congress, and believes that thinking injures the health, is not intended to represent Poe's belief. As usual, Poe himself leaves open the option that transcendentalism errs not in its mysticism, but in its failure to see that the mysteries are "simply true." For another passage in which Poe comments on the last three of these authors see "Marginalia" (Harrison edition, XVI, 100).

"St. Patrick . . . toad": The indexed edition of collected documents pertaining to St. Patrick includes no reference to toads. There is one to frogs: ". . . as Paradise is without beasts, without a snake, without a lion, without a dragon, without a scorpion, without a mouse, without a frog, so is Ireland in the same manner without any harmful animal. . . ." In folklore, however, it is said that St. Patrick's malediction cleared Ireland not only of snakes, but of toads and "all vermin" as well.

A 1569 document, unconnected to St. Patrick, claims that toads contain a stone which can warn the bearer of venom, perhaps thus "awakening him" etc.

8. *Khoda shefa midêhed:* The language is Persian, and Poe's translation is correct, though not literal. Literally, "God gives healing."

there were times . . . eyes: Poe used this joke again in "Fifty Suggestions" in the May-June 1845 *Graham's.*

9. hipped: depressed.

the transcendentals: Poe refers to the states of acute sensitivity which the transcendental authors say makes possible inspiration and communion with the world-spirit. Poe says, in effect, "Watch out when you get them: in dark covered bridges, you may wind up communing with the devil."

Merry-Andrewism: A Merry Andrew is a clown or buffoon.

Tom-Fool: An insane person used to be called Tom Fool. Poe is possibly making a private joke about a passage he read in *Noctes Ambrosianae* by Christopher North (John Wilson), a series of imaginary colloquies among *Blackwood's* personalities (principally North and James Hogg), in which "North" says, ". . . when devoid of all probability—nay, at war with possibility—fiction is falsehood, fun folly, mirth mere maundering, humor forsooth! idiotcy, would-be-wit 'wersh as parritch without saut,' James a merry-Andrew, and the Shepherd—sad and sorry I am to say it—a Buffoon!" Poe also connects Wilson with Carlyle, "rant and cant," Emerson and other authors he dislikes. See the passage from "Marginalia," mentioned in note 7, above.

pigeon-wing: a fancy dance step, jumping and clicking the feet together.

Carlyle: Poe repeatedly complains about Carlyle's style: he writes "sentences which are no sentences," he is "obscure only," etc. See note 7 above.

10. Quarterly Review . . . "Fudge": "Fudge" ties this to Thomas Moore (see "Some Passages in the Life of a Lion," note 17). John Lockhart (1792–1854) whom Poe knew because he was a *Blackwood's* author, edited the *Quarterly Review* from 1826 to 1853. A Tory magazine, it could have been "nonplused" by Moore's Whig politics.

11. Paixhan: Henri Joseph Paixhans (1783–1854) was a famous French artillery officer who invented Paixhans' gun which threw explosive shells.

"Poets and Poetry of America": In 1843 Poe used a review of Rufus Griswold's *The Poets and Poetry of America with an Historical Introduction* as an occasion for an attack on Griswold. For more on Griswold, see "The Angel of the Odd," note 2, and the General Preface.

12. As a ruse, pirate ships often ran up the flag of some appropriate nation.

13. stile: a pun (stile = style).

Mr. Lord: Poe reviewed *Poems* by William W. Lord in the May 24, 1845 *The Broadway Journal.* Poe thought Lord stupid.

dot-and-carry-one: an old-fashioned way of teaching addition; here, a stuffy old schoolteacher.

14. homœopathists: Doctors until fairly late in the nineteenth century tended to believe in one or another "system" of medicine, generally predicated on the false notion that all diseases were related, and so could be treated in the same way. A homeopathist believed that small doses of medicines which produced symptoms of the disease treated would also cure it. The successful and century-old use of cowpox to prevent smallpox gave them their chief support. The gag here has to do with the nature of Dammit's "ailment."

iron bar: Poe connects iron and the devil. See "Bon-Bon" (Bon-Bon is felled by an iron lamp), for instance.

15. in heraldry, a mark of bastardy. Its proper name is "baton sinister." The phrase refers back also to the passage early in the tale in which we are told of the evil consequences of being beaten by a left-handed mother—"sinister" also means "left."

A Tale of Jerusalem

1. "He suffered his grey beard to ascend his severe face." The lines are from Lucan's *Pharsalia,* though Poe changed Lucan's *descendere* to *ascendere.* The passage in *Pharsalia* refers to Marcus Porcius Cato. "Porcius" is a family cognomen which means, literally, "piggy," or "pertaining to pigs." So Poe's translation is a bilingual triple pun: the bearded characters in Smith's novel are bristly; Cato, with his shaggy beard ascending or descending his face is a boar-bore; so are those in *Zillah,* and a pig will close Poe's tale. See Section Preface. See also "Cicero's Puns" in Isaac Disraeli's *Curiosities of Literature.*

2. Abel-Phittim: In the first version of this tale, Poe indulged in the vulgar humor he seems to have enjoyed in his early work: the name was Abel-Shittim (Harrison; Thompson 2). It seems likely that "Shittim" was also intended as word-play: less the extra "t" and "i," it is a rearrangement of the letters in "Smith" (see Section Preface). The story is one of a group Poe submitted in 1831 to a contest sponsored by the *Philadelphia Saturday Courier.* It did not win, but was published in the *Courier* for June 9, 1832. Poe used it again in the *Southern Literary Messenger,* April 1836, in his 1840 *Tales of the Grotesque and Arabesque,* and finally in *The Broadway Journal,* September 20, 1845.

Buzi-Ben-Levi: This name does not appear in *Zillah,* but is not a total fabrication. "Buzi" is the family name of the prophet Ezekiel, and "Ben-Levi" means "the son of Levi"; "Levi" signifies a Levite, or keeper of the Temple.

Pharisee: Pharisees figure prominently in the Smith novel: Zillah's ambitious stepmother tries to arrange a marriage between her and a prominent and crafty Pharisee leader.

Tammuz: Tamuz is the tenth month of the Jewish calendar, mentioned, quite gratuitously, in *Zillah,* II, 200. The year 3941 would work out to about 181 C. E.

Pompey: Poe probably made an error in his arithmetic. The siege involving Pompey is earlier than the events of *Zillah,* and much earlier than the date Poe names for this episode. See Section Preface.

3. Gizbarim: Smith spelled it Gizbarin, I, 44. Here and elsewhere in the tale, Poe (correctly) alters Smith's Hebrew.

4. Literally, the Phoenician sun god or any of several other gods worshipped by various Semitic peoples, but as used here, a false god.

5. "true as the Pentateuch": See Section Preface. For an example of its use in *Zillah,* see I, 17 of the 1828 edition.

Adonai: "Lord." Adonai is one of several terms used in Judaism to avoid saying the name of God when one encounters it in prayers. Smith spells it Adonoye on II, 160 and III, 104.

Ammonites: See Deuteronomy 2:19: descendents of Ben Ammi, the son of Lot; Or worshippers of Ammon; loosely, idolators.

6. "Allow me to kiss the fifth corner of your . . . beard," says a character in Zillah, I, 103, and Smith explains in a footnote, "The Jews reckoned five corners to their beards—one on either cheek, one on either lip, and one below on the chin,—all of which a priest was forbidden to shave." Smith's account does not quite square with Jewish tradition, which speaks of five fringes of the beard, two by each ear and one at the chin.

The Dashers: ". . . the Dashing Pharisee[s], so called, because [t]he[y] crawled along apart and in humility, the heel of one foot touching the great toe of the other, and neither foot being lifted from the ground, so that . . . [their] toes were dashed against the stones. . . ." Smith, IV, 144.

7. Circumvallatory: Poe probably got this odd word (meaning an enclosing, a defensive rampart or trench) from Zillah, I, 81.

fosse: moat or defensive ditch.

"tower called Adoni-Bezek": See Judges 1:5, 6 and 7. The name is that of a Caananite king.

temple of Belus: In Poe's day, scholars debated whether Birs Nimroud, a huge mound 235 feet high, was on the site of part of ancient Babylon, or even the tower of Babel. Some maintained that the tower of Belus was built on the site of an ancient temple to Baal (the tower of Babel). Belus was the most important of the Babylonian gods. A description of the temple of Belus appears in Herodotus.

8. Valley of the King: probably the Valley of Kings—see II Samuel 8:13, Psalms 60:2, II Chronicles 25:11, II Kings 14:7.

Adommin: Edomites. But the word was often used to mean "Romans."

9. "from Aleph to Tau": from A to Z. Actually the last letter of the Hebrew alphabet is tav, not the Greek tau. Poe snipped this from Zillah, II, 156.

Jod: See Section Preface. "Jod" is a way of writing the Hebrew letter ⸜, a small letter, usually called "yod," because its sound is like the English "y." A small boy is said to be as small as a Jod in I, 14 of the 1828 Zillah.

10. Phoebus: Greek god of the sun. Why do Roman soldiers use the Greek form?

Ædepol!: in Zillah, II, 56. The word does not have Hebrew precedents. It is a Latin oath, probably street-Latin, meaning, "By Pollux!"

11. El Elohim!: Both words are substitutes for God's name; together their meaning is approximately "the Lord God."

Teraphim: small idols, statuettes, or gods, mentioned in Zillah, I, 79 and III, 37.

Nergal: See Jeremiah 39:3, 13.

Nergal, Ashimah, Nibhaz, Tartak, Adramalech, and Anamalech: all named in II Kings 17:30–31. They don't occur in Smith, so the biblical passage is probably Poe's source for this list of false gods.

Succoth-benith: This is in Smith (see below) and also in II Kings 17:30, and probably provided Poe his cue; looking up one false god gave him a list of a number of others. Smith writes, ". . . what is the exquisitely sculptured figure I see installed within . . . that splendid throne upon the stern of the vessel[?]" ". . . the figure is the Venus of the Sea, the Succoth Benoth [sic], the daughter of Assyria, to which this lewd idolator and his heathen fellow-worshippers doubtless pay their adorations" (Zillah, II, pp. 12–13).

Dagon: From Zillah, II, 41, 109 and 292; III, 205; IV, 68.

Belial: From Zillah, II, 41, 109 and III, 66.

Baal-Perith, Baal-Peor, Baal-Zebub: When Zillah urges her father the priest to be more tolerant of the prejudices and errors of the heathen Romans, he responds by speaking of their "brutal besotted ignorance" and concludes with a list of false gods: "Succoth-Benoth [sic] . . . Dagon, Belial, Baal-borith [sic], Baal-peor, and Baal-zebub himself, the very prince of devils!" (II, 109).

12. Katholim: Katholikin, overseers of the treasury in Zillah, I, 43. The title does not seem to exist in Jewish tradition.

13. frankincense: See I, 9 of the 1828 edition of Zillah.

loins girded up: Smith, who explains almost everything, explains that the everyday dress of the Hebrews included tunic and cloak, which ". . . were turned up and tucked into the girdle in riding or walking, or whenever the employment of the wearer rendered succinct garments more convenient: whence the phrase of girding up the loins. . . ." Poe must have been amused by Smith's pedantry.

14. A word used frequently in *Zillah*: II, 41 and 117, and many other instances. It is not Hebrew in origin; the "related" Hebrew root means "soft." See Isaiah 47:1, Proverbs 25:15 and Deuteronomy 28:56. It does, however, appear in the Christian testament; Jesus uses it in the Sermon on the Mount, Matthew 5:12. It is a strongly abusive word, meaning either "fool" or "braggart" (depending on from which language it was borrowed), but much more powerful than either.

15. See Section Preface. Smith uses this expression. Examples are in II, 110, 226. "Boosheh" as an expletive occurs in the Bible; it means "disgrace" (Jeremiah 15:9, 49:23, 50:12). "He" is an abbreviation for a circumlocution, "hashem," for God's name. The phrase would be said "Boosheh hashem," not "Booshoh he." "Boosheh hashem" would mean "a disgrace before God," but it does not occur in Smith nor the Bible, though it is probably what Smith intends.

16. Engedi: Smith refers in I, 185 to "the thickets of Engaddi."

Jehosaphat: See I Kings 22:41. In *Zillah*, see I, pp. 3, 166, and 241.

17. jewels of the Pectoral: Jewish tradition does not explain exactly how the breast-plate of the high priest was supposed to reflect God's will (see Exodus 28:4, 15, 17, 30), but Smith seems to believe that the jewels glowed —see II, 161–162 and IV, 125.

18. Bashan: an area east of the Jordan.

shawm, psaltery, harp, huggab, cythern, sackbut: See I, 31 of *Zillah*. Zillah, Smith tells us, is very musical and plays psaltery, harp, cythern and sacbut, all stringed instruments. Lilla, a minor female character, plays the sacbut also (IV, 139). The shawn is an ancient oboe-like double-reed instrument. Smith says that the huggub is a ". . . Hebrew organ—a rude instrument, resembling Pan's pipe" (I, 210).

19. a phrase deserving parody, because Smith uses it repeatedly. In *Zillah*, II, 41, a high priest from the Temple in Jerusalem eats a dish prepared of "prime oxen" which had been offered in sacrifice at a Roman temple. Smith's ignorance of Jewish law is considerable: none of the Jews at the dinner objects to oysters; indeed, one of them has deliberately procured them as a dish to please the priest. The priest, at any rate, objects vehemently to the sacrificial meat and calls it "the flesh of the unutterable animal itself." It is not, in short, from a pig. The priest, however, uses the same phrase in II, 269 to refer to a pig, and when, in III, 51, he is served a wild boar at a feast at Antony's villa, he says "El Elohim!—it is the unutterable flesh—the beast of abomination—. . . ." "El Elohim" means "God is with us" and is most familiar in its reversed form, "Emanu-El."

The Literary Life of Thingum Bob, Esq.

1. "Thingum Bob" is an alternative spelling for "thingamabob," something you've forgotten the name of. Poe's point is that his "author" is totally unimportant. Pollin shows that Poe's choice of Bob's name and profession could have been influenced by Thomas Moore's *The Fudges in England*. In Letter Three of Moore's work Fanny Fudge tells her cousin about "a literary man who edits 'live authors as if they were posthumous,'" and says "He was Lady Jane Thingumbob's last novel's editor" (Pollin 14). "Goosetherumfoodle" is probably nonsense. "Footle" (foodle), in fact, means "nonsense." This satire appeared first in the *Southern Literary Messenger*, December 1844, and again in *The Broadway Journal*, July 26, 1845. See Section Preface for the specific targets of Poe's satire and the referents of other "nonsense" words in this tale.

2. Richard "Pop" Emmons (1788–c. 1837) is a very minor writer at whom Melville also pokes fun. He was the author of "The Fredoniad," published in the *Western Monthly Review* 2:176. The point is that Thingum's literary intelligence is so low that he lumps Shakespeare and Pop Emmons together.

3. *very* remote ancestors: That is, Bob's origins are very obscure.

effusion . . . barbers: The bane of the publishing world in Poe's day was "puffing": over-praising the work of friends who would then do the same for you in *their* magazines. So Thingum Bob's introduction to literature involves "puffery"—his father rewards the editor-poet who praises his hair-oil. When Poe arrived in New York in 1844, he encountered all manner of puffery for Lewis Clark's edition of his brother's work (Whipple 3).

4. creative spirit or inspiration.

5. relative so surnamed: Willis Gaylord

Clark had been named after a rich uncle (Willis Gaylord), too (Whipple 3).

two birds with one stone: See Section Preface. This list of careers identifies Thingum with Fay as well as Clark (Pollin 14).

6. As Thingum Bob has no ancestry, so he has no education, failing to recognize Dante, Shakespeare, Homer, and Milton.

Ugolino: Ugolino della Gherardesca is the subject of a famous passage in Dante's *Inferno*; he is consigned to the ninth circle of hell, reserved for traitors, where the memory of how he, two sons, and two grandsons were starved to death drives him in his hatred to gnaw upon the skull of Archbishop Ruggieri degli Ubaldini, leader of the rival political party which defeated Ugolino's party and murdered him. Thingum Bob is too stupid to understand Ugolino's grief over the death of his children; hence Poe's allusion to "brats."

"angels" and "ministers . . .": At the entrance of the ghost of his father, in *Hamlet* (I, 4, 39–40), Hamlet says,

> Angels and ministers of grace defend us!
> Be thou a spirit of health or
>   goblin damn'd.

either a Greek or a Choctaw: Thingum Bob doesn't know a Creek from a Greek. The phrase shows racial condescension toward American Indians, who are assumed to be stupid and ignorant savages. To confuse Homer, a "Greek" (it was not yet clear in Poe's day that a poet actually named Homer had not literally "written" the *Iliad*) with an Indian is as strong evidence of ignorance as Poe can devise.

"Achilles' wrath" and "grease": The *Iliad* opens with an invocation; the goddess is asked to sing of the wrath of Achilles which brought, in the Chapman translation, "Infinite sorrowes on the Greekes.'" "Grease" is a bad pun on "Greece."

"hail" and "holy light": Book Three of Milton's *Paradise Lost* opens, "Hail, holy light! offspring of heav'n first-born" Homer is traditionally supposed to have been blind; Milton was blind.

7. Oppodeldoc: Willis Clark's pen name in the *Knickerbocker* magazine was "Ollapod," a name used by Poe in "A Predicament," and similar to "Oppodeldoc" (Whipple 3). Pollin (11) points out that "Op[p]odeldoc" is

the name of several very famous patent medicines based on an ages-old formula, and peddled vigorously in the U. S. in Poe's day. The tale contains a number of humorous turns based on that association: readers are "nauseated with a sad dose . . ." etc. Pollin (11) doubts Whipple's Ollapod-Oppodeldoc equation. Pollin (6) finds still another source for the name "Ollapod." See "A Predicament," note 7. Thackeray uses Opodeldoc as the name of a horse (the medicine was recommended, in one form, as a horse linament): referring to Club Snobs, in his *The Book of Snobs* (Thackeray had written on snobs as early as 1829, but his collection published under this title appeared in 1848) he writes, "They recollect the history of that short period in which they have been ornaments of the world by the names of winning-horses. As political men talk about 'the reform year,' 'the year the Whigs went out,' and so forth, these young sporting bucks speak of *Tarnation's* year, or *Opodeldoc's* year, or the year when *Catawampus* ran second for the Chester cup." Two other names shared by Poe in this tale and Thackeray in *The Book of Snobs* are "Daddy-Long-Legs" and "Lollipop." In Poe both are the names of journals. In Thackeray the former is another horse's name and the latter the surname of Lord Claude Lollipop, the Marquis of Sillabub's younger son. Poe's use of "Snob" as a pen-name later in this tale suggests some connection, though we don't know its precise nature.

the city of the transcendentals: Boston. Thingum Bob shows off his pretended erudition by using foreign terms whenever he can. The joke is double: first, that transcendentalists speak a language so lofty that it's foreign; second, Thingum mixes his metaphors: the "*coup-de-grâce*" is a death-blow, inappropriate to "nascent" hopes. The idea was introduced a paragraph earlier in the word-play about "abortions" and "labored in vain."

8. The central gag in this series of "notices" is that the magazine editors, like Thingum Bob, are too ignorant to recognize either the sources of the stolen poems or their worth. So the "Hum-Drum" says that Dante has no imagination. Clearly, "Poesy" refers to "Poe."

9. This phrase stuck in Poe's mind. He used it in numerous variations in his (1849) poem "The Bells" (See also "A Predicament,"

notes 3 and 5): "What a world of merriment their melody foretells!" . . . . "What a world of happiness their harmony foretells!" . . . . "What a gush of euphony voluminously wells!" . . . . "What a tale of terror, now, their turbulency tells!" . . . . "What a world of solemn thought their monody compels!"

10. Emperor so named: more ignorance. There never was, of course, an emperor by this name.

Nat Lee: Nathaniel Lee (c. 1649–1692) was an English tragic dramatist who spent five years (1684–1689) in Bedlam.

11. The *Knickerbocker* had run "Jack and Jill" in May 1843, though not, of course, as "original lyrics" (Whipple 3). All of the little literary magazines were stingy of pay, hence the frequent references to payment in this tale.

12. verbatim and literally.

13. Poe has some pet phrases which show up in both serious and satirical contexts. In "The Cask of Amontillado," we learn that Montresor's arms bear the motto, "*Nemo me impune lacessit*": "No one provokes me with impunity."

14. upon the *tapis*: up for consideration.

penny-a-liner: a cheap journalist; that is, a man who works for "a penny-a-line."

15. Some magazines did, in fact, boast that they paid well for contributions, though, as Poe well knew, most paid very little, and some not at all.

16. A lustrum is five years, so Thingum is only 14 or so.

17. hard cash.

18. Printer's code for a paid insertion— September 15, one time—of the same sort used today in many newspapers in the want-ads. It means that the item is paid for, and is to run just one time. Poe implies that editors themselves write the flattering accounts of their magazines and even pay to have the "puffery" printed. He is not exaggerating very much: for a good account of what passed for professional ethics among American magazinists, see Moss (3).

19. excellence . . . plates: Physical appearance sold magazines. Those which could afford plates showing exotic places, fashions, or sentimental scenes had larger circulations. Poe disliked steel plates and argued for simple and idiomatic woodcut engravings.

Hyperion . . . Satyr: In Greek mythology, "Hyperion" can mean one of the titans or, in later usage, Apollo, god of music and poetry. Poe probably intends the latter meaning, and contrasts Apollo with a satyr, an earthy woodland deity in more-or-less human form, with goat's legs, horns and pointed ears, noted for energetic and wanton sexuality.

100,000: literary journals struggled along on tiny circulations. The figures in these "notices" are absurdly exaggerated; editors were prone to exaggerate. When Poe worked for *Graham's Magazine,* one of the most prosperous, he and the proprietor spoke of building its circulation from 5,500 to 40,000. That was enormous for a literary magazine of the day, and probably somewhat exaggerated. *Graham's,* moreover, was not really all that literary—much of its contents was closer to what we would expect to find in a commercial magazine. Most literary periodicals had circulations more like that of Poe's *The Broadway Journal,* which had less than 1,000 subscribers. Even the great *Edinburgh Review* in Great Britain never had more than 14,000 paid subscribers.

20. pen-name (literally, "war-name").

21. Hardly an exaggeration. Poe wrote several articles about the poor pay for writers in his day, and there are sad letters from him to editors begging that they pay him the few dollars they promised for articles and reviews.

22. gem.

23. pronounced.

24. dishcloth.

25. "Boz" is the pen-name of Charles Dickens. "This linking of Willis Clark and Dickens may have been a covert allusion to Lewis's own reference to the likeness between Martin Chuzzlewit and Willis" (Whipple 3).

26. In a "puff" for the *Literary Remains of the Late Willis Gaylord Clark* in the July 1844 *Knickerbocker* appears the apparent source of Poe's gag: ". . . Clark was . . . as many-sided, to use an expressive German phrase, as almost any writer of whom we have knowledge" (Quoted by Whipple 3).

27. "Lord Brougham's Speeches": Henry Brougham (1778–1868), a most prominent editor and contributor to the *Edinburgh Review,* later Lord Chancellor. Poe would not have liked his reformist, Whig politics; his contentiousness was notorious. See "How to Write a Blackwood Article," note 4 and "The

System of Dr. Tarr and Professor Fether," note 18.

"Cobbett's Complete Works": William Cobbett (1766–1835) was a radical pamphleteer and agitator who cried out against social abuses prevalent in England. Fined, jailed, forced to flee to the United States as an exile, he returned to England to continue the fight, and became a member of Parliament. Poe, who shared the Tory fear of "the mob," was not sympathetic to radicals and reformers.

"New Slang-Syllabus": See "How to Write a Blackwood Article," note 6.

"Prentice's Billingsgate": Pollin (3) identifies George D. Prentice as an "abusive editor"; "Billingsgate" is vulgar slang. In one of his attacks on Poe (Knickerbocker, 22 [October 1843] 392), Lewis Gaylord Clark quotes George Denison Prentice of the Louisville Daily Journal instead of writing the attack himself. Moss (2) connects this to Poe's including a reference to Prentice and Clark in his revision of "The Literary Life of Thingum Bob, Esq." for The Broadway Journal version. Poe intends a list of intemperate and abusive writers.

gander's egg: There's no such thing, of course —a gander is a male goose. There is probably some slang expression involved which we've lost.

28. More bitterness about the tightwad policies of most magazines—not only the contributors, but members of the staff, too, are underpaid.

29. The Latin is faulty; aper is "wild boar." Poe is probably playing bilingual puns again; Thingum Bob calls his father an "old bore." Poe's point is that to be a successful magazinist you have to be the sort of person who would abuse his own (kindly) father.

30. rem: This is the accusative case of the Latin word res, "thing."

quocunque and modo: Apparently Poe means quocumque modo, "in whatever manner."

Poe is playing on the name "Thingum Bob" —Thingum doesn't even know his own name.

31. Thingum has now caught on to how the system works. If you want your work praised, you must be an editor with the power to praise in return. Now that he owns his own paper, his success is assured.

bouleversement: somersault.

32. "J'ai fait l'histoire": This is from Cha-

teaubriand's Mémoires d'outre-tombe, IV, Book 12.

33. Buffon: Georges Louis Leclerc, Compte de Buffon (1707–1788), the great French naturalist.

Hogarth: William Hogarth (1697–1764), the British artist. If they had anything to say about diligence, it is obviously inappropriate to Thingum Bob's case: it is not diligence, but crafty greed.

34. tête baissée: head lowered. It's French, of course, not Kickapoo.

whizz . . . now: This breathless—and careless —style, full of dashes, cheap rhetorical tricks and slang, was, as Poe implies, typical of a great deal of magazine prose. See "How to Write a Blackwood Article" for more on magazine styles.

The Duc De L'Omelette

1. Poe's motto is from William Cowper (1731–1800). Book One of The Task is called "The Sofa"; Poe quotes line 337, changing "stepp'd" to "stepped." This section deals with a walk in an estate; the preceding lines give the context:

Refreshing change! where now the
    blazing sun?
By short transition we have lost his glare,
And stepp'd at once into a cooler clime.

2. Keats: John Keats (1795–1821). In point of fact, Keats died of tuberculosis, but the poet did feel that critics had destroyed his chance of making a living through poetry, and Byron's scornful line about how he had let himself "be snuffed out by an article" perpetuated the idea of which Poe makes use. Poe used a paragraph very similar to this one in "Marginalia" (Godey's Lady's Book, September 1845) in which he says, a little more accurately, "Keats did (or did not) die of a criticism. . . ."

Poe's tale is early, first published in The Philadelphia Saturday Courier, March 3, 1832. He used it in the Southern Literary Messenger for February 1836, in the 1840 Tales of the Grotesque and Arabesque, and finally in The Broadway Journal, October 11, 1845. A shorter version was in both the London and New York editions of Bentley's Miscellany in October 1840. All versions after 1832 bear the present title; in 1832, "Duc" was spelled "Duke."

Who was it . . . "The Andromache?": Mont-fleury. The author of the *Parnasse Réformé* makes him speak in Hades:—*"L'homme donc qui voudrait savoir ce dont je suis mort, qu'il ne demande pas s'il fut de fièvre ou de podagre ou d'autre chose, mais qu'il entende que ce fut de 'L'Andromaque' "* [Poe's note]. Poe slightly misquotes Gabriel Guéret's *Le Parnasse Réformé* (1668), in which Montfleury (Zacharie Jacob Montfleury, 1600–1667) is made to say,

> *Qui voudra donc savoir de quoy je suis mort, qu'il ne demande point si c'est de la fièvre, de l'hydropisie, ou de la goutte, mais qu'il sache que c'est d'Andromaque.*

In English,

> The man then who would know of what I died, let him not ask if it were of the fever, the dropsy, or the gout; but let him know that it was of *the Andromache!* (Disraeli's translation)

Poe's version translates,

> The man then who would know of what I died, let him not ask if it were of fever or of gout (in the feet) or of something else, but let him understand that it was of *The Andromache.*

The translation given in the *Southern Literary Messenger* version, however, reads exactly the same as the Disraeli translation. Poe probably got the idea for this reference and note from Isaac Disraeli's article "Tragic Actors" in his *Curiosities of Literature*, in which his translation appears. We guess that Poe began with Disraeli's English, and translated it into French, without ever having seen the French original. Hence his *L'homme donc* etc. instead of *Qui voudra donc* etc. Probably he skipped "dropsy" because he didn't know the word; hence also the use of another word for "gout."

Andromaque: a tragedy (1667) by Jean Racine.

ortolan: Literally, a kind of European bunting and gourmet delicacy. But Poe is less interested in birds than in Nathaniel Parker Willis. Poe got the precious details about naked ortolans, soft music, etc. from a review of Benjamin Disraeli's *The Young Duke* (Hirsch). See Section Preface.

L'histoire en est brève: "The story of it is short."

Apicius. Marcus Flavius Apicius (fl. C.E. 14–

37), a Roman epicure who wrote a book on the ways of tempting an appetite; ". . . his own name is still proverbial in all matters of gastronomy."

3. *Chaussée D'Antin:* A street in Paris noted as the residence of *"gens à la mode"*— people of fashion. See Map of Poe's Paris in "The Murders in the Rue Morgue" for its location.

far Peru: See Section Preface. A Peruvian ortolan = a South American trullian.

La Bellissima: the most beautiful.

4. ottoman: Willis supposedly had a "copy of the ottoman in the Governor General's mansion in Quebec" (Daughrity). See Section Preface.

Cadêt: Pollin (3) says it might be Antoine Cadet de Vaux.

5. olive: See Section Preface.

"Horreur . . . papier": "Horror(s)! Dog! Baptiste! [Willis pretended he had a servant named Alphonse.] the bird! Oh, good God! this simple bird whose feathers you have removed and which you have served without paper frills." Willis' "Editor's Table" was filled with French, hence Poe's frequent use of it here.

6. haughtiness.

7. It is true.

8. Foie-Gras: *Pâté de foie gras* is a famous French gourmet food, a paste made of the liver of geese. As one of the Duc's titles, it suggests Willis' luxurious affectations. See Section Preface.

"Mazurkiad": apparently a made-up title. A "mazurka" is a Polish dance, and the suffix "iad" suggests an epic.

Academy: Daughrity thinks Poe may mean a famous Boston supper club which had as members two men from each of a number of professions; Willis was one of the two author-members.

Bourdon: Pollin (3) says this is the name of a bonafide tailor.

robe-de-chambre: See "The Murders in the Rue Morgue," note 15.

Rombêt: Pollin (3) says this name Poe made up.

9. Baal-Zebub: Beelzebub, Prince of demons, the devil, associated with the ancient Philistine deity who was worshipped as Lord of the Flies.

rose-wood . . . ivory: Willis said his office had a rosewood desk. See Section Preface.

curiously scented: Another dig at Willis, this time for his bottle of "perfumed Hungary water." See Section Preface.

Belial: In Milton's *Paradise Lost*, Beelzebub is the Prince of the Fallen Angels and Belial is another of the fallen angels.

10. another favorite phrase of Poe's. See "The Cask of Amontillado," note 8.

11. *bien comme il faut*: the way it should be.

parmi les nues: among the clouds. The dig at Boston is for its reputation as the capital of American arts, and particularly at the mystically tinged transcendentalist writers.

cresset: a metal holder for a light. Apparently, Poe means that the ruby is inside.

Gheber: a fire-worshiper or Parsee.

12. total effect.

13. Kupris: Cyprus, traditionally the birthplace of Aphrodite, whose worship there in ancient times is synonymous with licentiousness.

Astarte: In Phoenician mythology, Astarte is the goddess of love. She is associated with Aphrodite.

Astoreth: the same goddess as Astarte and Aphrodite.

Rafaelle: Raphael (1483–1520), the great Italian painter. The only "scandal" which seems strong enough to explain Poe's reference to damnation involves Raphael's use of his lovely mistress "La Fornarina" (the baker's daughter), whose real name was probably Margarita Luti, as his model for a number of paintings, among them two Madonnas—the face of the Sistine Madonna and the Madonna of Francis I in the Louvre, as well as in the Saint Cecilia in Bologna.

14. "It is true that he thought a good deal about these things—but!"

15. *Le pauvre Duc!*: The poor Duke!

petit-maître: fop.

et qui sourit: and who smiled.

si amèrement: so bitterly.

16. *Mais il faut agir*: But one must act.

B———: Daughrity thinks this is probably Joseph T. Buckingham, with whose *Courier* Willis had carried on a half-serious battle over Willis' affectations. See Section Preface.

See also "Some Passages in the Life of a Lion," note 26. Like that story, this one is too early to refer to Willis' experience with a duel.

il avait tué ses six hommes: He had killed his six men.

il peut s'échapper: He can escape.

17. *Mais il joue!*: But he gambles!

the "*Diable*" of the Abbé Gualtier: This allusion has eluded us (S.G.L.).

que le Diable n'ose pas refuser un jeu d'écarté: That the Devil doesn't dare refuse a game of *écarté* (a card game).

18. Père Le Brun: Possibly Le P. Laurent le Brun (1608–1663), a French Jesuit, author of *Virgilius Christianus* (1661). He was a classical theoretician, apparently well-known in his time. Another possibility is that Poe remembered the name "Le Brun" from Disraeli's article "Tragic Actors," mentioned in note 2 above. Two other possibilities: Pierre Antoine Lebrun (1785–1873), a lyric and dramatic poet, author of *Mary Stuart* (1820) and *Voyage en Grèce* (1827); Ponce Denis Ecouchard-Lebrun (1729–1807), a lyric and epigramatic poet, author of *A Buffon* and *Le Vengeur*. We lean to the first Le Brun because of an item about him in *The Southern Literary Messenger*, in the December 1835 issue, early in Poe's association with that magazine.

Si je perds: If I lose.

je serai deux fois perdu: I shall be doubly damned.

voilà tout!: That's all.

Si je gagne, je reviendrai à mes ortolans—que les cartes soient preparées!: If I win, I shall return to my ortolans—let the cards be made ready.

19. Francis I of France (1494–1547) reigned 1515–1547; Charles V (1500–1558), Holy Roman Emperor (1519–1556) and King of Spain (1516–1556). The two monarchs clashed repeatedly during a lengthy and complex series of confrontations.

20. *C'est à vous à faire*: It's your turn.

en présentant le Roi: while presenting the King.

21. "Had Alexander . . . Diogenes": See "Diddling," note 7.

"*que . . . Diable*": that if he hadn't been De L'Omelette he wouldn't have had any objection to being the Devil.

Some Passages in the Life of a Lion

1. Bishop Joseph Hall (1574–1656). See note 3 for the source and significance of Poe's motto.

2. the author . . . mask: Famous examples of hidden identities. The "Letters of Junius" appeared in the (London) *Public Advertiser* from 1769 to 1772. Since their mysterious author had access to secret ministerial information, enormous curiosity about the authorship was generated. The "man in the mask" refers to "The Man in the Iron Mask," a mysterious person imprisoned by Louis XIV for more than four decades. Whoever he was, he died in 1703 in the Bastille. His fame was kept alive long after his death by speculation, drama and fiction. See "The Man That Was Used Up," at note 16.

Fum-Fudge: London. See note 17.

3. Hungerford says that this is "A reference to Thomas Bartolin, the anatomist, 1616–1680, or to Gaspard Bartholin, 1655–1738, author of *Specimen historiae anatomicae partium corporis humani*." Pollin (3) lists Gaspar Bartholinus. We are quite certain Poe had in mind the Italian jurist Bartolus (Bartolo da Sassoferrate, 1314–1357), because of his use of the motto from Hall. Hall's Satire III, Book II of the *Virgidemiarum* attacks wealthy and unscrupulous lawyers who prey on trouble as flies on a wound, while genuine scholars go barefoot. Poe alters the lines he quotes. The original lines 19–22 read,

Genus *and* Species *long since
    barefoote went,
Vpon their ten-toes in wild wanderment:
Whiles father Bartoll on his
    footcloth rode
Vpon high pauement gayly siluer-strowd.*

Genus and *species* are logical terms used as nicknames for scholars; Bartoll is Bartolus, the jurist and professor of Civil Law at the University of Perugia; the footcloth is a rich, ornamented cloth laid on the back of one's horse, and the high pauement is the favored part of the street (Davenport). Older editions of Hall note Bartolus' "magnificence" and "liberality" and refer to accounts of "the gorgeous trappings of his horse, and of his scattering money among the people" as he rode through Bologna. Poe might have identified him with a nastier lawyer of the same name, the character Bartolus in John Fletcher and Philip Massinger's play *The Spanish Curate*

(1622), in which Bartolus is a greedy and unscrupulous lawyer. Poe uses Hall in the motto to suggest the parallel between the injustice he satirizes and the unjust situation in the magazine world where little men prey upon the talented. See also Isaac Disraeli's account of Gaspar Barthius in his article "Secret History of Authors who have Ruined their Booksellers" in *Curiosities of Literature*. Like Jones, Barthius was a prodigy and something of a charlatan. Poe knew the *Curiosities* well.

4. spirit or inspiration.

5. bluestocking. See "The Man That Was Used Up," note 13.

6. N. P. Willis, on arriving in London in 1834, looked up the Countess of Blessington, who became his hostess, and through whom he was introduced to her circle of celebrities. She, in short, made him a literary "lion" (Benton 3).

7. piece of *virtù*: rare or wonderful artifact; collector's item.

Jermyn street: a London street very near Piccadilly Circus, running from Haymarket to Albemarle.

8. choice or sought-after people.

9. a modern Platonist: Perhaps Thomas Taylor (1758–1835), referred to as "the Platonist" (Benton 3), an eminent English classicist, known as a great conversationalist and social butterfly, qualities which gained him the patronage of the wealthy and influential, in turn enabling him to publish his works.

Porphry: Neo-Platonic philosopher (233–304) and disciple of Plotinus.

Iamblicus: Iamblichus, pupil of Porphry (fl. 306–337) and also considered a Neo-Platonist.

Plotinus: Greek Neo-Platonic philosopher (204–270).

Proclus: another Neo-Platonist (412–485); disciple of Syrianus.

Hierocles: Platonist who headed a flourishing school in Alexandria in the fifth century.

Maximus Tyrius: Platonist born in Tyre in the second century; he wrote in Greek and lived in Athens and Rome.

Syrianus: Greek Neo-Platonist, died c. 450.

10. a human-perfectability man: Perhaps Edward Lytton Bulwer (Bulwer-Lytton, 1803–1873) (Benton 3).

Turgot: Anne Robert Jacques Turgot (1727–

1781), economic theorist of the French Enlightenment.

Price: Dr. Richard Price (1723–1792) was the author of a sermon in which he compared the French Revolution to the English Revolution of 1688, and congratulated the French for attaining freedom. His political liberalism had induced the Continental Congress to invite him to the colonies, then engaged in their war with England.

Priestly: Joseph Priestly (1733–1804) the scientist, theologian and philosopher whose perfectionist ideas and religious sentiments forced him to emigrate to the United States in 1794.

Condorcet: Marie Jean de Caritat, Marquis de Condorcet (1743–1794), French revolutionary social theorist.

De Staël: Anne Louis Germaine Necker (Madame de Staël) (1766–1817), French critic, essayist, and novelist who was liberal and romantic in sympathies.

"Ambitious Student in Ill Health": a reference to Bulwer's "Conversations with an Ambitious Student in His Last Illness," which "supports the doctrine of human perfectability" (Benton 3).

11. Poe liked this joke, and used it in "The Purloined Letter" (see that tale, note 9), substituting "poets" for "philosophers." That story appeared in 1845; "Lion-izing/A Tale" he published first in the Southern Literary Messenger for May 1835. He apparently thought well of it, using it in both the 1840 and 1845 collections of his stories, entering it in contests, planning to use it in several collections which he never succeeded in having printed, and publishing it one last time in The Broadway Journal for March 15, 1845, as "Some Passages in the Life of a Lion," the version which we follow. It is very different from the earlier versions: characters and authors who are alluded to appear in different order, the list of names included is somewhat altered, and most sentences have been moved, revised, or both. Basic ideas and events are unchanged.

12. Belief in the consubstantiality of the Trinity, or in a physics which is based upon a single essence or substance. The context suggests the latter meaning.

13. Theologos Theology: possibly Dionysius Lardner (1793–1859).

Eusebius: a leader in the Arian heresy, died 341.

Arianus: Arian, a presbyter of Alexandria in the fourth century who denied that Jesus was consubstantial with God.

Council of Nice (Nicaea): In this city in 325 a doctrine was adopted to counter the Arian heresy.

Puseyism: another name for the Tractarian movement in which Edward Bouverie Pusey (1800–1882) was a leader.

consubstantialism: Belief that Jesus is "substantial" in the Eucharistic elements, along with the bread and wine, which are felt to be unchanged.

Homoousios: the doctrine that the Father and Son are of like but not the same substance or essence.

Homoouioisios: the doctrine that Father, Son, and Holy Ghost are of the same essence. In his Curiosities of Literature Isaac Disraeli speaks of the confusion of the words "Homoousion" and "Homoiousion."

14. Rocher de Cancale: a famous Parisian restaurant.

Muriton: Miroton (?), a dish in which a sliced, cooked meat is warmed over sauteed onions, and served in a rich brown sauce.

velouté sauce; veal à la St. Menehoult: See "The System of Dr. Tarr and Professor Fether," note 5.

marinade à la St. Florentin: A marinade is a seasoned liquid in which food is steeped. "A la Florentine," a culinary term, is not applied to marinades.

orange jellies en mosaïques: See "How to Write a Blackwood Article," note 22.

15. Bibulus: For "bibulous," fond of drinking.

The other allusions in this paragraph are to types of wines. Poe repeats his own error (see "The Cask of Amontillado") about Sherry and Amontillado, and he leaves out the "t" in "Haut-Brion."

16. Tintontintino: a made-up name suggesting "tints" and Venetian painter Tintoretto.

Cimabué: Giovanni Cimabué (c. 1240–c. 1302), important Florentine painter.

Arpino: Giuseppe Cesari, "Il Cavaliere D'Arpino" (c. 1565–1640), Italian historical painter.

Carpaccio: Vittore Carpaccio, Italian painter born about 1450.

Argostino: Poe probably means either "Agostino dalle Prospettive," an early sixteenth-century Italian painter, or Agostino Veneziano, celebrated Italian engraver born c. 1490.

Caravaggio: Michelangelo Amerighi da Caravaggio (1569–1609), Italian painter.

Albano: Francesco Albani (1578–1660), Italian painter.

Titian: Tiziano Vecellio (c. 1477–1576), Venetian painter.

frows of Rubens: women of Peter Paul Rubens (1577–1640), Flemish painter.

Jan Steen: Dutch genre painter (c. 1626–1679).

17. President of the Fum Fudge University: a reference to Thomas Moore, author of the popular *The Fudge Family in Paris* (1818) which contained a political satire entitled "Fum and Hum, the Two Birds of Royalty," and which "led to a host of parodies" (Pollin 13). See also "Never Bet the Devil Your Head," note 9.

Bendis: a Thracian lunar goddess, worshipped also in Lemnos and Bithynia.

Bubastis . . . Artemis: Pollin (13) demonstrates that these references are from Thomas Moore's novel *The Epicurean* (1827). Bubastis is an Egyptian goddess symbolized by the cat and often identified with the Greek Artemis, goddess of the moon. The equivalent Roman goddess is Diana.

18. Stamboul: Istanbul.

angels . . . horns: Poe distorts lore from the Moslem religion for humorous effect. The *Dictionary of Islam* says,

> Our earth [one of seven] is said to be supported on the shoulders of an angel, who stands upon a rock of ruby, which rock is supported on a huge bull with four thousand eyes, and the same number of ears, noses, mouths, tongues, and feet; between every one of each is a distance of five hundred years' journey.

19. Aeschylus: great Greek tragic poet (525–456 B.C.E.).

Isaeus: Greek orator (fl. c. 400 B.C.E.).

Lysias: Athenian orator (458–c. 378 B.C.E.).

Theophrastus: Greek philosopher (c. 374–c. 286 B.C.E.). Some of his works are "Moral Characters," a "History of Plants," and "On the Causes of Plants."

Conic Sections of Apollonius: an allusion to geometric work by Apollonius Pergaeus, who flourished during the middle of the third century B.C.E., author of *Treatise on Conic Sections*, the eighth book of which is lost.

Pindar: great Greek lyric poet (c. 520–439 or 442 B.C.E.).

Homer Junior: "Homerus, one of the Pleiades" (Pollin 3), a school of French poets of the sixteenth century. We have been unable to identify him more precisely. The only epic poet among the Pleiades is Ronsard, whose epic is incomplete, but who was not a dramatist.

20. Almack's Assembly Rooms, King Street, St. James, London, "the center of splendid social functions during the first half of the nineteenth century" (Benton 3).

21. If the Freudian reading of this tale is correct (see Section Preface), this passage is exceedingly obscene.

22. *Diavolo!*: The Devil!

23. *Dios guarda*: Heaven help us!

24. *Mille tonnerres*: By thunder! By Jove!

25. *Tausend teufel*: Thousand devils. Poe's German is faulty.

Bluddennuff: i.e., of aristocratic lineage.

26. Chalk-Farm: It would seem logical here that Poe refers to Willis' famous argument with Captain Frederick Marryat, which led to a challenge to a duel (though friends intervened and the duel never took place). As Daughrity points out, however, Poe published the story before news of the feud became current. There had, however, been a famous duel in 1806 at the Chalk Farm between the editor of *The Edinburgh Review*, Francis Jeffrey (1773–1850), and Thomas Moore (1779–1852); and Poe, whose tale incorporates allusions to Moore, probably had it in mind (Pollin 13, Thompson 1).

27. Beast!

Devil in the Belfry

1. first published in the Philadelphia *Saturday Chronicle and Mirror of the Times*, May 18, 1839; included in *Tales of the Grotesque and Arabesque* (1840); used again in *The Broadway Journal*, November 8, 1845.

2. derivation: *Sartor Resartus* is saturated

with comic parodies of etymology. See Section Preface.

"Vondervotteimittiss . . . Blitzen": "Wonder what time it is—Wonder, read Thunder—What time it is, as if, and Bleitziz—Bleitziz obsolete: for Blitzen (Lightning)." This non-sensical mixture of German and Latin adds up to "thunder and lightning." The usage provides another tie to Carlyle. In William Maginn's humorous sketch of Carlyle in *Gallery of Illustrious Literary Characters* (items which ran in *Fraser's* in the 1830s and were collected in an 1873 book), Maginn speaks of Carlyle: ". . . donner-und-blitzen-izing it like a northwester." See comments in the Preface to Section Nine in "A Tale of Jerusalem" concerning Poe's familiarity with Maginn.

"Oratiunculae de Rebus Praeter-Veteris," of Dundergutz: "Little Oration on Matters Older than Old." The Latin is faulty. "Dundergutz" is probably a play on "Thunder gut."

Catch-work and No Cypher: In printing, "catch-word" is the first word of the following page inserted at the lower right-hand corner of each page. Cypher means number; hence, pages have the catchword but no number.

3. sixty yards: Poe's geometry is more approximate than he intends. One-quarter mile is 440 yards. If the radius of the perfectly round valley is 60 yards, its circumference is about 377 yards.

cabbage: Whipple (2) suggests that the frequent allusions to cabbages in this tale would tip off contemporary readers to the object of Poe's satire. Whig slogans urged Van Buren, who was Dutch and from Kinderhook, to return there and raise cabbages. Book II, Chapter 2 of *Sartor Resartus* also contains a reference to cabbages.

4. repeater: A watch that repeats the last hour; also a voter who is paid to vote several times (see Section Preface). Striking clocks, burghers, something tied to a dog's tail and other very similar details appear in Book II, Chapter 3 of *Sartor Resartus*.

quiz: practical joke or prank.

5. *papillotes*: curlers.

kerseymere: "a twilled fine woollen cloth of a peculiar texture."

chapeau-de-bras: See Section Preface. See also Book III, Chapter 8 of *Sartor Resartus*, wherein Teufelsdröckh speaks of "Space-annihilating" and "Time-annihilating" hats.

6. Note that the intruder does *not* keep time.

7. *chassez*: See "Landor's Cottage," note 3. *balancez*: a step performed in place, a balancing step in ballet.

pirouette: See "Loss of Breath," note 20.

pas-de-zéphyr: See "Loss of Breath," note 6.

pigeon-winged: See "Never Bet the Devil Your Head," note 9. The pigeon-wing is another tie to Carlyle. See "Never Bet the Devil Your Head," where Poe makes the connection specific.

8. wife (*vrouw*).

9. Devil. See "The Angel of the Odd," notes 6 and 12. The Angel uses similar language.

10. old Nick: another name for the Devil.

"Judy O'Flannagan and Paddy O'Raferty": In his article "On Irish Songs," William Maginn says of the heroine of a chant, "Miss Judy O'Flannikin, who is evidently transmuted from O'Flannegan" [sic]. For Poe's familiarity with Maginn's work, see Preface to Section Nine under "A Tale of Jerusalem." A tune called "Paddy O'Rafferty" appears in Washington Irving's *Tales of a Traveller* (1824).

Bon-Bon

1. An early story which Poe evidently liked, "Bon-Bon" appeared first in *The Saturday Courier* (Philadelphia) for December 1, 1832, under the title "The Bargain Lost." Bon-Bon was called Pedro Garcia and lived in Venice; there was a different motto, and the receipt for the soul of "A——" spelled out the name "Francois Marie Arouet" (Voltaire). Poe used "Bon-Bon" under its present title in the *Southern Literary Messenger*, August 1835, the 1840 *Tales of the Grotesque and Arabesque*, and in the April 19, 1845 *The Broadway Journal*.

The name "Bon-Bon" means, literally, a kind of candy and "good, good" in French; it appears repeatedly in English plays of Poe's period, in the mouths of French characters. Now Poe had Carlyle in mind in this story (see notes 3 and 7 below), and years later wrote in his "Marginalia,"

The Carlyle-ists should adopt, as a motto, the inscription on the old bell from whose metal were cast the Great Tom, of Oxford—"In **Thomæ** *laude resono 'Bim! Bom!' sine fraude!*"

[I sound forth in praise of Thomas
Bim! Bom! Without false promise.]

and "Bim! Bom" in such case, would be
a marvellous "echo of sound to sense."

Since Teufelsdröckh looks like a belfry, he
seems a likely source of Pierre Bon-Bon and
a tale about the devil, and "Bim! Bom!" is
close enough to "Bon-Bon" to constitute one
of those almost-private jokes Poe loved, and
which are scattered throughout his satiric
tales. Poe may even have had in mind the
following lines which appear in Disraeli's
Curiosities of Literature:

> *Voyant le portrait de Corneille,*
> *Gardez-vous de crier merveille;*
> *Et dans vos transports n'allez pas*
> *Prendre ici* **Pierre** *pour* **Thomas.**

Disraeli was quoting an "impromptu" under
the portrait of Thomas Corneille, the less famous brother of Pierre, but Poe may have
seen and recalled these lines when choosing
a suitable name for his character. Poe knew
Disraeli's *Curiosities* almost by heart.

2. The motto may be translated,

> *When a good wine furnishes*
> *my stomach*
> *I am more learned than Balzac*
> *Wiser than Pibrac*
> *Single-handed, I could attack*
> *The whole Cossack nation*
> *And plunder it.*
> *I would cross Charon's lake*
> *While sleeping in his boat.*
> *I would go to the proud Eac*
> *Without even getting excited*
> *And offer him tobacco.*

Balzac: Jean Louis Guez de Balzac (1597–
1654), French "pre-classicist" considered one
of the developers of French prose style.

Pibrac: Gui du Faur de Pibrac (1529–1584),
French poet, orator, and lawyer, author of
a popular poem called "Fifty Quatrains, containing Useful Precepts" (1574).

Charon: See "Shadow," note 3.

Eac: Probably Aeacus, son of Zeus and Aegina
(in some versions Europa). Zeus made him a
"judge of the dead from Europe in Hades with
Minos and Rhadamanthys."

See also Poe's "Pinakidia" (Harrison, Vol.
XIV, p. 68).

3. *restaurateur:* Poe probably got the idea
of a purveyor of food and ideas from Carlyle's essay "Biography," which appeared just
a few months before this tale. In it, Carlyle
calls modern historians "Historical Restaurateurs," and says they are "little better than
high priests of Famine," an idea which might
be connected with Poe's decision to dress the
devil as a priest, and to tuck a Catholic holy
book in his pocket. Moreover, Poe in some
editions capitalized "Restaurateur," following
Carlyle. Disraeli in his article "Ancient
Cookery, and Cooks" also refers to the ancients' concept of philosopher-cook.

pâtés à la foie: Poe means *pâté du foie (foie*
is masculine) liver paste.

sur la Nature: on Nature.

sur l'Ame: on the Soul.

sur l'Esprit: on the Spirit.

fricandeaux: stews in sauce, generally made
with veal.

savants: wise men.

dicta: pronouncements.

Academy . . . Lyceum: places in Athens associated with Plato and Aristotle, respectively.
Plato is believed to have acquired land at the
Academy, and to have taught there; the site
became home to scholars for centuries. Aristotle's walks in the Lyceum gave name to the
Peripatetic or "walking" school of philosophers.

Kant: See "Mellonta Tauta," note 8 and
"How to Write a Blackwood Article," note
10.

Leibnitz: Gottfried Wilhelm von Leibnitz
(1646–1716) German philosopher and mathematician.

facili gradu: by an easy step.

à priori: See "The Imp of the Perverse,"
note 1.

à posteriori: See "The Imp of the Perverse,"
note 3 and "The Murders in the Rue
Morgue," note 20.

George of Trebizond: A celebrated scholar
born in the isle of Crete (1396–1486), who
translated works from Greek to Latin and
wrote in Latin "Commentary on the Philip-
pics and Other Orations of Cicero" and
"Comparison between Plato and Aristotle."

Bossarion: Poe means Basilius Bessarion (c.
1395–1472) archbishop of Nicaea, religious
diplomat, cardinal, patron of learning and
scholar. Poe connects him with George of
Trebizond because his *Adversus Calumnia-*

torem Platonis attacks a work by that author, who was an Aristotelian.

4. diaphragm: Φρένες [Poe's note]. Should be φρένες.

alto rilievo: alto-relievo, a term in sculpture meaning that the figures project by more than half their depth from the background; high relief.

5. *essais*: essays.

Vin de Bourgogne: Burgundy.

Côtes du Rhone: wines from grapes grown on either bank of the Rhône along the 125 miles of its run from Lyon to Avignon.

Sauterne: white Bordeaux wine.

Médoc: See "The Cask of Amontillado," note 7.

"what Catullus was to Homer": i.e., frivolity in comparison to grandeur. Catullus wrote scurrilous and amusing verses.

St. Péray: a Côtes du Rhône wine, white and often sparkling.

Clos de Vougeot: See "The System of Dr. Tarr and Professor Fether," note 5.

Chambertin: a Burgundy.

diablerie: devilry.

6. sub-cook.

7. velvet of Genoa: an all-silk brocaded velvet.

aimable: Exhaustive search convinces us that if there was a fabric by this name, the usage was limited: no guide to fabrics we have seen lists it. Poe may simply mean by *"aimable"* a fabric one is fond of, or the term may have had only trade currency.

sky-blue cloak: Poe uses a number of tiny fat characters in unlikely clothes, usually in sky-blue cloaks: cf. "The Devil in the Belfry" and "Hans Pfaal." He probably has in mind Carlyle again; in *Sartor Resartus* Teufelsdröckh wears a light-blue cloak and looks "like a little blue Belfry."

tout ensemble: See "Landor's Cottage," note 6 and "The Duc De L'Omelette," note 12.

Benevenuta: Pollin (3) thinks Poe made up this name. Poe seems to be referring to a woman. She might be Benvenuta (Beata), a pious woman of the third Dominican order who died in Cividale del Friuli, Italy in 1295.

8. pâté: a little pie or pastry.

Œuvres de Bon-Bon: works of Bon-Bon.

9. canopy *à la Grecque*: Poe's reference to a Greek canopy is a reflection of neoclassical interior decorating; his use of a French fan suggests Empire or Directoire style.

bibliothèque: library.

duodecimo *mélanges*: Duodecimo is a book-collectors' term, meaning the page size obtained when a sheet is folded to make twelve pages. The French word *mélange* means "mixture," and is used to refer to a number of different dishes.

Eusebius: Poe probably means the leader of the Arian heresy. See "Some Passages in the Life of a Lion," note 13.

10. *des œufs à la Princesse: œufs princesse*, eggs arranged on fried croûtons, covered with Supreme sauce, garnished with asparagus tips and shreds of chicken breast with a sliver of truffle on each egg.

omelette à la Reine: possibly *œufs à la Reine*, eggs arranged in tartlets filled with chicken purée and covered with Supreme sauce.

11. "iron . . . approach": Poe associates iron and magnetism with evil or the devil in a number of places, apparently playing on ancient folk beliefs about the metal and its properties. The beliefs vary (some see iron as unholy and prohibit it in churches; others see it as a charm—in England, for instance, it was used to keep witches away). See "Never Bet the Devil Your Head," note 14.

12. ecclesiastic: See note 3 above.

Rituel Catholique: Poe plays on anti-Catholic sentiment. Actually, the official liturgical book to which he seems to refer is called not "Catholic Ritual" but *Roman Ritual*.

13. Mousseux: "sparkling," applied to wines and certain other liquids.

vis-à-vis: face-to-face.

14. *Register of the Condemned*: Poe liked inscriptions which changed; see "Silence," note 7.

Here and elsewhere in this tale we follow Harrison's corrections of Poe's French. *The Broadway Journal* had *regitre* without the accent.

15. We have not found this idea in Aristotle, but Montaigne, in Book II, chapter 6 of his *Essays*, says that people "kindly entertain" sneezes while frowning at the bodily exhalations: "Smile not at this subtlety; it is (as some say) Aristotle's." Sir Thomas Browne says that Aristotle feels sneezing to be a sign

of mental health (there is a folk-belief that idiots never sneeze). Browne writes that sneezing "being properly a motion of the brain expelling through the nostrils what is offensive to it" is therefore a good sign; for this reason, he says, Aristotle holds it sacred. We guess that Poe's source is "On the Custom of Saluting after Sneezing," an article in Disraeli's *Curiosities of Literature* which says, ". . . Aristotle has delivered some considerable nonsense on this custom: he says it is an honorable acknowledgement of the seat of good sense and genius—the head—to distinguish it from two other offensive eruptions of air, which are never accompanied by any benediction from by-standers."

16. ὁ νοῦς ἔστιν αὐλός: "The soul is a flute."

ὁ νοῦς ἔστιν αὐγός: "The soul is a gleaming light."

17. *Ils écrivaient sur la Philosophie* (Cicero, Lucretius, Seneca) *mais c'etait la Philosophie Grecque.*—(Condorcet) [Poe's note]. "They wrote on Philosophy, but it was Greek Philosophy." Poe altered a passage from Condorcet's *Esquisse d'un tableau historique des progrès de l'esprit humain* (1795). Condorcet actually wrote:

> Cicéron, Lucrèce et Sénèque écrivirent éloquemment dans leur langue sur la philosophie; mais c'était sur celle des Grecs. . . .

June Barraclough translates this passage,

> Cicero, Lucretius and Seneca wrote eloquently on philosophy in their own language, but the philosophy was Greek. . . .

The passage in Condorcet is connected to a number of allusions in "Bon-Bon." The "anarchy of five years" to which Poe's devil alludes seems related to a discussion of Roman jurisprudence which follows in Condorcet's next paragraph. The discussion of Epicurus which comes next in "Bon-Bon" is paralleled by a discussion of Epicurus in Condorcet which comes just *before* the passage Poe quotes.

Condorcet: Marie Jean Antoine Nicolas Caritat de Condorcet (1743–1794). See "The Domain of Arnheim," note 3.

18. eminent Greek philosopher, c. 340 B.C.E.–270 B.C.E.

19. See "Loss of Breath," note 25. Diogenes Laertius did in fact write about Epicurus.

20. A favorite word: See "Landor's Cot-

tage," note 6; "The Murders in the Rue Morgue," note 19; "The Mystery of Marie Rogêt," note 18; "The Spectacles," note 14; "The Business Man," note 2.

21. See the Devil's comments on Aristotle, above.

22. Cratinus: celebrated Athenian poet of the old comedy (c. 519 B.C.E.–422 B.C.E.), a rival of Aristophanes.

Aristophanes: Greek comic dramatist (c. 444–380 B.C.E.).

Plato the comic poet: an eminent Athenian comic poet of the old comedy, contemporary of Aristophanes. He flourished about 428–390 B.C.E.

Cerberus: the three-headed dog, in Greek myth, who guards the entrance to Hell.

Naevius: Cneius Naevius (c. 272–c. 204 B.C.E.), a Roman poet, author of an epic poem and several dramas.

Andronicus: Probably Marcus Livius Andronicus, a popular Roman dramatist and actor, who composed tragedies and comedies. He began his career as an author about 240 B.C.E.

Plautus: Titus Maccius Plautus (254?–184 B.C.E.), most celebrated of Roman comic poets.

Terentius: Publius Terentius Afer (c. 195–158 or 159 B.C.E.), celebrated Roman comic poet.

Lucilius: Caius Lucilius (c. 148–c. 100 B.C.E.), Roman satiric poet.

Catullus: Caius Valerius Catullus (c. 77–45? B.C.E.), eminent Latin poet.

Naso: Publius Ovidius Naso (Ovid—43–17 or 18 B.C.E.), a Roman poet.

Quintus Flaccus: Quintus Horatius Flaccus (Horace—65–8 B.C.E.), popular Latin poet.

seculare: Horace wrote *Carmen Seculare* for Augustus about 17 B.C.E. The *seculare* was a hymn for the secular games, a hymn to Apollo and Diana.

Quirite: a Roman citizen.

The Devil seems to have forgotten that he said he had only been in Rome once.

23. See "The System of Dr. Tarr and Professor Fether," note 9.

24. Horace: See note 22.

Menander: a Greek dramatic poet (341?–291? B.C.E.), called the originator of the new comedy.

Nicander: celebrated Greek physician and poet, supposed to have flourished about 175–135 B.C.E.

Virgilius: Publius Virgilius Maro (Virgil or Vergil—70–19 B.C.E.), the most illustrious of Latin poets.

Theocritus: one of the most famous pastoral poets, a native of Syracuse, flourished about 270 B.C.E.

Martial: Marcus Valerius Martialis, a famous Latin epigrammatic poet (c. 40–c. 98 A.C.E.).

Archilochus: An illustrious Greek lyric poet and satirist, flourished about 680 B.C.E.

Titus Livius: Livy, noted Roman historian (59 B.C.E.–17 A.C.E.).

Polybius: a celebrated Greek historian (c. 206–c. 122 B.C.E.).

Poe's point is the same made in note 17: that Roman culture is a weak restatement of Greek.

25. Hippocrates: the most eminent physician of antiquity, called "Father of Medicine" (460–377? B.C.E.).

asafoetida: asafetida, a fetid substance prepared from the juice of certain plants of the parsley family, used in medicines as an antispasmodic.

Styx: in Greek mythology one of the five rivers surrounding Hades, over which the souls of the dead had to pass.

cholera morbus: acute gastroenteritis.

26. "while the body is still living."

27. Cain: In the Bible the eldest son of Adam and Eve and murderer of his brother Abel (Genesis 4).

Nimrod: the "mighty hunter" mentioned in Genesis 10:8–9.

Nero: Nero Claudius Caesar Drusus Germanisus (37–68), the notoriously cruel Roman emperor from 54 until his suicide in 68.

Caligula: Another Roman emperor (12–41), reigned the last four years of his life until assassinated.

Dionysius: a celebrated tyrant of Syracuse (c. 430–367 B.C.E.).

Pisistratus: Athenian tyrant (c. 605–527 B.C.E.).

A——: Arouet (Voltaire). See note 1 above; "Hop-Frog," note 3; "William Wilson," note 5.

28. Machi: Machiavelli. See "The Purloined Letter," note 7.

Maza: Jules Mazarin? (1602–1661), the Cardinal under Louis XIV.

Robesp: Robespierre (1758–1794), the French Revolutionary leader.

George: King George III of England (1783–1820), reigned 1760–1820, during the American Revolution, hence a handy villain to any American author.

Elizabeth: Queen Elizabeth I (1533–1603), reigned 1558–1603, noted for ruthlessness.

29. Ragoût: a spicy stewed dish.

fricandeau: See note 3 above.

Why the Little Frenchman Wears His Hand in a Sling

1. Apparently Poe had difficulty selling this ethnic anecdote. His publishers inserted it as the only previously unpublished tale in the 1840 *Tales of the Grotesque and Arabesque;* Poe used it again in *The Broadway Journal* when he was editing that magazine himself (September 6, 1845). Between the two authorized publications, however, *Bentley's Miscellany,* one of a group of mass-circulation magazines which sprang up in England in the 1830s, swiped it and ran it (43, July 1, 1840) with a changed title: "The Irish Gentleman and the Little Frenchman" (Allen; A. H. Quinn). Heartman and Canny suspect an early, undiscovered periodical publication.

2. hot tun: *Haut ton,* high tone; elegance in fashion.

bog-throthing: bog trotting.

hopperer: opera.

Brisky: britzka, an open carriage.

three fut and a bit: another of Poe's tiny comic characters: see "Hans Pfaal," "Bon-Bon," and "The Devil in the Belfry."

spalpeen: a low or mean fellow, scamp or rascal.

summat: somewhat.

3. Connaught: province in Ireland. Sydney Owenson (Lady Morgan, 1775–1859) had published, in 1807, *Patriotic Sketches of Ireland, Written in Connaught* (see Section Preface).

mavourneen: my darling.

it's not . . . purliteness: I'm not one to be outdone in politeness.

purraty: We are not sure what Poe intends here. "Pretty" (i.e., a pretty girl) makes good sense, but elsewhere in the tale Poe spells it "purty." There is a Gaelic word "purradh," a shove, but the context seems to rule that out. Harold Orel writes, ". . . my guess is that "purraty" is an exaggerated form of 'pretty' . . . that is spelled differently from the earlier form because Londonderry is Northern Ireland (and always was, long before Partition), and speech forms in Londonderry and Belfast have always been strange to Irishmen in the southern provinces."

4. A Goose . . . Maiter-di-dauns: It is difficult to render Poe's Irish French. "A Goose," is certainly Auguste, but "Look-aisy" could be any of a number of French names, or even "Le Casey," which is to say, "no Frenchman at all." "Maiter-di-dauns" is *maître de danse*, dancing-master. In *Patriotic Sketches*, Lady Morgan speaks of the fondness of even poor Irishmen for dancing teachers (See note 3).

5. pully wou, woolly wou: probably *pouvez-vous, voulez-vous*, "can you, will you."

puncheon: penchant.

6. piano (pianoforte).

7. plump in the mud: another puzzle. We know no French phrase which makes sense here and which could be so mispronounced. Part of the difficulty may be that Poe's "equivalences" of this sort are very approximate—see, for example, "Zenobia's" treatment of "Blackwood's" Greek in "How to Write a Blackwood Article" and "A Predicament." One possibility is that the Frenchman is commenting on the elegance of Grandison's bow and says, "*Voulez-vous, pouvez-vous, plus à la mode . . . bien sûr*, Mrs. Tracle," which might mean "My, my (will you, can you [believe]), most elegant . . . quite sure, Mrs. Tracle."

8. alas! (Gaelic).

9. Frenchman.

10. conceited.

11. probably mouth, "pretty-trap." Early in the story we are told that the Frenchman is ". . . summat down in the mouth, and wears his lift hand in a sling" (see also note 3).

12. nun.

X-ing a Paragrab

1. First published in *The Flag of Our Union*, May 12, 1849.

2. Mr. . . . Bullet-head: In the September 1846 *Godey's Lady's Book* Poe, then engaged in a bitter literary exchange with Lewis Gaylord Clark, wrote a "Literati" item about him which included the following: "His forehead is, phrenologically, bad—round and what is termed 'bullety.' " Perhaps he is Poe's target.

Brownson: See "Mesmeric Revelation," note 2.

3. i.e. a Western town with a high-falutin name, such as Cincinnati. American identification with the classical past was extremely strong during the Federal period: witness architecture, women's dress, and the practice of naming new towns after figures or places in the Greek or Roman past.

4. i.e. "I started to say 'obstinacy.' "

5. fiery . . . salamander: In myth, the salamander was a monster able to live through fire.

6. Poe parodies "*O tempora! O mores!*" ("O the times! O the manners!").

7. *style:* Compare to "Mr. Blackwood's" comments on style in "How to Write A Blackwood Article."

Frogpondium: "The Frog-pond" in Poe means Boston. The key to cracking this tale would seem to be finding a Transcendentalist writer who moved west to a town with a classical name and became involved in an editorial war.

article . . . appearance: Such a piece is known as a lipogram. The author of a lipogram writes an essay, tale, or poem without using some letter, usually an important vowel. Variants exist, too: some writers have deliberately used only *one* vowel throughout a work.

8. See "Mellonta Tauta," note 5 and "Some Words with a Mummy," note 10.

9. Concord: another clue. Concord was the Transcendentalists' unofficial capital, home of Emerson, Thoreau, the Concord School of Philosophy, etc.

homo: Poe says "*homo*" to avoid the "a" in "man," though he uses several vowels other than "o" in other words in the tale.

log, dog, hog, or frog: a list which for some reason tickled Poe; he used it, for example, in "Thou Art the Man" (see note 7 of that tale). Possible meanings based on Poe's usage in other works are: log = Clark, dog = Carlyle, hog = James Hogg, frog = the Transcendentalists.

10. printer's devil, an apprentice or errand boy around a print shop.

11. his case of type.

12. Z's.

13. Poe plays with a slang phrase, "the Devil to pay and no pitch hot." The phrase "appears to be a corruption of the nautical expression, 'Hell's to pay,' etc., *hell* being . . . a portion of the hold of a smack . . . in which freshly-caught fish are thrown and . . . kept alive. It is . . . important that the bulkheads, etc. about 'hell' . . . be . . . water-tight . . . by calking with oakum and 'paying' with hot pitch . . ." (Walsh). Poe picked the expression to reinforce his line of diabolical imagery: hot pitch, printer's devil, the devil to pay, damn them, diabolical.

14. Poe knew well the writings of Lucian (c. 125–c. 200) in whose "Trial in the Court of Vowels" appears a paragraph in which "x's" are substituted for other letters (so rendered in the translation): "xympathizing with his xystem."

15. Brewers mark ales xx or xxx to suggest that the ales are extra strong.

10. Political Satires

Poe's satiric tales hit out in so many directions that calling one a political satire and the next a literary satire is to some extent arbitrary. The two in this section seem to us primarily political in intention, but their absurdity is part of Poe's game, too. And both should be compared to "The Devil in the Belfry," which also contains political elements.

Four Beasts in One/The Homo-Cameleopard. A Seleucid ruler of the second century B. C. E. who was strongly attracted to republicanism, who mingled democratically with the citizens of Antioch, yet whose ambitions were imperial and who identified himself with Zeus, provided Poe with a perfect platform from which to snipe at the kingly commoner Andrew Jackson.

The Man That Was Used Up. The object of this satire is Vice-President Richard M. Johnson, according to a convincing study by Whipple (2). There was a dreadful small-scale encounter in a swamp, part of the larger Battle of the Thames in 1813, in which Johnson fought with great bravery, killed Tecumseh, and was himself severely and repeatedly wounded. His courage, his stature as a national hero, and his wounds were potent campaign assets; Whipple quotes a contemporary who said he was "a man upon crutches; his frame all mutilated; moving with difficulty yet an object of patriotic interest with everybody." Any reader of Poe's tale at the time would have recognized Poe's target. Poe probably borrowed the idea of the "artificial man" from *The Devil upon Two Sticks* by Alain René Lesage (1668–1747) (Wetzel).

Note that General Smith admires "man-traps and spring-guns," means of inadvertent self-destruction, and that wherever the narrator goes to learn more about Smith, he meets more incidents of destruction or self-destruction: In church, man "cometh up and is cut down like a flower." At the theatre, Othello, having killed his wife, kills himself. At the card party, talk is of Captain Mann "who was either shot or hung" for a duel. Dancing, he hears of Byron's Manfred who, consumed with guilt, yearns not only for death but for eternal oblivion. The narrator's friend Sinivate brings up Captain Mann again, and the narrator responds, "Captain Mann be damned!" (See note 15.)

The Tales

FOUR BEASTS IN ONE THE HOMO-CAMELEOPARD[1]

Chacun a ses vertus.
Crébillon's Xerxes[2]

Antiochus Epiphanes is very generally looked upon as the Gog of the prophet Ezekiel. This honor is, however, more properly attributable to Cambyses, the son of Cyrus. And, indeed, the character of the Syrian monarch does by no means stand in need of any adventitious embellishment. His accession to the throne, or rather his usurpation of the sovereignty, a hundred and seventy-one years before the coming of Christ; his attempt to plunder the temple of Diana at Ephesus; his implacable hostility to the Jews; his pollution of the Holy of Holies; and his miserable death at Taba,[3] after a tumultuous reign of eleven years, are circumstances of a prominent kind, and therefore more generally noticed by the historians of his time, than the impious, dastardly, cruel, silly and whimsical achievements which make up the sum total of his private life and reputation.

* * *

Let us suppose, gentle reader, that it is now the year of the world three thousand eight hundred and thirty, and let us, for a few minutes, imagine ourselves at that most grotesque habitation of man, the remarkable city of Antioch. To be sure there were, in Syria and other countries, sixteen cities of that appellation, besides the one to which I more particularly allude. But *ours* is that which went by the name of Antiochia Epidaphne, from its vicinity to the little village of Daphne, where

stood a temple to that divinity. It was built (although about this matter there is some dispute) by Seleucus Nicanor, the first king of the country after Alexander the Great, in memory of his father Antiochus, and became immediately the residence of the Syrian monarchy. In the flourishing times of the Roman Empire, it was the ordinary station of the prefect of the eastern provinces; and many of the emperors of the queen city, (among whom may be mentioned especially, Verus and Valens,)[4] spent here the greater part of their time. But I perceive we have arrived at the city itself. Let us ascend this battlement, and throw our eyes upon the town and neighboring country.

"What broad and rapid river is that which forces its way, with innumerable falls, through the mountainous wilderness, and finally through the wilderness of buildings?"

That is the Orontes, and it is the only water in sight, with the exception of the Mediterranean, which stretches like a broad mirror, about twelve miles off to the southward. Every one has seen the Mediterranean; but let me tell you, there are few who have had a peep at Antioch. By few, I mean, few who, like you and me, have had, at the same time, the advantages of a modern education. Therefore cease to regard that sea, and give your whole attention to the mass of houses that lie beneath us. You will remember that it is now the year of the world three thousand eight hundred and thirty. Were it later—for example, were it the year of our Lord eighteen hundred and forty-five,[5] we should be deprived of this extraordinary spectacle. In the nineteenth century Antioch is—that is to say,

Antioch *will be*—in a lamentable state of decay. It will have been, by that time, totally destroyed, at three different periods, by three successive earthquakes. Indeed, to say the truth, what little of its former self may then remain, will be found in so desolate and ruinous a state that the patriarch shall have removed his residence to Damascus. This is well. I see you profit by my advice, and are making the most of your time in inspecting the premises—in

> ———— *satisfying your eyes*
> *With the memorials and the things*
> *of fame*
> *That most renown this city.* ————[6]

I beg pardon; I had forgotten that Shakespeare will not flourish for seventeen hundred and fifty years to come.—But does not the appearance of Epidaphne justify me in calling it *grotesque?*

"It is well fortified; and in this respect is as much indebted to nature as to art."

Very true.

"There are a prodigious number of stately palaces."

There are.

"And the numerous temples, sumptuous and magnificent, may bear comparison with the most lauded of antiquity."

All this I must acknowledge. Still there is an infinity of mud huts, and abominable hovels. We cannot help perceiving abundance of filth in every kennel, and, were it not for the overpowering fumes of idolatrous incense, I have no doubt we should find a most intolerable stench. Did you ever behold streets so insufferably narrow, or houses so miraculously tall? What a gloom their shadows cast upon the ground! It is well the swinging lamps in those endless colonnades are kept burning throughout the day; we should otherwise have the darkness of Egypt in the time of her desolation.

"It is certainly a strange place! What is the meaning of yonder singular building? See! it towers above all others, and lies to the eastward of what I take to be the royal palace."

That is the new Temple of the Sun, who is adored in Syria under the title of Elah Gabalah. Hereafter a very notorious Roman Emperor will institute this worship in Rome, and thence derive a cognomen, Heliogabalus.[7] I dare say you would like to take a peep at the divinity of the temple. You need not look up at the heavens; his Sunship is not there; at least not the Sunship adored by the Syrians. *That* deity will be found in the interior of yonder building. He is worshipped under the figure of a large stone pillar terminating at the summit in a cone or *pyramid*, whereby is denoted Fire.

"Hark!—behold!—who *can* those ridiculous beings be, half naked, with their faces painted, shouting and gesticulating to the rabble?"

Some few are mountebanks. Others more particularly belong to the race of philosophers. The greatest portion, however—those especially who belabor the populace with clubs—are the principal courtiers of the palace, executing, as in duty bound, some laudable comicality of the king's.

"But what have we here? Heavens! the town is swarming with wild beasts! How terrible a spectacle!—how dangerous a peculiarity!"

Terrible, if you please; but not in the least degree dangerous. Each animal, if you will take the pains to observe, is following, very quietly, in the wake of its master. Some few, to be sure, are led with a rope about the neck, but these are chiefly the lesser or timid species.—The lion, the tiger, and the leopard are entirely without restraint. They have been trained without difficulty to their present profession, and attend upon their respective owners in the capacity of *valets-de-chambre*.[8] It is true, there are occasions when Nature asserts her violated dominion;—but then the devouring of a man-at-arms, or the throttling of a consecrated bull, is a circumstance of too little moment to be more than hinted at in Epidaphne.

"But what extraordinary tumult do I hear? Surely this is a loud noise even for Antioch! It argues some commotion of unusual interest."

Yes—undoubtedly. The king has ordered some novel spectacle—some gladiatorial exhibition at the Hippodrome—or perhaps the massacre of the Scythian prisoners—or the conflagration of his new palace—or the tearing down of a handsome temple—or, indeed, a bonfire of a few Jews. The uproar increases. Shouts of laughter ascend the skies. The air becomes dissonant with wind instruments, and horrible with the clamor of a million throats. Let us descend, for the love of fun, and see what is going on! This way —be careful! Here we are in the principal street, which is called the street of Timarchus. The sea of people is coming this way, and we shall find a difficulty in stemming the tide. They are pouring through the alley of Heraclides, which leads directly from the palace;—therefore the king is most probably among the rioters. Yes;—I hear the shouts of the herald proclaiming his approach in the pompous phraseology of the East. We shall have a glimpse of his person as he passes by the temple of Ashimah. Let us ensconce ourselves in the vestibule of the sanctuary; he will be here anon. In the meantime let us survey this image. What is it? Oh, it is the god Ashimah in proper person. You perceive, however, that he is neither a lamb, nor a goat, nor a satyr; neither has he much resemblance to the Pan of the Arcadians.[9] Yet all these appearances have been given—I beg pardon—will be given —by the learned of future ages, to the Ashimah of the Syrians. Put on your spectacles, and tell me what it is. What is it?

"Bless me! it is an ape!"

True—a baboon; but by no means the less a deity.—His name is a derivation of the Greek *Simia*—what great fools are antiquarians! But see!—see! yonder scampers a ragged little urchin. Where is he going? What is he bawling about? What does he say? Oh! he says the king is coming in triumph; that he is dressed in state; that he has just finished putting to death, with his own hand, a thousand chained Israelitish prisoners! For this exploit the ragamuffin is lauding him to the skies!— Hark! here comes a troop of a similar description. They have made a Latin hymn upon the valor of the king, and are singing it as they go.

Mille, mille, mille,
Mille, mille, mille,
Decollavimus, unus homo!
Mille, mille, mille, mille, decollavimus!
Mille, mille, mille!
Vivat qui mille mille occidit!
Tantum vini habet nemo
Quantum sanguinis effudit![10]

Which may be thus paraphrased:

A thousand, a thousand, a thousand,
A thousand, a thousand, a thousand,
We, with one warrior, have slain!
A thousand, a thousand, a thousand,
a thousand,
Sing a thousand over again!
Soho!—let us sing
Long life to our king,
Who knocked over a thousand
so fine!
Soho!—let us roar,
He has given us more
Red gallons of gore
Than all Syria can furnish of wine!

"Do you hear that flourish of trumpets?"

Yes; the king is coming! See! the people are aghast with admiration, and lift up their eyes to the heavens in reverence. He comes;—he is coming;—there he is!

"Who?—where?—the king?—do not behold him;—cannot say that I perceive him."

Then you must be blind.

"Very possible. Still I see nothing but a tumultuous mob of idiots and madmen, who are busy in prostrating themselves before a gigantic cameleopard, and endeavoring to obtain a kiss of the animal's hoofs. See! the beast has very justly kicked one of the rabble over—and another—and another—and another. Indeed I cannot help admiring the animal for the excellent use he is making of his feet."

Rabble, indeed!—why these are the noble and free citizens of Epidaphne! Beast, did you say?—take care that you are not overheard. Do you not perceive that the animal has the visage of a man? Why, my dear sir, that cameleopard is no other than Antiochus Epiphanes Antiochus the Illustrious, King of Syria, and the most potent of all the autocrats of the East! It is true that he is entitled, at times, Antiochus Epimanes—Antiochus the madman—but that is because all people have not the capacity to appreciate his merits. It is also certain that he is at present ensconced in the hide of a beast, and is doing his best to play the part of a cameleopard; but this is done for the better sustaining his dignity as king. Besides, the monarch is of gigantic stature, and the dress is therefore neither unbecoming nor over large. We may, however, presume he would not have adopted it but for some occasion of especial state. Such, you will allow, is the massacre of a thousand Jews. With how superior a dignity the monarch perambulates on all fours! His tail, you perceive, is held aloft by his two principal concubines, Elline and Argelais;[11] and his whole appearance would be infinitely prepossessing, were it not for the protuberance of his eyes, which will certainly start out of his head, and the queer color of his face, which has become nondescript from the quantity of wine he has swallowed. Let us follow him to the hippodrome, whither he is proceeding, and listen to the song of triumph which he is commencing:

> Who is king but Epiphanes?
> Say—do you know?
> Who is king but Epiphanes?
> Bravo!—bravo!

> There is none but Epiphanes,
> No—there is none:
> So tear down the temples,
> And put out the sun!

Well and strenuously sung! The populace are hailing him "Prince of Poets," as well as "Glory of the East," "Delight of the Universe," and "most Remarkable of Cameleopards." They have encored his effusion, and—do you hear?—he is singing it over again. When he arrives at the hippodrome, he will be crowned with the poetic wreath, in anticipation of his victory at the approaching Olympics.

"But, good Jupiter! what is the matter in the crowd behind us?"

Behind us, did you say?—oh! ah!—I perceive. My friend, it is well that you spoke in time. Let us get into a place of safety as soon as possible. Here!—let us conceal ourselves in the arch of this aqueduct, and I will inform you presently of the origin of the commotion. It has turned out as I have been anticipating. The singular appearance of the cameleopard with the head of a man, has, it seems, given offence to the notions of propriety entertained, in general, by the wild animals domesticated in the city. A mutiny has been the result; and, as is usual upon such occasions, all human efforts will be of no avail in quelling the mob. Several of the Syrians have already been devoured; but the general voice of the four-footed patriots seems to be for eating up the cameleopard. "The Prince of Poets," therefore, is upon his hinder legs, running for his life. His courtiers have left him in the lurch, and his concubines have followed so excellent an example. "Delight of the Universe," thou art in a sad predicament! "Glory of the East," thou art in danger of mastication! Therefore never regard so piteously thy tail; it will undoubtedly be draggled in the mud, and for this there is no help. Look not behind thee, then, at its unavoidable degradation; but take courage, ply thy legs with vigor, and scud for the hippodrome! Remember that thou art

Antiochus Epiphanes Antiochus the Illustrious!—also " 'Prince of Poets,' " " 'Glory of the East,' " " 'Delight of the Universe,' " and " 'most Remarkable of Cameleopards!' " Heavens! what a power of speed thou art displaying! What a capacity for leg-bail thou art developing! Run, Prince!—Bravo, Epiphanes!—Well done, Cameleopard!—Glorious Antiochus! He runs!—he leaps!—he flies! Like an arrow from a catapult he approaches the hippodrome! He leaps!—he shrieks!—he is there! This is well; for hadst thou, "Glory of the East," been half a second longer in reaching the gates of the Amphitheatre, there is not a bear's cub in Epidaphne that would not have had a nibble at thy carcase. Let us be off—let us take our departure!—for we shall find our delicate modern ears unable to endure the vast uproar which is about to commence in celebration of the king's escape! Listen! it has already commenced. See!—the whole town is topsy-turvy.

"Surely this is the most populous city of the East! What a wilderness of people! what a jumble of all ranks and ages! what a multipilcity of sects and nations! what a variety of costumes! what a Babel of languages! what a screaming of beasts! what a tinkling of instruments! what a parcel of philosophers!"

Come let us be off!

"Stay a moment! I see a vast hubbub in the hippodrome; what is the meaning of it I beseech you!"

That?—oh nothing! The noble and free citizens of Epidaphne being, as they declare, well satisfied of the faith, valor, wisdom, and divinity of their king, and having, moreover, been eye-witnesses of his late superhuman agility, do think it no more than their duty to invest his brows (in addition to the poetic crown) with the wreath of victory in the foot-race—a wreath which it is evident he *must* obtain at the celebration of the next Olympiad, and which, therefore, they now give him in advance.

THE MAN THAT WAS USED UP

A Tale of the Late Bugaboo and Kickapoo Campaign

Pleurez, pleurez, mes yeux, et fondez-vous en eau!
La moitié de ma vie a mis l'autre au tombeau. CORNEILLE.[1]

I cannot just now remember when or where I first made the acquaintance of that truly fine-looking fellow, Brevet Brigadier General John A. B. C. Smith.[2] Some one *did* introduce me to the gentleman, I am sure—at some public meeting, I know very well—held about something of great importance, no doubt—at some place or other, I feel convinced,—whose name I have unaccountably forgotten. The truth is—that the introduction was attended, upon my part, with a degree of anxious embarrassment which operated to prevent any definite impressions of either time or place. I am constitutionally nervous—this, with me, is a family failing, and I can't help it. In especial, the slightest appearance of mystery—of any point I cannot exactly comprehend—puts me at once into a pitiable state of agitation.

There was something, as it were, remarkable—yes, *remarkable,* although this is but a feeble term to express my full meaning—about the entire individuality of the personage in question. He was, perhaps, six feet in height, and of a presence singularly commanding. There was an *air distingué* pervading the whole man, which spoke of high breeding, and hinted at high birth. Upon this topic—the topic of Smith's personal appearance—I have a kind of melancholy satisfaction in being minute. His head of hair would have done honor to a Brutus;—nothing could be more richly flowing, or possess a brighter gloss. It was of a jetty black;—which was also the color, or more properly the no color, of his unimaginable whiskers. You perceive I cannot speak of these latter without enthusiasm; it is not too much to say that they were the handsomest pair of whiskers under the sun. At all events, they encircled, and at times partially overshadowed, a mouth utterly unequalled. Here were the most entirely even, and the most brilliantly white of all conceivable teeth. From between them, upon every proper occasion, issued a voice of surpassing clearness, melody, and strength. In the matter of eyes, also, my acquaintance was pre-eminently endowed. Either one of such a pair was worth a couple of the ordinary ocular organs. They were of a deep hazel exceedingly large and lustrous; and there was perceptible about them, ever and anon, just that amount of interesting obliquity which gives pregnancy to expression.

The bust of the General was unquestionably the finest bust I ever saw. For your life you could not have found a fault with its wonderful proportion. This rare peculiarity set off to great advantage a pair of shoulders which would have called up a blush of conscious inferiority into the countenance of the marble Apollo. I have a passion for fine shoulders, and may say that I never beheld them in perfection before. The arms altogether were admirably modelled. Nor were the lower limbs less superb. These were, indeed, the *ne plus ultra* of good legs. Every connoisseur in such matters admitted the legs to be good. There was neither too much flesh nor too little,—neither rudeness nor fragility. I could not imagine a more graceful curve than that of the *os femoris*, and there was just that due gentle prominence in the rear of the *fibula* which goes to the conformation of a properly proportioned calf. I wish to God my young and talented friend Chiponchipino,[3] the sculptor, had but seen the legs of Brevet Brigadier General John A. B. C. Smith.

But although men so absolutely fine-looking are neither as plenty as reasons or blackberries, still I could not bring myself to believe that *the remarkable* something to which I alluded just now,—that

the odd air of *je ne sais quoi* which hung about my new acquaintance,—lay altogether, or indeed at all, in the supreme excellence of his bodily endowments. Perhaps it might be traced to the *manner;*—yet here again I could not pretend to be positive. There *was* a primness, not to say stiffness, in his carriage—a degree of measured and, if I may so express it, of rectangular precision, attending his every movement, which, observed in a more diminutive figure, would have had the least little savor in the world, of affectation, pomposity, or constraint, but which, noticed in a gentleman of his undoubted dimension, was readily placed to the account of reserve, *hauteur*[4]—of a commendable sense, in short, of what is due to the dignity of colossal proportion.

The kind friend who presented me to General Smith whispered in my ear some few words of comment upon the man. He was a *remarkable* man—a *very* remarkable man—indeed one of the *most* remarkable men of the age. He was an especial favorite, too, with the ladies—chiefly on account of his high reputation for courage.

"In *that* point he is unrivalled—indeed he is a perfect desperado—a downright fire-eater, and no mistake," said my friend, here dropping his voice excessively low, and thrilling me with the mystery of his tone.

"A downright fire-eater, and *no* mistake. Showed *that*, I should say, to some purpose, in the late tremendous swamp-fight away down South, with the Bugaboo and Kickapoo Indians."[5] [Here my friend opened his eyes to some extent.] "Bless my soul!—blood and thunder, and all that!—*prodigies* of valor!—heard of him of course?—you know he's the man——"

"Man alive, how *do* you do? why, how *are* ye? *very* glad to see ye, indeed!" here interrupted the General himself, seizing my companion by the hand as he drew near, and bowing stiffly, but profoundly, as I was presented. I then thought, (and I think so still,) that I never heard a clearer nor a stronger voice, nor beheld a finer set of teeth: but I *must* say that I was sorry for the interruption just at that moment, as, owing to the whispers and insinuations aforesaid, my interest had been greatly excited in the hero of the Bugaboo and Kickapoo campaign.

However, the delightfully luminous conversation of Brevet Brigadier-General John A. B. C. Smith soon completely dissipated this chagrin. My friend leaving us immediately, we had quite a long *tête-à-tête*,[6] and I was not only pleased but *really* —instructed. I never heard a more fluent talker, or a man of greater general information. With becoming modesty, he forebore, nevertheless, to touch upon the theme I had just then most at heart—I mean the mysterious circumstances attending the Bugaboo war—and, on my own part, what I conceive to be a proper sense of delicacy forbade me to broach the subject; although, in truth, I was exceedingly tempted to do so. I perceived, too, that the gallant soldier preferred topics of philosophical interest, and that he delighted, especially, in commenting upon the rapid march of mechanical invention. Indeed, lead him where I would, this was a point to which he invariably came back.

"There is nothing at all like it," he would say; "we are a wonderful people, and live in a wonderful age. Parachutes and railroads—man-traps and spring-guns! Our steam-boats are upon every sea, and the Nassau balloon packet is about to run regular trips (fare either way only twenty pounds sterling) between London and Timbuctoo. And who shall calculate the immense influence upon social life— upon arts—upon commerce—upon literature—which will be the immediate result of the great principles of electro-magnetics! Nor, is this all, let me assure you! There is really no end to the march of invention. The most wonderful—the most ingenious—and let me add, Mr.—Mr.— Thompson, I believe, is your name—let

me add, I say the most *useful*—the most truly *useful*—mechanical contrivances are daily springing up like mushrooms, if I may so express myself, or, more figuratively, like—ah—grasshoppers—like grasshoppers, Mr. Thompson—about us and ah—ah—ah—around us!"

Thompson, to be sure, is not my name; but it is needless to say that I left General Smith with a heightened interest in the man, with an exalted opinion of his conversational powers, and a deep sense of the valuable privileges we enjoy in living in this age of mechanical invention. My curiosity, however, had not been altogether satisfied, and I resolved to prosecute immediate inquiry among my acquaintances touching the Brevet Brigadier General himself, and particularly respecting the tremendous events *quorum pars magna fuit*,[7] during the Bugaboo and Kickapoo campaign.

The first opportunity which presented itself, and which (*horresco referens*) I did not in the least scruple to seize, occurred at the Church of the Reverend Doctor Drummummupp, where I found myself established, one Sunday, just at sermon time, not only in the pew, but by the side of that worthy and communicative little friend of mine, Miss Tabitha T. Thus seated, I congratulated myself, and with much reason, upon the very flattering state of affairs. If any person knew any thing about Brevet Brigadier General John A. B. C. Smith, that person, it was clear to me, was Miss Tabitha T. We telegraphed a few signals and then commenced, *sotto voce*,[8] a brisk *tête-à-tête*.

"Smith!" said she, in reply to my very earnest inquiry; "Smith!—why, not General A. B. C.? Bless me, I thought you *knew* all about *him!* This is a wonderfully inventive age! Horrid affair that!—a bloody set of wretches, those Kickapoos! —fought like a hero—prodigies of valor —immortal renown. Smith!—Brevet Brigadier General John A. B. C.!—why, you know he's the man——"

"Man," here broke in Doctor Drummummupp, at the top of his voice, and with a thump that came near knocking the pulpit about our ears—"man that is born of a woman hath but a short time to live; he cometh up and is cut down like a flower!" I started to the extremity of the pew, and perceived by the animated looks of the divine, that the wrath which had nearly proved fatal to the pulpit had been excited by the whispers of the lady and myself. There was no help for it; so I submitted with a good grace, and listened, in all the martyrdom of dignified silence, to the balance of that very capital discourse.

Next evening found me a somewhat late visitor at the Rantipole Theatre, where I felt sure of satisfying my curiosity at once, by merely stepping into the box of those exquisite specimens of affability and omniscience, the Misses Arabella and Miranda Cognoscenti. That fine tragedian, Climax, was doing Iago to a very crowded house, and I experienced some little difficulty in making my wishes understood; especially as our box was next the slips,[9] and completely overlooked the stage.

"Smith?" said Miss Arabella, as she at length comprehended the purport of my query; "Smith?—why, not General John A. B. C.?"

"Smith?" inquired Miranda, musingly, "God bless me, did you ever behold a finer figure?"

"Never, madam, but do tell me——"

"Or so inimitable grace?"

"Never, upon my word!—but pray, inform me——"

"Or so just an appreciation of stage effect?"

"Madam!"

"Or a more delicate sense of the true beauties of Shakespeare? Be so good as to look at that leg!"

"The devil!" and I turned again to her sister.

"Smith?" said she, "why, not General John A. B. C.? Horrid affair that, wasn't it?—great wretches, those Bugaboos—sav-

age and so on—but we live in a wonderfully inventive age!—Smith—O yes! great man!—perfect desperado—immortal renown—prodigies of valor! *Never heard!*" [This was given in a scream.] "Bless my soul!—why, he's the man——"

——mandragora
*Nor all the drowsy syrups of the world
Shall ever medicine thee to that
      sweet sleep
Which thou owd'st yesterday!*[10]

here roared out Climax just in my ear, and shaking his fist in my face all the time, in a way that I *couldn't* stand, and I *wouldn't*. I left the Misses Cognoscenti immediately, went behind the scenes forthwith, and gave the beggarly scoundrel such a thrashing as I trust he will remember till the day of his death.

At the *soirée* of the lovely widow, Mrs. Kathleen O'Trump, I was confident that I should meet with no similar disappointment. Accordingly, I was no sooner seated at the card table, with my pretty hostess for a *vis-à-vis*,[11] than I propounded those questions the solution of which had become a matter so essential to my peace.

"Smith?" said my partner, "why, not General John A. B. C.? Horrid affair that, wasn't it?—diamonds did you say?—terrible wretches those Kickapoos!—we are playing *whist*, if you please, Mr. Tattle—however, this is the age of invention, most certainly *the* age, one may say—*the* age *par excellence*—speak French?—oh, quite a hero—perfect desperado—*no hearts*, Mr. Tattle? I don't believe it!—immortal renown and all that—prodigies of valor! *Never heard!!*—why, bless me, he's the man——"

"Mann?—*Captain* Mann?" here screamed some little feminine interloper from the farthest corner of the room. "Are you talking about Captain Mann and the duel?—oh, I *must* hear—do tell—go on, Mrs. O'Trump!—do now go on!" And go on Mrs. O'Trump did—all about a certain Captain Mann, who was either shot or hung, or should have been both shot and hung. Yes! Mrs. O'Trump, she went on, and I—I went off. There was no chance of hearing any thing further that evening in regard to Brevet Brigadier General John A. B. C. Smith.

Still I consoled myself with the reflection that the tide of ill-luck would not run against me forever, and so determined to make a bold push for information at the rout of that bewitching little angel, the graceful Mrs. Pirouette.

"Smith?" said Mrs. P., as we twirled about together in a *pas de zéphyr*,[12] "Smith?—why, not General John A. B. C.? Dreadful business that of the Bugaboos, wasn't it?—terrible creatures, those Indians!—*do* turn out your toes! I really am ashamed of you—man of great courage, poor fellow!—but this is a wonderful age for invention—O dear me, I'm out of breath—quite a desperado—prodigies of valor!—*never heard!*—can't believe it—I shall have to sit down and enlighten you —Smith! why he's the man——"

"Man-*Fred*, I tell you!" here bawled out Miss Bas-Bleu, as I led Mrs. Pirouette to a seat. "Did ever anybody hear the like? It's Man-*Fred*, I say, and not at all by any means Man-*Friday*."[13] Here Miss Bas-Bleu beckoned to me in a very peremptory manner; and I was obliged, will I nill I, to leave Mrs. P. for the purpose of deciding a dispute touching the title of a certain poetical drama of Lord Byron's. Although I pronounced, with great promptness, that the true title was Man-*Friday*, and not by any means Man-*Fred*, yet when I returned to seek Mrs. Pirouette she was not to be discovered, and I made my retreat from the house in a very bitter spirit of animosity against the whole race of the Bas-Bleus.

Matters had now assumed a really serious aspect, and I resolved to call at once upon my particular friend, Mr. Theodore Sinivate;[14] for I knew that here at least I should get something like definite information.

"Smith?" said he, in his well-known peculiar way of drawling out his sylla-

bles; "Smith?—why, not General John A—B—C.? Savage affair that with the Kickapo-o-o-os, wasn't it? Say! don't you think so?—perfect despera-a-ado—great pity, pon my honor!—wonderfully inventive age!—pro-o-odigies of valor! By the by, did you ever hear about Captain Ma-a-a-n?"

"Captain Mann be d——d!" said I; "please to go on with your story."

"Hem!—oh well!—quite *la même cho-o-ose*,[15] as we say in France. Smith, eh? Brigadier General John A—B—C.? I say"—[here Mr. S. thought proper to put his finger to the side of his nose]—"I say, you don't mean to insinuate now, really and truly, and conscientiously, that you don't know all about that affair of Smith's, as well as I do, eh? Smith? John A—B—C.? Why, bless me, he's the ma-a-an——"

"*Mr.* Sinivate," said I, imploringly, "is he the man in the mask?"[16]

"No-o-o!" said he, looking wise, "nor the man in the mo-o-o-on."

This reply I considered a pointed and positive insult, and so left the house at once in high dudgeon, with a firm resolve to call my friend, Mr. Sinivate, to a speedy account for his ungentlemanly conduct and ill-breeding.

In the meantime, however, I had no notion of being thwarted touching the information I desired. There was one resource left me yet. I would go to the fountain head. I would call forthwith upon the General himself, and demand, in explicit terms, a solution of this abominable piece of mystery. Here at least, there should be no chance for equivocation. I would be plain, positive, peremptory—as short as pie-crust—as concise as Tacitus or Montesquieu.[17]

It was early when I called, and the General was dressing; but I pleaded urgent business, and was shown at once into his bedroom by an old negro valet, who remained in attendance during my visit. As I entered the chamber, I looked about, of course, for the occupant, but did not immediately perceive him. There was a large and exceedingly odd-looking bundle of something which lay close by my feet on the floor, and, as I was not in the best humor in the world, I gave it a kick out of the way.

"Hem! ahem! rather civil that, I should say!" said the bundle, in one of the smallest, and altogether the funniest little voices, between a squeak and a whistle, that I ever heard in all the days of my existence.

"Ahem! rather civil that, I should observe."

I fairly shouted with terror, and made off, at a tangent, into the farthest extremity of the room.

"God bless me! my dear fellow," here again whistled the bundle, "what—what—what—why, what *is* the matter? I really believe you don't know me at all."

What *could* I say to all this—what *could* I? I staggered into an arm-chair, and, with staring eyes and open mouth, awaited the solution of the wonder.

"Strange you shouldn't know me, though, isn't it?" presently re-squeaked the nondescript, which I now perceived was performing, upon the floor, some inexplicable evolution, very analogous to the drawing on of a stocking. There was only a single leg, however, apparent.

"Strange you shouldn't know me, though, isn't it? Pompey, bring me that leg!" Here Pompey handed the bundle a very capital cork leg, already dressed, which it screwed on in a trice; and then it stood up before my eyes.

"And a bloody action it *was*," continued the thing, as if in a soliloquy; "but then one mustn't fight with the Bugaboos and Kickapoos, and think of coming off with a mere scratch. Pompey, I'll thank you now for that arm. Thomas"[18] [turning to me] "is decidedly the best hand at a cork leg; but if you should ever want an arm, my dear fellow, you must really let me recommend you to Bishop." Here Pompey screwed on an arm.

"We had rather hot work of it, that you may say. Now, you dog, slip on my shoul-ders and bosom! Pettitt makes the best shoulders, but for a bosom you will have to go to Ducrow."

"Bosom!" said I.

"Pompey, will you *never* be ready with that wig? Scalping is a rough process after all; but then you can procure such a capital scratch at De L'Orme's."

"Scratch!"

"Now, you nigger, my teeth!" For a *good* set of these you had better go to Parmly's at once; high prices, but excellent work. I swallowed some very capital articles, though, when the big Bugaboo rammed me down with the butt end of his rifle."

"Butt end! ram down!! my eye!!!"

"Oh yes, by the by, my eye—here, Pompey, you scamp, screw it in! Those Kickapoos are not so very slow at a gouge; but he's a belied man, that Dr. Williams, after all; you can't imagine how well I see with the eyes of his make."

I now began very clearly to perceive that the object before me was nothing more nor less than my new acquaintance, Brevet Brigadier General John A. B. C. Smith. The manipulations of Pompey had made, I must confess, a very striking difference in the personal appearance of the man. The voice, however, still puzzled me no little; but even this apparent mystery was speedily cleared up.

"Pompey, you black rascal," squeaked the General, "I really do believe you would let me go out without my palate."

Hereupon the negro, grumbling out an apology, went up to his master, opened his mouth with the knowing air of a horse-jockey, and adjusted therein a somewhat singular-looking machine, in a very dexterous manner, that I could not altogether comprehend. The alteration, however, in the entire expression of the General's countenance was instantaneous and surprising. When he again spoke, his voice had resumed all that rich melody and strength which I had noticed upon our original introduction.

"D——n the vagabonds!" said he, in so

clear a tone that I positively started at the change, "D——n the vagabonds! they not only knocked in the roof of my mouth, but took the trouble to cut off at least seven eighths of my tongue. There isn't Bonfanti's[19] equal, however, in America, for really good articles of this description. I can recommend you to him with confidence," [here the General bowed,] "and assure you that I have the greatest plea-sure in so doing."

I acknowledged his kindness in my best manner, and took leave of him at once, with a perfect understanding of the true state of affairs, with a full comprehension of the mystery which had troubled me so long. It was evident. It was a clear case. Brevet Brigadier-General John A. B. C. Smith was the man—was *the man that was used up*.

Notes

Four Beasts in One

1. Poe probably had this title suggested to him by some rather obscure biblical passages in Daniel 7 and 8 which describe a series of visions and interpretations involving four beasts (one a four-headed, four-winged leopard). The passages contain several references to a "little horn" which has been traditionally associated with the wicked king Antiochus Epiphanes ("a type of the Beast," as biblical commentators call him) as well as with events other than those of Antiochus' reign. A cameleopard is a giraffe so, in a punning sense, a man-camel-leopard-giraffe is four beasts in one. In early publications of the tale the title was "Epimanes." See note 4 ("Daphne").

2. "Everybody has his virtues." The words are spoken by the villainous Artaban in Act 4, scene 2 of the tragedy *Xerxès* (1714) by Prosper Jolyot Crébillon (1674–1762). See "The Murders in the Rue Morgue," note 9.

3. Antiochus Epiphanes: Antiochus IV, King of Syria from 175 to 163 B.C.E. See Section Preface. He seized power after the assassination of Seleucus Philopater by Heliodorus in 175 B.C.E. Poe probably believed that Antiochus usurped the throne; he was the uncle of Demetrius, the legitimate heir, and Antiochus, a baby. Actually, though the usurping uncle came on from Greece with a borrowed army, he seems to have acted as king-regent "with" the baby at first. But the Book of Daniel repeats tales of his seizure of the crown

by guile. Epiphanes means "God Manifest," a blasphemy which made him seem an especially evil king. He is known to have been highly theatrical and very fond of pageantry and practical jokes.

Gog: In Ezekiel 38:2, God addresses Ezekiel, "Son of man, set thy face against Gog. . . ." Gog is identified (38:3) as "the chief prince of Rosh, Meshech and Tubal."

Cambyses: King of Persia, ruled c. 529–522 B.C.E.

Cyrus (The Great) died 529.

Diana at Ephesus: A famous temple to Artemis (Diana) was located at Ephesus, a Greek city in what is now Turkey. Actually, Antiochus attempted to plunder a temple at Elymais.

hostility to the Jews: Antiochus IV tried to suppress Judaism, and thus brought on the Maccabean war.

his miserable death at Taba: Assuming that by "Taba" Poe means "Tabae," he errs by a good many miles (see map). Antiochus IV died in Gabae in Media (Ispahan). He tried to sack a temple of Nanaia and was repelled by the natives, developed an illness which affected his mind, and so died miserably. Poe's error—if it is one—seems the result of following ancient sources other than those cited in modern histories, for there is "authority" for the location he gives in the writings of Polybius.

4. three thousand eight hundred and

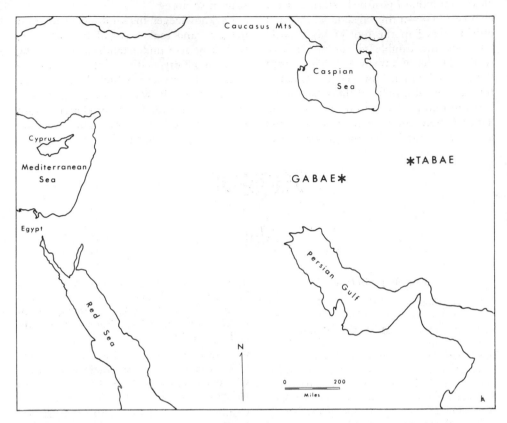

Figure Twelve. Location of Gabae and Tabae (see note 3). Map by Lewis Armstrong.

thirty: Poe wrote this story in 1833, but first published it in the March 1836 *Southern Literary Messenger*, and later in the 1840 *Tales of the Grotesque and Arabesque* and in *The Broadway Journal*, December 6, 1845. He gives the date of the events in the tale in this manner to suggest the parallel he intends between the foolish king and Andrew Jackson.

Antioch, Antiochia Epidaphne: Antioch is the ancient Syrian capital, now part of Turkey.

Daphne: In Greek mythology, Daphne was a nymph who was changed into a laurel tree to escape Apollo. The town called Daphne was near Antioch in ancient Syria. "Epi" means "near."

Seleucus Nicanor: Seleucus I or Seleucus Nicanor the Conqueror (c. 358–280 B.C.E.), ruled from 312.

Verus: Lucius Aurelius Verus, emperor from 161 to 169.

Valens: (c. 328–378), emperor of the Eastern Empire from 364 to 378.

5. Orontes: north-flowing river in present-day Syria and Turkey.

eighteen hundred and forty-five: Poe changed this date for *The Broadway Journal* version of the story to bring it up to date.

6. Poe's lines are from *Twelfth Night*, Act III, Scene 3, lines 22–24. Poe, as often, tinkers with the lines to fit his context. Sebastian speaks:

> *I pray you let us satisfy our eyes*
> *With....*

7. Marcus Aurelius Antoninus (204–222), ruled 218–222, a terrible Roman emperor who did, according to classical historians, institute worship of a conical pillar terminating in a point, as Poe says. Poe elsewhere uses

Elah Gabalah or Elah-Gabalus as an example of extreme debauchery and evil—see "William Wilson" at note 2, for example. "Heliogabalus" refers both to emperor and deity.

8. valets.

9. Timarchus: a provincial ruler under Antiochus Epiphanes. After Antiochus' death, he was to declare his realm independent, and himself "Great King of Babylon and Media."

Heraclides: descendents (or claimed descendents) of Hercules.

Ashimah: See II Kings 17:30. The precise identity of this god is not settled; some authorities think the word refers to the Semitic goddess Ashera. We think Poe has in mind Jacob Bryant's reference to Asamah (also written Asima), a deity among the Sarmatians and Syrians.

Pan of the Arcadians: god of forests, shepherds, etc., represented with goat's horns and hoofs. Arcadia is an area of Greece which gave its name to pastoralism, and is especially associated with Pan.

10. Flavius Vopiscus says that the hymn here introduced, was sung by the rabble upon the occasion of Aurelian, in the Sarmatic war, having slain with his own hand nine hundred and fifty of the enemy [Poe's note].

Flavius Vopiscus: Roman historian of the early fourth century, one of the Augustae Historiae Scriptores, six writers who wrote the lives of the emperors from 117 to 284.

Aurelian: Lucius Domitius Aurelianus (assassinated in 275), Roman emperor from 270 to 275, who succeeded in reuniting the Empire.

Sarmatic war: The Sarmatians were a people of the Near East who for years plagued Rome. Aurelian was only one of a number of emperors who had to contend with them.

Poe as usual tinkers with his source. Vopiscus writes,

> Mille mille mille decollavimus.
> unus homo mille decollavimus.
> mille bibat quisquis mille occidit.
> tantum vini nemo habet quantum
>   fudit sanguinus.

A translation of the passage Poe refers to follows:

> . . . over the course of several days he [the young Aurelian] slew over nine hundred and fifty, so that the boys even

composed in his honor the following jingles and dance-ditties, to which they would dance on holidays in soldier fashion:

> Thousand, thousand thousand we've
>   beheaded now.
> One alone, a thousand we've
>   beheaded now.
> He shall drink a thousand who a
>   thousand slew.
> So much wine is owned by no one as the
>   blood which he has shed.
>   Flavius Vopiscus, The Deified
>   Aurelian, VI, 4 and 5

Besides expanding these lines through repetitions, Poe changed *bibat*, so let him drink, to *vivat*, so let him live.

11. Whipple (2) uses the fact that Antiochus is tall and has two concubines to support his argument that Poe has Jackson in mind; there were nasty rumors about his involvement with Peggy Eaton. See Section Preface and "King Pest."

The Man That Was Used Up

1. Poe's citation is accurate; the lines are from *Le Cid*, by Pierre Corneille (1606–1684). They are spoken by the Cid's wife, Chimène. Poe translated them himself in the "Pinakidia" (*Southern Literary Messenger*, August 1836):

> "Weep, weep, my eyes! it is no time
>   to laugh
> For half myself has buried the
>   other half."

A more literal translation is Paul Landis's:

> "Weep, weep, my eyes, and drown
>   yourself in tears!
> One half my life has done to death
>   the other. . . ."

2. See Section Preface. "Smith" = "Johnson." Poe's sensitivity to common or "plebeian" last names appears elsewhere; (see "William Wilson"). Poe was an editor of *Burton's Gentleman's Magazine* when it published this tale in August 1839. The tale also appeared in the 1840 *Tales of the Grotesque and Arabesque*, in the 1843 *Prose Romances of Edgar Allan Poe*, and again in *The Broadway Journal*, August 9, 1845, during Poe's tenure as editor of that publication. The Mann trial (see note 15) was still in progress in August of 1839; Poe's tale is thus very topical (Varner).

3. *ne plus ultra:* perfection.

os femoris: the *femur* or thighbone.

fibula: the long or splint bone on the outer side of the leg.

Chiponchipino: a made-up name—a sculptor "chips away" chip on chip.

4. *je ne sais quoi:* I don't know just what.

hauteur: arrogance.

5. Tecumseh was actually a Shawnee.

6. private chat.

7. *quorum pars magna fuit:* "in which he bore a great part"—from Virgil's *Aeneid,* II, 6 (Norman).

8. *horresco referens:* "I shudder at the recollection"—from Virgil's *Aeneid,* II, 204 (Norman).

Drummummupp: Drum 'em up.

Tabitha T: Tabitha Titmouse is a character in *Ten Thousand a Year* by Samuel Warren (1807–1877), an extremely popular novel.

sotto voce: in whispers.

9. Here Poe makes fun, as he often does, of the over-acting fashionable in the theatre of his day. See "Loss of Breath," note 11. He may have had in mind a specific production of Shakespeare's *Othello, The Tragedy of the Moor of Venice,* perhaps the 1837 Philadelphia production starring Edwin Forrest, whose Iago was famous. There was no "Rantipole" theatre, but Forrest was often criticized for "ranting"; the production took place at the Chestnut Street Theatre. That year, however, Forrest played Othello, and E. S. Connor, Iago. Burton, Poe's employer in Philadelphia, was an actor himself.

Cognoscenti: "People in the know."

slips: the sides of the gallery in a theatre.

10. Iago's lines from Act III, scene 3 of *Othello:* Iago has just obtained Desdemona's handkerchief, which he plans to drop in Cassio's home to make Othello more jealous of Cassio. The sentence begins, "Not poppy, nor mandragora." Mandragora is mandrake, a narcotic plant which is important in folklore because its roots often resemble the figure of a man; that and its properties as a drug gave it considerable mystical importance. Poe's tale deals with the figure of a man who is not a real man either, though all manner of legend is attached to him. And the preceding paragraphs stress the figure of the actor "Climax."

11. face-to-face chat.

12. See "Loss of Breath," note 6.

13. Lord Byron's dramatic poem "Manfred" (1817). Again Poe's choice of allusions is interesting. Manfred, like Othello, comes to loathe himself for a crime against his beloved: "I loved her—and destroyed her."

Bas-Bleu: Bluestocking, a woman with literary pretensions.

Man-Friday: Robinson Crusoe's native sidekick in Daniel Defoe's *Strange Surprising Adventures of Robinson Crusoe* (1719).

14. In Cockney usage, "sinivate" means "insinuate" (Mabbott 7).

15. Mann: Captain Daniel Mann, who was on trial in a famous conspiracy case at the time Poe's tale was first published (Varner).

la même chose: the same thing.

16. See "Some Passages in the Life of a Lion," note 2.

17. Poe selects two terse, epigrammatic writers, one the Roman historian Cornelius Tacitus (c. 55–c. 117), who once summed up an emperor's career in a sentence: "*Omnium consensu capax imperii nisi imperasset*" ("By universal consent he was fit to rule only had he never ruled"); the other, the French philosopher, jurist, and essayist Charles de Secondat, Baron de la Brède et de Montesquieu (1689–1755), noted for point, irony, and economy of language.

18. scratch: slang for wig.

Thomas: See note 19 for this and other names in the next eleven paragraphs.

19. The names Poe mentions as specialists in artificial body parts are very obscure, and we have not located all of those in the paragraphs above.

Thomas: John F. Thomas of Philadelphia manufactured artificial limbs "on a plan the most correct and complicated" (Varner).

Bishop and Pettitt: We have been unable to locate these names.

Ducrow: Probably the great horseman mentioned in John Wilson's *Noctes Ambrosianae* (1822–1835). The character Shepherd ("James Hogg") says of Ducrow (d. 1842), "A silly thocht is a Centaur—a man and a horse in ane—in which the dominion o' the man is lost, and the superior incorpsed wi' the inferior natur! Ducraw 'rides on the whirlwind, and directs the storm.'" Shepherd speaks of him again later in the book, and a note tells us of his horsemanship and of his impersonations of statues. It is this that leads us to believe that Poe would recommend him as the man to make the best bosom. We are told that "His Mercury's beautifu'; but his Gladiawtor's shooblime."

Scratch: See above, for Poe's bad pun.

De L'Orme: Poe liked this name and used it repeatedly. There was a real person, a Negro who, during the French Revolution murdered more than 200 prisoners; there is also a Victor Hugo play, *Marion de Lorme* (1831).

Parmly: L. S. Parmley published on dentistry: *On the Natural History and Management of the Teeth* (1838).

Williams: We located a Dr. Williams, but he lived too late to have been Poe's referent, who was perhaps his father.

Bonfanti: another we've been unable to find.

11. Anti-Aristocratic Tales

These three stories could go elsewhere: "The Cask" and "The Masque" are tales of perception. Each contains a complex and "gothic" vision of the sort we have seen so frequently in other stories. "The Cask" could be grouped with the vengeance stories, such as "Hop-Frog." "Mystification" could be lumped together with Poe's many literary satires. But since Poe's social insecurity and snobbery are being heavily emphasized these days, we thought it wise to place these three together to suggest another side of Poe's social feelings. Resentment against aristocratic "privilege" of all kinds reached a peak in Jacksonian and post-Jacksonian America, while fascination with royalty and aristocracy, paradoxically, remained extremely strong. For all his fear of "mob" and for all his Southern-aristocratic pretensions, Poe at times revealed the same healthy democratic bias against the prerogatives of aristocrats.

Mystification. The early versions of "Mystification" contained a number of allusions to people and places in the United States ("Gotham" in particular) which Poe removed in the version printed here. Pollin (14) spells out the reasons behind those allusions: Poe was engaged in a verbal duel with Theodore Fay of the *New York Mirror* (the wine-of-insult in the tale is hurled, we note, not at Hermann, but at his image in the mirror), and built his tale around a very well-known episode in Fay's novel *Norman Leslie,* stocking it with allusions which would make his target clear. The duelling chapter in the novel, indeed, was one Fay had largely borrowed from another man's work, and Poe, ever alert to plagiarism real or imagined, had quite justly accused Fay of unoriginality. "Mystification," therefore, is another attack on puffery, third-class talents, and literary cliques. But since Poe's revisions make it a bit less specific, and since its plot will stand without the reader's knowledge of the literary feud, we chose to place it with the examples of "Poe on aristocracy." Poe's changes suggest that the feud had become old news, but that a tale about dissolute students and the stupid *code duello* still had market value for the copy-hungry little staff of *The Broadway Journal.*

The Masque of the Red Death. We are somewhat suspicious of Poe's intentions here. Since Prince Prospero and his courtiers can do nothing to combat

454

the disease, what is so immoral in their fleeing it? Moreover, what are they doing at the abbey of which we are supposed to disapprove? They have music, ballet, wine, and "Beauty"—all of which have favorable connotations in Poe's work—and don't seem to be misbehaving. We may well ask, as Marie Bonaparte did, where are the naked women? This is supposed to be a moral parable, but there seems little for a moralist to resent; the punishment is for no visible crime. To feel satisfaction in the moral, we must have what is usually called a puritan sensibility—a dislike of beauty for its own sake. And that is a position against which Poe fought all his life. How can we state a "moral" for this tale? Perhaps: "Death catches all, even the mighty, in the end." More likely: "Aristocracy is in itself sinful, and will be punished." Poe, in short, plays on the anti-aristocratic biases of his audience, another sign of his close ties to his country and time, especially in view of his own predilections for both aristocracy and beauty.

Prospero has all the signs of one of Poe's creators of elaborate beauty. "Some . . . would have thought him mad"; he loves the bizarre and the beautiful, and he directs the arrangements of the seven chambers of the masque himself.

Poe succeeded in "The Masque of the Red Death" in so controlling the rhythms of his sentences and the visual patterns of his decor that the story has thrilled readers into goosebumps for a century and more. But what is being *said* in those sinuous sentences will often not bear close examination. It is sometimes as nonsensical as the gothic absurdities he played with in "Metzengerstein." How, exactly, can we make sure, by touching him, that Prospero is not mad? Why take fifty words to tell us that the sound of the clock is "more emphatic" when you are close to it? We would urge readers to enjoy the thrills, as Poe no doubt did himself, but also to listen closely, in those silent moments when the music stops and the ebony clock speaks in brazen tones in the velvet room, for the sound of Edgar Poe, laughing.

The Cask of Amontillado. In structure, this is among Poe's tightest tales. Montresor is as mad as any of Poe's narrators, but Poe omits the usual passage revealing that men have called him mad or that he comes from a long line of monomaniacs. The plot itself tells us these things.

Like many of Poe's inspired madmen, however, Montresor creates a beautiful (if horrible) pattern which will take the adjectives Poe uses to describe the beautiful effect—strange, grotesque, outré, bizarre, complex. But there are none of the usual expository passages to explain why the narrator is mad or how he reached the state which enabled him to create the "beautiful" pattern; compare this to "Hop-Frog," a tale of vengeance which does explain these things.

Note also that our willingness to believe in this insane vengeance depends in large part on our anti-aristocratic prejudices. Poe's tale is related to innumerable articles in American magazines of the period about the scandalous goings-on of continental nobility.

The Tales

MYSTIFICATION[1]

*Slid, if these be your "passados" and
"montantes," I'll have none o' them.*
—NED KNOWLES.[2]

The Baron Ritzner Von Jung was of a noble Hungarian family, every member of
which (at least as far back into antiquity
as any certain records extend) was more
or less remarkable for talent of some description,—the majority for that species
of *grotesquerie* in conception of which
Tieck, a scion of the house, has given
some vivid, although by no means the
most vivid exemplifications. My acquaintance with Ritzner commenced at the magnificent Château Jung, into which a train
of droll adventures, not to be made public, threw me during the summer months
of the year 18—. Here it was I obtained
a place in his regard, and here, with
somewhat more difficulty, a partial insight into his mental conformation. In
later days this insight grew more clear, as
the intimacy which had at first permitted
it became more close; and when, after
three years separation, we met at G——n,[3]
I knew all that it was necessary to know
of the character of the Baron Ritzner Von
Jung.

I remember the buzz of curiosity which
his advent excited within the college precincts on the night of the twenty-fifth of
June. I remember still more distinctly,
that while he was pronounced by all parties at first sight "the most remarkable
man in the world," no person made any
attempt at accounting for this opinion.
That he was *unique* appeared so undeniable, that it was deemed impertinent to
inquire wherein the uniquity consisted.
But, letting this matter pass for the pres-

ent, I will merely observe that, from the
first moment of his setting foot within
the limits of the university, he began to
exercise over the habits, manners, persons, purses, and propensities of the whole
community which surrounded him, an
influence the most extensive and despotic,
yet at the same time the most indefinitive
and altogether unaccountable. Thus the
brief period of his residence at the university forms an era in its annals, and is
characterized by all classes of people appertaining to it or its dependencies as
"that very extraordinary epoch forming
the domination of the Baron Ritzner Von
Jung."

Upon his advent to G——n, he sought
me out in my apartments. He was then
of no particular age;—by which I mean
that it was impossible to form a guess
respecting his age by any data personally
afforded. He might have been fifteen or
fifty, and *was* twenty-one years and seven
months. He was by no means a handsome
man—perhaps the reverse. The contour
of his face was somewhat angular and
harsh. His forehead was lofty and very
fair; his nose a snub; his eyes large, heavy,
glassy and meaningless. About the mouth
there was more to be observed. The lips
were gently protruded, and rested the one
upon the other after such fashion that it
is impossible to conceive any, even the
most complex, combination of human
features, conveying so entirely, and so
singly, the idea of unmitigated gravity,
solemnity and repose.

It will be perceived, no doubt, from
what I have already said, that the Baron
was one of those human anomalies now
and then to be found, who make the science of *mystification* the study and the

business of their lives. For this science a peculiar turn of mind gave him instinctively the cue, while his physical appearance afforded him unusual facilities for carrying his projects into effect. I firmly believe that no student at G——n, during that renowned epoch so quaintly termed the domination of the Baron Ritzner Von Jung, ever rightly entered into the mystery which overshadowed his character. I truly think that no person at the university, with the exception of myself, ever suspected him to be capable of a joke, verbal or practical:—the old bull-dog at the garden-gate would sooner have been accused,—the ghost of Heraclitus,—or the wig of the Emeritus Professor of Theology. This, too, when it was evident that the most egregious and unpardonable of all conceivable tricks, whimsicalities, and buffooneries were brought about, if not directly by him, at least plainly through his intermediate agency or connivance. The beauty, if I may so call it, of his *art mystique*,[4] lay in that consummate ability (resulting from an almost intuitive knowledge of human nature, and a most wonderful self-possession,) by means of which he never failed to make it appear that the drolleries he was occupied in bringing to a point, arose partly in spite, and partly in consequence of the laudable efforts he was making for their prevention, and for the preservation of the good order and dignity of Alma Mater. The deep, the poignant, the overwhelming mortification which, upon each such failure of his praiseworthy endeavors, would suffuse every lineament of his countenance, left not the slightest room for doubt of his sincerity in the bosoms of even his most skeptical companions. The adroitness, too, was no less worthy of observation by which he contrived to shift the sense of the grotesque from the creator to the created—from his own person to the absurdities to which he had given rise. In no instance before that of which I speak, have I known the habitual mystific escape the natural consequence of his

manœuvres—an attachment of the ludicrous to his own character and person. Continually enveloped in an atmosphere of whim, my friend appeared to live only for the severities of society; and not even his own household have for a moment associated other ideas than those of the rigid and august with the memory of the Baron Ritzner Von Jung.

During the epoch of his residence at G——n it really appeared that the demon of the *dolce far niente*[5] lay like an incubus upon the university. Nothing, at least, was done, beyond eating and drinking, and making merry. The apartments of the students were converted into so many pot-houses, and there was no pot-house of them all more famous or more frequented than that of the Baron. Our carousals here were many, and boisterous, and long, and never unfruitful of events.

Upon one occasion we had protracted our sitting until nearly daybreak, and an unusual quantity of wine had been drunk. The company consisted of seven or eight individuals besides the Baron and myself. Most of these were young men of wealth, of high connection, of great family pride, and all alive with an exaggerated sense of honor. They abounded in the most ultra German opinions respecting the *duello*. To these Quixotic notions some recent Parisian publications, backed by three or four desperate, and fatal recontres at G——n, had given new vigor and impulse; and thus the conversation, during the greater part of the night, had run wild upon the all-engrossing topic of the times. The Baron, who had been unusually silent and abstracted in the earlier portion of the evening, at length seemed to be aroused from his apathy, took a leading part in the discourse, and dwelt upon the benefits, and more especially upon the beauties, of the received code of etiquette in passages of arms, with an ardor, an eloquence, an impressiveness, and an affectionateness of manner, which elicited the warmest enthusiasm from his hearers in general, and absolutely staggered even myself, who well knew him to be at heart a ridiculer of those very points for which he contended, and especially to hold the entire *fanfaronnade*[6] of duelling etiquette in the sovereign contempt which it deserves.

Looking around me during a pause in the Baron's discourse, (of which my readers may gather some faint idea when I say that it bore resemblance to the fervid, chanting, monotonous, yet musical, sermonic manner of Coleridge,) I perceived symptoms of even more than the general interest in the countenance of one of the party. This gentleman, whom I shall call Hermann, was an original in every respect —except, perhaps, in the single particular that he was a very great fool. He contrived to bear, however, among a particular set at the university, a reputation for deep metaphysical thinking, and, I believe, for some logical talent. As a duellist he had acquired great renown, even at G——n. I forget the precise number of victims who had fallen at his hands; but they were many. He was a man of courage undoubtedly. But it was upon his minute acquaintance with the etiquette of the *duello*, and the *nicety* of his sense of honor, that he most especially prided himself. These things were a hobby which he rode to the death. To Ritzner, ever upon the look-out for the grotesque, his peculiarities had for a long time past afforded food for mystification. Of this, however, I was not aware; although, in the present instance, I saw clearly that something of a whimsical nature was upon the *tapis*[7] with my friend, and that Hermann was its especial object.

As the former proceeded in his discourse, or rather monologue, I perceived the excitement of the latter momently increasing. At length he spoke; offering some objection to a point insisted upon by R., and giving his reasons in detail. To these the Baron replied at length (still maintaining his exaggerated tone of sentiment) and concluding, in what I thought very bad taste, with a sarcasm and a sneer

The hobby of Hermann now took the bit in his teeth. This I could discern by the studied hair-splitting *farrago*[8] of his rejoinder. His last words I distinctly remember. "Your opinions, allow me to say, Baron Von Jung, although in the main correct, are, in many nice points, discreditable to yourself and to the university of which you are a member. In a few respects they are even unworthy of serious refutation. I would say more than this, sir, were it not for the fear of giving you offence (here the speaker smiled blandly,) I would say, sir, that your opinions are not the opinions to be expected from a gentleman."

As Hermann completed this equivocal sentence, all eyes were turned upon the Baron. He became pale, then excessively red, then, dropping his pocket-handkerchief, stooped to recover it, when I caught a glimpse of his countenance, while it could be seen by no one else at the table. It was radiant with the quizzical expression which was its natural character, but which I had never seen it assume except when we were alone together, and when he unbent himself freely. In an instant afterward he stood erect, confronting Hermann; and so total an alteration of countenance in so short a period I certainly never saw before. For a moment I even fancied that I had misconceived him, and that he was in sober earnest. He appeared to be stifling with passion, and his face was cadaverously white. For a short time he remained silent, apparently striving to master his emotion. Having at length seemingly succeeded, he reached a decanter which stood near him, saying, as he held it firmly clenched—"The language you have thought proper to employ, Mynheer Hermann, in addressing yourself to me, is objectionable in so many particulars, that I have neither temper nor time for specification. That my opinions, however, are not the opinions to be expected from a gentleman, is an observation so directly offensive as to allow me but one line of conduct. Some courtesy, nevertheless, is due to the presence of this company, and to yourself, at this moment, as my guest. You will pardon me, therefore, if, upon this consideration, I deviate slightly from the general usage among gentlemen in similar cases of personal affront. You will forgive me for the moderate tax I shall make upon your imagination, and endeavor to consider, for an instant, the reflection of your person in yonder mirror as the living Mynheer Hermann himself. This being done, there will be no difficulty whatever. I shall discharge this decanter of wine at your image in yonder mirror, and thus fulfil all the spirit, if not the exact letter, of resentment for your insult, while the necessity of physical violence to your real person will be obviated."

With these words he hurled the decanter, full of wine, against the mirror which hung directly opposite Hermann; striking the reflection of his person with great precision, and of course shattering the glass into fragments. The whole company at once started to their feet, and, with the exception of myself and Ritzner, took their departure. As Hermann went out, the Baron whispered me that I should follow him and make an offer of my services. To this I agreed; not knowing precisely what to make of so ridiculous a piece of business.

The duellist accepted my aid with his stiff and *ultra recherché* air, and taking my arm, led me to his apartment. I could hardly forbear laughing in his face while he proceeded to discuss, with the profoundest gravity, what he termed "the refinedly peculiar character" of the insult he had received. After a tiresome harangue in his ordinary style, he took down from his bookshelves a number of musty volumes on the subject of the *duello*, and entertained me for a long time with their contents; reading aloud, and commenting earnestly as he read. I can just remember the titles of some of the works. There were the "Ordonnance of Philip le Bel on Single Combat;" the "Theatre of Honor," by

Favyn, and a treatise "On the Permission of Duels," by D'Audiguier. He displayed, also, with much pomposity, Brantôme's "Memoirs of Duels," published at Cologne, in 1666, in the types of Elzevir—a precious and unique vellum-paper volume, with a fine margin, and bound by Derôme. But he requested my attention particularly, and with an air of mysterious sagacity, to a thick octavo, written in barbarous Latin by one Hédelin, a Frenchman, and having the quaint title, "*Duelli Lex scripta, et non; aliterque.*" From this he read me one of the drollest chapters in the world concerning "*Injuriæ per applicationem, per constructionem, et per se,*"[9] about half of which, he averred, was strictly applicable to his own "refinedly peculiar" case, although not one syllable of the whole matter could I understand for the life of me. Having finished the chapter, he closed the book, and demanded what I thought necessary to be done. I replied that I had entire confidence in his superior delicacy of feeling, and would abide by what he proposed. With this answer he seemed flattered, and sat down to write a note to the Baron. It ran thus:

SIR,—My friend, M. P——, will hand you this note. I find it incumbent upon me to request, at your earliest convenience, an explanation of this evening's occurrences at your chambers. In the event of your declining this request, Mr. P. will be happy to arrange, with any friend whom you may appoint, the steps preliminary to a meeting.

With sentiments of perfect respect,

Your most humble servant,

JOHAN HERMANN.

To the Baron Ritzner Von Jung,

August 18th, 18—.

Not knowing what better to do, I called upon Ritzner with this epistle. He bowed as I presented it; then, with a grave countenance, motioned me to a seat. Having perused the cartel, he wrote the following reply, which I carried to Hermann.

SIR,

Through our common friend, Mr. P., I have received your note of this evening. Upon due reflection I frankly admit the propriety of the explanation you suggest. This being admitted, I still find great difficulty, (owing to the *refinedly peculiar* nature of our disagreement, and of the personal affront offered on my part,) in so wording what I have to say by way of apology, as to meet all the minute exigencies, and all the variable shadows of the case. I have great reliance, however, on that extreme delicacy of discrimination, in matters appertaining to the rules of etiquette, for which you have been so long and so preëminently distinguished. With perfect certainty, therefore, of being comprehended, I beg leave, in lieu of offering any sentiments of my own, to refer you to the opinions of the Sieur Hédelin, as set forth in the ninth paragraph of the chapter of *"Injuriæ per applicationem, per constructionem, et per se,"* in his *"Duelli Lex scripta, et non; aliterque."* The nicety of your discernment in all the matters here treated, will be sufficient, I am assured, to convince you *that the mere circumstance of me referring you to* this admirable passage, ought to satisfy your request, as a man of honor, for explanation.

With sentiments of profound respect,

Your most obedient servant,

VON JUNG.

The Herr Johan Hermann.
August 18th, 18——.

Hermann commenced the perusal of this epistle with a scowl, which, however, was converted into a smile of the most ludicrous self-complacency as he came to the rigmarole about *Injuriæ per applicationem, per constructionem, et per se.* Having finished reading, he begged me, with the blandest of all possible smiles, to be seated, while he made reference to the treatise in question. Turning to the passage specified, he read it with great care to himself, then closed the book, and desired me, in my character of confidential acquaintance, to express to the Baron Von Jung his exalted sense of his chivalrous behaviour, and, in that of second, to assure him that the explanation offered was of the fullest, the most honourable, and the most unequivocally satisfactory nature.

Somewhat amazed at all this, I made my retreat to the Baron. He seemed to receive Hermann's amicable letter as a matter of course, and after a few words of general conversation, went to an inner room and brought out the everlasting treatise *"Duelli Lex scripta, et non; aliterque."* He handed me the volume and asked me to look over some portion of it. I did so, but to little purpose, not being able to gather the least particle of meaning. He then took the book himself, and read me a chapter aloud. To my surprise, what he read proved to be a most horribly absurd account of a duel between two baboons. He now explained the mystery; showing that the volume, as it appeared *prima facie*, was written upon the plan of the nonsense verses of Du Bartas;[10] that is to say, the language was ingeniously framed so as to present to the ear all the outward signs of intelligibilty, and even of profundity, while in fact not a shadow of meaning existed. The key to the whole was found in leaving out every second and third word alternately, when there appeared a series of ludicrous quizzes upon a single combat as practised in modern times.

The Baron afterwards informed me that he had purposely thrown the treatise in Hermann's way two or three weeks before the adventure, and that he was satisfied, from the general tenor of his conversation, that he had studied it with the deepest attention, and firmly believed it to be a work of unusual merit. Upon this hint he proceeded. Hermann would have died a thousand deaths rather than ac-

Figure Thirteen. A woodcut of Londoners fleeing the plague of 1630: Poe was using a traditional subject in "The Masque of the Red Death." Reproduced courtesy of the New York Public Library, Astor, Lenox and Tilden Foundations.

knowledge his inability to understand anything and everything in the universe that had ever been written about the *duello*.

THE MASQUE OF THE RED DEATH[1]

The "Red Death" had long devastated the country. No pestilence had ever been so fatal, or so hideous. Blood was its Avatar[2] and its seal—the redness and the horror of blood. There were sharp pains, and sudden dizziness, and then profuse bleeding at the pores, with dissolution. The scarlet stains upon the body and especially upon the face of the victim, were the pest ban which shut him out from the aid and from the sympathy of his fellow-men. And the whole seizure, progress, and termination of the disease, were the incidents of half an hour.

But the Prince Prospero was happy and dauntless and sagacious. When his dominions were half depopulated, he summoned to his presence a thousand hale and light-hearted friends from among the knights and dames of his court, and with these retired to the deep seclusion of one of his castellated abbeys. This was an extensive and magnificent structure, the creation of the prince's own eccentric yet august taste. A strong and lofty wall gir-

dled it in. This wall had gates of iron. The courtiers, having entered, brought furnaces and massy hammers and welded the bolts. They resolved to leave means neither of ingress or egress to the sudden impulses of despair or frenzy from within. The abbey was amply provisioned. With such precautions the courtiers might bid defiance to contagion. The external world could take care of itself. In the meantime it was folly to grieve, or to think. The prince had provided all the appliances of pleasure. There were buffoons, there were improvisatori,[3] there were ballet-dancers, there were musicians, there was Beauty, there was wine. All these and security were within. Without was the "Red Death."

It was toward the close of the fifth or sixth month of his seclusion, and while the pestilence raged most furiously abroad, that the Prince Prospero entertained his thousand friends at a masked ball of the most unusual magnificence.

It was a voluptuous scene, that masquerade. But first let me tell of the rooms in which it was held. There were seven —an imperial suite. In many palaces, however, such suites form a long and straight vista, while the folding doors slide back nearly to the walls on either hand, so that the view of the whole extent is scarcely impeded. Here the case was very different; as might have been expected from the duke's love of the *bizarre*. The apartments were so irregularly disposed that the vision embraced but little more than one at a time. There was a sharp turn at every twenty or thirty yards, and at each turn a novel effect. To the right and left, in the middle of each wall, a tall and narrow Gothic window looked out upon a closed corridor which pursued the windings of the suite. These windows were of stained glass whose color varied in accordance with the prevailing hue of the decorations of the chamber into which it opened. That at the eastern extremity was hung, for example, in blue—and vividly blue were its windows. The second chamber was purple in its ornaments and tapestries, and here the panes were purple. The third was green throughout, and so were the casements. The fourth was furnished and lighted with orange—the fifth with white—the sixth with violet. The seventh apartment was closely shrouded in black velvet tapestries that hung all over the ceiling and down the walls, falling in heavy folds upon a carpet of the same material and hue. But in this chamber only, the color of the windows failed to correspond with the decorations. The panes here were scarlet—a deep blood color. Now in no one of the seven apartments was there any lamp or candelabrum, amid the profusion of golden ornaments that lay scattered to and fro or depended from the roof. There was no light of any kind emanating from lamp or candle within the suite of chambers. But in the corridors that followed the suite, there stood, opposite to each window a heavy tripod, bearing a brazier of fire, that projected its rays through the tinted glass and so glaringly illumined the room. And thus were produced a multitude of gaudy and fantastic appearances. But in the western or black chamber the effect of the fire-light that streamed upon the dark hangings through the blood-tinted panes, was ghastly in the extreme, and produced so wild a look upon the countenances of those who entered, that there were few of the company bold enough to set foot within its precincts at all.[4]

It was in this apartment, also, that there stood against the western wall, a gigantic clock of ebony. Its pendulum swung to and fro with a dull, heavy, monotonous clang; and when the minute-hand made the circuit of the face, and the hour was to be stricken, there came from the brazen lungs of the clock a sound which was clear and loud and deep and exceedingly musical, but of so peculiar a note and emphasis that, at each lapse of an hour, the musicians of the orchestra were constrained to pause, momentarily, in their performance, to hearken to the sound; and thus the waltzers perforce ceased their evolutions; and there was a brief disconcert of the whole gay company; and, while the chimes of the clock yet rang, it was observed that the giddiest grew pale, and the more aged and sedate passed their hands over their brows as if in confused revery or meditation. But when the echoes had fully ceased, a light laughter at once pervaded the assembly; the musicians looked at each other and smiled as if at their own nervousness and folly, and made whispering vows, each to the other, that the next chiming of the clock should produce in them no similar emotion; and then, after the lapse of sixty minutes, (which embrace three thousand and six hundred seconds of the Time that flies,) there came yet another chiming of the clock, and then were the same disconcert and tremulousness and meditation as before.

But, in spite of these things, it was a gay and magnificent revel. The tastes of the duke were peculiar. He had a fine eye for colors and effects. He disregarded the *decora*[5] of mere fashion. His plans were bold and fiery, and his conceptions glowed with barbaric lustre. There are some who would have thought him mad. His followers felt that he was not. It was necessary to hear and see and touch him to be *sure* that he was not.

He had directed, in great part, the moveable embellishments of the seven chambers, upon occasion of this great *fête;* and it was his own guiding taste which had given character to the masqueraders. Be sure they were grotesque. There were much glare and glitter and piquancy and phantasm—much of what has been since seen in "Hernani."[6] There were arabesque figures with unsuited limbs and appointments. There were delirious fancies such as the madman fashions. There were much of the beautiful, much of the wanton, much of the *bizarre,* something of the terrible, and not a little of that which might have excited disgust. To and fro in the seven chambers there stalked, in fact, a multitude of dreams. And these—the dreams—writhed in and about, taking hue from the rooms, and causing the wild music of the orchestra to seem as the echo of their steps. And, anon, there strikes the ebony clock which stands in the hall of the velvet. And then, for a moment, all is still, and all is silent save the voice of the clock. The dreams are stiff-frozen as they stand. But the echoes of the chime die away—they have endured but an instant—and a light, half-subdued laughter floats after them as they depart. And now again the music swells, and the dreams live, and writhe to and fro more merrily than ever, taking hue from the many-tinted windows through which stream the rays from the tripods. But to the chamber which lies most westwardly of the seven, there are now none of the maskers who venture; for the night is waning away; and there flows a ruddier light through the blood-colored panes; and the blackness of the sable drapery appals; and to him whose foot falls upon the sable carpet, there comes from the near clock of ebony a muffled peal more solemnly emphatic than any which reaches *their* ears who indulge in the more remote gaieties of the other apartments.

But these other apartments were densely crowded, and in them beat feverishly the heart of life. And the revel went whirlingly on, until at length there commenced the sounding of midnight upon the clock. And then the music ceased, as I have told; and the evolutions of the waltzers were quieted; and there was an uneasy cessation of all things as before. But now there were twelve strokes to be sounded by the bell of the clock; and thus it happened, perhaps, that more of thought crept, with more of time, into the meditations of the thoughtful among those who revelled. And thus, too, it happened, perhaps, that before the last echoes of the last chime had utterly sunk into silence, there were many individuals in the crowd who had found leisure to become aware of the presence of a masked figure which had arrested the attention of no single individual before. And the rumor of this new presence having spread itself whisperingly around, there arose at length from the whole company a buzz, or murmur, expressive of disapprobation and surprise—then, finally, of terror, of horror, and of disgust.

In an assembly of phantasms such as I have painted, it may well be supposed that no ordinary appearance could have excited such sensation. In truth the masquerade license of the night was nearly unlimited; but the figure in question had out-Heroded Herod,[7] and gone beyond the bounds of even the prince's indefinite decorum. There are chords in the hearts of the most reckless which cannot be touched without emotion. Even with the utterly lost, to whom life and death are equally jests, there are matters of which no jest can be made. The whole company, indeed, seemed now deeply to feel that in the costume and bearing of the stranger neither wit nor propriety existed. The figure was tall and gaunt, and shrouded from head to foot in the habiliments of the grave. The mask which concealed the visage was made so nearly to resemble the countenance of a stiffened corpse that the closest scrutiny must have had difficulty in detecting the cheat. And yet all this might have been endured, if not approved, by the mad revellers around. But the mummer had gone so far as to assume the type of the Red Death. His vesture was dabbled in *blood*—and his broad brow, with all the features of the face, was besprinkled with the scarlet horror.

When the eyes of Prince Prospero fell upon this spectral image (which with a slow and solemn movement, as if more fully to sustain its *rôle*, stalked to and fro among the waltzers) he was seen to be convulsed, in the first moment with a strong shudder either of terror or distaste; but, in the next, his brow reddened with rage.

"Who dares?" he demanded hoarsely of the courtiers who stood near him—"who dares insult us with this blasphemous mockery?[8] Seize him and unmask him— that we may know whom we have to hang at sunrise, from the battlements!"

It was in the eastern or blue chamber in which stood the Prince Prospero as he uttered these words. They rang throughout the seven rooms loudly and clearly —for the prince was a bold and robust man, and the music had become hushed at the waving of his hand.

It was in the blue room where stood the prince, with a group of pale courtiers by his side. At first, as he spoke, there was a slight rushing movement of this group in the direction of the intruder, who at the moment was also near at hand, and now, with deliberate and stately step, made closer approach to the speaker. But from a certain nameless awe with which the mad assumptions of the mummer had inspired the whole party, there were found none who put forth hand to seize him; so that, unimpeded, he passed within a yard of the prince's person; and, while the vast assembly, as if with one impulse, shrank from the centres of the rooms to the walls, he made his way uninterruptedly, but with the same solemn and measured step which had distinguished him from the first, through the blue chamber to the purple—through the purple to the green—through the green to the orange

—through this again to the white—and even thence to the violet, ere a decided movement had been made to arrest him. It was then, however, that the Prince Prospero, maddening with rage and the shame of his own momentary cowardice, rushed hurriedly through the six chambers, while none followed him on account of a deadly terror that had seized upon all. He bore aloft a drawn dagger, and had approached, in rapid impetuosity, to within three or four feet of the retreating figure, when the latter, having attained the extremity of the velvet apartment, turned suddenly and confronted his pursuer. There was a sharp cry—and the dagger dropped gleaming upon the sable carpet, upon which, instantly afterwards, fell prostrate in death the Prince Prospero. Then, summoning the wild courage of despair, a throng of the revellers at once threw themselves into the black apartment, and, seizing the mummer, whose tall figure stood erect and motionless within the shadow of the ebony clock, gasped in unutterable horror at finding the grave-cerements and corpse-like mask which they handled with so violent a rudeness, untenanted by any tangible form.

And now was acknowledged the presence of the Red Death. He had come like a thief in the night. And one by one dropped the revellers in the blood-bedewed halls of their revel, and died each in the despairing posture of his fall.[9] And the life of the ebony clock went out with that of the last of the gay. And the flames of the tripods expired. And Darkness and Decay and the Red Death held illimitable dominion over all.

THE CASK OF AMONTILLADO[1]

The thousand injuries of Fortunato I had borne as I best could, but when he ventured upon insult I vowed revenge. You, who so well know the nature of my soul, will not suppose, however, that I gave utterance to a threat. *At length* I would be avenged; this was a point definitely settled—but the very definitiveness with which it was resolved precluded the idea of risk. I must not only punish but punish with impunity.[2] A wrong is unredressed when retribution overtakes its redresser. It is equally unredressed when the avenger fails to make himself felt as such to him who has done the wrong.

It must be understood that neither by word nor deed had I given Fortunato cause to doubt my good will. I continued, as was my wont, to smile in his face, and he did not perceive that my smile *now* was at the thought of his immolation.

He had a weak point—this Fortunato—although in other regards he was a man to be respected and even feared. He prided himself on his connoisseurship in wine. Few Italians have the true virtuoso spirit. For the most part their enthusiasm is adopted to suit the time and opportunity, to practise imposture upon the British and Austrian *millionaires*. In painting and gemmary, Fortunato, like his countrymen, was a quack, but in the matter of old wines he was sincere. In this respect I did not differ from him materially;—I was skilful in the Italian vintages[3] myself, and bought largely whenever I could.

It was about dusk, one evening during the supreme madness of the carnival season, that I encountered my friend. He accosted me with excessive warmth, for he had been drinking much. The man wore motley. He had on a tight-fitting partistriped dress, and his head was surmounted by the conical cap and bells. I was so pleased to see him that I thought I should never have done wringing his hand.

I said to him—"My dear Fortunato, you are luckily met. How remarkably well you are looking to-day! But I have received a pipe[4] of what passes for Amontillado, and I have my doubts."

"How?" said he. "Amontillado? A pipe? Impossible! And in the middle of the carnival!"

"I have my doubts," I replied; "and I was silly enough to pay the full Amontillado price without consulting you in the matter. You were not to be found, and I was fearful of losing a bargain."

"Amontillado!"

"I have my doubts."

"Amontillado!"

"And I must satisfy them."

"Amontillado!"

"As you are engaged, I am on my way to Luchresi. If any one has a critical turn, it is he. He will tell me——"

"Luchresi cannot tell Amontillado from Sherry."[5]

"And yet some fools will have it that his taste is a match for your own."

"Come, let us go."

"Whither?"

"To your vaults."

"My friend, no; I will not impose upon your good nature. I perceive you have an engagement. Luchresi——"

"I have no engagement;—come."

"My friend, no. It is not the engagement, but the severe cold with which I perceive you are afflicted. The vaults are insufferably damp. They are encrusted with nitre."

"Let us go, nevertheless. The cold is merely nothing. Amontillado! You have been imposed upon. And as for Luchresi, he cannot distinguish Sherry from Amontillado."

Thus speaking, Fortunato possessed himself of my arm; and putting on a mask of black silk and drawing a *roquelaire*[6] closely about my person, I suffered him to hurry me to my palazzo.

There were no attendants at home; they had absconded to make merry in honour of the time. I had told them that I should not return until the morning, and had given them explicit orders not to stir from the house. These orders were sufficient, I well knew, to insure their immediate disappearance, one and all, as soon as my back was turned.

I took from their sconces two flambeaux, and giving one to Fortunato, bowed him through several suites of rooms to the archway that led into the vaults. I passed down a long and winding staircase, requesting him to be cautious as he followed. We came at length to the foot of the descent, and stood together on the damp ground of the catacombs of the Montresors.

The gait of my friend was unsteady, and the bells upon his cap jingled as he strode.

"The pipe?" said he.

"It is farther on," said I; "but observe the white web-work which gleams from these cavern walls."

He turned towards me, and looked into my eyes with two filmy orbs that distilled the rheum of intoxication.

"Nitre?" he asked, at length.

"Nitre," I replied. "How long have you had that cough?"

"Ugh! ugh! ugh!—ugh! ugh! ugh!— ugh! ugh! ugh!—ugh! ugh! ugh!—ugh! ugh! ugh!"

My poor friend found it impossible to reply for many minutes.

"It is nothing," he said, at last.

"Come," I said, with decision, "we will go back; your health is precious. You are rich, respected, admired, beloved; you are happy, as once I was. You are a man to be missed. For me it is no matter. We will go back; you will be ill, and I cannot be responsible. Besides, there is Luchresi——"

"Enough," he said; "the cough is a mere nothing; it will not kill me. I shall not die of a cough."

"True—true," I replied; "and, indeed, I had no intention of alarming you unnecessarily—but you should use all proper caution. A draught of this Medoc[7] will defend us from the damps."

Here I knocked off the neck of a bottle which I drew from a long row of its fellows that lay upon the mould.

"Drink," I said, presenting him the wine.

He raised it to his lips with a leer. He paused and nodded to me familiarly, while his bells jingled.

"I drink," he said, "to the buried that repose around us."

"And I to your long life."

He again took my arm, and we proceeded.

"These vaults," he said, "are extensive."

"The Montresors," I replied, "were a great and numerous family."

"I forget your arms."

"A huge human foot d'or, in a field azure; the foot crushes a serpent rampant whose fangs are imbedded in the heel."

"And the motto?"

"*Nemo me impune lacessit.*"[8]

"Good" he said.

The wine sparkled in his eyes and the bells jingled. My own fancy grew warm with the Medoc. We had passed through long walls of piled skeletons, with casks and puncheons intermingling, into the inmost recesses of the catacombs. I paused again, and this time I made bold to seize Fortunato by an arm above the elbow.

"The nitre!" I said; "see, it increases. It hangs like moss upon the vaults. We are below the river's bed. The drops of moisture trickle among the bones. Come, we will go back ere it is too late. Your cough——"

"It is nothing," he said; "let us go on. But first, another draught of the Medoc."

I broke and reached him a flagon of De Grâve.[9] He emptied it at a breath. His eyes flashed with a fierce light. He laughed and threw the bottle upward with a gesticulation I did not understand.

I looked at him in surprise. He repeated the movement—a grotesque one.

"You do not comprehend?" he said.

"Not I," I replied.

"Then you are not of the brotherhood."

"How?"

"You are not of the masons."

"Yes, yes," I said; "yes, yes."

"You? Impossible! A mason?"[10]

"A mason," I replied.

"A sign," he said, "a sign."

"It is this," I answered, producing a trowel from beneath the folds of my *roquelaire.*

"You jest," he exclaimed, recoiling a few paces. "But let us proceed to the Amontillado."

"Be it so," I said, replacing the tool beneath the cloak and again offering him my arm. He leaned upon it heavily. We continued our route in search of the Amontillado. We passed through a range of low arches, descended, passed on, and descending again, arrived at a deep crypt, in which the foulness of the air caused our flambeaux rather to glow than flame.

At the most remote end of the crypt there appeared another less spacious. Its walls had been lined with human remains, piled to the vault overhead, in the fashion of the great catacombs of Paris. Three sides of this interior crypt were still ornamented in this manner. From the fourth the bones had been thrown down, and lay promiscuously upon the earth, forming at one point a mound of some size. Within the wall thus exposed by the displacing of the bones, we perceived a still interior crypt or recess, in depth about four feet, in width three, in height six or seven. It seemed to have been constructed for no especial use within itself, but formed merely the interval between two of the colossal supports of the roof of the catacombs, and was backed by one of their circumscribing walls of solid granite.

It was in vain that Fortunato, uplifting his dull torch, endeavored to pry into the depth of the recess. Its termination the feeble light did not enable us to see.

"Proceed," I said; "herein is the Amontillado. As for Luchresi——"

"He is an ignoramus," interrupted my friend, as he stepped unsteadily forward, while I followed immediately at his heels. In an instant he had reached the extremity of the niche, and finding his progress arrested by the rock, stood stupidly bewildered. A moment more and I had fettered him to the granite. In its surface were two iron staples, distant from each other about two feet, horizontally. From one of these depended a short chain, from the other a padlock. Throwing the links about his waist, it was but the work of a few seconds to secure it. He was too much astounded to resist. Withdrawing the key I stepped back from the recess.

"Pass your hand," I said, "over the wall; you cannot help feeling the nitre. Indeed it is *very* damp. Once more let me *implore* you to return. No? Then I must positively leave you. But I must first render you all the little attentions in my power."

"The Amontillado!" ejaculated my friend, not yet recovered from his astonishment.

"True," I replied; "the Amontillado."

As I said these words I busied myself among the pile of bones of which I have before spoken. Throwing them aside, I soon uncovered a quantity of building stone and mortar. With these materials and with the aid of my trowel, I began vigorously to wall up the entrance of the niche.

I had scarcely laid the first tier of the masonry when I discovered that the intoxication of Fortunato had in a great measure worn off. The earliest indication I had of this was a low moaning cry from the depth of the recess. It was *not* the cry of a drunken man. There was then a long and obstinate silence. I laid the second tier, and the third, and the fourth; and then I heard the furious vibrations of the chain. The noise lasted for several minutes, during which, that I might hearken to it with the more satisfaction, I ceased my labours and sat down upon the bones. When at last the clanking subsided, I resumed the trowel, and finished without interruption the fifth, the sixth, and the seventh tier. The wall was now nearly upon a level with my breast. I again paused, and holding the flambeaux over the mason-work, threw a few feeble rays upon the figure within.

A succession of loud and shrill screams, bursting suddenly from the throat of the chained form, seemed to thrust me violently back. For a brief moment I hesitated, I trembled. Unsheathing my rapier,

I began to grope with it about the recess; but the thought of an instant reassured me. I placed my hand upon the solid fabric of the catacombs, and felt satisfied. I reapproached the wall. I replied to the yells of him who clamoured. I re-echoed, I aided, I surpassed them in volume and in strength. I did this, and the clamourer grew still.

It was now midnight, and my task was drawing to a close. I had completed the eighth, the ninth, and the tenth tier. I had finished a portion of the last and the eleventh; there remained but a single stone to be fitted and plastered in. I struggled with its weight; I placed it partially in its destined position. But now there came from out the niche a low laugh that erected the hairs upon my head. It was succeeded by a sad voice, which I had difficulty in recognizing as that of the noble Fortunato. The voice said—

"Ha! ha! ha!—he! he! he!—a very good joke, indeed—an excellent jest. We will have many a rich laugh about it at the palazzo—he! he! he!—over our wine—he! he! he!"

"The Amontillado!" I said.

"He! he! he!—he! he! he!—yes, the Amontillado. But is it not getting late? Will not they be awaiting us at the palazzo, the Lady Fortunato and the rest? Let us be gone."

"Yes," I said, "let us be gone."

"For the love of God, Montresor!"

"Yes," I said, "for the love of God!"

But to these words I hearkened in vain for a reply. I grew impatient. I called aloud—

"Fortunato!"

No answer. I called again—

"Fortunato!"[11]

No answer still. I thrust a torch through the remaining aperture and let it fall within. There came forth in return only a jingling of the bells. My heart grew sick; it was the dampness of the catacombs that made it so. I hastened to make an end of my labour. I forced the last stone into its position; I plastered it up. Against the new masonry I re-erected the old rampart of bones. For the half of a century no mortal has disturbed them. *In pace requiescat!*[12]

Notes

Mystification

1. Published first as "Von Jung, the Mystific," in the *American Monthly Magazine* (June 1837), then in *Tales of the Grotesque and Arabesque* (1840) as "Von Jung" and in *The Broadway Journal*, December 27, 1845 with the title "Mystification." For the nature of Poe's changes see Section Preface.

2. Poe's motto is from Ben Jonson's *Every Man in His Humour* (c. 1598). In Act IV, Scene V of this play, Edward Knowell, Junior, chides the foolish Bobadill, who, after bragging, is disarmed and thrashed by his enemy:

> '*Slid! an these be your tricks,*
> *your passadoes, and your*
> *montantos, I'll none of them.*'

A "passado" in fencing is a thrust forward made by moving the whole body; "montantos" are upward thrusts. "Slid" is a shortened form of "Gadslid" or "By God's blood." In his review of "Wakondah; the Master of Life" by Cornelius Matthews (*Graham's Magazine* for February 1842) Poe repeats this quotation. After calling the work "trash," he concludes " 'Slid, if these be your passados and montantes, we'll have none of them.' Mr. Matthews, you have clearly mistaken your vocation. . . ." The meaning of the motto here is simply "Duelling is stupid."

3. Tieck: Ludwig Tieck (1773–1853), a German romantic author noted, as Poe implies, for his gothicism. Poe probably knew Car-

lyle's *German Romances* (1827), which included folk-tales by Tieck. A guess at a line of association in Poe's mind: Ritzner = Richter. Carlyle wrote two essays titled "Richter" on Jean Paul Richter.

G——n: Göttingen, the great German university. Poe often played upon readers' preconceptions of universities; see "William Wilson" for similar passages. Students are dissolute young aristocrats in each tale.

4. Heraclitus: Greek philosopher (c. 540–c. 480 B.C.E.)

art mystique: mystical art.

5. agreeable idleness.

6. *duello:* the code of dueling. A number of books and articles in Poe's day attacked the custom as crude and barbarous.

rencontres: meetings.

fanfaronnade: blustering nonsense.

7. Coleridge: For Poe's feelings about Coleridge see "How to Write a Blackwood Article" and "Never Bet the Devil Your Head."

upon the *tapis:* under consideration.

8. hodgepodge.

9. *ultra recherché:* super-refined; ultra-affected.

Philip le Bel: Philip IV (1268–1314), a son of Philip III and Isabella of Aragon. He was a cruel, warlike king who persecuted the order of Templars and caused the court of the Pope to move to Avignon in 1308.

Favyn: André Favyn, French historical writer born in Paris between 1550 and 1590. Among his works were a "History of Navarre" (1612) and *Théâtre d'honneur et de la chevalerie ó Histoire des ordres militaires, duels, joutes et tournois* (1620). An English translation came out in 1623. Note that the French title speaks of duels, jousts, and tourneys.

D'Audiguier: Vital d'Audiguier (c. 1570–1625 or 1630), a French writer, extremely popular in his day. One of his works is *Le vrai et ancien usage des duels* (1617).

Brantôme: Abbé Pierre de Brantôme (c. 1535–1614), French chronicler. His *Memoires* appeared in 1665–1666.

Elzevir: Louis Elzevir (1540–1617), Dutch publisher noted for the excellence of the types his firm had designed and used, and for the high quality of its press-work. Elzevir is considered a pioneer in the production of good-quality inexpensive books, and the type

known in the United States and Great Britain as "old-style" is still called "Elzevir," in his honor, on the continent.

Derôme: A famous eighteenth-century family of French bookbinders, the best known of whom is Nicolas Denis (1731–1788).

Hédelin: François Hédelin Aubignac (1604–1676).

"Duelli Lex scripta, et non; aliterque": "The Law Written on Duelling, and Not, and Otherwise" (i.e., nonsense). The title is mispunctuated. The "semicolon after 'non' . . . destroys the force of the parallel 'written and non-written and otherwise' " (Pollin 14).

Injuriae per applicationem, per constructionem, et per se: Insults by application, by construction, and by themselves (meant to be obscure).

10. *prima facie:* at first appearance.

Du Bartas: Guillaume de Saluste, Seigneur du Bartas (1544–1590). Poe repeatedly spoke of his "nonsense verse" (see IX, 67, XI, 159 and XI, 259 of the Virginia Edition of Poe's works), sometimes putting the words in quotation marks to indicate that *he* considered it nonsense. He learned about it in Isaac Disraeli's *Curiosities of Literature,* which speaks of "nonsensical lines of Du Bartas" and then quotes some which are intended to imitate the song of a lark.

The Masque of the Red Death

1. Poe's disease seems to be of his own invention; its symptoms and incubation period match no known plague. But Poe was familiar with major epidemics in American cities in the recent past (Philadelphia had several cholera outbreaks in the 1790s, for instance) and in his own day (Baltimore in 1831; another, apparently brought in by immigrants, appeared in the United States in 1832). Shakespeare alludes to a "red plague" in *The Tempest,* I, 2, 363, and to a "red pestilence" in *Coriolanus,* IV, 1, 13, which commentators assume is the bubonic plague.

Poe also may have known of the famous case in which merchants from Genoa, pursued by Tartars in 1343, took refuge in a walled town. The Tartars besieged the town, and, when bubonic plague struck their ranks, threw the bodies of their dead over the walls. The entire town became infected, and the

Genoese survivors fled to various cities, infecting them in turn.

"The Masque of the Red Death" first appeared in *Graham's Magazine* for May 1842, then in *The Literary Souvenir*, June 4, 1842, and later in *The Broadway Journal* for July 19, 1845.

2. In Hindu myth, an avatar is an incarnation of a god in some earthly form.

3. people who improvise songs.

4. These are theatrical effects, based on contemporary stagecraft. The corridor serves no function except to provide a source of artificial light which can shine through the colored windows.

5. *decora*: decorum in the plural; proprieties.

6. play (1829) by Victor Hugo which Poe knew well—another sure sign that Poe's story is an attempt to recreate in prose a stage effect which impressed him.

7. See "William Wilson," note 10.

8. Another sign of the essential morality of the proceedings: Prospero sees mockery of the sufferings of the afflicted as blasphemous.

9. No "plague," of course, kills so suddenly. Poe is creating an operatic stage effect.

The Cask of Amontillado

1. Amontillado is a type of Spanish sherry. It's good stuff but not, as Poe implies, really rare. Poe published the story in *Godey's Lady's Book* in November 1846.

2. Fortunato: The name suggests both "good fortune" and "fated" (Mabbott 6; Pollin 5).

"*punish with impunity*": See note 8. Poe foreshadows a passage later in the tale by having Montresor paraphrase his family motto.

3. Poe apparently thinks Amontillado is an Italian wine.

4. a large cask.

5. neither can a taste-vin, since Amontillado *is* a sherry.

6. a short cloak. Poe's use of the word suggests that he has in mind an eighteenth-century setting, for that is when such cloaks were popular. See "The Man of the Crowd," note 12.

7. Médoc: a French red wine.

8. d'or: of gold.

"*Nemo me impune lacessit*": "No one insults me with impunity." Carlson (2) reports that this is the "motto of the Scottish royal coat of arms." In *Noctes Ambrosianæ* (see "Other Works Utilized" under "John Wilson" in the Bibliography), William Hazlitt is said to have composed a verse about Christopher North (Wilson's pen-name) in which he says that the thistle appears in North's crest because "*Nemo me* (is his motto) *Impune Lacesset*." Poe knew *Noctes Ambrosianæ* well. The change in spelling from "lacessit" to "lacesset" is just a change to the future tense. Certainly all of the writers for the Edinburgh-based *Blackwood's* who produced *Noctes Ambrosianæ* would have known the motto.

9. There is a wine called *Graves*. Poe is probably punning: Médoc (note 7) is supposed to be therapeutic, and this wine is "of the grave" (Pollin 5; Mabbott 6).

10. a member, that is, of the secret order of Freemasons.

11. Several critics have commented on the many repetitions in this tale: "impunity," "Amontillado," "nitre," "Luchresi"; the toasts, "A mason?" "A mason"; the blasphemous "For the love of God!"; and, finally, "Fortunato." Whether or not the tale is really a kind of Black Mass, it is strongly ritualistic in feel.

12. My heart grew sick . . . .: Poe teases us with the idea that Montresor's conscience is bothering him. But it's not conscience that makes his heart sick, only dampness. Rufus Griswold's edition reads, "My heart grew sick on account of the dampness of the catacombs."

In pace requiescat!: "Rest in peace!" The last heavy irony of a heavily ironic tale. Note Montresor's constant concern for Fortunato's health, and the incongruity of clowns' bells in the cap of a man descending into dank catacombs to his death. Pollin (5) points a further irony: an "*in pace*" was a very secure monastic prison.

12. Multiple Intention

Many of Poe's tales show "multiple intention": there are horror stories which snipe playfully at literary targets, philosophical stories which have, for the alert reader, political asides tucked within them, and so forth. The stories in this section are very different from one another, but seem especially strong examples of mixed artistic motivation. In truth one could devote perhaps a third of this edition to tales of multiple intention.

The Assignation. Numerous writers notice that Poe's early work is often Byronic, but here is more than the usual Byronism. Benton (1) argues that the tale is a hoax in which Poe deliberately played with notorious facets of Byron's biography. The "visionary" here who rescues the baby, like Byron, is (probably) an English poet living in a palazzo in Venice. Like Byron, he is in love with the young wife of a villainous old man (Countess Guiccioli and the Count, who actually threatened Byron). Even the narrator is identifiable: he is the Irish poet and friend of Byron, Thomas Moore.

   Yet though Benton is right and the hoaxing elements are present, we are not sure that "hoax" accurately describes Poe's intention: too many elements in the tale suggest serious purpose. Poe was capable of producing stories serious in intent yet filled with satiric or simply "hidden" allusions and referents: compare this tale, for instance, to "Ligeia." He was also a commercial journalist, and the idea of writing a story in which his readers would recognize Byron and his adventures would have been appealing. "Hoax" seems not quite the right word: the Irving-Hughes "autobiography" of 1971 was apparently a hoax; what Poe did in 1834 involves exploitation of a celebrity's notoriety, but is in no way an attempt to defraud or even fool anyone.

Loss of Breath. Freudian readings of "Loss of Breath" are plausible (see notes 4 and 9). We do not, however, feel that they show Poe compulsively revealing his fears and inadequacies. Rather, they show him making a sexual joke. Writers in his prudish age tended to mask such matters, sneaking them in so that only readers alert to them would "catch on." Poe's occasional sexual humor does have its own peculiar flavor, very different, for example, from the almost Elizabethan bawdiness of Herman Melville.

It is not accurate, however, to say that the dirty joke is the point of the tale. Most of the prose of "Loss of Breath" is devoted to Poe's whimsy and his playful associations of one thing with another. In the paragraphs marked by notes 10 and 11, for instance, Poe has fun with a sensationally popular play, a famous actor, and a theory of tragic acting which claimed that there was a limited number of great passions: *Metamora* was a virtuoso piece designed to allow Forrest to run through all of them. Poe's witty stringing-together of classical literary allusions, ancient history, current events, and contemporary theatre is as much "the point" as is the sexual joke.

"Loss of Breath" is also an interesting literary experiment, an attempt to use the effects and devices of a theatrical farce in fiction. When its hero escapes only to be mistaken for a condemned man, for example, we are seeing a piece of comic stage business (see Section Preface to "The Spectacles").

The Angel of the Odd. No single explanation will account for Poe's intention in "The Angel of the Odd." It contains enough literary horseplay to support Richard's contention that this is a literary satire (see notes 6 and 10 especially), but that is certainly not all it is. The surrealistic string of wild coincidences in the dream sequence is as much the "point" of Poe's story as is the literary play. This is, as Poe says, an "extravaganza," which reminds one of the wild humor of some silent film comedies or of the bizarre comedy attempted in the theatres of Poe's day.

Richard feels that "Poe's satire operates on two levels: the Angel may appear as a Transcendental critic using an abstruse, unintelligible German cant to justify the extravagant works of Boston writers whose romances are crowded with coincidence and unlikely events." He sees Poe parodying both the critics and their subjects. The list of works in the first paragraph names "examples of perverted or slipshod narrative techniques." Richard points out that two of the authors on the list, Tuckerman and Griswold, were genteel Boston critics, while Poe's tale was printed in John Inman's un-genteel, New York-based *Columbian Magazine,* an organ of the popularizing Young America literary clique. Richard feels that the satire is directed at two groups of New Englanders, the genteel Bostonians and the wild-eyed mystics of Concord. But even if Richard is correct, Poe's humor is not pointed merely at some American contemporaries. Other "bad" authors, rich food and drink, and an absurd—but true—newspaper article also help bring on the Angel of the Odd (see notes 2 and 10); one can't blame it all on Tuckerman and Griswold. In a sense, indeed, one can consider this a journalistic piece which says "The world is filled with curiosities, friends: beware of the Angel of the Odd."

The Tales

THE ASSIGNATION[1]

*Stay for me there! I will not fail
To meet thee in that hollow vale.*
[Exequy on the death of his wife,
by Henry King, Bishop
of Chicester.][2]

Ill-fated and mysterious man!—bewildered in the brilliancy of thine own imagination, and fallen in the flames of thine own youth! Again in fancy I behold thee! Once more thy form hath risen before me!—not—oh not as thou art—in the cold valley and shadow—but as thou *shouldst be*—squandering away a life of magnificent meditation in that city of dim visions, thine own Venice—which is a star-beloved Elysium of the sea, and the wide windows of whose Palladian[3] palaces look down with a deep and bitter meaning upon the secrets of her silent waters. Yes! I repeat it—as thou *shouldst be.* There are surely other worlds than this—other thoughts than the thoughts of the multitude—other speculations than the speculations of the sophist. Who then shall call thy conduct into question? who blame thee for thy visionary hours, or denounce those occupations as a wasting away of life, which were but the overflowings of thine everlasting energies?

It was at Venice, beneath the covered archway there called the *Ponte di Sospiri,*[4] that I met for the third or fourth time the person of whom I speak. It is with a confused recollection that I bring to mind the circumstances of that meeting. Yet I remember—ah! how should I forget?—the deep midnight, the Bridge of Sighs, the beauty of woman, and the Genius of Romance that stalked up and down the narrow canal.

It was a night of unusual gloom. The great clock of the Piazza had sounded the fifth hour of the Italian evening. The square of the Campanile lay silent and deserted, and the lights in the old Ducal Palace were dying fast away. I was returning home from the Piazetta, by way of the Grand Canal. But as my gondola arrived opposite the mouth of the canal San Marco,[5] a female voice from its recesses broke suddenly upon the night, in one wild, hysterical, and long continued shriek. Startled at the sound, I sprang upon my feet: while the gondolier, letting slip his single oar, lost it in the pitchy darkness beyond a chance of recovery, and we were consequently left to the guidance of the current which here sets from the greater into the smaller channel. Like some huge and sable-feathered condor, we were slowly drifting down towards the Bridge of Sighs, when a thousand flambeaux flashing from the windows, and down the staircases of the Ducal Palace, turned all at once that deep gloom into a livid and preternatural day.

A child, slipping from the arms of its own mother, had fallen from an upper window of the lofty structure into the deep and dim canal. The quiet waters had closed placidly over their victim; and, although my own gondola was the only one in sight, many a stout swimmer, already in the stream, was seeking in vain upon the surface, the treasure which was to be found, alas! only within the abyss. Upon the broad black marble flagstones at the entrance of the palace, and a few steps above the water, stood a figure which none who then saw can have ever since forgotten. It was the Marchesa Aphrodite—the adoration of all Venice—the gayest

KEY

1. Ponte di Sospiri (Bridge of Sighs)
2. Piazza di San Marco
3. Campanile
4. Piaz[z]etta
5. Canale Grande
6. Canale di San Marco
7. Palazzo Ducale (Ducal Palace)
8. Prigioni (prison)
9. Ponte di Rialto
10. Palazzo Mocenigo (Byron's home, see note 11)
X   Approximate spot where narrator hears cry and gondolier loses oar
●●●●▶ ●●●●▶   Route of narrator's gondola

Figure Fourteen. Poe's Venice, from a map roughly contemporary with Poe's tale, published in 1835 by the Society for the Diffusion of Useful Knowledge (see "How to Write a Blackwood Article," note 4).

Figure Fifteen. The Piazzetta, looking in from the juncture of the Grand Canal and the Canal San Marco toward the Piazza San Marco. The Ducal Palace is on the right and the Campanile is in the left middle distance. Despite the 1835 caption, St. Mark's Church (San Marco) is hidden by the palace. Figures 16–20 show other places mentioned in "The Assignation," and come from the same 1835 map used to locate the sites in the story.

Prigioni.

Figure Sixteen.
The prison.

St Marco.

Figure Seventeen.
San Marco.

The Palace.

Figure Eighteen.
The Ducal Palace.

Ponte di Rialto.

Figure Nineteen.
Ponte di Rialto.

Piazza di Rialto.

Figure Twenty.
Building facade,
Piazza di Rialto.

of the gay—the most lovely where all were beautiful—but still the young wife of the old and intriguing Mentoni, and the mother of that fair child, her first and only one, who now deep beneath the murky water, was thinking in bitterness of heart upon her sweet caresses, and exhausting its little life in struggles to call upon her name.

She stood alone. Her small, bare, and silvery feet gleamed in the black mirror of marble beneath her. Her hair, not as yet more than half loosened for the night from its ball-room array, clustered, amid a shower of diamonds, round and round her classical head, in curls like those of the young hyacinth. A snowy-white and gauze-like drapery seemed to be nearly the sole covering to her delicate form; but the mid-summer and midnight air was hot, sullen, and still, and no motion in the statue-like form itself, stirred even the folds of that raiment of very vapor which hung around it as the heavy marble hangs around the Niobe. Yet—strange to say!—her large lustrous eyes were not turned downwards upon that grave wherein her brightest hope lay buried—but riveted in a widely different direction! The prison of the Old Republic[6] is, I think, the stateliest building in all Venice —but how could that lady gaze so fixedly upon it, when beneath her lay stifling her only child? Yon dark, gloomy niche, too, yawns right opposite her chamber window— what, then, *could* there be in its shadows —in its architecture—in its ivy-wreathed and solemn cornices—that the Marchesa di Mentoni had not wondered at a thousand times before? Nonsense!—Who does not remember that, at such a time as this, the eye, like a shattered mirror, multiplies the images of its sorrow, and sees in innumerable far off places, the wo which is close at hand?

Many steps above the Marchesa, and within the arch of the water-gate, stood, in full dress, the Satyr-like figure of Mentoni himself. He was occasionally occupied in thrumming a guitar, and seemed

ennuyé[7] to the very death, as at intervals he gave directions for the recovery of his child. Stupefied and aghast, I had myself no power to move from the upright position I had assumed upon first hearing the shriek, and must have presented to the eyes of the agitated group a spectral and ominous appearance, as with pale countenance and rigid limbs, I floated down among them in that funereal gondola.

All efforts proved in vain. Many of the most energetic in the search were relaxing their exertions, and yielding to a gloomy sorrow. There seemed but little hope for the child; (how much less than for the mother!) but now, from the interior of that dark niche which has been already mentioned as forming a part of the Old Republican prison, and as fronting the lattice of the Marchesa, a figure muffled in a cloak, stepped out within reach of the light, and, pausing a moment upon the verge of the giddy descent, plunged headlong into the canal. As, in an instant afterwards, he stood with the still living and breathing child within his grasp, upon the marble flagstones by the side of the Marchesa, his cloak, heavy with the drenching water, became unfastened, and, falling in folds about his feet, discovered to the wonderstricken spectators the graceful person of a very young man, with the sound of whose name the greater part of Europe was then ringing.[8]

No word spoke the deliverer. But the Marchesa! She will now receive her child —she will press it to her heart—she will cling to its little form, and smother it with her caresses. Alas! *another's* arms have taken it from the stranger—*another's* arms have taken it away, and borne it afar off, unnoticed, into the palace! And the Marchesa! Her lip—her beautiful lip trembles: tears are gathering in her eyes—those eyes which, like Pliny's acanthus,[9] are "soft and almost liquid." Yes! tears are gathering in those eyes—and see! the entire woman thrills throughout the soul, and the statue has started into life! The pallor of the marble countenance, the swelling of the marble bosom, the very purity of the marble feet, we behold suddenly flushed over with a tide of ungovernable crimson; and a slight shudder quivers about her delicate frame, as a gentle air at Napoli about the rich silver lilies in the grass.

Why *should* that lady blush! To this demand there is no answer—except that, having left, in the eager haste and terror of a mother's heart, the privacy of her own *boudoir*, she has neglected to enthrall her tiny feet in their slippers, and utterly forgotten to throw over her Venetian shoulders that drapery which is their due. What other possible reason could there have been for her so blushing?—for the glance of those wild appealing eyes? for the unusual tumult of that throbbing bosom?—for the convulsive pressure of that trembling hand?—that hand which fell, as Mentoni turned into the palace, accidentally, upon the hand of the stranger. What reason could there have been for the low—the singularly low tone of those unmeaning words which the lady uttered hurriedly in bidding him adieu? "Thou hast conquered—" she said, or the murmurs of the water deceived me— "thou hast conquered—one hour after sunrise—we shall meet—so let it be!"

* * *

The tumult had subsided, the lights had died away within the palace, and the stranger, whom I now recognized, stood alone upon the flags. He shook with inconceivable agitation, and his eye glanced around in search of a gondola. I could not do less than offer him the service of my own; and he accepted the civility. Having obtained an oar at the water-gate, we proceeded together to his residence, while he rapidly recovered his self-possession, and spoke of our former slight acquaintance in terms of great apparent cordiality.

There are some subjects upon which I take pleasure in being minute. The person of the stranger—let me call him by this title, who to all the world was still a stran-ger—the person of the stranger is one of these subjects. In height he might have been below rather than above the medium size: although there were moments of intense passion when his frame actually *expanded* and belied the assertion. The light, almost slender symmetry of his figure, promised more of that ready activity which he evinced at the Bridge of Sighs, than of that Herculean strength which he has been known to wield without an effort upon occasions of more dangerous emergency. With the mouth and chin of a deity—singular, wild, full, liquid eyes, whose shadows varied from pure hazel to intense and brilliant jet—and a profusion of curling, black hair, from which a forehead of unusual breadth gleamed forth at intervals all light and ivory—his were features than which I have seen none more classically regular, except, perhaps, the marble ones of the Emperor Commodus.[10] Yet his countenance was, nevertheless, one of those which all men have seen at some period of their lives, and have never afterwards seen again. It had no peculiar—it had no settled predominant expression to be fastened upon the memory; a countenance seen and instantly forgotten—but forgotten with a vague and never-ceasing desire of recalling it to mind. Not that the spirit of each rapid passion failed, at any time, to throw its own distinct image upon the mirror of that face—but that the mirror, mirror-like, retained no vestige of the passion, when the passion had departed.

Upon leaving him on the night of our adventure, he solicited me, in what I thought an urgent manner, to call upon him *very* early the next morning. Shortly after sunrise, I found myself accordingly at his Palazzo, one of those huge structures of gloomy, yet fantastic pomp, which tower above the waters of the Grand Canal in the vicinity of the Rialto. I was shown up a broad winding staircase of mosaics, into an apartment whose unparalleled splendor burst through the opening door with an actual glare, mak-

Figure Twenty-one. The "classically regular" features of the Emperor Commodus. Left: The emperor as shown in a plate from M. Brunus, *Romanorum imperatorum effigies* (1617). Right: As he appears in Jacobus de Strada, *Imperatorum romanorum omnium orientalium et occidentalium verissimae imagines ex antiquis numismatibus* (1559). Both woodcuts are based on Roman coins. From the Summerfield Collection, Spencer Research Library, University of Kansas. Used by permission.

ing me blind and dizzy with luxuriousness.[11]

I knew my acquaintance to be wealthy. Report had spoken of his possessions in terms which I had even ventured to call terms of ridiculous exaggeration. But as I gazed about me, I could not bring myself to believe that the wealth of any subject in Europe could have supplied the princely magnificence which burned and blazed around.

Although, as I say, the sun had arisen, yet the room was still brilliantly lighted up. I judge from this circumstance, as well as from an air of exhaustion in the countenance of my friend, that he had not retired to bed during the whole of the preceding night. In the architecture and embellishments of the chamber, the evident design had been to dazzle and astound. Little attention had been paid to the *decora* of what is technically called *keeping*, or to the proprieties of nationality. The eye wandered from object to object, and rested upon none—neither the *grotesques* of the Greek painters, nor the sculptures of the best Italian days, nor the huge carvings of untutored Egypt. Rich draperies in every part of the room trembled to the vibration of low, melancholy music, whose origin was not to be discovered. The senses were oppressed by mingled and conflicting perfumes, reeking up from strange convolute censers, together with multitudinous flaring and flickering tongues of emerald and violet fire. The rays of the newly risen sun poured in upon the whole, through windows formed each of a single pane of crimson-tinted glass. Glancing to and fro, in a thousand reflections, from curtains which rolled from their cornices like cataracts of molten silver, the beams of natural glory mingled at length fitfully with the artificial light, and lay weltering in subdued masses upon a carpet of rich, liquid-looking cloth of Chili gold.[12]

"Ha! ha! ha!—ha! ha! ha!"—laughed the proprietor, motioning me to a seat as I entered the room, and throwing himself back at full length upon an ottoman. "I see," said he, perceiving that I could not immediately reconcile myself to the *bienséance* of so singular a welcome—"I see you are astonished at my apartment—at my statues—my pictures—my originality of conception in architecture and upholstery—absolutely drunk, eh? with my magnificence? But pardon me, my dear sir, (here his tone of voice dropped to the very spirit of cordiality,) pardon me for my uncharitable laughter. You appeared so *utterly* astonished. Besides, some things are so completely ludicrous that a man *must* laugh or die. To die laughing must be the most glorious of all glorious deaths! Sir Thomas More—a very fine man was Sir Thomas More—Sir Thomas More died laughing, you remember. Also in the *Absurdities* of Ravisius Textor, there is a long list of characters who came to the same magnificent end. Do you know, however," continued he musingly, "that at Sparta (which is now Palæochori), at Sparta, I say, to the west of the citadel, among a chaos of scarcely visible ruins, is

a kind of *socle,* upon which are still legible the letters ΛΑΣΜ. They are undoubtedly part of ΓΕΛΑΣΜΑ. Now at Sparta were a thousand temples and shrines to a thousand different divinities. How exceedingly strange that the altar of Laughter should have survived all the others! But in the present instance," he resumed, with a singular alteration of voice and manner, "I have no right to be merry at your expense. You might well have been amazed. Europe cannot produce anything so fine as this, my little regal cabinet. My other apartments are by no means of the same order; mere *ultras*[13] of fashionable insipidity. This is better than fashion—is it not? Yet this has but to be seen to become the rage—that is, with those who could afford it at the cost of their entire patrimony. I have guarded, however, against any such profanation. With one exception you are the only human being besides myself and my *valet,* who has been admitted within the mysteries of these imperial precincts, since they have been bedizened as you see!"

I bowed in acknowledgment; for the overpowering sense of splendor and perfume, and music, together with the unexpected eccentricity of his address and manner, prevented me from expressing, in words, my appreciation of what I might have construed into a compliment.

"Here," he resumed, arising and leaning on my arm as he sauntered around the apartment, "here are paintings from the Greeks to Cimabue, and from Cimabue to the present hour. Many are chosen, as you see, with little deference to the opinions of Virtû. They are all, however, fitting tapestry for a chamber such as this. Here too, are some *chefs d'œuvre*[14] of the unknown great—and here unfinished designs by men, celebrated in their day, whose very names the perspicacity of the academies has left to silence and to me. What think you," said he, turning abruptly as he spoke—"what think you of this Madonna della Pietà?"

"It is Guido's[15] own!" I said with all the

enthusiasm of my nature, for I had been poring intently over its surpassing loveliness. "It is Guido's own!—how *could* you have obtained it?—she is undoubtedly in painting what the Venus is in sculpture."

"Ha!"[16] said he thoughtfully, "the Venus—the beautiful Venus?—the Venus of the Medici?—she of the diminutive head and the gilded hair? Part of the left arm (here his voice dropped so as to be heard with difficulty), and all the right are restorations, and in the coquetry of that right arm lies, I think, the quintessence of all affectation. Give *me* the Canova! The Apollo, too!—is a copy—there can be no doubt of it—blind fool that I am, who cannot behold the boasted inspiration of the Apollo! I cannot help—pity me!—I cannot help preferring the Antinous. Was it not Socrates who said that the statuary found his statue in the block of marble? Then Michæl Angelo was by no means original in his couplet—

> 'Non ha l'ottimo artista alcun concetto
> Chè un marmo solo in se non
>   circonscriva.' "[17]

It has been, or should be remarked, that, in the manner of the true gentleman, we are always aware of a difference from the bearing of the vulgar, without being at once precisely able to determine in what such difference consists. Allowing the remark to have applied in its full force to the outward demeanor of my acquaintance, I felt it, on that eventful morning, still more fully applicable to his moral temperament and character. Nor can I better define the peculiarity of spirit which seemed to place him so essentially apart from all other human beings, than by calling it a *habit* of intense and continual thought, pervading even his most trivial actions—intruding upon his moments of dalliance—and interweaving itself with his very flashes of merriment—like adders which writhe from out the eyes of the grinning masks in the cornices around the temples of Persepolis.[18]

I could not help, however, repeatedly observing, through the mingled tone of levity and solemnity with which he rapidly descanted upon matters of little importance, a certain air of trepidation—a degree of nervous *unction* in action and in speech—an unquiet excitability of manner which appeared to me at all times unaccountable, and upon some occasions even filled me with alarm. Frequently, too, pausing in the middle of a sentence whose commencement he had apparently forgotten, he seemed to be listening in the deepest attention, as if either in momentary expectation of a visiter, or to sounds which must have had existence in his imagination alone.

It was during one of these reveries or pauses of apparent abstraction, that, in turning over a page of the poet and scholar Politian's beautiful tragedy "The Orfeo," (the first native Italian tragedy,) which lay near me upon an ottoman, I discovered a passage underlined in pencil. It was a passage towards the end of the third act[19]—a passage of the most heart-stirring excitement—a passage which, although tainted with impurity, no man shall read without a thrill of novel emotion—no woman without a sigh. The whole page was blotted with fresh tears, and, upon the opposite interleaf, were the following English lines, written in a hand so very different from the peculiar characters of my acquaintance, that I had some difficulty in recognising it as his own.

> Thou wast that all to me, love,
>   For which my soul did pine—
> A green isle in the sea, love,
>   A fountain and a shrine
> All wreathed with fairy fruits
>   and flowers;
>   And all the flowers were mine.
>
> Ah, dream too bright to last;
>   Ah, starry Hope that didst arise
> But to be overcast!
>   A voice from out the Future cries
> "Onward!"—but o'er the Past
>   (Dim gulf!) my spirit hovering lies,
> Mute, motionless, aghast!

For alas! alas! with me
   The light of life is o'er.
"No more—no more—no more,"
   (Such language holds the solemn sea
   To the sands upon the shore,)
Shall bloom the thunder-blasted tree,
   Or the stricken eagle soar!

Now all my hours are trances;
   And all my nightly dreams
Are where the dark eye glances,
   And where thy footstep gleams,
In what ethereal dances,
   By what Italian streams.

Alas! for that accursed time
   They bore thee o'er the billow,
From Love to titled age and crime,
   And an unholy pillow—
From me, and from our misty clime,
   Where weeps the silver willow!

That these lines were written in English —a language with which I had not believed their author acquainted[20]—afforded me little matter for surprise. I was too well aware of the extent of his acquirements, and of the singular pleasure he took in concealing them from observation, to be astonished at any singular discovery; but the place of date, I must confess, occasioned me no little amazement. It had been originally written *London*, and afterwards carefully overscored—not, however, so effectually as to conceal the word from a scrutinizing eye. I say this occasioned me no little amazement; for I well remember that, in a former conversation with my friend, I particularly inquired if he had at any time met in London the Marchesa di Mentoni, (who for some years previous to her marriage had resided in that city,) when his answer, if I mistake not, gave me to understand that he had never visited the metropolis of Great Britain. I might as well here mention, that I have more than once heard, (without of course giving credit to a report involving so many improbabilities,) that the person of whom I speak was not only by birth, but in education, an *Englishman*.

*   *   *

"There is one painting," said he, without being aware of my notice of the tragedy—"there is still one painting which you have not seen." And throwing aside a drapery, he discovered a full length portrait of the Marchesa Aphrodite.

Human art could have done no more in the delineation of her superhuman beauty. The same ethereal figure which stood before me the preceding night upon the steps of the Ducal Palace, stood before me once again. But in the expression of the countenance, which was beaming all over with smiles, there still lurked (incomprehensible anomaly!) that fitful stain of melancholy which will ever be found inseparable from the perfection of the beautiful. Her right arm lay folded over her bosom. With her left she pointed downward to a curiously fashioned vase. One small, fairy foot, alone visible, barely touched the earth—and, scarcely discernible in the brilliant atmosphere which seemed to encircle and enshrine her loveliness, floated a pair of the most delicately imagined wings. My glance fell from the painting to the figure of my friend, and the vigorous words of Chapman's *Bussy D'Ambois* quivered instinctively upon my lips:

      "He is up
There like a Roman statue! He
   will stand
Till Death hath made him marble!"[21]

"Come!" he said at length, turning towards a table of richly enamelled and massive silver, upon which were a few goblets fantastically stained, together with two large Etruscan vases, fashioned in the same extraordinary model as that in the foreground of the portrait, and filled with what I supposed to be Johannisberger.[22] "Come!" he said abruptly, "let us drink! It is early—but let us drink. It is *indeed* early," he continued, musingly, as a cherub with a heavy golden hammer, made the apartment ring with the first hour after sunrise—"It is *indeed* early, but what matters it? let us drink! Let us pour out an offering to yon solemn sun which these gaudy lamps and censers are so eager to subdue!" And, having made me pledge him in a bumper, he swallowed in rapid succession several goblets of the wine.

"To dream," he continued, resuming the tone of his desultory conversation, as he held up to the rich light of a censer one of the magnificent vases—"to dream has been the business of my life. I have therefore framed for myself, as you see, a bower of dreams. In the heart of Venice could I have erected a better? You behold around you, it is true, a medley of architectural embellishments. The chastity of Ionia is offended by antediluvian devices, and the sphynxes of Egypt are outstretched upon carpets of gold. Yet the effect is incongruous to the timid alone. Proprieties of place, and especially of time, are the bugbears which terrify mankind from the contemplation of the magnificent. Once I was myself a decorist: but that sublimation of folly has palled upon my soul. All this is now the fitter for my purpose. Like these arabesque censers, my spirit is writhing in fire, and the delirium of this scene is fashioning me for the wilder visions of that land of real dreams whither I am now rapidly departing." He here paused abruptly, bent his head to his bosom, and seemed to listen to a sound which I could not hear. At length, erecting his frame, he looked upwards and ejaculated the lines of the Bishop of Chichester:—

> Stay for me there! I will not fail
> To meet thee in that hollow vale.[23]

In the next instant, confessing the power of the wine, he threw himself at full length upon an ottoman.

A quick step was now heard upon the staircase, and a loud knock at the door rapidly succeeded. I was hastening to anticipate a second disturbance, when a page of Mentoni's household burst into the room, and faltered out, in a voice choking with emotion, the incoherent words, "My mistress!—my mistress!—poisoned!—poi-

soned! Oh beautiful—oh beautiful Aphrodite!"

Bewildered, I flew to the ottoman, and endeavoured to arouse the sleeper to a sense of the startling intelligence. But his limbs were rigid—his lips were livid—his lately beaming eyes were riveted in *death*. I staggered back towards the table—my hand fell upon a cracked and blackened goblet—and a consciousness of the entire and terrible truth flashed suddenly over my soul.

LOSS OF BREATH

A Tale Neither In Nor Out of "Blackwood"[1]

O breathe not, &c.
—MOORE'S MELODIES[2]—

The most notorious ill-fortune must in the end, yield to the untiring courage of philosophy—as the most stubborn city to the ceaseless vigilance of an enemy. Salmanezer, as we have it in the holy writings, lay three years before Samaria; yet it fell. Sardanapalus—see Diodorus—maintained himself seven in Nineveh; but to no purpose. Troy expired at the close of the second lustrum; and Azoth, as Aristæus declares upon his honor as a gentleman, opened at last her gates to Psammiticus,[3] after having barred them for the fifth part of a century.   *   *   *   *   *

"Thou wretch!—thou vixen!—thou shrew!" said I to my wife on the morning after our wedding, "thou witch!—thou hag!—thou whipper-snapper!—thou sink of iniquity!—thou fiery-faced quintessence of all that is abominable!—thou—thou—" here standing upon tiptoe, seizing her by the throat, and placing my mouth close to her ear, I was preparing to launch forth a new and more decided epithet of opprobrium, which should not fail, if ejaculated, to convince her of her insignificance, when, to my extreme horror and astonishment, I discovered that *I had lost my breath.*[4]

The phrases "I am out of breath," "I have lost my breath," &c., are often enough repeated in common conversation; but it had never occurred to me that the terrible accident of which I speak could *bona fide* and actually happen! Imagine—that is if you have a fanciful turn—imagine, I say, my wonder—my consternation—my despair!

There is a good genius, however, which has never entirely deserted me. In my most ungovernable moods I still retain a sense of propriety, *et le chemin des passions me conduit*—as Lord Edouard in the "Julie" says it did him—*à la philosophie véritable.*[5]

Although I could not at first precisely ascertain to what degree the occurrence had affected me, I determined at all events to conceal the matter from my wife, until further experience should discover to me the extent of this my unheard of calamity. Altering my countenance, therefore, in a moment, from its bepuffed and distorted appearance, to an expression of arch and coquettish benignity, I gave my lady a pat on the one cheek, and a kiss on the other, and without saying one syllable, (Furies! I could not), left her astonished at my drollery, as I pirouetted out of the room in a *Pas de Zéphyr.*[6]

Behold me then safely ensconced in my private *boudoir*, a fearful instance of the ill consequences attending upon irascibility—alive, with the qualifications of the dead—dead, with the propensities of the living—an anomaly on the face of the earth—being very calm, yet breathless.

Yes! breathless. I am serious in asserting that my breath was entirely gone. I could not have stirred with it a feather if my life had been at issue, or sullied even the delicacy of a mirror. Hard fate!—yet there was some alleviation to the first overwhelming paroxysm of my sorrow. I found, upon trial, that the powers of utterance which, upon my inability to proceed in the conversation with my wife, I then concluded to be totally destroyed, were in fact only partially impeded, and I discovered that had I at that interesting crisis, dropped my voice to a singularly deep guttural, I might still have continued to her the communication of my sentiments; this pitch of voice (the guttural) depending, I find, not upon the current of the breath, but upon a certain spasmodic action of the muscles of the throat.

Throwing myself upon a chair, I remained for some time absorbed in meditation. My reflections, be sure, were of no consolatory kind. A thousand vague and lachrymatory fancies took possession of my soul—and even the idea of suicide flitted across my brain; but it is a trait in the perversity of human nature to reject the obvious and the ready, for the far-distant and equivocal. Thus I shuddered at self-murder as the most decided of atrocities while the tabby cat purred strenuously upon the rug, and the very waterdog wheezed assiduously under the table; each taking to itself much merit for the strength of its lungs, and all obviously done in derision of my own pulmonary incapacity.

Oppressed with a tumult of vague hopes and fears, I at length heard the footsteps of my wife descending the staircase. Being now assured of her absence, I returned with a palpitating heart to the scene of my disaster.

Carefully locking the door on the inside, I commenced a vigorous search. It was possible, I thought that, concealed in some obscure corner, or lurking in some closet or drawer, might be found the lost object of my inquiry. It might have a vapory—it might even have a tangible form. Most philosophers, upon many points of philosophy, are still very unphilosophical. William Godwin, however, says in his "Mandeville," that "invisible things are the only realities," and this all will allow, is a case in point. I would have the judicious reader pause before accusing such asseverations of an undue quantum of absurdity. Anaxagoras,[7] it will be remembered, maintained that snow is black, and this I have since found to be the case.

Long and earnestly did I continue the investigation: but the contemptible reward of my industry and perseverence proved to be only a set of false teeth, two pair of hips, an eye, and a bundle of *billets-doux*[8] from Mr. Windenough to my wife. I might as well here observe that this confirmation of my lady's partiality for Mr. W. occasioned me little uneasiness. That Mrs. Lacko'breath should admire anything so dissimilar to myself was a natural and necessary evil. I am, it is well known, of a robust and corpulent appearance, and at the same time somewhat diminutive in stature. What wonder then that the lath-like tenuity of my acquaintance, and his altitude, which has grown into a proverb, should have met with all due estimation in the eyes of Mrs. Lacko'breath. But to return.

My exertions, as I have before said, proved fruitless. Closet after closet—drawer after drawer—corner after corner—were scrutinized to no purpose. At one time, however, I thought myself sure of my prize, having in rummaging a dressing-case, accidentally demolished a bottle of Grandjean's Oil of Archangels[9]—which, as an agreeable perfume, I here take the liberty of recommending.

With a heavy heart I returned to my *boudoir*—there to ponder upon some method of eluding my wife's penetration, until I could make arrangements prior to my leaving the country, for to this I had already made up my mind. In a foreign climate, being unknown, I might, with some probability of success, endeavor to conceal my unhappy calamity—a calamity calculated, even more than beggary, to estrange the affections of the multitude, and to draw down upon the wretch the well-merited indignation of the virtuous and the happy. I was not long in hesitation. Being naturally quick, I committed to memory the entire tragedy of "Metamora."[10] I had the good fortune to recollect that in the accentuation of this drama, or at least of such portion of it as is allotted to the hero, the tones of voice in which I found myself deficient were altogether unnecessary, and that the deep guttural was expected to reign monotonously throughout.

I practised for some time by the borders of a well frequented marsh;—herein, however, having no reference to a similar proceeding of Demosthenes,[11] but from a design peculiarly and conscientiously my own. Thus armed at all points, I determined to make my wife believe that I was suddenly smitten with a passion for the stage. In this, I succeeded to a miracle; and to every question or suggestion found myself at liberty to reply in my most frog-like and sepulchral tones with some passage from the tragedy—any portion of which, as I soon took great pleasure in observing, would apply equally well to any particular subject. It is not to be supposed, however, that in the delivery of such passages I was found at all deficient in the looking asquint—the showing my teeth—the working my knees—the shuffling my feet—or in any of those unmentionable graces which are now justly considered the characteristics of a popular performer. To be sure they spoke of confining me in a straight-jacket—but, good God! they never suspected me of having lost my breath.

Having at length put my affairs in order, I took my seat very early one morning in the mail stage for ——, giving it to be understood, among my acquaintances, that business of the last importance required my immediate personal attendance in that city.

The coach was crammed to repletion; but in the uncertain twilight the features of my companions could not be distinguished. Without making any effectual resistance, I suffered myself to be placed between two gentlemen of colossal dimensions; while a third, of a size larger, requesting pardon for the liberty he was about to take, threw himself upon my body at full length, and falling asleep in an instant, drowned all my guttural ejaculations for relief, in a snore which would have put to blush the roarings of the bull of Phalaris.[12] Happily the state of my respiratory faculties rendered suffocation an accident entirely out of the question.

As, however, the day broke more distinctly in our approach to the outskirts of the city, my tormentor arising and adjusting his shirt-collar, thanked me in a very friendly manner for my civility. Seeing that I remained motionless, (all my limbs were dislocated and my head twisted on one side,) his apprehensions began to be excited; and arousing the rest of the passengers, he communicated in a very decided manner, his opinion that a dead man had been palmed upon them during the night for a living and responsible fellow-traveller; here giving me a thump on the right eye, by way of demonstrating the truth of his suggestion.

Hereupon all, one after another, (there were nine in company), believed it their duty to pull me by the ear. A young practising physician, too, having applied a pocket mirror to my mouth, and found me without breath, the assertion of my persecutor was pronounced a true bill; and the whole party expressed a determination to endure tamely no such impositions for the future, and to proceed no farther with any such carcasses for the present.

I was here, accordingly, thrown out at the sign of the "Crow," (by which tavern the coach happened to be passing,) without meeting with any farther accident than the breaking of both my arms, under the left hind wheel of the vehicle. I must besides do the driver the justice to state that he did not forget to throw after me the largest of my trunks, which, unfortunately falling on my head, fractured my skull in a manner at once interesting and extraordinary.

The landlord of the "Crow," who is a hospitable man, finding that my trunk contained sufficient to indemnify him for any little trouble he might take in my behalf, sent forthwith for a surgeon of his acquaintance, and delivered me to his care with a bill and receipt for ten dollars.

The purchaser took me to his apartments and commenced operations immediately. Having cut off my ears, however, he discovered signs of animation. He now rang the bell, and sent for a neighboring apothecary with whom to consult in the emergency. In case of his suspicions with regard to my existence proving ultimately correct, he, in the meantime, made an incision in my stomach, and removed several of my viscera for private dissection.

The apothecary had an idea that I was actually dead. This idea I endeavored to confute, kicking and plunging with all my might, and making the most furious contortions—for the operations of the surgeon had, in a measure, restored me to the possession of my faculties. All, however, was attributed to the effects of a new galvanic battery, wherewith the apothecary, who is really a man of information, performed several curious experiments, in which, from my personal share in their fulfilment, I could not help feeling deeply interested. It was a source of mortification to me nevertheless, that although I made several attempts at conversation, my powers of speech were so entirely in abeyance, that I could not even open my mouth; much less then make reply to some ingenious but fanciful theories of which, under other circumstances, my minute acquaintance with the Hippocratian[13] pathology would have afforded me a ready confutation.

Not being able to arrive at a conclusion, the practitioners remanded me for farther examination.[14] I was taken up into a garret; and the surgeon's lady having accommodated me with drawers and stockings, the surgeon himself fastened my hands, and tied up my jaws with a pocket handkerchief—then bolted the door on the outside as he hurried to his dinner, leaving me alone to silence and to meditation.

I now discovered to my extreme delight that I could have spoken had not my mouth been tied up by the pocket handkerchief. Consoling myself with this reflection, I was mentally repeating some passages of the "Omnipresence of the Deity," as is my custom before resigning myself to sleep, when two cats, of a greedy and vituperative turn, entering at a hole in the wall, leaped up with a flourish à la Catalani,[15] and alighting opposite one another on my visage, betook themselves to indecorous contention for the paltry consideration of my nose.

But, as the loss of his ears proved the means of elevating to the throne of Cyrus, the Magian or Mige-Gush of Persia, and as the cutting off his nose gave Zopyrus[16] possession of Babylon, so the loss of a few ounces of my countenance proved the salvation of my body. Aroused by the pain, and burning with indignation, I burst, at a single effort, the fastenings and the bandage.—Stalking across the room I cast a glance of contempt at the belligerents, and throwing open the sash to their extreme horror and disappointment, precipitated myself, very dexterously, from the window.

The mail-robber W——, to whom I bore a singular resemblance, was at this moment passing from the city jail to the scaffold erected for his execution in the suburbs. His extreme infirmity, and long continued ill health, had obtained him the privilege of remaining unmanacled; and habited in his gallows costume—one very similar to my own—he lay at full length in the bottom of the hangman's cart (which happened to be under the windows of the surgeon at the moment of my precipitation) without any other guard than the driver who was asleep, and two recruits of the sixth infantry, who were drunk.

As ill-luck would have it, I alit upon my feet within the vehicle. W——, who was an acute fellow, perceived his opportunity. Leaping up immediately, he bolted out behind, and turning down an alley, was out of sight in the twinkling of an eye. The recruits, aroused by the bustle, could not exactly comprehend the merits

of the transaction. Seeing, however, a man, the precise counterpart of the felon, standing upright in the cart before their eyes, they were of opinion that the rascal (meaning W——) was after making his escape, (so they expressed themselves,) and, having communicated this opinion to one another, they took each a dram, and then knocked me down with the buttends of their muskets.

It was not long ere we arrived at the place of destination. Of course nothing could be said in my defence. Hanging was my inevitable fate. I resigned myself thereto with a feeling half stupid, half acrimonious. Being little of a cynic, I had all the sentiments of a dog. The hangman, however, adjusted the noose about my neck. The drop fell.

I forbear to depict my sensations upon the gallows; although here, undoubtedly, I could speak to the point, and it is a topic upon which nothing has been well said. In fact, to write upon such a theme it is necessary to have been hanged. Every author should confine himself to matters of experience. Thus Mark Antony composed a treatise upon getting drunk.[17]

I may just mention, however, that die I did not. My body was, but I had no breath to be suspended; and but for the knot under my left ear (which had the feel of a military stock) I dare say that I should have experienced very little inconvenience. As for the jerk given to my neck upon the falling of the drop, it merely proved a corrective to the twist afforded me by the fat gentleman in the coach.

For good reasons, however, I did my best to give the crowd the worth of their trouble. My convulsions were said to be extraordinary. My spasms it would have been difficult to beat. The populace encored. Several gentlemen swooned; and a multitude of ladies were carried home in hysterics. Pinxit availed himself of the opportunity to retouch, from a sketch taken upon the spot, his admirable painting of the "Marsyas[18] flayed alive."

When I had afforded sufficient amusement, it was thought proper to remove my body from the gallows;—this the more especially as the real culprit had in the meantime been retaken and recognized; a fact which I was so unlucky as not to know.

Much sympathy was, of course exercised in my behalf, and as no one made claim to my corpse, it was ordered that I should be interred in a public vault.

Here, after due interval, I was deposited. The sexton departed, and I was left alone. A line of Marston's "Malcontent"—

Death's a good fellow and keeps
    open house—[19]

struck me at that moment as a palpable lie.

I knocked off, however, the lid of my coffin, and stepped out. The place was dreadfully dreary and damp, and I became troubled with *ennui*. By way of amusement, I felt my way among the numerous coffins ranged in order around. I lifted them down, one by one, and breaking open their lids, busied myself in speculations about the mortality within.

"This," I soliloquized, tumbling over a carcass, puffy, bloated, and rotund—"this has been, no doubt, in every sense of the word, an unhappy—an unfortunate man. It has been his terrible lot not to walk, but to waddle—to pass through life not like a human being, but like an elephant—not like a man, but like a rhinoceros.

"His attempts at getting on have been mere abortions, and his circumgyratory proceedings a palpable failure. Taking a step forward, it has been his misfortune to take two towards the right, and three towards the left. His studies have been confined to the poetry of Crabbe. He can have had no idea of the wonder of a *pirouette*. To him a *pas de papillon* has been an abstract conception. He has never ascended the summit of a hill. He has never viewed from any steeple the glories of a metropolis. Heat has been his mortal enemy. In the dog-days his days have been

the days of a dog. Therein, he has dreamed of flames and suffocation—of mountains upon mountains—of Pelion upon Ossa. He was short of breath—to say all in a word, he was short of breath. He thought it extravagant to play upon wind instruments. He was the inventor of self-moving fans, wind-sails, and ventilators. He patronized Du Pont the bellows-maker,[20] and died miserably in attempting to smoke a cigar. His was a case in which I feel a deep interest—a lot in which I sincerely sympathize.

"But here," said I—"here"—and I dragged spitefully from its receptacle a gaunt, tall, and peculiar-looking form, whose remarkable appearance struck me with a sense of unwelcome familiarity—"here is a wretch entitled to no earthly commiseration." Thus saying, in order to obtain a more distinct view of my subject, I applied my thumb and fore-finger to its nose, and causing it to assume a sitting position upon the ground, held it thus, at the length of my arm, while I continued my soliloquy.

—"Entitled," I repeated, "to no earthly commiseration. Who indeed would think of compassionating a shadow? Besides, has he not had his full share of the blessings of mortality? He was the originator of tall monuments—shot-towers—lightning-rods—lombardy poplars. His treatise upon "Shades and Shadows" has immortalized him. He edited with distinguished ability the last edition of "South on the Bones." He went early to college and studied pneumatics. He then came home, talked eternally, and played upon the French-horn. He patronized the bag-pipes. Captain Barclay, who walked against Time, would not walk against *him*. Windham and Allbreath were his favorite writers.—his favorite artist, Phiz. He died gloriously while inhaling gas—*levique flatu corrumpitur*, like the *fama pudicitiæ* in Hieronymus.[21] He was indubitably a"
————
"How *can* you?—how—*can*—you?"—interrupted the object of my animadver-

sions, gasping for breath, and tearing off, with a desperate exertion, the bandage around its jaws—"how *can* you, Mr. Lack-o'breath, be so infernally cruel as to pinch me in that manner by the nose? Did you not see how they had fastened up my mouth—and you *must* know—if you know anything—how vast a superfluity of breath I have to dispose of! If you do *not* know, however, sit down and you shall see.—In my situation it is really a great relief to be able to open one's mouth—to be able to expatiate—to be able to communicate with a person like yourself, who do not think yourself called upon at every period to interrupt the thread of a gentleman's discourse.—Interruptions are annoying and should undoubtedly be abolished—don't you think so?—no reply, I beg you,—one person is enough to be speaking at a time.—I shall be done by-and-by, and then you may begin.—How the devil, sir, did you get into this place? —not a word I beseech you—been here some time myself—terrible accident!—heard of it, I suppose—awful calamity! —walking under your windows—some short while ago—about the time you were stage-struck—horrible occurrence!—heard of "catching one's breath," eh?—hold your tongue I tell you!—I caught somebody else's!—had always too much of my own—met Blab at the corner of the street—wouldn't give me a chance for a word—couldn't get in a syllable edgeways —attacked, consequently, with epilepsis—Blab made his escape—damn all fools! —they took me up for dead, and put me in this place—pretty doings all of them! —heard all you said about me—every word a lie—horrible!—wonderful!—outrageous! — hideous! — incomprehensible! —et cetera—et cetera—et cetera—et cetera—" ——

It is impossible to conceive my astonishment at so unexpected a discourse; or the joy with which I became gradually convinced that the breath so fortunately caught by the gentleman (whom I soon recognized as my neighbor Windenough)

was, in fact, the identical expiration mislaid by myself in the conversation with my wife. Time, place, and circumstance rendered it a matter beyond question. I did not, however, immediately release my hold upon Mr. W.'s proboscis—not at least during the long period in which the inventor of lombardy-poplars continued to favor me with his explanations.

In this respect I was actuated by that habitual prudence which has ever been my predominating trait. I reflected that many difficulties might still lie in the path of my preservation which only extreme exertion on my part would be able to surmount. Many persons, I considered, are prone to estimate commodities in their possession—however valueless to the then proprietor—however troublesome, or distressing—in direct ratio with the advantages to be derived by others from their attainment, or by themselves from their abandonment. Might not this be the case with Mr. Windenough? In displaying anxiety for the breath of which he was at present so willing to get rid, might I not lay myself open to the exactions of his avarice? There are scoundrels in this world, I remembered with a sigh, who will not scruple to take unfair opportunities with even a next door neighbor, and (this remark is from Epictetus)[22] it is precisely at that time when men are most anxious to throw off the burden of their own calamities that they feel the least desirous of relieving them in others.

Upon considerations similar to these, and still retaining my grasp upon the nose of Mr. W., I accordingly thought proper to model my reply.

"Monster!" I began in a tone of the deepest indignation, "monster; and double-winded idiot!—dost *thou*, whom for thine iniquities it has pleased heaven to accurse with a two-fold respiration—dost *thou*, I say, presume to address me in the familiar language of an old acquaintance? —"I lie," forsooth! and "hold my tongue," to be sure!—pretty conversation indeed, to a gentleman with a single breath!—all this, too, when I have it in my power to relieve the calamity under which thou dost so justly suffer—to curtail the superfluities of thine unhappy respiration."

Like Brutus,[23] I paused for a reply—with which, like a tornado, Mr. Windenough immediately overwhelmed me. Protestation followed upon protestation, and apology upon apology. There were no terms with which he was unwilling to comply, and there were none of which I failed to take the fullest advantage.

Preliminaries being at length arranged, my acquaintance delivered me the respiration; for which (having carefully examined it) I gave him afterwards a receipt.

I am aware that by many I shall be held to blame for speaking, in a manner so cursory, of a transaction so impalpable. It will be thought that I should have entered more minutely into the details of an occurrence by which—and this is very true —much new light might be thrown upon a highly interesting branch of physical philosophy.

To all this I am sorry that I cannot reply. A hint is the only answer which I am permitted to make. There were *circumstances*—but I think it much safer upon consideration to say as little as possible about an affair so delicate—*so delicate*, I repeat, and at the time involving the interests of a third party whose sulphurous resentment I have not the least desire, at this moment, of incurring.

We were not long after this necessary arrangement in effecting an escape from the dungeons of the sepulchre. The united strength of our resuscitated voices was soon sufficiently apparent. Scissors,[24] the Whig Editor, republished a treatise upon "the nature and origin of subterranean noises." A reply—rejoinder—confutation —and justification—followed in the columns of a Democratic Gazette. It was not until the opening of the vault to decide the controversy, that the appearance of Mr. Windenough and myself proved both parties to have been decidedly in the wrong.

I cannot conclude these details of some very singular passages in a life at all times sufficiently eventful, without again recalling to the attention of the reader the merits of that indiscriminate philosophy which is a sure and ready shield against those shafts of calamity which can neither be seen, felt, nor fully understood. It was in the spirit of this wisdom that, among the Ancient Hebrews, it was believed the gates of Heaven would be inevitably opened to that sinner, or saint, who, with good lungs and implicit confidence, should vociferate the word *"Amen!"* It was in the spirit of this wisdom that, when a great plague raged at Athens, and every means had been in vain attempted for its removal, Epimenides, as Laertius[25] relates in his second book of that philosopher, advised the erection of a shrine and temple "to the proper God."

LYTTLETON BARRY.

THE ANGEL OF THE ODD

An Extravaganza[1]

It was a chilly November afternoon. I had just consummated an unusually hearty dinner, of which the dyspeptic *truffe* formed not the least important item, and was sitting alone in the dining room, with my feet upon the fender, and at my elbow a small table, which I had rolled up to the fire, and upon which were some apologies for dessert, with some miscellaneous bottles of wine, spirit and *liqueur*. In the morning I had been reading Glover's "Leonidas," Wilkie's "Epigoniad," Lamartine's "Pilgrimage," Barlow's "Columbiad," Tuckerman's "Sicily," and Griswold's "Curiosities;" I am willing to confess, therefore, that I now felt a little stupid. I made effort to arouse myself by aid of frequent Lafitte,[2] and, all failing, I betook myself to a stray newspaper in despair. Having carefully perused the column of "houses to let," and the column of "dogs lost," and then the two columns of "wives and apprentices runaway," I attacked with great resolution the editorial matter, and, reading it from beginning to end without understanding a syllable, conceived the possibility of its being Chinese, and so re-read it from the end to the beginning, but with no more satisfactory result. I was about throwing away in disgust,

This folio of four pages, happy work
Which not even critics criticise,[3]

when I felt my attention somewhat aroused by the paragraph which follows:

"The avenues to death are numerous and strange. A London paper mentions the decease of a person from a singular cause. He was playing at 'puff the dart,' which is played with a long needle inserted in some worsted, and blown at a target through a tin tube. He placed the needle at the wrong end of the tube, and drawing his breath strongly to puff the dart forward with force, drew the needle into his throat. It entered the lungs, and in a few days killed him."[4]

Upon seeing this I fell into a great rage, without exactly knowing why. "This thing," I exclaimed, "is a contemptible falsehood—a poor hoax—the lees of the invention of some pitiable penny-a-liner —of some wretched concoctor of accidents in Cocaigne.[5] These fellows, knowing the extravagant gullibility of the age, set their wits to work in the imagination of improbable possibilities—of odd accidents, as they term them; but to a reflecting intellect (like mine," I added, in parenthesis, putting my forefinger unconsciously to the side of my nose,) "to a contemplative understanding, such as I myself possess, it seems evident at once that the marvellous increase of late in these 'odd accidents' is by far the oddest accident of all. For my own part, I intend to believe nothing henceforward that has anything of the 'singular' about it."

"Mein Gott, den, vat a vool you bees for dat!"[6] replied one of the most remarkable voices I ever heard. At first I took it for a rumbling in my ears—such as a man sometimes experiences when getting very drunk—but, upon second thought, I considered the sound as more nearly resembling that which proceeds from an empty barrel beaten with a big stick; and, in fact, this I should have concluded it to be, but for the articulation of the syllables and words. I am by no means naturally nervous, and the very few glasses of Lafitte which I had sipped served to embolden me no little, so that I felt nothing of trepidation, but merely uplifted my eyes with a leisurely movement, and looked carefully around the room for the intruder. I could not, however, perceive any one at all.

"Humph!" resumed the voice, as I continued my survey, "you mus pe so dronk as de pig, den, for not zee me as I zit here at your zide."

Hereupon I bethought me of looking immediately before my nose, and there, sure enough, confronting me at the table sat a personage nondescript, although not altogether indescribable. His body was a wine-pipe, or a rum puncheon, or something of that character, and had a truly Falstaffian air. In its nether extremity were inserted two kegs, which seemed to answer all the purposes of legs. For arms there dangled from the upper portion of the carcass two tolerably long bottles, with the necks outward for hands. All the head that I saw the monster possessed of was one of those Hessian canteens which resemble a large snuff-box with a hole in the middle of the lid. This canteen (with a funnel on its top, like a cavalier cap slouched over the eyes) was set on edge upon the puncheon, with the hole toward myself; and through this hole, which seemed puckered up like the mouth of a very precise old maid, the creature was emitting certain rumbling and grumbling noises which he evidently intended for intelligible talk.

"I zay," said he, "you mos pe dronk as de pig, vor zit dare and not zee me zit ere;

and I zay, doo, you mos pe pigger vool as de goose, vor to dispelief vat iz print in de print. 'T iz de troof—dat it iz—eberry vord ob it."

"Who are you, pray?" said I, with much dignity, although somewhat puzzled; "how did you get here? and what is it you are talking about?"

"As vor ow I com'd ere," replied the figure, "dat iz none ob your pizziness; and as vor vat I be talking apout, I be talk apout vat I tink proper; and as vor who I be, vy dat is de very ting I com'd here for to let you zee for yourzelf."

"You are a drunken vagabond," said I, "and I shall ring the bell and order my footman to kick you into the street."

"He! he! he!" said the fellow, "hu! hu! hu! dat you can't do."

"Can't do!" said I, "what do you mean? —I can't do what?"

"Ring de pell;" he replied, attempting a grin with his little villainous mouth.

Upon this I made an effort to get up, in order to put my threat into execution; but the ruffian just reached across the table very deliberately, and hitting me a tap on the forehead with the neck of one of the long bottles, knocked me back into the arm-chair from which I had half arisen. I was utterly astounded; and, for a moment, was quite at a loss what to do. In the meantime he continued his talk.

"You zee," said he, "it iz te bess vor zit still; and now you shall know who I pe. Look at me! zee! I am te *Angel ov te Odd*."

"And odd enough, too," I ventured to reply; "but I was always under the impression that an angel had wings."

"Te wing!" he cried, highly incensed, "vat I pe do mit te wing? Mein Gott! do you take me vor a shicken?"

"No—oh no!" I replied, much alarmed, "you are no chicken—certainly not."

"Well, den, zit still and pehabe yourself, or I'll rap you again mid me vist. It iz te shicken ab te wing, und te owl ab te wing, und te imp ab te wing, und te head-teuffel[7] ab te wing. Te angel ab *not*

te wing, and I am te *Angel ov te Odd*."

"And your business with me at present is—is"—

"My pizziness!" ejaculated the thing, "vy vat a low pred buppy you mos pe vor to ask a gentleman und an angel apout his pizziness!"

This language was rather more than I could bear, even from an angel; so, plucking up courage, I seized a salt cellar which lay within reach, and hurled it at the head of the intruder. Either he dodged, however, or my aim was inaccurate; for all I accomplished was the demolition of the crystal which protected the dial of the clock upon the mantel piece. As for the Angel he evinced his sense of my assault by giving me two or three hard consecutive raps upon the forehead as before. These reduced me at once to submission, and I am almost ashamed to confess that either through pain or vexation, there came a few tears into my eyes.

"Mein Gott!" said the Angel of the Odd, apparently much softened at my distress; "mein Gott, te man is eder ferry dronk or ferry zorry. You mos not trink it so strong—you mos put te water in te wine. Here, trink dis, like a good veller, und don't gry now—don't!"

Hereupon the Angel of the Odd replenished my goblet (which was about a third full of Port) with a colorless fluid that he poured from one of his hand bottles. I observed that these bottles had labels about their necks, and that these labels were inscribed "Kirschenwasser."[8]

The considerate kindness of the Angel mollified me in no little measure; and, aided by the water with which he diluted my Port more than once, I at length regained sufficient temper to listen to his very extraordinary discourse. I cannot pretend to recount all that he told me, but I gleaned from what he said that he was the genius who presided over the *contretemps* of mankind, and whose business it was to bring about the *odd accidents* which are continually astonishing the sceptic. Once or twice, upon my venturing to express my total incredulity in respect to his pretensions, he grew very angry indeed, so that at length I considered it the wiser policy to say nothing at all, and let him have his own way. He talked on, therefore, at great length, while I merely leaned back in my chair with my eyes shut, and amused myself with munching raisins and filliping the stems about the room. But, by and bye, the Angel suddenly construed this behavior of mine into contempt. He arose in a terrible passion, slouched his funnel down over his eyes, swore a vast oath, uttered a threat of some character which I did not precisely comprehend, and finally made me a low bow and departed, wishing me, in the language of the archbishop in Gil-Blas, "*beaucoup de bonheur et un peu plus de bon sens.*"⁹

His departure afforded me relief. The very few glasses of Lafitte that I had sipped had the effect of rendering me drowsy, and I felt inclined to take a nap of some fifteen or twenty minutes, as is my custom after dinner. At six I had an appointment of consequence, which it was quite indispensable that I should keep. The policy of insurance for my dwelling house had expired the day before; and, some dispute having arisen, it was agreed that, at six, I should meet the board of directors of the company and settle the terms of a renewal. Glancing upward at the clock on the mantel-piece, (for I felt too drowsy to take out my watch), I had the pleasure to find that I had still twenty-five minutes to spare. It was half past five; I could easily walk to the insurance office in five minutes; and my usual post prandial siestas had never been known to exceed five and twenty. I felt sufficiently safe, therefore, and composed myself to my slumbers forthwith.

Having completed them to my satisfaction, I again looked toward the time-piece and was half inclined to believe in the possibility of odd accidents when I found that, instead of my ordinary fifteen or twenty minutes, I had been dozing only

three; for it still wanted seven and twenty of the appointed hour. I betook myself again to my nap, and at length a second time awoke, when, to my utter amazement, it *still* wanted twenty-seven minutes of six. I jumped up to examine the clock, and found that it had ceased running. My watch informed me that it was half past seven; and, of course, having slept two hours, I was too late for my appointment. "It will make no difference," I said; "I can call at the office in the morning and apologize; in the meantime what can be the matter with the clock?" Upon examining it I discovered that one of the raisin stems which I had been filliping about the room during the discourse of the Angel of the Odd, had flown through the fractured crystal and lodging, singularly enough, in the keyhole, with an end projecting outward, had thus arrested the revolution of the minute hand.

"Ah!" said I, "I see how it is. This thing speaks for itself. A natural accident, such as *will* happen now and then!"

I gave the matter no farther consideration, and at my usual hour retired to bed. Here, having placed a candle upon a reading stand at the bed head, and having made an attempt to peruse some pages of the "Omnipresence of the Deity,"¹⁰ I unfortunately fell asleep in less than twenty seconds, leaving the light burning as it was.

My dreams were terrifically disturbed by visions of the Angel of the Odd. Methought he stood at the foot of the couch, drew aside the curtains, and, in the hollow, detestable tones of a rum puncheon, menaced me with the bitterest vengeance for the contempt with which I had treated him. He concluded a long harangue by taking off his funnel-cap, inserting the tube into my gullet, and thus deluging me with an ocean of Kirschenwasser, which he poured, in a continuous flood, from one of the long-necked bottles that stood him instead of an arm. My agony was at length insufferable, and I awoke just in time to perceive that a rat had run off with the lighted candle from the stand, but *not* in season to prevent his making his escape with it through the hole. Very soon, a strong suffocating odor assailed my nostrils; the house, I clearly perceived, was on fire. In a few minutes the blaze broke forth with violence, and in an incredibly brief period the entire building was wrapped in flames. All egress from my chamber, except through a window, was cut off. The crowd, however, quickly procured and raised a long ladder. By means of this I was descending rapidly, and in apparent safety, when a huge hog, about whose rotund stomach, and indeed about whose whole air and physiognomy, there was something which reminded me of the Angel of the Odd—when this hog, I say, which hitherto had been quietly slumbering in the mud, took it suddenly into his head that his left shoulder needed scratching, and could find no more convenient rubbing post than that afforded by the foot of the ladder. In an instant I was precipitated and had the misfortune to fracture my arm.

This accident, with the loss of my insurance, and with the more serious loss of my hair, the whole of which had been singed off by the fire, predisposed me to serious impressions, so that, finally, I made up my mind to take a wife. There was a rich widow disconsolate for the loss of her seventh spouse, and to her wounded spirit I offered the balm of my vows. She yielded a reluctant consent to my prayers. I knelt at her feet in gratitude and adoration. She blushed and bowed her luxuriant tresses into close contact with those supplied me, temporarily, by Grandjean.[11] I know not how the entanglement took place, but so it was. I arose with a shining pate, wigless; she in disdain and wrath, half buried in alien hair. Thus ended my hopes of the widow by an accident which could not have been anticipated, to be sure, but which the natural sequence of events had brought about.

Without despairing, however, I undertook the siege of a less implacable heart. The fates were again propitious for a brief period; but again a trivial incident interfered. Meeting my betrothed in an avenue thronged with the *élite* of the city, I was hastening to greet her with one of my best considered bows, when a small particle of some foreign matter, lodging in the corner of my eye, rendered me, for the moment, completely blind. Before I could recover my sight, the lady of my love had disappeared—irreparably affronted at what she chose to consider my premeditated rudeness in passing her by ungreeted. While I stood bewildered at the suddenness of this accident, (which might have happened, nevertheless, to any one under the sun), and while I still continued incapable of sight, I was accosted by the Angel of the Odd, who proffered me his aid with a civility which I had no reason to expect. He examined my disordered eye with much gentleness and skill, informed me that I had a drop in it, and (whatever a "drop" was) took it out, and afforded me relief.

I now considered it time to die, (since fortune had so determined to persecute me,) and accordingly made my way to the nearest river. Here, divesting myself of my clothes, (for there is no reason why we cannot die as we were born), I threw myself headlong into the current; the sole witness of my fate being a solitary crow that had been seduced into the eating of brandy-saturated corn, and so had staggered away from his fellows. No sooner had I entered the water than this bird took it into his head to fly away with the most indispensable portion of my apparel. Postponing, therefore, for the present, my suicidal design, I just slipped my nether extremities into the sleeves of my coat, and betook myself to a pursuit of the felon with all the nimbleness which the case required and its circumstances would admit. But my evil destiny attended me still. As I ran at full speed, with my nose up in the atmosphere, and intent only upon the purloiner of my property, I suddenly perceived that my feet rested no longer upon *terra-firma;* the fact is, I had thrown myself over a precipice, and should inevitably have been dashed to pieces but for my good fortune in grasping the end of a long guide-rope which depended from a passing balloon.

As soon as I sufficiently recovered my senses to comprehend the terrific predicament in which I stood, or rather hung, I exerted all the power of my lungs to make that predicament known to the æronaut overhead. But for a long time I exerted myself in vain. Either the fool could not, or the villain would not perceive me. Meantime the machine rapidly soared, while my strength even more rapidly failed. I was upon the point of resigning myself to my fate, and dropping quietly into the sea, when my spirits were suddenly revived by hearing a hollow voice from above, which seemed to be lazily humming an opera air. Looking up, I perceived the Angel of the Odd. He was leaning, with his arms folded, over the rim of the car; and with a pipe in his mouth, at which he puffed leisurely, seemed to be upon excellent terms with himself and the universe. I was too much exhausted to speak, so I merely regarded him with an imploring air.

For several minutes, although he looked me full in the face, he said nothing. At length removing carefully his meerschaum from the right to the left corner of his mouth, he condescended to speak.

"Who pe you?" he asked, "und what ter teuffel you pe do dare?"

To this piece of impudence, cruelty and affectation, I could reply only by ejaculating the monosyllable "Help!"

"Elp!" echoed the ruffian—"not I. Dare iz te pottle—elp yourself, und pe tam'd!"

With these words he let fall a heavy bottle of Kirschenwasser which, dropping precisely upon the crown of my head, caused me to imagine that my brains were entirely knocked out. Impressed with this idea, I was about to relinquish my hold and give up the ghost with a good grace, when I was arrested by the cry of the Angel, who bade me hold on.

"Old on!" he said; "don't pe in te urry —don't! Will you pe take de odder pottle, or ave you pe got zober yet and come to your zenses?"

I made haste, hereupon, to nod my head twice—once in the negative, meaning thereby that I would prefer not taking the other bottle at present—and once in the affirmative, intending thus to imply that I *was* sober and *had* positively come to my senses. By these means I somewhat softened the Angel.

"Und you pelief, ten," he inquired, "at te last? You pelief, ten, in te possibility of te odd?"

I again nodded my head in assent.

"Und you ave pelief in *me,* te Angel of te Odd?"

I nodded again.

"Und you acknowledge tat you pe te blind dronk und te vool?"

I nodded once more.

"Put your right hand into your left hand preeches' pocket, ten, in token ov your vull zubmizzion unto te Angel ov te Odd."

This thing, for very obvious reasons, I found it impossible to do. In the first place, my left arm had been broken in my fall from the ladder, and, therefore, had I let go my hold with the right hand, I must have let go altogether. In the second place, I could have no breeches until we came across the crow. I was therefore obliged, much to my regret, to shake my head in the negative—intending thus to give the Angel to understand that I found it inconvenient, just at that moment, to comply with his very reasonable demand! No sooner, however, had I ceased shaking my head than—

"Go to der teuffel, ten!" roared the Angel of the Odd.

In pronouncing these words, he drew a sharp knife across the guide-rope by which I was suspended, and as we then happened to be precisely over my own house, (which, during my peregrinations,

had been handsomely rebuilt,) it so occurred that I tumbled headlong down the
ample chimney and alit upon the dining-
room hearth.

Upon coming to my senses, (for the fall
had very thoroughly stunned me,) I found
it about four o'clock in the morning. I
lay outstretched where I had fallen from
the balloon. My head grovelled in the
ashes of an extinguished fire, while my
feet reposed upon the wreck of a small
table, overthrown, and amid the fragments of a miscellaneous dessert, intermingled with a newspaper, some broken
glasses and shattered bottles, and an
empty jug of the Schiedam Kirschenwasser. Thus revenged himself the Angel
of the Odd.

Notes

The Assignation

1. When Poe published this first in the
January 1834 *Godey's Lady's Book,* and later
in the July 1835 *Southern Literary Messenger*
and in the 1840 *Tales of the Grotesque and
Arabesque,* it was called "The Visionary."
For *The Broadway Journal* (June 7, 1845) he
changed the name to "The Assignation," referring to the lovers' meeting in death.

2. See note 22.

3. Elysium: See "Shadow," note 3.

Palladian: a modified classicism in the style
of Italian architect Andrea Palladio (1518–
1580).

4. *Ponte di Sospiri:* The "Bridge of Sighs"
which Byron made famous in his lines

*I stood in Venice on the Bridge of Sighs
A palace and a prison on each hand*
                                        (Benton 1).

5. For the location of places in this tale,
see the map, "Poe's Venice."

6. the Niobe: the mother whom Zeus
turned to a stone after her children were
killed. Tears flowed from the stone.

prison of the Old Republic: See map.

7. bored.

8. Although the episode of rescuing the
baby has no parallels in Byron's career, the
poet was known as an excellent swimmer
and brags playfully in *Don Juan* of having
swum the Hellespont.

9. None of the many references to acanthus in Pliny's *Natural History* seems to
match Poe's "soft and almost liquid" description. The plant's leaves provide a decorative
motif in Corinthian columns, for example.
Pliny describes its medicinal qualities in Book
IV, ch. 34 (see also XXIV, 66; XXV, 38), and
talks of a place named Acanthus (IV, 38; V,
104; V, 151). Poe is faking, mistranslating, or
confused; perhaps he has in mind a passage
from another classical author.

10. Lucius Aelius Aurelius Commodus
(161–192), emperor from 180 to 192. See
Figure 21.

11. Byron lived in the Palazzo Mocenigo
on the Grand Canal below the Rialto Bridge,
and in describing it, Thomas Moore used language similar to that of this paragraph (Benton 1). See map.

12. *grotesques . . .* painters: The term "grotesques" refers to a type of decorative wall
painting and is Roman, not Greek.

Chili gold: This could be a trade name for
a textile in Poe's day, but we did not find it
in catalogs or histories of textiles. Two possible reasons for the name: (1) Chilean gold
is found in long tenuous strands in the ore.
A fabric made of long strands of imitation
gold might have been known as "Chile gold."
(2) The province of Chihli, in northern
China, was famous for its rugs. Perhaps it
produced a characteristic gold rug with the
"liquid" texture Poe describes.

13. *bienséance:* propriety, decorum.

Sir Thomas More: Poe probably has in mind
Robert Southey's account of More's death in
The Doctor as it appeared in 1834: "It is one
thing to jest, it is another to be mirthful. Sir

Thomas More jested as he ascended the scaffold." Poe reviewed *The Doctor* in 1836. See Section Preface on "Shadow." Benton (1) thinks Poe has "Byron" introduce the idea to help the reader identify the narrator; he intends a pun on Sir Thomas More (c. 1478–1535, canonized in 1935) and Thomas Moore (the Irish poet, 1779–1852). Moore was Byron's friend.

Absurdities of Ravisius Texter: Jean Tixier, Seigneur de Ravisy, French humanist (1430–1524). We have found many references to Tixier's work, but no mention of his *Absurdities*. However, in *The Doctor*, Southey presents Textor's works as absurd and retells two of his dialogues which involve men making merry in defiance of Death.

Sparta . . . Palæochori: Poe is only approximately right: a town called Sparta still stands on the site of ancient Sparta. One portion of it is labelled "Palaiopolis," "the old town," on tourist maps; it contains the area in which Sparta's acropolis stood. The important excavations were not begun until 1906, however, so Poe may not have known these details. His word "Palæochori" means "the old place" and might well refer to the same area.

socle: a base or pedestal. See next item.

ΓΕΛΑΣΜΑ: laughter. Poe got this information from Chateaubriand's *Itinéraire de Paris à Jérusalem* (1811) (Engstrom). The passage in the *Itinéraire* also used the word *socle*, and Poe probably italicized it because he figured it was French. It is, but the same word is used in English architectural terminology.

ultras: Poe's intention seems to be "extreme examples." The Oxford English Dictionary reports instances of "ultras" used to refer to people (the meaning is "extremists"), but no examples of the word used as Poe employs it here.

14. Cimabue: Giovanni Cimabue (Cenni di Pepo), the great Florentine painter (c. 1240–c. 1302), and a logical breaking-point in art history: for his departure from the Byzantine tradition, he is often called the father of modern European painting.

Virtù: connoisseurship.

chefs d'oeuvre: masterworks.

15. Poe probably refers to Guido da Siena (active c. 1250–c. 1275), who produced a large and important Virgin and Child, and is felt to be the founder of a new and important

neo-Byzantine school, but about whom little is known. Hence a work by him would be exceedingly rare. There is another late thirteenth-century "Guido" about whom Poe might have read scholarly speculation: Guido Graziano. Little is known of him, though he is intriguing because he is mentioned in contemporary sources.

16. A letter from Byron to his publisher which Poe probably knew because Moore published it in his 1830 *Letters and Journals of Lord Byron, With Notices of His Life* contains a passage very similar to the following paragraph. Moreover, when Moore visited Byron in his Venice palazzo (see note 11 above), the two discussed art, and Byron expressed his unconventional views in much this manner (Benton). There is also the familiar couplet from *Don Juan* ii, 118:

> *I've seen much finer women, ripe*
> *and real*
> *Than all the nonsense of their*
> *stone ideal.*

17. Venus of the Medici: See Figure 22. The statue is now in Florence.

Canova: Antonio Canova (1757–1822), Italian sculptor of great influence, called by some the key figure in the neoclassical school. His "Venus" was placed on the pedestal of the "Medici Venus" when that work was moved to Paris.

Apollo: Byron is supposed to have looked much like the Vatican Apollo. To have him dislike it here is, Benton (1) feels, a humorous device on Poe's part.

Antinous: Antinoüs (fl. c. 110–130) was a favorite of the emperor Hadrian. After his death in Egypt in 130, Hadrian honored him through a religious cult, by naming cities after him and commanding statues showing him as an ideal of youthful beauty.

the quotation: Poe's attribution of the lines to Michaelangelo is correct. Isaac Disraeli translates them,

> *The sculptor never yet conceived*
> *a thought*
> *That yielding marble has refused*
> *to aid.*

But a more literal translation in Carlson (2) is more to Poe's point: "The best artist has no concept which the marble itself does not contain."

18. Persepolis: The ancient Persian capital.

Figure Twenty-two. The Venus of the Medici: Our photo shows a version by Massimiliano Soldani, a bronze from about 1710. The position of the arms to which Poe's Byronic hero objects is clear enough. Courtesy of the Nelson Gallery-Atkins Museum, Kansas City, Missouri. (Acquired through the Elmer F. Pierson Foundation.)

19. Angelo Poliziano (Ambrogini, 1454–1494), Florentine humanist, dramatist, and poet. Politian's brief play *La Favola d'Orfeo* (1480) is not divided into acts and scenes. It concerns the descent of Orfeo into the underworld to plead for the return of his love. Poe probably refers to Orfeo's pleading at the gates of hell, where his grief is so intense and his poem so beautiful they halt the various hellish activities. The play *could* be divided into three parts, but the "third part" deals just with the Baccantes gloating after cruelly killing Orfeo and sacrificing him to Bacchus for pursuing his other-worldly love.

20. Byron, of course, *is* an English poet; Poe is joking. This poem is generally known as "To One in Paradise." Basler feels Poe's poem is inspired by Byron's famous love affair with Mary Chaworth; indeed, he says that that affair may be a source of the story itself. The poem seems to predate the tale: Poe printed it as "To Ianthe in Heaven" in the July 1839 *Gentleman's Magazine*, the 1841 *American Melodies*, the February 25 and March 4, 1843 *Saturday Museum*, the May 10, 1845 *The Broadway Journal*, the 1845 *The Raven and Other Poems*, the *New York Daily Tribune* for November 29, 1845, and the 1849 *Poets and Poetry of America*.

21. Chapman's *Bussy D'Ambois*: The *Tragedie of Busye D'Amboise* (1607). The lines Poe has in mind are in Act V, scene iv, 95–97, but he altered or mis-remembered them. Bussy speaks:

> . . . I am up
> *Here like a Roman statue! I will stand*
> *Till death hath made me marble. . . .*

Bussy, an ambitious and unscrupulous courtier, has been shot, and determines to prop himself up with his sword, and thus die standing. The passage is appropriate, for Bussy D'Ambois' murder is the result of his illicit affair with Tamyra, the wife of Count Montsurry. See "The System of Dr. Tarr and Professor Fether," note 1.

22. wine from Johannisberg, Hessen, Germany, on the Rhine.

23. Bishop of Chicester: (Henry King, 1592–1669). The lines are from his "Exequy on the Death of a Beloved Wife" (1657).

Loss of Breath

1. Poe's original title for this piece when it was published on November 10, 1832, in *The Philadelphia Saturday Courier* was "A Decided Loss." He used it again in an expanded version (which we follow) in the *Southern Literary Messenger* for September 1835, in the 1840 *Tales of the Grotesque and Arabesque*, and in *The Broadway Journal*, January 3, 1846.

2. The motto is from a poem in a series by Thomas Moore (1779–1852) called "Irish Melodies," meant to be sung to traditional Irish tunes:

> *Oh, breathe not his name! let it sleep in*
> *   the shade,*
> *Where cold and unhonored his relics*
> *   are laid;*
> *Sad, silent, and dark be the tears that*
> *   we shed,*
> *As the night-dew that falls on the grass*
> *   o'er his head.*
>
> *But the night-dew that falls, though in*
> *   silence it weeps,*
> *Shall brighten with verdure the grave*
> *   where he sleeps;*

And the tear that we shed, though in
secret it rolls,
Shall long keep his memory green in
our souls.

Pollin (13) adds that the poem is in memory of Moore's friend Robert Emmet, leader of the United Irishmen, hanged in 1803. See Section Preface and note 17.

3. Salmanezer: Shalmaneser IV, King of Samaria (727–722 B.C.E.) laid siege to Samaria (II Kings 17). He died in the siege, and his successor, Sargon, actually took it after a three-year siege.

Sardanapalus: King of Assyria (668–626 B.C.E.). Nineveh, his capital, withstood a siege during his reign. Contrary to popular belief, the city didn't fall until 608 or 606, under the reign of his son.

Diodorus: a Greek historian of the second half of the first century B.C.E. In his "Historical Library" is an account of Sardanapalus.

Troy: the city besieged in the *Iliad*.

lustrum: five years.

Aristaeus: (or Aristeas) the supposed author of a document known as *Aristeas to Philocrates*. He seems to have been a courtier in the service of Ptolemy II Philadelphus (reigned 285–247 B.C.E.). Moses Hadas argues convincingly that the author was instead a Jew writing at about 130 B.C.E.

Azoth . . . Aristaeus . . . Psammitticus: Azoth (or Azotus, or Ashdod) is one of the five cities of the Philistine confederacy, located between Jaffa and Gaza. Hadas' edition of *Aristeas to Philocrates* is confusing on the matter; it mentions Azotus as a district, but locates Ascalon, not Azotus, between Jaffa and Gaza. We have not located an account in it of a siege of the city, though other historical sources show that Psammetichus besieged Ashdod for 29 years as part of his attempt to conquer Asia, starting in 666 B.C.E.

4. The Freudian critics equate "loss of breath" with loss of sexual potency, and suggest that the phrase traditionally has that meaning. If so, this paragraph seems crucial. Note the position of the narrator in relation to his wife, the fact that this occurs on the morning after the wedding night, that it takes place upstairs (as we learn seven paragraphs later), and that Poe chooses to use the word "ejaculated" to express what the narrator intended to do if he had not lost his "breath." The business about "insignificance" makes

sense, too, if one acknowledges the strong folk tradition which sees human coitus not as mutually pleasurable, but as an aggressive act by the male which debases the female.

5. Poe refers to Letter 3, Part 2 of *Julie ou la Nouvelle Héloïse* by Jean Jacques Rousseau, in which "Milord Edouard" writes ". . . and the route of passion leads me to the true philosophy." In chapter 23 of *Pelham*, one of Poe's favorite sources of ideas and allusions, Bulwer-Lytton cites this same passage and translates it: "It is the path of the passions which has conducted me to philosophy." See "The Murders in the Rue Morgue," note 24.

6. *Pas de Zéphire:* a step in which the dancer stands on one leg and sways the other backwards and forwards.

7. "Mandeville": *Mandeville: A Tale of the Seventeenth Century in England* by William Godwin (1756–1836). The passage Poe quotes is from III, 48 of the 1817 London edition. Without summarizing the complex novel, suffice it to say that the context in which the quotation appears is very serious. There is evidence that *Mandeville* influenced Poe in a number of ways; Pollin (5) discusses the importance of this quotation for Poe's philosophy. We have, then, another instance of Poe making fun of ideas he elsewhere takes seriously.

Anaxagoras: Athenian philosopher (c. 500–428 B.C.E.) who argues as part of a complex philosophical account of the nature of matter and the structure of the cosmos, that snow is, in a special sense too complex for brief summary, black and warm; at least, it contains particles of blackness and warmth as well as whiteness and coldness.

8. See "The Spectacles," note 24.

9. presumably a hairdressing product produced by Auguste Grandjean (see "The Angel of the Odd," note 11). If the tale is based on a sexual joke, this paragraph and the one preceding it again seem crucial.

10. *Metamora*, a famous play written by John Augustus Stone for the actor Edwin Forrest, first produced in 1829. Poe's joke has to do with Forrest's stage manner of representing Indian speech. Commentators on Forrest's portrayal of Metamora speak of "the deep and vigorous gutterals flung out from the muscular base of the abdomen. . . ." and of ". . . a dull monotony of manner. . . ."

11. a well frequented marsh . . . Demosthenes: Forrest was known to have taught

himself to act in a gloomy part of a forest near Covington, Kentucky, land which he later purchased for sentimental reasons. Poe seems to have in mind a comparison between this and the story of Demosthenes, the Athenian patriot (384–322) who, in the famous story told to schoolboys, became a great orator by practicing, with a mouthful of pebbles, against the roar of the sea. Poe pokes fun at the theatrical theory of the time (see Section Preface).

12. a tyrant of Agrigentum in Sicily from about 570 to about 554 or 549 B.C.E., notorious for his cruelty, notably his human sacrifices in a heated brazen bull.

13. the system of diagnosis of Hippocrates (c. 460–c. 377 B.C.E.), based upon the simple idea that every disease has a natural cause.

14. The innkeeper sells the "cadaver" to a doctor, who begins to dissect it at once. The apothecary and the doctor apply electricity to parts of the body. Poe makes fun of the process here, but in fact was, like all romantic authors, fascinated by the idea that electricity could produce responses in the human body. See "Some Words with a Mummy," at the passage indicated by note 11, and "The Premature Burial," at the passage indicated by note 7.

15. "Omnipresence of the Deity": See "The Angel of the Odd," note 10.

à la Catalani: probably a reference to Angelica Catalani (1779–1849), a successful Italian singer. See also "The Purloined Letter," note 15.

16. throne of Cyrus: Cambyses, cruel king of Persia, son of Cyrus, suspicious of his brother Smerdis, had him secretly executed. When Cambyses was killed in an accident, some of the magi installed one of their number, who looked like Smerdis, as king. He had no ears, however, and when this was discovered, he was murdered. Poe tells the tale backwards—his lack of ears cost the Magian the throne.

Zopyrus: one of Darius' officers at the siege of the rebellious city of Babylon. He cut off his nose and ears, said Darius had treated him cruelly, "defected" to the enemy, and became the Babylonian commander. He then showed his true colors and delivered the city to Darius.

17. I forbear . . . hanged: a joke Poe made elsewhere. See "How to Write a Blackwood Article."

Mark Antony: Plutarch characterizes Marc Antony as prone to drunken brawls. As for composing a treatise on getting drunk, in Horace Smith's Zillah, III, 40, Antony says he wrote such a treatise, and in a footnote, Smith says, "Bayle says it was published before the battle of Actium." For Poe's familiarity with Zillah, see "A Tale of Jerusalem."

On Pompey's galley, during a drinking bout, Shakespeare's Antony invites his companions,

Come, let's all take bowls,
Till that the conquering wine hath
    steeped our sense
In soft and delicate Lethe.

And before a crucial battle, he says,

Come,
Let's have one other gaudy night: call
    to me
All my sad captains; fill our bowls
    once more:
Let's mock the midnight bell.

That Poe had Shakespeare in mind is clear; see note 23.

18. Pinxit: Under the poem "Written Under the Engraving of A Portrait of Rafael Painted By Himself When He Was Young," in The Examiner for November 17, 1816 appears the line, "Leigh Hunt, pinxit," which probably suggested to Poe the idea of using Pinxit as the name of a painter. "Pinxit" is Latin for "he painted it." Poe knew and attacked Hunt's work in his criticism. See "The Angel of the Odd," where Poe alludes to the "Cockney School" of poetry; Hunt was referred to as "King of the Cockneys."

Marsyas: a satyr who found the flute the goddess Athena had invented and discarded. He played it beautifully, challenged Apollo to a contest, lost, and was flayed.

19. John Marston (1576–1634). Poe has the right author but the wrong play. The lines are from the third act of Marston's Antonio and Mellida (1602):

Each man take hence life, but no
    man death:
Hee's a good fellow, and keepes
    open house:
A thousand waies lead to his gate,
To his wide-mouthed porch: when
    niggard life
Hath but one little, little wicket through.

20. Crabbe: George Crabbe (1757–1832), grim, monotonous and realistic poet of outcasts and underdogs. Poe may also intend a pun on his name, alluding to the movements of the fat man.

pirouette: a full turn of the body accomplished on one leg with the point of the other leg at the knee.

pas de papillon: a springing movement in which one foot jumps over the other, executed on the diagonal.

Pelion upon Ossa: In Greek mythology, the Giants piled Ossa on Pelion. Otus and Ephialtes, Giants of a latter time, sons of Poseidon, threatened to pile Mt. Pelion on Mt. Ossa.

Du Pont the bellows-maker: Poe tended to use names of real tradesmen and craftsmen in his tales. We have not located Du Pont, but suspect that he will turn up, perhaps in a newspaper advertisement. Accounts of the American family Du Pont show no bellows-making. A French songwriter, Pierre Dupont (1821–1870), about whom Baudelaire wrote in 1849, is a possibility.

21. "Shades and Shadows": Pollin (3) thinks this title is Poe's coinage.

"South on the Bones": We are unable to identify Poe's allusion.

Captain Barclay: Robert Barclay Allardice (1779–1854), British officer and pedestrian, famous for having walked, in 1809, one mile each of 1,000 successive hours.

Windham: Pollin (3) thinks Poe might mean the antiquary Joseph Windham.

Allbreath: We have been unable to identify an author by this name.

"Phiz": Hablot K. Browne (1815–1882), the artist who illustrated Charles Dickens' *Pickwick Papers* (1836–1837). Poe added the allusion in the revised version of this tale. Poe's pun is on Phiz = fizz.

"Tenera res in feminis fama pudicitæ, et quasi flos pulcherrimus, cito ad levem marcessit auram, levique flatu corrumpitur, maxime, &c."—Hieronymus ad Salvinam. [Epist. LXXXV.] [Poe's note]. Poe's quotation is from St. Jerome (Hieronymus), *Ad Salvinam,* Epistle LXXIX, not LXXXV. He misremembered or miscopied. The original, *"Tenera res in feminis fama pudicitiae est: et quasi flos pulcherrimus cito ad leuem marcescit auram, leuique flatu corrumptur maxime. . . ."* translates, "It is a delicate thing, this reputation for chastity in women, and like a beautiful flower, which withered at the light breeze, and is destroyed wholly by the wind." "Marcessit" is a subjunctive, from another

verb meaning the same thing, so Poe's error does not change the meaning.

22. A search of the work of this Greek Stoic philosopher (c. 60–c. 120) failed to turn up "this remark."

23. Poe alludes to the passage in Shakespeare's *Julius Caesar* in which, having explained why he and the other conspirators slew Caesar, Brutus permits Mark Antony to speak, and leaves the hall. Antony speaks with great eloquence, turning the people against the conspirators. If Poe still had the actor Forrest in mind (see note 10), he might have connected Brutus with a famous play, John Howard Payne's *Brutus, or the fall of Tarquin,* in which the actor had starred as Titus and later as Brutus.

24. For editors who might be nicknamed "Scissors," see "How to Write a Blackwood Article" and "The Literary Life of Thingum Bob, Esq." Poe had numerous dealings with George Colton, editor of *The American (Whig) Review,* in which magazine he published a number of times.

25. Epimenides . . . Laertius: Laertius (Diogenes Laertium, c. 200), historian and biographer, author of the *Lives of Eminent Philosophers.* In section 3 (not 2) of his "Life of Epimenides," Laertius relates how Epimenides had sheep turned loose and followed. ". . . wherever any one of them lay down they were to sacrifice him to the God who was the patron of the spot, and so the evil [plague] was stayed. . . ." Epimenides was a Cretan poet and prophet of the seventh century B.C.E.

The Angel of the Odd

1. Poe published this in the *Columbian Magazine,* October 1844 (see Section Preface).

2. *truffe:* truffle.

Glover's "Leonidas": Richard Glover (1712–1785), author of a politically inspired epic poem, *Leonidas* (1737), which attained great popularity in its own day, then faded into obscurity.

Wilkie's "Epigoniad": Scottish poet William Wilkie (1721–1772) wrote another epic, *The Epigoniad* (1757), which was a critical failure in England.

Lamartine's "Pilgrimage": Alphonse Marie Louis de Prat de Lamartine (1790–1869), French romantic poet, produced a "last canto" to Byron's *Childe Harold's Pilgrimage,* dealing with Byron's death: "Le dernier Chant du pèlerinage d'Harold" ("The Last Canto of Harold's Pilgrimage"). Richard, however, believes Poe refers to Lamartine's *Le Voyage en Orient.*

Barlow's "Columbiad": Joel Barlow (1754–1812), American poet and political figure, one of a group of writers referred to as the "Connecticut Wits." The "Columbiad" was one of numerous attempts to provide the new nation with an epic poem. Built upon an earlier poem, "The Vision of Columbus," it views the French and American revolutions as the dawn of a new day for mankind. Barlow's political radicalism made him ugly to conservatives, but won him a diplomatic post in France. Poe would have been hostile to much of what he stood for.

Tuckerman's "Sicily": Henry T. Tuckerman (1813–1871), American writer who produced, out of his years in Italy, *The Italian Sketch-Book; Isabel or Sicily, a Pilgrimage* (1839). We would guess that the work popped into Poe's mind as he made up the list because the word "Pilgrimage" in its title is also in the title of Lamartine's poem on Byron.

Griswold's "Curiosities": A puzzle to your editors and to Richard, because Rufus Griswold (1815–1857) did not publish *The Curiosities of American Literature,* so far as we knew, until 1847; in 1853 it appeared as an appendix to Isaac Disraeli's *Curiosities of Literature* which Poe knew well in earlier editions and borrowed from often. But Bandy has solved the mystery: there is an 1844 edition of Disraeli-Griswold.

Lafitte: Chateau Lafite is a fine red Bordeaux wine, but Richard points out that Poe spells it wrong and leaves out the word "Chateau," suggesting a pun and a literary dig: Poe had reviewed unfavorably the popular novel *Lafitte: The Pirate of the Gulf* by Joseph Ingraham.

3. Poe quotes lines 50–51 from "The Winter Evening" by William Cowper (1731–1800).

4. a real incident; the paragraph is quoted from an 1844 newspaper (Mabbott 2).

5. penny-a-liner: a commercial journalist paid by the amount of his copy printed.

Cocaigne: *Blackwood's* word for the literary capital of the Cockneys, which they used to attack "the Cockney School of poetry." Allen gives a good account of why Poe was attracted to the regional feuding in British literary

magazines. Poe probably uses the word here also for a pun ("cocaine"), to suggest that the miserable Cockney hack must have been drugged to invent such a tale, and for the word play "concocter . . . Cocaigne."

6. Richard feels the phony accent is to suggest the Germanic influence on the Concord transcendentalists. Richard mentions William Ellery Channing II (see "How to Write a Blackwood Article," note 11). We note two facets of Poe's (1843) review of Channing's poems which suggest the specificity of Poe's satire: (1) Poe writes, ". . . the grammar . . . *may* be Dutch, but is not English." (2) Poe quotes Channing's lines

> To them the silver bells of
>   tinkling streams
> Seem brighter than an angel's laugh
>   in dreams.

Since Poe often alludes, by way of semi-private jokes, to his own writings, and since the review precedes the tale, it is possible that Poe had young Channing in mind. This tale is about "an angel's laugh in dreams."

7. head-devil.

8. a dry brandy.

9. *contre-temps:* contretemps, a mishap.

"*beaucoup . . . sens*": "Lots of luck and a little better judgment." The passage Poe has in mind in Le Sage's (1668–1747) *Gil Blas* comes when Gil Blas, a favorite copyist for the Archbishop of Granada, follows the Archbishop's instructions and tells him when he notes a failure in the Archbishop's style. Priding himself on his style, the Archbishop refuses to believe Gil Blas and fires him. He says "*Adieu, monsieur Gil Blas; je vous souhaite toutes sortes de prospérités, avec un peu plus de goût.*" ("Goodby, Mr. Gil Blas; I wish you all kinds of prosperity and a little better judgment.")

10. Poe probably means Robert Montgomery (1807–1855), *The Omnipresence of Deity.* Poe had probably read Macaulay's merciless attack (1830) on this work, and would have thought of it as a well-known example of bad poetry. Though Richard is probably right in suggesting that Poe to some extent had in mind some American colleagues, it makes good sense to read "The Angel of the Odd" as a tale with a simple moral: "This is what happens to you if you read rotten books and drink too much."

11. Auguste Grandjean, a New York hair treatment specialist (Pollin 3).

13. *Popular Journalism*

Here are five pieces of popular journalism set in the form of the spoof. The fictional frame is present less to enable Poe to make significant editorial comment than as a box in which he can place a series of interesting tidbits.

The Thousand-and-Second-Tale of Scheherazade. Here, for instance, Poe describes a group of wonders of the modern world. Any reader of popular magazines of Poe's day or our own knows the genre. Though Scheherazade's tale costs her her life, all is in fun, and clearly Poe is as interested in the accumulation of scientific curiosities and as proud of the mechanical accomplishments of his age as any booster of progress.

Although he elsewhere lambasted and satirized Dionysus Lardner, an extremely popular and successful lecturer on science, in this story Poe was in his debt: much of the miscellaneous scientific information came out of Dr. Lardner's *Course of Lectures* (1842) (Mabbott 4). Thirty-four of the footnotes (which begin on page 537) are Poe's own, many taken quite literally from Lardner. In general, we have not explicated them beyond identifying the works Poe cites.

Some Words With a Mummy. This tale and "The Thousand-and-Second Tale of Scheherazade," written at about the same time, are similar in intention. Both are journalistic, providing the author fictional frameworks in which he can present interesting and unusual information, the sort of material one still sees in Sunday supplements and the *Reader's Digest*. In one, examples of scientific wonders and modern technology are presented as "stranger than fiction"—the king, though accustomed to magical tales, refuses to believe them. In the other, the same sort of material appears routine to the Egyptian, because his civilization produced greater wonders. Both tales bear on the old argument about whether Poe had strong ties to his time and place. They suggest that he was both fascinated by the things that fascinated his readers and that he had a certain detachment from them. Like Twain, he was at once caught up in the excitement of new technology and new science, and, in another mood, skeptical that "progress" meant anything.

Diddling. Here is a popular magazine piece of the sort one still encounters in Sunday supplements: articles about ingenious frauds are good copy. In its first publication, it had in its favor an additional factor: the very recent performance in Philadelphia (where it was published) of James Kenney's farcical comedy "Raising the Wind" (1803), in which the character Jeremy Diddle is introduced. Pollin (4) reports that Poe does not really borrow much from the play beyond the personality of the character. He probably dropped the first part of the title (see note 1) because a few years had gone by and he could not expect readers to know what "Raising the Wind" (i.e., making money) meant.

The Business Man. The basic idea of this tale (assuming we do not have one of Poe's patented literary undercurrents) is that a stupid man—one who has been relieved of his intelligence by a blow on the head—equates intelligence with insanity. A "genius," anyone who pursues an even moderately useful or skilled profession, is an "ass," while a scoundrel and parasite is a "business-man." Poe simply takes a tendency which he has observed and carries it to extremes. The result reminds us just a little of an Art Buchwald column, and the comparison is probably apt. Poe would have made a good syndicated columnist, turning news items into whimsical satires.

Both this tale and "Diddling" are extremely urban in flavor; the reader might want to compare them to Poe's most serious urban story, "The Man of the Crowd."

Three Sundays in a Week. Poe probably got the idea for this anecdotal tale from an item in the *Philadelphia Public Ledger* for October 29, 1841, "Three Thursdays in One Week" (A. H. Quinn, F. N. Cherry). Poe ran it first under the title "A Succession of Sundays" in the *Saturday Evening Post* for November 27, 1841, shortly after the article appeared, and probably selected his title to avoid sounding too similar to the article. When he ran it again, in *The Broadway Journal* for May 10, 1845, he used the present title, perhaps figuring that enough time had elapsed to use one more like the original, or perhaps having forgotten his source, and recalling only that he had a catchier title in the back of his mind.

The scientific oddity at the heart of this anecdote should have a familiar ring to modern readers, for our journalists are still fond of such matters. The number of such curiosities in newspapers and magazines of Poe's day is remarkable, and Poe was as fascinated by them as were any of his contemporaries.

Yet it is likely that, minor as this piece of journalistic copy may be, it is as autobiographically significant as are the more emotional stories upon which more attention has been focused: see note 6.

The Tales

THE THOUSAND-AND-SECOND TALE OF SCHEHERAZADE

Truth is stranger than fiction.
Old Saying

Having had occasion, lately, in the course of some oriental investigations, to consult the *Tellmenow Isitsoörnot,* a work which (like the Zohar of Simeon Jochaides) is scarcely known at all, even in Europe, and which has never been quoted to my knowledge, by any American—if we except, perhaps, the author of the "Curiosities of American Literature;"—having had occasion, I say, to turn over some pages of the first-mentioned very remarkable work, I was not a little astonished to discover that the literary world has hitherto been strangely in error respecting the fate of the vizier's daughter, Scheherazade, as that fate is depicted in the "Arabian Nights,"[1] and that the *dénouement* there given, if not altogether inaccurate, as far as it goes, is at least to blame in not having gone very much farther.

For full information on this interesting topic, I must refer the inquisitive reader to the "Isitsoörnot" itself: but, in the mean time, I shall be pardoned for giving a summary of what I there discovered.

It will be remembered that, in the usual version of the tales, a certain monarch, having good cause to be jealous of his queen, not only puts her to death, but makes a vow, by his beard and the prophet, to espouse each night the most beautiful maiden in his dominions, and the next morning to deliver her up to the executioner.[2]

Having fulfilled this vow for many years to the letter, and with a religious punctuality and method that conferred great credit upon him as a man of devout feelings and excellent sense, he was interrupted one afternoon (no doubt at his prayers) by a visit from his grand vizier, to whose daughter, it appears, there had occurred an idea.

Her name was Scheherazade, and her idea was, that she would either redeem the land from the depopulating tax upon its beauty, or perish, after the approved fashion of all heroines, in the attempt.

Accordingly, and although we do not find it to be leap-year, (which makes the sacrifice more meritorious,) she deputes her father, the grand vizier, to make an offer to the king of her hand. This hand the king eagerly accepts—(he had intended to take it at all events, and had put off the matter from day to day, only through fear of the vizier)—but, in accepting it now, he gives all parties very distinctly to understand that, grand vizier or no grand vizier, he has not the slightest design of giving up one iota of his vow or of his privileges. When, therefore, the fair Scheherazade insisted upon marrying the king, and did actually marry him despite her father's excellent advice not to do anything of the kind—when she would and did marry him, I say, will I nill I, it was with her beautiful black eyes as thoroughly open as the nature of the case would allow.

It seems, however, that this politic damsel (who had been reading Machiavelli, beyond doubt,) had a very ingenious little plot in her mind. On the night of the wedding she contrived, upon I forget what specious pretence, to have her sister occupy a couch sufficiently near that of the royal pair to admit of easy conversation from bed to bed; and, a little before cock-crowing, she took care to awaken the good monarch, her husband, (who bore her none the worse will because he intended to wring her neck on the morrow,)—she managed to awaken him, I say, (although, on account of a capital conscience and an easy digestion, he slept well,) by the profound interest of a story (about a rat and a black cat,[3] I think,) which she was narrating (all in an under-tone, of course,) to her sister. When the day broke, it so happened that this history was not altogether finished, and that Scheherazade, in the nature of things, could not finish it just then, since it was high time for her to get up and be bowstrung—a thing very little more pleasant than hanging, only a trifle more genteel.

The king's curiosity, however, prevailing, I am sorry to say, even over his sound religious principles, induced him for this once to postpone the fulfilment of his vow until next morning, for the purpose and with the hope of hearing that night how it fared in the end with the black cat (a black cat I think it was) and the rat.

The night having arrived, however, the lady Scheherazade not only put the finishing stroke to the black cat and the rat, (the rat was blue,) but before she well knew what she was about, found herself deep in the intricacies of a narration, having reference (if I am not altogether mistaken) to a pink horse (with green wings) that went, in a violent manner, by clockwork, and was wound up with an indigo key. With this history the king was even more profoundly interested than with the other, and as the day broke before its conclusion, (notwithstanding all the queen's endeavours to get through with it in time for the bowstringing,) there was again no resource but to postpone that ceremony as before, for twenty-four hours. The next night there happened a similar accident with a similar result; and then the next —and then again the next; so that, in the end, the good monarch, having been unavoidably deprived of all opportunity to

keep his vow during a period of no less than one thousand and one nights, either forgets it altogether by the expiration of this time or gets himself absolved of it in the regular way, or, (what is more probable) breaks it outright as well as the head of his father confessor. At all events, Scheherazade, who, being lineally descended from Eve, fell heir, perhaps, to the whole seven baskets of talk which the latter lady, we all know, picked up from under the trees in the garden of Eden—Scheherazade, I say, finally triumphed, and the tariff upon beauty was repealed.

Now, this conclusion (which is that of the story as we have it upon record) is, no doubt, excessively proper and pleasant— but, alas! like a great many pleasant things, is more pleasant than true; and I am indebted altogether to the "Isitsöornot" for the means of correcting the error. "Le mieux," says a French proverb, "est l'ennemi du bien,"[4] and, in mentioning that Scheherazade had inherited the seven baskets of talk, I should have added that she put them out at compound interest until they amounted to seventy-seven.

"My dear sister," said she, on the thousand-and-second night, [I quote the language of the "Isitsöornot," at this point, verbatim,] "my dear sister," said she, "now that all this little difficulty about the bowstring has blown over, and that this odious tax is so happily repealed, I feel that I have been guilty of great indiscretion in withholding from you and the king (who, I am sorry to say, snores—a thing no gentleman would do) the full conclusion of the history of Sinbad the sailor. This person went through numerous other and more interesting adventures than those which I related; but the truth is, I felt sleepy on the particular night of their narration, and so was seduced into cutting them short—a grievous piece of misconduct, for which I only trust that Allah will forgive me. But even yet it is not too late to remedy my great neglect, and as soon as I have given the king a pinch or two in order to wake him up so far that he may stop making that horrible noise, I will forthwith entertain you (and him if he pleases,) with the sequel of this very remarkable story."

Hereupon the sister of Scheherazade, as I have it from the "Isitsöornot," expressed no very particular intensity of gratification; but the king having been sufficiently pinched, at length ceased snoring, and finally said "hum!" and then "hoo!" when the queen understanding these words, (which are no doubt Arabic) to signify that he was all attention, and would do his best not to snore any more,—the queen, I say, having arranged these matters to her satisfaction, re-entered thus, at once, into the history of Sinbad the sailor.

" 'At length in my old age,' [these are the words of Sinbad himself, as retailed by Scheherazade,]—'at length, in my old age, and after enjoying many years of tranquility at home, I became once more possessed with a desire of visiting foreign countries; and one day, without acquainting any of my family with my design, I packed up some bundles of such merchandize as was most precious and least bulky, and, engaging a porter to carry them, went with him down to the seashore, to await the arrival of any chance vessel that might convey me out of the kingdom into some region which I had not as yet explored.

" 'Having deposited the packages upon the sands, we sat down beneath some trees and looked out into the ocean in the hope of perceiving a ship, but during several hours we saw none whatever. At length I fancied that I could hear a singular buzzing or humming sound, and the porter, after listening awhile, declared that he also could distinguish it. Presently it grew louder, and then still louder, so that we could have no doubt that the object which caused it was approaching us. At length, on the edge of the horizon, we discovered a black speck, which rapidly increased in size until we made it out to be a vast monster, swimming with a great part of its body above the surface of the

sea. It came towards us with inconceivable swiftness, throwing up huge waves of foam around its breast, and illuminating all that part of the sea through which it passed, with a long line of fire that extended far off into the distance.

" 'As the thing drew near we saw it very distinctly. Its length was equal to that of three of the loftiest trees that grow, and it was as wide as the great hall of audience in your palace, O most sublime and munificent of the Caliphs. Its body, which was unlike that of ordinary fishes, was as solid as a rock, and of a jetty blackness throughout all that portion of it which floated above the water, with the exception of a narrow blood-red streak that completely begirdled it. The belly, which floated beneath the surface, and of which we could get only a glimpse now and then as the monster rose and fell with the billows, was entirely covered with metallic scales, of a colour like that of the moon in misty weather. The back was flat and nearly white, and from it there extended upwards six spines, about half the length of the whole body.

" 'This horrible creature had no mouth that we could perceive; but, as if to make up for this deficiency, it was provided with at least four score of eyes, that protruded from their sockets like those of the green dragonfly, and were arranged all around the body in two rows, one above the other, and parallel to the blood-red streak, which seemed to answer the purpose of an eyebrow. Two or three of these dreadful eyes were much larger than the others, and had the appearance of solid gold.

" 'Although this beast approached us, as I have before said, with the greatest rapidity, it must have been moved altogether by necromancy—for it had neither fins like a fish nor web-feet like a duck, nor wings like the sea-shell which is blown along in the manner of a vessel; nor yet did it writhe itself forward as do the eels. Its head and its tail were shaped precisely alike, only, not far from the latter, were two small holes that served for nostrils, and through which the monster puffed out its thick breath with prodigious violence, and with a shrieking disagreeable noise.

" 'Our terror at beholding this hideous thing was very great; but it was even surpassed by our astonishment when, upon getting a nearer look, we perceived upon the creature's back a vast number of animals about the size and shape of men, and altogether much resembling them, except that they wore no garments (as men do), being supplied (by nature no doubt) with an ugly, uncomfortable covering, a good deal like cloth, but fitting so tight to the skin as to render the poor wretches laughably awkward and put them apparently to severe pain. On the very tips of their heads were certain square-looking boxes, which, at first sight, I thought might have been intended to answer as turbans, but I soon discovered that they were excessively heavy and solid, and I therefore concluded they were contrivances designed, by their great weight, to keep the heads of the animals steady and safe upon their shoulders. Around the necks of the creatures were fastened black collars, (badges of servitude, no doubt,) such as we keep on our dogs, only much wider and infinitely stiffer, so that it was quite impossible for these poor victims to move their heads in any direction without moving the body at the same time; and thus they were doomed to perpetual contemplation of their noses—a view puggish and snubby in a wonderful, if not positively in an awful degree.

" 'When the monster had nearly reached the shore where we stood, it suddenly pushed out one of its eyes to a great extent, and emitted from it a terrible flash of fire, accompanied by a dense cloud of smoke and a noise that I can compare to nothing but thunder. As the smoke cleared away, we saw one of the odd man-animals standing near the head of the large beast with a trumpet in his hand, through which (putting it to his mouth) he pres-

ently addressed us in loud, harsh and disagreeable accents, that, perhaps, we should have mistaken for language had they not come altogether through the nose.

" 'Being thus evidently spoken to, I was at a loss how to reply, as I could in no manner understand what was said; and in this difficulty I turned to the porter, who was near swooning through affright, and demanded of him his opinion as to what species of monster it was, what it wanted, and what kind of creatures those were that so swarmed upon its back. To this the porter replied, as well as he could for trepidation, that he had once before heard of this sea-beast; that it was a cruel demon, with bowels of sulphur and blood of fire, created by evil genii as the means of inflicting misery upon mankind; that the things upon its back were vermin, such as sometimes infest cats and dogs, only a little larger and more savage; and that these vermin had their uses, however evil—for, through the torture they caused the beast by their nibblings and stingings, it was goaded into that degree of wrath which was requisite to make it roar and commit ill, and so fulfil the vengeful and malicious designs of the wicked genii.

" 'This account determined me to take to my heels, and, without once even looking behind me, I ran at full speed up into the hills, while the porter ran equally fast, although nearly in an opposite direction, so that, by these means, he finally made his escape with my bundles, of which I have no doubt he took excellent care—although this is a point I cannot determine, as I do not remember that I ever beheld him again.

" 'For myself, I was so hotly pursued by a swarm of the men-vermin (who had come to the shore in boats) that I was very soon overtaken, bound hand and foot, and conveyed to the beast, which immediately swam out again into the middle of the sea.

" 'I now bitterly repented my folly in quitting a comfortable home to peril my life in such adventures as this; but regret being useless, I made the best of my condition and exerted myself to secure the good-will of the man-animal that owned the trumpet, and who appeared to exercise authority over his fellows. I succeeded so well in this endeavour that, in a few days, the creature bestowed upon me various tokens of its favour, and, in the end, even went to the trouble of teaching me the rudiments of what it was vain enough to denominate its language; so that, at length, I was enabled to converse with it readily, and came to make it comprehend the ardent desire I had of seeing the world.

" 'Washish squashish squeak, Sinbad, hey-diddle diddle, grunt unt grumble, hiss, fiss, whiss,' said he to me, one day after dinner—but I beg a thousand pardons, I had forgotten that your majesty is not conversant with the dialect of the Cock-neighs,[5] (so the man-animals were called; I presume because their language formed the connecting link between that of the horse and that of the rooster.) With your permission, I will translate. 'Washish squashish,' and so forth:—that is to say, 'I am happy to find, my dear Sinbad, that you are really a very excellent fellow; we are now about doing a thing which is called circumnavigating the globe; and since you are so desirous of seeing the world, I will strain a point and give you a free passage upon the back of the beast.' "

When the Lady Scheherazade had proceeded thus far, relates the "Isitsöornot," the king turned over from his left side to his right, and said—

"It is, in fact, very surprising, my dear queen, that you omitted, hitherto, these latter adventures of Sinbad. Do you know I think them exceedingly entertaining and strange?"

The king having thus expressed himself, we are told, the fair Scheherazade resumed her history in the following words:—

"Sinbad went on in this manner, with his narrative to the caliph—'I thanked the man-animal for its kindness, and soon found myself very much at home on the beast, which swam at a prodigious rate through the ocean; although the surface of the latter is, in that part of the world, by no means flat, but round like a pomegranate, so that we went—so to say—either up hill or down hill all the time.' "

"That, I think, was very singular," interrupted the king.

"Nevertheless, it is quite true," replied Scheherazade.

"I have my doubts," rejoined the king; "but, pray, be so good as to go on with the story."

"I will," said the queen. " 'The beast,' continued Sinbad to the caliph, 'swam, as I have related, up hill and down hill, until, at length, we arrived at an island, many hundreds of miles in circumference, but which, nevertheless, had been built in the middle of the sea by a colony of little things like caterpillars.' "[6]

"Hum!" said the king.

" 'Leaving this island,' said Sinbad—(for Scheherazade, it must be understood, took no notice of her husband's ill-mannered ejaculation)—'leaving this island, we came to another where the forests were of solid stone, and so hard that they shivered to pieces the finest-tempered axes with which we endeavoured to cut them down.' "[7]

"Hum!" said the king, again; but Scheherazade, paying him no attention, continued in the language of Sinbad.

" 'Passing beyond this last island, we reached a country where there was a cave that ran to the distance of thirty or forty miles within the bowels of the earth, and that contained a greater number of far more spacious and more magnificent palaces than are to be found in all Damascus and Bagdad. From the roofs of these palaces there hung myriads of gems, like diamonds, but larger than men; and in among the streets of towers and pyramids and temples, there flowed immense rivers as black as ebony and swarming with fish that had no eyes.' "[8]

"Hum!" said the king.

" 'We then swam into a region of the sea where we found a lofty mountain, down whose sides there streamed torrents of melted metal, some of which were twelve miles wide and sixty miles long;[9] while from an abyss on the summit, issued so vast a quantity of ashes that the sun was entirely blotted out from the heavens, and it became darker than the darkest midnight; so that, when we were even at the distance of a hundred and fifty miles from the mountain, it was impossible to see the whitest object, however close we held it to our eyes.' "[10]

"Hum!" said the king.

" 'After quitting this coast, the beast continued his voyage until we met with a land in which the nature of things seemed reversed—for we here saw a great lake, at the bottom of which, more than a hundred feet beneath the surface of the water, there flourished in full leaf a forest of tall and luxuriant trees.' "[11]

"Hoo!" said the king.

" 'Some hundred miles farther on brought us to a climate where the atmosphere was so dense as to sustain iron or steel, just as our own does feathers.' "[12]

"Fiddle de dee," said the king.

" 'Proceeding still in the same direction, we presently arrived at the most magnificent region in the whole world. Through it there meandered a glorious river for several thousands of miles. This river was of unspeakable depth, and of a transparency richer than that of amber. It was from three to six miles in width; and its banks, which arose on either side to twelve hundred feet in perpendicular height, were crowned with ever-blossoming trees and perpetual sweet-scented flowers that made the whole territory one gorgeous garden; but the name of this luxuriant land was the kingdom of Horror, and to enter it was inevitable death.' "[13]

"Humph!" said the king.

" 'We left this kingdom in great haste, and, after some days, came to another, where we were astonished to perceive myriads of monstrous animals with horns resembling scythes upon their heads. These hideous beasts dig for themselves vast caverns in the soil, of a funnel shape, and line the sides of them with rocks, so disposed one upon the other that they fall instantly, when trodden upon by other animals, thus precipitating them into the monsters' dens, where their blood is immediately sucked, and their carcases afterwards hurled contemptuously out to an immense distance from the caverns of death.' "[14]

"Pooh!" said the king.

" 'Continuing our progress, we perceived a district abounding with vegetables that grew not upon any soil but in the air.[15] There were others that sprang from the substance of other vegetables;[16] others that derived their sustenance from the bodies of living animals;[17] and then, again, there were others that glowed all over with intense fire;[18] others that moved from place to place at pleasure,[19] and what is still more wonderful, we discovered flowers that lived and breathed and moved their limbs at will, and had, moreover, the detestable passion of mankind for enslaving other creatures, and confining them in horrid and solitary prisons until the fulfilment of appointed tasks.' "[20]

"Pshaw!" said the king.

" 'Quitting this land, we soon arrived at another in which the bees and the birds are mathematicians of such genius and erudition, that they give daily instructions in the science of geometry to the wise men of the empire. The king of the place having offered a reward for the solution of two very difficult problems, they were solved upon the spot—the one by the bees, and the other by the birds; but the king keeping their solutions a secret, it was only after the most profound researches and labor, and the writing of an infinity of big books, during a long series of years, that the men-mathematicians at length arrived at the identical solutions which had been given upon the spot by the bees and by the birds.' "[21]

"Oh my!" said the king.

" 'We had scarcely lost sight of this empire when we found ourselves close upon another, from whose shores there flew over our heads a flock of fowls a mile in breadth and two hundred and forty miles long; so that, although they flew a mile during every minute, it required no less than four hours for the whole flock to pass over us—in which there were several millions of millions of fowls.' "[22]

"Oh fy!" said the king.

" 'No sooner had we got rid of these birds, which occasioned us great annoyance, than we were terrified by the appearance of a fowl of another kind, and infinitely larger than even the rocs which I met in my former voyages; for it was bigger than the biggest of the domes upon your seraglio, oh, most Munificent of Caliphs. This terrible fowl had no head that we could perceive, but was fashioned entirely of belly, which was of a prodigious fatness and roundness, of a soft looking substance, smooth, shining and striped with various colors. In its talons, the monster was bearing away to his eyrie in the heavens, a house from which it had knocked off the roof, and in the interior of which we distinctly saw human beings, who, beyond doubt, were in a state of frightful despair at the horrible fate which awaited them. We shouted with all our might, in the hope of frightening the bird into letting go of its prey; but it merely gave a snort or puff, as if of rage, and then let fall upon our heads a heavy sack which proved to be filled with sand.' "[23]

"Stuff!" said the king.

" 'It was just after this adventure that we encountered a continent of immense extent and of prodigious solidity, but which, nevertheless, was supported entirely upon the back of a sky-blue cow that had no fewer than four hundred horns.' "[24]

"*That*, now, I believe," said the king, "because I have read something of the kind before, in a book."

" 'We passed immediately beneath this continent, (swimming in between the legs of the cow,) and, after some hours, found ourselves in a wonderful country indeed, which, I was informed by the man-animal, was his own native land, inhabited by things of his own species. This elevated the man-animal very much in my esteem; and in fact, I now began to feel ashamed of the contemptuous familiarity with which I had treated him; for I found that the man-animals in general were a nation of the most powerful magicians, who lived with worms in their brains,[25] which, no doubt, served to stimulate them by their painful writhings and wrigglings to the most miraculous efforts of imagination.' "

"Nonsense!" said the king.

" 'Among the magicians, were domesticated several animals of very singular kinds; for example, there was a huge horse whose bones were iron and whose blood was boiling water. In place of corn, he had black stones for his usual food; and yet, in spite of so hard a diet, he was so strong and swift that he would drag a load more weighty than the grandest temple in this city, at a rate surpassing that of the flight of most birds.' "[26]

"Twattle!" said the king.

" 'I saw, also, among these people a hen without feathers, but bigger than a camel; instead of flesh and bone she had iron and brick; her blood, like that of the horse, (to whom in fact she was nearly related,) was boiling water; and like him she ate nothing but wood or black stones. This hen brought forth very frequently, a hundred chickens in the day; and, after birth, they took up their residence for several weeks within the stomach of their mother.' "[27]

"Fal lal!" said the king.

" 'One of this nation of mighty conjurors created a man out of brass and wood, and leather, and endowed him with such ingenuity that he would have beaten at chess, all the race of mankind with the exception of the great Caliph, Haroun Alraschid.[28] Another of these magi constructed (of like material) a creature that put to shame even the genius of him who made it; for so great were its reasoning powers that, in a second, it performed calculations of so vast an extent that they would have required the united labor of fifty thousand fleshly men for a year.[29] But a still more wonderful conjuror fashioned for himself a mighty thing that was neither man nor beast, but which had brains of lead intermixed with a black matter like pitch, and fingers that it employed with such incredible speed and dexterity that it would have had no trouble in writing out twenty thousand copies of the Koran in an hour; and this with so exquisite a precision, that in all the copies there should not be found one to vary from another by the breadth of the finest hair. This thing was of prodigious strength, so that it erected or overthrew the mightiest empires at a breath; but its power was exercised equally for evil and for good.' "[30]

"Ridiculous!" said the king.

" 'Among this nation of necromancers there was also one who had in his veins the blood of the salamanders; for he made no scruple of sitting down to smoke his chibouc[31] in a red-hot oven until his dinner was thoroughly roasted upon its floor.[32] Another had the faculty of converting the common metals into gold, without even looking at them during the process.[33] Another had such delicacy of touch that he made a wire so fine as to be invisible.[34] Another had such quickness of perception that he counted all the separate motions of an elastic body, while it was springing backwards and forwards at the rate of nine hundred millions of times in a second.' "[35]

"Absurd!" said the king.

" 'Another of these magicians, by means of a fluid that nobody ever yet saw, could make the corpses of his friends brandish their arms, kick out their legs, fight, or even get up and dance at his will.[36] Another had cultivated his voice to so great an extent that he could have made himself heard from one end of the earth to the other.[37] Another had so long an arm that he could sit down in Damascus and indite a letter at Bagdad—or indeed at any distance whatsoever.[38] Another commanded the lightning to come down to him out of the heavens, and it came at his call; and served him for a plaything when it came. Another took two loud sounds and out of them made a silence. Another constructed a deep darkness out of two brilliant lights.[39] Another made ice in a red-hot furnace.[40] Another directed the sun to paint his portrait, and the sun did.[41] Another took this luminary with the moon and the planets, and having first weighed them with scrupulous accuracy, probed into their depths and found out the solidity of the substance of which they are made. But the whole nation is, indeed, of so surprising a necromantic ability, that not even their infants, nor their commonest cats and dogs have any difficulty in seeing objects that do not exist at all, or that for twenty thousand years before the birth of the nation itself, had been blotted out from the face of creation.' "[42]

"Preposterous!" said the king.

" 'The wives and daughters of these incomparably great and wise magi,' " continued Scheherazade, without being in any manner disturbed by these frequent and most ungentlemanly interruptions on the part of her husband—" 'the wives and daughters of these eminent conjurors are everything that is accomplished and refined; and would be everything that is interesting and beautiful, but for an unhappy fatality that besets them, and from which not even the miraculous powers of their husbands and fathers has, hitherto, been adequate to save. Some fatalities come in certain shapes, and some in others—but this of which I speak, has come in the shape of a crotchet.' "

"A what?" said the king.

" 'A crotchet,' " said Scheherazade. " 'One of the evil genii who are perpetually upon the watch to inflict ill, has put it into the heads of these accomplished ladies that the thing which we describe as personal beauty, consists altogether in the protuberance of the region which lies not very far below the small of the back.—Perfection of loveliness, they say, is in the direct ratio of the extent of this hump. Having been long possessed of this idea, and bolsters being cheap in that country, the days have long gone by since it was possible to distinguish a woman from a dromedary—' "

"Stop!" said the king,—"I can't stand that, and I won't. You have already given me a dreadful headache with your lies. The day, too, I perceive, is beginning to break. How long have we been married? —my conscience is getting to be troublesome again. And then that dromedary touch—do you take me for a fool? Upon the whole you might as well get up and be throttled."

These words, as I learn from the "Isitsöornot," both grieved and astonished Scheherazade; but, as she knew the king to be a man of scrupulous integrity, and quite unlikely to forfeit his word, she submitted to her fate with a good grace. She derived, however, great consolation, (during the tightening of the bowstring,) from the reflection that much of the history remained still untold, and that the petulance of her brute of a husband had reaped for him a most righteous reward, in depriving him of many inconceivable adventures.

SOME WORDS WITH A MUMMY

The symposium of the preceding evening had been a little too much for my nerves. I had a wretched head-ache, and was desperately drowsy. Instead of going out, therefore, to spend the evening as I had proposed, it occurred to me that I could not do a wiser thing than just eat a mouthful of supper and go immediately to bed.

A *light* supper of course. I am exceedingly fond of Welsh rabbit. More than a pound at once, however, may not at all times be advisable. Still, there can be no material objection to two. And really between two and three, there is merely a single unit of difference. I ventured, perhaps, upon four. My wife will have it five;—but, clearly, she has confounded two very distinct affairs. The abstract number, five, I am willing to admit; but, concretely, it has reference to bottles of Brown Stout, without which, in the way of condiment, Welsh rabbit is to be eschewed.[1]

Having thus concluded a frugal meal, and donned my night-cap, with the serene hope of enjoying it till noon the next day, I placed my head upon the pillow, and through the aid of a capital conscience, fell into a profound slumber forthwith.

But when were the hopes of humanity fulfilled? I could not have completed my third snore when there came a furious ringing at the street-door bell, and then an impatient thumping at the knocker, which awakened me at once. In a minute afterward and while I was still rubbing my eyes, my wife thrust in my face a note from my old friend, Doctor Ponnonner.[2] It ran thus:

> Come to me by all means, my dear good friend, as soon as you receive this. Come and help us to rejoice. At last, by long persevering diplomacy, I have gained the assent of the Directors of the City Museum,[3] to my examination of the Mummy—you know the one I mean. I have permission to unswathe it and open it, if desirable. A few friends only will be present—you, of course. The Mummy is now at my house, and we shall begin to unroll it at eleven to-night.
>
> Yours ever,
>
> PONNONNER.

By the time I had reached the "Ponnonner," it struck me that I was as wide awake as a man need be. I leaped out of bed in an ecstacy, overthrowing all in my way; dressed myself with a rapidity truly marvellous; and set off, at the top of my speed, for the Doctor's.

There I found a very eager company assembled. They had been awaiting me with much impatience; the Mummy was extended upon the dining table; and the moment I entered, its examination was commenced.

It was one of a pair brought, several years previously, by Captain Arthur Sabretash, a cousin of Ponnonner's, from a tomb near Eleithias, in the Lybian Mountains, a considerable distance above Thebes on the Nile. The grottoes at this point, although less magnificent than the Theban sepulchres, are of higher interest, on account of affording more numerous illustrations of the private life of the Egyptians.[4] The chamber from which our specimen was taken, was said to be very rich in such illustrations; the walls being completely covered with fresco paintings and bas-reliefs, while statues, vases, and Mosaic work of rich patterns, indicated the vast wealth of the deceased.

The treasure had been deposited in the Museum precisely in the same condition in which Captain Sabretash had found it; —that is to say, the coffin had not been disturbed. For eight years it had thus stood, subject only externally to public inspection. We had now, therefore, the complete Mummy at our disposal; and to those who are aware how very rarely the unransacked antique[5] reaches our shores, it will be evident, at once, that we had great reason to congratulate ourselves upon our good fortune.

Approaching the table, I saw on it a large box, or case, nearly seven feet long, and perhaps three feet wide, by two feet and a half deep. It was oblong—not coffin-shaped. The material was at first supposed to be the wood of the sycamore (platanus), but, upon cutting into it, we found it to be pasteboard, or more properly, papier mâché, composed of papyrus. It was thickly ornamented with paintings, representing funeral scenes, and other mournful subjects, interspersed among which in every variety of position, were certain series of hieroglyphical characters intended, no doubt, for the name of the departed. By good luck, Mr. Gliddon formed one of our party; and he had no difficulty in translating the letters, which were simply phonetic, and represented the word, Allamistakeo.[6]

We had some difficulty in getting this case open without injury, but, having at length accomplished the task, we came to a second, coffin-shaped, and very considerably less in size than the exterior one, but resembling it precisely in every other respect. The interval between the two was filled with resin, which had, in some degree, defaced the colors of the interior box.

Upon opening this latter (which we did quite easily,) we arrived at a third case, also coffin-shaped, and varying from the second one in no particular, except in that of its material, which was cedar, and still emitted the peculiar and highly aromatic odor of that wood. Between the second and the third case there was no interval; the one fitting accurately within the other.

Removing the third case, we discovered and took out the body itself. We had expected to find it, as usual, enveloped in frequent rolls, or bandages, of linen, but, in place of these, we found a sort of sheath, made of papyrus, and coated with a layer of plaster, thickly gilt and painted. The paintings represented subjects connected with the various supposed duties of the soul, and its presentation to different divinities, with numerous identical human figures, intended, very probably, as portraits of the persons embalmed. Extending from head to foot, was a columnar, or perpendicular inscription in phonetic hieroglyphics, giving again his name and titles, and the names and titles of his relations.

Around the neck thus ensheathed, was a collar of cylindrical glass beads, diverse in color, and so arranged as to form images of deities, of the scarabæus, etc., with the winged globe.[7] Around the small of the waist was a similar collar, or belt.

Stripping off the papyrus, we found the flesh in excellent preservation, with no perceptible odor. The color was reddish. The skin was hard, smooth and glossy. The teeth and hair were in good condition. The eyes (it seemed) had been removed, and glass ones substituted, which were very beautiful and wonderfully lifelike, with the exception of somewhat too determined a stare. The finger and toe nails were brilliantly gilded.

Mr. Gliddon was of opinion, from the redness of the epidermis, that the embalmment had been effected altogether by asphaltum; but, on scraping the surface with a steel instrument, and throwing into the fire some of the powder thus obtained, the flavor of camphor and other sweet-scented gums became apparent.

We searched the corpse very carefully for the usual openings through which the entrails are extracted, but, to our surprise, we could discover none. No member of the party was at that period aware that entire or unopened mummies are not unfrequently met. The brain it was customary to withdraw through the nose; the intestines through an incision in the side; the body was then shaved, washed, and salted; then laid aside for several weeks, when the operation of embalming, properly so called, began.

As no trace of an opening could be found, Doctor Ponnonner was preparing his instruments for dissection, when I observed that it was then past two o'clock. Hereupon it was agreed to postpone the internal examination until the next evening; and we were about to separate for the present, when some one suggested an experiment or two with the Voltaic pile.[8]

The application of electricity to a Mummy three or four thousand years old at the least, was an idea, if not very sage, still sufficiently original, and we all caught at it at once. About one tenth in earnest and nine tenths in jest, we arranged a battery in the Doctor's study, and conveyed thither the Egyptian.

It was only after much trouble that we succeeded in laying bare some portions of the temporal muscle which appeared of less stony rigidity than other parts of the frame, but which, as we had anticipated, of course, gave no indication of galvanic susceptibility when brought in contact with the wire. This the first trial, indeed, seemed decisive, and, with a hearty laugh at our own absurdity, we were bidding each other good night, when my eyes, happening to fall upon those of the Mummy, were there immediately riveted in amazement. My brief glance, in fact, had sufficed to assure me that the orbs which we had all supposed to be glass, and which were originally noticeable for a certain wild stare, were now so far covered by the lids that only a small portion of the *tunica albuginea*[9] remained visible.

With a shout I called attention to the fact, and it became immediately obvious to all.

I cannot say that I was *alarmed* at the phenomenon, because "alarmed" is, in my case, not exactly the word. It is possible, however, that, but for the Brown Stout, I might have been a little nervous. As for the rest of the company, they really made no attempt at concealing the downright fright which possessed them. Doctor Ponnonner was a man to be pitied. Mr. Gliddon, by some peculiar process, rendered himself invisible. Mr. Silk Buckingham,[10] I fancy, will scarcely be so bold as to deny that he made his way, upon all fours, under the table.

After the first shock of astonishment, however, we resolved, as a matter of course, upon farther experiment forthwith. Our operations were now directed against the great toe of the right foot. We made an incision over the outside of the exterior *os sesamoideum pollicis pedis*, and thus got at the root of the *abductor* muscle. Re-adjusting the battery, we now applied the fluid[11] to the bisected nerves —when, with a movement of exceeding life-likeness, the Mummy first drew up its right knee so as to bring it nearly in contact with the abdomen, and then, straightening the limb with inconceivable force, bestowed a kick upon Doctor Ponnonner, which had the effect of discharging that gentleman, like an arrow from a catapult, through a window into the street below.

We rushed out *en masse* to bring in the mangled remains of the victim, but had the happiness to meet him upon the staircase, coming up in an unaccountable hurry, brimfull of the most ardent philosophy, and more than ever impressed with the necessity of prosecuting our experiments with rigor and with zeal.

It was by his advice, accordingly, that we made, upon the spot, a profound incision into the tip of the subject's nose, while the Doctor himself, laying violent hands upon it, pulled it into vehement contact with the wire.

Morally and physically—figuratively and literally—was the effect electric. In the first place, the corpse opened its eyes and winked very rapidly for several minutes, as does Mr. Barnes[12] in the pantomime; in the second place, it sneezed; in the third, it sat upon end; in the fourth, it shook its fist in Doctor Ponnonner's face; in the fifth, turning to Messieurs Gliddon and Buckingham, it addressed them, in very capital Egyptian, thus:

"I must say, gentlemen, that I am as much surprised as I am mortified, at your behaviour. Of Doctor Ponnonner nothing better was to be expected. He is a poor little fat fool who *knows* no better. I pity and forgive him. But you, Mr. Gliddon—and you, Silk—who have travelled and resided in Egypt until one might imagine you to the manor born—you, I say, who have been so much among us that you speak Egyptian fully as well, I think, as you write your mother tongue—you, whom I have always been led to regard as the firm friend of the mummics—I really did anticipate more gentlemanly conduct from *you*. What am I to think of your standing quietly by and seeing me thus unhandsomely used? What am I to suppose by your permitting Tom, Dick and Harry to strip me of my coffins, and my clothes, in this wretchedly cold climate? In what light (to come to the point) am I to regard your aiding and abetting that miserable little villain, Doctor Ponnonner, in pulling me by the nose?"

It will be taken for granted, no doubt, that upon hearing this speech under the circumstances, we all either made for the door, or fell into violent hysterics, or went off in a general swoon. One of these three things was, I say, to be expected. Indeed each and all of these lines of conduct might have been very plausibly pursued. And, upon my word, I am at a loss to know how or why it was that we pursued neither the one or the other. But, perhaps, the true reason is to be sought in the spirit of the age, which proceeds by the rule of contraries altogether, and is now usually admitted as the solution of everything in the way of paradox and impossibility. Or, perhaps, after all, it was only the Mummy's exceedingly natural and matter-of-course air that divested his words of the terrible. However this may be, the facts are clear, and no member of our party betrayed any very particular trepidation, or seemed to consider that any thing had gone very especially wrong.

For my part I was convinced it was all right, and merely stepped aside, out of the range of the Egyptian's fist. Doctor Ponnonner thrust his hands into his breeches' pockets, looked hard at the Mummy, and grew excessively red in the face. Mr. Gliddon stroked his whiskers and drew up the collar of his shirt. Mr. Buckingham hung down his head, and put his right thumb into the left corner of his mouth.

The Egyptian regarded him with a severe countenance for some minutes, and at length, with a sneer, said:

"Why don't you speak, Mr. Buckingham? Did you hear what I asked you, or not? *Do* take your thumb out of your mouth!"

Mr. Buckingham, hereupon, gave a slight start, took his right thumb out of

the left corner of his mouth, and, by way
of indemnification, inserted his left thumb
in the right corner of the aperture above-
mentioned.

Not being able to get an answer from
Mr. B., the figure turned peevishly to Mr.
Gliddon, and, in a peremptory tone, demanded in general terms what we all
meant.

Mr. Gliddon replied at great length, in
phonetics; and but for the deficiency of
American printing-offices in hieroglyphical type, it would afford me much pleasure to record here, in the original, the
whole of his very excellent speech.

I may as well take this occasion to remark, that all the subsequent conversation in which the Mummy took a part,
was carried on in primitive Egyptian,
through the medium (so far as concerned
myself and other untravelled members of
the company)—through the medium, I
say, of Messieurs Gliddon and Buckingham, as interpreters. These gentlemen
spoke the mother-tongue of the mummy
with inimitable fluency and grace; but I
could not help observing that (owing, no
doubt, to the introduction of images entirely modern, and, of course, entirely
novel to the stranger,) the two travellers
were reduced, occasionally, to the employment of sensible forms for the purpose of conveying a particular meaning.
Mr. Gliddon, at one period, for example,
could not make the Egyptian comprehend
the term "politics," until he sketched
upon the wall, with a bit of charcoal,
a little carbuncle-nosed gentleman, out at
elbows, standing upon a stump, with his
left leg drawn back, his right arm thrown
forward, with the fist shut, the eyes rolled
up toward Heaven, and the mouth open
at an angle of ninety degrees. Just in the
same way Mr. Buckingham failed to convey the absolutely modern idea, "wig,"
until, (at Doctor Ponnonner's suggestion,)
he grew very pale in the face, and consented to take off his own.

It will be readily understood that Mr.
Gliddon's discourse turned chiefly upon

the vast benefits accruing to science from
the unrolling and disembowelling of
mummies; apologizing, upon this score,
for any disturbance that might have been
occasioned him, in particular, the individual Mummy called Allamistakeo; and
concluding with a mere hint, (for it could
scarcely be considered more,) that, as
these little matters were now explained,
it might be as well to proceed with the
investigation intended. Here Doctor Ponnonner made ready his instruments.

In regard to the latter suggestions of
the orator, it appears that Allamistakeo
had certain scruples of conscience, the nature of which I did not distinctly learn;
but he expressed himself satisfied with
the apologies tendered, and, getting down
from the table, shook hands with the
company all round.

When this ceremony was at an end, we
immediately busied ourselves in repairing
the damages which our subject had sustained from the scalpel. We sewed up the
wound in his temple, bandaged his foot,
and applied a square inch of black plaster
to the tip of his nose.

It was now observed that the Count,
(this was the title, it seems, of Allamistakeo,) had a slight fit of shivering—no
doubt from the cold. The doctor immediately repaired to his wardrobe, and soon
returned with a black dress coat, made in
Jennings' best manner, a pair of sky-blue
plaid pantaloons with straps, a pink ging-
ham *chemise*, a flapped vest of brocade, a
white sack overcoat, a walking cane with
a hook, a hat with no brim, patent-leather
boots, straw-colored kid gloves, an eye-
glass, a pair of whiskers, and a waterfall
cravat.[13] Owing to the disparity of size between the Count and the doctor, (the proportion being as two to one,) there was
some little difficulty in adjusting these
habiliments upon the person of the Egyptian; but when all was arranged, he might
have been said to be dressed. Mr. Gliddon, therefore, gave him his arm, and led
him to a comfortable chair by the fire,
while the doctor rang the bell upon the

spot and ordered a supply of cigars and wine.

The conversation soon grew animated. Much curiosity was, of course, expressed in regard to the somewhat remarkable fact of Allamistakeo's still remaining alive.

"I should have thought," observed Mr. Buckingham, "that it is high time you were dead."

"Why," replied the Count, very much astonished, "I am little more than seven hundred years old! My father lived a thousand, and was by no means in his dotage when he died."

Here ensued a brisk series of questions and computations, by means of which it became evident that the antiquity of the Mummy had been grossly misjudged. It had been five thousand and fifty years, and some months, since he had been consigned to the catacombs at Eleithias.

"But my remark," resumed Mr. Buckingham, "had no reference to your age at the period of interment; (I am willing to grant, in fact, that you are still a young man,) and my allusion was to the immensity of time during which, by your own showing, you must have been done up in asphaltum."

"In what?" said the Count.

"In asphaltum," persisted Mr. B.

"Ah, yes; I have some faint notion of what you mean; it might be made to answer, no doubt,—but in my time we employed scarcely anything else than the Bichloride of Mercury."[14]

"But what we are especially at a loss to understand," said Doctor Ponnonner, "is how it happens that, having been dead and buried in Egypt five thousand years ago, you are here to-day all alive, and looking so delightfully well."

"Had I been, as you say, *dead*," replied the Count, "it is more than probable that dead I should still be; for I perceive you are yet in the infancy of Galvanism,[15] and cannot accomplish with it what was a common thing among us in the old days. But the fact is, I fell into catalepsy,[16] and it was considered by my best friends that I was either dead or should be; they accordingly embalmed me at once—I presume you are aware of the chief principle of the embalming process?"

"Why, not altogether."

"Ah, I perceive;—a deplorable condition of ignorance! Well, I cannot enter into details just now: but it is necessary to explain that to embalm, (properly speaking,) in Egypt, was to arrest indefinitely *all* the animal functions subjected to the process. I use the word "animal" in its widest sense, as including the physical not more than the moral and *vital* being. I repeat that the leading principle of embalmment consisted, with us, in the immediately arresting, and holding in perpetual *abeyance,* all the animal functions subjected to the process. To be brief, in whatever condition the individual was, at the period of embalmment, in that condition he remained. Now, as it is my good fortune to be of the blood of the Scarabæus, I was embalmed *alive,* as you see me at present."

"The blood of the Scarabæus!" exclaimed Doctor Ponnonner.

"Yes. The Scarabæus was the *insignium,* or the "arms," of a very distinguished and a very rare patrician family. To be "of the blood of the Scarabæus," is merely to be one of that family of which the Scarabæus is the *insignium.* I speak figuratively."

"But what has this to do with your being alive?"

"Why it is the general custom, in Egypt, to deprive a corpse, before embalmment, of its bowels and brains; the race of the Scarabæi alone did not coincide with the custom. Had I not been a Scarabæus, therefore, I should have been without bowels and brains; and without either it is inconvenient to live."

"I perceive that;" said Mr. Buckingham, "and I presume that all the *entire* mummies that come to hand are of the race of Scarabæi."

"Beyond doubt."

"I thought," said Mr. Gliddon very

meekly, "that the Scarabæus was one of the Egyptian gods."

"One of the Egyptian *what?*" exclaimed the Mummy, starting to its feet.

"Gods!" repeated the traveler.

"Mr. Gliddon I really am astonished to hear you talk in this style," said the Count, resuming his chair. "No nation upon the face of the earth has ever acknowledged more than *one god*. The Scarabæus, the Ibis, etc., were with us, (as similar creatures have been with others) the symbols, or *media*, through which we offered worship to the Creator too august to be more directly approached."

There was here a pause. At length the colloquy was renewed by Doctor Ponnonner.

"It is not improbable, then, from what you have explained," said he, "that among the catacombs near the Nile, there may exist other mummies of the Scarabæus tribe, in a condition of vitality."

"There can be no question of it," replied the Count; "all the Scarabæi embalmed accidentally while alive, are alive now. Even some of those *purposely* so embalmed, may have been overlooked by their executors, and still remain in the tombs."

"Will you be kind enough to explain," I said, "what you mean by 'purposely so embalmed?' "

"With great pleasure," answered the Mummy, after surveying me leisurely through his eye-glass—for it was the first time I had ventured to address him a direct question.

"With great pleasure," said he. "The usual duration of man's life, in my time, was about eight hundred years. Few men died, unless by most extraordinary accident, before the age of six hundred; few lived longer than a decade of centuries; but eight were considered the natural term. After the discovery of the embalming principle, as I have already described it to you, it occurred to our philosophers that a laudable curiosity might be gratified, and, at the same time, the interests

of science much advanced, by living this natural term in instalments. In the case of history, indeed, experience demonstrated that something of this kind was indispensable. An historian, for example, having attained the age of five hundred, would write a book with great labor and then get himself carefully embalmed; leaving instructions to his executors *pro tem.*, that they should cause him to be revivified after the lapse of a certain period—say five or six hundred years. Resuming existence at the expiration of this time, he would invariably find his great work converted into a species of hap-hazard note-book—that is to say, into a kind of literary arena for the conflicting guesses, riddles, and personal squabbles of whole herds of exasperated commentators. These guesses, etc., which passed under the name of annotations or emendations, were found so completely to have enveloped, distorted, and overwhelmed the text, that the author had to go about with a lantern to discover his own book. When discovered, it was never worth the trouble of the search. After rewriting it throughout, it was regarded as the bounden duty of the historian to set himself to work, immediately, in correcting from his own private knowledge and experience, the traditions of the day concerning the epoch at which he had originally lived. Now this process of re-scription and personal rectification, pursued by various individual sages, from time to time, had the effect of preventing our history from degenerating into absolute fable."

"I beg your pardon," said Doctor Ponnonner at this point, laying his hand gently upon the arm of the Egyptian—"I beg your pardon, sir, but may I presume to interrupt you for one moment?"

"By all means, *sir*," replied the Count, drawing up.

"I merely wished to ask you a question," said the Doctor. "You mentioned the historian's personal correction of *traditions* respecting his own epoch. Pray, sir, upon an average, what proportion of these Kabbala were usually found to be right?"

"The Kabbala,[17] as you properly term them, sir, were generally discovered to be precisely on a par with the facts recorded in the un-re-written histories themselves; —that is to say, not one individual iota of either, was ever known, under any circumstances, to be not totally and radically wrong."

"But since it is quite clear," resumed the Doctor, "that at least five thousand years have elapsed since your entombment, I take it for granted that your histories at that period, if not your traditions, were sufficiently explicit on that one topic of universal interest, the Creation, which took place, as I presume you are aware, only about ten centuries before."[18]

"Sir!" said Count Allamistakeo.

The Doctor repeated his remarks, but it was only after much additional explanation, that the foreigner could be made to comprehend them. The latter at length said, hesitatingly:

"The ideas you have suggested are to me, I confess, utterly novel. During my time I never knew any one to entertain so singular a fancy as that the universe (or this world if you will have it so) ever had a beginning at all. I remember, once, and once only, hearing something remotely hinted, by a man of many speculations, concerning the origin *of the human race;* and by this individual the very word *Adam,* (or Red Earth)[19] which you make use of, was employed. He employed it, however, in a generical sense, with reference to the spontaneous germination from rank soil (just as a thousand of the lower *genera* of creatures are germinated)—the spontaneous germination, I say, of five vast hordes of men, simultaneously upspringing in five distinct and nearly equal divisions of the globe."

Here, in general, the company shrugged their shoulders, and one or two of us touched our foreheads with a very significant air. Mr. Silk Buckingham, first glanc-ing slightly at the occiput and then at the sinciput[20] of Allamistakeo, spoke as follows:—

"The long duration of human life in your time, together with the occasional practice of passing it, as you have explained, in instalments, must have had, indeed, a strong tendency to the general development and conglomeration of knowledge. I presume, therefore, that we are to attribute the marked inferiority of the old Egyptians in all particulars of science, when compared with the moderns, and more especially with the Yankees, altogether to the superior solidity of the Egyptian skull."

"I confess again," replied the Count with much suavity, "that I am somewhat at a loss to comprehend you; pray, to what particulars of science do you allude?"

Here our whole party, joining voices, detailed, at great length, the assumptions of phrenology and the marvels of animal magnetism.

Having heard us to an end, the Count proceeded to relate a few anecdotes, which rendered it evident that prototypes of Gall and Spurzheim had flourished and faded in Egypt so long ago as to have been nearly forgotten, and that the manœuvres of Mesmer were really very contemptible tricks when put in collation with the positive miracles of the Theban *savans,*[21] who created lice and a great many other similar things.

I here asked the Count if his people were able to calculate eclipses. He smiled rather contemptuously, and said they were.

This put me a little out, but I began to make other inquiries in regard to his astronomical knowledge, when a member of the company, who had never as yet opened his mouth, whispered in my ear that, for information on this head, I had better consult Ptolemy, (whoever Ptolemy is) as well as one Plutarch *de facie lunæ.*[22]

I then questioned the Mummy about burning-glasses and lenses, and, in general, about the manufacture of glass; but I had not made an end of my queries before the silent member again touched me quietly on the elbow, and begged me for God's sake to take a peep at Diodorus Siculus.[23] As for the Count, he merely asked me, in the way of reply, if we moderns possessed any such microscopes as would enable us to cut cameos in the style of the Egyptians. While I was thinking how I should answer this question, little Doctor Ponnonner committed himself in a very extraordinary way.

"Look at our architecture!" he exclaimed, greatly to the indignation of both the travelers, who pinched him black and blue to no purpose.

"Look," he cried with enthusiasm, "at the Bowling-Green Fountain in New York! or if this be too vast a contemplation, regard for a moment the Capitol at Washington, D. C.!"—and the good little medical man went on to detail very minutely the proportions of the fabric to which he referred. He explained that the portico alone was adorned with no less than four and twenty columns, five feet in diameter, and ten feet apart.

The Count said that he regretted not being able to remember, just at that moment, the precise dimensions of any one of the principal buildings of the city of Aznac, whose foundations were laid in the night of Time, but the ruins of which were still standing, at the epoch of his entombment, in a vast plain of sand to the westward of Thebes. He recollected, however, (talking of porticoes) that one affixed to an inferior palace in a kind of suburb called Carnac, consisted of a hundred and forty-four columns, thirty-seven feet each in circumference, and twenty-five feet apart. The approach of this portico, from the Nile, was through an avenue two miles long, composed of sphinxes, statues and obelisks, twenty, sixty, and a hundred feet in height. The palace itself (as well as he could remember) was, in one direction, two miles long, and might have been, altogether, about seven in cir-

cuit. Its walls were richly painted all over, within and without, with hieroglyphics. He would not pretend to *assert* that even fifty or sixty of the Doctor's Capitols might have been built within these walls, but he was by no means sure that two or three hundred of them might not have been squeezed in with some trouble. That palace at Carnac was an insignificant little building after all. He, (the Count) however, could not conscientiously refuse to admit the ingenuity, magnificence, and superiority of the Fountain at the Bowling-Green, as described by the Doctor. Nothing like it, he was forced to allow, had ever been seen in Egypt or elsewhere.

I here asked the Count what he had to say to our rail-roads.

"Nothing," he replied, "in particular." They were rather slight, rather ill-conceived, and clumsily put together. They could not be compared, of course, with the vast, level, direct, iron-grooved causeways,[24] upon which the Egyptians conveyed entire temples and solid obelisks of a hundred and fifty feet in altitude.

I spoke of our gigantic mechanical forces.

He agreed that we knew something in that way, but inquired how I should have gone to work in getting up the imposts on the lintels of even the little palace at Carnac.

This question I concluded not to hear, and demanded if he had any idea of Artesian wells; but he simply raised his eyebrows; while Mr. Gliddon, winked at me very hard, and said, in a low tone, that one had been recently discovered by the engineers employed to bore for water in the Great Oasis.

I then mentioned our steel; but the foreigner elevated his nose, and asked me if our steel could have executed the sharp carved work seen on the obelisks, and which was wrought altogether by edge-tools of copper.

This disconcerted us so greatly that we thought it advisable to vary the attack to Metaphysics. We sent for a copy of a book called the "Dial,"[25] and read out of it a chapter or two about something which is not very clear, but which the Bostonians call the Great Movement or Progress.

The Count merely said that Great Movements were awfully common things in his day, and as for Progress it was at one time quite a nuisance, but it never progressed.

We then spoke of the great beauty and importance of Democracy, and were at much trouble in impressing the Count with a due sense of the advantages we enjoyed in living where there was suffrage *ad libitum*, and no king.

He listened with marked interest, and in fact seemed not a little amused. When we had done, he said that, a great while ago, there had occurred something of a very similar sort. Thirteen Egyptian provinces determined all at once to be free, and so set a magnificent example to the rest of mankind. They assembled their wise men, and concocted the most ingenious constitution it is possible to conceive. For a while they managed remarkably well; only their habit of bragging was prodigious. The thing ended, however, in the consolidation of the thirteen states, with some fifteen or twenty others,

Figure Twenty-three. The fountain at the Bowling Green. The Count admits that even Egypt has nothing to match "the ingenuity, magnificence and superiority" of this edifice. The fountain was nicknamed "the riprap fountain" after the way the irregular stones are built up "riprap style." The fire is irrelevant to Poe's tale. Repeated funny references were made to the fountain in the press; they became especially frequent in the 1850s. The plate is from a Currier Lithograph (New York, 1845) reproduced from the Eno Collection, Prints Division, courtesy of the New York Public Library, Astor, Lenox and Tilden Foundations.

in the most odious and insupportable despotism that ever was heard of upon the face of the Earth.

I asked what was the name of the usurping tyrant.

As well as the Count could recollect, it was *Mob.*

Not knowing what to say to this, I raised my voice, and deplored the Egyptian ignorance of steam.

The Count looked at me with much astonishment, but made no answer. The silent gentleman, however, gave me a violent nudge in the ribs with his elbows—told me I had sufficiently exposed myself for once—and demanded if I was really such a fool as not to know that the modern steam engine is derived from the invention of Hero, through Solomon de Caus.[26]

We were now in imminent danger of being discomfited; but, as good luck would have it, Doctor Ponnonner, having rallied, returned to our rescue, and inquired if the people of Egypt would seriously pretend to rival the moderns in the all-important particular of dress.

The Count, at this, glanced downward to the straps of his pantaloons, and then, taking hold of the end of one of his coattails, held it up close to his eyes for some minutes. Letting it fall, at last, his mouth extended itself very gradually from ear to ear; but I do not remember that he said anything in the way of reply.

Hereupon we recovered our spirits, and the Doctor, approaching the Mummy with great dignity, desired it to say candidly, upon its honor as a gentleman, if the Egyptians had comprehended, at *any* period, the manufacture of either Ponnonner's lozenges, or Brandreth's pills.[27]

We looked, with profound anxiety, for an answer;—but in vain. It was not forthcoming. The Egyptian blushed and hung down his head. Never was triumph more consummate; never was defeat borne with so ill a grace. Indeed I could not endure the spectacle of the poor Mummy's mortification. I reached my hat, bowed to him stiffly, and took leave.

Upon getting home I found it past four o'clock, and went immediately to bed. It is now ten, A. M. I have been up since seven, penning these memoranda for the benefit of my family and of mankind. The former I shall behold no more. My wife is a shrew. The truth is, I am heartily sick of this life and of the nineteenth century in general. I am convinced that every thing is going wrong. Besides, I am anxious to know who will be President in 2045. As soon, therefore, as I shave and swallow a cup of coffee, I shall just step over to Ponnonner's and get embalmed for a couple of hundred years.

DIDDLING

Considered as One of the Exact Sciences[1]

Hey, diddle diddle,
The cat and the fiddle.

Since the world began there have been two Jeremys. The one wrote a Jeremiad about usury, and was called Jeremy Bentham. He has been much admired by Mr. John Neal, and was a great man in a small way. The other gave name to the most important of the Exact Sciences,[2] and was a great man in a *great* way—I may say, indeed, in the very greatest of ways.

Diddling—or the abstract idea conveyed by the verb to diddle—is sufficiently well understood. Yet the fact, the deed, the thing *diddling,* is somewhat difficult to define. We may get, however, at a tolerably distinct conception of the matter in hand, by defining—not the thing, diddling, in itself—but man, as an animal that diddles. Had Plato but hit upon this, he would have been spared the affront of the picked chicken.

Very pertinently it was demanded of Plato, why a picked chicken, which was clearly a "biped without feathers," was not, according to his own definition, a man?[3] But I am not to be bothered by any similar query. Man is an animal that diddles, and there is *no* animal that diddles *but* man. It will take an entire hen-coop of picked chickens to get over that.

What constitutes the essence, the nare, the principle of diddling is, in fact, peculiar to the class of creatures that wear coats and pantaloons. A crow thieves; a fox cheats; a weasel outwits; a man diddles. To diddle is his destiny. "Man was made to mourn,"[4] says the poet. But not so:—he was made to diddle. This is his aim—his object—his *end*. And for this reason when a man's diddled we say he's "done."

Diddling, rightly considered, is a compound, of which the ingredients are minuteness, interest, perseverance, ingenuity, audacity, *nonchalance*, originality, impertinence, and *grin*.

Minuteness:—Your diddler is minute. His operations are upon a small scale. His business is retail, for cash, or approved paper at sight. Should he ever be tempted into magnificent speculation, he then, at once, loses his distinctive features, and becomes what we term "financier." This latter word conveys the diddling idea in every respect except that of magnitude. A diddler may thus be regarded as a banker *in petto*—a "financial operation," as a diddle at Brobdignag. The one is to the other, as Homer to "Flaccus"[5]—as a Mastodon to a mouse—as the tail of a comet to that of a pig.

Interest:—Your diddler is guided by self-interest. He scorns to diddle for the mere *sake* of the diddle. He has an object in view—his pocket—and yours. He regards always the main chance. He looks to Number One. You are Number Two, and must look to yourself.

Perseverance:—Your diddler perseveres. He is not readily discouraged. Should even the banks break, he cares nothing about it. He steadily pursues his end, and

> Ut canis a corio nunquam
> absterrebitur uncto,[6]

so he never lets go of his game.

Ingenuity:—Your diddler is ingenious. He has constructiveness large. He understands plot. He invents and circumvents. Were he not Alexander he would be Diogenes.[7] Were he not a diddler, he would be a maker of patent rat-traps or an angler for trout.

Audacity:—Your diddler is audacious. —He is a bold man. He carries the war into Africa. He conquers all by assault. He would not fear the daggers of the Frey Herren. With a little more prudence Dick Turpin would have made a good diddler; with a trifle less blarney, Daniel O'Connell; with a pound or two more brains, Charles the Twelfth.[8]

Nonchalance:—Your diddler is *nonchalant*. He is not at all nervous. He never *had* any nerves. He is never seduced into a flurry. He is never put out—unless put out of doors. He is cool—cool as a cucumber. He is calm—"calm as a smile from Lady Bury." He is easy—easy as an old glove, or the damsels of ancient Baiæ.[9]

Originality:—Your diddler is original— conscientiously so. His thoughts are his own. He would scorn to employ those of another. A stale trick is his aversion. He would return a purse, I am sure, upon discovering that he had obtained it by an unoriginal diddle.

Impertinence:—Your diddler is impertinent. He swaggers. He sets his arms a-kimbo. He thrusts his hands in his trowsers' pockets. He sneers in your face. He treads on your corns. He eats your dinner, he drinks your wine, he borrows your money, he pulls your nose, he kicks your poodle, and he kisses your wife.

Grin:—Your *true* diddler winds up all with a grin. But this nobody sees but himself. He grins when his daily work is done —when his allotted labors are accomplished—at night in his own closet, and altogether for his own private entertainment. He goes home. He locks his door. He divests himself of his clothes. He puts out his candle. He gets into bed. He places his head upon the pillow. All this done, and your diddler *grins*. This is no hypothesis. It is a matter of course. I reason *à priori*,[10] and a diddle would be *no* diddle without a grin.

The origin of the diddle is referrible to the infancy of the Human Race. Perhaps the first diddler was Adam. At all events, we can trace the science back to a very remote period of antiquity. The moderns, however, have brought it to a perfection never dreamed of by our thick-headed progenitors. Without pausing to speak of the "old saws," therefore, I shall content myself with a compendious account of some of the more "modern instances."

A very good diddle is this. A housekeeper in want of a sofa, for instance, is seen to go in and out of several cabinet warehouses. At length she arrives at one offering an excellent variety. She is accosted, and invited to enter, by a polite and voluble individual at the door. She finds a sofa well adapted to her views, and, upon inquiring the price, is surprised and delighted to hear a sum named at least twenty per cent. lower than her expectations. She hastens to make the purchase, gets a bill and receipt, leaves her address, with a request that the article be sent home as speedily as possible, and retires amid a profusion of bows from the shop-keeper. The night arrives and no sofa. The next day passes, and still none. A servant is sent to make inquiry about the delay. The whole transaction is denied. No sofa has been sold—no money received—except by the diddler who played shop-keeper for the nonce.

Our cabinet warehouses are left entirely unattended, and thus afford every facility for a trick of this kind. Visiters enter, look at furniture, and depart unheeded and unseen. Should any one wish to purchase, or to inquire the price of an article, a bell is at hand, and this is considered amply sufficient.

Again, quite a respectable diddle is this. A well-dressed individual enters a shop; makes a purchase to the value of a dollar; finds, much to his vexation, that he has left his pocket-book in another coat pocket; and so says to the shop-keeper—

"My dear sir, never mind!—just oblige me, will you, by sending the bundle home? But stay! I really believe that I have nothing less than a five dollar bill, even *there*. However, you can send four dollars in change *with* the bundle, you know."

"Very good, sir," replies the shop-keeper, who entertains, at once, a lofty opinion of the high-mindedness of his customer. "I know fellows," he says to himself, "who would just have put the goods under their arm, and walked off with a promise to call and pay the dollar as they came by in the afternoon."

A boy is sent with the parcel and change. On the route, quite accidentally, he is met by the purchaser, who exclaims:

"Ah! this is my bundle, I see—I thought you had been home with it, long ago. Well, go on! My wife, Mrs. Trotter, will give you the five dollars—I left instructions with her to that effect. The change you might as well give to *me*—I shall want some silver for the Post Office. Very good! One, two,—is this a good quarter? —three, four—quite right! Say to Mrs. Trotter that you met me, and be sure now and *do* not loiter on the way."

The boy doesn't loiter at all—but he is a very long time in getting back from his errand—for no lady of the precise name of Mrs. Trotter is to be discovered. He consoles himself, however, that he has not been such a fool as to leave the goods without the money, and re-entering his shop with a self, satisfied air, feels sensibly hurt and indignant when his master asks him what has become of the change.

A very simple diddle, indeed, is this. The captain of a ship which is about to sail, is presented by an official looking person, with an unusually moderate bill of city charges. Glad to get off so easily, and confused by a hundred duties pressing upon him all at once, he discharges the claim forthwith. In about fifteen minutes, another and less reasonable bill is handed him by one who soon makes it evident that the first collector was a diddler, and the original collection a diddle.

And here, too, is a somewhat similar thing. A steamboat is casting loose from the wharf. A traveller, portmanteau in hand, is discovered running towards the wharf at full speed. Suddenly, he makes a dead halt, stoops, and picks up something from the ground in a very agitated manner. It is a pocket book, and—"Has any gentleman lost a pocket book?" he cries. No one can say that he has exactly lost a pocket-book; but a great excitement ensues, when the treasure trove is found to be of value. The boat however, must not be detained.

"Time and tide wait for no man," says the captain.

"For God's sake, stay only a few minutes," says the finder of the book—"the true claimant will presently appear."

"Can't wait!" replies the man in authority; "cast off there, d'ye hear?"

"What *am* I to do?" asks the finder, in great tribulation. "I am about to leave the country for some years, and I cannot conscientiously retain this large amount in my possession. I beg your pardon, sir," [here he addresses a gentleman on shore,] "but you have the air of an honest man. *Will* you confer upon me the favor of taking charge of this pocket-book —I *know* I can trust you—and of advertising it? The notes, you see, amount to a very considerable sum. The owner will, no doubt, insist upon rewarding you for your trouble—"

"*Me!*—no, *you!*—it was *you* who found the book."

"Well, if you *must* have it so—I will take a small reward—just to satisfy your scruples. Let me see—why these notes are all hundreds—bless my soul! a hundred is too much to take—fifty would be quite enough, I am sure—"

"Cast off there!" says the captain.

"But then I have no change for a hundred, and upon the whole, *you* had better—"

"Cast off there!" says the captain.

"Never mind!" cries the gentleman on shore, who has been examining his own pocket-book for the last minute or so— "never mind! *I* can fix it—here is a fifty on the Bank of North America—throw me the book."

And the over-conscientious finder takes the fifty with marked reluctance, and throws the gentleman the book, as desired, while the steamboat fumes and fizzes on her way. In about half an hour after her departure, the "large amount" is seen to be a "counterfeit presentment," and the whole thing a capital diddle.

A bold diddle is this. A camp-meeting, or something similar, is to be held at a certain spot which is accessible only by means of a free bridge. A diddler stations himself upon this bridge, respectfully informs all passers by of the new county law, which establishes a toll of one cent for foot passengers, two for horses and donkeys, and so forth, and so forth. Some grumble but all submit, and the diddler goes home a wealthier man by some fifty or sixty dollars well earned. This taking a toll from a great crowd of people is an excessively troublesome thing.

A neat diddle is this. A friend holds one of the diddler's promises to pay, filled up and signed in due form, upon the ordinary blanks printed in red ink. The diddler purchases one or two dozen of these blanks, and every day dips one of them in his soup, makes his dog jump for it, and finally gives it to him as a *bonne bouche*. The note arriving at maturity, the diddler, with the diddler's dog, calls upon the friend, and the promise to pay is made the topic of discussion. The friend produces it from his *escritoire*,[11] and is in the act of reaching it to the diddler, when up jumps the diddler's dog and devours it forthwith. The diddler is not only surprised but vexed and incensed at the absurd behavior of his dog, and expresses his entire readiness to cancel the obligation at any moment when the evidence of the obligation shall be forthcoming.

A very minute diddle is this. A lady is insulted in the street by a diddler's accomplice. The diddler himself flies to her assistance, and, giving his friend a comfortable thrashing, insists upon attending the lady to her own door. He bows, with his hand upon his heart, and most respectfully bids her adieu. She entreats him, as her deliverer, to walk in and be introduced to her big brother and her papa. With a sigh, he declines to do so. "Is there no way, then, sir," she murmurs, "in which I may be permitted to testify my gratitude?"

"Why, yes, madam, there is. Will you be kind enough to lend me a couple of shillings?"

In the first excitement of the moment the lady decides upon fainting outright. Upon second thought, however, she opens her purse-strings and delivers the specie. Now this, I say, is a diddle minute—for one entire moiety of the sum borrowed has to be paid to the gentleman who had the trouble of performing the insult, and who had then to stand still and be thrashed for performing it.

Rather a small, but still a scientific diddle is this. The diddler approaches the bar of a tavern, and demands a couple of twists of tobacco. These are handed to him, when, having slightly examined them, he says:

"I don't much like this tobacco. Here, take it back, and give me a glass of brandy and water in its place."

The brandy and water is furnished and imbibed, and the diddler makes his way to the door. But the voice of the tavern-keeper arrests him.

"I believe, sir, you have forgotten to pay for your brandy and water."

"Pay for my brandy and water!—didn't I give you the tobacco for the brandy and water? What more would you have?"

"But sir, if you please, I don't remember that you paid for the tobacco."

"What do you mean by that, you scoundrel?—Didn't I give you back your tobacco? Isn't that your tobacco lying there?

Do you expect me to pay for what I did not take?"

"But, sir," says the publican, now rather at a loss what to say, "but sir—"

"But me no buts, sir," interrupts the diddler, apparently in very high dudgeon, and slamming the door after him, as he makes his escape.—"But me no buts, sir, and none of your tricks upon travellers."

Here again is a very clever diddle, of which the simplicity is not its least recommendation. A purse, or pocket-book, being really lost, the loser inserts in *one* of the daily papers of a large city a fully descriptive advertisement.

Whereupon our diddler copies the *facts* of this advertisement, with a change of heading, of general phraseology, and *address*. The original, for instance, is long, and verbose, is headed "A Pocket-Book Lost!" and requires the treasure, when found, to be left at No. 1 Tom street. The copy is brief, and being headed with "Lost" only, indicates No. 2 Dick, or No. 3 Harry street, as the locality at which the owner may be seen. Moreover, it is inserted in at least five or six of the daily papers of the day, while in point of time, it makes its appearance only a few hours after the original. Should it be read by the loser of the purse, he would hardly suspect it to have any reference to his own misfortune. But, of course, the chances are five or six to one, that the finder will repair to the address given by the diddler, rather than to that pointed out by the rightful proprietor. The former pays the reward, pockets the treasure and decamps.

Quite an analogous diddle is this. A lady of *ton* has dropped, somewhere in the street, a diamond ring of very unusual value. For its recovery, she offers some forty or fifty dollars reward—giving, in her advertisement, a very minute description of the gem, and of its settings, and declaring that, upon its restoration to No. so and so, in such and such Avenue, the reward will be paid *instanter*, without a single question being asked. During the lady's absence from home, a day or two afterwards, a ring is heard at the door of No. so and so, in such and such Avenue; a servant appears; the lady of the house is asked for and is declared to be out, at which astounding information, the visitor expresses the most poignant regret. His business is of importance and concerns the lady herself. In fact, he had the good fortune to find her diamond ring. But, perhaps it would be as well that he should call again. "By no means!" says the servant; and "By no means!" says the lady's sister and the lady's sister-in-law, who are summoned forthwith. The ring is clamorously identified, the reward is paid, and the finder nearly thrust out of doors. The lady returns, and expresses some little dissatisfaction with her sister and sister-in-law, because they happen to have paid forty or fifty dollars for a *fac-simile* of her diamond ring—a *fac-simile* made out of real pinchbeck[12] and unquestionable paste.

But as there is really no end to diddling, so there would be none to this essay, were I even to hint at half the variations, or inflections, of which this science is susceptible. I must bring this paper, perforce, to a conclusion, and this I cannot do better than by a summary notice of a very decent, but rather elaborate diddle, of which our own city was made the theatre, not very long ago, and which was subsequently repeated with success, in other still more verdant localities of the Union. A middle-aged gentleman arrives in town from parts unknown. He is remarkably precise, cautious, staid, and deliberate in his demeanor. His dress is scrupulously neat, but plain, unostentatious. He wears a white cravat, an ample waistcoat, made with an eye to comfort alone; thick-soled cosy-looking shoes, and pantaloons without straps. He has the whole air, in fact, of your well-to-do, sobersided, exact, and respectable "man of business," *par excellence*—one of the stern and outwardly hard, internally soft, sort of people that we see in the crack high comedies[13]—fellows whose words are so many bonds,

and who are noted for giving away guineas, in charity, with the one hand, while, in the way of mere bargain, they exact the uttermost fraction of a farthing, with the other.

He makes much ado before he can get suited with a boarding house. He dislikes children. He has been accustomed to quiet. His habits are methodical—and then he would prefer getting into a private and respectable small family, piously inclined. Terms, however, are no object —only he must insist upon settling his bill on the first of every month, (it is now the second) and begs his landlady, when he finally obtains one to his mind, *not* on any account, to forget his instructions upon this point—but to send in a bill, *and* receipt, precisely at ten o'clock, on the *first* day of every month, and under no circumstances to put it off to the second.

These arrangements made, our man of business rents an office in a reputable rather than in a fashionable quarter of the town. There is nothing he more despises than pretence. "Where there is much show," he says, "there is seldom anything very solid behind"—an observation which so profoundly impresses his landlady's fancy, that she makes a pencil memorandum of it forthwith, in her great family Bible, on the broad margin of the Proverbs of Solomon.

The next step is to advertise, after some such fashion as this, in the principal business sixpennies of this city—the pennies are eschewed as not "respectable"—and as demanding payment for all advertisements in advance. Our man of business holds it as a point of his faith that work should never be paid for until done.

WANTED.—The advertisers, being about to commence extensive business operations in this city, will require the services of three or four intelligent and competent clerks, to whom a liberal salary will be paid. The very best recommendations, not so much for capacity, as for integrity, will be expected. Indeed, as the duties to be performed, involve high responsibilities, and large amounts of money must necessarily pass through the hands of those engaged, it is deemed advisable to demand a deposit of fifty dollars from each clerk employed. No person need apply, therefore, who is not prepared to leave this sum in the possession of the advertisers, and who cannot furnish the most satisfactory testimonials of morality. Young gentlemen piously inclined will be preferred. Application should be made between the hours of ten and eleven, A. M., and four and five, P. M., of Messrs.

BOGS, HOGS, LOGS, FROGS,
& Co.[14]
No. 110 Dog Street.

By the thirty-first day of the month, this advertisement has brought to the office of Messrs. Bogs, Hogs, Logs, Frogs and Company, some fifteen or twenty young gentlemen piously inclined. But our man of business is in no hurry to conclude a contract with any—no man of business is *ever* precipitate—and it is not until the most rigid catechism in respect to the piety of each young gentleman's inclination, that his services are engaged and his fifty dollars receipted for, *just* by way of proper precaution, on the part of the respectable firm of Bogs, Hogs, Logs, Frogs and Company. On the morning of the first day of the next month, the landlady does *not* present her bill according to promise—a piece of neglect for which the comfortable head of the house ending in *ogs*, would no doubt have chided her severely, could he have been prevailed upon to remain in town a day or two for that purpose.

As it is, the constables have had a sad time of it, running hither and thither, and all they can do is to declare the man of business most emphatically, a "hen knee high"—by which some persons imagine them to imply that, in fact, he is n. e. i.— by which again the very classical phrase *non est inventus*,[15] is supposed to be understood. In the meantime the young gen-

tlemen, one and all, are somewhat less piously inclined than before, while the landlady purchases a shilling's worth of the best Indian rubber, and very carefully obliterates the pencil memorandum that some fool has made in her great family Bible, on the broad margin of the Proverbs of Solomon.

THE BUSINESS MAN[1]

Method is the soul of business.
Old Saying

I am a business man. I am a methodical man. Method is *the* thing, after all. But there are no people I more heartily despise, than your eccentric fools who prate about method without understanding it; attending strictly to its letter, and violating its spirit. These fellows are always doing the most out-of-the-way things in what they call an orderly manner. Now here—I conceive—is a positive paradox. True method appertains to the ordinary and the obvious alone, and cannot be applied to the *outré*.[2] What definite idea can a body attach to such expressions as "methodical Jack o' Dandy," or "a systematical Will o' the Wisp"?

My notions upon this head might not have been so clear as they are, but for a fortunate accident which happened to me when I was a very little boy. A goodhearted old Irish nurse (whom I shall not forget in my will) took me up one day by the heels, when I was making more noise than was necessary, and, swinging me round two or three times, d——d my eyes for "a skreeking little spalpeen," and then knocked my head into a cocked hat against the bedpost. This, I say, decided my fate and made my fortune. A bump arose at once on my sinciput, and turned out to be as pretty an organ of *order*[3] as one shall see on a summer's day. Hence that positive appetite for system and regularity which has made me the distinguished man of business that I am.

If there is anything on earth I hate, it

is a genius. Your geniuses are all arrant asses—the greater the genius the greater the ass—and to this rule there is no exception whatever. Especially, you cannot make a man of business out of a genius, any more than money out of a Jew, or the best nutmegs out of pineknots. The creatures are always going off at a tangent into some fantastic employment, or ridiculous speculation, entirely at variance with the "fitness of things," and having no business whatever to be considered as a business at all. Thus you may tell these characters immediately by the nature of their occupations. If you ever perceive a man setting up as a merchant, or a manufacturer; or going into the cotton or tobacco trade, or any of those eccentric pursuits; or getting to be a dry-goods dealer, or soap-boiler, or something of that kind; or pretending to be a lawyer, or a blacksmith, or a physician—anything out of the usual way—you may set him down at once as a genius, and then, according to the rule-of-three,[4] he's an ass.

Now I am not in any respect a genius, but a regular business man. My Day-book and Ledger will evince this in a minute. They are well kept, though I say it myself; and, in my general habits of accuracy and punctuality, I am not to be beat by a clock.—Moreover, my occupations have been always made to chime in with the ordinary habitudes of my fellowmen. Not that I feel the least indebted, upon this score, to my exceedingly weak-minded parents, who, beyond doubt, would have made an arrant genius of me at last, if my guardian angel had not come, in good time, to the rescue. In biography the truth is everything, and in autobiography it is especially so—yet I scarcely hope to be believed when I state, however solemnly, that my poor father put me, when I was about fifteen years of age, into the counting-house of what he termed "a respectable hardware and commission merchant doing a capital bit of business!" A capital bit of fiddlestick! However, the consequence of this folly was, that in two or three days, I had to be sent home to my button-headed family in a high state of fever, and with a most violent and dangerous pain in the sinciput, all round about my organ of order. It was nearly a gone case with me then—just touch-and-go for six weeks—the physicians giving me up and all that sort of thing. But, although I suffered much, I was a thankful boy in the main. I was saved from being a "respectable hardware and commission merchant, doing a capital bit of business," and I felt grateful to the protuberance which had been the means of my salvation, as well as to the kind-hearted female who had originally put these means within my reach.

The most of boys run away from home at ten or twelve years of age, but I waited till I was sixteen. I don't know that I should have gone, even then, if I had not happened to hear my old mother talk about setting me up on my own hook in the grocery way. The *grocery* way!—only think of that! I resolved to be off forthwith, and try and establish myself in some *decent* occupation, without dancing attendance any longer upon the caprices of these eccentric old people, and running the risk of being made a genius of in the end. In this project I succeeded perfectly well at the first effort, and by the time I was fairly eighteen, found myself doing an extensive and profitable business in the Tailor's Walking-Advertisement line.

I was enabled to discharge the onerous duties of this profession, only by that rigid adherence to system which formed the leading feature of my mind. A scrupulous *method* characterised my actions, as well as my accounts. In my case, it was method—not money—which made the man: at least all of him that was not made by the tailor whom I served. At nine, every morning, I called upon that individual for the clothes of the day. Ten o'clock found me in some fashionable promenade or other place of public amusement. The precise regularity with which I turned my handsome person about, so as to bring successively into view every portion of the suit upon my back, was the admiration of all the knowing men in the trade. Noon never passed without my bringing home a customer to the house of my employers, Messieurs Cut and Comeagain. I say this proudly, but with tears in my eyes—for the firm proved themselves the basest of ingrates. The little account about which we quarreled and finally parted, cannot, in any item, be thought overcharged, by gentlemen really conversant with the nature of the business. Upon this point, however, I feel a degree of proud satisfaction in permitting the reader to judge for himself. My bill ran thus:

niences could be got out of a sheet of foolscap. But it is needless to say that I stood upon the *principle* of the thing. Business is business, and should be done in a business way. There was no *system* whatever in swindling me out of a penny—a clear fraud of fifty per cent.—no *method* in any respect. I left, at once, the employment of Messieurs Cut and Comeagain, and set up in the Eye-Sore line by myself—one of the most lucrative, respectable, and independent of the ordinary occupations.

My strict integrity, economy, and rigorous business habits, here again came into play. I found myself driving a flourishing trade, and soon became a marked

Messrs. Cut and Comeagain, Merchant Tailors.

	To Peter Proffit, Walking Advertiser,	Drs.
July 10.	To promenade, as usual, and customer brought home,	$00 25
July 11.	To do do do	25
July 12.	To one lie, second class; damaged black cloth sold for invisible green,	25
July 13.	To one lie, first class, extra quality and size; recommending milled sattinet as broadcloth,	75
July 20.	To purchasing bran new paper shirt collar or dickey, to set off gray Petersham,[5]	2
Aug. 15.	To wearing double-padded bobtail frock, (thermometer 106 in the shade,)	25
Aug. 16.	Standing on one leg three hours to show off new-style strapped pants at 12½ cts. per leg, per hour,	37½
Aug. 17.	To promenade, as usual, and large customer brought (fat man,)	50
Aug. 18.	To do do do (medium size,)	25
Aug. 19.	To do do do (small man and bad pay,)	6
		$2 95½

The item chiefly disputed in this bill was the very moderate charge of two pennies for the dickey. Upon my word of honor, this *was not* an unreasonable price for that dickey. It was one of the cleanest and prettiest little dickeys I ever saw; and I have good reason to believe that it effected the sale of three Petershams. The elder partner of the firm, however, would allow me only one penny of the charge, and took it upon himself to show in what manner four of the same sized conve-

man upon 'Change.[6] The truth is, I never dabbled in flashy matters, but jogged on in the good old sober routine of the calling—a calling in which I should, no doubt, have remained to the present hour; but for a little accident which happened to me in the prosecution of one of the usual business operations of the profession. Whenever a rich old hunks, or prodigal heir, or bankrupt corporation, gets into the notion of putting up a palace, there is no such thing in the world as stopping either of them, and this every intelligent person knows. The fact in question is indeed the basis of the Eye-Sore trade. As soon, therefore, as a building-project is fairly afoot by one of these parties, we merchants secure a nice corner of the lot in contemplation, or a prime little situation just adjoining or right in front. This done, we wait until the palace is half way up, and then we pay some tasty architect to run us up an ornamental mud hovel, right against it; or a Down-East or Dutch Pagoda, or a pig-sty, or an ingenious little bit of fancy work, either Esquimau, Kickapoo, or Hottentot. Of course, we can't afford to take these structures down under a bonus of five hundred per cent. upon the prime cost of our lot and plaster. *Can* we? I ask the question. I ask it of business men. It would be irrational to suppose that we can. And yet there was a rascally corporation which asked me to do this very thing—this *very thing!* I did not reply to their absurd proposition, of course; but I felt it a duty to go that same night, and lamp-black the whole of their palace. For this the unreasonable villains clapped me into jail; and the gentlemen of the Eye-Sore trade could not well avoid cutting my connexion when I came out.

The Assault and Battery business, into which I was now forced to adventure for a livelihood, was somewhat ill-adapted to the delicate nature of my constitution; but I went to work in it with a good heart, and found my account, here as heretofore, in those stern habits of methodical accuracy which had been thumped into me by that delightful old nurse—I would indeed be the basest of men not to remember her well in my will. By observing, as I say, the strictest system in all my dealings, and keeping a well regulated set of books, I was enabled to get over many serious difficulties, and, in the end, to establish myself very decently in the profession. The truth is, that few individuals, in any line, did a snugger little business than I. I will just copy a page or so out of my Day-

Book; and this will save me the necessity of blowing my own trumpet—a contemptible practice, of which no high-minded man will be guilty. Now, the Day-Book is a thing that don't lie.

"Jan. 1.—New Year's day. Met Snap in the street, groggy. Mem—he'll do. Met Gruff shortly afterwards, blind drunk. Mem—he'll answer too. Entered both gentlemen in my Ledger, and opened a running account with each.

"Jan. 2.—Saw Snap at the Exchange, and went up and trod on his toe. Doubled his fist, and knocked me down. Good!—got up again. Some trifling difficulty with Bag, my attorney. I want the damages at a thousand, but he says that, for so simple a knock-down, we can't lay them at more than five hundred. Mem—must get rid of Bag—no *system* at all.

"Jan. 3.—Went to the theatre, to look for Gruff. Saw him sitting in a side box, in the second tier, between a fat lady and a lean one. Quizzed[7] the whole party through an opera glass, till I saw the fat lady blush and whisper to G. Went round, then, into the box, and put my nose within reach of his hand. Wouldn't pull it—no go. Blew it, and tried again—no go. Sat down then, and winked at the lean lady, when I had the high satisfaction of finding him lift me up by the nape of the neck, and fling me over into the pit. Neck dislocated, and right leg capitally splintered. Went home in high glee, drank a bottle of champagne, and booked the young man for five thousand. Bag says it'll do.

"Feb. 15.—Compromised the case of Mr. Snap. Amount entered in Journal—fifty cents—which see.

"Feb. 16.—Cast by that villain, Gruff, who made me a present of five dollars. Costs of suit, four dollars and twenty-five cents. Nett profit—see Journal—seventy-five cents."

Now, here is a clear gain, in a very brief period, of no less than one dollar and twenty-five cents—this is in the mere cases of Snap and Gruff; and I solemnly assure the reader that these extracts are taken at random from my Day-Book.

It's an old saying, and a true one, however, that money is nothing in comparison with health. I found the exactions of the profession somewhat too much for my delicate state of body; and, discovering, at last, that I was knocked all out of shape, so that I didn't know very well what to make of the matter, and so that my friends, when they met me in the street, couldn't tell that I was Peter Profit at all, it occurred to me that the best expedient I could adopt, was to alter my line of business. I turned my attention, therefore, to Mud-Dabbling, and continued it for some years.

The worst of this occupation, is, that too many people take a fancy to it, and the competition is in consequence excessive. Every ignoramus of a fellow who finds that he hasn't brains in sufficient quantity to make his way as a walking advertiser, or an eye-sore-prig, or a salt and batter man, thinks, of course, that he'll answer very well as a dabbler of mud. But there never was entertained a more erroneous idea than that it requires no brains to mud-dabble. Especially, there is nothing to be made in this way without *method*. I did only a retail business myself, but my old habits of *system* carried me swimmingly along. I selected my street-crossing, in the first place, with great deliberation, and I never put down a broom in any part of the town *but that*. I took care, too, to have a nice little puddle at hand, which I could get at in a minute. By these means I got to be well known as a man to be trusted; and this is one-half the battle, let me tell you, in trade. Nobody ever failed to pitch *me* a copper, and got over *my* crossing with a clean pair of pantaloons. And, as my business habits, in this respect, were sufficiently understood, I never met with any attempt at imposition. I wouldn't have put up with it, if I had. Never imposing upon any one myself, I suffered no one to play the possum with me. The frauds

of the banks of course I couldn't help. Their suspension put me to ruinous inconvenience. These, however, are not individuals, but corporations; and corporations, it is very well known, have neither bodies to be kicked, nor souls to be damned.

I was making money at this business, when, in an evil moment, I was induced to merge it in the Cur-Spattering—a somewhat analogous, but, by no means, so respectable a profession. My location, to be sure, was an excellent one, being central, and I had capital blacking and brushes. My little dog, too, was quite fat and up to all varieties of snuff. He had been in the trade a long time, and, I may say, understood it. Our general routine was this:—Pompey, having rolled himself well in the mud, sat upon end at the shop door, until he observed a dandy approaching in bright boots. He then proceeded to meet him, and gave the Wellingtons a rub or two with his wool. Then the dandy swore very much, and looked about for a boot-black. There I was, full in his view, with blacking and brushes. It was only a minute's work, and then came a sixpence. This did moderately well for a time;—in fact, I was not avaricious, but my dog was. I allowed him a third of the profit, but he was advised to insist upon half. This I couldn't stand—so we quarreled and parted.

I next tried my hand at the Organ-Grinding for a while, and may say that I made out pretty well. It is a plain, straightforward business, and requires no particular abilities. You can get a music-mill for a mere song, and, to put it in order, you have but to open the works, and give them three or four smart raps with a hammer. It improves the tone of the thing, for business purposes, more than you can imagine. This done, you have only to stroll along, with the mill on your back, until you see tan-bark in the street, and a knocker wrapped up in buck skin.[8] Then you stop and grind; looking as if you meant to stop and grind till doomsday.

Presently a window opens, and somebody pitches you a sixpence, with a request to "Hush up and go on," &c. I am aware that some grinders have actually afforded to "go on" for this sum; but for my part, I found the necessary outlay of capital too great, to permit of my "going on" under a shilling.

At this occupation I did a good deal; but, somehow, I was not quite satisfied, and so finally abandoned it. The truth is, I labored under the disadvantage of having no monkey—and American streets are so muddy, and a Democratic rabble is so obtrusive, and so full of demnition mischievous little boys.

I was now out of employment for some months, but at length succeeded, by dint of great interest, in procuring a situation in the Sham-Post. The duties, here, are simple, and not altogether unprofitable. For example:—very early in the morning I had to make up my packet of sham letters. Upon the inside of each of these I had to scrawl a few lines—on any subject which occurred to me as sufficiently mysterious—signing all the epistles Tom Dobson, or Bobby Tompkins, or anything in that way. Having folded and sealed all, and stamped them with sham postmarks —New Orleans, Bengal, Botany Bay, or any other place a great way off—I set out, forthwith, upon my daily route, as if in a very great hurry. I always called at the big houses to deliver the letters, and receive the postage. Nobody hesitates at paying for a letter—especially for a double one—people are such fools—and it was no trouble to get round a corner before there was time to open the epistles. The worst of this profession was, that I had to walk so much and so fast; and so frequently to vary my route. Besides, I had serious scruples of conscience. I can't bear to hear innocent individuals abused —and the way the whole town took to cursing Tom Dobson and Bobby Tompkins, was really awful to hear. I washed my hands of the matter in disgust.

My eighth and last speculation has been in the Cat-Growing way. I have found this a most pleasant and lucrative business, and, really, no trouble at all. The country, it is well known, has become infested with cats—so much so of late, that a petition for relief, most numerously and respectably signed, was brought before the legislature at its last memorable session. The assembly, at this epoch, was unusually well-informed, and, having passed many other wise and wholesome enactments, it crowned all with the Cat-Act. In its original form, this law offered a premium for cat-*heads*, (fourpence a-piece) but the Senate succeeded in amending the main clause, so as to substitute the words "*tails*" for "heads." This amendment was so obviously proper, that the house concurred in it *nem. con.*[9]

As soon as the Governor had signed the bill, I invested my whole estate in the purchase of Toms and Tabbies. At first, I could only afford to feed them upon mice (which are cheap) but they fulfilled the Scriptural injunction at so marvellous a rate, that I at length considered it my best policy to be liberal, and so indulged them in oysters and turtle. Their tails, at the legislative price, now bring me in a good income; for I have discovered a way, in which, by means of Macassar oil,[10] I can force three crops in a year. It delights me to find, too, that the animals soon get accustomed to the thing, and would rather have the appendages cut off than otherwise. I consider myself, therefore, a made man, and am bargaining for a country seat on the Hudson.

THREE SUNDAYS IN A WEEK

"You hard-hearted, dunder-headed, obstinate, rusty, crusty, musty, fusty, old savage!" said I in fancy, one afternoon, to my grand uncle Rumgudgeon[1]—shaking my fist at him in imagination.

Only in imagination. The fact is, some trivial discrepancy *did* exist, just then, between what I said and what I had not the courage to say—between what I did and what I had half a mind to do.

The old porpoise, as I opened the drawing-room door, was sitting with his feet upon the mantel-piece, and a bumper of port in his paw, making strenuous efforts to accomplish the ditty,

> Remplis ton verre vide!
> Vide ton verre plein![2]

"My *dear* uncle," said I, closing the door gently, and approaching him with the blandest of smiles, "you are always so *very* kind and considerate, and have evinced your benevolence in so many—so *very* many ways—that—that I feel I have only to suggest this little point to you once more to make sure of your full acquiescence."

"Hem!" said he, "good boy! go on!"

"I am sure, my dearest uncle [you confounded old rascal!] that you have no design really, seriously, to oppose my union with Kate. This is merely a joke of yours, I know—ha! ha! ha!—how *very* pleasant you are at times."

"Ha! ha! ha!" said he, "curse you! yes!"

"To be sure—of course! I *knew* you were jesting. Now, uncle, all that Kate and myself wish at present, is that you would oblige us with your advice as—as regards the *time—you* know, uncle—in short, when will it be most convenient for yourself, that the wedding shall—shall—come off, you know?"

"Come off, you scoundrel!—what do you mean by that? Better wait till it goes on."

"Ha! ha! ha!—he! he! he!—hi! hi! ·hi! —ho! ho! ho!—hu! hu! hu!—oh, that's good!—oh, that's capital—*such* a wit! But all we want, just *now*, you know, uncle, is that you would indicate the time precisely."

"Ah!—precisely?"

"Yes, uncle—that is, if it would be quite agreeable to yourself."

"Wouldn't it answer, Bobby, if I were to leave it at random—some time within

a year or so, for example?—*must* I say precisely?"

"*If* you please, uncle—precisely."

"Well, then, Bobby, my boy—you're a fine fellow, aren't you?—since you *will* have the exact time, I'll—why, I'll oblige you for once."

"Dear uncle!"

"Hush, sir!" [drowning my voice]—"I'll oblige you for once. You shall have my consent—and the *plum*,[3] we mus'n't forget the plum—let me see! when shall it be? To-day's Sunday—isn't it? Well, then, you shall be married precisely—*precisely*, now mind!—*when three Sundays come together in a week!* Do you hear me, sir! *What* are you gaping at? I say, you shall have Kate and her plum when three Sundays come together in a week—but not *till* then—you young scapegrace—not *till* then, if I die for it. You know me—*I'm a man of my word*—now be off!" Here he swallowed his bumper of port, while I rushed from the room in despair.

A very "fine old English gentleman," was my grand-uncle Rumgudgeon, but unlike him of the song, he had his weak points. He was a little, pursy, pompous, passionate, semicircular somebody, with a red nose, a thick scull, a long purse, and a strong sense of his own consequence. With the best heart in the world, he contrived, through a predominant whim of *contradiction*, to earn for himself, among those who only knew him superficially, the character of a curmudgeon.[4] Like many excellent people, he seemed possessed with a spirit of *tantalization*, which might easily, at a casual glance, have been mistaken for malevolence. To every request, a positive "No!" was his immediate answer; but in the end—in the long, long end—there were exceedingly few requests which he refused. Against all attacks upon his purse he made the most sturdy defence; but the amount extorted from him at last was, generally, in direct ratio with the length of the siege and the stubbornness of the resistance. In charity no one gave more liberally or with a worse grace.

For the fine arts, and especially for the belles lettres he entertained a profound contempt. With this he had been inspired by Casimir Périer, whose pert little query *"A quoi un poète est-il bon?"* he was in the habit of quoting, with a very droll pronunciation, as the *ne plus ultra* of logical wit. Thus my own inkling for the Muses had excited his entire displeasure. He assured me one day, when I asked him for a new copy of Horace, that the translation of *"Poeta nascitur non fit"* was "a nasty poet for nothing fit"—a remark which I took in high dudgeon. His repugnance to "the humanities" had, also, much increased of late, by an accidental bias in favor of what he supposed to be natural science. Somebody had accosted him in the street, mistaking him for no less a personage than Doctor Dubble L. Dee, the lecturer upon quack physics. This set him off at a tangent; and just at the epoch of this story—for story it is getting to be after all—my grand-uncle Rumgudgeon was accessible and pacific only upon points which happened to chime in with the caprioles of the hobby he was riding. For the rest, he laughed with his arms and legs, and his politics were stubborn and easily understood. He thought, with Horsley,[5] that "the people have nothing to do with the laws but to obey them."

I had lived with the old gentleman all my life. My parents, in dying, had bequeathed me to him as a rich legacy. I believe the old villain loved me as his own child—nearly if not quite as well as he loved Kate—but it was a dog's existence that he led me, after all. From my first year until my fifth, he obliged me with very regular floggings. From five to fifteen, he threatened me, hourly, with the House of Correction. From fifteen to twenty, not a day passed in which he did not promise to cut me off with a shilling. I was a sad dog, it is true—but then it was a part of my nature—a point of my faith. In Kate, however, I had a firm friend, and I knew it. She was a good girl, and told me very sweetly that I might have her

(plum and all) whenever I could badger my grand-uncle Rumgudgeon into the necessary consent. Poor girl!—she was barely fifteen, and without this consent, her little amount in the funds was not come-at-able until five immeasurable summers had "dragged their slow length along." What, then, to do? At fifteen, or even at twenty-one [for I had now passed my fifth olympiad] five years in prospect are very much the same as five hundred. In vain we besieged the old gentleman with importunities. Here was a *pièce de résistance* (as Messieurs Ude and Carême would say) which suited his perverse fancy to a T. It would have stirred the indignation of Job[6] himself, to see how much like an old mouser he behaved to us two poor wretched little mice. In his heart he wished for nothing more ardently than our union. He had made up his mind to this all along. In fact, he would have given ten thousand pounds from his own pocket (Kate's plum was *her own*) if he could have invented anything like an excuse for complying with our very natural wishes. But then we had been so imprudent as to broach the subject *ourselves*. Not to oppose it under such circumstances, I sincerely believe was not in his power.

I have said already that he had his weak points; but, in speaking of these, I must not be understood as referring to his obstinacy: which was one of his strong points—*"assurément ce n'était pas son faible."* When I mention his weakness I have allusion to a bizarre old-womanish superstition which beset him. He was great in dreams, portents, *et id genus omne* of rigmarole. He was excessively punctilious, too, upon small points of honor, and, after his own fashion, was a man of his word, beyond doubt. This was, in fact, one of his hobbies. The *spirit* of his vows he made no scruple of setting at naught, but the *letter* was a bond inviolable. Now it was this latter peculiarity in his disposition, of which Kate's ingenuity enabled us, one fine day, not long after our interview in the dining room, to take a very unexpected advantage; and, having thus, in the fashion of all modern bards and orators, exhausted, in *prolegomena*,[7] all the time at my command, and nearly all the room at my disposal, I will sum up in a few words what constitutes the whole pith of the story.

It happened then—so the Fates ordered it—that among the naval acquaintances of my betrothed, were two gentlemen who had just set foot upon the shores of England, after a year's absence, each, in foreign travel. In company with these gentlemen, my cousin and I, preconcertedly, paid uncle Rumgudgeon a visit on the afternoon of Sunday, October the tenth, —just three weeks after the memorable decision which had so cruelly defeated our hopes. For about half an hour the conversation ran upon ordinary topics; but at last, we contrived, quite naturally, to give it the following turn:

Capt. Pratt. "Well, I have been absent just one year.—Just one year to-day, as I live—let me see! yes!—this is October the tenth. You remember, Mr. Rumgudgeon, I called, this day year, to bid you good-bye. And by the way, it *does* seem something like a coincidence, does it not—that our friend Captain Smitherton, here, has been absent exactly a year also—a year to-day?"

Smitherton. "Yes! just one year to a fraction. You will remember, Mr. Rumgudgeon, that I called with Capt. Pratt on this very day, last year, to pay my parting respects."

Uncle. "Yes, yes, yes—I remember it very well—very queer, indeed! Both of you gone just one year. A very strange coincidence, indeed! Just what Doctor Dubble L. Dee would denominate an extraordinary concurrence of events. Doctor Dub—"

Kate. (Interrupting.) "To be sure, papa, it *is* something strange; but then Captain Pratt and Captain Smitherton didn't go altogether the same route, and that makes a difference, you know."

Uncle. "I don't know any such thing, you huzzey! How should I? I think it only makes the matter more remarkable. Doctor Dubble L. Dee"—

Kate. "Why, papa, Captain Pratt went round Cape Horn, and Captain Smitherton doubled the Cape of Good Hope."

Uncle. "Precisely!—the one went east and the other went west, you jade, and they both have gone quite round the world. By the bye, Doctor Dubble L. Dee"—

Myself, (hurriedly.) "Captain Pratt, you must come and spend the evening with us to-morrow—you and Smitherton—you can tell us all about your voyage, and we'll have a game of whist, and"—

Pratt. "Whist, my dear fellow—you forget. To-morrow will be Sunday. Some other evening"—

Kate. "Oh no, fie!—Robert's not *quite* so bad as that. To-*day's* Sunday."

Uncle. "To be sure—to be sure!"

Pratt. "I beg both your pardons—but I can't be so much mistaken. I know to-morrow's Sunday because"—

Smitherton, (much surprised.) "What *are* you all thinking about? Wasn't *yesterday* Sunday, I should like to know?"

All. "Yesterday, indeed! you *are* out!"

Uncle. "To-day's Sunday, I say—don't *I* know?"

Pratt. "Oh no!—to-morrow's Sunday."

Smitherton. "You are *all* mad—every one of you. I am as positive that yesterday was Sunday as I am that I sit upon this chair."

Kate, (jumping up eagerly.) "I see it—I see it all. Papa, this is a judgment upon you, about—about you know what. Let me alone, and I'll explain it all in a minute. It's a very simple thing, indeed. Captain Smitherton says that yesterday was Sunday: so it was; he is right. Cousin Bobby, and uncle and I say that to-day is Sunday: so it is; we are right. Captain Pratt maintains that to-morrow will be Sunday: so it will; he is right too. The fact is, we are all right, and thus *three Sundays have come together in a week.*"

Smitherton, (after a pause.) "By the bye,

Pratt, Kate has us completely. What fools we two are! Mr. Rumgudgeon, the matter stands thus: the earth, you know, is twenty-four thousand miles in circumference. Now this globe of the earth turns upon its own axis—revolves—spins round —these twenty-four thousand miles of extent, going from west to east, in precisely twenty-four hours. Do you understand, Mr. Rumgudgeon?"

Uncle. "To be sure—to be sure—Doctor Dub"—

Smitherton, (drowning his voice.) "Well, sir; that is at the rate of one thousand miles per hour. Now suppose that I sail from this position a thousand miles east. Of course, I anticipate the rising of the sun here at London, by just one hour. I see the sun rise one hour before you do. Proceeding, in the same direction, yet another thousand miles, I anticipate the rising by two hours—another thousand, and I anticipate it by three hours, and so on, until I go entirely round the globe, and back to this spot, when, having gone twenty-four thousand miles east, I anticipate the rising of the London sun by no

less than twenty-four hours; that is to say, I am a day *in advance* of your time. Understand, eh?"

Uncle. "But Dubble L. Dee"—

Smitherton, (speaking very loud.) "Captain Pratt, on the contrary, when he had sailed a thousand miles west of this position, was an hour, and when he had sailed twenty-four thousand miles west, was twenty-four hours, or one day, *behind* the time at London. Thus, with me, yesterday was Sunday—thus, with you, to-day is Sunday—and thus, with Pratt, to-morrow will be Sunday. And what is more, Mr. Rumgudgeon, it is positively clear that we are *all right;* for there can be no philosophical reason assigned why the idea of one of us should have preference over that of the other."

Uncle. "My eyes!—well, Kate—well, Bobby!—this *is* a judgment upon me, as you say. But I am a man of my word— *mark that!* you shall have her, boy (plum and all,) when you please. Done up, by Jove! Three Sundays all in a row! I'll go, and take Dubble L. Dee's opinion upon *that.*"

Notes

The Thousand-and-Second Tale of Scheherazade

1. *Tellmenow Isitsoörnot:* "Tell me now, is it so or not?"

the Zohar of Simeon Jochaides: The *Zohar* is a "commentary on the Pentateuch . . . in reality by Moses de Leon" (Pollin 3).

"Curiosities of American Literature": The author is Rufus Griswold. See "Angel of the Odd," note 2. Poe probably also had in mind his favorite treasure-trove of literary ideas, Isaac Disraeli's *Curiosities of Literature,* in which a passage speaks of "the fairy tales and the Arabian Nights' entertainments of science."

"Arabian Nights": A little over a hundred years had passed since the *Arabian Nights* had first been translated into European languages. Poe probably knew E. W. Lane's annotated translation (1839–1841); his tale was first published in the February 1845 *Godey's Lady's Book.* He used it again in *The Broadway Journal* (October 25, 1845).

2. "Shahriyár caused his wife to be beheaded . . . and thenceforth he made it his regular custom, everytime that he took a virgin to his bed, to kill her at the expiration of the night" (Lane translation).

3. specious pretence: "When the King . . . introduced himself to her, she wept; and he said to her, What aileth thee? She answered,

O King, I have a young sister, and I wish to take leave of her" (Lane translation).

he slept well: In the *Arabian Nights*, the king is sleepless.

a rat and a black cat: The first tale which Shahrazád (Scheherazade) tells is actually about "The Merchant and the Jinnee," though it contains subsidiary tales about animals—a gazelle, cow, calf, two black hounds and a mule.

4. "Better is the enemy of good," or, loosely, "Leave well enough alone."

5. In a literary magazine of Poe's day, "Cockney" meant more than a native of London's East End. See "The Angel of the Odd," note 5. The nonsense has to do with magazine style.

6. The coralites [Poe's note]. Poe means "coral-forming animals." His word, so spelled, is his invention; the *OED* lists corallite, a fossil coral.

7. "One of the most remarkable natural curiosities in Texas is a petrified forest, near the head of Pasigno river. It consists of several hundred trees, in an erect position, all turned to stone. Some trees, now growing, are partly petrified. This is a startling fact for natural philosophers, and must cause them to modify the existing theory of petrifaction." —*Kennedy*. [Poe's note]. He refers to *The Rise, Progress, and Prospects of the Republic of Texas* (London, 1841) by William Kennedy (I, p. 220).

Current atlases and gazetteers list no Pasigno river, though there is a Paisano Creek near the Glass Mountains. Poe continues:

This account, at first discredited, has since been corroborated by the discovery of a completely petrified forest, near the head waters of the Chayenne, or Chienne river, which has its source in the Black Hills of the Rocky chain.

There is scarcely, perhaps, a spectacle on the surface of the globe more remarkable, either in a geological or picturesque point of view, than that presented by the petrified forest, near Cairo. The traveller, having passed the tombs of the caliphs, just beyond the gates of the city, proceeds to the southward, nearly at right angles to the road across the desert to Suez, and after having travelled some ten miles up a low barren valley, covered with sand, gravel, and sea shells, fresh as if the tide had retired but yesterday, crosses

a low range of sandhills, which has for some distance run parallel to his path. The scene now presented to him is beyond conception singular and desolate. A mass of fragments of trees, all converted into stone, and when struck by his horse's hoof ringing like cast iron, is seen to extend itself for miles and miles around him, in the form of a decayed and prostrate forest. The wood is of a dark brown hue, but retains its form in perfection, the pieces being from one to fifteen feet in length, and from half a foot to three feet in thickness, strewed so closely together, as far as the eye can reach, that an Egyptian donkey can scarcely thread its way through amongst them, and so natural that, were it in Scotland or Ireland, it might pass without remark for some enormous drained bog, on which the exhumed trees lay rotting in the sun. The roots and rudiments of the branches are, in many cases, nearly perfect, and in some the worm-holes eaten under the bark are readily recognisable. The most delicate of the sap vessels, and all the finer portions of the centre of the wood, are perfectly entire, and bear to be examined with the strongest magnifiers. The whole are so thoroughly silicified as to scratch glass and be capable of receiving the highest polish.—*Asiatic Magazine* [Poe's note]. *Asiatic Journal*, III (August 1844), p. 359.

8. The Mammoth Cave of Kentucky [Poe's note].

9. In Iceland, 1783 [Poe's note].

10. "During the eruption of Hecla, in 1766, clouds of this kind produced such a degree of darkness that, at Glaumba, which is more than fifty leagues from the mountain, people could only find their way by groping. During the eruption of Vesuvius, in 1794, at Caserta, four leagues distant, people could only walk by the light of torches. On the first of May, 1812, a cloud of volcanic ashes and sand, coming from a volcano in the island of St. Vincent, covered the whole of Barbadoes, spreading over it so intense a darkness that, at mid-day, in the open air, one could not perceive the trees or other objects near him, or even a white handkerchief placed at the distance of six inches from the eye."—*Murray*, p. 215, *Phil. edit.* [Poe's note]. He refers to the *Encyclopaedia of Geography* (London, 1834) by Hugh Murray (1779–1846), which he knew in the American edition, revised by Thomas G. Bradford (Philadelphia, 1843).

11. "In the year 1790, in the Caraccas, during an earthquake, a portion of the granite soil sank and left a lake eight hundred yards in diameter, and from eighty to a hundred feet deep. It was a part of the Forest of Aripao which sank, and the trees remained green for several months under the water."—*Murray*, p. 221 [Poe's note]. See note 10. The passage apparently refers to Venezuela; there is a small populated place called Aripao at 7° 22 N., 65° 05 W.

12. The hardest steel ever manufactured may, under the action of a blow-pipe, be reduced to an impalpable powder, which will float readily in the atmospheric air [Poe's note]. A blowpipe is a tube used to direct air or gas under pressure on a flame, to produce extremely high temperatures.

13. The region of the Niger. See *Simmond's "Colonial Magazine"* [Poe's note].

14. The *Myrmeleon*—lion-ant. The term "monster" is equally applicable to small abnormal things and to great, while such epithets as "vast" are merely comparative. The cavern of the myrmeleon is *vast* in comparison with the hole of the common red ant. A grain of silex is, also, a "rock" [Poe's note].

15. The *Epidendron, Flos Aeris*, of the family of the *Orchideæ*, grows with merely the surface of its roots attached to a tree or other object, from which it derives no nutriment —subsisting altogether upon air [Poe's note]. See "How to Write a Blackwood Article," note 16.

16. The *Parasites*, such as the wonderful *Rafflesia Arnoldi* [Poe's note].

17. *Schouw* advocates a class of plants that grow upon living animals—the *Plantæ Epizoæ*. Of this class are the *Fuci* and *Algæ*.

Mr. J. B. Williams, of Salem, Mass., presented the "National Institute," with an insect from New Zealand, with the following description:—" 'The Hotte,' a decided caterpillar, or worm, is found growing at the foot of the *Rata* tree, with a plant growing out of its head. This most peculiar and most extraordinary insect travels up both the *Rata* and *Puriri* trees, and entering into the top, eats its way, perforating the trunk of the tree until it reaches the root, it then comes out of the root, and dies, or remains dormant, and the plant propagates out of its head; the body remains perfect and entire, of a harder substance than when alive. From this insect the natives make a coloring for tattooing" [Poe's note].

Joachim Frederic Schouw: Danish botanist (1789–1852).

18. In mines and natural caves we find a species of cryptogamous *fungus* that emits an intense phosphorescence [Poe's note].

19. The orchis, scabius and vallisneria [Poe's note].

Pollin (9) believes that the reference to "vallisneria" (which Poe spelled "valisneria" in the original text) is from Bernardin's *Etudes* in the 1797 edition of Hunter's translation.

20. "The corolla of this flower, (*Aristolochia Clematitis,*) which is tubular, but terminating upwards in a ligulate limb, is inflated into a globular figure at the base. The tubular part is internally beset with stiff hairs, pointing downwards. The globular part contains the pistil, which consists merely of a germen and stigma, together with the surrounding stamens. But the stamens, being shorter than even the germen, cannot discharge the pollen so as to throw it upon the stigma, as the flower stands always upright till after impregnation. And hence, without some additional and peculiar aid, the pollen must necessarily fall down to the bottom of the flower. Now, the aid that Nature has furnished in this case, is that of the *Tipula Pennicornis*, a small insect, which entering the tube of the corolla in quest of honey, descends to the bottom, and rummages about till it becomes quite covered with pollen; but, not being able to force its way out again, owing to the downward position of the hairs, which converge to a point like the wires of a mouse-trap, and being somewhat impatient of its confinement, it brushes backwards and forwards, trying every corner, till, after repeatedly traversing the stigma, it covers it with pollen sufficient for its impregnation, in consequence of which the flower soon begins to droop and the hairs to shrink to the side of the tube, effecting an easy passage for the escape of the insect."—*Rev. P. Keith*—*"System of Physiological Botany"* [Poe's note]. Patrick Keith, *Physiological Biology* (London, 1816).

21. The bees—ever since bees were—have been constructing their cells with just such sides, in just such number, and at just such inclinations, as it has been demonstrated (in a problem involving the profoundest mathe-

matical principles) are the very sides, in the very number, and at the very angles which will afford the creatures the most room that is compatible with the greatest stability of structure.

During the latter part of the last century, the question arose among mathematicians— "to determine the best form that can be given to the sails of a windmill, according to their varying distances from the revolving vanes, and likewise from the centres of revolution." This is an excessively complex problem; for it is, in other words, to find the best possible position at an infinity of varied distances, and at an infinity of points on the arm. There were a thousand futile attempts to answer the query on the part of the most illustrious mathematicians; and when, at length, an undeniable solution was discovered, men found that the wings of a bird had given it with absolute precision, ever since the first bird had traversed the air [Poe's note].

22. He observed a flock of pigeons passing betwixt Frankfort and the Indiana territory, one mile at least in breadth; it took up four hours in passing; which, at the rate of one mile per minute, gives a length of 240 miles; and, supposing three pigeons to each square yard, gives 2,230,272,000 pigeons. "*Travels in Canada and the United States*," by Lieut. F. Hall [Poe's note]. Francis Hall (1793–1868), journalist, editor and part owner of the New York *Commercial Advertiser* (see "The Mystery of Marie Rogêt"). His trip to visit Indian missions in Canada resulted in his book *Travels in Canada and the United States in 1816 and 1817* (1818).

23. Poe is describing a balloon. The "house" with its roof off is the gondola; the sand dropped is ballast.

24. "The earth is upheld by a cow of a blue color, having horns four hundred in number."—*Sale's Koran* [Poe's note]. Sale is George Sale (Pollin 3), English orientalist (1680–1736), who published a fine annotated translation of the *Koran* in 1734. Though the cow supporting the earth is in Moslem lore (see "Some Passages in the Life of a Lion," note 18), we have not found it, curiously, in Sale's *Koran*.

25. "The *Entozoa*, or intestinal worms, have repeatedly been observed in the muscles, and in the cerebral substance of men." —*See Wyatt's Physiology*, p. 143 [Poe's note].

26. On the great Western Railway, between London and Exeter, a speed of 71 miles per hour has been attained. A train weighing 90 tons was whirled from Paddington to Didcot (53 miles,) in 51 minutes [Poe's note].

27. The *Eccaleobion* [Poe's note]. "'. . . a machine heated by steam . . . for the hatching of birds by artificial heat'" (Varner).

28. Maelzel's Automaton Chess-player [Poe's note]. Haroun Alraschid was a famous caliph (born c. 766), best known as the hero in *The Arabian Nights*. Poe's note refers to a famous and ingenious fraud about which he wrote an article; the automaton chess player had, as one would suspect, a little man hidden inside.

29. Babbage's Calculating Machine [Poe's note]. Charles Babbage (c. 1790–1871) was an English mathematician who invented a calculating machine, but who failed to complete its construction because the government stopped its financial support of the project.

30. Poe is describing the printing press.

lead: type.

black matter: ink.

31. salamanders: See "X-ing a Paragrab," note 5.

chibouc: pipe.

32. *Chabert*, and since him, a hundred others [Poe's note]. John Xavier Chabert, "a charlatan of London" (Pollin 3). A passage in *Noctes Ambrosianæ* (1822–1835) explains the connection between Chabert and heat. "Shepherd" (James Hogg, the "Ettrick Shepherd") speaks in the supposedly Scottish dialect assigned to him: "I carena if the fermometer war at aught hunder and aughty. I'll eat het [hot broth on a hot day] hotchpotch against Mosshy Shaubert—only I'll no gae intil the oven. . . ." In a note, Shelton Mackenzie (see Bibliography under John Wilson) explains that "Shaubert" means "Monsieur Chabert, who, in those days appeared to have perfect impunity as far as the effects of heat were concerned."

33. The Electrotype [Poe's note]. This refers to a plating method used in printing: a wax, or lead mold type is coated electrically with copper or nickel; melted type metal is poured over the coating, but the printing surface is the copper or nickel.

34. *Wollaston* made of platinum for the field of views in a telescope a wire one eighteen-thousandth part of an inch in thickness.

It could be seen only by means of the microscope [Poe's note].

William Hyde Wollaston (1776–1828): An important British chemist and physicist. The wire Poe speaks of was a byproduct of Wollaston's development of a way to make platinum malleable.

35. Newton demonstrated that the retina beneath the influence of the violet ray of the spectrum, vibrated 900,000,000 of times in a second [Poe's note].

36. The Voltaic pile [Poe's note]; a battery. The "fluid" is electricity.

37. The Electro Telegraph transmits intelligence instantaneously—at least so far as regards any distance upon the earth [Poe's note].

38. The Electro Telegraph Printing Apparatus [Poe's note].

39. Common experiments in Natural Philosophy. If two red rays from two luminous points be admitted into a dark chamber so as to fall on a white surface, and differ in their length by 0.0000258 of an inch, their intensity is doubled. So also if the difference in length be any whole-number multiple of that fraction. A multiple by 2¼, 3¼, &c., gives an intensity equal to one ray only; but a multiple by 2½, 3½, &c., gives the result of total darkness. In violet rays similar effects arise when the difference in length is 0.000[0]157 of an inch; and with all other rays the results are the same—the difference varying with a uniform increase from the violet to the red.

Analogous experiments in respect to sound produce analogous results [Poe's note].

Poe's knowledge of physics is somewhat shaky. He tries to describe a demonstration of interference but fails to grasp certain concepts; the experiment is considerably more complex and sophisticated than he implies. The "two rays" must come from the same source, be split, and then relayed to a screen ("white surface") by mirrors. By "length," we must understand not the "wavelength" (of the red Poe describes, for example), but the relationship of that wavelength to the differences in the lengths of the paths which the rays travel from source to screen. If the path lengths differ by certain ratios of the wavelength, the effects of which Poe speaks occur. For example:

1. If the path lengths are equal, the intensity at the screen will be 4 times as great as the combined intensity of both beams.

2. If they differ by ½ (.0000129", for example, in the case of Poe's red rays), the screen receives no light (0 intensity). This is also true if they differ by 1½, 2½, 3½, etc.

3. If they are *equal*, or differ by ratios of 1, 2, 3, etc., the screen receives the full intensity of both beams.

4. If they differ by ¼, ¾, 1¼, 1¾, 2¼, 2¾, etc., the screen receives the same intensity as a *single* beam.

Light energy has not, as Poe implies, disappeared or multiplied: a diagram of the phenomena shows that in the second case above, for example, the light is "interferred" with and deflected elsewhere. Poe's figure for the violet rays, 0.000157, is a typographical error. He means 0.0000157. Only the first sentence of Poe's note appeared in *The Broadway Journal*. The rest (as well as expansions of other notes) saw print first in the posthumous Griswold edition (see the Introduction). The new material is supposed to be by Poe. The error appears first in Griswold, and is copied in subsequent editions.

40. Place a platina crucible over a spirit lamp, and keep it a red heat; pour in some sulphuric acid, which, though the most volatile of bodies at a common temperature, will be found to become completely fixed in a hot crucible, and not a drop evaporates—being surrounded by an atmosphere of its own, it does not, in fact touch the sides. A few drops of water are now introduced, when the acid immediately coming in contact with the heated sides of the crucible, flies off in sulphurous acid vapor, and so rapid is its progress, that the caloric of the water passes off with it, which falls a lump of ice to the bottom; by taking advantage of the moment before it is allowed to re-melt, it may be turned out a lump of ice from a red-hot vessel [Poe's note]. Poe used the obsolete chemical concept of caloric, or "stuff of heat."

41. The Daguerreotype [Poe's note]: an early photographic process.

42. Although light travels 200,000 miles in a second, the distance of what we suppose to be the nearest fixed star (Sireus) is so inconceivably great, that its rays would require *at least* three years to reach the earth. For stars beyond this 20—or even 1000 years—would be a moderate estimate. Thus, if they had

been annihilated 20 or 1000 years ago, we might still see them to-day, by the light which *started* from their surfaces, 20 or 1000 years in the past time. That many which we see daily are really extinct, is not impossible —not even improbable [Poe's note].

Some Words With a Mummy

1. Poe's device of providing a "margin of credibility" by having his narrator in an unusual state of mind even appears in humorous tales in which the credibility really isn't necessary. But the fact that it is just a device is good corrective to those who insist on seeing Poe's art as compulsive: for every narrator whose vision is induced by madness or fever, there exists one whose bad dreams are the result of too much cheese and stout.

Poe published "Some Words . . ." in the April 1845 *American (Whig) Review,* and used it again in *The Broadway Journal,* November 1, 1845. Much of the technical information about mummies he took from the *Encyclopedia Americana* (King).

2. Pollin (11) suggests that Dr. Ponnonner, the one who always swears upon his honor, is "just such a character as 'Dr. Swaim' or 'Dr. Brandreth,' whose very name suggests hypocritical rascality." See note 27 below.

3. Pollin (8) believes this is a reference to Barnum's New York Museum.

4. Sabretash: Poe probably picked this name out of *Fraser's Magazine,* in which a "Captain Orlando Sabertash"—a made-up name, of course—"wrote" letters to "Oliver Yorke" (one of William Maginn's pen names). A sabretache, sabretasch[e] or sabretash is a leather satchel which a cavalry officer wears hung from long straps from the left side of his sword-belt.

Egyptians: A burst of exciting Egyptological archeology and scholarship followed Napoleon's campaigns in Egypt. Interesting new information was newsworthy for decades—to a lesser extent, it is so even today. So Poe is playing on a topic he knows will interest his readers.

5. Nineteenth-century Egyptologists often complained that sites not already plundered in the past yielded treasures which were plundered by local assistants or in transit.

6. *platanus:* Poe either has his trees confused or is telling us that the sarcophagus is

a hoax. *Platanus* refers to the American sycamore; the Egyptian tree is *Ficus sycomorus.*

Mr. Gliddon: a real person, George Robins Gliddon (1809–1857), whom Poe had mentioned in his 1837 review of Stephens' *Arabia Petraea.* He spent much of his life in Egypt and served as U. S. Consul there, and a couple of years before Poe's story, published a work on Egypt, *Ancient Egypt* (1843). Pollin (8) points out many items in the Poe story which suggest Gliddon's *Ancient Egypt* as one probable source of story and details.

Allamistakeo: All-a-mistake—more evidence that Poe is telling us the mummy is fake.

7. scarabæus: a sacred beetle, symbol of resurrection to ancient Egyptians. See next item.

winged globe: Poe means the winged disk, an Egyptian motif thought to represent the sun. Both it and the scarabaeus are in fact symbols connected with burial.

8. a battery.

9. the white fibrous coat of the eye.

10. See "Mellonta Tauta," note 5. Pollin (8) notices Poe's "scornful picture" of Buckingham whom, after an early (1837) noncommittal reference, Poe deprecates in several later references. Pollin feels that Poe's hostility may have stemmed from his notice of Buckingham's *The Slave States of America* and from his jealousy of Buckingham's success as a lecturer.

11. *os sesamoideum pollicis pedis:* sesamoid bone of the big toe.

abductor muscle: a muscle which draws any part of the body from its normal position, or from the median line.

the fluid: electricity.

12. John Barnes (1761–1841) of the Park theatre, New York, an extremely popular actor who had come to America in 1816 and was still on the stage in the 1830s. Noted for his "gagging," his skill at stepping out of character for laughs, he is called "one of the funniest of entertainers."

13. Jennings: a tailor, apparently. We have been unable to identify him.

waterfall cravat: waterfall neckcloth or Mail-Coach necktie, a large, usually white neckcloth with folds spreading down over the knot like a waterfall. It was common from 1818 to the 1830s.

14. See "The Gold-Bug," note 11. Poe's

choice of embalming fluid is poor for reasons explained in Pollin (8).

15. electricity.

16. A popular topic for writers of the day; the technical term they used is "Catochus," "a peculiar form of catalepsy, in which the patient retains the use of his various senses, while the power of motion is entirely suspended, and presents an appearance which may easily be mistaken for death." W. W. Story, "Catochus," *The Boston Miscellany of Literature and Fashion* I, vi (June 1842), 248–251.

17. The Cabala is a system of traditional rabbinical interpretations of the Bible. When used as a synonym for "tradition," Cabala is a singular word.

18. Poe plays here on an extremely topical subject. Those sciences which deal with data which could reveal the age of the earth or the length of human existence upon it—geology, archeology, to some extent chemistry, etc.—underwent radical transformations in the few decades before this story was written. Estimates based on the Bible, compiled primarily by adding up the "begats," suggested a "Creation" 5,000 or 6,000 years ago. The new scientific data suggested far greater age, ultimately, millions of years. The change in thinking was enormously important to people of Poe's generation, coming with a shock comparable to that produced by the Copernican and Galilean revolution in astronomy three centuries before.

19. Adam (or Red Earth): The association of "Adam" with "earth" is traditional—see I Corinthians 15:20–22, 42–58. Poe's derivation is based on the Hebrew meaning. The word appears in both Hebrew characters and corresponding heiroglyphics in Gliddon's *Ancient Egypt* (Pollin 8).

20. occiput: back part of the head.

sinciput: front part of the head.

21. Gall and Spurzheim: See "The Imp of the Perverse," note 2.

Mesmer: Friedrich (or Franz) Anton Mesmer (1733?–1815), German physician who developed the system of treatment through hypnotism called mesmerism. See "The Facts in the Case of M. Valdemar," Section Preface.

Theban *savans*: Forrest cites a Biblical source —Ex. 8:16–18.

22. Ptolemy: It is not clear why Poe refers to Ptolemy (fl. 127–141 or 151) here, because

he lived far too late for the count. He did, however, summarize the findings of earlier astronomy.

de facie lunae: Concerning the phases of the moon. It is doubtful that the work is Plutarch's.

23. historian, first century B.C.E.

24. A famous Egyptian causeway from the Nile to the site of the Giza pyramids, 60 feet wide and ⅝ mile long is mentioned repeatedly, but we find no mention of its use of iron. Moreover, iron was practically unknown in Egypt until long after the period to which Poe refers.

25. The organ of the New England Transcendentalists, against whom Poe waged an unrelenting literary war.

26. Hero: (or Heron) of Alexandria (dates unknown—probably between the second century B.C.E. and the third century B.C.E.) is supposed to have built a kind of steam engine. His dates are, of course, far too late for Poe's count, who was entombed 5,050 years.

Solomon de Caus: Norman engineer (Pollin 3) who did pioneering work on the theory of steam power (1576–1626).

27. Ponnonner's lozenges: Pollin (11) feels that Ponnonner is probably based on a real name—possibly that of a patent medicine—not yet determined. He suggests a pun on "Upon my honor." See note 2 above.

Brandreth's pills: A well-known patent laxative, and something of a popular joke. Melville says, "How to cure . . . a whale's dyspepsia it were hard to say, unless by administering three or four boat loads of Brandreth's pills, and then running out of harm's way, as laborers do in blasting rocks."

Diddling

1. The original title, when Poe published this first in the October 14, 1843 *Saturday Courier*, was "Raising the Wind; or Diddling Considered as One of the Exact Sciences." He shortened it for republication in *Lloyd's Entertaining Journal*, January 14, 1845, and in *The Broadway Journal* of September 13, 1845. See Section Preface.

2. Jeremy Bentham (1748–1832): the English jurist and economic philosopher.

John Neal: "The allusion is to John Neal's *The Yankee; and Boston Literary Gazette*, a periodical whose No. 79 (July 1829) contained a picture and eulogistic notice of Jeremy Bentham, with a motto from Bentham's writings" (Harrison). Neal (1793–1876) is, in a curious sense, the "author" of this tale: this was one of the Folio Club tales (see Section Nine, "Literary Satires," page 351) and was to be told by "Mr. Snap." As Hammond and others note, "Mr. Snap is a caricature of John Neal."

"gave name . . . Exact Sciences": i.e., Jeremy Diddle. See Section Preface and note 1.

3. Plato says in the *Politicus*, Section 266, "Man is the plumeless genus of bipeds, birds are the plumed."

4. The line is from Robert Burns's "Man Was Made to Mourn":

> *Nature's law*
> *That man was made to mourn.*

5. *in petto:* in secret. See "The System of Dr. Tarr and Professor Fether," note 24.

at Brobdignag: on a huge scale. In Swift's *Gulliver's Travels*, Brobdignag is the land of giants.

as Homer to "Flaccus": "Flaccus" is the penname of Thomas Ward (1807–1873), whom Poe had boiled in oil in a March 1843 review of his *Passaic, a Group of Poems touching that river* (1842). Poe feels that Ward's poems, while not entirely devoid of merit, are near enough to being so that only the influence of a literary clique could have gotten them published. En route, Poe accuses Ward of stealing a poetic idea from an author who lives in Philadelphia (Poe himself).

6. The line is from Horace S. 2, 5, 83; Poe added the word "Ut" ("as") to create the parallel in his sentence: [As] a dog can't be scared away from a greasy hide.

7. Poe contrasts the great conqueror (356–323 B.C.E.) with the Cynic philosopher (c. 412–323 B.C.E.) who is supposed to have used a lantern to search for an honest man at noon. Alexander is supposed to meet Diogenes and ask him what he (Alexander) can do for him. Diogenes says, "Stand out of my light." Alexander is delighted, and says "If I were not Alexander . . . etc."

8. Frey Herren: Poe's allusion has eluded scholars. There is internal evidence that Poe knew the *Historia del famoso predicator Fray Gerundio de Campazas, alias Zotes* (1758) by José Francisco de Isla (1703–1781). This is a hilarious book about an intensely stupid priest whose name in English is Frey Gerund.

Had Poe heard the Spanish name "Gerundio" pronounced (the "G" is similar to the English "H"), he might have misremembered its English form as Herren. But if our conjecture is correct, there remains the problem of the daggers. Friar Gerund is a butcher of Latin and a murderer of history, but does not literally knife anyone, though he delivers a richly absurd sermon in praise of scourging. Invited to deliver a lucrative funeral sermon for a rascally scrivener, Friar Gerund asks his friend and advisor Friar Blas how to praise an unworthy man. Blas tells him to fake erudition, make the scrivener's faults sound like virtues, and praise the traditional skills of Letters and Arms: "behold him continually with his penknife in his hands cutting off the heads of quills as he might have done of Moors, Turks, Jews, and Infidels!"

Dick Turpin: Richard Turpin (1706–1739), English highwayman.

Daniel O'Connell: Irish nationalist (1775–1847) who used his organizational and oratorical skills at great mass meetings to agitate for reforms in British laws affecting Catholics. Poe's comments on O'Connell (Harrison IX, 59–60; 77) are not unsympathetic.

Charles the Twelfth: The forceful and resourceful king of Sweden (1682–1718; reigned 1697–1718). Poe's comment about brains seems odd. Perhaps Poe refers to his too-ambitious plan to invade Russia, which resulted in a serious defeat in 1709, or to his attempt to inspire his troops by his personal courage, which resulted in a bullet in his head at the siege of Halden. Perhaps Poe had been reading popular history books, in which this bright and cultured ruler was sometimes described as a simple-minded militarist.

9. Lady Bury: Lady Charlotte Susan Maria Bury (1775–1861), beauty, sentimental novelist, diarist, poetess, and lady-in-waiting to Princess (later Queen) Caroline. We have not located a source which says that Lady B's calmness is proverbial, but there is ample evidence that as faithful confidante of a princess accused of adultery and tried publically, she behaved with great restraint. One writer says she loved Caroline, but was perhaps *too* calm for the circumstances: she "expected this harassed and persecuted woman [*i.e.* Caroline] to be consistently calm, dignified and prudent. . . ." Lady B. counselled her

mistress in "appearances," urging her to stay in England and in the public eye, and thus avoid gossip; the Princess had apparently been involved sexually with a servant in Italy. Most of our data, however, comes ultimately from Lady B.'s *Diary*, and Poe's allusion might be ironic.

Baiæ: The classical name of Baia, a port in Italy, known in antiquity as a resort and noted for its luxury and licentiousness; allusions to it are common in imperial age writers.

10. *à priori:* See "The Imp of the Perverse," note 1 and "Bon-Bon," note 3.

11. *bonne bouche:* a good taste in the mouth.

escritoire: writing desk.

12. *ton:* tone, manners, breeding. If Poe had, in fact, been reading Lady Bury (see note 9), he would have encountered her comments about "that mysterious quality known as *ton*" in her novel *The Exclusives* (1830).

instanter: immediately.

pinchbeck: an alloy of copper, zinc and tin, used to imitate gold.

13. Compare this diddler to Charlie Goodfellow in the tale "Thou Art the Man" Charlie not only looks and behaves like him, but is also a swindler, and is compared to the hearty stage character.

14. Compare to Hoggs, Frogs, Bogs and Co. in "Thou Art the Man." See note 13 above. See also "X-ing a Paragrab," note 9.

15. "hen knee high" . . . *non est inventus:* It is not found, i.e., not to be found.

The Business Man

1. Poe's first title for this tale, in *Burton's Gentleman's Magazine* for February 1840, was "Peter Pendulum, the Business Man." In *The Broadway Journal* (August 2, 1845), he shortened it. Peter Pendulum suggests care and measurement; see "The Devil in the Belfry" for a similar humorous device, also involving clocks and method.

2. positive paradox: a hint that there *is* a literary joke lurking beneath this tale. There is a character by this name in "Some Passages in the Life of a Lion"—see that tale at note 11.

outré: see "Landor's Cottage," note 6.

3. spalpeen: See "Why the Little Frenchman . . . ," note 2.

sinciput: front part of the skull.

organ of *order:* Poe uses phrenological terminology—the blow gave the narrator a new bump, hence changed his faculties. See "Murders in the Rue Morgue," note 6, and "The Imp of the Perverse," note 1.

4. a mathematics term. If one knows three parts of a proportion, one can apply the "rule" to find the fourth.

5. milled sattinet (satinet): A cheap imitation satin.

Petersham: A good-quality heavy woolen cloth.

6. 'Change: slang for "The Exchange."

7. Quizzed = scrutinized. This is considered very rude; see "The Spectacles."

8. "tan bark in the street, and a knocker wrapped up in buck skin": i.e., a sick person's home. The door knocker is wrapped to quiet it, and tanbark spread in the street —tanbark is the soft bruised residue of tree bark which has been used in dyeing or tanning.

9. See "Thou Art the Man," note 9.

10. a kind of hair-oil.

Three Sundays in a Week

1. Rumgudgeon: "Rum" is contemporary slang for "bad" or "rotten." It can also mean "queer." "Gudgeon" has three meanings, each appropriate: a bait-fish ("Rotten fish"); a pivot at the end of the shaft in a wagon or carriage on which the wheel turns ("Rotten link," approximately); a person easily fooled or cheated (combined with "queer," it would mean a "queer, gullible fellow").

For information about publications of this tale in Poe's lifetime, see Section Preface.

2. Fill your empty glass! Empty your full glass!

3. Kate's money.

4. "fine . . . gentleman": The *Oxford Song Book* gives words and music to this traditional song about the hearty, brave, and hospitable gentleman who "feasted all the great," but "ne'er forgot the small."

scull: skull.

curmudgeon: See note 5 below.

5. Casimir Pierre Périer (1777–1832): illiberal French banker, statesman, and premier of France (1831–1832) under Louis Philippe. He worked to repress republicanism and re-

fused aid to the Polish revolutionists, though he helped Belgium gain independence.

"A quoi un poète est-il bon?": What's a poet good for?

Ne plus ultra: summit (thus far and no farther).

Horace: Quintus Horatius Flaccus, 65–68 B.C.E., Roman poet.

"Poeta nascitur non fit": The poet is born, not made. The quotation is from Florus (fl. 148–173?), *De Qualitate Vitae*, fragment 8.

dudgeon: Poe engages in some word-play—Rumgudgeon, curmudgeon, dudgeon.

Doctor Dubble L. Dee: i.e., LL. D. Mabbott (4) identifies him for us as Dionysius Lardner. See "The Thousand-and-Second Tale of Scheherazade."

Horsley: Samuel Horsley (1733–1808), English bishop and scientist, remembered especially for his controversy with theologically liberal Joseph Priestly. Poe uses the same quotation in "Fifty Suggestions," (Harrison, XIV, 184). Poe said, "I am beginning to think with Horsley—that. . . ."

6. The narrator's situation is sufficiently similar to Poe's to bear comment. Both are orphans brought up by an "Uncle" whose relation to his ward was strained. In each case, the guardian is wealthy but tight-fisted, and each marries an unusually young cousin. Poe's marriage took place in 1836, when Virginia was still under 14.

"dragged . . . along": Poe quotes a familiar passage in Alexander Pope's "Essay on Criticism": Pope illustrates a "needless Alexandrine" (at the end of a bad poem):

> That, like a wounded snake, drags
>   its slow length along.

Poe changed a word to make his sentence agree, and probably thought of the Pope passage because it is about "Numbers"—that is, poetic meter.

pièce de résistance: the main dish of the meal.

Ude: Louis Eustache Ude, once chef of Louis XVI, founder of the modern French school in England, and author of *French Cook* (1822). Poe may have seen Ude's book or have learned the chef's name from one of two favorite sources: Carlyle's *Sartor Resartus* (see Section Preface to "The Devil in the Belfry") or Edward Bulwer-Lytton's *Pelham* (see "The Man of the Crowd," note 2). Carlyle's Teufelsdröckh mentions Ude in a passage about definitions of man—before concluding that man is a "tool-using Animal," he shows that he is not necessarily a laughing animal;

> Still less do we make of that other French Definition of Cooking Animal. . . . Or how would Monsieur Ude prosper among the Orinoco Indians . . . ?

The passage in *Pelham* is simpler: "Oh Lady C—— —— is going to write a 'commentary on Ude'. . . ." Later in that novel the epicure Guloseton speaks of "the venerable Ude," whom he highly respects.

Carême: Marie Antoine Carême (1784–1833), a famous French gastronomist, chef to Talleyrand, Tsar Alexander, and George IV.

Job: The biblical Job is proverbial for his patient and submissive suffering.

7. *"assurément ce n'était pas son faible"*: Assuredly that was not his weakness.

et id genus omne: and all this kind (Poe just translates an English phrase into Latin).

in *prolegomena*: by way of introduction.

14. Science, Technology, Oddities

By grouping these stories we stress their journalistic qualities. Their topics sound like "good copy": a transatlantic flight, a trip to the moon, a look at our world from a thousand years ahead, reform in the treatment of the insane, and the artificial creation of gold. The tales have other characteristics as well. Satirical allusions are present in several; certainly, for instance, "The System of Dr. Tarr and Prof. Fether" is in large part a political satire and could be so categorized. But we thought it therapeutic to stress the side of Poe which responded quickly and commercially—though probably also with genuine interest—to oddities, technology, and science.

The Balloon-Hoax. Although Poe's two flying stories are similar in many details, they are different in intention. "Hans Pfaal" frankly admits that it is a joke, while "The Balloon-Hoax" pretends to be news. Both tales are strong evidence of Poe's involvement in popular interests of his day and his excellent sense of journalistically exciting topics. The carefully contrived balloon hoax, especially the portions "by" Mr. Ainsworth, is obviously exciting to its author, who probably hoped someone would take his lead and try the journey. It appeared as an "extra" of the *New York Sun.* The front page of *The Extra Sun* (see Figure 24) also carries an article on Egyptology, not an unusual topic for an American paper of this period. For details about the hoax, see notes 1 and 2.

Hans Pfaal. If the satirical opening and conclusion of this tale seem somewhat diffuse in object, we think the reason is that satire is not Poe's main purpose. His imagination is deeply engaged in the science fiction adventure which forms the middle of the story. The Hans of this central portion seems so different from the Hans of the "frame" portions that one can only conclude that Poe was embarrassed by his own enthusiasm for the possibilities of the technology, exploration, and adventure, and sought to mock it by enclosing Hans's trip in parentheses of burlesque.

Mellonta Tauta. In one sense, "Mellonta Tauta" is a "savage attack . . . upon contemporary civilization, especially as represented by the city and by modern democratic government" (Pollin 10). It is filled with unflattering allusions to nineteenth-century technology and politics, especially to American government and leaders. In another sense, it is a philosophical tale, in which Poe divides savants into two groups, those who understand the role of the intuitive imagination and those who don't. Pundita, his wacky "antiquarian" of the future, generally botches the names of those Poe doesn't like, but is accurate about the "genuinely great." Thus, in the paragraph marked by note 11, she is accurate about Isaac Newton, Johannes Kepler, and Jean François Champollion. It is not accurate to say simply that Poe was hostile to science. He was hostile to grubbing for facts. The great scientists, Poe believed, were also artists and seers who used imagination and intuition to perceive the "consistency" of the universal order. So even Pundita's society remembers them accurately. In the same passage, Poe drops in a word about cryptography—the deciphering of codes—to help make his point that it takes intuition, not just mere logic, to solve difficult problems. He himself published on cryptography and even offered to decipher samples of difficult codes which readers were urged to send to him.

In a third sense, Poe attacks "progress," though he is not fully consistent. The people of 2848 are our children and share some of our faults. Although Pundita's world has learned to theorize imaginatively on the basis of the unity of the cosmos, there are things wrong with her society: Pundita is ignorant and a snob; historical knowledge remains spectacularly imperfect, and the balloon crashes into the sea.

One could also classify "Mellonta Tauta" as science fiction, for we know Poe's genuine fascination with the possibilities of contemporary technology. If these factors seem somewhat contradictory, well and good: Poe's attitudes are complex, and any system of classifying his tales is somewhat arbitrary.

The System of Dr. Tarr and Prof. Fether. Critics debate the target of Poe's satire: William Whipple (1) believes Poe has Dickens in mind; Richard Benton (2) is quite sure it's Nathaniel Parker Willis. Both had written about the new kind of asylum, and both had recently offended Poe.

Poe knew something of then-contemporary theories of treating the insane and had a medical acquaintance who had served at asylums run according to the more humane principles coming into use. Poe even visited such an institution, but disapproved of what he saw—and of humanitarian reform in general.

Poe's usual contempt for reformers is evident throughout the tale. The repeated references to the "South," where people are, according to "Parisians," "peculiarly eccentric;" the obvious failure of reform; the idea that using tar and feathers is the proper way to treat "inmates;" and the inmates' band playing "Yankee Doodle" all suggest that Poe has in mind the American South and the slave problem, on which subject his views are reactionary. The prevailing Southern fear of a slave uprising seems present, too. The "inmates" have, in fact, taken over, and they treat their former masters cruelly. They are not their keepers' equals, but are "cunning"—cunning enough to create the hoax on the stupid narrator. Southern accounts of slave personality stress characteristics such as cunning, childlike behavior, and eccentric aping of elite white-folks' ways. "Paris" seems intended to represent the North.

Von Kempelen and His Discovery. The revealing connections pointed out in the notes to this story rest largely on the patient work of Burton Pollin (5). Added together, they might make Poe's last hoax seem less hoax than satire. We think that Poe did intend a hoax, but that in searching around for fictitious names and places, he naturally thought of issues and people he was concerned with or troubled by. He lays down an unusually dense smoke screen of plausible but elusive allusions and references, and inserts picky quarrels about points no reader could be expected to follow because they are generated primarily out of his professional experience and memory. An annotated edition should explain such references, but we do not want to give the impression that they are what the story is about; it is still just a little hoax. Lurking in it are some private jokes for those very familiar with Poe's life and works, but for almost all readers even in his own day, the smoke screen is present for the same reason as the dense fog in "A Tale of the Ragged Mountains."

The Tales

THE BALLOON-HOAX

ASTOUNDING NEWS BY EXPRESS, *via* NORFOLK! THE ATLANTIC CROSSED IN THREE DAYS! SIGNAL TRIUMPH OF MR. MONCK MASON'S FLYING MACHINE!— ARRIVAL AT SULLIVAN'S ISLAND, NEAR CHARLESTON, S.C., OF MR. MASON, MR. ROBERT HOLLAND, MR. HENSON, MR. HARRISON AINSWORTH, AND FOUR OTHERS, IN THE STEERING BALLOON, "VICTORIA," AFTER A PASSAGE OF SEVENTY-FIVE HOURS FROM LAND TO LAND! FULL PARTICULARS OF THE VOYAGE![1]

The great problem is at length solved! The air, as well as the earth and the ocean, has been subdued by science, and will become a common and convenient highway for mankind. *The Atlantic has been actually crossed in a Balloon!* and this too without difficulty—without any great apparent danger—with thorough control of the machine—and in the inconceivably brief period of seventy-five hours from shore to shore! By the energy of an agent at Charleston, S.C., we are enabled to be the first to furnish the public with a detailed account of this most extraordinary voyage, which was performed between Saturday, the 6th instant, at 11, A.M., and 2, P.M., on Tuesday, the 9th instant, by Sir Everard Bringhurst; Mr. Osborne, a nephew of Lord Bentinck's; Mr. Monck Mason and Mr. Robert Holland, the well-known æronauts; Mr. Harrison Ainsworth, author of "Jack Sheppard," &c.; and Mr. Henson, the projector of the late unsuccessful flying machine—with two seamen from Woolwich—in all, eight persons. The particulars furnished below may be relied on as authentic and accurate in every respect, as, with a slight exception, they are copied *verbatim* from the joint diaries of Mr. Monck Mason and Mr. Harrison Ainsworth, to whose politeness our agent is also indebted for much verbal information respecting the balloon itself, its construction, and other matters of interest. The only alteration in the ms. received, has been made for the purpose of throwing the hurried account of our agent, Mr. Forsyth,[2] in a connected and intelligible form.

The Balloon

Two very decided failures, of late—those of Mr. Henson and Sir George Cayley—had much weakened the public interest in the subject of aerial navigation. Mr. Henson's scheme (which at first was considered very feasible even by men of science,) was founded upon the principle of an inclined plane, started from an eminence by an extrinsic force, applied and continued by the revolution of impinging vanes, in form and number resembling the vanes of a windmill. But, in all the experiments made with models at the Adelaide Gallery, it was found that the operation of these fans not only did not propel the machine, but actually impeded its flight. The only propelling force it ever exhibited, was the mere *impetus* acquired from the descent of the inclined plane; and this *impetus* carried the machine farther when the vanes were at rest, than when they were in motion—a fact which sufficiently demonstrates their inutility; and in the absence of the propelling, which was also the *sustaining* power, the whole fabric would necessarily descend. This consideration led Sir George Cayley to think only of adapting a propeller to some machine having of itself an independent power of support—in a word, to a balloon; the idea, however, being novel, or original, with Sir George, only so far as regards the mode of its application to practice. He exhibited a model of his invention at the Polytechnic Institution.[3] The propelling principle, or power, was here, also, applied to interrupted surfaces,

or vanes, put in revolution. These vanes were four in number, but were found entirely ineffectual in moving the balloon, or in aiding its ascending power. The whole project was thus a complete failure.

It was at this juncture that Mr. Monck Mason (whose voyage from Dover to Weilburg in the balloon, "Nassau," occasioned so much excitement in 1837,) conceived the idea of employing the principle of the Archimedean screw for the purpose of propulsion through the air—rightly attributing the failure of Mr. Henson's scheme, and of Sir George Cayley's, to the interruption of surface in the independent vanes. He made the first public experiment at Willis's Rooms,[4] but afterwards removed his model to the Adelaide Gallery.

Like Sir George Cayley's balloon, his own was an ellipsoid. Its length was thirteen feet six inches—height, six feet eight inches. It contained about three hundred and twenty cubic feet of gas, which, if pure hydrogen, would support twenty-one pounds upon its first inflation, before the gas has time to deteriorate or escape. The weight of the whole machine and apparatus was seventeen pounds—leaving about four pounds to spare. Beneath the centre of the balloon, was a frame of light wood, about nine feet long, and rigged on to the balloon itself with a network in the customary manner. From this framework was suspended a wicker basket or car.

The screw consists of an axis of hollow brass tube, eighteen inches in length, through which, upon a semi-spiral inclined at fifteen degrees, pass a series of steel wire radii, two feet long, and thus projecting a foot on either side. These radii are connected at the outer extremities by two bands of flattened wire—the whole in this manner forming the framework of the screw, which is completed by a covering of oiled silk cut into gores, and tightened so as to present a tolerably uniform surface. At each end of its axis this screw is supported by pillars of hollow brass tube descending from the hoop. In

Figure Twenty-four. *The Extra Sun*, April 13, 1844. Here is Poe's "Balloon Hoax" as it originally appeared. The picture is a careful copy of an engraving which appears on the frontispiece of *Remarks on the Ellipsoidal Balloon*, from which many technical passages of the story are copied almost verbatim (Wilkinson). Note the article on Egyptology following the hoax. This was big news in Poe's day. See "Some Words with a Mummy" and "Mellonta Tauta." Plate used courtesy of the American Antiquarian Society.

the lower ends of these tubes are holes in which the pivots of the axis revolve. From the end of the axis which is next the car, proceeds a shaft of steel, connecting the screw with the pinion of a piece of spring machinery fixed in the car. By the operation of this spring, the screw is made to revolve with great rapidity, communicating a progressive motion to the whole. By means of the rudder, the machine was readily turned in any direction. The spring was of great power, compared with its dimensions, being capable of raising forty-five pounds upon a barrel of four inches diameter, after the first turn, and gradually increasing as it was wound up. It weighed, altogether, eight pounds six ounces. The rudder was a light frame of cane covered with silk, shaped somewhat like a battledoor, and was about three feet long, and at the widest, one foot. Its weight was about two ounces. It could be turned *flat*, and directed upwards or downwards, as well as to the right or left; and thus enabled the æronaut to transfer the resistance of the air which in an inclined position it must generate in its passage, to any side upon which he might desire to act; thus determining the balloon in the opposite direction.

This model (which, through want of time, we have necessarily described in an imperfect manner,) was put in action at the Adelaide Gallery, where it accomplished a velocity of five miles per hour; although, strange to say, it excited very little interest in comparison with the previous complex machine of Mr. Henson —so resolute is the world to despise anything which carries with it an air of simplicity. To accomplish the great desideratum of ærial navigation, it was very generally supposed that some exceedingly complicated application must be made of some unusually profound principle in dynamics.

So well satisfied, however, was Mr. Mason of the ultimate success of his invention, that he determined to construct immediately, if possible, a balloon of suf-

ficient capacity to test the question by a voyage of some extent—the original design being to cross the British Channel, as before, in the Nassau balloon. To carry out his views, he solicited and obtained the patronage of Sir Everard Bringhurst and Mr. Osborne, two gentlemen well known for scientific acquirement, and especially for the interest they have exhibited in the progress of ærostation. The project, at the desire of Mr. Osborne, was kept a profound secret from the public— the only persons entrusted with the design being those actually engaged in the construction of the machine, which was built (under the superintendence of Mr. Mason, Mr. Holland, Sir Everard Bringhurst, and Mr. Osborne,) at the seat of the latter gentleman near Penstruthal, in Wales. Mr. Henson, accompanied by his friend Mr. Ainsworth, was admitted to a private view of the balloon, on Saturday last—when the two gentlemen made final arrangements to be included in the adventure. We are not informed for what reason the two seamen were also included in the party—but, in the course of a day or two, we shall put our readers in possession of the minutest particulars respecting this extraordinary voyage.

The balloon is composed of silk, varnished with the liquid gum caoutchouc.[5] It is of vast dimensions, containing more than 40000 cubic feet of gas; but as coal gas was employed in place of the more expensive and inconvenient hydrogen, the supporting power of the machine, when fully inflated, and immediately after inflation, is not more than about 2500 pounds. The coal gas is not only much less costly, but is easily procured and managed.

For its introduction into common use for purposes of ærostation, we are indebted to Mr. Charles Green. Up to his discovery, the process of inflation was not only exceedingly expensive, but uncertain. Two, and even three days, have frequently been wasted in futile attempts to procure a sufficiency of hydrogen to fill a balloon, from which it had great tendency to escape owing to its extreme subtlety,[6] and its affinity for the surrounding atmosphere. In a balloon sufficiently perfect to retain its contents of coal-gas unaltered, in quality or amount, for six months, an equal quantity of hydrogen could not be maintained in equal purity for six weeks.

The supporting power being estimated at 2500 pounds, and the united weights of the party amounting only to about 1200, there was left a surplus of 1300, of which again 1200 was exhausted by ballast, arranged in bags of different sizes, with their respective weights marked upon them—by cordage, barometers, telescopes, barrels containing provision for a fortnight, water-casks, cloaks, carpet-bags, and various other indispensable matters, including a coffee-warmer, contrived for warming coffee by means of slacklime,[7] so as to dispense altogether with fire, if it should be judged prudent to do so. All these articles, with the exception of the ballast, and a few trifles, were suspended from the hoop over head. The car is much smaller and lighter, in proportion, than the one appended to the model. It is formed of a light wicker, and is wonderfully strong, for so frail looking a machine. Its rim is about four feet deep. The rudder is also very much larger, in proportion, than that of the model; and the screw is considerably smaller. The balloon is furnished besides, with a grapnel, and a guide-rope; which latter is of the most indispensable importance. A few words, in explanation, will here be necessary for such of our readers as are not conversant with the details of aerostation.

As soon as the balloon quits the earth, it is subjected to the influence of many circumstances tending to create a difference in its weight; augmenting or diminishing its ascending power. For example, there may be a deposition of dew upon the silk, to the extent, even, of several hundred pounds; ballast has then to be thrown out, or the machine may descend.

This ballast being discarded, and a clear sunshine evaporating the dew, and at the same time expanding the gas in the silk, the whole will again rapidly ascend. To check this ascent, the only resource is, (or rather *was*, until Mr. Green's invention of the guide-rope,) the permission of the escape of gas from the valve; but, in the loss of gas, is a proportionate general loss of ascending power; so that, in a comparatively brief period, the best constructed balloon must necessarily exhaust all its resources, and come to the earth. This was the great obstacle to voyages of length.

The guide-rope remedies the difficulty in the simplest manner conceivable. It is merely a very long rope which is suffered to trail from the car, and the effect of which is to prevent the balloon from changing its level in any material degree. If, for example, there should be a deposition of moisture upon the silk, and the machine begins to descend in consequence, there will be no necessity for discharging ballast to remedy the increase of weight, for it is remedied, or counteracted, in an exactly just proportion, by the deposit on the ground of just so much of the end of the rope as is necessary. If, on the other hand, any circumstances should cause undue levity, and consequent ascent, this levity is immediately counteracted by the additional weight of rope upraised from the earth. Thus, the balloon can neither ascend or descend, except within very narrow limits, and its resources, either in gas or ballast, remain comparatively unimpaired. When passing over an expanse of water, it becomes necessary to employ small kegs of copper or wood, filled with liquid ballast of a lighter nature than water. These float, and serve all the purposes of a mere rope on land. Another most important office of the guide-rope, is to point out the *direction* of the balloon. The rope *drags*, either on land or sea, while the balloon is free; the latter, consequently, is always in advance, when any progress whatever is made: a comparison, therefore, by means of the compass, of the relative positions of the two objects, will always indicate the *course*. In the same way, the angle formed by the rope with the vertical axis of the machine, indicates the *velocity*. When there is *no* angle—in other words, when the rope hangs perpendicularly, the whole apparatus is stationary; but the larger the angle, that is to say, the farther the balloon precedes the end of the rope, the greater the velocity; and the converse.

As the original design was to cross the British Channel, and alight as near Paris as possible, the voyagers had taken the precaution to prepare themselves with passports directed to all parts of the Continent, specifying the nature of the expedition, as in the case of the Nassau voyage, and entitling the adventurers to exemption from the usual formalities of office: unexpected events, however, rendered these passports superfluous.

The inflation was commenced very quietly at daybreak, on Saturday morning, the 6th instant, in the Court-Yard of Wheal-Vor House, Mr. Osborne's seat, about a mile from Penstruthal, in North Wales; and at 7 minutes past 11, every thing being ready for departure, the balloon was set free, rising gently but steadily, in a direction nearly South; no use being made, for the first half hour, of either the screw or the rudder. We proceed now with the journal, as transcribed by Mr. Forsyth from the joint MSS. of Mr. Monck Mason, and Mr. Ainsworth. The body of the journal, as given, is in the hand-writing of Mr. Mason, and a P. S. is appended, each day, by Mr. Ainsworth, who has in preparation, and will shortly give the public a more minute, and no doubt, a thrillingly interesting account of the voyage.

The Journal

Saturday, April the 6th.—Every preparation likely to embarrass us, having been made over night, we commenced the inflation this morn-ing at daybreak; but owing to a thick fog, which encumbered the folds of the silk and rendered it unmanageable, we did not get through before nearly eleven o'clock. Cut loose, then, in high spirits, and rose gently but steadily, with a light breeze at North, which bore us in the direction of the British Channel. Found the ascending force greater than we had expected; and as we arose higher and so got clear of the cliffs, and more in the sun's rays, our ascent became very rapid. I did not wish, however, to lose gas at so early a period of the adventure, and so concluded to ascend for the present. We soon ran out our guide-rope; but even when we had raised it clear of the earth, we still went up very rapidly. The balloon was unusually steady, and looked beautifully. In about ten minutes after starting, the barometer indicated an altitude of 15,000 feet. The weather was remarkably fine, and the view of the subjacent country—a most romantic one when seen from any point,—was now especially sublime. The numerous deep gorges presented the appearance of lakes, on account of the dense vapors with which they were filled, and the pinnacles and crags to the South East, piled in inextricable confusion, resembled nothing so much as the giant cities of eastern fable. We were rapidly approaching the mountains in the South; but our elevation was more than sufficient to enable us to pass them in safety. In a few minutes we soared over them in fine style; and Mr. Ainsworth, with the seamen, were surprised at their apparent want of altitude when viewed from the car, the tendency of great elevation in a balloon being to reduce inequalities of the surface below, to nearly a dead level. At half-past eleven still proceeding nearly South, we obtained our first view of the Bristol Channel; and, in fifteen minutes afterwards, the line of breakers on the coast appeared immediately beneath us, and we were fairly out at sea. We now resolved to let off enough gas to bring our guide-rope, with the buoys affixed, into the water. This was immediately done, and we commenced a gradual descent. In about twenty minutes our first buoy dipped, and at the touch of the second soon afterwards, we remained stationary as to elevation. We were all now anxious to test the efficiency of the rudder and screw, and we put them both into requisition forthwith, for the purpose of altering our direction more to the eastward, and in a line for Paris. By means of the rudder we instantly effected the necessary change of direction, and our course was brought nearly at right angles to that of the wind; when we set in motion the spring of the screw, and were rejoiced to find it propel us readily as desired. Upon this we gave nine hearty cheers, and dropped in the sea a bottle, enclosing a slip of parchment with a brief account of the principle of the invention. Hardly, however, had we done with our rejoicings, when an unforeseen accident occurred which discouraged us in no little degree. The steel rod connecting the spring with the propeller was suddenly jerked out of place, at the car end, (by a swaying of the car through some movement of one of the two seamen we had taken up,) and in an instant hung dangling out of reach, from the pivot of the axis of the screw. While we were endeavoring to regain it, our attention being completely absorbed, we became involved in a strong current of wind from the East, which bore us, with rapidly increasing force, towards the Atlantic. We soon found ourselves driving out to sea at the rate of not less, certainly, than fifty or sixty miles an hour, so that we came up with Cape Clear, at some forty miles to our North, before we had secured the rod, and had time to think what we were about. It was now that Mr. Ainsworth made an extraordinary, but to my fancy, a by

no means unreasonable or chimerical proposition, in which he was instantly seconded by Mr. Holland—viz.: that we should take advantage of the strong gale which bore us on, and in place of beating back to Paris, make an attempt to reach the coast of North America. After slight reflection I gave a willing assent to this bold proposition, which (strange to say) met with objection from the two seamen only. As the stronger party, however, we overruled their fears, and kept resolutely upon our course. We steered due West; but as the trailing of the buoys materially impeded our progress, and we had the balloon abundantly at command, either for ascent or descent, we first threw out fifty pounds of ballast, and then wound up (by means of a windlass) so much of the rope as brought it quite clear of the sea. We perceived the effect of this manœuvre immediately, in a vastly increased rate of progress; and, as the gale freshened, we flew with a velocity nearly inconceivable; the guide-rope flying out behind the car, like a streamer from a vessel. It is needless to say that a very short time sufficed us to lose sight of the coast. We passed over innumerable vessels of all kinds, a few of which were endeavoring to beat up, but the most of them lying to. We occasioned the greatest excitement on board all—an excitement greatly relished by ourselves, and especially by our two men, who, now under the influence of a dram of Geneva,[8] seemed resolved to give all scruple, or fear, to the wind. Many of the vessels fired signal guns; and in all we were saluted with loud cheers (which we heard with surprising distinctness) and the waving of caps and handkerchiefs. We kept on in this manner throughout the day, with no material incident, and, as the shades of night closed around us, we made a rough estimate of the distance traversed. It could not have been less than five hundred miles, and was probably much more. The propeller was kept in constant operation, and, no doubt, aided our progress materially. As the sun went down, the gale freshened into an absolute hurricane, and the ocean beneath was clearly visible on account of its phosphorescence. The wind was from the East all night, and gave us the brightest omen of success. We suffered no little from cold, and the dampness of the atmosphere was most unpleasant; but the ample space in the car enabled us to lie down, and by means of cloaks and a few blankets, we did sufficiently well.

P.S. (by Mr. Ainsworth). The last nine hours have been unquestionably the most exciting of my life. I can conceive nothing more sublimating than the strange peril and novelty of an adventure such as this. May God grant that we succeed! I ask not success for mere safety to my insignificant person, but for the sake of human knowledge and—for the vastness of the triumph. And yet the feat is only so evidently feasible that the sole wonder is why men have scrupled to attempt it before. One single gale such as now befriends us—let such a tempest whirl forward a balloon for four or five days (these gales often last longer) and the voyager will be easily borne, in that period, from coast to coast. In view of such a gale the broad Atlantic becomes a mere lake. I am more struck, just now, with the supreme silence which reigns in the sea beneath us, notwithstanding its agitation, than with any other phenomenon presenting itself. The waters give up no voice to the heavens.[9] The immense flaming ocean writhes and is tortured uncomplainingly. The mountainous surges suggest the idea of innumerable dumb gigantic fiends struggling in impotent agony. In a night such as is this to me, a man *lives*—lives a whole century of ordinary life—nor would I forego this rapturous delight for that of a whole century of ordinary existence

Sunday, the seventh. [Mr. Mason's MS.] This morning the gale, by 10, had subsided to an eight or nine knot breeze, (for a vessel at sea,) and bears us, perhaps, thirty miles per hour, or more. It has veered however, very considerably to the north; and now, at sundown, we are holding our course due west, principally by the screw and rudder, which answer their purposes to admiration. I regard the project as thoroughly successful, and the easy navigation of the air in any direction (not exactly in the teeth of a gale) as no longer problematical. We could not have made head against the strong wind of yesterday; but, by ascending, we might have got out of its influence, if requisite. Against a pretty stiff breeze, I feel convinced, we can make our way with the propeller. At noon, to-day, ascended to an elevation of nearly 25,000 feet, by discharging ballast. Did this to search for a more direct current, but found none so favorable as the one we are now in.[10] We have an abundance of gas to take us across this small pond, even should the voyage last three weeks. I have not the slightest fear for the result. The difficulty has been strangely exaggerated and misapprehended. I can choose my current, and should I find *all* currents against me, I can make very tolerable headway with the propeller. We have had no incidents worth recording. The night promises fair.

P.S. [By Mr. Ainsworth.] I have little to record, except the fact (to me quite a surprising one) that, at an elevation equal to that of Cotopaxi, I experienced neither very intense cold, nor headache, nor difficulty of breathing; neither, I find, did Mr. Mason, nor Mr. Holland, nor Sir Everard. Mr. Osborne complained of constriction of the chest —but this soon wore off. We have flown at a great rate during the day, and we must be more than half way across the Atlantic. We have passed over some twenty or thirty vessels of various kinds, and all seem to be delightfully astonished. Crossing the ocean in a balloon is not so difficult a feat after all. *Omne ignotum pro magnifico.*[11] *Mem:* at 25,000 feet elevation the sky appears nearly black, and the stars are distinctly visible; while the sea does not seem convex (as one might suppose) but absolutely and most unequivocally concave.[12]

Monday, the 8th. [Mr. Mason's MS.] This morning we had again some little trouble with the rod of the propeller, which must be entirely remodelled, for fear of serious accident—I mean the steel rod not the vanes. The latter could not be improved. The wind has been blowing steadily and strongly from the northeast all day; and so far fortune seems bent upon favoring us. Just before day, we were all somewhat alarmed at some odd noises and concussions in the balloon, accompanied with the apparent rapid subsidence of the whole machine. These phenomena were occasioned by the expansion of the gas, through increase of heat in the atmosphere, and the consequent disruption of the minute particles of ice with which the network had become encrusted during the night.[13] Threw down several bottles to the vessels below. Saw one of them picked up by a large ship—seemingly one of the New York line packets. Endeavored to make out her name, but could not be sure of it. Mr. Osborne's telescope made it out something like "Atalanta." It is now 12, at night, and we are still going nearly west, at a rapid pace. The sea is peculiarly phosphorescent.

P.S. [By Mr. Ainsworth.] It is now 2, A. M., and nearly calm, as well as I can judge—but it is very difficult to determine this point, since we move *with* the air so completely. I have not slept since quitting Wheal-Vor, but can stand it no longer, and must take a nap. We cannot be far from the American coast.

Tuesday, the 9th. [Mr. Ainsworth's MS.] *One, P. M. We are in full view of the low coast of South Carolina.* The great problem is accomplished. We have crossed the Atlantic—fairly and *easily* crossed it in a balloon! God be praised! Who shall say that anything is impossible hereafter?

The Journal here ceases. Some particulars of the descent were communicated, however, by Mr. Ainsworth to Mr. Forsyth. It was nearly dead calm when the voyagers first came in view of the coast, which was immediately recognised by both the seamen, and by Mr. Osborne. The latter gentleman having acquaintances at Fort Moultrie,[14] it was immediately resolved to descend in its vicinity. The balloon was brought over the beach (the tide being out and the sand hard, smooth, and admirably adapted for a descent,) and the grapnel let go, which took firm hold at once. The inhabitants of the island, and of the fort, thronged out, of course, to see the balloon; but it was with the greatest difficulty that any one could be made to credit the actual voyage—*the crossing of the Atlantic.* The grapnel caught at 2, P. M., precisely; and thus the whole voyage was completed in seventy-five hours; or rather less, counting from shore to shore. No serious accident occurred. No real danger was at any time apprehended. The balloon was exhausted and secured without trouble; and when the MS. from which this narrative is compiled was despatched from Charleston, the party were still at Fort Moultrie. Their farther intentions were not ascertained; but we can safely promise our readers some additional information either on Monday or in the course of the next day, at farthest.

This is unquestionably the most stupendous, the most interesting, and the most important undertaking, ever accomplished or even attempted by man. What magnificent events may ensue, it would be useless now to think of determining.

HANS PFAAL[1]

With a heart of furious fancies,
  Whereof I am commander,
*With a burning spear **and a horse of air**,*
To the wilderness I wander.
                    Tom O' Bedlam's Song.[2]

By late accounts from Rotterdam, that city seems to be in a high state of philosophical excitement. Indeed, phenomena have there occurred of a nature so completely unexpected—so entirely novel—so utterly at variance with preconceived opinions—as to leave no doubt on my mind that long ere this all Europe is in an uproar, all physics in a ferment, all reason and astronomy together by the ears.

It appears that on the —— day of ——, (I am not positive about the date,) a vast crowd of people, for purposes not specifically mentioned, were assembled in the great square of the Exchange in the well-conditioned city of Rotterdam. The day was warm—unusually so for the season—there was hardly a breath of air stirring; and the multitude were in no bad humor at being now and then besprinkled with friendly showers of momentary duration, that fell from large white masses of cloud profusely distributed about the blue vault of the firmament. Nevertheless, about noon, a slight but remarkable agitation became apparent in the assembly; the clattering of ten thousand tongues succeeded; and, in an instant afterwards, ten thousand faces were upturned towards the heavens, ten thousand pipes descended simultaneously from the corners of ten thousand mouths,[3] and a shout, which could be compared to nothing but the roaring of Niagara, resounded long, loudly and furiously, through all the city and through all the environs of Rotterdam.

The origin of this hubbub soon became sufficiently evident. From behind the huge bulk of one of those sharply defined masses of cloud already mentioned, was seen slowly to emerge into an open area of blue space, a queer, heterogeneous, but apparently solid substance, so oddly shaped, so whimsically put together, as not to be in any manner comprehended, and never to be sufficiently admired, by the host of sturdy burghers who stood open-mouthed below. What could it be? In the name of all the devils in Rotterdam, what could it possibly portend? No one knew; no one could imagine; no one —not even the burgomaster Mynheer Superbus Von Underduk—had the slightest clew by which to unravel the mystery; so, as nothing more reasonable could be done, every one to a man replaced his pipe carefully in the corner of his mouth, and maintaining an eye steadily upon the phenomenon, puffed, paused, waddled about, and grunted significantly—then waddled back, grunted, paused, and finally —puffed again.

In the meantime, however, lower and still lower towards the goodly city, came the object of so much curiosity, and the cause of so much smoke. In a very few minutes it arrived near enough to be accurately discerned. It appeared to be—yes! it *was* undoubtedly a species of balloon; but surely no *such* balloon had ever been seen in Rotterdam before. For who, let me ask, ever heard of a balloon manufactured entirely of dirty newspapers? No man in Holland certainly; yet here, under the very noses of the people, or rather at some distance *above* their noses, was the identical thing in question, and composed, I have it on the best authority, of the precise material which no one had ever before known to be used for a similar purpose.—It was an egregious insult to the good sense of the burghers of Rotterdam. As to the shape of the phenomenon, it was even still more reprehensible. Being little or nothing better than a huge fool's-cap turned upside down. And this similitude was regarded as by no means lessened, when upon nearer inspection, the crowd saw a large tassel depending from its apex, and, around the upper rim or base of the cone, a circle of little instruments, resembling sheep-bells, which kept up a continual tinkling to the tune of

Betty Martin. But still worse.—Suspended by blue ribbons to the end of this fantastic machine, there hung, by way of car, an enormous drab beaver hat, with a brim superlatively broad, and a hemispherical crown with a black band and a silver buckle. It is, however, somewhat remarkable that many citizens of Rotterdam swore to having seen the same hat repeatedly before; and indeed the whole assembly seemed to regard it with eyes of familiarity; while the vrow Grettel Pfaal,[4] upon sight of it, uttered an exclamation of joyful surprise, and declared it to be the identical hat of her good man himself. Now this was a circumstance the more to be observed, as Pfaal, with three companions, had actually disappeared from Rotterdam about five years before, in a very sudden and unaccountable manner, and up to the date of this narrative all attempts at obtaining intelligence concerning them had failed. To be sure, some bones which were thought to be human, mixed up with a quantity of odd-looking rubbish, had been lately discovered in a retired situation to the east of the city; and some people went so far as to imagine that in this spot a foul murder had been committed, and that the sufferers were in all probability Hans Pfaal and his associates.— But to return.

The balloon (for such no doubt it was) had now descended to within a hundred feet of the earth, allowing the crowd below a sufficiently distinct view of the person of its occupant. This was in truth a very singular somebody. He could not have been more than two feet in height; but this altitude, little as it was, would have been sufficient to destroy his *equilibrium*, and tilt him over the edge of his tiny car, but for the intervention of a circular rim reaching as high as the breast, and rigged on to the cords of the balloon. The body of the little man was more than proportionally broad, giving to his entire figure a rotundity highly absurd. His feet, of course, could not be seen at all. His hands were enormously large. His hair was gray, and collected into a *queue* behind. His nose was prodigiously long, crooked and inflammatory; his eyes full, brilliant, and acute; his chin and cheeks, although wrinkled with age, were broad, puffy, and double; but of ears of any kind there was not a semblance to be discovered upon any portion of his head. This odd little gentleman was dressed in a loose surtout of sky-blue satin, with tight breeches to match, fastened with silver buckles at the knees. His vest was of some bright yellow material; a white taffety cap was set jauntily on one side of his head; and, to complete his equipment, a blood-red silk handkerchief enveloped his throat, and fell down, in a dainty manner, upon his bosom, in a fantastic bow-knot of super-eminent dimensions.

Having descended, as I said before, to about one hundred feet from the surface of the earth, the little old gentleman was suddenly seized with a fit of trepidation, and appeared disinclined to make any nearer approach to *terra firma*. Throwing out, therefore, a quantity of sand from a canvas bag, which he lifted with great difficulty, he became stationary in an instant. He then proceeded in a hurried and agitated manner, to extract from a side-pocket in his surtout a large morocco pocket-book. This he poised suspiciously in his hand; then eyed it with an air of extreme surprise, and was evidently astonished at its weight. He at length opened it, and, drawing therefrom a huge letter sealed with red sealing-wax and tied carefully with red tape, let it fall precisely at the feet of the burgomaster Superbus Von Underduk. His Excellency stooped to take it up. But the æronaut, still greatly discomposed, and having apparently no further business to detain him in Rotterdam, began at this moment to make busy preparations for departure; and, it being necessary to discharge a portion of ballast to enable him to reascend, the half dozen bags which he threw out, one after another, without taking the trouble to empty their contents, tumbled, every one of them, most unfortunately, upon the back of the burgomaster, and rolled him over and over no less than half a dozen times, in the face of every individual in Rotterdam. It is not to be supposed, however, that the great Underduk suffered this impertinence on the part of the little old man to pass off with impunity. It is said, on the contrary, that during each of his half dozen circumvolutions, he emitted no less than half a dozen distinct and furious whiffs from his pipe, to which he held fast the whole time with all his might, and to which he intends holding fast, (God willing,) until the day of his decease.

In the meantime the balloon arose like a lark, and, soaring far away above the city, at length drifted quietly behind a cloud similar to that from which it had so oddly emerged, and was thus lost forever to the wondering eyes of the good citizens of Rotterdam. All attention was now directed to the letter, the descent of which, and the consequences attending thereupon, had proved so fatally subversive of both person and personal dignity to his Excellency, Von Underduk. That functionary, however, had not failed, during his circumgyratory movements, to bestow a thought upon the important object of securing the epistle, which was seen, upon inspection, to have fallen into the most proper hands, being actually addressed to himself and Professor Rubadub, in their official capacities of President and Vice-President of the Rotterdam College of Astronomy. It was accordingly opened by those dignitaries upon the spot, and found to contain the following extraordinary, and indeed very serious, communication:—

To their Excellencies Von Underduk and Rubadub, President and Vice-President of the States' College of Astronomers, in the city of Rotterdam.

Your Excellencies may perhaps be able to remember an humble artizan, by name Hans Pfaal, and by occupation a mender of bellows, who, with three others, disappeared from Rotterdam, about five years ago, in a manner which must have been considered unaccountable. If, however, it so please your Excellencies, I, the writer of this communication, am the identical Hans Pfaal himself. It is well known to most of my fellow-citizens, that for the period of forty years I continued to occupy the little square brick building, at the head of the alley called Sauerkraut, in which I resided at the time of my disappearance. My ancestors have also resided therein time out of mind—they, as well as myself, steadily following the respectable and indeed lucrative profession of mending of bellows: for, to speak the truth, until of late years, that the heads of all the people have been set agog with politics, no better business than my own could an honest citizen of Rotterdam either desire or deserve. Credit was good, employment was never wanting, and there was no lack of either money or good will. But, as I was saying, we soon began to feel the effects of liberty, and long speeches, and radicalism, and all that sort of thing. People who were formerly the very best customers in the world, had now not a moment of time to think of us at all. They had as much as they could do to read about the revolutions, and keep up with the march of intellect and the spirit of the age. If a fire wanted fanning, it could readily be fanned with a newspaper; and as the government grew weaker, I have no doubt that leather and iron acquired durability in proportion—for, in a very short time, there was not a pair of bellows in all Rotterdam that ever stood in need of a stitch or required the assistance of a hammer. This was a state of things not to be endured. I soon grew as poor as a rat, and, having a wife and children to provide for, my burdens at length became intolerable, and I spent hour after hour in reflecting upon the most convenient method of putting an end to my life. Duns, in the meantime, left me little leisure for contemplation. My house was literally besieged from morning till night. There were three fellows in particular, who worried me beyond endurance, keeping watch continually about my door, and threatening me with the law. Upon these three I vowed the bitterest revenge, if ever I should be so happy as to get them within my clutches; and I believe nothing in the world but the pleasure of this anticipation prevented me from putting my plan of suicide into immediate execution, by blowing my brains out with a blunderbuss. I thought it best, however, to dissemble my wrath, and to treat them with promises and fair words, until, by some good turn of fate, an opportunity of vengeance should be afforded me.

One day, having given them the slip, and feeling more than usually dejected, I continued for a long time to wander about the most obscure streets without object, until at length I chanced to stumble against the corner of a bookseller's stall. Seeing a chair close at hand, for the use of customers, I threw myself doggedly into it, and, hardly knowing why, opened the pages of the first volume which came within my reach. It proved to be a small pamphlet treatise on Speculative Astronomy, written either by Professor Encke of Berlin, or by a Frenchman of somewhat similar name. I had some little tincture of information on matters of this nature, and soon became more and more absorbed in the contents of the book—reading it actually through twice before I awoke to a recollection of what was passing around me. By this time it began to grow dark, and I directed my steps toward home. But the treatise (in conjunction with a discovery in pneumatics, lately communicated to me as an important secret, by a cousin from Nantz,[5]) had made an indelible impression on my mind, and, as I sauntered along the dusky streets, I revolved carefully over in my memory the wild and sometimes unintelligible reasonings of the writer. There are some particular passages which affected my imagination in an extraordinary manner. The longer I meditated upon these, the more intense grew

the interest which had been excited within me. The limited nature of my education in general, and more especially my ignorance on subjects connected with natural philosophy, so far from rendering me diffident of my own ability to comprehend what I had read, or inducing me to mistrust the many vague notions which had arisen in consequence, merely served as a farther stimulus to imagination; and I was vain enough, or perhaps reasonable enough, to doubt whether those crude ideas which, arising in ill-regulated minds, have all the appearance, may not often in effect possess all the force, the reality, and other inherent properties of instinct or intuition.

It was late when I reached home, and I went immediately to bed. My mind, however, was too much occupied to sleep, and I lay the whole night buried in meditation. Arising early in the morning, I repaired eagerly to the bookseller's stall, and laid out what little ready money I possessed, in the purchase of some volumes of Mechanics and Practical Astronomy. Having arrived at home safely with these, I devoted every spare moment to their perusal, and soon made such proficiency in studies of this nature as I thought sufficient for the execution of a certain design with which either the devil or my better genius had inspired me. In the intervals of this period, I made every endeavor to conciliate the three creditors who had given me so much annoyance. In this I finally succeeded—partly by selling enough of my household furniture to satisfy a moiety of their claim, and partly by a promise of paying the balance upon completion of a little project which I told them I had in view, and for assistance in which I solicited their services. By these means (for they were ignorant men) I found little difficulty in gaining them over to my purpose.

Matters being thus arranged, I contrived, by the aid of my wife, and with the greatest secrecy and caution, to dispose of what property I had remaining, and to borrow, in small sums, under various pretences, and without giving any attention (I am ashamed to say) to my future means of repayment, no inconsiderable quantity of ready money. With the means thus accruing I proceeded to procure at intervals, cambric muslin, very fine, in pieces of twelve yards each; twine; a lot of the varnish of caoutchouc; a large and deep basket of wicker-work, made to order; and several other articles necessary in the construction and equipment of a balloon of extraordinary dimensions. This I directed my wife to make up as soon as possible, and gave her all requisite information as to the particular method of proceeding. In the meantime I worked up the twine into net-work of sufficient dimensions; rigged it with a hoop and the necessary cords; and made purchase of numerous instruments and materials for experiment in the upper regions of the upper atmosphere. I then took opportunities of conveying by night, to a retired situation east of Rotterdam, five iron-bound casks, to contain about fifty gallons each, and one of a larger size; six tin tubes, three inches in diameter, properly shaped, and ten feet in length; a quantity of a *particular metallic substance, or semimetal* which I shall not name, and a dozen demijohns of *a very common acid.* The gas to be formed from these latter materials is a gas never yet generated by any other person than myself—or at least never applied to any similar purpose. I can only venture to say here, that it is *a constituent of azote*,[6] so long considered irreducible, and that its density is about 37.4 times *less than that of hydrogen.* It is tasteless, but not odorless; burns, when pure, with a greenish flame, and is instantaneously fatal to animal life. Its full secret I would make no difficulty in disclosing, but that it of right belongs (as I have before hinted) to a citizen of Nantz, in France, by whom it was conditionally communicated to myself. The same individual submitted to me, without being at all aware of my intentions, a method of

constructing balloons from the membrane of a certain animal, through which substance any escape of gas was nearly an impossibility. I found it, however, altogether too expensive, and was not sure, upon the whole, whether cambric muslin with a coating of gum caoutchouc, was not equally as good. I mention this circumstance, because I think it probable that hereafter the individual in question may attempt a balloon ascension with the novel gas and material I have spoken of, and I do not wish to deprive him of the honor of a very singular invention.

On the spot which I intended each of the smaller casks to occupy respectively during the inflation of the balloon, I privately dug a small hole; the holes forming in this manner a circle twenty-five feet in diameter. In the centre of this circle, being the station designed for the large cask, I also dug a hole of greater depth. In each of the five smaller holes, I deposited a canister containing fifty pounds, and in the larger one a keg holding one hundred and fifty pounds of cannon powder. These—the keg and the canisters—I connected in a proper manner with covered trains; and having let into one of the canisters the end of about four feet of slow-match,[7] I covered up the hole, and placed the cask over it, leaving the other end of the match protruding about an inch, and barely visible beyond the cask. I then filled up the remaining holes, and placed the barrels over them in their destined situation.

Besides the articles above enumerated, I conveyed to the *dépôt,* and there secreted, one of M. Grimm's[8] improvements upon the apparatus for condensation of the atmospheric air. I found this machine, however, to require considerable alteration before it could be adapted to the purposes to which I intended making it applicable. But, with severe labor and unremitting perseverance, I at length met with entire success in all my preparations. My balloon was soon completed. It would contain more than forty thousand cubic feet of gas; would take me up easily, I calculated, with all my implements, and, if I managed rightly, with one hundred and seventy-five pounds of ballast into the bargain. It had received three coats of varnish, and I found the cambric muslin to answer all the purposes of silk itself, being quite as strong and a good deal less expensive.

Everything being now ready, I exacted from my wife an oath of secrecy in relation to all my actions from the day of my first visit to the bookseller's stall; and promising, on my part, to return as soon as circumstances would permit, I gave her what little money I had left, and bade her farewell. Indeed I had no fear on her account. She was what people call a notable woman, and could manage matters in the world without my assistance. I believe, to tell the truth, she always looked upon me as an idle body—a mere make-weight—good for nothing but building castles in the air—and was rather glad to get rid of me. It was a dark night when I bade her good bye, and taking with me, as *aides-de-camp*, the three creditors who had given me so much trouble, we carried the balloon, with the car and accoutrements, by a roundabout way, to the station where the other articles were deposited. We there found them all unmolested, and I proceeded immediately to business.

It was the first of April.[9] The night, as I said before, was dark; there was not a star to be seen; and a drizzling rain, falling at intervals, rendered us very uncomfortable. But my chief anxiety was concerning the balloon, which, in spite of the varnish with which it was defended, began to grow rather heavy with the moisture; the powder also was liable to damage. I therefore kept my three duns working with great diligence, pounding down ice around the central cask, and stirring the acid in the others. They did not cease, however, importuning me with questions as to what I intended to do with all this apparatus, and expressed much dissatisfaction at the terrible labor I made them undergo. They could not per-

ceive (so they said) what good was likely to result from their getting wet to the skin, merely to take a part in such horrible incantations. I began to get uneasy, and worked away with all my might; for I verily believe the idiots supposed that I had entered into a compact with the devil, and that, in short, what I was now doing was nothing better than it should be. I was, therefore, in great fear of their leaving me altogether. I contrived, however, to pacify them by promises of payment of all scores in full, as soon as I could bring the present business to a termination. To these speeches they gave of course their own interpretation; fancying, no doubt, that at all events I should come into possession of vast quantities of ready money; and provided I paid them all I owed, and a trifle more, in consideration of their services, I dare say they cared very little what became of either my soul or my carcass.

In about four hours and a half I found the balloon sufficiently inflated. I attached the car, therefore, and put all my implements in it—a telescope; a barometer, with some important modifications; a thermometer; an electrometer; a compass; a magnetic needle; a seconds watch; a bell; a speaking trumpet, etc. etc., etc.—also a globe of glass, exhausted of air, and carefully closed with a stopper—not forgetting the condensing apparatus, some unslacked lime, a stick of sealing wax, a copious supply of water, and a large quantity of provisions, such as pemmican, in which much nutriment is contained in comparatively little bulk. I also secured in the car a pair of pigeons and a cat.

It was now nearly daybreak, and I thought it high time to take my departure. Dropping a lighted cigar on the ground, as if by accident, I took the opportunity, in stooping to pick it up, of igniting privately the piece of slow match, the end of which, as I said before, protruded a little beyond the lower rim of one of the smaller casks. This manœuvre was totally unperceived on the part of the three duns;

and, jumping into the car, I immediately cut the single cord which held me to the earth, and was pleased to find that I shot upwards with inconceivable rapidity, carrying with all ease one hundred and seventy-five pounds of leaden ballast, and able to have carried up as many more. As I left the earth, the barometer stood at thirty inches, and the centigrade thermometer at 19°.

Scarcely, however, had I attained the height of fifty yards, when, roaring and rumbling up after me in the most tumultuous and terrible manner, came so dense a hurricane of fire, and gravel, and burning wood, and blazing metal, and mangled limbs, that my very heart sunk within me, and I fell down in the bottom of the car, trembling with terror. Indeed, I now perceived that I had entirely overdone the business, and that the main consequences of the shock were yet to be experienced. Accordingly, in less than a second, I felt all the blood in my body rushing to my temples, and, immediately thereupon, a concussion, which I shall never forget, burst abruptly through the night, and seemed to rip the very firmament asunder. When I afterwards had time for reflection, I did not fail to attribute the extreme violence of the explosion, as regarded myself, to its proper cause—my situation directly above it, and in the line of its greatest power. But at the time, I thought only of preserving my life. The ballon at first collapsed, then furiously expanded, then whirled round and round with sickening velocity, and finally, reeling and staggering like a drunken man, hurled me over the rim of the car, and left me dangling, at a terrific height, with my head downward, and my face outward, by a piece of slender cord about three feet in length, which hung accidentally through a crevice near the bottom of the wicker-work, and in which, as I fell, my left foot became most providentially entangled. It is impossible—utterly impossible—to form any adequate idea of the horror of my situation. I gasped convul-

sively for breath—a shudder resembling a fit of the ague agitated every nerve and muscle in my frame—I felt my eyes starting from their sockets—a horrible nausea overwhelmed me—and at length I lost all consciousness in a swoon.

How long I remained in this state it is impossible to say. It must, however, have been no inconsiderable time, for when I partially recovered the sense of existence, I found the day breaking, the balloon at a prodigious height over a wilderness of ocean, and not a trace of land to be discovered far and wide within the limits of the vast horizon. My sensations, however, upon thus recovering, were by no means so replete with agony as might have been anticipated. Indeed, there was much of madness in the calm survey which I began to take of my situation. I drew up to my eyes each of my hands, one after the other, and wondered what occurrence could have given rise to the swelling of the veins, and the horrible blackness of the finger nails. I afterwards carefully examined my head, shaking it repeatedly, and feeling it with minute attention, until I succeeded in satisfying myself that it was not, as I had more than half suspected, larger than my balloon. Then, in a knowing manner, I felt in both my breeches pockets, and, missing therefrom a set of tablets and a tooth-pick case, endeavored to account for their disappearance, and, not being able to do so, felt inexpressibly chagrined. It now occurred to me that I suffered great uneasiness in the joint of my left ankle, and a dim consciousness of my situation began to glimmer through my mind. But, strange to say! I was neither astonished nor horror-stricken. If I felt any emotion at all, it was a kind of chuckling satisfaction at the cleverness I was about to display in extricating myself from this dilemma; and never, for a moment, did I look upon my ultimate safety as a question susceptible of doubt. For a few minutes I remained wrapped in the profoundest meditation. I have a distinct recollection of frequently compressing my lips, putting my fore-finger to the side of my nose, and making use of other gesticulations and grimaces common to men who, at ease in their arm-chairs, meditate upon matters of intricacy or importance. Having, as I thought, sufficiently collected my ideas, I now, with great caution and deliberation, put my hands behind my back, and unfastened the large iron buckle which belonged to the waistband of my pantaloons. This buckle had three teeth, which, being somewhat rusty, turned with great difficulty on their axis. I brought them, however, after some trouble, at right angles to the body of the buckle, and was glad to find them remain firm in that position. Holding within my teeth the instrument thus obtained, I now proceeded to untie the knot of my cravat. I had to rest several times before I could accomplish this manœuvre; but it was at length accomplished. To one end of the cravat I then made fast the buckle, and the other end I tied, for greater security, tightly around my wrist. Drawing now my body upwards, with a prodigious exertion of muscular force, I succeeded, at the very first trial, in throwing the buckle over the car, and entangling it, as I had anticipated, in the circular rim of the wicker-work.

My body was now inclined towards the side of the car, at an angle of about forty-five degrees; but it must not be understood that I was therefore only forty-five degrees below the perpendicular. So far from it, I still lay nearly level with the plane of the horizon; for the change of situation which I had acquired, had forced the bottom of the car considerably outward from my position, which was accordingly one of the most imminent peril. It should be remembered, however, that when I fell, in the first instance, from the car, if I had fallen with my face turned toward the balloon, instead of turned outwardly from it as it actually was—or if, in the second place, the cord by which I was suspended had chanced to hang over the upper edge, instead of through a crevice near the bottom of the car—I say it may readily be conceived that, in either of these supposed cases, I should have been unable to accomplish even as much as I had now accomplished, and the disclosures now made would have been utterly lost to posterity. I had therefore every reason to be grateful; although, in point of fact, I was still too stupid to be any thing at all, and hung for, perhaps, a quarter of an hour, in that extraordinary manner, without making the slightest farther exertion, and in a singularly tranquil state of idiotic enjoyment. But this feeling did not fail to die rapidly away, and thereunto succeeded horror, and dismay, and a sense of utter helplessness and ruin. In fact, the blood so long accumulating in the vessels of my head and throat, and which had hitherto buoyed up my spirits with delirium, had now begun to retire within its proper channels, and the distinctness which was thus added to my perception of the danger, merely served to deprive me of the self-possession and courage to encounter it. But this weakness was, luckily for me, of no very long duration. In good time came to my rescue the spirit of despair,[10] and, with frantic cries and struggles, I jerked my way bodily upwards, till, at length, clutching with a vice-like grip the long-desired rim, I writhed my person over it, and fell headlong and shuddering within the car.

It was not until some time afterward that I recovered myself sufficiently to attend to the ordinary cares of the balloon. I then, however, examined it with attention, and found it, to my great relief, uninjured. My implements were all safe, and, fortunately, I had lost neither ballast nor provisions. Indeed, I had so well secured them in their places, that such an accident was entirely out of the question. Looking at my watch, I found it six o'clock. I was still rapidly ascending, and the barometer gave a present altitude of three and three-quarter miles. Immediately beneath me in the ocean, lay a small black object, slightly oblong in shape, seemingly about the size of a domino, and in every respect bearing a great resemblance to one of those toys. Bringing my telescope to bear upon it, I plainly discerned it to be a British ninety-four gun ship, close-hauled, and pitching heavily in the sea with her head to the W. S. W. Besides this ship, I saw nothing but the ocean and the sky, and the sun, which had long arisen.

It is now high time that I should explain to your Excellencies the object of my voyage. Your Excellencies will bear in mind that distressed circumstances in Rotterdam had at length driven me to the resolution of committing suicide. It was not, however, that to life itself I had any positive disgust, but that I was harassed beyond endurance by the adventitious miseries attending my situation. In this state of mind, wishing to live, yet wearied with life, the treatise at the stall of the bookseller, backed by the opportune discovery of my cousin of Nantz, opened a resource to my imagination. I then finally made up my mind. I determined to depart, yet live—to leave the world, yet continue to exist—in short, to drop enigmas, I resolved, let what would ensue, to force a passage, if I could, *to the moon*. Now, lest I should be supposed more of a madman than I actually am, I will detail, as well as I am able, the considerations which led me to believe that an achievement of this nature, although without doubt difficult, and full of danger, was not absolutely, to a bold spirit, beyond the confines of the possible.

The moon's actual distance from the earth was the first thing to be attended to. Now, the mean or average interval between the *centres* of the two planets is 59.9643 of the earth's equatorial *radii*, or only about 237,000 miles.[11] I say the mean or average interval;—but it must be borne in mind, that the form of the moon's orbit being an ellipse of eccentricity amounting to no less than 0.05484 of the major semi-axis of the ellipse itself, and the earth's centre being situated in its focus, if I could, in any manner, contrive to meet the moon in its perigee, the above-mentioned distance would be materially diminished. But to say nothing, at present, of this possibility, it was very certain that, at all events, from the 237,000 miles I would have to deduct the *radius* of the earth, say 4000, and the radius of the moon, say 1080, in all 5080, leaving an actual interval to be traversed, under average circumstances, of 231,920 miles. Now this, I reflected, was no very extraordinary distance. Travelling on the land has been repeatedly accomplished at the rate of sixty miles per hour; and indeed a much greater speed may be anticipated. But even at this velocity, it would take me no more than 161 days to reach the surface of the moon. There were, however, many particulars inducing me to believe that my average rate of travelling might possibly very much exceed that of sixty miles per hour, and, as these considerations did not fail to make a deep impression upon my mind, I will mention them more fully hereafter.

The next point to be regarded was one of far greater importance. From indications afforded by the barometer, we find that, in ascensions from the surface of the earth we have, at the height of 1000 feet, left below us about one-thirtieth of the entire mass of atmospheric air; that at 10,600, we have ascended through nearly one-third; and that at 18,000, which is not far from the elevation of Cotopaxi, we have surmounted one-half the material, or, at all events, one-half the *ponderable* body of air incumbent upon our globe. It is also calculated, that at an altitude not exceeding the hundredth part of the earth's diameter—that is, not exceeding eighty miles—the rarefaction would be so excessive that animal life could in no manner be sustained, and, moreover, that the most delicate means we possess of ascertaining the presence of the atmosphere, would be inadequate to assure us of its existence. But I did not fail to perceive that these latter calculations are founded altogether on our experimental knowledge of the properties of air, and the mechanical laws regulating its dilation and compression, in what may be called, comparatively speaking, *the immediate vicinity* of the earth itself; and, at the same time, it is taken for granted that animal life is and must be, essentially *incapable of modification* at any given unattainable distance from the surface. Now, all such reasoning and from such *data*, must of course be simply analogical. The greatest height ever reached by man was that of 25,000 feet, attained in the æronautic expedition of Messieurs Gay-Lussac and Biot.[12] This is a moderate altitude, even when compared with the eighty miles in question; and I could not help thinking that the subject admitted room for doubt, and great latitude for speculation.

But, in point of fact, an ascension being made to any given altitude, the ponderable quantity of air surmounted in any *farther* ascension, is by no means in proportion to the additional height ascended, (as may be plainly seen from what has been stated before,) but in a *ratio* constantly decreasing. It is therefore evident that, ascend as high as we may, we cannot, literally speaking, arrive at a limit beyond which *no* atmosphere is to be found. It *must exist*, I argued; although it *may* exist in a state of infinite rarefaction.

On the other hand, I was aware that arguments have not been wanting to prove the existence of a real and definite limit to the atmosphere, beyond which there is absolutely no air whatsoever. But a circumstance which has been left out of view by those who contend for such a limit, seemed to me, although no positive refutation of their creed, still a point worthy very serious investigation. On comparing the intervals between the successive arrivals of Encke's comet at its perihelion, after giving credit, in the most exact manner, for all the disturbances due to the attractions of the planets, it appears that the periods are gradually diminishing; that is to say, the major axis of the comet's ellipse is growing shorter, in a slow but perfectly regular decrease. Now, this is precisely what ought to be the case, if we suppose a resistance experienced from the comet from an extremely *rare ethereal medium* pervading the regions of its orbit. For it is evident that such a medium must, in retarding the comet's velocity, increase its centripetal, by weakening its centrifugal force. In other words, the sun's attraction would be constantly attaining greater power, and the comet would be drawn nearer at every revolution. Indeed, there is no other way of accounting for the variation in question. But again:—The real diameter of the same comet's nebulosity, is observed to contract rapidly as it approaches the sun, and dilate with equal rapidity in its departure toward its aphelion. Was I not justifiable in supposing, with M. Valz, that this apparent condensation of volume has its origin in the compression of the same ethereal medium I have spoken of before, and which is dense in proportion to its vicinity to the sun? The lenticular-shaped phenomenon, also, called the zodiacal light, was a matter worthy of attention. This radiance, so apparent in the tropics, and which cannot be mistaken for any meteoric lustre, extends from the horizon obliquely upwards, and follows generally the direction of the sun's equator. It appeared to me evidently in the nature of a rare atmosphere extending from the sun outwards, beyond the orbit of Venus at least, and I believed indefinitely farther.[13] Indeed, this medium I could not suppose confined to the path of the comet's ellipse, or to the immediate neighborhood of the sun. It was easy, on the contrary, to imagine it pervading the entire regions of our planetary system, condensed into what we call atmosphere at the planets themselves, and perhaps at some of them modified by considerations purely geological; that is to say, modified, or varied in its proportions (or absolute nature) by matters volatilized from the respective orbs.

Having adopted this view of the subject, I had little farther hesitation. Granting that on my passage I should meet with atmosphere *essentially* the same as at the surface of the earth, I conceived that, by means of the very ingenious apparatus of M. Grimm,[14] I should readily be enabled to condense it in sufficient quantity for the purposes of respiration. This would remove the chief obstacle in a journey to the moon. I had indeed spent some money and great labor in adapting the apparatus to the object intended, and confidently looked forward to its successful application, if I could manage to complete the voyage within any reasonable period.— This brings me back to the *rate* at which it would be possible to travel.

It is true that balloons, in the first stage of their ascensions from the earth, are known to rise with a velocity comparatively moderate. Now, the power of elevation lies altogether in the superior gravity of the atmospheric air compared with the gas in the balloon; and, at first sight, it does not appear probable that, as the balloon acquires altitude, and consequently arrives successively in atmospheric *strata* of densities rapidly diminishing—I say, it does not appear at all reasonable that, in this its progress upward, the original velocity should be accelerated. On the other hand, I was not aware that, in any recorded ascension, a *diminution* had been proved to be apparent in the absolute rate of ascent; although such should have been the case, if on account of nothing else, on account of the escape of gas through balloons ill-constructed, and varnished with no better material than the ordinary varnish. It seemed, therefore, that the effect of such escape was only sufficient to counterbalance the effect of the acceleration attained in the diminishing of the balloon's distance from the gravitating centre. I now considered that, provided in my passage I found the *medium* I had imagined, and provided it should prove to be *essentially* what we denominate atmospheric air, it could make comparatively little difference at what extreme state of rarefaction I

should discover it—that is to say, in regard to my power of ascending—for the gas in the balloon would not only be itself subject to similar rarefaction, (in proportion to the occurrence of which, I could suffer an escape of so much as would be requisite to prevent explosion,) but, *being what it was*, would, at all events, continue specifically lighter than any compound whatever of mere nitrogen and oxygen. Thus there was a chance—in fact, there was a strong probability—that, *at no epoch of my ascent, I should reach a point where the united weights of my immense balloon, the inconceivably rare gas within it, the car, and its contents, should equal the weight of the mass of the surrounding atmosphere displaced;* and this will be readily understood as the sole condition upon which my upward flight would be arrested. But, if this point were even attained, I could dispense with ballast and other weight to the amount of nearly 300 pounds. In the meantime, the force of gravitation would be constantly diminishing, in proportion to the squares of the distances, and so, with a velocity prodigiously accelerating, I should at length arrive in those distant regions where the force of the earth's attraction would be superseded by that of the moon.

There was another difficulty, however, which occasioned me some little disquietude. It has been observed, that, in balloon ascensions to any considerable height, besides the pain attending respiration, great uneasiness is experienced about the head and body, often accompanied with bleeding at the nose, and other symptoms of an alarming kind, and growing more and more inconvenient in proportion to the altitude attained. This was a reflection of a nature somewhat startling. Was it not probable that these symptoms would increase until terminated by death itself? I finally thought not. Their origin was to be looked for in the progressive removal of the *customary* atmospheric pressure upon the surface of the body, and consequent distention of the superficial blood-vessels—not in any positive disorganization of the animal system, as in the case of difficulty in breathing, where the atmospheric density is *chemically insufficient* for the due renovation of blood in a ventricle of the heart.[15] Unless for default of this renovation, I could see no reason, therefore, why life could not be sustained even in a *vacuum;* for the expansion and compression of chest, commonly called breathing, is action purely muscular, and the *cause,* not the *effect,* of respiration. In a word, I conceived that, as the body should become habituated to the want of atmospheric pressure, these sensations of pain would gradually diminish—and to endure them while they continued, I relied with confidence upon the iron hardihood of my constitution.

Thus, may it please your Excellencies, I have detailed some, though by no means all, the considerations which led me to form the project of a lunar voyage. I shall now proceed to lay before you the result of an attempt so apparently audacious in conception, and, at all events, so utterly unparalleled in the annals of mankind.

Having attained the altitude before mentioned—that is to say, three miles and three quarters—I threw out from the car a quantity of feathers, and found that I still ascended with sufficient rapidity; there was, therefore, no necessity for discharging any ballast. I was glad of this, for I wished to retain with me as much weight as I could carry, for the obvious reason that I could not be *positive* either about the gravitation or the atmospheric density of the moon. I as yet suffered no bodily inconvenience, breathing with great freedom, and feeling no pain whatever in the head. The cat was lying very demurely upon my coat, which I had taken off, and eyeing the pigeons with an air of *nonchalance.* These latter being tied by the leg, to prevent their escape, were busily employed in picking up some grains of rice scattered for them in the bottom of the car.

At twenty minutes past six o'clock, the barometer showed an elevation of 26,400 feet, or five miles to a fraction. The prospect seemed unbounded. Indeed, it is very easily calculated by means of spherical geometry, how great an extent of the earth's area I beheld. The convex surface of any segment of a sphere is, to the entire surface of the sphere itself, as the versed sine of the segment to the diameter of the sphere.[16] Now, in my case, the versed sine —that is to say, the *thickness* of the segment beneath me—was about equal to my elevation, or the elevation of the point of sight above the surface. "As five miles, then, to eight thousand," would express the proportion of the earth's area seen by me. In other words, I beheld as much as a sixteen-hundredth part of the whole surface of the globe. The sea appeared unruffled as a mirror, although, by means of the telescope, I could perceive it to be in a state of violent agitation. The ship was no longer visible, having drifted away, apparently, to the eastward. I now began to experience, at intervals, severe pain in the head, especially about the ears—still, however, breathing with tolerable freedom. The cat and pigeons seemed to suffer no inconvenience whatsoever.

At twenty minutes before seven, the balloon entered a long series of dense cloud, which put me to great trouble, by damaging my condensing apparatus, and wetting me to the skin. This was, to be sure, a singular *rencontre,* for I had not believed it possible that a cloud of this nature could be sustained at so great an elevation. I thought it best, however, to throw out two five-pound pieces of ballast, reserving still a weight of one hundred and sixty-five pounds. Upon so doing, I soon rose above the difficulty, and perceived immediately, that I had obtained a great increase in my rate of ascent. In a few seconds after my leaving the cloud, a flash of vivid lightning shot from one end of it to the other, and caused it to kindle up, throughout its vast extent, like a mass of ignited charcoal. This, it must be remembered, was in the broad light of day. No fancy may picture the sublimity which might have been exhibited by a similar phenomenon taking place amid the darkness of the night. Hell itself might then have found a fitting image. Even as it was, my hair stood on end, while I gazed afar down within the yawning abysses, letting imagination descend, and stalk about in the strange vaulted halls, and ruddy gulfs, and red ghastly chasms of the hideous and unfathomable fire. I had indeed made a narrow escape. Had the balloon remained a very short while longer within the cloud—that is to say had not the inconvenience of getting wet, determined me to discharge the ballast—my destruction might, and probably would, have been the consequence. Such perils, although little considered, are perhaps the greatest which must be encountered in balloons. I had by this time, however, attained too great an elevation to be any longer uneasy on this head.

I was now rising rapidly, and by seven o'clock the barometer indicated an altitude of no less than nine miles and a half. I began to find great difficulty in drawing my breath. My head, too, was excessively painful; and, having felt for some time a moisture about my cheeks, I at length discovered it to be blood, which was oozing quite fast from the drums of my ears. My eyes, also, gave me great uneasiness. Upon passing the hand over them they seemed to have protruded from their sockets in no inconsiderable degree; and all objects in the car, and even the balloon itself, appeared distorted to my vision. These symptoms were more than I had expected, and occasioned me some alarm. At this juncture, very imprudently, and without consideration, I threw out from the car three five-pound pieces of ballast. The accelerated rate of ascent thus obtained, carried me too rapidly, and without sufficient gradation, into a highly rarefied *stratum* of the atmosphere, and the result had nearly proved fatal to my expedition and to myself. I was suddenly seized with a spasm which lasted for more than five

minutes, and even when this, in a measure, ceased, I could catch my breath only at long intervals, and in a gasping manner, —bleeding all the while copiously at the nose and ears, and even slightly at the eyes. The pigeons appeared distressed in the extreme, and struggled to escape; while the cat mewed piteously, and, with her tongue hanging out of her mouth, staggered to and fro in the car as if under the influence of poison. I now too late discovered the great rashness of which I had been guilty in discharging the ballast, and my agitation was excessive. I anticipated nothing less than death, and death in a few minutes. The physical suffering I underwent contributed also to render me nearly incapable of making any exertion for the preservation of my life. I had, indeed, little power of reflection left, and the violence of the pain in my head seemed to be greatly on the increase. Thus I found that my senses would shortly give way altogether, and I had already clutched one of the valve ropes with the view of attempting a descent, when the recollection of the trick I had played the three creditors, and the possible consequences to myself, should I return, operated to deter me for the moment. I lay down in the bottom of the car, and endeavored to collect my faculties. In this I so far succeeded as to determine upon the experiment of losing blood. Having no lancet, however, I was constrained to perform the operation in the best manner I was able, and finally succeeded in opening a vein in my left arm, with the blade of my penknife. The blood had hardly commenced flowing when I experienced a sensible relief, and by the time I had lost about half a moderate basin-full, most of the worst symptoms had abandoned me entirely. I nevertheless did not think it expedient to attempt getting on my feet immediately; but, having tied up my arm as well as I could, I lay still for about a quarter of an hour. At the end of this time I arose, and found myself freer from absolute *pain* of any kind than I had been during the last hour and a quarter of my ascension. The difficulty of breathing, however, was diminished in a very slight degree, and I found that it would soon be positively necessary to make use of my condenser. In the meantime, looking towards the cat, who was again snugly stowed away upon my coat, I discovered, to my infinite surprise, that she had taken the opportunity of my indisposition to bring into light a litter of three little kittens. This was an addition to the number of passengers on my part altogether unexpected; but I was pleased at the occurrence. It would afford me a chance of bringing to a kind of test the truth of a surmise, which, more than any thing else, had influenced me in attempting this ascension. I had imagined that the *habitual* endurance of the atmospheric pressure at the surface of the earth was the cause, or nearly so, of the pain attending animal existence at a distance above the surface. Should the kittens be found to suffer uneasiness *in an equal degree with their mother*, I must consider my theory in fault, but a failure to do so I should look upon as a strong confirmation of my idea.

By eight o'clock I had actually attained an elevation of seventeen miles above the surface of the earth. Thus it seemed to me evident that my rate of ascent was not only on the increase, but that the progression would have been apparent in a slight degree even had I not discharged the ballast which I did. The pains in my head and ears returned, at intervals, with violence, and I still continued to bleed occasionally at the nose: but, upon the whole, I suffered much less than might have been expected. I breathed, however, at every moment, with more and more difficulty, and each inhalation was attended with a troublesome spasmodic action of the chest. I now unpacked the condensing apparatus, and got it ready for immediate use.

The view of the earth, at this period of my ascension, was beautiful indeed. To the westward, the northward, and the southward, as far as I could see, lay a boundless sheet of apparently unruffled ocean, which every moment gained a deeper and deeper tint of blue. At a vast distance to the eastward, although perfectly discernible, extended the islands of Great Britain, the entire Atlantic coasts of France and Spain, with a small portion of the northern part of the continent of Africa. Of individual edifices not a trace could be discovered, and the proudest cities of mankind had utterly faded away from the face of the earth.

What mainly astonished me, in the appearance of things below, was the seeming concavity of the surface of the globe. I had, thoughtlessly enough, expected to see its real *convexity*[17] become evident as I ascended; but a very little reflection sufficed to explain the discrepancy. A line, dropped from my position perpendicularly to the earth, would have formed the perpendicular of a right-angled triangle, of which the base would have extended from the right-angle to the horizon, and the hypothenuse from the horizon to my position. But my height was little or nothing in comparison with my prospect. In other words, the base and hypothenuse of the supposed triangle would, in my case, have been so long, when compared to the perpendicular, that the two former might have been regarded as nearly parallel. In this manner the horizon of the æronaut appears always to be *upon a level* with the car. But as the point immediately beneath him seems, and is, at a great distance below him, it seems, of course, also at a great distance below the horizon. Hence the impression of concavity; and this impression must remain, until the elevation shall bear so great a proportion to the prospect, that the apparent parallelism of the base and hypothenuse, disappears.

The pigeons about this time seeming to undergo much suffering, I determined upon giving them their liberty. I first untied one of them, a beautiful gray-mottled pigeon, and placed him upon the rim of the wicker-work. He appeared extremely uneasy, looking anxiously around him, fluttering his wings, and making a loud cooing noise, but could not be persuaded to trust himself from the car. I took him up at last, and threw him to about half-a-dozen yards from the balloon. He made, however, no attempt to descend as I had expected, but struggled with great vehemence to get back, uttering at the same time very shrill and piercing cries. He at length succeeded in regaining his former station on the rim, but had hardly done so when his head dropped upon his breast, and he fell dead within the car. The other one did not prove so unfortunate. To prevent his following the example of his companion, and accomplishing a return, I threw him downwards with all my force, and was pleased to find him continue his descent, with great velocity, making use of his wings with ease, and in a perfectly natural manner. In a very short time he was out of sight, and I have no doubt he reached home in safety. Puss, who seemed in a great measure recovered from her illness, now made a hearty meal of the dead bird, and then went to sleep with much apparent satisfaction. Her kittens were quite lively and so far evinced not the slightest sign of any uneasiness.

At a quarter-past eight, being able no longer to draw breath without the most intolerable pain, I proceeded, forthwith, to adjust around the car the apparatus belonging to the condenser. This apparatus will require some little explanation, and your Excellencies will please to bear in mind that my object, in the first place, was to surround myself and car entirely with a barricade against the highly rarefied atmosphere in which I was existing, with the intention of introducing within this barricade, by means of my condenser, a quantity of this same atmosphere sufficiently condensed for the purposes of respiration. With this object in view I had prepared a very strong, perfectly air-tight, but flexible gum-elastic bag. In this bag, which was of sufficient dimensions, the entire car was in a manner placed. That

is to say, it (the bag) was drawn over the whole bottom of the car, up its sides, and so on, along the outside of the ropes, to the upper rim or hoop where the net-work is attached. Having pulled the bag up in this way, and formed a complete enclosure on all sides, and at bottom, it was now necessary to fasten up its top or mouth, by passing its material over the hoop of the net-work,—in other words, between the net-work and the hoop. But if the net-work were separated from the hoop to admit this passage, what was to sustain the car in the meantime? Now the net-work was not permanently fastened to the hoop, but attached by a series of running loops or nooses. I therefore undid only a few of these loops at one time, leaving the car suspended by the remainder. Having thus inserted a portion of the cloth forming the upper part of the bag, I refastened the loops—not to the hoop, for that would have been impossible, since the cloth now intervened,—but to a series of large buttons, affixed to the cloth itself, about three feet below the mouth of the bag; the intervals between the buttons having been made to correspond to the intervals between the loops. This done, a few more of the loops were unfastened from the rim, a farther portion of the cloth introduced, and the disengaged loops then connected with their proper buttons. In this way it was possible to insert the whole upper part of the bag between the net-work and the hoop. It is evident that the hoop would now drop down within the car, while the whole weight of the car itself, with all its contents, would be held up merely by the strength of the buttons. This, at first sight, would seem an inadequate dependence; but it was by no means so, for the buttons were not only very strong in themselves, but so close together that a very slight portion of the whole weight was supported by any one of them. Indeed, had the car and contents been three times heavier than they were, I should not have been at all uneasy. I now raised up the hoop again within the covering of gum-elastic, and propped it at nearly its former height by means of three light poles prepared for the occasion. This was done, of course, to keep the bag distended at the top, and to preserve the lower part of the net-work in its proper situation. All that now remained was to fasten up the mouth of the enclosure; and this was readily accomplished by gathering the folds of the material together, and twisting them up very tightly on the inside by means of a kind of stationary *tourniquet.*

In the sides of the covering thus adjusted round the car, had been inserted three circular panes of thick but clear glass, through which I could see without difficulty around me in every horizontal direction. In that portion of the cloth forming the bottom, was likewise a fourth window, of the same kind, and corresponding with a small aperture in the floor of the car itself. This enabled me to see perpendicularly down, but having found it impossible to place any similar contrivance overhead, on account of the peculiar manner of closing up the opening there, and the consequent wrinkles in the cloth, I could expect to see no objects situated directly in my zenith. This, of course, was a matter of little consequence; for, had I even been able to place a window at top, the balloon itself would have prevented my making any use of it.

About a foot below one of the side windows was a circular opening, three inches in diameter, and fitted with a brass rim adapted in its inner edge to the windings of a screw. In this rim was screwed the large tube of the condenser, the body of the machine being, of course, within the chamber of gum-elastic. Through this tube a quantity of the rare atmosphere circumjacent being drawn by means of a *vacuum* created in the body of the machine, was thence discharged, in a state of condensation, to mingle with the thin air already in the chamber. This operation being repeated several times, at length filled the chamber with atmosphere proper for all

the purposes of respiration. But in so confined a space it would, in a short time, necessarily become foul, and unfit for use from frequent contact with the lungs. It was then ejected by a small valve at the bottom of the car,—the dense air readily sinking into the thiner atmosphere below. To avoid the inconvenience of making a total *vacuum* at any moment within the chamber, this purification was never accomplished all at once, but in a gradual manner,—the valve being opened only for a few seconds, then closed again, until one or two strokes from the pump of the condenser had supplied the place of the atmosphere ejected. For the sake of experiment I had put the cat and kittens in a small basket, and suspended it outside the car to a button at the bottom, close by the valve, through which I could feed them at any moment when necessary. I did this at some little risk, and before closing the mouth of the chamber, by reaching under the car with one of the poles before mentioned to which a hook had been attached. As soon as dense air was admitted in the chamber, the hoop and poles became unnecessary; the expansion of the enclosed atmosphere powerfully distending the gum-elastic.

By the time I had fully completed these arrangements and filled the chamber as explained, it wanted only ten minutes of nine o'clock. During the whole period of my being thus employed, I endured the most terrible distress from difficulty of respiration; and bitterly did I repent the negligence, or rather fool-hardiness, of which I had been guilty, of putting off to the last moment a matter of so much importance. But having at length accomplished it, I soon began to reap the benefit of my invention. Once again I breathed with perfect freedom and ease—and indeed why should I not? I was also agreeably surprised to find myself, in a great measure, relieved from the violent pains which had hitherto tormented me. A slight headache, accompanied with a sensation of fulness or distention about the wrists, the ankles, and the throat, was nearly all of which I had now to complain. Thus it seemed evident that a greater part of the uneasiness attending the removal of atmospheric pressure had actually *worn off*, as I had expected, and that much of the pain endured for the last two hours should have been attributed altogether to the effects of a deficient respiration.

At twenty minutes before nine o'clock —that is to say, a short time prior to my closing up the mouth of the chamber, the mercury attained its limit, or ran down, in the barometer, which, as I mentioned before, was one of an extended construction. It then indicated an altitude on my part of 132,000 feet, or five-and-twenty miles, and I consequently surveyed at that time an extent of the earth's area amounting to no less than the three-hundred-and-twentieth part of its entire superficies. At nine o'clock I had again lost sight of land to the eastward, but not before I became aware that the balloon was drifting rapidly to the N. N. W. The ocean beneath me still retained its apparent concavity, although my view was often interrupted by the masses of cloud which floated to and fro.

At half past nine I tried the experiment of throwing out a handful of feathers through the valve. They did not float as I had expected, but dropped down perpendicularly, like a bullet, *en masse,* and with the greatest velocity,—being out of sight in a very few seconds. I did not at first know what to make of this extraordinary phenomenon; not being able to believe that my rate of ascent had, of a sudden, met with so prodigious an acceleration. But it soon occurred to me that the atmosphere was now far too rare to sustain even the feathers; that they actually fell, as they appeared to do, with great rapidity; and that I had been surprised by the united velocities of their descent and my own elevation.

By ten o'clock I found that I had very little to occupy my immediate attention. Affairs went on swimmingly, and I believed the balloon to be going upwards with a speed increasing momently, although I had no longer any means of ascertaining the progression of the increase. I suffered no pain or uneasiness of any kind, and enjoyed better spirits than I had at any period since my departure from Rotterdam; busying myself now in examining the state of my various apparatus, and now in regenerating the atmosphere within the chamber. This latter point I determined to attend to at regular intervals of forty minutes, more on account of the preservation of my health, than from so frequent a renovation being absolutely necessary. In the meanwhile I could not help making anticipations. Fancy revelled in the wild and dreamy regions of the moon. Imagination, feeling herself for once unshackled, roamed at will among the ever-changing wonders of a shadowy and unstable land. Now there were hoary and time-honored forests, and craggy precipices, and waterfalls tumbling with a loud noise into abysses without a bottom. Then I came suddenly into still noonday solitudes, where no wind of heaven ever intruded, and where vast meadows of poppies, and slender, lily-looking flowers spread themselves out a weary distance, all silent and motionless for ever. Then again I journeyed far down away into another country where it was all one dim and vague lake, with a boundary-line of clouds. But fancies such as these were not the sole possessors of my brain. Horrors of a nature most stern and most appalling would too frequently obtrude themselves upon my mind, and shake the innermost depths of my soul with the bare supposition of their possibility. Yet I would not suffer my thoughts for any length of time to dwell upon these latter speculations, rightly judging the real and palpable dangers of the voyage sufficient for my undivided attention.

At five o'clock, P. M., being engaged in

regenerating the atmosphere within the chamber, I took that opportunity of observing the cat and kittens through the valve. The cat herself appeared to suffer again very much, and I had no hesitation in attributing her uneasiness chiefly to a difficulty in breathing; but my experiment with the kittens had resulted very strangely. I had expected, of course, to see them betray a sense of pain, although in a less degree than their mother; and this would have been sufficient to confirm my opinion concerning the habitual endurance of atmospheric pressure. But I was not prepared to find them, upon close examination, evidently enjoying a high degree of health, breathing with the greatest ease and perfect regularity, and evincing not the slightest sign of any uneasiness. I could only account for all this by extending my theory, and supposing that the highly rarefied atmosphere around, might perhaps not be, as I had taken for granted, chemically insufficient for the purposes of life, and that a person born in such a *medium* might, possibly, be unaware of any inconvenience attending its inhalation, while, upon removal to the denser *strata* near the earth, he might endure tortures of a similar nature to those I had so lately experienced. It has since been to me a matter of deep regret that an awkward accident, at this time, occasioned me the loss of my little family of cats, and deprived me of the insight into this matter which a continued experiment might have afforded. In passing my hand through the valve, with a cup of water for the old puss, the sleeve of my shirt became entangled in the loop which sustained the basket, and thus, in a moment, loosened it from the button. Had the whole actually vanished into air, it could not have shot from my sight in a more abrupt and instantaneous manner. Positively, there could not have intervened the tenth part of a second between the disengagement of the basket and its absolute disappearance with all that it contained. My good wishes followed it to the earth, but, of course, I had no hope that either cat or kittens would ever live to tell the tale of their misfortune.

At six o'clock, I perceived a great portion of the earth's visible area to the eastward involved in thick shadow, which continued to advance with great rapidity, until, at five minutes before seven, the whole surface in view was enveloped in the darkness of night. It was not, however, until long after this time that the rays of the setting sun ceased to illumine the balloon; and this circumstance, although of course fully anticipated, did not fail to give me an infinite deal of pleasure. It was evident that, in the morning, I should behold the rising luminary many hours at least before the citizens of Rotterdam, in spite of their situation so much farther to the eastward, and thus, day after day, in proportion to the height ascended, would I enjoy the light of the sun for a longer and a longer period. I now determined to keep a journal of my passage, reckoning the days from one to twenty-four hours continuously, without taking into consideration the intervals of darkness.

At ten o'clock, feeling sleepy, I determined to lie down for the rest of the night; but here a difficulty presented itself, which, obvious as it may appear, had escaped my attention up to the very moment of which I am now speaking. If I went to sleep as I proposed, how could the atmosphere in the chamber be regenerated in the *interim*? To breathe it for more than an hour, at the farthest, would be a matter of impossibility; or, if even this term could be extended to an hour and a quarter, the most ruinous consequences might ensue. The consideration of this dilemma gave me no little disquietude; and it will hardly be believed, that, after the dangers I had undergone, I should look upon this business in so serious a light, as to give up all hope of accomplishing my ultimate design, and finally make up my mind to the necessity of a descent. But this hesitation was only momentary. I reflected that man is the veriest slave of custom, and that many points in the routine of his existence are deemed *essentially* important, which are only so *at all* by his having rendered them habitual. It was very certain that I could not do without sleep; but I might easily bring myself to feel no inconvenience from being awakened at intervals of an hour during the whole period of my repose. It would require but five minutes at most, to regenerate the atmosphere in the fullest manner—and the only real difficulty was, to contrive a method of arousing myself at the proper moment for so doing. But this was a question which, I am willing to confess, occasioned me no little trouble in its solution. To be sure, I had heard of the student who, to prevent his falling asleep over his books, held in one hand a ball of copper, the din of whose descent into a basin of the same metal on the floor beside his chair, served effectually to startle him up, if, at any moment, he should be overcome with drowsiness. My own case, however, was very different indeed, and left me no room for any similar idea; for I did not wish to keep awake, but to be aroused from slumber at regular intervals of time. I at length hit upon the following expedient, which, simple as it may seem, was hailed by me, at the moment of discovery, as an invention fully equal to that of the telescope, the steam-engine, or the art of printing itself.

It is necessary to premise, that the balloon, at the elevation now attained, continued its course upwards with an even and undeviating ascent, and the car consequently followed with a steadiness so perfect that it would have been impossible to detect in it the slightest vacillation. This circumstance favored me greatly in the project I now determined to adopt. My supply of water had been put on board in kegs containing five gallons each, and ranged very securely around the in-

terior of the car. I unfastened one of these, and taking two ropes, tied them tightly across the rim of the wicker-work from one side to the other; placing them about a foot apart and parallel, so as to form a kind of shelf, upon which I placed the keg, and steadied it in a horizontal position. About eight inches immediately below these ropes, and four feet from the bottom of the car, I fastened another shelf —but made of thin plank, being the only similar piece of wood I had. Upon this latter shelf, and exactly beneath one of the rims of the keg, a small earthen pitcher was deposited. I now bored a hole in the end of the keg over the pitcher, and fitted in a plug of soft wood, cut in a tapering or conical shape. This plug I pushed in or pulled out, as might happen, until, after a few experiments, it arrived at that exact degree of tightness, at which the water, oozing from the hole, and falling into the pitcher below, would fill the latter to the brim in the period of sixty minutes. This, of course, was a matter briefly and easily ascertained, by noticing the proportion of the pitcher filled in any given time. Having arranged all this, the rest of the plan is obvious. My bed was so contrived upon the floor of the car, as to bring my head, in lying down, immediately below the mouth of the pitcher. It was evident, that, at the expiration of an hour, the pitcher, getting full, would be forced to run over, and to run over at the mouth, which was somewhat lower than the rim. It was also evident, that the water, thus falling from a height of more than four feet, could not do otherwise than fall upon my face, and that the sure consequence would be, to waken me up instantaneously, even from the soundest slumber in the world.[18]

It was fully eleven by the time I had completed these arrangements, and I immediately betook myself to bed, with full confidence in the efficiency of my invention. Nor in this matter was I disappointed. Punctually every sixty minutes was I aroused by my trusty chronometer, when, having emptied the pitcher into the bung-hole of the keg, and performed the duties of the condenser, I retired again to bed. These regular interruptions to my slumber caused me even less discomfort than I had anticipated; and when I finally arose for the day, it was seven o'clock, and the sun had attained many degrees above the line of my horizon.

April 3d. I found the balloon at an immense height indeed, and the earth's convexity had now become strikingly manifest. Below me in the ocean lay a cluster of black specks, which undoubtedly were islands. Overhead, the sky was of a jetty black, and the stars were brilliantly visible; indeed they had been so constantly since the first day of ascent. Far away to the northward I perceived a thin, white, and exceedingly brilliant line, or streak, on the edge of the horizon, and I had no hesitation in supposing it to be the southern disc of the ices of the Polar sea. My curiosity was greatly excited, for I had hopes of passing on much farther to the north, and might possibly, at some period, find myself placed directly above the Pole itself. I now lamented that my great elevation would, in this case, prevent my taking as accurate a survey as I could wish. Much, however, might be ascertained. Nothing else of an extraordinary nature occurred during the day. My apparatus all continued in good order, and the balloon still ascended without any perceptible vacillation. The cold was intense, and obliged me to wrap up closely in an overcoat. When darkness came over the earth, I betook myself to bed, although it was for many hours afterwards broad daylight all around my immediate situation. The water-clock was punctual in its duty, and I slept until next morning soundly, with the exception of the periodical interruption.

April 4th. Arose in good health and spirits, and was astonished at the singular change which had taken place in the appearance of the sea. It had lost, in a great measure, the deep tint of blue it had hitherto worn, being now of a grayish-white, and of a lustre dazzling to the eye. The convexity of the ocean had become so evident, that the entire mass of the distant water seemed to be tumbling headlong over the abyss of the horizon, and I found myself listening on tiptoe for the echoes of the mighty cataract. The islands were no longer visible; whether they had passed down the horizon to the south-east, or whether my increasing elevation had left them out of sight, it is impossible to say. I was inclined, however, to the latter opinion. The rim of ice to the northward was growing more and more apparent. Cold by no means so intense. Nothing of importance occurred, and I passed the day in reading, having taken care to supply myself with books.

April 5th. Beheld the singular phenomenon of the sun rising while nearly the whole visible surface of the earth continued to be involved in darkness. In time, however, the light spread itself over all, and I again saw the line of ice to the northward. It was now very distinct, and appeared of a much darker hue than the waters of the ocean. I was evidently approaching it, and with great rapidity. Fancied I could again distinguish a strip of land to the eastward, and one also to the westward, but could not be certain. Weather moderate. Nothing of any consequence happened during the day. Went early to bed.

April 6th. Was surprised at finding the rim of ice at a very moderate distance, and an immense field of the same material stretching away off to the horizon in the north. It was evident that if the balloon held its present course, it would soon arrive above the Frozen Ocean, and I had now little doubt of ultimately seeing the Pole. During the whole of the day I continued to near the ice. Towards night the limits of my horizon very suddenly and materially increased, owing undoubtedly to the earth's form being that of an oblate spheroid, and my arriving above the flattened regions in the vicinity of the Arctic circle. When darkness at length overtook me, I went to bed in great anxiety, fearing to pass over the object of so much curiosity when I should have no opportunity of observing it.

April 7th. Arose early, and to my great joy, at length beheld what there could be no hesitation in supposing the northern Pole itself. It was there, beyond a doubt, and immediately beneath my feet; but, alas! I had now ascended to so vast a distance, that nothing could with accuracy be discerned. Indeed, to judge from the progression of the numbers indicating my various altitudes, respectively, at different periods, between six, A. M., on the second of April, and twenty minutes before nine, A. M., of the same day, (at which time the barometer ran down,) it might be fairly inferred that the balloon had now, at four o'clock in the morning of April the seventh, reached a height of *not less*, certainly, than 7254 miles above the surface of the sea. This elevation may appear immense, but the estimate upon which it is calculated gave a result in all probability far inferior to the truth. At all events I undoubtedly beheld the whole of the earth's major diameter; the entire northern hemisphere lay beneath me like a chart orthographically projected; and the great circle of the equator itself formed the boundary line of my horizon. Your Excellencies may, however, readily imagine that the confined regions hitherto unexplored within the limits of the Arctic circle, although situated directly beneath me, and therefore seen without any appearance of being foreshortened, were still, in themselves, comparatively too diminutive, and at too great a distance from the point of sight, to admit of any very accurate examination. Nevertheless, what could be seen was of a nature singular and exciting. Northwardly from that huge rim before mentioned, and which, with slight qualification, may be called the limit of human discovery in these regions, one unbroken, or nearly unbroken sheet of ice continues to extend. In the first few degrees of this its progress, its surface is

very sensibly flattened, farther on depressed into a plane, and finally, becoming *not a little concave*, it terminates, at the Pole itself, in a circular centre, sharply defined, whose apparent diameter subtended at the balloon an angle of about sixty-five seconds, and whose dusky hue, varying in intensity, was at all times darker than any other spot upon the visible hemisphere, and occasionally deepened into the most absolute blackness.[19] Farther than this, little could be ascertained. By twelve o'clock the circular centre had materially decreased in circumference, and by seven, P. M., I lost sight of it entirely; the balloon passing over the western limb of the ice, and floating away rapidly in the direction of the equator.

April 8th. Found a sensible diminution in the earth's apparent diameter, besides a material alteration in its general color and appearance. The whole visible area partook in different degrees of a tint of pale yellow, and in some portions had acquired a brilliancy even painful to the eye. My view downwards was also considerably impeded by the dense atmosphere in the vicinity of the surface being loaded with clouds, between whose masses I could only now and then obtain a glimpse of the earth itself. This difficulty of direct vision had troubled me more or less for the last forty-eight hours; but my present enormous elevation brought closer together, as it were, the floating bodies of vapor, and the inconvenience became, of course, more and more palpable in proportion to my ascent. Nevertheless, I could easily perceive that the balloon now hovered above the range of great lakes in the continent of North America, and was holding a course, due south, which would soon bring me to the tropics. This circumstance did not fail to give me the most heartfelt satisfaction, and I hailed it as a happy omen of ultimate success. Indeed, the direction I had hitherto taken, had filled me with uneasiness; for it was evident that, had I continued it much longer, there would have been no possibility of my arriving at the moon at all, whose orbit is inclined to the ecliptic at only the small angle of 5° 8′ 48″. Strange as it may seem, it was only at this late period that I began to understand the great error I had committed, in not taking my departure from earth at some point *in the plane of the lunar ellipse.*

April 9th. To-day, the earth's diameter was greatly diminished, and the color of the surface assumed hourly a deeper tint of yellow. The balloon kept steadily on her course to the southward, and arrived, at nine, P. M., over the northern edge of the Mexican Gulf.

April 10th. I was suddenly aroused from slumber, about five o'clock this morning, by a loud, crackling, and terrific sound, for which I could in no manner account. It was of very brief duration, but, while it lasted, resembled nothing in the world of which I had any previous experience. It is needless to say that I became excessively alarmed, having, in the first instance, attributed the noise to the bursting of the balloon. I examined all my apparatus, however, with great attention, and could discover nothing out of order. Spent a great part of the day in meditating upon an occurrence so extraordinary, but could find no means whatever of accounting for it. Went to bed dissatisfied, and in a state of great anxiety and agitation.

April 11th. Found a startling diminution in the apparent diameter of the earth, and a considerable increase, now observable for the first time, in that of the moon itself, which wanted only a few days of being full. It now required long and excessive labor to condense within the chamber sufficient atmospheric air for the sustenance of life.

April 12th. A singular alteration took place in regard to the direction of the balloon, and although fully anticipated, afforded me the most unequivocal delight. Having reached, in its former course, about the twentieth parallel of southern latitude, it turned off suddenly, at an acute angle, to the eastward, and thus proceeded throughout the day, keeping nearly, if not altogether, *in the exact plane of the lunar ellipse.* What was worthy of remark, a very perceptible vacillation in the car was a consequence of this change of route,—a vacillation which prevailed, in a more or less degree, for a period of many hours.

April 13th. Was again very much alarmed by a repetition of the loud crackling noise which terrified me on the tenth. Thought long upon the subject, but was unable to form any satisfactory conclusion. Great decrease in the earth's apparent diameter, which now subtended from the balloon an angle of very little more than twenty-five degrees. The moon could not be seen at all, being nearly in my zenith. I still continued in the plane of the ellipse, but made little progress to the eastward.

April 14th. Extremely rapid decrease in the diameter of the earth. To-day I became strongly impressed with the idea, that the balloon was now actually running up the line of apsides[20] to the point of perigee,—in other words, holding the direct course which would bring it immediately to the moon in that part of its orbit the nearest to the earth. The moon itself was directly overhead, and consequently hidden from my view. Great and long continued labor necessary for the condensation of the atmosphere.

April 15th. Not even the outlines of continents and seas could now be traced upon the earth with distinctness. About twelve o'clock I became aware, for the third time, of that appalling sound which had so astonished me before. It now, however, continued for some moments, and gathered intensity as it continued. At length, while, stupefied and terror-stricken, I stood in expectation of I knew not what hideous destruction, the car vibrated with excessive violence, and a gigantic and flaming mass of some material which I could not distinguish, came with a voice of a thousand thunders, roaring and booming by the balloon. When my fears and astonishment had in some degree subsided, I had little difficulty in supposing it to be some mighty volcanic fragment ejected from that world to which I was so rapidly approaching, and, in all probability, one of that singular class of substances occasionally picked up on the earth, and termed meteoric stones for want of a better appellation.

April 16th. To-day, looking upwards as well as I could, through each of the side windows alternately, I beheld, to my great delight, a very small portion of the moon's disc protruding, as it were, on all sides beyond the huge circumference of the balloon. My agitation was extreme; for I had now little doubt of soon reaching the end of my perilous voyage. Indeed, the labor now required by the condenser, had increased to a most oppressive degree, and allowed me scarcely any respite from exertion. Sleep was a matter nearly out of the question. I became quite ill, and my frame trembled with exhaustion. It was impossible that human nature could endure this state of intense suffering much longer. During the now brief interval of darkness a meteoric stone again passed in my vicinity, and the frequency of these phenomena began to occasion me much apprehension.

April 17th. This morning proved an epoch in my voyage. It will be remembered, that, on the thirteenth, the earth subtended an angular breadth of twenty-five degrees. On the fourteenth, this had greatly diminished; on the fifteenth, a still more rapid decrease was observable; and, on retiring for the night of the sixteenth, I had noticed an angle of no more than about seven degrees and fifteen minutes. What, therefore, must have been my amazement, on awakening from a brief and disturbed slumber, on the morning of this day, the seventeenth, at finding the surface beneath me so suddenly and wonderfully *augmented* in volume, as to subtend no less than thirty-nine degrees in apparent angular diameter! I was thunderstruck! No words can give any adequate idea of the extreme, the absolute horror

and astonishment, with which I was seized, possessed, and altogether overwhelmed. My knees tottered beneath me —my teeth chattered—my hair started up on end. "The balloon, then, had actually burst!" These were the first tumultuous ideas which hurried through my mind: "The balloon had positively burst!—I was falling—falling with the most impetuous, the most unparalleled velocity! To judge from the immense distance already so quickly passed over, it could not be more than ten minutes, at the farthest, before I should meet the surface of the earth, and be hurled into annihilation!" But at length reflection came to my relief. I paused; I considered; and I began to doubt. The matter was impossible. I could not in any reason have so rapidly come down. Besides, although I was evidently approaching the surface below me, it was with a speed by no means commensurate with the velocity I had at first conceived. This consideration served to calm the perturbation of my mind, and I finally succeeded in regarding the phenomenon in its proper point of view. In fact, amazement must have fairly deprived me of my senses, when I could not see the vast difference, in appearance, between the surface below me, and the surface of my mother earth. The latter was indeed over my head, and completely hidden by the balloon, while the moon—the moon itself in all its glory—lay beneath me, and at my feet.

The stupor and surprise produced in my mind by this extraordinary change in the posture of affairs, was perhaps, after all, that part of the adventure least susceptible of explanation. For the *bouleversement*[21] in itself was not only natural and inevitable, but had been long actually anticipated, as a circumstance to be expected whenever I should arrive at that exact point of my voyage where the attraction of the planet should be superseded by the attraction of the satellite—or, more precisely, where the gravitation of the balloon towards the earth should be less powerful than its gravitation towards the moon. To be sure I arose from a sound slumber, with all my senses in confusion, to the contemplation of a very startling phenomenon, and one which, although expected, was not expected at the moment. The revolution itself must, of course, have taken place in an easy and gradual manner, and it is by no means clear that, had I even been awake at the time of the occurrence, I should have been made aware of it by any *internal* evidence of an inversion—that is to say, by any inconvenience or disarrangement, either about my person or about my apparatus.

It is almost needless to say, that, upon coming to a due sense of my situation, and emerging from the terror which had absorbed every faculty of my soul, my attention was, in the first place, wholly directed to the contemplation of the general physical appearance of the moon. It lay beneath me like a chart—and although I judged it to be still at no inconsiderable distance, the indentures of its surface were defined to my vision with a most striking and altogether unaccountable distinctness. The entire absence of ocean or sea, and indeed of any lake or river, or body of water whatsoever, struck me, at the first glance, as the most extraordinary feature in its geological condition. Yet, strange to say, I beheld vast level regions of a character decidedly alluvial, although by far the greater portion of the hemisphere in sight was covered with innumerable volcanic mountains, conical in shape, and having more the appearance of artificial than of natural protuberances. The highest among them does not exceed three and three-quarter miles in perpendicular elevation; but a map of the volcanic districts of the Campi Phlegræi[22] would afford to your Excellencies a better idea of their general surface than any unworthy description I might think proper to attempt. The greater part of them were in a state of evident eruption, and gave me fearfully to understand their fury and their power, by the repeated thunders of the mis-called meteoric stones, which now rushed upwards by the balloon with a frequency more and more appalling.

April 18th. To-day I found an enormous increase in the moon's apparent bulk—and the evidently accelerated velocity of my descent, began to fill me with alarm. It will be remembered, that, in the earliest stage of my speculations upon the possibility of a passage to the moon, the existence, in its vicinity, of an atmosphere dense in proportion to the bulk of the planet, had entered largely into my calculations; this too in spite of many theories to the contrary, and, it may be added, in spite of a general disbelief in the existence of any lunar atmosphere at all. But, in addition to what I have already urged in regard to Encke's comet and the zodiacal light, I had been strengthened in my opinion by certain observations of Mr. Schroeter, of Lilienthal. He observed the moon, when two days and a half old, in the evening soon after sunset, before the dark part was visible, and continued to watch it until it became visible. The two cusps appeared tapering in a very sharp faint prolongation, each exhibiting its farthest extremity faintly illuminated by the solar rays, before any part of the dark hemisphere was visible. Soon afterwards, the whole dark limb became illuminated. This prolongation of the cusps beyond the semicircle, I thought, must have arisen from the refraction of the sun's rays by the moon's atmosphere. I computed, also, the height of the atmosphere (which could refract light enough into its dark hemisphere, to produce a twilight more luminous than the light reflected from the earth when the moon is about 32° from the new,) to be 1356 Paris feet; in this view, I supposed the greatest height capable of refracting the solar ray, to be 5376 feet. My ideas upon this topic had also received confirmation by a passage in the eighty-second volume of the Philosophical Transactions, in which it is stated, that, at an occultation of Jupiter's satellites, the third disappeared after having been about

1″ or 2″ of time indistinct, and the fourth became indiscernible near the limb.[23]

Upon the resistance, or more properly, upon the support of an atmosphere, existing in the state of density imagined, I had, of course, entirely depended for the safety of my ultimate descent. Should I then, after all, prove to have been mistaken, I had in consequence nothing better to expect, as a *finale* to my adventure, than being dashed into atoms against the rugged surface of the satellite. And, indeed, I had now every reason to be terrified. My distance from the moon was comparatively trifling, while the labor required by the condenser was diminished not at all, and I could discover no indication whatever of a decreasing rarity in the air.

April 19th. This morning, to my great joy, about nine o'clock, the surface of the moon being frightfully near, and my apprehensions excited to the utmost, the pump of my condenser at length gave evident tokens of an alteration in the atmosphere. By ten, I had reason to believe its density considerably increased. By eleven, very little labor was necessary at the apparatus; and at twelve o'clock, with some hesitation, I ventured to unscrew the *tourniquet*, when, finding no inconvenience from having done so, I finally threw open the gum-elastic chamber, and unrigged it from around the car. As might have been expected, spasms and violent headache were the immediate consequences of an experiment so precipitate and full of danger. But these and other difficulties attending respiration, as they were by no means so great as to put me in peril of my life, I determined to endure as I best could, in consideration of my leaving them behind me momently in my approach to the denser *strata* near the moon. This approach, however, was still impetuous in the extreme; and it soon became alarmingly certain that, although I had probably not been deceived in the expectation of an atmosphere dense in proportion to the mass of the satellite, still I had

been wrong in supposing this density, even at the surface, at all adequate to the support of the great weight contained in the car of my balloon. Yet this *should* have been the case, and in an equal degree as at the surface of the earth, the actual gravity of bodies at either planet supposed in the ratio of the atmospheric condensation. That it *was not* the case, however, my precipitous downfall gave testimony enough; *why* it was not so, can only be explained by a reference to those possible geological disturbances to which I have formerly alluded. At all events I was now close upon the planet, and coming down with the most terrible impetuosity. I lost not a moment, accordingly, in throwing overboard first my ballast, then my water-kegs, then my condensing apparatus and gum-elastic chamber, and finally every article within the car. But it was all to no purpose. I still fell with horrible rapidity, and was now not more than half a mile from the surface. As a last resource, therefore, having got rid of my coat, hat, and boots, I cut loose from the balloon *the car itself,* which was of no inconsiderable weight, and thus, clinging with both hands to the net-work, I had barely time to observe that the whole country, as far as the eye could reach, was thickly interspersed with diminutive habitations, ere I tumbled headlong into the very heart of a fantastical-looking city, and into the middle of a vast crowd of ugly little people, who none of them uttered a single syllable, or gave themselves the least trouble to render me assistance, but stood, like a parcel of idiots, grinning in a ludicrous manner, and eyeing me and my balloon askant, with their arms set a-kimbo. I turned from them in contempt, and, gazing upwards at the earth so lately left, and left perhaps for ever, beheld it like a huge, dull, copper shield, about two degrees in diameter, fixed immovably in the heavens overhead, and tipped on one of its edges with a crescent border of the most brilliant gold. No traces of land or water could be discovered, and the whole was clouded with variable spots, and belted with tropical and equatorial zones.

Thus, may it please your Excellencies, after a series of great anxieties, unheard-of dangers, and unparalleled escapes, I had, at length, on the nineteenth day of my departure from Rotterdam, arrived in safety at the conclusion of a voyage undoubtedly the most extraordinary, and the most momentous, ever accomplished, undertaken, or conceived by any denizen of earth. But my adventures yet remain to be related. And indeed your Excellencies may well imagine that, after a residence of five years upon a planet not only deeply interesting in its own peculiar character, but rendered doubly so by its intimate connection, in capacity of satellite, with the world inhabited by man, I may have intelligence for the private ear of the States' College of Astronomers of far more importance than the details, however wonderful, of the mere *voyage* which so happily concluded. This is, in fact, the case. I have much—very much which it would give me the greatest pleasure to communicate. I have much to say of the climate of the planet; of its wonderful alternations of heat and cold; of unmitigated and burning sunshine for one fortnight, and more than polar frigidity for the next; of a constant transfer of moisture, by distillation like that *in vacuo*, from the point beneath the sun to the point the farthest from it; of a variable zone of running water; of the people themselves; of their manners, customs, and political institutions; of their peculiar physical construction; of their ugliness; of their want of ears, those useless appendages in an atmosphere so peculiarly modified; of their consequent ignorance of the use and properties of speech; of their substitute for speech in a singular method of inter-communication; of the incomprehensible connection between each particular individual in the moon, with some particular individual on the earth—a connection analogous with, and depending upon that of the orbs of the planet and the satellite, and by means of which the lives and destinies of the inhabitants of the one are interwoven with the lives and destinies of the inhabitants of the other; and above all, if it so please your Excellencies—above all of those dark and hideous mysteries which lie in the outer regions of the moon,—regions which, owing to the almost miraculous accordance of the satellite's rotation on its own axis with its sidereal revolution about the earth, have never yet been turned, and, by God's mercy, never shall be turned, to the scrutiny of the telescopes of man. All this, and more—much more—would I most willingly detail. But, to be brief, I must have my reward. I am pining for a return to my family and to my home: and as the price of any farther communications on my part—in consideration of the light which I have it in my power to throw upon many very important branches of physical and metaphysical science—I must solicit, through the influence of your honorable body, a pardon for the crime of which I have been guilty in the death of the creditors upon my departure from Rotterdam. This, then, is the object of the present paper. Its bearer, an inhabitant of the moon, whom I have prevailed upon, and properly instructed, to be my messenger to the earth, will await your Excellencies' pleasure, and return to me with the pardon in question, if it can, in any manner, be obtained.

I have the honor to be, &c., your Excellencies' very humble servant,

HANS PFAAL.

Upon finishing the perusal of this very extraordinary document, Professor Rubadub, it is said, dropped his pipe upon the ground in the extremity of his surprise, and Mynheer Superbus Von Underduk having taken off his spectacles, wiped them, and deposited them in his pocket, so far forgot both himself and his dignity, as to turn round three times upon his heel in the quintessence of astonishment and admiration. There was no doubt about the matter—the pardon should be obtained. So at least swore, with a round oath, Professor Rubadub, and so finally thought the illustrious Von Underduk, as he took the arm of his brother in science, and without saying a word, began to make the best of his way home to deliberate upon the measures to be adopted. Having reached the door, however, of the burgomaster's dwelling, the professor ventured to suggest that as the messenger had thought proper to disappear—no doubt frightened to death by the savage appearance of the burghers of Rotterdam—the pardon would be of little use, as no one but a man of the moon would undertake a voyage to so vast a distance. To the truth of this observation the burgomaster assented, and the matter was therefore at an end. Not so, however, rumors and speculations. The letter, having been published, gave rise to a variety of gossip and opinion. Some of the over-wise even made themselves ridiculous by decrying the whole business as nothing better than a hoax. But hoax, with these sort of people, is, I believe, a general term for all matters above their comprehension. For my part, I cannot conceive upon what data they have founded such an accusation. Let us see what they say:

Imprimis. That certain wags in Rotterdam have certain especial antipathies to certain burgomasters and astronomers.

Secondly. That an odd little dwarf and bottle conjurer, both of whose ears, for some misdemeanor, have been cut off close to his head, has been missing for several days from the neighboring city of Bruges.

Thirdly. That the newspapers which were stuck all over the little balloon, were newspapers of Holland, and therefore could not have been made in the moon. They were dirty papers—very dirty—and Gluck,[24] the printer, would take his bible oath to their having been printed in Rotterdam.

Fourthly. That Hans Pfaal himself, the drunken villain, and the three very idle gentlemen styled his creditors, were all seen, no longer than two or three days ago, in a tippling house in the suburbs, having just returned, with money in their pockets, from a trip beyond the sea.

Lastly. That it is an opinion very generally received, or which ought to be generally received, that the College of Astronomers in the city of Rotterdam, as well as all other colleges in all other parts of the world,—not to mention colleges and astronomers in general,—are, to say the least of the matter, not a whit better, nor greater, nor wiser than they ought to be.

NOTE.—Strictly speaking, there is but little similarity between the above sketchy trifle, and the celebrated "Moon-Story" of Mr. Locke; but as both have the character of *hoaxes,* (although the one is in a tone of banter, the other of downright earnest,) and as both hoaxes are on the same subject, the moon—moreover, as both attempt to give plausibility by scientific detail—the author of "Hans Pfaal" thinks it necessary to say, in *self-defence,* that his own *jeu d'esprit*[25] was published, in the "Southern Literary Messenger," about three weeks before the commencement of Mr. L.'s in the "New York Sun." Fancying a likeness which, perhaps, does not exist, some of the New York papers copied "Hans Pfaal," and collated it with the "Moon-Hoax," by way of detecting the writer of the one in the writer of the other.

As many more persons were actually gulled by the "Moon-Hoax" than would be willing to acknowledge the fact, it may here afford some little amusement to show why no one should have been deceived —to point out those particulars of the story which should have been sufficient to establish its real character. Indeed, however rich the imagination displayed in this ingenious fiction, it wanted much of the force which might have been given it by a more scrupulous attention to facts and to general analogy. That the public were misled, even for an instant, merely proves the gross ignorance which is so generally prevalent upon subjects of an astronomical nature.

The moon's distance from the earth is, in round numbers, 240,000 miles. If we desire to ascertain how near, apparently, a lens would bring the satellite, (or any distant object,) we, of course, have but to divide the distance by the magnifying, or more strictly, by the space-penetrating power of the glass. Mr. L. makes his lens have a power of 42,000 times. By this divide 240,000 (the moon's real distance,) and we have five miles and five-sevenths, as the apparent distance. No animal at all could be seen so far; much less the minute points particularized in the story. Mr. L. speaks about Sir John Herschel's perceiving flowers (the Papaver rhœas, &c.,) and even detecting the color and the shape of the eyes of small birds. Shortly before, too, he has himself observed that the lens would not render perceptible objects of less than eighteen inches in diameter; but even this, as I have said, is giving the glass by far too great power. It may be observed, in passing, that this prodigious glass is said to have been moulded at the glass-house of Messrs. Hartley and Grant,[26] in Dumbarton; but Messrs. H. and G.'s establishment had ceased operations for many years previous to the publication of the hoax.

On page 13, pamphlet edition, speaking of "a hairy veil" over the eyes of a species of bison, the author says—"It immediately occurred to the acute mind of Dr. Herschel that this was a providential contrivance to protect the eyes of the animal from the great extremes of light and darkness to which all the inhabitants of our side of the moon are periodically subjected." But this cannot be thought a very "acute" observation of the Doctor's. The inhabitants of our side of the moon have, evidently, no darkness at all; so there can be nothing of the "extremes" mentioned. In the absence of the sun they have a light from the earth equal to that of thirteen full unclouded moons.

The topography, throughout, even when professing to accord with Blunt's Lunar Chart,[27] is entirely at variance with that or any other lunar chart, and even grossly at variance with itself. The points of the compass, too, are in inextricable confusion; the writer appearing to be ignorant that, on a lunar map, these are not in accordance with terrestrial points; the east being to the left, &c.

Deceived, perhaps, by the vague titles, *Mare Nubium, Mare Tranquillitatis, Mare Fæcunditatis*, &c., given to the dark spots by former astronomers, Mr. L. has entered into details regarding oceans and other large bodies of water in the moon; whereas there is no astronomical point more positively ascertained than that no such bodies exist there. In examining the boundary between light and darkness (in the crescent or gibbous moon) where this boundary crosses any of the dark places, the line of division is found to be rough and jagged; but, were these dark places liquid, it would evidently be even.

The description of the wings of the man-bat, on page 21, is but a literal copy of Peter Wilkins'[28] account of the wings of his flying islanders. This simple fact should have induced suspicion, at least, it might be thought.

On page 23, we have the following: "What a prodigious influence must our thirteen times larger globe have exercised upon this satellite when an embryo in the womb of time, the passive subject of chemical affinity!" This is very fine; but it should be observed that no astronomer would have made such remark, especially to any Journal of Science; for the earth, in the sense intended, is not only thirteen, but forty-nine times *larger* than the moon. A similar objection applies to the whole of the concluding pages, where, by way of introduction to some discoveries in Saturn, the philosophical correspondent enters into a minute schoolboy account of that planet:—this to the Edinburgh Journal of Science!

But there is one point, in particular, which should have betrayed the fiction.

Let us imagine the power actually possessed of seeing animals upon the moon's surface;—what would *first* arrest the attention of an observer from the earth? Certainly neither their shape, size, nor any other such peculiarity, so soon as their remarkable *situation*. They would appear to be walking, with heels up and head down, in the manner of flies on a ceiling. The *real* observer would have uttered an instant ejaculation of surprise (however prepared by previous knowledge) at the singularity of their position; the *fictitious* observer has not even mentioned the subject, but speaks of seeing the entire bodies of such creatures, when it is demonstrable that he could have seen only the diameter of their heads!

It might as well be remarked, in conclusion, that the size, and particularly the powers of the man-bats (for example, their ability to fly in so rare an atmosphere—if, indeed, the moon have any)—with most of the other fancies in regard to animal and vegetable existence, are at variance, generally, with all analogical reasoning on these themes; and that analogy here will often amount to conclusive demonstration. It is, perhaps, scarcely necessary to add, that all the suggestions attributed to Brewster and Herschel,[29] in the beginning of the article, about "a transfusion of artificial light through the focal object of vision," &c., &c., belong to that species of figurative writing which comes, most properly, under the denomination of rigmarole.

There is a real and very definite limit to optical discovery among the stars—a limit whose nature need only be stated to be understood. If, indeed, the casting of large lenses were all that is required, man's ingenuity would ultimately prove equal to the task, and we might have them of any size demanded. But, unhappily, in proportion to the increase of size in the lens, and, consequently, of space-penetrating power, is the diminution of light from the object, by diffusion of its rays. And for

this evil there is no remedy within human ability; for an object is seen by means of that light alone which proceeds from itself, whether direct or reflected. Thus the only *"artificial"* light which could avail Mr. Locke, would be some artificial light which he should be able to throw—not upon the *"focal object of vision,"* but upon the real object to be viewed—to wit: *upon the moon*. It has been easily calculated that, when the light proceeding from a star becomes so diffused as to be as weak as the natural light proceeding from the whole of the stars, in a clear and moonless night, then the star is no longer visible for any practical purpose.

The Earl of Ross telescope, lately constructed in England, has a *speculum*[30] with a reflecting surface of 4071 square inches; the Herschel telescope having one of only 1811. The metal of the Earl of Ross' is 6 feet diameter; it is 5½ inches thick at the edges, and 5 at the centre. The weight is 3 tons. The focal length is 50 feet.

I have lately read a singular and somewhat ingenious little book, whose title page runs thus:—"L'Homme dans la lvne, ou le Voyage Chimerique fait au Monde de la Lvne, nouuellement decouuert par Dominique Gonzales, Aduanturier Espagnol, autremèt dit le Courier volant. Mis en notre langve par J. B. D. A. Paris, chez Francois Piot, pres la Fontaine de Saint Benoist. Et chez J. Goignard, au premier pilier de la grand' salle du Palais, proche les Consultations, MDCXLVIII." pp. 176.[31]

The writer professes to have translated his work from the English of one Mr. D'Avisson (Davidson?) although there is a terrible ambiguity in the statement. "I'en ai eu," says he, "l'original de Monsieur D'Avisson, medecin des mieux versez qui soient aujourd'huy dans la cònoissance des Belles Lettres, et sur tout de la Philosophie Naturelle. Je lui ai cette obligation entre les autres, de m'auoir non seulement mis en main ce Livre en anglois, mais encore le Manuscrit du Sieur

Thomas D'Anan, gentilhomme Eccossois, recommandable pour sa vertu, sur la version duquel j'advoue que j'ay tiré le plan de la mienne."[32]

After some irrelevant adventures, much in the manner of Gil Blas,[33] and which occupy the first thirty pages, the author relates that, being ill during a sea voyage, the crew abandoned him, together with a negro servant, on the island of St. Helena. To increase the chances of obtaining food, the two separate, and live as far apart as possible. This brings about a training of birds, to serve the purpose of carrier-pigeons between them. By and by these are taught to carry parcels of some weight —and this weight is gradually increased. At length the idea is entertained of uniting the force of a great number of birds, with a view to raising the author himself. A machine is contrived for the purpose, and we have a minute description of it, which is materially helped out by a steel engraving. Here we perceive the Signor Gonzales, with point ruffles and a huge periwig, seated astride something which resembles very closely a broomstick, and borne aloft by a multitude of wild swans (ganzas) who had strings reaching from their tails to the machine.

The main event detailed in the Signor's narrative depends upon a very important fact, of which the reader is kept in ignorance until near the end of the book. The ganzas, with whom he had become so familiar, were not really denizens of St. Helena, but of the moon. Thence it had been their custom, time out of mind, to migrate annually to some portion of the earth. In proper season, of course they would return home; and the author, happening, one day, to require their services for a short voyage, is unexpectedly carried straight up, and in a very brief period arrives at the satellite. Here he finds, among other odd things, that the people enjoy extreme happiness; that they have no law; that they die without pain; that they are from ten to thirty feet in height; that

they live five thousand years; that they have an emperor called Irdonozur; and that they can jump sixty feet high, when, being out of the gravitating influence, they fly about with fans.

I cannot forbear giving a specimen of the general *philosophy* of the volume.

"I must now declare to you," says the Signor Gonzales, "the nature of the place in which I found myself. All the clouds were beneath my feet, or, if you please, spread between me and the earth. As to the stars, *since there was no night where I was, they always had the same appearance; not brilliant, as usual, but pale, and very nearly like the moon of a morning.* But few of them were visible, and these ten times larger (as well as I could judge,) than they seem to the inhabitants of the earth. The moon which wanted two days of being full, was of a terrible bigness.

"I must not forget here, that the stars appeared only on that side of the globe turned towards the moon, and that the closer they were to it the larger they seemed. I have also to inform you that, whether it was calm weather or stormy, I found myself *always immediately between the moon and the earth.* I was convinced of this for two reasons—because my birds always flew in a straight line; and because whenever we attempted to rest, *we were carried insensibly around the globe of the earth.* For I admit the opinion of Copernicus, who maintains that it never ceases to revolve *from the east to the west,* not upon the poles of the Equinoctial, commonly called the poles of the world, but upon those of the Zodiac, a question of which I propose to speak more at length hereafter, when I shall have leisure to refresh my memory in regard to the astrology which I learned at Salamanca when young, and have since forgotten."

Notwithstanding the blunders italicised, the book is not without some claim to attention, as affording a naïve speci-

men of the current astronomical notions of the time. One of these assumed,
that the "gravitating power" extended
but a short distance from the earth's surface, and, accordingly, we find our voyager "carried insensibly around the globe,"
&c.

There have been other "voyages to the
moon," but none of higher merit than the
one just mentioned. That of Bergerac is
utterly meaningless. In the third volume
of the "American Quarterly Review" will
be found quite an elaborate criticism
upon a certain "Journey" of the kind in
question;—a criticism in which it is difficult to say whether the critic most ex-
poses the stupidity of the book, or his own
absurd ignorance of astronomy. I forget
the title of the work; but the *means* of the
voyage are more deplorably ill conceived
than are even the *ganzas* of our friend the
Signor Gonzales. The adventurer, in digging the earth, happens to discover a peculiar metal for which the moon has a
strong attraction, and straightway con-
structs of it a box, which, when cast loose
from its terrestrial fastenings, flies with
him, forthwith, to the satellite. The
"Flight of Thomas O'Rourke," is a *jeu
d'esprit* not altogether contemptible, and
has been translated into German. Thomas,
the hero, was, in fact, the game-keeper of
an Irish peer, whose eccentricities gave
rise to the tale. The "flight" is made on
an eagle's back, from Hungry Hill, a lofty
mountain at the end of Bantry Bay.[34]

In these various *brochures* the aim is
always satirical; the theme being a description of Lunarian customs as compared with ours. In none, is there any
effort at *plausibility* in the details of the
voyage itself. The writers seem, in each
instance, to be utterly uninformed in respect to astronomy. In "Hans Pfaal" the
design is original, inasmuch as regards an
attempt at *verisimilitude*, in the application of scientific principles (so far as the
whimsical nature of the subject would
permit,) to the actual passage between
the earth and the moon

MELLONTA TAUTA[1]

To the Editor
of the Lady's Book:—

I have the honor of sending you,
for your magazine, an article which
I hope you will be able to comprehend rather more distinctly than I
do myself. It is a translation, by my
friend, Martin Van Buren Mavis,
(sometimes called the "Toughkeepsie Seer,") of an odd-looking MS.
which I found, about a year ago,
tightly corked up in a jug floating
in the *Mare Tenebrarum*—a sea well
described by the Nubian geographer,[2] but seldom visited, now-a-
days, except by the transcendentalists and divers for crotchets.

Truly yours,

Edgar A. Poe

———————

ON BOARD BALLOON "SKYLARK,"
April 1, 2848.[3]

Now, my dear friend—now, for your
sins, you are to suffer the infliction of a
long gossiping letter. I tell you distinctly
that I am going to punish you for all your
impertinences by being as tedious, as discursive, as incoherent, and as unsatisfactory as possible. Besides, here I am, cooped
up in a dirty balloon, with some one or
two hundred of the *canaille*,[4] all bound
on a *pleasure* excursion (what a funny
idea some people have of pleasure!) and I
have no prospect of touching *terra firma*
for a month at least. Nobody to talk to.
Nothing to do. When one has nothing to
do, then is the time to correspond with
one's friends. You perceive, then, why it
is that I write you this letter—it is on account of my *ennui* and your sins.

Get ready your spectacles and make up
your mind to be annoyed. I mean to
write at you every day during this odious
voyage.

Heigho! when will any *Invention* visit
the human pericranium? Are we forever
to be doomed to the thousand inconve-
niences of the balloon? Will *nobody*

contrive a more expeditious mode of progress? The jog-trot movement, to my thinking, is little less than positive torture. Upon my word, we have not made more than a hundred miles the hour since leaving home! The very birds beat us—at least some of them. I assure you that I do not exaggerate at all. Our motion, no doubt, seems slower than it actually is—this on account of our having no objects about us by which to estimate our velocity, and on account of our going *with* the wind. To be sure, whenever we meet a balloon we have a chance of perceiving our rate, and then, I admit, things do not appear so very bad. Accustomed as I am to this mode of traveling, I cannot get over a kind of giddiness whenever a balloon passes us in a current directly overhead. It always seems to me like an immense bird of prey about to pounce upon us and carry us off in its claws. One went over us this morning about sunrise, and so nearly overhead that its drag-rope actually brushed the network suspending our car, and caused us very serious apprehension. Our captain said that if the material of the bag had been the trumpery varnished "silk" of five hundred or a thousand years ago, we should inevitably have been damaged. This silk, as he explained it to me, was a fabric composed of the entrails of a species of earth-worm. The worm was carefully fed on mulberries—a kind of fruit resembling a water-melon—and, when sufficiently fat, was crushed in a mill. The paste thus arising was called *papyrus* in its primary state, and went through a variety of processes until it finally became "silk." Singular to relate, it was once much admired as an article of *female dress!* Balloons were also very generally constructed from it. A better kind of material, it appears, was subsequently found in the down surrounding the seed-vessels of a plant vulgarly called *euphorbium*, and at that time botanically termed milk-weed. This latter kind of silk was designated as silk-buckingham, on account of its superior durability, and was usually prepared

for use by being varnished with a solution of gum caoutchouc—a substance which in some respects must have resembled the *gutta percha* now in common use. This caoutchouc was occasionally called India rubber or rubber of whist, and was no doubt one of the numerous *fungi.*[5] Never tell me again that I am not at heart an antiquarian.

Talking of drag-ropes—our own, it seems, has this moment knocked a man overboard from one of the small magnetic propellers that swarm in ocean below us —a boat of about six thousand tons, and, from all accounts, shamefully crowded. These diminutive barques should be prohibited from carrying more than a definite number of passengers. The man, of course, was not permitted to get on board again, and was soon out of sight, he and his life-preserver. I rejoice, my dear friend, that we live in an age so enlightened that no such a thing as an individual is supposed to exist. It is the mass for which the true Humanity cares. By the by, talking of Humanity, do you know that our immortal Wiggins is not so original in his views of the Social Condition and so forth, as his contemporaries are inclined to suppose? Pundit assures me that the same ideas were put, nearly in the same way, about a thousand years ago, by an Irish philosopher called Furrier, on account of his keeping a retail shop for cat-peltries and other furs. Pundit *knows*, you know; there can be no mistake about it. How very wonderfully do we see verified, every day, the profound observation of the Hindoo Aries Tottle (as quoted by Pundit)— "Thus must we say that, not once or twice, or a few times, but with almost infinite repetitions, the same opinions come round in a circle among men."[6]

April 2.—Spoke to-day the magnetic cutter in charge of the middle section of floating telegraph wires. I learn that when this species of telegraph was first put into operation by Horse, it was considered quite impossible to convey the wires over sea; but now we are at a loss to comprehend where the difficulty lay! So wags the world. *Tempora mutantur*—excuse me for quoting the Etruscan.[7] What *would* we do without the Atalantic telegraph? (Pundit says Atlantic was the ancient adjective.) We lay to a few minutes to ask the cutter some questions, and learned, among other glorious news, that civil war is raging in Africia, while the plague is doing its good work beautifully both in Yurope and Ayesher. Is it not truly remarkable that, before the magnificent light shed upon philosophy by Humanity, the world was accustomed to regard War and Pestilence as calamities? Do you know that prayers were actually offered up in the ancient temples to the end that these *evils* (!) might not be visited upon mankind? Is it not really difficult to comprehend upon what principle of interest our forefathers acted? Were they so blind as not to perceive that the destruction of a myriad of individuals is only so much positive advantage to the mass!

April 3.—It is really a very fine amusement to ascend the rope-ladder leading to the summit of the balloon-bag, and thence survey the surrounding world. From the car below you know the prospect is not so comprehensive—you can see little vertically. But seated here (where I write this) in the luxuriously-cushioned open piazza of the summit, one can see everything that is going on in all directions. Just now, there is quite a crowd of balloons in sight, and they present a very animated appearance, while the air is resonant with the hum of so many millions of human voices. I have heard it asserted that when Yellow or (Pundit *will* have it) Violet, who is supposed to have been the first æronaut, maintained the practicability of traversing the atmosphere in all directions, by merely ascending or descending until a favorable current was attained, he was scarcely hearkened to at all by his cotemporaries, who looked upon him as merely an ingenious sort of madman, because the philosophers (?) of the day declared the thing impossible. Really now it

does seem to me *quite* unaccountable how anything so obviously feasible could have escaped the sagacity of the ancient *savans*. But in all ages the great obstacles to advancement in Art have been opposed by the so-called men of science. To be sure, *our* men of science are not quite so bigoted as those of old:—oh, I have something *so* queer to tell you on this topic. Do you know that it is not more than a thousand years ago since the metaphysicians consented to relieve the people of the singular fancy that there existed but *two possible roads for the attainment of Truth!* Believe it if you can! It appears that long, long ago, in the night of Time, there lived a Turkish philosopher (or Hindoo possibly) called Aries Tottle. This person introduced, or at all events propagated what was termed the deductive or *à priori* mode of investigation. He started with what he maintained to be *axioms* or "self-evident truths," and thence proceeded "logically" to results. His greatest disciples were one Neuclid and one Cant. Well, Aries Tottle flourished supreme until advent of one Hog, surnamed the "Ettrick Shepherd,"[8] who preached an entirely different system, which he called the *à posteriori* or inductive. His plan referred altogether to Sensation. He proceeded by observing, analyzing and classifying facts —*instantiæ naturæ*, as they were affectedly called—into general laws. Aries Tottle's mode, in a word, was based on *noumena*; Hog's on *phenomena*. Well, so great was the admiration excited by this latter system that, at its first introduction, Aries Tottle fell into disrepute; but finally he recovered ground, and was permitted to divide the realm of Truth with his more modern rival. The *savans* now maintained that the Aristotelian and *Baconian* roads were the sole possible avenues to knowledge. "Baconian," you must know, was an adjective invented as equivalent to Hog-ian and more euphonious and dignified.

Now, my dear friend, I do assure you, most positively, that I represent this matter fairly, on the soundest authority; and you can easily understand how a notion so absurd on its very face must have operated to retard the progress of all true knowledge—which makes its advances almost invariably by intuitive bounds. The ancient idea confined investigations to *crawling*; and for hundreds of years so great was the infatuation about Hog especially, that a virtual end was put to all thinking, properly so called. No man dared utter a truth to which he felt himself indebted to his *Soul* alone. It mattered not whether the truth was even *demonstrably* a truth, for the bullet-headed *savans* of the time regarded only *the road* by which he had attained it. They would not even *look* at the end. "Let us see the means," they cried, "the means!" If, upon investigation of the means, it was found to come under neither the category Aries (that is to say Ram)[9] nor under the category Hog, why then the *savans* went no farther, but pronounced the "theorist" a fool, and would have nothing to do with him or his truth.

Now, it cannot be maintained, even, that by the crawling system the greatest amount of truth would be attained in any long series of ages, for the repression of *imagination* was an evil not to be compensated for by any superior *certainty* in the ancient modes of investigation. The error of these Jurmains, these Vrinch, these Inglitch, and these Amriccans (the latter, by the way, were our own immediate progenitors,) was an error quite analogous with that of the wiseacre who fancies that he must necessarily see an object the better the more closely he holds it to his eyes. These people blinded themselves by details. When they proceeded Hoggishly, their "facts" were by no means always facts—a matter of little consequence had it not been for assuming that they *were* facts and must be facts because they appeared to be such. When they proceeded on the path of the Ram, their course was scarcely as straight as a ram's horn, for they *never had* an axiom which was an axiom at all. They must have been very blind not to see this, even in their own day; for even in their own day many of the long- "established" axioms had been rejected. For example—"*Ex nihilo nihil fit;*" "a body cannot act where it is not;" "there cannot exist antipodes;" "darkness cannot come out of light"—all these, and a dozen other similar propositions, formerly admitted without hesitation as axioms, were, even at the period of which I speak, seen to be untenable. How absurd in these people, then, to persist in putting faith in "axioms" as immutable bases of Truth! But even out of the mouths of their soundest reasoners it is easy to demonstrate the futility, the impalpability of their axioms in general. Who *was* the soundest of their logicians? Let me see! I will go and ask Pundit and be back in a minute. * * * Ah, here we have it! Here is a book written nearly a thousand years ago and lately translated from the Inglitch —which, by the way, appears to have been the rudiment of the Amriccan. Pundit says it is decidedly the cleverest ancient work on its topic, Logic. The author (who was much thought of in his day) was one Miller, or Mill; and we find it recorded of him, as a point of some importance, that he had a mill-horse called Bentham.[10] But let us glance at the treatise!

Ah!—"Ability or inability to conceive," says Mr. Mill, very properly, "is in no case to be received as a criterion of axiomatic truth." What *modern* in his senses would ever think of disputing this truism? The only wonder with us must be, how it happened that Mr. Mill conceived it necessary even to hint at any thing so obvious. So far good—but let us turn over another page. What have we here?— "Contradictories cannot both be true— that is, cannot co-exist in nature." Here Mr. Mill means, for example, that a tree must be either a tree or not a tree—that it cannot be at the same time a tree and not a tree. Very well; but I ask him *why*. His reply is this—and never pretends to be any thing else than this—"Because it is impossible to conceive that contradictories can both be true." But this is no answer at all, by his own showing; for has he not just admitted as a truism that "ability or inability to conceive is *in no case* to be received as a criterion of axiomatic truth?"

Now I do not complain of these ancients so much because their logic is, by their own showing, utterly baseless, worthless and fantastic altogether, as because of their pompous and imbecile proscription of all *other* roads of Truth, of all *other* means for its attainment than the two preposterous paths—the one of creeping and the one of crawling—to which they have dared to confine the Soul that loves nothing so well as to *soar*.

By the by, my dear friend, do you not think it would have puzzled these ancient dogmaticians to have determined by *which* of their two roads it was that the most important and most sublime of *all* their truths was, in effect, attained? I mean the truth of Gravitation. Newton owed it to Kepler. Kepler admitted that his three laws were *guessed at*—these three laws of all laws which led the great Inglitch mathematician to his principle, the basis of all physical principle—to go behind which we must enter the Kingdom of Metaphysics. Kepler guessed—that is to say *imagined*. He was essentially a "theorist"—that word now of so much sanctity, formerly an epithet of contempt. Would it not have puzzled these old moles, too, to have explained by which of the two "roads" a cryptographist unriddles a cryptograph of more than usual secrecy, or by which of the two roads Champollion[11] directed mankind to those enduring and almost innumerable truths which resulted from his deciphering the Hieroglyphics?

One word more on this topic and I will be done boring you. Is it not *passing* strange that, with their eternal prattling about *roads* to Truth, these bigoted people missed what we now so clearly perceive to be the great highway—that of

Consistency? Does it not seem singular how they should have failed to deduce from the works of God the vital fact that a perfect consistency *must* be an absolute truth! How plain has been our progress since the late announcement of this proposition! Investigation has been taken out of the hands of the ground-moles and given, as a task, to the true and only true thinkers, the men of ardent imagination. These latter *theorize*. Can you not fancy the shout of scorn with which my words would be received by our progenitors were it possible for them to be now looking over my shoulder? These men, I say, *theorize*; and their theories are simply corrected, reduced, systematized—cleared, little by little, of their dross of inconsistency—until, finally, a perfect consistency stands apparent which even the most stolid admit, because it *is* a consistency, to be an absolute and an unquestionable truth.

April 4.—The new gas is doing wonders, in conjunction with the new improvement with gutta percha. How very safe, commodious, manageable, and in every respect convenient are our modern balloons! Here is an immense one approaching us at the rate of at least a hundred and fifty miles an hour. It seems to be crowded with people—perhaps there are three or four hundred passengers—and yet it soars to an elevation of nearly a mile, looking down upon poor us with sovereign contempt. Still a hundred or even two hundred miles an hour is slow traveling after all. Do you remember our flight on the railroad across the Kanadaw[12] continent?—fully three hundred miles the hour—*that* was traveling. Nothing to be seen, though—nothing to be done but flirt, feast and dance in the magnificent saloons. Do you remember what an odd sensation was experienced when, by chance, we caught a glimpse of external objects while the cars were in full flight? Everything seemed unique—in one mass. For my part, I cannot say but that I preferred the traveling by the slow train of a hundred miles the hour. Here we were permitted to have glass windows—even to have them open—and something like a distinct view of the country was attainable. * * * Pundit says that *the route* for the great Kanadaw railroad must have been in some measure marked out about nine hundred years ago! In fact, he goes so far as to assert that actual traces of a road are still discernible—traces referable to a period quite as remote as that mentioned. The track, it appears, was *double* only; ours, you know, has twelve paths; and three or four new ones are in preparation. The ancient rails are very slight, and placed so close together as to be, according to modern notions, quite frivolous, if not dangerous in the extreme. The present width of track—fifty feet—is considered, indeed, scarcely secure enough. For my part, I make no doubt that a track of some sort *must* have existed in very remote times, as Pundit asserts; for nothing can be clearer, to my mind, than that, at some period—not less than seven centuries ago, certainly—the Northern and Southern Kanadaw continents were *united*; the Kanawdians, then, would have been driven, by necessity, to a great railroad across the continent.

April 5.—I am almost devoured by *ennui.* Pundit is the only conversible person on board; and he, poor soul! can speak of nothing but antiquities. He has been occupied all the day in the attempt to convince me that the ancient Amriccans *governed themselves!*—did ever anybody hear of such an absurdity?—that they existed in a sort of every-man-for-himself confederacy, after the fashion of the "prairie dogs" that we read of in fable. He says that they started with the queerest idea conceivable, viz: that all men are born free and equal—this in the very teeth of the laws of *gradation* so visibly impressed upon all things both in the moral and physical universe. Every man "voted," as they called it—that is to say, meddled with public affairs—until, at length, it was discovered that what is everybody's business

is nobody's, and that the "Republic" (so the absurd thing was called) was without a government at all. It is related, however, that the first circumstance which disturbed, very particularly, the self-complacency of the philosophers who constructed this "Republic," was the startling discovery that universal suffrage gave opportunity for fraudulent schemes, by means of which any desired number of votes might at any time be polled, without the possibility of prevention or even detection, by any party which should be merely villainous enough not to be ashamed of the fraud. A little reflection upon this discovery sufficed to render evident the consequences, which were that rascality *must* predominate—in a word, that a republican government *could* never be anything but a rascally one. While the philosophers, however, were busied in blushing at their stupidity in not having foreseen these inevitable evils, and intent upon the invention of new theories, the matter was put to an abrupt issue by a fellow of the name of *Mob*, who took every thing into his own hands and set up a despotism, in comparison with which those of the fabulous Zeros and Hellofagabaluses[13] were respectable and delectable. This Mob (a foreigner, by the by) is said to have been the most odious of all men that ever encumbered the earth. He was a giant in stature—insolent, rapacious, filthy; had the gall of a bullock with the heart of a hyena and the brains of a peacock. He died, at length, by dint of his own energies, which exhausted him. Nevertheless, he had his uses, as every thing has, however vile, and taught mankind a lesson which to this day it is in no danger of forgetting—never to run directly contrary to the natural analogies. As for Republicanism, no analogy could be found for it upon the face of the earth —unless we except the case of the "prairie dogs," an exception which seems to demonstrate, if anything, that democracy is a very admirable form of government—for dogs.

April 6.—Last night had a fine view of Alpha Lyræ, whose disk, through our captain's spy-glass, subtends an angle of half a degree, looking very much as our sun does to the naked eye on a misty day. Alpha Lyræ, although so *very* much larger than our sun, by the by, resembles him closely as regards its spots, its atmosphere, and in many other particulars. It is only within the last century, Pundit tells me, that the binary relation existing between these two orbs began even to be suspected. The evident motion of our system in the heavens was (strange to say!) referred to an orbit about a prodigious star in the centre of the galaxy. About this star, or at all events about a centre of gravity common to all the globes of the Milky Way and supposed to be near Alcyone in the Pleiades, every one of these globes was declared to be revolving, our own performing the circuit in a period of 117,000,000 of years! *We,* with our present lights, our vast telescopic improvements and so forth, of course find it difficult to comprehend *the ground* of an idea such as this. Its first propagator was one Mudler. He was led, we must presume, to this wild hypothesis by mere analogy in the first instance; but, this being the case, he should have at least adhered to analogy in its development. A great central orb[14] *was,* in fact, suggested; so far Mudler was consistent. This central orb, however, dynamically, should have been greater than all its surrounding orbs taken together. The question might then have been asked —"Why do we not see it?"—*we,* especially, who occupy the mid region of the cluster—the very locality *near* which, at least, must be situated this inconceivable central sun. The astronomer, perhaps, at this point, took refuge in the suggestion of non-luminosity; and here analogy was suddenly let fall. But even admitting the central orb non-luminous, how did he manage to explain its failure to be rendered visible by the incalculable host of glorious suns glaring in all directions about it? No doubt what he finally maintained was merely a centre of gravity common to all the revolving orbs—but here again analogy must have been let fall. Our system revolves, it is true, about a common centre of gravity, but it does this in connection with and in consequence of a material sun whose mass more than counterbalances the rest of the system. The mathematical circle is a curve composed of an infinity of straight lines; but this idea of the circle—this idea of it which, in regard to all earthly geometry, we consider as merely the mathematical, in contradistinction from the practical, idea—is, in sober fact, the *practical* conception which alone we have any right to entertain in respect to those Titanic circles with which we have to deal, at least in fancy, when we suppose our system, with its fellows, revolving about a point in the centre of the galaxy. Let the most vigorous of human imaginations but attempt to take a single step toward the comprehension of a circuit so unutterable! It would scarcely be paradoxical to say that a flash of lightning itself, traveling *forever* upon the circumference of this inconceivable circle, would still *forever* be traveling in a straight line. That the path of our sun along such a circumference— that the direction of our system in such an orbit—would, to any human perception, deviate in the slightest degree from a straight line even in a million of years, is a proposition not to be entertained; and yet these ancient astronomers were absolutely cajoled, it appears, into believing that a decisive curvature had become apparent during the brief period of their astronomical history—during the mere point—during the utter nothingness of two or three thousand years! How incomprehensible, that considerations such as this did not at once indicate to them the true state of affairs—that of the binary revolution of our sun and Alpha Lyræ around a common centre of gravity!

April 7.—Continued last night our astronomical amusements. Had a fine view of the five Neptunian asteroids, and watched with much interest the putting up of a huge impost on a couple of lintels in the new temple at Daphnis in the moon.[15] It was amusing to think that creatures so diminutive as the lunarians, and bearing so little resemblance to humanity, yet evinced a mechanical ingenuity so much superior to our own. One finds it difficult, too, to conceive the vast masses which these people handle so easily, to be as light as our own reason tells us they actually are.

April 8.—Eureka! Pundit is in his glory. A balloon from Kanadaw spoke us to-day and threw on board several late papers; they contain some exceedingly curious information relative to Kanawdian or rather Amriccan antiquities. You know, I presume, that laborers have for some months been employed in preparing the ground for a new fountain at Paradise, the Emperor's principal pleasure garden. Paradise, it appears, has been, *literally* speaking, an island time out of mind—that is to say, its northern boundary was always (as far back as any record extends) a rivulet, or rather a very narrow arm of the sea. This arm was gradually widened until it attained its present breadth—a mile. The whole length of the island is nine miles; the breadth varies materially. The entire area (so Pundit says) was, about eight hundred years ago, densely packed with houses, some of them twenty stories high; land (for some most unaccountable reason) being considered as especially precious just in this vicinity. The disastrous earthquake, however, of the year 2050, so totally uprooted and overwhelmed the town (for it was almost too large to be called a village) that the most indefatigable of our antiquarians have never yet been able to obtain from the site any sufficient data (in the shape of coins, medals or inscriptions) wherewith to build up even the ghost of a theory concerning the manners, customs, &c., &c., &c., of the aboriginal inhabitants. Nearly all that we have hitherto known of them is, that they were a portion of the Knickerbocker tribe

of savages infesting the continent at its first discovery by Recorder Riker, a knight of the Golden Fleece.[16] They were by no means uncivilized, however, but cultivated various arts and even sciences after a fashion of their own. It is related of them that they were acute in many respects, but were oddly afflicted with monomania for building what, in the ancient Amriccan, was denominated "churches"—a kind of pagoda instituted for worship of two idols that went by the names of Wealth and Fashion. In the end, it is said, the island became, nine-tenths of it, church. The women, too, it appears, were oddly deformed by a natural protuberance of the region just below the small of the back—although, most unaccountably, this deformity was looked upon altogether in the light of a beauty. One or two pictures of these singular women have, in fact, been miraculously preserved. They look very odd, *very*—like something between a turkey-cock and a dromedary.

Well, these few details are nearly all that have descended to us respecting the ancient Knickerbockers. It seems, however, that while digging in the centre of the Emperor's garden (which, you know, covers the whole island,) some of the workmen unearthed a cubical and evidently chiseled block of granite, weighing several hundred pounds. It was in good preservation, having received, apparently, little injury from the convulsion which entombed it. On one of its surfaces was a marble slab with (only think of it!) *an inscription —a legible inscription.* Pundit is in ecstasies. Upon detaching the slab, a cavity appeared, containing a leaden box filled with various coins, a long scroll of names, several documents which appear to resemble newspapers, with other matters of intense interest to the antiquarian! There can be no doubt that all these are genuine Amriccan relics belonging to the tribe called Knickerbocker. The papers thrown on board our balloon are filled with fac-similes of the coins, MSS., typography, &c., &c. I copy for your amusement the Knickerbocker inscription on the marble slab:—

> This Corner Stone of a Monument
> to the
> Memory of
> GEORGE WASHINGTON,
> was laid with appropriate ceremonies
> on the
> 19TH DAY OF OCTOBER, 1847,
> the anniversary of the surrender of
> Lord Cornwallis
> to General Washington at Yorktown,
> A. D. 1781,
> under the auspices of the
> Washington Monument Association
> of the city of New York.[17]

This, as I give it, is a verbatim translation done by Pundit himself, so there *can* be no mistake about it. From the few words thus preserved, we glean several important items of knowledge, not the least interesting of which is the fact that a thousand years ago *actual* monuments had fallen into disuse—as was all very proper—the people contenting themselves, as we do now, with a mere indication of the design to erect a monument at some future time; a corner stone being cautiously laid by itself "solitary and alone" (excuse me for quoting the great Amriccan poet Benton!) as a guarantee of the magnanimous *intention*. We ascertain, too, very distinctly, from this admirable inscription, the how, as well as the where and the what, of the great surrender in question. As to the *where*, it was Yorktown (wherever that was), and as to the *what*, it was General Cornwallis (no doubt some wealthy dealer in corn). *He* was surrendered. The inscription commemorates the surrender of—what?—why, "of Lord Cornwallis." The only question is what could the savages wish him surrendered for. But when we remember that these savages were undoubtedly cannibals, we are led to the conclusion that they intended him for sausage. As to the *how* of the surrender, no language can

be more explicit. Lord Cornwallis was surrendered (for sausage) "under the auspices of the Washington Monument Association"—no doubt a charitable institution for the depositing of corner-stones.—— But, Heaven bless me! what is the matter? Ah, I see—the balloon has collapsed, and we shall have a tumble into the sea. I have, therefore, only time enough to add that, from a hasty inspection of the facsimiles of newspapers, etc., etc., I find that *the* great men in those days among the Amriccans, were one John, a smith, and one Zacchary, a tailor.[18]

Good-bye, until I see you again. Whether you ever get this letter or not is point of little importance, as I write altogether for my own amusement. I shall cork the MS. up in a bottle, however, and throw it into the sea.

Yours everlastingly,

Pundita.

THE SYSTEM OF DR. TARR AND PROF. FETHER

During the autumn of 18—, while on a tour through the extreme Southern provinces of France, my route led me within a few miles of a certain *Maison de Santé*, or private Mad-House, about which I had heard much, in Paris, from my medical friends. As I had never visited a place of the kind, I thought the opportunity too good to be lost; and so proposed to my traveling companion, (a gentleman with whom I had made casual acquaintance, a few days before,) that we should turn aside, for an hour or so, and look through the establishment. To this he objected— pleading haste, in the first place, and, in the second, a very usual horror at the sight of a lunatic. He begged me, however, not to let any mere courtesy toward himself interfere with the gratification of my curiosity, and said that he would ride on leisurely, so that I might overtake him during the day, or, at all events, during the next. As he bade me good-bye, I be-

thought me that there might be some difficulty in obtaining access to the premises,
and mentioned my fears on this point. He
replied that, in fact, unless I had personal
knowledge of the superintendent, Monsieur Maillard,[1] or some credential in the
way of a letter, a difficulty might be found
to exist, as the regulations of these private
mad-houses were more rigid than the public hospital laws. For himself, he added,
he had, some years since, made the acquaintance of Maillard, and would so far
assist me as to ride up to the door and introduce me; although his feelings on the
subject of lunacy would not permit of his
entering the house.

I thanked him, and, turning from the
main-road, we entered a grass-grown by-
path, which, in half an hour, nearly lost
itself in a dense forest, clothing the base
of a mountain. Through this dank and
gloomy wood we rode some two miles,
when the *Maison de Santé* came in view.
It was a fantastic *château*, much dilapi-
dated, and indeed scarcely tenantable
through age and neglect. Its aspect inspired me with absolute dread, and, check-
ing my horse, I half resolved to turn back.
I soon, however, grew ashamed of my
weakness, and proceeded.

As we rode up to the gate-way, I perceived it slightly open, and the visage of
a man peering through. In an instant afterward, this man came forth, accosted
my companion by name, shook him cordially by the hand, and begged him to
alight. It was Monsieur Maillard himself.
He was a portly, fine-looking gentleman
of the old school, with a polished manner, and a certain air of gravity, dignity,
and authority which was very impressive.

My friend, having presented me, mentioned my desire to inspect the establishment, and received Monsieur Maillard's
assurance that he would show me all attention, now took leave, and I saw him
no more.

When he had gone, the superintendent
ushered me into a small and exceedingly
neat parlor, containing, among other indications of refined taste, many books,
drawings, pots of flowers, and musical instruments. A cheerful fire blazed upon
the hearth. At a piano, singing an aria
from Bellini,[2] sat a young and very beautiful woman, who, at my entrance, paused
in her song, and received me with graceful courtesy. Her voice was low, and her
whole manner subdued. I thought, too,
that I perceived the traces of sorrow in
her countenance, which was excessively,
although, to my taste, not unpleasingly
pale. She was attired in deep mourning,
and excited in my bosom a feeling of mingled respect, interest, and admiration.

I had heard, at Paris, that the institution of Monsieur Maillard was managed
upon what is vulgarly termed the "system
of soothing"—that all punishments were
avoided—that even confinement was seldom resorted to—that the patients, while
secretly watched, were left much apparent liberty, and that most of them were
permitted to roam about the house and
grounds, in the ordinary apparel of persons in right mind.

Keeping these impressions in view, I
was cautious in what I said before the
young lady; for I could not be sure that
she was sane; and, in fact, there was a
certain restless brilliancy about her eyes
which half led me to imagine she was
not. I confined my remarks, therefore, to
general topics, and to such as I thought
would not be displeasing or exciting even
to a lunatic. She replied in a perfectly rational manner to all that I said; and even
her original observations were marked
with the soundest good sense; but a long
acquaintance with the metaphysics of
mania, had taught me to put no faith in
such evidence of sanity, and I continued
to practice, throughout the interview, the
caution with which I commenced it.

Presently a smart footman in livery
brought in a tray with fruit, wine, and
other refreshments, of which I partook,
the lady soon afterwards leaving the room.
As she departed I turned my eyes in an
inquiring manner toward my host.

"No," he said, "oh, no—a member of my family—my niece, and a most accomplished woman."

"I beg a thousand pardons for the suspicion," I replied, "but of course you will know how to excuse me. The excellent administration of your affairs here is well understood in Paris, and I thought it just possible, you know—"

"Yes, yes—say no more—or rather it is myself who should thank you for the commendable prudence you have displayed. We seldom find so much of forethought in young men; and, more than once, some unhappy *contre-temps*[3] has occurred in consequence of thoughtlessness on the part of our visiters. While my former system was in operation, and my patients were permitted the privilege of roaming to and fro at will, they were often aroused to a dangerous frenzy by injudicious persons who called to inspect the house. Hence I was obliged to enforce a rigid system of exclusion; and none obtained access to the premises upon whose discretion I could not rely."

"While your *former* system was in operation!" I said, repeating his words—"do I understand you, then, to say that the 'soothing system' of which I have heard so much, is no longer in force?"

"It is now," he replied, "several weeks since we have concluded to renounce it forever."

"Indeed! you astonish me!"

"We found it, sir," he said, with a sigh, "absolutely necessary to return to the old usages. The *danger* of the soothing system was, at all times, appalling; and its advantages have been much overrated. I believe, sir, that in this house it has been given a fair trial, if ever in any. We did every thing that rational humanity could suggest. I am sorry that you could not have paid us a visit at an earlier period, that you might have judged for yourself. But I presume you are conversant with the soothing practice—with its details."

"Not altogether. What I have heard has been at third or fourth hand."

"I may state the system then, in general terms, as one in which the patients were *menagés,* humored. We contradicted *no* fancies which entered the brains of the mad. On the contrary, we not only indulged but encouraged them; and many of our most permanent cures have been thus effected. There is no argument which so touches the feeble reason of the madman as the *argumentum ad absurdum*.[4] We have had men, for example, who fancied themselves chickens. The cure was, to insist upon the thing as a fact —to accuse the patient of stupidity in not sufficiently perceiving it to be a fact—and thus to refuse him any other diet for a week than that which properly appertains to a chicken. In this manner a little corn and gravel were made to perform wonders."

"But was this species of acquiescence all?"

"By no means. We put much faith in amusements of a simple kind, such as music, dancing, gymnastic exercises generally, cards, certain classes of books, and so forth. We affected to treat each individual as if for some ordinary physical disorder; and the word 'lunacy' was never employed. A great point was to set each lunatic to guard the actions of all the others. To repose confidence in the understanding or discretion of a madman, is to gain him body and soul. In this way we were enabled to dispense with an expensive body of keepers."

"And you had no punishments of any kind?"

"None."

"And you never confined your patients?"

"Very rarely. Now and then, the malady of some individual growing to a crisis, or taking a sudden turn of fury, we conveyed him to a secret cell, lest his disorder should infect the rest, and there kept him until we could dismiss him to his friends —for with the raging maniac we have nothing to do. He is usually removed to the public hospitals."

"And you have now changed all this—and you think for the better?"

"Decidedly. The system had its disadvantages, and even its dangers. It is now, happily, exploded throughout all the *Maisons de Santé* of France."

"I am very much surprised," I said, "at what you tell me; for I made sure that, at this moment, no other method of treatment for mania existed in any portion of the country."

"You are young yet, my friend," replied my host, "but the time will arrive when you will learn to judge for yourself of what is going on in the world, without trusting to the gossip of others. Believe nothing you hear, and only one half that you see. Now, about our *Maisons de Santé*, it is clear that some ignoramus has misled you. After dinner, however, when you have sufficiently recovered from the fatigue of your ride, I will be happy to take you over the house, and introduce to you a system which, in my opinion, and in that of every one who has witnessed its operation, is incomparably the most effectual as yet devised."

"Your own?" I inquired—"one of your own invention?"

"I am proud," he replied, "to acknowledge that it is—at least in some measure."

In this manner I conversed with Monsieur Maillard for an hour or two, during which he showed me the gardens and conservatories of the place.

"I cannot let you see my patients," he said, "just at present. To a sensitive mind there is always more or less of the shocking in such exhibitions; and I do not wish to spoil your appetite for dinner. We will dine. I can give you some veal *à la Mene-hoult*, with cauliflowers in *velouté* sauce —after that a glass of *Clos de Vougeot*[5]— then your nerves will be sufficiently steadied."

At six, dinner was announced; and my host conducted me into a large *salle à manger*, where a very numerous company were assembled—twenty-five or thirty in all. They were, apparently, people of rank —certainly of high breeding—although their habiliments, I thought, were extravagantly rich, partaking somewhat too much of the ostentatious finery of the *vieille cour*.[6] I noticed that at least two-thirds of these guests were ladies; and some of the latter were by no means accoutred in what a Parisian would consider good taste at the present day. Many females, for example, whose age could not have been less than seventy, were bedecked with a profusion of jewelry, such as rings, bracelets, and ear-rings, and wore their bosoms and arms shamefully bare. I observed, too, that very few of the dresses were well made—or, at least, that very few of them fitted the wearers. In looking about, I discovered the interesting girl to whom Monsieur Maillard had presented me in the little parlor; but my surprise was great to see her wearing a hoop and farthingale, with high-heeled shoes, and a dirty cap of Brussels lace,[7] so much too large for her that it gave her face a ridiculously diminutive expression. When I had first seen her she was attired, most becomingly, in deep mourning. There was an air of oddity, in short, about the dress of the whole party, which, at first, caused me to recur to my original idea of the "soothing system," and to fancy that Monsieur Maillard had been willing to deceive me until after dinner, that I might experience no uncomfortable feelings during the repast, at finding myself dining with lunatics; but I remembered having been informed, in Paris, that the southern provincialists were a peculiarly eccentric people, with a vast number of antiquated notions; and then, too, upon conversing with several members of the company, my apprehensions were immediately and fully dispelled.

The dining-room itself, although perhaps sufficiently comfortable, and of good dimensions, had nothing too much of elegance about it. For example, the floor was uncarpeted; in France, however, a carpet is frequently dispensed with. The windows, too, were without curtains; the shutters, being shut, were securely fastened with iron bars, applied diagonally, after the fashion of our ordinary shop-shutters. The apartment, I observed, formed, in itself, a wing of the *château*, and thus the windows were on three sides of the parallelogram; the door being at the other. There were no less than ten windows in all.

The table was superbly set out. It was loaded with plate, and more than loaded with delicacies. The profusion was absolutely barbaric. There were meats enough to have feasted the Anakim.[8] Never, in all my life, had I witnessed so lavish, so wasteful an expenditure of the good things of life. There seemed very little taste, however, in the arrangements; and my eyes, accustomed to quiet lights, were sadly offended by the prodigious glare of a multitude of wax candles, which, in silver *candelabra*, were deposited upon the table, and all about the room, wherever it was possible to find a place. There were several active servants in attendance; and, upon a large table, at the farther end of the apartment, were seated seven or eight people with fiddles, fifes, trombones, and a drum. These fellows annoyed me very much, at intervals, during the repast, by an infinite variety of noises, which were intended for music, and which appeared to afford much entertainment to all present, with the exception of myself.

Upon the whole, I could not help thinking that there was much of the *bizarre* about every thing I saw—but then the world is made up of all kinds of persons, with all modes of thought, and all sorts of conventional customs. I had traveled, too, so much as to be quite an adept in the *nil admirari*,[9] so I took my seat very coolly at the right hand of my host, and, having an excellent appetite, did justice to the good cheer set before me.

The conversation, in the mean time, was spirited and general. The ladies, as usual, talked a great deal. I soon found that nearly all the company were well educated; and my host was a world of good-humored anecdote in himself. He seemed quite willing to speak of his position as superintendent of a *Maison de Santé*; and, indeed, the topic of lunacy was, much to my surprise, a favorite one with all present. A great many amusing stories were told, having reference to the *whims* of the patients.

"We had a fellow here once," said a fat little gentleman, who sat at my right—"a fellow that fancied himself a tea-pot; and, by the way, is it not especially singular how often this particular crotchet has entered the brain of the lunatic? There is scarcely an insane asylum in France which cannot supply a human tea-pot. *Our* gentleman was a Britannia-ware[10] tea-pot, and was careful to polish himself every morning with buckskin and whiting."

"And then," said a tall man, just opposite, "we had here, not long ago, a person who had taken it into his head that he was a donkey—which, allegorically speaking, you will say, was quite true. He was a troublesome patient; and we had much ado to keep him within bounds. For a long time he would eat nothing but thistles; but of this idea we soon cured him by insisting upon his eating nothing else. Then he was perpetually kicking out his heels —so—so—"

"Mr. De Kock![11] I will thank you to behave yourself!" here interrupted an old lady, who sat next to the speaker. "Please keep your feet to yourself! You have spoiled my brocade! Is it necessary, pray, to illustrate a remark in so practical a style? Our friend, here, can surely comprehend you without all this. Upon my word, you are nearly as great a donkey as the poor unfortunate imagined himself. Your acting is very natural, as I live."

"*Mille pardons! mam'selle!*" replied Monsieur De Kock, thus addressed—"a thousand pardons! I had no intention of offending. Mam'selle Laplace[12]—Monsieur De Kock will do himself the honor of taking wine with you."

Here Monsieur De Kock bowed low,

kissed his hand with much ceremony, and took wine with Mam'selle Laplace.

"Allow me, *mon ami*," now said Monsieur Maillard, addressing myself, "allow me to send you a morsel of this veal *à la St. Menehoult*—you will find it particularly fine."

At this instant three sturdy waiters had just succeeded in depositing safely upon the table an enormous dish, or trencher, containing what I supposed to be the *"monstrum, horrendum, informe, ingens, cui lumen ademptum."*[13] A closer scrutiny assured me, however, that it was only a small calf roasted whole, and set upon its knees, with an apple in its mouth, as is the English fashion of dressing a hare.

"Thank you, no," I replied; "to say the truth, I am not particularly partial to veal *à la St.*—what is it?—for I do not find that it altogether agrees with me. I will change my plate, however, and try some of the rabbit."

There were several side-dishes on the table, containing what appeared to be the ordinary French rabbit—a very delicious *morceau*,[14] which I can recommend.

"Pierre," cried the host, "change this gentleman's plate, and give him a side-piece of this rabbit *au-chat*."[15]

"This what?" said I.

"This rabbit *au-chat*."

"Why, thank you—upon second thoughts, no. I will just help myself to some of the ham."

There is no knowing what one eats, thought I to myself, at the tables of these people of the province. I will have none of their rabbit *au-chat*—and, for the matter of that, none of their *cat-au-rabbit* either.

"And then," said a cadaverous looking personage, near the foot of the table, taking up the thread of the conversation where it had been broken off—"and then, among other oddities, we had a patient, once upon a time, who very pertinaciously maintained himself to be a Cordova cheese, and went about, with a knife in his hand, soliciting his friends to try a small slice from the middle of his leg."

"He was a great fool, beyond doubt," interposed some one, "but not to be compared with a certain individual whom we all know, with the exception of this strange gentleman. I mean the man who took himself for a bottle of champagne, and always went off with a pop and a fizz, in this fashion."

Here the speaker, very rudely, as I thought, put his right thumb in his left cheek, withdrew it with a sound resembling the popping of a cork, and then, by a dexterous movement of the tongue upon the teeth, created a sharp hissing and fizzing, which lasted for several minutes, in imitation of the frothing of champagne. This behavior, I saw plainly, was not very pleasing to Monsieur Maillard; but that gentleman said nothing, and the conversation was resumed by a very lean little man in a big wig.

"And then there was an ignoramus," said he, "who mistook himself for a frog; which, by the way, he resembled in no little degree. I wish you could have seen him, sir"—here the speaker addressed myself—"it would have done your heart good to see the natural airs that he put on. Sir, if that man was *not* a frog, I can only observe that it is a pity he was not. His croak thus—o-o-o-o-gh—o-o-o-o-gh! was the finest note in the world—B flat; and when he put his elbows upon the table thus—after taking a glass or two of wine—and distended his mouth, thus, and rolled up his eyes, thus, and winked them, with excessive rapidity, thus, why then, sir, I take it upon myself to say, positively, that you would have been lost in admiration of the genius of the man."

"I have no doubt of it," I said.

"And then," said somebody else, "then there was Petit Gaillard, who thought himself a pinch of snuff, and was truly distressed because he could not take himself between his own finger and thumb."

"And then there was Jules Desoulières,[16] who was a very singular genius, indeed, and went mad with the idea that he was a pumpkin. He persecuted the cook to make him up into pies—a thing which the cook indignantly refused to do. For my part, I am by no means sure that a pumpkin pie *à la Desoulières*, would not have been very capital eating, indeed!"

"You astonish me!" said I; and I looked inquisitively at Monsieur Maillard.

"Ha! ha! ha!" said that gentleman— "he! he! he!—hi! hi! hi!—ho! ho! ho!— hu! hu! hu!—very good indeed! You must not be astonished, *mon ami;* our friend here is a wit—a *drôle*[17]—you must not understand him to the letter."

"And then," said some other one of the party, "then there was Bouffon Le Grand —another extraordinary personage in his way. He grew deranged through love, and fancied himself possessed of two heads. One of these he maintained to be the head of Cicero; the other he imagined a composite one, being Demosthenes' from the top of the forehead to the mouth, and Lord Brougham[18] from the mouth to the chin. It is not impossible that he was wrong; but he would have convinced you of his being in the right; for he was a man of great eloquence. He had an absolute passion for oratory, and could not refrain from display. For example, he used to leap upon the dinner-table, thus, and —and—"

Here a friend, at the side of the speaker, put a hand upon his shoulder, and whispered a few words in his ear; upon which he ceased talking with great suddenness, and sank back within his chair.

"And then," said the friend, who had whispered, "there was Boullard, the tee-totum.[19] I call him the tee-totum, because, in fact, he was seized with the droll, but not altogether irrational crotchet, that he had been converted into a tee-totum. You would have roared with laughter to see him spin. He would turn round upon one heel by the hour, in this manner—so—"

Here the friend whom he had just interrupted by a whisper, performed an exactly similar office for himself.

"But then," cried an old lady, at the top of her voice, "your Monsieur Boullard was a madman, and a very silly madman at best; for who, allow me to ask you, ever heard of a human tee-totum? The thing is absurd. Madame Joyeuse[20] was a more sensible person, as you know. She had a crotchet, but it was instinct with common sense, and gave pleasure to all who had the honor of her acquaintance. She found, upon mature deliberation, that, by some accident, she had been turned into a chicken-cock; but, as such, she behaved with propriety. She flapped her wings with prodigious effect—so—so—so—and, as for her crow, it was delicious! Cock-a-doodle-doo!—cock-a-doodle-doo!—cock-a-doodle-de-doo-doo-dooo-do-o-o-o-o-o-o-!"

"Madame Joyeuse, I will thank you to behave yourself!" here interrupted our host, very angrily. "You can either conduct yourself as a lady should do, or you can quit the table forthwith—take your choice."

The lady, (whom I was much astonished to hear addressed as Madame Joyeuse, after the description of Madame Joyeuse she had just given,) blushed up to the eye-brows, and seemed exceedingly abashed at the reproof. She hung down her head, and said not a syllable in reply. But another and younger lady resumed the theme. It was my beautiful girl of the little parlor!

"Oh, Madame Joyeuse *was* a fool!" she exclaimed; "but there was really much sound sense, after all, in the opinion of Eugénie Salsafette. She was a very beautiful and painfully modest young lady, who thought the ordinary mode of habiliment indecent, and wished to dress herself, always, by getting outside, instead of inside of her clothes. It is a thing very easily done, after all. You have only to do so—and then so—so—so—and then so— so—so—and then—"

"Mon dieu! Mam'selle Salsafette!" here cried a dozen voices at once. "What *are* you about?—forbear!—that is sufficient! —we see, very plainly, how it is done!— hold! hold!" and several persons were al ready leaping from their seats to withhold Mam'selle Salsafette from putting herself upon a par with the Medicean Venus,[21] when the point was very effectually and suddenly accomplished by a series of loud screams, or yells, from some portion of the main body of the château.

My nerves were very much affected, indeed, by these yells; but the rest of the company I really pitied. I never saw any set of reasonable people so thoroughly frightened in my life. They all grew as pale as so many corpses, and, shrinking within their seats, sat quivering and gibbering with terror, and listening for a repetition of the sound. It came again—louder and seemingly nearer—and then a third time very loud, and then a fourth time with a vigor evidently diminished. At this apparent dying away of the noise, the spirits of the company were immediately regained, and all was life and anecdote as before. I now ventured to inquire the cause of the disturbance.

"A mere bagatelle,"[22] said Monsieur Maillard. "We are used to these things, and care really very little about them. The lunatics, every now and then, get up a howl in concert; one starting another, as is sometimes the case with a bevy of dogs at night. It occasionally happens, however, that the concerto yells are succeeded by a simultaneous effort at breaking loose; when, of course, some little danger is to be apprehended."

"And how many have you in charge?"

"At present, we have not more than ten, altogether."

"Principally females, I presume?"

"Oh, no—every one of them men, and stout fellows, too, I can tell you."

"Indeed! I have always understood that the majority of lunatics were of the gentler sex."

"It is generally so, but not always. Some time ago, there were about twenty-seven patients here; and, of that number, no less than eighteen were women; but, lately, matters have changed very much, as you see."

"Yes—have changed very much, as you see," here interrupted the gentleman who had broken the shins of Mam'selle Laplace.

"Yes—have changed very much, as you see!" chimed in the whole company at once.

"Hold your tongues, every one of you!" said my host, in a great rage. Whereupon the whole company maintained a dead silence for nearly a minute. As for one lady, she obeyed Monsieur Maillard to the letter, and thrusting out her tongue, which was an excessively long one, held it very resignedly, with both hands, until the end of the entertainment.

"And this gentlewoman," said I, to Monsieur Maillard, bending over and addressing him in a whisper—"this good lady who has just spoken, and who gives us the cock-a-doodle-de-doo—she, I presume, is harmless—quite harmless, eh?"

"Harmless!" ejaculated he, in unfeigned surprise, "why—why what can you mean?"

"Only slightly touched?" said I, touching my head. "I take it for granted that she is not particularly—not dangerously affected, eh?"

"Mon Dieu! what is it you imagine? This lady, my particular old friend, Madame Joyeuse, is as absolutely sane as myself. She has her little eccentricities, to be sure—but then, you know, all old women —all very old women are more or less eccentric!"

"To be sure," said I—"to be sure—and then the rest of these ladies and gentlemen—"

"Are my friends and keepers," interrupted Monsieur Maillard, drawing himself up with hauteur[23]—"my very good friends and assistants."

"What! all of them?" I asked—"the women and all?"

"Assuredly," he said—"we could not do at all without the women; they are the best lunatic-nurses in the world; they have a way of their own, you know; their bright eyes have a marvellous effect;—

something like the fascination of the snake, you know."

"To be sure," said I—"to be sure! They behave a little odd, eh?—they are a little *queer*, eh?—don't you think so?"

"Odd!—queer!—why, do you *really* think so? We are not very prudish, to be sure, here in the South—do pretty much as we please—enjoy life, and all that sort of thing, you know—"

"To be sure," said I—"to be sure."

"And then, perhaps, this *Clos de Vougeot* is a little heady, you know—a little *strong*—you understand, eh?"

"To be sure," said I—"to be sure. By-the-bye, monsieur, did I understand you to say that the system you have adopted, in place of the celebrated soothing system, was one of very rigorous severity?"

"By no means. Our confinement is necessarily close; but the treatment—the medical treatment, I mean—is rather agreeable to the patients than otherwise."

"And the new system is one of your own invention?"

"Not altogether. Some portions of it are referable to Professor Tarr, of whom you have, necessarily, heard; and, again, there are modifications in my plan which I am happy to acknowledge as belonging of right to the celebrated Fether, with whom, if I mistake not, you have the honor of an intimate acquaintance."

"I am quite ashamed to confess," I replied, "that I have never even heard the name of either gentleman before."

"Good Heavens!" ejaculated my host, drawing back his chair abruptly, and uplifting his hands. "I surely do not hear you aright! You did not intend to say, eh? that you had never *heard* either of the learned Doctor Tarr, or of the celebrated Professor Fether?"

"I am forced to acknowledge my ignorance," I replied; "but the truth should be held inviolate above all things. Nevertheless, I feel humbled to the dust, not to be acquainted with the works of these no doubt extraordinary men. I will seek out their writings forthwith, and peruse them

with deliberate care. Monsieur Maillard, you have really—I must confess it—you have *really* made me ashamed of myself!"

And this was the fact.

"Say no more, my good young friend," he said kindly, pressing my hand—"join me now in a glass of Sauterne."

We drank. The company followed our example, without stint. They chatted—they jested—they laughed—they perpetrated a thousand absurdities—the fiddles shrieked—the drum row-de-dowed—the trombones bellowed like so many brazen bulls of Phalaris—and the whole scene, growing gradually worse and worse, as the wines gained the ascendancy, became at length a sort of Pandemonium *in petto*.[24] In the meantime, Monsieur Maillard and myself, with some bottles of Sauterne and Vougeot between us, continued our conversation at the top of the voice. A word spoken in an ordinary key stood no more chance of being heard than the voice of a fish from the bottom of Niagara Falls.

"And, sir," said I, screaming in his ear, "you mentioned something, before dinner, about the danger incurred in the old system of soothing. How is that?"

"Yes," he replied, "there was, occasionally, very great danger, indeed. There is no accounting for the caprices of madmen; and, in my opinion, as well as in that of Doctor Tarr and Professor Fether, it is *never* safe to permit them to run at large unattended. A lunatic may be 'soothed,' as it is called, for a time, but, in the end, he is very apt to become obstreperous. His cunning, too, is proverbial, and great. If he has a project in view, he conceals his design with a marvellous wisdom; and the dexterity with which he counterfeits sanity, presents, to the metaphysician, one of the most singular problems in the study of mind. When a madman appears *thoroughly* sane, indeed, it is high time to put him in a strait-jacket."

"But the *danger*, my dear sir, of which you were speaking—in your own experience—during your control of this house —have you had practical reason to think liberty hazardous, in the case of a luna-tic?"

"Here?—in my own experience?—why, I may say, yes. For example:—no *very* long while ago, a singular circumstance occurred in this very house. The 'sooth-ing system,' you know, was then in opera-tion, and the patients were at large. They behaved remarkably well—especially so —any one of sense might have known that some devilish scheme was brewing from that particular fact, that the fellows behaved so *remarkably* well. And, sure enough, one fine morning the keepers found themselves pinioned hand and foot, and thrown into the cells, where they were attended, as if *they* were the lunatics, by the lunatics themselves, who had usurped the offices of the keepers."

"You don't tell me so! I never heard of anything so absurd in my life!"

"Fact—it all came to pass by means of a stupid fellow—a lunatic—who, by some means, had taken it into his head that he had invented a better system of govern-ment than any ever heard of before—of lunatic government, I mean.[25] He wished to give his invention a trial, I suppose— and so he persuaded the rest of the pa-tients to join him in a conspiracy for the overthrow of the reigning powers."

"And he really succeeded?"

"No doubt of it. The keepers and kept were soon made to exchange places. Not that exactly either—for the madmen had been free, but the keepers were shut up in cells forthwith, and treated, I am sorry to say, in a very cavalier manner."

"But I presume a counter revolution was soon effected. This condition of things could not have long existed. The country people in the neighborhood—visiters com-ing to see the establishment—would have given the alarm."

"There you are out. The head rebel was too cunning for that. He admitted no vis-iters at all—with the exception, one day, of a very stupid-looking young gentleman of whom he had no reason to be afraid. He let him in to see the place—just by

way of variety—to have a little fun with him. As soon as he had gammoned[26] him sufficiently, he let him out, and sent him about his business."

"And *how* long, then, did the madmen reign?"

"Oh, a very long time, indeed—a month certainly—how much longer I can't pre-cisely say. In the mean time, the lunatics had a jolly season of it—that you may swear. They doffed their own shabby clothes, and made free with the family wardrobe and jewels. The cellars of the *château* were well stocked with wine; and these madmen are just the devils that know how to drink it. They lived well, I can tell you."

"And the treatment—what was the par-ticular species of treatment which the leader of the rebels put into operation?"

"Why, as for that, a madman is not necessarily a fool, as I have already ob-served; and it is my honest opinion that his treatment was a much better treat-ment than that which it superseded. It was a very capital system, indeed—simple —neat—no trouble at all—in fact it was delicious—it was—"

Here my host's observations were cut short by another series of yells, of the same character as those which had previ-ously disconcerted us. This time, however, they seemed to proceed from persons rap-idly approaching.

"Gracious Heavens!" I ejaculated—"the lunatics have most undoubtedly broken loose."

"I very much fear it is so," replied Mon-sieur Maillard, now becoming excessively pale. He had scarcely finished the sen-tence, before loud shouts and impreca-tions were heard beneath the windows; and, immediately afterward, it became evident that some persons outside were endeavoring to gain entrance into the room. The door was beaten with what ap-peared to be a sledge-hammer, and the shutters were wrenched and shaken with prodigious violence.

A scene of the most terrible confusion

ensued. Monsieur Maillard, to my excessive astonishment, threw himself under the side-board. I had expected more resolution at his hands. The members of the orchestra, who, for the last fifteen minutes, had been seemingly too much intoxicated to do duty, now sprang all at once to their feet and to their instruments, and, scrambling upon their table, broke out, with one accord, into "Yankee Doodle,"[27] which they performed, if not exactly in tune, at least with an energy superhuman, during the whole of the uproar.

Meantime, upon the main dining-table, among the bottles and glasses, leaped the gentleman who, with such difficulty, had been restrained from leaping there before. As soon as he fairly settled himself, he commenced an oration, which, no doubt, was a very capital one, if it could only have been heard. At the same moment, the man with the tee-totum predilections, set himself to spinning around the apartment, with immense energy, and with arms outstretched at right angles with his body; so that he had all the air of a tee-totum in fact, and knocked every body down that happened to get in his way. And now, too, hearing an incredible popping and fizzing of champagne, I discovered, at length, that it proceeded from the person who performed the bottle of that delicate drink during dinner. And then, again, the frog-man croaked away as if the salvation of his soul depended upon every note that he uttered. And, in the midst of all this, the continuous braying of a donkey arose over all. As for my old friend, Madame Joyeuse, I really could have wept for the poor lady, she appeared so terribly perplexed. All she did, however, was to stand up in a corner, by the fire-place, and sing out incessantly, at the top of her voice, "Cock-a-doodle-de-dooooooh!"

And now came the climax—the catastrophe of the drama. As no resistance, beyond whooping and yelling and cock-a-doodleing, was offered to the encroachments of the party without, the ten windows were very speedily, and almost simultaneously, broken in. But I shall never forget the emotions of wonder and horror with which I gazed, when, leaping through these windows, and down among us *pêle-mêle*, fighting, stamping, scratching, and howling, there rushed a perfect army of what I took to be Chimpanzees, Ourang-Outangs, or big black baboons of the Cape of Good Hope.[28]

I received a terrible beating—after which I rolled under a sofa, and lay still. After lying there some fifteen minutes, however, during which time I listened with all my ears to what was going on in the room, I came to some satisfactory *dénouement*[29] of this tragedy. Monsieur Maillard, it appeared, in giving me the account of the lunatic who had excited his fellows to rebellion, had been merely relating his own exploits. This gentleman had, indeed, some two or three years before, been the superintendent of the establishment; but grew crazy himself, and so became a patient. This fact was unknown to the traveling companion who introduced me. The keepers, ten in number, having been suddenly overpowered, were first well tarred, then carefully feathered, and then shut up in underground cells. They had been so imprisoned for more than a month, during which period Monsieur Maillard had generously allowed them not only the tar and feathers (which constituted his "system") but some bread, and abundance of water. The latter was pumped on them daily. At length, one escaping through a sewer, gave freedom to all the rest.

The "soothing system," with important modifications, has been resumed at the *château;* yet I cannot help agreeing with Monsieur Maillard, that his own "treatment" was a very capital one of its kind. As he justly observed, it was "simple—neat—and gave no trouble at all—not the least."

I have only to add that, although I have searched every library in Europe for the works of Dr. *Tarr* and Professor *Fether,* I have, up to the present day, utterly failed in my endeavors at procuring an edition.

VON KEMPELEN AND HIS DISCOVERY

After the very minute and elaborate paper by Arago, to say nothing of the summary in "Silliman's Journal," with the detailed statement just published by Lieutenant Maury, it will not be supposed, of course, that in offering a few hurried remarks in reference to Von Kempelen's discovery, I have any design to look at the subject in a *scientific* point of view. My object is simply, in the first place, to say a few words of Von Kempelen[1] himself (with whom, some years ago, I had the honor of a slight personal acquaintance,) since every thing which concerns him must necessarily, at this moment, be of interest; and, in the second place, to look in a general way, and speculatively, at the *results* of the discovery.

It may be as well, however, to premise the cursory observations which I have to offer, by denying, very decidedly, what seems to be a general impression (gleaned, as usual in a case of this kind, from the newspapers,) viz.: that this discovery, astounding as it unquestionably is, is *unanticipated.*

By reference to the "Diary of Sir Humphry Davy,"[2] (Cottle and Munroe, London, pp. 150,) it will be seen at pp. 53 and 82, that this illustrious chemist had not only conceived the idea now in question, but had actually made *no inconsiderable progress, experimentally,* in the very *identical analysis* now so triumphantly brought to an issue by Von Kempelen, who although he makes not the slightest allusion to it, is, *without doubt* (I say it unhesitatingly, and can prove it, if required,) indebted to the "Diary" for at least the first hint of his own undertaking. Although a little technical, I cannot refrain from appending two passages from the "Diary," with one of Sir Humphry's

equations. [As we have not the algebraic signs necessary, and as the "Diary" is to be found at the Athenæum Library, we omit here a small portion of Mr. Poe's manuscript.—Ed.][3]

The paragraph from the "Courier and Enquirer," which is now going the rounds of the press, and which purports to claim the invention for a Mr. Kissam, of Brunswick, Maine,[4] appears to me, I confess, a little apocryphal, for several reasons; although there is nothing either impossible or very improbable in the statement made. I need not go into details. My opinion of the paragraph is founded principally upon its *manner.* It does not *look* true. Persons who are narrating *facts,* are seldom so particular as Mr. Kissam seems to be, about day and date and precise location. Besides, if Mr. Kissam actually *did* come upon the discovery he says he did, at the period designated—nearly eight years ago—how happens it that he took no steps, *on the instant,* to reap the immense benefits which the merest bumpkin must have known would have resulted to him individually, if not to the world at large, from the discovery? It seems to me quite incredible that any man, of common understanding, could have discovered what Mr. Kissam says he did, and yet have subsequently acted so like a baby—so like an owl—as Mr. Kissam *admits* that he did. By-the-way, who *is* Mr. Kissam? and is not the whole paragraph in the "Courier and Enquirer" a fabrication got up to "make a talk"? It must be confessed that it has an amazingly moon-hoax-y air. Very little dependence is to be placed upon it, in my humble opinion; and if I were not well aware, from experience, how very easily men of science are *mystified,* on points out of their usual range of inquiry, I should be profoundly astonished at finding so eminent a chemist as Professor Draper,[5] discussing Mr. Kissam's (or is it Mr. Quizzem's?) pretensions to this discovery, in so serious a tone.

But to return to the "Diary" of Sir Humphry Davy. This pamphlet was *not* designed for the public eye, even upon the decease of the writer, as any person at all conversant with authorship may satisfy himself at once by the slightest inspection of the style. At page 13, for example, near the middle, we read, in reference to his researches about the protoxide of azote: "In less than half a minute the respiration being continued, diminished gradually and *were* succeeded by analogous to gentle pressure on all the muscles." That the *respiration* was not "diminished," is not only clear by the subsequent context, but by the use of the plural, "were." The sentence, no doubt, was thus intended: "In less than half a minute, the respiration [being continued, these feelings] diminished gradually, and were succeeded by [a sensation] analogous to gentle pressure on all the muscles."[6] A hundred similar instances go to show that the MS. so inconsiderately published, was merely a *rough note-book*, meant only for the writer's own eye; but an inspection of the pamphlet will convince almost any thinking person of the truth of my suggestion. The fact is, Sir Humphry Davy was about the last man in the world to *commit himself* on scientific topics. Not only had he a more than ordinary dislike to quackery, but he was morbidly afraid of *appearing* empirical; so that, however fully he might have been convinced that he was on the right track in the matter now in question, he would never have spoken *out*, until he had every thing ready for the most practical demonstration. I verily believe that his last moments would have been rendered wretched, could he have suspected that his wishes in regard to burning this "Diary" (full of crude speculations) would have been unattended to; as, it seems, they were. I say "his wishes," for that he meant to include this note-book among the miscellaneous papers directed "to be burnt," I think there can be no manner of doubt. Whether it escaped the flames by good fortune or by bad, yet remains to be seen. That the passages quoted above, with the other similar ones referred to,

gave Von Kempelen *the hint*, I do not in the slightest degree question; but I repeat, it yet remains to be seen whether this momentous discovery itself (*momentous* under any circumstances,) will be of service or disservice to mankind at large. That Von Kempelen and his immediate friends will reap a rich harvest, it would be folly to doubt for a moment. They will scarcely be so weak as not to "*realize*," in time, by large purchases of houses and land, with other property of *intrinsic* value.

In the brief account of Von Kempelen which appeared in the "Home Journal," and has since been extensively copied, several misapprehensions of the German original seem to have been made by the translator, who professes to have taken the passage from a late number of the Presburg "Schnellpost." "*Viele*" has evidently been misconceived (as it often is,) and what the translator renders by "sorrows," is probably "*leiden*," which, in its true version, "sufferings," would give a totally different complexion to the whole account; but, of course, much of this is merely guess, on my part.[7]

Von Kempelen, however, is by no means "a misanthrope," in appearance, at least, whatever he may be in fact. My acquaintance with him was casual altogether; and I am scarcely warranted in saying that I know him at all; but to have seen and conversed with a man of so *prodigious* a notoriety as he has attained, or *will* attain in a few days, is not a small matter, as times go.

"The Literary World" speaks of him, confidently, as a *native* of Presburg (misled, perhaps, by the account in the "Home Journal,") but I am pleased in being able to state *positively*, since I have it from his own lips, that he was born in Utica, in the State of New York, although both his parents, I believe, are of Presburg descent. The family is connected, in some way, with Maelzel, of Automaton-chess-player memory. [If we are not mistaken, the name of the *inventor* of the chess-player was either Kempelen, Von Kempelen, or something like it.—ED.] In person, he is short and stout, with large, *fat,* blue eyes, sandy hair and whiskers, a wide but pleasing mouth, fine teeth, and I think a Roman nose. There is some defect in one of his feet. His address is frank, and his whole manner noticeable for *bonhomie.* Altogether, he looks, speaks and acts as little like "a misanthrope" as any man I ever saw. We were fellow-sojourners for a week, about six years ago, at Earl's Hotel, in Providence, Rhode Island; and I presume that I conversed with him, at various times, for some three or four hours altogether. His principal topics were those of the day; and nothing that fell from him led me to suspect his scientific attainments. He left the hotel before me, intending to go to New York, and thence to Bremen; it was in the latter city that his great discovery was first made public; or, rather, it was there that he was first suspected of having made it. This is about all that I personally know of the now immortal Von Kempelen;[8] but I have thought that even these few details would have interest for the public.

There can be little question that most of the marvellous rumors afloat about this affair, are pure inventions, entitled to about as much credit as the story of Aladdin's lamp; and yet, in a case of this kind, as in the case of the discoveries in California,[9] it is clear that the truth *may be* stranger than fiction. The following anecdote, at least, is so well authenticated, that we may receive it implicitly.

Von Kempelen had never been even tolerably well off during his residence at Bremen; and often, it was well known, he had been put to extreme shifts, in order to raise trifling sums. When the great excitement occurred about the forgery on the house of Gutsmuth & Co., suspicion was directed towards Von Kempelen, on account of his having purchased a considerable property in Gasperitch Lane, and his refusing, when questioned, to explain how he became possessed of the purchase money. He was at length arrested, but

nothing decisive appearing against him, was in the end set at liberty. The police, however, kept a strict watch upon his movements, and thus discovered that he left home frequently, taking always the same road, and invariably giving his watchers the slip in the neighborhood of that labyrinth of narrow and crooked passages known by the flash-name of the "Dondergat." Finally, by dint of great perseverance, they traced him to a garret in an old house of seven stories, in an alley called Flatzplatz; and, coming upon him suddenly, found him, as they imagined, in the midst of his counterfeiting operations. His agitation is represented as so excessive that the officers had not the slightest doubt of his guilt. After handcuffing him, they searched his room, or rather rooms; for it appears he occupied all the *mansarde.*[10]

Opening into the garret where they caught him, was a closet, ten feet by eight, fitted up with some chemical apparatus, of which the object has not yet been ascertained. In one corner of the closet was a very small furnace, with a glowing fire in it, and on the fire a kind of duplicate crucible—two crucibles connected by a tube. One of these crucibles was nearly full of *lead* in a state of fusion, but not reaching up to the aperture of the tube, which was close to the brim. The other crucible had some liquid in it, which, as the officers entered, seemed to be furiously dissipating in vapor. They relate that, on finding himself taken, Von Kempelen seized the crucibles with both hands (which were encased in gloves that afterwards turned out to be asbestic), and threw the contents on the tiled floor. It was now that they hand-cuffed him; and, before proceeding to ransack the premises, they searched his person, but nothing unusual was found about him, excepting a paper parcel, in his coat pocket, containing what was afterwards ascertained to be a mixture of antimony and some *unknown substance,* in nearly, but not quite, equal proportions. All attempts at analyzing the unknown substance have, so far, failed, but that it will ultimately be analyzed, is not to be doubted.[11]

Passing out of the closet with their prisoner, the officers went through a sort of ante-chamber, in which nothing material was found, to the chemist's sleeping-room. They here rummaged some drawers and boxes, but discovered only a few papers, of no importance, and some good coin, silver and gold. At length, looking under the bed, they saw *a large, common hair trunk, without hinges, hasp, or lock,* and with the top lying carelessly *across* the bottom portion.[12] Upon attempting to draw this trunk out from under the bed, they found that, with their united strength (there were three of them, all powerful men), they "could not stir it one inch." Much astonished at this, one of them crawled under the bed, and looking into the trunk, said:

"No wonder we couldn't move it—why, it's full to the brim of old bits of brass!"

Putting his feet, now, against the wall, so as to get a good purchase, and pushing with all his force, while his companions pulled with all theirs, the trunk, with much difficulty, was slid out from under the bed, and its contents examined. The supposed brass with which it was filled was all in small, smooth pieces, varying from the size of a pea to that of a dollar; but the pieces were irregular in shape, although all more or less flat—looking, upon the whole, "very much as lead looks when thrown upon the ground in a molten state, and there suffered to grow cool." Now, not one of these officers for a moment suspected this metal to be anything *but* brass. The idea of its being *gold* never entered their brains, of course; how *could* such a wild fancy have entered it? And their astonishment may be well conceived, when next day it became known, all over Bremen, that the "lot of brass" which they had carted so contemptuously to the police office, without putting themselves to the trouble of pocketing the smallest scrap, was not only gold—real

gold—but gold far finer than any employed in coinage—gold, in fact, absolutely pure, virgin, without the slightest appreciable alloy!

I need not go over the details of Von Kempelen's confession (as far as it went) and release, for these are familiar to the public. That he has actually realized, in spirit and in effect, if not to the letter, the old chimera of the philosopher's stone, no sane person is at liberty to doubt. The opinions of Arago are, of course, entitled to the greatest consideration; but he is by no means infallible; and what he says of *bismuth,* in his report to the academy, must be taken *cum grano salis.*[13] The simple truth is, that up to this period, *all* analysis has failed; and until Von Kempelen chooses to let us have the key to his own published enigma, it is more than probable that the matter will remain, for years, *in statu quo.* All that yet can fairly be said to be known, is, that "*pure gold can be made at will, and very readily, from lead, in connection with certain other substances, in kind and in proportions, unknown.*"

Speculation, of course, is busy as to the immediate and ultimate results of this discovery—a discovery which few thinking persons will hesitate in referring to an increased interest in the matter of gold generally, by the late developments in California; and this reflection brings us inevitably to another—the exceeding *inopportuneness* of Von Kempelen's analysis. If many were prevented from adventuring to California, by the mere apprehension that gold would so materially diminish in value, on account of its plentifulness in the mines there, as to render the speculation of going so far in search of it a doubtful one—what impression will be wrought *now,* upon the minds of those about to emigrate, and especially upon the minds of those actually in the mineral region, by the announcement of this astounding discovery of Von Kempelen? a discovery which declares, in so many words, that beyond its intrinsic worth for manufacturing purposes, (whatever that worth may be), gold now is, or at least soon will be (for it cannot be supposed that Von Kempelen can *long* retain his secret) of no greater *value* than lead, and of far inferior value to silver. It is, indeed, exceedingly difficult to speculate prospectively upon the consequences of the discovery; but one thing may be positively maintained—that the announcement of the discovery six months ago, would have had material influence in regard to the settlement of California.

In Europe, as yet, the most noticeable results have been a rise of two hundred per cent. in the price of lead, and nearly twenty-five per cent. in that of silver.

Notes

The Balloon-Hoax

1. Poe's story was a true hoax, published as an "extra" by the *New York Sun* on April 13, 1844 *(The Extra Sun).* Poe says it sold out repeatedly and that scalpers sold copies at inflated prices. When it appeared, after Poe's death, in the Griswold edition, a new note by Poe had been added. It reads: The subjoined *jeu d'esprit* [joke, witticism] with the preceding heading in magnificent capitals, well interspersed with notes of admiration, was originally published, as matter of fact, in the "New York Sun," a daily newspaper, and therein fully subserved the purpose of creating indigestible aliment for the *quidnuncs* [busybodies] during the few hours intervening between a couple of the Charleston mails. The rush for the "sole paper which had the news," was something beyond even the prodigious; and, in fact, if (as some assert) the "Victoria" *did* not absolutely accomplish the voyage recorded, it will be difficult to assign a reason why she *should* not have accomplished it.

2. "By the energy of an agent at Charleston, S. C.": In February 1844, a ship had made a remarkably fast trip from New York to Charleston, beating the U. S. mail by three days. Poe inserts this matter to explain the *Sun's* scoop: presumably, the other papers, relying on the mail service, don't yet have the story (Scudder, from Mabbott).

Sir Everard Bringhurst: probably a made-up name (Scudder).

Mr. Osborne, a nephew of Lord Bentinck's: Laughton Osborn (Pollin 3) (c. 1809–1878), poet and dramatist.

Mr. Monck Mason: A famous British aeronaut who had made a famous flight to Weilburg, Germany, had built a working model of a powered balloon, and had written a pamphlet, republished in America, *Account of the late Aeronautical Expedition from London to Weilburg, Accompanied by Robert Hollond, Esq., Monck Mason, Esq., and Charles Green, Aeronaut.* The flight occurred in 1836; the U. S. printing of the pamphlet is dated 1837. Poe borrowed heavily from it. Mason is the probable author of another pamphlet, *Remarks on the Ellipsoidal Balloon, propelled by the Archimedean Screw, described as the New Aerial Machine* (London, 1843) from which Poe lifted whole passages (Wilkinson). Mason died in 1889.

Mr. Robert Holland: a spelling error: Robert Hollond, M. P., suggested the flight, paid for it, and went along. The spelling error first appears in a note to the U. S. edition of Mason's pamphlet (Scudder); it is also present in Poe's *Sun* hoax.

Mr. Harrison Ainsworth: William Harrison Ainsworth (1805–1882), a novelist. See "Thou Art the Man," note 6.

Mr. Henson: William Samuel Henson (Pollin 3), who had "planned a heavier-than-air machine to be driven by steam," and who had tried to get parliamentary support for his Aerial Steam Transportation Company (Scudder).

Woolwich: A municipal borough of London, situated south of the Thames. It became an important naval station and, until 1869, a dockyard.

Mr. Forsyth: Pollin (3) thinks Poe made up this name.

3. Sir George Cayley: Scudder reports that Cayley is considered "the most important contributor to the science of aeronautics . . . during the first half of the nineteenth century."

Adelaide Gallery: Wilkinson says that "in 1843 Monck Mason exhibited a model dirigible balloon, of his own construction, at the Royal Adelaide Gallery in London."

Polytechnic Institution: Poe is using more information from *Remarks on the Ellipsoidal Balloon . . .* (Wilkinson).

4. Dover to Weilburg: Dover is on the coast of England, very close to France. Weilburg was where Mason's crew landed.

Archimedean screw: To Archimedes (287–212 B.C.E.) is attributed a continuous screw inside a cylinder, forming a spiral chamber. If the lower end is placed in water and the "screw" turned, water can be raised; the idea is used also in spiral conveyors and high-speed tools. Mason's device lacks the cylinder.

Willis's Rooms: a later name of Almack's Assembly-rooms in London.

From this point in Poe's tale to the words "in the opposite direction" Poe copies almost verbatim the *Ellipsoidal Balloon* pamphlet (Wilkinson).

5. caoutchouc: See "Mellonta Tauta," note 5; "The Man of the Crowd," note 14; "Hans Pfaal," note 6.

6. Mr. Charles Green: One of Mason's crew for the Weilburg flight. See note 2, above. Green wanted to cross the Atlantic and built a model of an "Atlantic Balloon." His work was reported in the United States (Scudder).

subtlety: In old chemistry terminology, "subtlety" was a characteristic of certain gases and "fluids." It carried implications that they were hard to detect, handle, or contain, and often that they had unusual characteristics. Phlogiston, for instance, the "stuff of fire" in which good scientists before the 1790s believed, had negative weight, which explained why some substances weighed more after combustion than before: they had given off their phlogiston. By Poe's day, modern chemistry was securely in being, but some older terms hung on with their meanings used rather loosely.

7. slaked lime (calcium hydroxide), lime to which water is added.

8. beat: tack into the wind.

lying to: staying as stationary as possible, bow into the wind.

Geneva: gin.

9. Poe has in mind a passage from Psalm 93:

The waters lift up their voices, O Lord,
The mighty waters, breakers of the sea;
Yet above the voices of the waters
Thou, O Lord, art mighty on high.

See also "The Conversation of Eiros and Charmion," note 2.

10. Poe's science here is sound. Wind velocities and even directions vary at different altitudes.

11. Cotopaxi: See "Hans Pfaal," note 12.

Omne ignotum pro magnifico: The phrase is from Tacitus, *Agricola,* XXX, and means, "What is unknown is always thought magnificent."

12. Mr. Ainsworth has not attempted to account for this phenomenon, which, however, is quite susceptible of explanation. A line dropped from an elevation of 25,000 feet, perpendicularly to the surface of the earth (or sea), would form the perpendicular of a right-angled triangle, of which the base would extend from the right angle to the horizon, and the hypothenuse from the horizon to the balloon. But the 25,000 feet of altitude is little or nothing, in comparison with the extent of the prospect. In other words, the base and hypothenuse of the supposed triangle would be so long when compared with the perpendicular that the two former may be regarded as nearly parallel. In this manner the horizon of the æronaut would appear to be *on a level* with the car. But, as the point immediately beneath him seems, and is, at a great distance below him, it seems, of course, also, at a great distance below the horizon. Hence the impression of *concavity;* and this impression must remain, until the elevation shall bear so great a proportion to the extent of prospect, that the apparent parallelism of the base and hypothenuse disappears—when the earth's real convexity must

become apparent [Poe's note]. Compare this note to the nearly identical passage in "Hans Pfaal" from which note 19 depends.

13. Hans Pfaal hears the same noises—see page 579 of that story.

14. A place Poe knew well, having served there. He used it in "The Gold-Bug." See note 4 for that story.

Hans Pfaal

1. Poe's first title for this tale (*Southern Literary Messenger*, June 1835) was "Hans Pfaall—A Tale." In his 1840 *Tales of the Grotesque and Arabesque*, he called it "Hans Pfaal." In the Griswold edition it assumed its usual title, "The Unparalleled Adventure of One Hans Pfaal."

2. Poe's motto is from "A Tom-O'-Bedlam Song" quoted in Disraeli's *Curiosities of Literature*. Disraeli gives his source as follows: "I discovered the present in a very scarce collection, entitled 'Wit and Drollery,' 1661; an edition, however, which is not the earliest of this once fashionable miscellany."

3. Dutchmen, their pipes, and their conformity are a favorite joke to Americans of Poe's day. See "The Devil in the Belfry" for similar material, and Washington Irving's Diedrich Knickerbocker's *History of New York*, especially Book III, chapter 3, for the best-known example of the *genre*.

4. Betty Martin: a song with traditional words and tune called "High, Betty Martin" played as a fiddle tune for country dances: The words (Linscott):

> High, Betty Martin
> Tip toe, tip toe
> High, Betty Martin
> Tip toe fine
> Never found a man
> To suit her fancy
> Never found a man
> To suit her mind.

Grettel Pfaal: Poe plays with names: Pfaal (which he also spelled "Pfaall" and "Phaal") suggests, of course, "fall," an unlucky name for an astronaut; his first name and his wife's suggest Hansel and Gretel, which is to say, "This is all a fairy-tale." Reiss points out that the Latin word *follis* means "bellows"; Hans is a bellows-mender. In later Latin usage, it meant "windbag" and the word is the origin of the French word "fou" and the English "fool."

5. Encke: Professor Johann Franz Encke (Pollin 3) (1791–1865), German astronomer.

Nantz: Nantes, in France.

6. caoutchouc: See "Mellonta Tauta," note 5; "The Man of the Crowd," note 14.

particular metallic substance: The substance Poe has in mind is "lunarium." He got the idea of a secret substance, as well as a number of other details, from a story called "A Voyage to the Moon" in the March 1828 *American Quarterly Review* (Posey).

azote: the old chemical name for nitrogen. Nitrogen is an element, and so Poe's character is wrong about having extracted a "constituent."

7. covered trains: lines of gunpowder.

slow-match: fuse.

8. Pollin (3) guesses he is a physicist.

9. Hans's voyage begins on April Fool's Day.

The private joke has to do with British magazines: *Blackwood's Edinburgh Magazine* had published its first number on April 1, 1817. In verse and prose, *Blackwood's* and *Fraser's Magazine* connect magazine journalism with April Fool's Day. See also "Mellonta Tauta," note 3.

10. See "A Descent into the Maelström," note 20 and "The Pit and the Pendulum," note 3.

11. From this point on in the story, Poe borrows very heavily from a number of sources, sometimes merely using them for data, but often copying technical passages almost verbatim (Posey; Nicolson).

12. Cotopaxi: a volcano in Ecuador. Modern sources list its height as 19,344 feet. The comparison is from Herschel (Posey).

Gay-Lussac and Biot: Jean Baptiste Biot (1774–1862) accompanied Joseph Louis Gay-Lussac (1778–1850) in his ascension by balloon in August 1804. They reached a height of 13,000 feet. The following month Gay-Lussac ascended alone and reached 23,040 feet. The figure 25,000 is from Herschel's *A Treatise on Astronomy* (Posey).

13. *rare ethereal medium:* The existence of an "ether" in deep space was important for the cosmology which Poe invented in *Eureka*. Poe argued that the universe is a unified whole which responds to every human action and thought and that ether is the physical basis for such influence. His effort was part

of the general Romantic attempt to provide scientific proof of mystical belief. Such thinking is embodied in "The Power of Words." In "Hans Pfaal," on the other hand, a degree of scientific credibility is more important to him than are the philosophical implications of the existence of an ether.

M. Valz: Jean Exix Benjamin Valz (1787–1867). Poe probably refers to his *"Essai sur la détermination des densités de l'ether"* (1831).

The zodiacal light is probably what the ancients called Trabes. *Emicantet trabes quas docos vocant.*—Pliny lib. 2, p. 26 [Poe's note]. Pliny is Gaius Plinius Secundus (23–79 A.C.E.), author of the *Natural History*.

Poe's "p." means "paragraph," not page, and he altered the original in several ways: *"Emicantet"* is probably just a typographical error; it should read *"Emicant et."* Poe omitted the words *simili modo* from the original; they mean, "similarly," and his decision was correct; the passage would be confusing with them. His word *docos* replaces the Greek word δοκούς in the original, and is probably his transliteration of it. As altered, his Latin may be translated, "These are also heavenly lights which they [the Greeks] call 'beams.' " The context: Pliny argues that spectacular natural phenomena are caused by natural forces as yet imperfectly understood.

14. See note 8 above.

15. Since the original publication of Hans Pfaall, I find that Mr. Green, of Nassau-balloon notoriety, and other late aeronauts, deny the assertions of Humboldt, in this respect, and speak of a *decreasing* inconvenience,—precisely in accordance with the theory here urged [Poe's note]. Charles Green (1785–1870), English inventor and aeronaut, was the first to use coal-gas to inflate balloons; he also invented the guide-rope Poe mentions in this tale. Alexander von Humboldt (1769–1859) was probably the most famous scientist of his day. Best known as a geographer, he was also influential in meteorology and other fields.

Their origin . . . of the heart: Poe's physiology is faulty.

16. In trigonometry, the versed sine is the function of an angle, equal to 1 minus the cosine.

17. Poe changed his mind on this point a number of times. In one version of this tale, Hans at this point begins to notice the earth's

convexity. In "The Balloon-Hoax" Poe adds a footnote (note 12) repeating this passage.

18. Poe forgets what he has said about gravity. Hans's water-clock is not going to work in space. There are numerous other impossibilities in this tale (getting to the moon in a balloon, condensing an adequate supply of air, etc.), but at least Poe has Hans offer a theoretical basis for each.

19. The ancient idea that the earth is open at the poles is the basis for Poe's playful cop-out here. The idea was still seriously entertained in the nineteenth century; an American Congress voted funds for an expedition one of whose functions was to check out that concept. Poe uses it again in the closing lines of *The Narrative of Arthur Gordon Pym.*

20. The apsides of an eccentric orbit are those points which are nearest to and furthest from the center of attraction, in this case, the earth. (When referring to planets, astronomers generally use the words "aphelion" and "perihelion.")

21. somersault.

22. the Phlegraean Fields, in Italy, a volcanic region of low craters, hot springs, and fumaroles.

23. Mr. Schroeter: Johann H. Schroeter (Pollin 3) (1745–1816), a German astronomer. Again the information is from Herschel (Posey).

"Paris feet": A "Paris foot" is 12.8 inches.

But, in addition . . . limb: Hevelius writes that he has several times found, in skies perfectly clear, when even stars of the sixth and seventh magnitude were conspicuous, that, at the same altitude of the moon, at the same elongation from the earth, and with one and the same excellent telescope, the moon and its maculae did not appear equally lucid at all times. From the circumstances of the observation, it is evident that the cause of this phenomenon is not either in our air, in the tube, in the moon, or in the eye of the spectator, but must be looked for in something (an atmosphere ?) existing about the moon.

Cassini frequently observed Saturn, Jupiter, and the fixed stars, when approaching the moon to occultation, to have their circular figure changed into an oval one; and, in other occultations, he found no alteration of figure at all. Hence it might be supposed, that *at some times,* and not at others, there is a dense matter encompassing the moon wherein the rays of the stars are refracted [Poe's note]. Poe copied the material in this note almost verbatim from *Rees's Cyclopedia* (Posey).

Johannes Hevelius (1611–1687) was an astronomer and pioneer in the study of the moon's surface. Giovanni Domenico Cassini (1625–1712) was an astronomer who organized the observatory at Paris, discovered four satellites of Saturn and divisions in its ring, and determined Mars' rotation period.

24. Pollin (3) thinks Poe invented this name.

25. Locke: Richard Adams Locke, the editor of *The New York Sun*, who had made the paper famous by writing an elaborate hoax about a trip to the moon. In the October 1846 *Godey's Lady's Book*, Poe published an essay on Locke as part of his "Literati" column, and reviewed the affair, being, in general, flattering to Locke, to whom he gives principal credit for making the penny press (the *Sun* sold for 1¢) successful. ". . . 'The Sun' was revolving in a comparatively narrow orbit when, one fine day, there appeared in its editorial columns a prefatory article announcing very remarkable astronomical discoveries. . . . This preparatory announcement took very well (there had been no hoaxes in those days) and was followed by full details of the reputed discoveries. . . ." Poe's "Note" and his article on Locke share a good many identical passages. The "Note" was not in the 1835 version of Poe's tale. (See note 34 below.)

jeu d'esprit: a witticism.

26. Sir John F. W. Herschel (1790–1871): Poe said he read Herschel's *A Treatise on Astronomy* (1834) in the Harpers edition (1835), and that it gave him the idea for his tale. He also lifted quite a bit of data, and sometimes whole passages, from this book.

Hartley and Grant: Grant is possibly the astronomer James William Grant (1788–1865). Hartley we have been unable to identify.

27. the work of George W. Blunt (1802–1878), important American chart and map maker and publisher.

28. the title character in a play, "Peter Wilkins; or, the Flying Islanders, a melodramatic spectacle, in two acts." The work was apparently widely known in Poe's time. There is, for instance, a long review of it by Leigh Hunt, which appears in *The Seer* (1840–1841), a selection of Hunt's earlier articles.

29. Sir David Brewster (1781–1868), Scottish physicist. For Herschel, see notes 12, 23, and 26 above.

30. Earl of Ross telescope: William Parsons, Earl of Rosse, (1800–1867), was a British astronomer who in 1839 completed a famous 36-inch reflecting telescope.

speculum: the mirror portion of a telescope.

31. "L'Homme. . . . MDCXLVIII.": "The Man in the Moon, or the Chimerical Voyage made to the World of the Moon, newly discovered by Dominique Gonzales, Spanish Adventurer, otherwise called the Flying Courier. Put into our language by J. B. D. A. Paris, in the home of Francois Piot, near the Fountain of Saint Benoist. And at the home of J. Goignard at the first pillar of the great hall of the Palace near the 'Consultations,' MDCXLVIII."

Dominique Gonzales: Domingo Gonsales, pseudonym of Francis Godwin (1562–1633). The book is mentioned at the start of the *American Quarterly Review* article (see note 34) under a shortened title and with Godwin's name spelled "Goodwin." A French edition of 1648 does exist as Poe says; it was translated by J. Baudoin. *The Man in the Moon* had been originally published in 1638, after Godwin's death.

32. "I had," says he, "the original of Mr. D'Avisson, among the best versed doctors today in knowledge of Fine Arts and especially of Natural Philosophy. I have this obligation to him among others, of having not only put in my hand that book in English, but besides the Manuscript of Sir Thomas D'Anan, Scotch gentleman, recommendable for his virtue, on whose version I admit I drew the plan of mine." We have not attempted to verify the French source, but are somewhat suspicious because of what Poe says about "terrible ambiguity" and D'Avisson—Davidson. Thomas Davison was the printer of the first two cantos of Byron's *Don Juan* (1819). The name of the publisher, John Murray, a "Scottish gentleman," did not appear on the title page—only Davison's. We think it likely that Poe is playing games.

33. See "The Angel of the Odd," note 9.

34. Bergerac: Savinien Cyrano de Bergerac (c. 1620–1655), who did in fact write a "Comic History of the Nations and Empires

of the Moon" (published posthumously in 1656).

"American Quarterly Review": The review to which Poe refers appears in III (March 1828), pp. 61–88. It is a discussion of Joseph Atterley's *A Voyage to the Moon: with some account of the Manners and Customs, Science and Philosophy, of the People of Morosofia and other Lunarians* (New York, 1827). Atterley may be a pseudonym for George Tucker (Posey, citing H. Allen). We think it likely that the *American Quarterly Review* article had even more influence on Poe than suggested by Posey; there is, for example, a reference to Daniel O'Rourke (see below).

Thomas O'Rourke . . . eagle's back: Poe means Daniel, not Thomas, O'Rourke. In a poem by "Sir Morgan O'Doherty" (William Maginn's pseudonym), Dan O'Rourke

> Mounted an eagle, and so reached the moon.

The poem appears in *Fraser's* XX (October 1839), p. 512, too late for Poe to have used it in the first version of "Hans Pfaal," but in time for the second—see notes 1 and 25 above.

Bantry Bay: a bay in extreme southwest Ireland.

Mellonta Tauta

1. Those things that are to be, or, as Poe translated it, "These things are in the future." Pollin (10) identifies these words as part of the reply of the messenger to Creon at the end of Sophocles' *Antigone*. They also appear as the motto added to the 1845 version of "The Colloquy of Monos and Una."

2. Mavis: Poe is playing a game with names. A well-known New York architect, Andrew Jackson Davis, was a close associate of the influential Andrew Jackson Downing, the popularizer of the idea of "cottage style" homes in the suburbs. *The Broadway Journal,* the magazine Poe actually owned for a brief period, had ridiculed Downing's ideas, so Poe would have been familiar with both men. Andrew Jackson, of course, was president before Martin Van Buren, who was to some extent his protégé, and Van Buren would have been in the public eye again when Poe wrote the story—the Free Soil party nominated him for the Presidency in 1848, and he did live near ["T"]Poughkeepsie. So Andrew

Jackson Davis = Martin Van Buren Mavis. Later editors "corrected" "Toughkeepsie"; given the word play here, we think it likely that Poe *meant* "T," not "P."

the Nubian geographer: one of Poe's favorite allusions. See "A Descent into the Maelström," note 3. Poe means, in effect, "Never-never Land."

3. Skylark: "to engage in hilarious or boisterous frolic." Note the date of Pundita's first letter. Cf. "Hans Pfaal," note 9.

4. the rabble or mob—literally, "dogs." The casual tossing around of the numbers of passengers is for shock value. Pundita isn't sure whether there are one or two hundred people on board, which is to say, in 2848 big balloons are common. Poe uses the future date and the science fiction to make his satire possible, but his interest in technology was genuine. He did not believe it would improve human nature, but it did catch his imagination; other stories involve flights across the ocean and a moon-shot. One wonders, incidentally, where Pundita and her fellow passengers are going. A month-long trip at 100 miles per hour would take one at least 72,000 miles, too far for a trip on earth, and not far enough for the space travel she mentions later.

5. "silk": the first of Pundita's near-misses in explaining the "past." Poe is making fun of our knowledge of history by suggesting that the future will badly misunderstand the past.

euphorbium: an obsolete word for Euphorbia, which can mean either a "gum resin obtained from certain . . . species of Euphorbia," or a family of plants commonly known as milkweed. Pundita's facts are straight, for a change.

silk-buckingham: There was an author of books of travel named James Silk Buckingham; Poe makes a cheap gag of his name (Carlson 2). See "Some Words with a Mummy," note 10.

caoutchouc . . . *fungi:* Caoutchouc is rubber, and *gutta-percha* is a rubber-like material made from the juice of Malayan trees, so Pundita is reasonable in her first guess, but of course neither is a fungus. If she is "at heart an antiquarian," she's not a very good one. "Whist" is a card game, the predecessor of bridge. Like bridge, it uses the term "rubber," hence the word-play.

6. drag-ropes: For Poe's explanation of how these work, see "The Balloon-Hoax," pages 553–554.

I rejoice. . . . cares: Poe's suspicions of the merits of democracy show here; he carries popular democratic thought to what he takes to be a logical conclusion, a society in which the individual does not count.

Furrier: She means Fourier (1772–1837), French social theorist whose schemes aroused great interest in the United States in Poe's day. Several of the socialistic communities set up in Poe's lifetime operated on modified Fourieristic principles.

Aries Tottle: Fourier comes out Irish and Aristotle Hindu. One wonders how funny the readers of Godey's Lady's Book (February 1849) thought humor of this sort. For the modern reader, one suspects, the gag quickly goes stale, though undoubtedly we miss some of the topical jokes which a reader in 1849 might have responded to.

"Thus . . . men": The lines are from Aristotle's Meteorologica, I, III (339 b 28–30).

7. Horse: Samuel F. B. Morse (1791–1872), the painter-turned-inventor who built the first practical telegraph.

Etruscan: It's Latin, of course—"times change." Eric Carlson (2) thinks that by "the Etruscan" Poe means Virgil, and that Pundita's error is in attributing to Virgil a quotation from Matthias Borbonius' Deliciae Poetarum Germanorum. It seems likely that Poe's joke is simpler—just that Pundita doesn't know what Latin is—but either way, the point is that Pundita's facts are shaky. The phrase does, in point of fact, appear in a number of Latin writers.

8. Violet: Carlson (2) thinks Poe was referring to Girond de Villette, an associate of the first man to make a balloon ascent (1783), François Pilatre de Rosier. Elsewhere, it has been suggested that this is a reference to Charles Green (see "Hans Pfaal," note 15).

savan[t]s: Poe consistently used the old spelling (savans) of this word in the Godey's version which we follow. Most editors modernize it to savants.

Neuclid . . . Cant: She means Euclid, the Greek mathematician, and Immanuel Kant (1724–1804), the German philosopher. Poe's humor is based on the dates involved: to one writer in 2848, presumably, Greece of the

third century B.C.E. and Germany of 1800 do not seem significantly far apart.

Hog: Francis Bacon (1561–1626), British essayist and philosopher who argued for an analytical and inductive approach to knowledge and who believed that such pooled learning would in fact produce progress. Pundita makes another of her double errors here. Having called Bacon "Hog," she then confuses him with James Hogg (1770–1835), who was called "the Ettrick Shepherd," and whose name would have been familiar to magazine readers from his work in Blackwood's Edinburgh Magazine, his narrative poems, and his novels.

instantiæ naturæ: Latinists translate it as "instances of nature," and report that it does occur, starting in Medieval Latin, with the meaning Poe gives it. It is likely that it occurs in Bacon (see "Hog" above). We did find plentiful examples of both instantiæ and of naturæ, but even our Latinist consultants could not find the two together in Bacon or in any of the Latin word-lists or dictionaries of Bacon's period.

noumena . . . phonomena: Pundita's contrast comes from Kant ("Cant"), who opposed noumena, objects understood through intellectual intuition, with phonomena, one's "precepts or experiences of objects in the world" about one.

9. true knowledge . . . bounds: Poe means this seriously. Knowledge progresses through intuitive inspiration, not through reasoning from given premises (Aristotle) or from sorting, classifying, analyzing (Bacon). Examine the Dupin stories to see how Poe's detective reaches his truths, and Eureka for Poe's own attempt to intuit scientific truths.

Ram: In astrology, Aries the Ram is the first sign of the Zodiac. Having called Aristotle "Aries Tottle," Poe now makes a bad pun by allowing Pundita to try her hand, inaccurately, at etymology.

10. Amriccans . . . progenitors: Poe is saying that the logical outcome of American influence will be Pundita's world, long on technology, short on historical accuracy, cocky, and concerned with the masses, not the individual. Yet Pundita herself is contemptuous of "the mob" (see note 4) and very much a snob. Moreover, some of the things she says Poe believes are right (see note 9), so Poe's satire is not entirely consistent.

Ex . . . fit: "Out of nothing comes nothing." The phrase comes from Lucretius (c. 95–55 B.C.E.), whose *De rerum natura* Poe clearly knew.

Miller, or Mill: John Stuart Mill (1806–1873). His *System of Logic* (1843) is an analysis of the process of inductive logic. See next item.

Bentham: Jeremy Bentham (1748–1832), utilitarian philosopher. Mill *was* deeply influenced by Bentham, particularly by the doctrine of the greatest happiness for the greatest number, but his independence from him is shown in his opinion of Bentham: "He was not a great philosopher but a great reformer in philosophy." The political causes for which Mill fought would not have been sympathetic to Poe: Negro rights, women's suffrage, working class rights.

11. Kepler . . . Newton . . . cryptograph: See Section Preface.·

Champollion: Jean François Champollion (1790–1832), using the Rosetta Stone, learned to decipher Egyptian hieroglyphics. The stone, found in 1799, bore an inscription in two different forms of hieroglyphics and in Greek. "Solving" it was a great scholarly feat, one Poe respects for the intuition involved by spelling "Champollion" correctly.

12. balloons: Having just lectured us on consistency, Pundita is now inconsistent. She opened, we recall, by complaining that travel by balloon was a drag; now she likes it.

Kanadaw: Canada, but Poe doesn't seem to mean the country—see the end of the paragraph. If he means the continents North and South America, and implies that they broke apart at some time between ours and Pundita's, then Pundita's talk about travelling *across* the continent is puzzling. So is his spelling of the word "Kanawdians" late in the paragraph. Perhaps he moved the "w" to keep it in the word; "Kanadians" would not have looked as odd.

13. The Roman emperors Nero (37–68, emperor 54–68) and Heliogabalus (204–222, emperor 218–222).

14. binary . . . suspected: Poe is making up his astronomy (Carlson 2). He's surprisingly consistent in these matters; he says the same thing about this star in "Ligeia." See below, "central orb."

Mudler: Johann H. von Madler (Pollin 3), German astronomer (1794–1872).

central orb: the idea of the rotation of stars around a common center appears in the writing of various theorists in the period; its most famous exposition, perhaps, is in Immanuel Kant (see note 8 above). The "analogy" Poe probably has in mind comes from Kant: stars move around a center as the planets move around the sun. They would have to be in motion, Kant reasoned, or gravity would draw them together and the universe would "collapse." Pundita's idea of a special relationship between Alpha Lyræ and the sun is pure stardust: all celestial bodies interact with one another, but Alpha Lyræ is too immensely distant to be in significant relationship with the sun. Carlson (2) notes, incidentally, that "there are two binary stars in the constellation of the Lyre," though this is not what Pundita claims.

15. In Greek mythology, Daphnis is a shepherd, the son of Hermes and the inventor of bucolic poetry. Daphnis and Chloe are the famous lovers in a Greek pastoral romance and many later works. But the moonmen, the "Neptunian asteroids," and so on are fun and games for Poe. If this nonsense is intended to mean anything, perhaps it is that, as nineteenth-century accomplishments are petty, as American ideas of politics are transient, so all human pride is benighted— i.e., there are rational creatures superior to us in given ways.

16. Paradise: "Paradise" turns out to be Manhattan Island. Poe's imagery comes from Coleridge's "The Pleasure Dome of Kubla Khan."

Knickerbocker . . . Riker . . . Golden Fleece: More of Pundita's scrambled history. Richard Riker (1773–1842) was Recorder of the City of New York (Pollin 3, Carlson 2), and "Knickerbocker" is a nickname often applied to New Yorkers (from Washington Irving's satirical *A History of New York* by "Diedrich Knickerbocker"). There may be a topical joke implied in calling Riker a knight of the Golden Fleece (in Greek legend, the fleece of gold sought by Jason and the Argonauts). If Riker were a friend of Poe, the author might just have been kidding him. If there had been financial scandal in the city government involving Riker, "fleece" would be intended as a pun.

17. The Washington Monument Association of New York in 1847 held a ceremony

to lay the cornerstone of a monument to be erected later. The monument was never erected, but continued to be a topic of current interest (Pollin 10).

18. Benton: Pollin (10) thinks it most likely that Poe refers to Senator Thomas Hart Benton (1782–1858, senator 1821–1851). He demonstrates that the expression "solitary and alone" was identified with Benton, an antagonist of Jackson. Pundita's calling him a poet probably reflects Poe's scorn for his optimistic and nationalistic writings on topics such as how Americans would civilize the Orient, the importance of a transcontinental road, absorbing California and Oregon, and so on.

Yorktown . . . Cornwallis. . . . sea: Having insulted national pride as deeply as he can by showing that even the culminating military victory of the Revolutionary War is so totally forgotten in 2848 that Pundita thinks Cornwallis is a corn-dealer and Americans were cannibals, Poe now tells us that even Pundita's world can't make a safe balloon.

John a smith: Carlson (2) thinks Poe means "John Smith, the average man." That makes sense in terms of Poe's mockery of democracy. Or he might have meant Captain John Smith (1580–1631), the Virginia colonial leader, in which case Pundita would be up to her old trick of telescoping dates to help Poe make his point about the insignificance of our history.

Zacchary, a tailor: The President at the time the story was published, Zachary Taylor (1784–1850).

The System of Dr. Tarr and Prof. Fether

1. Some guesses about the source of this name: (1) There is a game similar to blindman's bluff called colin-maillard. The idea matches the story line nicely. (2) In George Chapman's play The Revenge of Bussy D'Ambois (c. 1613) is a character named Maillard who uses treachery in what he feels is a good cause. (3) A feared judge in a French revolutionary tribunal was named Huisser Maillard. Poe, who feared the mob and had little sympathy with French revolutionary ideals, might have chosen the name for another misguided reformer. The story was first published in Graham's Magazine, November 1845.

2. See "The Spectacles," notes 17 and 18. Poe, who attended plays and operas frequently, seems to have known some of Bellini's works very well.

3. mischance.

4. in logic, the technique of demonstrating the falsity of a proposition by carrying it to its full (and absurd) consequences.

5. veal à la Menehoult: Sainte-Menehould is a district of the Marne noted for its fine pork products. The inmates have, in short, roasted a calf as you would a pig, and as we see later, the narrator isn't having any.

velouté sauce: A white wine sauce.

Clos de Vougeot: A delicate, fine white wine.

6. salle à manger: Dining room.

vieille cour: Old court.

7. hoop and farthingale: The old-fashioned hoopskirt such as one sees in Elizabethan portraits.

Brussels lace: A net lace to which designs are appliquéd.

8. In the Bible, the sons of Anak were a race of giants dwelling in southern Palestine.

9. "To wonder at nothing," the art, that is, of not being surprised. In Horace's Epistolae I, 6, 1 (Norman). The phrase was common in Poe's day; we encountered it frequently in his favorite books and magazines.

10. Whipple (1) thinks Britannia-ware is included to help point the satire at Charles Dickens.

11. Much of the foreign impression of what Parisian life was like in this period came from the crude and bawdy popular serial novels of Paul de Kock (1794–1871). They probably put this name in Poe's mind.

12. Mille pardons! mam'selle: "A thousand pardons, miss."

Laplace: another French name, probably suggested to Poe by his reading. Pierre Antoine de la Place (1749–1827) was a French writer to whom Poe alludes in a review of "The Canons of Good Breeding" and in "Pinakidia."

13. "monstrum . . . ademptum": "a monster, horrible, unshapely, gigantic, and eyeless," from Virgil.

14. morsel.

15. rabbit au-chat: Cat-meat tastes much like rabbit-meat, and has been used for food in times of siege or famine. Many Frenchmen believe that cook-shops often substitute cat for rabbit in preparing rabbit dishes.

16. Pollin (3) feels that this and several other names are of Poe's invention.

17. A rascal.

18. Bouffon Le Grand: Some of the names Poe uses suggest substantive connotations. Thus "Petit Gaillard," four paragraphs up, suggests a small man in sturdy good health, and this name, a great joker.

Cicero: Roman statesman (106–43 B.C.E.).

Demosthenes: The Athenian statesman and orator (c. 384–322 B.C.E.).

Lord Brougham: See "How to Write a Blackwood Article," note 4 and "The Literary Life of Thingum Bob, Esq.," note 27.

19. Boul = ball; the "ard" suggests a pejorative; tee-totum = a top. See note 18.

20. Cheerful.

21. the Venus de Medici—that is, nude.

22. trifle.

23. haughtiness.

24. bulls of Phalaris: See "Loss of Breath," note 12.

Pandemonium in petto: Pandemonium, in Milton, is Satan's palace in Hell. In petto means "concealed within the breast;" it is applied to Roman Catholic cardinals who hold no bishopric or benefice.

25. See Section Preface.

26. tricked.

27. See Section Preface.

28. pêle-mêle: pell-mell.

"there . . . Hope": i.e., the staff, tarred and feathered.

29. conclusion.

Von Kempelen and His Discovery

1. Arago: François Arago (1786–1853), an important French scientist.

"Silliman's Journal": popular nickname for the leading American scientific periodical of the period, the American Journal of Science and Arts, edited by Benjamin Silliman (1779–1864).

Lieutenant Maury: Matthew Maury (1806–1873), an American scientist best known in this period for his important work in charting ocean currents and winds as an aid to navigation.

Von Kempelen: Poe published, in 1836, an article purporting to uncover the trick which enabled an "automated" chess-playing machine to work (there was a little man inside).

The machine had been invented by a Baron Von Kempelen, and was a clever piece of "magic."

2. Sir Humphry Davy (1778–1829), the great English scientist. The "Diary" is probably Poe's invention (Pollin 3, 5).

3. This "editorial note" is by Poe. Pollin (5) reports that the Baltimore Athenaeum Library as of 1827 had no such volume.

4. "Courier and Enquirer": a New York paper. Poe had sent its favorable review of Eureka to Eveleth (see next item).

Mr. Kissam of Brunswick, Maine: Pollin (5) thinks that Poe's target here is G. W. Eveleth, a medical student in Brunswick with whom Poe corresponded. The reasons for Poe's grudge against Eveleth-Kissam are complicated, and have to do with Eveleth's "presumption" regarding Eureka, and his correspondence with Professor Draper (see note 5).

5. moon-hoax-y air: The "Moon-Hoax" was a celebrated journalistic hoax; for details see "The Balloon-Hoax."

Professor Draper: John William Draper (1811–1882), a New York University professor "distinguished in chemical and physical research" (Pollin 5). In 1845, he had been attacked by the New England-oriented North American Review, and Poe had defended him, but Pollin (5) points out that Poe came to bear a grudge against him, too.

6. A passage very similar to this does appear in Davy (Pollin 5, Hall). Poe doctored it to produce the errors.

The "protoxide of azote" is laughing gas; the source is Davy's Researches, Chemical and Philosophical, chiefly concerning Nitrous Oxide and its Respiration (1799).

7. "Home Journal": Another real periodical, owned by Nathaniel Willis (See "The Duc De L'Omelette").

"Schnellpost": A made-up periodical. Poe got the word "Schnellpost" from the title of a German paper published in New York, and Presburg, he says in "Maelzel's Chess-Player," was the home of the Von Kempelen who invented the chess-playing machine.

Viele: many. Since Poe doesn't give us the context, we can't tell how it was "misconceived."

This paragraph seems irrelevant to the tale. Pollin (5) thinks it a private reference: Nathaniel Willis, during the sad days of Virginia

Poe's illness and death, had printed a famous plea for help for the Poes in his *Home Journal*, and Poe's passage about misunderstanding the "German original" could refer to that. Poe had spoken often during the last year of his life (this is a very late tale which appeared first in the April 14, 1849 *Flag of Our Union*) of the need to make lots of money, and it is tempting to speak of, as Pollin (5) puts it, "the transmutation of Poe into the successful gold-maker, Von Kempelen." Hence the allusions to Von Kempelen's suffering and Willis' periodical link the tale to Willis and to Virginia's death.

8. "The Literary World": Poe attempted to publish this tale in *The Literary World*; it was apparently rejected (Pollin 5).

bonhomie: good nature.

Earl's Hotel, in Providence, Rhode Island: The site of a lecture Poe gave on December 20, 1848, and of an unfortunate alcoholic incident (A. H. Quinn) which was partially responsible for the breaking of Poe's engagement to Mrs. Helen Whitman. We think Pollin's (5) connection of these episodes with this tale is correct.

the now immortal Von Kempelen: probably a little day-dreaming on Poe's part: "I'll be an immortal author."

9. Poe had gold and riches on his mind; as Pollin (5) and others point out, his poem "Eldorado" is from this same period. The "discoveries" are those which set off the California gold-rush.

10. Gutsmuth; Gasperitch: Made-up names, but Pollin (5) has solved them: Poe had referred to Johan Christoph F. Gutsmuths (1759–1838) in a "Marginalia" item in 1845 (and left the "s" off his name there, too); Gutsmuths was a geographer who also wrote on children's education. The "Marginalia" piece also mentions, in the same list, the German statistician and geographer Adam Christian Gaspari (1752–1830), which Poe, who didn't know much German, tried to Teutonize by making it "Gasperitch."

flash-name: Poe uses "flash" to signify "showy," "slang-y" or "temporary." In "The Man of the Crowd," for instance, he refers to insubstantial financial firms as "flash-houses." See "The Man of the Crowd," note 6.

Dondergat: "Thunderpass," roughly (Pollin 5).

Flatzplatz: Griswold altered it to Flätplatz. Pollin (5) thinks it simply a made-up name. It seems to suggest "a place where there are flats or apartments," though Poe probably liked the comical sound of it in English.

mansarde: attic.

11. Poe plays here on popular conceptions of the pseudoscience of alchemy, which was supposed to be the age-old attempt to "transmute" lead into gold using a mysterious stuff (Poe's "unknown substance") often called "the philosopher's stone." In point of fact, alchemy was an occult system founded on belief in the unity of all things.

12. Compare the method of concealment in "The Purloined Letter."

13. "with a grain of salt." Salts of bismuth have long been used in medicine; Poe is punning.

15. The Beginning and the End

A very early and a very late tale are juxtaposed to allow the reader to compare Poe's prose of the early thirties with that of the late forties, and to suggest certain continuities of topic and technique.

Each is more or less a sea story. Adventure on the ocean is probably the single most popular genre of fiction in Poe's day. Continental writers had been fishing these waters for years; Poe, in "A Descent into the Maelström," *Pym,* and other fiction, tried his hand at it, too; Melville's most commercially successful novels of sea-adventure had already been published before Poe began working on "The Light-House," and *Moby-Dick* was only two years in the future. So pairing these tales shows Poe, as usual, responding to current interests and trends in fiction.

Each tale is told by a somewhat nervous and moody isolated aristocrat; apparently (one tale is incomplete) each narrator is to experience a weird adventure, made at least partially credible by his psychological instability. The reader has the option of considering it a "vision." The narrator of "MS. Found in a Bottle" has been reading works of "eloquent madness"; perhaps we were to learn that the man in the lighthouse read them too. Clearly, though, the pattern of perception-of-the-wild-beauty was to figure in each tale, as it figures in so many others. And, as always, the reader has the option of considering that pattern either a commercial writer's pet formula, or a means by which a philosophically oriented author sought to embody his visions in fiction. Or both.

MS. Found in a Bottle. Poe combines two old legends: the Flying Dutchman and the belief that the earth is open at the poles (see "Hans Pfaal," note 19, and the closing scene of Poe's novel, *The Narrative of Arthur Gordon Pym*). Moreover, in a curious sense, the hero of this tale may be Columbus, for Poe knew well the books of Bernardin de Saint-Pierre, and in his *Etudes* Columbus uses a bottle to secure a message. Saint-Pierre was exceedingly popular, and readers in Poe's day would have had Columbus in mind as soon as they saw the title (Pollin 9). For another bottled message, see "Mellonta Tauta."

Though the narrator takes pains to tell us how rational he is, how prone to explain everything in physical and scientific terms, he has been reading "eloquent" German "madness," is temperamentally restless and nervous, cut off from family and country, and ill-used: enough like the usual Poe narrator to lead us to conclude that Poe's most frequent formula for keeping a fantasy at least reasonably credible occurred to him very early in his career.

The Light-House. This tale will do very well as an emblem of Poe's career: having achieved a government job (Poe always wanted one, and never got one) which gives him the license to do his "book," this nobleman (recall Poe's pseudo-aristocratic airs) finds himself dissatisfied and fears his nerves even as he experiences the high delight of solitude. His tower is supposed to be secure, yet he worries: its base is chalk, and clearly something is to happen to it. The "nerves" and the "artistry" are probably there to make credible his journal account of fantastic adventures. And the tale is fragmentary, only hinting at what it might have been.

The Tales

MS. FOUND IN A BOTTLE[1]

*Qui n'a plus qu'un moment à vivre
N'a plus rien à dissimuler.*
                    —Quinault—Atys[2]

Of my country and of my family I have little to say. Ill usage and length of years have driven me from the one, and estranged me from the other. Hereditary wealth afforded me an education of no common order, and a contemplative turn of mind enabled me to methodize the stores which early study very diligently garnered up.—Beyond all things, the study of the German moralists gave me great delight; not from any ill-advised admiration of their eloquent madness, but from the ease with which my habits of rigid thought enabled me to detect their falsities. I have often been reproached with the aridity of my genius; a deficiency of imagination has been imputed to me as a crime; and the Pyrrhonism of my opin-

ions has at all times rendered me notorious. Indeed, a strong relish for physical philosophy has, I fear, tinctured my mind with a very common error of this age—I mean the habit of referring occurrences, even the least susceptible of such reference, to the principles of that science. Upon the whole, no person could be less liable than myself to be led away from the severe precincts of truth by the *ignes fatui*[3] of superstition. I have thought proper to premise thus much, lest the incredible tale I have to tell should be considered rather the raving of a crude imagination, than the positive experience of a mind to which the reveries of fancy have been a dead letter and a nullity.

After many years spent in foreign travel, I sailed in the year 18—, from the port of Batavia, in the rich and populous island of Java, on a voyage to the Archipelago of the Sunda islands.[4] I went as passenger—having no other inducement than a kind of nervous restlessness which haunted me as a fiend.

Our vessel was a beautiful ship of about four hundred tons, copper-fastened, and built at Bombay of Malabar teak. She was freighted with cotton-wool and oil, from the Lachadive islands. We had also on board coir, jaggeree, ghee, cocoa-nuts, and a few cases of opium. The stowage was clumsily done, and the vessel consequently crank.[5]

We got under way with a mere breath of wind, and for many days stood along the eastern coast of Java, without any other incident to beguile the monotony of our course than the occasional meeting with some of the small grabs[6] of the Archipelago to which we were bound.

One evening, leaning over the taffrail, I observed a very singular, isolated cloud, to the N. W. It was remarkable, as well for its color, as from its being the first we had seen since our departure from Batavia. I watched it attentively until sunset, when it spread all at once to the eastward and westward, girting in the horizon with a narrow strip of vapor, and looking like a long line of low beach. My notice was soon afterwards attracted by the dusky-red appearance of the moon, and the peculiar character of the sea. The latter was undergoing a rapid change, and the water seemed more than usually transparent. Although I could distinctly see the bottom, yet, heaving the lead, I found the ship in fifteen fathoms. The air now became intolerably hot, and was loaded with spiral exhalations similar to those arising from heated iron. As night came on, every breath of wind died away, and a more entire calm it is impossible to conceive. The flame of a candle burned upon the poop without the least perceptible motion, and a long hair, held between the finger and thumb, hung without the possibility of detecting a vibration. However, as the captain said he could perceive no indication of danger, and as we were drifting in bodily to shore, he ordered the sails to be furled, and the anchor let go. No watch

was set, and the crew, consisting principally of Malays, stretched themselves deliberately upon deck. I went below—not without a full presentiment of evil. Indeed, every appearance warranted me in apprehending a Simoom.[7] I told the captain my fears; but he paid no attention to what I said, and left me without deigning to give a reply. My uneasiness, however, prevented me from sleeping, and about midnight I went upon deck.—As I placed my foot upon the upper step of the companion-ladder, I was startled by a loud, humming noise, like that occasioned by the rapid revolution of a mill-wheel, and before I could ascertain its meaning, I found the ship quivering to its centre. In the next instant, a wilderness of foam hurled us upon our beam-ends, and, rushing over us fore and aft, swept the entire decks from stem to stern.

The extreme fury of the blast proved, in a great measure, the salvation of the ship. Although completely water-logged, yet, as her masts had gone by the board, she rose, after a minute, heavily from the sea, and, staggering awhile beneath the immense pressure of the tempest, finally righted.

By what miracle I escaped destruction, it is impossible to say. Stunned by the shock of the water, I found myself, upon recovery, jammed in between the stern-post and rudder. With great difficulty I gained my feet, and looking dizzily around, was, at first, struck with the idea of our being among breakers; so terrific, beyond the wildest imagination, was the whirlpool of mountainous and foaming ocean within which we were engulfed. After a while, I heard the voice of an old Swede, who had shipped with us at the moment of our leaving port. I hallooed to him with all my strength, and presently he came reeling aft. We soon discovered that we were the sole survivors of the accident. All on deck, with the exception of ourselves, had been swept overboard; —the captain and mates must have perished as they slept, for the cabins were deluged with water. Without assistance, we could expect to do little for the security of the ship, and our exertions were at first paralyzed by the momentary expectation of going down. Our cable had, of course, parted like pack-thread, at the first breath of the hurricane, or we should have been instantaneously overwhelmed. We scudded with frightful velocity before the sea, and the water made clear breaches over us. The frame-work of our stern was shattered excessively, and, in almost every respect, we had received considerable injury; but to our extreme joy we found the pumps unchoked, and that we had made no great shifting of our ballast. The main fury of the blast had already blown over, and we apprehended little danger from the violence of the wind; but we looked forward to its total cessation with dismay; well believing, that, in our shattered condition, we should inevitably perish in the tremendous swell which would ensue. But this very just apprehension seemed by no means likely to be soon verified. For five entire days and nights—during which our only subsistence was a small quantity of jaggeree, procured with great difficulty from the forecastle—the hulk flew at a rate defying computation, before rapidly succeeding flaws of wind, which, without equalling the first violence of the Simoom, were still more terrific than any tempest I had before encountered. Our course for the first four days was, with trifling variations, S. E. and by S.; and we must have run down the coast of New Holland.[8]—On the fifth day the cold became extreme, although the wind had hauled round a point more to the northward.—The sun arose with a sickly yellow lustre, and clambered a very few degrees above the horizon—emitting no decisive light.—There were no clouds apparent, yet the wind was upon the increase, and blew with a fitful and unsteady fury. About noon, as nearly as we could guess, our attention was again arrested by the appearance of the sun. It gave out no light, properly so called, but a dull and sullen glow without reflection, as if all its rays were polarized. Just before sinking within the turgid sea, its central fires suddenly went out, as if hurriedly extinguished by some unaccountable power. It was a dim, silver-like rim, alone, as it rushed down the unfathomable ocean.

We waited in vain for the arrival of the sixth day—that day to me has not arrived —to the Swede, never did arrive. Thenceforward we were enshrouded in pitchy darkness, so that we could not have seen an object at twenty paces from the ship. Eternal night continued to envelop us, all unrelieved by the phosphoric sea-brilliancy to which we had been accustomed in the tropics. We observed too, that, although the tempest continued to rage with unabated violence, there was no longer to be discovered the usual appearance of surf, or foam, which had hitherto attended us. All around were horror, and thick gloom, and a black sweltering desert of ebony.—Superstitious terror crept by degrees into the spirit of the old Swede, and my own soul was wrapped up in silent wonder. We neglected all care of the ship, as worse than useless, and securing ourselves, as well as possible, to the stump of the mizen-mast, looked out bitterly into the world of ocean. We had no means of calculating time, nor could we form any guess of our situation. We were, however, well aware of having made farther to the southward than any previous navigators, and felt great amazement at not meeting with the usual impediments of ice. In the meantime every moment threatened to be our last—every mountainous billow hurried to overwhelm us. The swell surpassed anything I had imagined possible, and that we were not instantly buried is a miracle. My companion spoke of the lightness of our cargo, and reminded me of the excellent qualities of our ship; but I could not help feeling the utter hopelessness of hope itself, and prepared myself gloomily for that death which I thought nothing could defer beyond an hour, as, with every knot of way the ship made, the swelling of the black stupendous seas became more dismally appalling. At times we gasped for breath at an elevation beyond the albatross—at times became dizzy with the velocity of our descent into some watery hell, where the air grew stagnant, and no sound disturbed the slumbers of the kraken.[9]

We were at the bottom of one of these abysses, when a quick scream from my companion broke fearfully upon the night. "See! see!" cried he, shrieking in my ears, "Almighty God! see! see!" As he spoke, I became aware of a dull, sullen glare of red light which streamed down the sides of the vast chasm where we lay, and threw a fitful brilliancy upon our deck. Casting my eyes upwards, I beheld a spectacle which froze the current of my blood. At a terrific height directly above us, and upon the very verge of the precipitous descent, hovered a gigantic ship of, perhaps, four thousand tons. Although up-reared upon the summit of a wave more than a hundred times her own altitude, her apparent size still exceeded that of any ship of the line or East Indiaman in existence. Her huge hull was of a deep dingy black, unrelieved by any of the customary carvings of a ship. A single row of brass cannon protruded from her open ports, and dashed from their polished surfaces the fires of innumerable battle-lanterns, which swung to and fro about her rigging. But what mainly inspired us with horror and astonishment, was that she bore up under a press of sail[10] in the very teeth of that supernatural sea, and of that ungovernable hurricane. When we first discovered her, her bows were alone to be seen, as she rose slowly from the dim and horrible gulf beyond her. For a moment of intense terror she paused upon the giddy pinnacle, as if in contemplation of her own sublimity, then trembled and tottered, and—came down.

At this instant, I know not what sudden self-possesssion came over my spirit. Staggering as far aft as I could, I awaited fearlessly the ruin that was to overwhelm. Our own vessel was at length ceasing from her struggles, and sinking with her head to the sea. The shock of the descending mass struck her, consequently, in that portion of her frame which was already under water, and the inevitable result was to hurl me, with irresistible violence, upon the rigging of the stranger.

As I fell, the ship hove in stays, and went about; and to the confusion ensuing I attributed my escape from the notice of the crew. With little difficulty I made my way unperceived to the main hatchway, which was partially open, and soon found an opportunity of secreting myself in the hold. Why I did so I can hardly tell. An indefinite sense of awe, which at first sight of the navigators of the ship had taken hold of my mind, was perhaps the principle of my concealment. I was unwilling to trust myself with a race of people who had offered, to the cursory glance I had taken, so many points of vague novelty, doubt, and apprehension. I therefore thought proper to contrive a hiding-place in the hold. This I did by removing a small portion of the shifting-boards,[11] in such a manner as to afford me a convenient retreat between the huge timbers of the ship.

I had scarcely completed my work, when a footstep in the hold forced me to make use of it. A man passed by my place of concealment with a feeble and unsteady gait. I could not see his face, but had an opportunity of observing his general appearance. There was about it an evidence of great age and infirmity. His knees tottered beneath a load of years, and his entire frame quivered under the burthen. He muttered to himself, in a low broken tone, some words of a language which I could not understand, and groped in a corner among a pile of singular-looking instruments, and decayed charts of navigation. His manner was a wild mixture of the peevishness of second childhood, and the solemn dignity of a God. He at length went on deck, and I saw him no more.

*   *   *   *   *   *   *   *

A feeling, for which I have no name,

has taken possession of my soul—a sensation which will admit of no analysis, to which the lessons of by-gone times are inadequate, and for which I fear futurity itself will offer me no key. To a mind constituted like my own, the latter consideration is an evil. I shall never—I know that I shall never—be satisfied with regard to the nature of my conceptions. Yet it is not wonderful that these conceptions are indefinite, since they have their origin in sources so utterly novel. A new sense—a new entity is added to my soul. * * * *

It is long since I first trod the deck of this terrible ship, and the rays of my destiny are, I think, gathering to a focus. Incomprehensible men! Wrapped up in meditations of a kind which I cannot divine, they pass me by unnoticed. Concealment is utter folly on my part, for the people *will not* see. It was but just now that I passed directly before the eyes of the mate—it was no long while ago that I ventured into the captain's own private cabin, and took thence the materials with which I write, and have written. I shall from time to time continue this journal. It is true that I may not find an opportunity of transmitting it to the world, but I will not fail to make the endeavour. At the last moment I will enclose the MS. in a bottle, and cast it within the sea. * *

An incident has occurred which has given me new room for meditation. Are such things the operation of ungoverned Chance? I had ventured upon deck and thrown myself down, without attracting any notice, among a pile of ratlin-stuff and old sails, in the bottom of the yawl. While musing upon the singularity of my fate, I unwittingly daubed with a tar-brush the edges of a neatly-folded studding-sail which lay near me on a barrel. The studding-sail is now bent[12] upon the ship, and the thoughtless touches of the brush are spread out into the word DIS-COVERY. * * * * * * * * * * * * *

I have made many observations lately upon the structure of the vessel. Although well armed, she is not, I think, a ship of war. Her rigging, build, and general equip-

ment, all negative a supposition of this kind. What she *is not*, I can easily perceive—what she *is* I fear it is impossible to say. I know not how it is, but in scrutinizing her strange model and singular cast of spars, her huge size and overgrown suits of canvass, her severely simple bow and antiquated stern, there will occasionally flash across my mind a sensation of familiar things, and there is always mixed up with such indistinct shadows of recollection, an unaccountable memory of old foreign chronicles and ages long ago. * *

I have been looking at the timbers of the ship. She is built of a material to which I am a stranger. There is a peculiar character about the wood which strikes me as rendering it unfit for the purpose to which it has been applied. I mean its extreme *porousness*, considered independently of the worm-eaten condition which is a consequence of navigation in these seas, and apart from the rottenness attendant upon age. It will appear perhaps an observation somewhat over-curious, but this wood would have every characteristic of Spanish oak, if Spanish oak were distended by any unnatural means.

In reading the above sentence a curious apothegm of an old weather-beaten Dutch navigator comes full upon my recollection. "It is as sure," he was wont to say, when any doubt was entertained of his veracity, "as sure as there is a sea where the ship itself will grow in bulk like the living body of the seaman." * * * * *

About an hour ago, I made bold to thrust myself among a group of the crew. They paid me no manner of attention, and, although I stood in the very midst of them all, seemed utterly unconscious of my presence. Like the one I had at first seen in the hold, they all bore about them the marks of a hoary old age. Their knees trembled with infirmity; their shoulders were bent double with decrepitude; their shrivelled skins rattled in the wind; their voices were low, tremulous and broken; their eyes glistened with the rheum of years; and their gray hairs streamed terribly in the tempest. Around them, on every part of the deck, lay scattered mathematical instruments of the most quaint and obsolete construction. * * * * * *

I mentioned some time ago the bending of a studding-sail. From that period the ship, being thrown dead off the wind, has continued her terrific course due south, with every rag of canvass packed upon her, from her trucks to her lower studding-sail booms, and rolling every moment her top-gallant yard-arms into the most appalling hell of water which it can enter into the mind of man to imagine. I have just left the deck, where I find it impossible to maintain a footing, although the crew seem to experience little inconvenience. It appears to me a miracle of miracles that our enormous bulk is not swallowed up at once and forever. We are surely doomed to hover continually upon the brink of Eternity, without taking a final plunge into the abyss. From billows a thousand times more stupendous than any I have ever seen, we glide away with the facility of the arrowy sea-gull; and the colossal waters rear their heads above us like demons of the deep, but like demons confined to simple threats and forbidden to destroy. I am led to attribute these frequent escapes to the only natural cause which can account for such effect. —I must suppose the ship to be within the influence of some strong current, or impetuous under-tow. * * * * * * * *

I have seen the captain face to face, and in his own cabin—but, as I expected, he paid me no attention. Although in his appearance there is, to a casual observer, nothing which might bespeak him more or less than man—still a feeling of irrepressible reverence and awe mingled with the sensation of wonder with which I regarded him. In stature he is nearly my own height; that is, about five feet eight inches. He is of a well-knit and compact frame of body, neither robust nor remarkably otherwise. But it is the singularity of the expression which reigns upon the face —it is the intense, the wonderful, the thrilling evidence of old age, so utter, so

extreme, which excites within my spirit a sense—a sentiment ineffable. His forehead, although little wrinkled, seems to bear upon it the stamp of a myriad of years.—His gray hairs are records of the past, and his grayer eyes are Sybils[13] of the future. The cabin floor was thickly strewn with strange, iron-clasped folios, and mouldering instruments of science, and obsolete long-forgotten charts. His head was bowed down upon his hands, and he pored, with a fiery unquiet eye, over a paper which I took to be a commission, and which, at all events, bore the signature of a monarch. He muttered to himself, as did the first seaman whom I saw in the hold, some low peevish syllables of a foreign tongue, and although the speaker was close at my elbow, his voice seemed to reach my ears from the distance of a mile. * * * * * * * * * * * * *

The ship and all in it are imbued with the spirit of Eld. The crew glide to and fro like the ghosts of buried centuries; their eyes have an eager and uneasy meaning; and when their fingers fall athwart my path in the wild glare of the battle-lanterns, I feel as I have never felt before, although I have been all my life a dealer in antiquities, and have imbibed the shadows of fallen columns at Balbec, and Tadmor, and Persepolis,[14] until my very soul has become a ruin. * * * * *

When I look around me I feel ashamed of my former apprehensions. If I trembled at the blast which has hitherto attended us, shall I not stand aghast at a warring of wind and ocean, to convey any idea of which the words tornado and simoom are trivial and ineffective? All in the immediate vicinity of the ship is the blackness of eternal night, and a chaos of foamless water; but, about a league on either side of us, may be seen, indistinctly and at intervals, stupendous ramparts of ice, towering away into the desolate sky, and looking like the walls of the universe. * * * * *

As I imagined, the ship proves to be in a current; if that appellation can properly be given to a tide which, howling and shrieking by the white ice, thunders on to the southward with a velocity like the headlong dashing of a cataract. * * * *

To conceive the horror of my sensations is, I presume, utterly impossible; yet a curiosity to penetrate the mysteries of these awful regions, predominates even over my despair, and will reconcile me to the most hideous aspect of death. It is evident that we are hurrying onwards to some exciting knowledge—some never-to-be-imparted secret, whose attainment is destruction. Perhaps this current leads us to the southern pole itself. It must be confessed that a supposition apparently so wild has every probability in its favor. * *

The crew pace the deck with unquiet and tremulous step; but there is upon their countenances an expression more of the eagerness of hope than of the apathy of despair.

In the meantime the wind is still in our poop, and, as we carry a crowd of canvass, the ship is at times lifted bodily from out the sea—Oh, horror upon horror! the ice opens suddenly to the right, and to the left, and we are whirling dizzily, in immense concentric circles, round and round the borders of a gigantic amphitheatre, the summit of whose walls is lost in the darkness and the distance. But little time will be left me to ponder upon my destiny—the circles rapidly grow small—we are plunging madly within the grasp of the whirlpool—and amid a roaring, and bellowing, and thundering of ocean and of tempest, the ship is quivering, oh God! and——going down.[15]

THE LIGHT-HOUSE[1]

Jan. 1—1796. This day—my first on the light-house—I make this entry in my Diary, as agreed on with DeGrät. As regularly as I *can* keep the journal, I will—but

"The Light-House" reprinted courtesy of Henry W. and Albert A. Berg Collection, The New York Public Library, The Astor, Lenox and Tilden Foundations.

there is no telling what may happen to a man all alone as I am—I may get sick or worse. . . . So far well! The cutter had a narrow escape—but why dwell on that, since I am *here,* all safe? My spirits are beginning to revive already, at the mere thought of being—for once in my life at least—thoroughly *alone;* for, of course, Neptune, large as he is, is not to be taken into consideration as "society." Would to Heaven I had ever found in "society" one half as much *faith* as in this poor dog:—in such case I and "society" might never have parted—even for a year. . . . What most surprises me, is the difficulty De-Grät had in getting me the appointment —and I a noble of the realm! It could not be that the Consistory had any doubt of my ability to manage the light. *One* man has attended it before now—and got on quite as well as the three that are usually put in. The duty is a mere nothing; and the printed instructions are as plain as possible. It would never have done to let Orndoff accompany me. I never should have made any way with my book as long as he was within reach of me, with his intolerable gossip—not to mention that everlasting meërschaum. Besides, I wish to be *alone.* . . . It is strange that I never observed, until this moment, how dreary a sound that word has—"alone"! I could half fancy there was some peculiarity in the echo of these cylindrical walls—but oh, no!—that is all nonsense. I do believe I am going to get nervous about my insulation. *That* will never do. I have not forgotten DeGrät's prophecy. Now for a scramble to the lantern and a good look around to "see what I can see." . . . . To see what I can see indeed!—not very much. The swell is subsiding a little, I think—but the cutter will have a rough passage home, nevertheless. She will hardly get within sight of the Norland[2] before noon to-morrow—and yet it can hardly be more than 190 or 200 miles.

Jan. 2. I have passed this day in a species of ecstasy that I find it impossible to describe. My passion for solitude could scarcely have been more thoroughly gratified. I do not say *satisfied;* for I believe I should never be satiated with such delight as I have experienced to-day.[3] . . . The wind lulled after day-break, and by the afternoon the sea had gone down materially. . . . Nothing to be seen, with the telescope even, but ocean and sky, with an occasional gull.

Jan. 3. A dead calm all day. Towards evening, the sea looked very much like glass. A few sea-weeds came in sight; but besides them absolutely *nothing* all day —not even the slightest speck of cloud. . . . Occupied myself in exploring the light-house. . . . It is a very lofty one—as I find to my cost when I have to ascend its interminable stairs—not quite 160 feet, I should say, from the low-water mark to the top of the lantern. From the bottom *inside* the shaft, however, the distance to the summit is 180 feet at least:—thus the floor is 20 feet below the surface of the sea, even at low-tide. . . . It seems to me that the hollow interior at the bottom should have been filled in with solid masonry. Undoubtedly the whole would have been thus rendered more *safe:*—but what am I thinking about. A structure such as this is safe enough under any circumstances. I should feel myself secure in it during the fiercest hurricane that ever raged—and yet I have heard seamen say that, occasionally, with a wind at South-West, the sea has been known to run higher here than any where with the single exception of the Western opening of the Straits of Magellan. No mere sea, though, could accomplish anything with this solid iron-riveted wall—which, at 50 feet from high-water mark, is four feet thick, if one inch. . . . The basis on which the structure rests seems to me to be chalk. . . .

Jan. 4. [Here Poe's manuscript breaks off.]

Notes

MS. Found in a Bottle

1. This early tale had a long publication history in Poe's lifetime. He entered it in a *Baltimore Saturday Visiter* contest, won, and saw it in print in the October 19, 1833 issue. That prize was Poe's first pay as an author, and most writers feel it was instrumental in making him decide to pursue writing as a profession. *The People's Advocate* of Newburyport, Mass. reprinted it almost instantly (October 26, 1833), probably without Poe's knowledge or consent. He used it again in the *Southern Literary Messenger* December 1835. It showed up, to Poe's annoyance, in *The Gift* for 1836; Poe had wanted the editors to run "Siope" ("Silence") or "Epimanes" ("Four Beasts in One"). It was in the 1840 *Tales of the Grotesque and Arabesque,* and in the October 11, 1845 *The Broadway Jour-*nal. At Poe's death on October 7, 1849, it came out one last time, in the *Richmond Semi-Weekly Examiner* for October 10.

2. Carlson (2) translates the motto:

He who has only a moment longer to live Has no longer anything to conceal.

Philippe Quinault: French dramatist (1635–1688).

Atys: an opera libretto which Quinault wrote for Lully.

3. Pyrrhonism: skepticism.

ignes fatui: tantalizing but misleading attractions.

4. The old name for Borneo, Celebes, Java, Sumatra, the Molucca Islands and Nusa Tenggara.

5. Lachadive islands: Now spelled "Lacccadive," these are located in the Indian Ocean

off the southwest coast of India.

coir: fiber from coconut husk.

jaggeree: jaggery, a kind of coarse sugar made from the sap of a variety of palm tree.

ghee: a foodstuff made by processing the butterfat of buffalo milk.

crank: a nautical term meaning "liable to heel or capsize" (Carlson 2).

6. East Indian coasting vessels (Carlson 2).

7. a meteorological term usually used to refer to a hot, dry desert wind. Poe means a big storm.

8. Our cable: Poe refers to the anchor cable. Seeing that the ship was drifting toward shore, the captain had anchored it.

New Holland: The old name for Australia (Carlson 2).

9. a legendary Norse sea monster.

10. gigantic ship: In the legend of the Flying Dutchman, the ghost ship is supposed to appear when a ship is going down. Poe's ghost ship is right on schedule, as the ensuing paragraphs reveal.

ship of the line: a large warship.

East Indiaman: "a ship of large tonnage engaged in East Indian trade" (OED).

press of sail: Sailing ships in storms normally run under light storm sails, designed to provide some control in the high winds and to minimize the dangers of capsizing, or damage to sails, masts, and rigging.

11. hove in stays: "A vessel in the act of tacking is said to be . . . hove in stays" (OED).

went about: headed into the wind.

shifting-boards: partitions in a ship's hold to keep cargo from shifting.

12. yawl: a small boat.

studding sail: a sail set beyond the leeches

of any of the principal sails during a fair wind (OED).

bent: in use.

13. Sybils: Sibyls.

14. Eld: antiquity.

Balbec, and Tadmor, and Persepolis: ruined cities of the Near East (Carlson 2).

15. NOTE.—The "Ms. Found in a Bottle" was originally published in 1831, and it was not until many years afterwards that I became acquainted with the maps of Mercator, in which the ocean is represented as rushing, by four mouths, into the (northern) Polar Gulf, to be absorbed into the bowels of the earth; the Pole itself being represented by a black rock, towering to a prodigious height [Poe's note]. If the tale was printed in 1831, no scholar has yet found it in a periodical for that year. See note 1. Poe's episodic novel *The Narrative of Arthur Gordon Pym* also ends with the hero plunging to an unknown fate at the South Pole.

The Light-House

1. Poe's "last," unfinished tale was discovered in 1942 by the late Thomas Ollive Mabbott who first published it in the English *Notes & Queries* (1942). Mabbott guessed from the handwriting that it was very late, probably the last thing Poe worked on before his death.

2. Norland: A term used generally to refer to the north of Scotland. "Orndoff" and "De Grät," however, are not Scottish sounding names. Perhaps Poe wants the exact locale vague, and intends "Norland" in a general sense to mean the north of some northern European country.

3. Compare this "journal entry" in language and tone with those by Ainsworth in "The Balloon-Hoax."

Index

	Preface	Text	Notes
Angel of the Odd, The	472	489	500
Assignation, The	471	473	495
Balloon-Hoax, The	547	549	611
Berenice	63	71	100
Black Cat, The	251	254	290
Bon-Bon	356	398	431
Business Man, The	503	528	545
Cask of Amontillado, The	455	464	470
Colloquy of Monos and Una, The	108	119	146
Conversation of Eiros and Charmion, The	108	116	146
Descent into the Maelström, A	39	40	59
Devil in the Belfry, The	355	393	430
Diddling Considered As One of the Exact Sciences	503	522	543
Domain of Arnheim, The	4	5	32
Duc De L'Omelette, The	354	388	425
Eleonora	64	76	101
Facts in the Case of M. Valdemar, The	112	134	150
Fall of the House of Usher, The	64	88	104
Four Beasts in One/The Homo-Cameleopard	438	439	449
Gold-Bug, The	152	155	244
Hans Pfaal	547	558	613
Hop-Frog	251	262	290
How to Write a Blackwood Article	351	357	414
Imp of the Perverse, The	252	268	290
Island of the Fay, The	3	18	36
King Pest	294	296	319
Landor's Cottage	4	21	37
Ligeia	64	79	103

	Preface	Text	Notes
Light-House, The	623	629	631
Literary Life of Thingum Bob, Esq., The	353	376	422
Loss of Breath	471	482	497
Man of the Crowd, The	253	283	292
Man That Was Used Up, The	438	443	451
MS. Found in a Bottle	622	623	630
Masque of the Red Death, The	454	461	469
Mellonta Tauta	547	588	616
Mesmeric Revelation	114	139	151
Metzengerstein	294	303	320
Morella	63	68	99
Morning on the Wissahiccon	4	29	38
Murders in the Rue Morgue, The	152	175	244
Mystery of Marie Rogêt, The	153	197	246
Mystification	454	456	468
Never Bet the Devil Your Head	352	368	417
Oblong Box, The	154	236	249
Oval Portrait, The	62	65	99
Philosophy of Furniture, The	3	14	35
Pit and the Pendulum, The	39	50	60
Power of Words, The	107	114	145
Predicament, A	352	363	417
Premature Burial, The	295	308	321
Purloined Letter, The	154	225	248
Shadow	109	124	147
Silence	110	126	148
Some Passages in the Life of a Lion	354	390	428
Some Words with a Mummy	502	512	542
Spectacles, The	323	333	348
Sphinx, The	295	316	322
System of Dr. Tarr and Prof. Fether, The	548	596	619
Tale of Jerusalem, A	352	374	420
Tale of the Ragged Mountains, A	112	128	150
Tell-Tale Heart, The	251	259	290
Thou Art the Man	323	324	347
Thousand-and-Second Tale of Scheherazade, The	502	504	537
Three Sundays in a Week	503	533	545
Von Kempelen and His Discovery	549	607	620
Why the Little Frenchman Wears His Hand in a Sling	356	407	435
William Wilson	253	271	291
X-ing a Paragrab	357	410	436